THE WOODCUTTER

Reginald Hill is a native of Cumbria and former resident of Yorkshire, the setting for his novels featuring Superintendent Dalziel and DCI Pascoe, 'the best detective duo on the scene bar none' (*Daily Telegraph*). Their appearances have won him numerous awards including a CWA Gold Dagger and the Diamond Dagger for Lifetime Achievement. They have also been adapted into a hugely popular BBC TV series.

REGINALD HILL

The Woodcutter

HarperCollins*Publishers*

HarperCollins*Publishers*
77–85 Fulham Palace Road, London W6 8JB

www.harpercollins.co.uk

Published by HarperCollins 2010

1

A catalogue record for this book
is available from the British Library

ISBN 978-0-00-734387-4

Typeset in Meridien by Palimpsest Book Production Limited,
Falkirk, Stirlingshire
Printed in Great Britain by
Clays Ltd, St Ives plc

For John Lennard
a poet among critics
a true friend to writers
and a fountain of knowledge
who by imagining what he knows
helps us to know what we imagine

*'Insensé, dit-il, le jour où j'avais résolu de me venger,
de ne pas m'être arraché le coeur!"*

Alexander Dumas: *Le Comte de Monte-Cristo*

"I must have been mad,' he said, 'the day I started planning revenge, not to have
ripped my heart out!'

PROLOGUE

necessity

I am sworn brother, sweet,
To grim Necessity, and he and I
Will keep a league till death.

Shakespeare: Richard II (v.i)

1

Summer 1963; Profumo disgraced; Ward dead; The Beatles' *Please please me* top album; Luther King having his dream; JFK fast approaching the end of his; the Cold War at its chilliest; the Wind of Change blowing ever more strongly through Colonial Africa, with its rising blasts already being felt across the Gate of Tears in British-controlled Aden.

But the threat of terrorist activity is not yet so great that an eleven-year-old English boy cannot enjoy his summer holiday there before returning to school.

There are restrictions, however. His diplomat father, aware of the growing threat from the National Liberation Front, no longer lets him roam free, but sets strict boundaries and insists he is always accompanied by Ahmed, a young Yemeni gardener cum handyman who has become very attached to the boy.

In Ahmed's company he feels perfectly safe, so when a scarred and dusty Morris Oxford pulls up alongside them with its rear door invitingly open, he feels surprise but no alarm as his friend urges him inside.

There are already two people on the back seat. The boy finds himself crushed not too comfortably between Ahmed and a stout bald man who smells of sweat and cheap tobacco.

The car roars away. Soon they reach one of the boundaries laid down by his father. The boy looks at Ahmed queryingly, but already they are moving into one of the less salubrious areas of the city.

Oddly this isn't his first visit. The previous year, in safer times, having overheard one of the British clerks refer smirkingly to its main thoroughfare as *The Street of a Thousand Arseholes*, he had persuaded Ahmed to bring him here. The street in question had been something of a disappointment, offering the boy little clue as to the origin of its entertaining name. Ahmed had responded to his questioning by saying with a grin, 'Too young. Later maybe, when you are older!'

Now the Morris turns into this very street, slows down, and almost before it has come to a halt the boy finds himself bundled out by the bald man and pushed through a doorway.

But he is not yet so frightened that he does not observe the number 19 painted on the wall beside the door.

He is almost carried up some stairs and taken into a room empty of furniture but full of men. Here he is dumped on the floor in a corner. He tries to speak to Ahmed. The young man shakes his head impatiently, and after that will not meet his gaze.

After ten minutes or so a new man arrives, this one wearing a European suit and exuding authority. The others fall silent.

The newcomer stands over the boy and stoops to peer into his face.

'So, boy,' he says. 'You are the son of the British spymaster.'

'No, sir,' he replies. 'My father is the British commercial attaché.'

The man laughs.

'When I was your age, I knew what my father was,' he says. 'Come, let us speak to him and see how much he values you.'

He is dragged to his feet by the bald man and marched into another room where there is a telephone.

The man in the suit dials a number, the boy hears him speak his father's name, there is a pause, then the man says, 'Say nothing. I speak for the Front for the Liberation of South Yemen. We have your son. He will speak to you so that you know I do not lie.'

He makes a gesture and the boy is forced forward.

The man says, 'Speak to your father so he may know it is you,' and puts the phone to the boy's mouth.

4

The boy chants, *'Mille ani undeviginti.'*

The man snatches the phone away and grabs the boy by the throat.

'What did you say?' he screams.

'You said he had to know it was me,' gabbles the boy. 'It's a song we sing together about Paddy McGinty's Goat. Ask him, he'll tell you.'

The man speaks into the phone: 'What is this Ginty goat?'

Whatever is said to him seems to satisfy him and, at a nod from the man, the boy is dragged back to the first room.

Here he lies in the corner, ignored. Men come and go. There is an atmosphere of excitement as though everything is going well. Ahmed, who receives many congratulatory slaps and embraces, still refuses to look at him. He grows increasingly fearful and sinks towards despair.

Then from below comes a sudden outburst of noise.

First the splintering of wood as though a locked door is being broken down, then a tumult of upraised voices followed almost instantly by the rattle of small-arms fire.

All the men rush out. Left alone, the boy looks for a place to hide but there is nowhere. The room's one window is too small for even a small eleven-year-old to wriggle through.

The din is getting louder, nearer. The door bursts open. The bald man rushes in with a pistol in his hand. The boy falls to the floor. The man screams something unintelligible and aims the weapon. Before he can fire, Ahmed comes in behind and jumps on his back. The gun goes off. The bullet hits the floor between the boy's splayed legs.

The two men wrestle briefly. The gun explodes again.

And the bald man slumps against the wall, his hands holding his stomach. Blood seeps through his fingers.

Ahmed stands over him, clutching the pistol. Now at last his eyes meet the boy's and he tries to smile, but it doesn't quite work. Then he turns to the door that has been slammed shut in the struggle.

5

The boy cries, 'Ahmed, wait!'

But the young Yemeni is already opening the door.

He hardly takes one pace over the threshold before he is driven back into the room by a hail of bullets that shatter his chest.

Their eyes meet once more as he lies on the floor. This time the smile makes it to his lips. Then he dies.

Folded in his father's arms, the boy finally lets himself cry.

His father says, 'You did well, you kept your head; the apple doesn't fall far from the tree, eh? And didn't I tell you that doing your Latin homework would come in useful some day!'

Two years later his father will be killed when his car is blown up by a FLOSY bomb, so the boy never has the chance to sit down with him as an adult and ask what the subversives wanted him to do as the price of his son's safety.

Nor what his answer would have been if his own young wits had not been quick enough to reveal the street and the building number where he was being held.

But before he went back to school he did ask how it was that his friend Ahmed, who had loved him enough to save his life and give up his own in the process, could have put him in that perilous position in the first place.

And his father had answered, 'When love is in opposition to grim necessity, there is usually only one winner.'

He had not understood then what he meant. But he was to understand later.

2

Autumn 1989; the world in turmoil; the Berlin Wall crumbling; Chris Rea's *The Road to Hell* top album; Western civilization watching with bated breath the chain of events that will lead to the freeing of Eastern Europe and the end of the Cold War.

In a Cumbrian forest in a glade dappled by the midday sun, a man sits slumped against a twisted rowan, his weathered face more deeply scored by the thoughts grinding through his bowed head, his eyes fixed upon but not seeing the unopened flask and sandwich box between his feet. A little way apart, a second man stands and watches, his long brown hair edged wolf-grey, his troubled face full of a compassion he knows it is vain to express, while at his back a young girl too regards the sitting man with unblinking gaze, though her expression is much harder to read. And over the wide woodland tract, so rarely free of the wind's soughing music above, and the pizzicato of cracking twigs below, a silence falls as if trees and sky and surrounding mountains too were bating their breath for fear of intruding on grief.

Three hundred miles to the south in an East London multi-storey car park, five hoodies who probably wouldn't bate a breath if Jesus Christ crash-landed on St Paul's in a chariot of fire are breaking into a car.

But they've done it once too often, and suddenly cops spring up all around as if someone had been sowing dragon's teeth. The hoodies scatter and run, only to find there's no place to run to.

Except for one. He heads for a ten-foot concrete wall with a one-foot gap at the top. To the cops' amazement, he goes up the wall like a lizard. Then, to their horror, he rolls through the gap and vanishes.

They are on the fifth level and there's nothing beyond that gap but a sixty-foot drop to the street below.

The cops radio down to ask their waiting colleagues to go round the back of the multi-storey and pick up the corpse.

A few minutes later word comes back – no corpse at the foot of the wall, just a young hoodie who tried to run off as soon as he spotted them.

At the station he tells them he is John Smith, age eighteen, no fixed abode.

After that he shuts up and stays shut up.

They print him. He's not in the records.

His fellow hoodies claim never to have seen him before. They also claim never to have seen each other before. One of them is so doped up he's uncertain whether he's ever seen himself before.

Two are clearly juveniles. A social worker is summoned to sit in on their questioning. The other two have police records. One is eighteen, the other nineteen. The duty solicitor deals with them.

John Smith's age they're still not sure about, and something about the youth, some intangible aura of likeability, makes them share their doubts with the duty solicitor.

He starts his interview by pointing out to Smith that as a juvenile he would be dealt with differently, probably getting a light, non-custodial sentence. Smith sticks to his story, refusing to add details about his background though his accent is clearly northern.

The solicitor guesses he's lying about his age and name to keep his family out of the picture. Hoping to scare the boy into honesty by over-egging the adult consequences of his crime, he turns his attention to the case against him and quickly perceives it isn't all that strong. Identification via the grainy CCTV tape in the dimly lit multi-storey is a long way this side of reasonable doubt. And could anyone really have shinned down the sheer outer wall in under a minute as the police evidence claims?

8

As they talk, the boy relaxes as long as no questions are asked about his origins, and the solicitor finds himself warming to his young client. On his way home he diverts to take a photo of the outer wall of the multi-storey to show just how sheer it is. Next day he shows it to the boy, who is clearly touched by this sign of concern, but becomes panicky when told he has to appear before a magistrate that same morning. The solicitor assures him this is just a committal hearing, not a trial, but warns him that as he is officially an adult of no fixed abode, he will almost certainly be remanded in custody.

This is what happens. As the boy is led away, the solicitor tells him not to worry, he will call round at the Remand Centre later in the day. But he has other work to deal with that keeps him busy well into the evening. He remembers the boy as he makes his way home and eases his guilt with the thought that a night in a Remand Centre without sight of a friendly face might be just the thing Smith needs to make him see sense.

He talks to his wife about the boy. She regards him with surprise. He is not in the habit of getting attached to the low-life criminals who form his customary clientele.

He goes to bed early, exhausted. In the small hours when his wife awakens him, whispering she thinks someone is trying to break in through the living-room window, he reckons she must be having a nightmare as their flat is on the tenth floor of a high rise.

But when they go into the living room and switch on the light, there perched on the narrow window box outside the window is the figure of a man.

Not a man. A boy. John Smith.

The solicitor tells his wife it's OK, opens the window and lets Smith in.

You said you would come, says the boy, half tearfully, half accusingly.

How did you get out of the Centre? asks the solicitor. *And how did you find me?*

Through a window, says the boy. *And your office address was on that*

9

card you gave me, so I got in through a skylight and rooted around till I found your home address. I tidied up after, I didn't leave a mess.

His wife, who has been listening to this exchange with interest, lowers the bread knife she is carrying and says, *I'll make a cup of tea.*

She returns with a pot of tea and a large sponge cake which Smith demolishes over the next hour. During this time she gets more out of the boy than the combined efforts of her husband and the police managed in two days.

When she's satisfied she's got all she can, she says, *Now we'd better get you back.*

The boy looks alarmed and she reassures him, *My husband's going to get you off this charge, no problem. But absconding from custody's another matter, so you need to be back in the Remand Centre before reveille.*

We can't just knock at the door, protests her husband.

Of course not. You'll get back in the way you came out, won't you, ducks?

The boy nods, and half an hour later the couple sit in their car distantly watching a shadow running up the outer wall of the Remand Centre.

Nice lad, says the wife. *You always did have good judgment. When you get him off you'd better bring him back home till we decide what to do with him.*

Home! exclaims the solicitor. *Our home?*

Who else's?

Look, I like the lad, but I wasn't planning to adopt him!

Me neither, says his wife. *But we've got to do something with him. Otherwise what does he do? Goes back to thieving, or ends up flogging his arsehole round King's Cross.*

So when the case is dismissed, Smith takes possession of the solicitor's spare room.

But not for long.

The wife says, *I've mentioned him at the Chapel. JC says he'd like to meet him.*

The solicitor pulls a face and says, *King's Cross might be a better bet.*

The wife says, *No, you're wrong. None of that with a kid he takes under his wing. In any case, the boy needs a job and who else can we talk to?*

The meeting takes place in a pub after the lunchtime crush has thinned out. To start with the boy doesn't say much, but under the influence of a couple of halves of lager and the man, JC's, relaxed undemanding manner he becomes quite voluble. Voluble enough to make it clear he's not too big on hymn-singing, collection-box rattling or any of the other activities conjured up in his mind by references to the Chapel.

The man says, *I expect you'd prefer something more active and out of doors, eh? So tell me, apart from running up and down vertical walls, what else is it that you do?*

The boy thinks, then replies, *I can chop down trees.*

JC laughs.

A woodcutter! Well, curiously at the Chapel we do have an extensive garden to tend and occasionally a nimble woodcutter might come in handy. I'll see what I can do.

The boy and the woman look at each other and exchange smiles.

And the man, JC, looks on and smiles benevolently too.

3

Winter 1991; Terry Waite freed; 264 Croats massacred at Vukovar; Freddy Mercury dies of AIDS; Michael Jackson's *Dangerous* top album; the Soviet Union dissolved; Gorbachev resigns.

And in a quiet side street in the 20th arrondissement of Paris, a man with a saintly smile relaxes in the comfortable rear seat of a Citroën CX. Through the swirling mist above the trees on the far side of a small park he can just make out the top three storeys of a six-storey apartment block. He imagines he sees a shadow moving rapidly down the side of the building, but it is soon out of sight, and in any case he is long used to the deceptions of the imagination on such a night as this. He returns his attention to Quintus Curtius's account of the fall of Tyre, and is soon so immersed that he is taken by surprise a few minutes later when the car door opens and the boy slips inside.

'Oh hello,' he says, closing the book. 'Everything all right?'

'Piece of cake,' says the boy. 'Bit chilly on the fingers though.'

'You ought to wear gloves,' says the man, passing over a thermos flask.

'Can't feel the holds the same with gloves,' replies the boy, drinking directly from the flask.

The man regards him fondly and says, 'You're a good little wood-cutter.'

In the front of the car a phone rings. The driver answers it,

12

speaking in French. After a while, he turns and says, 'He's on his way, JC. But there's a problem. He diverted to the Gare d'Est. He picked up a woman and a child. They think it's his wife and daughter. They're in the car with him.'

Without any change of expression or tone the man says softly, *'Parles Français, idiot!'*

But his warning is too late.

The boy says, 'What's that about a wife and daughter? You said he lived by himself.'

'So he does,' reassures the man. 'As you doubtless observed, it's a very small flat. Also he's estranged from his family. If it is his wife and daughter, and that's not definite, he is almost certainly taking them to a hotel. Would you like something to eat? I have some chocolate.'

The boy shakes his head and drinks again from the flask. His face is troubled.

The man says quietly, 'This is a very wicked person, I mean wicked in himself as well as a dangerous enemy of our country.'

The boy says, 'Yeah, I know that, you explained that. But that doesn't mean his wife and kid are wicked, does it?'

'Of course it doesn't. And we do everything in our power not to hurt the innocent; I explained that too, didn't I?'

'Yes,' agrees the boy.

'Well then.'

They sit in silence for some minutes. The phone sounds again.

The driver answers, listens, turns his head and says, *'Ils sont arrivés. La femme et l'enfant aussi. Il demande, que voudrais-vous?'*

The man said, *'Dites-lui, vas'y.'*

The boy's face is screwed up as if by sheer concentration he can make sense of what's being said. On the far side of the park the mist above the trees clears for a moment and the apartment block is visible silhouetted against a brightly starred sky.

A light comes on in one of the uppermost chambers. At first it is an ordinary light, amber against an uncurtained window.

And then it turns red. It is too distant for any sound to reach inside the well-insulated car, but in that moment they see the glass dissolve and smoke and debris come streaming towards them like the fingers of a reaching hand.

Then the mist swirls back and the man says, 'Go.'

Back in their apartment, the boy goes to his room and the man sits by a gently hissing gas fire, encoding his report. When it is finished, he pours himself a drink and opens his *History of Alexander the Great*.

Suddenly the door opens and the boy, naked except for his brief underpants, bursts into the room.

He says in a voice so choked with emotion he can hardly get the words out, 'You lied to me, you fucking bastard! They were still with him, both of them, it's on the news, it's so fucking terrible it's on the British news. You lied! Why?'

The man says, 'It had to be done tonight. Tomorrow would have been too late.'

The boy comes nearer. The man is very aware of the young muscular body so close he can feel the heat off it.

The boy says, 'Why did you make me do it? You said you'd never ask me to do anything I didn't want to do. But you tricked me. Why?'

The man for once is not smiling. He says quietly, 'My father once said to me, when love and grim necessity meet, there is only one winner. You probably don't understand that now any more than I did then. But you will. In the meantime all I can say is I'm very sorry. I'll find a way to make it up to you, I promise.'

'How? How can you possibly make it up to me?' screams the boy. 'You've made me a murderer. What can you do that can ever make up for that! There's nothing! Nothing!'

And the man says, rather sadly, like one who pronounces a sentence rather than makes a gift, 'I shall give you your heart's desire.'

BOOK ONE

wolf and elf

After the hunters trapped the wolf, they put him in a cage where he lay for many years, suffering grievously, till one day a curious elf, to whom iron bars were no more obstacle than the shadows of grasses on a sunlit meadow, took pity on his plight, and asked, 'What can I bring you that will ease your pain, Wolf?'

And the wolf replied, 'My foes to play with.'

Charles Underhill (tr): *Folk Tales of Scandinavia*

Wolf

Once upon a time I was living happily ever after.

That's right. Like in a fairy tale.

How else to describe my life up till that bright autumn morning back in 2008?

I was the lowly woodcutter who fell in love with a beautiful princess glimpsed dancing on the castle lawn, knew she was so far above him that even his fantasies could get his head chopped off, nonetheless when three seemingly impossible tasks were set as the price of her hand in marriage threw his cap into the ring and after many perilous adventures returned triumphant to claim his heart's desire.

Here began the *happily ever after*, the precise extent of which is nowhere defined in fairy literature. In my case it lasted fourteen years.

During this time I acquired a fortune of several millions, a private jet, residences in Holland Park, Devon, New York, Barbados and Umbria, my lovely daughter, Ginny, and a knighthood for services to commerce.

Over the same period my wife Imogen turned from a fragrant young princess into an elegant, sophisticated woman. She ran our social life with easy efficiency, made no demands on me that I could not afford, and always had an appropriate welcome waiting in whichever of our homes I returned to after my often extensive business trips.

Sometimes I looked at her and found it hard to understand how I could deserve such beauty, such happiness. She was my piece of perfection, my heart's desire, and whenever the stresses and strains of my hugely active life began to make themselves felt, I just had to think of my princess to know that, whatever fate brought me, I was the most blessed of men.

Then on that autumn day – by one of those coincidences that only a wicked fairy can contrive, our wedding anniversary – everything changed.

At half past six in the morning we were woken in our Holland Park house by an extended ringing of the doorbell. I got up and went to the window. My first thought when I saw the police uniforms was that some joker had sent us an anniversary strip-aubade. But they didn't look as if they were about to rip off their uniforms and burst into song, and suddenly my heart contracted at the thought that something could have happened to Ginny. She was away at school – not by my choice, but when the lowly wood-cutter marries the princess, there are some ancestral customs he meekly goes along with.

Then it occurred to me they'd hardly need a whole posse of plods to convey such a message.

Nor would they bring a bunch of press photographers and a TV crew.

Imogen was sitting up in bed by this time. Even in these fraught circumstances I was distracted by sight of her perfect breasts.

She said, 'Wolf, what is it?' in her usual calm manner.

'I don't know,' I said. 'I'll go and see.'

She said, 'Perhaps you should put some clothes on.'

I grabbed my dressing gown and was still pulling it round my shoulders as I started down the stairs. I could hear voices below. Among them I recognized the Cockney accent of Mrs Roper, our housekeeper. She was crying out in protest and I saw why as I reached the half landing. She must have opened the front door and policemen were thrusting past her without ceremony. Jogging up the stairs towards me was a short fleshy man in a creased blue suit flanked by two uniformed constables.

He came to a halt a couple of steps below me and said breathlessly, 'Wolf Hadda? *Sorry*. Sir *Wilfred* Hadda. Detective Inspector Medler. I have a warrant to search these premises.'

He reached up to hand me a sheet of paper. Below I could hear people moving, doors opening and shutting, Mrs Roper still protesting.

I said, 'What the hell's going on?'

His gaze went down to my crotch. His lips twitched. Then his eyes ran up my body and focused beyond me.

He said, 'Maybe you should make yourself decent, unless you fancy posing for Page Three.'

I turned to see what he was looking at. Through the half-landing window overlooking the garden, I could see the old rowan tree I'd transplanted from Cumbria when I bought the house. It was incandescent with berries at this time of year, and I was incandescent with rage at the sight of a *paparazzo* clinging to its branches, pointing a camera at me. Even at this distance I could see the damage caused by his ascent.

I turned back to Medler.

'How did he get there? What are the press doing here anyway? Did you bring them?'

'Now why on earth should I do that, sir?' he said. 'Maybe they just happened to be passing.'

He didn't even bother to try to sound convincing.

He had an insinuating voice and one of those mouths which looks as if it's holding back a knowing sneer. I've always had a short fuse. At six thirty in the morning, confronted by a bunch of heavy-handed plods tearing my home to pieces and a paparazzo desecrating my lovely rowan, it was very short indeed. I punched the little bastard right in his smug mouth and he went backwards down the stairs, taking one of his constables with him. The other

19

produced his baton and whacked me on the leg. The pain was excruciating and I collapsed in a heap on the landing.

After that things got confused. As I was half dragged, half carried out of the house, I screamed at Imogen, who'd appeared fully dressed on the stairs, 'Ring Toby!'

She looked very calm, very much in control. Princesses don't panic. The thought was a comfort to me.

Cameras clicked and journalists yelled inanities as I was thrust into a car. As it sped away, I twisted round to look back. Cops were already coming down the steps carrying loaded bin bags that they tossed into the back of a van. The house, gleaming in the morning sunlight, seemed to look down on them with disdain. Then we turned a corner and it vanished from sight.

I did not realize – how could I? – that I was never to enter it again.

ii

My arrival at the police station seemed to take them by surprise. My arrest at that stage can't have been anticipated. Once the pain in my leg subsided and my brain started functioning again, I'd worked out that I must be the subject of a Fraud Office investigation. Personal equity companies rise on the back of other companies' failures and Woodcutter Enterprises had left a lot of unhappy people in its wake. Also the atmosphere on the markets was full of foreboding and when nerves are on edge, malicious tongues soon start wagging.

So being banged up was my own fault. If I hadn't lost my temper, I would probably be sitting in my own drawing room, refusing to answer any of Medler's impertinent questions till Toby Estover, my solicitor, arrived. I would have liked to see Medler's expression when he heard the name. *Mr Itsover* his colleagues call him, because that's what the prosecution says when they hear Toby's acting for the defence. Barristers may get the glory but there are many dodgy characters walking free because they were wise enough and rich enough to hire Toby Estover when the law came calling.

I was treated courteously – I even thought I detected the ghost of a smile on the custody sergeant's lips when told I'd been arrested for thumping Medler – then put in a cell. Pretty minimalist, but stick a couple of Vettriano prints on the wall and it could have passed for a standard single in a lot of boutique hotels.

I don't know how long I sat there. I hadn't been wearing my watch when they arrested me. In fact I hadn't been wearing anything but my dressing gown. They'd taken that and given me an off-white cotton overall and a pair of plastic flip-flops.

I was just wondering whether to start banging on the door and making a fuss when it opened and Toby came in. It was good to see him, in every sense. As well as having one of the smartest minds I've ever known, he dresses to match. Same age as me but slim and elegant. Me, I can make a Savile Row three-piece look like a boiler suit in twenty minutes; Toby would look good in army fatigues. In his Henry Poole threads and John Lobb shoes he looked smooth enough to talk Jesus off the Cross which, had he been in Jerusalem at the time, I daresay he would have done.

I said, 'Toby, thank God. Have you brought me some clothes?'

He looked surprised and said, 'No, sorry, old boy. Never crossed my mind.'

'Damn,' I said. 'I thought Imo might have chucked a few things together.'

'I think she may have other things to occupy her,' he observed. 'Let's sit down and have a chat.'

'Here?' I said.

'Here,' he said firmly, sitting on the narrow bed. 'Less chance of being overheard than in an interview room.'

The idea that the police might try to eavesdrop on a client/lawyer conversation troubled me less than the implication that it could contain something damaging to me.

I said, 'Frankly, I don't give a damn what they hear. I've got nothing to hide.'

'It's certainly true that by now you're unlikely to have anything you think may be hidden,' he said sardonically. 'I understand they are still searching the house. But it's your computers we need to concentrate on. Wolf, we won't have much time so let's cut to the chase. I've had a word with DI Medler . . . is it true you hit him, by the way?'

'Oh yes,' I said with some satisfaction. 'You'll probably see the picture in the tabloids. I'd like to buy the negative and have it blown up for my office wall, if you can fix that. Did Imogen tell you the media were all over the place? There must have been a tip-off from the police. I want you to chase that up vigorously, Toby. There's been far too much of that kind of thing recently and no one's ever called to account . . .'

'Wolf, for fuck's sake, shut up.'

I stopped talking. Toby was normally the most courteous of men. OK, he'd heard me on one of my favourite hobby horses before, but there was an urgency in his tone that went far beyond mere exasperation. For the first time I started to feel worried.

I said, 'Toby, what's going on? What are the bastards looking for? For God's sake, I may have cut a few corners in my time, but the business is sound, believe me. Does Johnny Nutbrown know about this? I think we ought to give him a call . . .'

Nutbrown was my closest friend and finance director at Woodcutter. He was mathematically eidetic. If Johnny and a computer calculation differed, I'd back Johnny every time.

Toby said, 'Johnny's not going to be any use here. Medler's not Fraud. He's on what used to be called the Vice Squad. Specifically his area is paedophilia. Kiddy porn.'

I laughed in relief. I really did.

I said, 'In that case, the only reason I'm banged up here is because I hit the smarmy bastard. They've had plenty of time to realize they've made a huge booboo, and they're just hoping the media will get tired and go away before I emerge. No chance! I'll have my say if I've got to rent space on TV!'

I stopped talking again, not because of anything Toby said to me but because of the way he was looking at me. Assessingly. That was the word for it. Like a man looking for reassurance and not being convinced he'd found it.

22

He said, 'From what Medler said, they feel they have enough evidence to proceed.'

I shook my head in exasperation.

I said, 'But they'll have squeezed my hard drive dry by now. What's the problem? Some encryptions they haven't been able to break? God, I'm happy to let them in for a quick glance at anything, so long as I'm there . . .'

Toby said, 'He spoke as if they'd found . . . stuff.'

That stopped me in my tracks.

'Stuff?' I echoed. 'You mean kiddy porn? Impossible!'

He just looked at me for a long moment. When he spoke, his voice had taken on its forensic colouring.

'Wolf, I need to be clear so that I know how to proceed. You are assuring me there is nothing of this nature, no images involving paedophilia, to be found on any computer belonging to you?'

I felt a surge of anger but quickly controlled it. A friend wouldn't have needed to ask, but Toby was more than my friend, he was my solicitor, and that was how I had to regard him now, in the same way that he was clearly looking at me purely as a client.

I said, 'Nothing.'

He said, 'OK,' stood up and went to the door.

'So let's go and see what DI Medler has to say,' he said.

So hell begins.

iii

I'll say this for Medler, he didn't mess around.

He showed me some credit-card statements covering the past year, asked me to confirm they were mine. I said that as they had my name and a selection of my addresses on them, I supposed they must be. He asked me to check them more closely. I glanced over them, identified a couple of large items on each – hotel bills, that kind of thing – and said yes, they were definitely mine. He then drew my attention to a series of payments – mainly to an Internet company called InArcadia – and asked me if I could recall what these were for. I said I couldn't offhand, which wasn't surprising as I paid for just about everything in my extremely busy life by one of the vast selection of cards I'd managed to accumulate, but no doubt if I sat down with my secretary we could work out exactly what each and every payment covered.

He shuffled the statements together, put them in a folder, and smiled. His split lip must have hurt but it didn't stop his smile from being as slyly insinuating as ever.

'Don't think we'll need to involve your secretary, Sir Wilfred,' he said. 'We can give your memory a jog by showing you some of the stuff you were paying for.'

Then he opened a laptop resting on the table between us, pressed a key and turned it towards me.

There were stills to start with, then some snatches of video. All involved girls on the cusp of puberty, some displaying themselves provocatively, some being assaulted by men. Years later those images still haunt me.

Thirty seconds was enough. I slammed the laptop lid shut. For a moment I couldn't speak. I looked towards Toby. Our gazes met. Then he looked away.

I said, 'Toby, for God's sake, you don't think . . .'

Then I pulled myself together. Whatever was going off here, getting into a public and recorded row with my solicitor wasn't going to help things.

I said to Medler, 'Why the hell are you showing me this filth?'

He said, 'Because we found it on a computer belonging to you, Sir Wilfred. On a computer protected by your password, in an encrypted program accessed by entering a twenty-five digit code and answering three personal questions. Personal to you, I mean. Also, the images in question, and many more, both still and moving, were acquired from the Internet company InArcadia and paid for with various of your credit cards, details of which you have just confirmed.'

The rest of the interview was brief and farcical. Medler made no effort to be subtle. Perhaps the little bastard disliked me so much

24

he didn't want me to cooperate! He simply fired a fusillade of increasingly offensive questions at me – How long had I been doing this? How deeply involved was I with the people behind InArcadia? Had I ever personally taken part in any of the video sessions? and so on, and so on – never paying the slightest heed to my increasingly vehement denials.

Toby sat there silent as a statue during all this and in the end I forgot my resolve not to have a public row and screamed, 'For fuck's sake, man, say something! What the hell do you think I'm paying you for?'

He didn't reply. I saw him glance at Medler. Maybe I was so wrought up I started imagining things but it seemed to me Toby was looking almost apologetic as if to say, I really don't want to be here doing this, and Medler gave him a little sympathetic smile as if to reply, yes, I can see how tough it must be for you.

I was at the end of my admittedly short tether. It was a toss up whether I took a swing at my lawyer or the cop. If I had to rationalize I'd say it made more sense to opt for the latter on the grounds that my relationship with him was clearly beyond hope whereas I was still going to need Toby.

Whatever, I gave Medler a busted nose to add to his split lip.

And that brought the interview to a close.

iv

My second journey to my cell was handled less courteously than the first.

The two cops who dragged me there then followed me inside were experts. I lay on the floor, racked with pain for a good half hour after the door crashed shut behind them. But when I recovered enough to examine my body, I realized there was precious little visual evidence of police brutality.

I banged at the door till a constable appeared and told me to shut up. I demanded to see Toby. He went away and came back a few minutes later to say that Mr Estover had left the station. I then said I wanted to make the phone call I was entitled to. How entitled I was, I'd no idea. Like most people my knowledge of criminal law was garnered mainly from TV and movies. The cop went away again and nothing happened for what felt like an hour. I was just about to launch another assault on the door when it opened to reveal Medler. His nose was swollen and he had a couple of stitches in his lip. In his hand was a grip that I recognized as mine. He tossed it towards me and said, 'Get yourself dressed, Sir Wilfred.'

I opened the bag to see it contained clothing.

I said, 'Did my wife bring this? Is she here?'

He said, 'No. She's gone to stay with a Mrs Nutbrown at her house, Poynters, is it? Out near Saffron Walden.'

I sat down on the bed. OK, so Johnny Nutbrown's wife, Pippa, was Imogen's best friend, but the notion that she was running for cover without even attempting to contact me filled me with dismay. And disappointment.

It must have showed, for Medler said roughly, as though he hated offering me any consolation, 'She had to go. Your daughter was being taken there. The press would have been sniffing round her school in no time. They're already camped outside your house.'

'Yes, and whose fault is that?' I demanded.

'Yours, I think,' he said shortly.

I didn't argue. What was the point? And if Imo and Ginny needed to seek refuge, there were few better places than Poynters. Johnny had bought the half-timbered Elizabethan mansion a couple of years earlier. It must have cost him a fortune. I recall saying to him at the time, *I'm obviously paying you too much!* He claimed it had once belonged to the Nutbrowns back in the eighteenth century and he'd always known it would come back. The great thing in the present situation was that it was pretty remote and Pippa, who was a bit of a hi-tech nerd, had installed a state-of-the-art security system.

I tipped the clothes he'd brought on to the bed. The jacket trousers and shirt weren't a great match, which meant they hadn't been selected by Imogen. Presumably Medler or one of his minions had flung them together. I ripped off the paper overall.

26

Medler stood watching me.

'Looking for bruises?' I said.

He didn't reply and I turned my back on him. As I pulled on my underpants, there was a brief flash of light. I looked round to see Medler holding a mobile phone.

'Did you just take a photo?' I demanded incredulously.

I got that knowing smirk, then he said, 'That's a nasty scar you've got on your back, Sir Wilfred.'

'So I believe,' I said, controlling my temper again. 'I don't see a lot of it.'

A man doesn't spend much time watching his back. Perhaps he ought to. The scar in question dated from when I was thirteen and running wild in the Cumbrian fells. I slipped on an icy rock on Red Pike and tobogganed three hundred feet down into Mosedale. By the time I came to a halt, my clothing had been ripped to shreds and my spine was clearly visible through the torn flesh on my back. Fortunately my fall was seen and the mountain rescue boys stretchered me out to hospital in a relatively short time.

First assessment of the damage offered little hope I would ever walk again. But gradually as they worked on me over several days, their bulletins grew cautiously more optimistic, till finally, much to their amazement, they declared that, while the damage was serious, I had a fair chance of recovery. Six months later, I was back on the fells with nothing to show for my adventure other than a firm conviction of my personal immortality and a lightning-jag scar from between my shoulder blades to the tip of my coccyx.

Was it legal for Medler to take a photo of my naked body without my permission? I wondered.

Whatever, I was determined not to let him think he had worried me, so I carried on dressing and when I was finished I said, 'Right, now I'd like to phone my wife.'

'First things first. Sergeant, bring Sir Wilfred along to the charge room.'

Things were moving quickly. Too quickly, perhaps. Arrest, questioning, police custody, these were stages a man could come out of with his reputation intact. There were time limits that applied. Eventually that moment so beloved of TV dramatists would arrive when a solicitor says, 'Either charge my client or let him go, Inspector.'

But Medler was pre-empting all that.

Foolishly when I realized I was being charged with assault on a police officer in the execution of his duty, I felt relieved. I took this to mean they were still uncertain about their child pornography case. I'd passed through disbelief and outrage to indignation. Either the cops had made a huge mistake or someone was trying to drop me in the shit. Either way, I felt certain I could get it sorted. After all, wasn't I rich and powerful? I could pay for the best investigators, the best advisors, the best lawyers, and once they got on the case I felt confident that all these obscene allegations would quickly be shown for the nonsense they were.

After the formalities were over, I was about to re-assert my right to call Imogen when Medler took the wind out of my sails by saying, 'Right, Sir Wilfred, let's get you to a phone.'

He took me to a small windowless room containing a chair and a table with a phone on it.

'This is linked to a recorder, I take it?' I said mockingly.

'Why? Are you going to say something you don't want us to hear?' he asked.

He always slipped away from my questions, I realized.

But what did I expect him to say anyway?

I sat down and Medler went out of the door. It took a few seconds for me to recall the Nutbrowns' Essex number. I dialled. After six or seven rings, a woman's voice said cautiously, 'Yes?'

'Pippa? Is that you? It's Wolf.'

She didn't reply but I heard her call, 'Imo, it's him.'

A moment later I heard Imogen's voice saying, 'Wolf, how are you?'

She sounded so unworried, so normal that my spirits lifted several degrees. This was not the least of her many qualities, the ability to provide an area of calm in the midst of turbulence. She was always at the eye of the storm.

I said, 'I'm fine. Don't worry, we'll soon get this nonsense sorted out. How about you? Is Ginny with you? How is she?'

'Yes, she's here. She's fine. We're all fine. Pippa's being marvellous. There've been a couple of calls from the papers. I think that once they realized I'd gone, and Ginny had been taken out of school, they started checking out all possible contacts. They really are most assiduous, aren't they?'

She sounded almost admiring. I was alarmed.

'Jesus! What did Pippa say?'

'She was great. Pretended not to have heard anything about the business, then drove them to distraction by asking them endless silly questions till finally they were glad to ring off.'

'Good. But it means you'll have to keep your heads down in case they send someone to take a look for themselves. I blame that little shit Medler for this, he obviously alerted the press in the first place . . .'

She said, 'Perhaps. But it was Mr Medler who suggested I got Ginny out of school, then helped smuggle me out of the house without the press noticing.'

This got a mixed reaction from me. Naturally I was pleased my family were safe, but I didn't like having to feel grateful to Medler. Still, I comforted myself, it was good to know that Imogen's powers of organization included the police.

I said, 'I'm glad to hear Medler's got a conscience. And if the media turn up mob-handed at Pippa's door, we'll definitely know who to blame, won't we?'

'Yes,' she said. 'We'll know who to blame. Wolf, I need to ring off now. I'm expecting a call. I rang home to let them know what was going on. I didn't want them to start hearing things through the media. I spoke to Daddy but Mummy was out. She's expected back for lunch, so Daddy said he'd get her to ring me then.'

I bet she'll enjoy that! I thought savagely. My mother-in-law, Lady Kira Ulphingstone, had never been my greatest fan, though things improved slightly after the birth of Ginny. I suspect she vowed to herself that her granddaughter wasn't going to make

29

the same ghastly mistake as her mother, and she was clever enough to know that pissing me off all the time might put Ginny outside her sphere of influence. So superficially she thawed a little, but underneath I knew it was the same impenetrable permafrost.

My father-in-law, Sir Leon, on the other hand, though he was a Cumbrian landowner of the old school with political views that erred towards the feudal, had demonstrated the pragmatism of his class by making the best of a bad job. Unlike my own father, Fred. He and Sir Leon had been united in absolute opposition to the marriage, the difference being that Fred's disapproval survived the ceremony. I can't blame Dad. After putting him through the wringer by vanishing for five years with only the most minimal attempt at contact, I'd returned, and while he was still trying to get his head round that, I had once more set my will in opposition to his. Any hope of getting back to our old relationship had died then and things had never been the same between us since. That had been the highest price I paid for my fairy-tale happy ending. For four-teen years I had judged it a price worth paying. I was wrong. And though I didn't know it yet, I was never going to get the chance to tell him so.

I said, 'Well, we can't have Mummy getting the engaged signal, can we? But if the journalists start bothering them up there, do try to stop Leon setting the dogs on them. Listen, you couldn't give Fred a ring, could you? The bastards are likely to have him in their sights too. I'd do it myself soon as I get out of here, but I'm not sure how long that will take.'

'I asked Daddy to make sure Fred knows,' she said.

God, she was efficient, I thought admiringly. Even at moments of crisis, she took care of all the details.

She went on, 'You're expecting to be out . . . when?'

'I don't know exactly, but it can't be long,' I said confidently. 'You know Toby. He's helped get serial killers, billion-dollar fraud-sters and al-Qaeda terrorists off. I'm sure he can sort out my bit of bother.'

I was exaggerating a bit, less about Toby's CV than my confidence in his ability to sort out my problem. I recalled the way he'd looked at me. Perhaps he was just too high powered for something like this.

'Is he there with you now?' said Imogen.

'No, he left after . . . after my interview.'

I hesitated to tell Imogen that I'd assaulted Medler a second time. She'd find out soon enough, but no need to give her extra worry now.

'Then I'll hear from you later,' she said.

'Of course. Listen, don't ring off, I'd like a quick word with Ginny.'

There was a pause then she said, 'I don't think that would be a good idea. She's very bewildered by everything that's happened, naturally. So I gave her a mild sedative and she's having a rest now.'

I said, 'OK. Then give her my love and tell her I'll see her very soon.'

'Of course,' she said. 'Goodbye, Wolf.'

'Bye,' I said. 'I love you.'

But she'd already rung off.

I put the phone down. The fact that Imogen hadn't felt it necessary to refer to the monstrous allegations being made against me should have been a comfort. But somehow I didn't feel comforted.

Medler came into the room a moment later, confirming my suspicion he'd probably been listening in.

I said, 'Look, I need to get Mr Estover back here so that he can speed up whatever rigmarole you people put me through before my release.'

He said, 'We've kept Mr Estover in the picture. He'll be waiting at the court.'

I said, 'The court? Which court?'

He said, 'The magistrate's court. The hearing's in half an hour.'

And again, I was relieved!

Magistrate's court, assault charge, slap on the wrist, hefty fine,

I could be out in a couple of hours organizing my own super-investigation into what the fuck was going on here.

'So what are we hanging about for?' I said. 'Let's go!'

v

When we reached West End Magistrates Court, the media were already there in force.

I looked at Medler and said, 'I expect they were just passing, huh?'

He said wearily, 'You'd better get used to it. You're in the system now and the system is accessible. Wherever you're headed, there'll always be someone ready to make a quick buck by tipping the mob.'

Curiously, this time I believed him.

Inside I was shown into a small windowless room furnished with two chairs and a table. Toby was waiting there. He quickly disabused me of my notion that I'd be in and out in the time it took to sign a cheque.

He said, 'You're being charged with assaulting a police officer in the execution of his duty and occasioning actual bodily harm. The magistrate can deal with this himself or decide it's serious enough to commit you to the Crown Court for a jury trial.'

I said, 'Which is best for me? I mean, which will get me on my way home quickest?'

He regarded me gloomily and said, 'There are problems either way. The magistrate has the power to jail you for six months . . .'

'Six months for hitting a cop?' I interrupted. 'There's people murder their mothers and get less than that, especially when they've got you on a retainer!'

He ignored the flattery and said. 'If on the other hand the beak decides you're a Crown Court job, then the question of bail arises. Medler would certainly oppose it.'

'On what grounds?' I demanded.

'On the grounds that you are being investigated on more serious

32

charges and that, with your wealth and international connections, there's a serious risk you might abscond.'

This incensed me as much as anything I'd heard on this increasingly surreal day.

'Abscond? Why would I? From what, for God's sake? From these ludicrous kiddy-porn allegations? Give me twenty-four hours to have those properly investigated and they'll vanish like snow off a dyke. And how the hell can Medler claim they're more serious anyhow? You said I could get six months for punching his stupid face. That pop singer they sent down for having child abuse images on his computer only got three months, didn't he?'

Toby said, 'There have been developments. I'm far from sure exactly what's going on, but they've raided your offices. Also we're getting word that simultaneous raids are being carried out on your other premises worldwide, domestic and commercial.'

I think that was the moment when I first felt a chill of fear beneath the volcano of anger and indignation that had been simmering inside me since I met Medler coming up my stairs.

I sank heavily on to a chair.

'Toby,' I said, 'what the fuck's going on?'

Before he could answer, the door opened and Medler's face appeared.

'Nearly done, Mr Estover?' he said.

'Give us another minute,' said Toby.

Medler glanced at me. What he saw in my face seemed to please him.

He gave me one of his smug smiles and said, 'OK. One minute.'

It was the smile that provoked me to my next bit of stupidity. To me it seemed to say, Now you're starting to realize we've really got you by the short and curlies!

I said to Toby, 'Give me your mobile.'

He said, 'Why?'

I said, 'For fuck's sake, just give it to me!'

In the *Observer* profile when I got my knighthood, they talked about what they called my in-your-face abrasive manner. When I

33

read the draft, I rang up to request, politely I thought, that this phrase should be modified. After I'd been talking to the feature writer for a few minutes, he said, 'Hang on. Something I'd like you to listen to.' And he played me back a tape of what I'd just been saying.

When it finished, I said, 'Jesus. Print your piece the way it is. And send me a copy of that tape.'

I made a genuine effort to tone down my manner after that, but it wasn't easy. I paid my employees top dollar and I didn't expect to have to repeat anything I said to them. That included solicitors, even if they happened to be friends.

I thrust my hand out towards Toby. It took him a second or two, but in the end he put his mobile into my palm.

I thumbed in 999.

When the operator asked, 'Which service?' I said, 'Police.'

Toby's eyes widened.

When he heard what I said next, it was a wonder they didn't pop right out of their sockets.

'The Supreme Council of the People's Jihad has spoken. There is a bomb in West End Magistrate's Court. In three and a half minutes all the infidel gathered there will be joining their accursed ancestors in the fires of Hell. *Allahu Akbar!*'

Toby's face was grey.

'For God's sake, Wolf, you can't . . .'

'Shut up,' I said, putting the phone in my pocket. 'Now we'll see just how efficient all these new anti-terrorist strategies really are.'

They were pretty good, I have to admit.

Within less than a minute I heard the first sounds of activity outside the door.

Toby said, 'This is madness. We've got to tell them . . .'

I poked him hard in the stomach.

It served a double purpose. It shut him up and when the door opened and Medler said, 'Come on, we've got to get out of here,' I was able to reply, 'Mr Estover's not feeling well. I think we ought to get a doctor.'

34

'Not here, outside!' commanded Medler.

I got one of Toby's arms over my shoulder and began moving him through the door. I looked appealingly at Medler. He didn't look happy, but to give him credit he didn't hesitate. He hooked Toby's other arm over his shoulder and we joined the flood of people pouring down the corridor towards the exit.

To create urgency without causing panic is no easy task and I think the police and court officers did pretty well. But of course the last people to get the message are very aware that there's a large crowd between them and safety, and they want it to move a lot faster than it seems to be doing. Two men dragging a third along between them forms a pretty effective bung and all I had to do as the lobby came in sight was to cease resisting the growing pressure behind me and let myself be swept towards the exit on the tide.

I don't know at what point Medler realized I was no longer with him. I didn't look back but burst out of the building into the sunlight to be confronted by a uniformed constable who shouted at me. For a second I thought my escape was going to be very short lived. Then I realized that what he was shouting was, 'Get away from the building! Run!'

I ran. Everyone was running. I felt a surge of exhilaration. It must feel like this to start a marathon, I thought. All those months of training and now the moment was here to put your fitness to the test.

My marathon lasted about a quarter of a mile, firstly because I was now far enough away from the court for a running man to attract attention and secondly because I was knackered. I still tried to keep reasonably fit but clearly the days when I could roam twenty miles across the Cumbrian fells without breaking sweat were long past.

I was beginning to feel anything but exhilarated. My sense of self-congratulation at getting away was being replaced by serious self-doubt. What did I imagine I was going to do with my freedom? Head up to Poynters to see Imogen and Ginny? That would be the first place Medler would set his dogs to watch. Or was my plan to set about proving my innocence like they do all the time in the movies? I'd need professional help to do that and no legitimate investigator was going to risk his licence aiding and abetting a fugitive. OK, the promise of large sums of money might make one or two of them bend the rules a little, but only if they believed I still had easy access to large sums of money.

And now I came to think about it, I didn't even have access to small sums of money. In fact, I had absolutely nothing in my pockets except for Toby's phone. I was an idiot. I should have made him hand over his wallet as well!

My horizons had shrunk. Without money I wasn't going anywhere I couldn't reach on my own two feet. The obvious places to lay my hands on cash – home in Holland Park, my offices in the City – were out because they were so obvious.

Well, as my Great Aunt Carrie was fond of saying, if the mountain won't come to Mohammed, Mohammed must go to the mountain. Probably saying that would get you stuck on the pointed end of a fatwa nowadays. But Carrie lived all her life in Cumberland where they knew a lot about the intractability of mountains and bugger all about the intractability of Islam.

I took out Toby's phone and rang Johnny Nutbrown on his mobile.

When he answered I said, 'Johnny, it's me. Meet me in twenty minutes at the Black Widow.'

I thought I was being clever when I said that. No reason why anybody should be listening in to Johnny, but even if they were, unless the Met was recruiting Smart Young Things, even less reason for them to know this was how habitués referred to The Victoria pub in Chelsea. Not that I was ever a Smart Young Thing, but Johnny had taken me there once and been greeted as an old chum by the swarming Dysons, i.e. vacuums so empty they don't even contain a bag. I'd committed the place to my memory as somewhere I'd no intention of visiting again.

Circumstances change cases. It's being nimble on your feet that keeps you ahead of the game in business and in life.

I soon realized that I was going to need to be exceedingly nimble on my feet if I was going to make the Widow in twenty minutes. Being chauffeured around in an S-class Merc tends to make you insensitive to distances. Might have done it if I'd started running again but neither my legs nor my need for discretion permitted that. Not that it mattered. Johnny would wait. In fact, come to think of it, he too would be hard pushed to make it through the lunchtime traffic in much under half an hour.

I took thirty-five minutes. As I entered the crowded bar my first thought was that we were going to have to find somewhere a lot quieter to have a chat. I couldn't see Johnny. At six feet seven, he was usually pretty easy to spot, even in a crowd, but I pushed a little further into the room just to make sure.

No sign, but I did notice a man at the bar, not because he was tall, though he was; nor because he had the kind of face that defies you to make it smile, though he did. No, it was just that somehow he looked out of place. That is, he looked like an ordinary guy who'd just dropped in for a quick half in his lunch break. Except that this was the kind of bar that ordinary guys in search of a quick half reversed out of at speed. He was raising a bottle of Pils to his mouth. As he did so his gaze met mine for a moment and registered . . . something. Maybe he'd just realized how much he'd had to pay for the Pils. He drank, lowered his head, and I saw his lips move. Nowadays everyone knows what men speaking into their lapels are doing.

I didn't turn back to the main door. If I'd got it right, the guys he was talking to would be coming in through there pretty quickly. Instead I followed a sign reading Toilets and found myself in a dead-end corridor. I peered into the Gents. Windowless. I pushed open the door of the Ladies. That looked better. A frosted-glass pane about eighteen inches square. There was a bin for the receipt of towels. I stood on it and examined the catch. It didn't look as if it had been opened in years and the frame was firmly painted in place. I stepped down, picked up the bin and hit the glass hard. Cheap stuff, it shattered easily. Behind me I heard a door open. I swung round but it was only a woman coming out of one of the cubicles. I'll say this for the Dysons, they don't do swoons or hysterics.

She said, 'About time they aired this place out.'

I rattled the bin around the frame to dislodge the residual shards, put the bin on the floor once more, stood on it and launched myself through the window. As I did so, I heard another door open and male voices shouting.

I felt my trousers tear, then my leg, so my clear-up technique hadn't been all that successful. I hit the ground awkwardly, doing something to my shoulder. I was dazed but able to see that I was in a narrow alley. One way it ran into a brick wall, the other on to a busy street. I staggered towards the street.

Behind me, voices. Ahead, a crowded pavement. I could vanish into the crowd, I told myself. I glanced back. Two men coming very quick. I commanded my legs to move faster and the old in-your-face-abrasive technique worked.

I erupted on to the pavement at a fair rate of knots, decided that turning left or right would slow me down, so kept on going.

The thing about London buses is you can wait forever when you want one in a hurry, but if you don't want one . . .

I saw it coming, even saw the driver's shocked face, almost saw the number . . .

Then I saw no more.

Elf

'It's . . . interesting,' said Alva Ozigbo cautiously.

Wolf Hadda smiled. It was like a pale ray of winter sunshine momentarily touching a dark mountain. In all the months she'd been treating him, this was only the second time she'd seen his smile, but even this limited observation had hinted at its power to distract attention from the sinister sunglasses and the corrugated scars, inviting you instead to relate to the still charming man beneath.

Charm was perhaps the most potent weapon a pederast could possess.

But it was a weapon Hadda could hardly be conscious of possessing or surely he would have brought it out before now to reinforce his lies?

He said, 'I remember interesting. That's the word they use out there to describe things they don't understand, don't approve of, or don't like, without appearing ignorant, judgmental or lacking in taste.'

She noted the intensity of *out there*.

She said, 'In here I use it to describe things I find interesting.'

They sat and looked at each other across the narrow table for a while. At least she presumed he was looking at her; his wrap-around glasses made it difficult to be certain. She could see herself reflected in the mirrored lenses, a narrow ebon face, its colouring inherited from her Nigerian father, its bone structure from her Swedish mother. Also her hair, straight and pale as bone. Many people assumed it was a wig, worn for effect. She was dressed in black jeans and a white short-sleeved sweater that neither obscured nor drew attention to her breasts. *Don't be provocative in your dress,* the Director had advised her when she started the job. *But no point in over-compensating. If you turned up in a burka, they'd still mentally undress you.*

Did Hadda mentally undress her? she wondered. Up to their last session she'd have judged not. But what had happened then had stayed with her for the whole of the intervening seven days.

It had started in the usual way. She was already seated at her side of the bare wooden table when the door on the secure side of the interview room opened. Prison Officer Lindale, young and compassionate, had smiled and nodded his head at her, then stood aside to let Wilfred Hadda enter.

He limped laboriously into the room and sat down on the basic wooden chair that always seemed too small for him. Her fanciful notion that his rare smile was like wintry sunshine on a mountain probably rose from the sense of mountainous stillness he exuded. A craggy mountain, its face bearing the scars of ancient storms, its brow streaked with the greyish white of old snows.

It was well over a year since their first meeting, and despite her own extensive research that had been added to the file inherited from Joe Ruskin, her predecessor at Parkleigh, she did not feel she knew much more about Hadda. Ruskin's file was in Alva's eyes a simple admission of failure. All his attempts to open a dialogue were simply ignored and in the end the psychiatrist had set down his assessment that in his view the prisoner was depressed but stable, and enforced medication would only be an option if his behaviour changed markedly.

Alva Ozigbo had read the file with growing exasperation. The system it seemed to her had abandoned Hadda to deal with his past himself, and the way he was choosing to do it was to treat his sentence as a kind of hibernation.

The trouble with hibernation was when the bat or the hedgehog or the polar bear woke up, it was itself again.

Hadda, she read, had never admitted any of his crimes, but unlike many prisoners he did not make a thing of protesting his innocence either. According to his prison record, verbal abuse simply bounced off his monumental indifference. Isolation in the Special Unit had meant that there was little opportunity for other prisoners to attack him physically, but on the couple of occasions when, hopefully by accident, the warders let their guard down and an assault had been launched, his response had been so immediate and violent, it was the attackers who ended up in hospital.

But that had been in the early days. For five years until Alva's appointment in January 2015 he had been from the viewpoint of that most traditional of turnkeys, Chief Officer George Proctor, a model prisoner, troubling no one and doing exactly what he was told.

The Chief Officer, a well-fleshed man with a round and rubicund face that gave a deceptive impression of Pickwickian good humour, was by no means devoid of humanity, but in his list of penal priorities it came a long way behind good order and discipline. So when he concluded his verdict on Hadda by saying, 'Can't understand what he's doing in here', Alva was puzzled.

'But he was found guilty of very serious crimes,' she said.

'Yeah, and the bugger should be locked up for ever,' said Proctor. 'But look around you, miss. We got terrorists and subversives and serial killers, the bloody lot. That's what this place is for. Hadda never done any serious harm to no one.'

It was a point Alva would usually have debated fiercely, but she had already wasted too much time beating her fists against Proctor's rock-hard shell of received wisdom and inherited certainties. Also she knew how easy it would be for him to make her job even harder than it was, though in fairness he had never done anything to block or disrupt what he called her *tête-à-têtes*, which he pronounced *tit-a-tits* with a face so blank it defied correction.

After a year in post, she wasn't sure how much good she'd done in relation to the killers and terrorists, but as far as Hadda was concerned, she felt she'd made no impression whatsoever. They brought him along to see her, but he simply refused to talk. After a while she found that her earlier exasperation with what she had judged to be her predecessor's too easy abandonment of his efforts was modifying into a reluctant understanding.

And then one day when she turned up at Parkleigh, the Director had sent for her.

'Terrible news,' he said. 'It's Hadda's daughter. She's dead.'

Alva had studied the man's file so closely she did not need reminding of the facts. The girl, Virginia, had been thirteen when her father was sentenced. She had never visited him in prison. A careful check was kept of prisoners' mail in and out. He had written letters to her c/o his ex-wife in the early days. There had been no known reply and the letters out had ceased though he persevered with birthday and Christmas cards.

Joe Ruskin had recorded that Hadda's reaction to any attempt to bring up the subject of his relationship with his daughter had been to stand up and head for the door. Grief or guilt? the psychiatrist speculated. Hadda's predilection for pubescent girls had led the more prurient tabloids to speculate whether she might have been an object of his abuse, but there had been no suggestion of this either in the police investigation nor in the case for the prosecution. Ruskin had demanded full disclosure of all information relevant to the man's state of mind and crimes, but nowhere had he found anything to indicate that details had been kept secret to protect the child.

Now the Director filled in the details of Ginny's life after her father's downfall.

'Her mother sent her to finish her education abroad, out of the reach of the tabloids. Her grandmother, that's Lady Kira Ulphingstone, has family connections in Paris, and that's where the girl seems to have settled. She was, by all accounts, pretty wild.'

'With her background, why wouldn't she be?' said Alva. 'How did she die?'

'The worst way,' said the Director. 'There was a party in a friend's flat, drugs, sex, the usual. She was found early this morning in an alley behind the apartment block. She'd passed out, choked on her own vomit. Nineteen years old. What a waste! Alva, he's got to be told. It's my job, I know, but I'd like you to be there.'

She'd watched Hadda's face as he heard the news. There'd been no reaction that a camera could have recorded, but she had felt a reaction the way you feel a change of pressure as a plane swoops down to land, and you swallow, and it's gone.

He hadn't been wearing his sunglasses and his monoptic gaze had met hers for a moment. For the first time in their silent encounters, she felt her presence was registered.

Then he had turned his back on them and stood there till the Director nodded at the escorting officer and he opened the door and ushered the prisoner out.

'I've put him on watch,' said the Director. 'It's procedure in such circumstances.'

'Of course,' she said. 'Procedure.'

He looked at her curiously.

'You don't think he's a risk?'

'To himself, you mean? No. But there has to be some sort of reaction.'

There was, but its nature surprised her.

He started talking.

Or at least he started responding to her questions. He was always reactive, never proactive. Only once did he ask a question.

He looked up at the CCTV camera in the interview room and said, 'Can they hear us?'

She replied, 'No. As I told you when we first met, the cameras are on for obvious security reasons, but the sound is switched off. This is a condition of my work here.'

The question had raised hopes that in the weeks that followed were consistently disappointed. He began to talk more but he never said anything that came close to the confessional. References to his daughter were met by the old blankness. She asked why he hadn't

43

applied to go to the funeral. He said he wouldn't see his daughter there but he would see people he didn't want to see. What people? she asked. The people who put me here, he said. But he didn't even assert his innocence with any particular passion. Again the mountain image came into her mind. Climbers talk of conquering mountains. They don't. Sometimes the mountain changes them, but they never change the mountain.

But she persevered and after a few more months of this, there came a session when, as soon as he came into the room, she had felt something different in him. As the door closed behind Prison Officer Lindale, she got a visual clue as to what it was.

Usually when he sat down, he placed his hands palm up on the table, the right one black gloved, the left bare, its life and fate lines deep etched, as though he expected his fortune to be read.

This day his hands were out of sight, as though placed on his knees.

She said, 'Good morning, Mr Hadda. How are you today?'

He said in his customary quiet, level tone, 'Listen, you black bitch, and listen carefully. I have a shiv in my hand. Show any sign of alarm and I'll have one of your eyes out before they can open the door.'

Shock kept her brave. Only once had she been attacked, shortly after she'd started work here. A client (she refused to talk of them as prisoners), a mild-mannered little man who hadn't even come close to the kind of innuendo by which some of the men tried to imply a sexual relationship with her, suddenly lunged across the table, desperate to get his hands on some part of her, *any* part of her. The best he'd managed was to brush her left wrist before the door slid open and a warder gave him a short burst with a taser.

Since then there'd been no trouble. Only Alva knew how frightened she'd been. When Parliament passed the Act a year ago permitting prison officers to carry tasers after the great Pentonville riot of 2014 she had been one of those who protested strongly against it. Now her certainty that if she pushed back her chair and screamed, the taser would be pumping 50kV into Hadda's back long before the shiv could get anywhere near her eyes, gave her the strength to respond calmly, 'What is it you want, Mr Hadda?'

He said, 'What I want is to fuck you till you faint, but we don't have time for that. So I'll have to make do with you kicking your left shoe off, stretching your leg under the table, placing your bare foot against my crotch, and rubbing it up and down till I come.'

The part of her mind not still in shock thought, You poor sad bastard! You're banged up with all the other deviants. Can't you find someone in there to service you?

She was still wondering if she could bring this situation to a conclusion without testing what level of voltage was necessary to subdue a mountain when Hadda smiled – that was the first time – and placed his empty hands palm up on the table and said, 'I think if they were going to come they'd have been here by now, don't you agree?'

It took a second or two to get it. He'd been testing her assurance that the watching officers could not hear what was being said. Her mind was already exploring the implications of this, and she did not realize that her body was shaking in reaction until the door slid open and Officer Lindale said, 'You OK, miss?'

'Yes, thank you,' she said. 'Just got something stuck in my throat.' And subsumed her trembling into a bout of coughing.

He said, 'Like some water, miss?'

She shook her head and said, 'No thanks. I'll be OK.'

When the door was closed again, Hadda said, 'Sorry about my little charade. What you need is a stiff brandy. I suggest we cut this session short so you can go and get one.'

She was still struggling with the after-effects of the shock and now she had to adjust to the new tone of voice in which he was addressing her.

Somehow she managed to keep her own voice level as she replied, 'No, if you're so keen to be sure we're not being listened to, I presume that means you've got something you'd like to say.'

'Not now,' he said. 'What I've got is something for you to read. OK, I'm convinced you're telling the truth when you say there's nobody listening to us. Now I'd like your reassurance that nobody else will read this or anything else I give to you.'

As he spoke, he pulled from his prison blouse a blue school exercise book.

This was a shock different in nature from the threat of a shiv attack but in its way almost as extreme.

With many of her clients, she suggested that if they felt like putting any of their feelings or thoughts down on paper before their next meeting, this could only be to the good. Nobody but herself would see what they wrote, she assured them, an assurance some took advantage of to lay before her in graphic detail their sexual fantasies.

Hadda had simply blanked her out when she first suggested he might like to write something. She'd repeated the suggestion over several weeks, then at last she had given up.

So this came completely out of the blue. It should have felt like a breakthrough, but she didn't have the energy to exult.

She realized Hadda was right. What she wanted to do now was get away to somewhere quiet and have a stiff drink.

She said, 'I promise you. No one will read anything of yours, unless you give permission. All right?'

'It will have to be,' he said, handing her the book.

She took it and held it without attempting to open it.

'And this is . . .?' she said.

'You keep saying you want to understand how I ended up in here. Well, this is the story. First instalment anyway.'

She stood up, glanced at one of the cameras, and said as the door opened, 'I look forward to reading it.'

Then she'd headed straight back to her flat, had the longed-for stiff drink after which, rather to her surprise, she was violently sick.

When she was done, she had a very hot shower. Dried and wrapped in a heavy white bathrobe, she sat at her dressing table and stared back at herself out of the mirror.

Behind her, through the open door into the living room, she could see the exercise book lying on a table where she'd thrown it on entering the flat.

46

Opening it was going to be the first step on a journey that could take her to some very dark places. No darker, she guessed, than many others she'd visited already. But somehow going there in the company of Wilfred Hadda seemed particularly unappealing.

Why was that? she asked herself.

Not because of any horrors that might possibly be revealed. They came with the territory. So it must have something to do with the man they would be revealed about.

This was a measure of his power. This was why she must be on her guard at all times, not against the physical threat which he had used to test her assurance of confidentiality, but against a much more insinuating mental and emotional onslaught.

She recalled her father's words when she told him about the job offer.

'Elf,' he had boomed, 'you sure you're not biting off more than you can chew?'

'Trust me,' she had replied. 'I'm a psychiatrist.'

And they had shared one of those outbursts of helpless laughter that had her mother looking at them in affectionate bewilderment.

But now, alone, in her mind's eye she conjured up an image of the menacing bulk of Parkleigh Prison printed against the eastern sky and shuddered at the thought of driving towards it in the morning.

ii

Parkleigh Prison was built in the 1850s on a marshy greenfield site in Essex just outside London. As if determined that it would be to penology what cathedrals were to religion, its architect incorporated into the design a single massive tower, visible for miles around in that flat landscape, a reassurance to the virtuous and a warning to the sinful.

Rapidly overtaken by the capital's urban sprawl, it continued pretty well unchanged until the 1980s when even the Thatcher hardliners had to accept it was no longer fit for purpose. Closed, it languished as a menacing monument to Victorian values for a decade or more. Everyone expected that eventually the building would be demolished and the site redeveloped for housing, but then it was announced, in the face of considerable but unavailing local protest, that under the Private Finance Initiative, Parkleigh was going to be refurbished as a maximum-security category A private prison.

It would be a prison for all seasons, enthused the developers. Outside dark and forbidding enough to please the floggers and hangers, inside well ahead of the game in its rehabilitatory structures and facilities.

Its clientele was to be category A prisoners, those whom society needed to be certain stayed locked up until they had served out their usually lengthy sentences. In 2010 Wolf Hadda was sent there to popular acclaim. Five years later he was joined by Alva Ozigbo, to far from popular acclaim.

There were two main strikes against her.

As a psychiatrist, she was too young.

And as a woman, she was a woman.

Outwardly Alva treated such objections with the contempt they deserved.

Inwardly she acknowledged that both had some merit.

At twenty-eight she was certainly a rising star, a rise commenced when she'd worked up her PhD thesis on the causes and treatment of deviant behaviour into a book with the catchy title of *Curing Souls*. This attracted attention, mainly complimentary, though the word *precocious* did occur rather frequently in the reviews. But it was a chance meeting that brought her to Parkleigh.

Giles Nevinson, a lawyer friend who hoped by persistence to become more, had invited her to a formal dinner in the Middle Temple. While she had no intention of ever becoming more, she liked Giles. Also, through his job with the Crown Prosecution Service, he was a useful source of free legal advice and information. So she accepted.

Giles spent much of the dinner deep in conversation about the breeding of Persian cats with the rather grand-looking woman on his left. As he explained later, it was ambition rather than ailurophilia that caused him to neglect his guest. The other woman was Isa Toplady, the appropriately named wife of a High Court judge rumoured to be much influenced by his spouse's personal opinions.

Alva, obliged to turn to her right for conversational nourishment, found herself confronted by a slightly built man in his sixties, with wispy blond hair, pale blue eyes, and that expression of rather vapid benevolence with which some painters have attempted to indicate the indifference of saints to the scourges they are being scourged with, arrows they are being pierced with, or flames they are being roasted with.

He introduced himself as John Childs and when he heard her name, he said, 'Ah, yes. *Curing Souls*. A stimulating read.'

Suspecting that, for whatever reason, he might have simply done a little basic pre-prandial homework, she tried him out with a few leading questions and was flattered to discover that not only had he actually read the book but he did indeed seem to have been stimulated by it.

Some explanation of his interest came when he told her that he had a godson, Harry, who was doing A-level psychology and hoping to pursue his studies at university. Childs then set himself to pick Alva's brain about the best way forward for the boy. It is always flattering to be consulted as an expert and it wasn't till well through the dinner that she managed to turn the conversation from herself to her interlocutor.

His own job he described as *a sort of Home Office advisor, I suppose,* a vagueness that from any other nationality Alva would have read as an attempt to conceal unimportance, but which from this kind of Englishman probably meant he was very important indeed.

When they parted he said how much he'd enjoyed her company, and she replied that the feeling was mutual, realizing, slightly to her surprise that this was no more than the truth. He was certainly very good to talk to, meaning, of course, that he was an excellent listener!

Next morning she was surprised but not taken aback when he rang to invite her to take tea with him in Claridge's. Curious as to his motives, and also (she always tried to confront her own motivations honestly) because she'd never before been invited to take tea at Claridge's, she accepted. The hotel lived up to her expectations. Childs couldn't because she had none. They chatted easily, moving from the weather through the ghastliness of politicians to more personal matters. She learned that he came from Norfolk yeoman stock, lived alone in London, and was very fond of his godson, whose parents, alas, had separated. Childs had clearly done all he could to minimize the damage done to the boy. He seemed keen to get her approval for the way he'd responded to the situation, and once again Alva enjoyed the pleasure of being deferred to.

Later she also had a vague feeling with no traceable source that she was being assessed.

But for what? The notion that this might be an early stage of some rather old-fashioned seduction technique occurred and was dismissed.

Then a couple of days later he asked her to lunch at a Soho restaurant she didn't know. When on arrival she found she had to knock to get admittance, the seduction theory suddenly presented itself again. Might this be the kind of place where elderly gentlemen entertained their lights-of-love in small private rooms decorated in high Edwardian kitsch? If so, what might the menu consist of?

She knocked and entered, and didn't know whether to be pleased or disappointed when she was escorted into an airy dining room with very well spaced tables. Any residual suspicions were finally dissipated by the sight of a second man at the table she was led towards.

Childs said, 'Dr Ozigbo, hope you don't mind, I invited Simon Homewood along. Homewood, this is Alva Ozigbo that I was telling you about.'

'Dr Ozigbo,' said the newcomer, reaching out his hand. 'Delighted to meet you.'

Not as delighted as me, she thought as they shook hands. This had to be the Simon Homewood, Director of Parkleigh Prison, whose liberal views on the treatment of prisoners, widely aired when appointed to the job six years earlier, had met with scornful laughter or enthusiastic applause, depending on which paper you read.

Or maybe, she deflated herself as she took her seat, maybe it was *another* Simon Homewood, the Childs family trouble-shooter, come to cast an assessing eye over this weird young woman bumbling old John had taken a fancy to.

One way to settle that.

'How are things at Parkleigh, Mr Homewood?' she enquired.

He smiled broadly and said, 'Depends whether you're looking in or out, I suppose.'

The contrast with Childs couldn't have been stronger. There was nothing that you could call retiring or self-effacing about Homewood. In his late thirties with a square, determined face topped by a thatch of vigorous brown hair, he fixed her with an unblinking and very unmoist gaze as he talked to her. He asked her about her book, prompted her to expatiate on her ideas, outlined some of the problems he was experiencing in the management of long-term prisoners, and invited her opinion.

Am I being interviewed? she asked herself. Unlikely, because if she were, it could only be for one job. Ten days previously, the chief psychiatrist at Parkleigh Prison, Joe Ruskin, had died in a pile-up on the M5. She'd had only a slight acquaintance with the man, so her distress at the news was correspondingly slight and soon displaced by the thought that, if this had happened four or five years later, she might well have applied to fill the vacancy. Parkleigh held many of the most fascinating criminals of the age. For someone with her areas of interest, it was a job to die for.

But at twenty-eight, she was far too young and inexperienced to be a candidate. And they'd want another man anyway. But she enjoyed the conversation, in which Childs took little part, simply sitting, watching, with a faintly proprietorial smile on his lips.

At the end of lunch she excused herself and made for the Ladies.

Away from the two men, her absurdity in even considering the possibility seemed crystal clear.

'Idiot,' she told her reflection in the mirror.

As she returned to the table she saw the two men in deep conversation. It stopped as she sat down.

Then Homewood fixed her with that gaze which probably declared to everyone he spoke to, *You are the most interesting person in the room*, and as if enquiring where she was spending her holidays this year, he said, 'So how would you like to work at Parkleigh, Dr Ozigbo?'

iii

Fortified with a large scotch and water accompanied by a bowl of bacon-flavoured crisps, Alva at last felt up to opening Hadda's exercise book.

She went through the narrative three times, the first time swiftly, to get the feel of it; the second slowly, taking notes; the third intermittently, giving herself plenty of time for reflection and analysis.

She was as disappointed at the end of the third reading as she had been by the first.

The narrative had panache, it was presented with great clarity of detail and emphatic certainty of recollection, it rang true.

All of which meant only one thing: Wilfred Hadda was still in complete denial.

This was not going to be easy, but surely she'd never expected it would be?

She knew from both professional experience and wide study how hard it was to lead some men to the point where they could confront their own crimes. When child abuse was involved, the journey was understandably long and tortuous. At its end was a moment of such self-revulsion that the subconscious decided the cure was worse than the disease and performed gymnastics of Olympic standard to avoid it.

This was why the narrative rang so true. Hadda wasn't trying to

52

deceive her. He'd had years to convince himself he was telling the truth. Plus, of course, so far as the events described were concerned, she knew from her close reading of all the trial and associated media material, he never deviated from the known facts. Only the implied motivation had changed. He was a man of wealth and power, used to getting his own way, and while he clearly had a very sharp mind, he was a man whose physical responses were sometimes so urgent and immediate that reason lagged behind. It wasn't outraged innocence that made him assault Medler but the challenge to his authority. And once he realized that, by doing this, he had provided the police with an excuse for keeping him in custody while they delved into his private business at their leisure, he had made a desperate bid to get within reach of the sources of wealth and influence he felt could protect him.

The important thing was that her relationship with Hadda had advanced to the point where he clearly wanted to get her on his side. She knew she had to proceed very carefully from here on in. To let him see how little credit she gave to his account would almost certainly inhibit him from writing any more. There was still much to be learned even from evasions and downright lies.

As she drove towards Parkleigh next morning, she found herself wondering as she did most mornings why she wasn't feeling a lot happier at the prospect of going to work. Was it cause or effect that, when she met older, more experienced colleagues, particularly those who had been close to her predecessor, Joe Ruskin, she had to bite back words of explanation and apology? What had she to feel sorry for? She hadn't been responsible for the lousy driving that killed him!

As for explanation, she still hadn't explained things satisfactorily to herself. Had she been deliberately sought out or was she just lucky enough to be in the right place at the right time? After the euphoria of being offered the post died down, she'd asked Giles very casually who'd invited John Childs to the dinner. Not casually enough, it seemed. His barrister sensors had detected instantly the thought behind the question and he had teased her unmercifully about her alleged egotism in imagining she might have been head-hunted. Next day he had renewed the attack when he rang to say that Childs had been the guest of the uxorious Mr Justice Toplady, whose cat-loving wife was always on the lookout for elderly bachelors to partner her unmarried sister.

'Though that might be described as the triumph of hope over experience,' he concluded.

'That sounds rather sexist even for a dedicated male chauvinist like yourself,' said Alva.

'Why so? I refer not to the sister's unattractiveness, although it is great, but Childs' predilections.'

'You mean he's gay?'

'Very likely, though in his case he seems to get his kicks out of moulding and mentoring personable young men, then sitting back to watch them prosper in their adult careers. Geoff Toplady was one such, I believe, and he's certainly prospered. Word is that he'll be lording it in the Court of Appeal by Christmas. Oh yes. Hitch your wagon to John Childs and the sky's the limit.'

'Meaning what? That he's buying their silence?'

'Good Lord, what a mind you have! Still, if you spend your time dabbling in dirt, I suppose some of it must stick. No, on the whole Childs' young men seem to be very positively heterosexual types, and the fact that most of them seem perfectly happy to continue the relationship in adult life suggests that he never tried to initiate them into the joys of buggery as boys. A form of sublimation, I expect you'd call it.'

'Giles, if you don't try any analysis, I won't try any cases,' said Alva acidly, stung more than she cared to show by the dabbling-in-dirt crack. 'Would Simon Homewood have been one of his mentored boys?'

'I believe he was. Of course, it could be Childs is going blind and mistook you for a testosteronic young man in need of a helping hand. Whatever, you simply hit lucky, Alva. No subtle conspiracy to take a closer look at you. Even the seating plan at these do's is purely a random thing so you don't get all the nobs clumping together.'

Alva didn't believe the last – nothing lawyers did was ever random – but she more or less accepted that fate alone had been responsible for her advancement. Which, she assured herself, she didn't mind. The world was full of excellent young psychiatrists; far better to be one of the lucky ones!

Still it would have been nice to be headhunted! Or perhaps she meant it would have made her feel more confident that she was the right person in the right job.

She met Chief Officer Proctor as she went through the gate. He greeted her with his usual breezy friendliness, but as always she felt those sharp eyes were probing in search of the weakness that would justify his belief that this wasn't a suitable job for a woman.

She put all these negative thoughts out of her mind as she sat and waited for Hadda to be brought into the interview room.

His face was expressionless as he sat down, placing his hands on the table before him with perhaps a little over emphasis.

Then he let his gaze fall slowly to the exercise book she'd laid before her and said, 'Well?'

And she said, with a brightness that set her own teeth on edge, 'It's very interesting.'

And this led to the brief exchange that ended with them trying to outstare each other.

This was not how she'd planned to control the session.

She said abruptly, 'Tell me about Woodcutter Enterprises.'

Her intention was to distract him by focusing not on his paedophilia, which was her principal concern, but on the fraudulent business activities that had got him the other half of his long sentence.

He looked at her with an expression that suggested he saw through her efforts at dissimulation as easily as she saw through his, but he answered, 'You know what a private equity company is?'

She nodded and he went on, 'That's what Woodcutter was to start with. We identified businesses that needed restructuring because of poor management and organization which often made

55

them vulnerable to take-over as well. When we took charge, we restructured by identifying the healthy profit-making elements and getting rid of the rest. And eventually we'd move on, leaving behind a leaner, healthier, much more viable business.'

'So, a sort of social service?' she said, smiling.

'No need to take the piss,' he said shortly. 'The aim of business is to make profits and that's what Woodcutter did very successfully and completely legitimately.'

She said, 'And you called yourselves Woodcutter Enterprises because you saw your job as pruning away deadwood from potentially healthy business growth?'

He smiled, not the attractive face-lightening smile she had already remarked upon but a teeth-baring grimace that reminded her that his nickname was Wolf.

'That's it, you're right, as usual. And eventually as time went by with some of our more striking successes we retained a long-term interest, so anyone saying we were in for a quick buck then off without a backward glance ought to check the history.'

Interesting, she thought. His indignation at accusation of business malpractice seems at least as fervent as in relation to the sexual charges.

She said, 'I think the relevant government department has done all the checking necessary, don't you?'

For a moment she thought she might have provoked him into another outburst, but he controlled himself and said quietly, 'So where are we now, Dr Ozigbo? I've done what you asked and started putting things down on paper. I've told you how things happened, the way they happened. I thought someone in your job would have an open mind, but it seems to me you've made as many prejudgments as the rest of them!'

The reaction didn't surprise her. The written word gave fantasy a physical existence and, to start with, the act of writing things down nearly always reinforced denial.

'This isn't about me, it's about you,' she said gently. 'I said it was very interesting, and I really meant that. But you said it was just the first instalment. Perhaps we'd better wait till I've had the whole oeuvre before I venture any further comment. How does that sound, Wilfred? May I call you Wilfred? Or do you prefer Wilf? Or Wolf? That was your nickname, wasn't it?'

She had never moved beyond the formality of Mr Hadda. To use any other form of address when she was getting no or very little response would have sounded painfully patronizing. But she needed to do something to mark this small advance in their relationship.

He said, '*Wolf*. Yes, I used to get Wolf. Press made a lot of that, I recall. I was named after my dad. Wilfred. He got Fred. And I got Wilf till . . . But that's old history. Call me what you like. But what about you? I'm tired of saying *Doctor*. Sounds a bit clinical, doesn't it? And you want to be my friend, don't you? So let me see . . . Your name's Alva, isn't it? Where does that come from?'

'It's Swedish. My mother's Swedish. It means *elf* or something.'

The genuine non-lupine smile again. That made three times. It was good he doled it out so sparingly. Forewarned was forearmed.

'Wolf and elf, not a million miles apart,' he said. 'You call me Wolf, I'll call you Elf, OK?'

Elf. This had been her father's pet name for her since childhood. No one else ever used it. She wished she hadn't mentioned the meaning, but thought she'd hidden her reaction till Hadda said, 'Sure you're OK with that? I can call you madam, if you prefer.'

'No, *Elf* will be fine,' she said.

'Great. And elves perform magic, don't they?'

He reached into his tunic and pulled out another exercise book.

'So let's see you perform yours, Elf,' he said, handing it over. 'Here's Instalment Two.'

Wolf

You open your eye.

The light is so dazzling, you close it instantly.

Then you try again, this time very cautiously. The process takes two or three minutes and even then you don't open it fully but squint into the brightness through your lashes.

You are in bed. You have wires and tubes attached to your body, so it must be a hospital bed. Unless you've been kidnapped by aliens.

You close your eye once more to consider whether that is a joke or a serious option.

Surely you ought to know that?

It occurs to you that somehow you are both experiencing this and at the same time observing yourself experiencing it.

Neither the observer nor the experiencer is as yet worried.

You open your eye again.

You're getting used to the brightness. In fact the observer notes that it's nothing more than whatever daylight is managing to enter the room through the slats of a Venetian blind on the single window.

The only sound you can hear is a regular beep.

This is reassuring to both of your entities as they know from the hospital soaps it means you're alive.

Then you hear another sound, a door opening.

58

You close your eye and wait.

Someone enters the room and approaches the bed. Everything goes quiet again. The suspense is too much. You need to take a look.

A nurse is standing by the bedside, writing on a clipboard. Her gaze moves down to your face and registers the open eye. Hers round in surprise.

It is only then that it occurs to you that they usually come in pairs.

You say, 'Where's my other eye?'

At least that's your intention. To the observer and presumably to the nurse what comes out sounds like a rusty hinge on a long unopened door.

She steps back, takes a mobile out of her pocket, presses a button and says, 'Tell Dr Jekyll he's awake.'

Dr Jekyll? That doesn't sound like good news.

You close your eye again. Until you get a full report on the spare situation, it seems wise not to overtax it.

You hear the door open and then the nurse's voice as she assures the newcomer that your eye was open and you'd tried to talk. A somewhat superior male voice says, 'Well, let's see, shall we?'

A Doubting Thomas, you think. Feeling indignant on the nurse's behalf you give him a repeat performance. He responds by producing a pencil torch and shining it straight into your precious eye.

Bastard!

Then he asks, 'Do you know who you are?'

You could have done with notice of this question.

Does it mean he has no idea who you are?

Or is he merely wanting to check on your state of awareness?

You need time to think. Not just about how you should respond tactically, but simply how you should respond.

You are beginning to realize you're far from certain if you know who you are or not.

You check with your split personality.

The observer declares his best bet is that you're someone called Wilfred Hadda, that you've been in an accident, that leading up to the accident you'd been in some kind of trouble, but no need to

59

worry about that just now as it will probably all come back to you eventually.

The experiencer ignores all this intellectual stuff. You're a one-eyed man in a hospital bed, he says, and all that matters is finding out just how much of the rest of you is missing.

You make a few more rusty hinge noises and Dr Jekyll demonstrates that the tens of thousands spent on his training have not been altogether misused by saying, 'Nurse, I think he needs some water.'

He presses a button that raises the top half of the bed up to an angle of forty-five degrees. For a moment the change of viewpoint is vertiginous and you feel like you're about to tumble off the edge of a cliff.

Then your head clears and the nurse puts a beaker of water to your lips.

'Careful,' says Jekyll. 'Not too much.'

Bastard! He's probably one of those mean gits who put optics on spirit bottles so they know exactly how much booze they're giving their dinner guests.

When at last you get enough liquid down your throat to ease your clogged vocal cords, you don't try to speak straight away. First you need a body check.

You try to waggle fingers and toes and feel pleased to get a reaction. But that means nothing. You've read about people still having pain from a limb that was amputated years ago. With a great effort you raise your head to get a one-eyed view of your arms.

First the left. That looks fine. Then the right. Something wrong there. You're sure you used to have more than two fingers. But a man can get by on two fingers. Missing toes would be more problematical.

You say, 'Feet.'

Jekyll looks blank but the nurse catches on quickly.

'He wants to see his feet,' she says.

Jekyll still looks puzzled. Perhaps he had a hangover when they did feet on his course. But the nurse slowly draws back the sheet and reveals your lower body.

The Boy David it isn't, but at least everything seems to be there even if your left leg does look like it's been badly assembled by a sculptor who felt that Giacometti was a bit too profligate with his materials. There's a tube coming out of your cock and someone's been shaving your pubic hair. So far as you can see, your scrotum's still intact.

You try for something a little more complicated than wiggling your toes but an attempt to bend your knees produces nothing more than a slow twitch and you give up.

You say, 'Mirror.'

Nurse and doctor exchange glances over your body.

They're both wearing name tags. The nurse is called Jane Duggan.

The doctor claims to be Jacklin, not Jekyll. A misprint, you decide.

Jekyll shrugs as if to say he doesn't care one way or the other, mirrors are a nurse thing.

Nurse Duggan leaves the room. Jekyll takes your pulse and does a couple of other doctorly things you're too weak to stop him from doing. Then Jane comes back in carrying a small shaving mirror.

She holds it up before your face.

You look into it and observer and experiencer unite in a memory of what you used to look like.

You never were classically handsome; more an out-of-doors, rough-hewn type.

Rough-hewn falls a long way short now. You look as if you've been worked over by a drunken chain-saw operator.

Where your right eye used to be is a hollow you could sink a long putt in.

Out of your left eye something liquid is oozing.

You realize you are starting to cry.

You say, 'Fuck off.'

And to give Nurse Duggan and Dr Jekyll their due, off they fuck.

ii

It turns out you have been in a coma for nearly nine months.

During the next nine you come to regard that as a blessed state.

61

There is some good news. You've slept through another lousy winter.

Your memories are as fragmented as your body. You've little recall of the accident, but someone must have described it in detail for later you know exactly what happened.

It seems you'd been very unlucky.

Normally in the middle of the day Central London traffic proceeds at a crawl. Occasionally, however, there occur sudden pockets of space, stretches of open road extending for as much as a hundred metres. Most drivers respond by standing on the accelerator in their eagerness to reconnect with the back of the crawl.

You'd emerged in the middle of one of these pockets. The bus had lumbered up to close on thirty miles an hour. You were flung through the air diagonally on to the bonnet of an oncoming Range Rover whose superior acceleration had got him up to near sixty. From there you bounced on to a table set on the pavement outside a coffee shop, and from there through the shop's plate-glass window.

By this time your body was in such a mess that it wasn't till they got you into an ambulance that someone noticed there was a coffee spoon sticking out of your right eye.

Both your legs were fractured, the left one in several places. You also broke your left arm, your collarbone, your pelvis and most of your ribs. You suffered severe head trauma and fractured your skull. And you'd left half of your right hand somewhere in the coffee shop, but unfortunately no one handed it in to Lost Property.

As for your internal organs, you get the impression the medics crossed their fingers and hoped.

Not that it can seem to have mattered all that much. Until you opened your eye, the smart prognosis was that sooner or later you'd have to be switched off.

At first you have almost as little concept of the passage of time as in your coma. You exist in a no-man's land between waking and sleeping, and the pain of treatment and the pain of dreams merge indistinguishably. Brief intervals of lucidity are occupied with trying to come to terms with your physical state. You are totally self-centred with your mental faculties so fragmented that information comes in fluorescent flashes, making it impossible to distinguish between memory and nightmare. So you do what non-nerds do when a computer goes on the blink: you switch off and hope it will have put itself right by the time you switch on again.

But though you have no sense of progress, progress there must be for eventually in one of the lucid intervals you find that you're certain you have a wife and family.

But no one comes visiting. Your room is not bedecked with get-well cards, you receive no bouquets of flowers or bottles of bubbly to mark your return to life. *Perhaps the nursing staff are hoarding them,* is your last lucid thought before drifting off into no-man's land once more.

Next time you awake, you have a visitor. Or a vision.

He stands at the end of your bed, a fleshy little man wearing a beach shirt with the kind of pattern you make on the wall after a bad chicken tikka. You think you recognize his sun-reddened face but no name goes with it.

He doesn't speak, just stands there looking at you.

You close your eye for a second. Or a minute. Or longer.

When you open it again, he's gone.

But the space he occupied, in reality or in your mind, retains an after-image.

Or rather an after-impression.

Though still unable to separate memory from nightmare, you've always had a vague sense of some unpleasantness in the circumstances leading up to your accident. But even if real, you don't feel that this is anything to worry about. It's as if a deadline had passed. OK, you regret not being able to meet it, but once it has actually passed, your initial reaction is simply huge relief that you no longer have to worry about it!

But the appearance of Medler destroyed this foolish illusion.

Medler!

There, you remember the name without trying, or perhaps because you didn't try.

And with the name come other definite memories.

Medler, with his sly insinuating manner.

Medler whose mealy-mouth you punched. Twice.

Medler who raided your house, drove your wife and child into hiding, accused you of being a paedophile.

That at least must be sorted out by now, you reckon. Even the slow creaky mills of the Met must have ground the truth out of that ludicrous allegation after all these months.

Nurse Duggan comes in. You ask her how long since you came out of your coma.

She says, 'Nearly a fortnight.'

'A fortnight!' you echo, looking round at the flowerless, cardless room.

She takes your point instantly and smiles sympathetically. She is, you come to realize, a truly kind woman. And she's not alone. OK, a couple of the nurses treat you like dog-shit, but most are thoroughly professional, even compassionate. Good old NHS!

Nurse Duggan now tries to soothe your disappointment with an explanation.

'It's not policy to make a general announcement until they think it's time.'

Meaning until they're sure your resurgence hasn't just been a fleeting visit before you slip back under for ever. But surely your nearest and dearest, Imogen and Ginny, would have been kept informed of every change in your condition? Why weren't they here by your bedside?

You take a drink of water, using your left hand. The two fingers remaining on the right come in useful when words fail you in conversation with Dr Jekyll, but you're a long way from trusting a glass to their tender care.

Your vocal cords seem to be getting back to full flexibility, though your voice now has a sort of permanent hoarseness.

You say, 'Any phone calls for me? Any messages?'

Nurse Duggan says, 'I think you need to talk to Mr McLucky. I'll have a word.'

She leaves the room. Mr McLucky, you assume, is part of the hospital bureaucracy and you settle back for a long wait while he is summoned from his palatial office. But after only a few seconds, the door opens and a tall, lean man in tight jeans and a grey sweat-shirt comes in. About thirty, with a mouthful of nicotine-stained teeth in a long lugubrious face, he doesn't look like your idea of a hospital administrator.

You say, 'Mr McLucky?'

He says, 'Detective Constable McLucky.'

You stare at him. You feel you've seen him before, not like Medler, much more briefly . . . across a crowded room? Later you'll work out this was the out-of-place drinker in the Black Widow who alerted you to the fact that the police were waiting for you.

You say, 'What the hell are you doing here?'

He says, 'My job.'

You say, 'And what is your job, Detective Constable McLucky?'

He says, 'Making sure you don't bugger off again, Sir Wilfred.'

You would have laughed if you knew which muscles to use.

You say, 'You mean you're sitting outside the door, guarding me? How long have you been there?'

'Since you decided to wake,' he says. 'The nurse said you wanted to talk to me.'

He has a rough Glasgow accent and a manner to go with it.

You say, 'I wanted to know if there's been any messages for me. Or any visitors. But I'm not clear why this information should come through you.'

He says, 'Maybe it's something to do with you being in police custody, facing serious charges.'

It comes as a shock to hear confirmed what Medler's visit has made you suspect, that nothing has changed in the time you've spent out of things.

You are wrong there, of course. A hell of a lot of things have changed.

You feel mad but you're not in a position to lose your rag, so you say, 'Messages?'

He shrugs and says, 'Sorry, none.'

That's enough excitement for one day. Or one week. Or whatever period of time it is that elapses before you feel strong enough to make a decision.

You get Nurse Duggan to summon DC McLucky again.

You say, 'I'd like to make a phone call. Several phone calls.'

He purses his lips doubtfully, an expression his friends must find very irritating. You want to respond with some kind of legalistic threat, but a man not yet able to wipe his own arse is not in a position to be threatening. The best you can manage is, 'Go ask DI Medler if you must. That will give him time to make sure all his bugs are working.'

He says laconically, 'Medler? No use asking him. Early retirement back in January. Bad health.'

That confirms what you suspected. You were hallucinating. Funny thing, the subconscious. Can't have been much of an effort for it to have conjured up Imo in all her naked glory, but instead it opted for that little shit.

You squint up at McLucky, difficult as that is with one eye. He still looks real.

You say, 'Please,' resenting sounding so childish. But it does the trick.

McLucky leaves the room. You hear his voice distantly. You presume he is ringing for instructions.

Then a silence so long that you slip back into no-man's land. As you come out of it again, you wouldn't be surprised to find you'd imagined DC McLucky too.

But there he is, sitting at the bedside. Has he been there for a minute or for an hour? Seeing your eye open, he picks up a phone from the floor and places it on the bed.

'Can you manage?' he asks.

'Yes,' you say. It might be a lie.

He goes out of the room.

You pick up the phone with difficulty, then realize you can't recall a single number. Except, thank God, Directory Enquiries.

Asking for your own home number seems a sad admission of failure, so you say, 'Estover, Mast and Turbery. Solicitors in Holborn.'

They get the number and put you through. You give your name and ask for Toby. After a delay a woman's voice says, 'Hello, Sir Wilfred. It's Leila. How can I help you?'

Leila. The name conjures up a picture of a big blonde girl with a lovely bum. Rumour has it that when Toby enters his office in the morning, his mail and Leila are both lying open on his desk. You've always got on well with Leila.

'Hi, Leila,' you say. 'Could you put me through to Toby.'

'I'm sorry, Sir Wilfred, but I can't do that,' she says.

'Why not, for God's sake? Isn't he there?' you say.

'I mean I've consulted Mr Estover and he does not think it would be appropriate to talk with you,' she says, sounding very formal, as if she's quoting verbatim.

'Not appropriate?' You can't raise a bellow yet, but you manage a menacing croak. 'So when did sodding lawyers start thinking it wasn't appropriate to talk to their clients?'

She says, still formal, 'I'm sorry, Sir Wilfred, I assumed it had been made clear to you that you are no longer Mr Estover's client.'

Then her voice changes and she reverts to her usual chatty tone, this time tinged with a certain worrying sympathy.

'In the circumstances, it wouldn't really be appropriate, you must see that.'

You get very close to a bellow now.

'What circumstances, for fuck's sake?'

'Oh hell. Look, I'm sorry,' she says, now sounding really concerned. 'I just assumed you'd know. It shouldn't be me who's telling you this, but the thing is, Toby's acting for your wife in the divorce.'

Elf

i

Now this really *was* interesting, thought Alva Ozigbo.

He'd moved from the first person past to the second person present.

Did this bring him closer or move him further away?

Closer in a sense. The first instalment had been a pretty straight-forward piece of storytelling. The detail he recalled, the emotional colouring he injected, all suggested this was a version of that distant morning frequently rehearsed in his mind. In fact, *rehearsed* was the *mot juste*. Like a dedicated actor, he had immersed himself so deeply in his role of innocent victim that he was actually living the part.

She'd done some serious research since she took over Hadda's case. In fact, when she looked at her records, she was surprised to see just how much research she'd done. She'd turned her eye inwards to seek out the reason for this special interest. Like her analysis of Hadda, that too was still work in progress.

She recalled Simon Homewood's advice when she had started here on that dark January day in 2015. It had surprised her.

'Many of them will tell you they are innocent. Believe them. Carry on believing them as you study their cases. Examine all the evidence against them with an open, even a sceptical mind. You understand what I'm saying?'

'Yes, but I don't understand why you're saying it,' she'd said.

He smiled and said, 'Because that's what I do with every prisoner who comes into my care at Parkleigh. Until I'm absolutely convinced of their guilt, I cannot help them. I want it to be the same for you.'

'And how often have you not been convinced?' she'd asked boldly.

'Twice,' he said. 'One was freed on appeal. The other killed himself before anything could be done. I am determined that will never happen again.'

So she'd gone over the evidence against Hadda in the paedophile case with a fine-tooth comb. And she'd persuaded Giles Nevinson of the prosecutor's office to do the same. 'Tight as a duck's arse,' he'd declared cheerfully. 'And that's water-tight. Why so interested in this fellow?'

'Because he's ... interesting,' was all she could reply. 'Psychologically, I mean.'

Why did she need to add that? How else could she be interested in a man like this, a convicted sexual predator and fraudster with a penchant for violence? It was on record that in his early days at Parkleigh he'd come close enough to 'normal' prisoners for them to attempt physical assault. His crippling leg injury limited his speed of movement, but he retained tremendous upper body strength and he had hospitalized one assailant. Transfer to the Special Wing had put him out of reach of physical attack, and verbal abuse he treated with the same massive indifference as he displayed to all other attempts to make contact with him. In the end a kind of contract was established with the prison management. He made no trouble, he got no trouble.

He also got no treatment. While he wasn't one of those prisoners who staged roof-top demonstrations to protest their innocence or had outside support groups mounting appeals, he never took the smallest step towards acknowledging his guilt. Perhaps it was this sheer intractability that caught her attention.

With the Director's permission, she had visited Hadda's cell at a time he and all the other prisoners were in the dining hall. Even by prison standards it was bare. A reasonable amount of personalization was allowed, but all that Hadda seemed to have done to mark his occupancy was to Blu-Tack to the wall a copy of a painting that looked as if it had been torn out of a colour supplement. It showed a tall upright figure, his right hand resting on a lumberjack's axe, standing under a turbulent sky, looking out over a wide landscape of mountains and lakes. Alva studied it for several minutes.

'Like paintings, do you, miss?' enquired Chief Officer Proctor, who'd escorted her into the cell.

'I like what they tell me about the people who like them,' said Alva. 'And of course the people who paint them.'

If there were a signature on the painting, the reproduction wasn't good enough to show it. She made a note to check and turned her attention to the rest of the cell. Only its emptiness said anything about the personality of its inmate. It was as if Hadda had resolved to leave no trace of his passing. She did find one book, a dog-eared paperback copy of *The Count of Monte-Cristo*. Seeing her looking at it, Proctor said sardonically, 'It's all right, miss. We check regularly under the bed for tunnels.'

Later in the prison library she asked for a record of Hadda's borrowings and found there were none. Years of imprisonment with little but his own thoughts for company. He was either a man of great inner resources or of no inner life whatsoever.

Giles Nevinson during his trawl through the case files on her behalf had come up with an inventory of all the material removed from Hadda's house at the time of the initial raid. It was the books and DVDs confiscated that she was interested in. There was nothing here that the prosecution had been able to use to support their case, but they suggested that, pre-accident, Hadda's taste had been for the kind of story in which a tough, hard-bitten protagonist fought his way through to some kind of rough justice despite the fiendish plots and furious onslaughts of powerful enemies.

This could account for his choosing to present the police raid and its sequel in the form of the opening chapters of a thriller with himself as the much put-upon hero.

But in Alva's estimate the form disguised its true function.

For Hadda this wasn't fiction, it was revelation, it was Holy Writ! If ever any doubts about the rightness of his cause crept into his consciousness, all he had to do was refer back to this ur-text and all became simple and straightforward again.

But he hadn't been able to keep it up when it came to writing about his emergence from the coma. Here the tight narrative control was gone. Even after the passage of so many years, that sense of confusion on waking into a new and alien landscape remained with him. His account of it was immediate, not historical. Hindsight usually allows us to order experience, but here it was still possible to feel him straining to make sense of blurred images, broken lines, shifting foci.

There was some shape. Each of the two sections climaxed at a moment of violent shock. The first, his recognition of physical change; the second, his discovery of his wife's defection. Nowhere in his account of his waking confusion, nor in the aftermath of these systemic shocks, was there the slightest indication that he was moving out of denial towards recognition.

But these were early days. She was pretty certain she now had every scrap of available information about Wolf Hadda, but what did it add up to? Very little. The significant narrative of the mental and emotional journey that had brought him to Parkleigh could only come from within.

Her hope had to be that, by coaxing him to provide it, she might be able to lead him to a moment of self-knowledge when, like a mountain walker confronted by a Brocken Spectre, he would draw back in horror from the monstrous apparition before him, then recognize it as a projection of himself.

She liked that image, and it was particularly apt in Hadda's case. From her study of his background she knew he'd grown up in the Lake District where his father had been head forester on the estate of his father-in-law, Sir Leon Ulphingstone. Lots of fascinating possibilities there. Perhaps the almost idealized figure in the painting on his cell wall was saying something about his relationship with his father. Or perhaps it was there as a reminder to himself of what he had been and what he now was.

With the help of an artistic friend, she'd identified the artist as the American, Winslow Homer. The painting was called *The Woodcutter*. She'd tracked down an image on her computer. It was accompanied by an old catalogue blurb.

In Winslow Homer's painting, the Woodcutter stands looking out on a panorama of mountains and lakes and virgin forest. He is tall and muscular, brimful of youthful confidence that he can see no peak too high to climb, no river too wide to cross, no tree too tall to fell. This land is his to shape, and shape it he will, or die in the attempt.

She could see what the writer meant. And of course Woodcutter had been the name of Hadda's business organization. Significant?

Everything is significant, her tutor used to reiterate. You cannot know too much.

I'm certainly still a long way from knowing too much about you, Wolf Hadda, she thought as she watched him limp slowly into the interview room. She'd wondered in George Proctor's presence if it might not be possible to equip him with a walking stick. The Chief Officer had laughed and said, 'Yeah, and I'll put in a requisition for a supply of shillelaghs and assegais while I'm at it!'

He seemed even slower than usual today. As he settled on to his chair, she looked for signs that he was impatient to discuss the second episode. That would have been indicative; she wasn't sure of what. But there were no signs, which was also indicative, though again she wasn't sure what of.

His face was expressionless, the dark glasses blanking out his good eye. For all she knew, it could be closed and he could be asleep.

She said loudly, 'How do you feel now about your disfigure-ment?'

If she'd thought to startle him by her sudden bluntness, she was disappointed.

He said reflectively, 'Now let me see. Do you mean the Long

John Silver limp, or the Cyclopean stare, or the fact that I'll never play the violin again?'

She nodded and said, 'Thank you,' and made a note on her pad.

'What for? I didn't answer your question.'

'I think you did. By hyperbole in respect of your leg and your eye. Silver was a murderous cutthroat who'd lost his entire leg, and the Cyclops were vile cannibalistic monsters. As for your hand, nothing in your file suggests you ever could play the violin, so that was a dismissive joke.'

'Indicating?'

'That you're really pissed off by being lame and one-eyed, but you've managed to adapt to the finger loss.'

'Maybe that's because I don't get the chance to play much golf in this place. Mind you, I'll be able to cap Sammy Davis Junior's answer when asked what his handicap was.'

'I'm sorry, I'm not into golf.'

'He said, "I'm a black, one-eyed Jew." I'd be able to say, I'm a one-eyed, one-handed, lame, paedophiliac fraudster.'

'And how much of that would be true?'

He frowned and said, 'You don't give up, do you? Eighty per cent at most. The physical stuff is undeniable. As for the fraud, I walked some lines that seemed to get re-drawn after the big crash and I'm willing to accept that maybe I ended up on the wrong side of the new line. But I'm not in word or thought or deed a paedophile.'

She decided to let it alone. Accepting he might have been guilty of fraud had to be some kind of advance, though from her reading of the trial transcripts, the evidence against him here had looked far from conclusive. Perhaps his lawyer had got it right when he tried to argue that the huge publicity surrounding his conviction on the paedophilia charges made it impossible for him to get a fair hearing at the fraud trial. The judge had slapped him down, saying that in his court he would be the arbiter of fairness. But by all accounts Hadda had cut such an unattractive and non-responsive figure in the dock, if they'd accused him of membership of al-Qaeda, too, he'd probably have been convicted.

She knew how the jury felt. He had made no effort to project a positive image of himself. Even after he started talking to her, all she got was a sense of massive indifference. This in itself did not bother her. It was a psychiatrist's job to inspire trust, not affection. But it did puzzle her if only because in jail her clients usually fell into two categories – those who resented and feared her, and those who saw her as a potential ally in their campaigns for parole.

Hadda was different. Though he had by now served enough time to be eligible for parole he had made no application nor shown the slightest interest in doing so.

Not of course that there was much point. A conviction like his made it very hard to persuade the parole board to release you back into the community, particularly when your application was unsupported by any admission of guilt or acceptance of treatment.

But at least he had started writing these narratives. That had to be progress.

And there was something about him today, something only detectable once he'd started talking. An undercurrent of restlessness; or, if that was too strong, at least a sense of strain in his self-control.

She said, 'Wilfred . . . Wilf . . .'

Both versions of his name felt awkward on her lips, smacking of the enforced familiarity of the hospital ward or the nursing home. His expression suggested he was enjoying her problem.

She said, '. . . Wolf.'

He nodded as if she'd done well and said, 'Yes, Elf?'

Her sobriquet came off his tongue easily, almost eagerly, as though she were an old friend whose words he was anxious to hear.

She said, 'How do you feel about Imogen now?'

He frowned as if this wasn't the question he'd been looking for.

'About the fact that she divorced me? Or the fact that she subsequently married my former solicitor and friend, Toby Estover? Wonder how that worked out?'

He spoke casually, almost mockingly. A front, she guessed. And she also guessed he might have a pretty good idea how it had

74

worked out. Modern prisons had come a long way from the Bastille and the Chateau d'If, where a man could linger, forgotten and forgetting, oblivious to the march of history outside. She'd checked on the happy pair, telling herself she had a professional interest. Estover was now, if not a household name, at least a name recognized in many households. He was so sought after he could pick and choose his clients, and the fact that he seemed to pick those involved in cases that attracted maximum publicity could hardly be held against him.

As for the lovely Imogen, she was certainly as lovely as ever. Alva had seen a recent photo of her in the Cumbrian churchyard where her daughter's ashes were being placed in the family tomb. Not an event that drew the world's press, but a local reporter had been there and taken a snap on his mobile. By chance he'd got a combination of light, angle, and background that lent the picture a kind of dark, brooding Brontë-esque quality, and the *Observer* had printed it for its atmospheric impact rather than its news value.

She said, 'I just wondered what you feel when I mention her name?'

'Hate,' he said.

This took her aback.

He said, 'You look surprised. That I should feel it, or that I should say it?'

'Both. It's such an absolute concept . . .'

'It's not a bloody concept!' he interrupted. 'It has nothing to do with intellectual organization. You asked what I felt. What else should I reply? Contempt? Revulsion? Anger? Dismay? A bit of all of those, I suppose. But hate does it, I think. Hate folds them all neatly into a single package.'

'But what has she done to deserve this?' she asked.

'She has believed the lies they told about me,' he said. 'And because she believed them, my lovely daughter is dead.'

All Alva's previous attempts to get him to talk about his daughter had been met with his mountainous blankness, but now for a moment she saw the agony that seethed beneath the rocky surface.

75

She said in her most neutral tone, 'You blame her for Ginny's death?'

He was back in control but within his apparent calm she sensed a tension like that intense stillness of air when an electric storm is close to breaking.

'Maybe,' he said. 'But not so much as I blame her bitch of a mother.'

She noted that, despite the intensity of the negative feelings he'd expressed about Imogen, he was reluctant to lay full responsibility for the girl's death upon her. Whatever bonds there had been between him and his wife must have been unusually strong for this ambiguity of feeling to have survived.

'You hold Lady Kira responsible?'

'Oh yes. Everything tracks back to her. She never wanted me to have her daughter. And now she has helped deprive me of mine.'

'And she did this, how? By helping with the arrangements for her to finish her education in France, out of reach of our prurient press?'

She deliberately let a trace of doubt seep into her voice, hoping to provoke further revelation of what was going on inside his mind, but all she succeeded in doing was bring down the defences even further.

He said indifferently, 'If you'd ever met her, you'd understand.'

This for the moment was a dead end. Leave the mother-in-law, get back to the wife, she told herself.

She said, 'If, as you claim, you are innocent, then someone must have framed you. Do you have any idea who?'

The question seemed to amuse him.

'I have a short list of possibilities, yes.'

'Is Imogen on it?'

The question seemed to surprise him. Or perhaps he simply didn't like it. She really must find a way to get into this key relationship.

'What does it matter?' he demanded. 'Which is worse? That she went along with a plot to frame me? Or that she actually believed I was guilty as charged?'

'Be fair,' said Alva. 'The evidence was overwhelming; the jury took twenty minutes to find you guilty . . .'

'Twelve strangers!' he interrupted. 'Twelve citizens picked off the street! In this world we're unfortunate enough to live in, and especially in this septic isle we live on, where squalid politicians conspire with a squalid press to feed a half-educated and wholly complacent public on a diet of meretricious trivia, I'm sure it would be possible to concoct enough evidence to persuade twelve strangers that Nelson Mandela was a cannibal.'

Wow! she thought as she studied him closely. That rolled off your tongue so easily, it's clearly been picking up momentum in your mind for years!

His voice was still controlled, but his single eye sparkled with passion. What was it he said he felt about his ex-wife's behaviour?

Contempt.

Revulsion.

Anger.

Dismay.

These were all necessary elements of that condition of self-awareness she was trying to draw him to. Perhaps by transferring these emotions away from himself to his ex-wife, he was showing her he was closer than she'd thought. His strained parallel with Mandela was also significant. A man of dignity and probity, imprisoned by a warped regime, and finally released and vindicated after long years to become a symbol of peace and reconciliation. It was as if Hadda's denial could only be sustained by going to the furthermost extreme in search of supportive self-images.

Hopefully, if he continued far enough in that direction, he would eventually come upon himself unawares. And then it would be up to her to direct him away from self-hatred into more positively remedial channels.

Meanwhile it would be good if she could nudge him into a memory of Imogen in her fairy-tale princess phase. It was possible that by reliving that period when she had become the unique and obsessive object of his adoration, he might come to wonder whether it was in fact his idol that had fallen or himself.

Even if that admittedly ideal outcome didn't materialize, this was the part of his life she had least information about, for there were few living sources but himself.

Now the passion had faded and he was looking at her assessingly.

He's got something else for me, she thought. She knew how habit-forming this business of writing about your past could be. In many clients, it went beyond habit into compulsion. So of course since their last meeting he'd carried on writing.

But as what he wrote came closer to the most intimate details of his being, he naturally became less and less sure of sharing it with her.

So, show no eagerness. Do not press.

She said, 'Wolf, time's nearly up. I was wondering, is there anything I can get for you? Books, journals, that sort of thing? I should have asked before. Or something more personal. Something in the food line? Or proper linen handkerchiefs, silk socks, perhaps?'

He shook his head as if impatient at her change of subject, or perhaps at the silly notion that there could be something he might enjoy receiving, and said, 'We were talking about Imo. I got to thinking about her after I wrote that last piece.'

She said, 'Yes?'

He said, 'That stuff about feeling hate, I mean it. Or part of me means it. But there's also a part of me that hates me for feeling it. Does that make sense?'

She nodded and said gravely, 'What wouldn't make sense is for you not to feel it.'

That was the right answer. He pulled another exercise book out of his blouson.

'You might like to see this,' he said.

'Thank you,' she said, taking the book. She opened it and glanced at the first page.

And she knew at once she'd got what she wanted.

Wolf

I was a wild boy, in just about every sense.

My mam, God bless her, died when I was only six. Brain fever, they called it locally. Probably some form of meningitis, spotted too late.

We had my dad's Aunt Carrie living with us. Or rather we were living with her in her farmhouse, Birkstane. Up there in Cumbria they still expect the young to take care of the old. Not that Carrie can have been all that old when we moved in with her. Birkstane was all that remained, plus a couple of small fields, of her husband's farm. Widowed in her mid forties, already in her early fifties she was getting a bit forgetful. Also she had arthritis which gave her mobility problems. Normally up there supportive neighbours would have kept her going quite happily till her dotage, but she was a bit isolated, several miles from Mireton, the nearest village, right on the edge of the Ulphingstone estate.

Dad was her only living relative so when word reached him that there was a social worker snooping around, he knew something had to be done. I was still in nappies at the time, so I can only speculate, but I suspect it suited him to move into Birkstane. As head forester to Sir Leon, Dad had a tied cottage on the estate but as I often heard him say later, only a fool lives in a house another

79

fool can throw him out of any time he likes. Not that he thought Sir Leon was a fool. In fact they got on pretty well, and far from dividing them, my liaison with Leon's daughter only brought them closer together.

They both thought it was a lousy idea.

But that was a long way in the future.

Everything seems to have worked fine to start with. Birkstane was almost as handy for Dad's work as the tied cottage had been. Mam got to work on the old farmhouse and dragged it back from the edge of dereliction, while Carrie, in familiar surroundings with someone constantly present to keep an eye on her, got a new lease of life.

All this I picked up later. Like I say, I was so young that my memory of those early years in Birkstane is generally non-specific, but I know how blissfully happy I must have been, for I recall all too clearly how I felt when they told me Mam was dead. No, not when they told me; I mean when it finally got through to me that being dead meant gone for good, meant I would never ever see her again.

I was in my second year at school. It had taken a whole year for me to come to terms with the daily separation from Mam; this new and permanent separation was a loss beyond all reach of consolation. I was far too young and far too immersed in my own pain to observe what this blow did to my father, but as I have no recollection of him finding the strength to try and comfort me, I'd guess he too was rendered completely helpless by the loss. I suppose if I'd drawn attention to myself, someone might have tried to do something about me, but I think I must have moved in a bubble of grief through which everyone could see and hear me behaving apparently normally – in fact I suspect that many people observed what a blessing it was that I was clearly too young to take it all in and the best thing was for everyone to treat me as if nothing important had happened.

What they didn't realize was that within that bubble I too was as good as dead, and as I slowly came back to life, I think I unconsciously resolved that never again would I be in a position where the loss of any single individual could cause me such pain.

Because there was still a woman in the house, no thought was given to the need to make any special arrangements for me. And because of Carrie's apparent return to her old self during the five years of having us to live with her, nobody doubted that she was a fit guardian and housekeeper.

The reality was very different. Her mobility problems made it hard for her to keep up with a wild young boy, and without my mam's corrective presence, the old memory lapses (the result, it was later diagnosed, of early-onset Alzheimer's) now became much more significant. As for Fred, my dad, he went out to work and rarely came home till it was time for his tea. This is the generic term we gave to the early evening meal. As Carrie got more forgetful, the combinations of food offered to us grew increasingly eccentric, but neither of us took much notice – me because I was too young to make comparisons, Dad because he prefaced the meal with a couple of bottles of strong ale and washed it down with another two before driving down to the Black Dog in Mireton. He success-fully avoided the attention of the local constabulary by driving his old Defender along the forest tracks, which he knew like the back of his hand, and leaving it on the edge of the estate and walking the last quarter mile to the Dog.

Sorry, I've gone on a lot more than I intended about all this early trauma stuff and I know all you really wanted was an account of how me and Imogen got together. But I started off trying to explain the kind of youngster I was, and to understand that, you need to know the rest.

To cut a long story short, because of my instinctive reluctance to get close to anybody and because of the almost total lack of any meaningful supervision at home, I ran wild. Literally. Every free moment I had I spent roaming the countryside. Some streak of natural cunning made me realize the dangers of too much truancy, and I trod a line between being an internal nuisance and an external problem. But I usually turned up late and when I could I bunked off early. As I said, Aunt Carrie was ill-equipped physically or mentally to cope with me. Indeed, as I grew older and wiser, if that's the right word, a combination of self-interest and I hope fondness for the old lady made me cover up for her as best I could.

Of course my behaviour did not go unremarked, but unlike in the towns where suspicion of child neglect prompts people either to look the other way or at best to ring Social Services anonymously, in the countryside they deal with such problems in-house, so to speak. Looking back, I see that I was probably watched over much more carefully than I understood then. The postman was the eyes and ears of the district, the vicar dropped by a couple of times a week, and there was a steady stream of local ladies who found a reason to call on Carrie, and help with a bit of tidying up. Also for some reason I never really understood, everyone, teachers and locals alike, seemed ready to show a remarkable degree of tolerance towards my aberrant behaviour.

Maybe I'd have turned out better if someone had been ready to skelp my ear a bit more frequently!

Sir Leon was another one who missed the chance to sort me out. I remember when I was eight or nine I got caught by his gamekeeper. I was never a serious poacher, though if the odd trout or rabbit came my way, I regarded it as the peasant's tithe. The day I got caught peering into Sir Leon's newly stocked tarn, it was the fact that I had no criminal intent that made me vulnerable. I was stretched out on the bank, raptly viewing the tiny fry at their play, when a heavy hand landed on my shoulder and I was hauled upright by Sir Leon's head keeper.

When he realized who he'd got, he threw me into his pick-up and drove me through the forest to where my father was supervising a gang of loggers. Sir Leon was there too, and after the situation had been explained, he stared down at me and said, 'This your brat then, Fred? What's your name, boy?'

'Wilf,' I blurted.

'Wilf?'

Then he squatted down beside me, ran his fingers through my hair, opened my mouth and peered in like he was checking out a horse, then winked at me and said, 'Sure you don't mean Wolf?

Looks to me like you've been suckled by wolves. That might explain things! Suckled by wolves, and here's me thinking they were all dead.'

He stood up, laughing at his own joke, and everyone else laughed, except me and Dad.

Thereafter every time Sir Leon saw me he called me Wolf and gradually the name stuck. I rather like the notion of being suckled by wolves, maybe because Sir Leon with his long nose and great mane of grey-brown hair looked like he might have a bit of wolf in him too. His name, Ulphingstone, certainly did.

Dad, however, hadn't cared to be shown up in front of his workers and his boss. That night he stayed home and paid me more attention than I think he had since Mam died, and he didn't much like what he saw. When I responded surlily to his remonstrations, he skelped me round the left ear, and when I responded angrily to that, he skelped me round the right.

After that I was obliged to mend my ways for a while, but as well as developing a taste for the wild life, I was already well grounded in the art of deception, and I continued on my independent way pretty much as before, only taking a little more care.

I suppose I was a bit of a loner, but that was through choice. At junior school I never had any problem getting on with the other boys; in fact most of them seemed keen to be friends with me, but I always felt myself apart from them. Maybe it was because I didn't give a toss about who was going to win the Premier League, maybe it was something deeper than that. A lot of the girls were keen to be friendly too, but I reckoned they were a waste of space. At least with the boys you could run around and jump on top of each other and have a bit of a wrestle. It was a long time before I realized you could do that with girls too.

Then came secondary school. There was the usual bullying, but I've always had a short fuse. Neither size nor number made any difference – if you messed with me, I lived up to my name and reacted like a wild beast, wading in with fists, feet, teeth, and head till someone lay bleeding on the schoolyard floor. Eventually the physical bullying stopped, but there were still scores to settle. One day, aged about twelve, I found someone had broken into my locker and sprayed car paint all over the stuff I kept there. I had a good idea who it was. Next morning I smuggled in the cut-down lumber axe my dad was teaching me to use and I demolished my chief suspect's locker and everything in it. All the kids thought I'd be expelled or at least excluded for that, but the Head just settled for giving me a long lecture and getting Dad to pay for the damage.

I didn't get a lecture from Fred, but an ear-ringing slap which he made clear wasn't for damaging the other boy's gear but for ruining a perfectly good axe!

After that, helped by the fact that I got bigger and stronger every month, I was left strictly alone by the would-be bullies. I wasn't thick, I did enough work to keep my head above water, and for some reason the teachers cut me a lot of slack. I never sucked up to any of them but most of them seemed to like me and I suspect I got away with stuff another kid might have been pulled up for. I never made any particular friends because the kind of thing I liked to do away from school, I liked to do alone. But I was always one of the first to get picked when my class was split up for school-yard games.

The only significant contacts I made was age thirteen when I had my accident. You must have heard about my accident, Elf, the one that left me with the scars on my back that the bastards at my trial tried to claim established I was in those filthy videos. It was a real accident, not carelessness or anything on my part. A boulder that had been firmly anchored for a couple of thousand years decided to give way the same moment I put my weight on it. I fell off on to a sheet of ice and went bouncing and slithering down the fellside for a couple of hundred feet, and when the mountain rescue team reached me, they reckoned I was a goner. Didn't I mention this in one of my other scribblings? I think I did, so you'll know that fortunately there was no permanent damage and a few months later I was back on the fells with nothing worse than a heavily scarred back.

But what the experience did do was let me see close-up what a

84

great bunch of guys the mountain rescue team was. They were really good to me. I was too young to join officially, but none of them objected when I started hanging out with them, and a couple of them really took me under their wing and taught me all about proper climbing.

Mind you, I did sometimes have a quiet laugh when they roped me up to do some relatively easy ascent that I'd been scampering up like a monkey all by myself for years, but I was learning sense and kept my gob shut.

Now at last we're getting to Imogen.

I was fifteen when I first saw her, she was – is – a year younger.

I knew Sir Leon had a daughter and I daresay I'd glimpsed her before, but this was the first time I really noticed her.

Like I said, after that first encounter with Sir Leon, whenever our paths crossed he greeted me as Wolf and always asked very seriously how the rest of the pack was getting on. I'd grunt some response, the way boys do. Once when Dad told me to speak proper, Sir Leon said, 'No need for that, Fred. The boy's talking wolf and I understand him perfectly,' then he grunted something back at me, and smiled so broadly I had to smile back as if I'd understood him. After that he always greeted me with a grunt and a grin.

There was of course no socialization between us peasants and the castle, not even in the old feudal sense: no Christmas parties for the estate staff, no village fêtes in the castle grounds, nothing like that. Sir Leon was a good and fair employer, but his wife, Lady Kira, my dear ma-in-law, called the shots at home.

Scion of a White Russian émigré family, Kira was more tsarist than her ancestors in her social attitudes. She believed servants were serfs, and anything that encouraged familiarity diminished efficiency. For her the term servant covered everyone in the locality. In her eyes we all belonged to the same sub-class, related by frequently incestuous intermarriage, and united in a determination to cheat, rob and, if the opportunity rose, rape our superiors.

I don't think anyone actually doffed their cap and tugged their forelock as she passed, but she made you feel you ought to.

So when Sir Leon suggested to my dad I might like to come up to the castle one summer day to 'play with the young 'uns' as he put it, we were both flabbergasted.

It turned out they had some house guests who between them had five daughters and one son, a boy of my own age, and Sir Leon felt he needed some male company to prevent his spirit being crushed by the 'monstrous regiment' (Sir Leon's phrase again).

I didn't want to go, but Dad dug his heels in and said that it was time I learnt some manners and Sir Leon had always been good to me and if for once I didn't do what he wanted, he'd make bloody sure I didn't do what I wanted for the rest of the summer holidays and lots of stuff like that, so one bright sunny afternoon I clambered over the boundary wall behind Birkstane and walked through the forest to the castle.

As castles go, it's not much to write home about, no battlements or towers, not even a moat. It had been a proper castle once, way back in the Middle Ages, I think, but somewhere along the line it got bashed about a bit, whether by cannon balls or just general neglect and decay I don't know, and when the family started rebuilding, they downsized and what they ended up with was a big house.

But that's adult me talking. As I emerged from the trees that day, the building loomed ahead as formidable and as huge as Windsor!

Everyone was scattered around the lawn in front of the house. With each step I took, it became more apparent that the Sunday-best outfit that Dad had forced me to wear was entirely the wrong choice. Shorts, jeans, T-shirts abounded, not a hot tweed suit in sight. I almost turned and ran away, but Sir Leon had spotted me and advanced to meet me.

'Uggh grrr,' he said in his pretended wolf-speak. 'Wolf, my boy, so glad you could make it. You look like you could do with a nice cold lemonade. And why don't you take your jacket and tie off – bit too hot for them on a day like this.'

Thus he managed to get me looking slightly less ridiculous by the time he introduced me to the 'kids'.

The girls, ranging from eleven to fifteen, more or less ignored me. The boy, stretched out on the grass apparently asleep, rolled over as Sir Leon prodded him with his foot, raised himself on one elbow, and smiled at me.

'Johnny,' said Leon, 'this is Wolf Hadda. Wolf, this is Johnny Nutbrown. Johnny, why don't you get Wolf a glass of lemonade?'

Then he left us.

Johnny said, 'Is your name really Wolf?'

'No. Wilf,' I said. 'Sir Leon calls me Wolf.'

'Then that's what I'll call you, if that's all right,' he said with a smile.

Then he went and got me a lemonade.

I got no real impression of Johnny from that first encounter. The way he looked, and moved, and talked, he might have been a creature from another planet. As for him, I think even then he was as unperturbed by everything, present, past or future, as I was to find him in later life. He took the arrival of this inarticulate peasant in his stride. I think he was totally unaware that I'd been brought along to keep him company. I can't believe that being the sole boy among all those girls had troubled him for a moment. That was Sir Leon imagining how he might have felt in the same circumstances.

A tall woman, slim and athletic with a lovely figure and a face whose features were almost too perfect to be beautiful came and looked at me for a second or two with ice-cold eyes, then moved away. That was Lady Kira. The ice-cold look and the accompanying silence set the pattern for most of our future encounters.

I've little recollection of any of the other adults. As for the girls, they were just a blur of bright colours and shrill noises. Except for Imogen. Not that I knew it was Sir Leon's daughter to start with. She was just part of the blur until they started dancing.

Most of the adults had moved off somewhere. Johnny, after two or three attempts at conversation, had given up on me and gone back to sleep. The girls had got hold of a radio or it might have been a portable cassette player, I don't know. Anyway it was beating out the pop songs of the time and they started dancing. Disco dancing, I suppose it was – it could have been classical ballet for all it meant to me – the music scene, as they term it, was an area of teenage life that entirely passed me by.

But presently as they went through their weird gyrations, one figure began to stand out from the half-dozen, not because she was particularly shapely or anything – in fact she was the skinniest of the lot – but because while the others were very aware of this as a competitive group activity, she was totally absorbed in the music. You got the feeling she would have been doing this if she'd been completely alone in the middle of a desert.

The difference eventually made itself felt even among her fellow dancers, and one by one they slowed down and stopped, till only this single figure still moved, rhythmically, sinuously, as though in perfect harmony not only with the music but with the grass beneath her feet and the blue sky above, and the gently shimmering trees of the distant woodland that formed the backdrop from my viewpoint. Unlike the others, she was wearing a white summer dress of some flimsy material that floated around her as she danced, and her long golden hair wreathed about her head like a halo of sunbeams.

I was entranced, in the strictest sense of the word; drawn into her trance; totally absorbed. I didn't know what it meant, only that it meant something hugely significant to me. I didn't want it to stop. I wanted to sit here and watch this small and still totally anonymous figure dancing forever.

Then Johnny who, unseen by me, had woken and sat up, said, 'Oh God, there goes Imo again. Turn on the music and it sets her off like a monkey on a stick!'

His tone was totally non-malicious, but that didn't save him.

I punched him on the nose. I didn't even think about it. I just punched him.

Blood fountained out; one of the remaining adults – maybe it was Johnny's mother – had been looking our way, and she screamed. Johnny sat there, stock-still, staring down at his cupped hand as it filled with blood.

I just wanted to be as far away from all this as I could get.

Again without thought, I found myself on my feet and heading as fast as I could run towards the welcome shelter of the distant woodland.

My shortest line took me past Imogen. She had stopped dancing and her eyes tracked me towards her and past her and I imagined I could feel them on me still as I covered the couple of hundred yards or so to the sanctuary of the trees.

That is my first memory of Imogen. I think even then, uncouth and untutored though I was, I knew I was hers and she was mine forever.

Just shows how wrong you can be, eh, Elf?

ii

I've just read over what I've written.

It strikes me this is just the kind of stuff you want, Elf. Childhood trauma, all that crap.

Except maybe I haven't made it clear: I *enjoyed* my childhood. It was a magical time. Do you read poetry? I don't. Rhyme or reason, isn't that what they say? Well, I'm a reason man. At school I learnt some stuff by rote to keep the teachers happy but I also learnt the trick of instant deletion the minute I'd spouted it. The only bit that's stuck doesn't come from my schooldays but from my daughter, Ginny's.

It was some time in that last summer, '08 I mean, it was raining most of the time I recall, perhaps that's why Ginny got stuck into her holiday assignments early.

At her posh school, they reckoned poetry was important, and one of the things she had to do was write a paraphrase of some lines of Wordsworth. She assumed because I was a Cumbrian lad, I'd know all about him. A father doesn't like to disappoint his daughter, so I glanced at the passage. A lot of the language was daft and he went all round the houses to say something, but to my amazement I found myself thinking, this bugger's writing about me!

He was talking about himself as a kid, the things he got up to, climbing steep cliffs, moonlight poaching, going out on the lake, but the lines that stuck were the ones that summed it all up for him.

Fair seed-time had my soul and I grew up
Fostered alike by beauty and by fear.

That was me. I don't mean fear of being clouted or abused, anything like that. I mean the kind of fear you feel when you're hanging over a hundred-foot drop by your fingernails or when the night's so black you can't see your hand in front of your face and you hear something snuffling in the dark, the fear that makes your sense of being alive so much sharper, that lets you feel the life-blood pounding through your heart, that makes you want to dance and shout when you beat it and survive!

Do you know what I'm talking about, Elf? Or are you stuck in all that Freudian clart, where everything's to do with sex, even if you're dealing with kids before they know what sex is all about?

Me, I was never much interested in sex, not even after my balls dropped. Maybe I was leading such a physical life, I was just too knackered. Of course my cock stood up from time to time and I'd give it a pull and I enjoyed the spasm of pleasure that eventually ensued. But I didn't have much time for the dirty jokes and mucky books and boasting about what they'd done with girls that most of my schoolmates went in for.

Not that I didn't have the chance to learn on the job, so to speak. Despite me ignoring them as much as I could, most of the girls seemed more than willing to be friendly, but I couldn't see any point in wasting time with them that I could have spent scrambling up a wet rock face!

So what you'd likely call significant sexual experience didn't come my way until . . . well, let me tell you about it.

Or rather, let me tell myself. I'm not at all sure I shall ever let you see this, Elf, which means I can be completely frank as I'm reserving the right to tear it all to pieces, if that's what I decide.

90

So let's go back to me taking off into the woods, leaving Imogen staring after me, Johnny Nutbrown bleeding from the nose, his parents puce with indignation, Sir Leon hugely disappointed and Lady Kira flaring her nostrils in her favourite *what-did-you-expect* expression.

Of course I'm just guessing at most of that, apart from Johnny's nose. What I'm certain I left behind was the jacket and tie I'd taken off at Sir Leon's suggestion.

He came round to Birkstane with them that evening.

I was in my bedroom. Naturally I'd said nothing about the events of the day to either Dad or Aunt Carrie, just muttered something in reply to their question as to whether I'd had a good time.

I heard the car pull up outside and when I looked out and recognized Sir Leon's Range Rover, I thought of climbing out of the window and doing a bunk.

Then I saw there was still someone in the car after Sir Leon had climbed out of the driver's seat.

It was Imogen, her pale face pressed against the window, staring up at me.

For a moment our gazes locked. I don't know what my face showed but hers showed nothing.

Then Dad roared, 'Wilf! Get yourself down here!'

The time for flight was past. I went down and met my fate.

It wasn't as bad as I'd feared. Sir Leon was very laid back about things. He said boys always fight, it's in their genes, and he was sure my blow had been more in sport than in earnest, and Johnny's nose wasn't broken, and he was sure a little note of apology would set all things well.

Dad stood over me while I wrote it.

Dear Johnny, I'm really sorry I made your nose bleed, I didn't mean to, it was an accident. Yours sincerely Wilfred Hadda.

Dad also wanted me to write to Lady Kira, but Sir Leon said that wouldn't be necessary, he'd pass on my verbal apologies.

As he left, he punched me lightly on the arm and said, 'Us wolves need to pick our moments to growl, eh?'

91

I expected Dad to really whale into me after Sir Leon had gone, but he just looked at me and said, 'So that's a lesson to us both, lad, one I thought I'd learned a long time back. My fault. Folks like us and folks like the Ulphingstones don't mix.'

'Because they're better than us?' I asked.

'Nay!' he said sharply. 'The Haddas are as good as any bugger. But if you put banties in with turtle doves, you're going to get ructions!'

And that was it. He obviously felt in part responsible. Me, I suppose I should have been delighted to get off so lightly, but as I lay in bed that night, all I could think of was Imogen, and why she'd accompanied her father to Birkstane.

I found out the next day. She wanted to be sure she knew how to get there by herself. I left the house as usual straight after break-fast, i.e. about seven a.m. Dad got up at six and so did Aunt Carrie. Breakfast was the one meal of the day she could be relied on for, so long as you were happy to have porridge followed by scrambled egg, sausage and black pudding all the year round. If I decided to have a lie-in, the penalty was I had to make my own, so usually I got up.

It was a beautiful late July morning. The sun had been up for a good hour and a half and the morning mists were being sucked up the wooded fellside behind the house, clinging on to the tall pines like the last gauzy garments of a teasing stripper.

I hadn't any definite plan, it might well turn into a pleasant pottering-about, basking kind of day with a dip in the lake at the end of it, but in case I got the urge to do a bit of serious scram-bling, I looped a shortish length of rope over my rucksack and clipped a couple of karabiners and slings to my belt.

I hadn't gone a hundred yards before Imogen stepped out from behind a tree and blocked my path.

I didn't know what to say so said nothing.

She was wearing a T-shirt, shorts and trainers. On her back was a small pack, on her head a huge sunhat that shaded her face so I could not see her expression.

She said, 'Johnny says you punched him 'cos he was rude about my dancing. He said if I saw you to tell you he's OK and it was a jolly good punch.'

I remember feeling surprise. In Nutbrown's shoes I don't think I'd have been anywhere near as gracious. In fact I know bloody well I wouldn't!

I said, 'Is that what you've come to tell us? Grand. Then I'll be off.'

I pushed by her rudely and strode away. I thought I'd left her standing but after a moment I heard her voice behind me saying, 'So where are we going?'

I spun round to face her and snapped, 'I'm going climbing. Don't know where you're going. Don't care either.'

In case you're wondering, Elf, how come I was talking like this to the same girl I'd fallen for so utterly and irreversibly just the day before, you should recall I was a fifteen-year-old lad, uncouth as they came, with even fewer communication skills than most of the breed because there were so very few people I wanted to communicate with.

Also, let's be honest, standing still in shorts and trainers with her golden hair hidden beneath that stupid hat, it was hard to believe this was the visionary creature I'd seen dancing on the lawn.

My mind was in a whirl so I set off again because that seemed the only alternative to standing there, looking at her.

She fell into step beside me when the terrain permitted, a yard behind me when it didn't. I set a cracking pace, a lot faster than I would have done if I'd been by myself, but it didn't seem to trouble her. When I got to the lake, that's Wastwater, I deliberately headed along the path on the south-east side, the one at the foot of what they call the Screes, a thousand feet or so of steep, unstable rock that only an idiot would mess with. Even the so-called path that tracks the lake's edge is a penance, involving a tedious mile or so of scrambling across awkwardly placed boulders. I thought that would soon shake her off, but she was still there at the far end. So now I crossed the valley and went up by the inn at Wasdale Head into Mosedale, not stopping until I reached Black Sail Pass between Kirk Fell and Pillar.

This was a good six miles over some pretty rough ground and she was still with me, no more out of breath than I was. Now I found I had a dilemma. The further I went, particularly if as usual I wandered off the main well-trodden paths, the more I'd be stuck with her. But she could easily retrace the path we'd come by back to the valley road, and on a day like this, there would be plenty of walkers tracking across Black Sail, so I felt I could dump her here without too much trouble to my conscience.

I sat down and took a drink from the bottle of water I carried in my sack. She produced a can of cola and drank from that.

I said, 'That's stupid.'

'Why's that?' she said, not sounding offended but genuinely interested.

'Because you can't seal it up again like a bottle. You've got to drink the lot.'

'So I'll drink the lot.'

'What happens when you get thirsty again?'

'I'll open another one,' she said, grinning and shaking her rucksack till I could hear several cans rattling against each other. 'Like a drink?'

She offered me the can. I shook my head. I wouldn't have minded, but drinking out of a can that had touched her mouth seemed a bit too intimate when I was planning to dump her.

I said, 'Won't your mam and dad be worrying about you?'

She said, 'No. They think I'm out walking up Greendale with Jules and Pippa.'

These it emerged were two of the other girls I'd seen the previous day. Imogen had proposed they all went out walking today, but when she revealed her plan involved getting up really early, two of them had dropped out. It said much for her powers of persuasion that she'd persuaded the other two to go along with her. It said even more that she'd got them to agree to cover up for her when she announced she was taking off on her own the moment they were out of sight of the castle.

'I've arranged to meet them at five,' she said, 'so that gives us plenty of time.'

'To do what?' I was foolish enough to ask.

'Whatever you're going to do,' she said expectantly. 'Sounds like it could be fun. A lot better than anything that was likely to happen with Jules and Pippa.'

It turned out she'd made enquiries about me, of Sir Leon and also of some of the locals who worked at the castle.

From them she'd learned that I spent most of my spare time roaming the countryside, 'getting up to God knows what kind of mischief'. She heard the story of my accident, my miraculous survival, and my subsequent exploits with some of the mountain rescue team. She'd also learned that I was usually up with the lark, so when she resolved to tag along with me, she knew she had to contrive an early start.

The trouble was, in letting her explain all this to me, I had taken a significant step towards the role of fellow conspirator. If I tried to dump her, I could now see that she was quite capable of following at a distance. I could have tried to take her back to the castle, but I had no way to compel her. And one thing I knew for certain, if ever it became known that she hadn't spent the day with her friends, no way would my pleas of complete innocence cut any ice with Lady Kira.

So I was stuck with her. The best plan looked to be to keep her occupied a couple of hours and above all make sure that she kept her rendezvous with the other two girls.

'Right,' I said. 'Time to move.'

We stood up. I noticed she just left her Coke can lying on the ground. I gave it a kick. She looked down at it, looked up at me, thought for a moment, then grinned and picked it up and stuffed it into her sack.

Daft, but somehow that acknowledgement that I was the boss

gave me a thrill, so rather than simply lead her up the main track on to Pillar, I decided to take her round by the High Level route that winds above Ennerdale and eventually leads to the summit by a steep scramble at the back of Pillar Rock.

It was a bad mistake. It turned out she'd heard of Pillar Rock because a friend's brother had had a fall there in the spring and broken both his legs.

'Yeah,' I said. 'I remember. I know a couple of the guys who brought him down. They said him and his mates were real wankers, didn't know what they were doing.'

'My friend said her brother had been climbing in the Alps,' she protested.

'Oh yeah? Can't have been all that good if he managed to come off the Slab and Notch,' I declared, annoyed that my mountain rescue friends' verdict should be called in doubt. 'It's nowt but a scramble. Don't even need a rope.'

This was laying it on a bit thick. OK, in terms of climbing difficulty, this most popular route up the Rock really is classed as a Grade-3 scramble. But it's got tremendous exposure. If you come off, you fall a long way. Only real climbers, or real idiots, go up there without a rope. The guy they brought down in the spring was lucky to get away with nothing worse than a couple of smashed legs.

She said, 'You've been up it then?'

'Couple of times.'

'By yourself?'

'Yeah.'

It was true. The first time I'd been ten and back then I suppose I was a real idiot. I was like a spider, scuttling up rock faces that give me vertigo now just thinking about them. How the hell I never got cragfast, I don't know.

I'd got a bit more sense since my close encounter with the mountain rescue, but I still liked climbing by myself. The second time I went up Pillar Rock had been the previous spring. After I heard my mountain rescue friends talking about the accident, some ghoulish subconscious impulse took me back there. I remember pausing in the Notch and looking down and picturing the guy tumbling through the air. I wondered what it must feel like. All I had to do to find out was let go.

Don't worry, it wasn't a serious thought. If I was going to fall, it would be off something that would impress my rescue mates! But dismissing the Slab and Notch as a 'mere' scramble now got me into more bother.

'Let's go up there then,' she said.

'With you? No way!'

'Why not? You just said it was dead easy.'

'Yeah, but not for someone like you.'

'What do you mean, like me? We do climbing at my school. I've been on the wall at the sports centre.'

This was true, though, as I learned later, Imogen's desire to take up rock climbing seriously had provoked a loud and unified negative from her parents, and the school had been instructed to make sure she didn't get near the wall again.

Well, her parents might have got their way, but with me it was no contest.

In my defence, she did make it clear that she was going to have a go with or without me, and by going along with her at least I could make sure she was on the end of my rope.

And to tell the truth, this readiness of hers to go spidering up a rock face the way I'd been doing for years had an effect on me like the sight of her dancing on the lawn.

So up we went, me first, then Imogen after I'd got her belayed. There were no problems, and she clearly wasn't in the slightest fazed by having several hundred feet of air beneath her at the most exposed points.

It was worth it just to see her face as she stood on the top of the rock.

It's a marvellous place to be, beautifully airy in three directions with the huge bulk of Pillar Fell itself looming behind.

She drank it all in then she turned towards me, a wide smile on her face.

'Thanks,' she said, pulling her hat off so that her golden hair once more floated in the gentle breeze.

Then in one fluid movement she pulled her T-shirt over her head, kicked off her trainers, pushed down her shorts and stepped out of them.

'Would you like to fuck me?' she said.

I stood staring at her, dumbfounded.

Part of me was thinking that anyone on their way up the path to the summit of Pillar has a perfect view of the top of the rock.

Another part was thinking there was next to nothing of her! She was so skinny her ribs showed, her breasts looked like they'd just begun to form, she looked more like ten than fourteen. She was as far as you could get from those pneumatic images in the porn mags that got passed around at school.

But despite the danger of being overlooked, despite her lack of any obvious feminine attractiveness, my heart and my soul and, yes, my body was crying out in answer to her question: Oh yes, I'd like to fuck you very much!

And I did.

What was it like? It was a first for me, and for her too. I knew that because I ended up with blood on my cock. So, a pair of raw virgins, but we meshed like we'd been doing it for years, and unless they ran lessons in faking it at that expensive boarding school of hers, she enjoyed it every bit as much as I did. I can't take any credit for that. While it was happening I was totally absorbed in my own feelings. But afterwards as we lay wrapped in each other's arms, I knew I wanted this to be for ever.

In the end it was her who pushed me away and stood up.

'Mustn't be late,' she said, 'or those two will run scared and give the game away.'

She got dressed as quickly as she'd stripped, but not through any modest need to cover up. I've never met anyone as unself-conscious as Imogen.

I lay there and watched her, then followed suit. She would have done the descent unroped, but I wouldn't let her.

On the long walk back I don't think we exchanged more than half a dozen words. There was lots I wanted to say but, like I told you, communication wasn't my thing.

With about a quarter mile to go she halted and put her hand on my chest.

'I'm OK from now on,' she said.

I said, 'Yeah. When . . . how . . .?'

'Don't worry,' she said. 'I'll find you when I want you.'

And she was gone.

So there you have it, Elf. Sex, rites of passage, teenage trauma, all the steamy stuff you people like to paddle your inquisitive little fingers in.

Watch out that you don't find yourself touching something nasty!

But that's what turns you on, isn't it?

That's what turns you on!

Elf

When she was thirteen Alva Ozigbo's English teacher had asked her class to write about what they wanted to be when they grew up.

That night Alva sat so long over the assignment that both her parents asked if there was something they could help with.

She regarded them long and assessingly before shaking her head.

Her father, Ike, big, black and ebullient, was a consultant cardiologist at the Greater Manchester Teaching Hospital. Her mother, Elvira, slender, blonde and self-contained, had been an actress. She'd left her native Sweden in her teens to study in London in the belief that the English-speaking world would offer far greater opportunities. For a while her Scandinavian looks had got her parts that required Scandinavian looks, but it soon became clear that her best future lay on the stage. The nearest she got to a film career was being screentested for a Bergman movie. She still talked of it as a missed opportunity but the truth was the camera didn't love her. On screen she became almost transparent, and by her mid-twenties she was resigned to a career of secondary roles in the theatre. She was Dina in *The Pillars of the Community* at the Royal Exchange when she met Ike Ozigbo. When they married six months later, she made a rare joke as they walked down the aisle together after the ceremony.

'I always knew I'd get a starring role one day.'

To which he'd romantically replied, 'And it's going to be a record-breaking run!'

So it had proved.

Thirteen-year-old Alva was proud of her father, but it had always been her mother she pestered for stories of her life on the stage. Now, after vacillating for a good hour between the two main exemplars in her life, it was not without a small twinge of disloyalty that she finally wrote that what she wanted to be was an actress.

At the time she meant it. But somewhere over the next few years that urge to get inside the skin of a character had changed from interpretation to analysis. She discovered that wanting to understand was not the same as wanting to be. The actress had to lose herself in the part; Alva found that she wanted to preserve herself, to remain the detached observer even as all the intricate wirings of personality and motivation were laid bare.

Psychiatry gave her that option, but she soon discovered that the observer had to be an actor too. When she read Hadda's account of his first encounters with Imogen, she felt a great surge of excitement. To be sure, there was a deal of hyperbole here. The bolder the picture he painted of himself as the victim of a grand passion for one woman, the dimmer his sense of that other degrading and disgusting passion became. But in his effort to stress that his love for Imogen was based on some collision of mind and spirit rather than simply a natural adolescent lust, he had fallen into a trap of his own setting.

What did he say? Here it was . . . *there was next to nothing of her! She was so skinny her ribs showed, her breasts looked like they'd just begun to form, she looked more like ten than fourteen . . .* Yet he'd been sexually roused by this prepubescent figure, and sexually satisfied too. This was probably what he saw in his fantasies thereafter, this was the source of those desires that had brought about his downfall.

She recalled a passage in the first piece he'd written for her, when he was in his best hard-nosed thriller mode.

Imogen was sitting up in bed by this time. Even in these fraught circumstances I was distracted by sight of her perfect breasts.

Stressing his red-blooded maleness, trying to distract her attention,

101

and his own, away from the fact that it was unformed new-budding bosoms that really turned him on.

And now she knew she would need to call upon her acting skills when next she saw him. She must give no hint that she saw in this narrative anything more than an honest and moving account of first love. Indeed, it might be well to give him a quick glimpse of that Freudian prurience he was accusing her of. He was, she judged, a man who liked to be right, who was used to having his assessments of people and policies confirmed. No way could she hope to drive such a man to that final climactic confrontation with his own dark inner self, but with care and patience she might eventually lead him there.

Another spur to caution was the fact that he'd obviously got the writing bug. She'd seen this happen in other cases. The people she dealt with were more often than not obsessive characters and this was something she liked to use to her advantage. Her guess was that he'd have another exercise book ready for her, but if she annoyed him, he'd punish her by not handing it over.

That was his weapon.

Hers of course was his desire that what he wrote should be read! Withholding it might punish her, but only at the expense of punishing himself.

So she prepared for her next session with more than usual care.

ii

'Wolf,' she said. 'Tell me about your father.'

'What?'

She'd wrong-footed him, she could tell. He'd expected her to home in on that first sexual engagement on top of Pillar Rock.

'Fred, your father. Is he still alive?'

'Ah. I see where we're going. Oedipus stuff, right? No, I didn't blame him for my mother's death; no, I didn't want to kill him; and no, just in case you're too shy to ask, he never abused me in any way. Unless you count the odd clip around the ear, that is.'

'In some circumstances, I might indeed count that,' she said, smiling. 'I was just wondering about his attitude to what's happened, that's all. You do indicate that when it came to your marriage with Imogen, he wasn't all that keen.'

That got the flicker of a smile. The smiles, though hardly regular, came more frequently now. She took that as a sign of progress, though, paradoxically, in physical terms her goal was tears, not smiling.

'That's putting it mildly,' he said. 'He was even more opposed than Sir Leon. He at least in the end gave his daughter away. Dad wouldn't even come to the wedding.'

'Did that hurt you very much?'

'Of course it bloody hurt me,' he said angrily. 'But I was ready for it, I suppose. He wasn't exactly supportive when I started bettering myself. I thought he'd be proud of me, but he made it quite clear that he thought I'd have done better to follow in his footsteps and become a forester.'

'Did he have any reason to think that was what you were going to do?'

Hadda shrugged and said, 'Yeah, I suppose so. I'd always gone along with the assumption that I'd leave school as soon as I could and start working under him on the estate. I mean, why wouldn't I? I loved working with him, I'd been wielding an axe almost since I was big enough to pick up a teddy bear without falling over. And working outdoors in the countryside I loved seemed the best way of carrying on the way I was.'

'So what changed?'

'Don't act stupid. You know what changed. I met Imogen.'

'You carried on meeting after that first time?'

'Obviously. All that summer, whenever we could. She needed to keep quiet about it of course. Me too. It was easier in my case, I just went on as normal, taking off in the morning with my walking and climbing gear. She had to make excuses. She was good at that, I guess. She couldn't manage every day, but if three days went by without her showing up, I started getting seriously frustrated.'

'You continued having sex?'

'Why wouldn't we?'

'She was under age. And the danger of pregnancy. Did you start using condoms?'

'No, she said she'd taken care of all that. As for her age, I suppose I was under age too to start with. Anyway, it never crossed my mind. We were at it all the time. Always out of doors and in all weathers. On the fellside, in the forest.'

He smiled reminiscently.

'There was this old rowan tree that had survived among all the conifers that had been planted commercially on the estate. We often used to meet there early morning or late evening if one of us couldn't manage to get away for the whole day. Imo would slip out of the castle and I would go over the wall behind Birkstane, and be there in twenty minutes or so. We didn't even have to make a special arrangement. It was like we both knew the other would be there under the tree.'

'This was the rowan you had dug up and transplanted to your London garden?'

He said, 'You remembered! Yes, the very same. They were harvesting the conifers in that part of the forest and it looked as if the rowan would simply be mowed down to give the big machines access. So I saved it. A romantic gesture, don't you think?'

'More sentimental, I'd say. Men in particular look back fondly on their adolescent encounters. Pleasure without responsibility, I can see its attraction. So you'd meet under this tree, have a quick bang, then go home?'

This was a deliberate provocation. The clue to what he'd become had to lie in this first significant sexual relationship.

He looked at her coldly.

'It wasn't like that. We drew each other like magnets. I felt her presence wherever I was, whatever I was doing. She was always with me. Under the rowan we were in total union, but no matter how far apart physically, she was always with me.'

She was tempted to probe how he felt now, whether he still

believed that Imogen had genuinely shared that intensity of feeling. But she judged this wasn't the right moment. Concentrate on getting the facts.

'So when did it end?'

'How do you know it ended?'

'Because it had to. From what you say of Lady Kira, she wasn't going to be fooled for ever. Also that first piece you wrote, the one about living in a fairy tale, in it you talk about the woodcutter's son being given three impossible tasks and going away and performing them. That implies an ending – and a new beginning, of course.'

'Did I write that? Yes, I did, didn't I? It seems a long time ago, somehow.'

'Three weeks,' she said.

'Is that all? We've come a long way.'

He spoke neutrally and she was tempted to probe but decided against it. The more progress you made, the more dangerous the ground became.

'So, the end,' she said.

'It was in the Christmas holidays,' he said slowly. 'We'd both gone back to school in the autumn, her to her fancy ladies' college in the south, me to the comp. I couldn't wait for the term to finish.'

'You didn't think she might have had second thoughts about your relationship during those months apart?'

'Never crossed my mind,' he said wearily. 'Not vanity, if that's what you're thinking. It was just a certainty, like knowing the sun would rise. But when we met in December, it was harder for us to get whole days together when the weather was bad. I mean, a teenage girl wanting to go for a solitary stroll in the summer sunshine is one thing. In a winter gale it's much more suspicious. We met more and more often under the rowan tree. A blizzard blew up, it was practically a white-out. We sheltered among the trees till things improved a bit, then I insisted on accompanying her back through the grounds till the castle was in sight. Sir Leon had got worried and organized a little search party that included my dad. We met them on the estate drive. I'd have tried to bluff it out, say I'd run into Imogen somewhere and offered to see her home, but she didn't bother. I think she was right. They weren't going to believe us. I went home with Fred, she went home with Sir Leon to face her mother.'

'What did Fred say?'

'He asked me what I thought I was doing. I told him we were in love, that I was going to marry her as soon as I legally could. He said, "Forget the law, there's no law ever passed that'll let you marry that lass!" I said, "Why not? There's nowt anyone can say that'll make a difference." And he laughed, more snarl than a laugh, and he said that up at the castle the difference had been made a long time back. I didn't know what he meant, not until the next day.'

'You saw Imogen again?' guessed Alva.

'Oh yes. Sir Leon brought her down to Birkstane. They left us alone together. I grabbed hold of her and began gabbling about it making no difference, we could still do what we planned, we could run away together, and so on, lots of callow adolescent stuff. She pushed me away and said, sort of puzzled, "Wolf, don't talk silly. We never planned anything." And she was right, I realized later. All the plans had been in my head.'

'And was this when she set you the three impossible tasks?' asked Alva.

'Who's a clever little shrink then?' he mocked. 'Yes, suddenly this girl every bit of whose body I knew as well as my own turned into something as cold and distant as the North Pole. She said she was sorry, it had been great fun, but she'd assumed I knew as well as she did that it would have to come to an end eventually. I managed to stutter, "Why?" And she told me. With brutal frankness.'

His face darkened at the memory, still potent after all these years.

Alva prompted, 'What did she say?'

'She said surely I could see how impossible it would be for her to marry someone who couldn't speak properly, had neither manners nor education, and was likely to remain on a working man's wage all his life.'

Jesus! thought Alva. They really do bring their princesses up differently!

'So these were the three impossible tasks?' she said. 'Get elocution lessons, get educated, get rich. And you resolved you would amaze everyone by performing them?'

'Don't be silly. I had a short fuse, remember? I went into a right strop, told her she was a stuck-up little cow just like her mam, that I weren't ashamed to talk the way everyone else round here talked, that a Hadda were as good as an Ulphingstone any day of the week, and that my dad said all a man needs is enough money to buy what's necessary for him to live. She smiled and said, "Clearly you don't put me in that category. That's good. I'll see you around." And she went.'

'She sounds very self-contained for a fourteen-year-old,' said Alva.

'She was fifteen by then,' he said, as if this made a difference. 'And I was sixteen.'

'What did you do?'

'I moped all over Christmas. Must have been unliveable with. Dad headed off to the Dog as often as he could. Then New Year came. Time for resolutions about changing your life, according to the guys on the telly. I started fantasizing about leaving home, having lots of adventures, striking it rich by finding a gold mine or something, then returning, all suave and sexy like one of them TV presenters, to woo Imogen. Only she wouldn't know it was me till she'd been overcome by my manly charms. Pathetic, eh?'

'We all have our dreams,' said Alva, recalling her teenage fantasies of collecting a best actress Oscar.

'Yeah. I'd like to say I set off to chase mine, but it wouldn't be true. I just knew that, whatever I wanted, I wasn't going to get it hanging around in Cumbria. So I set off to school one morning with everything I owned in my sports bag and all the money I could raise in my pocket. And I just kept on going. The rest as they say is history.'

'I'd still like to hear it,' said Alva.

'Come on!' he said. 'You strike me as a conscientious little researcher. The meteoric rise of Wilfred Hadda from uncouth Cumbrian peasant to multi-millionaire master of the universe has been charted so often you must have got it by heart!'

'Indeed,' she said, reaching into her document case. 'I've got copies of most of the articles here. There's general agreement on events after your return. But their guesses at what you did between running away as a poor woodcutter's son and coming back with your rough edges smoothed and enough money in the bank to launch your business career make speculation about Lord Lucan read like a Noddy story. Anyone get close?'

'How would I know? I never read them. Which looks best to you?'

'Well, I'm torn between the South American diamond mine and the Mexican lottery. But on the whole I'd go for the *Observer* writer, who reckons you probably got kidnapped by the fairies, like True Thomas in the ballad.'

That made him laugh, a rare sound, the kind of laugh that made you want to join in.

'Yeah, go with that one,' he said. 'Away with the fairies, that's about right. Did he have a good time, this Thomas fellow?'

'It was a strange place they took him too,' said Alva. 'Hang on, he quotes from the ballad in his article. You'll have to excuse my Scots accent.'

She opened the file and began to read.

> *'It was mirk mirk night, there was nae stern light,*
> *And they waded through red blude to the knee;*
> *For a' the blude that's shed on earth*
> *Rins through the springs o' that countrie.'*

When she finished he nodded vigorously and said, 'Oh yes, that guy knows what he's talking about. So how did Thomas make out when he got back?'

'Well, he had a bit of a problem, Wolf,' she said. 'The one condition of his return was that thereafter he was never able to tell a lie.'

Their gazes locked. Then he smiled, not his attractive winning smile this time, but something a lot more knowing, almost mocking.

'Just like me then, Elf,' he said. 'That old lie-detector mind of yours must have spotted long ago that you're getting nothing but gospel truth from me!'

'Gospel? Somehow I doubt if your runaway years had much of religion in them!'

'You're so wrong, Elf,' he said with a grin. 'I was a regular attender at chapel.'

'Chapel?' she said. 'Not church? That's interesting. None of the speculation in the papers suggested a religious dimension to your disappearance.'

'For God's sake,' he said, suddenly irritated. 'Can we get away from what those fantasists dream up? Look, Elf, I'm trying to be honest with you, but if I say there's something I don't want to talk about, you've got to accept it, OK?'

'OK, OK,' she said making a note. 'Let's cut to the chase. Age twenty-one, you're back with a suitcase full of cash, talking like a gent, no longer sucking your peas off your knife, and able to tell a hawk from a handsaw. How did Imogen greet you?'

'She asked me to dinner at the castle. There were two or three other guests. Sir Leon was very polite to me. Lady Kira watched me like the Ice Queen but hardly spoke. I joined in the conversation, managed to use the right cutlery and didn't knock over any wine glasses. After dinner Imogen took me out into the garden, allegedly to cast my so-called expert eye over a new magnolia planted to replace one that hadn't made it through the winter. Out of sight of the house she stopped and turned to face me. "Well, will I do?" I asked. "Let's see," she said. And stepped out of her dress with the same ease that she'd stepped out of her shorts and trainers on Pillar Rock all those years ago. When we finished, she said, "You'll do." Couple of months later we married.'

'Despite all the family objections?'

'We had a trump card by then. Imo was pregnant. With Ginny. Made no difference to Dad and Sir Leon. They still stood out against the marriage. But Lady Kira seemed to see it made sense and that was enough. She calls the shots at the castle. Always did. So poor Leon had no choice but to give his blessing, and shake the moth-balls out of his morning dress to give the bride away.'

'Poor Leon?' she echoed. 'You sound as if you have some sympathy for him.'

'Why not? He's married to the Ice Queen, isn't he? No, fair do's, he may not have wanted me for his son-in-law, but I always got on well with Leon. And he went out of his way to try to make things right between me and my dad. Just about managed it the first two times. Third time was beyond human help.'

'I'm sorry . . .?'

Hadda said bleakly, 'Think about it. They say things come in threes, don't they? They certainly did for Fred. One, I disappeared for five years. Two, I came back and married Imogen against his wish and his judgment. Three, I got sent down for fraud and messing with young girls. Three times I broke his heart. The last time it didn't mend.'

And who do you blame for that? wondered Alva. But this wasn't the time to get aggressive, not when she'd got him talking about what had to be one of the most significant relationships in his life.

She said, 'But the first two times, you say Leon tried to help?'

'Oh yes. I think he recognized Dad and me were carved from the same rock. Left to our own devices, we'd probably never have spoken again! Don't know what he said to Fred about me, but he told me that, after I vanished, often he'd go into the forest with Imogen, and they'd find Dad just sitting slumped against the old rowan, staring into space, completely out of it. Sometimes there'd be tears on his cheeks. It cracked me up, just hearing about it. So whenever I felt like telling Dad that if he wanted to be a stubborn old fool, he could just get on with it, I'd think of what Leon had told me and try to bite my tongue. Gradually things got better between us. And when Ginny was born . . .'

110

He stopped abruptly and glared at her as if defying her to question him further about his daughter.

She said, 'So did Fred attend the wedding?'

'Oh no,' said Wolf, relaxing. 'That would have been too much. I hoped right up till the ceremony started he'd show up. Then, once it started, I was scared he might!'

'Why?'

'That bit when the vicar asks if anyone knows of any impediment, I imagined the church door bursting open and Fred coming in with his axe and yelling, "How's this for an impediment?" I remember, after the vicar asked the question he seemed to pause for ever. Then Johnny glanced round to the back of the church and shouted, "Speak up then" and that set everyone laughing.'

'Johnny . . .?'

'Johnny Nutbrown. He was my best man.'

'A large step from being the nose-bleeding object of your anger,' she said. 'How did that come about?'

'You mean, how come I didn't have any old friends of my own to take on the job? Simple. I was always a loner and the few half friendships I formed at school didn't survive my transformation, as you call it.'

'But didn't you make any new ones during this transformation period?' she asked. 'Even lowly woodcutters on a quest to perform three impossible tasks probably need a bit of human contact on the way.'

'I don't know, I didn't meet any others,' he said shortly.

Then he pushed back his chair and stood up, reaching into his blouson as he did so.

'You're curious about me and Johnny Nutbrown?' he said. 'Well, I think you'll find all you need to know in here.'

And there it was, the next exercise book just as she'd hypothesized.

But by producing it he had once again stepped aside from talking about those missing years, so as she took the book, she felt it less as a triumph than an evasion.

Wolf

i

Let's move on from our little diversion into childhood trauma and adolescent sexuality, shall we? Where was I before you nudged me down that fascinating side road?

Oh yes.

I'd been in a coma for the best part of nine months.

During the early stages of my so-called recovery, I've no idea what proportion of my time I spent out of things. All I do know is that every period of full lucidity seemed to provide the opportunity for a new piece of shit to be hurled at me.

I rapidly came to see that, far from things going away while I lay unconscious, they had got immeasurably and by now irrecoverably worse.

Let me lay them out, not in any particular order.

The charges against me had multiplied and intensified.

It seems that during the panic caused by my false terrorist attack warning to the Magistrates Court, several people had been injured and one had died. Didn't matter that like me he was a prisoner waiting to face committal proceedings, that he too tried to escape in the panic, slipped on the stairs, and suffered a heart attack from a long-standing condition, the bastards still added a charge of

112

manslaughter to the offence of making a hoax terrorist call which was worth a long jail sentence in itself.

In addition, the bus driver had been severely traumatized, several of his passengers had been hurt, two patrons of the pavement café had been hospitalized, and the driver of the Range Rover turned out to be a barrister, and he was orchestrating a whole battery of civil claims against me.

But these were the least of my troubles. In face of these charges there was nothing to do but put my hand up and plead guilty, only offering in mitigation the tremendous strain the manifestly ludicrous allegations of paedophilia had put me under.

Except they were no longer manifestly ludicrous. In fact they had moved on from the passive downloading of pornographic images to devastating accusations that I was actively involved in the whole revolting business, both as commercial organizer and active participant.

The InArcadia website, it was alleged, had been set up and maintained by money channelled through one of my off-shore companies. Some of the video footage obtained from InArcadia was identified as having been shot at various of my overseas properties. And in several scenes of a particularly revolting nature, there were glimpses of a naked back that bore a scar similar to mine.

There had been a steady leak of much of this material into the public domain and I'd already been tried, judged and condemned by the media, a verdict that must have seemed confirmed by the news that Imogen had started divorce proceedings.

And was this the end?

No, Elf, you bet your sweet life it wasn't!

Back in 2008 we could all hear the rumblings of the approaching economic storm. I admit I was rather smug about it and arrogantly assumed Woodcutter was soundly enough rigged to ride it out. When I woke from my trance, I found the tempest had struck with even greater force than anyone had anticipated and the economies of the Western world were in tatters.

Had I been around, I might have been able to do something to limit the damage to Woodcutter.

Or, as the *Financial Times* put it, 'Possibly if Sir Wilfred's grubby paw had still been on the helm, he might have been able to steer the most seaworthy of his piratical fleet into some extrajudicial haven, but left unmanned in those desperate seas, they either sank with all hands or were boarded and taken in tow by the local excise men.'

In times of crisis, journalists often erupt in flowery excrescence.

To continue in the same vein, as far as I could make out many of my old shipmates had leapt overboard clutching whatever portable pillage they could, while others had surrendered to the invading officers and saved their own worthless carcases from the yard-arm by offering them mine!

My initial assumption had been that the morning raid on my house was part of a Fraud Office investigation, and I recalled my airy reassurance to Toby that there was nothing for them to find.

Now I had the Fraud Office crawling all over my affairs and finding all kinds of crap! The worst of it was that I couldn't remember in most instances whether I knew it was there or not. The trauma of the accident had left so many gaps both physical and mental that my degree of recovery was always in doubt. But *I can't remember* is not a line of defence that wins much sympathy from a stony-faced financial investigator.

But none of these events and accusations hit me like the news that Imogen was planning to divorce me. And even that wasn't the end of the trauma. The very next day they broke the news to me that Fred had suffered a serious stroke and while I had been lying in my coma, he'd been lying in the twilight state of the stroke victim.

I was desperate to see him, but I wasn't fit to travel even if the authorities had given me permission. DC McLucky was very helpful here, bringing me the phone and getting me connected to the Northern hospital where Dad was a patient. According to the consultant I spoke to, Dad's condition was still extremely serious. He wasn't willing to even estimate just how far any recovery process might take him.

Fred and I had slowly moved back towards each other after the rift over my marriage. Ginny made the difference. In a way I'm glad he wasn't around to hear of her death.

Back then I was devastated by the prospect that I might never see him again.

McLucky did his best to reassure me in his forthright Glaswegian way. He it was who ran a check on the hospital and discovered that it had possibly the best stroke unit in the north of England, and that Fred was there as a private patient funded by no less a person than my dear old father-in-law, Sir Leon! It was a strange irony that their shared opposition to a Hadda–Ulphingstone marriage had turned their strong employer/employee bond into something like friendship and ultimately Fred had graduated from being the estate's head forester to more of an overall estate manager.

For several days, I could think about nothing else but my sick father and my estranged wife. I had plenty of time for thinking as, apart from the medical staff and DC McLucky, I saw no one.

As I've said, I'd never been a particularly sociable man and as I became rich and powerful, I put little faith in the pretensions of new acquaintance to genuine affection. But people seemed to like me and I did form a small circle of friends to whom I would once have applied the old-fashioned designation of *faithful and true*.

Not one of the faithful and the true made an effort to contact me or turned up to see me in hospital. Wankers! I thought. But why should any of them prove more faithful and true than my own wife and my good friend and solicitor, Toby Estover?

The only one I felt confident would show me some loyalty was Johnny Nutbrown.

As I've already told you, my first encounter with Johnny age fifteen was far from auspicious. On my return after my years away with the fairies, I was rather surprised to find him still around. While Johnny is always at ease everywhere, he never gives an impression of actually belonging anywhere. Of course he'd been to the same school as some of the others, including Estover, and also he had a bad case of the hots for Imo's best friend, Pippa Thursby.

115

So they were good enough reasons for him to be on the fringe of their magic little circle.

But I never counted him as being truly in it, which was a plus for me.

I'm sure Imogen had to put up with a lot of crap from her friends when she announced she was going to marry me. She never passed any of it on, and it wouldn't have bothered me if she had. Frankly, I thought most of them were a waste of space that could have been more usefully occupied by a flock of Herdwicks. All the interest most of them showed in me was a prurient curiosity about the parameters of the sexual performance they were sure must be the basis of Imogen's interest. I think I could probably have shagged the lot of them, men and women, if I'd been so inclined.

But Johnny saw me differently. Later, when we got close enough for honesty, he told me with that cynical grin of his, 'The others looked at you and thought *big fucks*; I looked at you and thought *big bucks*. This guy is going where the money is.'

I couldn't complain about this economic basis for our relationship as initially I only became interested in him when I realized he'd got the sharpest mind for figures of anyone I'd ever met. If it had been allied to an entrepreneurial spirit, he would have been a master of the commercial universe in his own right.

I soon realized we were made for each other.

The thing was that Johnny could do just about anything, so long as someone told him what to do.

An old schoolmate of his – in fact, Toby Estover my former solicitor, and former friend – told me about Johnny's first appearance on a rugby field. As he evinced neither interest nor talent, they stuck him on the wing for a practice game. The first time the ball was passed to him, he caught it one-handed and was standing still, examining it with mild curiosity, when most of the opposing team jumped on top of him. When he'd got back on his feet, the games master expostulated, 'For heaven's sake, Nutbrown, I don't expect you to do much when you get the ball, but I do expect you to do *something*!'

116

'Yes, sir. What exactly?' replied Johnny.

'Well, ideally I'd like to see you run forward as fast as you can, not letting anyone touch you, until you reach those two tall posts sticking out of the ground, and then place the ball gently between them. Failing that, as I'm sure you will, just kick it as far as you can!'

'Yes, sir,' said Johnny.

And next time he received the ball, he jinked and sidestepped his way the length of the field without anyone laying a hand upon him and touched down between the posts. The only trouble was the *next* time he took a pass he chose the alternative instruction and kicked it as far as he could, this being sideways over the line of poplars separating the ground from a river into which the ball plopped, never to be seen again.

That was the thing about Johnny. You had to tell him what to do, you had to be clear what you were telling him, and you had to tell him every time. We suited each other perfectly. I had the ambition, the energy and the imagination; and he had a mind that could run over my proposals, detect flaws, point out short-cuts, and calculate risks, often in the time it took to down the two large vodka martinis that were the inevitable precursor to lunch and dinner.

Without Johnny, I don't doubt I would have still managed to become stinking rich, but with him, the sweet stink of success came a lot quicker.

Without me, Johnny might well have degenerated into a sort of old-fashioned lounge-lizard, charming enough money to get by on out of a succession of susceptible women. I took some pride in having saved him from this fate, but rather less in having been responsible for his marriage.

Pippa Thursby, like many best friends, was all the things that Imogen wasn't.

While Imogen defied friends and family to marry the man she loved, Pippa never made any secret of the fact that though she found Johnny to be hugely attractive, highly entertaining, and a maestro of the mattress, he was merely (as she put it) stopping her gap until she could get her hands on some seriously wealthy old guy who would set her up for life by either death or divorce. She had her sights set on the MD of the advertising company for which she worked. Pippa was no featherbrain, she had excellent IT skills and could have carved out a successful career for herself, but she saw no reason to catch a train into work every day when she could get somebody else to do that on her behalf.

So Johnny was fun but marriage to someone so feckless simply wasn't an option. Then he and I got together, and things changed as it dawned on Pippa that my eruption towards the financial stratosphere was dragging Johnny in its wake.

Johnny himself was more than happy with his long-standing no-strings relationship, but he was dead meat once Pippa decided that life as Mrs Nutbrown could be a five-star arrangement after all. So three years after my own wedding, I was standing as best man at Johnny's.

As my closest colleague and my closest friend, I had hoped, nay I had believed, he would stand by me in turn.

I put it to the back of my mind as I set about trying to make sense of what was happening in my marriage.

DC McLucky had proved to be a rough diamond with a heart of gold. He even apologized obliquely for not being allowed to leave the phone permanently plugged in by my bedside, but he fetched it without demur whenever I asked for it. I tried without success to talk with Imogen. I rang Pippa but she told me bluntly that she couldn't help me and put the phone down. I rang my office and found the number was disconnected. When I got on to BT to complain, there was a long silence then I found myself connected to a DI in the Fraud Squad. I told him all the money was buried in a dead man's chest on a South Sea island but I'd lost the map, which wasn't very clever but I was getting beyond clever. I rang just about everyone I knew and found they were either uncommunicative or unavailable. A call from me clearly sounded like the tinkle of a leper's bell.

But I made no attempt to contact Johnny Nutbrown. I didn't mention him even when I spoke to his wife. I think it was superstition. If Johnny deserted me, then I was truly fucked. He would surely come to see me of his own accord. And in his own time, of course, for one thing you soon found out about Johnny was that his own time was not as other people's time.

But as the days passed and he didn't appear, I was ready to sink into despair.

Then one afternoon I woke up from yet another involuntary nap to find a lean, rangy figure sitting by my bed. His face was hidden behind a copy of the *Racing Times* but I didn't need to see his face to know who it was.

I felt a huge surge of happiness.

If you're interested in drawing a detailed map of my emotional progress, Elf, here is a significant moment to sketch in.

That is the last time I can recall feeling happy. I mean, what the fuck have I had to be happy about in the last seven years?

But, moron that I was, I felt happy then.

Johnny had come at last.

ii

As I fixed my one eye on Johnny, a second emotion came to join happiness.

It was relief.

The thing was he looked so relaxed, so completely unchanged from the man I had last seen many months earlier, or indeed from the elegant figure who'd winked at me as I passed him his wedding ring all those years ago, that it seemed impossible there could be anything seriously wrong with my life or my business.

'My dear old Wolf,' he said. 'So glad you've decided to join us.'

I pressed the button that raised the top end of the bed.

'Johnny, good to see you,' I croaked. 'Have you been here long?'

'Ten minutes or so. Chap in the corridor with a speech defect wanted to stop me, but I managed to talk him round.'

119

It was a comfort to know that not even DC McLucky was immune to the Nutbrown charm.

He said, 'Brought you a bunch of grapes. Could only get them processed, I'm afraid.'

He was wearing what he called his poacher's jacket. I don't think it was altogether a joke. Johnny would much rather help himself to a neighbour's birds than accept an invitation to an organized shoot. From one of the deep internal pockets he drew a bottle of red wine and from the other two goblets.

'Thank God for screw tops, eh?' he said, opening the bottle and filling the glasses. 'Bottoms up.'

We drank. It was my first alcohol and it tasted foul, but symbolically it was nectar. Despite everything I found myself thinking, with Johnny here, things must be on the up.

I said, 'So how're things looking, Johnny?'

For a moment my heart leapt as he said, 'Not so bad if you like lots of blue sky.'

Then he added with a grin, 'Of course, not much else to see when you've gone belly-up.'

It was then I recalled that never in any crisis situation, professional or personal, had I seen Johnny anything but relaxed! Here was a mind that could make sense of a vast acreage of figures at a glance but had no more concept of tomorrow than a gadfly.

'It can't be as bad as that, surely?' I said, still scrabbling for some scrap of hope.

'You weren't there,' he said. 'Might have been different if you had been. Did what I could but it was *sauve qui peut* with the rest of them. That arse Massie in charge of Off-shore just vanished. Even helped himself to those rather nice Gillray prints from his office wall. Then those awful Fraud Squad people started crawling all over the place. I stopped going in after that. Nothing to do and they've got absolutely no conversation.'

I was genuinely bewildered by this indication of just how serious my business worries were.

I said, 'What the hell's going on, Johnny? Hell, we pushed the boundaries like everyone else, but we didn't step over them, or at least not very far.'

He shrugged and said, 'You know what they say, Wolf. When the tide goes out, that's when all the crap shows up on the beach. Not a lot of sympathy around for anyone just now, and with this other business, you are pretty well at the bottom of the list.'

'You mean the kiddy-porn stuff? For God's sake, Johnny, they can't make that stick.'

'No? Well, if anyone can beat the rap, I'd back you, Wolf.'

I didn't like the way he phrased that.

I said sharply, 'Johnny, you don't believe any of that crap, do you? I shouldn't need to tell you that it's just not true!'

He shrugged again and said, 'Whatever you say. Doesn't matter what I think, does it? Like my great uncle Nigel. Had this thing about sheep, no one in the family gave a damn, they were his sheep, weren't they? But when it hit the papers, that was different. Had to resign from his clubs. What the papers are saying about you, Wolf, well, all I can say is, if you can prove it's not true, no need to worry about the business. You'll be able to live like a lord on your profits from libel actions!'

I looked at him aghast. I'd always known Johnny lived in a different world from the rest of us, now I saw he lived in another dimension.

At least if he was giving me the truth as he saw it here, he was my best bet to get the truth about what took pride of place at the top of my mountain of worries.

I said, 'Is Imogen still staying with you?'

'Good lord, no. Moved out a few months back. Went up to Cumbria, easier to set mantraps for the press boys up there.'

'And Ginny?'

'Went with her, I think. Some talk of sending her off to this school in Paris, all the top people have their kids there so they've got better security than the Pentagon. Don't know whether she's gone yet or not, though.'

'Have you talked to her at all – Imogen, I mean? About the divorce?'

I don't know what I was looking for. Perhaps I had some faint hope that what Imogen was doing was in some way tactical, a legal move to put herself and some of our fortune beyond the reach of the circling sharks while I lay in a coma.

I wanted truth from Johnny. I got it.

'Yes, I had a chat when Pippa told me that was the way Imo was thinking. Nothing else for her to do really. I mean, it's a no-brainer. I expect Toby told her the same. Husband either a vegetable, or if he wakes, a convicted kiddy-fucker and fraudster. Either way, no point hanging about, get out quick as you can with as much as you can. Though the way things are looking, you've really got to be sorry for the poor old girl.'

'*Poor old girl . . .!* You've lost me, Johnny,' I said tightly.

'Think about it. If she'd divorced you, say, a year ago, she'd have scooped the pot! Kind of settlements our courts have been giving, even the Yanks were flocking here from Reno. She'd have walked away with God knows how many millions. Now . . . well . . .'

He made a wry face.

I said bitterly, 'If you see her, tell her I'm really sorry about that, Johnny.'

'Yes, I will,' he said. 'She'll appreciate that. Here, let me top you up.'

I shook my head. As we talked my initial euphoria had wilted and died, leaving me in a worse state than before. Johnny, I realized, had been my last best hope of relief, the only basket left for me to place my eggs in. Not his fault for not being able to give me what I wanted. My need had bulled him up to saviour status. And in any case the eggs were probably cracked and addled already. There was nothing he could do for me, I realized. All I wanted now was to be left alone.

'No thanks,' I said. 'Actually, I'm feeling a bit tired. I suppose I'm not used to visitors. Sorry.'

'No, it's me who should be sorry. Should have known better than to overtire you. I'll leave the bottle in your locker here. Don't want the nurses taking a swig, do we?'

He disposed of the bottle and stood up. At six foot seven, he'd always had a good four inches on me. Now he seemed to tower like some visitor to Lilliput, free from malicious intent but unable to avoid giving the tiny figures around his ankles the occasional painful kick.

I said, 'If you get a chance to talk to Ginny, tell her I love her.'

'Of course I will,' he said. 'I'll be in touch when you're feeling a bit more up to snuff. Take care now.'

He left. Before the door could swing shut, DC McLucky came through.

'Enjoy your wine, did you?' he said.

This for him was a subtle way of letting me know he'd been listening in on our conversation. Curiously the sight of his lugubrious face and the sound of his aggressive voice raised my spirits a bit. To say his manner had softened would be going too far – I don't think he did soft – but at least he seemed to regard me as a human being, unlike some of the medical staff who could hardly conceal their distaste. I realized later this was because as news of my recovery circulated, the papers had decided this was too good a story to miss. 'The Kraken Wakes' was an *Observer* headline. 'IT'S BACK!' was the *Sun*'s.

But DC McLucky treated me, if not like a man innocent till proven guilty, at least like a PoW under the protection of the Geneva Convention.

I said, 'Not a lot. Help yourself, if you fancy a glass. Won't keep now it's opened.'

'Thanks,' he said, taking the bottle out of the locker and filling my water tumbler. 'Cheers. Very nice.'

'This mean you're not on duty?' I asked.

He said, 'Read a lot of detective stories, do you? But I suppose you're right. I'm on my break. Till I finish this anyway.'

He was regarding me with an expression I couldn't quite identify.

He said, 'Buddy of yours, that Mr Nutbrown?'

I said, 'Yes, he is. A close friend and business colleague. Why?'

123

He drank some more wine then said, 'No reason. Must be a comfort to have such a close friend and colleague walking around free and watching your back.'

He finished the wine as I let the implications of what he was saying sink in.

If the Fraud Squad investigation was probing so deep, why wasn't my closest business associate at its heart?

It was at this point another bubble of memory floated to the surface of my mind.

Before my accident, I'd been rendezvousing with Johnny at the Black Widow, but it was the cops who were waiting for me there.

McLucky was at the door.

I said, 'Mr McLucky.'

He said warningly, 'I'm back on duty now.'

I said, 'I'd just like the telephone, if I could. I think I should get myself a lawyer.'

He nodded, and it came to me that the elusive expression was not a million miles from pity.

He said, 'First good idea you've had since you woke up, Sir Wilfred.'

iii

It was six months from my awakening before I was fit enough to stand trial and even then I entered court leaning heavily on a stick. I'd been told I would have a permanent limp, by which I think they meant stagger. Add to that my scarred face, black eye-patch, and the leather glove on my right hand, and you'd think that perhaps the change from what I used to be might have provoked some pangs of sympathy in the great British public.

No chance. The abuse and catcalls, not to mention stones and spit that were hurled my way by the crowd gathered for my first appearance, indicated that to a man and woman they'd taken their lead from the tabloids. The *Mirror* described me as lower than vermin while the *Mail* had photos of me before and after the accident with the headline 'Now We See Him as He Really Is!'

The so called quality press weren't much better. The *Guardian* developed the *Mail*'s theme in a cartoon showing two policemen struggling up the steps of the Bailey with an ornate picture frame containing what was obviously a painting of me with the caption 'Dorian Gray Comes Down from the Attic'. The *Telegraph*, not to be outdone in the literary stakes, published a photo that could have been a still from a Frankenstein movie accompanied by the tag-line 'He must be wicked to deserve such pain'. They didn't, however, trust their readers sufficiently not to give chapter and verse of the quotation's source.

Meant nothing to me, but I'd guess a well-educated girl like you didn't need to be told, Elf.

But worst of all was the way they treated Dad's stroke. Responsibility was laid entirely at my door. The sins of the child being visited on the father was the burden of every reference to Fred. My pleas to be allowed to visit him continued to be disregarded on the grounds that (a) his condition was not presently life-threatening and (b) such a visit might cause public unrest if not disorder. When I pressed my solicitor to make waves, he said laconically, 'Not worth the bother. Even if we did get permission, they'd leak it to the press and the whole fucking thing would turn into a circus parade with you as the main attraction.'

Getting a new solicitor hadn't been as easy as I envisaged. Toby Estover's defection had dropped me in the mire and none of the other legal firms I knew proved keen to dig me out. I quickly realized the problem wasn't moral repugnance but money. What the financial crash had left of my fortune, the divorce courts took, and it was soon made clear to me that there was a mile-long queue of investors with writs in their hands, all eager to sue me for the pittance I was likely to earn sewing mailbags or whatever gainful employment was available in HM Prisons these days. In the end I would have had to take pot luck with the legal aid system if I hadn't remembered Edgar Trapp, a small-time solicitor with an East End practice, who I'd once done a favour for. He had two great merits, one was availability, the other was frankness. Not once either in the run-up to or during the course of my trials did he hold out any hope of an acquittal.

I had to fall back on Legal Aid for a barrister and when I heard that the court had appointed Andrew Stoller QC, my spirits lifted for a moment. Stoller was a radical crusading lawyer with a growing reputation for taking on lost causes and sometimes winning them. But Trapp shook his head and said gloomily, 'It just means the CPS are so sure of their case, they've pulled strings to make sure you get the best defence possible so there'll be no leeway for an appeal.'

I said, 'For Christ's sake, Ed! If I were paying you, I'd sack you!'

He gave one of his rare smiles and said, 'If you were paying me, I'd have probably resigned long since.'

It was a joke, but I knew it couldn't be easy for someone like Ed Trapp to be my legal representative. I was the perfect hate figure. The high-flying bankers who'd brought the country to the edge of ruin were on the whole still flying high, some of them buoyed up by the kind of pension packet that would have kept a dozen or more families out of the dole queue. No way to touch them. But I was in the public's sights and in their reach, a ruthless financial fraudster with a taste for molesting children. I suspect the general public gave Ed a pretty rough time. Not that they'd get much change if Ed's wife and assistant, Doll, was around. Only a very brave or very stupid man messed with Doll!

These were the thoughts that I consoled myself with when I thought of the trouble I might be bringing Ed. Not that I thought of it all that much. To be honest, I had little emotional energy left to worry about anyone else's woes. As the months rolled by, my physical improvement was matched by a mental deterioration. My early confident belief that nobody could place any credence in any of these accusations, sexual or financial, was worn away by the unremitting drip of evidence from the investigators. After a couple of months it was plain they had enough to drown me in. Trapp said they were showing their hand so clearly because it would save time and money if I pleaded guilty on all charges. This was particularly true in the fraud case, which recent experience had shown could run on for months.

'Let it run!' was my first reaction. 'They'll run out of steam before I do.'

Ed shook his head and said lugubriously, 'Doubt it. Anyway, you'll almost certainly be in jail by then. That's why they've scheduled the other thing first.'

He usually referred to the kiddy-porn case as *the other thing*.

It soon became clear Stoller, my brief, was as pessimistic as Trapp about my chances in the porn case. He asked me how I was thinking of pleading.

I exploded, 'Not guilty, of course!'

He drew in his breath like a plumber you've asked for a quote and said, 'Let's not be too hasty. Not before we examine the options . . .'

I said, 'The only option for me is not guilty, because that's what I am. No one who's known me for any length of time could possibly think I'd get off on this filth. And if you don't believe that, maybe I should look for another lawyer.'

He smiled and said, 'Of course I believe everything you tell me, Sir Wilfred. I could not function else. But the evidence appears strong. And I fear that by now the Great British Public has grown so accustomed to the notion that sexual deviancy may lurk behind even the most respectable façade that Jesus Christ himself at the second coming might be well advised to drop that *suffer the little children to come unto me* stuff.'

I got the message. He'd studied the prosecution case and what he'd found there had left him a long way short of absolute faith in my innocence.

I think that was when the fight began to go out of me. As long as I'd been able to think that, no matter what evidence the cops dug up or what kind of crap the papers printed, most people who actually knew me, even those who didn't like me much, would find the porn charges impossible to believe, I'd had something to cling to.

Now, looking at myself through Stoller's eyes, I saw that most of my acquaintance, far from declaring, *Wolf Hadda? No way he could*

127

be into that stuff! were probably saying, *Hadda, eh? Who'd have thought it? Mind you, there was always something . . .*

And, as I've indicated earlier, that readiness to believe the worst of people which has been the inevitable consequence of the downward spiral of modern standards was only reinforced by the change in my appearance.

Stoller was looking to do a deal with the CPS. He reckoned that in return for a plea of guilty to the charge of possessing illegal downloaded images he could persuade them to shelve the related charges of helping to finance InArcadia, the pornographic website, and of taking part in one of its videos.

'Their evidence is much shakier here,' he said. 'And on the surface there would be some illogicality in your downloading stuff from the site if you were not only one of its organizers but also an active participant in its videos.'

I jumped on this eagerly, saying that as my defence was that this was all a set-up, surely this looked like a weakness we could exploit.

He said patiently, 'It's a very small weakness and we could only attempt to exploit it by encouraging them to bring the more serious charges. As it is, you could get away with a relatively short period of jail time for the downloading, particularly if you put your hand up for it and promised to sign up for the aversion course. But if they throw the book at you, then we could be talking five or six years.'

I wouldn't listen. Whatever else happened, no way was I going to admit to being into that filth.

It's a matter of history now that I got found guilty on all counts. I can't even say I went down fighting. I was deeply depressed on the eve of the trial but still deluded myself that when I stepped out into the spotlight and the directors called *Action!* I'd be up for it.

Then, at the end of our last pre-trial consultation, Stoller and Trapp looked at each other and exchanged what seemed to me a reluctant nod of agreement.

I said, 'What?'

Stoller said, 'There's something you need to know, Sir Wilfred.

Better you hear it from us than from someone shouting it out during the trial. It's your wife, I mean your former wife . . .'

I remember feeling a real shock of fear that he was going to tell me something bad had happened to Imogen. Instead, and even more shocking, that was the first time I learned that Imo was going to remarry, and the intended groom was my ex-solicitor and ex-friend, Toby Estover.

Stoller and Trapp tried to play down the implications of the news. What concerned them of course was that to the Great British Public, including the twelve on my jury, my beloved wife and my dear friend might as well have put out an advert on prime-time television declaring that they knew beyond all doubt that I was guilty as charged.

But I was way beyond such practical forensic concerns. Somewhere deep down beyond the reach of reason I must have nursed a hope that the divorce was tactical, a temporary measure devised by Toby to put Imo out of reach of the media and my creditors. Now I was unable to ignore the full enormity of their betrayal.

After a sleepless night retreading every inch of the past till my heavy feet must have obliterated all traces of truth, I turned up at court like a zombie. My face and bearing spoke guilt, and in the end Stoller didn't even bother to put me on the witness stand.

In prison, I was put in the relative safety of the exclusion wing from the start, but that didn't stop me being viciously abused whenever the so-called normal prisoners got within shouting and spitting distance. When the time of my second trial arrived, I was past caring about its outcome. I wouldn't plead guilty, but I couldn't be bothered to make much effort to prove I wasn't guilty. No surprise then that they found me guilty.

So that's how it ended, my fairy tale.

A year after I came out of the coma, I was locked up for a total of twelve years.

That feels like forever after in anyone's language.

Like that guy Thomas in the poem, I told nothing but the truth. Those fairies knew a thing or two. The truth doesn't set you free, it gets you banged up for ever!

I had no friends. Johnny never came back. The only time I saw him again was when he appeared as a witness in the fraud case. To give him his due, he was clearly reluctant to say anything that told against me, but his airy evasions just managed to suggest there was a helluva lot of stuff to hide, and the fact that he kept glancing across at me with a look of rueful bewilderment and saying, 'Sorry, Wolf', didn't help much either.

Just when you think things can't get worse, they do. Six months after I'd started my sentence, Ed Trapp came to see me. I could tell it was bad news. Typically he didn't muck about.

'Your dad's dead,' he said. 'Sorry.'

I never got to see Fred. I just assumed that soon as he was fit to travel he'd come down to see me. News had begun to sound a bit more promising. Progress continued, very slow but steady. And then he'd had another stroke, so massive that despite being where he was, they could do nothing.

I didn't bother to apply to be allowed to go to the funeral. What was the point? He'd be laid to rest in St Swithin's up at Mireton. Everyone would be there. He was well liked. All that my presence would do would be to attract the media swarm, all pointing their cameras to see how I would react as they lowered into the ground the father that I'd killed.

That's how I felt, Elf, that's how I feel. I don't need the papers to say it. One way or another, I killed Fred, I acknowledge it.

And that's not all. Fill your boots, this is payday for you.

After I heard about Fred, I sat down and wrote a letter to Ginny. I'd written to her several times in the period leading up to the trial. No reply, either because she didn't want to, or maybe she never got my letters. After I was sentenced, I wrote again, and again nothing came back. I didn't blame her. It's a lot for a young kid to get her head around, being told her father's a pervert and a fraud-ster. Give her time, I thought, let her grow up. Christmas cards, birthday cards, let her know I was still alive. But she'd been close to her granddad, and I wanted her to know . . . I don't know what I wanted her to know, except that I loved her. When I finished the letter I read it through, once, twice, three times. Then I tore it up, because in my mind's eye that's what I could see her doing.

Another mistake. I should have had the courage to send it. I should have moved heaven and earth to make contact with her. Maybe if I'd been able to talk to her, maybe I could have persuaded her I was innocent, maybe she wouldn't have let them pack her off out of the country like they did . . .

Maybe she would still be alive.

But now I look back on her childhood I see how rarely I'd been there for her. I'd always thought of myself as a loving dad, but thinking about her after my sentence, I realized the last time I'd seen her before everything blew up was early in that last summer vacation when she asked me to help her with her Wordsworth assignment. Shortly afterwards I'd shot off on a business trip and by the time I returned she'd gone back to school. In fact that had been the pattern of our contact for the past few years: me away a lot of the time, only getting to see her if my presence in England coincided with one of her school vacations. OK, I always came back loaded with expensive presents from exotic parts, but what kind of compensation was that for my neglect?

What do you make of that, Elf? Some great dad, eh?

Whatever responsibility others share for putting me in this place and for putting Ginny in the way of harm over there in France, I know the truth of it. She was my responsibility and I failed her. I failed her all along. There's a long trail leading back from that filthy Parisian alleyway she died in, and it starts at my feet.

Is that what you're after, Elf? Is that what you want to hear?

Then you've got it, girl.

Whatever else I may have been framed for, I make a full and frank confession here.

You've got me bang to rights. I let my daughter down and I let my father down.

I killed them both. I killed them both.

Elf

i

This was it. The breakthrough!

She liked to watch sport on television. She got real pleasure out of the grace and athleticism of those involved, and she also learned a lot from observing with clinical detachment the range of human reaction to triumph and failure, to victory and defeat. She had written a paper on the subject for a psychological journal. It was judged to have such popular appeal that a national paper had offered a handsome fee for the right to publish it, but she had refused, mainly because they wanted to make some significant cuts but also because in retrospect her initial delight at the offer felt like taking a step away from a spectating objectivity towards the condition of those in the sporting arena.

But now as she read Hadda's narrative for a second time, she knew at last what it was to feel the impulse to punch the air and let out a scream of *YES!*

This was the crack in the dam that could . . . should . . . might . . . *must* lead to a breach of the huge defensive wall he had thrown up around his actions.

Its form had changed again, this time more subtly. It was back to first-person historical narrative, but it was now addressed directly

132

and specifically to herself. It was a statement that went a good way to being one half of a dialogue.

And its concluding admission that he had failed his daughter and his father beyond any mitigation of circumstance or outside interference was monumental. Even the derisive snarl of *Is that what you want to hear? . . . Then you've got it, girl!* was significant. It showed that he recognized and, albeit with reluctance and distaste, accepted their relationship of patient and therapist.

Of course he was still in denial . . . *whatever else I've been framed for . . .* but the more aggressive he became, the more it demonstrated his inner turmoil as he felt his defences hard pressed.

It wasn't surprising. All the evidence suggested his predilection was for girls in the early pubertal stages. He blamed the Ulphingstones for his daughter's banishment to boarding school, but from his point of view it put her safely out of the way during this dangerous stage of her development for a good two-thirds of the year. And his complaint that business trips frequently took him away from home during her holidays fitted the pattern perfectly. He knew what he was, didn't trust himself round his own young daughter, and protected her and himself by keeping her at a physical distance as much as possible.

It wasn't just guilt at her neglect that he was confessing to; it was the much greater guilt that had caused it!

Now was the time for her to press on – but with very great care. In the long hunt the most dangerous time is when the quarry turns at bay. So she prepared the ground for their next meeting even more meticulously than usual. But in the event she was frustrated.

He refused to see her.

There was nothing she could do.

These sessions were voluntary. No point in trying to work with a prisoner who had to be brought kicking and screaming before you.

The following week it was the same.

She guessed that he was regretting having gone so far to meet her. He felt he had given too much away, put himself in her power.

133

And perhaps he was fearful of what more might come. This was good. But only if somehow she could gain access to him.

The third week he didn't show either. But Officer Lindale, one of the few she didn't automatically assume would report everything back to Chief Officer Proctor, chose a moment when they were alone to say, 'Hadda asked me to give you this, miss.'

He handed her an exercise book.

She took it and glanced inside.

'Did you read this?' she asked.

'Looked through it, miss. In case it was, you know, offensive.'

And what would you have done if in your judgment it had been? she wondered.

But she knew that Hadda must have chosen Lindale as his messenger because he too trusted him, so all she said was, 'Thank you very much.'

She couldn't wait till she got home. As soon as she slipped into the driving seat of her car, she took out the book and began to read.

Wolf

i

Dear Dr Ozigbo, I won't be seeing you again, not unless they bring me under restraint. At first I thought I'd simply just not turn up any more, but that lets you down too easily, and I've decided to write to you just so you'll know that I know exactly what you've been up to.

You must have been really pleased with yourself when you read what I wrote about Johnny's visit and seen that you'd managed to stir up all kinds of feelings I didn't understand. And when you started in at me about Imogen I guess you didn't have to be Sigmund Freud to spot you'd touched a very sensitive spot. I know you'll say it's your job and everything you're trying to do is for my benefit, and I daresay you half believe it. I was ready to believe it myself to start with, but not any longer. Now I've come to realize you're little more than an interfering busybody poking around in matters you don't understand on the basis of gross misinformation and all you've managed to do is disturb whatever equilibrium I've achieved to see me safe through my sentence.

This writing business, for instance – you said the point of it was to get me to externalize my memories and feelings about what happened so that I could stand back and take it all in and come to terms with it – OK, you'd probably wrap it up in some trick cyclist's

135

mumbo-jumbo but that's what it amounts to – right? Clarity. It's meant to give me clarity, but all it's done is create utter confusion.

When I started, I thought I'd get you off my back by giving you a blow-by-blow account of what happened to me and my take on the reasons why it happened. Instead I've ended up doubting my own memories. Is that your job – to leave your patients more fucked up than when you found them?

Take sleeping, for instance. I used to sleep OK. I used to sleep sound. But ever since I started seeing you I've started having broken nights, bad dreams, the cold sweats, and it's got steadily worse. Recently my dreams have been getting really terrible, I do some really bad stuff in them, I won't tell you what because I know you'd just seize on it to support whatever it is you imagine you're doing with me. But I know what you're really doing. I've been reading about it in the library; false memory syndrome, they call it, which is when some trick cyclist is so obsessed with the notion that their patient has been abused in childhood that they keep on and on at the poor sod till he or she starts agreeing with them, and then the psych says *Hooray! This is a repressed memory brought to the surface through my clever therapy* when all it is is a disgusting idea that he or she has actually planted there!

I think this is what you've been doing to me, drip drip drip, going on at me about the paedophilia stuff, till you've got inside my head and put these false memory nightmares there. Look, I'll give you the benefit of the doubt and accept that this probably wasn't your intention. You read the trial transcripts and decided I was guilty and never once did you let it enter your head that maybe the stuff I was writing was the truth and you'd got it all wrong. No, from the start you reckoned I was in denial, isn't that what you people say? That my accounts were just my effort to hide from the knowledge of my own perverted crimes.

Well, congratulations, Dr Ozigbo. I'd never looked at images of kids being sexually abused till Medler showed me those that had been planted on my computer. I thought I'd cleansed them out of my memory. But now, thanks to you, I'm seeing them all the time.

136

They're in my mind, in my dreams, in my nightmares, exactly where you've put them!

That's what you've done to me. I was in control, eating my porridge, ticking down the minutes and hours and days till I got out of here.

Now I'm in hell.

Thanks a bunch.

And goodbye for ever.

Elf

i

As soon as she'd read Hadda's letter, Alva Ozigbo asked to see the Director.

During her time at Parkleigh she had come to admire Simon Homewood. He was by no means the bleeding-heart liberal the right-wing papers liked to caricature him as. There was a strength in him that even George Proctor had to respect, though the Chief Officer made no secret of his belief that all this syrupy-therapy stuff, as he called it, was a waste of time that could more usefully have been spent picking oakum. But after some preliminary tussles, Proctor had come to realize that unless the prison was run the way the Director wanted it run, he might as well start looking for a new post.

Homewood asserted that his primary duty was one of care for the prisoners in his charge. Get that right and all the other penal issues of punishment, rehabilitation and public safety could be resolved. So now when Alva spoke to him about Hadda, she simply stated that in her judgment the prisoner had reached a stage in his journey to self-awareness where the burden of recognition might be stressful enough to provoke self-harm.

The Director had never made any attempt to pressurize her for confidential details of exchanges between herself and Hadda or any other prisoner, and nor did he now.

He asked, 'Do you think he needs to be hospitalized?'

'No,' said Alva firmly. 'It's best if what's going on inside him works itself out inside. If he becomes aware he is an object of concern, this will allow him to externalize his fears and doubts once more. As it is, I'm the sole external target for his redirection of blame. At the moment he is asserting vehemently that he never wants to see me again. Eventually his turmoil will come to a climax which he can only resolve by demanding to see me. But it is not an outcome that he will admit willingly, and it may be that, as he approaches it, he'll look for a way of avoiding it.'

'Suicide, you mean?'

'I think he might see it as an attempt to re-enter the comatose state he existed in for nine months,' said Alva slowly. 'When he came out of it, the medical concentration was, quite naturally, on his physical condition. I wish there'd been more attention paid to what was actually going on in his mind, both before and after recovery. As far as I can make out from the records, the head trauma itself wasn't serious enough to explain such a long period of unconsciousness.'

'You think he might have somehow been seeking it out for himself?'

'Perhaps. He certainly talked of feeling a kind of nostalgia for the coma period in the months after his recovery.'

'If it was such a desirable state, why did he ever wake up?' enquired Homewood.

'Because there probably came a point where whatever element of choice was left to him had to opt between living and dying,' said Alva.

'And now you fear the decision might be reversed,' said Homewood, frowning. 'OK, I'll put Hadda on suicide watch.'

'With maximum discretion,' said Alva. 'It's best if he isn't aware he's giving concern to anyone except me.'

As the Director picked up his phone and summoned George Proctor to make the arrangements, she glanced over her notes. When she looked up, she caught Homewood watching her. As their eyes met, he gave her a faintly embarrassed smile and looked away.

This was the only flaw in their otherwise excellent working relationship. At first she'd been slightly amused when she detected that she aroused him sexually. In her experience a dash of unreciprocated sexual attraction, openly acknowledged, could lead to a fruitful relationship like that between herself and Giles Nevinson. Now and then he would try to pounce, of course, and when rejected accuse her of being a common-or-garden prick teaser. 'Are you saying you don't like your prick teased?' she'd respond. And they'd laugh and fall back into their easy friendship till next time.

There wasn't going to be any of that with Homewood. His arousal was clearly a deep trouble to him. He was, she gathered, a highly moral man, happily married with a deep-rooted Christian faith. She guessed he probably rationalized these pangs of lust by treating them as a strengthening test of his beliefs.

It was clear he believed he'd successfully concealed all signs of their effect, and Alva in her turn was eternally vigilant not to let him see that she was aware of his feelings. The only person she'd mentioned it to was John Childs, whom she still met from time to time. *Their* relationship was completely asexual; indeed she found it hard to categorize it as friendship; yet she rarely refused his invitations to have lunch or occasionally go to a concert.

Their meetings all took place on such neutral territory until one evening after a concert she invited him back to her flat for coffee, she wasn't sure why except that perhaps after more than a year she felt completely safe with him. The following Sunday, as if he felt the need for balance (or perhaps, she joked with herself, he now felt completely safe with *her*!), he invited her to his 'little place' for tea. This 'little place' turned out to be a three-storeyed house overlooking Regent's Park. She found out later he'd inherited it from his grandmother. He seemed to live in it alone. She did not feel their relationship permitted her to ask any direct questions about his private life, but she did ask if she could take a look around while he was seeing to the tea. In his study on the top floor looking out on the park, one wall was lined with framed photographs. One showed a man in tropical kit glaring at the camera as if he did not

140

care to be photographed. He had a look of Childs, as did the boy in the next one who stood smiling shyly alongside a dark-skinned youth in Arab dress who had a much wider smile on his face and his arm draped familiarly over the boy's shoulders.

The other pictures were all of young men, one of whom she recognized as Simon Homewood. She presumed that these were the fortunate recipients of Childs's friendship that Giles Nevinson had told her about. A gap in the line suggested that things did not always work out well. The last and newest, an unsmiling young man with a great mop of black hair blowing across and half obscuring his face, she guessed was his godson, Harry, the tyro psychiatrist who provided the topic for a great deal of their conversation. His ambitions, her expertise, these she'd decided explained Childs's evident desire to keep their relationship going. Giles, however, insisted it was a strong masculine streak in her character, the one enabling her to resist his own advances, that formed the attraction.

'I thought we might have our tea in here,' said Childs, coming in with a tray. 'For London, it's a fine view.'

He set the tray down on the desk, nudging over a thick stack of manuscript sheets to make room.

'You're not writing a novel, are you?' she said, smiling.

He looked at her blankly and for a moment she thought she might have gone a familiarity too far, then as her smile faded, his arrived and he said, 'Oh, this stuff, you mean? No, just a little thing I'm trying to put together on the Phoenicians.'

'Not so little, from the look of it,' she said. 'Why the Phoenicians?'

'Perhaps because they were not unlike the British. Great traders, fine ship-builders, hugely ingenious in matters of practical technology. Same stubbornness too. When their principal city, Tyre, was taken by Alexander, none of the men under arms took advantage of Alexander's offer of mercy to any who sought sanctuary in the temples. Rather they chose to die defending their own homes.'

'And you think that's what would happen here?'

'Perhaps,' he said, smiling. 'But it does us good to seek help and refuge in the deep past sometimes, don't you think?'

'I think you're right,' she said. Then, encouraged by his easy reception of her inquisitiveness, she went on, 'I was looking at your photos. Is the boy you?'

'Yes,' he said. 'And that's Father.'

'I can see the likeness,' she said. 'I notice Simon's here, too. Looking very attractive. Still does, of course. Though I could wish that he wasn't attracted to me.'

She wasn't quite sure why she said it. Perhaps she was looking for advice. Or perhaps she simply wanted to test the continuing strength of the psychological links between the man and his protégés.

Childs did not respond straight away but regarded her seriously for a moment with those mild blue eyes.

He should have been a saint, thought Alva, beginning to feel a little guilty. Or a priest, maybe. Not one of your hellfire brigade, but one of those who sought to lead his flock to heaven through love, not drive them there by fear. Which was a strange judgment coming from a devout atheist who earned her crust digging for the roots of human evil!

Then he smiled and said, 'Frankly, my dear, I don't see a problem. Nice to know that Simon's human. His one fault perhaps is that he can be a bit of a boy scout. But as Baden Powell was not unaware, even boy scouts can fall into temptation. BP's remedy was cold showers, but I'm sure with your professional skills we won't need to turn on the water! Now, let's have tea.'

Alva didn't feel this was the greatest compliment she'd ever received, but it did confirm her feeling that, unfair as it might seem, though the problem wasn't hers, the solution had to be.

She made sure that her relationship with Homewood never became too informal; not always easy, as she liked him a lot. It was in some ways easier for her to deal with George Proctor, who now came into the office and performed his customary semi-military halt before the Director's desk.

He then accepted an invitation to sit down, which he did, disapprovingly, perching himself right on the edge of his chair. For the next minute or so he listened carefully to Homewood's detailed and comprehensively glossed instructions, at the end of which he nodded and said, 'So, suicide watch but we don't let him know we're watching, right?'

Homewood, long used to Proctor's reductionism, smiled and said, 'I think that just about sums it up, George. Anything to add, Dr Ozigbo?'

'Only that if ever Hadda asks to see me, please try to get in touch immediately, no matter what time of day.'

'You think that time could be of the essence here?' said Homewood.

'The disturbed mind is constantly opening and closing windows. It's important not to miss the opportunity when the right opening comes,' she said.

'I understand. You got that, George?'

'Yes, sir. Buzz Dr Ozigbo's pager any time of day or night. Best make sure you keep it switched on then, miss.'

'Oh, I will, George. I will.'

Proctor got up to go and Alva rose too. Homewood hardly seemed to notice she was leaving, busying himself with some papers on his desk. A gentleman in the old-fashioned sense, he normally would have risen and escorted her to the door. But in the presence of Proctor or any of his officers, he had taken to making a conscious effort to show that he classified her simply as a staff member like any other.

As they walked together down the corridor, Proctor said, 'Fancy a cuppa, miss?'

This was a first. She knew Proctor had a little office of his own next to the warders' common room, but she'd never been inside it.

Intrigued by the motives for this sudden attack of sociability, she said, 'That would be nice.'

The room was small and functional. Its furnishings consisted of a desk, two hard chairs and a filing cabinet on top of which stood a portable radio.

Proctor said, 'Have a seat, miss, while I pop next door. Milk and sugar?'

'Just milk,' she said.

'Right. Won't be a sec. Like some music while I'm gone?'

Without waiting for an answer he turned the radio on. It was tuned to a non-stop music station that seemed to specialize in hard rock. The music bounced off the walls at a level just short of painful but she didn't want to risk marring this moment of rapprochement by turning it down.

Proctor returned from the common room carrying two mugs of tea. He placed one in front of her and took his seat at the other side of the table.

'Cheers,' he said.

'Cheers.'

They both drank. The tea was extremely strong. Alva was glad she'd asked for milk.

'You and Mr Homewood seem to get on well,' said Proctor.

Alva had to lean across the table to catch his words above the noise of the radio but long usage had presumably inured the Chief Officer to the din.

'Yes, I'd say we have a good working relationship,' said Alva carefully. She sensed that Proctor was not just making casual conversation, so care seemed a good policy till she knew where he was leading. Her first guess was that he'd detected Homewood's feelings for her and for some reason felt it incumbent on him to warn her not to lead him on. Which, if the case, was a bloody cheek!

'Funny places, prisons,' he resumed. 'Ups and downs, lots of atmosphere, easy to get funny ideas.'

Was he perhaps a nonconformist preacher in his spare time, lumbering towards a stern moral reproof?

She said, 'Yes, I suppose it is, George. You should know that better than anyone. Because of your long service, I mean.'

'Very true,' he said. 'Bound to be the odd disagreement, though. Between you and the Director, I mean.'

'Not really,' she said firmly. 'I think we're very much on the same wavelength.'

144

'That's good. Mind you, Dr Ruskin and the Director were like that too, until they fell out.'

There had of course been various references made to her predecessor during Alva's time in the post, but this was the first mention of a dispute.

'I didn't know they'd fallen out,' she said.

'Oh yes. I mean, that's why the job came vacant.'

This was even more of a surprise.

'No, surely it was because of the car accident?' she said.

'Yeah, well, him dying like that meant they didn't have to say he'd resigned. Best to keep quiet about that, Mr Homewood said.'

'Why did he need to say that to you, George?' said Alva.

'Because I was waiting outside his office with my daily report when they had the row. Couldn't help noticing, there was a deal of shouting, Dr Ruskin mainly. Then he came through the door yelling, "You'll have my resignation in writing by the end of the day." I gave it five minutes before I went in, but the Director knew I was there. That's why two days later, when Dr Ruskin had his accident, he brought it up with me. Said best to keep quiet about Dr Ruskin wanting to resign. That way it would make things straightforward with Dr Ruskin's widow for the pension and such.'

Alva digested this, then said, 'So why aren't you keeping quiet about this now, George?'

'Oh, you don't count, miss. You're one of the family. No secrets in a family, or it just leads to bother, eh? How's your tea, miss? Like a top-up?'

'No thanks, George. I'll have to be on my way now,' said Alva, recognizing that the significant part of the conversation was at an end.

But what did it signify? she asked herself as she walked away.

She felt she'd received a warning, but Proctor's motive in offering it was obscure. Could be kindness, so her sense of being on the same wavelength as Homewood wouldn't lead her into dangerous areas of over-presumption. Or maybe it was just a malicious need to insert a small wedge in what he saw as a wrongheaded liberal alliance.

Time would probably reveal all. It usually did. She focused her attention instead on the delicate stage she had reached in her treatment of Wolf Hadda. She had a feeling that something was going to happen in the next couple of weeks. At least it seemed likely that George Proctor's new friendliness meant he would live up to his promise of giving her a buzz as soon as it happened.

ii

The buzz came sooner than she expected.

Three days later at half past four in the morning, to be precise. She picked up her bedside phone and dialled. Proctor answered instantly.

'Tried to slit his wrist, miss,' he said. 'And as they took him off to the hospital wing, he kept saying your name.'

'I'm on my way.'

She walked through the shower to wake herself up. As she towelled dry, she glimpsed herself in the full-length wall mirror. There was, she thought, a great deal more to her than her prison outfit promised. If Homewood could see her like this, the poor man would probably burst out of his trousers!

She excised the narcissistic thought, pinned up her hair and pulled on her prison kit.

She arrived at the prison at the same time as Homewood. He'd been told first about the suicide attempt, of course, but he had slightly further to come. She'd heard he had wanted to live close to his place of work but his wife had insisted that, in choosing a home for herself and her three children, other considerations came first. Alva sympathized. Homewood's devotion to his job probably meant he took it home with him. That must be bad enough without having the looming gothic reality of the place just around the corner.

He said, 'You were right.'

It sounded as much an accusation as a compliment.

Proctor was waiting for them.

146

As they walked with him towards the hospital block, he told them what had happened.

'He got into bed at lights out, settled down, seemed to go to sleep, but some time in the night he slashed his right wrist with a razor blade. Normally he's a very restless sleeper, and he's been a lot worse lately, tossing and turning all night, sometimes just lying there with his eyes wide open like he didn't want to go back to sleep. Fortunately Lindale was on duty. He's got a good nose for anything different and it struck him that Hadda was lying unusually still, so he took a closer look.'

'How the hell did he get a razor blade into bed with him?' demanded Homewood.

Proctor said woodenly, 'Looking into that, sir.'

Alva guessed he was thinking, If we ran this prison on my lines, not yours, there'd have been a lot less chance of this happening.

On admittance to the hospital block, they found the doctor waiting for them. His name was Martens. According to his own account, he'd been a star student and he couldn't disguise his sense that fate had played him a dirty trick by leaving him high and dry as a prison doctor in early middle age. He was certainly no great fan of forensic psychiatry, but her first glimpse of him this morning was reassuring. He had the weary, irritated look of a man eager to get back to his bed rather than the sad resigned expression of someone who's just lost a patient.

'Oh good. You're here at last, *Doctor*,' he said in the faintly sneering tone with which he always used her title.

Homewood frowned and asked brusquely, 'How's Hadda?'

'Hadda is fine,' said Martens. 'In fact, he might well have been fine even if he hadn't been found till breakfast. Despite what one may glean from sensational literature, wrist-slitting is a pretty inefficient way of committing suicide. Most people slash, as Hadda did, across the wrist, and few go deep enough to get to the artery. If your blood is normal, the body's pretty efficient at sealing up a severed vein. Opening it up longitudinally rather than laterally gives you a much better chance of success . . .'

147

'But he's going to live?' interrupted Homewood impatiently.

'Oh yes,' said the doctor. 'Still, I suppose it's the thought that counts.'

'Is he conscious?' asked Alva.

'Indeed he is. He became quite agitated when I tried to sedate him. He's mentioned your name several times, *Dr* Ozigbo. Not always in the most complimentary of terms.'

He said this not without satisfaction. Clearly, in his eyes, for a psychiatrist's patient to attempt suicide was prima facie evidence of failure.

And in mine . . .? she asked herself.

She moved forward into the ward. Homewood was going to follow her but she put her hand on his chest.

'Just me,' she said.

Hadda was watching her as she approached his bed. He looked pale so far as it was possible to tell on that scar-crossed face. His right wrist was heavily bandaged but it was the ungloved hand that drew her eyes. It was the first time she'd seen it plain. She understood now why he usually wore the black protective glove. The absence of two fingers was a disfigurement more startling than the facial scars or even that suggested by the eye-patch.

He said, 'Come to gloat?'

'I'm sorry?'

'Don't play not understanding,' he said. 'Everyone's entitled to an I-told-you-so, even psychiatrists.'

'You need to spell it out, Wolf,' she said. 'What is it you think I told you so?'

His gaze drifted away from hers and his expression froze as though his facial muscles were resisting his brain's command. Then, with a perceptible effort of will he brought his eye back to focus on her face.

He said, softly at first but with growing strength, 'Everything they said about me at the trial, the paedophile trial, I mean, was true. And a lot more besides. I know the dreadful things I did. I

148

know the dreadful person I was, the dreadful person I still am. I'll spell it out to you, chapter and verse, if that's what you want. I know it, I admit it, I acknowledge it.'

Now she saw his eyes filling with the tears that she'd been hoping to see from the start of her involvement in his case, but the sight filled her with pity not pleasure.

Whether it was her pity or his pain that made things unbearable she could not know, but now he broke eye contact with her and turned his head away and buried his face in the pillow. But he was still talking and she lowered her head close to his to catch what he was saying.

Distant, muffled, half sobbed, half spoken, she made out the words.

'Help me . . . help me . . . help me . . .'

BOOK TWO

the beautiful trees

Ich habe die friedlichste Gesinnung. Meine Wünsche sind: eine bescheidene Hütte, ein Strohdach, aber ein gutes Bett, gutes Essen, Milch und Butter, sehr frisch, vor dem Fenster Blumen, vor der Tür einige schöne Bäume, und wenn der liebe Gott mich ganz glücklich machen will, lässt er mich die Freude erleben, dass an diesen Bäumen etwa sechs bis sieben meiner Feinde aufgehängt werden.

Mit gerührtem Herzen werde ich ihnen vor ihrem Tode alle Unbill verzeihen – die sie mir im Leben zugefügt – ja, man muss seinen Feinden verzeihen, aber nicht früher, als bis sie gehenkt werden.[†]

Heinrich Heine: *Gedanken und Einfälle*

[†] I am the most easygoing of men. All I ask from life is a humble thatched cottage, so long as there's a good bed in it, and good victuals, fresh milk and butter, flowers outside my window, and a few beautiful trees at my doorway; and if the dear Lord cares to make my happiness complete, he might grant me the pleasure of seeing six or seven of my enemies hanging from these trees.

From the bottom of my compassionate heart, before they die I will forgive then all the wrongs they have visited on me in my lifetime – yes, a man ought to forgive his enemies, but not until he sees them hanging.

1

The ruts on the lonning up to Birkstane Farm were frozen hard.

Even at low speed, the old Nissan Micra advanced like a small boat in a rough sea and Luke Hollins, its driver, winced at each plunge into a new trough. His only consolation was that if the track hadn't been frozen, he'd have been walking through ankle-deep mud for a quarter mile. On the other hand it might have been wiser to walk. As a country vicar with four parishes to cover, he couldn't afford serious damage to his suspension. Not in any sense. Four parishes, one stipend. The Church of England in the Year of Our Lord 2017 did not require its priests to take a vow of poverty. No need when it was a built-in condition of the job!

In sight of the house his way was barred by a rickety old gate. He got out, forced it open a few feet and decided to walk the rest of the way. As he approached he could see signs of the attack that had brought him here. Smashed windows roughly patched with squares of cardboard, scorch marks up the barn door, and across the wall of the main house in red paint the words *Fuck off peedofile!*

Was there anything he could have done to stop this? He doubted it, but he still felt guilty that he'd found reasons to put off visiting his new and controversial parishioner ever since news had run round the area two weeks earlier that, seven years after Fred had died, there was a Hadda back in Birkstane.

No one had gone out to tie yellow ribbon round the old oak tree.

Jimmy Frith, landlord of the Black Dog and the kind of conservative who made Torquemada look like an equal-opportunities counsellor, spoke longingly of the rack and the stake. Many of the local women whipped themselves into a frenzy of indignation. Even Hollins' wife, a determinedly counter-traditional vicar's spouse, made it clear that in this case she was at one with the Mothers' Union. Hollins himself had acted disappointment, but beneath his plea for compassionate understanding he couldn't suppress an instinctive sympathy with the scripturally endorsed view that the best treatment for paedophilia involved millstones.

Then the previous evening at a parish council meeting he'd learned that twenty-four hours earlier a gang of young hotheads had mounted an attack against Birkstane with a view to letting Wolf Hadda know he wasn't wanted.

'Would have burnt the barn down, and not much bothered if he were in it,' said Len Brodie, his churchwarden, father of three daughters. 'Only that sudden hail shower put the fire out and sent them scuttling back to the Dog. Daresay you'd call that divine intervention, Vicar.'

He wouldn't, but he'd certainly felt it as a firm reminder that the cure of souls did not contain any opt-out clauses.

So now he approached the vandalized house with the reluctant determination of Roland coming to the Dark Tower.

Tentatively he tapped on the solid oak of the front door.

There was no sound from within and he'd raised his fist to deal a firmer blow when behind him he heard a deep-throated growl.

He spun round and found himself confronting a big man with a deeply scarred face not improved by an empty socket where his right eye should have been. His right hand was missing two fingers and his left leg looked as if it had been removed by force and stuck back on with plastic filler.

He noticed the ruined hand because the man's remaining fingers were wrapped around the handle of a tree-feller's axe, and the ruined leg because the man was stark naked. Alongside the damaged leg, and presumably the source of the growl, was what looked like a wolf badly disguised as a Border Collie.

Stepping back so quickly he collided with the door, the vicar exclaimed, 'Jesus Christ!'

'Wolf Hadda,' said the man. 'Glad to meet you, Mr Christ. Thought for a moment you might be one of them yobs, come back for more.'

'No, I'm sorry, my name isn't . . . I mean . . . I was just a bit surprised . . .'

He caught a gleam of amusement in the man's one eye, which was a relief. Mockery was fine. It came with the job. Axes were something else.

Recovering he said, 'I'm Luke Hollins, your vicar. I thought I'd drop by to see how you were settling in. I'm sorry about this . . . it's youngsters who can't hold their drink . . .'

He gestured towards the graffiti and the broken windows.

'Just letting off a bit of steam then?' said Hadda. 'With Jimmy Frith stoking the boiler, I'd guess. It's still Jimmy running the Dog, is it? How he's survived as his own best customer for forty years, God knows. It was always a high price to pay for a pint, listening to him putting the world to right. Do they still call him Jimmy Froth?'

'Not to his face,' said Hollins. 'Can we go inside, Mr Hadda? You're looking a bit cold. Do you always walk around naked?'

'No. I was just taking my morning shower. I get my water piped from the beck behind the house, but it comes in such a slow trickle it's quicker to step outside and wash at source. There's a little fall I can sit under. I heard your car and after the other night . . .'

He turned away round the side of the house, swinging the axe and burying its head in a chopping block as he passed. He did this one-handed with an ease that made Hollins glad he hadn't done anything to provoke attack. If ever that did happen, best strategy would be to run, he decided. The man's damaged left leg seemed

155

to be locked at the knee, producing a laboured rolling gait. That, combined with the facial disfigurement, should have produced a totally ogreish effect but, walking behind him, Hollins found himself enjoying the play of muscles in that broad scarred back. He dropped his gaze to the tight smooth buttocks, then quickly raised it to the sky.

Careful, boy! he admonished himself. You're a happily married C of E parson!

Inside, the house wasn't much warmer than out. There was a log fire laid in the open fireplace in the kitchen.

Hadda said, 'Stick a match in that, will you? Sneck, lie by.'

The dog settled down across the hearth, producing the deep growl once more as Hollins gingerly reached over him to light the fire. It caught quickly and he sat down at the old table and took in his surroundings.

The room didn't look as if it had changed much in the last couple of hundred years. There were ham hooks in the black ceiling beam, the small window panes had swirls and gnarls in them, and the woodwork had that bleached, weathered look you only get from long use or large expense. The rough plaster on the walls followed the swells and hollows of the granite stones from which they were constructed. Almost at ceiling height an ancient bracket clock hung from a six-inch nail driven into the crack where two stones met. Below it a shorter nail driven into the same crack supported a lettered sampler rendered illegible by an accretion of cobwebs. The room's furniture consisted of a square oak table that looked as old as the house, a trio of kitchen chairs perhaps a couple of centuries younger, and a bum-polished rocker by the fire. The twentieth century was represented by an ancient electric oven and the twenty-first by a streamlined jug kettle standing by the sink.

A surreal note was struck by the presence in one corner of a small deflated rubber dinghy and a foot pump.

Hollins stared down at this for a moment then turned his attention to the sampler. Unwilling to brush aside the cobwebs, he had to peer close to make out beneath their silvery threads the Gothic lettering painstakingly sewn by some human hand.

It was the Lord's Prayer.

'Don't get your hopes up, Padre,' said Hadda drily from the inner door. 'I think it hides a patch of damp.'

He moves very quietly for a big lame man, thought Hollins, noting with some relief that his host was now wearing a heavy polo-neck sweater, old cords, and boots. He'd also covered his empty eye socket with a black patch and pulled on a black leather right-hand glove.

'Is it fear of damp that's making you prepare an ark?' said Hollins, glancing at the dinghy.

'What? Oh that. I used to trawl the local tarns when I was a boy. I came across it stored away with a lot of other childish stuff, thought it might be worth getting it seaworthy again in case I need to go foraging for my own victuals. Talking of which, you'd like a coffee?'

'Yes, please.'

Hadda ran some water into the kettle, switched it on, put several spoonfuls of ground coffee into a pot jug, then sat down and studied his guest.

Luke Hollins had grown used to being studied, usually with disbelief.

He had a close-shaved head and an unshaved chin. He wore a bright red fleece with a full-length zip, khaki trousers that could be turned into shorts by zipping off the bottom half of the legs, and Nike trainers. His only sartorial concession to his calling was the reversed collar visible under the fleece, and even that had acquired a greenish tinge.

'Lady Kira must love you,' said Hadda.

'Sorry?'

'The castle's in your parish, isn't it? I'm sure Sir Leon still does his Lord of the Manor thing and invites the parson up to lunch after morning service from time to time.'

'Once to date,' said Hollins. 'I'm not holding my breath for the next invite.'

'It'll come. The Old Guard deals with tradition breakers by kettling them inside the tradition,' said Hadda. 'How long have you been here?'

'Six months,' said Hollins, thinking, How come I'm not asking the questions?

'As long as that? They must be desperate.'

'The only other candidate was a woman,' Hollins heard himself explaining.

'Must have been a close call. So, what can you do for me, Padre?'

'Sorry?'

'You know, if you listen to the words that are spoken to you and ascribe to them their conventional meaning, then maybe you'll find it unnecessary to say "Sorry?" all the time. You've come knocking at my door. I presume you don't want to borrow a pound of sugar or ask for a donation to the Church Missionary Society. So, likely you've come to offer your services. Not literally, I hope. I don't do prayer. So what can you do for me?'

'I can offer a sympathetic ear . . .' began Hollins.

'Really? You a pervert then?'

'Sorry . . . I mean . . . sorry?'

The kettle boiled. Hadda switched it off, waited till the water had stopped bubbling, then poured it into the jug, stirring vigorously.

'That's what I am, isn't it? Therefore a sympathetic ear implies . . . sympathy. But that's your problem. Listen, I don't want you sneaking up on my soul from behind, so let's get down to it and ask the big question. Do you get Tesco deliveries?'

He poured coffee into two heavy pot mugs and passed one across. No milk or sugar.

Biting back another 'sorry?', Hollins said, 'Yes, I mean . . . yes, we do.'

'Good. They won't deliver here, say the lonning's too rough. And even if I do a bit of fishing and so on, I'm still going to need stuff. So if I give you a list from time to time, you can add it to your order, right? Then ferry it out to Birkstane.'

158

'Well, yes, I suppose so . . .' said Hollins, thinking of his wife's probable reaction.

'Come on! Don't worry, I'll pay my whack. Anyway, I thought feeding the poor came under your job description.'

'Of course. It will be a pleasure.'

'A pleasure, is it? Maybe I shouldn't pay you. Right, jot your phone number down and I'll be in touch.'

He glanced up at the bracket clock on the wall, then rose to his feet.

'Got to leave you now,' he said. 'Appointment with my probation officer in Carlisle. That and reporting my movements regularly to the local fuzz in Whitehaven are the highlights of my social life. You stay and finish your coffee. Oh, and next Sunday when you get up in your pulpit you can tell those moronic parishioners of yours two things. The first is, I'm no threat to their kids, I've taken the cure, swallowed the medicine both literally and metaphorically, I'm fit to retake my place in society – and if they don't believe you, they can ask Dr Ozigbo.'

'Ozigbo? That sounds . . . unusual.'

'Foreign, you mean?' Hadda grinned. 'I forgot, they still think folk from Westmorland are foreign round here. Nigerian stock, I believe, but she's British born and bred. And educated too, better than thee and me, I daresay. Yes. Dr Ozigbo's my psychiatric saviour. And I'm one of her great successes. Wouldn't surprise me if she'd put me in a book by now. So tell the dickheads that. Now I'm off. If I'm late I may get detention. I'll be in touch. Sneck!'

Leaning heavily on a stout walking stick he limped slowly out of the door. The dog, with a promissory growl at the vicar, rose and followed.

After a moment Hollins tipped his coffee into the sink – he was a two sugars and a dollop of cream man – and rinsed the mug in a trickle of peaty brown water. It occurred to him that this might be a good opportunity to have a poke around, but not even radical C of E priests did that.

He went outside. The scorched barn door was open and the

159

sound of an engine clanking to life emerged, followed shortly by an ancient Defender. As it drew up alongside him he saw that Sneck occupied the passenger seat.

'That your Dinky toy?' said Hadda through the open window, nodding towards the bright blue Micra by the gate.

'Yes.'

'Next time, leave it at the top of the lonning. You were lucky to get as close as you did. And if you want to last the winter, I'd trade it in for one of these beauties.'

As the Defender's engine growled as if in appreciation of the compliment, Hollins shouted, 'You said there were two things I should tell my congregation?'

'Nice to see you were paying attention,' Hadda shouted back. 'The second is, I may be no threat to their kids, but next time Jimmy Froth sends any of his hotheads from the Dog up here, they'll find my axe will be a threat to them. End of lesson. A-fucking-men!'

2

Davy McLucky had bought a *Glasgow Herald* to read on the train. Automatically he opened it at the classifieds to check his ad was there.

> *Got a problem?*
> *GET McLUCKY!*
> *Confidential enquiries*
> *Security*
> *Debt Collection*

In fact he rarely did any debt collection, it required a level of hardness he didn't aspire to, but Glaswegians hiring a PI liked to think they were getting someone hard. It was a front he'd learned to adopt from an early age. *Your blether's aye been tae near your eyeballs*, his father had said when he came home with a tear-stained face after a hard day in the school playground. *You need to stand up for yersel'.*

I don't want you teaching wee Davy to be hard, his mother had protested.

I'm no teaching him tae be *hard*, said his father. *I'm teaching him tae* act *hard!*

He'd learned the lesson and it had helped him survive childhood and adolescence in parts of Glasgow that somehow didn't quite make it into the European City of Culture. And it had helped him when

161

he moved South and joined the Met. Conditioned by the telly, his new London acquaintance, both colleagues and crooks, were ready to be impressed by a hard-talking Glaswegian. But in that unrelenting atmosphere where every day brought new tests of what you really were, his basic soft-centeredness did not go undetected, and in the end it was made clear to him that detective constable was his limit. In his mid-thirties, divorced and disillusioned, he'd decided that he'd had enough of both the Met and the metropolis and resigned from the service. Back in Glasgow, living with his mother, he had got a job with a private security firm. Then his mother had died suddenly and he found himself the owner of the small family house on the edge of Bishopbriggs. Amazed to discover how much it was worth, he sold up and used the money to start his own PI business.

GET McLUCKY! Not a bad slogan, he thought complacently. After a sticky start, his reputation for reliable service and reasonable prices had started bringing in a steady stream of work, enough in a good season to give him scope to be a bit picky, turning down jobs he didn't like the look of, beginning with debt collection.

So why was he travelling down to Carlisle to meet a notorious ex-con?

This was the question that had made him raise his eyes from the ads section of the *Herald* and sit staring out at the frost-bound Border landscape as he headed back towards England for the first time since he'd handed in his badge.

Hadda's phone call had taken him by surprise.

'You the McLucky used to work in the Met?'

'That's me.'

'This is Wolf Hadda. Remember me?'

'Aye.'

'I'd like to hire you.'

'To do what?'

'We'll talk about it when we meet. Thursday next, two o'clock, the Old Station Hotel, Carlisle. I'll pay you for your journey time and fare before we start talking, OK?'

'Now hang about, I'd like a bit more . . .'

'When we meet. Goodbye, Mr McLucky.'

And that had been it. He'd thought about it a lot before opting to make the trip. And he was still thinking about it as he sat with his unread newspaper on his lap, staring out at the passing landscape, oblivious to its lunar beauty under the winter sun.

He had almost two hours to spare when he arrived in Carlisle. After locating the Old Station Hotel, he went for a walk around the town to see the sights.

A mini cathedral and a low squat castle, both in red sandstone, seemed to do the job. He felt no great impulse to enter either and there was a razor-edged wind following him round the quiet streets so he headed back to the hotel and was sitting in the bar, nursing a Scotch, when Hadda limped slowly in, looking warm in a long field jacket and leaning heavily on his stick.

He came straight to the table, cleared a space to stretch out his left leg, and sat down.

'You're early,' he said.

'You too.'

'Yes. My probation officer decided I'd been a good boy and didn't keep me long. First things first. What do I owe you for your train ticket and associated expenses?'

He pulled out a wallet as he spoke. McLucky noted it looked well filled.

He said, 'That'll keep. If I don't take your job, I'll not take your money.'

'Why's that?'

'Because if I don't take your job, it will likely be because it's something I don't want to be associated with, so I'll not be seen to have taken any money from you either.'

'I like your thinking,' said Hadda. 'Why'd you leave the Met?'

'Because it had nothing more to give me. And maybe I had nothing more to give it. How did you get on to me?'

'I made enquiries. I was told you'd retired and gone back home to Glasgow. I asked myself, what do old detectives do? And I got McLucky.'

163

'Fine. That's the how. Let's move on to the why.'

'Hold on. My turn to ask a question, I think. You were still a DC when you left, right? Did that have anything to do with your decision?'

'Yes and no,' said the Scot. 'If you're asking whether I felt being a detective constable in some way demeaned me, the answer's no. It was a decent enough job. If you mean, did I get pissed off seeing little gobshites with worse records and no more brains heading up the slippery pole, the answer's yes.'

'DI Medler, was he one of the aforementioned little gobshites?'

'Could be,' said McLucky, finishing his drink. 'There's a train back I could catch in half an hour. So maybe we could move things along?'

A waitress had brought some sandwiches for a couple on a nearby table. Hadda summoned her with a wave of his stick.

'Another drink? And a sandwich? You can pay for your own if I ask you to smuggle me out to Thailand.'

McLucky didn't reply and Hadda ordered anyway.

'Taxpayers picking up the tab for this?' wondered McLucky.

'What makes you think I haven't got a job?'

The PI ran his dispassionate gaze over Hadda and said, 'Well, I canna see you doing much in the world of international finance, so what else are you qualified for?'

Hadda gave a grin that matched his sobriquet.

'Back to basics, maybe. You don't forget what you learned at your father's knee.'

'So what does that make you?'

'A woodcutter,' said Wolf Hadda. 'Something you can help me with. Did Medler ever come to see me in hospital?'

The Scot nodded.

'Aye. Not long after you woke up. Just the once.'

'I'm glad about that,' said Hadda. 'I was never quite sure whether I was in or out of my mind back then. My recollection is he looked lightly grilled and he was wearing a Hawaiian shirt that looked like it had been made for some other life form.'

'Aye. He'd gone to live in Spain after he retired, so maybe that accounts for it.'

'I daresay. So when he retired, what was the word?'

'Eh?'

'Come on. I'm sure your squad was as gossipy as an all-girls marching band. What were people saying?'

McLucky thought for a moment before replying, 'They were saying that a guy who knew all the moves must have had good reason for moving out.'

'And what reason did he give?'

'Health problems, stress-related.'

'Staying in would have got him where?'

The Scot shrugged.

'Up to commander, maybe. But walking the high wire, it only takes a fart to blow you off.'

'You saying he was bent?' said Hadda.

'If I'd thought that and done nothing about it, then I'd have been bent myself. He wasn't my best buddy, guys like him don't have best buddies. Maybe he was a bit self-centred and cut a few corners, but that doesn't make him a bent cop. Look, where's all this leading?'

'I'm not sure,' said Hadda. 'He can't have been all that self-centred, though. He did come back to check me out even though he was long gone from the case. That has to mean something. What do you think, Mr McLucky?'

'Well, he could have been driven by compassion for a fellow human being in trouble.'

His expression was deadpan, his tone neutral.

Hadda said, 'Maybe. And he must have been really concerned about me to ask one of his old colleagues to keep him posted about any change in my condition.'

'Could have read about it in the papers.'

Now Hadda shook his head.

'No. The info wasn't released to the public until two weeks after I woke up. I checked.'

165

The sandwiches and drinks arrived. A scotch was put in front of McLucky.

Hadda, he noticed, was on orange juice.

He said, 'I can still catch that train if I move quick, so say something to make me stay.'

'All right. It's bothered you, hasn't it, something about my case?'

'Why do you say that?'

'Because in the hospital all those years ago, you started by doing your job conscientiously, but you ended doing it compassionately. Nothing dramatic, but by the time I got transferred to the Remand Centre, you were treating me like a human being.'

'You look after a scabby rat long enough, you can become fond of it,' said McLucky.

'Maybe. But there's something else.'

'What?'

'You're here. How many ex-detectives do you know would travel a hundred miles just for the pleasure of having a drink with a recently released fraudster and paedophile?'

'You saying I've fallen in love with you, Sir Wilfred?' said the Scot mockingly.

'Mr Hadda, please. Don't you recall, once I was convicted, they looked to see if there was anything else they could take away from me after my family, my fortune, my friends and my future, and someone said, he's still got his title, I expect Her Majesty would like that back. So they took it. No, unless your tastes are even more perverted than mine are reputed to be, you have no special feeling for me. I, on the other hand, do have a special feeling for you.'

'You do? Mind if I have the smoked salmon sandwich? It's likely from the Highlands and I'm starting to feel homesick.'

'By all means. Yes, my special feeling is based on you being a member of a very exclusive club. You see, Mr McLucky, I think that despite the fact that you only knew me for a few short weeks, and unlike my friends and colleagues who'd known me forever, or my psychiatrist who knew me in depth probably better than anyone else, or for that matter the Great British Public who knew bugger all about me – as I say, despite that and unlike them, you found it hard to be absolutely one hundred per cent sure that I was guilty as charged. Yes, that qualifies you for a very exclusive club indeed.'

McLucky swallowed the mouthful of salmon he was chewing, washed it down with whisky, and said, 'Tell me what you want, Mr Hadda, or I'm out of here soon as I finish this sandwich.'

'Thank God for the Scottish hatred of waste, eh? All right, I tried to contact you via the Met in the hope you could be persuaded to answer a few questions about DI Medler. Then I found you'd retired into the private sector, and it occurred to me that maybe we could put our relationship on a proper business footing.'

'A job, you mean? Doing what exactly?' asked McLucky, placing the last piece of the sandwich in his mouth.

Hadda said, 'To start with I'd like some basic information about the people on this list: where they are, what they're doing.'

He handed over a folded sheet of paper.

The Scot glanced down it and whistled.

'What are you after, Mr Hadda?' he asked.

'I told you. Information. To start with.'

'Aye? And to finish with?'

'A little practical assistance, maybe. Always within the bounds of legality, after making allowances for the necessary deceptions of your profession.'

McLucky gave him a hard stare then said, 'Talking of legality, last I heard, you were bankrupt. This kind of stuff could pile up the hours, not to mention the expenses. You'd need to be doing a lot of woodcutting to afford my bills.'

For answer Hadda reached inside his field jacket. This time it wasn't a wallet he produced but a bulging A5 envelope.

'There's a thousand in there,' he said, laying it on the table. 'Also my mobile number. Keep a running total and when the thousand looks like running out, give me a ring.'

'And you'll do what?' asked McLucky. 'Go into the forest and chop some more trees?'

'Like I say, you never forget what you learn as a kid,' said Hadda.

McLucky picked some crumbs from his plate and asked, 'What's the time?'

Hadda glanced at his watch. When he looked up, the envelope had vanished.

'I think you've missed that train,' he said.

'No problem. There's another in an hour. Any time scale on this?' Hadda shook his head.

'I want it done well. Take as long as it needs. All winter, if necessary.'

'All winter,' echoed the Scot. 'And what will you be doing all winter, Mr Hadda?'

'Sharpening my axe,' said Wolf Hadda.

3

Imogen Estover awoke and lay still, trying to identify what had woken her.

Old buildings have their own language as meaningful to the initiate as the singing of whales and the howling of wolves. Imogen could interpret just about every sigh and creak of her Holland Park house. She'd had plenty of time to learn in the two decades since she and Wolf Hadda had first moved in here.

Toby Estover had wanted to sell. It was strange, she'd said to him, that a man who had no scruples about taking possession of his friend's wife should balk at taking possession of his friend's property. She loved the house. She saw no reason to leave it.

So they had stayed. There had been changes. Wolf had known what he liked and seen no reason why his home should not reflect his tastes as well as his wife's. All traces of his rough masculinity had long since vanished and as Toby had shown no interest in leaving his own scent marks on the house, it was now redolent of Imogen alone.

Toby shifted heavily beside her and threw an arm across her chest.

He was getting fat, she thought. She knew that Wolf had changed physically. She had seen him during the trial. His face, his hand, his leg. And the years of imprisonment had doubtless wrought other changes. But she was certain he would never let himself become fat.

Would she still find him as magnetically attractive as she had way back? He had tried to describe to her the effect she'd had on him when he first saw her dancing on the castle lawn. She'd made no attempt to let him know the effect he'd had on her, either then or later. Attraction exerted was power. Attraction felt was weakness. Life was a struggle if you left yourself at the mercy of feelings. She had learnt that from her mother.

By now she had isolated what had woken her. It was a distant sound, very regular, part thud, part crack. It hovered on the edge of familiarity without spilling over into recognition.

She moved her husband's arm and slipped out of bed.

Toby grunted, 'What?'

She didn't reply but went to the door. The sound was too faint to have come from the front of the house which their bedroom overlooked. Out on the landing she could hear it much more distinctly. She looked towards the tall arched window that stretched from the first floor to the half-landing. It overlooked the garden and she was sure the sound was coming from out there. To get close to the window she had to descend to the half-landing. As she moved forward, she felt the cold air caress her naked body. If Toby had his way, the central heating would have stayed full on all over the house throughout the winter. She'd told him to wear bed-socks and a thicker nightshirt.

She reached the half-landing and looked out into the garden.

It was a murky night. The air was full of dank vapours dense enough in patches to negate even the perpetual half-light of the sleeping metropolis. Slowly her eyes adjusted to the outer darkness and began to etch shape, trace movement.

A big shape – the old rowan tree.

A smaller shape – a figure standing beside it.

And now a movement.

Over the figure's head something caught what little light drifted between the vapours. Bright, metallic, swift.

And then the sound again. Now it was unmistakable. How many times had she heard it in the estate forest surrounding Ulphingstone Castle?

The sound of sharp steel biting deep into wood.

She recalled the rowan standing proud among the dreary conifers of Ulphingstone forest, much smaller than these foreign invaders but large for its kind and brighter far. It had been one of their favourite trysting spots in that first crazy year when they had roamed the countryside together, making love on fellside and in forest whenever the urge took them. And often the urge had been so strong that they had not moved from beneath the rowan's shade before their first coupling.

When Wolf had learned from his father that this section of forest was scheduled for harvesting and realized that almost inevitably the rowan would be flattened along with its tall neighbours, he'd said, 'No way!' and at vast expense arranged for it to be dug up, roots and all, and transported three hundred miles to begin a new life in their London garden.

In defiance of Fred Hadda's assurance that it was an insane waste of money and the tree would be dead in a fortnight, the rowan had flourished and blossomed and fruited. Imogen recalled how her daughter, Ginny, had been tempted to feast on the bright red berries. Refusing to be put off by the bitter taste she had persevered till she'd been sick. Granddad Fred had laughed when the girl told him the story and assured her that at Christmas they'd reckoned nowt to a roast goose unless accompanied by a dollop of his Aunt Carrie's rowanberry jelly. After that Ginny hadn't rested till a recipe was found, by which time the birds had eaten all the berries. But the following autumn she'd remembered and, under Mrs Roper's supervision, she'd boiled up the berries with slices of apple and cloves and grated cinnamon and triumphantly burst in upon her mother a couple of hours later flourishing a small jar of what turned out to be a surprisingly tasty relish.

Thereafter it became an annual event, with the jelly saved for Christmas Day. When this was celebrated up in Cumbria, Sir Leon declared it was the finest rowan jelly he'd ever tasted and even Lady Kira compared it favourably with the crab-apple relish served by her family with the festive roast suckling pig. Everyone had

171

smiled at the little girl trying in vain to look modest in face of such praise, and for a few moments they had felt like a real united family.

All because of a crop of blood-red berries from this same rowan tree that someone was now chopping down.

She drew in her breath.

As if hearing the sound, the figure paused and turned to look towards the house. The air was far too opaque for her to make out features. She had the impression he was looking straight at her, but if she could only see him dimly, he would not be able to see her at all.

Slowly he raised his right arm, stretched it out, placed the palm of his hand against the trunk of the tree, and pushed.

In the same moment Toby's voice grumbled, 'Jesus, it's like an ice-box out here. Imo, what are you doing?'

And the landing light came on, wiping the garden from her sight.

She knew to the man in the garden she would be framed naked in the window, but she did not move.

There was noise outside once more, different, no single sound this time but a drawn-out creaking, tearing noise accompanied by a confusion of groans and cracks all climaxing in a single thud.

Then silence.

'Toby,' she said calmly, 'put the light out.'

'What? Oh, all right. What the hell's going on?'

The light went out.

It took a few moments for her night sight to return, but in her mind she already knew what she was going to see.

The figure was gone. And after all those long years of growth, first in Cumbria where it had come to maturity in her father's forest, then here in London where it had put on new strength in this milder clime, the rowan tree lay overturned across the ravaged lawn.

She found she was weeping.

For what, she wasn't sure.

4

A week after his first meeting with Hadda, Luke Hollins had found a message on his mobile dictating a grocery list. He turned up at Birkstane with the supplies a couple of days later.

It occurred to him that if Hadda had to drive to Carlisle from time to time to see his probation officer, there was nothing to stop the man picking up his groceries at one of the big supermarkets. Perhaps he didn't care to stump around the aisles, leaning on his trolley like a Zimmer frame. Or perhaps, despite his declaration of unsociability, he needed some human contact locally, some line of communication with what was going on around him, how people were feeling about him.

Hadda gave no evidence of such curiosity. His grunted greeting made even Sneck's rumbling growl sound more welcoming. Hollins had parked the Micra at the head of the lonning, not wanting to risk his suspension again. There were too many boxes to carry on one trip so he had to go back for the second instalment. Hadda did not offer to accompany him and the vicar tried charitably to put it down to his disability, but it was hard to keep resentment out.

On his return, very much out of puff and slightly out of temper, he found Hadda transferring the contents of the first load to his kitchen cupboards. On the table he'd placed a bag of sugar, a carton of cream, and a packet of dog chews.

'What's them?' he said. 'Not on my order.'

'Not on your bill either,' said Hollins. 'A gift.'

'Oh aye? You'll not get round Sneck that easy.'

Or me, was the implication.

Hollins opened the chews and tossed one to the dog, who caught it, nibbled it cautiously, then swallowed it whole.

'How did you find him?' he asked.

'Didn't. He found me. Takes a one to know a one.'

Meaning outcast, the vicar assumed.

'Why Sneck?'

''Cos with a dog like him you don't need one. If that hail storm hadn't started when it did, I'd have turned him loose on those idiots who came up from the village the other night.'

A sneck, Hollins had discovered in his time here, was Cumbrian for a door- or gate-latch.

He tossed the dog another chew. A sop for Cerberus.

Hadda, who'd resumed putting the shopping away, said, 'Make yourself useful then. Brew us a coffee.'

Hollins obeyed, careful to follow his host's procedure on his previous visit as closely as possible.

When he'd filled the same two mugs as before and sat down at the table, Hadda pushed the sugar and cream towards him.

'Care to try your gift?' he said sardonically.

He drank his own black and unsweetened.

'Not bad,' he said. 'A teaspoon short, I'd say.'

'You're very precise.'

'One thing I missed inside. I think they used gravy browning. The other cons were mostly trying to get smack smuggled into the jail. With me it was coffee.'

'Did you have a hard time? I've heard that people with your kind of conviction . . .'

'At first, yeah. Fortunately, at least it seems that way now, I wasn't registering all that much to start with, so it mostly bounced off me. When I began to take notice, I hit back. Didn't matter who it was. Got me a lot of trouble, but eventually the message got round. They could have their fun but they'd always have to pay for it.'

'Sounds a bit Old Testament,' said Hollins.

'You reckon? Well, that's where all the best bits are, isn't it? Including rules for survival in a primitive society.'

'And you survived.'

'I suppose so. Time helped. Good old Time. Either makes or breaks, even in prison. You stay inside long enough, you start getting treated for the way you are, not the reason you ended up there.'

Over the next few weeks, Hollins saw something of the same process taking place locally. The initial outrage faded and there were no more vigilante attacks. Perhaps the news that Sneck had adopted him helped. It turned out the dog was well known locally as an unapproachable renegade, more elusive than a fox, and as vicious a killer. He would have been shot long since if any of the local farmers had been able to get him in their sights. Hadda's own comment of *takes a one to know a one* was often repeated.

It also helped that no one could complain that the returned and unforgiving prodigal was provocative. Hadda steered well clear of the village, though occasional reports of sightings of his solitary figure trudging round the countryside came in. No one cared to approach him. Even had they wanted to, Sneck and the fact that he often carried a lumber axe were considerable disincentives. Occasionally the noise of an axe at work in some remote piece of woodland cracked through the chill air.

'Sounds more like a man attacking something he hates than just cutting down a tree,' opined Joe Strudd, his nearest neighbour.

'Does it not bother you, having him living so close to thy farm, Joe?' enquired Len Brodie, the churchwarden.

Strudd, a pillar of the chapel who reckoned that Anglicans were papists in mufti, said, 'God looks after his own, Len Brodie. Now if you were the bastard's neighbour, then I'd be worried!'

If ever a note of sympathy did enter a reported sighting, contrasting the energetic athletic young man Hadda had once been with the shambling, stooped, scarred and limping figure he had become, it was quickly countered with the stern asseveration that this was no more than just payment for his foul sins.

175

'Fifty years from now, mothers will be frightening their naughty kids with a bogeyman called The Hadda,' forecast Hollins.

'Let's hope he doesn't start frightening them a lot sooner than that,' said his wife, Willa, sourly.

It was odd, thought the vicar. Willa, childless and, in the eyes of many of his flock, outrageously liberal in her views, was the most determinedly unrelenting in her attitude to Hadda. He sometimes got the disturbing impression that she'd almost welcome an attack on a young girl to prove how right she'd been.

Hollins's grocery deliveries were of course common knowledge almost as soon as he started them. He soon realized that the price he was paying for the message of tolerance and understanding he preached was that he'd been elected Hadda's keeper.

'How's he doing then, Vicar?' he'd be asked – very few people actually spoke the name.

'Going on steady,' was the reassuring reply they wanted. 'Very quiet, that's the way he wants things.'

Only at the castle did he find this kind of bromidic response inadequate.

He could not believe it a coincidence that after he started his regular visits to Birkstane, lunch invitations to the castle became almost regular as well.

The first time he was summoned, Lady Kira ignored him till he was looking down at his plateful of steamed duff and custard. Lady Kira never touched it herself, but as a keen traditionalist, once she'd established this was as essential a part of the Sabbath to Sir Leon as Communion wine and wafers, she'd made it a permanent feature of the castle menu.

Hollins was aware that her attention had turned to him even though he wasn't looking at her. She had that kind of presence. The years that had turned Sir Leon into a white-haired patriarch had been much kinder to her, and now the twenty-two-year gap between looked as if it might be twice as much. At sixty she was still a very attractive woman, if you liked your women lean and predatory. Occasionally Hollins had felt that penetrating gaze

176

running up and down him as he ascended into the pulpit to deliver his Sunday sermon. His wife had laughed and said, 'Wishful thinking' when he told her that now he understood what women meant when they talked of some men stripping them with their eyes. But he knew what he meant.

Waiting till he was raising the first spoonful of duff to his mouth, she said, 'So how is our resident monster, Mr Collins?'

Her determined Anglophilia had made her a keen fan of Jane Austen (Dickens, except on Christmas, being far too radical) and on the few occasions she addressed the vicar direct, she always called him Mr Collins. Sir Leon did this too, but in his case, it seemed possible it was a genuine mistake. Not in Lady Kira's.

For a moment he thought of exacting a mild revenge by pretending not to know who she was talking about, but it hardly seemed worth it.

Lowering his spoon, he said in a measured tone, 'While I wouldn't call Mr Hadda a fit man, he seems determined to be independent. Apart from the loss of an eye and a few fingers, his upper body seems in good working order, and he certainly gets plenty of shoulder-muscle exercise by wielding an axe. But I regret to say that it appears as if his damaged leg still gives him considerable pain. Perhaps the cold weather doesn't help.'

'Considerable pain?' echoed Lady Kira, visibly savouring the words. 'Well, that's something. And his state of mind, how do you judge his state of mind, Mr Collins?'

'He seems to bear his lot with some equanimity, Lady Kira.'

'Indeed. Well, that's more than I've enjoyed since they permitted him to camp on our doorstep.'

'The chap's entitled to live in his own house, my dear,' protested her husband.

'There wouldn't have been a house if you'd bulldozed it down while he was enjoying his incredibly short holiday in prison,' spat Lady Kira. 'And how is it that he has a house anyway when all his other properties had to be sold off to pay for his fraudulent transactions, virtually putting our daughter on the streets!'

'Bit of an exaggeration there, I think, my dear,' said Sir Leon, glancing apologetically at Hollins. 'Point is, as I've explained before, by the time Fred died, the Woodcutter finances had all been sorted out so no one had a claim on Birkstane when Wolf inherited it. All above board and by the law.'

'The law!' exclaimed his wife. 'I thought the law banned these perverts from taking up residence anywhere near children. What about the village school?'

This was the first time she'd ever shown the slightest interest in the village school, despite Hollins's efforts to get the castle involved in opposing the council's education 'rationalization' policy which proposed closing Mireton Primary and bussing the couple of dozen local kids fifteen miles to a larger school.

He said, 'Birkstane is seven miles from the village, Lady Kira. In any case, unless we can persuade the council to change their minds, the school will be closing next summer.'

Sir Leon shifted uneasily in his chair. Poor devil feels guilty he hasn't done enough to support the campaign, guessed Hollins. But nobody in the county had any doubts who called the shots at the castle.

'Lot of fuss about nothing, eh, Vicar? They'd hardly have let Wolf out before his time was up if he hadn't been cured.'

'Cured?' cried Lady Kira. 'You mean they took a pair of gelding shears to him?'

Hollins had a flashback to his first sighting of Hadda and restrained a smile as he said, 'I don't think any actual surgery was involved, Lady Kira, but I gather he was and probably still is under psychiatric care and supervision. I'm sure Sir Leon's right, he wouldn't have been released on licence unless he'd satisfied experts that he was no longer a menace.'

'While he's still a man, he's a menace,' said Lady Kira. 'Where do these experts live, eh? Not round here, that's for sure. Take that axe of his and cut it off, that's the only way to guarantee we are safe.'

With that, she seemed to lose interest in both the topic and her

178

guest, and with evident relief Sir Leon said, 'Thought I might take a gun out in the Long Spinney this afternoon. Do you shoot, Collins?'

And Hollins, who'd been asked this question several times already, replied again, 'No, Sir Leon,' but he no longer added the word *sorry*.

5

Even nature seems occasionally nostalgic, and this year just when the English had become resigned to a future of dank wet winters, the season went retro with day after day and week after week of old-fashioned dazzling sunshine following nights of biting frost.

Not just in England either. This bracing weather stretched across the Channel and down the Bay of Biscay, till even the heliotropic ex-pats along the Spanish *costas* found they were given unwelcome reminders of what they thought they'd left behind. Tiled floors, so deliciously cool in summer, now felt icy beneath bare feet and stored luggage was ransacked in search of carpet slippers.

Arnie Medler drove carefully down from his mountain villa into Marbella. At least at this time of year, and in these conditions, there was no problem parking right outside the Hotel Gaviota, which for his money provided the most authentic Full English Breakfast to be had the length and breadth of the Costa del Sol. In the summer he was happy enough with cereal and fruit juice, but from time to time during the dark months he felt the need for cholesterol shock, and Tina, his wife, had made it clear that she hadn't come to Spain to slave over a hot frying pan.

This winter had turned him into a regular customer and he was greeted by name as he entered the restaurant. He took his usual seat at a corner table by a window overlooking the hotel pool, deserted now. The restaurant was only half full. The hotel ticked over during the off-season by offering reduced rates, mainly taken up by UK pensioners keen to escape the latest flu bug. Medler amused himself by listening to their often surprisingly intimate conversations. Many things had changed in this twenty-first-century world, but the English still headed into Europe like eighteenth-century aristos, treating Johnny Foreigner as a kind of moving wallpaper, and after a decade here the sun had burnt his skin brown enough and his Spanish had become good enough for him to pass as a native to anyone who wasn't a native.

This morning those nearest to him were couples who seemed to have said all they had to say to each other half a lifetime ago and he let his gaze wander round the room. A man was being shown to a table at the far end.

With a mild shock, more of surprise than alarm, Medler registered that his face looked familiar.

Better safe than sorry. Changing politics and economics meant that the costas were no longer the refuge of choice for British crooks, but there were still enough of them about to make a retired cop proceed with caution.

He raised his napkin to his lips and held it there till the man had been seated with his back towards him.

When he'd finished his meal, he left the restaurant by the kitchen entrance. The head waiter was in there and he looked at him in surprise.

'Señor Medler,' he said, 'is there something wrong?'

He was proud of his English and Medler knew he would smile sympathetically and wrinkle his brow if he tried to reply in Spanish.

He said, 'José, could you help me? There's a gentleman by himself, over there . . .'

He pointed through the circular window of the kitchen door.

'. . . I think I may know him. Could you find out who he is?'

He was known as a generous tipper and José had no problem in cooperating.

A couple of minutes later, by the reception desk, Medler learnt that the solitary man was his former colleague, David McLucky,

181

that he was booked into a double room but he'd turned up alone, and that he was here for another five nights.

So, not a crook who might feel like banging him on the nose for old time's sake.

But the question remained: of all the gin joints in all the towns in all the world, was it just coincidence he'd booked into this one, and alone?

'Thanks,' said Medler, peeling off a twenty-euro note.

'Is he your friend, señor?'

'We'll see. No need to mention my interest, eh?'

Another note.

'Of course not, Señor Medler. I hope we see you again soon.'

'Perhaps.'

In fact it was the following morning that the head waiter saw Medler return to the restaurant. McLucky was already at his table, talking into a mobile phone with what looked like increasing exasperation.

Medler strode confidently towards his own table, glanced towards McLucky as he passed, did a double take, then diverted.

'Davy McLucky, is that you?' he said.

The Scot looked up and said, 'Who's asking?'

'Come on, Davy. Should auld acquaintance and all that!'

'Fuck me, is it Medler?' said McLucky without any noticeable enthusiasm.

'It most certainly is! What the hell are you doing here?'

'Trying to get out and not having much luck.'

There was a tinny voice coming out of the phone.

McLucky barked, 'Sod off!' into the mouthpiece and switched it off.

'Problems?'

'I'm trying to get a flight out and not getting any joy, not without coughing up a small fortune.'

'Perhaps I can help, if it's a language thing,' said Medler, pulling out a chair. 'Mind if I sit down?'

'You never used to be so polite.'

182

'Never needed to be, when I could pull rank,' laughed Medler. 'So how are you, Davy? Still with the Met?'

'No. Asked for my cards years back.'

'Followed my good example, eh?'

'Not exactly. They said you were sick. Me, I was just sick of the fucking job.'

'You always were a bit of a loner, Davy. So what are you up to now?'

'Security,' said McLucky shortly.

'Oh Christ. What's that mean then? Nightwatchman at a building site?'

The slightly jeering tone seemed to provoke the Scot.

'No! I run my own enquiry firm in Glasgow.'

'Oh yes? And are you here on business?'

'I wish,' said McLucky. 'It would be nice to think some other poor bastard was paying me to be in this dump.'

'Oh dear. Is the wife with you? What's her name . . . Jenny, right?'

'Jeanette. No, took off with her hairdresser couple of years before I left the Met. Helped me make up my mind. You can imagine the jokes.'

'I'm sorry,' said Medler. 'So you're here by yourself?'

McLucky stared at him aggressively for a moment, then shrugged and said, 'Aye, that's right, I'm a real sad bastard, eh? Not the plan, but that's how it turned out. Me and a friend – a former friend! – we thought we'd take a break away from the blizzards back in Scotland. Picked this cheap last-minute deal on the Internet. Then I got a call at the airport: she couldn't make it, family emergency. Bitch! Got a better offer, I reckon. I thought I might as well come anyway, it was a no-refund deal. But I wish to hell I hadn't bothered. It's almost as bad here as back in Glasgow! That's what I was trying to do, get an early flight back home. There must be any amount of spare space on the charters, but no, it's scheduled or nothing, the bastards tell me.'

He looked at Medler calculatingly and said, 'You really think you could help? I'd appreciate it.'

He offered his phone.

'Maybe,' said Medler, smiling. 'But tell you what. Why don't we have some breakfast first, chew the fat about old times? Then we'll see.'

6

As the days shortened and winter bit deeper and deeper into the earth as though determined to give global warming a good run for its money, the Reverend Luke Hollins's thoughts turned to Christmas. While naturally his main focus was on the spiritual dimension and he lost no opportunity to decry the unrelenting commercialization of the festival, there was a part of his mind preoccupied with more mundane questions, such as which was more likely to get a result? – a plea to the bishop for a new heating boiler in the vicarage or a letter to Father Christmas at the North Pole?

Most of his parishioners, including Hadda, seemed impervious to the cold. Cumbrians, he decided, had a strong proportion of ice water in their veins. Only at Ulphingstone Castle did he find someone who longed for heat as much as he did and as that person was Lady Kira, this coincidence of feeling brought little mutual warmth.

The lunches, and Lady Kira's questions about Hadda (now punctuated by strident and abusive commands to servants, her husband and occasionally the vicar himself to pile more logs on the fire) continued throughout the winter.

There was, however, no reciprocal curiosity at Birkstane. If there had been, Hollins would probably have been as discreet in his replies to Hadda as he was in those he offered Kira. But the man's apparent indifference to news from the outside world in general and the castle in particular was somehow provocative. So some time in mid-December, the vicar heard himself saying as he placed the last grocery box on the kitchen floor, 'Sir Leon was telling me his daughter's coming up for Christmas.'

Hadda, who was pouring hot water into the coffee jug, paused and said slowly, 'Now why should you imagine that bit of information holds the slightest interest for me?'

'Well, she did used to be your wife, didn't she? And I thought I'd mention it just to give you a forewarning against a potentially distressing and embarrassing chance encounter . . .'

He was waffling, he realized, and he brought himself to a halt.

Hadda stirred the coffee vigorously.

Then he smiled.

'That shows Christian foresight, Padre. Lead me not into temptation, eh? Talking of which, is that a bottle of Shiraz I see sticking out of that box? I don't recollect putting that on my list.'

'Sorry . . . I mean it's a gift, it was on offer and I thought you might like it.'

The addition of a packet of chews to the order had come to be accepted, and though Hollins would not have cared to put his relationship with Sneck to the test, the dog's growl when he arrived was now anticipatory rather than minatory.

For a moment the scowl on Hadda's face made him fear the wine was going to be a gift too far.

Then his features cleared and he said, 'Thank you kindly. Much appreciated. But I really must ask you not to repeat the generosity. On the pittance the State allows me, I can't afford to develop expensive habits.'

'Come on, it only cost four quid,' protested Hollins.

'Nevertheless . . .'

He poured the coffee and they drank in silence for a while.

'So what are you doing for Christmas?' asked Hollins.

Hadda let out a snort of laughter.

'Ask me again after I've had time to sort through all my many invitations. But, like I say, definitely no more gifts, eh? I'll save the

Shiraz for Christmas Day. As for a Christmas tree, well, I've got several thousand of those just over the wall in the estate.'

The vicar looked at him in alarm and he said, 'Relax. Only joking. Now look at the time. Got to dash off to see my PO, it's have-you-been-a-good-boy? time again. Stick the rest of this stuff in the cupboard, will you?'

He was on his feet and limping towards the door as he spoke. His parting request was tossed almost casually over his shoulder and suddenly Hollins felt himself greatly irritated. What he wanted to say was, 'I'm not your bloody valet!' but what he heard himself asking somewhat aggressively was, 'Is that really how you feel about these sessions with your probation officer?'

Hadda paused and looked back at him in surprise.

'To coin a phrase . . . sorry?'

'You always seem to refer to your meetings frivolously, as though they were nothing more than a necessary chore.'

'Didn't realize I did. Though, come to think about it, what else should they be?'

'I don't know. A time for self-assessment, perhaps. A time to quantify progress.'

'Progress? From what? To what?'

Hollins hesitated before replying. He hadn't planned to go down this road at this stage in their relationship, but now he'd started, it would be cowardly to turn back.

He said slowly, 'From what and to what isn't for me to say. But I do know what I'd call the actual journey. Repentance.'

'Re-pen-tance,' said Hadda, as though trying to commit to memory a new word in a foreign language he was learning.

'Yes. I'm sure your prison psychiatrist, Dr whatsername . . .'

'Ozigbo.'

'. . . Ozigbo would have other terms for it, but that's what the Church calls it. I should have thought it was an essential element in whatever process you went through to get here – outside, I mean, back in the community. To be honest, there are a lot of things I've seen in you during our short acquaintance. Fortitude,

187

self-control, temperance, resolution. But I can't say I've detected much evidence of repentance.'

'So how would it show itself then?' asked Hadda. 'Hair shirts? Self-flagellation? Prayer and fasting? I think I could put my hand up for the fasting. Some nights I can't be bothered to make myself anything more than a mug of coffee and a hunk of cheese. Does that count, Holy Father?'

'You see, there you go,' said Hollins wearily. 'Putting up a front's fine, but do it too much and the front becomes a fixture that no one, not even yourself, can look behind.'

'Let me guess, that must be New Testament,' said Hadda. 'Nothing like that in the OT among all the smiting and begatting. I'm a bit disappointed, Padre. I was almost beginning to think you were a real post-modern priest – you know, to hell with old-fashioned preaching, let's treat people like people. But if you're going to revert to type, then you can sod off out of here and take your cut-price Shiraz with you! Think about it while you're stacking my shelves.'

He left the kitchen. Sneck, with what seemed almost like an apologetic glance back, followed him. A few minutes later, Hollins heard the Defender start up.

After its clatter had faded down the lonning, he began to put the groceries away. Eventually only the wine bottle remained. If he left it, Hadda would think he'd caved in. But if he took it, then that could be the end of their regular contact. He half regretted his outburst, but only half. He'd found himself coming to like the man but he felt the danger in that, especially when the relationship was developing very much on Hadda's terms. He recalled a seminar on the paedophile threat to the Church given by an elderly priest during his training course.

'Never forget,' the tutor had said, 'paedophiles are among the most cunning creatures on God's earth.'

The man had spoken with the voice of experience. Currently he was serving two years for indecent assault on an altar boy.

So he'd been right to confront Hadda, even if it was only to draw a line in the sand.

But every particle of reason and judgment in him said that the man was OK, that his past was a closed book that would never be opened again. In fact, come to think of it, those medieval manifestations of repentance that Hadda had mockingly cited, weren't they all around him? Living in this cold damp cheerless house, bathing each morning in the icy beck, surviving on the pathetic groceries that Hollins brought every couple of weeks, and which Hadda always paid for in full out of his social security pittance, weren't these the modern forms of hair shirt and self-flagellation?

Somewhere a mobile rang.

His own was in his pocket. This had to be in the house. Upstairs, he worked out. Hadda must have forgotten it. Would be furious if it turned out to be his probation officer, cancelling their meeting.

He started up the stairs to answer it but the ringing stopped before he was halfway up. It seemed as easy to continue as turn on the narrow staircase and he carried on up to the landing. Through a half-open door he saw the mobile lying on an unmade bed.

After a moment's hesitation, he went into the room and picked it up. The display said *1 message*.

He pressed the call button without thinking. Or without letting himself think.

Listen to message?

If it was his PO cancelling, he thought, maybe I can think of a way to intercept the Defender.

He didn't give himself time to deconstruct this piece of irrationality, but pressed again.

The voice that spoke had a strong Scots accent.

Hi. I'm at the villa! Dinner invite turned to 'Stay as long as you like'. Christ. He's done well for himself. All mod cons, swimming pool, jacuzzi. Very security conscious, big gate, high fence with what looks like razor wire on the top. All windows and doors fitted with metal security shutters that come down sharp when he presses the button. Could do with them to keep his wife at bay! She's a nice little package of simmering hormones. After the second bottle of Rioja, she started eyeing me up like she was contemplating inviting me to share her paella. Wish I'd got one of them shutters

*on my bedroom door! I'm out of here soon as I can! I'll stop off in London,
see if there are any developments on the home front. It'll be good to get
back somewhere with a bit of life. You can keep the Costa Geriatica for me.
I'm glad you're paying for it. I'll be in touch. Maybe I'll even beard the
Wolf in his lair on my way home. Cheers!*

What was that all about? wondered Hollins.

He switched the phone off and laid it on the bed.

Then he looked around the room.

Not much furniture but maybe that was all there'd ever been.
A bedside table, an ancient Lloyd Loom chair, a picture of what
looked like a lumberjack on the wall, a wardrobe that looked as
old as the rough-plastered wall it stood against.

The door was ajar.

Peering inside without opening it any further wasn't poking
around, was it?

You should have been a Jesuit! he told himself pulling the door
wide.

Couple of rough shirts and two pairs of heavy trousers. And on
the floor a cardboard wine box.

He checked its contents.

Half a dozen of Gevrey-Chambertin plus a couple of bottles of
fifteen-year-old Glen Morangie.

He thought of his four-quid bottle of Shiraz on the kitchen table.
The cheeky sod had said he'd save it for Christmas! So where had
this lot come from? Perhaps with the economy soaring to record
levels once more, social security were being unusually generous
with the Christmas bonuses.

He looked round the room for other signs of unexplained affluence.

Nothing obvious, but the blankets draped over the bed had been
caught by something pushed underneath.

He knelt down and pulled out an old metal chest, rusting at the
corners, painted in flaking black enamel, with the initials W.H. sten-
cilled on the lid in white.

It felt quite heavy.

190

There was a key in the lock.

So, nothing to hide there, not with the key left in the lock . . .

Why am I still looking for excuses? he asked himself.

Surely that wine box is justification enough?

He was still debating the point mentally as he turned the key and opened the box.

It was full of money. Bundles of fifty-pound notes, neatly laid out four times six, and at least five layers of them, with a couple of bundles missing from the top layer.

Oh hell! thought Luke Hollins, sitting heavily on the bed.

Now at last he had something to take his mind off the vicarage boiler.

7

Wolf Hadda realized he'd forgotten his phone when he was halfway to Carlisle.

Old age, he thought. Not that it mattered. The call he wanted to make was perhaps better made from the anonymous security of a landline rather as part of the babbling traffic of the air.

Public boxes were thin on the ground these days and he was on the edge of the city before he spotted one. It occurred to him that in the years since he'd rung this number, it might well have changed. In fact it was answered almost immediately.

'Chapel Domestic Agency, how can I help you?' said a bright young voice.

He said, 'I'm looking for a woodcutter.'

'Hold on.'

There was a long silence then a man's voice said, 'Good day.'

'And a good day to you too, JC.'

'How nice to hear your voice. What can I do for you?'

'I need something.'

'Really? And what makes you imagine I may be in a giving mood?'

'The fact that I've not been pestered by hordes of journalists lurking in the undergrowth. Only reason I can think of for that is editors have had their arms twisted. Only one old twister with that kind of strength I can think of.'

'I'm almost flattered. But if I have already done so much for you, why do you think I should want to do more?'

'Because having done so much suggests there's a bit of guilt there, JC. How much, I'm not sure. Eventually I'll find out, but till then you might feel the need to establish a bit more goodwill.'

'Have you never heard of simple altruism?'

Hadda replied with a silence more telling than laughter.

'All right. What do you want?'

'A couple of kilos of coke.'

'I see. Any chance of giving a reason?'

'Call it necessity.'

'In that case, give me a moment.'

'I'm in Cumbria, on the western outskirts of Carlisle, if you're running a trace.'

'Of course you are,' said the man. 'Which may in fact be pertinent. So, let me see . . . Ah, yes. Here we are. Now I think a couple of kilos might be difficult.'

'A kilo might do, at a pinch.'

'No, the problem is in the other direction. If you could make do with a hundred kilos, I might be able to help. In fact, geographically speaking, you are particularly well placed. Interested? If so, ring off and I'll get back to you in a few minutes.'

Hadda rang off and went to sit in the Defender. Three minutes later the phone rang.

He answered it, listened, made a note, and said, 'Thanks.'

'Be careful. These are professional people. And you are not as young as you were.'

'I'm not as anything as I was,' said Hadda harshly and rang off.

He got back into the Land Rover and drove away.

As he negotiated the increasing traffic into the heart of the ancient city, he said to himself, 'Now that was very easy. Just how guilty do you feel, JC?'

8

With her parentage, Alva Ozigbo felt she ought to be able to switch seasonally from a stoic indifference to the chills of winter to a sensuous enjoyment of summer heat.

The truth was her slim Scandinavian mother hated to be cold and enjoyed nothing more than luxuriating in the scorching rays of a southern sun, while her bulky Nigerian father strode around in sub-zero temperatures wearing a short-sleeved shirt and at the first sign of milder weather started mopping his perspiring brow and turning up the air conditioning.

Alva felt she'd got the worst of both worlds. She was no sun-worshipper and she hated the pervasive chill of the wintry city.

This evening as she returned home from work, the east wind that had been pursuing her like a determined stalker ever since she got out of her car managed to squeeze enough of its presence into the entrance hall of her apartment block to keep her shivering as she paused to check her mail box. It contained only one letter and as she saw the postmark, she shivered again.

Cumbria.

As far as she knew, she had only one connection with Cumbria. But she didn't recognize this handwriting.

Quickly she ran up the stairs to her second-floor flat. The central heating had already switched itself on and she turned her electric fire up high to give herself the thermal boost she needed.

Then she sat down and opened the envelope.

St Swithin's Vicarage
Mireton
Cumbria
Dear Dr Ozigbo
*I am sorry to trouble you but I need advice and, so far as
I can judge at the moment, you are the best person to
give it to me. I am vicar of St Swithin's here in West
Cumbria and since last November Wilfred Hadda has
been one of my parishioners. Let me say at once I know
that as he is a former, perhaps indeed a current, patient
of yours, the usual strict rules of medical confidentiality
will apply and I'm not about to ask you to do anything
that may break them. All I can do is provide you with
some information and ask for your expert guidance on
what, if anything, I should do about it.*

*I visit Mr Hadda every couple of weeks or so. While I
can't say his return was welcomed locally, after some
initial violent reaction things have settled down considerably, helped by both the relative remoteness of Birkstane,
his house, and also by Mr Hadda's own self-prescribed
remoteness. So far as I know, he has made no attempt to
communicate with anyone in the parish. My own conversations with him have, on the whole, been at a fairly
social level, but I haven't evaded the subject of his
offence and its consequences. While I've got the impression of a pretty calm and well-ordered personality (and
to my surprise a rather engaging one, too), I am very
aware that the baggage he carries must at times weigh
heavy. One thing I didn't spot, however, was any overt
sign of remorse or repentance. When I put this to him he
more or less told me to mind my own business.*

*Now, in a very real sense, this is my business, and I
cannot let my generally good impression of Mr Hadda*

and my respect for his rights come before my responsibilities to the rest of my parishioners. I want to be able to assure them with no reservation that I've found nothing in Mr Hadda's attitude or behaviour to suggest he could ever be a threat to their families. I suppose it could be argued that the fact that he doesn't wear remorse on his sleeve is a good sign. I mean, a paedophile still seeking the opportunity to offend would be at pains to advertise his change of heart, wouldn't he? I'd be interested to hear what you have to say about that. But the reason I'm writing to you is that, whatever the state of his libido, I've come across something that suggests in his other sphere of crime, financial fraud, he may still be adept at concealment.

Mr Hadda claims to be surviving on state benefit alone. But by chance when I was alone in his house yesterday I came across a crate of expensive wine and a box full of money. A lot of money. I didn't count it, but it must have amounted to several hundred thousand pounds, in bundles of forty £50 notes, two of which seemed to be missing (= £4,000).

I've thought about this and a possible explanation seems to be that when he was in business, knowing the risks he was running, he put aside an emergency fund, and hid it so well that the Fraud Squad investigation didn't manage to turn it up. This implies a level of fore-planning and powers of deception that trouble me. I don't know what to do. To talk to the authorities opens up the possibility that this has been a breach of his probation conditions, which would mean an instant return to jail. I don't want that on my conscience. But if it is symptomatic of a naturally deceitful character, and if at some stage it turned out he was also concealing his old urges, and these burst out and resulted in damage to any of my parishioners, I could not easily forgive myself.

*I could of course confront him and demand to know
where the money came from, and what he has spent
£4,000 on since his release. But this would certainly
shatter our delicate relationship and I doubt if I have the
skills to sort the wheat from the chaff in any explanation
he cares to offer.*

*So in my dilemma, I'm turning to you, Dr Ozigbo. Mr
Hadda has mentioned your name and your job, lightly
but affectionately I felt, and I've tracked down your
address via the Internet. No such thing as privacy these
days! And what I want to ask you is this. As the psychiatric expert who supervised his progress through the
regeneration course (sorry, don't know what you call it,
but that's how I think of it!) how convinced are you that
he is no longer a menace to the community?*

*Obviously you must have been very convinced last
autumn or you wouldn't have recommended his release
on licence. But in the light of what I've just told you,
how convinced are you now?*

*We are both employed in the cure of souls, Dr Ozigbo,
though not in the same sense of the term. Your concern
is individual; you try to repair damaged psyches. Mine is
pastoral; I try to look after the welfare of my flock. If you
do not feel able to reply to this letter, or if in your reply
you are not able to offer total reassurance, then my duty
will be clear and I'll have to report what I know to the
authorities even though I fear that the consequences for
Mr Hadda might be severe.*

I look forward to hearing from you.

Yours sincerely

Luke Hollins

After she'd read the letter, Alva went into the kitchen, took a
prepared chicken salad out of the fridge, poured herself a glass of
white wine, carried food and drink into the living room and sat

down by the fire. Before she started eating, she switched her radio on to catch the six o'clock news.

Its burden was familiar. The world was in a mess. Not quite the same mess it had been in when Wilfred Hadda started his sentence – the worry now was that the economy was overheating again rather than bumping along the bottom – but the same wars were being fought, the same groups were blowing people up in the name of the same gods, the ice-mass was a little lower, the sea levels were a little higher, a couple more species had been declared extinct – no, on the whole Hadda would probably not have noticed any significant change on his release.

She brought to mind their last meeting, some three months earlier. She had met him as he came out of the prison. The only other person there was a small bespectacled man in a battered Toyota. She recognized him as Mr Trapp, the solicitor. They hadn't met, but she had glimpsed him when he was acting for Hadda as his probation hearing approached. He wasn't the most impressive representative of the legal profession she'd met, but he seemed to know his business.

It occurred to her it must have been a pretty big favour he owed Hadda to still be paying it off after all this time. Or maybe it was Hadda's capacity to inspire personal loyalty that she saw working here. She'd felt it herself and there were suggestions in Luke Hollins's letter that he'd come under the influence.

It was a dangerous quality in a man with his sexual predilections.

There was no such thing as a cure, of course, not unless you went a lot further down the chemical road than she was able to contemplate. All you could do was try and restore that barrier between impulse and action that keeps most of us within the bounds of socially acceptable behaviour. First of all you had to strip away all the excuses and evasions, the explanations and deceptions, and once you had got the patient to see what he was, then you could start building up a positive image of what he might be.

It was a tortuous road that you trod with great care, for at the end of it lay the question, Is it safe to let this man out into the world again?

She had of course discussed progress with Simon Homewood at regular intervals. He had been consistently helpful and supportive. And always he had talked about the final recommendation for parole as being their joint decision. Technically this was true, but nothing Homewood said could blur Alva's awareness that ultimately the responsibility for Hadda's release would be hers.

She'd also spoken of the case in general terms with John Childs. Curiously she derived much more comfort from her non-specific chats with him than she did from her much more detailed discussions with the Director. Perhaps this was because his response was tinged with a gentle cynicism against which she was forced to test her own conclusions and intuitions.

'Is it inevitable,' he asked, 'that recognition of the evil of one's actions is accompanied by regret for performing them?'

'Not in certain extreme cases of sociopathic behaviour,' she replied. 'But I do not categorize my client as a sociopath.'

'Then what?'

'A man with a compulsion he deplores so much he could only deal with it by denying it completely. Like some alcoholics.'

'Isn't that a rather easy judgment? I mean, alcoholics don't hurt other people. Except their families. And they have the AA to help them. And I doubt the public would tolerate a support organization called Paedophiles Pseudonymous.'

'The Law makes judgments,' said Alva. 'My job is to assess and, where possible, adjust.'

'And ultimately to advise,' said Childs. 'It's a huge responsibility.'

'And you think I should duck it by leaving my client banged up for ever?'

'Good Lord, no. I'm sure you wouldn't dream of letting him loose if you had the slightest fear he'd still be a danger to young girls. Whether, of course, he might be a danger to anyone else hardly falls within the brief of your terms of employment.'

He smiled as he spoke, so she decided he was making what in the Home Office passed for a joke and smiled back, and the conversation then moved on to young Harry's imminent enrolment at university.

By the time of Hadda's parole hearing, she entertained no doubts about his fitness to return to society, and her certainty carried the day with the panel. Nor did she feel any pang of unease as she saw him emerge from the jail and stand for a moment, looking up at the sky.

She got out of her Fiesta and advanced to meet him. Trapp had remained in his car.

'Elf,' said Hadda, 'it's good of you to come. Good to see you exist outside.'

'That's the point,' she said. 'You've got to know that my concern for you doesn't stop at the prison gate. It never did.'

'I appreciate that. And I know I thanked you inside, but now I want to thank you outside for all you've done for me. Without you . . . well, I don't know what I'd be. I certainly know where I'd be! Thank you. And I'm sorry for all that crap I fed you.'

She shook her head and said, 'You were in denial. Anyway, it was full of truths; not always the truths you imagined, but without them, I'd never have known how to move forward.'

This amused him enough for the transforming smile to flicker briefly across his lips, and he said, 'So a diet of crap can do you good? Must remember that whenever I hear myself moaning about prison food. Now I'd best be on my way. I'm due at the hostel at ten. Don't want to start my new life by being late.'

She knew he was booked into a halfway house, knew also that when he moved out of there after a couple of weeks, he planned to return to his family home in Cumbria.

She'd said, 'Good luck. The probation service will keep me updated on how things are going, but if you ever feel the need to get in touch direct, don't hesitate.'

He had smiled and for a moment she'd thought he was going to lean forward and kiss her goodbye. But in the event he only gave the kind of head bob men give to royalty, then went across to the old Toyota, got in and was driven away without glancing back.

A job well done, she'd thought. Not necessarily a job finished.

When you're dealing with the human mind, you can never say the job's finished. But so far, so good.

And now there was this letter.

She made herself finish her meal and wine before she picked it up again.

Luke Hollins was worried and so was she. Even though the syndrome Hadda had presented with predicated great powers of deception, this firm evidence of their continuance was disturbing.

Even more than the source of the money, she shared Hollins's concern about the missing four thousand.

A man with Hadda's record spending that kind of money in a few months . . . her heart sank.

She knew what she ought to do and that was drop this lock, stock and barrel into the lap of the probation service. And she knew that the almost inevitable result would be a revocation of Hadda's licence and a return to custody, at least until his case was reviewed.

These things she knew.

At the same time she realized that, without spending long hours in soul-searching and mental debate, she knew exactly what she was going to do.

9

Drigg Beach on the Cumbrian coast is a heavenly spot on a fine
summer day. A couple of miles of level sand, skylarks above the
dunes, oyster-catchers at the water's edge, the Irish Sea sparkling
all the way to the Isle of Man, to the south the bulk of Black Combe
looming benevolently over the land, to the north St Bees Head
staring thoughtfully out to sea, all combine to provide a setting in
which even the prospect of Sellafield Nuclear Power Station
slouching in the sunshine can attain something of a festive air.

But in the darkness of a cold December night with scorpion tails
of sleet riding on the back of a strong nor'wester that drives the
white-maned waves up the shore like ramping hosts of warrior
horse, it can feel as remote and perilous as the edge of the Barents
Sea.

Tonight, however, there was human presence here, on the shore
and on the water.

A motor-powered rubber dinghy came riding up the beach till
it grounded on the sand. Two men in wet suits jumped out carrying
between them a large leather grip. At the same time two more men
climbed out of a Toyota Land Cruiser parked on the shore and ran
down to the water's edge where the first pair deposited the grip.
As they returned to the dinghy, the men from the Land Cruiser
carried the grip to the car. They were ill matched in build, one large
and lumbering, the other much slighter though with an athletic

rhythm of movement that gave promise of strength. He certainly seemed to take his share of the load as they hoisted their burden into the Toyota's load space.

Meanwhile the dinghy men had unloaded a second grip on to the sand. They then climbed into the dinghy, the helmsman put the engine into reverse for a few metres then swung round and accelerated out to sea.

By the time the shore men had carried the second grip to the Toyota, the dinghy had vanished into the darkness.

Once more the two men bent their backs to swing their burden up into the load space.

'I shouldn't bother,' said a voice.

From the landward side of the vehicle stepped a figure. He was tall, broad-shouldered; his features were hard to make out but they could see that over one eye he wore a piratical patch; and in his hands he carried a long-handled axe.

The smaller man reacted first, releasing his hold on the grip handle, and reaching into his jacket. The shaft of the axe swung and caught him under the jaw and he collapsed to the ground without a sound.

The taller man had been unbalanced by having to take the full weight of the grip and by the time he let go and straightened up, he found the blade of the axe was six inches from his neck. It stayed steady even when the axeman took his gloved right hand off the shaft and reached down to pluck a gun from the unconscious man's jacket.

'Makarov,' he said dismissively. 'Just an old sentimentalist then.'

He tossed it behind him, then nodded down at the grip.

'Open it,' he said.

The big man obeyed.

The grip was full of transparent packs of white powder.

'Lay them along the sand,' said the axeman. 'In a straight row.'

When that was done he pointed to the grip already loaded.

'Again,' he said.

The man repeated the process except that this time when there

203

were only a couple of the packs left, the axeman said, 'That'll do. Now walk slowly along the row.'

The man started to walk. Suddenly he cried out in terror as the axe-blade whistled past his ear. Then it buried itself in the first of the packs, splitting it open so that the powder spilt out across his shoes.

The process was repeated till all the packs had been burst. By the time they returned to the car, the tide was already running up over the line.

'The fish will be happy tonight,' said the axeman. 'See if you can revive your mate.'

He laid his axe on the sand, took an empty rucksack off his back and placed the remaining two white powder packs in it. The big man knelt by his companion.

'Hey, Pudo, Pudo, you OK?'

There was no response, so the big man tried slapping his face. Perhaps he meant to be gentle, but he wasn't built for refinement. With a scream of pain, the recumbent man tried to roll away from his companion.

'I'd say if poor old Pudo's jaw wasn't broken before, it certainly is now,' said the axeman. 'See if you can get him on his feet without breaking anything else.'

He shrugged the rucksack on to his broad shoulders, retrieved his axe, raised it high and brought the broad back of the head down on the pistol barrel. He then picked up the weapon and chucked it into the back of the Land Cruiser.

'I wouldn't recommend trying to use it,' he said. 'But what I would recommend is for you to get your mate into your car and drive away as fast as you can. If you're tempted to hang around this neck of the woods, just remember that, next time we meet, I may not be in such a generous mood. Tell whoever sent you that he should find himself another landing spot. This coast is out of bounds. You got that?'

The big man nodded. His injured companion was now upright. He still looked as if his knees would buckle without the support of the other's arms, but the gaze that he fixed on the axeman was lively enough. His eyes were black and glittered with hatred. He tried to speak but the damage to his jaw made this impossible.

'No need for thanks, Pudo,' said the axeman. 'Get him aboard.'

The big man half carried, half dragged the other to the passenger door and pushed him on to the seat. Then he walked round to the driver's side. Here he paused by the door, looking round, as if expecting further instruction.

But the axeman had vanished just as completely as the white powder scattered along the beach had disappeared beneath the onward surging waves.

10

Imogen Estover arrived at Ulphingstone Castle four days before Christmas. She parked her sky-blue Mercedes E-Class coupé, sounded the horn, and strode through the main entrance confident that her mother's well-trained staff would take care of her luggage without need of any further instruction.

'Darling, you're early. How nice,' said Lady Kira, offering the double air kiss that was the nearest she permitted to physical contact when her make-up was on.

'London's hideous. You can smell the fug in Oxford Street three miles away,' said Imogen. 'I thought of the fells in the sunshine and had to escape. I can't wait to get out.'

Lady Kira wrinkled her nose. Though occasionally she might affect nostalgia for the great swathes of Caucasian wilderness her family had allegedly once owned, or even join a shooting party on the estate – usually proving herself a better shot than most of the men – she was no lover of the Great Outdoors. Fell walking was, in her vocabulary, a euphemism for trespass, and all that could be said for rock climbing was that from time to time it killed one of the idiots who indulged in it.

Her daughter's enjoyment of these pursuits she treated as a sort of venereal infection resulting from her marriage to the wood-cutter's son. But if the years of motherhood had taught her anything it was that Imogen had a will as strong as her own, so she passed no comment but said, 'Where's Toby?'

'Probably clearing his desk so he can roger his fat secretary on it,' said Imogen. 'He'll be up tomorrow on the train.'

Kira screwed up her mouth and for a surprised moment Imogen thought the reference to Toby's infidelities had disconcerted her, but she was quickly reassured.

'On the train?' said Kira in disbelief. 'Pasha's driving up tomorrow, or rather being driven up in that lovely Bentley of his. I'm sure he'd be delighted to give Toby a lift.'

'I think Toby would prefer the train.'

Her mother frowned.

'Prefer travelling with hoi polloi rather than with someone who is his very important client, my relative, and everyone's friend?' she said. 'Why would he prefer that?'

Imogen said, 'I really can't imagine, Mummy. Can you?'

Her father appeared.

He said, 'There you are, my dear. Saw the car,' and gave her a hug.

'Hello, Daddy,' she said. 'You're looking well.'

'Am I?' said Sir Leon doubtfully. 'Nice of you to say so. Staying long?'

'Well, till after Christmas anyway.'

'Ah, Christmas. Toby with you?'

'He's coming tomorrow. And I gather we're having the pleasure of cousin Pasha's company too.'

'What? Oh yes. Nicotine,' said Sir Leon with no sign of enthusiasm.

'*Nik-EE-tin*,' said his wife in an exasperated tone.

Imogen smiled at her father and patted his arm gently.

'I'll go and get unpacked,' she said.

Her parents watched her leave the room then Sir Leon said, 'She know that Wolf's back at Birkstane?'

'I expect so,' said his wife.

'But you didn't mention it?'

'If she knows, why would I remind her?' asked Lady Kira. 'And if she doesn't, why would I tell her?'

They stood and looked at each other, she with indifference and he with the blank incomprehension that had quickly replaced that now almost mythic sense of pride he had felt when, aged forty, he had turned to see his beautiful eighteen-year-old bride processing up the aisle towards him.

Upstairs, their daughter stood in the wide bay of her dressing room and looked out over the lawn to the forest. Frost still sparkled on those shaded areas of grass that the sun couldn't reach. The air was so clear she could pick out the individual branches and trunk markings of the first line of trees and in the distance she could make out some of the great Lakeland fell tops whose names were as familiar to her as those of most of her friends.

She knew her Cumbrian weather. Meaning she knew there was no way of knowing what was going to greet her when she woke the following morning. When you see what you want, don't hesitate, had long been her philosophy. Ignoring her unopened cases, she went downstairs to the drying room where she'd dumped her gear last time she was here. Boots, cleaned and waxed, stood neatly on low shelves, jackets and waterproofs hung from their pegs. Who was responsible for the cleaning and tidying she'd no idea, except that it was unlikely to be her mother. She slipped on a pair of lightweight boots, grabbed a jacket at random and went out of a side door.

She met her father at the corner of the terrace.

'Hullo,' he said. 'Off for a stroll?'

'Shame to waste this weather,' she said, not pausing in her easy, deceptively fast stride.

He watched her go. She had matured into an elegant, shapely woman, but as she walked away from him now, she didn't look all that different from the young teenager who'd run wild around the estate a quarter of a century ago. The thought took him somewhere he didn't care to go. Suddenly it was his granddaughter he was seeing . . . Ginny . . . lovely lost Ginny. At her christening he'd sworn to himself that he'd do everything in his power to protect her, and he'd failed. As usual, the women in his life had had their way and she'd been whisked out of his sight to France . . . and finally out of his sight for ever . . .

He shook the pain from his head and refocused on his daughter. From the direction she was taking across the garden he guessed where she was headed. Nothing to be done about it, he thought as she vanished into the wood.

Nothing that ever could be done about it.

Half an hour later, Imogen was standing on the far edge of the forest looking out at the back of Birkstane Farm. The boundary wall was tumbledown here and she stepped easily over the moss-wigged stones. Through the kitchen window she glimpsed movement. She was not a woman who hesitated action and she went straight up to the back door and pushed it open without knocking.

Her face rarely registered surprise, but it did now.

It wasn't Wolf Hadda she found sitting at the kitchen table but a slim black woman with high cheek bones and fine shoulder-length hair of a curious ochrous shade that didn't look artificial.

Imogen said, 'Hello.'

The woman replied, 'Hello.'

Imogen's gaze moved round the room. Unwashed dishes in the sink, one cup, one bowl, one plate. Wolf, alone, never washed up after a meal, always before the next one. So breakfast for one.

She said, 'Wolf not home then?'

The black woman said, 'Evidently not.'

'You're waiting for him?'

'For a while.'

Imogen liked the non-aggressive way she refused to initiate an exchange of information. At the moment, in the unspoken contest to establish who had the greater right to be in Wolf's kitchen, honours were pretty even.

In the fireplace paper and kindling had been laid and several dry logs were stacked ready on the hearth.

She said, 'Too nice a day to waste indoors, but if you're going to sit here long, I'd put a match to the fire.'

Then she turned and left, not bothering to close the door behind her.

11

You should have closed the door, thought Alva Ozigbo.

She'd known this was Hadda's former wife as soon as the woman stepped into the kitchen, and not merely because her files on the man contained photographs. In fact, to identify her from the photos wouldn't have been easy. They all showed her in urban mode, elegant, composed. The figure that stepped through the door in her boots and ancient jacket, her face flushed from walking fast in the cold air, and with bits of twig and bark in her hair from ducking under low branches, was very different. But Alva had recognized her at once. Perhaps it was the composure. That was still very much there.

But she hadn't closed the door behind her. Probably because she did not want to risk even the suggestion of a slam.

They must have made a magnificent couple, thought Alva. Both tall, strong-featured, blue-eyed, blond-haired, with the poise that comes from physical athleticism and psychological certainty. Both qualities vanished in Hadda's case, but from this one brief glimpse, as present as ever in his ex-wife.

She glanced up at the old bracket clock hanging on the wall.

Half past three. She'd wait another half hour, she decided. Luke Hollins had said that if Hadda was out and the Defender was in the barn, that meant there was a good chance he'd be back before dusk, which began to fall about four o'clock this time of year.

She looked up and he was there, standing in the open doorway.

'You should have lit the fire,' he said.

'That's what your ex-wife said.'

He showed no surprise but moved across the kitchen with that slow limping gait she remembered so well, stooped over the hearth, struck a match and set it to the paper. Behind him a dog paused in the doorway to study her, then, growling softly in its throat and never shifting its gaze, padded across to the fireplace and lay down.

'You knew she'd been here?' she said.

'I saw her leaving.'

'But you didn't speak?'

'No,' he said indifferently. 'For the time being, I've nothing to say to her. Anyway, I can't manage a conversation with two women at the same time and I wanted to talk to you first.'

'How did you know I was here?'

'I saw your car at the end of the lonning.'

'You saw a car. How did you know it was mine?'

'I saw you in it outside of the prison, remember? Grey Fiesta, very anonymous, a real psychiatrist's car. Hollins tell you not to try to bring it all the way up?'

'Yes. He said there were ruts you could lose a sledge team down.'

Hadda smiled.

'Nice turn of phrase for a parson. I keep telling him he ought to dump that Dinky he drives, but he says he can't afford a four by four.'

'Perhaps you could loan him the money. I gather you're quite flush at the moment.'

She saw no reason to dance around the reason she was there. If he'd worked out that Hollins must have been responsible in some way for her visit, then he must also suspect – or have deduced from some trace the vicar had left of his search – that the money box had been discovered.

'Perhaps I could. I feel guilty that the poor devil has got to carry my groceries the last quarter mile. So what did you and Imogen find to talk about?'

If this was evasion, he disguised it very well as indifference.

'Absolutely nothing. We didn't even introduce ourselves.'

'No need,' said Hadda. 'Clearly you recognized her. And she'll be able to find out everything she needs to know about you.'

'How?' asked Alva, puzzled.

'Striking black woman arrives at vicarage then drives out to Birkstane. Every detail will have been noted and analysed by the locals. Hollins and his wife will be quizzed. No need to tell you how much can be given away by even the most noncommittal of answers. Add to this your car. Even anonymous psychiatrists' cars have numbers. When Imogen left she headed out up the lonning so she'll have had a good peer around it too. Did you lock it?'

'I'm not sure. No, I didn't. Somehow, leaving it out here . . .'

'. . . in the middle of nowhere, it didn't seem necessary,' he finished her sentence. 'You'll learn. Leave anything lying around in there?'

Alva said, 'My case is in the boot.'

Hadda whistled.

'Hope you didn't pack it with confidential files. So you're not staying at the vicarage?'

Very quick, she thought. Perhaps his emotional turmoil during most of their later sessions in the prison had obscured just how sharp his mind was.

'Mr Hollins did ask, but I'd booked a room at the village inn. Only, when I got there, it turned out there'd been a mix-up. The landlord said he was sorry, it must have been the girl who took my order, but they were full.'

'That would be Jimmy Frith, better known as Froth,' said Hadda. 'Big fat man, in his sixties, sharp intake of breath when he saw you, smiled a lot as he told you to sod off?'

'Are you suggesting he lied because I'm black?' said Alva. She'd suspected it herself, but couldn't be bothered to make a fuss.

'Hard to prove,' said Hadda. 'For a start, it's against the law, and you need to get up very early in the morning to catch our Jimmy breaking the law.'

213

'Then perhaps someone ought to get up early in the morning,' she said, irritated at what seemed a rural complacency in the face of prejudice.

'Maybe somebody will,' he said, smiling. 'So you didn't head back to the vicarage to take up the padre's offer?'

'No, I thought if I came straight out here, maybe I could take a good step south this evening.'

He said, 'You can stay here if you like.'

The offer took her by surprise.

She said, 'Thanks, but I don't think . . .'

'It's all right, you don't have to brush up your transference theory, I haven't taken a sudden strange fancy to you,' he said. 'It will be getting dark soon, the mist will be rising, the frost falling, and you don't want to be driving round our narrow roads in those conditions.'

'It's not dark yet,' she said.

'No, but it will be by the time you interrogate me about the money,' he said.

I was right, she thought. He knows exactly why Hollins contacted me. This is not a good start!

He went on, 'Also you'd be doing me a favour.'

'How so?'

'Imo won't come back if she thinks you're still around and, to be honest, I don't think I'm ready yet to meet her face to face.'

This was indeed honest. One thing you learned to distrust in patients like Hadda was a show of honesty.

Delaying her decision, Alva said, 'But having me here one night wouldn't be much help. Surely she'll be staying at the castle for the entire holiday?'

He said, 'Someone more suspicious than me might think you were fishing for an invite to spend all of Christmas at Birkstane.'

'Someone couldn't be more wrong,' she said. 'My parents are expecting me.'

'And you want to spend Christmas with them?' He sounded genuinely curious.

She said, 'Certainly I do.'

'Touching,' he said, regarding her expectantly.

Why am I delaying this decision? she asked herself. She knew it ought to be *No*. But she also knew it was going to be *Yes*.

She said, 'Thank you, I will stay here tonight.'

'Great. Off you go and get your case. I'd offer myself but you'll be twice as quick. And lock the car this time. Oh, hang on a sec.'

He went out of the kitchen and returned with a couple of heavy blankets.

'Here,' he said. 'Take these.'

For a moment she thought he was inviting her to make herself a bed on the kitchen floor, or out in the barn. Her uncertainty must have shown for he grinned and said, 'Drape them over the bonnet of your car. It's going to be a bloody cold night and we don't want your radiator to freeze up, do we?'

She took the blankets and left the house. When she returned, she saw he'd been busy. Logs had been piled on to the kitchen fire, the washed dishes were draining by the sink, and an electric kettle came to the boil and switched itself off as she entered the room.

He must have heard her come in. From somewhere above, his voice called, 'Up here.'

She left the kitchen and went up a steep flight of worn stone stairs.

Sound and an open door led her into a bedroom where she found Hadda shaking a fresh white sheet out over a bed.

'Tuck that side in, will you?' he said.

She obeyed. As she helped him with the second sheet, she noticed a pile of bedding on the floor by the door.

'This is your bedroom,' she said.

'That's right.'

'But I can't move you out of your own bed,' she protested.

'No problem. There are two other rooms with perfectly good beds in them,' he said, swiftly and efficiently piling blankets on top of the sheets. 'But they'll need a bit of airing.'

'I'd be perfectly happy . . .'

'I wouldn't,' he interrupted. 'I can guarantee your virtue is safe under my roof, but I can't do the same for your respiratory system if you don't use this room.'

'But what about you?'

'You forget where I've spent most of the last decade,' he said. 'Her Majesty's hospitality either wrecks you or leaves you with the constitution of a polar bear. The speed I move, I've had to develop highly efficient heat-conservation circuits. There, if you need more blankets, you'll find them in that chest. I've laid a fire in the grate to take the chill off the air. There should be plenty of space in the wardrobe unless that bag of yours holds a lot more than it looks to.'

He stooped to set a match to the fire as Alva put her bag on the bed and unzipped it. Then she went to the wardrobe to check if Hadda's notion of plenty of room matched hers.

It did, though the wine box on the wardrobe floor might impede the hang of the one long dress she'd packed – not in any expectation of needing it but because her actress mother had taught her what she claimed as an old touring adage, *When packing, try to anticipate the extremes which are, sleeping on your dressing-room floor or dining with a duke.*

'Yes,' said Hadda behind her. 'That's the secret booze hoard I'm sure Hollins has told you he chanced upon. And seeing as you know about it, we might as well spare ourselves Tesco's cut-price Shiraz.'

He stooped down and drew out a bottle.

'He told me he chanced upon your money chest too,' said Alva.

'Is that how he put it?' said Hadda. 'Well, if like a timid old maid, you check under the bed before you get into it, you'll work out that he must also have chanced to get down on his knees, pull it out, turn the key and raise the lid.'

'I might have done the same, out of curiosity,' she said.

'So you might. But you are my guest and this is your room, and therefore you have certain rights of access.'

Then he laughed and said, 'But don't worry, I'll practise what I

216

presume Hollins preaches and forgive him. Now, have you got everything?'

'I think so. Let me see . . .' She looked around. A stack of books on the deep sill of the small window caught her eye. '. . . Yes, even bedtime reading. Hello, I thought I recognized that lurid green jacket . . .'

She went to the window and picked up a copy of *Curing Souls*.

'Now this is very flattering,' she said lightly. 'What happened? You got a psychic message that I might be coming, so thought you would try to impress me?'

'Something like that,' he said, smiling as he took the book from her hand.

'At least let me sign it.'

'Later perhaps,' he said firmly. 'Oh, one thing I forgot. Bathroom is first left. Water pressure is pathetic, hot water is in short supply, but don't be put off by the faintly brown tinge, it makes a lovely cup of tea which will be awaiting you when you're ready to come down.'

He left her.

She thought of only unpacking what she'd need for tonight to make a statement. But it would only be a statement if at some point he came into the room to notice.

She unpacked everything. As she hung her clothes up, her thoughts kept turning to the box. Should she open it or not? He'd more or less given her permission. More or less. In any case, no need to admit to opening it. Unless there was some way he could tell if it had been touched, some little trick he'd picked up in prison, a hair across the lid, for instance . . .

This is silly, she told herself. Open it, and if he asks, admit to it.

She knelt on the floor by the bed, reached under and drew the tin chest out.

It scraped along the bare floorboards.

She had a picture of Hadda standing directly underneath, looking up at the ceiling, and smiling.

She turned the key, lifted the lid.

The bundles of banknotes were there as Hollins had described. But there was also a scrap of paper lying on top of them.

On it was written *Your tea's getting cold.*

So it's games time, she thought.

That was fine. He might think he was good at game-playing, but she had degrees in it.

She shut the box and went downstairs.

12

At two thirty that afternoon Toby Estover had not been rogering his secretary on his cleared desk as his wife had theorized.

He'd completed that task mid-morning, shortly after his arrival in the office. In the years since his marriage he had started to put on weight and now his elegant suits were cut to disguise his middle-age spread rather than show off his youthful figure. Also he'd been diagnosed with a slight heart problem, which meant he ended up post-coitally slightly more breathless than his doctor would have cared to see, even though the secretary, Morag Gray, an obliging Scottish girl built on the same generous lines as all her predecessors, made sure he had little to do other than lie back and think of England (who, incidentally, were also feeling slightly breathless as they received yet another comprehensive thrashing in their final one-day game in distant Mumbai).

After a lengthy recovery period, hindered rather than helped by several cups of strong coffee which did nothing for his blood pressure, he had asked Morag if there'd been anything in the morning mail that required his attention before he began his extended festive break.

She replied, 'Not really. A few Christmas cards.'

She scattered them on his desk. He made a dismissive movement and she began to gather them together again. Then he reached forward, eased one of them out of the pack with his forefinger, and impatiently waved the rest of them away.

She observed him curiously as he studied the card at length.

In her eyes, it wasn't at all Christmassy. It showed a tall figure wearing a floppy hat and some form of overall. His right hand rested on the haft of a long lumberjack's axe, and he was standing on a ridge looking out over a mountainous landscape. The sky was filled with dark lowering clouds. It was a composition in blues and browns. The only touch of brightness lay in an edging of red along the blade of the axe.

Now Estover picked up the card and opened it. There was an inscription printed in a bold red font.

May your Christmas be merry
and New Year bring you all that you deserve.

There was no signature.

He said, 'Where's the envelope?'

'Shredded,' she said. 'Why?'

'No reason. See if you can get Mr Nutbrown on the phone . . . no, on second thoughts, forget that. Some things are better face to face.'

'Aye, I know what you mean,' she said huskily.

He looked at her blankly. Please yourself, thought Morag. Her employer didn't do sexy small-talk. She knew this, but she was basically a sweet girl and kept on trying.

He stood up and headed for the door, slipping the card into his inside pocket.

There was something there already and he pulled it out. He paused, turned, said, 'Nearly forgot. Merry Christmas, Morag. See you next year.'

After he'd left, Morag checked the plain buff office envelope he'd handed to her. No writing on it. She opened it. Bank notes, used, not in sequence. Generous, but no accompanying message. It would have been ironic if this year Estover had made some more personal gesture, but now into her third year in his employ, like the absence of intimate chit-chat, this was what she'd come to expect. This was the measure of his trust.

She picked up her phone and dialled.

'Hi, Mr Murray,' she said. 'It's Morag. He saw the card and he's away out. I think he's going to see Mr Nutbrown.'

'Guid girl,' said a man's voice.

Their shared nationality had certainly made it easier to accept this man's proposal, though she assured herself she would never have betrayed her boss if there'd been the slightest hint of any emotional connection in their sex. But not once in the two and a half years she'd worked for Estover had he given her anything but money, which made her . . . well, she didn't care to think what it made her, but it didn't make her loyal, that was for sure.

She slipped the envelope into her bag and put Toby Estover out of her mind. Christmas and Oxford Street were just around the corner. What with her bonus and her new Scottish friend's contribution, she could do full justice to both.

13

Toby Estover was not much given to flights of fancy, and he had long since forgotten all of his classical education save some scraps about Roman Law, but as he eased his Lexus out of the gloomy underground car park up into the bright winter sunshine it occurred to him that this must have been how it felt to emerge from Hades.

Except of course that London's traffic as the modern Saturnalia raged to its climax was just another form of hell. As he progressed slowly northwards, he was tempted to abandon his plan and use the car phone to contact Johnny. But he'd tried that several times recently, he reminded himself. He had an uneasy feeling that, despite all his urgings that whatever they did, they must do it in unison, Pippa Nutbrown was plotting some independent action. He needed to see for himself.

Finally with huge relief he joined the M11, still very busy but at least he was able to spend more time with his foot on the accelerator than the brake for forty miles till he turned off towards Saffron Walden.

His destination, Poynters, Johnny Nutbrown's country retreat, wasn't easy to find even for a frequent visitor, and now Estover drove slowly by choice to make sure he didn't miss the unclassified road that eventually led him to the old stone gateway marking the entrance to the grounds.

'Well, well, well,' he murmured, bringing the car to a halt.

There was a *For Sale* sign by the gate.

He sat and studied it. The agent was Skinners of Mayfair. He knew them. They specialized in top-of-the-market country estates. Claimed to get the highest prices. Which was just as well, as they charged the highest commission.

Approached up the drive, the house sold itself. Warm red brick below, black timbers against dazzling white mortar above, not one of your great rambling Tudor mansions, relatively small but perfectly formed, all bathed in the brightness of winter sunshine that either reveals flaws pitilessly or, as in this case, emphasizes every perfect detail of line and contour. It looked like most Englishmen's unachievable dream of a place in the country.

Johnny had achieved it, and Estover knew how much he loved it. Which made it all the more worrying that he was trying to sell it.

He parked the car and tugged at the old bell-pull at the side of the almost square front door.

After a few moments it opened and a woman looked out at him with little sign of enthusiasm.

'Pippa,' said Estover, smiling. 'The house looks so well that, if I had bucolic longings, I might be tempted to buy it myself.'

Pippa Nutbrown in her youth had always had a faint look of dissatisfaction even at moments of great pleasure, as though the peach she was eating could be juicier, or the music she was hearing could be better played, or the sex she was enjoying could be more ecstatic. But youthful beauty, good skin tone and a lively manner had obscured the expression, or else merely inspired the men in her life to attempt to do better next time.

Now, however, time, which had made this house look more beautiful, had in her case merely eroded everything else and left her looking permanently and unmistakably dissatisfied.

'Toby,' she said coldly. 'I hope you're not expecting lunch.'

'Why should a man need lunch who has your beauty to feast upon?' he asked.

'If I want a combination of meaningless noise and crap, I'll take a walk through the rookery,' she said.

223

She turned away and he followed her into the house.

Her arse, he remarked with the eye of a connoisseur, was the only feature that age had improved. Once a tad angular for his taste, it had broadened into a saddle fit for a champion jump jockey. Perhaps this was the best angle of approach. He had sampled Pippa face on in their shared youth, but had not been tempted to repeat the experiment. He liked to see his own rapture mirrored in the eyes of the women he screwed, not a pair of scoring discs reading five point two.

But she had other attractions, one of them being an almost complete lack of any moral sense, and another an almost complete control over her husband. She would have needed that to persuade him to put Poynters on the market.

She pushed open the door of a small sitting room and said, 'Johnny, here's Toby.'

Johnny Nutbrown was relaxing on a huge Chesterfield that must have cost half a herd of cattle their skin. He was eating a piece of pie, presumably the end of the lunch Estover had been told not to expect.

'Toby!' he said. 'Marvellous. Just the man. Good to see you.'

His enthusiasm did not impress. Estover had known him long enough to suspect that if Adolf Hitler himself had goose-stepped into the room, Nutbrown's greeting would probably have been unchanged.

'And you,' he said. 'You're a hard man to get hold of these days. In fact, you both seem pretty inaccessible.'

The Nutbrowns exchanged glances, his interrogative, hers monitory.

'Busy busy,' said Johnny. 'Sit down, try this claret. Pippa, bring the man a glass. And one for yourself.'

Pippa obeyed. Her husband took the wine bottle from the table by his elbow and poured.

'Here's health,' he said.

They drank, Nutbrown deep, Estover a sip, Pippa a moistening of her lips.

224

'I didn't realize you were thinking of moving,' said Estover.

Pippa didn't reply but turned a gaze like a remote control on her husband.

'You know how it is,' said Johnny. 'Old bones, English winters, as easy to move on lock stock and barrel as pack up all the gear needed for a couple of months in the sun.'

He spoke the words like a schoolboy repeating a rote-learned formula.

'You're going abroad then?'

Pippa said, 'California. We like it there.'

'Very nice.' He set down his glass. 'And the Americans are so fussy about who they let in, aren't they? One strike and you're shut out.'

'That's right,' said Pippa. 'You got a problem with that, Toby?'

'No, indeed. Oh, by the by, I received an interesting Christmas card at the office. Wondered whether you got one too?'

He produced the card.

Pippa scarcely glanced at it before saying, 'Yes, we did.'

Johnny said, 'Did we? Don't recall. Nice picture, though. I'm sure I've seen it somewhere before.'

Estover looked at Pippa and raised his eyebrows.

The doorbell rang.

She didn't move. Her husband didn't even look as if he'd heard it.

There was another ring, more protracted this time.

Now without a word she rose and left the room.

As the door closed behind her, Estover said, 'So tell me, Johnny, has Wolf tried to contact you?'

'No. Why should he?'

'Because you are, you were, his very dear friend.'

'You too, Toby.'

'I married his ex-wife, remember?' said Estover grimly. 'That puts me a little further beyond the pale, I think. And you might say that chopping down our rowan tree was a form of contact.'

'Yes. You ever do anything about that?'

'No. I wanted to get the police, Imo said no. No way to prove it was Hadda, but some cop would certainly make a bob or two by tipping off the press and we'd have those bastards crawling all over us.'

'Probably right. Imo usually is,' said Nutbrown. 'Wish you hadn't mentioned it to Pippa though. Last straw for her, I think. She'd been fussed ever since we heard Wolf was getting out early. Funny how you got that wrong, Toby. What was your forecast? Good for the whole stretch, you said! You really must tell me what you fancy for the George on Boxing Day.'

He smiled as he spoke but Estover was reminded that, though Pippa might pull the strings, Johnny Nutbrown's limbs could still kick independently.

'Give it a rest, will you?' he said wearily. 'I assume this move's mainly down to Pippa, right? How about you, Johnny? Not worried Wolf might come calling?'

'Not likely, is it? I mean, we've really lost touch. OK, I know there was a good reason for that, but it happens even if you don't go to jail. Look at you and me, sometimes months go by without us meeting up.'

'It's certainly been hard to contact you recently,' said Estover. 'I've tried several times. I'm particularly surprised I didn't hear from you professionally when you decided to put your house on the market. Unless you're doing your own conveyancing?'

'Pippa's handling all that,' said Nutbrown. 'Not your sort of thing, conveyancing, is it, Toby? You're far too important for that. No, it made sense to go local.'

'So you were just going to pack up and leave all this behind you without so much as a word?'

Nutbrown's gaze went slowly round the room as if for the first time the reality of leaving all this behind him had struck.

Estover pressed on.

'Johnny, isn't this a bit of an over-reaction? OK, we need to take stock, but as long as we stick together, what do we have to worry about?'

'That's what I said to Pippa,' said Nutbrown. 'Wolf's out, so what? In fact, I was jolly glad to hear the news. Being banged up all that time, it makes me shudder just to think about it. Which is why I try not to. Incidentally, any idea how he managed to get out so early?'

'I put out some feelers. Discreetly, of course. Seems he put his hand up for everything, took the cure,' said Estover.

'Good lord, why would he do that?'

'To get out, of course,' said Estover irritably. 'Was a time when a prison sentence meant what it said. Now they employ people to help the bastards work the system! They've got some black bitch trick cyclist at Parkleigh, evidently. Pity she didn't stay in the wood-pile.'

Nutbrown grimaced and said, 'Pippa says he's gone back up to Cumbria. Is that right?'

'Pippa's always right. Yes, he's up there, and I'm keeping a close check on him, believe me.'

'Let me guess: the ineluctable Lady Kira?'

'Yes. And from what I hear, he's leading a hermitic existence, he's a physical wreck, he exists on his social security hand-outs and, as for his state of mind, well, perhaps religion really has reared its ugly head as the only person he talks to is the local vicar.'

'There you are then,' said Johnny. 'What's to worry about? How's Imo? You two heading off to Frog-land for Christmas?'

The Estovers had a farmhouse in Gascony.

'No. Imo's been rather off France since Ginny died. She doesn't show it, but she took it really hard. So we're going up to the castle. Imo's there already. I'm joining her tomorrow.'

'Wow,' said Nutbrown, impressed. 'Bearding Wolf in his lair, eh? Sounds more Imo's style than yours, Toby.'

'It is not, I assure you, my intent to do any bearding,' said Estover. 'You know Kira. She so loves an old-fashioned English house-party.'

'Sounds grisly. Anyone I know?'

'Nikitin's going to be there, I believe.'

'Pasha? He can be fun.'

'Depends how you define fun.'

'Still sniffing around Imo, is he?' said Nutbrown sympathetically. 'Still, the fees he pays you, I daresay he feels he has a big share in what's yours. Only joking, old boy. And he is family, after all.'

'He's a cousin so often removed that Kira wouldn't have paid the slightest heed to him if he hadn't turned up in England trailing a few billion roubles,' said Toby sourly. 'Now I catch her watching me all the time, and I can almost hear her thinking: If only I'd trodden water a little longer, rather than encouraging Imo to marry this nobody, I could have had the fabulously rich Pavel Nikitin for my son-in-law. I'm sometimes tempted to tell her how he makes his money!'

'You think it would make a difference?' said Johnny. 'At least she helped you get him as a client, so not all bad. Anyway, my love to all. And if you do bump into old Wolf, give him my best.'

Estover shook his head in bafflement. Talking to Johnny was like swimming in a goldfish bowl: you never ended up very far from where you'd begun. Except when you moved from words to figures. Ask Nutbrown how much they were worth and where it all was, and suddenly you were out in the open sea, only too glad to have this instinctive navigator leading you to Treasure Island. But on most other matters, to change the metaphor, it was like going down the rabbit hole.

As he rose to leave he said, 'So how's the sale going? Any interest?'

'Nothing close to the asking price,' declared Johnny, not bothering to hide his pleasure. 'And you know Pippa, she likes her pound of flesh.'

'Yes, I remember,' said Estover, smiling reminiscently.

'I daresay you do,' said Nutbrown, returning the smile. 'Though, from what I hear, in your case a pound might be stretching things a bit.'

Yes, when Johnny's limbs moved independently, he could manage a fair old kick, thought Estover as he left the room.

In the hall he heard voices and tracked them to the kitchen where he found Pippa drinking coffee with a long thin man with a slightly lugubrious face. She was smiling and looked very like her young self till she became aware he'd entered the room.

'Toby, you off then?' she said brusquely.

'Yes. If I could have a quick word . . .'

He glanced at the man, who stood up and offered his hand.

'Donald Murray,' he said in a Scots accent. 'Not here to look at the house, I hope?'

'No, just a friend.'

'Good! This is my second viewing and it's looking even better than on the first! No appointment this time, but Mrs Nutbrown's such a welcoming kind of body, I thought as I was in the area . . .'

'No problem, Mr Murray,' said Pippa, smiling again. 'Look, why don't you wander around by yourself while I talk to my . . . friend. I won't be long.'

The Scot nodded at Estover and left the room.

'High hopes there, then?' murmured the solicitor.

'Hopes,' said Pippa. 'So what can I do for you, Toby?'

'Nothing, it seems. I just wanted to wish you a Merry Christmas.'

'What? No wise words? No little lecture?'

'No. You've clearly made a decision.'

'Yes, I have. If I had any doubts, that card removed them.'

'You think it's from Wolf?'

She laughed and said, 'You know it is. It's that bloody picture he was so fond of he had a copy in his office at work and another in his study at home. *The Woodcutter*, it's called. But you know that, don't you, Toby?'

'Perhaps. But so what? Perhaps these are some cards that survived from the old days. Perhaps the poor chap can't afford to buy new Christmas cards.'

She shook her head and said, 'Do people really pay you thousands to talk such bollocks, Toby? What's the problem? You can't drop everything and leave the country and you'd rather we didn't either? Safety in numbers, that what you think?'

'Safety from what? It's a Christmas card, not a threat.'

Pippa said, 'Take another look, Toby. I checked it out on the

229

Internet just to be sure. In the original painting, the blade of the axe doesn't have any red on it.'

Estover examined the card, frowning, and said, 'Just a poor reproduction, perhaps. I noticed you don't seem to have shared any of your concerns with Johnny.'

She shook her head impatiently and said, 'Of course I haven't. You know Johnny. He can't take too much reality. You haven't been upsetting him, I hope?'

'Upset Johnny?' Estover laughed. 'You're joking, of course. You know what he said to me as I left? *If you run into Wolf in Cumbria, give him my best!*'

She said, 'And that didn't convince you we were wise to be getting away?'

'On the contrary. If Wolf did have any notion of coming after us, Johnny in the witness box would be worth at least six jury votes.'

She said incredulously, 'You think Wolf would be using the law? Jesus!'

'What else would he do?'

Pippa shook her head and said, 'You may be a great lawyer, Toby, but it's real life out here, not just words. Didn't having your tree chopped down teach you anything? I doubt if Wolf Hadda is looking to get himself a good brief. He's a dangerous man.'

'You think so?' said Estover. 'Well, I have some dangerous friends too. But it bothers me to see you reacting like this, Pippa. I've always regarded you as a rock. Why would you think Wolf might be truly dangerous? I understand he's pretty well a broken reed after all those years inside.'

'I just don't care to be around if and when he puts himself together again,' she said. 'You can rely on your dangerous friends for protection, Toby. From my memories of Wolf, I prefer distance.'

Estover observed her thoughtfully for a moment, then began to smile.

'Now what memories would they be? Let me guess. I often wondered why you were such a non-fan of Wolf's. I'm guessing

230

that, back in the golden days when we were all such dear friends together, you tried your charms on him and he turned you down. He must have given you a real scare for you to be still feeling the aftermath!'

She didn't react to his gibe but said quietly, 'Right as always, Toby. He said, "I'll screw you if you really want it, Pippa. But I'm sure that, even while you were hitting the high notes, you'd be thinking of half a dozen good moral imperatives for confessing to Imo. So I'd probably have to kill you soon as we finished. So what do you say? Still up for it?"'

'And you actually believed him?' said Toby.

'I'm selling the house, aren't I? And I'd better get on with it. By the way, you got your card at your office, did you?'

'That's right. Why?'

'Interesting he didn't send it to your house. Perhaps he's got some other form of greeting in mind for Imo. Have yourself a merry little Christmas, Toby.'

She walked out of the kitchen. When Estover followed, she was halfway up the stairs.

She didn't look back.

14

A noise woke Alva Ozigbo in the middle of the night and for a second she experienced that heart-stopping feeling of not knowing where the hell she was.

Then she remembered, and in her confused mind *where?* was pushed aside by *how?* and *why?*

Professionally, there was nothing wrong in a psychiatrist accepting overnight hospitality from a patient. As long as they didn't share a bed, of course, and she had minimized any danger of this by wedging a chair against the door. Not that anything in Hadda's manner had suggested he regarded her as desirable. Indeed, as her analysis had probed deeper and deeper after that first impassioned cry for help, he had revealed that his sexual urges seemed to have gone into hibernation during his prison sentence.

'I don't even wake up with an erection now,' he told her. 'But of course you'll probably have to take my word for that.'

And this, apart from the time he had tested her assurance that the sound channels of the CCTV system were turned off, was the only time he had come close to suggestiveness.

But hibernation was not a permanent state, and better safe than sorry, so in lieu of a lock, the chair had been jammed up against the door handle, though she couldn't avoid a sense that her motives for such a melodramatic gesture were at best muddied.

She set that aside for later consideration and concentrated on examining how she'd come to be staying at Birkstane.

Her practical reasons were those urged by her host. Dusk had been fast approaching, the first swirls of mist were already rising, and she needed more time to talk to him about the money. Pretty feeble. The mist had proved little more than a frost haze, she would have had no difficulty in driving slowly back to the village, and even with the pub a no-go area, the vicar would hardly have turned her away.

In the event, the fact that she stayed had turned into a reason for denying her the object of her staying.

Their simple dinner had been accompanied by a far from simple bottle of excellent burgundy. She'd examined the label and felt this was a good cue to bring up the subject of the money chest. As soon as she started, Hadda had put one of the two fingers on his right hand to his lips and said, 'Football and finance are banned topics at civilized dinner tables.'

'I thought it was religion and politics,' she said.

'Not in Cumbria,' he said.

Afterwards, mellowed by the wine plus a shot of whisky in her coffee, she had not resisted when in reply to her attempt to return to the subject he said, 'Let's leave the dénouement till tomorrow, like in the *Arabian Nights*, OK?'

It was only as she was on the point of slipping into sleep that it occurred to her that in the *Arabian Nights* it was Scheherazade who kept on postponing the conclusion of her tale because she knew that, when it was finished, she would be put to death.

Now, waking, it struck her that the bedroom was remarkably light. Her last impression just before she closed the curtains had been of complete and utter darkness, the kind of dark that anyone used to the permanent half-light of the modern city never sees. So the square of brightness marking the small window made her wonder if some intruder had triggered a security light, though somehow the ideas of Birkstane and modern technology didn't sit well together.

She slipped out of bed and drew back the curtains.

Not modern technology; more like ancient mythology.

The evening mist had vanished and the moon had risen. Its pearly light suffused the sky and the countryside, exploding to brilliance, like gunpowder scattered over embers, wherever it touched the hard hoar frost clinging to twigs and branches and blades of grass and the ribs and furrows of ancient stone walls.

It wasn't a human landscape she looked out upon, it was the land of faerie, a land where human *why's* and *how's* didn't apply. It was magic that bound her here. Her only safety lay in flight from the enchanter, but her books of knowledge held no elfish charms to see her safe through these fields of light.

Her gaze drifted down to the farmyard below her window. There were marks on the whitened cobbles as if something had moved across them since the frost fell. She remembered that a noise had awoken her but she couldn't remember what it was.

She went back to bed, and must have slipped back into sleep immediately for it seemed only a few seconds till she was woken again, this time by a fist banging on the bedroom door and Hadda's voice calling, 'Breakfast in fifteen minutes. After that it's DIY!'

She rose. Perhaps the remnants of the fire in the grate had still been warming the air when she got up in the night as she hadn't noticed the cold then, but now it was freezing. She dragged on her clothes. Through the window the countryside still looked magical, but only in a glitzy Christmas card kind of way. She removed the chair from the door and headed out to the bathroom. There was a trickle of warm water. Getting enough to fill the ancient tub would have taken half an hour, by which time she would probably have contracted pneumonia, so she settled for a perfunctory splash in the cracked basin. Then after dragging a comb through her hair, she descended to the kitchen.

Here there was warmth from the crackling fire and the smell of frying bacon. Hadda greeted her with, 'Perfect timing, Elf. Sleep all right?'

This was the first time since her arrival that he'd used the nickname. Last night he'd called her ... in fact, he hadn't called her anything, and she realized now that this sense of a barrier raised had distressed her.

'Yes, thanks. Anything I can do?'

'Make the coffee, if you like.'

His face had a healthy ruddy glow that made the scars on it stand out like ribs of quartz in a granite boulder. His hair, she noticed, was damp and looked as if it had been roughly ordered by drawing his fingers through it.

As she made the coffee she said, faintly accusing, 'You look as if you've had a shower.'

He said, 'What?'

Then he put his hand to his head and smiled and said, 'Of course. Didn't I mention the shower facilities?'

'No, you didn't,' she said.

'Well, no time now, but after breakfast if you still want one, just go out of the door, head towards the estate boundary wall, you'll meet a beck. Turn left and follow it upstream about twenty yards and beneath a little waterfall you'll see a pool, just room enough for one. I'll get you a towel.'

It took a moment to realize he wasn't joking. She thought of that frost-bound world out there and shuddered.

He took some plates out of the oven where they'd been warming, put the bacon on them, quickly scrambled some eggs in the remaining fat, spooned them alongside the rashers and said, 'Grub up.'

The plate looked to hold more calories than she usually consumed in a day, but she cleared it without any noticeable difficulty.

He sliced a loaf thickly, impaled one slice on a toasting fork, another on the bread knife and said, 'Now it really is do-it-yourself time.'

They sat before the fire, toasting bread, spreading it thick with butter and marmalade, then washing it down with coffee.

'Enough,' she said after three slices.

'Eat,' he commanded. 'Lunch is a moveable feast at Birkstane.'

She remarked, but didn't remark upon, the assumption that she'd be staying for lunch.

Their breakfast conversation was desultory in an easy domestic sort of way, touching on how old the house was (500 years, give or take); who had embroidered the Lord's Prayer sampler hanging on the wall (Great Aunt Carrie); why toast done on an open fire was so much better than under a grill or in a toaster (how could it not be?); but finally she felt it was time to say, 'So, Wolf, this matter of the money . . .'

'Not before the dishes are washed,' he said firmly.

'This another old Cumbrian custom?'

'Oh yes. We always washed up before going out to kill the Scots or the Irish. Whichever happened to be invading at the time.'

You can't have been in a Celticidal mood yesterday, she thought, recalling the sinkful of dirty dishes.

She stood up and went to the sink.

'Let's get to it,' she said. 'Washing-up liquid?'

'I seem to be out,' he said, coming to stand beside her. 'Look, it's a bit crowded by this little sink. Why don't you wander off and check that your car's survived the night. Sneck, you go with Elf.'

In other circumstances she might have replied that she didn't mind a bit of crowding. Instead, obediently she slipped on her jacket and set out gingerly across the yard which the frost had turned into a frozen sea.

Sneck, equally obedient, followed her. Whether his function was to watch over or simply watch her, she didn't know, and she didn't care to test it by diverting from the direct route along the lonning to her car.

The blankets were still in place, stiff in their folds. She sat in the car and turned the key. The engine started first time and she let it run while she opened the boot. She took out her walking boots. Had it been some kind of vanity that prevented her from changing from her smart trainers when she arrived yesterday? She did a quick self-analysis. A psychiatrist was as susceptible to mixed motives as anyone else, but needed to be a lot clearer about them! No, she decided. Yesterday afternoon the frost had thawed enough for the surface of the lonning to be tacky rather than polished.

This morning, however, a bit of substantial ankle support was very much in order. An immobilizing sprain was the last thing she wanted.

Could it be that Hadda had considered the possibility when he suggested she went out to the car?

Now she was really being paranoid!

She was roused from her reverie by Sneck letting out a bark.

After a while she heard what he'd already heard, an approaching car, and a moment later a blue Micra that she'd last seen outside the vicarage came into view.

To her surprise, Sneck advanced to meet it, wagging his tail.

Luke Hollins got out and reached out his open hand to the dog with something on the palm that Sneck removed with surprising gentleness.

'That's a pretty convincing demonstration of the power of faith,' said Alva.

'Just the power of food, I'm afraid,' replied Hollins. 'I always bring a packet of treats with the groceries. No groceries today, but fortunately I remembered to fill my pocket with Sugar Puffs. How about you? What have you done to tame the beast?'

Sneck had returned to Alva's side and was lying down on the icy ground with his shoulder warm against her leg.

'Nothing, really. I used to have a dog, when I was a child. Not as wolfish as this one, but pretty crazy. Spot, I called him, but my father said I should have called him Sufficient.'

Hollins looked puzzled and Alva laughed and said, 'Don't you do the Bible any more in the modern church? *Sufficient is the evil!* Spot used to terrorize the neighbourhood, dig up the garden and chew the furniture if he was left in the house by himself.'

'So you're used to dealing with wild things,' he said.

He glanced toward the house as he spoke.

She frowned then said lightly, 'So, if no groceries, what brings you here?'

'I just wanted to check that everything was OK. I called in at the Dog first thing. They were in a bit of a tizz. Jimmy Frith, that's the landlord, always likes a glass of ale with his breakfast but when he drew it, it came out foaming.'

'Isn't that what ale is meant to do?'

'No, I mean really foaming. It was the same in all the pumps and when he checked he found someone had got down in the cellar and put washing-up liquid in all the casks.'

Instantly she thought of the noise that had woken her, the spoor on the frost whitened yard, the lack of washing-up liquid in the cottage. Could Hadda have gone down to the village in the night to exact revenge on the pub landlord for his racist rudeness? It didn't seem likely. Getting into the cellar and doctoring the beer would have required a dexterity quite beyond a man who walked like a wounded bear. But somehow the idea made her feel warm.

Hollins was offering his own much more reasonable explanation:

'Serves Jimmy right for letting the kids who come in drink more than they should. His nickname's Jimmy Froth, so as practical jokes go, it was pretty apt!'

He grinned as he spoke, then, as if realizing that the discomfiture of one of his parishioners was not a proper subject for mirth, he overcompensated into a tone of deep concern as he said, 'Anyway, when I found you hadn't stayed there, I got really worried and thought I'd better head out here straight away.'

'Thinking Wolf might have murdered me?' she said. 'Well, as you can see, he didn't.'

'But you did spend the night here at Birkstane?' He said it with a casualness more significant than reproach.

'Yes. His wife . . . his ex-wife showed up while I was waiting for Wolf. We chatted briefly then she went. Wolf seemed to think my presence would deter her from coming back.'

It rang pretty unconvincingly in her own ears but the vicar seemed ready to accept it was reasonable.

He said, 'So what was his explanation of the money?'

'He hasn't offered one yet,' said Alva. 'But he has worked out where I got my information from. I was just on my way back to the house for a heart to heart. Why don't you join us?'

Hollins looked doubtful.

'Don't know if that would be a good idea. If he knows it was me who . . .'

But the issue was resolved by a cry of, 'Is that you, Padre? Didn't they teach you at your seminary not to keep a lady standing in the cold? Come along to the house, for God's sake!'

Hadda had appeared at the bottom of the lonning.

He whistled and turned away. Sneck, with an appreciative glance at Hollins, raced after him and was alongside the slow-moving figure in an instant.

'There you are,' said Alva. 'All is forgiven.'

As they walked together down the lonning, Hollins said, 'So how did you find him?'

Alva said, 'As my host or as my patient? Not that it matters. Good manners prevent me from commenting on him in the first capacity, and professional ethics in the second. I'm sorry, but as you said in your letter, our concerns here are rather different. I'm very glad however to have you present to hear his explanation about the money. In this case I think that four ears may definitely be better than two.'

Hadda was brewing more coffee when they entered the kitchen. She saw his gaze take in her change of footwear and foolishly felt glad that her boots had the well-worn, well-cared-for look that showed they belonged to a serious walker.

'Car all right?' he said.

'Yes, thanks. I'm glad you suggested the blankets, though. They're frozen solid.'

'It was a hard night. I had to break some icicles off the fall this morning else I might have been speared as I showered. How about you, Padre? That vicarage still an ice-box?'

'The boiler heats the cellar perfectly adequately but then seems to deny the basic law of physics that says heat rises,' said Hollins.

'It's the Church of England's subtle technique for keeping its priests moral,' said Hadda. 'Here we are. Coffee. Sorry, no cream, Padre. My guest polished off the last of your little store last night.

239

By the way, I suggest you keep on feeding my dog whatever it is you've got him hooked on, else you're going to lose your jacket.'

Hollins fed another handful of Sugar Puffs to Sneck, who was sitting alongside him with his nose pressed close to the provender-bearing pocket.

'Right,' said Hadda. 'Now I think it's time we dealt with the main item on both your agendas, which I take to be, am I complying with the letter and the spirit of my licence, or should I be man-acled and fettered and cast back into the deepest oubliette the state can provide? So, if you are sitting comfortably, then I'll begin.'

15

It was, thought Alva, either a consummate performance or a consummate act.

In her vocabulary the term *performance* was neutral. It did not imply dissimulation or dishonesty. Long jail sentences turn most of those who suffer them into performers in some degree or other. Ultimately, survival in jail can depend on working out what disparate groups of people want and giving it to them. The face a man presents to his fellow prisoners will probably differ from the face he presents to the warders, or his visitors, or the governor, or the parole board.

Or the prison psychiatrist.

But performing is not the same as acting a part. Or it need not be. It can simply mean emphasizing one aspect of personality over others. A performer can be the sum of his performances while an actor is rarely the sum of his parts.

So, performance or act?

It occurred to her that she probably knew more about Wolf Hadda than anyone else in the world. But she also knew that in the mental as in the physical sciences, conventional knowledge could only take you so far; after that you were into quantum theory where none of your carefully tabulated laws applied.

Yet she'd been confident enough of her judgment that he was no longer a threat to recommend his release on licence as power-fully as she'd ever made any recommendation.

Which of course was why she was here now. A question had been raised. If she turned out to have been wrong, the damage to her reputation would be large but survivable. But if some young girl were harmed . . .

So, performance or act? He had certainly started by establishing himself as an almost theatrical presence, taking a position in front of the fireplace, resting most of his weight on his good leg, and looming over them like a soloist on a concert platform. Even Sneck turned from his absorption with the vicar's pocket to look up attentively as his master started to speak. Alva established her own parameters by interrupting him to take her notebook out of her purse and poising her pencil over it.

Then she smiled at him and nodded permission to continue.

'I'll come straight to the point,' he said. 'Out of the goodness of my heart, and not because I feel any compulsion to do so, moral or legal, let me give you an account of how I come to have a chestful of banknotes in my bedroom. Or would either of you like to hazard a guess?'

He paused expectantly.

The vicar looked uncomfortable, Alva's pencil scrawled shorthand hieroglyphics across her notepad. What she wrote was, *How rarely people who say they are coming straight to the point do! Now he'll answer his own question.*

'Come on! Don't be shy,' said Hadda. 'I bet the proceeds of some old fraud was top of your list. Some account I'd cleverly concealed from the Fraud Squad. Or a pay-off from some of my confederates for keeping my mouth shut. Or maybe I robbed a bank. The police are looking for a man with a badly scarred face, a marked limp, and a vicious-looking dog. There are no suspects.'

Another pause. Another silence. Alva made a note.

'Oh, all right,' he said, affecting disappointment. 'I'll put you out of your misery. I inherited the money. There! You look surprised, Padre. Or should I rather say incredulous? And you, Alva, have that look of concerned neutrality, if that's not a contradiction, that I know so well. OK. Here are the facts. Way back in the dark ages

242

when I returned from my quest for self-improvement and claimed my bride, I told my father that I wanted him to have a share in my new and ever-increasing affluence. Fred, in any circumstances, would have found it hard to feel beholden, even to his own flesh and blood. In the circumstance that he was seriously pissed off with me about my choice of bride, he said he wanted no part of my money. He told me I should keep it, and where, in a very precise anatomical way.'

His lips faked a smile but it didn't get beyond his mouth as he turned to the stone mantel shelf where he'd placed his coffee mug. He raised the mug, but Alva could tell he wasn't drinking.

Then he turned back to them and continued briskly, 'Yes, he was a cussed old sod. Some folk reckon I take after him, though I can't see it myself. But I do admit I can be a bit cussed too on occasion, so I simply arranged for a thousand quid a month to be paid into his bank account. It was his to do with what he wanted. I was very willing to make it a lot more if necessary and I kept an eye on him, but he never showed any sign of being strapped for cash, and I knew that to mention money would just get us into a row, so for all the years of my prosperity, Fred was getting his monthly thousand. And what was he doing with it, do you think?'

Luke Hollins spoke, almost with relief.

'He was drawing it out as fast as it was paid in, and storing it in that tin chest.'

'Spot on, Padre. I reckon he didn't want it in his account, polluting his hard-earned wages. As for letting it lie to gather a bit of very useful interest, perish the thought! No, he drew it out and stored it away, and when he died, his will declared me the sole heir of all his estate. As you probably know, both of you, because he died after all the dust had settled around the ruin of my business, and my creditors had reluctantly agreed that they'd screwed me for every penny they could, then I was able to inherit that estate free of charge, which is how I come to be living in these palatial surroundings.'

'You seem to find them comfortable enough,' said Alva.

243

'Indeed I do. I'm not complaining. After my years as a guest of Her Majesty, bedding down with Sneck in the barn would have seemed comfortable. Anyway, to cut a long story short, poking around in the attic to rid myself of a couple of rats' nests, I came across Dad's old tin chest. Imagine my surprise when I opened it to see it was full of money. I rapidly worked out what it was. A quick check of Dad's old bank statements confirmed my guess. I took legal advice as to what to do . . .'

'Mr Trapp?' wondered Alva.

'The same. He confirmed there was no obstacle to my hanging on to the money.'

'The Inland Revenue and Social Services might not agree,' said Alva.

'Only if I didn't inform them,' he replied. 'Or perhaps I mean only if I did. Anyway, there you are. Any questions?'

Alva looked at Hollins. The vicar looked at the ground.

'Quite a lot of the money seems to have gone,' she said. 'What have you been spending it on?'

'Good question. This time I won't enquire after possible answers as one of you might say something that would cause us to fall out. I've provided myself with a stock of decent liquor, as you've both observed. My ancient Defender is surprisingly sophisticated under her rustic bonnet. Don't let the noise fool you. I left a few loose bits to create a good rattle, and they're pretty noisy beasts anyway!'

'And that's all? Doesn't add up to a great deal, it seems to me.'

'An accountant as well as a lawyer and a psychiatrist!' he mocked. 'There have been other expenses. For instance, I like to make donations where I think the money might do some good.'

Hollins now raised his eyes and said, 'There was a couple of hundred quid stuffed into the church donations box last month . . .'

'Mea culpa,' said Hadda.

The vicar said, 'Well . . . thank you. I'm very grateful.'

He looked, thought Alva, rather less surprised than he should that somehow this crippled man, this self-defined hermit, this local ogre, had entered the village and visited the church unobserved.

244

'So, good wine and good works,' she murmured. 'It seems a reasonable balance.'

'Yes, indeed,' said Hollins.

And Sneck let out a low rumbling growl that might have been taken for approval.

'I'm glad you think so,' said Hadda. 'Now, I daresay you'd like to talk among yourselves and, as I have things to do, I'll leave you to it for a while.'

He drained his coffee and headed for the door, Sneck at his heels.

'That went well, I thought,' said the vicar.

'Yes. Thank you for joining me in quizzing him about what he might have been doing with the money,' said Alva tartly.

'I thought he'd take it better from you, being his psychiatrist,' said Hollins apologetically. 'He doesn't care much for me coming the old C of E parson with him, as he puts it. But you have to admit, he did give a perfectly logical explanation.'

'You're not letting yourself be influenced by his donation to church funds, I hope,' said Alva.

'Of course not,' he said indignantly.

'But it didn't seem to surprise you much that a man in his condition had been able to visit the church unobserved?'

'No. The truth is, when I found the money, my first thought was of Mr Hadda,' admitted Hollins. 'That same morning I noticed that someone had planted a couple of rowan sprigs, heavy with berries, in the churchyard. One was on his father's grave, the other in front of the Ulphingstone tomb where his daughter is interred.'

'Why rowan?' wondered Alva, recalling that Hadda had referred to a rowan tree in the garden of his Holland Park house.

'My wife knows about such things,' said Hollins. 'She told me that in folklore the mountain ash is considered a strong defence against evil spirits, and also it can prevent the dead from rising and walking the earth. But I couldn't be certain it was Mr Hadda, until now. So what do you think, Dr Ozigbo? Are you happy with his explanation?'

What Alva was thinking was that if Hadda had planted the rowan in his London garden as a defence against evil, it hadn't been very effective. Also that in her eyes he'd once more become a prime suspect in the case of the foaming beer!

What she said was, 'I think Mr Hadda is maybe even more complex than we'd thought. For instance, I think the real reason he's left us to have a chat by the fireside is that Sneck told him he had another visitor.'

She put her theory to the test by rising and going out into the yard.

She was right. He was standing by the open gate in deep conversation with a tall thin man. The visitor spotted her and said something. Hadda turned, saw Alva watching them, said something to the newcomer, then the two men walked towards her across the yard.

'Elf, we have a traveller in distress,' said Hadda. 'Mr . . . sorry, I don't know your name?'

'Murray,' said the man, in a distinctive Scots accent. 'Donald Murray. Sorry to trouble you. My sat nav's gone on the blink.'

'Never trust technology, eh? Let's get you into the warm and I'll show you the way on a good old-fashioned map. Padre, this will be a busy time for you. I'll not be needing an order till after the festive dust has settled. So, Merry Christmas.'

Hollins, who'd followed Alva into the yard, took his dismissal with Christian fortitude.

'Thank you . . .'

Rather hesitantly he reached into the capacious pocket of his heavy cagoule and produced a rectangular packet wrapped in red-and-green Christmas paper.

'I came across this,' he said. 'Thought you might like it. A Merry Christmas to you, too.'

'A present? Well, thank you, Padre. I'm touched.'

Alva said to Hollins, 'I'll walk you back to your car.'

They walked up the lonning in the kind of silence that gradually magnifies sound. The crunch of the frozen grass beneath their feet, the eerie whistle of a circling buzzard scanning the earth for the corpse of any creature that hadn't made it through the night, the baa-ing of a distant sheep, the rustle as the morning sun thawed the first tiny icicles from the upmost branches of the hedgerow hollies and sent them slithering through the frosted leaves; these and a myriad other small indistinguishable sounds united and increased till Hollins shrank them all back to near nothingness by speaking.

'That man . . .'

'Mr Murray?'

'Yes, him. You recall the reason I chanced upon the money chest was I went upstairs because his mobile rang?'

'But it stopped as you got into the bedroom . . .'

'Yes. But there was a message. I listened to it.'

'Ah. You chanced to listen to it,' said Alva, gently mocking the priest's defensiveness about prying into Hadda's affairs. She smiled to show she didn't blame him. Crimes such as Hadda's meant a forfeiture of trust which in turn could provoke acts that were at least intrusive.

'It was a man speaking. He had a Scots accent. He sounded very like Mr Murray.'

'An accent can be deceptive.'

Hollins said, 'You mean all Scots sound the same? Sounds a touch racist to me, Dr Ozigbo.'

She glanced at him and saw that now he was smiling. Getting his own back. She'd reserved judgment on Hollins, but she found she was quite liking him.

'I take it your fine ear detects distinctions?' she said.

'No, but one of my best mates at college was from Glasgow. So is Mr Murray, and so was the man on the phone.'

'And so are a million other people. You'll need to fine it down a little.'

'Well, it certainly wasn't my mate,' he said. 'Look, all I'm saying is they sounded very much the same.'

And if they're the same, why is Wolf Hadda trying to hide the fact that he knows this man? Alva asked herself. His behaviour in bringing him into the house to show him the way had already struck her as atypical. And he'd only done it when he'd realized it wasn't going to be possible to avoid a meeting with her.

'So what did the message say?' she enquired.

'Something about making contact and going to a villa,' said Hollins. 'I think it was from abroad as he said he'd stop off in London on the way back and check things there. He didn't much like where he was, called it an elephants' graveyard and said he was glad that Hadda was paying for it.'

Alva, keeping anger but not reproach out of her voice, said, 'And you didn't think this was worth telling me till now? You must have looked at the possible implications.'

'In my business, when you rush to judgment, you end up crucifying people,' said Hollins.

'You were worried enough about the money to contact me,' she said.

'The money was a fact. It needed explaining. Contacting you was, I don't know, more a way of giving myself some extra thinking time. I thought at best you might write, or email, or even phone. I didn't expect you to turn up personally. When you did, I thought I'd wait and see what transpired – about the money, I mean.'

'And you found his explanation satisfactory enough to still your doubts, even though you knew for sure he was lying?'

'What do you mean?'

'You'd heard the message. You knew that whatever the man on the phone, that man back there possibly, is doing, Hadda is paying him to do it. So there's something more than good wine and good works going on here. The fact that he slipped a couple of hundred pounds into your poor box doesn't make him a saint, Mr Hollins. Suppose rather than making a charitable gesture it was more like purchasing an indulgence? Was that what you gave him just now? A papal indulgence?'

They had reached her car. Parked behind it was the vicar's Micra, and behind that a black BMW.

'Got the wrong church there, I think, Dr Ozigbo,' Hollins said.

'Look, there may be a perfectly reasonable explanation for that phone message. And you've only got my not-too-reliable memory to suggest that it was whatsisname? Donald Murray, who left it.'

'We've got Sneck. He doesn't accept strangers without his master's say so, and he looked pretty comfortable with Mr Murray out there.'

As she spoke, Alva peered into the BMW. Recalling her readiness to leave her car unlocked in such a remote area she tried the door. Mr Murray wasn't so trusting. On the back seat she saw a document case, embossed in faded gilt with the initials D.M.

Donald Murray. Right initials, but was that really his name? Something in the way he'd said it when prompted by Hadda had rung a false note. Of course it might be that too many hours spent straining to detect false notes had over-sensitized her. Sometimes she wondered if she would ever again hear someone say something she could take at face value.

'What will you do?' asked the vicar.

'What will *you* do?' she retorted.

He said, 'Sorry, I wasn't trying to offload responsibility. I'll pray, and then I'll decide. I meant, what will you do now? If you want to stay another night but not here at Birkstane, you're very welcome to a bed at the vicarage. And we have a real shower.'

She felt reproved. She should be able to tell the difference between a man trying to marshal all known facts before making a decision and a man trying to duck responsibility.

She said, 'That's kind, but if I do decide to stay another night, I'll be all right here. The shower apart, that is. I'll ring you before I leave.'

'I'd appreciate that.'

They shook hands and she watched as he did a three-point turn.

As he drove away, her phone started ringing.

Her mother said, 'Alva, you are not to worry . . .' and instantly she started worrying.

Hadda and Murray looked up in surprise as she burst into the kitchen and Sneck was on his feet in a flash, crouched low, teeth bared.

She said, 'I've got to go. My father's ill. Heart attack. Fortunately it happened at work.'

'Fortunately?' said Hadda.

'He's a surgeon in Manchester. I'll just grab my things and be on my way.'

When she came down a couple of minutes later, Hadda wasn't in the kitchen.

Murray said, 'He's outside. I hope your dad's OK.'

No false note there. He sounded genuinely concerned.

She said, 'Thanks,' and left. Hadda was sitting in the Defender.

'Don't want you cracking your ankle running up the lonning,' he said.

She scrambled in beside him. As he drove he said, 'Leave me your mobile number. I'd like to be able to check on you.'

Something wrong with that picture, she thought as she scribbled it on the cover of a road map. When they got to her car, he reached into the back seat and handed her a flask.

'Coffee,' he said. 'Drive for an hour and a half, stop and drink it, then drive on.'

The precision of the instruction was oddly comforting.

She got into her car. The engine again started first time. He took the blankets off the bonnet and tossed them into the Land Rover.

She turned the car, looked up at him through the open window and said, 'Thanks.'

'You're welcome,' he said. 'Good luck, Elf.'

He stooped to the window and his lips brushed her cheek.

It was, she realized, the first physical contact they'd ever had. What did she feel about it? Was it significant? If so, how?

There might be a time to consider these questions but it certainly wasn't now.

Now all she could think about was her father, that huge bear of a man whose sloe-black skin seemed to pulsate with energy, lying helpless on a bed in his own hospital.

She put her lights full on and sent the car hurtling along the narrow country road.

BOOK THREE

unions and reunions

Christmas was close at hand, in all his bluff and hearty honesty; it was the season of hospitality, merriment, and open-heartedness . . . How many families, whose members have been dispersed and scattered far and wide, in the restless struggles of life, are then reunited, and meet once again in that happy state of companionship and mutual goodwill, which is a source of such pure and unalloyed delight . . . How many old recollections, and how many dormant sympathies, does Christmas time awaken! . . . Happy, happy Christmas, that can win us back to the delusions of our childish days . . .

Charles Dickens: *The Pickwick Papers*

1

Like most men, ex-DI Medler imagined that he'd once enjoyed Christmas.

In his case the enjoyment must have been brief and infantile, for that miasma of disillusion, disappointment, cynicism and scepticism which men call maturity descended early on the boy, Arnie.

Indeed he was only six when he decided that a year of fulltime education was more than enough for the cultural, spiritual and intellectual needs of a growing boy and resolved to hand in his resignation from Wapping C of E First School with immediate effect.

He first shared this resolution with his gran, Queenie Medler, who appeared to Arnie as a benevolent old lady full of wisdom and insight, and to her many admirers across the bar of the China Clipper on Wapping Wall as a right little cracker, game for anything.

Queenie advised him to sleep on it. He flew into a childish tantrum, the burden of which was that he found the prospect of another ten years of education unbearable and wished passionately that he could be grown up and rich enough to lie in bed as long as he fucking well liked, answerable to no man.

Queenie had chuckled at the same time as she lightly clipped his ear and told him to watch his language and be careful what he wished for as the gods who like a laugh might just make it come true.

Well, they had, and now, forty years on, he thought gloomily that the bastards must really be laughing.

Early retirement to a sunny clime with a pension pot sufficiently deep to keep him in comfort till the end of his days. That was all he'd wanted. That was his adult version of his childhood wish. And that was what he'd got.

He'd also got boredom. And he'd got a wife who saw no reason why not being married to a football star should stop her spending like a WAG. And he found that in ex-pat social circles, the crooks treated him as a cop and the straights treated him as a crook.

He'd never been a man who made friends easily, or indeed thought he needed them, but he'd come to realize the truth of what some cynical Frog philosopher probably said, that it wasn't enough to get what you wished for, there had to be someone around who envied you for it.

Tina's friends and relatives didn't count – they were, on the whole, a bunch of wankers. As to his own acquaintance from the old days, in the beginning one or two, lured by the thought of a freebie in the sun, came to stay and confirmed that he'd got it made, which was good, but rarely came a second time, which was puzzling.

His encounter with Davy McLucky had turned into a real ego-titillating treat, all the better because it had started so unpromisingly, with the ex-DC naturally showing little enthusiasm at running across an ex-boss who'd never done him any favours. But after reluctantly accepting an invite to come out to the villa, McLucky had not been able to conceal his growing envy as he was taken on the grand tour. Even Tina had played a part. Roused from her customary domestic lethargy by the sight of a new man, she'd led the way, waggling her bum and shaking her tits in a manner that certainly caught McLucky's attention.

His tongue loosened by a couple of bottles of Rioja, McLucky had bemoaned the contrast between his fate after retirement – *gloomy fuckin' Glasgae 'n' squalid fuckin' divorce cases!* – and Medler's – *sunshine 'n' tottie 'n' fuck all tae do but booze 'n' fornicate yer fuckin' life awa'!* Medler had rubbed it in by assuring him that this life could be his too, presenting a balance sheet of property values and living expenses as if they were dirt cheap, knowing full well that they were a million miles outside of McLucky's range.

Maybe he'd overdone it. Maybe he always overdid it. Certainly the next day his guest had shown no enthusiasm when pressed to stay longer, not even when the pressure had been applied by Tina's melonic breasts.

Arnie hardly knew the guy, he'd only invited him to the villa to parade his comparative wealth, yet when McLucky said he was going home, he'd felt utterly bereft.

That had been more than a week ago. He was used to troughs of depression but usually he managed to drag himself back to the surface in a couple of days. This time, however, he felt himself sinking in darkness deeper and deeper, beyond all hope of day.

Now it was Christmas Eve, the season for friends and family and universal jollity, and here he was, sitting on the terrace overlooking his pool, with a fag in one hand and a glass of cognac in the other, wondering how the hell he was going to spend the rest of his life.

Tina wasn't here. Far from a devout Christian, she nevertheless adhered to the superstitious patterns of her upbringing by attending services at the English Church on Easter morning and at midnight on Christmas Eve. Afterwards no doubt she would be inveigled into having a festive drink with some of her friends. People liked Tina, and they liked her all the more he guessed, when he wasn't around.

Well, that didn't bother him. He didn't know how far she strayed, but he knew she wasn't going to risk straying so far she couldn't find her way back to the source of all comforts. There were plenty of guys out there who'd like to give her one, but not many who'd want her to stay on in the morning to give her another. Perhaps it might be a good thing if she did find an alternative bankroll. Perhaps that would give him the incentive to change his life around.

He almost wished it would happen, that something, *anything* would happen, to jerk him out of this state of enervating depression.

Be careful what you wish . . .

'Hello, Mr Medler. And a happy Christmas to you.'

255

On to the terrace stepped a figure of nightmare. Literally in that he saw it occasionally in his nightmares. The scarred face, the eye-patch, the gloved right hand . . .

Only the gloved left hand differed significantly from his guilty imaginings.

There it was sometimes pointed at him accusingly.

Here it carried a small and shining axe.

Two hours later, Tina Medler's taxi drew up at the main gate of the villa. She'd had to pay a small fortune to get the guy to come all the way out here, and he'd insisted on having the fare upfront. The least the bastard could do was get out from behind the wheel and open the door for her.

On the other hand, if he did that he might notice that she'd been comprehensively sick all over the rear seat. Fortunately the racket of his clapped-out engine had covered her discomfiture. She pushed open the door, pulled her already short skirt up even higher and managed a not too undignified debouchment. The driver was clocking her lacy briefs.

'Not for you, *compadre*,' she said. 'I've left you a tip in the back. *¡Felices Pascuas!*'

She slammed the door so hard the glass shook. The driver made a rude gesture then sent the cab rattling away into the dark.

Seeing a light on in the villa, she pressed the bell-push and waited for the gates to be unlocked. Nothing happened. Arnie must have got himself pissed again and passed out. Stupid sod. At least she never reached that state. Always knew what she was doing, though sometimes she didn't know why she was doing it.

She dug through the junk in her purse till she found the remote, pointed and pressed, and the gates swung open. Would have been a bugger if she'd forgotten it. Arnie was big on security and even with her skirt round her bum she wouldn't have fancied trying to scale the garden walls with their coronet of razor wire. Best she could have hoped for was to trigger the alarm system and hope that the din roused the useless piss-artist.

She closed the gates behind her, slipped off her designer sling-backs, which were giving her gip, and walked up the smoothly paved driveway in her bare feet. Cup of coffee, fall into bed, wake up around midday tomorrow, couple of corpse-revivers, and then it would be prezzie time! Arnie tended to be a bit mean on the present front, but never mind, she'd made a couple of purchases on his behalf, and he could hardly complain so long as she showed her gratitude in the usual way, always supposing he wasn't still too pissed to get it up.

As she approached the villa she realized the light she'd spotted was the light on the pool terrace, so that's where she headed. She noticed to her surprise that all the metal security shutters were down. As she rounded the corner she saw the empty lounger, the low table on which stood an almost empty bottle of cognac, and shards from a shattered glass all over the tiles. One of her best crystal set, from the look of it. Useless bastard! Christmas or not she'd tear him limb from limb when she laid hands on him.

But first she had to lure him out of hiding.

She called, 'Honey, I'm home!'

Nothing.

The bastard must really have tied one on tonight. Suddenly, fearful that he might have been stupid enough to go for a drunken swim, she peered into the pool.

Just a lilo on the surface and nothing underneath.

She felt a pang of relief. Arnie wasn't much, but he wasn't so little she could be indifferent to his death. The relief was already morphing back to irritation as she turned to face the villa.

Something caught her eye, lying on the tiles at the foot of the heavy security shutter that protected the patio door. Some things.

She went forward.

There were two of them.

Gloves, she thought. Odd. These December nights got chilly, even here on the Costa del fucking Sol, but surely it wasn't so cold that Arnie, with enough alcohol in him to fuel a rocketship, would need to wear gloves? She herself, fearing to damage her long, beautifully manicured and lacquered fingernails wouldn't dream of wearing them; she didn't even know Arnie owned a pair of gloves . . .

And why had he placed them so neatly, almost flush up against the metal shutter . . .?

Finally her mind gave up the effort to conceal beneath this tangle of irrelevant thought the truth of what her eyes were telling her.

Not gloves.

Hands.

Severed from their arms, which were presumably on the far side of the patio shutter.

She recognized the signet ring on one of the fingers, and went down on her knees, not to look more closely but because her legs refused to support her.

She'd thought she had left all that there was to bring up on the back seat of the taxi, but now she found she was wrong.

And when she stopped retching, she raised her head to the Christmas stars and started to scream.

2

After matins on Christmas Day, most members of St Swithin's congregation were eager to head off home to their secular celebrations. There was a good smell of roast fowl rising over Mireton, and Luke Hollins was looking forward as much as anyone to closing his front door and stretching his legs under his own well-laden table.

This was his first Christmas in the parish and by chance it was also going to be the first that he and Willa had spent alone. Usually her parents joined them, and sometimes his sister and her family. But a new baby in the latter case, and reluctance to make the long journey from Devon in the former, had left them with no one to please but themselves. And of course any members of his parochial flock who cared to put their needs before the vicar's relaxation.

As he exchanged greetings by the door with the last of the worshippers, he saw that the castle party was still in the churchyard, over by the Ulphingstone family tomb. This was by far the most prominent sepultural monument, resembling in Hollins's democratic eyes one of those blockhouses still visible on parts of the UK's sea coast out of which the aged eyes of Dad's Army peered in fearful expectation of seeing cohorts of Nazi storm-troopers goosestepping out of the waves.

The tomb was marked off from its populist neighbours by a metal fence, its uprights shaped like Zulu assegais, its interstices filled by curlicues of cast iron in a Celtic knot-pattern, all enamelled black except for the spear blades, which were picked out in gold. Whether its function was to keep the living out or the dead in, Hollins didn't know. But he did know he found it as offensive to good taste as it was to democratic principle.

The most recent entrant to the tomb had been, according to the lapidary inscription, Virginia, beloved daughter of Imogen, and granddaughter of Sir Leon and Lady Kira Ulphingstone.

Hollins thought of how Wolf Hadda must have felt when he came down here in the dark of night to lay his bough of rowan before the tomb and saw that his name didn't get a mention.

The girl's death had predated Hollins's own arrival in Mireton. He had referred to it once at the lunch table, but had been blanked out by Kira, while Leon's face had twisted into such a mask of grief that Hollins had found himself babbling about the church-tower restoration fund in an attempt at distraction.

The castle party were being lectured by Lady Kira, who took her family responsibilities very seriously and expected her guests to do the same. There were half a dozen of them beside the elder Ulphingstones. Quite a small house-party by Kira's standards if this were all, which presumably it was, as you didn't stay at the castle without processing down to the church for morning service. In fact he'd discovered soon after arrival that the verger didn't start ringing the calling bell until he had the castle party in his sights even if this meant delaying the start of things by four or five minutes.

Lady Kira was equally imperious at the other end of the service. Today, in her haste to illustrate the antiquity of the Ulphingstones by close reference to the tomb, she had ushered her party straight by him without a glance as he stood at the door to wish his home-going congregants Merry Christmas.

Well, good luck to them! he thought as he turned to go back into the church, looking forward to getting out of his canonicals and home to his turkey. Then Sir Leon's voice came drifting through the clear air.

'Vicar, hold on a tick.'

If he hadn't had one foot across the threshold of God's house, he might have muttered, 'Oh fuck!' but he nipped the profanity in the bud and turned with a smile.

'Yes, Sir Leon?'

'Don't think you've met my daughter,' called the old man.

Chance would have been a fine thing, he thought as he advanced towards the tomb.

The woman he'd already identified from the pulpit as being Wolf Hadda's ex-wife turned towards him at a touch from her father's hand. Almost of an age with her ex-husband, she seemed to have marked time while time was marking him. She was serenely beautiful with a lovely fair complexion, blue eyes, golden hair – a very English kind of beauty, he thought, that must have come from Sir Leon's side of the family as it had little to do with the high-cheek-boned dark-eyed good looks of her mother.

'Imogen, this is, er, Mark . . .'

'Luke.'

'That's the fellow, knew it was something religious. Luke Collins, been with us six months. Settling in well. Considering.'

'Hollins,' said the vicar. 'Glad to meet you.'

She took his proffered hand and shook it firmly. He looked at her with a mixture of curiosity and compassion. The compassion came from his knowledge of the crap life had chucked at her. Young woman with everything – lovely home, wealth, comfort, a beautiful daughter – discovers that her apparently devoted and hugely successful husband is in fact a pervert and a fraud. He goes to jail, she remarries, tries to rebuild her life, and her daughter dies in tragic, sordid circumstances.

As for the curiosity, well, a measure of how well he was settling into his new job – *considering!* – was the degree to which many of his parishioners were now dropping their guard. They no longer stopped conversations short at his approach. He might be an odd bugger but he was *their* odd bugger. Now when they went all feudal and closed ranks to protect the Ulphingstones from the intrusive gaze of nosey off-comers, he found himself included in the closed ranks. And he soon found out that feudal loyalty earned you the ancient feudal right of close observation and closer analysis of *them up at the castle.*

According to local lore, *that lass Imogen* from the castle had a mind of her own. From an early age she'd led Fred Hadda's lad, Wilf, by the balls. Tossed him aside like a shit-sac from a spring nest when her dad found out, but sat up and took notice when he turned up five years on with a walletful of money and his manners mended.

Then comes the trouble and she divorces him while he's still on trial and marries his lawyer! And when the daughter she's dumped on the Continent in the care of a bunch of foreigners goes to the dogs and dies, she brings her body back to be laid to rest at St Swithin's, then doesn't show up more than once a year to pay her respects!

In other words, though there was next to no sympathy for Hadda himself, there was a lot less for his former wife than might have been expected.

She was still holding his hand after the conventional shaking period had elapsed.

She said in a loud clear voice, with that indifference to being overheard no matter how personal the topic that marks the ruling class, 'Mr Hollins, I understand you're the main point of contact locally with my ex-husband.'

He noted she gave him his correct name with sufficient aspiration to let him know that she was aware she was doing so.

He said cautiously, 'I do see Mr Hadda from time to time, yes.'

'Then I wonder if you know where he is just now?'

He said, 'To the best of my knowledge, he's up at Birkstane.'

She let go his hand and frowned.

'Then the best of your knowledge isn't worth much, Mr Hollins. I called there last week and all I found was a black woman who, I gather, is his psychiatrist. When I called again yesterday, there was still no sign of him, and his vehicle wasn't in the barn.'

'He is not, so far as I know, constrained to stay within the house,' he said.

The rest of the party were still peering at the tomb, apparently taking no interest in the conversation, though Hollins suspected Kira was recording it verbatim. A small, thin-faced dark-complexioned man, wearing only an exquisitely cut lightweight suit despite the cold, came to stand alongside Imogen. The second husband? guessed Hollins. He had noticed him sitting close to her and sharing a hymn book in the castle pew.

'In my country he would be constrained to stay in a prison cell,' he said.

While Hollins was wondering why an English solicitor should talk like a foreigner, Sir Leon said punctiliously, 'Don't think you've met. Paddle Nicotine, cousin of my wife's, Mark Collins, our vicar.'

Hollins for once didn't mind Sir Leon's cavalier way with his name when he saw the small man wince and heard him say, 'Pavel Nik-EET-in.'

Now another member of the castle party, a slightly florid man beginning to run to fat, got in on the act and declared somewhat officiously, 'If you do know where he is, Vicar, and it turns out he's breaking the terms of his licence, you realize you too would be guilty in the eyes of the law?'

Imogen frowned at the interrupter then said apologetically to Hollins, 'My husband. He's a solicitor, therefore sees everything in legal black and white. Toby, be civilized. Mr Hollins is our vicar, not a hostile witness.'

'Sorry,' said the man, offering his hand. 'Toby Estover. It's just that it's a bit worrying, Hadda wandering round loose. Of course we may find it's all been cut and dried with his probation officer. You don't happen to know who that is, do you?'

'I'm afraid not,' said Hollins.

'No?' said Estover dubiously. 'Thought you might have set up some kind of liaison with him, in the circumstances.'

'The circumstances being?'

'A man on the sex offenders' list living on your doorstep, a man who must presumably still be the cause of some concern to our probation service if his prison psychiatrist is making home visits; doesn't that concern you, pastorally if not personally?'

263

'It's the Law that let him out, Mr Estover, not the Church,' said Hollins. 'Maybe you should be talking to somebody else. Sorry I can't be more helpful, Mrs Estover. Now if you'll excuse me, I think I can smell my turkey burning.'

He moved back towards the church.

'Beat you on penalties, I reckon,' said Imogen to her husband.

Nikitin laughed and Estover said sharply, 'I think he's more worried than he's letting on, which suggests he may have more to worry about than he's letting on.'

Lady Kira, accepting that the tomb was played out as a focal topic, now joined in.

'I've been telling Leon to get rid of him ever since I first saw him,' she declared.

'Keep telling you, the living's not in the castle's gift, not for a century and a half,' said Leon. 'As for Wolf, why all the fuss? You complain when he's on your doorstep and you complain when he's not. Can't see why you'd want to see him anyway, Imo.'

'Can't you, Daddy?' said Imogen. 'Let's go home. I wonder what's for lunch?'

She moved away. Pavel Nikitin hurried to catch up with her.

'Imo OK, is she?' Sir Leon said to his son-in-law.

'As far as it is possible for anyone ever to say,' said Estover. He turned his head slowly, taking in the landscape beyond the church and the scatter of village houses. The fells lay sharp as wolf fangs against the cold blue sky, their edges gleaming white, their craggy lower slopes like diseased gums smudged with black where the frost had lost its grip. He longed to be back in London.

'Could be the bloody Caucasus,' he said with a shudder.

Lady Kira shrieked an unexpected laugh.

'Don't be stupid, Toby,' she said. 'It is nothing like. In the Caucasus, Mr Collins would have been dragged apart by wild horses long since.'

She set off after her daughter and cousin several times removed.

'Reads a lot,' said Sir Leon apologetically. 'Far as I know, she's never been nearer the Caucasus than Monte Carlo.'

The two men shared a rare moment of bonding, then gathered up the rest of their party and set out after Kira.

And finally the few villagers who'd lingered beyond the church-yard wall headed home to their dinners, satisfied that the raree-show was over for this Christmas Day.

3

Two days after Boxing Day Wolf Hadda moved slowly through the green channel at Luton Airport, hardly distinguishable from the geriatrics who accompanied him, leaning on their contraband-filled trolleys like Zimmer frames in an effort to win sympathy from any suspicious customs officer.

As he emerged he saw Edgar Trapp standing among the welcomers, most of whom advanced to greet their elderly relatives as if they'd just got back from the Thirty Year War. Before he could reach Trapp, a hatchet-faced woman in a pink jump suit and matching wimple with enough cigarettes on her trolley to carci-nomate a convent, flung her free arm round his neck and gave him a long sucking kiss.

'Lovely to meet you, Wally,' she said. 'You got my address safe? You be sure to keep in touch, dearie. Go safe with Jesus.'

He disengaged himself with difficulty and a promise of ever-lasting friendship.

Trapp said, 'Looks like you made an impression there. She really a nun?'

He said, 'If she is, God help us all! I don't know what the NHS is feeding these people, but it ought to be banned. Ed, what were you thinking of?'

'You said you wanted to blend in. Pensioners' package to Fuengirola seemed perfect.'

'I'll ignore that. How's Sneck been?'

'Growled once at Doll, but she spoke firmly to him and he's been good as gold since.'

Hadda nodded understandingly. If Doll Trapp had spoken firmly to him, he too would have been good as gold.

When they got into Trapp's old Toyota, Hadda, who felt his solicitor was a bad enough driver without distraction, did not speak till they were clear of the airport and running down the M1.

'Have a good Christmas?' he asked.

'Usual. You?'

'I think you're being cheeky, Ed.'

'I mean, the other.'

'Oh that. Yes, fine.'

'Bad as you thought then?'

'Bad as I thought.'

'I'm sorry. By the way, there's messages on your mobile from that Scotch geezer. Sounds a bit agitated. Or maybe it's just the accent.'

He'd bought a new PAYG mobile to use in Spain and left his old phone with Trapp. He didn't want any calls made abroad to register on the old one. The new one lay in several pieces in several litter bins in Fuengirola.

Traffic on the M25 was heavy and it was dark by the time they pulled up at Trapp's house in Chingford. It was a substantial pre-war semi, built well enough to have survived with dignity for the best part of a hundred years and now worth more than the whole street had cost back in the 1930s.

When Trapp opened the front door, they were met by Sneck, his back arched, his teeth bared in a long threatening growl. Then, reproof administered for his owner's callous dereliction of duty, he advanced to offer forgiveness by the vigorous application of wet tongue to Hadda's face.

'Dogs and nuns,' said Trapp. 'You got it made.'

Doll Trapp appeared, pushing Sneck aside unceremoniously to give Hadda a hug.

267

'Wives, too,' he said, giving Trapp a wink over the woman's head. 'Christ, Doll, don't crush me to death.'

Mrs Trapp was large enough to make two of her husband, with a broad face whose naturally stern expression she attempted, unsuccessfully, to soften by her choice of hair colouring. Today it was blush pink.

'You're skin and bones, Wolf,' she declared, releasing him. 'It's all that foreign muck. You must be starved. Come on through. Supper's ready.'

They went through into the dining room. There were things Hadda would rather have been doing, but when Doll spoke, obedience was the best policy.

They ate steak-and-kidney pudding followed by apple pie and custard, all washed down with strong tea. Alcohol wasn't an option in the Trapp household. Trapp had been on the wagon for a couple of decades now and Doll was determined that he would never be led into temptation in his own home.

It was a comfortable meal, the conversation such as it was led by Doll. Anyone seeing and hearing her might have set her down as a confirmed *Hausfrau*, her interests centred on kitchen and family, but Hadda knew better. Trapp's decisions, professional and personal, were all filtered through her. He wouldn't be sitting here at this table if she hadn't given the nod, and it was an endorsement he valued more than his lost title.

At the end of the meal Doll said, 'You with us long, Wolf?'

'Just tonight. I need to get up to Carlisle tomorrow to see my minder, so I'll be off early in the morning to beat the traffic. No need for you to get up.'

'Don't be daft. I'll want to say goodbye to old Sneckie, won't I? I'll really miss him.'

Hadda glanced down at the dog lying alongside his chair and got a return look which, if he'd been anthropomorphically inclined, he might have interpreted as, 'And what's so odd about that?'

Trapp said, 'I've put your phone in your room. And my update.'

He said, 'Thanks,' and excused himself.

On the bed lay the phone and a file.

First he checked his messages. There were a couple from Luke Hollins, hoping all was well and asking him to get in touch. And three from Davy McLucky, starting the previous day, growing increasingly imperative, the last left only a couple of hours earlier.

'Hadda, last fucking chance, whatever you're doing, give me a ring. We need to talk. Now!'

He pressed the return call key.

'McLucky.'

'Hadda. You left a message.'

'Where've you been?'

'Nowhere. Sorry not to get back to you sooner. Let my battery run down and I've just recharged it. So what's so urgent?'

A silence. The silence of disbelief? Maybe. But why should the Scot react to a very believable lie with such scepticism?

Now he spoke.

'The old mate from my Met days that I got Medler's address from gave me a bell. Said if I hadn't made contact yet, not to bother. The good life's over for Arnie. He's dead.'

'*What?*'

'You didn't know then?'

'No, I didn't. Has it been on the news?'

'No, and probably won't be. Yard's been notified because he was one of their own, but seems there's been a note to keep it under wraps as much as possible. Must have been a pretty heavy note as there's nothing the press likes more than a nice grisly human interest story over the festive season.'

'Grisly? What the hell happened?'

'Wife found him Christmas morning. He was in their lounge. His hands were on the patio. The security shutter had come down and chopped them off. He bled to death.'

'Jesus! Your mate tell you anything else?'

'That he had more booze in him than a cross-Channel ferry, and the local cops reckon he was so pissed that either by accident or design he pressed the shutter control then fell forward with his arms outstretched across the patio door.'

'That's terrible,' said Wolf.

'That's what I said. Then my mate asked me, dead casual, if it had been anything important I wanted to get in touch with Arnie about.'

'And what did you tell him, Davy?'

'Well,' said McLucky slowly, 'I know what I should have told him, being ex-job, not to mention a PI with his licence to worry about. I should have told him, I've been working for this guy, got form, been paying me good money to find out where Medler lived, his habits, the layout of his villa, all sorts of stuff. You might want to give him a pull, check how he spent Christmas . . .'

Now it was Hadda's turn to be silent.

He said, 'I think we should meet.'

'You don't expect me to go wandering round that fucking wilderness you live in again, do you?'

'I'll be in Carlisle tomorrow, could you manage that again? It's not like leaving the kingdom; it was once the capital of Scotland, they tell me.'

McLucky wasn't in the mood for lightness.

'Same time, same place. I'll be there.'

The phone went dead.

Hadda switched off and sat in thought for a few moments.

Then he picked up the file and opened it. It only took ten minutes to read. Trapp was not a man to waste words.

He finished, opened his grip, put the file inside and took out a large bottle of expensive perfume, a handsome gold-plated watch and a compact digital recorder. He was at the door when he remembered something and went to the wardrobe. From one of the shelves he took a package. It was Luke Hollins's Christmas gift that some atavistic superstition had prevented him from opening before Christmas.

Trapp and his wife were sitting before a glowing fire in a living room that could have been a tribute to the seventies.

Hadda said, 'I've got a little recording I'd like you both to listen to. Then I've got a sad and rather troubling story I need to tell you. But first things first. Christmas prezzie time! Sorry yours aren't wrapped.'

He handed Doll the watch and Ed the perfume, then said, 'Whoops, I was in prison a long time,' and swapped them round.

They both smiled and said thanks, then watched as Hadda unwrapped his parcel.

It was a postcard-size picture stuck in a gilt frame. It showed a bearded man with a halo. He carried what looked like a small tree in one hand and an axe in the other. There was a post-it note attached to the frame.

It read: *This is St Gomer or Gummarus. The double name may come in useful if you're ever asked to name three famous Belgians. He is the patron of woodcutters and unhappy husbands. Hope he might come in useful. LH*

Hadda began to smile and finally he laughed out loud.

'What?' said Doll.

'Nothing. Just my friendly local vicar. I told him I didn't care to be preached at, so I think he's decided, if you can't convert them with sermons, next best thing is to have a laugh with them!'

He looked at the picture again, then nodded, and added, 'You know, he could be right!'

4

The nearest Alva Ozigbo got to the pleasures of a traditional Christmas was the rather grisly festive atmosphere that hung over the hospital wards.

The balloons and decorations stopped short of Intensive Care but nowhere was beyond the reach of the sucrose notes of old Christmas hits seeping out of the in-house radio system. When she arrived, she'd found her father scheduled for angioplasty the following day and her mother in a state of near collapse. Alva was prepared for this, being aware since childhood that Elvira's way of dealing with bad situations was to anticipate the worst, as if by embracing it, she could avert it. Her gloomy prognostications were uttered in a tone which her husband and daughter had often theorized would surely have won her a part in that Bergmann movie if only she could have produced it at the audition.

The operation went well, and by Boxing Day patient and wife were both making a good recovery. Indeed, Ike Ozigbo already seemed bent on proving the truth of the old adage that doctors make the worst patients, and his surgeon, Ike's registrar, told Alva that her father should be ready to move back home by the New Year, adding 'and that's by popular appeal!'

Elvira's superstitious gloom having achieved its goal, she reverted to her usual brisk efficient self. Her husband's health naturally still preoccupied her mind, but other concerns were now allowed to surface, principle among them being a probing inquisitiveness about the state of her daughter's sex life.

Even in her time of deepest Scandinavian depression, she had registered that Alva was taking phone calls from a man. This was Wolf Hadda, who rang twice, once on the evening of her departure from Cumbria to check she'd reached Manchester safely, the second time a couple of days later. Moving out of range of her mother's hearing but not her speculation, Alva found herself going into what seemed later to be unnecessary detail about Elvira's behaviour. Hadda said, 'I'm with your ma here. Hope for the best, prepare for the worst, that's sound sense. Inside, we're all hoping for the best. So feed the hope and put up with the rest. But I'm teaching my granny to suck eggs.'

Alva said, 'None of my grannies was English. Do English grannies suck a lot of eggs?'

He said, 'It's a condition of service. Listen, I just wanted to say . . .'

What he just wanted to say was drowned in a burst of noise.

She said, 'Say again. I didn't get that.'

He said, 'Sorry, radio on. Look, I've got to dash. You take care.'

Then he was gone, leaving her looking at her phone and wondering whether she should check the radio schedules to see if there was anything on that might be broadcasting a noise like a loudspeaker announcement on a railway platform or in an airport.

Of course she didn't. Her life was too busy for luxuries like reading the *Radio Times*.

But she felt disappointed when he didn't ring again and found it difficult to analyse why.

Two days after Boxing Day, things (meaning Elvira) had settled down enough for Alva to think of accessing her London apartment phone to check on messages. She'd made sure everyone likely to want to contact her had known she'd be away, so there weren't many, and only one that held her attention. It had been left the previous day.

'Dr Ozigbo, this is Imogen Estover. I thought it might be useful

273

for us to talk. I'm up here at the castle for a few more days, then I'll be back in London.'

She left her mobile number and the message ended. Her voice had been cool, almost expressionless, but Alva would have recognized it even if she hadn't given her name.

Useful. To whom, she wondered as she saved the mobile number.

She thought of ringing back that same evening, but decided to sleep on it.

Next morning as she helped Elvira with the breakfast dishes, her phone rang.

The display showed a Cumbrian number. Either Hadda or his ex-wife, she guessed as she put it to her ear. But she was wrong. It was Luke Hollins.

She went out of the kitchen into the garden. It was chilly, but here she could keep an eye on her mother through the window with no risk of being overheard.

'Dr Ozigbo, hi, I've been meaning to ring to see how your father is, but it's been a busy time for me. So how are things?'

She'd rung him before Christmas to explain why she hadn't contacted him as promised before leaving Cumbria.

After she'd brought him up to date on Ike, he said, 'That's good to hear. You'll be staying on there for a while?'

'I was always planning to stay till the New Year,' she said, not adding her mental rider, unless my mother has driven me to flight with her catechism about my private life!

'Good. That's good.'

He wants to tell me something but is reluctant to pile more stuff on me during a family crisis, she thought. There was only one possible topic.

She said, 'How are things at Birkstane?'

That turned on the tap. He told her about his encounter with the Ulphingstones on Christmas Day.

'I got worried, so I called at the house on Boxing Day. Not a sign. I tried again yesterday. Still nothing. The Defender wasn't in the barn. Of course no reason why he couldn't have been out all day. So I was up there at the crack this morning. Nothing. There's no escaping it, he's not here, probably hasn't been here since before Christmas.'

'That doesn't mean anything,' said Alva. 'The terms of his licence don't preclude movement within the country.'

'Yes, I realize that, but he'd need to keep his probation officer informed, I should have thought? And definitely the police?'

'So have you checked?'

'Well, no,' said Hollins hesitantly. 'To tell the truth, I didn't want to stir things up unnecessarily. I thought maybe you . . .'

'I see,' said Alva.

What she saw was how yet again the priest's personal liking for Wolf was at odds with his pastoral concerns. She should have been irritated by his efforts to share the problem with her, but she realized she wasn't.

She could see Elvira behind the kitchen window, still at the sink, watching her as she dried and re-dried the same cup.

She's dying to know if there's a man in my life! thought Alva. How would she react if I told her there were two men, one a convicted pederast, the other a married vicar!

She waved at the watching woman and raised her face to catch the morning sun still low on the south-eastern horizon. It wasn't nine o'clock yet. The day stretched before her, full of hospital smells and Elvira's subtle questioning. The sky was cloudless. She took a deep breath of the sharp air and it seemed to scour her mind.

The motorway wouldn't be back to its normal overcrowded state yet. She could be back in Cumbria in a couple of hours. To do what?

Hollins said, 'Hello? Dr Ozigbo, are you still there?'

She said, 'Yes, sorry. Look, are you going to be around later this morning? I could come up . . .'

He said, 'Great. That would be helpful.'

She wanted to ask him, *How exactly?* but it didn't seem apt.

She said, 'Till later then,' switched off and went back into the kitchen.

'Mum,' she said, 'would you mind if I ducked out of the visits today?'

'Of course not, dear. You deserve a break. Is it something special you want to do?'

'I thought I might take a little drive and maybe look up an old friend.'

'Anyone I know?' said Elvira, very casual.

'I think you know all my old friends, Mum,' she said.

Her mother smiled but didn't press.

She's spotted that there's more going on than I'm saying, thought Alva, but naturally her interpretation's romantic. A date, an assignation, even an affair!

She gave her mother a hug and said, 'Great. Give my love to Daddy. I'll be home this evening some time. Don't wait supper for me.'

As she drove away from the house, she felt a pang of guilt at her own sense of release. It had come as a disappointment to her as a student to realize that understanding the often irrational origins of common emotions didn't stop you feeling them. When she told her father this, he'd boomed his great laugh and said, 'Even dentists get toothache!'

And even cardiologists have heart attacks, she told herself.

She set the guilt aside and concentrated on her driving as she swept down the slip road on to the motorway.

She soon realized she'd been wrong about the traffic, or perhaps everyone had made the same miscalculation. Her two-hour estimate rapidly stretched to three, giving her both the incentive and the time to ask herself precisely why she was doing this.

Striving for that complete honesty she looked for in her therapies, she systematically listed all her motivational springs.

First the professional: concern for a patient; concern for a community; Luke Hollins's request for help; Imogen Estover's desire to speak with her.

Then the personal: her fear that she might have got things wrong; her irritation at the feeling that Hadda was mucking her about; her

276

frustration in the presence of mysteries she'd not yet been able to disentangle; her simple need to have a break from her mother's company and hospital visits!

There it was. Can't get any honester than that, she told herself.

Except that, as her college tutor had loved to iterate, complete honesty is like clearing a cellar. When you've got all the clutter neatly laid out in the back yard, don't waste time congratulating yourself on a job well done. Head down those steps again and start digging up the concrete floor.

She dug. She knew already there was something to find. Something so deeply repressed that she couldn't be sure it wasn't a figment of her imagination, the crocodile under the sofa that had made her sit with her legs tucked up beneath her as a child, the trolls in Elvira's Swedish fairy tales who lived beneath the rockery in the garden. Unreal things, but her fear was real till she discovered that the simple way to dispose of them was to expose them to daylight and watch them shrivel away.

This was what she tried now. It didn't take long to find it, not because it wasn't buried deep but because she knew where to start digging. And there it was, hidden beneath all that stuff about his face-transforming smile, that dangerous charm which she had complimented herself on being so alert to.

She spoke it out loud so that there could be no fudging.

'Deeply repressed reason for driving north to Birkstane: I am sexually attracted to Wolf Hadda.'

Now she could submit it to the test of exposure to the clear light of day.

But it wasn't shrivelling.

Damn! But no need to panic. Such things happened. Usually the other way round, of course. And it seemed peculiarly perverse in every sense that her urges should have focused on a man who was physically scarred, psychologically damaged, and morally repugnant. But if human beings weren't perverse, she'd be out of a job.

She would deal with it, just as Simon Homewood dealt with his feelings for her.

Her self-examination had taken care of the time nicely. She saw a sign telling her that she was now in Cumbria.

She wasn't altogether sure what had started here all those years ago, but one way or another all journeys are circular. We never arrive anywhere that we haven't been before.

Where was Hadda now? she asked herself.

And where did he think he was heading?

She switched on her left indicator and prepared to turn off the motorway.

5

McLucky was late.

'Fucking trains,' he said. 'They couldn't run a raffle.'

'That's all right,' said Hadda. 'I'm just here myself. My probation officer was very keen to exchange notes on how we'd enjoyed our respective Christmases.'

'Me too,' said McLucky, sitting down heavily.

The lounge door opened and a young, pretty waitress backed in carrying a heavily laden tray.

'I ordered you a scotch,' said Hadda. 'And some smoked salmon sandwiches.'

'And I told you before, I'm choosy who I eat with.'

'If you don't stop snarling, the waitress will be thinking we're having a lovers' tiff.'

'Would it put her mind at rest if I gave you a thump?'

'She looks the happy-ending type to me, so she'd probably prefer if you gave me a kiss.'

That didn't make McLucky smile but his face relaxed a little and when the waitress reached their table and set down the plates and glasses, he picked up his glass.

'I'm not so choosy who I drink with,' he said. 'Cheers. Now, answers.'

'Yes, I've been to Spain,' said Hadda. 'Yes, I saw Medler. No, I didn't kill him.'

McLucky said, 'Jesus.'

'You did ask.'

'I didn't actually. I was hoping you were going to turn up with your clerical friend and he was going to swear on the Bible you'd not been out of the county all Christmas. How the hell did you manage it? I thought there were travel restrictions.'

'There are. I would have needed permission. If I'd asked.'

'But your passport . . . you'll be on record . . .'

'Mr Wally Hammond, widower, of Gloucestershire, is on record as having enjoyed a festive break with sixty other geriatrics at the Hotel Flamenco. I have a friend who knows how to arrange such things. He is, as you'll probably have gathered, a cricket fan.'

McLucky looked at him blankly, then said, 'Why are you telling me this?'

'Because I think the only way to persuade you I'm telling you everything is to do just that. I went to see Medler late on Christmas Eve, having seen his wife head off to the midnight service at the English Church. We had a long conversation. I left him a sadder and I hope a wiser man about twelve thirty. He was alive and well. Except for being pretty drunk. And he must have got drunker from the sound of what happened. Happy now?'

'Happy? You must be joking.'

'You've still got doubts? I thought that tape you brought me of Estover and the Nutbrowns chatting at Poynters would have cleared your mind.'

'It was suggestive, but a long way from conclusive,' said McLucky. 'Anyway, it just says something about what you maybe were. It's what you might have become that bothers me.'

'Fine.' Hadda sipped his orange juice. 'In your shoes, maybe I'd be cautious too. Why don't you see how suggestive you find this? Me, I'll just check that Sneck's all right in the van. Give me a ring when you've had time to listen to it.'

He pushed across the table a digital recorder with an earpiece attached.

McLucky studied it suspiciously for a moment then fixed the

device in his ear and pressed the start button. Hadda rose and, leaning heavily on his stick, made his way out of the lounge, smiling his gratitude at the young waitress who rushed forward to open the door for him.

In the car park he opened the Defender's tailgate.

'Out,' he said to Sneck.

The dog woke up, yawned as if thinking about it, then jumped down. Hadda locked the car, walked to the edge of the car park and sat down on a low wall bordering a patch of municipal greenery. Sneck jumped over the wall, sniffed around, cocked his leg against a tired-looking tree, then returned to lie across his master's feet and went back to sleep.

Hadda, leaning forward with both hands resting on his stick and his chin resting on his hands, closed his eyes too and let his mind go back to his encounter with Arnie Medler on Christmas Eve.

6

It had taken a minute or more for Medler to recover from his initial
shock. Hadda saw no reason to make things easier. He settled in a
chair opposite the man and stared at him fixedly as if able to read
the confusion of emotion running across the ex-policeman's mind.
Finally he reached forward with the axe and nudged the cognac
bottle towards the ex-cop.

'You look like you need a drink,' he said.

'Bloody right, I do,' croaked Medler. 'Seeing you there waving
that fucking hatchet around, wonder I didn't have a heart attack.'

'Can't have that,' said Hadda. 'Not before we talk.'

Medler topped up his glass, emptied it, filled it again then looked
at Hadda.

'You?'

'No thanks. I'm driving.'

The conventional response plus the drink seemed to help Medler's
recovery and his voice was stronger as he said, 'So how'd you find
me? McLucky, was it?'

'Might have been.'

'I knew there was something. First lesson in CID. Never trust a
coincidence.'

'So why did you go along with him?'

'Don't know. Could have snuck off home soon as I clocked him,
pulled down the shutters. I suppose I was just glad to see a face I

recognized from the old days. Any face. Someone to talk to who knew me when I was . . . someone.'

'A good honest cop,' said Hadda with savage irony.

'That's right! That's what I was. All right, I cut a few corners, took a couple of drinks, but only to help me get where I wanted to be.'

'You mean, like *here*?'

'*No!* I mean get a result. Saw no harm in letting a few sprats swim loose if they helped me catch a fucking great shark. And if I picked up a few backhanders on the way, that just increased my credibility, right? Come on, Sir Wilf, you were a financial whiz. All right, you may have taken the rap for stuff you didn't know about, but you can't have made all the money you did without dipping your fingers in places they shouldn't have been.'

'You trying to say I got what I deserved?' said Hadda incredulously.

Medler shook his head.

'No. Of course not.' He tried a laugh, but it didn't come out right. Nevertheless he pressed on: 'I'll tell you something funny, though. In one way it *was* your own fucking fault you got what you did. Ironic that. Like in Greek tragedy. That surprises you, eh? I'm not just a dumb plod, I got O-levels.'

Hadda leaned forward and said harshly, 'I'm not here for literary fucking criticism, Medler. Just tell me what happened. And quick. I don't want to be still here when the lovely Tina returns from her devotions.'

'Don't worry, one way or another I reckon she'll be on her knees for a couple of hours yet. But all right, here goes . . .'

He emptied his glass again. Refilled it. He was beginning to feel he had some control over the situation. Hadda didn't mind. It was a delusion easily remedied.

'Sure you won't? OK. Well, it started with a tip, an anonymous email, said we might like to take a close look at Sir Wilfred Hadda, mentioned a website, InArcadia. We knew about InArcadia. Clever buggers, they were. Everything heavily encrypted, more layers to get through than you'd find on an Eskimo whore, ducking and weaving all the time so that just when you thought you'd got a handle on them, they'd be over the hills and far away. It was only a matter of time, though, and we'd just had a big breakthrough when we got this tip about you. While we hadn't laid hands on the people running it – not surprising, they could be anywhere in the world – we'd got about twenty thousand client credit-card records.'

'Twenty thousand!'

'Tip of the fucking iceberg. There's a lot of weirdoes about. Anyway, among all these credit-card records we found a couple that we traced back to your company. That with the email allegations was enough to get a warrant to take a closer look. Maximum discretion. You were an important man.'

'Maximum discretion!' exclaimed Hadda. 'The media turned up mob-handed! You couldn't resist it, could you, Medler? A big hit, you wanted all the world to see you making it, right?'

The ex-cop was shaking his head vigorously.

'You're wrong, Hadda. Man like you with fancy-dan lawyers, we tread careful till we're sure. I played it by the book, need-to-know op, me the lowest rank needing to know. Nearly shit myself when I arrived and saw it was looking like a muck-rakers' convention.'

No reason for the man to lie, thought Hadda. Meant someone else wanted the world to be in on the act from the start . . .

'But I bet you enjoyed it, all the same.'

'Why not? Everyone likes taking a swipe at a tall poppy. Build 'em up, knock 'em down, that's what makes celebrity culture go round. And when I clocked that stuff on your computer, I thought, Hello! This case isn't going to do me any harm whatsoever.'

'Made your mind up straight away, did you?' said Hadda. 'Innocent till proved guilty doesn't apply, not when you've got yourself a big one.'

Medler laughed again and shook his head.

'That's where you're wrong again, Sir Wilf . . . sorry, Mr Hadda. That's the irony I was telling you about. If you hadn't reacted the way you did, punching me in the mouth, twice, and doing a runner

284

and getting yourself hospitalized, you know what you'd probably be doing now? You'd be relaxing in your Caribbean mansion, having a drink, looking forward to eating your Christmas turkey on the beach!'

'What the fuck are you talking about?'

'I'm talking about me being a good cop,' said Medler, suddenly animated. 'I'm talking about me doing the job I was paid for. We do a real job on sifting through evidence, and not just because we know rich bastards like you will be spending more than the department's annual budget on putting together a defence. We do it for rich and poor alike, because it's the right fucking thing to do!'

Hadda had come prepared for many things, but not moral indignation.

He's talking like he's still in the job! he thought.

But even as he looked he saw the indignation fade and awareness of the truth of his situation return to Medler's eyes.

He rubbed his hand over his face and said wearily, 'Yeah, that's right, Mr Hadda. If you'd just sat on your hands, protesting your innocence, and let us get on with the job of investigating the case, I reckon that a week or so later, I'd have been making a statement to the media saying Sir Wilfred's been the victim of a scurrilous attempt to smear his good name and, as far as the Met's concerned, he's being released without a stain on his character.'

He filled his glass again and regarded his visitor with a malicious glint in his eyes.

'But you couldn't sit still, could you? Not the great Wolf Hadda, the City's own action man. You had to hit out and make a run for it, and suddenly everything changed. You were lying on your back with lots of bits missing and enough machinery attached to you to run a small factory, and it was impossible to find a bookie who'd give odds on you lasting the week out. So, like you, the case was put on ice. We had plenty of living perverts to pursue without wasting too much time on the moribund. In fact, at the time, following up all these payment trails from InArcadia, things got really hectic.'

285

Wolf Hadda suddenly reached forward and seized the brandy bottle. He raised it to his lips and took a long swig. Finished, it took all his will power not to hurl the bottle against the villa wall. Instead he lowered it gently to the table and said, 'So when did you realize I was innocent, Mr Medler?'

'Month or so on. Most of the media boys had lost interest, they like their meat to be still on the hoof, so I was surprised when my boss asked for an update on your case. We went back a long way, him and me, so I told him I'd better things to do than investigate a living corpse, and he told me it wasn't his idea but there was "an interest". Now that's code for politics or security or both. Somebody somewhere wanted to know whether you'd been sticking it to little girls or not. You got any idea who, Mr Hadda?'

He was starting to sound far too like his old cocky self. And his old cocky self would be sifting through truths, weighing alternatives, looking for opportunities.

Wolf brought the hatchet blade down on the arm of the recliner just an inch from Medler's wrist, causing him to jerk away so violently his glass flew out of his hand and smashed on the tiled patio.

'Jesus Christ! What you do that for? You could have had my hand off!'

'Your hands are the least of your worries if you start jerking me around, Medler. We're not having a conversation. Just tell me what happened!'

'All right, all right, keep your hair on!'

He reached for the cognac and took a long pull straight from the bottle.

'What I did then was go away and do what I'd have done if you hadn't been such an action hero. I took a long hard look at the case notes and the evidence file. On the surface it all looked pretty sound, but once I started digging, it didn't take long to smell a rat.'

'Meaning, you started to suspect that I'd been fitted up? Why?'

'There were patterns I looked for. You got to understand, this wasn't the first time this kind of thing happened. You get everyone

286

from redundant employees to betrayed wives or even pissed-off kids thinking, Wouldn't it be neat to download some mucky images on to the old bastard's computer and give the pigs an anonymous tip? Often it sticks out like a sore thumb. Yours was a rather more sophisticated job. Whoever did it knew what they were doing. Took me the best part of a week, on and off, but in the end I got there.'

'Well, congratulations,' sneered Hadda. 'So why didn't you go to your superiors, tell them what you thought, get my name cleared publicly?'

Medler smiled bitterly, 'Oh, I was going to, believe me. But first – this'll make you laugh – I thought, wouldn't it be nice to get a line on the bastards who'd been shafting you? All right, you'd split my lip, twice, but that didn't mean you deserved this.'

'I'm very touched. So what did you do?'

'I went along to see Toby fucking Estover. He was still your solicitor then, of course. This was before he went public about banging your missus. Sorry. All I intended was to have a chat, see if he could give me any line on who was most likely to be responsible. But you know what? I hadn't been in his office two minutes when I realized I need look no further. Whatever was going on, whoever had initiated it, Mr Toby Estover was in it right up to his lily-white upper-class neck!'

Now as he regarded Hadda, his expression was no longer malicious but pitying.

'Come on, Hadda,' he said. 'You've had years to think about this. You must have suspected.'

'I suspected . . . lots of people,' said Hadda. Then he took a deep breath and demanded, 'So your super-sensitive copper's nose put Estover in the frame. What did you do about it?'

'Without evidence, what could I do except sit back and let him go on thinking that I'd come to talk to him because I was on to his little game? At this point all I was interested in was letting him incriminate himself so that I could bang him up! Estover, Mast and Turbery, in the Met they're high on most people's hate list! I'd be flavour of the month if I could throw a spanner in their well-oiled works. And when he began hinting a pay-off, I began rubbing my hands at the prospect of getting him on a bribery count as well.'

'But in the end he offered enough to make you change your mind,' said Hadda.

'Not exactly. Or at least, not straight away. After half an hour of me looking like I knew everything while really I knew fuck all and him giving off enough legal smog to contravene the Clean Air Act, we agreed to meet again the following day. I naturally took the chance to get myself wired. When the bribe was clearly offered, I wanted it on tape.'

'Still thinking like an honest cop,' mocked Hadda.

'Yeah, surprisingly, I was. But someone had been keeping tabs on me. I was sitting at my desk, writing up my report when my boss ushered this geezer into my office and said, "This is Mr Wesley. He'd like to talk to you about the Hadda case. He has full clearance." Then he left me with Mr sodding Wesley.'

'Wesley?' Hadda frowned. 'What did he look like?'

'Nothing special. Hard to say if he was fifty or seventy. Hair thinning, a bit wispy, sort of brown turning grey. Five foot ten, slim build, blue eyes, not much chin, nice smile, except it didn't always go with the things he was saying. Expensive suit, MCC tie. Softly spoken, posh but not grating, slight hint of East Anglia in there, maybe.'

'For someone nothing special, he seems to have made an impression,' said Wolf.

Medler shrugged and said, 'When I heard what he had to say, I made sure I'd know him again. What about you? Sounds familiar, does he?'

He hadn't lost his super-sensitive copper's nose, thought Hadda.

'Maybe. What did this Mr Wesley say?'

'I told him what was going off, what I suspected about Estover. He asked me who else knew what I was doing. I said my boss a bit, but not much. And nobody else. He said keep it that way. If Estover did offer me a bribe, push him to see how far he'd go. But don't take any action till I'd talked to him again. And nothing in

288

writing or in my computer. I said, "How do I get in touch?" and he smiled and said, "Don't worry about it."'

'And you didn't argue or talk this over with your boss?'

Medler shrugged and said, 'Not the kind of guy you want to argue with. But if he's a friend of yours, you'll know that. Anyway, I met Estover again. I could tell straight off he was easing towards a deal. He started by talking about you, showed me the latest medical report. Just one step back from a death certificate, he said. "And you can't harm the dead," he told me, "so why harm the living?" Trying to soften me up, I suppose. But he still didn't say anything like, Here's ten k, it's yours if you keep your mouth shut.'

'Ten k? You didn't get this place with ten k,' said Hadda.

'No. I played it like Mr nothing special Wesley told me and gave him a push.'

He smiled as if relishing the memory.

'Suddenly I stood up and said, all pompous like, "I hope you're not offering me an inducement, Mr Estover. Because if you are, I think you ought to know, I'm not the kind of cop who'd put his reputation on the line for a handful of silver." "How about a handful of gold?" he said, laughing to show it was just a joke. And I said, "What would I do with gold? No, I'm a man of simple needs. All I'm looking to do is to get enough years in to retire early to some-where sunny like Spain." Then I said we'd need to talk again, I'd give him a ring. And I left.'

'And not long after you left a car drew up and Mr Wesley invited you to take a ride with him,' said Hadda.

'Where were you? Hiding in the boot? Sorry. Yes, he took charge of the tape. Didn't bother to listen to it, but he seemed to know what had gone off. He asked me if there really was somewhere in Spain I had in mind. I said there were a couple of places. I'd always kept an eye on the Spanish house market. Most of the stuff I fancied was way out of my league normally, but I knew that with the banking crisis getting worse every day, a lot of overstretched ex-pats were going to be looking to sell cheap. I'd just got the details of this place. It was still only a pipe-dream. Even with a fifty per cent discount, I'd never be able to afford it. But now Wesley said, "Show it to Estover. Ask his advice."'

'Which you did when you met again?'

'Yeah. Next day. Not in his office this time. I chose the rendezvous, outside, down by the river. He was as cautious as me. The way we patted each other to make sure neither of us was wired, anyone watching must have thought we were a couple of poofs! Then I showed him the details of the villa, asked what he thought. He said it looked a good investment, how much of the cost would I be looking for? And I said, "Well, all of it. Plus I'd need a bit of a lump sum to cover maintenance and so on."'

He paused for effect. He was beginning to enjoy his narration again.

Hadda flourished the hatchet and snarled, 'For fuck's sake, get on with it!'

'Sorry, sorry,' said Medler, taking another swig of brandy. 'I expected him to start to haggle, but he didn't even blink. He said, leave it to him. He'd do the negotiating. And he'd get it all registered in my name. Plus a nice maintenance account.'

'And that was it?' said Hadda. 'Sounds like you were getting a helluva lot for not very much.'

'There was something else,' said Medler uneasily. 'Estover said, "We need guarantees. No come back. Whatever happens. Never."'

'So what did you have to do?' said Hadda softly, breathing on the hatchet blade and polishing it on his sleeve.

'He told me that, for both our sakes, I'd need to make sure that if ever anyone looked at the details of the charges again, they'd find a truly watertight case.'

'And then?'

'We shook hands and left. I met Wesley later. He told me to sit tight for a couple of days, mention nothing of this to no one. Later in the week he turned up in my office. Said it had been decided I should go along with Estover the whole way. I said, "What's that mean?" He said, cool as you like, "I mean let him buy the villa and make it over to you. Then you do what he asked and make sure that the case against Hadda is tighter than a duck's arsehole." I said, "What about the fraud case?"'

'Why'd you say that? You weren't anything to do with the Fraud Squad.'

Medler grinned and said, 'Everything's about sex or money, and this clearly wasn't about sex. Fitting you up on the porn charges had just been a way of making sure your name stank before the Fraud boys got their teeth into you. Stands to reason.'

'You reckon? And what did Mr Wesley say?'

'Told me to stick to my business and live happily ever after.'

'He said that? Interesting choice of phrase. And you said, all right, I'm yours body and soul for a place in the sun and a bottle of sangria.'

'No, I bloody well didn't! Listen, you got to believe me, Hadda, I didn't like where all this was going, and I said so.'

'So what precisely did you say, Arnie?' asked Hadda quietly.

'I said, the fraud stuff was one thing – way it looked to everyone back then, all you lot in high finance were on the fiddle and deserved every bit of shit that could be thrown at you – but the other stuff, to shovel that on to an innocent man, that just wasn't on.'

'Nice of you to be so concerned,' said Hadda. 'And your Mr Wesley replied . . .?'

'He said you were to all intents a dead man and dead men didn't mind whether you shovelled earth or shit over them. As for Estover, he would be more useful on the end of their string than relaxing in comfort at Her Majesty's expense. I said, "You mean this has all been for nothing?" And he laughed and said, "Hardly nothing. You've got yourself a nice retirement villa out of it, haven't you? Of course you might turn out to be the gabby type. In which case I don't think retirement would be an option." So what could I do?'

He looked at Hadda pleadingly. The bastard wants me to feel sorry for him in his sad predicament! he thought.

'You could have told him to get stuffed! But instead, you accepted a large bribe from Estover and his associates to conceal the fact that

291

they'd framed me. And in addition, before you left, you made sure their botched-up job was completely watertight, right?'

For a second, Medler looked ready to argue, then he shrugged and said, 'Yeah, more or less. Once I was happy with the way your case file looked, I went sick, made sure I got the maximum severance payments – why not? I'd worked all those years in a really shitty job, I reckon I'd earned it!'

Now he was looking defiant. As if this were a point really worth arguing.

Hadda said, 'So we've got Estover right in the middle of the frame. What about the others? You're a nosey little fox, I'll give you that. I bet you had a chat with your mates in Fraud. What were they saying?'

Medler said, 'They were pretty sure your finance guy, Nutbrown, had to be involved. Where'd you find him? Fell out of the moon, I'd guess! The Fraud boys said trying to get a line on him was like trying to get water out of a pond with your finger and thumb. In the end they were happy to have him on board as a fully cooperating witness! I'd say Estover was pulling his strings. And Nutbrown's wife too. I only met her the once, that was enough!'

'Anyone else?'

Now the man looked at him shrewdly and said, 'You're thinking about your ex-missus, aren't you?'

'Just answer my questions, Medler,' growled Hadda.

'Right, right, keep your hair on. Listen, she struck me as a very together lady, never showed no signs of falling apart despite everything. At the time I thought it was just that upper-class stiff-upper-lip thing, but when I heard later that she dumped you and married Estover, well, it speaks for itself, don't it? Come on, Hadda, you know her a lot better than me. Was she so thick that greasy bastard could take her in? I don't think so!'

He gave a knowing sneer, reminding Hadda of his manner on their first meeting.

It was a provocation too much.

He leaned forward, shoved the hatchet against Medler's crotch and snarled, 'So why'd you come to see me, fuck-face? Brought some poisoned grapes, did you?'

It was even more effective than he'd hoped. The man went pale, or at least his tan went sallow, and he shrank back as far as he could get in his chair.

'An old mate rang and told me you'd woke up,' he gabbled. 'I couldn't believe it. I mean, no one expected it, not after all those months . . .'

'And you were so relieved you had to come straight to my bedside?'

'I wasn't thinking straight,' admitted Medler. 'I had to see for myself. I mean, for all I knew you were a drooling idiot, right? At the hospital I talked my way past the guy on duty . . . come to think of it, it was McLucky, wasn't it? Yeah, it was. Jesus, how could I have forgotten that? After that I talked to Estover . . .'

'Did he contact you or did you contact him?'

'I don't know. It was him contacted me, I think . . . yeah, that's right . . . all he wanted to know was, had I really tidied things up? I said yes, I was sure. Then I said, did he understand, the way I'd left things, you could go down for a really long stretch? He said, "Too late to worry about that now." But I did worry, Hadda, you've got to believe me. I mean, I was just covering myself . . . I never thought . . . I believed you'd be dead!'

'Oh, I can tell you were really bothered,' said Hadda. 'That's why you went straight round to the Yard and told them everything.'

'I couldn't do that, I'd have ended up worse off than you!' he cried. 'I got a card wishing me a happy retirement. It was signed Wesley. Even if I'd given an anonymous tip-off, no way that smiling bastard wouldn't have traced it back to me. I'm sorry, I'm really sorry, there hasn't been a day since when I haven't thought about what was happening to you, how people must be thinking about you . . .'

'Wish I'd known,' said Hadda, standing up. 'It would have been such a comfort.'

'What are you going to do?' asked Medler, looking up at him fearfully.

'I'm going to go away and consider my options,' said Hadda. 'The two top ones are, I could come back here and chop your balls off with my axe and stick them in a highball glass and make you drink them down. Or I could take this along to the Yard and play it to your old colleagues and see what they have to say.'

He flourished a digital recorder in the air.

'Either way, Arnie, I reckon you're fucked. Merry Christmas!'

7

'Get a job!'

Wolf Hadda sat upright. A middle-aged woman with a laden shopping bag was scowling down at him. On the ground between Sneck's
paws someone had dropped a handful of change. Not her, he assumed.

His mobile rang.

The woman went puce with righteous indignation.

'My stockbroker,' said Hadda.

When he returned to the bar a few moments later, he saw that
McLucky had finished his drink. But the sandwiches were still
untouched.

'So?' he said, sitting down. 'Happy *now*?'

'You could have switched off, then dealt with Medler. You had
an axe, for God's sake!'

'Little hatchet. It was Medler's, actually. Picked it up from a
storage shed in the villa garden. Anyway his hands got chopped
off by the security shutter, wasn't that what your informant said?'

'You could have made it look that way.'

'Clever me,' said Hadda. 'So you're still not sure about me. Then
why aren't you ringing the cops?'

'Maybe because the little gobshite was definitely in line for a
good kicking after what he did to you. You'd be OK over there.
These Latinos understand revenge. Provocation, you didn't mean
him to die, manslaughter.'

295

'And how long do these sympathetic Latinos bang you up for that?'

'I don't know. You'd need to consult a lawyer.'

'I have done,' said Hadda, smiling. 'He reckons three, four years, maybe, if I got lucky. Then back here to serve the rest of my current sentence.'

'With this,' said McLucky, holding up the recorder, 'they'd surely quash that.'

'Without hard evidence?' said Hadda. 'Parole breaker. Responsible for the death of an ex-cop. Over here they don't make allowances for revenge. One way or another, I'd be back inside. Look, I could have gone to the Yard with this, but not now Medler's dead.'

McLucky regarded the other man speculatively.

'Don't know if you're fooling yourself, Hadda, but you don't fool me. I think I knew from the first time we talked. All this stuff you've been paying me for, you're not interested in proving your innocence, are you? You want to sort it out yourself.'

'You doing an extension course in psychology?'

'Maybe I should. Like I say, I'm not so easy to fool as that nice black lass that helped get you out of jail. Or is she in on this?'

Hadda shook his head.

'Absolutely not.'

'Very positive. Meaning you've either got a conscience about her or you're lying.'

'Lying? When have I ever lied to you?'

'How about every time I see you shuffling across a room like you couldn't raise a sprint if a randy gorilla was chasing you across the veldt with its cock at the ready?'

'Think your natural history might be a little rusty.'

'That's because I'm spending all my time on the psychology.'

'So where do we go from here?' said Hadda.

McLucky said, 'I don't know about you, but me, I can go any which way I fucking well like. I can still back away from all this shite with none of it sticking to me. What have I done? Gone to Spain, chatted to an old colleague. OK, I've pretended to be interested in buying your old mate's house, but I've not got any financial advantage out of that, so no crime.'

'Well, you did plant a couple of bugs so we could know what they're saying,' corrected Wolf. 'But of course I'd not expect you to break the law seriously. Not for the money I'm paying.'

He smiled as he spoke.

'Sounds like the start of a negotiation to me,' said McLucky. 'Listen, before I decide anything, I want to know what all this stuff about "an interest" means. What are we talking here? Whitehall? Spooks?'

Hadda shrugged.

'God knows. Probably DTI, worried about how my trial might affect British commercial interests. I was quite important, remember?'

McLucky bared his teeth and snarled, 'Don't bullshit me. This guy Wesley's no civil fucking servant. I listened to the tape, remember? The way you repeated *Wesley,* that sounded like it meant something to you. And Medler certainly thought so.'

'Just reminded me of someone I used to know,' said Hadda lightly.

'Aye? Old friend or old enemy? Mind you, with old friends like you've got, I dread to think what your old enemies must be like!'

'I do still have a few real friends,' said Wolf.

'You mean like this solicitor of yours and his guidwife? Aye, they sound like real chums to cover for you like they're doing. Or do you just know where they buried the bodies?'

'No, Ed and Doll are the real deal. Good people, too. I'd like you to meet them. Maybe I'll fix that up when you go back down to London. In fact, they could put you up. Be a damn sight cheaper than these fancy hotels you keep piling on your expense sheet.'

'Hold it there! You want someone to stay in fleapits, you should have sent that dog of yours. And who says I'm going back to London? I've got other clients to think of.'

'Name three,' said Wolf. 'While you're thinking, why don't you try a sandwich?'

297

McLucky studied his face for a moment, then selected a sandwich, opened it, sniffed the smoked salmon and took a bite.

'That's agreed then,' said Hadda. 'Now it's just a question of haggling over your fee and sorting out when you head back to the Smoke. That right, Davy?'

'Davy? You thinking of paying me enough to call me Davy?'

Hadda shook his head.

'I always call my friends by their first names, and I'd like to think that anyone I'm employing to do what I'm asking you to do was my friend.'

McLucky finished his sandwich, picked up another.

'I'm getting used to the smoked salmon, Wolf,' he said.

8

Mireton looked deserted but Alva felt herself observed as she drove through the village past the church to the vicarage.

Hollins came out the front door as she got out of the car.

Eager to greet her, or trying to pre-empt an encounter with his unfriendly wife?

He said, 'Dr Ozigbo, I'm so sorry. You've had a wasted journey.'

'You mean, he's back?'

'On his way. Like I said, I've left several messages on his phone. I thought I'd try him one more time just a few minutes ago, and he answered!'

'And where is he?' asked Alva.

'He's in Carlisle. Visiting his probation officer.'

'That's what he told you?' she said, trying to keep the doubt out of her voice.

'No. That's what his probation officer told me. Mr Hadda put him on. It seems he spent Christmas in London, staying with his solicitor and his wife.'

For a second Alva thought crazily he was referring to the Estovers.

Then she said, 'Mr Trapp, would that be?'

'That's it!' Hollins looked delighted that she knew the name, as if this confirmed all was well. 'And the arrangement had been made in advance, and Mr Cowper, that's the probation officer, had checked it out, and Hadda was sorry not to have replied to my calls but his

299

battery had gone flat and he hadn't noticed till he tried to use the phone himself last night.'

It was a good story, and one so easily checked it had to be water-tight, thought Alva.

So why didn't she feel as relieved as she ought to?

Maybe because part of her was resenting the knowledge that when Hadda had gone through the motions of pressing her to stay at Birkstane over Christmas, he had already made his other arrange-ments!

She really needed to get these distracting emotions sorted out. Head back to London, throw herself into her work at Parkleigh, remind herself that Hadda still legally belonged there, and of the reasons why. That should sort it.

'He sends his regards, by the way,' added Hollins.

'You told him I was coming?'

'Yes. Sorry, shouldn't I have done? I just wanted to make it clear that going off like that without a word had caused a lot of worry. He said he was really sorry, asked after your father, and said that if you wanted a bed for the night, Birkstane was at your disposal.'

'Big of him, but I don't think so,' said Alva drily, trying to conceal, not least from herself, how attractive the offer was.

'No, of course, you'll want to get back to your mother. I'm sorry you've had a wasted journey,' said Hollins. 'Look, why don't you come inside and have a spot of lunch before you set off back? Willa would love to see you again.'

Was this faith at work, or just a simple clerical lie? wondered Alva.

'Thanks, but no,' she said. 'But you can tell me how I get to Ulphingstone Castle.'

'You're going to the castle?' he said in surprise.

'Yes. It's all right. I'm expected, sort of. Mrs Estover said she wants to talk to me. I can only imagine it's something to do with her former husband, so naturally I'm curious. I hope she's still there.'

She wasn't certain why she was being so forthcoming with

Luke Hollins. Except of course that she liked him, and liked particularly the way he had responded to the arrival of Hadda on his parochial doorstep. Vicars generally she regarded as either inadequates compensating for poor human relationship skills by claiming a special relationship with God, or social workers in drag. Hollins fitted neither of these categories. He was a nice young guy who hadn't yet made his mind up where he wanted to be.

Perhaps his strong-willed wife would be able to steer him right.

Wasn't that what wives were for?

She doubted if Wolf Hadda would agree with her.

He said, 'Yes, she's there. I rang this morning when I heard from Mr Hadda. His disappearance over Christmas seems to have got them in a bit of a flap. For all the wrong reasons, of course. So I was pleased to be able to assure them that it had all been quite legal and above board.'

She was too kind to remind him it was his own 'flap' about the possible wrong reasons for Hadda's absence that had got her driving all the way here this morning. Instead she said, 'And how did she take the news?'

'I didn't actually speak to Mrs Estover. One of the house guests, Mr Nikitin, answered the phone. He said that the others had all gone down to the stables to see a new foal. He himself does not care for horses, I gather. But he promised to tell Mrs Estover when she got back. That was a couple of hours ago, so she should be back by now. How long does it take to look at a foal?'

'Depends whether you're buying or selling, I suppose,' said Alva. 'This Mr Nikitin, is that a Russian name?'

'I believe so. Some distant relative of Lady Kira, I understand.' He hesitated, then went on, 'I got the impression that he might be a bit stuck on Mrs Estover.'

Alva smiled at the old-fashioned phrase, which she suspected had been chosen for fear of offending her with something more modern like *got the hots for*.

'And Mrs Estover . . .?'

'Hard to tell what she is thinking. But I only met her briefly. Now, let me give you directions . . .'

His directions were brief, as indeed was the journey, and five minutes later she was turning through the rather grandiose gateway. The drive up to the castle along an avenue of old oaks was also quite impressive, as was the line of cars she parked alongside. A Bentley Continental in burgundy, a sky-blue Mercedes and a black Range Rover – maybe there was somewhere round the back for grey Fiestas! But the building itself might have been a disappointment if Hadda's description hadn't prepared her for it. A substantial mansion in dark granite, with not a battlement, moat or portcullis in sight, it didn't get anywhere close to being a castle.

For all that when she got out of her car and looked up at the forbidding three-storeyed front, she felt herself repulsed.

The main door opened as she approached and a man came out. Late seventies, early eighties, with a mane of grey hair swept back from his patrician head, he had the kind of looks a director of Roman epics would have given his script-writer's right hand for.

Had to be Sir Leon, she thought. Unless the baronetcy went in for look-alike butlers.

'Hello,' she said. 'My name's Alva Ozigbo. Mrs Estover left me a message inviting me to have a chat.'

Her clever wording looked to be a wasted subtlety. The man regarded her so blankly she began to wonder if she'd misunderstood the vicar's directions. Maybe half a mile further on there was a real castle with moat and portcullis.

She said, 'It is Sir Leon, isn't it?'

His name seemed to trigger awareness.

He said, 'Ozigbo? You the psycho thingy?'

'That's right. Is your daughter at home?'

'Glad to meet you,' he said, shaking her hand. 'Very glad. Imo? Think she's around, though you never know with that girl. Was the same when she was young. Came and went at her own sweet will. Moves like a ghost.'

302

'Ms Ozigbo, you got my message then. I really didn't expect the pleasure of seeing you in person. A phone call would have done.'

Imogen, as if to prove the accuracy of her father's simile, had materialized in the doorway. Last time Alva had seen her, she'd been wrapped up in winter walking gear. Even that hadn't been able to disguise how attractive she was. Now in a flowered skirt and a sleeveless top, she looked ready for a glossy photo-shoot.

'I thought it would be good to meet face to face. If you're not too busy, that is?'

'Not at all. Come in. Thank you, Daddy.'

Dismissing Sir Leon almost as if he *were* a look-alike butler!

Alva followed the woman into a hall that had a definite touch of the baronial about it, and up a staircase that might not have been sweeping enough for a coach and horses but could certainly have accommodated a couple of armoured knights side by side.

'In here,' said Imogen, opening a door.

Baronial stopped. They entered into a room that could have illustrated an article in a modern style and design magazine. Carpeted in pale ivory, with everything else in subtly varied shades of the same colour, it was a room for someone who moved like a ghost. The only strident note was sounded by the one painting, an abstract, an undulating line of bright green over a flat plane of glowing orange above another broader plane of fiery red underscored by a jagged band of pure black. Rothko, maybe? guessed Alva. What did having a Rothko on your wall indicate? Apart, of course, from a desire to say, Look at this, you peasants, and acknowledge we're stinking rich! From what she'd gathered about Lady Kira, this might well be her style.

She said, 'Lovely room. Is that a Rothko?'

Imogen said, 'Don't be silly. It's something I did years back to go with my room.'

Now that was much more interesting. Nothing to do with Lady Kira. Imogen's own painting in Imogen's own private room. No; more than that. Through a half-opened door, Alva glimpsed a bed. Her own private suite! Most children became very possessive about their own bedrooms. Not many had the ego – or the space – to demand and get their own private sitting room too. Or perhaps it was termed a dressing room?

She said, 'Is Mr Estover still here?'

'No. Toby had to go back to town yesterday. Business. All the Western world is closed down for a fortnight, but Toby still has business. Do sit down.'

The only seating available was a chaise longue with a chair set at its head.

Imogen indicated neither. There was a faint smile on her lips. She's waiting to see if I take the therapist's or the patient's option, thought Alva.

She moved the chair so that it was facing the chaise and sat down.

She expected Imogen to recline along the chaise but instead she perched on its edge, like a child nervously awaiting an interview with her head teacher.

'I hope you didn't have to come too far,' she said. 'Did you spend Christmas in Cumbria?'

It occurred to Alva that perhaps the woman had suspected her absence and Wolf's were connected.

'No. In Manchester.'

'That's far enough. But you wouldn't have come all this way just on the chance I'd be at home?'

'Hardly. I really just felt like a day away from home. My father's been ill and things have been quite fraught.'

'I'm sorry. Nothing too serious, I hope?'

'Heart. But he's doing well.'

'I'm glad. At least he's in the right job.'

She's been checking up on me, thought Alva. And she doesn't mind letting me know.

'Yes. Why did you want to talk to me, Mrs Estover?'

And now she's got me to open the bowling!

'Of course. Let me come straight to the point,' said Imogen, somehow making Alva feel it was her fault they hadn't come to the point a lot earlier. 'As you know, I tried to see Wolf. I didn't succeed. I called again twice, once in the evening, once early morning. He wasn't there.'

She paused as if inviting an intervention. She doesn't sound as if she's got Luke Hollins's message, thought Alva. Perhaps Mr Nikitin's English isn't so good.

Imogen nodded as if the intervention had been made, and went on, 'My reasons for wanting to see him are varied, if not to say confused. But I expect that, in your line of work, you are used to that.'

'I'm not used to people admitting it so readily,' said Alva.

'Perhaps that's because I'm not talking to you as a patient,' said Imogen with a faint smile.

No? In what capacity do you see yourself talking to me? wondered Alva.

Again the woman gave a little nod as if her guest had spoken.

'One of the reasons I wanted to see Wolf was to check if he were a threat to me or my family,' she said. 'It struck me that, in his absence, perhaps I could get the answer from you.'

The opening exchange was over, thought Alva. Now things should liven up.

'Why should you think he might be a threat?' she enquired.

'He was always a very ruthless man. You of all people should be able to tell me if and how prison has changed him.'

'By ruthless, are you implying he was violent?'

Imogen considered.

'Not to me, certainly. But in his drive to get what he wanted, I don't believe he ever excluded the option of violence. And his temper had a short fuse.'

'So, he'd lash out violently if provoked? And if he had time to think about something, and violence seemed the most productive way of proceeding, that's the way he'd go? Sounds like a pretty definitive description of a violent man to me, Mrs Estover.'

'Perhaps my fear is making me over-emphatic.'

Somehow fear and this woman didn't seem to go together. For the time being, though, it was best to go with her flow.

305

'You still haven't said why you feel afraid. He's confronted what he did. He's accepted he is solely responsible for the crimes that got him into prison. He's taken control of his life. What do you imagine he might blame you for?'

Imogen ran her hand down the side of her face, down her slender neck, down till it rested on her right breast. She had been sitting so still, the movement was almost a shock.

She said, 'Come now, Ms Ozigbo. Are you telling me he doesn't blame me for not standing by him? For marrying Toby? For my daughter's death?'

My daughter, Alva noted.

Alva said, 'If you really fear he might be a threat to you, going to see him unaccompanied in a lonely farmhouse doesn't strike me as the wisest move.'

Imogen said, 'When Wolf and I used to go climbing together, he taught me, when you're working at a line of ascent, look for the most hazardous route, the closer to impossible the better. Then resist the temptation to try it if you can.'

'I'm sorry. I don't get that.'

Imogen smiled as if unsurprised.

She said, 'Wolf used to say that rock climbing wasn't about getting to the top, it was about falling.'

'Conquering the fear of falling, you mean?'

Imogen shook her head impatiently.

'Conquering the desire to fall,' she said.

Alva ran this through her mind. Was she saying that meeting her ex alone was the most attractive option because she knew it was the most dangerous?

The psychology of rock climbing was interesting. But then so was the psychology of morris dancing.

Hoping by silence to draw the woman into further speech, she let her gaze run round the room. Strangely, despite the obvious differences of size, comfort and decoration, it put her in mind of Hadda's cell at Parkleigh. Apart from the painting, it contained nothing personal. No photographs, no books. Had it looked different

306

before the tragedies of first her husband's downfall and then their daughter's death?

Her gaze returned to Imogen. The woman gave no sign of wanting to say anything further. Whatever her reason for wanting this conversation, presumably it had been satisfied.

Alva looked at her watch and said, 'I ought to be going. Mrs Estover, all I can say in answer to your question is that if ever I feel Mr Hadda is a danger to anyone, I shall of course convey my feelings to the appropriate authority.'

She stood up.

Imogen said, 'Does he blame me for Ginny's death?'

Well, that had certainly done the trick. The question sounded as if it had burst out of her in contrast to the control that had marked the rest of her speech.

'Not as much, I gauge, as he blames himself,' said Alva.

'I see.' She fixed her eyes on her visitor as though in some doubt whether to proceed or not. But suddenly Alva knew there wasn't really any doubt. What the woman wanted to say to her was going to be said now.

Imogen said, almost casually, 'Then in your judgment would it make things better or worse if I told Wolf he wasn't Ginny's father?'

Jesus! What's she trying to do – use me as a messenger?

Before she could marshal her thoughts and come up with a response, the door opened. If there'd been a tap, it was too perfunctory to be noticed.

A woman came in, coldly beautiful with the kind of skin and bone structure that is hard to age, tall, supple, dressed in very English heather-mix tweed that didn't hinder her from exuding a sense of something dangerously exotic.

She said, 'Imogen, I did not know you had company,' not much bothering to make it sound unlike a lie.

'Mother,' said Imogen, unfazed, 'this is Ms Ozigbo, Wolf's therapist.'

'Not a job for a woman, I shouldn't have thought,' said Lady Kira coldly. 'And I suppose it's public money that pays your fees?'

Alva may have been fazed by Imogen's assertion about her child's parentage, but patrician rudeness she took in her stride.

'Nice to meet you,' she said, rising. 'Please don't apologize for disturbing us, I was just leaving.'

Lady Kira looked inclined to deny even the thought of apology, but Alva had turned back to Imogen.

'Goodbye, Mrs Estover,' she said. 'It's *Dr* Ozigbo, by the way. Do ring me if you'd like to talk again?'

Imogen said, 'I think we're done, *doctor.*'

She too rose and moved to face her red-and-orange painting.

From the doorway, Alva said, 'Your ex-husband seems to be fond of a painting by Winslow Homer. *The Woodcutter,* I think it's called. Is there any particular reason he's so fond of it?'

'Perhaps because it shows a man faced with simple problems that can be overcome by his own strength and resources,' said the woman, not turning round.

'That's an interesting idea,' said Alva. 'Your picture, by the way, what do you call it?'

'*Falling*,' said Imogen.

9

Alva closed the door behind her. It might be interesting to hear what mother and daughter had to say to each other, but the door was too heavy to make eavesdropping possible without pressing her ear to the keyhole.

At the foot of the staircase she found Sir Leon waiting.

'Got a moment, my dear?' he said.

Before she could reply, a door behind him opened and a smallish man, in his late thirties, handsome in a high-cheekboned, slightly toothy Slavic sort of way, came out.

His eyes ran up and down Alva's body with an almost insolent slowness.

He said, 'What a surprising county this Cumbria of yours is, Leon. I had not expected such rarities. Will you not introduce me?'

'What? Oh yes. Ms Ozigbo, friend of Imogen's. And this is Mr Nicotine who's staying with us.'

'Nik-EE-tin,' said the man. 'Pavel Nikitin. My friends call me Pasha. I'm pleased to meet you.'

He looked the type who might be inclined to take her hand and suck on her fingers, so Alva, who did not care to be called a rarity like some kind of ornithological specimen, put her arms behind her and nodded. One question had been answered. Whatever reason Nikitin had for not passing on Luke's message, there was no problem with language.

'If you'll excuse us,' said Sir Leon. 'Something I need to show Ms Ozigbo.'

He didn't wait for a response but took her elbow and urged her into a small alcove and through a door into what appeared to be a Hollywood producer's impression of an English gentleman's study.

'Foreigner,' he said, as if that were both apology and explanation. 'Wife's cousin or some such thing. *Pasha!* Do you think he gets called that because of the Nicotine connection? Sorry, probably far too young – you, I mean. Used to be a peculiarly foul cigarette my ma smoked during the war when she couldn't get anything else.'

Alva smiled at him. She could understand why Wolf was so fond of the old boy. He might live in a Wodehousian world of his own, but in his forays into the real world he seemed entirely without malice which was why she felt no inclination to remind *him* that she was *Dr* Ozigbo.

Now she took in the room. You could tell a lot from rooms.

A huge mahogany desk dominated, bedecked with silver photo frames, a pewter inkstand, and a black Bakelite dial telephone. One wall was almost filled by a huge bookcase in which Alva glimpsed bound copies of *Punch* and various shooting magazines as well as the transactions of the Cumbrian Archaeological Society dating back to a period itself worthy of research. The opposing wall held a locked gun case flanked by the head of a twelve-point stag and, most weird of all, that of a wolf.

'Last wolf shot in Cumberland,' said Sir Leon, following her gaze. 'Least, that's what the fellow she bought it from told Kira. Load of nonsense. Anyone can see it's a Canadian timber wolf, and pretty decrepit at that. Probably died of old age in some zoo.'

'Your wife has a taste for history?' ventured Alva.

'If that's what you call it,' said Sir Leon. 'Did this room up herself. Used to be a perfectly decent hideaway in the old man's day. Now look at it. I can hardly bear to come inside.'

'In that case . . .?' said Alva.

'What? Oh yes. Not likely to be interrupted. I wanted to ask you, how is Wolf?'

Her thoughts still on the mangy creature on the wall, Alva was thrown for a moment.

'Mr Hadda, you mean?'

'Yes, Wolf,' he said impatiently. 'I've thought of calling round at Birkstane, but it would just cause bother. Don't need security cameras out here in the sticks. Kira would hear about it before I got home! So how is he?'

'He was well when I saw him before Christmas,' said Alva slowly. 'Of course by comparison with the way you'll remember him, he moves rather slowly. And his face is scarred . . .'

Sir Leon was shaking his head.

'Poor boy, poor boy,' he said. 'But in himself, his state of mind, I mean, how are things there? He was always so full of life and high spirits.'

'I think, all things considered, that it's fair to say he's doing pretty well,' said Alva.

She was puzzled. This was not a kind of conversation that she could have imagined having with the father of a girl whose marriage to an undesirable had turned out even more badly than forecast.

'Good, good, I'm glad to hear it. Funny thing, life, what it does to you. But you'd know all about that in your job, my dear. All those years locked up. Don't think I could bear it myself.'

He turned away to the window as if to hide his emotion. Alva moved forward to stand by his side.

'Sir Leon, is there any message you'd like me to give to Wolf?'

'Just say I was asking after him.'

'I will. But if you don't mind me saying, I'm a little puzzled why you should be. I mean, so far as I know, you were absolutely opposed to the marriage, weren't you? You did everything you could to stop it.'

'I thought I did. But it wasn't enough. I should have tried harder.'

'And circumstances proved you right, and things worked out even worse for your daughter than you could have imagined, so why –'

'No, no,' he interrupted her. 'You're barking up the wrong tree.

I didn't want to stop the marriage for Imo's sake. She's always been perfectly capable of looking after herself. It was poor Wolf I was concerned for!'

This was truly bewildering.

'But why . . .?'

'Because the apple doesn't fall far from the tree. I love my daughter, Ms Ozigbo, but a father's love isn't blind. Fred Hadda was a decent man, a loyal worker and a good friend. I'd seen what it did to him when the boy vanished for all those years. That was down to what Wolf felt about Imogen. When he came back and I saw it was all going to start up again, I couldn't stand by and let Fred's boy destroy himself, could I? But in the end . . . Well, what's done's done. Better get you out of here before we get noticed.'

He feels spied upon in his own house, thought Alva. She still wasn't altogether clear what lay at the bottom of the old man's attitude. There was neither the time nor was he a suitable subject for subtle psychological questioning, so she took the direct route.

She said, 'Sir Leon, I'm still not sure what you're saying. Did you feel that this was a mismatch for social reasons? That Wolf would feel out of his depth by being transplanted from one class to another?'

She had learned that, even in twenty-first century England, class still mattered. *Cherchez la femme* might apply in France, in England it was usually *cherchez la classe!*

'What? No, of course not,' he replied, a touch indignantly. 'Used to be the case if you didn't go to the right school, you were always playing catch-up. Maybe there's still a bit of that around, but a chap like Wolf, he'd catch most of them up and be whizzing by in no time at all. In fact, that's what he did, wasn't it? No, this was personal. Imogen wasn't right for him. He was always going to get hurt.'

'And Imogen?'

'Imo? I love my daughter, Ms Ozigbo. Funny thing, though. In forty years I've never seen her cry. Not even as a baby. Funny.'

If true, this was pretty amazing. Though it might just be a physiological oddity.

She asked, 'And did you say anything about this to Wolf directly?'

'No point. He wasn't going to take any notice, was he? When the blood's bubbling along a boy's veins, first thing that goes is his hearing, eh?'

He turned her away from the window and for the first time she saw the photos in the silver frames. Lady Kira featured prominently. She obviously believed that family photos on the desk were as intrinsic a part of the traditional gent's study as hunting trophies on the wall.

In one of the photos she stood looking down possessively at a pretty girl leaning forward to blow out the candles on a birthday cake. The girl had such a look of Imogen, it had to be her daughter, thought Alva.

She picked up the photo and said gently, 'It must have been a terrible shock to you, losing your granddaughter.'

Immediately she wished she hadn't spoken. The old man's face, indeed his whole body, seemed to shrivel up as if in a desperate attempt to contain an emotion that might rip him apart if he let it out. Here was a man born into wealth and privilege, with all the attendant comforts and opportunities tossed into his cradle. Yet Alva felt she was looking at the kind of pain and despair you usually glimpsed on your TV screen after some momentous life-shattering natural disaster.

'I'm sorry, I'm sorry,' she said wretchedly. 'It's just that she looks so lovely in the photo.'

'What photo?' said Leon, taking refuge from his grief in irritation. 'Got no photo of Ginny here. Couldn't bear it.'

'But this one here,' said Alva, holding up the frame. 'Isn't that her?'

'Don't be silly. Of course not. That's Imo.'

'Imogen? Your daughter?' said Alva incredulously, trying to count the candles.

'That's right. Fourteenth birthday. Fourteen going on forty, isn't that what they say about young girls today, eh?'

Fourteen! Imo's age when she and Hadda first met.

There was only one thing wrong. She'd discounted the possibility that this might be Imo because this girl bore no resemblance whatsoever to her mental image of the skinny pre-pubertal creature who'd allegedly offered herself to Hadda on Pillar Rock. This was a healthy young teenager whose scoop-neck top revealed as she bent forward to blow out the candles a pair of very well-developed breasts.

There are times when even a psychiatrist can receive too much information.

Despite Sir Leon's obviously growing eagerness to get her out of the study and off the premises, she stood transfixed, staring at the photo.

She needed to talk further with the old man, she needed to talk again to Imogen, above all she needed to confront Hadda.

But in what order and in what manner she ought to do these things wasn't clear.

Then her phone rang. Sir Leon grimaced at the sound. She took it out and glanced at the display. It was Elvira.

Checking up on my putative date, she guessed. Well, she can leave a message!

Sir Leon now took a firm grip on the situation and her elbow, and a minute later she was outside the house with the door closing in her face.

She still hadn't got her thoughts in order. Not to ask Imogen more questions while she was here seemed a missed opportunity. Perhaps she should go back into the house and press for answers. But when she glanced back at the house to its general air of unwelcomingness were added the sight of Lady Kira's face peering down from an upper window and Mr Nikitin's from a lower.

She got into her car and let what she had learned scroll across her mind, trying to assess its significance and turn it into usable data.

The main items were:

One: Imogen said Ginny wasn't Hadda's child. True or false?

Two: Leon said he had objected to the marriage for Hadda's sake,

314

not for his daughter's, and class had nothing to do with it. Almost certainly true, she judged.

Three: at fourteen, Imogen was a mature girl with a well-developed bosom. Definitely true!

So what to do?

She could drive back to Manchester and ponder. She could get out of the car and bang on the door and demand readmittance. She could head round to Birkstane and lie in wait for Hadda. She could . . .

She shook her head impatiently. Choice is a largely delusional concept, her tutor used to say. Whether in politics, morals or shopping, we have far less than we imagine. In the end what we have to do often doesn't even figure on our list of pseudo-options.

She took out her phone and played her mother's message and was yet again reminded how right her tutor was.

'Alva! Where are you? You've got to get back here as soon as you can. Your father's much worse. They think he's going to die!'

10

Wolf Hadda liked to believe he had his feelings under tight control. You didn't survive a long stretch in jail by letting your imagination roam free. Deal with the minute and let the hour look after itself. A man can dig his way out with a teaspoon, but only if he takes it one scrape at a time. But if you let yourself relax too much, sometimes feelings and imagination can sneak up and take you by surprise.

He had spent a good part of the afternoon talking with Davy McLucky, then he had diverted on the way home to a supermarket. It was a couple of weeks now since he'd given Luke Hollins a Tesco order and fresh supplies would be running low. On the way back he stopped on a high fell road to give Sneck a bit of a run and it was getting on for eight o'clock as he approached Birkstane.

Perhaps it was the pleasure of heading back to the only place in the world he thought of as home that relaxed him, but he realized that somehow over the last few miles his mind had been playing such a lively picture of reaching the turn into the Birkstane lonning and finding Alva Ozigbo's grey Fiesta parked there that he felt a totally illogical shock of disappointment at its absence.

'Just thee and me then, Sneck,' he said to the dog as he brought the Defender to a halt in front of the closed barn door.

The dog jumped out and started quartering the yard, muzzle low, sniffing the cobbles and growling softly in its throat.

Wolf watched him for a moment, before climbing down stiffly. With his supermarket bag swinging from one hand and leaning heavily on his stick with the other, he limped slowly towards the house.

The kitchen felt cold and unwelcoming. He realized his fantasy had expanded insidiously to finding Alva had got the fire going and was brewing a pot of coffee. But now his earlier disappointment had turned to relief. As he closed the door, he saw a sheet of paper that must have been pushed beneath it.

He smoothed it out on the kitchen table and read the words scribbled across it.

I'm at the castle till the New Year. We ought to talk.

No signature. None needed.

He used it to help start the fire and while it got going he put the kettle on the hob, switched on the radio, turning it up loud. All this he did with a slow and laboured movement that would have caused Ed and Doll Trapp serious concern. When the kettle boiled he made himself a cup of coffee and sat at the table with his back to the small window. After a while he rose, shivering, and went to the window to draw the curtains, as if to keep out the draught.

But when he turned away he didn't sit down. Moving now with decisive swiftness, pausing only to pluck his long-handled axe from the wall, he headed out of the kitchen and up the stairs to the bedroom on the far side of the house from the yard. This was north facing and its window was small even by Cumbrian farmhouse standards but he went through it on his back, head first, reaching up to take a grip in a crack between two of the rough granite blocks, and hauling himself out till he stood on the sill. Then he dropped down till his arms rested on the sill, reached in and retrieved his axe.

Sneck stood alert, watching him.

He said, 'Guard!'

It was a stronger command than *Stay!* In Sneck's mind *Stay!* had a time-limitation clause. After ten minutes max, he'd reckon it had expired and start thinking independently. With *Guard!* he'd stay all night and attack anyone who came near.

Now, hanging one-handed, Hadda lowered his body full length then dropped the remaining five feet to the ground.

Picking himself up, he made for the old forest wall, climbed over it with silent ease and went a couple of yards into the trees. Here he turned south and moved parallel to the wall till he was opposite the side of the barn.

Now he emerged from the forest and climbed back over the wall and waited.

A man emerged from the barn and flitted silently across the yard. He was dressed in black and in his right hand he carried a gun.

Slowly he turned the handle of the kitchen door then flung it open and stepped inside.

A moment later he reappeared and made a signal. A second man came out of the barn as the first went back into the house.

So, two of them. The first had expected to surprise him in the kitchen. That having failed, he was now going to search the house, and he'd called up the second to watch his back.

Could there be a third? Doubtful. If so, a pair of them would probably have made the initial sortie.

He didn't waste time debating the point, reaching his conclusion and the second man crouched by the kitchen door almost simultaneously.

The man must have heard something, for he turned – which was unfortunate for him. Instead of the stunning blow to the base of the neck that was intended, he took the full force of the axe's shaft across his Adam's apple. There was usually only one result of such a blow, but Hadda was in too much of a hurry to check it out.

The kitchen was empty, the living room too. The second man had gone up the stairs. If he opened the door of the bedroom which Sneck was guarding, the dog would attack. And a bullet moves quicker than even the fastest dog.

Hadda went up the stairs not bothering to try for silence. The

318

man was pushing open the bedroom door. He glanced round as he heard Hadda's approach. Then Sneck hit him with such force he was driven back across the narrow landing. He'd instinctively raised his left arm to ward off the attack and he screamed as Sneck's fangs tore through the fabric of his tight-fitting top and dug into the flesh beneath. But his right arm was still free and he raised his weapon to put the muzzle to the dog's head at the same time as the axe blade drove down through his skull.

The gun went off.

The man slid to the ground, blood and brains trickling down his face. Sneck lay on top of him, his teeth still fixed in his arm. Hadda dropped the axe and knelt down beside the dog. There was a smell of scorched hair coming from a burn line between his ears, as though someone had laid a hot poker there. But the eyes that looked up at Hadda were as bright as ever.

'OK, you can let go now,' he said, and turned his attention to the man.

'Damn,' he said. Then he looked closer. Death, especially when caused by a blow from an axe, changes features somewhat, but there was something familiar about the face.

He stood up and went back down stairs. When he checked out the second man in the yard, he said, 'Damn,' again.

It seemed a long long time ago that he'd driven down the lonning, buoyed with a foolish hope that he'd find Alva Ozigbo waiting to welcome him.

Instead he had two dead men on his hands. He wasn't sure yet how he felt about that. Disappointed didn't seem to do it.

'Good job you're not here, Elf,' he said to the dark sky. 'I don't have time for psycho-analysis right now!'

He set to work. The living first.

He checked Sneck's burn mark. It didn't look too bad. He smeared some antiseptic cream along the line of the bullet, then commanded the dog to lie down in the kitchen.

Then the dead.

He went through their pockets and found nothing, but in the

barn he found a small back-pack containing two mobile phones, a Toyota key, and the OS sheet for the area. The key he pocketed, the phones he set aside for later examination, the map he opened. There was a cross on the unclassified road about half a mile north of where the Birkstane lonning turned off. He brought the place to his mind. There was an old track there, no longer used, leading to one of the sad heaps of stones that marked where a thriving hill farm had once stood. Some scrubby woodland offered good temporary shelter for a vehicle. Then they would have walked back along the road and down the lonning and, realizing he wasn't home, settled to wait.

But that implied they knew he was coming home.

He put that problem aside with the phones.

There were lots of old plastic sheets in the barn, remnants of better days.

He set about parcelling up the bodies, placing large rocks alongside them before securing the plastic with baler twine and wire. He then loaded the grisly packages into the Defender and returned to the house to clean up the mess on the landing. The blade of his axe he washed beneath the running tap in the kitchen.

The bullet that had burned Sneck was buried in the bedroom wall. He would dig it out later.

He went back to the barn and opened the lid of an ancient but still solid metal feed box. It was in here that he'd found on his return, neatly packaged and labelled, all the stuff that had been his as a boy. At some point during his runaway years, his father must have collected all his gear together and set out to make sure it would still be to hand and serviceable on his return. It had made him weep to see the care with which the task had been carried out, and to imagine Fred's state of mind as he went about the job.

Of course when he came back he'd been, in his own eyes at least, a man and far beyond childish things. Looking back now, he found it unforgivable that his fixation on Imogen, and his euphoria at winning her, had deadened him completely to any real appreciation of what he'd put his father through. It wasn't till he himself

320

experienced the gut-searing pain of loss all those years later that he came, too late, to understand.

Now he lifted out of the box the inflatable dinghy that had been in the kitchen on the occasion of Luke Hollins's first visit. It had required very little work to render it serviceable. Look after your gear and your gear will look after you, was a lesson Fred had drummed into him, and he practised what he preached. The rubber had been heavily oiled and the inflation nozzle coated in a thick layer of protective grease. How many times had his father renewed it over the years – as if by preserving it he also preserved the hope that somehow the young boy who had left him would return unchanged?

He put the dinghy and the foot pump in the back of the Defender. Then he went into the kitchen, stoked up the fire and set the kettle to boil again.

He didn't have much of an appetite, but he knew he had a long night ahead and his body needed fuel. So he opened a can of stew, heated it up and ate it straight out of the pan, wiping the sides clean with a hunk of bread. Sitting drinking tea and chewing on a muesli bar, he checked out the mobile phones. No messages. He brought up their phone books. None of the numbers was familiar. Next he checked their photo stores. One specialized in close-ups of female genitalia. Maybe it was some kind of trophy thing. They did nothing for Hadda. The other had shots of a family picnic, a handsome woman with an Eastern European look and a couple of young kids, sitting on a sunny hillside overlooking the sea. This did something for him. It made him feel bad.

He looked at his watch. It was eleven o'clock. Three hours had passed since he came home. But it was still too early. He fed Sneck, who seemed none the worse for his close encounter with the intruder's gun, then he settled in the wooden rocker by the fire and closed his eyes.

In Parkleigh he had learned to sleep almost at will and to wake at whatever hour he ordained, but sleep came hard now. When he finally nodded off he went straight into a dream in which he was being pursued through a dark forest by two men whom he couldn't shake off no matter how he twisted and turned. Then in the space of a single stride he was no longer the pursued but the pursuer, his quarry not two men but a single woman whose skin as she ran naked through the moon's shadows gleamed first white as pearl then dark as ebony.

He awoke to find he was sexually aroused.

'What the hell was that all about?' he asked the dog who lay at his feet, watching him.

It was one o'clock. He stood up, made another pot of tea and drank a burning mugful. The rest he poured into a thermos flask which he put into his backpack with a couple of bars of chocolate. He changed into his warmest mountain gear and pulled on his walking boots.

'Right, Sneck, how are you feeling?' he asked.

The dog rose instantly.

'OK, if you're sure. But we could face a long walk.'

The Defender, as ready it seemed as the dog, burst into life at first time of asking and he set it bumping back up the frozen lonning.

He found the intruder's car exactly where he'd estimated. It was a Toyota Land Cruiser. Now he knew where he'd seen the first dead man before. But he was pretty sure the other body wasn't that of the other man on Drigg Beach, the one called Pudo. Probably still recovering from a broken jaw.

The Land Cruiser had a capacious boot so there was plenty of room to transfer his grisly cargo and the rest of his gear. As an afterthought, he took the jerry can of petrol he always carried in the Defender and tossed it into the back of the Toyota.

'OK, Sneck, here we go,' he said.

The narrow winding road he followed ran up the remote western valley of Wasdale. It ended at the valley head, so unless there was anyone heading late for the tiny hamlet situated there, or the old inn, he was unlikely to have company at this hour of a freezing winter night. It wasn't just the remoteness that attracted him. It was Wastwater, the darkest and deepest of all Cumbria's lakes, lying between the road and the Screes, the awful precipitous slopes plunging down from the long ridge between Ill Gill and Whin Rigg.

He parked as close to the edge of the lake as possible and set about inflating the dinghy. As far as he could make out in the near pitch darkness, his father had done an excellent job of storage and the rubber expanded and tautened and held its shape when he finally stopped pumping.

He lifted the topmost body out of the car and laid it in the dinghy. As expected, there was only room for one of the bundles. Indeed, there was scarcely room for himself and he had to kneel with his knees resting against the dead man as he began to paddle the vessel out from the bank. An unimaginable distance above him the sky was crowded with stars but the light that had set out earthward so many millennia ago seemed to fail and lose heart as it was sucked into the terrestrial black hole of Wasdale's lake.

Ahead was darkness, behind was darkness, all around was darkness. He struck with the paddle and struck again. The temptation to push the body over the side then turn to regain the shore was strong, but he knew he had to go much closer to the furthermost side. At its deepest the lake measured more than two hundred and fifty feet, well below the safety limit for the district's recreational divers. But it was the Screes ahead that plunged to this forbidding depth and to deposit his burden too soon might mean it would come to rest on the much shallower northern shelf.

Now it seemed to him at last that the view ahead was mottled with different intensities of blackness and a couple of strokes later he began to make out the detail of the precipitous slopes soaring two thousand feet above his head.

He laid the paddle in the dinghy and tried to ease the body over the side. Lifting it in and out of the car had been hard enough. Moving it all in the unstable confines of this small craft was back-breaking and perilous. For a moment one side dipped down beneath the surface and water came slopping in. He had no illusions. Weighed down with boots and clothing as he was, he would find it hard to survive long enough in water at this temperature even to struggle to the visible shore. Then he'd have to walk all the way along the boulder strewn track to one end of the lake or the other and back along the road to the car.

It would take the best part of a couple of hours, he would be wet, cold, and exhausted, and he'd still have the second body to deal with.

The thought steadied him. Human beings are better at avoidance than achievement. When things are bad, don't look for a good to struggle to, look for something worse to struggle from!

He wondered how this downbeat view of the human psyche would appeal to Alva. All that mattered now was that it worked for him. At last he got more of the plastic-wrapped package out of the dinghy than was in it and suddenly, as though it too had made a choice and opted for a peaceful rest in the dark deeps, it slid easily over the side and was gone.

Without that dead weight, it now seemed to him that the dinghy moved like an elfin pinnace (where did that phrase come from?) under his strong even strokes and what had felt like an immeasurable distance on the way out was behind him in no time and Sneck was welcoming him back on dry land with a wild oscillation of the tail.

But now it was all to do again.

He didn't take a rest because he feared that if he did his heart might fail him.

They say that having performed a difficult task once gives you confidence and makes the second time easier.

As usual, the bastards lie!

The lake seemed wider, the night seemed darker, the dinghy rode even lower in the water, and at one point he felt so totally disorientated he could not with any confidence say in what direction he was paddling.

Then he got guidance, but in a form that was more frightening than the situation it rescued him from.

A car's headlights came splitting the darkness along the road, heading up the valley.

It seemed to slow momentarily as it approached the point where he'd left the Toyota. And then, perhaps theorizing that the most likely reason for a car to be parked so late at night in such a remote situation was that the inmates were engaged in a very private activity, the driver speeded up again and soon the light faded as he wound his way to the distant inn.

This brief interlude of illumination deepened the resurgent blackness to impenetrability, but Hadda had once again got his bearings. A few more strokes, then, careless of the water he was shipping, he rolled the second body over the side and began to paddle back to the shore.

No elfin pinnace now, the dinghy felt heavy and wallowed through rather than cut across the water. But finally he made it. He was tempted to puncture the inflatable and let it sink, but that would be stupid. It wouldn't go to the bottom, it would easily be spotted, people would get worried, the car driver might recall the parked vehicle, and even if his belief that the bodies were sunk too deep for retrieval turned out to be true, the incident might be picked up by someone anxious to know what had happened to the two men he had sent out on a murderous mission . . .

He deflated the dinghy, jumping up and down on it to remove the last bit of air, and flung it into the back of the Land Cruiser.

'Right, Sneck,' he said. 'Let's go!'

He drove through the hills, past dark farms sleeping under ancient stars, meeting no traffic till he reached a main road. Even here at this hour there was only the very occasional car. Eventually he turned off again and was soon back on the single-track fell road where he'd paused on his way home to let Sneck have a run before the light faded completely from the sky. At its highest point he bumped off the tarmac on to the frozen grass, keeping going till the engine finally stalled. Now he got out of the car with the dog at his heel. From the load space he retrieved his rucksack and the jerry can.

The dinghy he left lying there.

He unscrewed the jerry can and soaked the vehicle's interior with petrol. His thinking was simple. Leave an empty car in the Lake District and eventually someone would report it, mountain rescue might be called out to do a search of the nearby hills while the police concentrated on tracing the owner of the vehicle.

What was relatively commonplace, however, was for a gang of local tearaways to help themselves to a car after a night on the beer, enjoy a bit of wild joy-riding on the quiet country roads, and finish up by torching the vehicle in some remote spot before heading off home.

So a burnt-out wreck would draw far less attention because it carried with it its own built-in explanation.

He laid a trail of petrol across the ground for some twenty feet or so from the car, then returned to hurl the jerry can into the back. Picking up his sack, he shrugged it on to his shoulder and made his way back to the end of the petrol trail.

Now he took out a box of matches, struck one and tossed it on to the ground.

'Heel,' he said to Sneck, and set off at a steady pace that would have surprised those who only ever saw him limping slowly across the ground.

Behind him he heard a whoomph! as the line of fire reached the car.

He didn't look back until a few minutes later he heard the explosion that told him the car's tank had gone up.

Now he stopped and turned.

He'd already covered a quarter-mile and climbed a couple of hundred feet.

Below him he could see the flames from the burning car licking the darkness out of the air. Two thousand years ago people would have taken it for a funeral pyre. In a way, it was. He thought of the two men anchored for ever (he hoped) to the bed of the cold lake. He knew from experience how long it took for the human mind to come to terms with responsibility for a human death. Eventually factors in mitigation would loom larger – they had, after all, been out to kill him – but for the moment their innocence or guilt did not signify. They were just two lives that he had brought to a sudden end. The man with the mucky pictures on his mobile and the man with the loving family were equally dead.

It would take a long time for him to deal with it, but seven years in prison had taught him how to compartmentalize his thoughts.

He turned his back on the accusing flames. It was five o'clock in the morning and he had a long walk ahead of him.

To start with his way lay east and already, though dawn was still hours away, he thought he could see the line of the dark hills before him beginning to be outlined against a paler sky.

There was always a growing light to walk towards as well as a dying light to leave behind.

And the ground he walked on was holy. His great mistake had been ever to leave it.

'Come on, Sneck,' he said. 'Let's go home.'

BOOK FOUR

the noise of wolves

Meanwhile abroad
Incessant rain was falling, or the frost
Raged bitterly, with keen and silent tooth;
And, interrupting oft that eager game,
From under Esthwaite's splitting fields of ice
The pent-up air, struggling to free itself,
Gave out to meadow grounds and hills a loud
Protracted yelling, like the noise of wolves
Howling in troops along the Bothnic Main.

William Wordsworth: *The Prelude* (Book 1)

1

Johnny Nutbrown was truly a man of the moment, indifferent alike to future fears or past regrets. To him, each day was a box that closed at bedtime. During the night it was taken away, marked *not wanted on voyage*, and stored in some deep dark hold. Thus he never woke to a new day without feeling happy to greet it, and on the odd occasion when returning consciousness brought with it the awareness of some threat serious enough to ripple even his equanimity, the disturbance rarely survived a hearty breakfast.

One that did sometimes stay with him through lunch was the proposed sale of Poynters and the move to California. Toby Estover's visit had rattled his cage more than he cared to admit, but as the Christmas holiday dragged its grossly inflated length towards New Year it was easy to fall back into his usual insouciance.

Every year the Nutbrowns gave a much-anticipated Hogmanay party and as usual Johnny was the perfect host. Booze, food, entertainment were the best money could buy, while the scag and coke he supplied for the delectation of his most trusted guests was of such a quality that many of them pestered him to learn the source of his supply. But the vagueness that had stood Johnny in such good stead throughout all his life was certainly not going to fail him in this instance. He knew there was a link that led from his supplier to Toby Estover's client Pavel Nikitin, and that was not a man he cared to irritate.

'Oh, just a chap I met at some club,' he said. 'Harold, I think his name was. Or George. Gosh, look at the time! Everyone into the Great Hall!'

And a few minutes later he was standing on a chair, leading the raucous midnight countdown as though he truly longed to ring out the old and ring in the new, though to tell the truth he'd never seen much reason to distinguish between the last day of December and the first of January.

So when a neighbour sighed, 'Another great party, Johnny. Hard to believe it will be the last,' he just looked at the woman blankly till she added, 'Sorry, I thought Pippa said you'd found a buyer, or at least someone so interested he was paying for a survey.'

'Ah, that,' he said without much enthusiasm. 'Yes, there was some Scottish fellow Pippa thought might be good for the asking price.'

'That would be very good news,' said the woman, too tipsy to recognize how this contradicted her recent expression of regret at the possibility of losing her neighbours.

In fact there were mixed feelings but there was no insincerity here. It was the local consensus that the Nutbrowns would have to come down a couple of hundred k at least to make a sale this side of summer. On the other hand, while no one likes to be proved wrong, if by some miracle they did get what they were asking, the implication for all neighbourhood values would more than compensate for the loss of *Schadenfreude.*

In the early hours, after speeding the last of their departing guests with affectionate farewells and promises of eternal friendship, the Nutbrowns surveyed the melancholy relics of their passing.

'Can't say I'm sorry I shan't be seeing any of that ghastly crew again,' said Pippa.

It was part of Pippa's capacity for disappointment that all social gatherings, including her own, left her with feelings of deep antipathy towards the guests.

'Let's go to bed,' said her husband, ignoring this oblique reference to their possible departure. 'Hope Mrs P and her crew don't make too much row.'

332

This was Mrs Parkin, their cleaner, who traditionally came mob-handed on New Year's Day to restore order.

'Can't lie in too long,' said Pippa. 'Need to be up to see Parkin doesn't skimp. I want the house to be looking its best when Mr Murray comes on the third.'

'Who?'

'Murray who's interested in buying the house. So interested he's bringing his own surveyor to look the place over this time. I did tell you.'

She hadn't, but she knew her husband wouldn't argue the point.

'Good God,' he said in some agitation. 'I thought these Scots spent the first week after Hogmanay in a drunken stupor.'

'Don't be racist. And come to bed.'

It was quickly apparent that despite the lateness of the hour Pippa wasn't ready for sleep. Parties always left her with a residue of nervous energy which would keep her awake all night if she didn't dissipate it. She stepped out of her clothes, helped her husband out of his, then fell back on the bed, pulling him on top of her.

Johnny's great virtue as a sexual partner was that he was rarely importunate but when called upon was always ready and able to do exactly what was wanted in the proportions and for the length of time that Pippa wanted it. Five minutes did the trick tonight. After she came, she pushed him off, rolled over and went to sleep. Johnny lay awake a little longer, staring into the darkness, not exactly thinking but aware that there were thoughts in the room that might keep him awake were he foolish enough to think them. Finally he too fell asleep.

The day of Donald Murray's visit was a perfect selling day. New Year had blown in on a sleet-filled easterly straight from the Steppes, but after two days this had died away to leave clear skies and bright sunshine that touched the property with the delicate skill of a Hollywood lighting engineer, every shadow and every highlight making the director's point, which was in this case *love me! buy me!*

Johnny had opted to head for the golf course. Ignoring the fact

333

that you were selling up was hard when you had a surveyor clunking around the property. He looked up in alarm when the doorbell rang just as they were finishing breakfast.

'Good God, is that them already?' he said.

'They're not due till ten,' said Pippa. 'Probably the post.'

She returned a few moments later bearing the morning mail, which included two identical parcels, about twelve by six by three, addressed one to him and one to her.

They removed the outer brown paper with a synchronicity that would have got them into an Olympic synchronized paper-removing team, only to find themselves confronted by a substantial layer of clear plastic wrapping. This too they removed. Now each of them had something like a shoebox.

Each removed a lid.

'Now why would anyone want to send me two Gideon Bibles?' wondered Johnny. 'What have you got, old girl?'

'The same,' said Pippa.

'Seriously weird. What do you think it means?'

'God and presumably Gideon knows, and I don't intend wasting time trying to puzzle it out,' said his wife.

She gathered together all the wrapping and the books, took them out of the kitchen into the utility room where their variously coloured recycling boxes stood, and returned saying, 'Rubbish to rubbish.'

'Good girl. I'll be off then,' said Nutbrown.

His wife was glad to see him go. Bargaining, she preferred to do alone, and even though she and Donald Murray had agreed a price, she had a feeling there was still a bit of negotiating to be done.

Dead on the stroke of ten, the doorbell rang again and she opened it to see the long spare figure of Mr Murray standing there, smiling down at her. Some way behind him, looking up at the façade of Poynters with the expression of traveller who has stumbled upon the House of Usher moments before its fall, lurked a second man who was summoned forward to be introduced as Duff, the surveyor. Whether this were forename or surname wasn't clear, but either way, Pippa guessed he too was a Scot.

Her guess was confirmed when in response to her bright, 'Well, you've brought the good weather with you,' he sniffed the air vigorously as though already scenting damp and dry rot, and said something in an accent so thick it might as well have been the Gaelic.

She glanced at Murray and he interpreted, 'Is it OK for Duff to have a poke around?'

'Of course,' she said. 'Go anywhere you like.'

They watched as he shuffled off, bent under the weight of a haversack that presumably held the tools of his trade.

'You brought him all the way down from Scotland, did you?' she asked wonderingly.

'Aye. When I'm paying for a service I like to know I've got someone I can trust.'

'It's your money,' she said. 'Now, while he's doing his job, is there anything you'd like to take a closer look at, Mr Murray?'

He gave her a quizzical smile and she feared for a moment he might lurch into a pass. Not that she had any objection in principle to being the object of a pass – accepted or rejected, it usually established a relationship with her on top. But mixing pleasure with business in Mr Murray's case would not, she intuited, be a good idea.

Happily she was wrong, or he decided against it.

'Aye,' he said. 'A wee trip round the policies again would be nice, to see if it's all as grand as I remember.'

They did the tour, outside and then in, seeing nothing of Duff but hearing creaks and clanks that suggested he was hard at his task.

They ended up in the kitchen, where she offered to make coffee. He said yes and she asked if he'd like to go through into the living room, but he said no, the kitchen suited him just fine, he always felt it was the centre of a house.

'Mr Nutbrown no' around?' he asked.

'No. Business, I'm afraid,' she lied.

'So you're left to deal with the sale, eh? Lucky man, to have such a capable wife,' he said.

335

He sounded as if he meant it.

She said, 'Would Mr Duff like a cup, do you think?'

'Duff's not a coffee man,' he said. 'Irn-Bru, with a whisky chaser. But never on the job. He's a man who likes to focus. He'd really hate it if he missed anything that came up later.'

'I hope he's not going to find much that need come up at all,' she said, a touch acidly.

He gave her that quizzical look again, then said, 'You needn't fear I'm setting up to stiff you, Mrs Nutbrown. Me, I'd rather be buying a house the way we do it in Scotland: I make an offer, you accept it, we shake hands and the thing's done. On the other hand, a wee reduction would be nice. Still, we've all got to live, even estate agents, eh? How much are Skinners charging you? Five per cent?'

'Six,' she said.

He whistled.

'They live up to their name. Six per cent's a mighty chunk of money once you get into the six-figure bracket.'

Here it comes, she thought. This was the kind of pass she'd been ready for ever since she met Murray.

She said, 'Would you like a slice of cake?'

He looked at the lemon drizzle sponge she'd set on the table.

'In a minute maybe,' he said. 'Talking of Skinners, what kind of agreement do you have with them anyway?'

'The kind I can easily terminate,' she said. 'I made sure of that when they told me their charges. They in return made sure they drew my attention to the fact that the terms of the agreement would hold even after termination if ultimately I sold the house to anyone they'd introduced.'

'Aye, that's normal practice,' he said. 'Else why would anyone ever pay the sharks, eh? On the other hand, suspecting and proving are very different things, as the minister said when he got caught coming out of the massage parlour.'

'Meaning?'

'Meaning, like the minister, I may have been a bit vague with my details when I made the appointment. And I did it on the phone, so I never actually met anyone from Skinners face to face. Also, for tax purposes, if we did reach an accord, Mrs Nutbrown, I'd probably do it through a wee holding company I use from time to time.'

He looked at her expectantly.

She said, 'Are you ready for that slice of cake now, Mr Murray?'

'Oh, I am,' he said. 'I am.'

2

It was the second week of January before Alva Ozigbo got back to London.

Her father's relapse had been serious but he had survived.

'The good thing,' his second-in-command had told her, 'is that perhaps now Ike will stop thinking he knows best and trying to treat himself.'

'I shouldn't bet on it,' said Alva.

By the time the New Year came, the prognosis was once again optimistic, but this time Elvira put no faith in it and Alva had realized there was no way she could leave her mother till she too had recovered from the shock. Early in the New Year Ike was pronounced fit enough to return home, but only if he had full-time nursing care. When he reacted angrily to this, Alva spoke to him severely.

'Stop being such a diva and think of Mum for a change,' she commanded. Then she softened her tone as she added, 'Anyway, give it a few days, and it will probably be Elvira who bumps the nurse.'

Which was more or less what happened, with Elvira assuring the nurse, a laid-back Oldham lass called Maggie Marley, that she was more than capable of managing her husband's health regime.

'Fair enough,' said Nurse Marley. 'But I'll still call round every other day just to check up, OK?'

Ike regarded this as a major victory.

'Who's a clever little psychiatrist then?' he said. 'So what now, Miss Motivator?'

'I leave you two to it,' said Alva. 'And God help you both!'

She'd been doing what she could by phone and Internet to reorganize her own work, but of course all her patient contact had to be either postponed or reallocated, both of which options were far from satisfactory. Her interest in Wolf Hadda's case was shelved completely. During this period leaving her mother to make another Cumbrian visit hadn't been an option, even if she'd wanted to. She'd phoned Luke Hollins to explain her situation, told him that it was her unofficial opinion that Hadda was no danger to anyone, but of course if the vicar had any further cause for concern, he must take whatever steps he thought appropriate, and implied without spelling it out that her own involvement in the case was over unless it were officially revived.

As for her visit to the castle and what had transpired there, she examined each seemingly significant element clinically.

Imo's assertion about the paternity of her daughter, true or not, meant nothing. Wolf's grief at her death was not likely to be diminished, while his pain at his wife's betrayal could hardly be intensified.

Sir Leon's claim that when he resisted the marriage it had been Wolf's well being he was concerned about rather than Imogen's was surprising till you considered what the poor old sod's life must have been like with a domineering wife and a wilful daughter. Also he'd been on the spot to see what the disappearance of Wolf had done to Fred Hadda, his loyal and loved head forester. The prospect of more pain being heaped on the poor devil's head by his son's insistence on what Fred saw as a foolish and potentially disastrous marriage must have affected him deeply. No wonder that he'd thrown all his feeble weight against the proposed union.

Finally the photo. Maybe the old man had got the birthday wrong. Maybe Wolf's memory had been at fault. Maybe in view of his subsequent sexual predilections, he had unconsciously been trying to stress that pubescent girls could be active temptresses.

Conclusion. Individually each of these 'significant' elements was explicable and disregardable. She had merely overreacted to their coincidence.

There was however another coincidence that surprisingly proved more resistant to clinical analysis.

Twice she had got herself involved in something that was no longer her business, twice she had found herself acting more like a private detective than a clinical psychiatrist.

Both times she had been interrupted by news that her father was dangerously ill.

She was not superstitious, but she knew superstition was the name people often gave to feelings and intuitions that conveyed useful warnings outside the sphere of rationality.

While not persuaded that Hadda was, in any sense that should alarm her professionally, dangerous, she had started to believe that there was danger in his proximity. So when she finally got back to London, in her mind she consciously, perhaps even a touch self-consciously, drew a line under the Hadda case.

As for those little stirrings of desire she felt when she thought of him, she assured herself they were no more troublesome than the small pangs of indigestion she got after eating blue cheese.

And just as easily treatable by giving it up.

She threw herself into her work. After her extended break there was a lot of it to throw herself into. At Parkleigh, Simon Homewood welcomed her enthusiastically.

'God, I've missed you,' he said.

His fervour sounded more than professional. He didn't look well and when she asked him how his Christmas had been, he said, 'Traditional,' and changed the subject.

A few days later she dropped into his office at the end of the day to give her customary updating on her work. During this she would pass on any particular concerns she had about individual prisoners, but she was scrupulous about not sharing any detail of her work with them that she would have classed as confidential had they been free agents.

When she had finished, to her surprise he opened a drawer in his desk and brought out a bottle of sherry and two glasses.

'You shot off so quickly before Christmas I never had time to offer you a festive drink,' he said.

Her reason for leaving so precipitately had been her decision to visit Hadda in Cumbria. She hadn't mentioned it then and saw no reason to do so now.

He poured and passed her a glass.

'Happy New Year,' he said. 'We both deserve it, I think, to make up for what sounds like a couple of rotten Christmases.'

He knew about her father, of course, but why his should be termed rotten she did not know.

'So what made your Christmas so bad?' she asked.

'Oh, domestic matters,' he said vaguely. Then he took a drink and said, 'Why am I being so coy? It will get out soon enough. Sally and I are splitting up.'

Selfishly her first thought was, *Oh shit!* This changed everything. With luck he might postpone making any move on her till he got his domestic problems in some kind of order, but after that . . .!

No doubt he'd try to take her rejection like an old-fashioned gent, but things were bound to change. She couldn't see him settling for the kind of open, friendly if occasionally prick-teasing relationship she had with Giles.

She said, 'I'm sorry to hear it.'

'Thank you,' he said, regarding her speculatively. She was suddenly fearful he might be about to jump the gun. Seeking a diversion, she heard herself saying brightly, 'By the way, I ran into Hadda over the holiday.'

He didn't look surprised.

'Ah yes. Hadda. And how is he getting on up there in his mountain fastness?'

Why the hell had she got into this? she asked herself.

'He seemed fine,' she said. 'Very domesticated. Quite a good cook, actually.'

'You had a meal with him?'

She said, 'More a snack, really.'

'Just the two of you?'

'Well, the local vicar was there for part of the time.'

As she said this, she was asking herself, Why am I feeling guilty? And what right does he have to question me like he was a Victorian father worried in case his daughter had compromised herself?

Or am I overreacting and is he just questioning me like a prison director discussing a parolee with his prison psychiatrist?

Homewood said, 'Hadda's the responsibility of the probation service now, Alva. Best to leave it to them, eh? You did marvels with him while he was here, and with your annual review due shortly, we don't want anything muddying the waters, do we?'

He said this with an emphasis she didn't care for. She was halfway through her four-year contract and she'd assumed the pattern for the built-in annual review had been set last year when it had taken the form of a casual chat followed by an assurance that the Director would be ticking all the right boxes. The unpleasant thought slid into her mind that maybe Homewood had brought the subject up to remind her that it was in her interests to stay on friendly terms with him!

No! She wouldn't believe that. But that didn't mean she had to sit down under his implied criticism.

She said defiantly, 'Just because a client leaves Parkleigh doesn't stop him being a client in my book. If I feel a patient needs help, that's what he gets from me.'

'And you felt that Hadda needed help? On what grounds, may I ask?'

She thought of telling him about Luke Hollins's letter, but that could lead to an unravelling of the whole visit to Birkstane and that was something she preferred to avoid.

She said, 'No particular reason. Just checking up that all was well.'

'Very conscientious of you,' he said. 'Though why this should involve a meal and an overnight stay, I don't quite see. Look, Alva, this isn't me talking as your boss, it's me talking as your friend.

You ought to be more careful. It's all right meeting these people in controlled conditions, but they can be unpredictable. Hadda might have been playing games when he was in prison, but that doesn't mean he hasn't been indulging in real sexual fantasies about you, and I doubt if they just involve your foot!'

Prat! she thought. If this was how you tried to control your wife, no wonder she dumped you.

She emptied her glass and stood up.

'I have to dash,' she said. 'Thanks for the drink. Good night.'

She left not quite at a run but fast enough not to give him time to protest.

As she approached the main gate, she saw another visitor being let out. She hurried to save the duty officer the bother of shutting and opening the gate again, but Chief Officer Proctor stepped out of the gatehouse and fell into step beside her. At the gate he nodded to the duty man and said, 'I'll see Dr Ozigbo out.'

He watched till the man vanished into the gatehouse, then said, 'Sorry to hear about your father, miss. Hope he's OK.'

She'd seen him distantly a couple of times since her return, but this was the first chance for conversation they'd had.

She said, 'Thank you, George. He's doing fine.'

'Good. And how are you doing, miss?'

'I'm fine too, George.'

'That's good. Mr Homewood missed you.'

'Did he? I hope you missed me too, George.'

She spoke rather sharply, her mind going back to that earlier occasion when she'd felt Proctor was trespassing on private ground. What was his motive? Perhaps he'd heard of Homewood's marital problems and was now trying to act as his pandar! No, that didn't really make sense . . .

'Did, as a matter of fact, miss. Know we don't always see eye to eye, but you're straight. Straight and discreet. Mr Ruskin, he was straight too. Maybe not quite so discreet. Anyway, like I say, we're all glad you're back. The Director especially. Lonely job, that. Needs to know everything, if he's to do it properly, that's why he takes such an interest. Mustn't hold you back, miss. I think we're in for a bit of rain. Goodnight now.'

What the hell was that all about? she asked herself as she walked the short distance to the visitors' car park. Standing by the entrance she saw the man who'd left the jail ahead of her. This time she recognized him. It was Wolf Hadda's solicitor, Mr Trapp.

They had never met formally but she had glimpsed him at the time of the probation hearings and when he'd picked up Hadda on his release.

A flurry of rain gave her an excuse to put her head down and hurry past without glancing his way. They only had one connection and her brief exchange with Homewood had made her realize how dangerously alive in her mind Wolf Hadda still was.

She got into her car. The rain was setting in now and she switched on the wipers. Each sweep of the running windscreen brought Trapp into view. Why on earth was he just standing there, hatless, umbrella-less, protected only by a thin raincoat that already looked as if it had reached saturation point?

Now she saw him, now she didn't. It was as if the wipers were offering her a choice. Or rather, as if a choice was being made for her. Like plucking petals off a flower . . . he loves me . . . he loves me not . . . She could just drive out of the exit. She didn't even have to go past him.

But the car was moving towards him. My choice, she told herself firmly. A humanitarian act, nothing more.

She wound down the window and said, 'Mr Trapp, isn't it?'

'Yes,' he said.

She said, 'You're getting wet.'

He said, 'Yes.'

Losing patience with herself more than him, she said, 'Well, get in, man!'

He hesitated then walked round the car and slid damply into the passenger seat.

He really was an unprepossessing-looking little man; not quite scruffy, but close to down-at-heel. She'd seen photos of Toby Estover.

From that smooth, sophisticated, immaculately tailored figure to Mr Trapp was an uncomputable distance. Put them side by side and you had a measure of Hadda's fall. Yet from what she read of the trial records, Trapp had done his job well. And hadn't Hadda, in one of his biographical pieces, said something that implied a previous acquaintance? Something about a favour, and something more than merely professional, she guessed, if Wolf had been a house guest of the Trapps at Christmas . . .

Careful, you're being a PI again, she warned herself.

She said, 'Alva Ozigbo.'

'Yes, I know,' he said. Then, as if feeling a need to offer explanation, he added, 'My wife's picking me up. She shouldn't be long. I finished earlier than expected.'

'Well, let's see if we can get you dry for her,' she said, turning the heater up full blast. 'It would be unjust if you caught a cold just because you were super efficient.'

He smiled, a gentle, not quite melancholy smile that lit up his face.

'Hardly that,' he said. 'When I told my client that in my judgment appealing against his sentence was a waste of time, money and energy, he indicated to me that sending him a bill for my services would enjoy much the same status, and if I cared to argue the toss, his brother would offer a few clinching arguments with a baseball bat.'

'He sounds a well-educated man.'

'That was the gist,' he said primly. 'His choice of words was more idiomatic.'

She laughed. There was clearly more to Mr Trapp than met the eye. Or rather, met her eye. Presumably not Hadda's.

As if merely thinking the name forced her to utter it, she heard herself asking, 'Did you know Mr Hadda before you acted as his solicitor at the time of his trial?'

I'm just making conversation, she assured herself. Till his wife arrives.

He took his time replying. Finally he said, 'We'd met.'

'Professionally?'

He smiled again and said, 'Yes. Our first meeting was professional.'

Our first meeting. She tried to imagine a situation in which Wolf Hadda, newly wed to his princess and striding forth to conquer the business world, would have needed a solicitor like Trapp. Not completely impossible, but very unlikely.

So this contact probably dated back to the five years between young Wolf running away from home and his return with his three impossible tasks accomplished.

The mystery years, the years of emerald mines, piracy, buried treasure . . .

A car turned into the car park, a muddy and dented Toyota. Trapp leaned across and pressed the horn, catching the Toyota driver's attention, and it drew up alongside.

Alva wound down her window and found herself looking at a broad-faced woman with rose-pink hair and a disconcertingly direct unblinking gaze.

Trapp said, 'Doll, this is Dr Ozigbo. She kindly offered me shelter till you came. Dr Ozigbo, my wife, Doll.'

'I'm pleased to meet you,' said Alva.

'Likewise,' said the woman. 'Hope he's not messed up your car.'

'Thanks a lot,' said Trapp, scurrying round to climb in alongside his wife.

In a moment we'll go our separate ways, thought Alva. Fate does much, but you've got to take a few steps to meet it.

She called, 'Mr Trapp, I meant to ask, how is Mr Hadda? A lot of people are concerned to learn how he's doing. I'd like to be sure everything's going well . . .'

'Fine, so far as I know. I'll tell him you were asking after him, shall I?' said Trapp.

'Thank you,' she said. She felt there was something else she ought to say but couldn't imagine what it might be.

The woman, who'd been staring fixedly at her during this exchange with her husband, now stuck her head out of the window as if to take an even closer look. Alva had to force herself not to flinch before that fierce, assessing gaze.

Doll said, 'That colour, how do you get it?'

It took a second to register the reference was to her hair not her skin, though in both cases the answer was the same.

'Actually, it's natural.'

'Oh. Pity. Wouldn't have minded giving it a try. Nice to meet you, dearie. You're ever in Chingford, give us a call.'

She handed Alva a card. Then the window wound up and the Toyota pulled away.

So what's happened here? wondered Alva. The card suggested that Doll Trapp anticipated meeting her again, and probably not to discuss the colour of her hair.

The one subject they had in common was Wolf Hadda.

If Homewood hadn't offered her a drink, she would have been in her car and on her way home before Trapp left the prison. She might even have escaped George Proctor's interception. So she'd have been home by now enjoying a pleasant evening in front of the telly instead of driving along, her thoughts moving in time with the screen wipers between Hadda and Proctor and Simon Homewood.

One thing her encounter with the Trapps had made her recognize was that the line she had drawn under Hadda had been for emphasis not closure.

By the time she drew up in front of her flat, a screech from her wipers as they swept drily over the screen told her the rain had stopped. It also did something else, bringing together the three men who'd been dividing her thoughts during the drive.

Proctor had said Homewood needed to know everything to do his job properly.

But now she'd had time to examine their encounter with the emotional temperature turned down, there were certain aspects of the Director's knowledge that puzzled her.

For a start, when she said she'd run into Hadda he'd instantly assumed it was in Cumbria rather than in Manchester, where he knew she had been staying with her parents.

OK, that might not be all that significant. But later he'd referred to her spending the night at Birkstane even though she'd deliberately avoided mentioning it.

A lucky guess, perhaps.

But the final thing couldn't be put down to guesswork. He'd mentioned her foot.

So how the hell did he know about the sexual charade Hadda had played with her to find out if the surveillance audio really was switched off?

3

Toby Estover was wondering whether it were time for a change of secretary.

It wasn't that Morag wasn't as efficient as ever in her professional duties and as obliging as ever in her personal services. The trouble was that in the first couple of weeks after his return to the office in the New Year she had shown signs of looking for something more from their relationship than a regular desktop bang.

To start with she had tried to engage him in an exchange of idle chit-chat about the Christmas holiday, giving him more details of her family celebrations than he needed to hear, then leaving a gap that he was clearly expected to fill with more details of his festive break than he cared to give.

Also after kneeling astride him and bringing him to climax, she no longer immediately rose with a friendly smile and retired to the washroom, emerging a few minutes later, perfectly composed and ready to take dictation. She had taken to sinking forward against him, offering her lips to be kissed and murmuring inanities like, 'Was that good for you, lover?'

When by his responses he made it clear that he wasn't in the market for either idle gossip or post-coital *tendresse*, she desisted, but the experience had not been pleasant. So, time for a change, perhaps. Not in terms of size, of course; he liked his office furniture well upholstered; but colouring was another matter. Morag was fair and freckled, her generous breasts milky pale and small nippled. He found himself fantasizing about a brown-skinned girl with nipples like thumbs set in a boss of plum-dark crushed velvet . . .

The thought made him languid and he looked with displeasure on Morag as she entered his office after a barely perfunctory knock and said, 'You're no' forgettin' you're lunching wi' Kitty Locksley?'

Was his hearing faulty or had her Scots accent grown more intrusive in the past few days? She really would have to go. He'd have a word with Miss Jenner, the office personnel manager. She would arrange for a transfer to general duties downstairs. No drop in pay, but they usually got the message and left of their own accord after a week or so.

He said irritably, 'Of course I haven't forgotten. Though why I'm lunching with the bitch, I've no idea. Still, always best to keep the press on board.'

Kitty Locksley was the news editor of one of the slightly more literate tabloids, the kind that people he knew sometimes admitted to reading.

He stood up and waited. Morag usually went into the cloakroom to fetch his overcoat and help him into it. Today she didn't move. That did it. She definitely had to go. He got the coat himself and as he struggled into it he said, 'I should be back by three. Ask Miss Jenner to come and see me then, will you?'

Morag waited till she heard the lift door close, then took out her mobile and dialled.

'Hi, Mr Murray,' she said. 'He's on his way.'

'Good girl. Got to go. Talk later.'

She put the phone down and strolled round Estover's expansive desk and settled into his very comfortable leather swivel chair. She prided herself on always trying to see things from other people's viewpoint and things certainly looked very different from here. Not that she was complaining. She'd come into the job with her eyes wide open. She'd have had to be very naïve indeed not to recognize what was on Toby Estover's mind as his eyes ran up and down her body at the interview. Well, that was fine, he seemed a nice enough guy, and she was a thoroughly modern girl with no hang-ups about enjoying sex for its own sake, plus there were all kinds of perks as well as the Christmas bonus. So it had merely amused her when some of the other girls felt it their bounden duty to tell her that on average Estover's secretaries lasted three years. There would come a time when Miss Jenner, the office manager, would approach her, shoot some shit about moving staff around to give them a variety of experience, then invite her to leave her comfortable ante-room outside Estover's lofty office and dive into the common pool below.

'That'll be nice,' she'd replied with a smile. 'I really look forward to seeing more of you guys.'

On her return to work after the Christmas break, she'd been almost immediately approached by her Scottish friend. He had a new proposition that took her aback. Keeping Murray apprised of Estover's movements was no more than a bit of harmless disloyalty. But, however you wrapped it up, accessing, copying and selling Estover's confidential records was unambiguously criminal.

The money Murray offered had been good. And she liked the guy. So she hadn't refused him out of hand. Next time they met, he brought up the proposition again, upping his offer from good to generous. Also he assured her he was working for the good guys and that nothing would happen to Estover as a result of her actions that he didn't deserve. Which, from her own knowledge of Toby's working practices, suggested the poor bastard was in for a very bad time indeed!

Still she hesitated. As well as being a thoroughly modern girl, Morag was also an old-fashioned sentimentalist. She didn't expect declarations of eternal love from Estover, still less did she have any hope or indeed desire that he should make an honest woman out of her. But she did feel that after what they'd been to each other for the past couple of years, there must be some affection there.

Since then she'd given Estover every chance to show his regard for her, to demonstrate he regarded her as something more than just a high-class wanking machine.

He hadn't taken the chance. So a few days earlier she'd taken the plunge. Next time she saw Murray she'd passed over the tiny flash drive he had given her.

'Everything's on there,' she said. 'A lot of it's encrypted.'

'No problem,' he said. 'I'm grateful.'

Then he'd leaned forward and looked into her eyes and she'd thought, here it comes – he's going to hit on me!

But instead all he said was, 'If you ever fancy a job back in Glasgow, I might be able to fix you up.'

She was surprised to realize how disappointed she was his proposition was commercial rather than personal!

'I'll think on it,' she said coolly.

'Good,' he said, sitting back. 'Now some time soon, a journalist called Kitty Locksley is probably going to want to fix up a meeting with your boss. Over lunch, I'd guess. I need to know where and when.'

Back to business, she thought. They're all the same! One way or another, they'll squeeze every last drop of use out of you, then it's *On your bike, girl!*

He was muttering something else that her irritation made her miss.

'Eh?' she said.

'I was just wondering,' he said rather awkwardly. 'Maybe you and me could meet for a drink some time, you know, just to meet.'

'Like a date, you mean?' she said, hiding her pleasure.

'Aye.'

'I'll think about it.'

Well, now she'd thought about it. A date seemed good. And as she had no intention of letting the bitches downstairs get in their cracks about her being rolled off Estover's desk a year earlier than the average, what Murray had said about working in Glasgow sounded good too. She'd had enough of the fucking Sassenachs – in every sense.

She picked up the desk phone and punched in Miss Jenner's number.

Estover, meanwhile, was finding his welcome at the restaurant more to his taste than his departure from the office. As the pretty blonde on reception helped him off with his coat, she said, 'Nice to see you again, Mr Estover. Miss Locksley's already at your table.'

'Thank you,' he said, giving her a warm smile. Pity she was so willowy. And fair-skinned too, so probably no crushed velvet there.

'Miss Locksley?' said a man's voice. 'That Miss Kitty Locksley?'

He turned to see a man in the courier's outfit of crash helmet and leather jacket standing behind him. He was lanky, what was visible of his face had an impatient expression on it, and he had a Scottish accent which at the moment Estover felt was a strong strike against him.

'Who are you?' he said in his most patrician fashion.

'Courier. Got a package for her. Here, chum, could you take it? The bike's on the pavement, probably being clamped by now!'

He thrust a small package into Estover's hand then turned and left.

Bloody cheek! thought Estover. The Celtic fringe seemed to be in a conspiracy to irritate him today.

'Shall I take that, sir?' said the receptionist.

'No, that's all right.'

At the table Kitty Locksley smiled up at him as he approached. He stooped to give her a perfunctory kiss. Small, fine-boned, with not enough flesh on her to feed a hungry bluebottle, she definitely wasn't his type.

As he sat down he said, 'This is for you.'

'A late Christmas present, Toby?' she mocked.

'No! Courier was leaving it as I came in.'

She slipped it into her bag down at her feet and said, 'You'd think they'd let me enjoy my lunch in peace!'

'But this is a working lunch, surely?' said Estover. 'You haven't just asked me out because you've taken a sudden fancy to me, have you, Kitty?'

'Definitely not,' said the woman, rather too emphatically for Estover's liking. Even where he did not desire, he liked to be found desirable.

A waiter interrupted them to ask if they'd like a drink and they chatted in a desultory fashion till her gin and tonic and his large scotch came. When he was talking to journalists, Estover liked to have a prop to hand, in every sense.

'So, Kitty, what's this all about?' he said. 'My secretary said you were quite mysterious.'

'I certainly didn't mean to be,' she said. 'It was just a rather odd thing. Does the name Arnie Medler mean anything to you?'

Now Estover was glad of his prop. He took a long pull at the scotch and said cautiously, 'It does ring a bell.'

'DI in the Met, till he retired to live in Spain.'

'Yes, of course. That's how I know the name. The fuzz. In my line one has to make contact from time to time.'

He was sounding a little too jolly, perhaps. He resisted the temptation to take another drink and said, 'So?'

'I'm glad he's not a friend,' she said. 'Because he's dead.'

'Good Lord!'

'Yes. He died in a rather macabre accident some time over Christmas. You didn't know?'

'No, why should I? Was it in the papers?'

'No. Not a trace. Mind you, so many good stories about rows over Christmas dinner turning into family massacres that an ex-pat's death in sunny Spain was hardly going to stop the presses. So what was your connection with him, Toby?'

By now Estover was fully back in control.

'More to the point, Kitty, as it's you who got me here, what's your interest?' he said.

She shrugged. 'Nothing sinister. Someone rang the desk with the story and said there was a link between you and the dead man that might be worth following up. Also they intimated it was something you'd prefer to discuss face to face, so, as a girl's got to eat, I thought why not get a lunch on the paper with my dear old chum?'

What the caller had actually said was, 'You might like to have Estover where you can watch his reaction, preferably some place he can't have his secretary primed to interrupt him with an urgent call.'

So far the watching had been interesting but a long way from suggestive.

He said, 'Well, as I say, I barely remember the name and I'd need to check back to see what the nature of my acquaintance with the man was.'

She said, 'The caller mentioned something about helping with Medler's purchase of a villa in Spain. Didn't know you went in for that kind of stuff, Toby.'

'Oh well, you know, seven years back, I was still making my way,' he said.

'Really?' she said, noting the clash between the claim of *barely remembering* and the precision of *seven years*. 'Just shows how wrong our records can be. They've got you down as top stud, legally speaking, back then. Didn't realize you were still picking up pennies with a bit of conveyancing.'

He ignored the sarcasm and said, 'So, delightful as it always is to see you, Kitty, I fear your well-known reputation for probity will make it hard for you to claim this lunch on expenses. Retired policeman dies in Spanish accident. London solicitor may have been acquainted with him. Even your ingenious editor would be hard pushed to work that up into a story! By the way, you described the accident as rather macabre. How so?'

He spoke casually. Why was it lawyers always spoke casually when they approached something they really wanted to know? wondered the journalist.

She watched his face carefully as she replied.

'It seems your old friend, sorry, acquaintance, Mr Medler, had taken to hitting the bottle quite hard in his retirement. His wife returned home early on Christmas morning to find he'd drunk himself silly and managed to fall in their villa. As he fell, he must somehow have triggered the mechanism that brought the heavy metal security shutters down over the sliding patio doors. Unfortunately, they were open and he fell with his arms stretched across the threshold. The first thing his wife saw when she got home was his severed hands lying on the patio, looking like they'd been chopped off with an axe.'

Now this was more interesting, thought Kitty Locksley. Either that detail had a special significance for Estover or maybe he just had a very weak stomach. Either way, she didn't think she was going to have to pick up too heavy a bill for his lunch.

And Davy McLucky, now helmetless and sitting in a car parked across the street from the restaurant, was so entertained by Toby Estover's expression that he took another photo to add to the ones he'd already shot of this fascinating encounter.

4

The Sunday after her conversation with the Trapps, Alva Ozigbo ate her frugal breakfast, pressed the mute button on her answer machine, and sat down on the floor of her flat surrounded by all the material she had gathered relating to the Hadda case.

The only thing scheduled for the day ahead was tea at John Childs's house. He'd rung the previous day to say that he'd bought his godson, Harry, a copy of *Curing Souls* for his birthday and hoped she'd be kind enough to sign it. She'd said of course she would and he had then wondered in his diffident manner if she might like to do this while having tea with him the following day.

So she had all morning to trawl through the Hadda files, and seeing them laid out neatly on her floor, it struck her she was going to need all morning!

There was a hell of a lot of material here.

More, she guessed, than normal with the majority of her clients.

But that was explicable, she reassured herself, by the complexity of the case rather than any special interest in Hadda.

She didn't feel all that reassured.

Taking a deep breath, she went back to the beginning.

Three hours later she emerged from her second complete review, poured herself a stiff gin, and in search of a temporary distraction checked her messages.

357

All were negligible except one from her mother sounding fraught and asking her to ring as soon as she had a moment. Since Ike had come home to convalesce, most messages from Elvira took this form, so she didn't let herself feel too anxious, but she rang straight back. To her relief it was the mixture as before.

'He won't eat what he should, won't rest when he should, says it's all a plot to keep him away from his work and claims I'm up to my neck in the conspiracy!' said Elvira.

As she spoke, Alva heard Ike's rich bass distantly demanding to know who was on the phone. Elvira ignored him, the voice got louder till finally she was cut off in mid syllable and Ike's voice cried, 'Elf! Thank God! Send for the SAS, I'm being held here against my will! Or if you can't do that, restore my sanity by saying something sensible.'

Alva laughed out loud, partly with relief at hearing that voice at its old decibel level, partly because she knew that this was the response her father wanted.

It was strange, she thought, that Elvira, the actress, never seemed to have caught on that her husband's outbursts were usually purely histrionic, and all that was required of his audience was appreciative applause.

Then she recalled her growing suspicion that she'd been played by Hadda and stopped feeling superior.

Her laughing response quickly reduced the performance to a more conventional discussion of Ike's progress. But after they'd been talking a few moments, he said, 'That's enough of me. How about you, Elf? You sound a bit strung out.'

He'd always been very sensitive to her moods.

'I'm fine,' she said. 'I've just realized a patient may have been fooling me, that's all.'

He said, 'Serious? I mean, you've not turned some nut loose who's going around cutting people's throats?'

'No. Nothing like that.'

'Then why so down? Being fooled's an occupational hazard in your business, I should have thought.'

'I know. It's just that I feel like I'd been fêted for translating the Rosetta Stone, only to find out later maybe I'd got it all wrong and the hieroglyphics were nothing but an Egyptian laundry list.'

He boomed a laugh and said, 'Think of it this way. You'd find out a lot more about the Egyptians from a laundry list than the kind of high-falutin' crap folk usually carve on monuments.'

'I suppose,' she said.

'You sound like you're taking it personally,' said Ike. 'Now why should that be? I seem to recall you once telling me that there was a line between professional and personal that your patients were always pressing up against and you had to make sure it was never crossed *either* way.'

God, but he was sharp!

She said lightly, 'Daddy, didn't we agree: you do no analysis and I'll do no surgery?'

'Never agreed to stand by and let my little girl get hurt,' he said.

'And if I want someone beaten up, you're still the first guy I'll call,' she said. 'But I need you back to full fighting fitness for that. So get back into bed and stop being an asshole to Mummy. You know she takes it personally even though it means nothing.'

'Yeah. Maybe that's where you get it from. Bad gene. Don't worry, I promise to be good. You take care, Elf. I love you.'

'Me too.'

She switched the phone off. Was Ike right? Was she taking personally something that meant nothing?

She returned to the notes she'd been making as she went through the Hadda files.

The way in which they differed from her original case notes was the input of new information. Not that this amounted to much.

Imogen Ulphingstone at fourteen hadn't been the skinny, early pubescent girl that Hadda had described having his first sexual encounter with on Pillar Rock. She had been a rapidly maturing young woman with a bosom already giving promise of the perfect breasts Hadda had been distracted by in his first piece of writing.

Sir Leon hadn't objected to the marriage to protect his daughter

359

from Hadda but to protect Hadda from his daughter, and by implication his wife.

So, not much. But it meant she'd needed to take a fresh look at what Wolf had actually written. And she had to admit that her own brief encounter with the two Ulphingstone women had left her with some sympathy for the old man's point of view.

And now the clarity of her original interpretation and analysis had been brought into doubt. The whole thing began to resemble one of those drawings in which a slight change of perception turns a goose into a rabbit. It was all a matter of focus. Her initial perception had been of a paedophile in denial gradually coming to a horrified awareness of what he had done. But change that to an innocent man coming to a realization that his only hope of getting early release was by faking the process, and the whole thing made just as much sense.

She cast her memory back to her developing relationship with Hadda. Her delight when he'd given her the first piece of writing. She had taken his racy description of the events leading up to the accident as clear evidence that he was still in denial. She had never for a second considered the possibility that this might in fact be the plain truth.

And she had almost certainly let her scepticism show.

She recalled the way he'd looked at her before producing his second piece, the description of waking from the coma.

She'd seen this as a definite step forward. And maybe this was exactly the way Hadda wanted her to see it. But only if her reaction to the first piece showed him there was no hope of convincing her he was innocent.

Once he'd taken this path there was no way back. He had played his part perfectly, written and spoken his lines in a way that persuaded her she was guiding him against his will to confront his Brocken spectre. Whereas all the time, he was leading and she was eagerly following . . .

She couldn't believe it, she wouldn't believe it. How could she, the professional, have been fooled by a . . . *woodcutter!* He'd surely have needed expert assistance as to which strings to pull . . .

Then she remembered finding a copy of *Curing Souls* in the bedroom at Birkstane, and the speed with which he'd removed it from her.

Why? A good reason would be that it was heavily annotated.

The bastard had used her own book to get inside her mind, her professional thought processes!

But why the hell was she so pissed off at the thought that this man she felt something for, even if she wasn't yet sure what, might turn out to be innocent of the disgusting crime he'd been sent down for? Wouldn't revelation of his innocence more than make up for the fact that he'd fooled her?

Or maybe of course he was simply even more cunning and manipulative than child molesters usually were.

Alva shook her head angrily.

She needed to put all that personal stuff out of her mind. She was a professional and she had a professional interest here. But even as she made the assertion, she knew she was not going to act professionally. That would mean taking her concerns to the proper authorities – the probation service and/or the police. And of course, if she had serious reason to believe a client was likely to commit a crime, she would have no choice.

But, she reassured herself, you don't! If anything, you're beginning to consider the possibility that a client may have been the object of a crime.

OK, she answered herself, then at least you ought to talk this over with someone whose informed judgment you respect.

Like who?

Her father would normally have been high on her list, but not in his present state. He'd already detected that something was worrying her. If once he got a sniff that what lay at the bottom of her problem was her inappropriate feeling for a convicted pederast . . .

No, Ike was out. Elvira was never in.

And not a colleague.

She knew only too well what another psychiatrist's advice would be. Go to the authorities, get them to initiate a formal investigation.

The trouble there was, whatever it produced in the long run, its first fruit would be the return of Hadda to custody. In her mind's eye she saw him drinking his strong black coffee in the kitchen at Birkstane, logs crackling in the hearth across which Sneck lies, gently snoring, while outside the winter wind sends volleys of hail against the panes . . .

Jesus! She was thinking Christmas-card sentimentality now! But she knew she could not be responsible for dragging him away from that without better reason than she had so far.

Not so long ago she might have contemplated an off-the-record chat with Homewood, but having already experienced the irritatingly proprietary attitude probably spawned by his new domestic situation, she had no desire to invite him further down the road of intimacy.

And also there was still the nagging question of how he seemed to know what he couldn't possibly know. She had gone over the exchange again and again and almost persuaded herself that she'd simply misinterpreted something quite insignificant.

Then an inner voice said, Just like all that stuff at Ulphingstone Castle? Right!

So who could she talk to?

One possibility remained and she was seeing him this afternoon!

At four o'clock precisely she rang the bell of Childs's front door. As always, he greeted her with an ego-stroking delight.

'Dr Ozigbo, hello. Come in, come in,' he said. 'It's lovely to see you.'

'And you too, Mr Childs,' she said.

Would their relationship ever move on to a more casual form of address? she wondered. After more than two years, she doubted it, and in fact she didn't mind. There was something pleasantly old fashioned in this friendly formality. It implied the closeness of equality without the dangers of intimacy, though to ask his advice in this instance might bring her perilously close to the borderline between the two.

362

'Let's go up to my study again,' he said. 'I always think the climb works up the appetite so well.'

On their way up the stairs, he said, 'So how are things going back at work? Settled comfortably into the routine again, are you?'

She said, 'Well, yes and no. Actually there's something I'd really like your advice about, if you don't mind me bringing my problems along to a Sunday tea-party.'

'You interest me strangely,' he said. 'And one good turn deserves another. Now, here we are.'

They had reached the top landing and entered the study. On his desktop lay a pristine copy of *Curing Souls*.

'Perhaps you would like to inscribe it while I get the tea,' he suggested. 'Then we can sit down together and mull over this problem of yours.'

'Of course,' she said. 'What would you like me to write in the book?'

'Oh, something encouraging,' he said vaguely. 'I know he will be so delighted to have your signature and your support.'

She must have looked a little doubtful, for he smiled mischievously and added, 'I daresay he will also be delighted to have my signature on the fat cheque I shall be enclosing with the volume.'

Alva smiled back at him and said, 'I'm relieved to hear it. Universities are full of books, but hard cash is always in short supply.'

She sat down at the desk as he excused himself and headed back down the stairs.

There was a pen in a small jug that acted as a desk tidy. She picked it up and opened the book and tried to think of something witty to write.

She recalled a remark of R. D. Laing's: *Few books today are forgivable*. Yes, that would do, followed by *I hope you will find something to forgive in this one. Good luck and Happy Birthday!*

She picked up the pen and started writing. Or at least tried to. The pen was dry. The only other writing implement in the tidy was a red pencil, which would hardly do.

Without thinking she pulled open the nearest drawer of the desk in search of a more suitable implement.

There were several pens in there. There was also a framed photograph.

She took it out and stared from it to the gap in the line of photos displayed on the wall, then back again.

It was a face she knew, though not like this.

She heard a distant clink of crockery on the stairs.

When the door opened, the desk drawer was shut and Alva was just putting the final flourish to her signature.

'All done?' said Childs, entering with the tea tray.

'Yes, all done,' she said brightly.

Too brightly? She hoped not. But she reckoned she'd done very well to answer him with even a semblance of normalcy while her mind was bubbling with the question: What the hell was John Childs doing with a photograph of the young Wolf Hadda hidden in his desk?

5

Davy McLucky was whistling as he turned into the quiet Chingford street where the Trapps' cosy suburban villa was located. He hadn't been too delighted when it turned out Hadda was serious in his suggestion that on his next trip to London he should stay with the solicitor, but it had turned out fine. The absence of alcohol apart, Ed and Doll were his kind of people, and the hip flask he always carried made up for that single deficiency.

But it wasn't pleasurable anticipation of the warming cup of cocoa and large wedge of chocolate cake awaiting him that put the bounce in his step and the music on his lips, it was the memory of the evening he'd just spent with Morag Gray.

He'd started by coming clean, or at least as clean as he felt he could. She'd shown no surprise when he told her his real name and profession. They'd exchanged biographical details over a couple of drinks, and then they'd gone back to her flat where the exchange became more biological.

Now here he was, striding along the quiet suburban street with a lightness of heart he hadn't experienced since he was a teenager.

He reached the Trapps' villa and turned in at the gate.

As he took the key out of his pocket and inserted it in the front door lock, he heard the sound of a footfall behind him. It had nothing of the menacing speed of attack, nevertheless he spun round, his forearms raised defensively.

'Good evening, Mr Murray,' said Alva Ozigbo. 'Why am I not as surprised as I should be to see you here? Or is your sat-nav on the blink again?'

Doll Trapp's reaction when she saw Alva following McLucky into the old-fashioned lounge where she and Ed Trapp were sitting reading the Sunday papers was to smile widely and say, 'Dr Ozigbo! I was hoping you'd show up. Take a seat, dearie. Ed, you make us a cup of tea. Davy, why don't you give Wolf a bell? See what he thinks, OK?'

Alva thought, *Davy*. There'd been a Scottish cop looking after Hadda in hospital. They had seemed to get on well. *Davy McLucky*. That was it: *D.M.*

The Scot followed Ed Trapp from the room.

Doll said, 'I know you said it was natural, but I thought I'd give it a go anyway. What do you think?'

She shook her head to draw attention to her hair, whose pink tinge had been replaced by pale straw.

'It's very nice,' said Alva.

'Yeah, but now I see you again, it's nothing close, is it? Hard to carry colours in your head. You buy a scarf thinking that'll go with my blue jacket and you get home and it clashes like a skullcap in a mosque. Why's it so hard, do you think?'

'Perception's an inexact thing. That's what makes witness evidence so dodgy. Mrs Trapp, is that man David McLucky who used to be a detective constable in the Met?'

'Now how on earth do you know that?' said Doll.

'Wolf wrote about him.'

'Oh yes. And you've put two and two together. He said you were sharp.'

'Not sharp enough, I'm beginning to think. Listen, Mrs Trapp –'

'Doll. Call me Doll. I think we're going to be friends. And leave the questions for a moment, Alva . . . I've got that right, I hope? Such a pretty name. How long does it take a man to make a pot of tea? No wonder it takes for ever to get a plumber. At last!'

The door opened and Ed Trapp entered carrying a tray that bore the tea things and a plateful of biscuits.

'Just look at the way he's arranged those biscuits,' scolded Doll. '"Arranged", did I say? I think he's stood at one end of the kitchen and thrown them at the plate.'

But even as she scolded him, she was smiling affectionately at her husband. This was a very close-knit couple, guessed Alva.

She noted there were only two cups on the tray. As Doll started to pour the tea, Murray/McLucky came into the room.

He said, 'It's OK.'

'Is that all? Come on, he must have said more than that!' protested Doll.

'Aye,' said the Scot. 'What he actually said was, you can either tie her up, gag her and keep her in the attic for a few weeks, or you can tell her anything she wants to know.'

'That Wolf, he's such a joker,' said Doll.

Alva felt she wouldn't have cared to be here if Doll hadn't thought it was a joke.

'Right, you two, off you go and watch some footie or something,' the woman continued. 'Me and Alva have got things to sort out.'

Obediently the two men left.

'Milk? Sugar? Bikky?' said Doll. 'No? No wonder you keep your lovely figure. Too late for me.'

She added a couple of teaspoons of sugar to her tea and helped herself to a biscuit which she dipped into her cup.

'So what made you decide to come round to see us?' she said.

Because I want answers, thought Alva. And because I couldn't think of anyone it's safe to ask except you, and I'm not all that sure about you!

But a good psychiatrist never reveals the depths of her own ignorance. She'd impressed this woman with her identification of McLucky. Build on that.

She said, 'I need to fill in some gaps in my files before I decide whether to go to the authorities or not.'

Doll gave her a wry grin as if she didn't believe a word of it and said, 'Then we have a problem, dearie, as I can't tell you anything without your assurance that nothing you hear here will go any further. Like you were listening to one of your patients.'

Alva said, 'If one of my patients told me he was planning to blow up Parliament, and I believed him, I'd have to tell someone.'

Doll let out a cockatoo screech of laughter and said, 'Me, I'd ask the bugger if he wanted any help! But I take your point. Makes things difficult, though. Up to you, dearie.'

She ate another biscuit, regarding her guest expectantly.

Alva blanked her out and focused on her problem. With everything she did it seemed the gap between the professional and the personal was widening. Her reaction to Luke Hollins's letter had started the rot. Instead of taking it straight to the probation service, she had shot off to Cumbria. All very unprofessional.

On the other hand, until very recently the authorities she was threatening to go to would have included Homewood and Childs, so what was she hesitating for? She'd returned to her flat from tea at Childs's house, her mind sparking with speculation that she knew could lead nowhere except a restless night. She needed more information and the number of people she could approach in search of it was very limited. In fact, the only ones in reach were the Trapps.

Pointless wasting more time on futile thought. She'd dug out Doll's card and headed straight for Chingford, arriving there just in time to see Murray/McLucky walking along the pavement towards the house.

She said, 'If you tell me unequivocally that a crime is about to be committed, then I'll have to speak. Otherwise you'll get maximum discretion.'

Doll screwed up her face and said, 'I suppose that'll do to be going on with. All right, dearie, sitting comfortable? Then I'll begin right at the beginning. Here's how Ed and me first met Wolf. He was just sixteen and me, God help us, I was just turned thirty!'

When Doll fell silent twenty minutes later, Alva said, 'I'd just like to make sure I'm not missing anything. You're saying Ed met Wolf in his capacity as duty solicitor, guessed the boy was under age, believed he was guilty as charged, knew he'd absconded from a Remand Centre and broken into his office . . . And despite this, Ed made no attempt to involve Social Services, got him off the charge, and covered up the absconding and the break-in. Then you took him into your home and found him a job. Have I got it right?'

'Word perfect, ducks,' said Doll. 'Though, I got to admit, hearing you spell it out so precise, it does sound a bit weird.'

'Weird!' said Alva. 'It sounds . . . I'm not sure how it sounds, except I've had patients whose fantasies came over as more down to earth than this.'

'Yes, well, the thing is, you *are* missing something, dearie. Though the fact that you're here at all makes me think maybe you're not really missing it at all, you're just not facing up to it. The thing is, Wolf was . . . is . . . very attractive, I mean, not just in the usual boy–girl way, though that too. But most people just *like* him! Even the cops put in a bit of effort with him. And Ed was full of him when he came back from their first meeting at the nick. I recall saying, "I hope you're not on the turn, Ed!" He just laughed and said, "If you met the lad, you'd see what I mean." Never thought I would meet him, of course. But I did. And I saw. This making any sense to you, dearie?'

It was. Alva thought of what she knew of Wolf's childhood. A loner, yes. But through *his* choice, not other people's exclusion.

In fact (why hadn't she spotted this before?) it was the fact that he was so attractive that had permitted him to go his own way so merrily. The evidence was all there: his teachers cutting him an enormous amount of slack at school; the girls trying to date him; Sir Leon ruffling his hair and talking to him in wolf-language; the mountain rescue men taking him under their wing; Johnny Nutbrown not taking offence when this uncouth yokel punched him on the nose; Imogen pulling her clothes off on the mountain and inviting him to fuck her; and even after his disgrace, a hard-nosed cop like Davy McLucky finding something in this damaged paedophile to like and sympathize with. And Luke Hollins clearly took a more than pastoral interest in his new parishioner.

Then there was herself . . .

Doll, as if following her thoughts, said, 'Yes, and he might have lost an eye, a few fingers and his good looks, but it's still there, isn't it? Don't be ashamed of admitting it, dearie. Impossible not to like him, right? Well, imagine what he was like way back, a young lad adrift and in danger on the streets of wicked old London. Even if I hadn't liked him, it would have been hard to throw him back. But we couldn't keep him living with us for ever. It was before we bought this place. Tight little high-rise flat in Whitechapel. Lots of temptations there for the idle young. He needed a real job.'

'So what was it you found for him to do, Doll?' asked Alva, glad of a diversion from her own feelings for Hadda.

'Thing is,' said Doll, 'to get some idea about Wolf's job, you'll need to know a little about mine. As it was back then, I mean. Now, of course, I work with Ed. But my first connection with the law was I started out as a secretary to a barristers' clerk. Meaning I was mainly an office skivvy. Made a lovely cup of tea, though.'

She smiled reminiscently.

Alva said disbelievingly, 'You're not saying you got Wolf a job in a law office?'

'Not quite the way you mean it,' said Doll. 'Though he'd probably have done better than me eventually. To start with, I had ambitions to become a fully fledged clerk in a top chambers. Lot of money in that game, if you play your cards right. And despite them trying to keep me at the tea urn, I set out to learn the job; after a few years, I reckoned I was good enough to start applying for real clerks' jobs. Some hope! Talk about glass ceilings. This one was bulletproof and electrified at that! After a year of getting nowhere, I was ready to relocate to a cash desk in Tesco's. You ever feel like that, dearie?'

'I've been very lucky,' said Alva. 'But you kept out of Tesco's?'

'Yeah. That was down to Geoff Toplady. He was the one barrister in chambers I really got on with. At first I thought he was just after squeezing my tits. Didn't mind that, so long as he listened to my moans as he squeezed. One day he said if I fancied being more appreciated there was this outfit he knew about who were always looking for talent. I said, I don't fancy lap dancing, and he laughed and said no, this was very respectable, sort of the civil service really. Sorry, dearie, you want to say something?'

'This barrister, Geoff Toplady, he's not a judge now, is he?'

'The very same. Done well for himself, has Geoff. Up in the Appeal Court now. Sky's the limit for Geoff. You know him?'

'Not exactly. Sorry. Do go on.'

'Can't say I fancied being a civil servant, but anything was better than going nowhere, so I attended an interview Geoff set up. I soon realized I wasn't being invited to work in a Whitehall department, I was being recruited into something a lot less high profile. They knew everything about me. I'd filled in a form, told the usual lies, made the usual omissions. They picked them all out one by one, but they didn't seem to care. In fact they asked me if there was anything they'd missed that I'd managed to get past them!

'I was told if I got the job I'd need to sign the Official Secrets Act. They stressed this wasn't just a formality. If I contravened the Act, the consequences would be severe. Very severe. I believed them, and I've never stepped out of line. But I'm stepping across it now, ducks, so I hope your guide's honour is still intact!'

It wasn't Alva's honour that was being troubled, it was her credulity.

'You're telling me you were a spy or something glamorous like that?' said Alva with a scepticism that another woman might have found offensive.

All it got from Doll was another cockatoo screech.

'Glamorous, me? Don't be daft!! Worked in a run-down office in Clerkenwell. Can't tell you exactly where, or I'd have to kill you, but we referred to it as the Chapel, 'cos the building was converted from a disused Methodist chapel.'

'And Wolf worked in the office with you?' asked Alva, wondering what kind of undercover department took sixteen-year-old runaways on as office boys.

'Of course not,' said Doll impatiently. 'Just listen, will you? Like I said, where I sat, the Chapel wasn't at all glamorous. But then,

I wasn't out in the big wide world doing an Indiana Jones. I just sat at a computer, putting together bits and pieces of information.'

'What kind of information?' asked Alva.

'Oh, this and that,' said Doll vaguely. 'Pay wasn't all that good, but on the whole I enjoyed the work. We all like knowing things that other people don't. Must be the same in your job, dear. Maybe that's why we understand each other.'

'I wish,' said Alva. 'Did your husband work there too?'

'Ed? No. But it was through the Chapel we got together. After I'd been working for them a year, my boss, JC (not that one, ducks, nothing religious about the Chapel), told me the Chapel needed a solicitor they could use for the occasional job, someone too low profile to be noticed. He wondered if I'd come across anyone who might fit the bill during my time running errands at the chambers. Ed came into my mind, I don't know why. He was very small beer, but even small beer solicitors have clients who need big-time barristers occasionally. Specially the kind of clients Ed specialized in.'

'What kind was that?'

'Bankers *manqués*, Ed calls 'em. People who think other folks' money is better off in their pockets. Anyway, JC had him checked out. Later, when I got interested in Ed personally, I took a peek at the results. God help me, I suppose I knew more about the man I eventually married than any other woman in history!

'But you don't want a blow-by-blow account of our courting. Eventually I told JC we wanted to get married. He said he was fine with that, Ed had signed the Act too, and it was better for me not to have to lie about my job.

'We'd been married a couple of years when Wolf came along. You've heard that story. Upshot was, I told JC all about the boy, said I wanted to find him a job, asked if JC had any advice. He said he'd like to meet Wolf, so one lunch hour we met up in a pub. JC was good at getting people to talk to him. He soon had Wolf eating out of the palm of his hand. And Wolf . . . well, as you know, he didn't have to work at being liked.

'A couple of days later JC told me it was fixed, said he'd arrange

372

for Wolf to be picked up the following morning. And that's what happened. Next morning he packed the few bits and pieces we'd got for him while he was staying with us, thanked us both very much, and left. And that was the last we heard from him for a dozen years or more.'

Doll fell silent. Was it a painful memory? Or was she just trying to work out how much more she could tell?

Alva said casually, 'This JC, your boss. Were those his real initials by any chance?'

Doll gave her that shrewd look again and said, 'Can't tell you that, dearie. I'm already telling you a lot more than I should.'

Casual isn't going to get me anywhere, thought Alva. So let's try direct!

'OK,' she said. 'In order not to trouble your conscience, and in case we're being bugged, let me declare here and now that you have never told me anything to make me think this man JC's full name might be John Childs.'

For the first time, she felt she'd laid a glove on Doll Trapp.

'Well, you really are full of surprises,' she said. 'Interesting theory. I'd be careful who you share it with. Now, where was I?'

That's all the confirmation I'm going to get, thought Alva.

She said, 'You were telling me you got a boy you were concerned about a job with what sounds a very morally ambiguous organization run by a man whose sexual tastes incline to the Greek. Then you managed to lose contact with him for over a decade.'

She didn't try too hard not to sound accusatory.

Doll said defiantly, 'No moral ambiguity about the Chapel, ducks. That's for plonkers who don't care to know what the security services are doing, but are bloody glad to know they're doing it. As for the Greek stuff, no worries there. All in the mind with JC. Sublimation, isn't that what you people call it?'

She spoke with utter certainty. Alva felt she'd need several close consultations with Childs before she shared it. And in view of her growing suspicion just how completely she'd been deceived by Hadda, perhaps even that wouldn't be enough!

She said, 'You must surely have asked how Wolf was getting on?'

'Of course I did. JC would just smile and say, "Fine, fine. He's doing well."'

'And you were happy with that? What about records? They must have kept track of what their employees were up to.'

Doll grinned and said, 'I can see you're as nosey as I am, dear. That's why we get on so well. Yes, I did take the odd peek in some well-hidden corners of my computer.'

'And?'

'I can't be sure, they used codenames at the Chapel – claimed it was good security, but I reckon it was mainly like little boys liking nicknames! After a while I noticed references to someone tagged the Woodcutter. Could that be Wolf? I wondered. I recalled how it had amused my boss when he asked Wolf what else he could do besides climb vertical walls, and he said he could chop down trees.'

'Is that all? You didn't probe deeper?'

'Not wise in the Chapel, going where you didn't oughter,' said Doll. 'If you really want to know what he did in his Chapel years, you'll have to ask him yourself.'

'I may do that,' said Alva. 'How did you and Wolf make contact again?'

Doll said, 'It was 2001. We'd been really busy in the Chapel since Labour got in and Tony started brown-nosing the Yanks. I worked longer and longer hours without really noticing. And that meant I didn't notice what was happening with Ed.

'His clients were always demanding. I don't know which were worse, the out-and-out villains or the poor bastards that life and circumstance were pushing under. He still got work from the Chapel from time to time, but that wasn't exactly stress-free either.

'To cut a long story short, Ed had a booze problem. I knew he liked a drink. OK, that's a long way from needing a drink, but there's an unbroken thread running between them, and I was too busy to see it being spun out.

'As he got more and more stressed out by his case-load, Ed turned to the booze to help him out. My wake-up call was finding a bottle of vodka hidden in the lavatory cistern. I confronted Ed with it. He denied all knowledge at first, but when that wouldn't wash, he denied it meant anything sinister. But now a whole pattern of behaviour began to make sense. I screamed at him like a fishwife. Not the clever thing to do. Knowing I knew meant he just didn't have to bother to hide the problem any more. After a particularly bad binge, I got him to promise he'd turn himself in to Alcoholics Anonymous. I stood over him while he rang up and arranged to go to a meeting with a counsellor. I'd have taken him there myself, but there was so much on at work. Big mistake. On his way to the meeting, he remembered he was representing a client at the magistrates' court.

'Hardly need tell you the rest. He took a couple of drinks to steady his nerves. Then several more for no good reason other than he was a helpless piss-artist.

'Unfortunately no one spotted how rat-arsed he was before he got into the court. He made a real idiot of himself. When the magistrate told him to sit down, he became abusive. And when the court bailiff tried to escort him out, he became violent.

'It made all the papers. Looked like the end of his career. He'd be charged, fined, even imprisoned, certainly disbarred. I think he was suicidal. I know I was.

'And then this fifty-thousand-pound car pulls up outside our house and out steps this smart young fellow in a three-thousand-pound suit and when I open the door he takes me in his arms, gives me a big kiss and says, "Hello, Doll. You're looking great."

'It was Wolf. Or as he was now, Sir Wilfred Hadda. He'd read about Ed in the morning papers, cancelled everything and headed straight round to see us.

'I still can't believe what he did, I still don't know how he did it. But in a couple of days it had ceased to be a scandal. Ed was some kind of modern saint who'd broken down under the pressure of too many good works; the magistrate was happy, the Law Society was happy, and best of all Ed was shut away in the country's top addiction clinic, receiving film-star-level treatment for his alcoholism.

'So there you are, my dear,' concluded Doll Trapp. 'If you can't see now why we know Wolf has to be totally innocent of all those dreadful things they sent him down for, then maybe you should retrain for another line of work!'

6

John Childs sat in his study working on his book.

At the head of a fresh sheet of paper he wrote *Chapter 97* in the same immaculate hand with which he had inscribed *Chapter 1* nearly forty years ago. Sometimes he looked back a trifle ruefully at his chosen title, *A Brief History of the Phoenician People,* but a delicate sense of irony prevented him from changing it.

A man as meticulous in thought as in script, he calculated that his *Brief History* would take another seventeen years to complete. If he, and the market for books like his, survived till then, he did not anticipate troubling the best-seller lists. In fact it amused him to think that his largest readership might prove to be those colleagues from departments cognate with his own who had been clandestinely checking out the script from time to time just to make sure he wasn't composing a *roman à clef.*

Something scratched against the window pane. He rose to draw back the curtains and open the French window leading on to a small balcony overlooking Regent's Park.

'You could just have rung the bell,' he said.

Wolf Hadda stepped into the room.

'Hello, JC,' he said. 'I needed the exercise.'

The two men looked at each other critically.

'You've aged,' said Hadda.

'And you have . . . well, you look better than you ought to,' said

377

Childs. 'From all accounts you are extremely fit. Does your training regime permit alcohol?'

'In moderation.'

'Then let me get you a moderate scotch. Have a seat.'

Hadda sank into a recliner chair and spun round to take in the whole room. His gaze ran along the photos on the wall – Childs Senior in tropical kit, looking very serious; a boy he knew to be John Childs standing with a young Arab who had his arm round his shoulder; and then the young men, some casual, some formal; and among them a gap.

'*Et tu Brute,*' he said. 'I see I've been banished.'

'What? Ah, yes. A temporary security precaution. Here, let me remedy it.'

He handed Hadda a glass and opened a drawer in his desk. Then he paused, frowning for a moment as if something about the contents had caught his eye. Finally he took out a framed photograph and went to hang it in the space on the wall.

'There,' he said. 'All as it should be.'

'Yes, nothing changed. A few more photos, of course. And the manuscript pile looks a little thicker. The Phoenicians doing well, are they?'

'Steady progress,' said Childs, returning to his seat. 'You always had a good memory, Wolf.'

'Better than ever now, I find.'

'Then you will remember that I have never wished you anything but good.'

Hadda smiled and said, 'If wishes were horses, beggars would ride.'

'Is that one of your old Cumbrian saws?' said Childs. 'I hope so. It seems to imply a recognition that grim necessity takes precedence over all things.'

'A heavy interpretation of one of my Great Aunt Carrie's favourite catchphrases. But, now I come to think of it, I seem to recall you pleaded grim necessity the first time the good you always wished me didn't come through.'

'True. Though in recompense I did help you instead to get your heart's desire.'

'And look how that turned out.'

Childs wrinkled his brow as though contemplating a close philosophical analysis of this proposition, but before he could speak, a mobile trembled in Hadda's pocket.

'Sorry,' he said, taking it out.

He examined the display then said, 'Excuse me,' and stepped back out on the balcony, pulling the window to behind him.

'Hi, Davy,' he said.

He listened for a few moments then smiled.

'She's nobody's fool. I'm sorry I had to make her mine. What to do? Well, you could gag her and lock her in the attic, I suppose. But failing that, I think the best thing is for you and Doll to tell her everything she wants to know. And you won't forget to withdraw your offer for Poynters? Good man. Cheers, Davy.'

He switched off and came back into the room.

'Sorry about that,' he said.

'That's OK. Especially as it seems to have been good news.'

'Still so easy to read, am I? Even with my rearranged face! Ah well.'

He sat down again and took a sip of his drink.

'Now what were we talking about? Oh yes. Grim necessity. Which I presume was your reason for your decision not to intervene, even when you knew for certain I'd been fitted up. In fact, you chose to connive at making the cover up water-tight. Necessity must have been really grim that week.'

'You were in an apparently moribund state. What good would it have done you to set about proving your innocence?'

'And when I came out of my moribund state?'

'Believe me, no one was happier to hear of your recovery than I,' said Childs. 'But once we'd started dabbling, there was no going back, you must see that. All I could do was keep a watchful eye on you. And a caring eye too.'

'You mean you were working behind the scenes for my release?' mocked Hadda.

'Pointless till you wanted to be released. And once you decided on that, you seemed quite capable of making your own ingenious arrangements.'

'You seem very well up on my activities,' said Hadda, frowning.

'Like I say, old acquaintance should not be forgot. And after your release, I was pleased to be able to squeeze a few journalistic scrota to keep the jackals from nipping too closely at your heels.'

'Yes, I did notice. I wondered why you should feel so obligated. Then of course I talked to Medler and found out just how great your obligation really was.'

Childs shrugged and said, 'It would have been easy to prevent your meeting Medler. But I felt you had a right to know everything, and you were more likely to believe what you heard from his lips than mine.'

'I suppose I was. Of course, once he'd talked to me, who knows who he might talk to next? But, happily for you, he had his accident. A form of accident that would put me in a poor light if ever I tried to make public anything poor Arnie might have told me.'

He stared at Childs significantly.

'Yes, there were certainly some at the Chapel who regarded that as a happy coincidence,' said the other man blandly.

'Not so happy for that poor bastard,' said Wolf. 'And are there perhaps some Chapel-goers who reckon it could be an even happier coincidence if I followed Medler in very short order?'

John Childs sipped his whisky and said slowly, 'You've had trouble? Professional, I mean, not just the local vigilantes?'

'A little.'

'Then I'm glad that you worked out I was unlikely to be directly concerned.'

'Did I? Why do you say that?'

'Because you did not come through my window swinging your axe. What?'

Childs's sharp eyes had detected a reaction.

'Nothing.'

380

'Let me guess. You had a visitor and you did welcome him with your axe?'

'Visitors,' said Hadda. 'Two of them.'

'That explains it. One you can take alive, two make that less of an option.'

'What makes you think I didn't take them alive?'

'The degree of uncertainty about their origin. While being *almost* sure they weren't Chapel, you still had to ask. If you'd kept one of them alive, I think you'd have known where they came from.'

'Maybe not,' said Hadda irritably. 'I'm not such a cold bastard as you.'

'Yet, despite your inner warmth, they're both dead. How does that work, I wonder? But tell me about them.'

Hadda didn't deny it but explained what had happened.

'One of them was definitely one of the pair I took the drugs from on Drigg Beach,' he concluded. 'OK, so it's understandable that they would want revenge, but how did they get on to me so easily, that's what puzzles me. But I see it doesn't puzzle you, JC.'

Childs smiled and said, 'No, but not for the reason you are clearly suspecting. There was no tip-off from the Chapel. There didn't need to be. Have you ever heard of a man called Pavel Nikitin? I see you have.'

Hadda thought, the old sod still doesn't miss much!

He lied easily, 'Only because when I was talking recently to Luke Hollins, my local padre who takes a strong parochial interest in my affairs, he brought me up to date on matters he thought might interest me. These included a list of people who'd been staying at Ulphingstone Castle over Christmas. And one of them was a man with a name that sounded rather like your chap, Nikitin.'

Childs nodded and said, 'The same. He's a Russian businessman, one of those who rose stinking rich out of the wreckage of the old Soviet Union. Eventually, however, fearing that there were too many ex-comrades back in dear old Moscow who still subscribed to Marxist principles about sharing wealth, about five years ago he opted to settle in the West. He is currently pursuing an application for UK citizenship. With strong political support, I may add. For the very best of reasons, of course.'

'Like, he'd add so much to our cultural diversity? No? Then it must be because once he is accepted as a Brit cit, his wealth too becomes acceptable as political donation.'

'Spot on, as always,' applauded Childs.

'But I don't see how the Ulphingstones fit in here,' said Hadda. 'Leon is the least political person I know, and Kira believes that anyone who relies on a public vote for his power is a dangerous radical. So how come this Nikitin gets invited to stay at the castle?'

'Politically he is very much in sympathy with Lady Kira,' said Childs. 'More importantly, he claims to be distantly related to her. And as he's rich, personable, moves in the top circles, and has important people to stay at his various villas and on his luxury yacht, Lady Kira is happy to acknowledge the relationship. I would guess she sees in him a personification of all the old tsarist values so sadly destroyed in 1917.'

'Sounds just her cup of tea. But if you know so much about him, JC, there has to be more.'

'You know me too well,' murmured Childs. 'The details of the dubious means by which Nikitin made his Russian fortune, I don't know, but I do know the kind of business he has been investing in since coming to the West. Alongside some conventional and legitimate commercial interests, he has a well-balanced criminal portfolio ranging from people-trafficking through drug-dealing to illegal arms sales.'

'Jesus! And Sir Leon lets him into his house!' exclaimed Hadda.

'Now you're being silly. Why should Sir Leon know anything of this? Nikitin can afford the very best lawyers. Any hint of criticism in the media gets sat upon with all the weight of a very well-upholstered legal bum, belonging, as I suspect you know, to our mutual friend, Toby Estover.'

Hadda didn't deny it but said, 'So the drugs I intercepted were Nikitin's?'

'Of course. I suspect that during one of his visits to the castle it occurred to him that parts of the Cumbrian coastline offered an ideal location for the safe landing of a not-too-bulky illicit cargo. I doubt he'll be using it again.'

'But it doesn't explain how he got on to me so quick. And I still don't understand what he was doing at the castle. OK, I can see Kira falling over herself backwards to get an invite to one of his swell parties. But why the hell would he be willing to accept her invitation to stay at the castle? I used to start yawning as I passed through the door!'

'You're forgetting the Estover connection.'

'You mean Toby introduced him? But that still doesn't explain . . .'

'There's more than one Estover,' said Childs.

It took a moment to sink in.

'What?'

'Oh dear. Now I'm really glad you didn't bring your axe. I'm not suggesting that the lovely Imogen was party to the attempt on your life, though why it should bother you so much if she were, I'm not quite sure . . .'

He looked invitingly at Hadda, who brushed aside the implied question and said, 'So what are you saying, JC?'

'Just that it seems Nikitin has taken a very strong fancy to Mrs Estover. Once he realized her mother's background was Russian, he doubtless dug till he discovered, or perhaps he even invented, the family connection. Once he met Kira and saw what she was, he set about making her an ally.'

'And Imogen, does she . . .?'

'I've no idea whether he is her lover or not. But he will know all about you, if not from one or both of the Estovers, certainly from Lady Kira, who is not averse to telling the world that letting you out of jail to settle in such close proximity to Ulphingstone Castle was an outrage to human decency. So Nikitin would have known more than he perhaps cared to know about this large, lame, one-eyed woodcutter who was presented as a threat to the woman he loves. And when his men reported to him that his drugs consignment had been hijacked and destroyed by a large, lame, one-eyed man with an axe . . . well, he knew exactly where to find you, and now he had two reasons, one commercial and one sentimental, for wanting to get rid of you.'

Wolf said, 'So why does the Chapel let this bastard wander around free?'

'Our concern is with national security, not supra-national criminality.'

'You could pass what you know to the police.'

Childs said, 'Who would do what with it? I doubt if it would even come to trial. He is well protected. Objections to his citizenship application have already been dealt with by Mr Estover with his usual silky efficiency, by his friends in high places with their usual winks and nods, and, where persistent, by Nikitin himself with ruthless brutality.'

'You could always fit him up,' said Hadda. 'You're good at that.'

'We'd need to catch him with a body at his feet and blood on his hands,' said Childs. 'Be careful of him, Wolf. He will not be happy that his men have not returned. And the man whose jaw you broke is still alive and he's the worst of the lot. His name is Pudovkin, known to his friends as Pudo. You did well to put him out of commission first, but you would have done better to put him out permanently. He is Nikitin's chief attack dog. You were lucky he was probably still recovering from his experience on Drigg Beach when Nikitin decided to have you taken out.'

Hadda shrugged indifferently and said, 'Maybe he was lucky. It occurs to me, JC, that maybe it's really Estover you're protecting here. That deal you did with him, the deal that put me in Parkleigh for seven years, remember? Access to all his confidential files on all his high-profile clients – how far would you go to protect that?'

'Not perhaps as far as you think,' said Childs. 'In my opinion, Estover is rather *passé* as a source. His loss would leave a very small hole that could easily be filled.'

'So if someone did move to sort him out, you wouldn't be too bothered?'

384

'Personally, not at all. So long as it was done with discretion.'

'Meaning the Chapel is kept right out of the frame,' laughed Wolf. 'How much do you think Imogen knows about Toby's work?'

'It's hard to say. She is not, so I gather, easy to read. But I need not tell you that. Have you spoken to her yet?'

'Why would I want to talk to her?'

'Wolf, I wish I could tell you how complicit she was in the plot to frame you, but I can't. You must find that out for yourself. To do that, you need perhaps to talk. Or are you afraid of what you might do? Or of what you might not be able to do . . .?'

'Don't try to play your old mind games, JC,' said Hadda.

'No? I thought you were quite partial to playing mind games, Wolf.'

Hadda looked at him sharply, but that bland, amiable face gave nothing away.

'I'll talk to Imogen when I'm ready,' he said.

'Of course you will,' said Childs. 'Now, before you go, is there anything more I can do for you? Don't be afraid to ask.'

Hadda regarded him dubiously then said, 'All right. Any chance of getting me details of the accounts where Nutbrown and Estover have stashed their ill-gotten gains?'

'Ah, the estimable Mrs Trapp is having a problem there, is she? Curious how lawyers protect their own secrets so much more vigorously than they do their clients'! Of course. Anything else?'

'You're being very helpful, JC. You must really be feeling guilty!'

Childs said, 'Perhaps. Though of course I shouldn't. My part in your troubles was late and slight, and based on the happily false intelligence that you were as good as dead. In a sense, we are both victims of accident and grim necessity.'

'Our old friends, eh? I recall what you said when you introduced them to me way back. Something about love always losing out, I think.'

'I believe I told you that one day you would understand what I meant. I suspect that day is now well behind you.'

'Why do you say that? Nothing's happened to me by accident,

385

except perhaps . . .' he raised his maimed hand to his scarred face and smiled '. . . my accident. As for grim necessity conflicting with love, that happily is a choice I shall never have to make.'

'Really? And how do you propose avoiding it?'

'By avoiding them. By controlling my life from now on in.'

'And you think that's possible? Perhaps it is, but only if you have extremely rare qualities . . . practically unique . . . let me see, I think I can lay my hands on it . . .'

He rose and went to his bookshelf, took down a volume and riffled through it.

'Yes, here it is: *Necessity and Chance approach not me, and what I will is Fate.*'

'That sounds about right,' said Hadda. 'You could have taken the words out of my mouth. Whose mouth did you take them out of?'

'Milton's,' said Childs, holding the volume up so that Hadda could read the title.

'*Paradise Lost,*' said Hadda. 'Never read it. But in my case, it seems pretty appropriate. And whose mouth did Milton put these words in?'

'You should be careful, Wolf,' said Childs. 'It was God's.'

7

There was so much to take in that Alva sat back in her chair and closed her eyes to concentrate on arranging it all into a meaningful pattern. But all she could see was Wolf Hadda laughing when she quoted the *Observer* article that suggested he'd been kidnapped by the fairies, then smiling mockingly as he claimed that, like True Thomas, he too came back unable to tell a lie.

Inside, he must have laughed quite a lot more as he led her along the fallacious road to his rehabilitation.

She opened her eyes. Doll Trapp's face wore an expression of serene confidence. She clearly believed that she had proved Hadda's innocence beyond all doubt. For a second Alva was tempted to point out that being very good in one area didn't preclude being very bad in another. Human beings were much more complex than that.

Instead she said, 'You'd never noticed that Sir Wilfred Hadda, the millionaire businessman, was one and the same as your own Wolf the Woodcutter?'

'No,' said Doll. 'Never paid much attention to the business news, or the gossip columns for that matter.'

Alva wasn't sure if she believed her.

'Fine,' she said. 'Funny though that Wolf didn't get in touch with you himself when he came to live in London.'

Doll laughed and said, 'Not really. I suspect JC had told him it wouldn't do me any good if he tried to renew the connection.'

'Why would he say that?'

'He's a very careful man,' said Doll.

'So why did Wolf renew the connection?' asked Alva.

'That's the kind of guy he is,' said Doll. 'Wolf might have stayed away from paying a social call because he was warned off for my sake, but it would have taken an SAS regiment to keep him away when he heard that Ed was in serious shit.'

'Couldn't your friends at the Chapel have helped sort it out?'

'JC was the first person I turned to,' said Doll grimly. 'He said they already had a watching brief on the situation and, if it got worse, the Chapel might have to protect itself. I got the message. They don't like publicity. Any sniff of Ed's connection with the Chapel, they'd treat like a gas leak: cut it off at the source. No, if it hadn't been for Wolf . . . Anyway when it was all done, I resigned. Didn't go down too well and I didn't get a leaving prezzie unless you count a blunt reminder that the Official Secrets Act was operative till the end of time! I didn't give a toss! I knew that Ed was going to need me close from now on in, so I went back to being a paralegal and kept his business ticking over till he came back to work.'

'And Wolf, how strong were his links with the Chapel at that point, do you think?'

'Don't know, didn't want to know. But, international businessman with contacts everywhere, I'm sure they'd have wanted to use him.'

'So how might they have reacted when his troubles started?'

Doll said, 'Their main concern would have been that something might come out that tracked back to them. Like with Ed, but Wolf was a lot more significant, of course.'

'You sound bitter,' said Alva, who saw no reason not to be as direct with Doll as she was with her.

'Do I? Then I'm being silly. No taste for sentimental mush at the Chapel.'

The kind of mush that made you help a kid in trouble, the kind that brought that same kid riding to the rescue when you and Ed got in trouble, thought Alva.

She said, 'They say in politics that loyalty's a one-way street. So you no longer have any contact with the Chapel?'

'Last time I heard from them was when Ed started acting for Wolf. Phone rang. It was JC. I thought at first he was going to try and warn us off acting for Wolf. Instead, when I told him how bad things were, what with the strong evidence and Wolf's state of mind, he sounded genuinely upset. I made it clear I believed absolutely in Wolf's innocence and he said, "So do I, Doll. So do I. But in this wicked world, innocence is sometimes not enough." And that was that.'

'No offer of assistance then?'

'No way! But at least after talking to him I felt sure it wasn't the Chapel who'd set Wolf up. Not directly, anyway. I know now they got their finger in the pie later.'

Alva made a note of that for future exploration, but she wanted to get the basic picture clear to start with.

'What made you consider the possibility that it was the Chapel setting him up?'

Doll shrugged and said, 'Wolf's a man who likes to make his own choices. Like he did with Ed. If he'd done something that really got their knickers in a twist, the Chapel would have been quite willing and able to put him out of commission. Only it would probably have been less round-the-houses. Car accidents – they were very good at car accidents. So maybe he was lucky.'

'Lucky? You call getting banged up for something you didn't do lucky?' said Alva.

Doll seemed to take this as a reproof.

'We did everything we could for him,' she said angrily. 'Trouble was, back then Wolf just didn't want to know. Imo divorcing him and marrying Estover, his friends deserting him, the accident crippling him. It was all too much. And it didn't stop when he got to jail. First his old dad died, then his daughter. It was like Wolf had died himself.'

'I believe Ginny's death was the trigger that brought him back to life,' said Alva.

'Oh yes? Well, that's your line of country, isn't it? Ed did all he could, and went on trying to find out what was really going on long after Wolf went down. But we're not detectives, and it's hard helping someone who doesn't want to be helped. We thought he was just going to rot inside for the whole length of his sentence. So when he got in touch and asked Ed to help him with the parole hearing, we were really delighted.'

'But weren't you surprised?' asked Alva. 'Ed must have told you that the whole basis of that hearing was his full and frank acknowledgement of his guilt and his willingness to undertake a course of remedial therapy.'

Doll laughed and asked, 'How else was he going to get out, dearie?'

Then she stopped laughing and looked at Alva pityingly.

'I'm sorry. It must have been a real shock to find out how he'd fooled you. But what else could he do when he realized the only way to get out early was getting you to testify that he was no longer a danger to anyone? He had to use you. You must see that.'

Alva nodded, unable to trust herself to speak. Being fooled was an occupational hazard; every therapy session with a patient was to some extent a contest in manipulation; but to feel personally betrayed was irrational, as if they'd been in some sort of relationship other than therapeutic.

Doll reached over and patted her on the shoulder.

'Don't take it to heart, dearie,' she said. 'He'd have tricked his own mother if that's what had been needed to get him out.'

Alva was back in control now.

She drew away and said, 'What bothers me is that he felt that getting out was worth admitting to the world he was as bad as he'd been painted. He's not interested in proving his innocence, is he? All he wants to do is take revenge on the people he blames for putting him inside.'

Looking uneasy for the first time, Doll said, 'It's not quite like that. What he wants is to find out the exact truth of what happened.'

390

'And then he'll apply to get his case reviewed, is that what you're telling me?'

Doll shook her head and said, 'No. You've met him, ducks. You know what he's like. And I don't blame him, whatever he does. So long as it's based on the facts.'

She spoke defiantly. She's got reservations too, thought Alva.

She said, 'So how does he intend to get these facts?'

'Oh, he's done that already,' said Doll. 'We're well in to phase two now.'

'Phase two! For God's sake, tell me about phase one before we go there!'

Doll said, 'We're really getting to the edge of girl scout country here, dearie.'

Here it comes! thought Alva. She'd known from the start that sooner or later they were going to leave the ambiguous territory in which she could still persuade herself that keeping silent was a matter of personal choice. Now she was at the border.

She said carefully, 'If Wolf has committed or is planning to commit an act of violence, then I will have no choice but to call in the authorities. But peccadilloes such as breaking the strict terms of his parole licence won't bother me.'

'Great,' said Doll. 'In that case it won't bother you to learn that Wolf went to Spain over Christmas. There was an ex-cop living there, the one who arrested him. He thought he might know something that could help.'

'You mean,' said Alva, 'that while Wolf was supposed to be staying with you over Christmas he was actually out of the country? And you helped him and covered up for him? You realize how much trouble you could be in?'

'Ed's a lawyer,' said Doll indifferently. 'Look, Wolf thought it might help if he talked to this ex-cop, Arnie Medler, who lived in Spain, so that's where Wolf had to go.'

Medler. The name rang a bell. This was the arresting officer that Hadda had assaulted. Twice.

'And did it help?' she asked.

'Oh yes. Wolf told Ed that Medler had been able to confirm a lot of what he suspected. And he got it all recorded. You can listen to the recording, if you like.'

'I will do,' said Alva. 'Me and the authorities too. That should do the trick.'

But Doll was shaking her head.

'Wish it was so simple, ducks. Thing is, not long after Wolf left him, this guy Medler had an accident and died. That's really muddied the water.'

This got worse. Hadda leaves the country illegally to visit an ex-cop he thinks might be withholding information and now the cop is dead. Alva knew how it sounded to her, so she didn't have to take time out to guess how it would sound to the authorities.

'How did Medler die?' she asked.

'His wife found him early on Christmas morning. He'd got so pissed he fell forward unconscious with his arm stretched out across the threshold of his patio door. He must have touched some control panel as he fell. Result, as he lay there some heavy security shutters came down. Chopped his hands right off. He'd bled to death.'

'Oh Jesus,' said Alva aghast. Just when you thought you'd hit rock bottom, the ground opened up again.

'Yeah, I know,' said Doll. 'You're thinking *Woodcutter*. But it's not Wolf's style, ducks. Might have chopped the bastard's head off, if he deserved it, but not his hands!'

She seemed to think this comment should be reassuring. Alva did not find it so.

She said, 'So what do you and Ed do when someone turns up with their head chopped off?'

Doll regarded her quizzically as if wondering whether the first of Wolf Hadda's suggested methods for dealing with her might not have been the better option.

The door opened and Ed Trapp looked in and tapped his watch significantly.

'I think that'll do to be going on with, dear,' said Doll. 'You'll want to get home to listen to that tape and I've got work to do.'

392

Ed was holding the door open invitingly.

'I'll walk you back to your car,' he said.

They walked to the Fiesta in silence. As she unlocked the door, Trapp said gently, 'Don't worry about Wolf, Dr Ozigbo. He'd never hurt anyone that was innocent.'

'How can you be so sure?'

'There's something in him, connected with something that happened a long time ago, I think. Maybe he did once. He won't do it again.'

'He shouldn't be thinking about hurting anyone, Mr Trapp. Innocence, guilt, punishment, that's the Law's job. You of all people should know that.'

He smiled at her rather sadly.

'Should I?' he said. 'When the Law kept an innocent man banged up for seven years despite anything I could do? When the only way he could get out was to deceive a woman he likes and respects? Should I? Good night, Dr Ozigbo.'

She got in her car and drove home.

She tried to put everything she had just heard into some sort of order, but every third thought took her back to Mr Trapp's parting words.

A woman he likes and respects.

That had to mean something!

But not, she thought, all that much. Not while the memory of Imogen Ulphingstone was still burnt on his soul like a shadow on a wall left by an atomic explosion.

8

Monday morning dawned bright and very cold, with frost scaling the window panes and highlighting the bare twigs and branches of the trees and shrubbery in the grounds of Poynters.

'Where are you going, Johnny?' demanded Pippa Nutbrown.

'Just for a stroll through the spinney,' said her husband. 'Thought I'd see if I could pick up a rabbit.'

Pippa looked in scorn at the shotgun he carried broken in the crook of his arm.

'As much chance of you coming back with a Siberian tiger,' she said.

'Sorry, old girl, was there something you wanted me to do?'

'Don't be stupid,' she snapped dismissively. 'What the hell would I want you to do that I can't do better myself?'

Nutbrown could think of one thing but he knew better than to say it. Best policy was to make yourself scarce when Pippa was in one of her moods, which she seemed to be most of the time recently. It was a couple of weeks since she'd announced that she'd given Skinners their marching orders and done a private deal with Donald Murray. The news had filled Nutbrown with a dismay that not even his wife's delight could compensate for. But as the days went by and she heard nothing more from Murray, her mood began to darken while her husband's spirits began to rise, though he was careful not to let her see this.

As he walked away from the house, he began to whistle 'Happy Days Are Here Again', though not till he was sure he was out of earshot. He had neither the will nor the guile to resist Pippa's insistence that they should sell Poynters and go to live abroad, but he did have a deep-rooted conviction that this was never going to happen. No logical basis, of course, but nothing new there! His motto had always been, Take the line of least resistance and generally speaking things would work out for the best.

He entered the spinney. The winter sun could hardly penetrate here and the temperature dropped by several degrees. He heard a twig crack and paused. All was silent again. Pity. It would be nice to surprise Pippa and actually come back with something in his game bag. The trouble was, on the odd occasion he'd managed to get something in his sights, he'd rarely been able to bring himself to shoot it. The wild creatures here were also inhabitants of Poynters and deserved as much as he did to pass their lives untroubled.

But not perhaps all of them.

Something growled, a deep threatening rumble, and standing at a bend in the track about fifty feet ahead he saw a dog.

Johnny Nutbrown quite liked dogs. (Pippa didn't, so there were none at Poynters.) But this didn't look like the kind of dog you called *Hey boy!* to and ruffled its ears when it came running up to you, tail wagging. It stood quite still. What light there was under the tree glinted off its yellowing teeth and from its eyes that seemed to have a reddish glow as they focused unblinkingly on the approaching man.

He clicked the shotgun barrel into place.

The beast's ears pricked. It let out one last growl that had something of a promissory note in it, then turned and vanished.

Slowly, still holding the gun at the ready, he advanced round the bend.

And halted.

The dog was there, lying across the feet of a man sitting on the trunk of a fallen tree. If anything, with his scarred face and a patch over his right eye, he looked even more menacing than the dog. Alongside him, resting against the trunk, stood a long-handled axe.

The man spoke.

'When I was a lad, I got taught never to point a gun at anything I wasn't going to use it on.'

Nutbrown took a step closer and said, 'Good God, is that you, Wolf?'

'Who else? Been a long time, Johnny.'

'Too long, Wolf,' said Nutbrown fervently, lowering the gun. 'It's great to see you!'

Wolf Hadda laughed. He hadn't been sure what reaction to expect; certainly not this one, but, now he'd heard it, nothing else seemed possible. He shifted to make room beside him on the trunk. The dog growled as Nutbrown sat down, but ceased at a warning nudge from his master's foot.

'Been here long?' asked Nutbrown, resting his shotgun against the fallen tree. 'Jesus, you must be frozen! You should have come up to the house.'

'I don't think so, Johnny.'

Nutbrown considered then nodded.

'Probably right. Pippa's got a bit of a bee in her bonnet about you, I'm afraid.'

'Really? Now why should that be, do you think?'

'Well, she seems to think there could be some bad blood between us, after everything that happened, don't you know?'

'Everything that happened,' echoed Hadda. 'That's really what I came to talk to you about, Johnny. Everything that happened. I'd just like to understand it from your point of view, if you've got the time, that is.'

'Of course. Gent of leisure these days. But let's not freeze altogether. Try a nip of this.'

He produced a hip flask, opened it and passed it to Hadda. He took a long pull of the liquor, rolled it round in his mouth, then swallowed.

'Still nothing but the best, Johnny.'

'What else is there? Cheers!'

'Cheers. So, from the beginning, Johnny.'

Nutbrown took another drink as if, despite his apparent ease of manner, he needed a little booster for an imminent ordeal. Or perhaps, thought Hadda, it simply is against the cold.

'Well, it was all that money swilling around,' he began. 'Those were golden days, do you remember, Wolf? And you had the golden touch. It was like taking buckets of water out of a bottomless pond. An endless supply. Impossible to leave a hole!'

'So you helped yourself, is that what you're saying, Johnny?'

'No. Well, yes. But not really. You always saw to it that I had plenty, Wolf. But Toby and Pippa, they felt that you weren't making the most of your opportunities. A wise man fills his boots while he's still got boots to fill, that was how Toby put it. And Pippa agreed. Toby took care of the legal side and Pippa's always been a whiz with computers.'

'And you, Johnny?'

'They needed me to run the figures. Complex business keeping things in balance, you see. My sort of thing. I could hardly say no when Pippa and Toby asked. And they would have brought you in, Wolf, really they would. Only Toby said that, despite you marrying Imo and all, you still had this working-class thing about wealth, and it was best to keep you out for your own sake. Me, I thought it was a load of bollocks, I knew you were one of us from the start, but they insisted that it was best for us to make sure you got your share without you knowing.'

'And you went along with them?'

'All got a bit complicated for me, Wolf. Figures, fine. But forward planning, not my scene. Though, way back in 2006, I did get a feeling things were going pear-shaped.'

'You foresaw the financial crisis as far back as that?' said Hadda. 'Didn't you think it might be worth mentioning it to me?'

'I did, I did,' said Nutbrown indignantly. 'But you were always busy busy busy, Wolf. And when you did listen, you just laughed and said we were in happy-ever-after land, these were the sunny uplands, no one was ever going to drive us out of here. And I thought, Good old Wolf, it's down to him that I'm so comfortably placed, he always gets things right.'

Hadda regarded him sadly and asked, 'Did I really say that, Johnny? Yes, I believe I did. That's what I thought back then. Maybe you should have kept on at me. Punched me in the nose, maybe. You owed me one.'

Nutbrown laughed, a merry note, and said, 'Yes, I did, didn't I? Still do, I suppose.'

'No, Johnny,' said Hadda gently. 'Not any more. So who else did you try to warn?'

'Pippa, of course. Not a warning as such, just chat over the break-fast table. Ignored me at first. What's new? But once the US housing bubble began to burst, anyone with any sense could see what was coming.'

'Pity you weren't Chancellor,' said Hadda. 'And Pippa started listening?'

'Still told me not to be stupid. But this time she gave Toby a bell and he came round and asked me what it was all about.'

'And what did you tell him, Johnny?'

'I said I thought it might be a good idea to do a bit of forward planning. First thing was to make sure that our little nest eggs were tucked away safe. I made a few suggestions, but he really sat up and took notice when I told him that he ought to have a word with you because, when the markets hit the skids, it was going to be impossible to carry on hiding what we'd been doing. Like I say, a few bucketfuls from a big pond no one notices, but once the pond starts drying up . . .'

'I've got the picture,' said Hadda. 'But Toby didn't take your advice.'

'About placing our money, he did,' said Johnny. 'But as to putting you in the picture, he said he'd need to think about it.'

'I bet. And what was the result of his thinking?'

'No idea,' said Johnny cheerfully. 'I mentioned it to Pippa, but she just said it was in hand. Toby too. When I mentioned you, he said everything was hunky-dory. Finally things began to slowly unravel, just like I'd said. I thought, Good old Wolf will be taking care of things as far as Woodcutter's concerned. Next thing I hear is that they're doing you for looking at mucky pictures on your computer or something.'

'No, Johnny,' said Hadda gently. 'I think the next thing you heard was me on the phone asking you to meet me at The Widow.'

'That's right. Only I was in the office and there was this cop there and he sort of listened in. He asked me where The Widow was and I said, "Everyone knows The Widow!" And he said he didn't, so naturally I told him. Then I got up to leave, but he said I shouldn't bother, it was best for you if one of their chaps went there to meet you. I wasn't all that happy about it, you understand, Wolf. But what could I do?'

Hadda took the flask from Nutbrown's hand and took another long pull. It wasn't against the cold.

'And then?' he said softly.

'Next thing, you're in hospital, on life support, bulletins lousy. Not long after, the banks start going bellyside up, shares drop like a donkey's bollocks, and the Fraud Squad's crawling all over Woodcutter like bluebottles round an open dustbin.'

'And they found . . .?'

For the first time, Nutbrown was looking a little uneasy.

'They found shortfalls, Wolf. I mean, they were bound to. Would have been all right if the good times had continued. We were always well ahead of the game. Would be all right now with everything back to where it was, more or less. But back then there was nowhere to hide.'

'Yet somehow you managed it, Johnny. You hid so well no one even came looking for you. How did you manage that?'

'Just lucky, I suppose.'

He sounded as if he really believed it, thought Hadda. Perhaps he did. And perhaps in his own terms he was lucky. Lucky to exist in an impermeable bubble where thoughts of loyalty, morality, friendship could not penetrate and in which the only reality was his own well being, comfort and survival. He felt no guilt about what had happened, just a touch of regret. While the news of his early release had clearly caused the others considerable disquiet,

Johnny's reaction was mild relief that his old friend was free again so no need to worry about that any more!

'But you and Toby must have got your story all neatly prepared,' he said.

Nutbrown nodded emphatically as he replied, 'Oh yes. Toby was marvellous. Had them eating out of his hands. Don't know what I'd have done without him beside me.'

'What a pity I didn't have him beside me as well,' said Hadda. 'When they piled all that shit on top of me, I mean.'

'What? Look, Wolf, I can see how it must look to you. But be fair, by then you were as good as dead, no point in trying to protect your good name, impossible to do that anyway without getting Toby sent down for yonks. Pippa too, maybe. Wouldn't have wanted to see Pippa in jail, would you? No allowances made for women these days!'

This attempt to appeal to his sense of chivalry almost brought a smile to Hadda's lips. He noted also that Nutbrown didn't offer as argument the certainty that he would have been sent down too. Could he really believe he was in some way invulnerable?

He said, 'You didn't say any of this when you came to see me, Johnny. You could see I was alive and breathing then. You had a chance to protect this good name of mine you were so worried about.'

'Not true,' said Nutbrown eagerly. 'Not with that other business hanging over you, and all the papers saying they'd got you bang to rights over that. Besides, everything was signed, sealed and delivered by then. Statements on tape, in writing, even video. And the books had been gone over with a fine-tooth comb, all done and dusted. Too late to turn back the clock, Wolf. Like Toby said, you were a cooked goose. But I did come to see you, didn't I? I really got a bollocking from Pippa when she found out. Toby wasn't best pleased either. But I told them, I owed you a lot, couldn't have lived with myself if I hadn't paid a visit.'

Just when you thought you'd reached the limits of Nutbrown's moral vacuity, you found you were still floating in space!

He said, 'Don't think I'm not grateful, Johnny. So, do you see much of Imo? How's she doing?'

'Oh, fine, fine,' said Johnny, relief at the change of subject manifest on his face. 'Don't see a lot of her, to tell the truth. Pippa and her have a girls' lunch from time to time. She always sends her love.'

'To you, you mean?'

'Well, yes . . . I mean she'd hardly send it to . . . oh, you're having a joke. Ha ha.'

'If you can't take a laugh, you shouldn't have joined, eh, Johnny? As a matter of interest, how much did Imo know about your special financial arrangements at Woodcutter before the tide went out and left all the shit visible on the shore?'

He spoke as casually as he could but a more perceptive man might have noticed the tension in his voice.

'Nothing, not at all, you've nothing to worry about there, Wolf,' said Nutbrown reassuringly. 'No, she wasn't in on any of that. But once we started looking for a way round things, then she had to be told, of course.'

'Why was that?' asked Hadda.

'Look, there was trouble coming, I could see that a long way off. Like I said, I had a hard time convincing Toby and Pippa; they're great at managing things, but when it comes to economics . . .'

He smiled tolerantly. To survive, everyone needs a viewpoint from which they can look down on everyone else, thought Hadda. With some it's intellect, with some it's beauty, with some it's religion.

What is it with me?

Vengeance, came the uncomfortable answer.

'I'm not quite sure I understand,' he said. 'Why Imo had to be told, I mean.'

'If you'd grown up around her like the rest of us did, you'd know,' said Johnny. 'Any plans we made, if Imo was for them, they worked; if she wasn't interested, they might limp along; but if she was against them, then you were in real shit.'

401

'So you invited my wife to join in the plot to offload all the blame on to me, right?'

'No, Wolf, it wasn't as simple as that,' said Nutbrown, eager to explain. 'I mean, it wasn't as if you weren't going to be right at the front when the shit hit the fan, was it?'

'I'm sorry?' said Hadda, not believing what he was hearing.

'Well, you were the man in charge, weren't you? Woodcutter was your baby. No way was anyone going to believe you didn't know what was going on. I remember thinking to myself, surely Wolf's got to notice what we're doing!'

There was a note of reproach in his voice. Don't let yourself be provoked! thought Wolf.

Perhaps he even had a point!

'Maybe because I trusted my friends just a little too much,' he said.

'Well, yes, there was that,' said Nutbrown, sounding a little uncomfortable but not too much. 'So look at it from our point of view, Wolf. You were going to get it in the neck anyway, you were the boss man, you were responsible. There didn't seem to be any point in the rest of us catching it too.'

'And Imo agreed with this?'

'Oh yes. After Toby and Pippa explained it to her.'

'You weren't there?'

'No. Didn't seem any point in crowding her.'

'Very considerate,' said Hadda. 'Did you get the impression she took a lot of persuading?'

'Not really. Not once she understood about the money.'

'Which money?'

'The money we'd put aside,' said Johnny patiently, as if explaining to a child. 'The point was, once the dropping markets left us exposed, Woodcutter was dead in the water. You were going to be the Fraud Squad's main man. All your assets would be seized and ultimately disposed of. The only money from the business that would survive were the funds that Toby and me had diverted.'

He said it as if expecting congratulation.

'And if the investigation had you and Toby in their sights, they

402

wouldn't rest till they got a line on that,' said Hadda slowly. 'And even if they couldn't, they'd make sure it was a hell of a long time before you could hope to enjoy it.'

'That's right. So you see, it was a no-brainer for Imo. Whatever happened, you were going down. At least if we stayed out of the frame, she wouldn't be destitute.'

'How much did she ask for?'

'Half. I think Pippa wanted to haggle, but Toby said there was no point.'

He was right, thought Hadda bitterly. They were lucky she left them anything.

And anyway, Toby was probably already mapping out the future. Mastermind the divorce first, then marry her. But if he thought that was going to regain him full access to his ill-gotten gains, he clearly didn't know her as well as he thought!

Unlike himself, who clearly didn't know her at all.

Or perhaps he knew her all too well but had never systematized his knowledge.

She had set him three goals as the price of her hand. A fortune, an education, a social polish. He'd gone away a poor ignorant clod and he'd come back, if not yet a wealthy civilized gent, certainly a piece of malleable clay she could mould into shape.

She'd kept her side of the bargain, more or less. And now she was told that he was reneging on his. Didn't matter that losing his wealth wasn't his fault, obtaining it had been part of the contract.

Was that all their marriage had ever amounted to? It hadn't felt like that. But what had it felt like?

It certainly hadn't felt like she was shagging away behind his back. Yet from the sound of it . . .

He said, 'So things fell out all right for her all round, didn't they? I mean, her and Toby getting together like they did. Things going well there, are they?'

'Seem to be,' said Nutbrown. 'They have their ups and downs, I expect. Don't we all? And you know Toby, he likes his office comforts. Pippa says she'd cut his balls off, but it doesn't seem to bother Imo. Of course, they've known each other a long time.'

'That's true. You were all chums together long before I came on the scene. So how long had they been at it, would you say?'

This time enough of his feelings came through to pierce even the Nutbrown carapace of insensibility.

'Come on, Wolf, no point dwelling on the past, all water under the bridge, eh?'

'Of course it is. Still, just as a point of interest, how long would you say?'

'I don't know. I suppose, off and on for as long as I've known them. Never meant anything, they'd been chums for ever, it was the same for all of us . . .'

All of us! Had they all been at it? Trying each other out, exchanging notes . . .

Don't go down that road. Not now.

'Of course it was. So whenever any two of you met, if you had time on your hands you'd jump over the hedge for a quick one, right? Perfectly understandable behaviour. Among pack rats!'

The snarl in which he uttered the last phrase got Nutbrown to his feet. At the sudden movement, the dog rose too, its teeth bared.

'Easy, Wolf. Don't lose your rag. I remember what you can be like. Don't want another bloody nose, eh?'

Hadda took a deep breath and even managed a smile as he stood up also.

'Don't worry, Johnny,' he said. 'I'm a changed man. We all are, aren't we? *Tempus fugit.* The past's dead, it's the future that matters.'

'You don't know how happy I am to hear you say that, Wolf,' said Nutbrown, looking genuinely relieved. 'Not that I had any doubt. I tried to tell the other two, there's nothing to worry about, let's just be glad Wolf's out of that dreadful place. Look, why don't you come back with me now, see Pippa, let her know that all this business about selling up and leaving the country's just a load of nonsense?'

'Very tempting,' said Hadda. 'But not today. Don't worry, I'll make sure that things are put right between me and Pippa some time very soon, OK? But maybe for the time being it's best not to mention you've met me. Let's pick our moment carefully.'

'If that's what you think best, Wolf,' said Johnny. 'Only, I was hoping it might put the kybosh on this sale thing. It's pretty near being all signed and sealed, you know.'

Wolf smiled and said, 'I shouldn't be too concerned about that, Johnny. I've got a feeling that your sale's going to fall through, and you'll be able to relax and enjoy Poynters and everything that's in it for a little time yet.'

'You think so? That would be great.'

His face lit up with a child's joy at the promise of a treat. The sight of it filled Hadda with a great sadness. He had come to see Nutbrown because the man had come to see him, and he felt he owed him a hearing. McLucky and the Trapps all told him it was pointless, but he'd insisted, even though he knew what he would find: a child in a man's body, a child whose responses were all based on his own immediate needs and appetites.

A child's punishments should be different from a man's. Or maybe a child's punishments always felt different.

'For you, Johnny, it will be like being sent to bed without any supper,' he murmured, half to himself.

'Sorry?'

'Nothing,' said Hadda. 'Here, don't forget your gun.'

He stooped to retrieve the weapon.

'Nice piece of kit. Nothing but the best, eh?'

He raised it to his shoulder, pointed it at Nutbrown, who stepped back in alarm.

Then he saw that Hadda was sighting down the barrel at him with his patched eye.

'Can't see a damn thing!' Wolf laughed. 'Catch!'

He threw the gun to Nutbrown, picked up his axe easily with one hand, slung it across his shoulder, then turned and limped slowly away, not looking back. But the dog who followed at his heels gave many a backward glance.

405

9

On his way home on Wednesday night, George Proctor knew he was being followed, and he knew who by, and he had a strong suspicion why.

Ahead was a long lay-by, usually packed with lorries there to enjoy the gourmet cuisine offered by The Even Fatter Duck, a mobile catering van that reputedly served the best bacon butties in Essex. But the Duck was long flown on this gloomy winter's evening and the lay-by was empty.

Proctor signalled and pulled in, not stopping till he was almost at the far end. In his mirror he saw the grey Fiesta come to a halt just inside the entrance. He got out of his car and waved imperiously.

After a moment, the Fiesta began to move slowly forward. He made a violent denying motion with his hand, and when the Fiesta stopped again, he jabbed his forefinger towards it two or three times then used the same finger to beckon.

Alva Ozigbo got the message.

She slid out of her car and advanced to meet the Chief Officer.

'What do you want, miss?' asked Proctor.

His breath hung visible in the freezing air. A cartoonist could have written his words upon it.

'I want to talk, George. Privately.'

Her breath balloon rose and merged with his.

'You could have come to my office, miss.'

'Oh, I did, George, remember? Three times I looked in on you this week.'

'And?'

'You wouldn't switch the radio on. In fact, once you switched it off.'

He looked at her frowningly for a moment then his face relaxed into a smile.

'Could tell from the start you was a sharp one, miss. And I tell you, you need to be sharp to survive at Parkleigh.'

'So why didn't you want to have another little confidential chat with me, George?'

'Because I didn't see no point. Anyway, we're talking now, so say what you want to say before we catch pneumonia.'

'We could talk in my car. Or yours.'

'Might be OK. Probably is. But better safe than sorry, eh? So?'

This really shocked her. But even hard-headed men could get bees in their bonnet.

'OK I'll be quick. I get the impression that whatever is said in Parkleigh is overheard.'

'Yeah?'

'And I think you've got that impression too.'

'Maybe.'

'And I think that maybe that was why my predecessor and the Director were having that row you told me about.'

'Could be.'

'For God's sake, George,' Alva said in exasperation. 'Are you going to keep this up till we freeze to death? I'm talking to you because the alternative is to go along and confront Mr Homewood.'

'I shouldn't do that, miss,' said Proctor, alarmed.

'Why not?'

He regarded her dubiously, then shrugged like a man who has counted the alternatives and found none.

'Look,' he said, 'I don't know nothing except that over a long period I started getting this feeling when I was talking with the

407

Director that occasionally he knew stuff before I told him, or sometimes he knew stuff I hadn't told him! I did a couple of little tests
and I wasn't happy to find out I was right. It's my guess that when
they refurbished Parkleigh, they fitted it up with a wall-to-wall
bugging system. Total non-privacy. Everything anyone says
anywhere gets heard. So I keep my radio turned up in my office.
Or I step outside the main gate when I fancy a bit of privacy.'

This is what Alva had asked for, this is what she'd expected. But
this blunt confirmation that her suspicions were shared still came
as a shock.

'But why?' she demanded, though she could guess the answer.

'Look at who they've got banged up there. Politicals, terrorists,
mega fraudsters, serial killers. Hearing what any of that lot have
got to say to their lawyers, their visitors, on the phone, in the yard,
anywhere, everywhere – just think how useful that could be. Stick
people in Parkleigh, everyone thinks it's like throwing them into
an old-fashioned dungeon. But it's really like putting them into the
most advanced listening post in the country!'

'You've obviously thought a lot about this, George. But you've
never said anything, I take it?'

'Me? No way! I'm not so green as cabbage looking as my old
gran used to say.'

'But you talked to me. A bit obliquely, I admit. But you talked.
Why was that?'

Proctor slapped his arms around his body to drive out the cold
and said, 'Getting soft in my old age, maybe. I just got the impression watching you dealing with Mr Homewood that you'd gone off
him a bit. Compared with how you started. Can't put my finger
on it, just sometimes talking to him you were coming over a bit
hesitant, like you didn't altogether trust him. And him with you
too. And the only reason I could think why was you'd got a hint
he knew things he didn't ought to, personal confidential stuff you
hear in your tits-a-tits.'

Which she had. But not till very recently.

Alva thought she could see what had happened. Her concern at picking up signals that Homewood was developing the hots for her had caused her to introduce a measure of circumspection into her dealings with him. But eagle-eyed Chief Officer Proctor, his sensors honed by a lifetime of dealing with violent men whose mood swings could be a matter of life or death, had detected something. Detected and misinterpreted.

What was especially worrying was that this hard-headed, down-to-earth, long-serving prison officer preferred to stand out here in the freezing air rather than take the risk of talking in his own car. Or hers, for that matter. A bad case of paranoia? She looked at the man standing before her and wished she could think it so.

She said, 'When you say you think the Director's attitude to me changed too, what do you mean?'

'Little things again. Thought he started being a bit more abrupt with you.'

Meaning he'd spotted as she had that Homewood, fighting against the attraction he felt to her, started over-emphasizing that she was just another member of staff.

But Proctor hadn't finished.

'And he was always asking how you were getting on, saying he hoped I was making sure that no obstacles got in your way, like he was concerned to give you a chance to do well. But I sometimes felt like I was being asked to spy on you. Then on Monday . . .'

He hesitated. Alva pressed.

'What happened, George?'

'He called me in and gave me a spiel about having to compile some kind of report on you for the Home Office by the end of the month.'

'That in fact is true, George,' she interrupted. 'More or less. My contract doesn't come up for renewal for another two years but there is this annual review written into it. Just a matter of ticking off the boxes.'

'Yeah? Well, it didn't sound to me like the Director was thinking about just ticking boxes,' said Proctor. 'He asked straight out how

I thought you were doing. Never asked me that before. What kind of effect did I think you were having on the prisoners' morale? Had it been a mistake to bring a female in? Hello, I thought, what's brought this on?'

'And you said?'

'I said I know I'd been against appointing you at the start, but now I'd had time to get to know you and see the way you worked, I thought you were doing a good job.'

This was the best unsolicited testimonial she'd ever had, thought Alva.

She said, 'Thanks, George.'

'Don't bother. I got to thinking later maybe I'd done you no favours.'

'I'm sorry?'

'Maybe if they just ease you out gently, unsuitable job for a woman, that sort of thing, no harm done to you professionally, or not much, everyone happy, that would be for the best.'

'So that was why you didn't want another confidential chat with me!' she said indignantly. 'You really don't want me around the place after all! Why didn't you just badmouth me to the Director in the first place?'

'Wasn't thinking, miss. But if he asks me again, I'll be ready.'

Her mind was whirling in search of a viewpoint that would bring all this into perspective.

There was no doubt that a negative report from Homewood, even unsupported by a thumbs-down from Proctor, could put her job in jeopardy. But why would he want to do that? And why should Proctor be so ready to shift his position from a reluctant recognition that she might be doing a decent job to reverting to his original attitude and wanting her out? It made no sense . . .

Unless the man was thinking there were worse ways to go than getting the sack!

But that was absurd! Wasn't it?

She said, 'You said way back when we talked in your room that my predecessor had a big row with the Director. Was that about these listening devices?'

'That's right, miss. Dr Ruskin had worked it out like you. Must be something in your training, I suppose. Makes you spot things. But he wasn't like you in most other ways. You're the calm rational sort. Dr Ruskin saw something he didn't like, he really let you know. I heard him screaming at the Director that it breached all medical ethics, it was an outrage and he reckoned it was his duty to let the whole country know how their hard-earned money was being spent.'

'And then he died. And I became his replacement. A bit of a shock for you, I seem to recall, George.'

'Maybe, at first, but when I came to think of it . . .' he tailed off.

'What?'

'Look, miss, don't be offended. At first I thought, bloody political correctness and all that garbage. Appoint a young woman and if she happens to be black, that's even better. But later I got to thinking . . .'

'What did you get to thinking, George?'

'I got to thinking if they'd just got shot of a shrink who turned out to be a trouble maker and hard to control, well, they wouldn't want another one of the same, would they?'

This was getting worse!

'You mean, they wouldn't want another independently minded, experienced, middle-aged man, they'd much prefer a young, inexperienced girl who'd be frightened to make waves, and would more likely to get blamed than listened to if she did.'

Proctor looked rather sheepish.

'Yeah, that's about it, miss. But when I started to see they'd picked wrong, that was when I got worried.'

'Because you felt I might end up having an accident like Ruskin?'

He looked alarmed and shook his head vigorously.

'Don't put words into my mouth, miss. I'm not saying for one moment there was a connection between him handing in his notice and what happened. I mean, the state of mind he was in, he was an accident ready to happen. But when I started worrying you were going down the same road . . .'

411

He stopped, as if fearful he might be straying into some unmasculine area like compassion. Or maybe the black humour of his metaphor had just occurred to him.

Alva stepped in.

'And this week, after thinking about it, you came to the conclusion that maybe the simplest thing would be to go along with seeing me edged out as not up to the job, an experiment that failed? Make your life a lot easier, would it?'

The bitterness she was feeling wasn't directed at him, but she couldn't keep it out of her voice.

He said stolidly, 'That's right, miss. Pure self-interest. Seeing you on your way, safe and free, that would suit me down to the ground. Thing is, I know accidents happen, we've all got to live with that. But an accident happens twice and I'd have to speak up. Don't know what good it would do, but I'm pretty sure it would be the end of my career. I'll say good night, miss.'

He turned away and started to walk back to his car.

Suddenly Alva felt ashamed of herself.

She called after him, 'George!'

He halted and looked back.

'Yes, miss?'

'I'm sorry. I've no right to say anything to you except thanks. You've acted like a friend. I'll not forget that. But I won't mention it, not unless they use the thumbscrews.'

That brought a smile.

'I reckon they'd need to screw them down real tight to make you talk, miss. You take care now.'

Alva watched him get into his car and drive away.

We probably disagree on most of the major political and social issues of the day, she thought. But there goes a truly moral man!

Whereas Homewood, with whom she'd have said she was in almost perfect philosophical agreement, and John Childs whom she'd come to respect and admire, these two had vetted her, not because she represented a new generation of psychiatrist, young, vital, open-minded, forward-looking, but because she was a novice,

412

easy to influence and divert, easy too to dispose of, if push came to shove . . .

Something in her demeanour at Childs's house must have warned him that she was starting to ask questions. He'd know about her special interest in Hadda from Homewood and perhaps she'd left some evidence that she'd found the photo. At the very least her prevarications when he made enquiry about the urgent matter she wanted to discuss with him must have rung false. She'd tried to pretend it was all about the danger of Homewood making an open pass at her now that his marriage was in trouble, and the problem this might cause in their working relationship. Treating him like a Lonely Hearts consultant! Jesus!

A chat with Homewood had probably confirmed his unease. Maybe Childs's queries had prompted the Director to realize he might have revealed a greater knowledge of her dealings with Hadda than he should have had.

Whatever, the very next day Homewood had started making enquiries about her job performance. He must have got a shock when Proctor hadn't given her an emphatic thumbs-down! At least it appeared they felt they could deal with the situation by terminating her contract rather than her life . . .

She pulled herself up short.

Without concrete evidence, she couldn't just make the leap from accepting Joe Ruskin's death as tragic accident to believing it was murder!

What kind of people were capable of treating human life so casually?

And in what capacity had Childs employed the young Hadda, *the woodcutter*?

I'm not cut out to be a PI! she told herself.

In fact she was beginning to wonder if she was really cut out to be a psychiatrist. She suddenly felt weary of being the seeker after hidden truths, the recipient of shadowy and sometimes shameful secrets. How much better if she'd followed in her mother's footsteps, exploring only fictional characters and wiping off their traumas with the greasepaint. Or her father's, getting your hands bloody from time to time but washing it off at the end of the day.

Suddenly she found herself fantasizing about life without Parkleigh. Walking away from the prison without looking back. Taking a long break with her family, then looking for some cosy teaching job in a university somewhere a long way from England, somewhere that they had real summers for a start!

But she wasn't going to turn her back on Wolf Hadda. She didn't know what he was planning but, whatever it was, one way or another she was involved in it.

She went back to her car. She'd left the engine running and the heater was full on.

Eventually she stopped shivering but as she drove away she felt that deep inside her being there was a coldness no amount of hot air could reach.

10

The following morning Simon Homewood called Alva into his office.

There was a severe-looking young woman there with a notepad. She wasn't the Director's regular secretary and Alva looked at her queryingly.

'This is Miss Leslie from the Home Office,' said Homewood. 'She'll be keeping a minute of our meeting.'

'That sounds ominous,' murmured Alva.

'Just bureaucracy,' said Homewood with an attempt at lightness. 'As you know, Dr Ozigbo, like everyone else on contract, your work is subject to an annual review process, and yours is due this month.'

'Yes, I know. The review happened last year too, but I don't recall this rigmarole.'

'No? Well, procedures are constantly updated, particularly in sensitive areas. So let's start, shall we?'

For the next half hour she was subjected to a barrage of questions about her work. Their tone was unremittingly polite but their unmistakable aim was to get her to admit to problems and confess difficulties. She fielded them with some ease but also with growing irritation. If they were trying to get her out, they would have to do a lot better than this!

Finally Homewood glanced at his watch and said, 'Let's take a break. Miss Leslie, perhaps you could have a word with my secretary and see if you can rustle up some coffee and a few choc biscuits to keep up our energy level.'

Miss Leslie did not look like the kind of woman who included waitressing in her job description but she rose without demur and left the room.

This is part of the game, thought Alva. In fact, this is probably where the game really starts.

She was right. But she was unprepared for just how brutal a game it was.

Homewood said, 'Alva, this is difficult, but I think we know each other well enough to be frank. Yours was always a somewhat controversial appointment and the opposition never really went away. I've always fought your corner, of course, and I'll continue to give you my full support. But sometimes in public life one has to box clever. A wise man picks his battles and only picks those he knows he can win.'

He paused. Alva had been listening with growing concern. This parade of clichés was, if anything, a greater insult to her intelligence than the unsubtle line of the official questioning. But Homewood was no fool and he was speaking with the quiet confidence of one who is certain of winning an argument.

She said, 'That may be what a wise man does. But I fight my own battles, Simon. And you ought to know, win, lose, I'll be fighting this one to the bitter end!'

She spoke with a confidence she no longer felt.

He said, 'I understand. I would expect no less. But there is something else you should know.'

She was experiencing once more the bone-deep chill that her conversation with Proctor had left her with the previous night. Now they were getting to it, the clinching argument, or threat, or bribe that would confirm her suspicions.

He had paused as if inviting her to prompt him with a question.

She kept silent and forced him to speak.

He said, 'Somehow one of the people who opposed your appointment has picked up a rumour about you and Hadda. An inappropriate relationship.'

'What?'

He gave her a reassuring smile.

416

'It's all right, I know it's absurd. But you did visit him in Cumbria. And spent the night at his house, too, I believe. I've told them I have no problem with that, perfectly understandable in the circumstances, but these things tend to develop a momentum of their own unless halted at the start . . .'

'Then let's halt it!' she exploded. 'This is outrageous. Who's saying this? Let me meet them face to face . . .'

'I don't think that would help,' said Homewood smoothly. 'In fact, it might be provocative. Look, the point I'm making is that nobody is using this ridiculous allegation as a reason for terminating your contract. Not yet, anyway. But look at it from the opposition's point of view. Your annual review provides an opportunity for you to withdraw with honour and dignity and professional reputation intact. But if this opportunity isn't taken, who can say what kind of allegations might fly around? You see where it might go? An improper relationship between a prisoner and the psychiatrist who is then almost single-handedly responsible for persuading the parole hearing to turn him loose . . . Everything would be cast in doubt. At the very least there would have to be a full-scale enquiry. God knows how long that might drag on – I'm sure you wouldn't take it lying down . . .'

'Of course I wouldn't!' she exclaimed. 'I'd fight it through every court in the land!'

'I'd expect no less. And you'd have my full support. But . . .'

She'd been fighting to control her feelings of outrage. That *but* did the job for her. Again she had a sense that, like the questions and the clichés, this was still a preliminary to the main event.

Now she was impatient to get to it and she gave him his prompt.

'But what?' she snapped.

'But,' he went on quietly, 'obviously, in view of the nature of the allegation, Hadda's parole would have to be revoked and until the enquiry, however prolonged, had reached its conclusion, he would be returned to custody.'

She opened her mouth to cry, 'But he is innocent.' And shut it.

The bastard was smiling at her sympathetically. He understood her dilemma. Any opposition she offered to the move to oust her was going to result in the revoking of Hadda's parole. And any protestations she made now of Hadda's innocence were just going to sound like confirmation of the improper relationship!

Homewood said urgently, 'Alva, the world of national security is a murkier place than even a criminal psychiatrist can know. Sometimes grim necessity overrides everything else: laws, loyalties, morality. I am your friend. I would have liked, as you know, to be more than your friend. That, I suspect, is going to be impossible now. But I hope something of our friendship can survive. And as a friend I say to you, there is no shame in moving on from this job. The pressures here are huge. And the external pressures you have been experiencing from your family situation can only have added to them. Spend some quality time with your father. Professionally the world is your oyster. And I promise you that any testimonial from me will do nothing but sing your praises. Now, shall we have our coffee and then get back to your review?'

Alva didn't reply. It was hard for a psychiatrist to admit it, but sometimes words are inadequate, only a blow will do.

After a couple of moments Miss Leslie returned with the coffee tray.

Has the bitch been listening? she wondered.

She realized she didn't care.

For suddenly her anger was swept away by a huge surge of euphoria! It took only a few seconds to identify its source.

Without any effort on her part she was going to get what nearly every inmate of Parkleigh dreamt of, what she herself had fantasized about the previous night – release! This place with all its restraints, its fears, its secrets, its sounds, its smells, its monstrous looming presence, would be behind her. She knew she would take some of it with her, in fact she wanted to take some of it with her. But where it mattered, in her power of decision, her freedom of choice, she would be her own mistress again.

She gulped down her coffee, smiled sweetly at Homewood, and said, 'Let's get to it.'

BOOK FIVE

a shocking light

...*then it befell that as they drew near safety, in the night's most secret hour, some hand in an upper chamber lit a shocking light, lit it and made no sound.*

For a moment it might have been an ordinary light, fatal as even that could very well be at such a moment as this; but when it began to follow them like an eye and to grow redder and redder as it watched them, then even optimism despaired.

And Sippy very unwisely attempted flight, and Slorg even as unwisely tried to hide . . .

Lord Dunsany: *Probable Adventure of the Three Literary Men*

1

There had been snow off and on all through January, with particularly heavy falls in the east. At the end of the month, day temperatures began to rise and soon the wind-planed drifts that had turned the gardens of Poynters into a surreal sculpture park began to thaw to a grubby slush. The landscape that for so many weeks had something other-worldly about it now had the look of a tract of no-man's land in some wintry war.

For some reason Johnny Nutbrown associated this deterioration with Wolf Hadda's visit. His sense of euphoria after the encounter had been reinforced the following day when Pippa had taken a call from their solicitor.

Johnny was still in bed when he heard her scream of rage from below.

'Bad news, dear?' he asked unnecessarily when she erupted into the bedroom.

'That Scotch git, he's backed out of the sale!' she yelled. 'Family problems. If I could get my hands on the bastard, I'd fix it so he never had any family problems again!'

Inside, Johnny was jubilant. Good old Wolf, he'd called it right. You could always rely on Wolf.

But he took great care not to let any of this show on his face.

He had resolved not to tell Pippa anything about his meeting with Wolf, but in the end, as she went on and on about the failed

421

sale as if it were the end of the world, he decided that describing the encounter with the stress on how well it had gone, how unthreatening Wolf had been, might reassure her.

He rapidly saw how wrong he had been.

'He was here? He was in our garden? Oh Jesus wept, you had your gun, why didn't you just shoot the bastard?'

'Steady on,' he said. 'Can't go around shooting people, even if I wanted to. Look, love, he was fine. And if he's fine, everything's fine, no need for us to sell up and head off into the sunset as if we had Interpol on our heels and we were running for our lives!'

She shook her head and said with an intensity that was worse than her screaming, 'You fucking moron. Can't you get it into your stupid head that's exactly what we're doing, and it's something a fucking sight worse than Interpol we're running from!'

After that she'd redoubled her efforts to sell the house, at the same time fixing a definite date early in spring for their move to the States, whether the house were sold or not.

As the days went by and the snow began to melt, Nutbrown found that his euphoria began to melt too. His wife's will had always been stronger than his. He'd been happy to accept this and come to regard it as a kind of protective barrier against the world's ills. Now at last he began to appreciate that if even her strength sank in face of this unspecified threat, perhaps there was something out there he ought to be afraid of too. Like a man who has never been ill, he found it hard to understand the meaning of the early symptoms of the potentially fatal disease that has infected him. Eventually, slowly, he came to recognize that for the first time in seven years he was feeling prickings of guilt at the way he'd treated his former boss and colleague and friend. Now the eight hours of untroubled sleep he'd enjoyed all his life started to decay like the snow. He awoke in the dark at one, two, or three o'clock in the morning, and that was the end of his night's rest. Fearful of waking Pippa if he lay there, tossing and turning, he took to slipping out of bed and going down to the kitchen to make a cup of tea laced with brandy and would sit there, thinking about things, till the dawn.

The closed book of the past now opened to him, not as a continuous narrative, but in disconnected fragments that were sometimes identifiable as his own memories, but frequently seemed to belong to someone else. One scene that played itself again and again was of Wolf being woken by the arrival of the police that autumn dawn all those years ago and being dragged from the home he was never to enter again.

So when one dark morning early in February he heard the ringing of a doorbell accompanied by a thunderous knocking, he sat some moments longer at the kitchen table, trying to work out whether the noise originated at his own front door or in his mind.

It was the sound of Pippa yelling his name from upstairs and demanding to know where the hell he was that put the disturbance firmly in the here and now.

He stood up and went to the front door and opened it.

He was just in time. There was a large uniformed police officer standing there wielding one of those battering rams Johnny had seen on the telly. He looked disappointed at being deprived of the chance to use it.

A man in plainclothes edged him aside. He held a warrant card and some printed papers before Johnny's eyes.

'DI O'Reilly,' he said. 'Mr Nutbrown, is it?'

'Yes?'

'I have a warrant to search these premises, Mr Nutbrown. Right, lads.'

He stepped into the hallway, not quite pushing but certainly edging Johnny aside.

Behind him came at least a dozen others, some in uniform, some in plainclothes. Slushy snow slid off their shoes on to the floor. Pippa's not going to like that, thought Johnny.

He was right. She came down the stairs like St Michael descending on the dragon. Perhaps if she'd started demanding explanations or questioning the legality of the warrant, DI O'Reilly would have been able to put up stronger resistance. But her focus was entirely on the state of the invaders' footwear.

423

Within half a minute she had them all out of the hall and queuing up to wipe their feet on the rug at the entrance before they came back in.

Only then did she take the warrant from the DI's hand and study it carefully.

When she'd finished reading it she said to her husband, 'You'd better ring Toby.'

He said, puzzled, 'Bit early, isn't it, old girl? He's probably not up. Anyway, not sure if Toby's going to be much use here.'

She let out a snort of fury and exasperation.

'For God's sake, Johnny! Don't you understand anything?' she said, and went to the phone herself.

For once she was wrong. It wasn't just Johnny's usual disconnection from reality that was at work here.

He couldn't have given her chapter and verse on how he understood it, but understand it he did: today something was ending, and something was starting, something that not even the cleverest of solicitors was going to be able to put right, something that meant nothing was ever going to be the same again.

2

Toby Estover mounted the scaffold unhesitatingly, not because he was brave but because his legs moved independently of his mind, which was screaming, *Run! Run for your life!*

Waiting by the block with his back to him was the executioner. His right hand, which had only two fingers, was resting lightly on the shaft of his long-handled axe and he was gazing out across a wide panorama of mountains and lakes and virgin forest that somehow looked familiar.

Through his terror, Estover felt a pang of indignation. Surely his imminent execution was more important than admiring the fucking view! But he couldn't get any words out, his mouth was totally preoccupied with trying to suck into his lungs all the air that should have been his over the next forty years, all the air that should have been anybody's, all the fucking air in the earth's atmosphere, fuck everybody else, fuck global warming, fuck every fucking thing!

When his legs reached the block, they came to a halt and his knees folded and he knelt. Then his back muscles dissolved and he fell forward, prone, his Adam's apple pressing against the nadir of the block's shallow dark-stained U.

Out of the corner of his eye he saw the executioner's feet turn, he saw the shining blade rise out of sight, he saw the mountains and the lakes and the forest.

Then he heard the *whoosh!* as the blade came sweeping down.

And as he died, he woke up and was surprised to find that all the sheets and pillow were soaked with was sweat, not blood.

Two other things he eventually registered.

He was alone and the telephone was ringing.

He was not surprised to find he was alone. After a fortnight he was getting used to it.

He'd come to bed one night to find that Imogen had moved all her stuff into another bedroom, the room that had once belonged to her daughter.

The move had coincided with his announcement that he had got a new secretary, but he couldn't believe it had anything to do with this. For seven years she had seemed happy to share the large master bedroom, despite the fact that their moments of sexual intimacy had become increasingly rare. This had been due to a combination of her growing indifference and his own health problems which meant that a regular desktop servicing in the office was more than enough to satisfy his sensual needs.

There had been no warning of the move, no dispute, no debate. He guessed something had happened during her stay in Cumbria. What, he couldn't guess, and he knew there was no point in asking. This was the way that Imogen worked. No drama attended her decisions, just a quiet inevitability. He'd barged into her new bedroom one morning and found her sitting on the bed, holding a rag doll that had been a favourite of Ginny's. She wasn't clutching it to her but holding it out before her and staring at it, as if she hoped it might start talking. She didn't even glance his way and after a moment he'd left. He hadn't entered the room since.

The phone stopped. Either it had rung long enough to switch over to the answer machine, or someone had answered it.

He rolled out of bed and headed for the bathroom.

Fifteen minutes later, showered and wrapped in a monogrammed towelling robe that Imogen said looked as if it had been stolen from a particularly pretentious hotel, he headed downstairs in search of breakfast.

Imogen was standing on the half-landing looking out of the

window. She had a cup of coffee in her hand and was completely naked. He was reminded of the night that bastard Hadda had chopped down the tree.

'Morning,' he said. 'What are you looking at?'

'I think it's sending out shoots,' she said.

He stood beside her.

Out in the garden in the still dim dawn light they could just make out the stump of the rowan.

After it had been chopped down, Estover had arranged for the trunk and brash to be cleared away, but Imogen had refused to let him have the stump dug out of the lawn.

'They are great survivors, rowans,' she said. 'They need to be. They cling on in places other trees would only be seen dead in. I've seen them growing out of north-facing rock faces at two thousand feet.'

'Maybe,' he said. 'But whatever it does, in our lifetime it will just be an eyesore!'

'It will still be alive,' she said. 'Wolf planted it to shelter us from evil.'

'Yeah? Well the bastard should have done the job properly when he chopped it down and dug up the roots too!' he said. 'Did you get the phone?'

'Yes.'

'Well? If you want to make me very happy, tell me it was a wrong number.'

She looked as if she might be considering the proposition, then said, 'It was Pippa.'

'Pippa? What the hell did she want at seven o'clock on a cold February morning?'

'She says they've got a houseful of policemen with a search warrant.'

'You're joking, I hope?'

She shook her head slightly.

'Jesus! What are they looking for?'

'Who knows? Pippa says she doesn't. She wants some legal advice, I think.'

427

'What did you say to her?'

'I said that you never gave legal advice till you'd had your breakfast. I suggested she should await the outcome of the search. Either nothing would be found and she'd be able to ring you to ask how to register a formal complaint. Or if they discovered Lord Lucan hiding in the cellar, they would no doubt transport Johnny and herself to some police station where you would join them as soon as you heard where it was.'

'Good girl,' he said. 'That's worth five hundred quid of anyone's money. Any more of that coffee downstairs?'

'I'm sure there will be. I've roused Mrs Roper to tell her you'll be breakfasting early as you may be driving to Cambridge pretty soon.'

'Cambridge?'

'That's probably where they'll take Pippa and Johnny, isn't it?'

'You seem pretty sure these cops are going to find what they're looking for.'

She said, 'In my limited experience of dawn raids, they usually do, don't they?'

He could think of no answer to this and continued on his way.

In the kitchen there was a pot of coffee standing on the stove. As he poured himself a cup, Mrs Roper appeared with the morning papers. The housekeeper was a hangover from the days when Wolf Hadda had been master here, and she had made it clear to Estover without overstepping any employee boundaries that she didn't reckon he was an improvement.

'Morning,' she said. 'The usual, is it?'

'Yes, thank you, Mrs Roper.'

As the woman began preparing the bacon, mushroom and scrambled eggs that comprised the usual, he turned his gaze to the pile of newspapers. It was high, containing as it did a copy of every national daily. At the office he had people who went through them all much more meticulously than he ever did. Forewarned is forearmed, he declared to his staff, and it was certainly true that a sharp eye could sometimes spot in a small para a hint of something that might ultimately affect the economy or equanimity of one of

428

his clients. He himself liked to do a quick scan of all the headlines, or sometimes to track through the various reportings of any case he was involved with in search of misrepresentation or bias or anything else of interest.

Today what he called the *titty tabloids* were at the top, and what he saw on the front page of the third of these made him exclaim, 'Shit!'

'Sorry, Mr Estover?' said the housekeeper.

'Nothing, nothing,' he grunted, opening the paper.

It was Kitty Locksley's rag, the news editor who had quizzed him about Arnie Medler a few weeks back. That had been easy enough to field, but what he read on the front page now filled him with foreboding.

The Russian Invasion. Is there more than snow on Pasha Nikitin's boots? See Page 6 for our Exclusive Report!

He found page six.

It was full of photos of Nikitin at receptions and parties, in the company of many well-known faces from the worlds of politics, or showbusiness, or sport. The headline above them all was *WHAT'S HE TREADING INTO THEIR CARPETS?*

The main copy started on the next page. He ran his eyes down the columns with the speed of long practice and under his breath he said, 'Oh shit!' again.

Kitty's journalists were past masters and mistresses in the art of blurring the boundary between speculation and accusation. But there was stuff here that went so far beyond that boundary that they would hardly have dared print it unless they believed they had the wherewithal to back it up under a legal challenge.

The feature finished with a promise that the next day's edition would contain some *really* shocking revelations.

We'll see about that! thought Estover grimly.

He was already working out the grounds of his application for an injunction. Kitty Locksley might have persuaded her bosses that she had enough to take a run at Nikitin, but that was very different from persuading a judge that she wasn't just flying kites. And while the paper's lawyers were preparing their case for a lifting of the injunction, Estover, who had files on all the major newspaper editors and owners, would be working out the combination of threat, bribe, and called-in favour best suited to getting the whole thing nipped in the bud.

Imogen, now wearing a pale blue kimono, came into the kitchen and refilled her mug. When she sat down opposite him, he pushed the paper across to her.

She glanced over it, then said, 'Is it as bad as it looks?'

'Not nice but manageable,' he said confidently. 'I'll slap an injunction on them to put a brake on tomorrow's edition. That will give us a breathing space to wheel the big guns into position.'

'Meaning?'

'As you know, Pasha's got friends. Important friends. Important enough to make even a newspaper owner take stock of how he sees the rest of his life.'

'So, suppression not rebuttal.'

'Always less risky,' he said. 'Thank you, Mrs Roper.'

The housekeeper had placed a crowded plate before him. He reached for the tomato ketchup and squirted his initials cursively across the fry-up.

'You won't forget Pippa and Johnny?'

'I don't even know if they'll need me yet.'

'They'll need you,' she said confidently. 'And they've contacted you. Pasha hasn't.'

'That's true,' he said, raising the first forkful of bacon to his mouth. 'I'm surprised. Perhaps he's had a hard night and his people are afraid to rouse him with bad news.'

'Perhaps,' she said, as if she thought this unlikely.

He finished his breakfast at a leisurely pace, drank more cups of coffee, browsed through more of the papers.

Imogen nibbled at a slice of toast and kept up a desultory conversation with Mrs Roper.

Finally he rose, said, 'Lovely breakfast as always, Mrs Roper,' and left the kitchen.

As he dressed, the phone rang again. It stopped almost immediately.

He continued dressing. It was eight fifteen and the sky was now bright. February was generally regarded as the most dismal of months, but sometimes it held the promise of spring, he thought.

In the kitchen he found Imogen doing the *Guardian* crossword.

He said, 'Pasha, or Pippa again?'

'Pippa.'

'And?'

'They've been arrested. They're taking them to Cambridge.'

'Good God!' he said. 'What for?'

'Drugs.'

She said it so casually that for a moment he didn't take it in.

'*Drugs*? I know Johnny usually has a small stash of coke around the place, just in case he ever feels reality is beginning to break in, but I can't believe they'd do a dawn raid for that.'

'No. I think they probably did it for what, from Pippa's account, looks like half a hundredweight of the stuff found under the cistern in their attic.'

'Jesus wept! You're joking? No, you're not. What did you tell them?'

'I told them you were on your way.'

'What? Look, I can't, not till I start the ball rolling on this Nikitin business.'

'He hasn't asked you to do anything, has he?'

'No, not yet, but there's probably a simple explanation . . .'

'There probably is,' said Imogen. 'But till you hear it, you have two of our oldest friends who are expecting you. Head to Cambridge, Toby. Stay there if you have to. It might be a good idea to stay there even if you don't have to.'

He looked at his wife in bewilderment. More and more these days he felt he understood her as little as her father understood her mother. But frequently she turned out to be right.

He said, 'I'll have to call in at the office first and make sure they're up to speed if or rather when Pasha calls.'

431

Imogen shrugged.

'If you must,' she said indifferently. 'By the way, if you do get to Cambridge, watch out for the media. Pippa said somehow the press and TV have got wind of the raid and they're all over the place. That seemed to worry her almost more than anything else.'

'Bastards,' he said. 'State the world's in, you'd think they'd have better things to occupy them.'

This won him a faintly mocking smile, then she returned her attention to the crossword.

'I'll be off then,' he said, stooping as if to kiss her then contenting himself with a squeeze of her shoulder.

She didn't look up but said, almost to herself, 'I think you're right about the rowan. It's going to be a long time before it grows big enough to shelter us.'

He said, 'Don't worry, my love. While we've got the Law to hide behind, there's nothing that can touch us.'

Now she looked up.

'But if you chop down the Law,' she said, 'how long does that take to grow again?'

3

Alva Ozigbo also woke early on that February morning. For a moment she lay in the darkness, in that birth moment when we don't know who or what or where we are.

Then memory switched on and joy flooded her mind and body like the midday sun.

This morning she did not have to rise and prepare herself for the drive east to the Dark Tower.

Yesterday she had left Parkleigh for the last time!

Against her expectations she hadn't felt any shame at her easy capitulation. Perhaps that would come later. She could, if she'd wanted to, have rehearsed the excellent reasons for her decision to go quietly – principally the threat to Wolf Hadda's freedom and the fact that she had no concrete evidence whatsoever for her belief that the refurbishment of the prison had given Childs's people an opportunity to embed surveillance devices in every nook and cranny. But she was too honest to give them pride of place over her recognition that she was simply relieved and delighted to be giving up her job.

Know thyself is a good if not an essential motto for a psychiatrist. And she was ready to admit she knew herself a lot better now than when she'd first started at Parkleigh.

Her father had resisted any temptation he felt to say *I told you so!* when she gave him the news, but he hadn't concealed his feeling that these were glad tidings.

'Don't you be rushing into any other job,' he said. 'Give yourself time to look around. And above all, Elf, give yourself time to come up here to rescue your poor old dad from this Swedish monster who's got him chained to the wall! I'm wasting away to nothing on a diet of lettuce leaves. If she had her way, I'd spend six hours a day in a sauna, whipping myself with willow twigs. It's my birthday this month and I bet she won't even let me have a cake unless you're here!'

The 'Swedish monster' had intervened at this point to say that she hoped her daughter would come as soon as possible as Ike was now even harder to keep under control than he'd been before his heart attack.

And Alva, hearing the love in their voices and the desire to see for themselves that she was OK, had difficulty in keeping her own voice bright and steady as she promised to come up for Ike's birthday and stay at least a week.

She had put her feelings about Hadda and her concern about his plans and his future to one side during the past couple of weeks. Once the decision to go had been taken, she had no desire to hang around, but at the same time she wanted to make sure that the files and notes she left her successor were comprehensive and up to date. She thought of leaving some form of warning that the confidentiality of his exchanges with the inmates was not guaranteed. The problem was, if it were too general it would be useless and if it were too explicit, it would provoke questions she could not answer. Or did not want to answer.

She knew that in life there were some battles you had to fight even if the odds were insuperable and defeat guaranteed. This did not feel like one of them. OK, it was part of the ongoing and important debate about prisoners' rights versus the general weal. But there was no torture involved here, no physical or mental abuse. This was more like the discussion of how admissible telephone tapping should be in criminal cases. People got heated about it, but no one sacrificed their own reputation or someone else's freedom because of it.

Was this simply a self-justifying rationalization? she asked herself after her waking delight at the realization of her freedom had faded. She didn't think so, but it was almost with relief that she moved from considering that moral question to the other and more personal issue of what she was going to do about Hadda.

She was convinced he was innocent. Her duty was therefore to make public her belief, argue the case, get the investigation reopened, mount an appeal . . .

All of which sounded very straightforward if it weren't for the fact that she could not rely on any of those who should have been her supporters – Doll and Ed Trapp, Davy McLucky, Wolf himself – to stand alongside her.

And this brought her to the next, even more pressing question.

What was Hadda planning to do – and what ought she to do about it?

To hell with it – enjoy your first morning as a free woman! she told herself.

She flung back the duvet and got out of bed.

Dawn was tinting the sky an ochrous pink. London was rumbling back to full consciousness. She washed and dressed then went into her kitchen.

The room could do with a good spring clean, she judged as she sat and ate her breakfast. One way and another with all the pressures she'd endured over the past couple of months, she'd let things go. In fact the whole flat needed a good going over. Her awareness of the symbolic implications of this decision did not make it any the less a factual truth. The place had a neglected look. Leave it much longer and it would be downright grubby! She imagined what Elvira, with her Nordic standards of hygiene, would say if she walked in now.

She'd promised her parents she would drive north in time for her father's birthday. That gave her three days to set her apartment to rights. And some good hard non-cerebral work was just what the psychiatrist had ordered!

By mid-morning she had reduced the relative order of the flat to chaos, but at least it was well on the way to being clean chaos.

When her doorbell rang, she was up a stepladder, dealing with a spider's web of Shelobian proportions. She thought of ignoring the bell, but it rang again insistently.

Grumbling, she descended and went to the door.

It was John Childs. He stood there, looking even more neat and tidy than usual by contrast with the confusion behind her, his sweet smile neither broadening nor fading as he took in her bedraggled appearance.

'I had pictured you taking your ease on your first day away from the toils of employment,' he said. 'Perhaps I should have known better.'

With Homewood it had been easier to maintain the pretence that her departure was by mutual agreement on reasonable grounds.

With Childs she saw no reason for such pretence.

'What do you want?' she asked coldly.

'To apologize,' he said. 'And to talk to you about Wolf.'

This, she acknowledged, was perhaps the only formula that could have got him into the flat. She suspected no matter whose door he knocked at he would always have the right formula.

She let him disinter a chair and she didn't offer him coffee, partly because she did not want to make him feel welcome, but mainly because until she shifted everything she'd taken out of her cupboards back into them, the kitchen was a no-go area.

'So, apologize,' she said.

'I am truly sorry to have recruited you to the job at Parkleigh under false pretences. I am sure that by now a combination of your own sharp intellect and the information supplied by the estimable Chief Officer Proctor will have filled in the picture. Any damage to your self-esteem from the discovery that you were recruited less for your positive qualities and more because of your youth and inexperience should be repaired by your own awareness, even more than my reassurance, that you have performed your duties in an exemplary fashion and with a skill far beyond your years. The glowing testimonial Simon Homewood will no doubt provide will be no less than the truth and no more than you deserve.'

436

He paused. She gave an ironic little clap that reminded her she was still wearing rubber gloves.

'Nice apology,' she said. 'Must have taken you half an hour off the Phoenicians to prepare it.'

'I'm sorry,' he said. 'I've never really mastered the art of sounding spontaneous, even when that's exactly what I'm being. I've truly enjoyed our ongoing relationship and I truly regret that it has probably come to an end.'

'Probably!' she exploded.

'Life is fuller of surprises than certainties,' he said. 'And the more I got to know you, the more I suspected you were going to surprise me. So, that's my apology. All of us are to some degree driven by grim necessity. In my job she is, alas, almost a permanent companion. Let's move on to Wolf.'

'Yes, let's,' she said.

'I assume you are pretty well au fait by now with the circumstances that led to his jail sentence?'

She nodded.

'Good. What happened was of course regrettable, but because of the way things worked themselves out, also inevitable, I fear. Had I been aware earlier what was going on, I might have been able to do something, but by the time I became involved, it was out of my hands.'

'Out of your hands!' she exclaimed. 'He was innocent, this man you feel some affection for – at least that's the conclusion I draw from his inclusion in your picture gallery . . .'

He nodded and said, 'Yes, indeed. I have always been very fond of Wolf.'

'Yet you let him be sent down for a long sentence on the most disgusting of charges! Jesus, Childs, what do you do to your enemies?'

He gave her the sweet smile and said, 'This is not the time or place to go into that. But as to those I'm fond of, I fear that from time to time in too many cases grim necessity has ordained that I should be complicit in their suffering far worse fates than poor Wolf.'

437

He was, she saw, deadly serious. Her head was in a whirl but she did not want to let this occasion to learn all she could about Hadda escape.

She said, 'When Doll Trapp brought him to you, what did you do with him?'

'I gave him a home and an education. He also received some special training, not that he needed much, his peculiar talent for scaling unscaleable obstacles was already highly developed. He could get in and out of almost anywhere.'

'You mean you used him as a burglar?' she asked incredulously.

'On occasion. But more often it was a matter of leaving rather than removing something.'

'Leaving what?' she demanded. She didn't want to know, but she had to ask.

'Surveillance devices,' he said. 'And occasionally, other devices.'

'Like bombs, you mean? You turned him into an assassin?'

'I fear so. Just on a couple of occasions. I did not send him in blind. He was fully briefed. On each occasion the details of the file we were able to show him on the targets were sufficiently powerful to persuade him that this was in the public good, a necessary execution rather than a wanton killing.'

Sneering is not a response that psychiatrists find much occasion to practise, but Alva managed it as to the manner born.

'You *persuaded* him! A boy, a naïve young man at the very most, in your employ, in your *care*, probably dependent upon you emotionally as well as economically! And you *persuaded* him to become a killer. I bet that called on all your Ciceronian skills!'

He said, 'If I gave you the details, I think you yourself might be persuaded that the world was a better place and our country more secure for the deaths of these men. But your reproach is not unjust. I had become very fond of young Wolf in the time I had known him. Rest quiet, Miss Ozigbo. There was nothing sexual in it, not overtly anyway. Wolf, you may be pleased to hear, is unswervingly straight in his appetites.'

He paused as if to allow response and Alva thought of bursting

438

out indignantly, 'Why do you think I should be particularly pleased to hear that?' But she didn't. She was beginning to understand that Childs rarely used words casually.

He resumed, 'So I myself had begun to have some misgivings about steering the boy down this road. I comforted myself with the thought that it was not too late to divert. Then a third occasion requiring his special talents presented itself. Definitely the last, I told myself. And I was right, but for the wrong reasons. Things went awry.'

'Awry?' echoed Alva, tiring of his prissy language. 'You mean there was a cock-up?'

'Yes and no. The target was killed. So unfortunately were some members of his family who were not expected to be there. His wife. And two children.'

'Good God,' said Alva aghast. 'And this was down to Wolf?'

'No, as I attempted to explain to him, it was down to grim necessity. These things happen. It is not a question of choice. As I told Wolf when last I saw him, only God can claim to be independent of accident and necessity.'

'You've seen Wolf recently? And you don't have any broken bones?'

'You sound regretful, Miss Ozigbo,' he said, smiling. 'So there are occasions when you might approve violence?'

'Never approve, Mr Childs,' she said coldly. 'But I'm a human being as well as a scientist. I have emotions. So, you were telling me how you took a young boy and broke him to pieces.'

'Yes. And then as best I could, I put him back together again. I offered him the only prize that could compensate for the damage I had done. You will know what that was from his interesting interchanges with you at Parkleigh.'

'You offered him Imogen Ulphingstone,' she said.

'In a manner of speaking. He'd told me all about his reasons for running away from home. I couldn't, of course, guarantee that Miss Ulphingstone would accept his proposal, and indeed, having made a few discreet enquiries about the lady, I had serious doubts as to whether it would be to Wolf's benefit if she did. But once again I had no choice. Had I offered Wolf anything else, he would have taken off, and God knows what would have happened to him.'

'He might have been able to carve out a perfectly happy life for himself!' she said. 'At least he would have been away from your malign influence!'

Childs grimaced.

'I'm sorry, I am being unnecessarily periphrastic. When I say God knows what would have happened, I am talking about details not outcome. A young man who had been privy to the sort of event I have just sketched out to you could hardly be allowed to run wild, could he? Loose cannons, if they cannot be tied down, must be tipped overboard. You must see that.'

'You mean, he would have been killed? What kind of monster are you, Childs?'

'The kind who saved Wolf's life. It was clear to me from the start that as well as huge personal charm, he had a surprising aptitude for business. In America they value these assets rather more highly than we do here and I saw to it that he received there the kind of higher education that made the most of them. Now all he needed was opportunity, and of course money. The latter was easy enough. Reward for services rendered and still to render. He returned to England a personable young man with his first million already in his account, and a great future before him. All the tests the young woman had set him he had passed with flying colours. She, alas, kept her end of the bargain.'

'You said, services still to render. Do you mean Wolf carried on working for you after he founded Woodcutter?'

'Not in the capacity you fear,' said Childs. 'But in his capacity as international businessman, he was welcome in circles that we were glad to get intelligence from. And people opened up to him in a wonderful way. Oh yes, he earned his keep. In fact, as he was soon so successful he didn't need to be underpinned by public monies, he proved to be huge value for our initial investment.'

'But you were still willing to let this valuable asset be destroyed?'

'Even if he had been saved, with the collapse of Woodcutter, he was considerably less of an asset. And there was no way that I could have prevented the defection of Imogen. His occupation gone, his wife untrue, he would have been as unstable as Othello. As I say, loose cannons must be tied down, and it was convenient in so many ways that the State did us this service.'

'He's not tied down now,' said Alva.

'Indeed. And after the apology, that is my second reason for intruding upon you today. The Woodcutter is running free. I am sure you have been experiencing some serious concerns as to what he may be planning to do.'

She said, 'Yes, I have. But I've no reason to believe whatever he's planning will have anything to do with his connection with Chapel. You say you've spoken to him. He must have made this clear, surely?'

'Because I have no broken bones?' He smiled. 'True. But I'm not here in my ringmaster capacity, Alva. I'm here as a friend of Wolf's.'

His use of her name was as shocking as anything else she'd heard from him. It signalled . . . she wasn't sure what it signalled, but it put her on maximum alert.

'His friend? You mean you want to save him from himself and scupper any plan he might have to take revenge?' she mocked. 'Of course it would be pure coincidence that this would probably involve protecting what sounds like another of your valuable assets, the unspeakable Toby Estover.'

'Too late for that, I fear,' he said.

The words trembled across her brain like a migraine.

'What do you mean?'

'There have been developments. You've probably been too preoc-cupied with your priestlike task of pure ablution to listen to the news, but if you had done so, you might have heard that the Nutbrowns' country residence was raided this morning and Johnny and Pippa Nutbrown have been taken into custody. Naturally they have summoned their solicitor, Mr Toby Estover. Unfortunately, he is nowhere to be found. His car is in its reserved spot in the

441

underground car park that serves his office block. But of Mr Estover himself, there is not a trace.'

'Oh Jesus,' said Alva, feeling the strength drain out of her muscles.

'Please, don't upset yourself,' said Childs. 'There's no reason to think that Wolf is involved in the disappearance, not physically anyway. He works much more subtly than that, and I'm sure at this moment he is safely alibi'd three hundred miles away in Cumbria. No, the fate of the Nutbrowns and of Estover is nothing to cause us concern.'

'You're saying that Wolf has nothing to do with this?' she asked incredulously.

'Don't be silly,' he said, with the first signs of impatience she'd ever seen him show. 'Of course I'm not saying that. But whatever connection there is will not be traceable, of that I'm sure. Forget these people, they're getting no more than they deserve. And as I do not think they deserve death, I shall do my utmost to ensure their fate stops short of that.'

'How nice to protect your conscience by making such delicate judgments!' she sneered.

'No, it is not my conscience I want to protect,' he said quietly. 'It is Wolf. Eventually I have hopes that we may be able to get his convictions overturned. I am not without influence. But the seeds of doubt must first be sowed. Meanwhile the best we can do for him is make sure he draws no attention to himself.'

'You think it's still possible to get the case reviewed?' said Alva. Despite her resolve never to trust Childs again, she found she was letting him give her hope.

'Anything is possible if you have the means to make it necessary,' he said. 'But let me speak plainly. Wolf so far has moved with stealth and care, but what I fear is that his final act might not be so meticulously planned, so remotely triggered as the first two. If Wolf seriously harms his former wife, he will certainly spend much of the rest of his life in jail. And that, I fear, might be the least of his worries. What such an act might do to his mental stability, you are better placed than I am to work out. This is why I have come to see you, Alva. I want Wolf to remain free, in body and in spirit. I think you want the same. What I can do, I have done. But I feel it may not be enough. He needs reasons other than any I can give him to stay his hand. If you think you can supply those reasons, then I beg you to make the attempt before it is too late.'

'For God's sake,' cried Alva. 'Can't Imogen be taken into protective custody?'

'To be protected from what?' said Childs. 'If the authorities get a hint that Wolf poses some kind of danger, it is he who will be returned to custody. Not that I would put money on them being able to find him if he decided to go to earth in that wilderness he so loves.'

'At least you can keep a watch to make sure there's plenty of warning if he looks like leaving home . . .'

'I don't think he has any intention of doing that. The good huntsman knows how his prey will react. He prepares his hide, and waits.'

'I don't understand,' said Alva. 'What do you think is going to happen?'

In an inner pocket of Childs's immaculate jacket, a phone trembled.

Murmuring an apology, he took it out, looked at it with distaste, then placed it close to but not touching his ear and said, 'Yes?'

He listened, said, 'I'm on my way,' replaced the phone in his pocket and stood up.

'I'm sorry,' he said. 'I must leave you. But in answer to your question, I think that in the very near future, Mrs Estover is going to find her home besieged by the media. The last time that happened she was able to take refuge at the Nutbrowns' house, Poynters, in leafy Essex. That is no longer an option, so I believe that, both because it is a good place to hide and also because I suspect that's where she will want to be, eventually she will head north to seek solace in the bosom of her family at Ulphingstone Castle. And from what I know of the lady, I would guess that Wolf will not need to go looking for her. She will come looking for him.'

443

4

They had transported the Nutbrowns to Cambridge Police HQ in separate vehicles with sirens ululating and lights oscillating in hope of outspeeding the media caravan. All they did of course was open up a traffic-free channel along which the motley gang of reporters and cameramen sped at supra-legal speeds a couple of hundred yards behind them.

In the station they were kept apart as they were booked in and fingerprinted.

Both refused to make statements until the arrival of their solicitor.

After two hours when Estover still hadn't arrived, DI O'Reilly rang the lawyer's London office to check if there were any known reason for the delay. He found the staff there in a state of mystified concern. Toby Estover's car was in its reserved bay in the car park, but of the man himself there was no sign.

His wife, when contacted, confirmed that her husband had set out early to the office with the intention of dealing with a pressing matter there before driving north to Cambridge to represent the Nutbrowns.

O'Reilly then informed the Nutbrowns separately that it did not look as if Mr Estover was going to turn up and invited them to nominate an alternative, failing which they could, of course, accept the services of the duty solicitor.

On hearing this, Pippa Nutbrown gave her opinion of her absentee

444

lawyer in such ripe terms that the DI observed drily that if he was even half those things, she was probably better off without him. Johnny Nutbrown asked what his wife was doing. In the end the man opted for the duty solicitor while the woman said that in order to get out of this shithole as quickly as possible, she'd answer just enough questions to let O'Reilly see what a dickhead he was being.

In the event, though for very different reasons, neither interview lasted long.

Pippa Nutbrown denied all knowledge of the packages of cocaine discovered in her attic. When asked how, in that case, her fingerprints came to be on the plastic wrapping, she shook her head violently and said, 'It's a lie.'

Next she was asked if it were true that there was always a plentiful supply of coke on offer at her parties.

She snapped, 'There might be the odd line for recreational purposes, but not fucking bucketsful!'

'So you're not in the business of actually dealing in the stuff?' enquired O'Reilly.

'Certainly not!'

'In that case, you'll have a perfectly reasonable explanation of your account in the Caymans that, according to my information, currently stands at something in excess of five million pounds in credit?'

And now she stopped talking altogether.

The same sequence of questions to her husband produced a rather different set of answers.

Asked about the packages found in the attic, he said, 'It's an old curiosity shop up there, wouldn't surprise me if you found Lord Lucan riding Shergar.'

When told his fingerprints were on the wrapping of one of the packages, he said, 'Suppose it must be mine then. Bit of a facer, finding I'd got all that gear up there when I think of the price I've been paying for a couple of bags in town.'

When asked if he supplied coke at his parties, he said, 'Doesn't everybody?'

And finally, asked about the Cayman account, he raised his eyebrows and said, 'Thought it would be more than that. Still, Pippa's a bright girl, she's probably got it spread about a bit.'

At which point DI O'Reilly enquired politely if Mr Nutbrown felt in need of some refreshment as he had a feeling this interview might take some little time.

Leaving Johnny to enjoy a breakfast-all-day from the canteen, he returned to Pippa.

'Mr Nutbrown is being most cooperative,' he said. 'Usually, in the case of co-defendants, the judge tends to look more favourably on the more cooperative.'

'Fuck off,' she said. 'Any sign of Estover?'

'I'm afraid not.'

She didn't look surprised.

'I hope the bastard rots in hell,' she said.

5

It is not often that a wish so malevolent as Pippa Nutbrown's is positively answered, but in figurative terms hell was certainly where Toby Estover had been spending the past couple of hours.

As he'd stepped out of his car in the underground car park, he was approached by a bulky figure he recognized as an associate of Pavel Nikitin. The kind of associate who fades into the background in polite society but looms menacingly in less friendly surroundings.

The man, who was definitely looming at the moment, said, 'Mr Nikitin would like to talk to you.'

'Yes, I thought he might,' said Estover. 'First thing I'll do when I get into my office is give him a ring.'

'He would like to talk now.'

'Yes, I said . . . oh, you mean face to face. Listen, there's something I've got to do, I'll ring him and make a firm appointment for later, if that's what he wants.'

Suddenly the man was looming very large indeed.

'Now,' he said.

And Estover felt his arm seized, he was spun round, marched forward a few steps, then thrust into the back seat of a car with windows tinted dark enough to hide an orgy.

In the front passenger seat sat a man he recognized. His name was Pudovkin, known familiarly as Pudo, though he did not invite familiarity. His precise function in Nikitin's entourage Toby had never discovered. Small and wiry, he lacked the intimidating bulk of the looming man. 'Make sure your bodyguards are wide enough to take the first bullet,' Pasha had once said to him in a lighter moment. So, not a bodyguard. But clearly a man of value to Nikitin who always called him Pudo and occasionally draped an arm round the smaller man's shoulders in a way that made Estover wonder if some of the services he provided might be very personal indeed. But the deference the big bodyguards showed him confirmed he was a lot more than just a best boy.

'Pudo,' said the lawyer, anger making him risk familiarity, 'what the hell's going on?'

The man turned and stared coldly at him and hissed, 'Sit still!' with hardly any movement of his mouth. Perhaps that was because his jaw was wired. Whatever, the effect was extremely scary, and increasingly, as the car sped through streets that, so far as he could tell through the darkened windows, did not lie on any route he knew to Nikitin's home or office, fear began to outweigh anger in Estover's mind.

Their destination turned out to be a riverside warehouse somewhere, he estimated, in Wapping. Pavel Nikitin was waiting for him here, seated behind a dilapidated desk in an office that did not look as if it had been occupied by anything but mice and spiders for a very long time.

'Jesus, Pasha, you're not back home in Russia, all you had to do was ring me,' said Estover, exaggerating his exasperation in order to cover his concern.

The looming man thrust him down on to a chair he would have preferred to brush with his handkerchief before settling his mohaired buttocks on it. Nikitin still didn't speak.

'Look,' said Estover, 'there's nothing to worry about, just because some gung-ho editor has a rush of blood to the head. They've all tried it before. We'll have an injunction on them by lunchtime and by the end of the week they'll be printing a grovelling apology and paying large sums to the charity of our choice.'

Now the Russian spoke.

'No,' he said. 'They have more, much more.'

'How much more? How do you know this? Have they been in touch?'

'Early this morning, just before the paper came out. They woke me to tell me what was going to be printed and asked if I had any comment. They said there would be at least three follow-ups. They told me what was likely to be in them also.'

'A bluff!' insisted Estover. 'They knew if they'd contacted you earlier, I'd have made damned sure even this first load of crap didn't see the light of day.'

Then, genuinely puzzled because Nikitin was no respecter of anyone's comfort or convenience, he asked, 'Why didn't you ring me straight away? I'd have come round, no matter what the hour.'

'Because I wanted to see you without anyone knowing I was seeing you,' said Nikitin.

For a moment the response seemed an impenetrable enigma.

Then the Russian drew an envelope out of his pocket and shook half a dozen photographs on to the desktop.

Estover stared down at them and the enigma began to dissolve.

They showed him at a restaurant table, handing a package to Kitty Locksley, the woman looking at it quizzically, the pair of them smiling as she slipped it unopened into her handbag.

'This was delivered to my house just before the paper phoned me,' said the Russian.

Professionally speaking, extreme situations had always made Toby Estover's mind go into overdrive. This was one of the reasons he was such a good lawyer. As he riffled through a client's options, he inevitably recited the reassuring mantra, 'Rest easy, there is always a way out.'

His mind worked fast enough now to grasp the implications of the pictures and the fact that nobody knew he was here with the Russian. The reassuring mantra did not seem quite appropriate, and he was saying, 'Come on, Pasha, you surely don't believe . . .' when the chair was pulled from under him and he sprawled on the floor.

449

He cried out in alarm then screamed in pain as the looming man's foot drove hard into his crotch.

They waited patiently till he was recovered sufficiently to push himself up into a sitting position.

'Now, Toby,' said Nikitin. 'Let's us talk.'

A couple of hours later, at just about the time Pippa Nutbrown was uttering her anathema, Pudovkin said to his master, 'I think perhaps he is telling the truth.'

Nikitin nodded and looked at the photos on the desk.

'I think so too, Pudo,' he said. 'This means we must look for explanations elsewhere. Go to this restaurant. See if you can find out anything about the taking of these pictures.'

Pudovkin nodded and left.

On the floor, Estover moved slightly and let out a groan.

'So what shall we do with him, boss?' said the looming man.

Nikitin made an impatient gesture and took out his cigarette case. He lit a cigarette and frowned down at the limp and bleeding figure on the floor. One eye was invisible beneath a mass of bloody flesh, the other peered out of the remaining narrow slit like a terrified hunted mouse that has squeezed into a minute crack in a wall. On the pulpy lips a pink bubble slowly grew, then burst in a soft, almost inaudible sigh.

He knew Estover. He was soft. No way he would have held out under this pressure. So someone had set this up. The question was why? To get at Estover, or to get at him?

He finished the first cigarette and lit another. Curiously, he found himself wanting to discuss the affair with the man at his feet. Soft, the solicitor might be, but when it came to working out moves and counter moves, Toby Estover was without doubt the best in the business.

Used to be the best in the business.

One thing was clear. They couldn't just pick him up, dust him down and send him home.

The looming man was looking at him expectantly.

He stubbed out the second cigarette and said, 'Make sure he is weighted down so much he does not come to the surface in your lifetime.'

'Guaranteed,' said the looming man with perfect confidence.

And whatever god the man worshipped smiled, knowing that this lifetime had something less than ninety seconds to go.

The door burst open, there was a cry of 'Armed police!' and the looming man reached inside his jacket. Two shots rang out, and he loomed no more but slumped on the floor, not yet as bloody as, but already stiller than the figure he joined there.

Pavel Nikitin stood perfectly still, his face impassive. When the new arrivals screamed at him to lie face down on the floor with his hands behind his head he obeyed instantly. Seconds later his arms were forced down behind his back, his wrists handcuffed, and he was dragged to his feet.

A well-dressed man with wispy, almost white hair and a benevolent smile stood gazing down at Estover. A pair of paramedics came into the room, took a quick look at the shot man, shook their heads, then moved John Childs aside to start working on the lawyer.

Childs turned his attention to the Russian.

'I'm so glad to meet you at last, Mr Nikitin,' he said.

The man regarded him blankly.

'Who the hell are you?'

'A friend. I think you're going to need a good lawyer, though after the way you seem to have treated your last one, you may find it difficult to hire a substitute. Whatever, it seems likely you are going to spend several years in one of our prisons. Parkleigh might suit you very well, it has all mod cons and is very handy for London. Of course, there is an alternative . . .'

'What?'

'Under the recent human rights reciprocation agreement, it may be possible to transfer you to Russian custody so that you can enjoy the solace of serving out your sentence under the tender care of your fellow countrymen.'

'Go to hell!' the Russian spat.

451

'I daresay I will. But I hope we may meet again before then. Who knows? We might even find a way of being mutually beneficial. Grim necessity makes strange bedfellows, Mr Nikitin. I'm sure there's an old Russian proverb that states as much.'

The man was back in control now. He even managed a smile as he said, 'You speak very well, *friend*. But how important are you really? You are an old man and I think I know all the truly important old men in this country. Yes, soon you will find I have other friends who speak better than you. This is just a misunderstanding, a small difficulty that can easily be resolved.'

'Of course,' said Childs. 'As you resolved the small difficulty of Mr Hadda, you mean?'

That got Nikitin's attention. He looked genuinely puzzled as he said, 'What has Hadda to do with this, old man?'

'Nothing,' said Childs, regretting the impulse that had made him mention Wolf. 'I just happen to know you had a small commercial problem with him. And a small emotional problem too, I gather. Neither of which your boasted expertise was able to clear up.'

But he could see that his efforts at diversion were not working. The man's gaze moved from the recumbent figure of Estover, still being worked on by the paramedics, to the photos on the table.

Childs thought, they must have worked on Estover enough to know it wasn't him who spilled the beans to the paper. Now, because of my foolish desire to display omniscience, this bastard is making a link to Wolf.

He turned away abruptly and signalled to the armed police standing in the doorway.

He watched as Nikitin was hustled out of the room, then turned his attention to Estover. The medics had done all they could for him on the spot and were now preparing to stretcher him out.

'Will he live?' enquired Childs.

'Probably,' said one of the men. 'But there'll be long-term damage. And he won't look pretty. One of his eyes is a goner.'

'Oh dear. The whirligig of time, eh?'

'Sorry?'

'Nothing. Don't let me hold you up.'

A few seconds later he was left alone with the dead bodyguard. A fatal-shooting enquiry would follow and the corpse wouldn't be shifted till it had been photographed from every possible angle.

In death we can all become stars, thought Childs.

Of course it would have been neater if it had been Toby Estover's body lying there. The lawyer still had the capacity to cause the Chapel some embarrassment, particularly if, as was not uncommon, his near-death experience turned him into some kind of blabber-mouth penitent.

On the other hand, he thought, studying the photographs lying on the desk, if the press were fed some tasty morsels about some of Estover's other clients who were then permitted to see these pictures, no one was ever going to believe a word he said again!

He slipped the photos into his pocket.

It was an ill wind that blew nobody any good, and he could either sell Nikitin to the Russians or he could bargain every last drop of useful information out of the man. And once a man had betrayed his associates, he was yours for ever.

Still, he would have to move carefully. Had this been purely a Chapel operation, Nikitin would have been rapidly removed from all possibility of contact with the outside world, but now he had entered the conventional legal system there was no way of keeping him incommunicado. The man wasn't lying when he said he had friends, both in high and in low places.

Would he among all his other concerns have time to do anything about the possibility that he had Wolf Hadda to thank for his predicament? The man Pudovkin was still free. He had been seen driving away from the warehouse not long before the police moved in. A couple of men had been sent to detain him once he was safely out of range of the operation, but they must have been careless or he had been extra alert, and he had slipped past them.

Nikitin would almost certainly get word to him of what had happened, and share his suspicions of who was behind it. Once this happened, and the attack dog was let loose, Wolf might find what it was to be the object as well as the agent of revenge.

Walking back to his car, Childs took out his mobile and dialled.

'Dr Ozigbo,' he said. 'John Childs. I wonder, if you should happen to see Wolf in the next few days, could you possibly give him a message from me?'

BOOK SIX

the world's edge

... but Slith, knowing well why that light was lit in that secret upper chamber, and who it was that lit it, leaped over the edge of the World, and is falling from us still through the unreverberate blackness of the abyss.
Lord Dunsany: *Probable Adventure of the Three Literary Men*

1

As Luke Hollins walked down Birkstane lonning, he heard the sound of an axe biting into wood. It came from beyond the house, over the boundary wall, in the Ulphingstone estate forest.

As he got nearer he could see the tall figure of Wolf Hadda swinging his axe with rhythmic ease, carving gobbets of bright white wood out of a young pine tree. The man was naked to the waist, his upper body glistening with sweat. In the reflecting sunlight, Hollins appreciated the play of muscles in his arms and chest as the axe rose and fell.

Michelangelo could have done something with this, thought Hollins as he called out, 'Hullo!'

The woodcutter's head turned slowly towards him. He wasn't wearing his eye patch and the sight of that scarred face with its one eye glaring at him turned the vicar's thoughts from Greek statuary to Greek monsters.

'I shouldn't stand there,' said Hadda, placing his hand against the trunk and pushing.

'What? Oh yes . . .'

He turned and ran backwards and sideways as the tree began to sway towards him. He could have sworn he felt the rush of displaced air as it passed close and he certainly felt the ground tremble as the trunk hit the earth. But when he turned he saw that in fact the tree had fallen many yards to the side of where he'd been standing and Hadda was grinning broadly.

'I doubt if a Cumbrian parson's moved so fast since they raided that knocking shop near Carlisle Cathedral,' he said as he strode forward, towelling himself down with his shirt before pulling it over his head.

'Very funny,' said Hollins, slightly out of breath. 'Does Sir Leon know you're stealing his trees?'

'I reckon he can spare one,' said Hadda indifferently. 'In fact, I reckon he probably owes my dad quite a few. But if he looks bothered when you mention it to him, tell him to send me a bill.'

'Even if I were inclined to act as a grass, I doubt if the occasion will arise in the near future,' said Hollins. 'I seem to have become *non grata* at the castle since Christmas. In fact, Lady Kira hasn't shown up at church for the past couple of Sundays, though that might have something to do with that unfortunate business with her Mr Nikitin.'

'Really? What's that all about then?' said Hadda, leading the way towards the house with Sneck walking at the vicar's side, trying to get his nose into his trouser pocket.

As Hollins produced the looked-for treats, he regarded Hadda sceptically. Even in his self-imposed isolation, could he really have missed the main topic of local interest for the last several days? It had got plenty of media space to start with.

He said, 'It sounds as if Lady Kira's distant cousin (the distance is increasing daily, I gather) attempted to murder her son-in-law. Surely even if you didn't hear about it on the news, you must have had journalists sniffing around to see if they could get a quote out of you. Everybody else in the parish has.'

And not everybody else in the parish is a notorious parolee who once employed the assaulted man as his solicitor and had subsequently been replaced by him in the marital bed, was the unspoken rider.

'Oh *that,*' said Hadda indifferently. 'There were a couple. Never found what they wanted. I chased them off with Sneck. Then I borrowed Joe Strudd's muck-spreader and parked it up the lonning. Next lot that came, I turned the spreader on as they were getting out of their car. After that they didn't seem to bother me any more.'

Hollis fixed on the most remarkable piece of this statement.

'Joe Strudd loaned you his muck-spreader?' he said incredulously.

Strudd, Hadda's nearest neighbour, was a Cumbrian farmer of the old school and a devout chapel-goer who regarded St Swithin's as an outpost of popish laxity.

'Aye. I found one of them Holsteins he's so proud of badly mired in Hillick Moss and I pulled it out. Someone must have seen me, but didn't want to risk contamination by actually helping me. One of your Anglican flock, I daresay. At least he told Joe, and he called round to say thanks. Would have said a few prayers too, but I told him I was already spoken for. And he said, "Aye, I can see how you'd feel more at home at St Swithin's." So you see what kind of reputation you've got, Padre!'

Hollins grinned and said, 'Yes, Strudd's usual greeting to me is "Give my regards to the whore of Babylon!" But all the same, Joe Strudd loaning you his muck-spreader . . . well, well. That's a step in the right direction.'

'They'll be inviting me to speak at the WI next,' said Hadda indifferently. 'So, to what do I owe the pleasure? I've not put in my Tesco order yet.'

They were in the kitchen now. Sneck, persuaded the treats were finished, had stretched himself out on the hearth. Hadda, having put the kettle on, was spooning coffee into the pot.

Hollins said, 'Mainly, like I say, to check you weren't being besieged by journalists, but I see I needn't have worried. In fact, you've never been much bothered by the media, have you? Not even when you first came back here. One might almost think you were under some kind of protection . . .?'

'Aren't we all, Padre? Surely that's part of your message.'

'I was thinking more of the terrestrial sphere,' said Hollins drily.

Hadda poured the coffee. He'd grown quite fond of the young vicar and it pleased him to note that Hollins's professional desire to see the best in people hadn't taken the edge off a sharp eye and a sharp ear.

'No cream, sorry. No, not really sorry. I still have hopes that I can convert you to agreeing black is best.'

459

'Perhaps we can look forward to a mutual conversion? Perhaps not! But on the subject of black being best, another thing that brought me here was I had a phone call from Ms Ozigbo.'

The mug paused momentarily in its arc to Hadda's lips, then he drank and said mildly, 'I'm trying to work out if that's racist or not.'

'Hardly, when it's not my intention to be discriminatory, inflammatory or offensive, any more than it's yours when you offer your little *bon mots* about the Church.'

Oh yes, thought Hadda. One might make much of the Reverend Luke Hollins if you caught him while he was still young!

He said, 'So what did Alva want? Checking up that I hadn't run amuck with my axe?'

'She told me several things. One was that she's left her job at Parkleigh.'

'Good lord. Any particular reason?'

'None given to me. She said that she was presently staying with her parents again in Manchester. Her father seems well on the road to full recovery, by the way.'

'I'm glad. Owt else?'

Hollins grinned. It was good to feel on top in a conversation with Hadda for a change. The man's effort to sound only casually interested wasn't all that convincing.

'She seemed particularly concerned to know if your ex-wife was at the Castle. I said in view of the reported condition of her husband, it hardly seemed likely.'

Hadda said indifferently, 'Don't see why not. Unless Imo's changed, I can't see her spending her waking hours sitting by a sickbed, mopping Estover's heated brow and squeezing his hand reassuringly.'

'It turns out you're right. When I checked with my church-warden, whose youngest daughter does a bit of cleaning at the castle, he said that Mrs Estover is expected there some time today.'

'You really are adapting to country life, Padre,' said Hadda. 'Impossible to survive here unless you've got a well-organized and highly motivated intelligence network. So did you relay this bit of news to Alva?'

'No. I thought it would keep till I talked to her face to face.'

That got his interest.

'Face to face?'

'Yes, she too is driving up today.'

Both your women on the road north, he thought; maybe they'll meet up for a coffee and a chat in a service station.

Hadda was regarding him sharply, as if he'd read the thought. Or maybe because he'd had it himself.

'And she's coming all this way just to see you?' said Wolf.

'She didn't indicate otherwise,' said Hollins. 'She said she had some information she needed to share with me.' He paused, counted to three, then added, 'Something to do with you, as far as I could make out.'

'So let's get this straight, my psychiatrist is driving up to Cumbria to talk with my local vicar about something that concerns me?'

Hadda sounded angry but only, it seemed to Hollins, to hide some other emotion.

'I suppose you could put it like that.'

'And tell me, Padre, why did you feel the need to share this information with me? Secret meetings to discuss a patient's state of mind are conventionally kept secret, I should have thought.'

'I expect so. But as Ms Ozigbo didn't indicate it was your state of mind she wanted to discuss, I don't think it applies here. I'm sure she will reveal all when she calls to see you.'

'But you said she wasn't going to try and see me.'

'No. I said she didn't say she was. But I would lay odds she does.'

'Oh yes? Turned you into a gambling man now, has she? So what am I supposed to do, hang around here all day on the off chance she drops by?'

'You must do as you will, Wolf,' said Hollins, standing up.

'Must I? Well, I suppose I should thank you for acting as go-between.'

'No, I'm not a go-between,' said Hollins sternly. 'Nor am I the confidant of either you or Ms Ozigbo. If you have secrets from each other, you should learn not to share them with me. Not unless, of course, either of you wish to confide in me as a priest.'

461

'Wow,' said Hadda. 'Nice speech. I'll pick the bones out of it later. There wasn't anything in there about not being a delivery man, was there? You might as well take my Tesco order while you're here.'

He took a pad out of a drawer, checked through a list written on it, scribbled a couple of extra items, and handed it over to Hollins.

'Nearly forgot your cream,' he said lightly. 'Wouldn't like to think I was driving you off by not pandering to your fleshly weaknesses. I like a few fleshly weaknesses in my priests.'

Hollins said, 'Just as I like small acts of generosity from my sinners. Incidentally, as a matter of curiosity, what exactly are you going to do with that tree you've stolen?'

'The ridge beam in one of the barns has a bit of a sag in it,' said Hadda. 'Probably been up there for three hundred years or so. It'll last a while yet, but I'd like to have another one, seasoned and ready, for when the time comes.'

'I see. You're planning to stay around then?'

'Not for three hundred years, perhaps,' laughed Hadda. 'But I can't think of anywhere else I'd want to go. Not wanting shut of me, are you?'

'Of course not.'

'And you, you'll be sticking around too?'

'Not wanting shut of me, are you?' retorted Hollins.

'Just when I'm breaking you in? No way. They might opt for a woman next time!'

'Now that does sound sexist.'

'No. It's just that I'm out of practice with women. Now, I'd better get my tree sorted and shifted before one of Leon's foresters notices it lying there.'

They went into the yard together. As they parted, Hadda said, 'By the way, tell Alva if she does decide to drop by and I'm not here, she should make herself at home. This time, she should light the fire.'

'I'll tell her,' said Hollins.

He made his way back up the hard rutted lonning, wondering how it was that every time he saw Hadda, it felt more and more like a meeting of friends.

2

Imogen Estover sat at the breakfast table, studying the morning paper. In front of her, hardly touched, was a bowl of muesli. Behind her the electric hot-plate on the sideboard was covered with the usual array of silver-domed dishes. The fact that the sole occupants of the castle at the moment were herself and her parents made no difference. Any suggestion that it hardly made sense to offer such a wide choice to so few people drew from Lady Kira the response, 'Why should I treat guests better than I treat myself?'

Imogen turned a sheet and let her eyes run down the next page. She wasn't so much reading the paper as grazing over it to check if there were any references to the assault on her husband and the arrest of Pavel Nikitin.

There were none. The Great British public likes its meat fresh and any successful editor knows that today's lie will always sell more papers than yesterday's truth. When Nikitin came to trial, it would all start up again, but a man locked away in a prison cell and another lying comatose on a hospital bed do not combine to generate very much of interest. Meanwhile a terrorist bomb in Paris, a premier league footballer accused of match-fixing, the suspicious death of a TV chat-show host, a scientist's claim that global warming was responsible for a plague of locusts in the Channel Isles, the first streaker in the House of Commons, the possibility of a consti-tutional crisis if the imminent royal twins both turned out to be

463

male, the launch of the first solar-powered sex toy – these and many other items of similar importance competed for the headlines.

'Good morning, darling.'

Her mother had come into the room.

'Good morning, Mummy. You're bright and early.'

It was barely light outside.

'I sleep badly these days. You too?'

'No. The days are short and I thought I might go for a walk.'

'Yes, I see you are dressed *au paysan*,' said Kira, her gaze taking in with distaste her daughter's woollen socks, cord breeks and checked shirt. 'Anything in the paper?'

'Not a word. I think it's probably safe for you to go out now.'

When Imogen had arrived the previous evening she discovered her mother hadn't been out of doors for nearly a fortnight.

The upsurge in media interest in the Ulphingstones that had occurred as a consequence of what was referred to as the Wapping Warehouse Shoot-out had put the castle under siege for a couple of days. Locking the main gates gave little protection as the estate perimeter was defined by little more than sheep-proof fences and decaying dry-stone walls. Lady Kira's initial response was to stroll around with a shotgun under her arm, ready to take a pot-shot at any stranger she came across. It had taken a formal warning from the Chief Constable after a couple of near misses to persuade her that she was not entitled to kill, maim or even seriously frighten trespassers.

'Then let them roam at will. They shall not see me!' she'd declared.

Now she helped herself to a generous plateful of bacon, sausage and eggs and sat down opposite her daughter.

'How do you stay so healthy?' she asked, looking disapprovingly at the muesli.

'I wonder the same about you,' said Imogen.

It was true. In her early sixties, Kira Ulphingstone weighed little more than when she'd arrived at the castle as a young bride more than four decades earlier. Nor had she controlled her weight in any way that had visibly affected her looks. The high cheeks might be more accentuated than they appeared in her wedding photographs, but her brow was still smooth, her skin tone was good, her eyes were still bright, and her figure, clothed at least, was still as seductively curvaceous.

What did seem to have changed from those old pictures was the difference in age between herself and her husband. Sir Leon was over twenty years her senior. On his wedding day it seemed less. Now when they appeared together, the difference looked to be nearer half a century.

'Will Daddy be breakfasting?' asked Imogen.

Lady Kira shrugged.

'Who knows? These days, I do not disturb him.'

It was many years since she and her husband had shared a bedroom. In fact, Imogen could not recall a time when they had. When she'd grown old enough to notice such things, she'd been aware that from time to time her father would walk down the corridor from his room to his wife's, then return a little later. Such excursions became rarer as she got older and had long since, to the best of her knowledge, ceased altogether.

This separation was not down to any frigidity on her mother's part, Imogen was sure. In fact, probably the contrary. She believed she'd inherited her own strong sexuality from Kira, and she guessed that, even as a young bride, she had never been satisfied by her middle-aged husband. At least, thought Imogen, with Wolf present, she had never had that problem, but his increasingly long absences had left a gap that needed to be filled . . .

She sometimes wondered how her mother had dealt with her needs, but their similarities had somehow never added up to a closeness that permitted her to ask. Or perhaps it was affection for her father that prevented her from wanting to know. It seemed to her that Leon had had a bad enough deal in life already. A wife he could not satisfy, a wife who did not care much for his friends and whose own friends he did not altogether approve, a wife who had set herself to change the traditional, easy-going squirearchical relationship between the castle and the locality to something the far side of feudal, a wife who had given him no male heir, only a daughter as wilful as her mother who, in the old phrase, had married to disoblige her family.

He did not deserve that this daughter should be privy to his cuckolding.

Her mother had no such inhibitions, it seemed.

After devouring a large forkful of sausage, Kira said, 'I am not sorry that Pasha has been found out. I always suspected that there must be something a little soiled about his money. And besides, he was a great disappointment in bed.'

Imogen felt a surprise that came close to shock.

She hoped she concealed it efficiently as she replied, 'And why do you imagine that this is of the slightest interest to me?'

'Do not be so disingenuous, dear. You know very well I had hopes that perhaps one day you and he might get together.'

'I hope you're not going to tell me that these hopes included encouraging him to try and murder Toby?'

'Now you're being silly. One way or another, it was clear to me that you and Toby are pretty well played out. When did you last have sex with him?'

'I shouldn't have thought that you rated marital sex as an essential element in a lasting marriage, Mother,' said Imogen.

'My case is different. A title and a castle are worth clinging on to. A fat lawyer who is notorious for fornicating with his secretaries is quite another matter. Anyway, that is beside the point now. What condition he will be in, if he recovers, I dread to think. But with Pasha out of the picture, we must look to your future. No real problem. You are still a desirable woman in many ways. There will be plenty of suitable candidates.'

Imogen said, 'And do you intend to vet them all as thoroughly as you did Pasha?'

Lady Kira shrugged.

'Pasha was here, feeling as always very frustrated by the way

466

you played with him. The poor boy needed an outlet. I needed – how shall I put it? – an inlet. Do not pretend to be shocked, my dear. You are my daughter, you know how these needs of ours work.'

'There is such a thing as discrimination,' said Imogen. 'As a matter of interest, how long have you been offering this in-depth maternal service? And who to? Good God, don't tell me, not you and Toby . . .?'

Kira waved her fork dismissively.

'A long time ago,' she said. 'He was better than I anticipated. After you and your peasant split up, I thought he might do quite nicely for you. Money, standing, a good school, an old family – there is a title, you know, but unfortunately he is at least three disgustingly healthy cousins away from it.'

Despite herself, Imogen could not restrain a small smile.

'Mother, I thought you had long ago lost the capacity to surprise me, but I see I was wrong. Well, at least I can be confident that my first choice was tested by no one but myself. No way would you demean yourself by making out with a peasant!'

'Come now, my dear. I am sure back in the old days our ancestors felt no shame in taking their pleasure with a well set-up *kulak*. And working as a woodcutter certainly seems to set a man up very well . . .'

She smiled as she said it with a kind of significant coyness that put her daughter on the alert.

She said, 'Mother, if you're trying to imply that you and Wolf . . . I don't believe you!'

'And if I had, how would that make you feel?' asked Kira. 'In fact, how *do* you feel about Hadda? It bothers me. You don't seem to hate him as you should. And what's worse, you don't seem to fear him as you should! For God's sake, you're not still lusting after him, are you?'

'What I feel about Wolf is nothing to do with you,' said Imogen.

Lady Kira looked at her daughter with the kind of icily reductive stare that in olden days had probably set serfs thinking nostalgically

467

of happier times working out in the fields in sub-zero temperatures till their frostbitten fingers fell off.

Then she relaxed and smiled a smile that was worse than the stare.

'Well, that's not precisely true, my love,' she said. 'Let me tell you a story . . .'

Fifteen minutes later, Kira stood by the window and watched her daughter's Mercedes go screaming down the drive.

Had that gone well or badly? she wondered. She wasn't sure, but she wasn't going to let it spoil her breakfast.

She took the congealing remnant of her first selection to the sideboard, set it down, and began to load another plate. She was not so arrogant that she did not count her blessings. High on the list alongside her ability not to get emotional about things she could not change was possession of the kind of body that could take in almost anything by way of food, or drink, or men, extract maximum enjoyment, and then move on with very little residual damage to show for it.

She lifted another domed lid and now she did give her emotions free rein.

No black pudding!

She was really going to have to have a serious talk with those incompetents in the kitchen!

3

Wolf Hadda stood under the icy waterfall and rubbed himself vigorously with a bar of kitchen soap.

He remained there long enough for the hissing water to sluice off the suds then moved out into the shallow pool.

There was someone on the bank. Sneck was standing by, watchful, but on the whole assessing the watcher as harmless.

Hadda said, 'I didn't have you down as a Peeping Tom.'

Alva Ozigbo said, 'I wanted to see whether you really did take a shower here at the crack of dawn every day, or if you were just trying to impress me.'

'Call this the crack of dawn, city girl? It must be nearly nine o'clock! I'm coming out now.'

'So what am I supposed to do? Blush and turn my back?'

'Of course not. A man should hide nothing from his psychiatrist. But if I stand here too long being admired, I'll start to form icicles. Let's get back to the house. Do you want to walk in front or behind?'

'In front, I think. Walking behind, I wouldn't know where to look.'

'Not a problem for me,' he said, falling into step behind her. 'Young Hollins was here yesterday. He told me you might be coming. When did you get here?'

'Last night. I stayed at the vicarage.'

'Draughty old place, as I recall. You'd have been better off here. What did his wife think about having a good-looking dolly bird from the big city landed on her?'

Why am I feeling such a glow of pleasure at being told I could have stayed at Birkstane and being referred to as a dolly bird? Alva asked herself.

She said, 'I don't think she likes me much.'

'Something else you and I have in common, I suspect.'

Something else . . .

She didn't spoil it by asking what, but led the way into the kitchen where she was glad to see flames licking out of a tall wigwam of logs in the old grate.

Hadda said, 'Excuse me a minute. Make yourself useful. You know where the coffee is.'

When he returned fully dressed, she said casually, 'Talking of Luke, I told him I was certain you'd been framed.'

'That must have been relief for him. Can't have been much fun, having to stand up for a pervert. He took your word for it, did he? No demand for incontrovertible evidence?'

'He just nodded as if I was confirming something he'd known all along.'

'Yeah, sure he did. That's why he got his canonicals in such a twist when he found the money. You going to pour that coffee or are you waiting for the maid?'

The brusque jollity confirmed what she'd felt from the moment their eyes had met at the pool. He was glad to see her! That was . . . she wasn't certain what it was, but it was certainly something.

But it was time to get serious.

She said, 'I nearly forgot. John Childs asked me to give you a message.'

'Jesus!'

That really did surprise him. Good! He needed to be surprised from time to time.

He sat down heavily and looked at her from under lowering brows.

470

'How the hell have you got involved with Childs?' he asked.

She told him, succinctly but not omitting any significant detail.

He listened intently and when she'd finished he said accusingly, 'Well, well. Pity you hadn't thought to mention his name a lot earlier.'

'Why should I?' she demanded.

He considered this, then relaxed and said, 'No reason. So what was this message?'

'Something about Nikitin knowing, and the man with the broken jaw being on the loose.'

'And that's it?' he said indifferently.

'That's it.'

'Very mysterious. Dear old JC always did like to speak in tongues. Knows what, I wonder?'

Alva said, 'I would guess, knows it was you who set up Estover so the Russian would do your dirty work for you.'

This was the second time she'd surprised him in a minute. A third success and she might get to keep him!

He said, 'Psychiatrists shouldn't make guesses. So all this time you've been a buddy of JC's. Got to give the old boy credit. Having your own personal prison with wall-to-wall wire, that's a real Chapel trick! Now if I'd known that, I might have done things differently.'

'You mean you might not have played your game with me?' she said, regarding him steadily over the brim of her coffee mug.

'My game?'

She said, 'Don't pretend you didn't enjoy playing me.'

He said, 'Of course I did. To start with, anyway. Who doesn't enjoy outwitting an expert? But then, I did have the best expert advice on how to go about it . . .'

He regarded her quizzically.

'My book, you mean? And I was foolish enough to feel slightly flattered when I saw it in your bedroom.'

'Sorry about that. I hadn't meant to be so careless.'

'Come to think of it, I didn't see it in your cell at Parkleigh. That was really a book-free zone. Except for *The Count of Monte-Cristo*.'

He grinned and said, 'I couldn't resist leaving that for you to find.'

'You knew I would be having a look?'

'It seemed likely if, as suggested by *Curing Souls*, you had a truly enquiring mind,' he said. 'So I rented storage space for the books I didn't want you to find from a guy in the next cell.'

'Books?'

'Yes. Sorry. Couldn't just rely on *Curing Souls*, could I? It was, after all – what was the word the reviewers used? – rather *precocious*. So I got hold of some more mainstream stuff.'

'Just as well. It would hardly have done for you to rely for your deception on the work of such a second-rate psychiatrist as I clearly am,' she said, unable to keep the bitterness out of her voice.

'Oh dear,' he said. 'And now you hate me more for being innocent than ever you did for being guilty? Don't you find that odd?'

'I don't hate you,' she said. 'I never did.'

'A child-abusing fraudster? Come on!'

It did not seem the time to tell him she'd felt attracted to him almost from the start, despite everything she'd thought she knew about him, despite his appearance, despite all her efforts to analyse this troubling reaction out of her psyche. Getting this back on a formal professional level was important.

'Hate the sin, not the sinner is the first line of the psychotherapist's creed,' she said. 'You can't help where you hate. I wanted to help you. I still do.'

'Really?' he said in mock surprise. 'But now you recognize that I'm innocent, that I was set up, what's to help?'

She regarded him sadly and said, 'Wolf, after all that has happened to you, there's no way you're not damaged goods, you're too bright not to see that.'

'Damaged's a bit strong, isn't it? I've taken a few knocks, yes, but in the circumstances, I think I've come through it all a lot less battered inside than out. Look, Elf, don't take it personally. I'm sorry you were the tool I used for getting out of jail. OK, I enjoyed fooling you to start with, but as I got to know you, I stopped enjoying.'

'Why didn't you just try to convince me you were innocent?'

He laughed and gave her much the same answer as Doll Trapp.

'How the hell could I do that when every protestation of innocence was just another symptom of denial in your eyes? Even if I'd succeeded, who was going to listen to you? The parole hearing would pay you the respect due to an expert if you told them I'd responded to treatment and was now fit to be turned loose. But tell them I was innocent and all they'd see was a dotty woman who'd been duped by a manipulative sociopath.'

She resisted the temptation to say that was a pretty good description of what had happened anyway, and replied, 'OK. So the end of the exercise was to get out and look for evidence of how you were fitted up. And you got it from Medler. So why didn't you go straight to the authorities and say, Have a listen to this?'

He laughed again.

'Don't be naïve, Elf,' he said. 'They don't want me to be innocent any more than you did. Fine, they'll look into it, but while they're doing that, I'll be back inside.'

'But not for long, surely, once they hear your recording.'

'You reckon? But how do I prove it really was Medler talking? Or that he wasn't under duress? After all, the poor sod was found dead not long afterwards. There'd be plenty of people eager to point the finger at me. And there's Ed to think of. I was supposed to be staying with him. The Law Society would be down on him like a ton of bricks for covering up for me. And if they managed to prove it was Ed and Doll that fixed me up with a fake passport, what do you imagine that would do to them?'

She didn't speak for a while, just sat there regarding him steadily.

Then she nodded and said, 'Good arguments. You've obviously thought it through. But I think that, even if none of them applied, you would still have found some equally convincing reasons for not taking that recording to the authorities and asking them to take another look at your conviction.'

He grew angry now, or perhaps, she thought, unconsciously echoing Hollins the day before, he was seeking refuge in anger.

473

'Haven't you learned anything about the way the world works?'
he demanded. 'To find evidence to support what Medler alleged,
they'd have to go after Estover and the Nutbrowns. Toby's one of
the smartest lawyers in the country. Pippa Nutbrown's as slippery
as a sackful of snakes. As for Johnny, following his thought processes
is like trying to count bubbles in a champagne glass. And remember,
they'd be outside crying foul! while I'd be sitting on my arse in a
cell.'

'Childs says he thinks he can help you get your name cleared
officially.'

'Does he? I shan't hold my breath.'

'I just meant, with him on your side, it seems to me there's a
real chance for justice to be done.'

'He let me go down in the first place,' said Hadda indifferently.
'I always knew, if I wanted justice, I had to look for it my way.'

'You call what's happened to the Nutbrowns justice?'

His expression turned cold.

'To be dragged out of your bed by a dawn raid, to lose everything you hold precious, oh yes, that sounds like justice to me.'

'And Estover?'

'I gather his professional reputation may take a bit of a nose-
dive, and if he seeks for consolation in the little pile of gold he's
got stashed away for a rainy day, he may be in for a big surprise.
So, no reputation, no money. Now who does that remind me of?
Of course I'm sorry to hear he's going to lose his youthful good
looks and may end up walking with a bit of a limp. Maybe we
could get together and do a double act round the halls?'

This was going to be even harder than she'd anticipated.

She said, 'So, an eye for an eye; that sounds a lot more like
revenge to me than justice.'

'Anything they get will be less than they deserve,' he said dismissively.

'Would you still have been able to say that if Estover had died?
You knew that was the likely outcome if it hadn't been for Childs's
intervention.'

474

He shrugged.

'It may still be that Toby will come to regard that as the better alternative,' he said. 'As for JC, I'll bottle my gratitude till I've got enough to make a grateful tear.'

'I think that, despite everything, he's helped you because he is fond of you.'

'And the same for you, no doubt. But John's god is Necessity, and that's an idol carved out of granite. Try not to come between it and anything you value.'

'He's genuinely worried about what you intend to do next,' she said.

'He needn't be. What's the point of worrying about fate?'

'He said you might be suffering from the delusion that you were the instrument of God. Wolf, believe me, if left too late, that's a delusion whose dissipation you might find too hard to bear.'

Suddenly he relaxed and let out a hoot of laughter.

'Jesus, Elf, we're beginning to sound like two characters in an old-fashioned melodrama! What do you think's going to happen? I'm not about to mount a rocket attack on Ulphingstone Castle or anything like that, believe me. I've got most of the revenge stuff out of my system now, honest. All I want's a bit of peace and quiet so that I can watch the spring arrive.'

She wanted to believe him. She had a feeling he wanted to believe himself. But she'd had it drummed into her that the truly effective psychiatrist always gets the couch warm for the client. Or, put another way, the first job is to look deep into yourself and make sure you start with a clean sheet.

Sneck suddenly rose from the hearth and went to the door, growling deep in this throat.

Hadda rose too.

'Excuse me,' he said.

Motioning Sneck to heel, he pulled the door open, waited a moment, then slipped outside. Alva found herself once more comparing the smooth, slightly rolling movement caused by his ruined knee with the laboured limp she remembered from Parkleigh.

475

She too stood up and went to the door.

She saw him in the barn doorway standing by the Defender. He plucked a spill of paper tucked in behind the wipers, unfolded it and began to read. Sneck turned and looked at Alva. Not wanting Wolf to think she was spying on him, she retreated and was sitting at the table once more, nursing her coffee mug, when he came back in.

'Problem?' she said.

'No,' he said, tossing a screwed-up ball of paper towards the fire. 'Might have been a deer. Sneck and me are both getting neurotic. We had a bit of trouble with reporters.'

'Yes, Luke Hollins told me about the muck-spreader. He seemed to find it rather poetic.'

'He's a good lad,' said Hadda, resuming his seat and picking up his mug. 'Now, where were we?'

He was trying to sound the same as he did before, but something had changed.

She said, 'You were telling me how content you were to relax in your own cosy little house, far away from the world's troubles, just waiting for the daffodils and swallows to return with the spring.'

'Was I? Sounds good to me. Why are you giving me that fish-eyed psychiatrist look?'

'Because I don't believe you,' she said.

'Hang about? Are you people allowed to call your patients liars?'

'I'm not talking to you as a patient but as a friend,' she said. 'And here's what I think. I think that everything you've done since you got out, all your clever planning and scheming, all your talk of justice and revenge, amounts to nothing more than delaying tactics. You don't really give a damn about Estover and Nutbrown. You don't give a damn about proving your innocence. The only thing that really matters to you is what you're going to do about Imogen. And the truth is, you've no idea what to do, no idea what you want to do. But now, with everything else out of the way, the big moment's getting near. So what's it to be, Wolf? Have you made up your mind yet?'

For a moment she thought she'd stung him to an honest reply. Then he let out a rather histrionic sigh, shook his head ruefully and said, 'There you go, Elf. Even when you're talking as a friend, you can't stop working out interesting little mental scenarios, can you? I always suspected that all this psycho-analysing stuff came down to storytelling in the end. You plot a little narrative to take everything in, make a few adjustments to let the action flow more smoothly, offer a couple of endings, one happy, one unhappy, then tell your client to make his choice, that'll be a hundred guineas please. Well, I'm sorry, Elf. I'm no longer a character in your fairy tale. I'm very happy in my own.'

She said, '*Once upon a time I was living happily ever after.* Those were the first words you wrote for me, remember? You were a character in your own fairy tale, Wolf, not mine. In fact, you were two characters. The wolf and the woodcutter. Bit of a conflict there. Maybe it's a good job that fairy tale's over. No way can you ever get back into it. But you're right. Even without paying a hundred guineas, you can still choose the ending.'

On the wall the old bracket clock struck the hour.

He stood up and said, 'That time already? Damn. And I was so enjoying our fireside chat. But I'm afraid I've got to go. Us licensed cons aren't masters of our lives, as I'm sure you know. I need to show my face at regular intervals, prove I'm still on the straight and narrow.'

'You mean you're driving to Carlisle to see your probation officer?'

'That's right,' he said. 'No need for you to rush off, sit here and finish your coffee. But don't feel you've got to wash up! Will I see you again before you go back down to Manchester, or are you heading off straight away?'

She looked up at him and said, 'I'm not sure.'

'OK,' he said, turning away to pluck his axe from where it stood in a corner. Then he turned to look at her, curiously indecisive. Finally he took a couple of steps forward till he was standing alongside her chair. She sat quite still, aware of the closeness of his body. And of his axe also.

He said, 'I never felt I could do this while you thought I was guilty. And now you don't, I'm finding all kinds of other reasons for being frightened of doing it. At this rate, I'll never do it! So here goes.'

He stooped, put his right hand behind her head and pressed his face to hers in a kiss that went on so long she felt herself becoming breathless, but she made no effort to break contact.

Finally he pulled away.

'For better or worse, that's done,' he said. 'First kiss? Last kiss? Who can ever tell?'

He made for the door. Sneck rose from the hearth but subsided reluctantly as his master commanded, 'Stay!'

Then he was gone. A moment later she heard the grating roar of the Defender. When that died away, the silence seemed like the silence of space.

She finished her coffee. She'd made it strong, the way she knew Hadda liked it, but far from being a stimulant, it seemed to act on her like an opiate. A strange lassitude stole over her limbs and she sat peering sightlessly and for the most part thoughtlessly into her empty mug. It was as if there were a problem she had to puzzle out, only it was so big her mind could not even begin to get to grips with it.

It was the wigwam of logs in the grate collapsing in a gentle sigh of heron-grey ash that roused her from her reverie.

She ran her tongue round her lips.

Better or worse? First or last?

Who can tell?'

She stood up to get some more logs from the basket. Sneck looked up at her hopefully. She said, 'Sorry,' and he returned his attention to something he was licking at between his paws. As she set the logs in the grate, she realized it was the piece of paper Hadda had balled up and thrown at the fire.

She tried to pick it up. The dog bared his teeth. She went to the kitchen cupboard and got a ginger biscuit. Sneck acknowledged this was fair exchange and let her retrieve the paper.

478

She smoothed it out on the kitchen table.

It was a handwritten note:

Is she a permanent fixture then? I think I'll take a stroll to Pillar Rock. Who says I'm not sentimental?

She didn't recognize the writing; she didn't need to.

He wasn't on his way to see his probation officer. She should have known that as soon as he took his axe from the corner. But the kiss had diverted her mind down other channels in search of its meaning.

One thing she was certain of: the kiss couldn't mean whatever she wanted it to mean while his problems with Imogen remained unresolved.

And she doubted whether a true resolution were possible while the woman was alive. But if she died, and if Wolf was responsible, then the problem would remain frozen in time for ever, and Wolf would be completely beyond her reach, emotionally, mentally, and almost certainly physically too.

She had no idea what she could do, but she knew that the possibility of solution did not lie in the maze of her mind but out there somewhere on the cold fell tops.

She made for the door. From the hearth came an enquiring growl.

She turned and looked at Sneck.

'Why not, boy?' she said. 'To tell you the truth, I'll be glad of company!'

4

Imogen stood on top of Pillar Rock looking down at the Liza winding its way along the valley bottom two thousand feet below and recalling the first time she had climbed up here more than a quarter of a century before.

Then she had simply trailed along beside Wolf, not certain where he was going, just knowing there was a life force in this young man that she wanted a share of.

Well, she'd certainly got her share, sucked him almost dry some might say, though he had got his fair share of all that she had to offer too.

No, not his *fair* share, because fairness didn't enter into it.

He had stepped out of his world into hers, but it had been both impossible and undesirable that he could step all the way.

Impossible because, despite all the social cosmetology of the modern democratic era, it remained as true as it had always been that the *arriviste* could never really arrive.

And undesirable because for Wolf to have completely adapted to the moral code of her circle, which was basically *do what thou wilt shall be all of the law*, he would have had to sacrifice so much of what made him Wolf that he'd no longer have been worth having.

The wind was blowing hard up here. She sat down with her back to it. She was well insulated by several layers of clothing, but its chilly fingers still probed through to her warm flesh. Suggesting the Rock as a rendezvous point had not been the cleverest idea she'd ever had. Why had she done it? In one sense it was typical of the way she'd conducted a great deal of her life, an instinctive decision made without reference to reason or consequence. But at the same time it was also atypical, a reaching out of the random in search of a pattern.

Here it had all started. Here it would all end.

How it would end, she could not foretell. Her efforts to see him at Christmas had been coloured by the assumption that she would still have power over him, based on her awareness that he still had power over her. Her sense that he was making a conscious effort not to see her had confirmed her assumption. But after what had happened to Toby and the Nutbrowns, things had moved on. A first step had been taken, and she knew from her own life how much easier a second step was.

Curiously, her increased sense of risk made her all the more determined to confront him head on. She enjoyed danger as long as it was in her face. What she didn't like was relaxing in her bath and hearing the buzz of an invisible wasp. Or to put it more poetically (she sometimes tried at poetry) all she wanted was to be able to stroll through the woodlands of her future without constantly straining her ears to catch the distant sound of an axe.

Was she a cold-hearted bitch, as a discarded lover had once called her? She'd examined the accusation closely and did not think so. Indeed, compared with her mother, she felt she was a creature of impulse and feeling. They had so much in common yet there were ways in which they were incomprehensible to each other. When Kira declared that the only thing better than having Wolf back in jail would be to have him buried deep in his grave, she was simply stating what she felt. To Imogen, neither of these was a desirable solution. What she wanted was to find a way for the pair of them to accept the collapse of their relationship and walk away from the wreckage comparatively unscathed.

There was a chance, albeit a small one, that her breakfast

481

exchange with Kira might have provided a faint hope of finding such a way.

And another hopeful factor was the possibility that Wolf might even have something to walk away *to* as well as from. Men traditionally fell in love with their nurses, so why not with their psychiatrists?

Finding the black woman at the house again had been a surprise. When Alva Ozigbo came to the castle after Christmas, Imogen hadn't considered the possibility that she might have any interest in Wolf other than a professional one. After all, from her point of view, he was a convicted paedophile/fraudster whom she had certified safe to return to the community, so naturally she had a vested interest in keeping a close eye on him.

Now Imogen wished she'd taken rather more notice of her as an individual. She was certainly striking. Attractive? Possibly. Imogen tried to see her through male eyes. She herself wasn't too sensitive to the sexual aura of other women. In the interest of total experience she and Pippa had once spent a night together, but while there had been certain advantages in relating to a body that had the same geography and responses as your own, it had not been something she wanted to do again.

But she could see how Alva Ozigbo, with that combination of black skin, ochrous hair and fine bone structure, might turn some men on. Wolf? She wasn't sure. He had been so totally fixated on herself that she had never heard him express even a theoretical interest in another woman. She was one hundred per cent sure he'd never been unfaithful to her, even when his travels had kept him away from home for months on end. The pent-up passion released on his return had given her some of the sensual highs of her life, though after he'd been at home a while, his attentions began to make her feel a touch claustrophobic.

Had he ever suspected this? She thought not.

And she was absolutely sure he'd never suspected her of being unfaithful. His reaction would have been, to say the least, extreme. She had been very lucky for fourteen years that no malicious tongue had sought to set him straight. Perhaps his natural unselfconscious likeability had protected him. It would have been like hurting a child.

Or perhaps it had been his other defining quality, the sense of raw power seething beneath the surface and looking for an outlet, that had kept him safe. If ever there was a man whose first reaction might be to kill the messenger, it was Wolf!

But eventually, inevitably, he would have found out.

She knew her friends.

They might hold their peace for years but in the end, like the scorpion in the fable, they would have to sting, because it was in their nature.

This certainty that the marriage was living on borrowed time had been one of the factors that made it easy to go along with Toby and Pippa when they'd revealed their survival scheme. When necessity rules, regret is as pointless as resistance.

One way or another, Wolf was going to jail and the marriage was finished.

One way, she would be penniless.

The other, she wouldn't be.

Where was the choice in that?

To say she saw him condemned without a pang would have been untrue. To say that this pang kept her awake at nights would have been untruer. Only two things kept her awake and they were sex and toothache.

No, that was the kind of smart untruth she'd grown too used to pushing away people with. After Ginny died, she hadn't slept soundly for months without the help of pills or alcohol. Though, curiously, she now found that since moving into Ginny's old room, she slept like a child.

And she felt a kind of childish diffidence now as she sat on top of the Rock and wondered if he would come, and if he did, what he would do. She felt a sense of danger but no real fear. If necessity drove him to harm her, then so be it. She was confident he would not want to disfigure her as he had been disfigured. Death was another matter. He had never spoken openly about the years of youthful absence, but there had been killing in there somewhere, she was sure. In the right cause, he had the power to kill.

She stared down into the valley and saw herself slowly tumbling through the air.

Of course it wouldn't really be slow. Thirty-two feet per second, something like that, she seemed to recollect. Which worked out at a lot of miles per hour!

But how slow might it feel in the mind? Climbing, she'd often wondered about this. How many recollections and regrets could be crushed between that moment when your fingers slipped from their hold and the next when your body broke against the rocks?

Perhaps there was just time for one clear revelation, one all-illuminating insight.

Or perhaps it would go on forever. She recalled a story her father used to read to her about a thief who escaped capture by jumping over the edge of the world. She used to lie in bed after Leon had put out the light, imagining how that would feel. And the words had often played through her mind as she was climbing . . . *falling from us still through the unreverberate blackness of the abyss* . . .

Falling . . . falling . . . falling . . .

A sound reached her that wasn't borne on the gusting wind. She rose to her feet and strained her ears.

There it was again, the sound of boot on rock, from far below.

He was coming. She'd never doubted that he would.

She settled down for the last minutes of waiting.

5

Pudo Pudovkin had all the attributes of a fine chess player: a mind that could sum up several moves ahead, an ability to read an opponent, and the patience not to make a move until he was happy it was the right one. Everything, in fact, except the capacity to accept defeat philosophically. And while being a bad loser doesn't necessarily make you a bad player, being the kind of bad loser who is likely to fly into a rage and attempt to make a winning opponent swallow his chessmen tends to leave you short of people willing to play with you.

His positive qualities, plus a large infusion of the negative one, combined to make him an excellent assassin. But on this dank February morning, he found his patience was being sorely tried.

Arriving early in the vicinity of Birkstane, he had left the anonymous grey Honda he was driving parked out of sight near the head of the lonning and made his way towards the house. He took up a position on a swell of ground about thirty yards from the building where a few scrubby gorse bushes gave him cover, and his elevation gave him a view into the yard through his compact Leika binoculars.

As the sky grew light, there'd been signs of activity within the house, and smoke had begun to rise from the chimney. Then to his amazement, the door opened and Hadda stepped out into the cold morning air, stark naked except for a towel flung over one

485

shoulder. He headed out of sight behind the barn buildings. The sound of running water revealed the presence of a stream some-where close. Presumably this madman was going to bathe in it!

Pudovkin shivered at the thought, but it made his job easy. The only fly in the ointment was the mangy dog trotting along at Hadda's heel. It looked a vicious beast. Pudovkin did not care for dogs. He'd once been bitten by one in childhood. Later he had returned with a piece of poisoned meat and had the pleasure of watching the beast die in agony. Hadda's dog would have a more merciful death. The first shot would take care of it. A naked cripple bathing in an icy stream would hardly be in any condition to take advantage of the brief respite offered by this diversion.

He was just beginning to move forward from his hiding place when he heard a distant engine. A few moments later, a black woman had come down the lonning and into the yard. Who the fuck was she? he wondered. Maybe she would leave when she found the house empty.

She opened the door and peered inside. For a moment she hesi-tated in the doorway. Then she turned and went in the lame man's footsteps.

'Fuck!' he muttered. A man and a dog were do-able, but this woman complicated matters. Who was going to miss her and how soon? There might even be someone waiting for her in her car. In cleaning operations escape routes were vital, and in this fucking wilderness time was an essential part of any escape plan. Pudo wanted to be long gone before the deed was discovered. He needed at least an hour to get on the south-bound motorway. Any pursuit that started sooner than that could have him road-blocked off with the peasants.

He settled back into his hide. After a few minutes he heard the sound of another car engine. Jesus, he thought. This is like Oxford fucking Street at Christmas!

Shortly afterwards another woman came strolling down the lonning. This one he recognized. It was the lawyer's wife, the good-looking blonde that Pasha Nikitin lusted after. As he'd worked on

486

Toby Estover in the warehouse, Pudo had been satisfied the lawyer knew nothing about the newspaper article long before his boss had signalled a halt. How much, he wondered, had this had to do with the lovely Imogen? And how was Pasha going to react to the news that she was still sniffing around her ex-husband?

With great indifference, if the said ex was dead, he guessed.

But her presence was a further unwelcome complication.

As she approached the gate, there was a sound of voices and the black woman came into view, heading towards the house. The blonde stepped sideways out of sight into the hedgerow that flanked the lonning. Hadda, still naked, and his dog appeared behind the black and the three of them went inside.

The blonde woman retreated up the lonning. Pudovkin listened for the sound of a car starting up but heard nothing. Then she reappeared. This time she passed through the gate and walked into the yard. She was holding a sheet of paper in her hand as she vanished from the Russian's line of sight into the barn, but when she reappeared a moment later, she was empty-handed.

Once more she went up the lonning, moving with an easy grace, but purposefully. This time he did hear a car start up.

Next Hadda, now fully dressed, came out of the house. He looked around carefully. Something must have alerted him, probably that fucking dog. Now he crossed the yard and went into the barn. The black woman stood in the doorway watching him for a moment before going back inside. Hadda followed shortly, in his hand a sheet of paper, presumably that left by his ex-wife, which he crumpled up as he passed through the door.

Now what was that all about? wondered Pudo. Not that he really gave a damn. His only concern was that he was freezing his nuts off stuck in this gorse bush with no way of working out how long it was going to be before he could have the pleasure of blowing Hadda's fucking head off!

Much longer and he would be too cold to pull a trigger. He was sorely tempted just to head down to the house, burst into the kitchen and blast away at everything that moved. But that was just the chill entering his brain. Time to head back to his nice warm car and review the situation.

He was almost at the head of the lonning when he heard the roar of an engine starting up somewhere behind him. He scuttled sideways through the hedgerow and was able to see the Land Rover Defender bumping over the rutted surface of the lane. He hurried after it, keeping on the blind side of the hedge. Where the lonning met the narrow road, if the vehicle turned west then it was heading towards what passed for the main road in this third world county and pursuit would be futile.

But if it turned east . . .

And east it had turned.

Pudo had studied his map before venturing into this wasteland and he knew that eastward, not far past the head of the long dark lake with the suggestive name of Wastwater, the road came to a dead end. Here stood a scatter of dwellings and an inn. A man wanting to go further than these would have to go on foot.

He sent the Honda hurtling along the narrow road till he could see the Defender up ahead, then slowed to its pace. Hadda kept going all the way to the inn and parked before it. Pudovkin brought the Honda to a halt with a light blue Merc coupé between it and the Defender. There weren't many other cars here. Big surprise. Who in his right senses would want to come here at this time of year?

If Hadda went into the inn, then he might be in for a long wait. But the big man was shrugging on a cagoule and slinging his fucking axe over his back. Pudo's jaw, still wired, ached at the sight of it. Even if Pasha hadn't sent commands, he'd have wanted to sort this bastard out on his own behalf.

Now Hadda was ready. He slammed the tailgate shut and set out past the inn.

A glance at his map confirmed to the Russian that there was nowhere to go except wilderness. This was excellent. One thing you could say for this benighted landscape was it offered the careful killer any number of good ambush positions, plus a superfluity of sites where a body could be dumped and not be found for days if not weeks.

He gave his prey a couple of minutes' start which he used to slip into a pair of trekking shoes and a fur-lined parka, congratulating himself on his foresight in coming prepared. Then he set out in pursuit.

He didn't anticipate any problem keeping pace with a lame man, and felt confident he'd have enough in reserve to overtake him when the moment and location seemed ripe to conclude the business. In his work, keeping fit was a condition of service. It could mean the difference between life and death. So he worked out daily at the activity centre when he was in London, with separate regimes for strength, for endurance, for agility. He could run for an hour, snatch a hundred and sixty kilos, and go up the climbing wall at a speed that made some of the serious mountaineering boys open their eyes. When, as occasionally happened, one of them suggested he might like to join them on a real rock face, he said, 'You must be fucking joking! I don't do this for pleasure.'

Hadda had vanished towards the rear of the inn. There was a broad stream here spanned by an ancient footbridge. Pudovkin started to cross it but paused when he could see no sign of Hadda on the open ground ahead. He glanced to his right, and there he was, still on the same side of the water.

Pudo followed. The path bore left, climbing above the stream. He lost sight of his prey but a solid stone wall to one side and a wire fence to the other cut down the chance of diversion. There were several gates to pass through. He didn't waste time by closing them behind him. The final one took him out into open countryside with the path descending into a broad valley. Now once more he could see Hadda. Despite his lameness, he was setting a spanking pace and the Russian soon had to revise his notion of being able to overtake the man at his ease.

As the path became steeper he revised it even more, discovering the considerable difference between gym fitness and the demands on your muscles made by hill climbing. He made up a bit of ground when his prey came to a halt beside a tumultuous stream and stooped to gather water in his hands and take a drink. He didn't look back. No need to worry if he had. At this distance recognition wasn't likely and the presence of another walker on the same well-trodden path was hardly going to be suspicious.

When Pudovkin reached the stream, he too paused to drink and briefly consult his map. The path crossed the stream (fittingly, in view of its spate, called Gatherstone Beck) and then bore right above it to the depression of Black Sail Pass between the mountain whose side he'd been traversing, Kirk Fell, and an even higher one ahead, named Pillar, though it didn't look to have much that was pillar-like about it.

Having no idea which of the routes on offer Hadda was planning to take when he reached the pass, the Russian forced himself to speed up. But despite his best efforts, the man had vanished by the time he got there.

Furious that all this expenditure of energy might have been in vain, Pudovkin checked out the options. To his right the track rose to what looked like a steep and rocky ascent of Kirk Fell. There was no one climbing it.

He went forward till he could see down into the next valley. He recalled its name: Ennerdale. If anything it looked even more godforsaken than the valley he had just climbed out of.

He scanned the possible lines of descent from the pass, but again spotted no movement.

He returned to the main cross path and started along it towards Pillar. Now once more he spotted his man, not on the main path but on a lower branch that skirted beneath the craggy north face of Pillar overlooking Ennerdale.

The short descent to this lower path was steep and slippery and he did most of it on his backside. His earlier notion of somehow overtaking and lying in ambush was now completely abandoned. Apart from the surprising speed at which the lame man was moving, this was a track that followed the best, indeed for most of the time the only possible line, and getting ahead of his prey was virtually

490

impossible. So now all he could hope for was to get close enough for a clear shot.

His weapon was a Makarov PM, similar to the one that Hadda had ruined on the beach. He'd really loved that gun. It had belonged to the first man he'd killed, and he felt a sentimental attachment towards it. So though there were more efficient modern weapons available, he'd chosen to replace it with the same.

Its drawback was that to guarantee deadliness of both aim and impact he needed to be within a range of no more than twenty metres and preferably nearer half of that. In his usual urban environment, this was fine. Out in this fucking wilderness, something with a long-range capability would have come in useful. On the other hand, closeness might bring the pleasure of being recognized. He was more than happy to shoot Hadda in the back, but the buzz of letting him know who was pulling the trigger would be a definite bonus.

The weather was changing. Clouds were gobbing up the clear blue sky, sinking low enough to obscure the mountain crests and send questing swirls of mist down the rocky slopes. Not normally a fanciful man, Pudovkin was surprised by the thought that it might be Hadda who was summoning these vapours to help conceal him, and when a huge raven swooped out of the crags and croaked mockingly just above his head, it felt like a visitation from an enemy spy.

He waved away these superstitious fancies, but they came flocking back a few minutes later when the track climbed to a prominent shoulder on which stood an imposing cairn.

Straight ahead of him, towering from the mountainside like the ruin of some ancient troll-king's stronghold was a huge jagged rock, dark and menacing, its front plunging precipitously to the valley below.

Here was an explanation of the name Pillar. The fell was named not for its height or bulk but for this single dominant feature. And it was toward this terrifying excrescence that the track was leading.

He could see Hadda clearly, striding onward at the same unrelenting pace. For the first time, doubt seeped into the Russian's mind. This creature he was pursuing was in its own hunting grounds. He was the intruder here.

Then he reminded himself that his quarry was a one-eyed cripple with a maimed hand and no weapon but a long axe. He felt the comforting weight of the Makarov in its shoulder holster and, leaving the cairn behind, he resumed his progress along the path.

Most of the snow had vanished from the track up to Black Sail but here on the north-facing flank of the fell, many of the cracks between the dark crags were still packed white, creating a savage pied beauty that might have appealed to a mind less focused than the Russian's. All he noticed was that the wind here was much stronger than it had been in Mosedale, blowing in gusts that rattled among the crags and bounced back with a resonance almost metallic. He drew his fur-lined hood up around his head. The din of the wind would conceal the sound of his approach and, even if Hadda did look round, the hood would delay recognition till it was too late.

Ahead the man was following the track up a steep slope across loose stones that scrunched and tinkled beneath his boots. Pudovkin lost sight of him in a swirl of mist. He expected to glimpse him again higher up the track but he didn't appear. Perhaps he was taking a rest. Surely there was nowhere to divert to in this rocky wilderness? This could be it, he thought, picturing coming upon his prey lying at his ease to catch what he didn't realize was his last breath.

He pressed on, but as he approached the spot where he'd last seen Hadda, there was no sign of the man. Indeed, it wasn't the kind of place anyone in their right senses would have paused to seek rest. At least while you were moving you didn't have too much time to take in the horror of your surroundings.

Above him, the track steepened up a scree slope. Up there, Hadda would surely have been in clear view. He looked for alternatives and spotted a tiny cairn. It seemed to indicate the start of a side path, not the kind of path anything but a demented sheep would follow, but he followed it anyway. It led down and round till at a bend he found himself gazing over a desolate gully that made the terrain he'd just crossed seem an oasis of calm and security.

On the far side of the gully, close now but diminished by the scale of the surrounding crags, he saw his prey again. He was picking his way gingerly up a great slab of rock that seemed to lead nowhere but the sheer face of the towering pillar above. The slowness of his movement encouraged Pudovkin to consider the possibility of a shot.

He pulled out his gun and took aim. Even as he did so, his mind was calculating the distance, and the wind, and coming almost instantaneously to the conclusion he'd be mad to take the risk. At the moment, if Hadda spotted him, he was just another idiot whose idea of fun was to risk life and limb crawling around this inhospitable place in the middle of winter. But a bullet bouncing off the rock he was clinging to would be a strong hint that there was trouble around!

He reholstered the gun. He had to get close enough to ensure his first shot at least disabled the guy.

Hadda had reached the top of the slab. He seemed to take a step down, moved a little to his right, and then began climbing straight up.

Now this was much more promising, thought Pudovkin. Get below him and he would present a perfect target with no scope for evasion.

As quickly as he could, he crossed the gully and pulled himself up on to the slab. Its angle wasn't so steep as to be much of an obstacle in itself and there were cracks and indentations that provided good footholds. But there was also a lot of ice and Pudovkin now appreciated why Hadda had been taking this so carefully.

His foot slipped and he went down heavily on his right knee.

He swore violently in Russian. His friends would have taken this as a signal to stand clear. He had a full range of English oaths at his disposal for everyday use, but at moments of extreme anger, he always reverted to his native language.

He was beginning to wish he'd just shot Hadda as he bathed in the stream behind his house, and the black woman too. And the dog as well, of course. Not so easy getting off three accurate shots at different targets, but if he'd known where his pursuit of Hadda was going to bring him, he might have taken the chance.

On the other hand, as he headed back to his car, he'd probably have met Estover's wife, and she'd have had to go too. That wouldn't have pleased Nikitin. OK, he might have accepted the argument of necessity, but resentment has a longer shelflife than gratitude, and in some dark recess of the future, when all the many services Pudovkin had done for him had faded from his memory, he would still recall that his faithful servant had killed the woman he loved.

So he bottled his anger. Here was where he was, and he did not intend to leave without accomplishing what he'd set out to do.

But his heart sank when he stepped off the end of the slab and moved along a narrow ledge to the right. He'd been hoping when he looked up to see his quarry exposed on the rock face above him. Instead he was just in time to see him moving out of sight to commence the next section of the ascent.

To get to him he was going to have to follow him.

Suddenly the indoor climbing wall which he was accustomed to running up like a spider diminished in his recollection to little more than a gentle slope liberally scattered with regular hand and foot-holds.

But where a fucking cripple could go, he could go too!

Not before he had a rest, though, and some refreshment.

He squatted down and pulled a small plastic bag out of an inner pocket. From it he took a pinch of white powder, set it to his right nostril and sniffed. Then he repeated the process with the left.

Now he sat for a couple of minutes till he felt strength and clarity return.

At last he was ready.

He took a deep breath, said a prayer to his birth-saint (who after so many years of neglect probably wrinkled her face and said, *Who?*) and began to climb.

6

'Hello, Wolf,' said Imogen.

Hadda looked up and saw her standing above him. She was in her forties now, but she still had the clear glowing skin and the fresh-faced beauty of a Botticelli angel.

If she wanted, she could drive her boot into his face and send him tumbling five hundred feet, give or take a bounce. End of all her worries. End of his too, and perhaps not the worst way to go, with those calmly lovely features the last thing he saw on earth.

She reached her hand towards him and he thought for a moment that maybe his fantasy was going to come true. Then she grasped his hand and hauled him up towards her.

They stood facing each other.

'So here we are,' she said.

'Again,' he said.

'Yes. Again. Only I didn't need a rope this time.'

'I don't think you needed a rope the first time.'

'But then you were worried about me,' she said. 'Funny, isn't it? All the climbing we did, we never came back here.'

'There was nothing to come back for. I mean, nothing that could be added to that first time. Not for me, anyway.'

'Oh, Wolf,' she said. 'You made a bad choice.'

'No,' he said. 'I never made any choice. Choosing didn't come into it. It was you who made the bad choice.'

She nodded gravely.

'You're right. I chose. And it was a selfish choice because I could see you had none.'

He realized he was still holding her hand and let it fall.

He said, 'Let's sit down.'

'Why? Have you brought a picnic?'

He said, 'No. I was thinking, violence is more difficult from a sitting position.'

'Ah.'

They moved away from the edge and sank on to a rib of dry rock. He'd unslung his axe and now he laid it between them. Then he reached into the pocket of his cagoule and produced a pewter flask.

'No picnic,' he said. 'But a drop of the Caledonian cream to keep the cold out. You could have frozen to death, waiting up here.'

'I'm like you, I don't feel the cold,' she said. 'And I haven't been waiting long. You must still move fast.'

'For a cripple, you mean.'

'No,' she said. 'For a geriatric.'

That almost made him smile. He unscrewed the flask and passed it over. She took a short drink. He took a slightly longer one.

'So, Wolf,' she said. 'Let's talk seriously. There's just me left, now that you've pronounced judgment on Johnny, Pippa and Toby.'

'Have I?' he said. 'I thought I'd just been sitting quietly up here in God's Own Country, minding my business.'

'That's what you were doing when you chopped our rowan tree down, was it?'

He said, 'Woodcutting's always been my business. But I doubt anyone will be able to link me with whatever's happened to the Nutbrowns and your husband.'

'I'm sure of it,' she said. 'Just as I'm sure that, if you wanted, you could arrange for me to be dealt with at a distance. But you're here.'

'Justice is like sex,' he said. 'Less satisfying at a distance. That could be my explanation for being here. What's yours?'

496

'Oh, you know me,' she said. 'Just an old-fashioned girl who prefers most things face to face. Especially a trial.'

'So you've come to make your defence?'

'No. No defence. Guilty as charged. But I would like to exercise my right to make a plea in mitigation.'

He took another drink, offered the flask. She shook her head.

'Plead away,' he said.

'Well, first of all, I have never lied to you.'

'You're saying you weren't screwing Estover before and during our marriage?'

'No, I'm not saying that. And not just Toby. There were others,' she said. 'You did spend a lot of time away from home, Wolf. If I say it meant nothing, I would be lying. But it meant no more or less than eating. Always a necessity, only occasionally a real pleasure. Never like it was when you came home.'

'So you were just keeping in practice, is that it?' he said harshly. 'And you don't count that as deceiving me?'

'I didn't say I didn't deceive you. I said I never lied to you. If you'd ever asked, I would have told you. But you never did. Was that because you trusted me, Wolf? Or because you were frightened to ask?'

'Forget the psychoanalysis,' he said. 'I'm done with that. If I were your brief, I'd advise that your plea in mitigation is getting off on the wrong foot. When are we going to get on to the disturbed childhood, the school bullying, the dysfunctional family stuff?'

'I had all of those,' she said evenly. 'The bullying stopped when those concerned found they suffered far more than I did. As for my family, well, you know my mother.'

'Ah yes. Kira. All her fault, is it?'

'To a large extent. Didn't you wonder why she stopped objecting to our marriage?'

'I always assumed it was because I got you pregnant and she didn't care to have a bastard for a grandchild.'

'The second part of that is certainly true,' said Imogen.

She spoke so calmly that it took several seconds for the implication to sink into Hadda's mind.

He scrambled to his feet and took a few steps back from her. His fists were clenched. He had clearly realized, she thought, that sitting down wasn't such a disincentive to violence as he'd imagined.

He said, 'Now you're lying.'

She said, 'No. I got confirmation I was pregnant about a week after your return. Far too early for it to have been you. But, if it's any consolation, I didn't know about it when I said I'd marry you.'

'And when you did know, you just let me think it was mine?'

'If you'd asked, I'd have told you the truth,' she said. 'But you didn't. So I didn't. Wolf, I'm sorry.'

'*Sorry!* For what particular lump of all this shit you've piled on me, may I ask?'

'I'm sorry I connived at keeping Ginny away from you after . . . after it happened. I told myself it didn't matter as she wasn't really yours. But that was wrong. I see that now. She was as much yours as . . .'

'As whose? Who was Ginny's real father? Estover?'

'I don't think so,' she said indifferently. 'Does it matter? You were the only father Ginny ever knew. That was a pain I had no right to inflict on either of you. For both your sakes, I should have let your letters reach her. I shouldn't have listened to Mother.'

'Ah, the bitch-queen. I knew she'd be in there somewhere. What did she advise then?'

'That now was the time to tell Ginny the truth about her parentage. I agreed because I thought it would make her feel better, less connected . . . She was very upset.'

'Jesus!' exclaimed Hadda, his face working with rage. 'Upset! You mess up her mind and then send her out of the country! No wonder the poor kid never got in touch with me, no wonder she went completely off the rails. Whatever else I blamed you for, I tried not to blame you for her death. But now . . . For Christ's sake, Imo, forget all this crap about a plea in mitigation for what you've done to me. How can you ever forgive yourself for what you did to Ginny?'

She said urgently, 'Wolf, I can't, I don't. Believe me, for a long time now, I've been frozen inside. When I melt I'm simply going to wash away. You and I are very much the same. We survive by not asking questions. We create a world we can live in because we have invented our own rules. We climb not because we want to reach the top but because deep down inside, what we really want is to fall. *We are the same!'*

Her voice had become increasingly agitated till the final words came out in a single breath. Her agitation seemed to calm him and when he replied it was in a low, even tone.

'What the hell are you talking about?' he asked. 'Don't try to tar me with your brush, Imo. All I ever wanted was to get into your world so I could have you, but it was a delusion, a madness, and I'm over it now. When I was a boy I always thought you were far beyond my dreams and now I see how right I was. But not beyond. Beneath! I thought I had to climb up to get to your world, now I see that all I did was let go of everything real and fall till I hit rock bottom!'

He had moved steadily forward as he spoke and now he stooped to pick up his axe.

She looked up at him and said softly, 'Oh, Wolf. It's not worlds I'm talking about. It's genes. We're sides of the same coin, that's what drew us together. You weren't the first woodcutter to feel the pull of the magic castle. Did you never wonder why we were so drawn to each other? And when we made love there was a darkness in it that made it all the better, don't say you never felt that.'

'What the hell are you talking about?' he repeated, this time more vehemently. *'The same coin? Darkness?* Come on, woman, speak plain while you've still got the chance!'

She regarded him sadly and said, 'Haven't you guessed? I thought you might have guessed long ago. We're brother and sister, Wolf. Fred was my father too.'

7

At Wasdale Head, Alva parked her car alongside Hadda's Defender. Next to it was a blue Mercedes. No way to identify it positively as Imogen's, but she recalled a similar car standing outside Ulphingstone Castle when she'd called there in January.

She took her small day-pack out of the boot and checked its contents. Waterproof, spare pullover, mint cake, isotonic orange juice, lightweight binoculars, map, compass, whistle, torch. Everything the wise psychiatrist should carry on the fells. All her Lake District walking had been done on the east side, so she opened her map to check the route to Pillar, but when she heard Sneck's bark, she realized she needn't have bothered. The dog was standing on the track that led past the side of the inn, looking back at her impatiently. As she went after him, he turned and ran ahead with a reassuring certainty.

Perhaps Hadda wasn't as far in front as she'd feared. Perhaps for some reason he'd diverted on his way here.

As she reached the main path running up the right-hand side of Mosedale along the flank of Kirk Fell, she glimpsed a figure far ahead and her heart leapt. But when she paused to focus her glasses, she quickly realized it wasn't Hadda. Just another walker, and one moving fast. She put the glasses away and settled into the long rangy stride that had been the envy of her college friends when they went hiking together. 'For God's sake, Alva, it's not a bloody

500

race!' they'd say. But, being a student psychiatrist, she'd known that it usually was.

Sneck knew exactly where he was going and in his eagerness often disappeared from view, but always he returned as if to reassure himself she was keeping up. She thought of urging him to take off by himself in the hope that he'd catch up with his master and let him know that she was following. But what good would that do?

And while the path ahead was perfectly clear at the moment, if ever she reached a point of divergence, she'd need the dog to guide her to the right choice.

As the angle of ascent steepened, the rangy stride became harder to maintain. At the crossing of Gatherstone Beck she paused and rested for a moment, looking up the slope towards the col and seeing the other walker silhouetted momentarily against the skyline. She'd made up ground on him but this was no guarantee she'd made up any on Hadda.

What the hell did she think she was doing here, anyway? Their rendezvous on top of Pillar Rock was probably going to put them out of her reach – she was no mountaineer, and from what she recalled of Wolf's description of the climb, it posed real problems for a novice.

But she'd come this far and wasn't about to turn back now.

Carefully she crossed the stream and then began the haul up to the pass.

She knew from the map that to approach the Rock she needed to move off the main track to the summit of the fell, but it was Sneck who showed her where the diversion began. Now she found herself in an airy craggy area that made the track up to the col seem homely by comparison. The river winding along the valley bottom far below seemed little more than a blue ribbon. She felt that surge of exhilaration which is the mountain walker's true reward for effort, and normally would have paused to savour the experience. But today she was walking not for pleasure but for something that she didn't quite understand, though she felt that somehow the meaning of her future lay in it.

She increased her speed along the narrow path. Increasingly the way ahead was obscured by mist. At a large cairn with a memorial plate screwed into a rock beneath it, she paused for another sweep ahead with the glasses. As if at a command, the mist cleared and for the first time she saw the Rock. It was an awe-inspiring sight. She couldn't make out anyone on top of it but when she lowered her sights to the approach path, the figure of the other walker swam into view.

This was good, she told herself. If he too was looking to climb the Rock, then surely the presence of a stranger would inhibit Wolf from offering any violence to his ex-wife?

She was about to lower the binoculars when the man ahead halted. He seemed to be pulling something out of his jacket. Now he was pointing it ahead . . .

Oh Jesus Christ! she thought. It's a gun!

John Childs's message erupted into her mind. *Tell him Nikitin knows. Tell him the man with the broken jaw is still on the loose.*

She couldn't see what the man was aiming at but assumed it was Hadda. She tried to scream a warning but the wind drove the sound back into her throat. All she could do was wait for the sound of the shot.

It didn't come. The man slipped the weapon out of sight and a moment later he too had vanished behind a crag.

She hurried on. She was taking risks now to move at speed, but she knew it was in vain. The gunman was too far ahead. If he got Wolf in his sights as he was climbing up the Rock, that would be an end to it. Her only hope was that Wolf would reach the top unharmed and she could somehow get a warning to him. How the hell she would do this, she didn't know, but as she scrambled up the track to a point where the side path the man had been on branched off, she began to get the glimmer of an idea. This diversion had to lead round the huge crag ahead of her to the foot of the climb. The main track ran up a steep scree slope to the top of the crag and presumably thereafter led all the way to the summit of the fell. From up there it must be possible to look out directly on to the top of the Rock.

She attacked the slope ferociously. After a moment or so she realized that Sneck had opted for the path taken by his master. For the first time she felt truly and frighteningly alone. At the top of the slope the path turned along a more gently inclined rock shelf that on her right side fell steeply into the valley. She fixed her gaze firmly ahead. A mountain rescue stretcher box came into view, more of a dreadful warning than a comfort. Now the track headed up another scree slope. The Rock loomed to her right, but she still wasn't high enough to view its top.

Soon, she told herself. Soon!

But what was she going to see when she got high enough to look down at it?

She recalled the shining blade of the axe that Wolf had carried out of Birkstane with him.

But he wasn't a killer, she told herself. It had been unnecessary killing that had made him fall out with JC.

Unnecessary.

There was the rub. The death of the innocent had filled him with rage.

But the death of the guilty . . .

She pushed herself still harder.

8

As Lady Kira told her story at the breakfast table, Imogen had noticed with a slight distaste how her voice grew mellow under the power of sensual recollection.

'It wasn't long after I came to the castle,' said her mother. 'Your father, well, let me put it this way, your father had a very English attitude to making love. He was the perfect gentleman, very concerned in case he hurt me, and anxious to make what he assumed might not be a very pleasing experience for me last as short a time as possible. I tried to let him know that I didn't care about being hurt as long as I was overwhelmed, but . . . anyway, things weren't going too well, and after a particularly unsatisfactory night, I wandered out in the morning, across the lawns and into the forest.

'I heard him before I saw him. The perfectly regular, powerful crash of an axe into the trunk of a tree. A rhythm that seemed to vibrate through my whole body. I walked towards it. Then in the light of the early-morning sun slanting down through the trees, I saw him at the edge of a clearing, tall, fair, naked to the waist, already sweating through his effort though the morning air was still cool.

'I sat down on an old stump and watched him, delighting in his strength, his vigour, his strong rhythmic movement. He paused to wipe his brow with a large red kerchief. And then, though I made no sound, he became aware of me.

504

'He stood and looked at me for a moment, then he came towards me. He was still carrying his axe. I remember the blade seemed huge close to my head and he himself looked like a giant towering over me.

'He said, "I shouldn't sit there, my lady. Tree 'ull be coming down shortly."

'I didn't say anything, but just drank in his closeness. His belt buckle was only a foot or so from my face. Almost without thinking, I reached up and began to undo it. For a moment he went tense and I thought he was going to pull back.

'Then he relaxed.

'And then I had the most ecstatic sex I had yet experienced.'

She'd fallen silent. Her features had softened, her body relaxed, and her eyes were focused elsewhere, elsewhen.

Imogen said coldly, 'And how was it for him, Lady Chatterley?'

Kira straightened up and was herself again.

'All right, I suppose. He didn't say. All he could do when it was over was apologize, as if he'd been the one who set things in motion! Men can be very arrogant, can't they? He stuttered a lot of stuff about his wife having a child a couple of months earlier, and things still not being right between them, and so on. What it added up to, I suppose, was he hadn't been getting any sex for some time before the birth and it didn't look as if he were likely to be getting any in the foreseeable future, and this state of frustration he offered as explanation for his unforgivable effrontery in screwing me. His main concern seemed to be that I might broadcast our encounter!

'Well, as you can imagine, I soon grew tired of this babble. I tidied myself up and said to him that I certainly had no intention of letting anyone know I'd demeaned myself with a woodcutter. And I further added that if ever I got the slightest hint by so much as a word or a look or a nod or a wink that he had mentioned it to anybody else, that would be the day he found himself out of work and out of his tied cottage.'

Imogen had stopped listening. Her mind was making calculations.

'You say this happened how many months after Wolf's birth?'

'Who said anything about Wolf?'

'The Haddas only had one child. How long?'

'Two, three months,' said Kira.

'And I'm almost exactly a year younger than Wolf . . . Christ, Mother, what are you trying to tell me? That you let me marry my half-brother?'

Interestingly the idea excited as much as it horrified her.

Lady Kira shrugged.

'Why not? In the old days, unions closer than that were winked at to keep the bloodline pure. Hardly applicable here, of course. To start with, while having no objection to you pleasuring yourself with a woodcutter as I had done, the idea of your actually marrying him struck me as positively obscene. Then you told me you were pregnant, but it wasn't his. And I thought, why not? It did mean the little bastard would have a name. And Hadda had come back to us with his manners mended and money in his pocket, and he looked to have the kind of ingratiating manner that could lead him to make a lot more. He might do reasonably well for a few years till you grew tired of him and someone better suited came along.'

Imogen said, 'But he was my brother!'

'Half-brother. And as you'd made it clear you weren't going to have any more children, I couldn't see how your possible relationship might be a problem.'

Imogen said, 'I bet it was a problem for poor old Fred though. I bet he put three and nine together and took a good look at me and saw my blonde hair and blue eyes and nothing whatsoever of Ulphingstone in me. No wonder he was so absolutely dead set against the marriage!'

'Perhaps,' said Kira indifferently. 'Or perhaps he just had the good sense to see it was an ill match. Anyway, he never said anything.'

'What could he say? *Excuse me, Sir Leon, I rogered your wife twenty years ago and it occurs to me that perhaps your beloved daughter is really mine?* And I was pregnant!'

'Oh, come on, dear. I think you're crediting the man with far too delicate a sensibility. He was a woodcutter, for God's sake!'

Not since her teens had Imogen felt frustrated enough to want to strike her mother, but the urge welled up in her now.

She'd controlled it, stood up and made for the door.

'Where are you going, dear?' called her mother.

'For a drive. Somewhere the air's a bit fresher.'

And she'd closed the door behind her with a gentleness more powerful than a slam.

All this Imogen recounted to Wolf plainly and simply, leaving nothing out, putting nothing in.

He listened, standing still as a statue, his features set in marble.

When she finished, he let silence fall like a barrier between them.

Finally he said quietly, 'So you and your family destroyed my father just as completely as you destroyed me.'

With an effort at lightness she said, 'You don't look too destroyed to me, Wolf. Look, why don't we just walk away from this? I've got money. My share of the Woodcutter loot that Toby and Johnny squirrelled away. It's safely stored in a Taiwanese bank. We can live any way you like. Brother and sister. Husband and wife.'

'Wipe the slate clean, you mean?' he said.

'As clean as you like,' she said. 'If you want to spend the rest of your life punishing me, that's all right too. Or perhaps not the rest. Seven years would seem about right.'

'And is this what you came here to tell me?' he said incredulously.

She shook her head vigorously.

'No. Far from it. I had some silly notion of trying to clear things up between us, then I'd walk away, leaving you to the tender mercies of your black beauty. But now, after seeing you, talking to you, I can see how wrong that would be. You don't want to tie yourself to a psychiatrist, Wolf! She'd be in your mind all the time, ferreting around, trying to set things straight. Me, I'm in your blood, I'm in your genes, I'm in your soul. And you're in mine. I think I've always known it. But I never wanted to admit it. Betraying you like I did, I made excuses to myself, put it all down to reason and necessity. But all I was really doing was trying to prove I was stronger than this dependency I felt. I wanted to prove I was myself. Now I know that I can't be that self without acknowledging you are part of it too. So what do you say?'

'You let me go to jail for a disgusting crime I was innocent of,' he cried. 'You let me take the blame for frauds I knew nothing about. You divorced me and married the bastard who framed me. You helped drive our daughter to distraction and my father to despair. And now you want me to run away with you?'

'Look at yourself, Wolf,' she commanded with a matching force. 'Think of the things you've done, or left undone. There's only one hard truth to hold on to in that fantasy world you built. You want me, I want you. We both knew that the first time we came here. We both know it still. Do I have to strip off like that first time and offer myself? I will if you want. Just say the word, Wolf. Just say the word!'

She looked up at him, imploringly, defiantly.

He loomed over her, holding the axe over her head as if to ward off her gaze. The polished blade mirrored her face beneath. She ripped the zip on her fleece jacket open, pulled on the buttons of her shirt till it too parted, revealing the soft white swell of her breasts.

A hundred feet away on the summit path, seeing the movement of the axe, Alva Ozigbo screamed, 'No!' but the gusting north-west wind blew the word back down her throat. She dived her hand into her pocket and pulled out her mobile phone. Somehow she had to let them know she was here. And then beyond the two figures who seemed bound together in a kind of all-excluding ecstasy, she saw the man she'd been following. He was on his hands and knees, having just pulled himself up the final few feet of the climb.

She opened her phone, sought and found Imogen's number that she'd put in there last month, prayed that its state-of-the-art technology would find a signal up here and that Imogen would have her phone switched on.

She pressed the speed-dial key.

Pudovkin pushed himself upright. It had been harder than he'd imagined. It wasn't at all like the climbing wall. All that space beneath his feet, and somewhere far below he kept imagining he could hear a dog barking angrily, like some hound of hell waiting to seize him if he fell. A couple of times he'd nearly lost his grip and even the coke he'd snorted couldn't stop him trembling. He'd need to get close to make sure of his shot.

And then he realized there were two of them. The lawyer's wife was here too. What the hell was that all about? He didn't want to kill her, but it was hard to see an alternative. At least her presence seemed to be such a distraction that Hadda was totally unaware of his arrival.

He took a step forward, gun raised.

Two things happened as he pressed the trigger.

A telephone rang.

And Hadda raised his axe.

The bullet glanced off the blade, making it ring like a bell, then rattled away among the fellside crags.

Hadda turned his one-eyed gaze on the Russian. Even safely distanced from any possible swing of the axe, and with a loaded pistol in his hand, Pudovkin felt himself paralysed. Only for a moment.

But in that moment Imogen had raised her phone to her ear and pushed herself upright so that she stood between Hadda and his assassin.

A shaft of sunshine broke through the lowering cloud as if to highlight a climactic scene.

She called, 'Pudo, it's Pasha. He'd like to speak to you.'

She advanced unhurriedly, a smile on her face, the phone outstretched.

Some part of his mind was yelling at him that Nikitin couldn't possibly know that he was up here on top of this fucking great rock with his fancy woman and her ex-husband.

Another part was registering that her jacket and shirt were open and she had really great tits.

And perhaps because of the normalcy of this reaction, yet another part assured him that the guy with the gun was always the guy in control, and he reached out his hand to take the phone.

He grasped it.

The woman kept on coming.

She wrapped herself around him in an embrace as fierce as a lover's and with an irresistible force drove him backwards.

Hadda and Alva screamed together in unconscious unison, 'No!'

Then they were gone.

Somewhere in mid air, they lost contact with each other and Imogen was falling alone, first through the bright air, then through the unreverberate blackness, as she had always dreamed.

Only Sneck was positioned to see the whole of the fall, and he, alone on the slab below, threw back his head and filled the valley with a mournful howl.

High above, Hadda turned and looked across to Alva in despair. Then he began to spin round, axe held out at arm's length, faster and faster, finally letting go and sinking to his knees as the axe hurtled so far through the air that it fell a thousand feet before landing in the valley below.

EPILOGUE

wait and hope

'*Il n'y a ni bonheur ni malheur en ce monde, il y a la comparaison d'un état à un autre, voilà tout. Celui-là seul qui a éprouvé l'extrême infortune est apte à ressentir l'extrême félicité. Il faut avoir voulu mourir pour savoir combien il est bon de vivre.*

'*Vivez donc et soyez heureux, enfants chéris de mon coeur, et n'oubliez jamais que, jusqu'au jour où Dieu daignera dévoiler l'avenir à l'homme, toute la sagesse humaine sera dans ces deux mots:*

'*Attendre et espérer!*'‡

Alexandre Dumas: *Le Comte de Monte-Cristo*

‡ 'There is neither happiness nor misery in the world, only the comparison of one state with another. Only the man who has plumbed the depths of misfortune is capable of scaling the heights of joy. To grasp how good it is to live you must have been driven to long for death.

'Live, then, and be happy, dear children of my heart, and never forget, until the day arrives when God in his mercy unveils the future to man, all of human wisdom lies in these two words:

'Wait and hope!'

1

Autumn 2018: nothing changes; the world continues as mixed up as ever, the same mélange of comic and tragic, triumph and disaster, sweet and sour, as in every age since humanity hauled itself upright and put on pants.

Nine months after the drama on Pillar Rock, Wolf Hadda tasted both the sweet and the sour as he heard the Court of Appeal (Right Hon. Lord Justice Toplady presiding) declare his convictions of 2010 unsafe.

Outside the Royal Courts of Justice, bathed in the noontide sunshine of an Indian summer, he stood in mountainous silence as Ed Trapp read a short bland statement to the waiting reporters. Then, cocooned by policemen, the two men made their way through the exploding flashbulbs and the strident questions to a waiting limo that pulled away so quickly the pursuing press didn't have time to register that there was already someone sitting in the darkened passenger compartment.

Nothing was said as the car sped along the Strand. As it approached Charing Cross, Trapp said, 'This'll do me.'

'You sure?'

'Yeah. I'm meeting Doll for a spot of lunch.'

'Give her my love,' said Wolf. 'And Ed – thank you.'

The car pulled over, the two men shook hands as Trapp got out, then Wolf settled back in his seat as the journey resumed.

'So all's well that ends well,' said John Childs. 'Justice prevails.'

'Justice!' exclaimed Hadda. 'Imogen dead, Arnie Medler dead, the Nutbrowns in jail for a crime they didn't commit, Estover half-blind and crippled and facing God knows what kind of future, me winning my appeal on new evidence that was just about as dodgy as the old evidence that got me sentenced in the first place – and that's what you call justice!'

'*Exitus acta probat*,' said Childs. 'The end justifies the means.'

'Does it? You once warned me about acting like God, JC. Maybe you should have listened to yourself.'

'My way is not so mysterious. All I did to steer you to this safe haven was call in a lot of favours, so much so that the favour bin is rather empty now. I do hope you are going to behave yourself in the foreseeable future.'

Hadda laughed and said, 'Worried in case I'm tempted to accept one of the tabloid offers for my unexpurgated memoirs?'

'Well, since you were so energetic in making sure all the recovered Woodcutter misappropriations were returned to those who suffered from the crash, the money must be very tempting.'

'Sure! And the Chapel would let me live to enjoy it? I don't think so. No, I've got a job offer I'm thinking about.'

'Your late lamented father's job, you mean, looking after the Ulphingstone estate? Start as a woodcutter, end as a woodcutter. Neat, but hardly progress.'

'Jesus! I don't know why I bother to open my mouth when you could speak all my lines for me!' said Wolf. 'Yes, Leon is keen to keep me close. I really thought that after what happened, he mightn't be able to stand the sight of me. Instead it seems to have brought us closer.'

'Without you he has lost everything,' said Childs. 'Though I cannot imagine his parting with Lady Kira tore his heartstrings.'

'Maybe not. I got her wrong, I think. Well, slightly wrong. She had a small stroke when she heard about Imo. But of course you know that. So she did care for someone more than herself. I only

514

saw her once before she left for Switzerland. It was a shock. She'd put on thirty years; she looks older than Leon now.'

'Will she come back, do you think? After the clinic has put her together again.'

'Leon says no. She told him she hated the castle, and Cumbria, and England. "In the end the dreadful, drab English always win," she said, "that is the lesson of European history."'

'I'm pleased to hear that she got something from her stay with us,' said JC.

'She got Imo. She got Ginny. She's lost everything.'

'It's all right to feel sorry for her,' said Childs gently. 'Only, don't let it turn into guilt. Not about her, or anyone. No one got more than they deserved.'

'Even Arnie Medler?'

'That was an accident, Wolf. Truly. These things happen. Think positive. Think of the good that has come out of all this. The Trapps, what friendship they've displayed. The estimable Mr McLucky who would never have met the delectable Morag without your intervention. Your good friend Luke Hollins who may yet bring religion to darkest Cumbria. And, of course, the wonderful Dr Ozigbo. Most relationships end in deceit. Yours began with it, so that bodes nothing but good.'

'What makes you think there's a relationship?'

'Well, I know for a fact that when she decided to pursue her career in an academic setting, opportunities arose at Warwick University, and Bath, and there was even talk of Cambridge. But she's opted for Lancaster.'

'That's because it's handy for her family,' Wolf asserted firmly.

'Perhaps. But the M6 goes north as well as south. Talking of motorways, should you really drive back today? You've had a trying morning.'

'Hardly that,' said Wolf. 'Not when so many favours had gone into ensuring the outcome. No, the sooner I'm out of this rat-run, the better. I'll be home before dark.'

'If you are sure.'

They relapsed into a silence that stretched till they pulled into the London Gateway service area at the foot of the M1.

There, parked in an area marked Staff Only, stood the Defender.

'It's been cleaned,' said Hadda accusingly.

'I'm sure by the time you get back to Birkstane it will have lost its shine,' said Childs. '*Au revoir*, Wolf.'

He offered his hand. Hadda looked at it for a moment then grinned and leaned forward and kissed Childs on the forehead.

'Let's make that goodbye, JC,' he said.

Childs sat and watched the Land Rover pull out of the service area, and continued to sit, still and silent, long after it had passed from his sight.

'Where now, sir?' asked his driver finally.

Childs considered for a moment before replying.

'Give me a moment to make a phone call,' he said. 'Then, I think, Phoenicia.'

2

It was dusk when the Defender arrived in Mireton.

Wolf knew he should have taken a break on the long drive home, but a need stronger than reason had made him let the motorway carry him north till the familiar outline of his beloved Cumbrian fells became visible, and then it had seemed silly to stop.

He parked outside St Swithin's and went into the churchyard. Something had changed since last he was here for Imogen's funeral. The defensive metal paling around the Ulphingstone tomb had been removed.

As he approached the tomb he saw there'd been other changes. A young rowan tree had been planted before it, its handful of berries shining bright in the twilight.

And the inscription now read *Here lies Virginia, beloved daughter of Wilfred and Imogen Hadda, and granddaughter of Sir Leon and Lady Kira Ulphingstone.*

Daughter. That was right, whatever Imo had said. She'd been his beloved daughter all those years. Nothing could ever change that.

He stood there for a moment then turned away.

A voice called, 'Wolf.'

Luke Hollins was standing in the church porch watching him.

'Great news, Wolf,' said the vicar. 'I was delighted. I thought I might preach on the prodigal son on Sunday.'

'Shouldn't bother,' said Wolf. 'The talents might be more appropriate. I'll see you, Padre.'

'In church, you mean?' said Hollins hopefully.

'When you bring my Tesco order.'

He went out of the churchyard. Opposite the church the lights of the Black Dog were already burning bright in the gathering dusk. Three men were strolling towards the pub entrance. He recognized them all as local farmers. One of them was Joe Strudd, his nearest neighbour.

Strudd looked across the street and called, 'How do, Wolf. What fettle?'

'Middling. How's yourself?'

'Not si bad. Coming in for a pint and a crack?'

'Later maybe.'

'See you, then.'

The trio raised their hands in salutation and vanished into the pub.

Wolf smiled as he drove out of the village. Luke Hollins still had much to learn about his parish. They didn't go in for fatted calves round here. An invitation to have a drink and a crack was as good as it got.

The turn-off down the lonning to Birkstane came into view. He swung the Defender into it without slowing and the judder of its wheels as it bumped over the old ruts and potholes felt like a caress. The gate was open and he could see a light in the farmhouse while out of the chimney a plume of grey smoke drifted across the star-studded sky.

Home. He recalled JC's words, half mocking, half envious. *Start as a woodcutter, end as a woodcutter.* Is that what he really wanted? In fact, is that really possible after . . . everything.

He brought the car to a halt and started to climb out. The house door opened and Sneck came hurtling towards him, eyes blazing, teeth bared, as if intent on tearing out his throat. Then the dog's paws were on his shoulders and its great rough tongue was sandpapering his face.

'Get down, you slobbery lump!' he commanded.

'Is that what you're going to say to me?' asked Alva from the doorway.

Childs must have rung her. Bless you for that at least, JC! he thought.

What the future held, he didn't know. What demons lay in wait to haunt him, he could only speculate. But this moment, this place, were too perfect for such considerations.

For the rest, wait and hope was all a man could do.

He went towards her, smiling, and said, 'Well, let's see, shall we?'

UTILIZATION OF THE SOUTHERN PINES

PETER KOCH

Agriculture Handbook No. 420

In two volumes:

I The Raw Material

II Processing

U.S. DEPARTMENT OF AGRICULTURE FOREST SERVICE
Southern Forest Experiment Station

The Author

Peter Koch is one of America's most eminent scientists in wood technology.

After gaining early experience in the design and manufacture of heavy-duty planers and matchers, he spent a year studying the effects of chip formation on cutterhead horsepower and quality of surfaces generated in peripheral milling. His Ph.D. thesis, accepted by the University of Washington in 1954, contained high-speed photos of chips forming under the action of knives and was basic to later work on the chipping headrig.

After 2 years of teaching and research at Michigan State University and 5 years of managing a New England lumber company, he wrote the book *Wood Machining Processes*.

For the past 9 years, he has been in charge of the Southern Forest Experiment Station's timber utilization laboratory at Pineville, in central Louisiana. Here, in 1963, he cooperated with two manufacturers of woodworking machines to construct three experimental versions of chipping headrigs. These headrigs square a log by converting the round sides into pulp chips without creating slabs or wasting material as sawdust. They are now in wide industrial use throughout North America and comprise one of the major wood-machining advances of the 20th century.

During 1964, when manufacture of southern pine plywood was in early stages of development, he provided data that were instrumental in the formulation of gluing practices for the industry. Next, he invented a system of gluing up single-species wooden beams by placing the most limber laminae in the center and the stiffest in the outer, most highly stressed regions. Beams thus assembled are stronger, stiffer, and more uniform than those made by conventional methods.

For these three developments Koch was awarded, in 1968, the Superior Service medal of the U.S. Department of Agriculture. He has received patents on the method of beam construction and on a system of making straight studs from southern pine veneer cores and boltwood. Patent application has been made on a process for drying southern pine studs in 24 hours under restraints that prevent warping.

Acknowledgments

In preparing a work of this scope, characterizing an important and variable resource in relation to its industrial use, an author receives essential assistance and services of many kinds. Especially significant contributions were made by the researchers who wrote the papers referred to in footnotes of many of the chapters. Most of these were prepared for the symposium "Utilization of the southern pines," presented by the Southern Forest Experiment Station and the Forest Products Research Society at Alexandria, La., November 6-8, 1968. Cooperating were the Louisiana Forestry Association, Southern Pine Association (now the Southern Forest Products Association), American Plywood Association, American Pulpwood Association, and American Wood Preservers' Association.

Special acknowledgment is due the more than 100 scientists who meticulously studied and criticized various chapters and sections.

I also wish to express my great appreciation for aid from within the Department of Agriculture. Indispensable knowledge and guidance were provided by the Forest Service's Division of Forest Products and Engineering Research and by the Forest Products Laboratory at Madison, Wis. The New Orleans office of the Southern Forest Experiment Station supplied unfailing support and counsel, including the most essential editorial and library services.

To members of the Forest Products Utilization Research Project at the Alexandria Forestry Center, Pineville, La., I owe particularly personal thanks. The scientists accelerated their research to fill many gaps in information, the technicians assisted them in ways that often went beyond the call of duty, and the administrative personnel efficiently handled infinite details of correspondence and text.

Since the book is a digest of research observations specific to the properties and utilization of the southern pines, a substantial effort was made to abstract, or to make reference to, all major work published prior to 1971. Some findings published or in process during 1971 were also included. Inevitably some worthwhile work has been overlooked; for such omissions, I apologize.

Peter Koch
Pineville, La.
January 1972

CONTENTS

VOLUME II—PROCESSING

PART V—PROCESSES

18

Storing

CONTENTS

18

Storing

18–1 LOGS AND VENEER BOLTS

Prior to World War II, southern pine logs were commonly protected against stain and decay by storing them in ponds. While in the water, only the exposed portion of each log—that part floating above the surface—suffered fungal infection. Safe storage time in the pond could be extended by periodically revolving each log to hold its light side immersed. The difficulty in keeping logs wet throughout, and the expenses of pond maintenance, recovery of sunken logs, and withdrawal of logs from storage caused discontinuance of this method of storage.

In the South today virtually all pine saw logs and veneer bolts are stored in 10- to 18-foot-high decks. Where such decks are held more than a week or 2 in summer or 1 to 3 months in winter, water spraying or sprinkling is desirable to control stain and decay (see secs. 16–1, 16–2, and 16–4). In addition to controlling plant organisms, water retards or prevents the development of checks in the ends of logs. A water **spray** applies water continuously (fig. 18–1); a **sprinkler** may rotate or oscillate so that water application is periodic but frequent. Evidence suggests that intermittent spraying or sprinkling will give good protection if the wetting is sufficiently frequent to keep log surfaces from getting noticeably dry. Sprays and sprinklers are commonly operated 365 days per year with shutdowns only when there is danger of system damage from freezing temperatures. Preferably, logs are put under sprays or sprinklers as soon as possible after felling and withdrawn on a "first in, first out" basis.

Logs may be sprayed or sprinkled from the top only, but water application from both top and sides is preferable. Top sprinkling wets more log surface and produces better water penetration into the interior of the deck than does end sprinkling. Sprinkling or spraying from the sides wets the log ends effectively to retard checking and growth of fungi (Lowery 1959).

Provision for recovery and recyling of the spray water is common. In the Midsouth, addition of 10 to 15 percent makeup water is commonly needed to replace water loss from evaporation during each circulation cycle. A concrete slab under the deck permits forklift access and reduces water seepage. Vick (1964) observed that effective sprays or sprinklers are a compromise between heads that produce low volume and a fine mist (subject to wind drift) and heads that produce large drops and high volume (requiring large pump capacity).

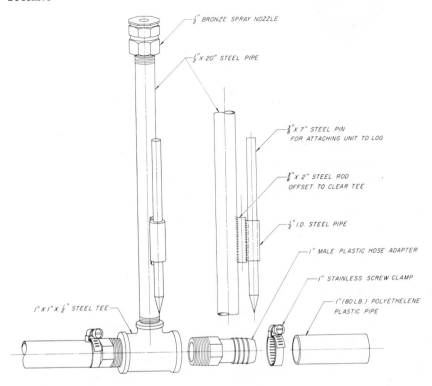

M–136314

Figure 18–1.—Water spraying equipment used to protect southern pine logs in storage. The spray nozzle, attached to plastic water supply pipe, is secured to the log pile with a sharpened pin. (Drawing after Scheffer 1969.)

Most sprinkler systems used on logs are the "impact" type, with heads that rotate in a pulsating manner; designs are available for a wide range of wetting areas and delivery rates. For example, sprinkler coverage may range from 60 to 400 feet in diameter with output per nozzle of 0.60 to 450 gallons per minute at water pressure from 20 to 80 pounds per sq. ft. Spray heads have lesser coverage—usually 20 to 45 feet in diameter— with outputs of about 0.05 to 3.5 gallons per minute at water pressures of 15 to 30 pounds per sq. ft. Water sprays used at one Louisiana mill are elevated on short pipes and conveniently attached along the top of the log deck by a steel pin (fig. 18–1). These "self-cleaning" nozzles are reported to spray a 24-foot circle at a delivery rate of 2.5 gallons per minute with a nozzle pressure of 15 pounds per sq. in. A plastic pipe connecting the nozzles extends down over one end of the deck and ends in a valve within reach of the ground; this valve is opened from time to time to flush out accumulated dirt (Scheffer 1969).

Thoroughly wetted logs can be safely stored for at least a year. There is some evidence that abnormally long storage of pine logs under water sprays may have side effects in addition to the increased permeability described in section 16–1. Lumber cut from such logs may be more subject to staining. Veneer cut from the logs sometimes turns a deep yellow when dried. Data from DeGroot and Scheld (1971) of the USDA Forest Service, Southern Forest Experimentation Station, Gulfport, Miss., indicate that lumber cut from southern pine logs stored under water sprinkling systems will be no more susceptible to decay than will lumber cut from freshly felled trees.

18–2 PULPWOOD

To control decay of pulpwood, storage conditions should keep the wood either wetter or drier than optimum for growth of decay organisms (see sec. 16–5). For peeled wood, open piles designed to afford maximum ventilation help minimize decay by fast reduction of moisture content. Rough (i.e., unpeeled) wood, on the other hand, is best stored in large, compact piles, affording minimum aeration. Decay is retarded by the high moisture levels and cooler temperatures maintained within such piles. In piles of unpeeled wood, long bolts of large diameter deteriorate more slowly than short bolts of small diameter. At best, however, considerable damage may be expected in warm weather, especially on the exterior of the pile (Lindgren 1953).

Water sprays that keep pulpwood wet during warm seasons of the year are highly effective in reducing damage and are widely used by pulp companies to safely store southern pine (Mason et al. 1963; Djerf and Volkman 1969). Volkman (1966) has described successful storage of 3,000 cords of southern pine pulpwood under water sprays at a kraft mill near Camden, Ark. The layout is shown in figure 18–2; storage began in July 1964. Moisture content of the roundwood remained at about 55 percent (of total weight) during the 12 months in spray storage. Mill and laboratory evaluations at intervals showed no appreciable loss in wood density, pulp yield, byproducts yield or pulp strength from wood stored under sprays for periods up to 12 months. The conclusion that water spraying of roundwood controls losses in wood density, pulp quality, and byproducts was further confirmed by Djerf and Volkman (1969), who also suggested spraying with pulpmill effluent to retard growth of slime.

Djerf and Volkman (1969) estimate that storage of pulpwood under water spray can eliminate 80 percent of the wood deterioration and handling costs involved in maintaining and rotating dry-stored pulpwood. Though less troublesome with pine than with hardwoods, the system is not without problems. Sprinkler heads are often plugged with fines, and grit or corrosion cause malfunction of oscillators. Maintaining the in-line filters needed to keep pipes from plugging is expensive. During pile breakdown, bark sloughing makes it difficult to get full grapple loads. Where wood is floated to barking drums, some spray-stored bolts may sink, while loose bark and grit may reduce production by plugging circulation pumps and drag-chain gratings.

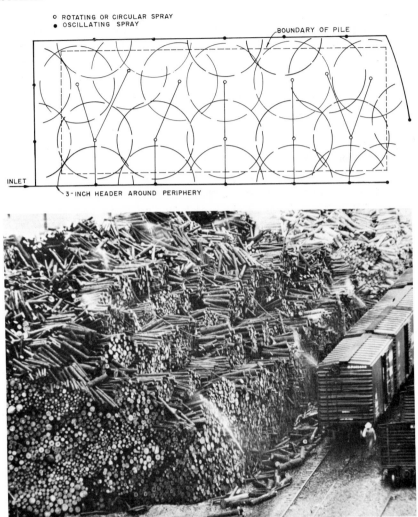

Figure 18–2.—(Top) Plan of 26 sprinkler locations on and around a 3,000-cord pile of southern pine pulpwood. The pile was approximately 240 feet long, 90 feet wide, and 30 feet high. Whole circles represent sprinklers mounted on top of the pile, and half circles designate sprayers covering the sides of the pile. (Bottom) Sprayed pulpwood showing placement of sprinklers on and around the pile. (Drawing and photo from Volkman 1966.)

As an alternative to the water-spray system, southern pine pulpwood may be successfully stored under water in large concrete ponds. Altman (1965) has described construction details and operating procedures for a 10,000-cord pond at Bastrop, La., which is 700 feet long, 150 feet wide, and 35 feet deep. The sides slope in so that the bottom measures 625 by 80 feet. Cranes equipped with orange-peel grapples move debarked wood into and out of the pond.

18–3 PULP CHIPS

Outside storage of wood in chip form has been practiced on the West Coast since about 1950 (Schmidt 1969). Increasingly in the South, wood is stored outside in chip piles rather than in roundwood form (Djerf and Volkman 1969). Advantages include better chip measurement, lower handling costs, reduced space requirements, and smoother operation in the woodyard and woodroom. In addition, chip piles solve storage problems arising from establishment of chip mills at the wood source. Finally, they simplify procedures for handling mixed species and sawmill residues.

Rothrock et al. (1961) took data on a pile of slash pine chips established May 28 and 29, 1959 at Fargo, Ga. The area under the pile had been graded, covered with 6 inches of lime rock, and topped with 1½ inches of asphalt. Chips from freshly cut trees were built into the pile and compacted with a crawler tractor. The top of the pile measured 21 feet wide by 42 feet long with sides sloped to a base width of 42 feet and length of 72 feet. Depth of the pile varied from 7 to 10 feet.

Chip deterioration was mostly in the outer shell of the pile (sec. 16–6). Loss of wood substance amounted to 1 to 1½ percent per month of storage. There was no loss in percentage of yield based on tonnage of wood charged to a kraft process digester. Loss of tear strength of pulp amounted to about 5 percent per month of storage. **Permanganate number** (a measure of bleach requirement) of pulps was not influenced by temperature and moisture fluctuations in the pile. The proportion of screen rejects was less from stored chips than from stored roundwood. Chips in piles are vulnerable to airborne contamination by dirt and fly ash.

Temperature inside a chip storage pile may increase as much as 60° F. in the first few weeks. Elevated temperature persists through 5 months' storage except in the outer shell. Successive waves of increasing temperature are characteristic, and the temperature in the pile bears no relationship to surrounding ambient temperature, i.e., the heat is generated in the pile (Rothrock et al. 1961). Springer and Hajny (1970) found that this initial release of heat to the pile results from respiration of the living ray parenchyma cells of the wood chips.

Moisture is driven out of the high-temperature zone in the center of the pile in the first weeks (fig. 18–3) and appears to condense in the cooler outer zones. When the initial high temperature subsides, rainfall seeps into the pile from the top, and the entire pile reaches a uniform moisture level higher than the original condition.

Schmidt's (1969) studies of redwood (*Sequoia sempervirens* (D. Don) Endl.) and Douglas-fir (*Pseudotsuga menziesii* (Mirb.) Franco) suggest that heat from biological activity in chip piles can trigger chemical reactions leading toward ultimate ignition. Pockets of chips, especially in fan-shaped areas high in the pile, in front of pneumatic delivery lines, reached temperatures of 150° to 180° F. He suggests positive plans for pile rota-

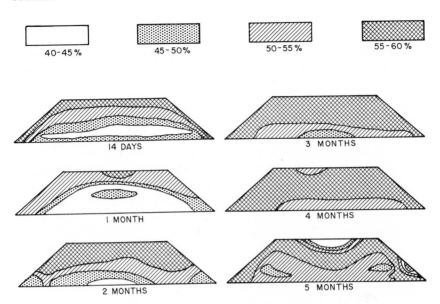

40-45%   45-50%   50-55%   55-60%

14 DAYS   3 MONTHS

1 MONTH   4 MONTHS

2 MONTHS   5 MONTHS

Figure 18–3.—Moisture in chips stored in a compacted pile 42 feet wide and 7 to 10 feet deep, expressed as percent of wet weight. (Drawing after Rothrock et al. 1961.)

tion, watering, and limiting pile height to 50 feet as means for maintaining quality and avoiding excessive temperatures.

Since chip storage in unsprayed piles results in quality of pulp and yields of byproducts about equal to those from dry roundwood storage, its chief advantage is efficiency in material handling. Djerf and Volkman (1969) tested water spraying as a means of improving quality of chips stored in piles. Their 1,200-cord pile of loblolly and shortleaf pine chips at Camden, Ark. measured 90 by 170 feet, was completed to a height of 25 feet in 3 weeks, and was then sprayed continuously for 12 months. Six sprinklers applied evaporator hot-well water (100 to 120° F., pH 9.0) at 270 gallons per minute. Samples from the pile were evaluated at 2-month intervals.

The moisture content of the spray-stored chips increased from 53 to 63 percent over the first 2 months of storage and then gradually increased to 66 percent of total weight at 12 months' storage. After 2 months in the pile, the chips began to turn dark brown and were covered by a thin layer of slime; after 12 months' storage, the chips were almost black. The change in color was believed attributable to generation of organic acids by micro-organisms other than decay-causing fungi.

Chip density was unaffected during the first 4 months of water-spray storage (fig. 18–4E). After 6 months, chip density was reduced by about 6 percent; it decreased uniformly thereafter to a total loss of 10 percent at 12 months. Kraft pulp yield declined in proportion to density loss. By comparison, dry-stored chips began to lose density very soon after being stored (Rothrock et al. 1961; Rhyne and Brinkley 1961), and the

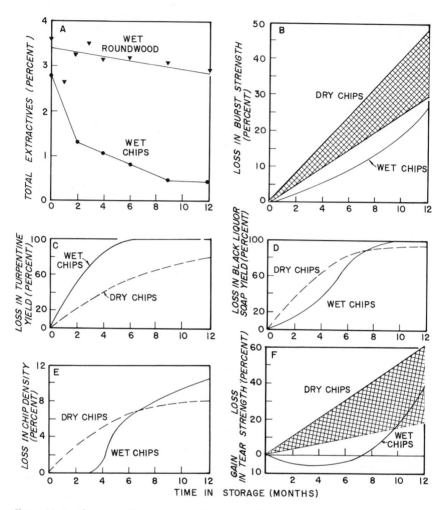

Figure 18–4.—Changes with storage time in wet-stored roundwood and in chips stored in piles with (wet) and without (dry) water spray. (A) Extractives content in water-sprayed chips compared to water-sprayed roundwood. (B) Loss of burst strength (Mullen) in kraft pulp (500 ml. Canadian Standard Freeness) made from chips stored wet and dry. Shaded areas show range of reported values. (C) Loss of turpentine yield from chips stored wet and dry. (D) Loss in yield of black liquor soap from chips stored wet and dry. (E) Loss in density of chips stored wet and dry. (F) Loss of tear strength in kraft pulp (500 ml. Canadian Standard Freeness) made from chips stored wet and dry. Shaded areas show range of reported values. (Drawings after Djerf and Volkman 1969; curves also reflect findings of Rothrock et al. 1961, Rhyne and Brinkley 1961, Saucier and Miller 1961, Somsen 1962, and Thornberg 1963.)

former found no loss in wood density of water-sprayed roundwood after 12 months' storage.

In contrast to water-sprayed roundwood, which produced pulp of un-diminished strength after 12 months' storage, strength properties of pulp from water-sprayed chips declined with storage time (Djerf and Volkman 1969). Deterioration was less rapid than for dry-stored chips, however, as evaluated by burst strength data (fig. 18–4B) from Rhyne and Brinkley (1961) and by tear strength data (fig. 18–4F) from these authors, Roth-rock et al. (1961) and Saucier and Miller (1961).

Water-spray chip storage accelerated the serious decline in byproduct yield which accompanies dry storage of chips; in both cases the large sur-face area probably exposes resinous materials to oxidation. Turpentine yields (fig. 18–4C) decreased by 50 percent after 2 months in storage, and after 4 months in storage virtually no turpentine was recovered. Turpen-tine losses with dry chip storage average about 10 percent per month in most cases (Rhyne and Brinkley 1961; Somsen 1962), and as high as 30 percent in extreme cases (Thornberg 1963). In contrast, roundwood stored for 12 months under water sprays shows little loss in turpentine yield (Volkman 1966).

After 6 months of chip storage, virtually no black liquor soap is recovered from either wet or dry stored chips (fig. 18–4D); roundwood stored under water sprays, however, has very little loss in soap yield over 12 months' storage.

Djerf and Volkman (1969) conclude that water spraying of chips during long-term storage offers no advantage over dry chip storage. Spray stor-age of chips for a month or less, however, may offer some economic bene-fits by decreasing loss of wood density and black liquor soap (fig. 18–4E, D).

Shields (1967) noted that compaction of southern pine chips in the storage pile reduces wood losses; blowing chips onto a pile reportedly pro-duces greater compaction than piling and packing by tractor. Chip de-terioration is also reduced if wood is removed from the pile on a "first in, first out" basis; systems for accomplishing such rotations have been de-scribed (e.g., Glassy 1969).

Various chemicals have been evaluated for their effectiveness in pre-venting wood loss from fungal action and spontaneous combustion. Springer et al. (1969, 1970, 1971) found that dipping of fresh pulp chips in a laboratory-prepared **green liquor** effectively prevented loss of wood substance from fungal action and prevented temperature rise in simulators of chip piles. Green liquor is derived from the smelt of spent kraft black liquor burned in chemical recovery furnaces; it is composed primarily of sodium carbonate and sodium sulfide. Smith and Hatton (1971) evalu-ated the economic feasibility of protecting chips by application of green liquor. King et al. (1971) noted that in small scale tests, application of SO_2 inhibited fungal growth on pulp chips for 3 months.

18–4 POLES, PILING, POSTS, AND TIMBERS

Bark-free green roundwood and sawn timbers are particularly vulnerable to stain and decay because they require long periods for air-drying. For outdoor storage, roundwood and timber should be in piles conforming as nearly as possible to the arrangements for air-drying recommended in chapter 20. Pile foundations should keep timber clear of the ground to avoid dampness from groundwater. Piles should be roofed to reduce wetting, warping, checking, and staining. Protection from rain is more essential for solid than for stickered piles, because water which enters solid piles is very slow to evaporate. Outdoor storage in solid piles is always hazardous.

Chemical protection from fungi and end coatings for prevention of seasoning checks are described in sections 16–7 and 20–1.

18–5 LUMBER AND MILLWORK

Exclusive of economic and materials handling aspects, the primary objectives of storage are to keep the lumber clean, undamaged, and to maintain it at a moisture content approximating that which it will reach in use. Solid-piled wood changes moisture content slowly if protected from the elements. Protection afforded commonly ranges from a simple roof to an enclosed and heated warehouse. Fluctuation of moisture content under various storage situations was measured in a few studies conducted a number of years ago; the data are still highly applicable.

OPEN SHEDS

In a limited study at Chicago, Ill., J. S. Mathewson and O. W. Torgeson[1] compared moisture changes in southern pine shiplap stored in covered yard piles and in an open-end shed with those in a closed shed heated an average of $5\frac{1}{2}°$ F. above outdoor temperature. The lumber was solid piled, well elevated above the ground, and its moisture content was 7 percent when storage started in May 1930. Normal equilibrium moisture content under prevailing outdoor conditions was 13 to 14 percent. Average moisture contents, plotted in figure 18–5, reached $11\frac{1}{2}$ and 10 percent, respectively, in the roofed yard piles and the open-end sheds by August 1931. At that time the lumber in the heated shed contained a little less than $9\frac{1}{2}$-percent moisture content.

A similar test was made in Chicago by J. S. Mathewson[1] with solid-piled 1- by 6-inch car lining and 1- by 4-inch, kiln-dried southern pine flooring. The test extended $21\frac{1}{2}$ months, from April 1930 to January 1932. Temperature in the unheated open shed averaged 2.7° F. above ambient and in the heated shed, 8° F. The lumber in covered yard storage changed from a moisture content of 10.2 percent to 13.5 percent. In the unheated shed the change was from 9.9 to 11.0 percent. In the heated shed, beginning moisture content was 10.3, and final was 10.6 percent.

Obviously the equilibrium moisture content of lumber stored in open sheds will vary according to the outside ambient temperature and relative

---

[1] Peck, E. C. Abstracts of numerous experiments on the change in moisture content of lumber in storage and in transit. Unpublished report, USDA Forest Serv., Forest Prod. Lab., Madison, Wis. (1961).

humidity. Loughborough and Torgeson (1929) found that climatic conditions in the southeastern States during November and December of 1928 would cause lumber (protected but exposed to exterior air) to reach a moisture content of about 13 percent.

UNHEATED CLOSED SHEDS

Closed sheds should be located on well-drained sites and be floored with planking, concrete, or asphalt. Ventilation should be provided by adjustable openings in the roof and walls.

If a closed shed is unheated, the temperature inside will be somewhat higher than outdoors because of heat from the sun. With proper ventilation, the mean relative humidity within the shed will be somewhat lower than that of the outdoor air. In theory an unheated closed shed full of thoroughly kiln-dried lumber should not be ventilated if there is no source of moisture within the shed except that contained within the lumber. As a practical matter, however, moisture is frequently introduced through the shed floor; in this situation ventilation is required. A vapor barrier installed as a soil cover will reduce ingress of moisture through the floor.

Kiln-dried lumber stored in an unheated shed will ordinarily absorb some moisture (fig. 18–5). An increase in moisture content from 7 percent to approximately 10 percent over a period of a year and a half in storage is common. Exposed ends, edges, and faces quickly attain a moisture content in balance with temperature and humidity in the shed. Moisture diffusion is most rapid along the grain inward from the ends. If there are spaces within the pile, created by milled patterns on lumber, the moisture pickup will proceed more rapidly to the interior of the pile.

Although average moisture content of kiln-dried lumber may increase during storage, moisture distribution within the pile may become more uniform. Longborough and Torgeson (1929) observed this effect in kiln-dried southern pine stored for 90 days in an unheated shed. Average moisture content increased from 7.1 to 9.4 percent, but moisture in the wettest boards decreased from 16.2 to 14.0 percent.

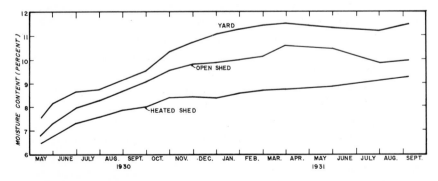

Figure 18–5.—Increase in moisture content of solid-piled, kiln-dried southern pine shiplap in Chicago, Ill. (Drawing after Peck 1961.)

HEATED SHEDS

The efficiency of a closed shed in maintaining a low moisture content can be considerably enhanced if it is heated as weather conditions require. Table 8–2 indicates combinations of temperature and humidity which will maintain specific equilibrium moisture contents.

Closed storage sheds may be heated with steam coils, radiators, or unit heaters. Open, unvented gas heaters should not be used, as combustion creates large amounts of water. The heating system need not have a large capacity. A shed temperature 10 to 20° above outdoor temperature is usually sufficient. Temperatures must be maintained above 32° F. to prevent freezing in traps and return lines if a steam or water system is used. Fans placed at strategic points will help keep conditions uniform.

PROTECTION OF LUMBER FOR SHIPMENT AND EXTERIOR STORAGE

Under some circumstances, particularly at building sites, it is impractical to store lumber in sheds. Two approaches to the problem are in frequent use, i.e., wrapping and dipping. While framing lumber may get extended exterior exposure during rail shipment, exposure at the building site is normally short. Preferably, kiln-dry finish and millwork should never be subjected to exterior exposure, but should be delivered only after a tight roof is in place.

Wrappings.—Protection of dry lumber by wrappings is common practice, but no data have been published on moisture changes in southern pine when so protected. Hickman [n.d.] wrapped solid-piled, 4-foot lengths of 4/4 kiln-dried (7.4-percent moisture content) ponderosa pine (*Pinus ponderosa* Laws.) in packages 4 feet square and about 3 feet high. These packages were stored outdoors in the vicinity of Portland, Ore. for 1 year. Four packages were wrapped—each in a different manner.

1. Covered on top, bottom, and all sides with a sheet of laminated, reinforced, wet-strength kraft paper consisting of two layers of 30-pound kraft paper with a 113-pound inner laminate of asphalt per 3,000 sq. ft.
2. Covered on top, sides and ends with a sheet of black, 4-mil (0.004-inch), polyethylene film.
3. Covered on top, sides, and ends with a prefabricated cover made of the same material used on package number -, except that the kraft paper was of standard quality.
4. Covered on top, sides and ends with a prefabricated cover made of material similar to that used on package number 1.

Moisture content of the top five courses varied considerably during the test, due mostly to leakage (fig. 18–6). Moisture in the main part of the packages increased about 2 percentage points, remaining well within limits required for satisfactory storage.

In a replicated test with kiln-dried soft maple (*Acer rubrum* L.) in

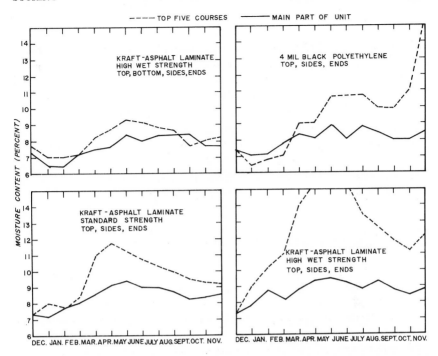

Figure 18–6.—Moisture content of 4-foot lengths of 4/4 ponderosa pine exposed in solid packages protected by wrappings. Test site was Portland, Ore. (Drawing after Hickman [n.d.].)

North Carolina (Applefield 1966), neither kraft paper, polyethylene film, nor metal pile roofs afforded acceptable protection. Wet spots, stain, and even incipient decay developed, especially in the upper courses. Leakage through breaks in the covering appeared to be responsible.

Obviously, the durability of the wrapping material affected these results. Multilayered, wet-strength, kraft paper is now available with interior laminae of glass-reinforced, waterproof material. These new wrapping materials have reinforced edges and can be expected to give good results when carefully applied.

In 1965, William H. Rae, Jr. reported (unpublished) on the effect of wind on lumber wrapped in paper for shipment on open cars and trucks. The wind—up to 115 miles per hour—was obtained by placing the lumber 12 feet behind a World War II P–51 fighter plane. He found that of three wrapping methods tested, that shown in figure 18–7 was best. The staple strap should be semirigid and nonstretchable. A flexible laminate is necessary to prevent damage to protective covers from wind whip during temperatures below 30° F.

Dip treatments.—Most lumber dips are primarily fungicides (see chs. 16 and 22). Some, however, are designed to help maintain moisture stability in storage and during construction. (End coatings are discussed in sec. 18–3.)

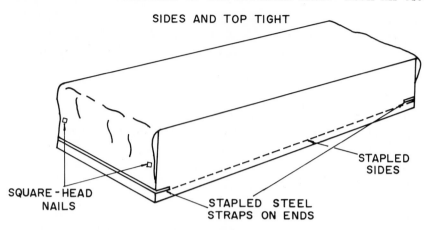

Figure 18–7.—Lumber wrapping system for shipment on open cars. Staples spaced 10 inches apart and driven through steel strap or cord embedded in the paper.

An evaluation was made of seven coatings (Koch 1966) to determine their effectiveness in excluding moisture pickup when lumber is exposed to exterior conditions. Several widely used commercial formulations were included. Studs cut from southern pine veneer cores were dried to 9-percent moisture content and treated as follows:

A. Control—no treatment.
B. 10-second dip in PAR [2], a clear, glossless, nonfungicidal, penetrating, water-repellent finish.
C. 10-second dip in Woodlife[2], a clear, penetrating, water-repellent preservative.
D. 10-second dip in Lumbrella[2], (9:1 ratio of water to concentrate).
E. 10-second dip in Convoy[2], (6:1 ratio of water to concentrate).
F. 10-second dip in experimental Millbrite[2], (9:1 ratio of water to concentrate).
G. Two brush coats of shellac (including ends of studs).
H. Two brush coats of aluminum paint (including ends of studs).

The dilutions in treatments D, E, and F are the manufacturer's recommendation. These three treatments are generically described as unpigmented, emulsified, semipenetrating, fungicidal water repellents in aqueous solution. The coating of treatment H is described as: aluminum pigment powder for paint Fed. Spec. TTA468, Type II, Class B; mixed with varnish (for mixing with aluminum paint) Fed. Spec. TTV–81D, Type I.

Studs were suspended in one of the following three atmospheres:

Exterior exposure under continuous water spray
90-percent relative humidity and 80° F.
42-percent relative humidity and 81° F.

After 8 weeks' exposure, average moisture contents were:

Under continuous water spray   22 percent
At 90-percent relative humidity   13 percent
At 42-percent relative humidity   9 percent

[2] These proprietary products are mentioned for information only; other water-repellent preparations are commercially available.

All humidity and treatment conditions considered, the most rapid change in moisture content occurred during the first 2 weeks (4.8 percent compared to an average of 2.0 percent for each of the following 2-week periods).

Figure 18–8 shows that none of the coatings tested was very effective in providing protection against moisture change over the 8-week period. Two brush coats of aluminum paint gave best protection under the water shower and at 90-percent humidity. Shellac was second best at 90-percent humidity but inferior to three other coatings under the shower. Some of the other treatments have value for very short-term protection from rainwetting during storage at a building site and during construction.

While this test was conducted with studs, the advisability of treating studs with a coating which blocks moisture movement may be questioned. If ends are trimmed during construction and become wetted in the completed structure, drying may be slowed enough to start decay.

18–6 PLYWOOD, PARTICLEBOARD, AND HARDBOARD

Because these panel products are hot-press formed, they come out of the manufacturing process at a moisture content well below 10 percent. When they are stacked in storage packages, the prevailing atmosphere has very limited access to the center of the pile; therefore, the moisture content in

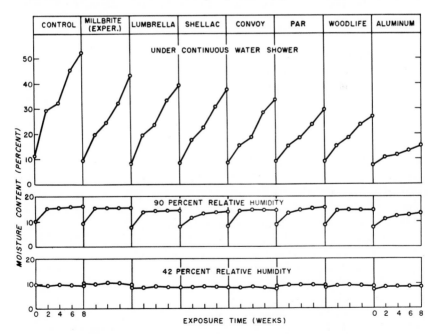

Figure 18–8.—Moisture content of coated and uncoated studs exposed to water spray, 90-percent humidity, and 40-percent humidity. Each curve represents average for 10 studs. (Drawing after Koch 1966.)

these stacked products changes slowly in response to changes in temperature and humidity of the surrounding air. Because the top and bottom panels in each storage package are so completely exposed on one side, however, it is highly desirable to store these products in a heated shed where conditions can be manipulated to keep the material at an equilibrium moisture content near the anticipated moisture content in use. It should be recognized that the equilibrium moisture content of these panel products—which incorporate varying percentages of resins and waxes—may differ significantly from the equilibrium moisture content of ordinary solid wood products exposed to the same atmospheric conditions. (See sec. 8–3, under heading EQUILIBRIUM MOISTURE CONTENT OF RECONSTITUTED WOOD.)

18–7 PAPER

Environmental deterioration of paper involves interactions of heat, light, moisture, and gases. Since papers are made by numerous processes and many contain a variety of additives, it is difficult to make generalized statements about optimum storage conditions.

Luner (1969) has reviewed factors affecting paper permanence and observed that presence of moisture accelerates the aging of paper, as does exposure to light or high temperature. It is concluded, therefore, that deterioration of many southern pine papers can be controlled by storing them in a regulated dry atmosphere (50-percent relative humidity or lower), in comparative darkness, and at a temperature of 72° F. or lower.

18–8 LITERATURE CITED

Altman, J. A.
    1965.   Wet storage of pulpwood.
            Amer. Pulpwood Assoc.
            Tech. Release 65–R–17,
            3 pp.

Applefield, M.
    1966.   Wrappings for protecting
            kiln-dried lumber stored
            in the open. Forest Prod.
            Res. Soc. News Dig.
            H–2.3, 2 pp.

DeGroot, R. C., and Scheld, H. W.
    1971.   Biodegradability of sapwood
            from southern pine logs
            stored under a continuous
            water spray. Forest Prod.
            J. 21(10): 53–55.

Djerf, A. C., and Volkman, D. A.
    1969.   Experiences with water
            spray wood storage.
            TAPPI 52: 1861–1864.

Glassy, M.
    1969.   Rader pneumatics reports
            new chip pile shape reduces decomposition.
            Amer. Plywood Assoc.
            Tech. Pap. 68–16, pp.
            3–4.

Hickman, L.
    [n.d.].   Protection of lumber for
            exterior storage. West.
            Pine Assoc. Res. Note
            6.711, 4 pp.

King, A. D., Stanley, W. L., Jurd, L.,
    and Boyle, F. P.
    1971.   Wood chip microbiological
            control with sulfur dioxide. TAPPI 54: 262.

Koch, P.
    1966.   Straight studs from southern pine veneer cores.
            USDA Forest Serv. Res.
            Pap. SO–25, 37 pp.
            Southern Forest Exp.
            Sta., New Orleans, La.

Lindgren, R. M.
  1953. Deterioration losses in stored southern pine pulpwood. TAPPI 36: 260–264.

Loughborough, W. K., and Torgeson, O. W.
  1929. Standard commercial moisture specifications for southern yellow pine lumber: Effect of present seasoning and storage practices on the moisture content of southern yellow pine at time of shipment. USDA Forest Serv. Forest Prod. Lab., 88 pp.

Lowery, D. P.
  1959. Management of log inventories. USDA Forest Serv. Intermountain Forest and Range Exp. Sta. Res. Note 63, 4 pp.

Luner, P.
  1969. Paper permanence. TAPPI 52: 796–805.

Mason, R. R., Muhonen, J. M., and Swartz, J. N.
  1963. Water sprayed storage of southern pine pulpwood. TAPPI 46: 233–240.

Peck, E. C.
  1961. Air drying of lumber. USDA Forest Serv. Forest Prod. Lab. Rep. 1657, 21 pp.

Rhyne, J. B., and Brinkley, A. W., Jr.
  1961. Seven months outside storage of pine and hardwood chips at the Panama City Mill of International Paper Company. Southern Pulp and Pap. Manufacturer 24(2): 86, 88, 116–117.

Rothrock, C. W., Jr., Smith, W. T., and Lindgren, R. M.
  1961. The effects of outside storage on slash pine chips in the South. TAPPI 44: 65–73.

Saucier, J. R., and Miller, R. L.
  1961. Deterioration of southern pine chips during summer and winter storage. Forest Prod. J. 11: 371–379.

Scheffer, T. C.
  1969. Protecting stored logs and pulpwood in North America. Mater. und Organismen 4: 167–199.

Schmidt, F. L.
  1969. Observations on spontaneous heating toward combustion of commercial chip piles. TAPPI 52: 1700–1701.

Shields, J. K.
  1967. Microbiological deterioration in the wood chip pile. Can. Dep. Forest. and Rural Develop. Dep. Pub. 1191, 29 pp.

Smith, R. S., and Hatton, J. V.
  1971. Economic feasibility of chemical protection for outside chip storage. TAPPI 54: 1638–1640.

Somsen, R. A.
  1962. Outside storage of southern pine chips. TAPPI 45: 623–628.

Springer, E. L., Eslyn, W. E., Zoch, L. L., and Hajny, G. J.
  1969. Control of pulp chip deterioration with kraft green liquor. USDA Forest Serv. Res. Pap. FPL–110, 4 pp. Forest Prod. Lab., Madison, Wis.

Springer, E. L., Eslyn, W. E., Zoch, L. L., and Hajny, G. J.
  1970. Want a chemical to protect chip quality? Look in "backyard". Pulp and Pap. 44: 151–152.

Springer, E. L., and Hajny, G. J.
  1970. Spontaneous heating in piled wood chips. I. Initial mechanism. TAPPI 58: 85–86.

Springer, E. L., Haslerud, E. J., Fries, D. M., Clark, I. T., Hajny, G. J., and Zoch, L. L.
  1971. An evaluation of four chemicals for preserving wood chips stored outdoors. TAPPI 54: 555–560.

Thornburg, W. L.
  1963. Effect of roundwood or chip storage on tall oil and turpentine fractions of slash pine. TAPPI 46: 453–455.

Vick, H.
  1964. Storage of hardwood logs by the water spray system. Southern Lumberman 209(2609): 198, 200, 202.

Volkman, D.
  1966. Water spray storage of southern pine pulpwood. TAPPI 49(7): 48A–53A.

19

Machining

CONTENTS

19

Machining

Since information on machining southern pine is available in forms requiring some understanding of basic woodworking processes, essential explanations are provided. Broader coverage of wood machining processes is available in Koch (1964b). In addition, a number of comprehensive literature reviews have been made (Forest Products Research Society 1959, 1960, 1961; Koch and McMillin 1966; Koch 1968b; McMillin 1970; Kollmann and Côté 1968, pp. 475–541). Historical reviews of the development of wood machining technology are also available (Mansfield 1952; Koch 1964b, pp. 3–6; Koch 1967b; Prokes 1966; Simons 1966; Thunell 1967; Wilkins 1966; Goodman 1964).

19–1 HISTORICAL BACKGROUND

Earliest southern pine sawmills applied waterpower to straight reciprocating saws only slightly modified from the primitive hand-operated pit saw. After their introduction in the early 1800's, large circular saws increased in popularity and by 1860 were in wide use as **headsaws**, cutting logs into boards and timbers. Smaller, specialized circular saws were developed as **edgers** to remove bark and wane from lumber, as **trimmers** to square up ends, and as **slashers** to cut waste pieces into short lengths.

While double circular saws, cutting from above and below, were developed as headrigs for very large logs, these began to be supplanted by bandsaws in the decades after 1870. By 1900 band headrigs, served by steam shotgun carriages, and supplemented by resaws to cut lumber from slabbed cants, and by edgers, trimmers, and fast lumber handling equipment, were featured in mills cutting up to 150 M b.f. per day.

Toward the end of the century demand for planed lumber stimulated development of practical planing machines. By 1907 most sawmills were equipped with single or double **surfacers**, planing one or both sides of a board simultaneously, and **matchers** to cut matching patterns in board edges, or combinations handling both functions. More specialized plants might also have **jointers** to plane precisely squared pieces for edge-gluing, or **moulders** which cut patterns in edges or surfaces of lumber. Versatility and efficiency of these machines improved in the early 1900's with the introduction of ball bearings, electric motors, and thin, high-speed steel knives in round, instead of square cutterheads.

The chainsaw, first introduced to North America in about 1915, was much improved in the late 1930's and has since gained almost complete acceptance for felling and bucking trees. It is probable that hydraulic shears, which have been in limited operation in the woods since 1960, will find increasing use—and to some extent—will perform harvesting work presently done with chainsaws.

Increasing consumption of pulp and paper, and hence increased need for bark-free wood, brought important developments in bark removal equipment during the 20 years from 1935 to 1955. Drum barkers developed for cordwood were not applicable to saw logs, so hydraulic and mechanical machines were invented to strip bark from sawmill slabs and whole logs.

The rotating-ring mechanical barker was invented in about 1950. It has proven to be a wood machining innovation of primary importance because it has vastly increased the supply (in the form of sawmill slabs and veneer mill clippings) of bark-free chippable wood available to the pulp industry.

By 1963, techniques for peeling and gluing southern pine veneer had been established, and the manufacture of southern pine plywood has since become a major industry.

The multiple-wide-belt sander that appeared in the United States after 1955 is now widely used to size and smooth southern pine particleboard and plywood.

The years from 1963 to 1966 have seen the invention of chipping headrigs for small logs. These new headrigs convert a log into a cant without forming either sawdust or slabs. In 1966 a tape-controlled routing and shaping machine was introduced, a development signalling the imminent application of computers to control various wood machining processes.

Prior to 1945 most advances in wood machining were the result of industrial trial and error; however, reviews of wood machining research published in recent years reflect results gained from formal laboratory research. It is expected that this new approach will accelerate change in the techniques of wood machining.

19–2 ORTHOGONAL CUTTING [1]

Wood is machined by removing chips that range in size from sanderdust to pulp chips or larger. There are two basic machining processes. In the first, known as **orthogonal cutting**, the cutting edge is perpendicular to the direction of the relative motion of tool and workpiece; the surface generated is a plane parallel to the original work surface. A carpenter's hand plane cuts orthogonally, as does a bandsaw. Rotary peeling of veneer approximates orthogonal cutting.

The second is a rotary-cutting process (**peripheral milling**) in which

---

[1] In sec. 19–2, the illustrations and cutting-force data specific to southern pine are all taken from Woodson and Koch (1970).

single chips are formed and removed by the intermittent engagement of knives carried on the periphery of a rotating cutterhead or saw. A rotary planer machines wood by the peripheral milling process.

To separate a chip from the workpiece during any wood machining process, it is first necessary to cause a structural failure at the juncture of chip and workpiece. Since the strength of wood varies with grain direction, chip configuration, cutting power, and surface quality are all strongly affected by the direction of cut (fig. 19–1), as well as the knife geometry.

A two-number notation used by McKenzie (1961) is useful in describing the orthogonal machining situation. With this system the first figure given is the angle the cutting edge makes with the grain of the wood; the second figure is the angle between direction of tool motion and grain (fig. 19–1).

DEFINITIONS

Figure 19–2 illustrates standard nomenclature of wood machining terms applicable to orthogonal cutting.

EFFECTS OF CUTTING VELOCITY

In the experimental data that follow in this chapter, cutting velocity is always stated because the effect of cutting velocity on cutting forces is not well established. Endersby (1965), when cutting in a near-orthogonal mode, found that in the range from 1,000 to 9,000 feet per minute (f.p.m.), cutting velocity had little effect on cutting forces; however, when velocity was reduced from 1,000 to 7 f.p.m., cutting force increased about 2½ times.

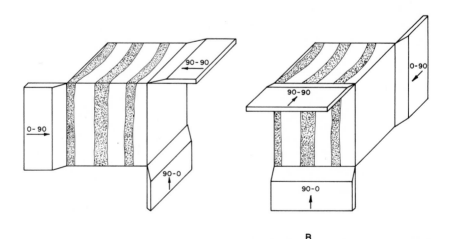

B

Figure 19–1.—Designation of the three major machining directions. The first number is the angle the cutting edge makes with the grain; the second is the angle between cutter movement and grain.

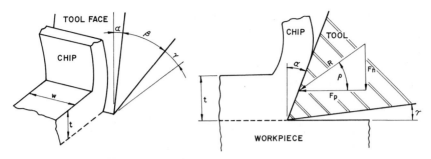

Figure 19–2.—Nomenclature in orthogonal cutting.

α   Rake angle: angle between the tool face and a plane perpendicular to the direction of tool travel.

β   Sharpness angle: angle between the tool face and back.

γ   Clearance angle: angle between the back of the tool and the work surface behind the tool.

t   Thickness of chip before removal from the workpiece.

w   Width of undeformed chip.

F_n Normal tool force: force component acting perpendicular to parallel tool force and perpendicular to the surface generated.

F_p Parallel tool force: force component acting parallel to tool motion relative to workpiece, i.e., parallel to cut surface.

R   Resultant tool force: the resultant of normal and parallel tool force components.

ρ   Angle of tool force resultant: the angle whose tangent is equal to the normal tool force divided by the parallel tool force.

Factors that may alter the cutting resistance of wood as cutting velocity is increased include the following:

- More force is required to accelerate the chip at high cutting velocity than at low.
- Strength of wood increases with increasing rate of deformation.
- Strength of wood decreases as temperature increases; there may be localized changes in workpiece temperature near the juncture of chip and workpiece.
- The coefficient of friction between tool and chip may change as cutting velocity is varied.
- When cutting wet wood, hydraulic action of water in proximity to the knife may alter cutting forces as velocity is changed.

It may be that in most situations these several factors are mutually counteracting so that the net effect of changing cutting velocity is minor.

As a final comment, high cutting velocity may sometimes assist in accomplishing clean severance of fibers because of chip inertia. This effect can be observed when cutting grass with a scythe or rotary power motor.

PARALLEL TO GRAIN: 90–0 DIRECTION

General discussions of orthogonal cutting parallel to the grain are available (Franz 1958; Koch 1964b, pp. 35–87). This text will be restricted to data specific to southern pine. Because the earlywood and latewood of southern pine are so different, the information presented here is organized to show cutting forces and chip types separately for earlywood and latewood.

Chip formation.—As described by Koch (1955, p. 261; 1956, p. 397) and enumerated by Franz (1958), three basic chip types (figs. 19–3, 19–5, and 19–6) may result when southern pine is machined parallel to the grain in the 90–0 mode. Type I chips are broken splinters formed by cleavage along the grain; Type II chips fail in shear and tend to form continuous spirals; Type III chips are severely compressed parallel to the grain and are more or less formless. Type II chips leave the best surface.

Type I chips are formed when cutting conditions are such that the wood splits ahead of the tool by cleavage until it fails in bending as a cantilever beam, as illustrated by dry wood in figure 19–3A. Type I chips from saturated specimens of both earlywood and latewood sometimes peel off in segmented spirals without breaking abruptly (fig. 19–3B). Factors leading to formation of Type I chips are:

- Low resistance in cleavage combined with high stiffness and strength in bending.
- Deep cuts (Type I chips can form with any depth of cut, depending on the other factors).
- Large rake angles (25° and more).
- Low coefficient of friction between chip and tool face.
- Low moisture content in the wood.

The Type I chip leaves a surface that exhibits **chipped grain**, i.e., the split ahead of the cutting edge frequently runs below the plane generated by the path of the cutting edge. The amount of roughness depends upon the depth to which the cleavage runs into the wood. Power consumed by a knife forming Type I chips is low because wood fails relatively easily in tension perpendicular to the grain, and the knife severs few fibers. Because it is seldom cutting, the knife edge dulls slowly.

Rake angles of 25 and 35° tend to cause Type I chips because the normal cutting force (F_n) is negative at all depths of cut for all moisture contents (fig. 19–4).

Type II chips occur under certain limited conditions which induce continuous wood failures extending from the cutting edge to the work surface ahead of the tool (fig. 19–5). The movement of the tool strains the wood ahead of the tool in compression parallel to the grain and causes diagonal shearing stresses; as the wood fails it forms a continuous, smooth spiral chip. The radius of the spiral increases as chip thickness increases. Quite frequently latewood chips display laminae or layers. The resultant surface ➤

F–520976

Figure 19–3.—Franz Type I chips from 0.045-inch cuts in 90–0 direction, 25° rake angle. (A) In loblolly pine earlywood at 7-percent moisture content. (B) In saturated loblolly pine latewood. Type I chips form less frequently in saturated than in dry wood. (Photos from Woodson and Koch 1970.)

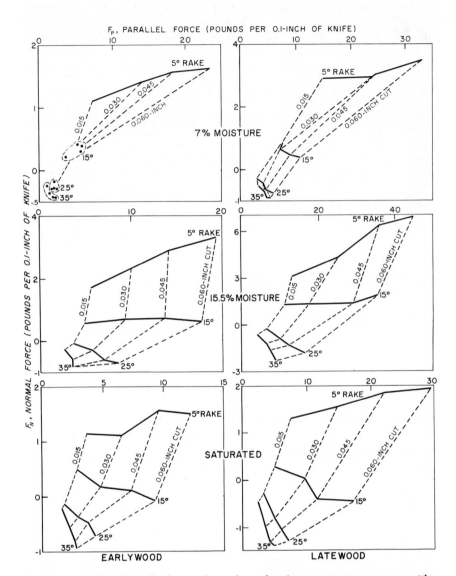

Figure 19–4.—Effect of depth of cut, rake angle, and moisture content on average cutting forces for earlywood and latewood of southern pine; 90–0 mode, orthogonal, 15° clearance angle, 2 inches per minute cutting velocity, wood at room temperature. (Drawing after Woodson and Koch 1970.)

is excellent. Thin chips, intermediate to high moisture content, and 5 to 10° rake angles favor formation of the Type II chip in excised earlywood or latewood. The cutting edge is in intimate contact with the wood at all times, and dulling may be rapid. Power demand is intermediate between that for Type I and Type III chips.

Type III chips tend to form in cycles. Wood ahead of the tool is stressed

F-520977

Figure 19–5.—Franz Type II chip from an 0.045-inch cut (90–0 direction) in loblolly pine latewood at 7-percent moisture content; 5° rake angle. (Photo from Woodson and Koch 1970.)

in compression parallel to the grain and ruptures in shear parallel to the grain and compression parallel to the grain. The chip does not escape freely up the tool, and the deformed wood is compacted against the tool face (fig. 19–6). Stresses are then transferred to undeformed areas that fail in turn. When the accumulation of compressed material becomes critical, the chip buckles and escapes upward, and the cycle begins again. Factors favorable to the formation of Type III chips include:

- Small or negative rake angles.
- Dull cutting edges (the rounded edge presents a negative rake angle at tool edge extremity).
- High coefficient of friction between chip and tool face.

Wood failures ahead of the tool establish the surface, frequently extending below the plane of the cut or leaving incompletely severed wood elements prominent on the surface. This machining defect is termed **fuzzy grain**. Power consumption is high, and dulling may be rapid.

Occurrence of the three chip types during orthogonal cutting of loblolly pine earlywood and latewood is summarized in table 19–1.

Effects of knife angles.—The angle between the tool face and a plane perpendicular to the direction of tool travel **(rake angle)** strongly affects tool forces as well as chip type and smoothness of cut; forces are negatively correlated with rake angle (fig. 19–7A and tables 19–2 through 19–6). Figure 19–4 shows the effect of rake angle of three moisture contents.

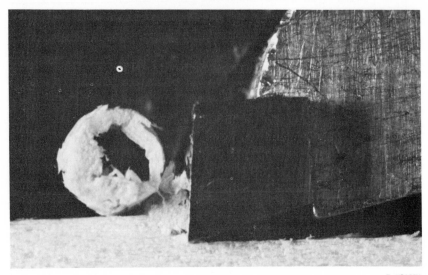

F–520978

Figure 19–6.—Franz type III chip from an 0.045-inch cut (90–0 direction) in loblolly pine earlywood at 7-percent moisture content; 5° rake angle. (Photo from Woodson and Koch 1970.)

TABLE 19–1.—*Chip types when loblolly pine wood is cut in the parallel-to-grain (90–0) mode* (Woodson and Koch 1970)[1]

Moisture content and rake angle (degrees)	Chip type[2]	
	In earlywood	In latewood
Saturated		
5	II(III)	II
15	II(III)	I(II)
25	I(II)	I
35	I	I
15.5 percent		
5	III(II)	II(III)
15	II(III)	II
25	I(II)	I(II)
35	I	I
7.0 percent		
5	III(I)	II(I)
15	I(III)	I
25	I	I
35	I	I

[1] Depths of cut ranged from 0.015 to 0.060 inch; cutting velocity was 2 inches per minute; clearance angle 15°.

[2] The first number in each entry is major chip type as classified by Franz (1958); a second number in parentheses indicates that a combination of chip types was observed.

TABLE 19–2.—*Average tool forces per 0.1 inch of knife when loblolly pine wood is cut in the parallel-to-grain (90–0) mode* (Woodson and Koch 1970)

Factor[1]	Parallel force	Normal force[2]
	– – – – – – *Pounds* – – – – –	
Cell type		
Earlywood	6.5	0.3
Latewood	12.5	.5
Moisture content, percent		
7 percent	8.3	.4
15.5 percent	12.9	.8
Saturated	7.3	.0
Depth of cut, inch		
0.015	5.2	.5
.030	8.3	.4
.045	10.8	.4
.060	13.7	.4
Rake angle, degrees		
5	18.0	2.6
15	10.9	.5
25	5.4	− .6
35	3.7	− .7

[1] Clearance angle constant at 15°.

[2] A negative normal force means that the knife tended to lift the workpiece; force was positive when the knife tended to push the workpiece away.

The angle between the tool face and back (**sharpness angle**) strongly affects the rate at which the cutting edge dulls. Minute fracturing of a freshly sharpened and honed knife edge occurs as the very first few chips are cut and continues until equilibrium is reached between the cutting edge—which grows thicker and more rigid as dulling proceeds—and the cutting forces; from this time, wear proceeds at a slower rate. Effective rake angle is decreased as wear proceeds (fig. 19–8); cutting forces rise, and chip formation is altered.

In one of the few studies of cutting-edge sharpness specific to southern pine, Bridges (1971) found that rate of dulling was positively correlated with specific gravity, resin content, and silica (grit) content in southern pine particleboard.

The angle between the back of the tool and the work surface behind the tool, i.e., **clearance angle**, does not have a critical effect on cutting force or chip formation; 15° is usual. As it is reduced below 15°, tool forces rise moderately. Dulling of the tool reduces the effective clearance angle, which may in fact become negative; a negative clearance angle increases the cutting forces exerted by the knife and usually adversely affects surface quality

TABLE 19–3.—*Parallel tool forces per 0.1 inch of knife when loblolly pine latewood is cut in the parallel-to-grain (90–0) mode* (Woodson and Koch 1970)[1][2]

Depth of cut and moisture content (percent)	Rake angle, degrees			
	5	15	25	35
	— — — — — — — — — — *Pounds* — — — — — — — — — — —			
0.015 inch				
7_____	14.4(26.6)	7.6(22.5)	3.0(16.7)	3.3(11.3)
15.5_____	13.0(17.1)	11.1(15.7)	6.3(11.0)	4.0(6.4)
Saturated_____	7.4(11.1)	5.0(7.8)	3.0(5.3)	2.4(3.7)
0.030 inch				
7_____	23.9(49.2)	7.1(39.9)	4.1(22.3)	4.4(15.7)
15.5_____	25.0(32.7)	17.5(28.7)	9.9(16.9)	6.4(10.3)
Saturated_____	14.8(19.2)	9.6(13.9)	5.0(8.1)	3.5(6.5)
0.045 inch				
7_____	24.4(62.4)	8.8(46.0)	4.5(31.6)	4.8(16.6)
15.5_____	36.1(46.0)	28.8(38.0)	11.8(26.2)	7.1(12.9)
Saturated_____	22.3(28.0)	11.5(19.5)	5.9(10.7)	4.2(7.8)
0.060 inch				
7_____	33.2(87.3)	10.3(52.6)	6.0(31.0)	5.2(21.6)
15.5_____	44.8(57.6)	35.5(51.8)	16.3(34.9)	9.2(15.3)
Saturated_____	29.6(35.8)	17.3(27.9)	7.1(14.5)	4.7(7.9)

[1] The first number in each entry is the average cutting force; the number in parentheses is the average of the maximum forces observed; both are based on five replications.
[2] Clearance angle 15°; cutting velocity 2 inches per minute.

by causing **raised grain**—a roughened condition in which dense latewood, after being depressed by the dull knife, swells subsequent to planing so that it is raised above the less dense (and therefore less swollen) earlywood. At the other extreme, if the clearance angle is made very large and rake angle is kept constant, then the cutting edge becomes thin, and resulting rapid dulling causes increased cutting forces. In the cutting force data presented in this section (19–2), the clearance angle is 15° unless otherwise stated.

Effects of width and depth of cut.—If the tool is wider than the workpiece, the cutting forces are directly proportional to width of cut; if width of cut is doubled, cutting forces are doubled.

In orthogonal cutting, depth of cut is synonymous with thickness of the undeformed chip. As Lubkin (1957) and others have observed, in a given cutting situation two types of parallel-force curves may develop with changing chip thickness. When chips are very thin, the parallel force varies according to a power curve, and F_p becomes zero at zero chip thickness.

$$F_p = Kt^m w \tag{19–1}$$

where:

F_p = parallel tool force
K = a constant

t = chip thickness

m = a constant between 1 and 0 (generally observed to be from 0.25 to 0.67)

w = width of chip

Beyond the region of very thin chips it is possible, with suitably chosen constants A and B, to approximate considerable portions of this curve with a straight-line function of t:

$$F_p = (A + Bt)w \qquad (19\text{--}2)$$

In some situations the experimentally determined parallel cutting force defined by equation 19–1 holds for the entire practical range of chip thicknesses. In other situations, however, the curve straightens beyond a certain chip thickness and continues linearly as described by equation 19–2.

If the data on parallel cutting force (tables 19–3 and 19–4) are averaged for both earlywood and latewood over all moisture contents and all rake angles, the cutting force-chip thickness relationship can be approximated by straight lines (fig. 19–7B). Figure 19–4 shows in more detail how cutting forces are related to chip thickness.

TABLE 19–4.—*Parallel tool forces per 0.1 inch of knife when loblolly pine earlywood is cut in the parallel-to-grain (90–0) mode* (Woodson and Koch 1970)[1][2]

Depth of cut and moisture content (percent)	Rake angle, degrees			
	5	15	25	35
	– – – – – – – – – – – *Pounds* – – – – – – – – – – – –			
0.015 inch				
7	7.3(10.6)	5.8(9.2)	2.0(6.2)	1.3(5.2)
15.5	5.5(7.4)	4.9(6.2)	3.7(5.3)	2.5(3.5)
Saturated	3.8(5.2)	2.9(4.0)	2.0(3.0)	1.6(2.4)
0.030 inch				
7	14.2(18.8)	5.9(16.5)	1.8(9.8)	1.8(7.3)
15.5	10.0(12.6)	9.3(11.1)	5.7(8.4)	3.5(5.8)
Saturated	6.6(8.7)	5.0(6.3)	2.9(.4.5)	2.2(3.8)
0.045 inch				
7	18.5(25.8)	3.7(20.6)	2.0(10.9)	2.2(9.1)
15.5	14.0(16.9)	13.6(15.7)	6.9(11.9)	3.6(8.5)
Saturated	9.7(11.9)	7.4(9.5)	3.8(5.7)	2.6(4.3)
0.060 inch				
7	23.4(33.9)	5.2(25.7)	2.2(13.4)	1.9(10.9)
15.5	18.3(22.7)	17.5(20.2)	8.5(14.5)	3.6(10.7)
Saturated	12.4(14.5)	9.3(11.5)	4.3(7.1)	2.9(5.3)

[1] The first number in each entry is the average cutting force; the number following in parentheses is the average of the maximum forces observed; both are based on five replications.

[2] Clearance angle 15°; cutting velocity 2 inches per minute.

TABLE 19–5.—*Normal tool forces per 0.1 inch of knife when loblolly pine latewood is cut in the parallel-to-grain (90–0) mode* (Woodson and Koch 1970)[1][2][3]

Depth of cut and moisture content (percent)	Rake angle, degrees			
	5	15	25	35
	Pounds			
0.015 inch				
7	2.8 (0.4 to 5.6)	0.8 (−0.3 to 2.5)	−0.3 (−1.8 to 0.5)	−0.5 (−2.5 to 0.4)
15.5	3.1 (1.6 to 4.5)	1.3 (−.4 to 2.6)	−.3 (−1.0 to .5)	−.6 (−1.3 to −.1)
Saturated	1.3 (.5 to 2.5)	.3 (−.4 to 1.1)	−.3 (−.8 to .4)	−.4 (−1.0 to .2)
0.030 inch				
7	2.9 (.4 to 6.1)	.7 (−1.1 to 2.7)	−.4 (−3.2 to .7)	−.7 (−3.9 to .4)
15.5	4.6 (2.6 to 7.7)	1.4 (−.2 to 3.0)	−.9 (−2.3 to .1)	−1.2 (−2.2 to −.2)
Saturated	1.6 (.6 to 2.9)	.0 (−1.0 to 1.1)	−.8 (−1.7 to .0)	−1.0 (−2.0 to .1)
0.045 inch				
7	3.0 (.6 to 7.7)	.4 (−1.8 to 2.5)	−.6 (−4.7 to .7)	−.9 (−4.3 to .5)
15.5	6.7 (4.7 to 9.6)	1.4 (−.7 to 3.1)	−1.3 (−3.2 to .0)	−1.5 (−3.1 to −.3)
Saturated	1.8 (.8 to 3.4)	−.4 (−1.8 to .5)	−1.0 (−2.2 to .0)	−1.3 (−2.8 to .0)
0.060 inch				
7	3.4 (.5 to 9.1)	.4 (−2.0 to 2.3)	−.8 (−5.6 to .6)	−.9 (−5.9 to .4)
15.5	7.0 (3.8 to 11.1)	1.7 (−.7 to 4.1)	−1.8 (−4.4 to .0)	−2.4 (−4.1 to −.6)
Saturated	2.0 (.6 to 3.7)	−.4 (−1.7 to .7)	−1.3 (−3.2 to −.1)	−1.4 (−3.1 to .1)

[1] The first number in each entry is the average normal cutting force; the numbers in parentheses are minimum and maximum forces; each number is based on five replications.

[2] Clearance angle 15°; cutting velocity 2 inches per minute.

[3] A negative normal force means that the knife tended to lift the workpiece; force was positive when the knife tended to push the workpiece away.

TABLE 19–6.—*Normal tool force per 0.1 inch of knife when loblolly pine earlywood is cut in the parallel-to-grain (90–0) mode* (Woodson and Koch 1970)[1][2][3]

Depth of cut and moisture content (percent)	Rake angle, degrees			
	5	15	25	35
	———————————————————————— Pounds ————————————————————————			
0.015 inch				
7	1.1 (0.4 to 1.9)	0.3 (−0.1 to 0.9)	−0.2 (−0.9 to 0.4)	−0.2 (−1.3 to 0.2)
15.5	1.7 (.7 to 2.7)	.6 (.1 to 1.4)	.0 (− .4 to .3)	− .3 (− .7 to .0)
Saturated	1.2 (.5 to 2.1)	.5 (.1 to 1.0)	− .1 (− .4 to .3)	− .2 (− .5 to .2)
0.030 inch				
7	1.4 (.3 to 2.6)	.4 (− .6 to 1.1)	− .3 (−1.7 to .4)	− .3 (−2.3 to .2)
15.5	2.3 (1.1 to 4.1)	.7 (.3 to 1.3)	− .3 (−1.0 to .3)	− .6 (−1.5 to .0)
Saturated	1.1 (.7 to 2.2)	.2 (− .1 to .7)	− .4 (− .7 to .0)	− .6 (−1.1 to − .1)
0.045 inch				
7	1.6 (.4 to 3.0)	.2 (−1.2 to 1.2)	− .3 (−2.2 to .4)	− .4 (−3.1 to .2)
15.5	2.9 (1.8 to 4.6)	.6 (.1 to 1.3)	− .6 (−1.7 to .2)	− .8 (−2.3 to .1)
Saturated	1.6 (1.0 to 2.9)	.1 (− .3 to .6)	− .5 (−1.0 to .1)	− .8 (−1.5 to − .2)
0.060 inch				
7	1.6 (.4 to 3.5)	.4 (−1.6 to 1.4)	− .3 (−2.9 to .3)	− .4 (−3.6 to .3)
15.5	3.3 (1.8 to 5.1)	.6 (.0 to 1.5)	− .7 (−2.4 to .2)	− .8 (−2.9 to .2)
Saturated	1.5 (.9 to 2.2)	− .1 (− .5 to .7)	− .7 (−1.5 to .1)	− .9 (−2.0 to .1)

[1] The first number in each entry is the average normal cutting force; the numbers in parentheses are minimum and maximum forces; each number is based on five replications.

[2] Clearance angle 15°; cutting velocity 2 inches per minute.

[3] A negative normal force means that the knife tended to lift the workpiece; force was positive when the knife tended to push the wood away.

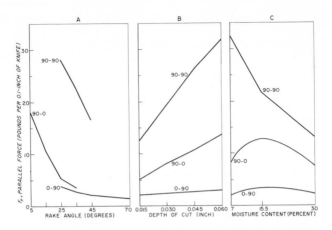

Figure 19–7.—Effect of moisture content of southern pine, rake angle, and depth of cut on average parallel cutting force for three modes of cutting. For these curves, data were pooled for both earlywood and latewood, at three moisture contents, four depths of cut, and at rake angles relevant to cutting direction. (Drawing after Woodson and Koch 1970.)

Effects of wood factors.—Specimens were cut on the radial face (fig. 19–1B, 90–0 direction) to develop the data here presented on orthogonal cutting parallel to the grain. It was observed that most Type I chips failed in the rays. Had the specimens been machined on the tangential face (fig. 19–1A), fewer Type I failures might have developed at the 25° rake angle. Orthogonal cutting data for edge-grain compared to flat-grain southern pine have not been published.

Cutting force is positively correlated with wood specific gravity. Data from Woodson and Koch (1970)—when averaged over all rake angles, all depths of cut, and all moisture contents—showed that latewood required much more cutting force per 0.1 inch of knife than earlywood, which is less dense.

Cell type	Specific gravity (ovendry volume and weight)	F_p	F_n
		– – Pounds – –	
Latewood	0.85	12.5	0.5
Earlywood	.34	6.5	.3

Woodson and Koch (1970) also found that maximum parallel cutting force per 0.1 inch of knife was inversely proportional to moisture content when averaged over all rake angles, all depths of cut, and both cell types.

Moisture content	Maximum F_p
Percent	Pounds
7	24.6
15.5	18.8
Saturated	10.5

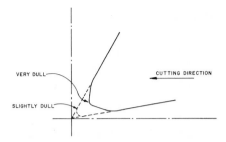

Figure 19–8.—Profile of a cutting edge as dulling proceeds. (Drawing after McKenzie and Cowling 1971.)

At low moisture contents, however, average parallel cutting force in the 90–0 mode is often positively correlated with moisture content (fig. 19–7C, tables 19–3 and 19–4). When dry wood is cut, the forming chip fails as a cantilever beam, and there are intervals when no force is required; hence the average is low even though the maximum force is high.

Kivimaa (1950), working with Finnish birch (*Betula* spp.), found that force required for cutting parallel to the grain, as well as for the other modes, decreases as wood temperature increases (fig. 19–9). It is probable that workpiece temperature interacts strongly with moisture content, chip thickness, and rake angle to affect chip formation and cutting forces. Wood is weakened by heat; steamed wood is softened more than wood subjected to dry heat. The plasticity of steamed wood is due mainly to softening of the middle lamella. Even at temperatures somewhat below 100° C., wood may be somewhat plastic; when wood has cooled completely, however, the original strong bond between the cell walls is nearly restored (Necesany 1965).

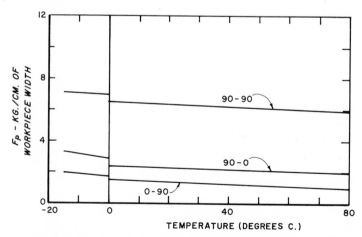

Figure 19–9.—Effect of temperature on parallel tool force. See figure 19–1 for explanation of cutting directions. Species, Finnish birch; chip thickness, 0.1 mm.; moisture content approximately 80 percent; rake angle, 35°; clearance angle, 10°. (Drawing after Kivimaa 1950.)

The mechanical properties of the wood being cut strongly influence the type of chip formed and the cutting forces. For example, Type I chips tend to form from wood that has low resistance to cleavage and high strength in bending. Strong southern pine latewood obviously requires more force to machine than weak earlywood. A summary of quantitative analyses by Franz (1958) and McKenzie (1961) of the effect of wood mechanical properties on chip formation can be found in Koch (1964b, pp. 79, 101).

A high coefficient of friction between workpiece and tool face is conducive to formation of a Type III chip; conversely, a low coefficient tends to promote Type I chips. Section 9–3 describes the frictional properties of southern pine wood sliding over a ground steel surface.

Woodson and Koch (1970) summarized the effect of the principal factors in 90–0 cutting; their earlywood and latewood data were pooled and multiple regression equations were developed to relate depth of cut (inch), rake angle (degrees), moisture content (decimal fraction of ovendry weight), and specific gravity (ovendry volume and weight) to average parallel (F_p) and normal (F_n) cutting forces (pounds) per 0.1-inch width of specimen.

When loblolly pine is cut parallel to the grain (90–0 mode) :

$$F_p = -6.996$$

$$+2,178.193 \left[\frac{(\text{specific gravity})(\text{depth of cut})}{\sqrt{\text{rake angle}}} \right] \qquad (19\text{--}3)$$

$$-274.182 \ (\text{specific gravity})(\text{depth of cut})$$
$$-409.777 \ (\text{moisture content})^2$$
$$+147.362 \ (\text{moisture content})$$

Within the limits of their experiment, equation 19–3 accounted for 75 percent of the variation with a standard error of the estimate of 4.7 pounds.

When loblolly pine is cut parallel to the grain (90–0 mode) :

$$F_n = -0.659$$
$$-6.610 \ (\text{moisture content})^2$$

$$+4.751 \left[\frac{1}{\sqrt{\text{rake angle}}} \right] \qquad (19\text{--}4)$$

$$-87.518 \ (\text{specific gravity})(\text{depth of cut})$$

$$+336.975 \left[\frac{(\text{specific gravity})(\text{depth of cut})}{\sqrt{\text{rake angle}}} \right]$$

Equation 19–4 accounted for 71 percent of the variation with a standard error of the estimate of 0.93 pound.

PERPENDICULAR TO THE GRAIN: 0–90 DIRECTION

To study cutting forces required for earlywood and latewood of loblolly pine, Woodson and Koch (1970) orthogonally cut room-temperature wood in the veneer peeling, or 0–90 mode. Their tests differed from commercial veneer peeling because the wood was cut at low temperature (unsteamed) and no restraint was applied above the knife (see sec. 19–10). This subsection is based primarily on the Woodson-Koch data.

Chip formation.—Under favorable conditions, chips formed by cutting in the 0–90 mode emerge as **continuous veneer,** defined by Leney (1960) as unbroken sheet in which the original wood structure is essentially unchanged by the cutting process. With a suitably sharp knife and a thin cut, continuous veneer with relatively smooth unbroken surfaces on both sides can be cut (fig. 19–10).

For 0–90 cutting, McMillin (1958) has accounted for the formation of veneer of various types in terms of the mechanical properties of the wood.

Following initial incision, the cells above the cutting edge must move upward along the face of the knife. Being restrained by the wood above them they are compressed, developing a force normal to the knife face, together with a frictional force along the face of the knife. As the cut proceeds, the forces reach a maximum when the veneer begins to bend as a cantilever beam. This bending deformation creates a zone of maximum tension above the cutting edge and causes compression near the top surface of the forming veneer.

As depth of cut is increased, rake angle decreased, or cutting edge dulled, critical zones of stress develop as depicted in figure 19–11. In Zone 1 maximum tension due to bending develops close to the cutting edge and at right angles to the long axis of the zone as drawn; failure occurs as a **tension check.** In Zone 2 the frictional force along the face of the knife may cause a more or less horizontal shear plane to develop between the compressed cells at the knife-chip interface and the resisting wood above them. In Zone 3 the cutting edge deflects the wood elements into a slight bulge preceding the edge, and the somewhat compacted cell walls may fail in tension either above or below the cutting plane (**compression tearing**).

Woodson and Koch (1970) found that compression tearing was prominent in earlywood cut with rake angles in the range from 25 to 70°. The degree of tearing ranged from moderate (fig. 19–12A) to severe (fig. 19–12C); in the latter case, the earlywood was torn away from the underlying latewood band. With rake angles of 45° and lower, latewood failed as a cantilever beam at all moisture contents (fig. 19–13). The knife with 70° rake and 0° clearance cut continuous veneer from saturated latewood with only an occasional failure as a cantilever beam (fig. 19–10C). With all knives (rake angles 25, 35, 45, and 70°), both earlywood and latewood developed deep tension checks when cut at 7-percent moisture content (figs. 19–13, 19–14). From these photographs it is evident that veneer

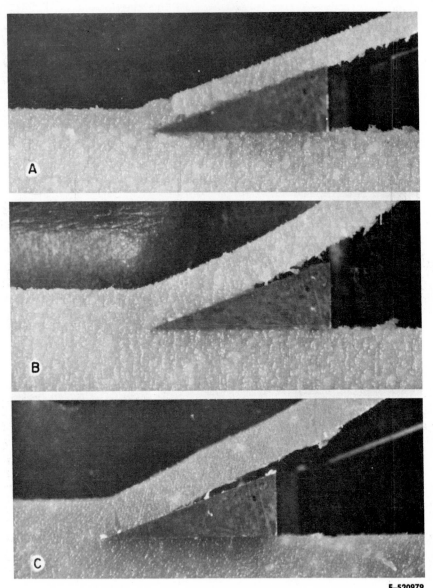

F-520979

Figure 19–10.—Continuous veneer cut from saturated loblolly pine in 0–90 mode; 70° rake angle, 20° sharpness angle; zero clearance angle. (A) Earlywood; 0.030-inch cut. (B) Earlywood; 0.060-inch cut. (C) Latewood; 0.060-inch cut. (Photos from Woodson and Koch 1970.)

cut in the 0–90 mode has a **loose** side containing numerous tension checks, and a **tight** side with few checks.

The knife with 70° rake angle cut the best veneer; saturated wood yielded the highest proportion of continuous veneer, although there was some compression tearing in earlywood. Generally, tension checks occurred

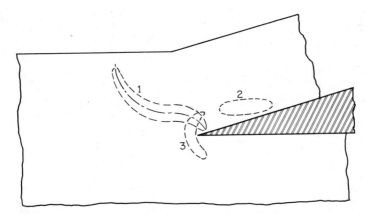

Figure 19–11.—Critical zones of stress in vener cut without a nosebar. 1, tension; 2, shear; 3, compression tearing.

when veneer was cut from wood dried to 15.5 or 7 percent. When studying figures 19–10, 12, 13, and 14, it should be remembered that the specimens were very narrow (about 0.1 inch) and that chip formation in wide specimens of mixed earlywood and latewood might develop somewhat differently (Woodson and Koch 1970). For a discussion of commercial practice in peeling veneer with a nosebar from heated logs see section 19–10.

Cutting forces.—Cutting forces are strongly affected by cell type, moisture content, depth of cut, and rake angle (table 19–7).

Woodson and Koch (1970) found that moisture content of loblolly pine cut in the 0–90 mode was negatively correlated with maximum parallel cutting force per 0.1 inch of width (but not with maximum normal force) when averaged over all rake angles, all depths of cut, and both cell types.

Moisture content	Maximum F_p
Percent	*Pounds*
7	9.8
15.5	8.2
Saturated	4.7

Average parallel cutting force, however, was highest at an intermediate moisture content (fig. 19–7C, 0–90). Figure 19–15 and tables 19–8 and 19–9 afford more details. When veneer is cut from dry wood, the forming chip fails as a cantilever beam, and there are intervals when no force is required; hence, the average is low. In more moist wood, however, continuous veneer is formed, and the average parallel force is high. Saturated wood, being softer, requires less force.

Parallel cutting force is negatively correlated with rake angle (figs. 19–7A, 19–15, and tables 19–8, 19–9). With the rake angles evaluated by Woodson and Koch (1970), the average normal force was always negative in latewood. With earlywood, however, the 25 and 35° rake angles

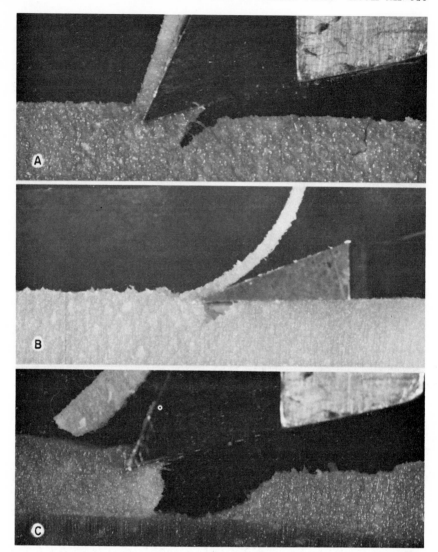

F-520980
Figure 19-12.—Compression tearing in veneer cut in the 0–90 mode from saturated loblolly pine earlywood. (A) Rake angle 25°, depth of cut 0.030-inch. (B) Rake angle 70°, depth of cut 0.015-inch. (C) Rake angle 25°, depth of cut 0.045-inch. (Photos from Woodson and Koch 1970.)

generally caused a positive normal force, i.e., the tool pushed on the work-piece (fig. 19–15 and tables 19–10 and 19–11).

Depth of cut had a relatively small effect on the average parallel cutting force; figure 19–7B (0–90) shows data averaged over all rake angles, all moisture contents, and both cell types. Figure 19–15 and tables 19–8 through 19–11 show the interactions for both normal and parallel forces.

Woodson and Koch (1970) summarized the effects of the major factors

F–520981

Figure 19–13.—Veneer fails as a cantilever beam when cut in 0–90 mode from loblolly pine latewood at 7-percent moisture content with a rake angle of 45° and clearance angle of 15°; veneer is 0.030-inch in top photo and 0.045-inch in bottom. (Photos from Woodson and Koch 1970.)

in 0–90 veneer cutting; their earlywood and latewood data were pooled, and multiple regression equations were developed to relate depth of cut (inch), rake angle (degrees), moisture content (expressed as a decimal fraction), and specific gravity (ovendry volume and weight) to average parallel (F_p) and normal (F_n) cutting forces (pounds) per 0.1-inch width of specimen.

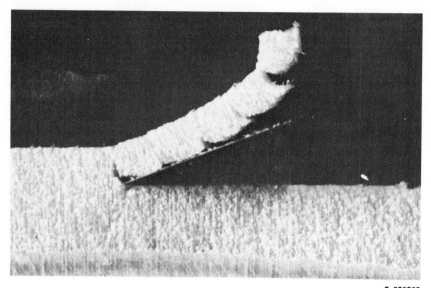

F–520982
Figure 19–14.—Tension checks in 0.060-inch veneer cut in 0–90 mode from loblolly pine earlywood at 7-percent moisture content. Rake angle 70°. Sharpness angle 20°. (Photo from Woodson and Koch 1970.)

For cutting loblolly pine veneer in the 0–90 mode:

$$F_p = -5.902 + 63.565 \left[\frac{1}{\text{rake angle}} \right] + 747.561 \left[\frac{\text{depth of cut}}{\text{rake angle}} \right]$$

$$-0.0338 \left[\frac{1}{\text{moisture content}^2} \right] + 3.318 \left[\frac{1}{\sqrt{\text{moisture content}}} \right] \qquad (19\text{–}5)$$

Within the limits of the Woodson-Koch experiment (1970), equation 19-5 accounted for 64 percent of the variation with a standard error of the estimate of 0.85.

For cutting loblolly pine veneer in the 0–90 mode:

$$F_n = -2.241 - 3.572 \left(\sqrt{\text{depth of cut}} \right) + 694.063 \left[\frac{1}{\text{rake angle}^2} \right] \qquad (19\text{–}6)$$

$$+1.296 \left[\frac{1}{\sqrt{\text{specific gravity}}} \right] + 0.0305 \ (\text{moisture content})(\text{rake angle})$$

Within the limits of the experiment, equation 19–6 accounted for 69 percent of the variation with a standard error of the estimate of 0.36 pound.

Tool forces for cutting in the 0–90 mode are influenced by the strength of wood in tension perpendicular to the grain, in shear perpendicular to

TABLE 19–7.—*Average tool forces per 0.1 inch of knife when veneer is cut from loblolly pine in the 0–90 mode* (Woodson and Koch 1970)[1]

Factor	Parallel force	Normal force[2]
	– – – – – – *Pounds* – – – – – –	
Cell type		
Earlywood	2.6	0.1
Latewood	2.7	−.8
Moisture content, percent		
7	2.2	−.5
15.5	3.5	−.4
Saturated	2.2	−.2
Depth of cut, inch		
0.015	2.2	−.1
.030	2.5	−.3
.045	2.7	−.4
.060	3.0	−.6
Rake angle, degrees		
25	3.9	.1
35	2.8	−.3
45	2.2	−.6
70	1.6	−.6

[1] Clearance angle 15°, except that knife with 70° rake had zero clearance. Cutting velocity 2 inches per minute, wood at room temperature.

[2] A negative normal force means that the knife tended to lift the workpiece; force was positive when the knife tended to push the workpiece away.

the grain, and in compression perpendicular to the grain. Because wood is relatively weak when so stressed, tool forces are substantially less for cutting in this mode than for orthogonal cutting in the 90–0 or 90–90 mode.

PERPENDICULAR TO GRAIN: 90–90 DIRECTION

Because gangsaws, bandsaws, and tenoners cut across the grain in the 90–90 direction (fig. 19–1), this mode of cutting is of practical interest to woodworkers.

Chip formation.—Optimum (Type I) chips in across-the-grain cutting are cleanly severed and undeformed except for shear along the grain (fig. 19–16A). Undesirable are chips (Type II) which in part have been torn rather than sharply cut from the workpiece, and which have been deformed by compression (fig. 19–17). Both types were observed in several woods by McKenzie (1961) and in southern pine by Woodson and Koch (1970). During formation of Type I chips, average cutting forces are relatively constant. Below the cutting plane, splits occur parallel to the grain. The splits may be minute and virtually invisible, in which case the surface is

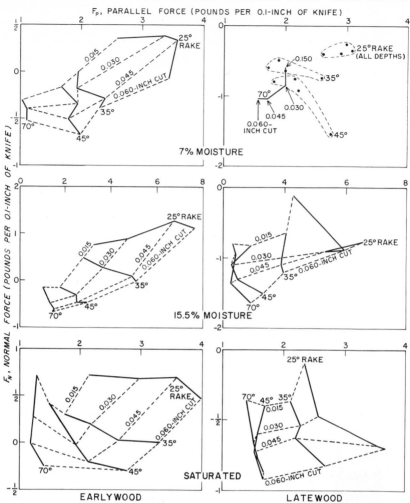

Figure 19–15.—Effect of depth of cut, rake angle, and moisture content on average cutting forces for earlywood and latewood of southern pine; 0–90 mode, orthogonal, 15° clearance angle, 2 inches per minute cutting velocity, wood at room temperature. (Drawing after Woodson and Koch 1970.)

quite good (fig. 19–16A) ; or they may be fairly frequent and deep, in which case the surface is poor (fig. 19–16C). Each subchip above the cutting plane is formed by shear along the grain.

When Type II chips are formed, average cutting forces tend to vary in cycles with successive cuts (visualize bandsaw teeth cutting successively). Failures occur perpendicular to the grain and at variable distances below the cutting plane (fig. 19–17). After the initial cut, therefore, a succeeding cutting edge may not be engaged in all portions of its path. The mechanics of these two chip formations are explained in McKenzie (1961) or Koch (1964b, pp. 93–109).

TABLE 19–8.—*Parallel tool forces per 0.1 inch of knife when veneer is cut from loblolly pine latewood in the 0–90 mode* (Woodson and Koch)[1][2]

Depth of cut and moisture content (percent)	Rake angle, degrees			
	25	35	45	70
	— — — — — — — — — *Pounds* — — — — — — — — — —			
0.015 inch				
7	2.9(14.7)	2.0(12.3)	2.1(8.8)	2.0(4.3)
15.5	4.3(8.7)	4.0(6.6)	2.9(4.7)	2.3(3.7)
Saturated	2.3(4.5)	2.1(3.6)	1.7(2.8)	1.4(1.9)
.030 inch				
7	3.0(20.7)	2.5(15.2)	1.8(11.4)	2.0(5.0)
15.5	5.9(14.8)	3.9(10.0)	2.3(7.2)	2.4(5.0)
Saturated	2.6(6.9)	2.3(6.1)	1.6(4.1)	1.5(2.5)
.045 inch				
7	3.1(25.6)	1.9(16.1)	2.2(15.9)	1.7(5.3)
15.5	5.5(17.7)	3.9(14.8)	2.5(9.2)	2.3(5.6)
Saturated	3.5(10.0)	2.2(7.8)	1.5(5.9)	1.6(2.9)
.060 inch				
7	2.6(26.9)	1.7(18.2)	2.8(17.9)	1.5(5.3)
15.5	6.6(21.5)	4.0(16.3)	3.3(11.7)	2.9(7.1)
Saturated	3.7(12.7)	2.7(10.3)	1.7(6.8)	1.7(3.7)

[1] The first number in each entry is the average cutting force; the number in parentheses is the average of the maximum forces observed; both are based on five replications.

[2] Clearance angle 15°, except that knife with 70° rake had zero clearance. Cutting velocity 2 inches per minute, wood at room temperature.

Type I chips and good surfaces can be achieved by cutting the wood at relatively high moisture content with a very sharp knife having a large rake angle, i.e., 45° (fig. 19–16A). Although supporting data are not published, it is probable that high cutting velocities, e.g., 10,000 f.p.m., are conducive to formation of Type I chips. Figure 19–18 suggests the idea that a high-velocity cutter might be resisted by the inertia of the fibers, and therefore could accomplish clean severance and a Type I chip. In comparative tests at low cutting speed, Type II chips were more frequent in earlywood than in latewood, particularly in wood of medium and low moisture content. In both latewood and earlywood, Type II chips were more frequent in wood of low moisture content (table 19–12).

Cutting forces.—Woodson and Koch (1970) have shown that when loblolly pine is cut orthogonally across the grain in the 90–90 mode, cutting forces are strongly affected by cell type, moisture content, depth of cut, and rake angle (table 19–13).

They found that when their data were averaged over all rake angles, all depths of cut, and both cell types, maximum cutting forces per 0.1 inch of specimen width were negatively correlated with wood moisture content.

TABLE 19–9.—*Parallel tool forces per 0.1 inch of knife when veneer is cut from loblolly pine earlywood in the 0–90 mode* (Woodson and Koch 1970)[1][2]

Depth of cut and moisture content (percent)	Rake angle, degrees			
	25	35	45	70
	— — — — — — — — — *Pounds* — — — — — — — — — — —			
0.015 inch				
7	2.6(5.5)	2.0(4.8)	1.7(4.1)	1.0(1.8)
15.5	3.3(5.1)	2.8(4.1)	1.8(3.7)	1.0(1.9)
Saturated	2.2(2.9)	1.8(2.6)	1.5(2.2)	1.3(1.9)
0.030 inch				
7	3.4(8.2)	1.9(6.3)	1.9(5.6)	1.1(2.2)
15.5	4.7(6.8)	3.6(6.7)	2.5(5.6)	1.4(2.8)
Saturated	3.0(4.5)	2.2(3.5)	1.9(3.2)	1.2(1.9)
0.045 inch				
7	3.5(10.1)	2.4(7.5)	1.8(6.0)	1.1(2.2)
15.5	6.7(10.1)	4.9(8.8)	2.5(6.1)	1.6(3.0)
Saturated	3.6(5.4)	2.6(4.7)	2.1(3.8)	1.2(1.9)
0.060 inch				
7	3.4(9.6)	2.3(8.1)	2.0(5.6)	1.1(2.4)
15.5	7.6(13.0)	5.1(10.2)	3.0(7.0)	1.4(2.6)
Saturated	4.0(6.0)	3.3(5.5)	2.8(4.7)	1.3(2.0)

[1] The first number in each entry is the average cutting force; the number in parentheses is the average of the maximum forces observed; both are based on five replications.

[2] Clearance angle 15°, except that knife with 70° rake had zero clearance. Cutting velocity 2 inches per minute, wood at room temperature.

Moisture content	F_p	F_n
Percent	*Pounds*	
7	43.3	6.8
15.5	29.0	1.6
Saturated	16.6	−1.7

Moisture content was also negatively correlated with average cutting force (fig. 19–7C, 90–90). Figure 19–19 and tables 19–14 through 19–17 give a more detailed view of interactions involving moisture content.

Rake angle was negatively correlated with both parallel (tables 19–13, 19–14, and 19–15) and normal tool forces (tables 19–13, 19–16, and 19–17).

Depth of cut had a positive linear correlation with parallel cutting force when data for earlywood and latewood were pooled over all moisture contents and rake angles (fig. 19–7B, 90–90). Figure 19–19 illustrates an interaction; normal force was unaffected by depth of cut only when dry earlywood was cut with a knife having a 45° rake angle.

Woodson and Koch (1970) summarized the effects of the major factors in 90–90 cutting; their earlywood and latewood data were pooled, and a

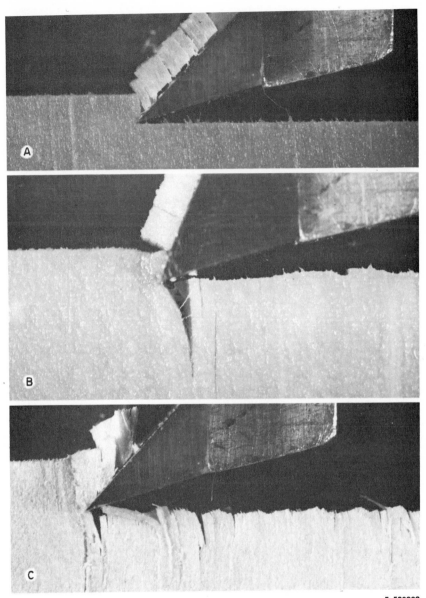

F–520983

Figure 19–16.—McKenzie type I chips from orthogonal cuts 0.060-inch deep across the grain of loblolly pine (90–90 mode). (A) Latewood, saturated, rake angle 45°. (B) Earlywood, saturated, rake angle 25°. (C) Latewood at 7-percent moisture content, rake angle 45°. (Photos from Woodson and Koch 1970.)

multiple regression analysis was made to relate depth of cut (inch), rake angle (degrees), moisture content (expressed as a decimal fraction), and specific gravity (ovendry volume and weight) to average parallel (F_p) and normal (F_n) cutting forces (pounds) per 0.1-inch width of specimen.

F–520984

Figure 19–17.—McKenzie type II chips from orthogonal cuts across the grain (90–90 mode) of loblolly pine earlywood of 7-percent moisture content. (A) Rake angle 45°; 0.060-inch cut. (B) Rake angle 25°; 0.045-inch cut. (Photos from Woodson and Koch 1970.)

When loblolly pine is cut across the grain (90–90 mode) :

$$F_p = +1.964$$

$$+561.346 \left[\frac{\text{specific gravity}}{\text{rake angle}} \right] \qquad (19\text{--}7)$$

$$+2{,}650.962 \left[\frac{(\text{specific gravity})(\text{depth of cut})}{(\text{rake angle})(\text{moisture content})} \right]$$

Within the limits of their experiment, equation 19–7 accounted for 87 percent of the variation with a standard error of the estimate of 6.8 pounds.

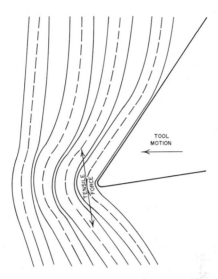

Figure 19–18.—In the 90–90 mode, failure
at the cutting edge is due to tension
across the cutting plane. (Drawing after
McKenzie 1961.)

TABLE 19–12.—*Typical chip types when loblolly pine
wood is cut in the across-the-grain (90–90) mode*
(Woodson and Koch 1970)[1]

Moisture content and rake angle (degrees)	Chip type[2]	
	In earlywood	In latewood
Saturated		
25	I	I
35	I	I
45	I	I
15.5 percent		
25	II(I)	I
35	II	I
45	II(I)	I
7 percent		
25	II	II(I)
35	II	II(I)
45	II	II(I)

[1] Depths of cut ranged from 0.015 to 0.060 inch. Cutting
velocity was 2 inches per minute, clearance angle 15°.

[2] The first number in each entry is major chip type as classified
by McKenzie (1961); a second number in parentheses indicates
that a combination of chip types was observed.

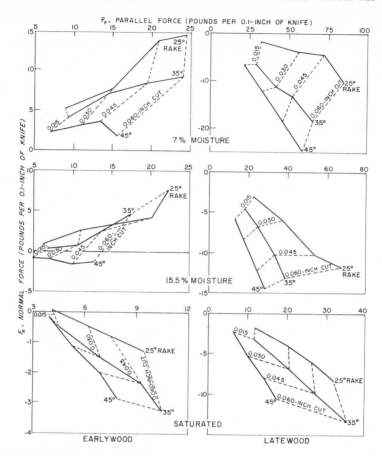

Figure 19–19.—Effect of depth of cut, rake angle, and moisture content on average cutting forces for earlywood and latewood of southerrn pine; 90–90 mode, orthogonal, 15° clearance angle, 2 inches per minute cutting velocity, wood at room temperature. (Drawing after Woodson and Koch 1970.)

When loblolly pine is cut across the grain (90–90 mode) :

$$F_n = -0.285$$
$$-180.253 \text{ (specific gravity)(depth of cut)}$$
$$+6.699 \left[\frac{\text{depth of cut}}{\text{moisture content}} \right] \quad\quad (19\text{–}8)$$
$$-50.615 \left[\frac{\text{(specific gravity)(depth of cut)}}{\text{moisture content}} \right]$$
$$+894.843 \left[\frac{\text{depth of cut}}{\text{(moisture content)(rake angle)}} \right]$$

TABLE 19–13.—*Average tool forces per 0.1 inch of knife when loblolly pine wood is cut in the across-the-grain (90–90) mode* (Woodson and Koch 1970)

Factor	Parallel force	Normal force[1]
	------ *Pounds* ------	
Cell type		
Earlywood_____	11.4	2.4
Latewood_____	33.6	−8.8
Moisture content, percent		
7_____	32.5	−2.1
15.5_____	21.9	−3.6
Saturated_____	13.1	−3.9
Depth of cut, inch		
0.015_____	12.4	−1.3
.030_____	19.5	−2.5
.045_____	26.2	−3.7
.060_____	31.9	−5.3
Rake angle, degrees[2]		
25_____	28.2	−0.7
35_____	22.8	−3.6
45_____	16.6	−5.4

[1] A negative normal force means that the knife tended to lift the workpiece; force was positive when the knife tended to push the workpiece away.

[2] All knives had a 15° clearance angle; cutting velocity 2 inches per minute.

Equation 19–8 accounted for 82 percent of the variation with a standard error of the estimate of 3.4 pounds.

FORCE COMPARISON FOR THREE CUTTING DIRECTIONS

Because chip formation when cutting in the 90–90 mode requires wood to be failed in tension parallel to the grain (fig. 19–18), parallel cutting forces are much higher than in the 0–90 and 90–0 mode. While the data in table 19–18 are restricted to a rake angle of 35° and one depth of cut, the trends shown in the table are valid for cuts from 0.015 to 0.060 inch deep and also for a rake angle of 25°.

The Woodson and Koch (1970) data on maximum and minimum cutting forces reveal some figures of interest to machine designers.

In the 90–0 (planing) direction, forces were most extreme (per 0.1 inch of knife) for 0.060-inch cuts in latewood:

F_p was maximum at 87.3 pounds for cuts with 5° rake angle in wood at 7-percent moisture content.

F_n was maximum at 11.1 pounds for cuts with 5° rake angle in wood at 15.5-percent moisture content.

F_n was minimum at −5.9 pounds for cuts with 35° rake angle in wood at 7-percent moisture content.

TABLE 19–14.—*Parallel tool forces per 0.1 inch of knife when loblolly pine latewood is cut in the across-the-grain (90–90) mode* (Woodson and Koch 1970)[1][2]

Depth of cut and moisture content (percent)	Rake angle, degrees		
	25	35	45
	– – – – – – – – – – – *Pounds* – – – – – – – – – – –		
0.015 inch			
7	32.4(42.8)	29.1(39.6)	21.7(31.7)
15.5	22.8(27.7)	18.2(22.9)	13.5(17.7)
Saturated	11.8(14.8)	11.7(14.3)	6.2(7.8)
0.030 inch			
7	56.6(73.5)	42.1(62.3)	33.6(51.8)
15.5	37.9(45.5)	24.5(32.2)	17.6(24.7)
Saturated	20.2(24.4)	20.4(24.9)	10.0(13.5)
0.045 inch			
7	71.9(81.7)	52.2(80.5)	46.1(66.7)
15.5	53.7(66.0)	33.8(43.7)	24.3(34.2)
Saturated	26.3(31.8)	27.3(32.4)	14.0(18.9)
0.060 inch			
7	85.9(119.7)	65.7(99.7)	59.1(87.1)
15.5	68.0(80.5)	38.4(53.4)	28.1(40.7)
Saturated	31.8(37.4)	35.6(42.0)	17.5(24.1)

[1] The first number in each entry is the average cutting force; the number in parentheses is the average of the maximum forces observed; both are based on five replications.
[2] Clearance angle 15°; cutting velocity 2 inches per minute.

In the 0–90 (veneer) direction, forces were most extreme (per 0.1 inch of knife) when cutting 0.060 inch deep:

F_p was maximum at 26.9 pounds for cuts with 25° rake angle in latewood at 7-percent moisture content.

F_n was maximum at 4.3 pounds for cuts with 25° rake angle in earlywood at 15.5-percent moisture content.

F_n was minimum at −9.5 pounds for cuts with 45° rake angle in latewood at 7-percent moisture content.

In the 90–90 (cross-cut) direction, forces (per 0.1 inch of knife) were most extreme when cutting 0.060-inch chips at 7-percent moisture content:

F_p was maximum at 119.7 pounds for cuts with 25° rake angle in latewood.

F_n was maximum at 28.7 pounds for cuts with 25° rake angle in earlywood.

F_n was minimum at −40.6 pounds for cuts with 45° rake angle in latewood.

TABLE 19–15.—*Parallel tool forces per 0.1 inch of knife when loblolly pine earlywood is cut in the across-the-grain (90–90) mode* (Woodson and Koch)[1][2]

Depth of cut and moisture content (percent)	Rake angle, degrees		
	25	35	45
	– – – – – – – – – – – *Pounds* – – – – – – – – – – – –		
0.015 inch			
7	8.9(11.0)	9.3(11.9)	7.1(10.2)
15.5	6.2(9.7)	7.0(9.2)	4.9(7.4)
Saturated	4.1(5.5)	4.5(5.5)	4.0(4.9)
0.030 inch			
7	15.0(19.5)	14.0(19.5)	11.0(14.8)
15.5	11.2(15.8)	10.8(14.9)	7.1(10.6)
Saturated	6.1 (8.2)	6.9(9.3)	5.3(6.6)
0.045 inch			
7	21.8(27.5)	19.6(27.3)	13.4(18.6)
15.5	20.3(25.2)	13.9(18.8)	9.9(14.6)
Saturated	7.6(10.6)	9.3(13.4)	6.8(9.2)
0.060 inch			
7	24.4(34.1)	24.0(32.5)	15.5(24.8)
15.5	22.4(31.4)	17.6(26.9)	12.8(22.8)
Saturated	9.5(13.0)	10.6(15.4)	7.8(10.8)

[1] The first number in each entry is the average cutting force; the number in parentheses is the average of the maximum forces observed; both are based on five replications.
[2] Clearance angle 15°; cutting velocity 2 inches per minute.

OBLIQUE AND INCLINED CUTTING

In strictly orthogonal cutting, the cutting edge is perpendicular to the motion of the tool over the workpiece. In some applications, the cutting edge is set obliquely to its direction of movement; the **deviation angle** between the edge and a line normal to the motion measures the degree of obliquity. Kivimaa (1950) has shown that when wood is cut parallel to the grain, parallel cutting force is negatively correlated with deviation angle; however, when cutting tangentially across the grain (as in veneer slicing) parallel cutting force stays the same or rises as deviation angle is increased.

If a cutting edge is drawn transversely during an otherwise orthogonal cutting operation (visualize bread being sliced with a long knife), the process is termed **inclined cutting**. It has been established that cutting forces can be reduced substantially and surface quality greatly improved by this means (fig. 19–20). No data specific to southern pine have been published; information on other species has been reported, however, by McKenzie (1961), Plough (1962), McKenzie and Franz (1964), St. Laurent (1965), Collins (1965), and McKenzie and Hawkins (1966). In the United States, the inclined cutting principle has had limited application to veneer lathes (see sec. 19–10).

TABLE 19–16.—*Normal tool forces per 0.1 inch of knife when loblolly pine latewood is cut in the across-the-grain (90–90) mode* (Woodson and Koch 1970)[1][2][3]

Depth of cut and moisture content (percent)	Rake angle, degrees		
	25	35	45
	Pounds		
0.015 inch			
7	− 1.7 (− 6.6 to 3.8)	− 6.7 (−12.0 to −1.6)	− 6.7 (−12.3 to −1.3)
15.5	− 3.1 (− 4.9 to − .9)	− 4.5 (− 6.4 to −1.4)	− 5.7 (− 8.1 to −2.6)
Saturated	− 1.6 (− 2.7 to − .5)	− 3.1 (− 4.2 to −1.4)	− 2.3 (− 3.6 to −1.0)
0.030 inch			
7	− 3.7 (−11.6 to 4.3)	−11.2 (−19.4 to −2.4)	−12.0 (−20.6 to −2.2)
15.5	− 6.0 (− 8.6 to −2.9)	− 6.7 (−10.3 to −2.5)	− 8.4 (−12.2 to −3.0)
Saturated	− 3.9 (− 5.6 to −2.1)	− 6.7 (− 8.7 to −3.7)	− 5.1 (− 7.9 to −2.0)
0.045 inch			
7	− 4.4 (−15.5 to 8.7)	−13.2 (−27.8 to −2.2)	−18.4 (−31.1 to −2.5)
15.5	−10.1 (−13.7 to −4.7)	−10.2 (−14.4 to −3.6)	−12.1 (−16.6 to −3.7)
Saturated	− 5.7 (− 7.9 to −3.2)	− 9.8 (−12.5 to −4.5)	− 7.9 (−11.1 to −3.1)
0.060 inch			
7	−10.4 (−24.4 to 1.9)	−18.4 (−35.9 to −4.2)	−25.0 (−40.6 to −4.4)
15.5	−11.7 (−16.1 to −4.5)	−13.0 (−18.7 to −4.4)	−14.5 (−21.9 to −4.7)
Saturated	− 8.1 (−10.1 to −4.4)	−13.4 (−16.7 to −7.5)	−10.5 (−14.8 to −3.6)

[1] The first number in each entry is the average normal cutting force; the numbers in parentheses show minimum and maximum forces; each number is based on five replications.

[2] Clearance angle 15°; cutting velocity 2 inches per minute.

[3] A negative normal force means that the knife tended to lift the workpiece; force was positive when the knife tended to push the workpiece away.

TABLE 19–17.—*Normal tool forces per 0.1 inch of knife when loblolly pine earlywood is cut in the across-the-grain (90–90) mode (Woodson and Koch 1970)*[1][2][3]

Depth of cut and moisture content (percent)	Rake angle, degrees		
	25	35	45
	Pounds		
0.015 inch			
7	5.3 (1.5 to 8.9)	4.1 (0.4 to 7.7)	2.2 (−1.0 to 6.3)
15.5	.8 (− .8 to 2.4)	.4 (−1.3 to 2.3)	− .9 (−2.1 to .4)
Saturated	.0 (− .4 to .6)	− .5 (−1.1 to .1)	− .1 (− .6 to .3)
0.030 inch			
7	8.8 (1.9 to 16.2)	7.4 (.5 to 14.9)	3.0 (−1.6 to 8.4)
15.5	2.7 (−1.0 to 6.5)	.7 (−3.0 to 4.8)	− .9 (−3.9 to 2.6)
Saturated	.5 (−1.3 to .3)	−1.5 (−2.6 to − .5)	−1.1 (−1.8 to − .3)
0.045 inch			
7	13.2 (2.7 to 20.7)	8.7 (.3 to 17.1)	3.8 (−2.4 to 10.0)
15.5	4.2 (−2.7 to 10.9)	2.5 (−2.8 to 8.7)	−1.5 (−5.8 to 4.2)
Saturated	− .8 (−1.9 to .2)	−2.4 (−4.2 to .9)	−2.0 (−3.5 to − .6)
0.060 inch			
7	14.6 (2.8 to 28.7)	9.5 (− .2 to 18.7)	1.9 (−4.5 to 8.6)
15.5	7.7 (−1.2 to 18.1)	4.7 (−3.2 to 13.1)	−1.4 (−6.9 to 4.5)
Saturated	−1.4 (−2.7 to .0)	−3.2 (−5.2 to −1.3)	−2.8 (−4.7 to −1.1)

[1] The first number in each entry is the average normal cutting force; the numbers in parentheses show minimum and maximum forces; each number is based on five replications.

[2] Clearance angle 15°; cutting velocity 2 inches per minute.

[3] A negative normal force means that the knife tended to lift the workpiece; force was positive when the knife tended to push the workpiece away.

TABLE 19–18.—*Average parallel tool force per 0.1 inch of knife when loblolly pine wood is cut in the three major modes with a rake angle of 35°; depth of cut 0.030 inch* (Woodson and Koch 1970)[1]

Moisture content and cell type	Average parallel tool force		
	0–90	90–0	90–90
	— — — — — — *Pounds* — — — — — —		
7 percent			
Earlywood_._ _ _ _ _ _ _ _	1.9	1.8	14.0
Latewood_ _ _ _ _ _ _ _ _ _	2.5	4.4	42.1
15.5 percent			
Earlywood_ _ _ _ _ _ _ _ _	3.6	3.5	10.8
Latewood_ _ _ _ _ _ _ _ _ _	3.9	6.4	24.5
Saturated			
Earlywood_ _ _ _ _ _ _ _ _	2.2	2.2	6.9
Latewood_ _ _ _ _ _ _ _ _ _	2.3	3.5	20.4

[1] Clearance angle, 15°; cutting velocity 2 inches per minute, wood at room temperature.

Cuts made by a knife having deviation angle are sometimes erroneously equated with cuts made by a longitudinally oscillating knife; a moment's thought about the pattern cut by a nicked knife should clarify the difference between the two situations. A knife given deviation angle has a slightly decreased effective sharpness angle, and therefore cutting forces

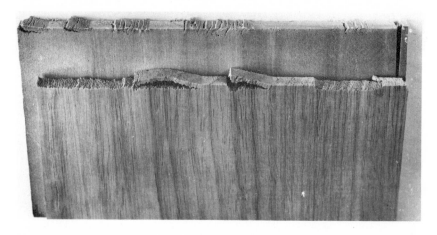

Figure 19–20.—Lateral vibration of the knife at 120 cycles per second improved surfaces of wood cut in the 90–90 mode at 0.5 inch per minute. (Top) Yellow poplar (*Liriodendron* L.). (Bottom) Common persimmon (*Diospyros virginiana* L.). The poorer surfaces shown resulted when lateral vibration was stopped. Rake angle, 25°; nominal chip thickness, 0.03 inch. (Photo from McKenzie 1961.)

are reduced when cutting orthotropic materials. An oscillating knife, however, has a substantially reduced effective sharpness angle. Also, the oscillating knife, because of slight imperfections in the cutting edge, exerts a toothed cutting action that is more effective than the simple pressure of a knife cutting with deviation angle (visualize drawing a toothed knife across a tomato skin compared to simply pressing the knife against the skin).

19–3   SHEARING AND CLEAVING [2]

These processes are distinguished from conventional orthogonal cutting because of the extreme depth of cut, i.e., the chip and the workpiece are equally massive, stiff, and difficult to deform (fig. 19–21).

SHEARING

When very great depths of cut are taken by a knife cutting in the 90–90 mode against an anvil or opposing knife (visualize rose stems cut with pruning shears), the process is described as shearing (fig. 19–21A). Tree-felling shears and shears to reduce long logs to shorter pulpwood lengths are in common use on southern pine. Most of the published research, however, has described work with other species (Erickson 1967; Kempe 1967; Wiklund 1967; Johnston 1967, 1968a, b, c, d; McIntosh and Kerbes 1969; Arola 1971).

This research has indicated that, in general, shear forces are less in warm than in frozen wood, less in clear than in knotty wood, less in heartwood than in sapwood, less in low-density wood than in dense wood, and less where the shearing direction is perpendicular to the annual rings than where the cut is parallel to the annual rings. Above the fiber saturation point, moisture content apparently makes little difference in the force required to shear.

Cutting velocity has little effect on shearing force. Shear force is least when the specimen is cut between opposing knives; if cut by a single knife against an anvil, a narrow anvil requires less force than a wide one.

The friction coefficient between a steel knife and green wood is approximately 0.2. Grease lubrication between knife and wood is not particularly effective in reducing shearing forces; Teflon surfaces on the cutter are more effective. Axial loads (simulating the weight of a standing tree) do not appreciably increase shearing forces. Lateral vibration of the cutter reduces shear forces required, as does tapering the cutter plate (fig. 19–21D) to give clearance between the plate and the wood. In a review of Russian

---

[2] In sec. 19–3, the text on shearing is condensed from Koch (1971), and that on cleaving from: Koch, P. Forces required to split green and dry southern pine bolts. USDA Forest Service, Southern Forest Experiment Station, Alexandria, La., Final Report FS-SO-3201-1.33 dated June 10, 1970.

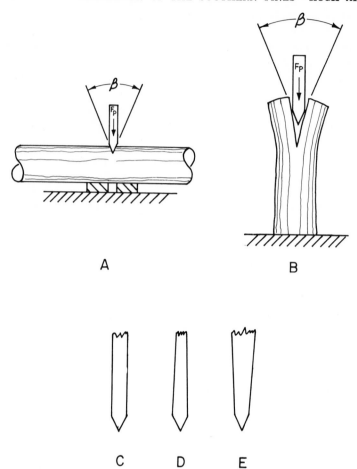

Figure 19–21.—(A) Shearing. (B) Cleaving. (C) Parallel-sided knife. (D) Tapered knife. (E) Knife with thick root.

work, Kubler (1960) reported that vibration in the feed direction also reduces shear forces required.

For parallel-sided cutters (fig. 19–21C), thin blades shear with less force than thick blades. Blades tapered so that the plate near the cutting edge is thin and the root thick (fig. 19–21E) require forces intermediate to thin and thick plates without taper. Sharp blades shear with less force than dull blades. Cutting edges in the shape of an open V do not appreciably lower forces required to shear logs.

The quality of sheared ends is impaired—i.e., knife-induced splits tend to be deep—if the wood is frozen, the knife dull, or the blade thick. An anvil that conforms to log curvature causes less crushing at the support point than a rigid straight anvil. McIntosh and Kerbes (1969) found that lumber losses from splitting were less than 1 percent when lodgepole pine (*Pinus contorta* Dougl.) and white spruce (*Picea glauca* var. *glauca*) trees less than 14 inches in diameter were sheared at 45° F. with a knife 1½ inches thick.

In trials (unpublished) of industrial shears with ½-inch-thick blades (45° sharpness angle) converging at the center of the tree, lumber loss from splitting in southern pine butt logs was more severe than indicated by McIntosh and Kerbes. In the test, 202 sheared butt logs scaling 7,280 board feet (Scribner standard rule) yielded 8,064 board feet of lumber when sawed. From production records, the mill estimated that, if the trees had been felled with a chainsaw, the butt logs would have yielded 8,820 board feet of lumber; i.e., the sheared logs produced 10.7 percent overrun as compared to the usual overrun of 20.1 percent.

The same mill (located in South Carolina) observed what appeared to be even more severe splitting when 30 longleaf pines were sheared with a single blade closing against a fixed anvil. The sheared butt logs were conventionally converted to lumber, dried, and planed—except that the butt ends of the boards were not trimmed. Length of shear-caused splits in the planed boards was positively correlated with stump diameter as follows:

Stump diameter	Split length		Logs cut	Boards measured
	Maximum	Average		
Inches	– – – – *Inches* – – – –		– – – *Number* – – –	
12	14	8.1	6	36
14	25	10.3	12	70
16	31	11.6	8	44
18	22	8.7	2	21
20	50	20.6	2	21

Mill management concluded that butt logs from sheared trees 16 inches and less in diameter would have to be cut back 24 inches before conversion to lumber; larger butt logs would require a 48-inch trim to eliminate most splits in the lumber. Such a trimming practice, although resulting in lumber loss, has some virtue; Hallock (1965) has reported that the portion of loblolly pine trees immediately adjacent to the ground yields lumber that frequently warps excessively when dried.

Koch (1971) has provided force data for slow-speed shearing of southern pine logs in diameter classes averaging 5.1, 9.7 and 13.6 inches; shearing was at 2 inches per minute with ⅜-inch-thick knives ground to 22½ and 45° sharpness angles. Thirty-six green logs, with bark in place, without regard to knots, and at a wood temperature of 60 to 80° F. were positioned horizontally and sheared against a flat anvil measuring 10¾ inches along the length of the log.

Data for logs of the three diameters and of two specific gravity classes are shown for each sharpness angle in table 19–19. Effects of primary variables are tabulated below; values significantly different (0.05 level) by analysis of variance appear below an asterisk:

Factor	Maximum force	Work to shear	Average check depth
	Pounds	Foot-pounds	Inches
Diameter of log	*	*	
5.1 inches_____	12,569	3,980	1.1
9.7 inches_____	33,121	18,594	1.2
13.6 inches_____	57,338	39,415	1.2
Specific gravity	*	*	
0.40-0.46_____	30,847	18,275	1.2
.47- .52_____	37,800	23,051	1.1
Sharpness angle	*	*	*
22-½°_____	30,935	19,409	.9
45°_____	37,750	21,918	1.3

Check depth was unaffected by bolt diameter; the significant interaction involving specific gravity and sharpness angle is shown in table 19–19. With the 22½° knife, specific gravity of the wood had little effect on check depth; with the 45° knife, however, check depth was greater (1.4 inch) in low-gravity wood than in high-gravity wood (1.2 inch).

Shearing force and work to shear were greatest for dense, 13.6-inch logs cut with a knife having a 45° sharpness angle (73,517 pounds, 49,838 foot-pounds); conversely, shear force and work were least for 5.1-inch bolts of low density when cut with a knife having 22½° sharpness angle (9,975

TABLE 19–19.—*Maximum shear force, work, and average check depth when bark-covered, round, green, southern pine logs were sheared with a ⅜-inch-thick knife closing against a flat anvil* (Koch 1971[1])

Average log diameter inside bark and specific gravity[2]	22½° sharpness angle			45° sharpness angle		
	Force	Work	Check depth	Force	Work	Check depth
	Pounds	Foot-pounds	Inch	Pounds	Foot-pounds	Inch
5.1 inches						
0.40-0.46____	9,975	2,885	0.8	12,466	4,191	1.4
.47- .52____	12,533	4,506	.8	15,300	4,339	1.1
9.7 inches						
0.40-0.46____	22,900	13,618	1.0	32,100	18,120	1.4
.47- .52____	36,300	20,637	1.0	41,183	22,001	1.3
13.6 inches						
0.40-0.46____	55,933[3]	37,822[3]	.9	51,933	33,016	1.4
.47- .52____	47,967	36,983	1.1	73,517	49,838	1.3

[1] Cutting velocity 2 inches per minute. Each value is an average of three replications.
[2] Based on green volume and ovendry weight.
[3] Values are high because these three low-gravity logs averaged 15.1 inches in diameter, whereas the three high-gravity logs cut with the 22½° knife averaged only 13.3 inches in diameter.

pounds, 2,885 foot-pounds). In shearing green southern pine, shear force builds to a maximum about three-fourths the way through the log; it then drops rapidly as the knife travels the remaining distance. Momentary peaks of force commonly occur near the three-quarter point (fig. 19–22).

At a cutting velocity of 2 inches per minute with cutter thickness constant at $\frac{3}{8}$-inch, shearing force (F_p, pounds) of green southern pine at 60 to 80° F. can be expressed in terms of bolt diameter inside bark (inches), sharpness angle (β, degrees), and wood specific gravity (ovendry weight and green volume).

For green southern pine logs sheared with bark in place:

$$
\begin{aligned}
F_p = &-76{,}268 \\
&+5{,}173 \text{ (diameter)} \\
&+104{,}485 \text{ (specific gravity)} \\
&+373 \text{ (sharpness angle)}
\end{aligned}
\tag{19-9}
$$

This equation is graphed in figure 19–22 (bottom). Within the range of the factors tested (sharpness angles $22\frac{1}{2}$ to 45°, bolt diameters 5 to 15 inches, and specific gravity on ovendry weight and green volume basis 0.40 to 0.52), equation 19–9 accounted for 81 percent of the variation with standard error of the estimate of 9,680 pounds (Koch 1971).

For green southern pine logs sheared with bark in place, work to shear (foot-pounds) is expressed:

$$
\begin{aligned}
\text{work} = &-71{,}538 \\
&+4{,}048 \text{ (diameter)} \\
&+102{,}589 \text{ (specific gravity)} \\
&+171 \text{ (sharpness angle)}
\end{aligned}
\tag{19-9a}
$$

Within the range of the study, equation 19–9a accounted for 93 percent of the variation with standard error of the estimate of 4,500 (Koch 1971).

Shears cause some checking in the severed ends (fig. 19–23). Koch (1971) found that sheared logs viewed in radial section showed a check at the earlywood-latewood boundary in each annual ring (fig. 19–23 Top right). Checks were least severe in the smallest logs sheared with the $22\frac{1}{2}°$ knife where they averaged 0.8 inch deep; they were most severe in the larger logs of low density sheared with the 45° knife where they averaged 1.4 inches deep.

In addition to the shallow checks shown in figure 19–23 (Top right), one rather lengthy check (fig. 12–23 Bottom) generally formed in each sheared log just prior to emergence of the knife.

Figure 19–24 (Top and center) illustrates a tree shear that cuts orthogonally; the anvil—hinged like tongs—closes around the back side of the tree before the $\frac{3}{4}$-inch-thick knife begins its shear stroke. As the tree falls away from the shear, the tonglike anvil is opened and—when the tree has fallen—is clamped to the butt; the tree, with branches in place, is then skidded by the shear-equipped tractor to a concentration point. A grapple skidder then forwards the bunched trees to a centralized limbing and loading area. It is reported that a skilled operator clear cutting on favorable terrain can shear 400 to 500 trees per 8-hour shift and bunch them for grapple skidding. Pines up to 22 inches in diameter at ground level can be cut with the shears illustrated. Other commercial models are available that cut in the manner of scissors or pruning shears; generally

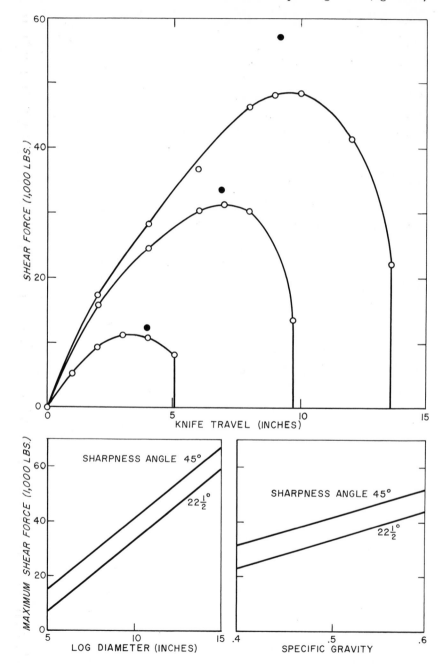

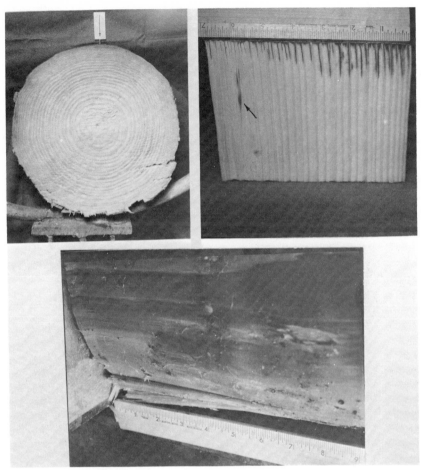

F–520985

Figure 19–23.—Checks in southern pine logs caused by shearing with a ⅜-inch-thick knife. (Top left) End-view of sheared surface. (Top right) Portion of radial section; arrow indicates pith. (Bottom) Typical longitudinal check near point of knife emergence (Photos from Koch 1971.)

in these designs, one hinged blade closes against a fixed anvil (fig. 19–24 Bottom).

◄
Figure 19–22.—Force to shear green southern pine logs. (Top) Force related to knife travel when shearing green southern pine logs in three diameter classes (5.1, 9.7, and 13.6 inches). Circles defining curves each represent information from 12 logs; i.e., data from both high- and low-gravity logs and from both 22½° and 45° knife angles were pooled. The solid point above each curve shows the average (and position of occurrence) of maximum peak forces that lasted only momentarily; they tended to occur when the knife was about three-quarters through each log. (Bottom) Relationships between maximum shearing force and factors of log diameter, specific gravity (basis of green volume and ovendry weight), and sharpness angle. Curves plotted from regression equation 19–9 by holding all factors but the one of interest at average value. Average log diameter was 9.51 inches; average specific gravity was 0.467. (Drawings after Koch 1971.)

Figure 19–24.—Tractor-mounted tree shears operating in southern pine. (Top and center) Orthogonal shear: felling, short-distance skidding, mechanism. (Bottom) Hinged shear: felling, mechanism. (Top and center photos from Rome Industries, Inc.; bottom photos from J. I. Case Company.)

CLEAVING

Longitudinal splitting of a short log in the 90–0 mode (as with a hatchet) is termed **cleaving** (fig. 19–21B). The parallel cutting force (F_p) is affected by numerous factors including width of cut, distance from cutting plane to periphery of the log, sharpness angle, straightness of grain, moisture content of the wood, and wood specific gravity. Length of log has only a minor effect on maximum force required.

Koch[2] has provided some data specific to southern pine. Saturated and dry (13-percent moisture content) southern pine bolts 14, 28, and 42 inches long and from 4.7 to 13.5 inches in diameter were split through their centers with a ⅜-inch-thick plate ground like a common screwdriver to sharpness angles of 22½ and 45°. Table 19-20 gives some typical values. The bolts were randomly selected without regard to knot structure or straightness of grain. Knife speed was 2 inches per minute.

In the following tabulation of effects of primary variables, those values found significantly different (0.01 level) by analysis of variance appear below double asterisks (Koch[2]).

Factor and level	Maximum force	Work to cleave
	Pounds	*Foot-pounds*
Moisture content	**	
Green	7,630	4,210
Kiln-dry (12.9 pct.)	12,140	4,190
Specific gravity		
0.44	9,440	3,970
0.49	10,330	4,440
Sharpness angle, degrees	**	**
22.5	8,120	3,230
45.0	11,650	5,180
Bolt length, inches		**
14	10,880	970
28	9,760	3,790
42	9,020	7,850
Diameter of bolt, inches	**	**
4.7	4,260	1,320
9.4	9,830	3,430
13.5	15,560	7,870

Each value in the foregoing tabulation is an average with all data pooled except for stratification by the indicated primary variable. The specific gravities given are based on green volume and ovendry weight.

Koch[2] found that splitting force (F_p) generally reached a maximum within the first inch of knife travel and diminished thereafter (fig. 19–25).

The 4.7-inch-diameter bolts required significantly less force and work to cleave than the 9.4- and 13.5-inch bolts (4,260 vs. 9,830 vs. 15,560 pounds, and 1,320 vs. 3,430 vs. 7,870 foot-pounds).

At a cutting velocity of 2 inches per minute with cutter thickness constant at ⅜-inch, peak cleaving force (F_p, pounds) of green southern pine at 60 to 80° F. can be expressed in terms of bolt diameter inside bark (inches), bolt length (inches), sharpness angle (β, degrees), and wood specific gravity (ovendry weight and green volume):

$$F_p = -13,317$$
$$+1,154.5 \text{ (diameter)}$$
$$+1.9156 \text{ (length)} \quad\quad (19\text{--}10)$$
$$+29.283 \text{ (sharpness angle)}$$
$$+19,545 \text{ (specific gravity)}$$

TABLE 19–20.—*Parallel tool force and work to longitudinally split green and dry southern pine bolts of low and high density with a ⅜-inch-thick knife*[1] [2] [3] [4] (Data from Koch; see text footnote[2])

Bolt diameter and length (inches)	22½° sharpness angle		45° sharpness angle	
	Force	Work	Force	Work
	Pounds	*Foot-pounds*	*Pounds*	*Foot-pounds*
GREEN				
4.7-inch diameter class				
14_____	2,020(2,930)	210(410)	2,830(2,540)	240(240)
28_____	2,160(3,090)	980(2,030)	2,410(2,710)	1,250(1,270)
42_____	1,830(2,960)	1,650(3,520)	3,900(2,680)	3,160(5,150)
9.4-inch diameter class				
14_____	6,550(9,280)	790(820)	7,790(6,120)	470(610)
28_____	7,010(8,480)	2,350(2,160)	7,030(7,030)	3,140(2,060)
42_____	6,200(6,610)	3,770(6,290)	7,810(6,240)	7,550(7,140)
13.5-inch diameter class				
14_____	12,580(13,880)	1,780(1,470)	11,120(13,510)	1,120(2,620)
28_____	13,890(14,050)	7,320(5,520)	12,530(13,090)	4,430(7,820)
42_____	13,470(11,110)	14,560(7,890)	10,950(16,230)	11,530(28,400)
DRY				
4.7-inch diameter class				
14_____	3,180(3,430)	130(190)	9,070(10,970)	240(610)
28_____	3,220(3,020)	700(670)	7,820(9,420)	860(1,040)
42_____	2,170(2,980)	1,210(1,750)	7,610(7,270)	2,220(1,880)
9.4-inch diameter class				
14_____	9,230(12,930)	585(1,080)	17,920(18,180)	830(1,790)
28_____	6,060(8,630)	1,190(3,770)	13,870(19,850)	3,180(6,620)
42_____	6,180(6,610)	3,430(4,910)	13,490(16,560)	5,870(11,810)
13.5-inch diameter class				
14_____	15,880(23,120)	1,600(1,950)	25,960(20,070)	2,690(880)
28_____	12,530(9,580)	4,990(2,460)	21,520(25,220)	15,680(9,450)
42_____	13,030(12,120)	11,730(10,260)	18,580(19,510)	19,320(13,350)

[1] Cutting velocity 2 inches per minute.

[2] The first number gives the force (or work) to split low-density bolts; the second number, in parentheses, gives the force (or work) required to split high-density bolts. Each number is an average of three replications.

[3] Average moisture content of the dry bolts was 12.9 percent.

[4] Average specific gravity of low-density bolts (basis of green volume and ovendry weight) was 0.44; that of high-density bolts was 0.49.

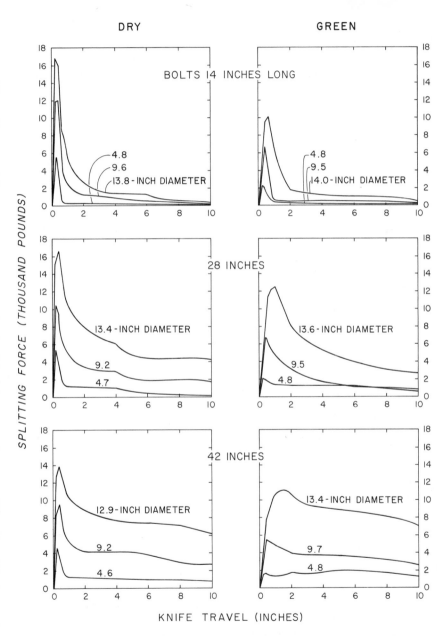

Figure 19–25.—Force to split (cleave) dry and green southern pine bolts of three diameters and three lengths as related to distance penetrated (to 10 inches) by the knife. Except at knot clusters, the force was more or less linear from the value shown at 10-inch penetration to 0 at emergence of the knife at the end of the bolt. Each curve is based on data from 12 bolts with data for both specific gravity classes and both sharpness angles pooled. (Drawing after Koch[2].)

Within the range of the factors tested (sharpness angles 22½ to 45°, bolt diameters 3.3 to 17.8 inches, bolt length 14 to 42 inches, and specific gravity on ovendry weight and green volume basis (0.40 to 0.53), equation 19–10 accounted for 89 percent of the variation with standard error of the estimate of 1,584 pounds. (See fig. 19–26.) Peak force to cleave average 7,627 pounds.

Force to cleave green was minimum if a 22½° knife was used on bolts that were short, of low gravity, and of small diameter.

For dry southern pine, moisture content (percent) was also a factor in determining peak cleaving force (F_p, pounds):

$$F_p = -23,230$$
$$+1,429.4 \text{ (diameter)}$$
$$-108.23 \text{ (length)} \tag{19–11}$$
$$+309.12 \text{ (sharpness angle)}$$
$$+30,850 \text{ (specific gravity)}$$
$$+35.943 \text{ (moisture content)}$$

Within the range of factors tested, equation 19–11 accounted for 85 percent of the variation with stadard error of the estimate of 2,854 pounds. (See fig. 19–26.) Peak force to cleave averaged 12,140 pounds; it was minimum for dry wood if a 22½° knife was used to cut bolts of low specific gravity and of small diameter.

When simple expressions with the form and factors of equations 19–10 and 19–11 were used to predict work to cleave green and dry bolts, percent of variation accounted for was low (53 and 72 percent). More complex models (see Koch[2]), however, provided equations that accounted for 73 percent of the observed variation in green bolts and 86 percent of the variation in dry bolts. The various interactions are illustrated in figure 19–27. Work to cleave green bolts averaged 4,215 foot-pounds, that for dry bolts averaged 2,069 foot-pounds.

For both green and dry bolts, regression analysis showed that work to cleave was lowest for short specimens of small diameter and low specific gravity cut with the 22½° knife. By regression analysis, work to cleave kiln-dried bolts proved positively correlated with moisture content in the range from 9 to 20 percent; analysis of variance, however, did not indicate that green bolts required more work to split than dry bolts.

Of the 216 bolts split by Koch[2], only a few were knot free. Only rarely, however, did split surfaces expose knots; typically they followed the pith closely, were irregular, and revealed some spiral grain close to the pith.

19–4 PERIPHERAL MILLING PARALLEL TO GRAIN [3]

Peripheral milling, or planing, may be defined as the removal of excess wood in the form of single chips formed by intermittent engagement with the workpiece of knives carried on the periphery of a rotating cutter-

---

[3] Sec. 19–4 is condensed from Koch (1954, 1955, 1956, 1964b).

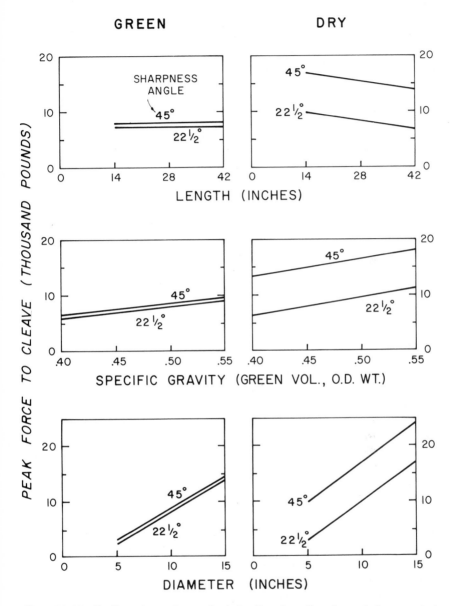

Figure 19–26.—Significant interactions and relationships that affect the peak force required to cleave green (left) and dry (right) southern pine logs or bolts with a ⅜-inch-thick knife travelling at 2 inches per minute. The curves were plotted from equations 19–10 and 10–11 by holding all values but one at their mean (or stated) values and allowing the factor named on the abscissa to vary throughout the range tested. (Drawing after Koch[2].)

head. The cutterhead usually carries several knives, removable for sharpening, which are precisely adjusted to cut in a common cutting circle. Final adjustment involves **jointing** the knives with an abrasive hone while the cutterhead revolves at operating speed. The finished surface therefore con-

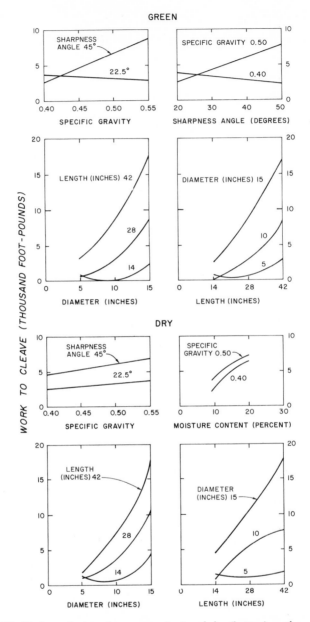

Figure 19–27.—Work required to cleave green (top) and dry (bottom) southern pine logs or bolts with a ⅜-inch-thick knife travelling at 2 inches per minute. The curves were plotted from regression equations by holding all values but one at their mean (or stated) values and allowing the factor named on the abscissa to vary throughout the range tested. (Drawings after Koch[2].)

sists of a series of individual knife traces generated by the successive engagement of each knife.

A detailed treatment of the kinematics, force systems, and chip severance phnomenon is available (Koch 1964b).

NOMENCLATURE

Figures 19–28 and 19–29 ilustrate nomenclature in peripheral milling.

KINEMATICS

In conventional planers, the engaged knives move counter to the movement of the workpiece—an action termed **up-milling** (fig. 19–30A); if the engaged knives move in the same direction as the workpiece, the process is called **down-milling** (fig. 19–30B).

The trochoidal path taken by each knife tip can be represented (fig. 19–30C) by considering the workpiece fixed in space and allowing the cutterhead to rotate about a roll circle of a diameter that gives a relative translatory velocity equal to the desired feed speed.

Feed per jointed knife (F_t) can be stated:

$$F_t = \frac{12F}{Tn} \tag{19–12}$$

The distance between knife marks can be reduced by decreasing the feed speed, increasing the number of jointed knives in the cutterhead, or by increasing the cutterhead speed.

If the knives are accurately jointed, for up-milling the wave height can be expressed:

$$h = \frac{F_t^2}{8\left(R + \dfrac{F_t T}{\pi}\right)} \tag{19–13}$$

Wave height can be reduced by increasing the radius of the cutterhead or by decreasing the feed per knife.

For up-milling the length of knife path engagement is as follows:

$$L = R \text{ arc cos} \left(1 - \frac{d}{R}\right) + \frac{F_t T}{\pi D} (Dd - d^2)^{1/2} \tag{19–14}$$

When up-milling, the average thickness of the undeformed chip can be stated:

$$t_{\text{avg}} = \frac{F_t d}{L} \tag{19–15}$$

The significance of these formulae can be visualized from a tabulation of the dimensions of chips and surfaces produced by two commonly used up-milling cutterheads. For purposes of comparison, it is assumed that both heads rotate at 3,450 revolutions per minute (r.p.m.) and take a ⅛-inch-deep cut.

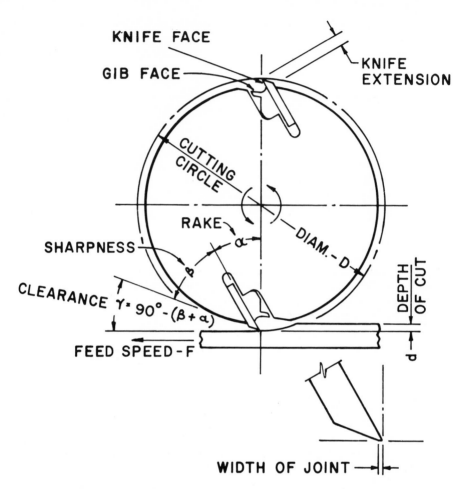

Figure 19–28.—Terminology for peripheral-milling cutterhead. Up-milling illustrated.

α   Rake angle, degrees
β   Sharpness angle, degrees
γ   Clearance angle, degrees
d   Depth of cut, inches
D   Cutting-circle diameter, inches
F   Feed speed of workpiece, feet per minute
(Drawing after Koch 1955.)

Dimension	T = eight knives D = nine inches F = 300 f.p.m.	T = 16 knives D = 11 inches F = 1,000 f.p.m.
	Inch	*Inch*
F_t	0.130	0.217
h	0.441×10^{-3}	0.891×10^{-3}
L	1.100	1.289
t_{avg}	0.015	0.021

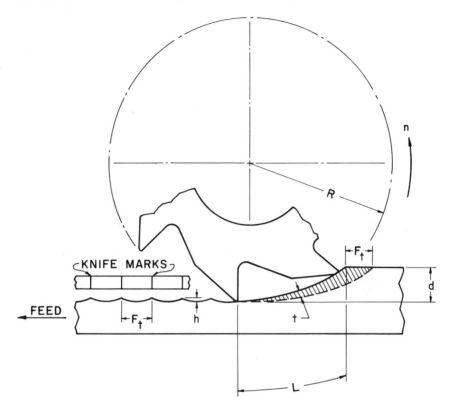

Figure 19–29.—Path generated by up-milling knife.

F_t Feed per knife; translation of the workpiece between engagement of successive knives, inch

h   Height of knife marks above point of lowest level, inch

L   Length of knife path during each engagement with the workpiece, inches

n   Revolutions per minute of cutterhead, r.p.m.

R   Cutting-circle radius, inches

$t_{avg.}$ Average thickness of undeformed chip, inch

T   Number of jointed knives in the cutterhead

d   Depth of cut, inch

(Drawing after Peter Koch 1964b, p. 113, WOOD MACHING PROCESSES Copyright © 1964 The Ronald Press Company, New York.)

CHIP FORMATION

Koch's (1954, 1955, 1956) high-speed photographs of up-milling knives cutting Douglas-fir, *Pseudotsuga Menziesii* (Mirb.) Franco (none for southern pine have been published) show the same chip formations observed in orthogonal cutting of southern pine in the 90-0 or planing direction (e.g., figs. 19–3, 19–5, 19–6). Peripheral up-milling differs in one important respect from 90-0 orthogonal cutting; while the initial up-milling cut is essentially parallel to the grain, the emerging cut may be at a considerable angle to the grain (fig. 19–31). Furthermore, in peripheral up-milling the undeformed chip thickness constantly changes from a

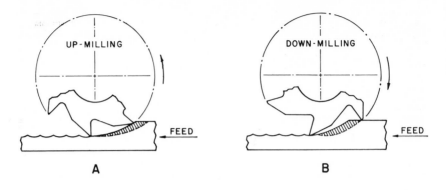

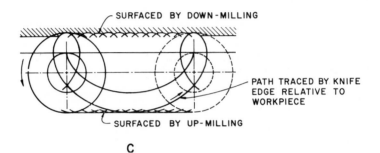

Figure 19–30.—(A) Up-milling. (B) Down-milling. (C) Knife path, relative to workpiece, is a curtate trochoid. (Drawings after Peter Koch, 1964b, WOOD MACHINING PROCESSES, Copyright © 1964, The Ronald Press Company, New York.)

minute value at contact to a maximum just prior to emergence; chips cut at emergence are frequently Franz Type I (fig. 19–31).

Fortunately, the part of the knife path that remains visible on the machined surface is the initial portion where chip thickness is minute; a Franz Type II failure can therefore be induced (figs. 19–32 and 19–44). With very low rake angles, Type III chips are common (fig. 19–33).

SURFACE QUALITY

Quality of the machined surface is primarily determined by the cutting geometry and the type of chip formed. In general, machined surfaces are improved by maintaining low values for F_t (feed per knife) and h (height of knife marks); this is accomplished by increasing the cutting-circle diameter and the number of jointed knives in the cutterhead and by reducing the feed speed. A good surface on dry southern pine requires an F_t of less than $\frac{1}{8}$-inch, and an h of less than 0.00044 inch. Cutterhead speed is commonly fixed at a nominal 3,600 r.p.m. because this is the synchronous speed of the usual motor mounted direct on the spindle; further, 3,600 r.p.m. is the highest speed at which knives can be consistently jointed so that they all track in the same path and share equally in the cut.

Figure 19–31.—An eight-knife, 9-inch cutterhead rotating at 3,450 r.p.m. taking ¼-inch depth of cut at 300 f.p.m. from flat-grain Douglas-fir. Moisture content, 10 percent; rake angle, 17°10′; clearance, 32°50′; surface quality, unsatisfactory. Net cutterhead horsepower required per inch of workpiece width, 3.70. (Data and photo from Koch 1954, p. 123.)

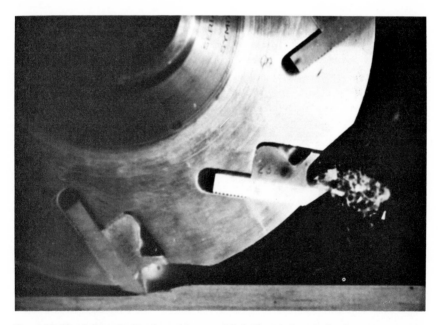

Figure 19–32.—A Type II chip formed by an eight-knife, 9-inch cutterhead turning at 3,450 r.p.m. taking a 3/16-inch depth cut at 307 f.p.m. on dry (9 percent) Douglas-fir of low specific gravity. Rake angle, 30°; clearance angle, 20°; net cutterhead power required per inch of workpiece width, 0.93 hp. (Data and photo from Koch 1954, p. 275.)

Figure 19–33.—Type III chip formed by up-milling dry Douglas-fir 3/32-inch deep with knife having a rake angle of —5°. Cutterhead speed, 3,500 r.p.m. (Photo from Koch 1954, p. 173.)

The best surfaces result when Type II chips are formed during the early part of knife engagement (fig. 19–32). For southern pine of varying moisture content, rake angles from 20 to 30° in combination with a clearance angle of about 20° (not less than 15°) are appropriate. Type II chips are more likely to occur with shallow cuts (less than ⅛-inch) than with deep cuts, but are difficult to form if wood is planed against a sloping grain.

Type III chips (fig. 19–33) tend to cause incomplete fiber severance and **fuzzy grain** (fig. 19–34); the defect is a particular problem when cutting wet wood with knives of low rake angle. Type I chips—if the splits run below the cutting plane—cause **chipped grain** (fig. 19–34).

Dull knives, knives that have been jointed too many times between sharpenings, and knives with insufficient clearance angle cause **raised grain** —a roughened condition in which hard latewood is raised above the softer springwood but not torn loose from it (fig. 19–34). The defect may show up subsequent to machining, as the wood swells when exposed to high humidity.

When a dry flat-grain southern pine board is planed with dull knives, impact of the knives may cause the latewood bands to separate from earlywood; this defect is called **loosened grain** (fig. 19–34 Top).

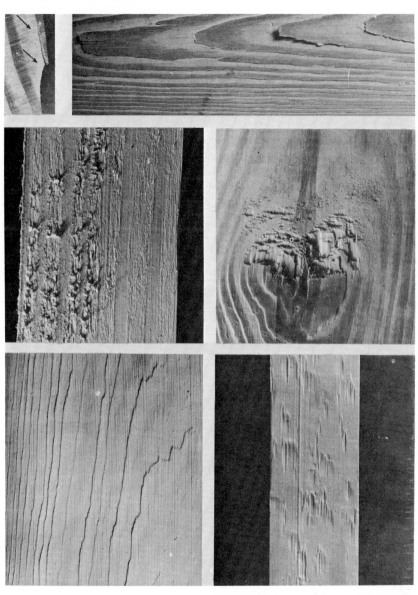

F–520986

Figure 19–34.—Typical machining defects in southern pine. (Top) Loosened grain; arrows at left indicate location of partially crushed wood and separation at earlywood-latewood border. (Middle left) Fuzzy grain. (Middle right) Chipped grain. (Lower left) Raised grain. (Lower right) Chipmarks.

The defect of **chip marks** is caused by shavings or fiber bundles that fold over and adhere to the cutting edge so that they are carried around and indented into the surface of the wood (fig. 19–34). Most pine is not particularly subject to this defect, but some pieces characteristically show

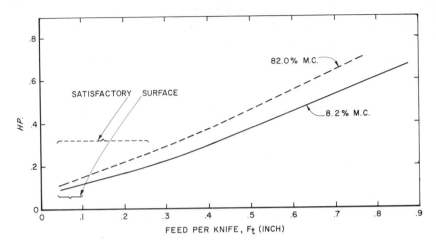

Figure 19–35.—Effect of moisture content on the net cutterhead power required per inch of workpiece width by a single knife cutting Douglas-fir at various feeds per knife. Rake angle, 30°; depth of cut, 1/16-inch; cutting-circle diameter 9.02 inches; nominal speed, 3,600 r.p.m. (Drawing after Peter Koch 1964b, p. 122, WOOD MACHINING PROCESSES, Copyright © 1964, The Ronald Press Company, New York.)

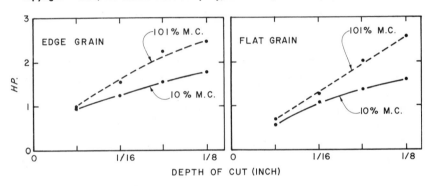

Figure 19–36.—Shallow cuts in flat-grain Douglas-fir require less net cutterhead horsepower per inch of workpiece width than in edge grain wood when cut with an eight-knife, 9-inch-diameter cutterhead rotating at 3,600 r.p.m.; rake angle, 30°; feed speed, 298 f.p.m. (Drawing after Peter Koch 1964b, p. 124, WOOD MACHINING PROCESSES, Copyright © 1964, The Ronald Press Company, New York.)

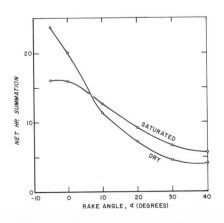

Figure 19–37.—In milling Douglas-fir, more power is required for saturated than for dry wood, except at very low or negative rake angles (data pooled for all depths of cut and all clearance angles). $F_t = 0.127$ inch with 9-inch-diameter cutterhead turning at 3,600 r.p.m. (Drawing after Koch 1955.)

chip marks. While a remedy is difficult to find, wiping each knife edge with a solvent-soaked rag sometimes helps. Inadequate suction in the blowpipe system aggravates the problem.

A well-illustrated and more detailed discussion of the causes and remedies for raised, loosened, torn, chipped, and fuzzy grain is available (USDA Forest Products Laboratory 1955).

For a greatly magnified view of a surface cut by a peripheral-milling cutterhead see figure 25–8.

FACTORS AFFECTING POWER

No information specific to southern pine has been published; trends apparent in Koch's (1954, 1955, 1956, 1964b) data on Douglas-fir, however, should be generally applicable to southern pine. Detailed discussion of the causes behind the effect of each factor are available (Koch 1964b, p. 121).

Workpiece factors.—With commonly used rake angles, more cutterhead power is required to plane wet wood than dry because of the power consumed accelerating heavy wet chips (figs. 19–35, 19–36). With very low or negative rake angles, however, dry wood takes more power than wet (fig. 19–37); this is reasonable inasmuch as knives with low rake angles form Type III chips by compressing the wood parallel to the grain, and dry wood is much stronger than wet when so loaded.

Flat-grain wood has more of a tendency to split ahead of the knife than does edge-grain wood; therefore, flat-grain wood may require less power to mill (fig. 19–36).

Because wood of high density is strong and the heavy chips require substantial energy for acceleration to cutting velocity, high-density wood requires more power to plane than that of low density (fig. 19–38).

Cutterhead factors.—Net power required for a cutterhead is affected by:

Cutting velocity
Cutting-circle diameter
Number of jointed knives cutting
Rake angle
Clearance angle
Sharpness of cutting edge

Width of joint
Knife extension beyond face of gib
Shape of gib face
Angle between rotational axis of
    cutterhead and direction of feed

Koch (1964b, p. 142) has calculated the power required to accelerate chips to commonly used cutting velocities. For example, if $\frac{1}{8}$-inch is planed from one face of saturated 2- by 12-inch planks at 1,000 f.p.m., with an 11-inch diameter cutterhead turning at 3,450 r.p.m., 10.1 hp. are required just to accelerate the chips to the cutting velocity of 182 feet per second.

A cutterhead of 11-inch-diameter cuts a better surface than a comparable one 9 inches in diameter because the wave height (h) is less. At the same speed of rotation, the larger head requires more power because of its greater cutting velocity; e.g., 3.4 percent more with dry Douglas-fir

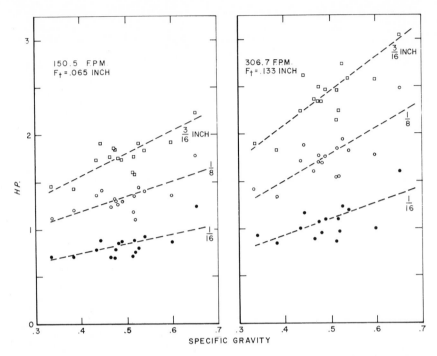

Figure 19–38.—Effect of specific gravity (basis of ovendry weight and volume) of Douglas-fir on net cutterhead horsepower per inch of workpiece width. Data are for two feed speeds (150.5 and 306.7 feet per minute) and three depths of cut with an eight-knife, 9-inch cutterhead turning at 3,600 r.p.m. Rake angle, 30°. Moisture content, 8.5 percent. (Drawing after Koch 1956.)

and 10.8 percent more with saturated fir (Koch 1956). Figure 19–39 illustrates the difference if data for green and dry wood are pooled.

At feed speeds below $F_t = 0.3$ inch and cuts less than ⅛-inch deep, horsepower demand increases with number of jointed knives cutting, although in no case does a doubling of the number of knives cause a doubling of power demand (see fig. 19–40 in the range from six to 12 knives). With deep cuts and values of F_t over 0.3, power demand may be negatively correlated with number of knives cutting because the large chips formed cannot readily escape from the knife; such clogging (fig. 19–41A) explains the high power demand for the two-knife, ⅛-inch cut in figure 19–40.

Net cutterhead power is inversely correlated with rake angle; figure 19–37 shows the interaction of rake angle with moisture content. Power required rises sharply with decreased rake angle, reaching a point of inflection between plus 15 and minus 5° (fig. 19–42); with dry wood a rake angle of 15° requires about half as much power as a 0° angle, and about twice as much as a 30° angle. With saturated wood, a rake angle of 25 to 30° requires about half the power required by a 0° angle. Application of this knowledge must be tempered by the fact that a 40° rake

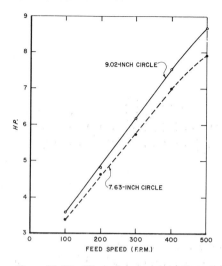

Figure 19–39.—Effect of cutting circle diameter and feed speed on net cutterhead horsepower (summed data for green and dry Douglas-fir and two-, four-, and eight-knife heads). For both diameters, rake angle was 30°, depth of cut 1/16-inch, and cutterhead speed 3,600 r.p.m. (Drawing after Koch 1956.)

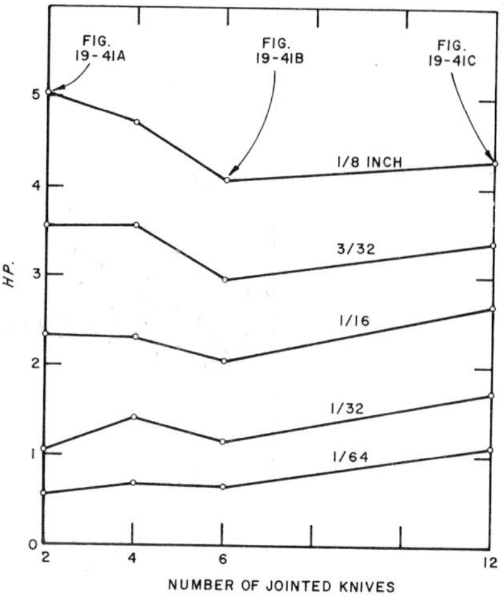

Figure 19–40.—Effect of number of knives and depths of cut on net cutterhead horsepower per inch of workpiece width. Feed speed, 500 f.p.m.; rake angle, 27½°; moisture content, 7.33 percent; cutting-circle diameter, 9.44 inches; nominal speed of cutterhead, 3,600 r.p.m.; species, Douglas-fir. (Drawing after Koch 1955.)

angle will probably cause chipped grain, and a zero or negative rake angle will cause fuzzy grain on saturated wood and raised grain on dry wood (fig. 19–34).

Clearance angle is negatively correlated with net cutterhead power required. The trend is not pronounced; tests have shown that a 5° clearance angle causes about 9 percent more power consumption than a 30° angle (Koch 1955). Practical limitations usually govern selection of clearance angle. For example, a clearance angle of 30° in combination with a rake angle of 40° results in a cutting edge too fragile for most applications. On the other hand, a 5° clearance angle causes an undesirable width of joint (fig. 19–28) after even the lightest of jointing operations. A small clearance angle in combination with a heavy joint causes raised grain (fig. 19–34).

Dull knives (fig. 19–8) increase power consumption in addition to causing fuzzy and raised grain as wear reduces effective rake angle. Knives that have been heavily jointed require extra power for the same reason as knives having small clearance angle, i.e., the feed of the workpiece pushes the cut surface against the back of the knife as it nears the end of its cutting path (fig 19–43).

Up to a certain critical value, the knife extension beyond the face of the gib (fig. 19–28) is negatively correlated with horsepower requirement of the cutterhead. For example, Koch (1956) has shown that with flat-face gibs (fig. 19–44), the knife edge should be extended at least 0.3 inch

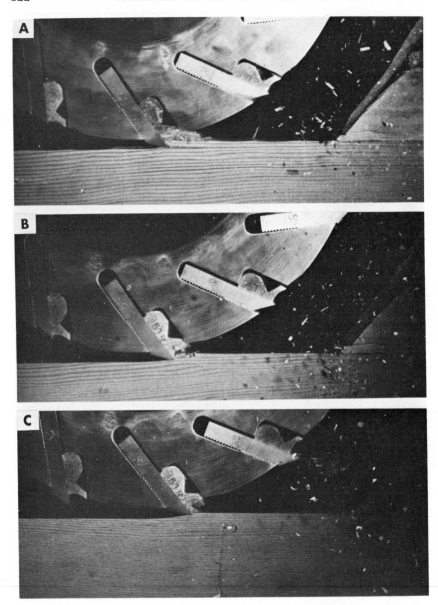

Figure 19–41.—Chips formed by ⅛-inch depth cut at 500 f.p.m. under conditions outlined in figure 19–40. (A) Two knives (every sixth knife cutting). (B) Six knives. (C) All 12 knives cutting. (Photos from Koch 1955.)

beyond the gib if power is to be minimized when making a ³⁄₃₂-inch cut at an F_t of 0.13 inch; under these conditions required power increases about 40 percent if the extension is reduced to 0.15 inch.

The flat-face gibs of figure 19–44 require 25 percent more cutterhead power than do concave gibs when making identical ⅛-inch cuts with

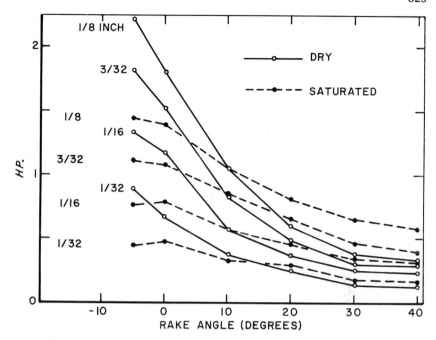

Figure 19–42.—Effect of rake angle and depth of cut on net cutterhead power requirement (per inch of workpiece width) for planing dry and saturated Douglas-fir. F_t, 0.127 inch; clearance angle, 20°; cutting circle diameter, 9.05 inches; nominal speed, 3,600 r.p.m. (Drawing after Peter Koch 1964b, p. 149, WOOD MACHINING PROCESSES, Copyright © 1964, The Ronald Press Company, New York.)

eight knives at 300 f.p.m. (Koch 1955). It is evident from figure 19–44 that very abrupt chip deformation is caused by the flat-faced gib. Figure 19–32 illustrates how the cutterhead body should be relieved to conform to gib shape.

If the cutterhead is slewed so that its rotational axis makes an angle other than 90° with the direction of feed, each element of each cutting edge cuts at an angle to the grain direction. The effective knife extension and rake angle are increased by an amount dependent on the angle through which slewed, the feed speed, and the cutterhead peripheral velocity; therefore cutterhead power is slightly reduced (fig. 19–45).

Feed factors.—In the special case where F_t is held constant while feed speed is increased (i.e., the number of knives in the cutterhead is doubled each time the feed speed is doubled), the horsepower requirement *per knife* is approximately constant within the feed speed range from 100 to 1,000 f.p.m.

In the more general case in which all other factors remain constant, an increase in feed speed increases the height of the individual knife marks and increases the distance between them, lowering surface quality and raising cutterhead power demand (fig. 19–46). With cuts less than ⅛-inch deep, the horsepower requirement does not double when F_t is doubled;

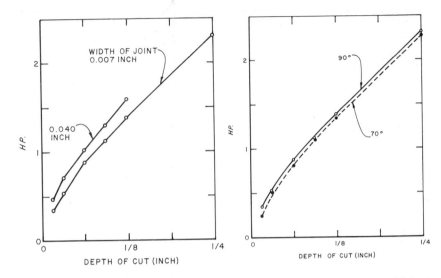

Figure 19–43.—Effect of width of joint on net horsepower requirement per inch of workpiece width. F_t, 0.0895 inch; rake angle, 30°; moisture content, 8.9 percent; cutting-circle diameter, 9.08 inches; nominal speed, 3,600 r.p.m.; species, Douglas-fir. (Drawing after Koch 1956.)

Figure 19–45.—Effect on net cutterhead horsepower (per inch of workpiece width) of changing angle between cutterhead axis and feed direction from 90 to 70°. Douglas-fir; 8.9-percent moisture content; eight-knife, 206-f.p.m., 3,600-r.p.m. cutterhead. (Drawing after Koch 1956.)

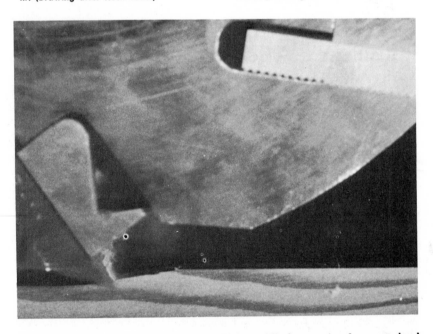

Figure 19–44.—Chips are severely deformed and have difficulty escaping from cutterheads equipped with flat-faced gibs. Curved gibs shown in figures 19–32 and 19–33, although not ideally contoured, permit chip to escape with less breakage. (Photo from Koch 1955.)

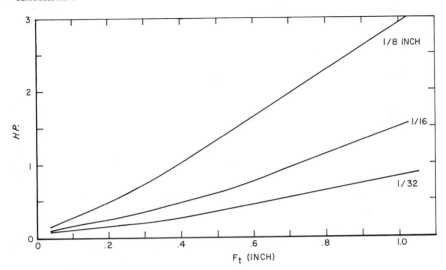

Figure 19–46.—Effect of feed per knife (F$_t$) on net cutterhead power (per knife per inch of workpiece width). Data for three depths of cut in Douglas-fir at 7.3-percent moisture content. Rake angle, 27½°; cutting-circle diameter, 9.44 inches; nominal speed, 3,600 r.p.m. (Drawing after Peter Koch 1964b, p. 157, WOOD MACHINING PROCESSES, Copyright © 1964, The Ronald Press Company, New York.)

in other words, it takes less energy to cut a given volume of wood into long chips than into short.

Depth of cut is positively correlated with cutterhead power demand. With conventional feeds per knife (F$_t$ of less than 0.2 inch) and relatively shallow cuts, cutterhead power demand falls short of doubling when depth of cut is doubled; under these conditions it generally requires less energy to remove a given volume of wood in a single cut than in two shallow cuts (fig. 19–40). Where F$_t$ exceeds 0.5 inch, however, some tests have shown that horsepower requirement per knife is approximately proportional to depth of cut, i.e., a ⅛-inch cut takes nearly twice as much power as a ¹⁄₁₆-inch cut and nearly four times as much as a ¹⁄₃₂-inch cut (fig. 19–46).

DOWN MILLING

Most conventional planing is accomplished by the up-milling process as described in the previous portion of this section. Some machining, however is performed in the down-milling mode (fig. 19–47). In addition, the development of the **chipping headrig,** which reduces logs to square or rectangular timbers plus pulp chips (no sawdust), has stimulated interest in down-milling (Koch 1964a).

As with up-milling, the feed per jointed knife is given by the equation:

$$F_t = \frac{12F}{Tn} \qquad (19\text{–}12)$$

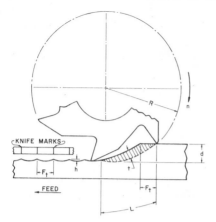

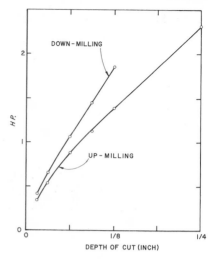

Figure 19–47.—Path generated by down-milling knife. The path of knife engagement is shorter than in up-milling because feed of workpiece shortens time knife is cutting.

d   Depth of cut, inch

F_t Feed per knife; translation of the workpiece between engagement of successive knives, inch

h   Height of knife marks above point of lowest level, inch

L   Length of knife path during each engagement with the workpiece, inches

n   Revolutions per minute of cutterhead, r.p.m.

R   Cutting-circle radius, inches

$t_{avg.}$ Average thickness of undeformed chip, inch

T   Number of jointed knives in the cutterhead

(Drawing after Peter Koch 1964b, WOOD MACHINING PROCESSES Copyright © 1964 The Ronald Press Company, New York.)

Figure 19–48.—Net cutterhead power per inch of workpiece width in up-milling, as compared to down-milling. F_t, 0.0895 inch; rake angle, 30°; feed speed, 206 f.p.m.; cutting-circle diameter, 9.08 inches; cutterhead speed, 3,600 r.p.m.; number of knives, eight; species, Douglas-fir at 8.9-percent moisture content. (Drawing after Koch 1956.)

The distance between knife marks is reduced by decreasing the feed speed, increasing the cutterhead speed, or by increasing the number of jointed knives carried in the cutterhead.

If the knives have been jointed to a common cutting circle, the wave height can be expressed:

$$h = \frac{R}{8}\left[\frac{F_t}{R - \dfrac{F_t T}{2\pi}}\right]^2 \qquad (19\text{–}16)$$

As in up-milling, wave height can be reduced by increasing the radius of the cutterhead and by decreasing the feed per knife.

For down-milling, the length of knife path engagement is as follows:

$$L = R \text{ arc cos } \frac{R-d}{R} - \frac{F_t T}{2\pi R}(2Rd - d^2)^{1/2} \qquad (19\text{--}17)$$

As with up-milling, the average thickness of the undeformed chip can be stated:

$$t_{avg} = \frac{F_t d}{L} \qquad (19\text{--}15)$$

Down-milling at 300 f.p.m. (⅛-inch-deep cut) with an eight-knife, 9-inch-diameter cutterhead turning at 3,600 r.p.m. can be compared with up-milling in similar circumstances:

Dimension	Down-milling	Up-milling
	— — — — — Inch — — — — —	
F_t	0.130	0.130
h	$.551 \times 10^{-3}$	$.441 \times 10^{-3}$
L	1.022	1.100
t_{avg}	.016	.015

In down-milling, wave height, average chip thickness, and maximum chip thickness are greater than in up-milling; however, length of tool path is shorter for down-milling.

Because down-milling cuts thicker chips than up-milling, it requires substantially more cutterhead power (fig. 19–48). The attitude of the knife at engagement in down-milling is less conducive to advance splitting (Type I chip formation).

With sharp knives and in the conventional range of rake angles, the up-milling knife exerts very little pressure on the workpiece or tends to lift it away from the bed plate. Down-milling, however, holds the workpiece strongly against the bed plate due to the manner of knife engagement (fig. 19–49A). While this force may be of some advantage, the accompanying horizontal force vector, tending to uncontrollably accelerate the rate of feed, is usually a disadvantage. Since less feed power is required, however, the down-milling process frequently requires less total power than up-milling.

Down-milling differs from up-milling in two additional respects. In down-milling the knife enters at the rough surface, thus wiping adhering bundles of fibers from the cutting edge before chip marks can be indented into the finished surface. Also, as figure 19–49 shows, down-milling chips are discharged horizontally along the workpiece.

19–5 BARKING

Bark removal is the first step in most conversion processes for southern pine. Pulpmills require bark-free wood because paper of good quality can contain neither dirt specks nor bark. The wood-treating industry removes

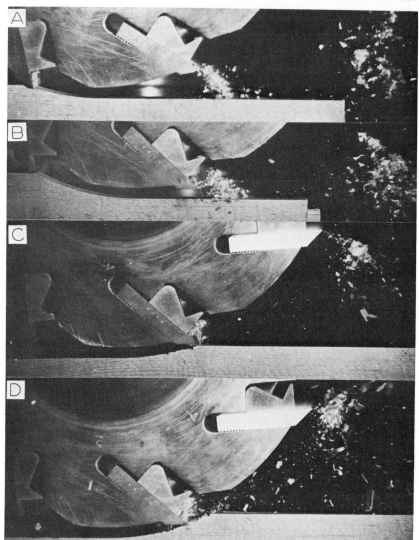

Figure 19–49.—Comparison of up-milling and down-milling at 175 f.p.m. with eight-knife cutterhead rotating at 3,600 r.p.m. and carrying knives with 30° rake. (A) Down-milling, ¼-inch cut. (B) Down-milling, ½-inch cut. (C) Up-milling, ¼-inch cut. (D) Up-milling, ½-inch cut. (Photos from Koch 1956.)

bark from posts, piles, and poles to accelerate drying and to facilitate treatment with chemicals. Sawmills and veneer plants remove the bark from logs so that their wood residues will be bark free and suitable for reduction into pulp chips; cutting bark-free logs extends service life of saws and veneer knives; also, bark-free logs are advantageously sawn because defects are visible. Finally, pine bark—some 10 percent of the volume of each tree—is beginning to have economic value for conversion into various agricultural, fiber, and chemical products.

The many and varied designs of barkers have been reviewed extensively (e.g., Koch 1964b, pp. 169–178; Holzhey 1969). Because southern pine bark is removed relatively easily by mechanical means—particularly if trees have been cut in the spring or if logs or bolts have been stored in ponds or under water sprays—there are only a few major types of barkers in common use. Mechanical removal of bark is commonly accomplished by one of three methods: rubbing or abrasion in a drum barker, shear at the cambium layer with tools cutting approximately in the 0–90 mode, and cutting in the 0–90 mode with sharp knives to remove all the bark plus a thin layer of wood.

DRUM BARKERS

Rotating-drum barkers are used to remove bark from pulpwood. The bolts tumble together forcibly and repeatedly in their passage through the drum, rubbing off bark against each other and against the corrugated interior of the drum (fig. 19–50). Barking drums may be as short as 45 feet or as long as 80 feet.

The 12- by 68-foot drum illustrated in figure 19–50 is rotated by a girth sprocket and two trunnion tires with supporting rollers. The drum has a corrugated interior that keeps the bolts tumbling as the drum rotates. The tumbling wood progresses through the rotating drum impelled by gravity and by the force of additional incoming bolts. A control gate facing the outlet of the drum, and headers within it with restricted openings control longitudinal progress of bolts and rate of discharge. Bark escapes through slots in the drum into a conveyor.

Barking drums should be operated about half full to obtain the greatest production of bark-free sticks with the least fiber damage from broomed ends. Table 19–21 shows productivity data. Tight-barked, winter-cut wood must be tumbled longer to remove bark than loose-barked pulpwood cut in spring or summer.

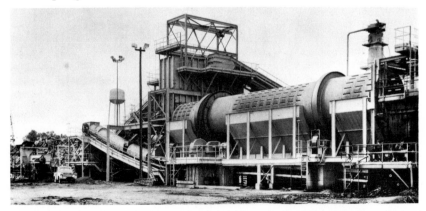

Figure 19–50.—Twelve-foot by 68-foot rotating drum barker designed to remove the bark from pulpwood 4 to 10 feet in length. (Photo from Manitowoc Shipbuilding, Inc.)

Table 19–21.—*Productivity of rotating drum barkers on southern pine pulpwood 4 to 10 feet in length* (data from Manitowoc Shipbuilding, Inc.)

Drum characteristics				Productivity in summer[1]	Productivity in winter[1]
Length	Diameter	Speed	Power		
Feet	*Feet*	*R.p.m.*	*Hp.*	– – – *Cords per hour* – – –	
45	12.0	6.9	150	28 (23)	23 (18)
68	12.0	6.2	250	55 (45)	45 (35)
75	12.0	6.2	250	60 (50)	50 (40)
80	14.5	5.5	500	85 (70)	70 (55)

[1] The first number in each entry is based on 85-percent bark removal; the number following in parentheses applies when 95-percent of the bark is removed.

RING BARKERS

Mechanical ring barkers are widely used to remove bark from saw logs and veneer bolts. The 26-inch machine illustrated in figure 19–51 is one of several models; for southern pine, ring diameters may range from a size suitable for 2½-inch fenceposts to a maximum of 40 inches. The infeeding conveyor advances the log longitudinally into the feed rolls. As shown in figure 19–51, the feed rolls automatically center the log in the rotating mechanical ring. The ring has five crescent-shaped tools which open automatically as the feed rolls force the log against them. As the log advances through the rotating ring, the sharp-edged tools shear off the bark in the 0–90 mode; separation takes place in or near the cambium layer. Pressure on the tools is furnished by heavy rubberbands connected to each tool shaft.

In some makes of ring barkers, tool pressure is regulated with air cylinders. Twenty-five to 50 pounds of force at each tool edge is usual.

Table 19–22 gives data on productivity of mechanical ring barkers on southern pine.

Table 19–22.—*Productivity of five-knife mechanical ring barkers on southern pine* (data from Soderhamn Machine Manufacturing Company)

Ring			Feed		Average logs		Productivity per 8-hour shift
Diameter	Speed	Power	Speed	Power	Length	Diameter	
Inches	*R.p.m.*	*Hp.*	*F.p.m.*	*Hp.*	*Feet*	*Inches*	*Number of logs*
14	440	30	150	5.0	7	5	7,000
18	423	50	250	7.5	12	9	6,500
21	242	40	120	5.0	9	9	4,150
26	222	50	187	5.0	28	11	1,800
30	221	75	226	10.0	15	11	4,700
35	123	75	140	10.0	16–20	15	1,600
40	120	75	156	10.0	16–20	15	1,600

Figure 19–51.—Mechanical ring barker. (Top) Log is centered in the ring, and the tools remove the bark by shearing the cambium layer (0–90 mode). (Bottom) Outfeed side of a 26-inch, five-knife, rotating-ring, mechanical barker. Knobby outfeed rolls are identical to infeed rolls; they automatically center each log. Typically, infeed chains are powered independently of the barker by a 5-hp., two-speed or variable-speed drive. The ring—mounted in ball bearings—is turned at 222 r.p.m. by a 50-hp. motor. Force is applied to the feedworks by air cylinders and to the tools by heavy rubber bands. (Drawing and photo from Soderhamn.)

POLE SHAVERS

Bark is commonly removed from poles, piling, and posts by machines with peripheral-milling cutterheads. The log is revolved as it is fed longitudinally past the rotating **rosser head.** If the knives are sharp and the cutterhead fixed, the log will be turned to a relatively smooth diameter and its taper eliminated with considerable loss of wood. If the knives are somewhat dull and the cutterhead is arranged to float over branch knots and other irregularities, taking a constant-depth cut gauged from the bark surface, the loss of wood is minimized and the natural taper retained.

Small machines of this type are used to peel fenceposts. Some are fixed in place, with highly mechanized handling equipment; more common are portable machines small enough to be towed by a light truck. If well supplied with posts, a portable machine carrying the cutterhead shown in figure 19–52 can peel 1,500 posts during an 8-hour day.

The heavy job of peeling poles and piling requires larger, more permanent installations with mechanized infeeding and outfeeding equipment (fig. 19–53). A typical pole shaver has a pair of four-knife rosser heads that revolve at 3,550 r.p.m. One is a 25-hp. roughing cutter, the other a 15-hp finishing head. Both cutterheads are similar to that shown in figure 19–28; their cutting action approximates the 0–90 mode.

The pole is rotated and driven past the rosser heads by angled, air-filled, rotating tires. Production is dependent on the efficiency of the handling system as well as the capabilities of the pole shaver. The machine illustrated in figure 19–53 can process Class 4, 40-foot southern pine poles at a rate of 50 per hour.

OTHER METHODS

Jets of high-pressure water will readily remove bark from coniferous wood, and hydraulic log barkers are much used to remove the thick bark typical of many western species. For the small, relatively thin-barked southern pine log, however, mechanical barkers are probably most economical.

The southern pine pulp industry has long desired an economical method of separating bark from wood chipped with bark in place. One method in limited use relies on the difference in specific gravity between saturated pine wood and bark; however, no method has been proven to be generally economically competitive with the system of mechanically removing bark from whole stems prior to chipping. Descriptions of investigations aimed at separating bark and wood chips have been provided by Harvin et al. (1952), Grondal (1956), Liiri (1960, 1961), Blackford (1961, 1965), Wesner (1962), and Einspahr et al. (1969).

19–6 CONVERTING WITH CHIPPING HEADRIGS [4]

The chipping headrig—a machine to convert logs into timbers (cants or flitches) without simultaneously producing slabs or sawdust—is probably the most important innovation in mechanical conversion since the invention of the mechanical ring barker. In most installations the resulting

---

[4] Sec. 19–6 is condensed from Koch (1968a).

ROSSER HEAD

Figure 19–52.—Trailer-mounted post peeler driven by gasoline engine. (Top) Rosser head; carbide teeth remove bark and branch stubs; planer knives then smooth the wood. Fixed infeed and outfeed shoes control the amount of wood removed. (Bottom) The post revolves as toothed feed wheels advance it over the rosser head. (Photos from Morbark Industries, Inc.)

Figure 19–53.—Pole shaver. (Top) The pole rotates as it passes under the rosser heads. (Middle) Feed wheels are mounted on turrets that control angularity of feedworks. (Bottom) Roughing head on left; finishing head on right. Depth of cut is controlled by shoes that ride on the rotating pole. (Photos from Nelson Electric.)

squared material is resawn into boards or dimension lumber. The machines, invented to eliminate sawdust from slabbing cuts on conventional head-rigs, are still under development. Events contributing to the development of the various configurations of chipping headrigs were reviewed by Koch (1967a).

Three modes of cutting have been developed for chipping headrigs: (a) cutting with a shaping-lathe configuration (fig. 19–54A), in which the knife edge is parallel to the grain but moves perpendicular to the grain, i.e., 0–90 mode; (b) end-milling (fig. 19–54B), with chip severance accomplished by cutting across the grain with the knife edge at right angles to the grain, i.e., 90–90 mode; (c) peripheral down-milling (plan-ing) with the knife edge perpendicular to the grain but traveling more or less parallel to the grain, i.e., approximately in the 90–0 mode (fig. 19–54C).

POWER REQUIREMENT

The horsepower driving any head of a chipping headrig is determined by properties of the wood, chip dimensions, volume of wood chipped per unit of time, cutter configuration, and cutting mode. As a common base for comparison, it is convenient to use the concept of **specific cutting energy,** i.e., the amount of energy required to remove a unit volume of wood. With green slash pine (84 to 106 percent in moisture content and from 0.50 to 0.58 in specific gravity on basis of ovendry weight and green volume) and the cutterheads illustrated in figure 19–54, energy require-ments have been measured (Koch 1964a):

Cutting configuration	Chip length along the grain	Specific cutting energy
	Inch	*Hp. min./cu. in. of wood removed*
End-milling (fig. 19–54B)___	¾	0.011
Planing (fig. 19–54C)_____	¾	.002
Shaping-lathe (fig. 19–54A)_	1 (and 0.015 inch thick)	.009

Specific cutting energy for the shaping-lathe configuration (fig. 19–54A, 0–90 cutting direction) would be less than for the other two modes if the flake thickness were increased from 0.015 inch tested to usual pulp chip thickness. A specific cutting energy for pulp chips of less than 0.002 hp. minute per cubic inch is probable.

The cutterhead in figure 19–54A had a rake angle of 45° with a clear-ance angle of 15°; diameter of the cutting circle was 13 inches. In figures 19–54B and C the rake angle was 45° with a clearance angle of 7½°; cutting-circle diameter was 11¹⁄₁₆ inches.

Cutterheads can be mounted to cut at intermediate angles with energy requirements intermediate to the extremes illustrated.

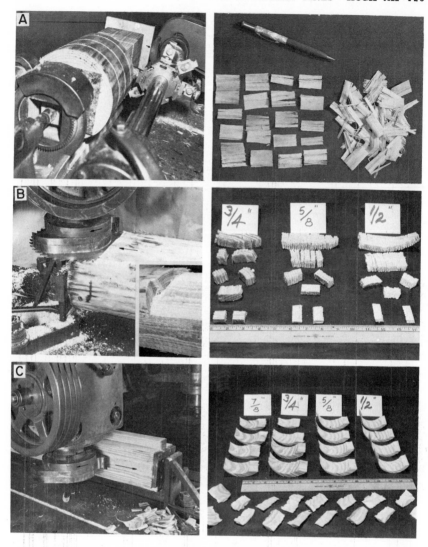

F–520987

Figure 19–54.—Three configurations of chipping headrigs and resulting chips. (A) Shaping lathe, 0–90 mode. (B) End-milling, 90–90 mode. (C) Down-milling, approximately 90–0 mode. Arrow in (A) points to cam and cam follower controlling shape of cant. The saw in the end-milling configuration (B) proved unnecessary and was later removed. (Photos from USDA Forest Service 1964, p. 60.)

COMMERCIAL DESIGNS

In 1964 there were no chipping headrigs operating on southern pine. By 1970 the machines were in wide use throughout the southern pine region.

Planing.—Two manufacturers have pioneered four-head machines that use the planing principle (fig. 19–54C) ; both handle random-length logs. In one design (fig. 19–55) the feedworks centers the log vertically and laterally to yield a pith-center cant. A top loader is provided to speed entry of each log into the feedworks, which characteristically runs at 183 f.p.m.—at which speed chips are ⅝-inch in length. Some operate at 250 f.p.m.

Purchasers of early models did not fully appreciate the productiveness

Figure 19–55.—Stetson-Ross Beaver chipping headrig. (Top left) Assembled cutterheads. (Top right) Method of holding knives in the heads. (Bottom) Logs, poised for instant delivery, may be fed from either side to the infeed chain. Production is over 100,000 bd. ft. of lumber per 8-hour shift. The four-head machine is equipped with hydraulic setworks with range of adjustment sufficient to square logs from 5 to 24 inches in diameter. Feed rate is commonly 180 f.p.m.; some machines, however, feed at 250 lineal f.p.m. (Photos from Stetson-Ross.)

of the equipment and failed to provide for a sufficiently rapid flow of logs. Figure 19–55 illustrates a well-designed installation in British Columbia that feeds at 250 f.p.m. and will accept logs up to 24 inches in diameter. Similar machines are installed in the South.

The first machines were followed (in straight line) by gang circular ripsaws to convert the S4S cants into dimension lumber. Some later installations employ single, dual, or even quad bandsaws in place of the circular saws. The initial canting operation need not produce only square-cornered timbers, but may turn out round-edge or wany cants for subsequent resawing.

In addition to the larger machines, a similar but much smaller chipping headrig is available for converting cordwood (up to 11 inches in diameter) into hexagonal fenceposts. This machine also feeds at 183 f.p.m.

The edger shown in figure 19–56 is designed to remove wane from boards and is a significant application of two chipping heads in the planing configuration. The guide for the lumber (straight-edge) shifts in relation to the fixed head to accommodate varying amounts of wane. The movable head shifts to accommodate lumber of varying width. Splitter saws can be installed in a modular section following the chipper heads. Machines are available that will accept lumber up to 24 inches wide and 4 inches thick.

A second widely used chipping headrig features a feedworks that employs the bottom platen as a reference for infeeding logs. The top and bottom cutterheads can profile each log—much as a moulder shapes a pattern—in a stepped pattern for subsequent resawing (fig. 19–57).

The manufacturer of this machine favors tipped cutterheads—intermediate between the 90–0 situation (fig. 19–54C) and the 0–90 situation (fig. 19–54A)—for side chipping heads. The headrig characteristically feeds at about 100 f.p.m. Machines are available in a wide range of sizes, with numerous combinations of cutterheads and resaws. The firm also manufactures a two-head chipping edger with tipped side chipping heads followed by a circular ripsaw.

End-milling.—There are a number of chipping headrigs and edgers that cut—with modification—in the mode shown in figure 19–54B. In one arrangement (fig. 19–58), the two opposed end-milling disks each carry several knives. Each chipping knife has two cutting edges, which join at an angle; one edge severs the fibers, and the other smooths the cant. Some end-milling disks carry scoring knives that make slits parallel to the grain before the chipping knives sever the chips. Chips are uniform in size and shape (fig. 19–58). A two-head, end-milling edger that operates on the same principle is also available.

A Swedish design available in this country has two end-milling heads carrying small knives mounted in a multiple helical pattern around cutterheads made in the shape of shallow truncated cones (fig. 19–59). The truncated end of the cone finishes the face of the cant and has spe-

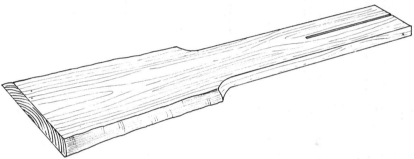

Figure 19–56.—(Top) Two-head chipping edger that converts wany edges of lumber into pulp chips. One head is fixed; the other (left center) is hydraulically positioned to suit lumber to be edged. Cutterheads resemble those shown in figure 19–55. To rip wide boards, saws are positioned as required. Feed rates from 180 to 500 lineal feet per minute are usual. (Bottom) Partially edged and ripped board stopped in cut. (Photo from Stetson-Ross.)

cial knives (conveniently replaceable as a plate-mounted unit) that impart an improved surface. A tong-type gripping mechanism feeds each incoming log in a straight line.

Figure 19–60 shows application of an end-milling chipping head to a conventional headrig. The cutterhead chips the slab from the log before the saw takes its first cut. The chipper head can be withdrawn after the log has been squared. To maintain a uniform chip length the carriage speed must be proportional to the chipper rotational speed. The eight-knife cutterhead illustrated is driven at 900 r.p.m. by a 200-hp. motor to cut ¾-inch-long chips at a carriage speed of 450 f.p.m. The manufacturer states that when cutting 6 inches deep to produce an 18-inch face, the specific cutting energy is 0.003 hp. minute per cubic inch.

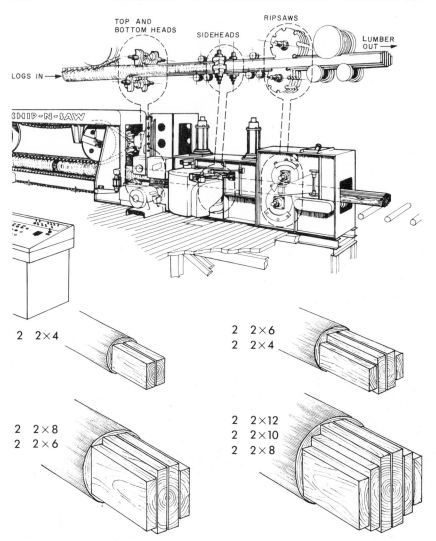

Figure 19–57.—(Top) Cutaway sketch of Chip-N-Saw profiling a log in the same way that mouldings are machined. Usual feed speed is 90 f.p.m. to produce ¾-inch chips. Motors total 603 hp. as follows: Drive, 28 hp. total; bottom chipping head, 50 hp; top chipping head, 125 hp.; each of two side heads, 50 hp.; (top saw arbor carrying five 22½-inch, ¼-inch-kerf saws), 150 hp.; bottom saw arbor (carrying five 19-inch saws), 150 hp. Saw arbors turn at 1,770 r.p.m. (Bottom) Profiling and ripping patterns. (Drawings after Canadian Car.)

Shaping lathe.—Considerable interest has been stimulated by descriptions (Koch 1964a, 1967c) of a headrig with shaping-lathe configuration, but no commercial version is yet available.

Although the model shown in figure 19–54A cuts only $3\frac{9}{16}$ inches per rotation of the log, the production machine would carry a 104-inch cutterhead—sufficient to machine an 8-foot log. It is envisaged that the

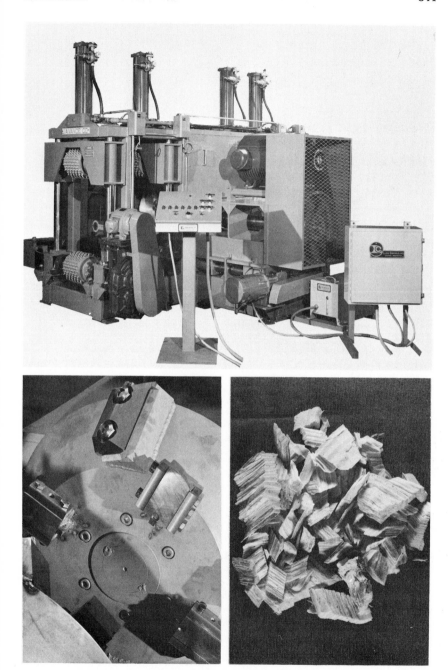

Figure 19–58.—Vance Chip-O-Matic log canter. (Top) Side view of headrig. Logs, controlled by spiked feed rolls, are machined flat on two sides only. (Bottom left) One of the two opposed end-milling cutterheads. Four scoring and four chip-severing knives are mounted on each 150-hp. head. (Bottom right) Pulp chips for headrig. (Bottom left and top photos from J. A. Vance Co.; bottom right photo from Koch 1967a.)

Figure 19–59.—Soderhamn H–P Canter. Knives are mounted in a spiral. Cutterheads open to 16 inches to admit logs up to 18 inches in diameter. Logs are machined flat on two sides only. With heads closed, logs as large as 12 inches can be entirely chipped. Bottom bedplate is fixed. One-hundred-fifty horsepower drives both cutterheads at 700 r.p.m. Feed speed is 117 f.p.m. with two spirals per head or 175 f.p.m. with three. (Photo from Soderhamn.)

head would be 13 inches in diameter and would be turned at 2,880 r.p.m. by a pair of 150-hp. motors, one at either end. Rake angle of the knives would be 45°, sharpness angle 30°, and clearance 15°.

The log would revolve only once to be fully machined. Adjusting the cutterhead spindle axis to parallel the surface of the log prior to machining would enable the headrig to taper-machine. The cutterhead force, tangent to the cutting plane, may be sufficient to cause deflections in logs smaller than 3 to 4 inches in diameter or more than 100 inches long.

The shaping-lathe headrig produces an accurately sized cant with a superior surface and sharp, well-defined corners. By modifying the shape of the cam (see fig. 19–54A), it is possible to produce cylindrical fence-posts, cants with chamfered corners, crossties of trapezoidal sections, or other polygonal shapes. The ability of the headrig to taper-machine—i.e., to make cants that are square or rectangular in cross section but tapered along the length to parallel the bark—would permit remanu-facture on a linebar resaw for maximum recovery of clear lumber.

Flakes cut on the experimental machine (fig. 19–54A) have dimen-sions suitable for manufacturing flakeboards with superior mechanical properties. Flake thickness is controlled by adjusting the speed of either the cutterhead or the log. Flake length is controlled by the length of the

Figure 19–60.—End-milling chipping head installed in conjunction with a conventional carriage. The cutterhead is equipped with setworks and can be used alone or in tandem with a circular saw or bandsaw. The sawyer's box can be as shown or elevated above the chipping head. (Photo from Chipper Machines and Engineering Corporation.)

cutting edge on the individual knives, or by suitably placed scoring knives. At some sacrifice of surface quality on the cants, the headrig can produce pulp chips with a minimum amount of damage to individual fibers. The design would appear to be applicable to the utilization of crooked trees. Short logs, straight enough for the headrig, could be cut from such trees. Production is estimated at five cants per minute.

PRODUCTIVITY

An idea of the potential of chipping headrigs can be obtained by reading trade journal articles describing existing installations. By the end of 1969 many such articles were in print; 41 have been abstracted and assembled in convenient form (Koch 1967a, 1968b; McMillin 1970).

Because logs flow continuously through it, the chipping headrig has more in common with a four-side timber sizer than with a conventional sawmill. Production is reduced by the time required for the push-button-operated setworks to adjust for incoming logs. If incoming wood is sorted into runs by diameter classes as is always done with timber sizers, the logs can be more nearly butted end-to-end for increased production (Dobie 1970).

A few examples illustrate potential productivity. They also show how output is lost if logs are not available, if maintenance problems cause downtime, or if setup time for each log is excessive.

Given:

T_1 = minutes per shift that logs are available and headrig is running
V = gross lineal feed speed, feet per minute
L_{avg} = length of average log, feet
T_2 = time lost between logs (seconds) for setup

$$L_e = \text{effective length of log, feet} = L_{avg} + \left[\frac{V}{60}\right](T_2)$$

Then:

$$n = \text{number of logs per shift} = T_1\left[\frac{V}{L_e}\right]$$

and: Production in board feet of lumber per shift = $\left[\dfrac{bd}{12}\right](L_{avg})(n)$

Where: b = width of average cant, inches
d = depth of average cant, inches

In the tabulation below (based largely on personal observation), mill A has the lowest productivity because incoming random-diameter logs are short (12 feet), gross feed rate is slow (100 f.p.m.), and cants produced are small (average 4 by 4 inches). In contrast, hypothetical mill D has very high production resulting from several factors: logs are longer (14 feet), are of diameters to yield cants averaging 6 by 8 inches, and are fed butted end-to-end at high speed (250 f.p.m.) in prescribed diameter classes.

Mill	Shift length	T_1	V	L_{avg}	T_2	b	d	n	Production per shift
	Hr.	Min.	F.p.m.	Ft.	Sec.	In.		Logs per shift	M b f.
A_____	8	384	100	12	7	4	4	1,620	26
B_____	10	400	187	14	7	6	8	2,088	117
C_____	8	384	250	14	7	6	8	2,222	124
D (Hypothetical)_	8	384	250	14	0	6	8	6,857	384

Small, crooked logs yield more chips and less lumber than large straight ones. Mills cutting only square-edge cants make more chips at the headrig than mills cutting round-edge cants for later resawing. Unpublished yield data on chipping-headrig conversion of 462 southern pine logs in Mississippi indicated that percentage of gross log volume (inside bark) recovered as rough green lumber was positively correlated with log diameter; percentage recovery was 32.3, 33.7, 42.8, 49.4, 60.1, and 53.5 for logs averaging 6.6, 7.8, 8.7, 9.9, 11.7, and 15.1 inches in diameter.

Yield of chips per thousand board feet of lumber cut is inversely proportional to the diameter of logs processed through a chipping headrig; yield of lumber per thousand board feet of logs (M b.f. Doyle scale) is also negatively correlated with log diameter (Kaiser and Jones 1969).

Log size class	Lumber yield per M.b.f. Doyle scale	Yield of green chips per M.b.f. of lumber sawn
Inches	Bd. ft.	Tons
5.5– 6.4	4,650	3.9
6.5– 7.4	3,390	2.6
7.5– 8.4	2,630	2.0
8.5– 9.4	2,200	1.7
9.5–10.4	2,000	1.4
10.5–11.4	1,850	1.3
11.5–12.4	1,740	1.2
12.5–13.4	1,630	1.2
13.5–14.4	1,560	1.1

While information specific to southern pine is not published, data taken from Dobie et al. (1967) and summarized in table 19–23 give a comparison between three methods of log conversion, a chipping headrig followed by resaws, a sash gangsaw mill without band headrig, and a scrag mill which reduces logs to cants with multiple circular saws. The sawmill built around a chipping headrig converts 95 percent of the cubic volume into useable products, whereas the scrag mill with circular saws turns 22 percent of the log into sawdust. The feed rate tabulated for the chipping headrig is very low—a result of inadequate supply of logs, insufficient barker capacity, time lost adjusting setworks to each succeeding logs, and downtime for maintenance. Newer mills should be able to increase the effective feed rate greatly. Lumber and chip production is high, and even at the inefficient feed rates studied by Dobie, productivity per man-hour is impressive.

ADVANTAGES AND DISADVANTAGES

Chipping headrigs have several disadvantages. These newly-designed machines are expensive and need considerable maintenance. Rarely can the chipping headrig be installed as the only headrig (machines are available that will accept logs up to 24 inches in diameter), for very large, very crooked, or flared-butt logs are better handled by a conventional saw. (If tapered, crooked logs are processed through a four-head chipping headrig, the concave side should be turned up and the small end admitted to the machine first.) In some designs, severe tear-out around knots leaves a poor surface that normal planing cannot remedy. As the log enters or leaves some machines, great care is needed to avoid sniping the ends of cants. There is some loss in ability to grade-saw in a chipping headrig mill. The amount of this loss depends on the type of resaws installed and the extent to which round-edge cants are produced at the headrig.

TABLE 19–23.—*Performance of chipping headrigs, sash gangsaws, and scrag mills in western Canada* (Dobie et al. 1967)

Performance statistics	Chipping headrig[1]	Sash gangsaw[2]	Scrag mill[3]
Percent of cubic log volume converted to:			
Lumber	54	56	52
Sawdust	5	13	22
Chips	41	31	26
Average top diameter of logs, inches	7.3	12.5	9.6
Lumber production per man-hour, bd. ft.	1,400–4,000	1,270–2,460	350–1,240
Lineal feet of logs per hour	1,700–4,900	1,080–1,380	900–1,800
Number of logs per hour	99–266	64–79	58–107
Effective feed rate, f.p.m.	26–81	18–23	15–30

[1] Followed by resaws.

[2] No other headrig or resaws.

[3] The scrag mill is a headrig carrying multiple circular saws which reduce a log to cants and planks in a single pass. Edgers and circular gangsaws then convert the cants and planks to wane-free lumber.

More than offsetting these disadvantages are several advantages. Sawdust from headrigs and edgers is greatly reduced and pulp chips proportionately increased. Less sawdust means less material going to the burner and, thus, less atmospheric pollution. The labor and danger of handling slabs and edgings are eliminated. Mill conveyors can be simpler and, since no slab or edging space is needed behind machines, mill length can be reduced. The straight-line flow plan of the mill built around a chipping headrig boosts production with less manpower (table 19–23). Some of the economic factors motivating the rapid acceptance of chipping headrigs have been reviewed by Hobbs and Thomason (1967), Koch (1969, 1970), Kaiser and Jones (1969), Anderson and Kaiser (1970), and Sampson and Fasick (1970).

For southern pine operators the advantages outweigh the disadvantages. It is anticipated that the chipping headrig will find an increasingly important place in the southern pine sawmill industry.

SAW-KERF PULP CHIPS

Prior to the development of the chipping headrig, there was considerable interest in modifying circular-saw headrigs to produce a pulpable sawdust. Tests of inserted-tooth circular saws indicated that a ⅓-inch feed per tooth produced pulpable chips from the kerf.

Malcolm et al. (1961) sawed southern pine at extreme feeds to evaluate both the sawdust produced and the surface quality of resultant boards; he used inserted-tooth, 48-inch diameter, circular saws with 5⁄16-inch kerf.

Surface quality was negatively correlated with feed per tooth, and tear-out along the annual rings and at board corners was severe at large feeds per tooth (fig. 19–61). Large feeds per tooth also caused board thickness to vary excessively; variation of 95 percent of the boards was $25\!/_{64}$ at $\frac{1}{3}$-inch feed per tooth and $12\!/_{64}$ at $\frac{1}{4}$-inch compared to $4\!/_{64}$ at a feed per tooth of $\frac{1}{8}$-inch. Table 19–24 gives an idea of the size of sawdust particles formed.

Fassnacht (1966) prepared charts to help operators decide whether a board or its chips yield a greater return. Because board prices are so much higher than chip prices (tonnage basis), most pine mills have continued to use relatively low feeds per tooth.

TABLE 19–24.—*Retention of saw-kerf chips on $\frac{3}{16}$-inch screen*[1] (Malcolm et al. 1961)

Feed per tooth (inch)	12-tooth saw[2]	36-tooth saw[2]
	– – – – – *Percent* – – – –	
$\frac{1}{8}$	36	49
$\frac{1}{4}$	49	58
$\frac{1}{3}$	59	72

[1] Oscillating screen with $\frac{3}{16}$-inch round holes spaced $\frac{9}{16}$-inch apart.
[2] Saw diameter, 48 inches; kerf, $\frac{5}{16}$-inch.

19–7 SAWING

The kinematics and cutting forces in sawing have been described by Koch (1964b, pp. 179–284); techniques of saw fitting and sharpening were described by Hanchett (1946). Here the sawing process is briefly described as necessary to present the available information specific to sawing southern pine.

Common to all saws are multiple teeth arranged to cut in sequence. The teeth may be formed into, or attached to, the periphery of round flat plates (circular saws), chains (chainsaws), thin continuous metal bands (bandsaws), or long flat rectangular plates or webs arranged in multiples (sash gangsaws).

Saw teeth are designed to make ripping cuts parallel to the grain for headrigs, gangsaws, resaws, and edgers; they are made to cut across the grain for chainsaws, log cut-off saws, and trim saws.

Headrigs designed to saw logs into timbers, cants, dimension lumber and boards usually have log carriages with reciprocating motion, and lumber is ripped from each log one board at a time with a single circular saw or bandsaw.

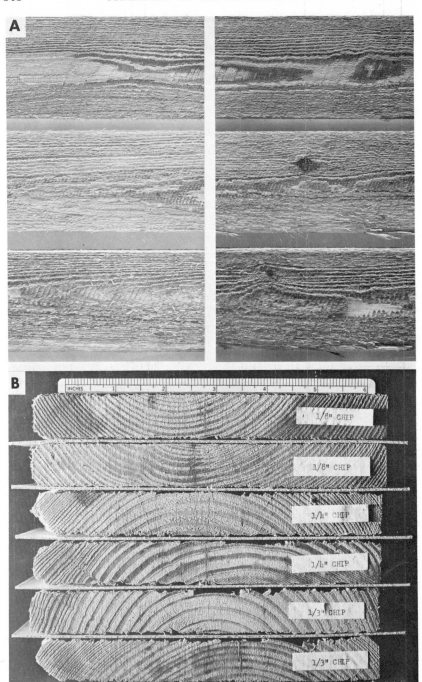

M–118697, M–118696, M–117605

Figure 19–61.—Effect of saw feed per tooth on surface of flat-grain 1- by 7-inch southern pine boards. (A) Boards representative of the best (left) and poorest (right) surfaces produced by feeds per tooth of ⅛-inch (top), ¼-inch (center), and ⅓-inch (bottom). (B) Cross sections of boards cut at three different feeds per tooth. (Photos from Malcolm et al. 1961.)

Less frequently used are headrigs that saw logs into wany-edged cants or lumber in a single pass through the machine, e.g., with multiple circular saws (scrag mills), multiple-band saws (quad bandmills), or multiple oscillating web saws (sash gangsaws).

Cants produced on the headrig are resawn into lumber of smaller dimension by multisaw ripsaws (sash gangsaws or gangsaws carrying circular saws); alternatively, a band resaw (usually a vertical linebar resaw) is used to give greater flexibility in resawing. By adjustment of the distance between linebar (guide) and bandsaw, lumber of any thickness can be ripped from a cant; cants that will yield several boards are conveyed back to the infeed end of the linebar resaw for additional cuts as required.

Except for chainsaws, crosscut saws in mills are virtually all circular. The design of ripping and crosscutting teeth is controlled by the size of timber to be sawn, feed speed, moisture content and density of the wood, and smoothness of surface desired.

BANDSAWING

Bandsaw teeth cut orthogonally (fig. 19–62B). When rip sawing the length of a log or timber, the teeth cut across the grain in the 90–90 mode (fig. 19–1). In general, **swage-set** wide bandsaws (figs. 19–62C, 19–63A,D) are used for longitudinal cutting in primary manufacturing because they make less sawdust (have a narrower **kerf**), and can cut wider boards than circular saws. In the woodworking shop, **spring-set** narrow bandsaws (fig. 19–63E) are used because they can cut curves and irregular shapes that are difficult to cut with other tools. All saw teeth require clearance between kerf wall and saw plate; the swaged tooth (fig. 19–63D) is formed by upsetting the tooth tip against an anvil, and teeth are spring set (fig. 19–63E) by bending alternate teeth sideways.

Nomenclature for bandsaws is indicated in figures 19–62 and 19–63.

Cutting edge velocity is:

$$v = \sqrt{c^2 + f^2} \tag{19–18}$$

Feed per tooth, or **bite,** is:

$$t = \frac{pf}{c} \tag{19–19}$$

The volume of wood V (cubic inches) removed by each swaged tooth as it travels through the workpiece of depth d (inches) is:

$$V = tdk = \frac{pfdk}{c} \tag{19–20}$$

Swaged-tooth wide bandsaws for primary manufacture.—To resist the feeding forces and stay on the saw wheels (fig. 19–64) bandsaws require **tension** making them tightest on the cutting edge and stiff throughout their width. Hanchett (1946) gives detailed instructions for tensioning bandsaws with power-driven stretcher rolls.

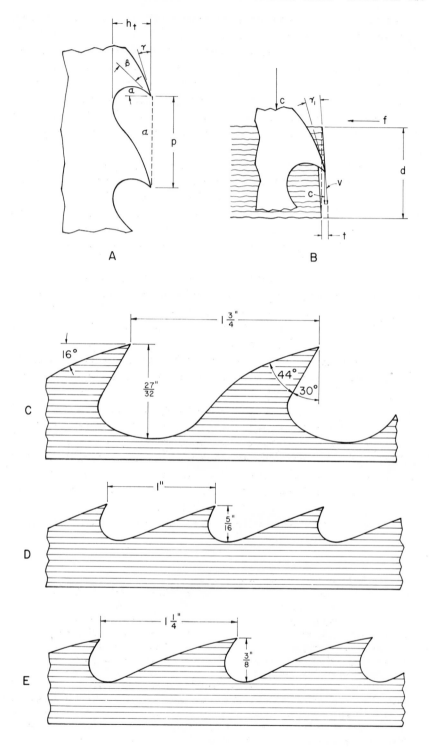

In ripping, cutting force on a bandsaw tooth is positively correlated with the thickness of the undeformed chip, i.e., feed per tooth (table 19–13). Cutting energy per unit volume of wood removed is smallest when feed per tooth is fairly large—a bite of one-half the width of swage (k in fig. 19–63A) is reasonable. Power is consumed severing the fibers in the 90–90 direction, shearing the chips from the kerf boundary, dragging the expanded chip past the kerf boundary, chambering the sawdust in the gullet space, and accelerating the sawdust to ejection velocity (fig. 19–65).

As an approximate rule of thumb, a bandsaw can operate efficiently at a feed per tooth of one-fourth the width of swage but will saw with less specific cutting energy at a feed of one-half the width of swage. As swage width is normally about twice the blade thickness plus 1 gauge, it increases as thicker and wider blades over larger wheels are employed to increase depth of cut; optimum cut per tooth increases proportionally (table 19–25).

Practical strength considerations make a 44° sharpness angle fairly standard; sharpening, swaging, and shaping tools are designed with this in mind. The tooth proportions shown in figure 19–62C are in general use; gullets are rounded, and the back of the teeth are full to give maximum strength. Rake angle is commonly 30°, clearance angle 16°. For band headrigs, tooth pitches of 1¾ or 2 inches matched with gullet depths of 2⁷⁄₃₂- and 1⁵⁄₁₆-inch are in common use. In the South, frozen wood is not ordinarily a problem.

Teeth are first swaged, next lightly faced on a grinding machine, then side-dressed with a pressure-type swage shaper, and finally ground on the face. Teeth should be straight, and swaged with 4° clearance behind the side-cutting edges. Cutting corners should be perfectly formed, sharp, and shaped to have 6° side clearance (fig. 19–63A and D). Teeth are commonly swaged to twice blade thickness plus 1 gauge; for example, a 14-gauge blade would be swaged to 9 gauge.

The force (**strain**) between the wheels (fig. 19–64) required to prop-

←

Figure 19–62.—(A and B) Bandsaw nomenclature.

α	Rake angle, degrees	p	Tooth. pitch, i.e., distance between teeth, inches
β	Sharpness angle, degrees		
γ	Clearance angle, degrees	h_t	Depth of gullet, inches
c	Saw velocity, f.p.m.	a	Area of tooth gullet, square inches
f	Feed speed, f.p.m.	d	Depth of workpiece, inches
v	Resultant velocity of cutting edge with respect to workpiece, f.p.m.	t	Tooth bite, i.e., depth of cut per tooth, inch

(C) Tooth form suitable for headrigs or linebar resaws cutting southern pine; a tooth pitch of 2 inches with depth of 15/16-inch is also in common use. (D) Box factory saw (usually 19 to 21 gauge) for dry pine. (E) Commonly used tooth for resawing dry southern pine. (Drawings A and B after Peter Koch 1964b, p. 179, WOOD MACHINING PROCESSES, Copyright © 1964, The Ronald Press Company, New York.)

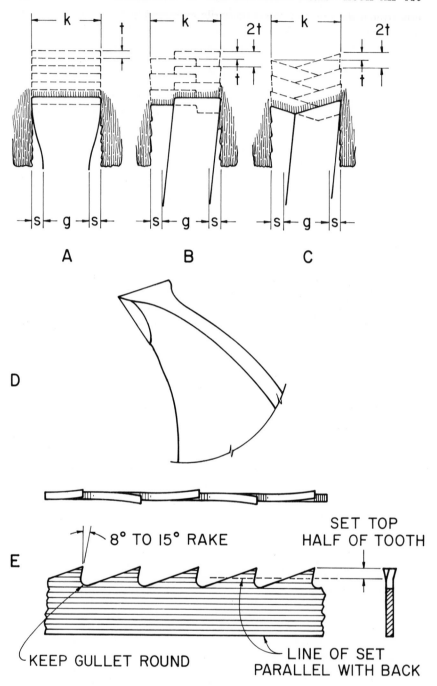

A   B   C

D

E

8° TO 15° RAKE

SET TOP HALF OF TOOTH

KEEP GULLET ROUND

LINE OF SET PARALLEL WITH BACK

erly stretch the saw can be satisfactorily expressed in terms of blade width and thickness (Koch 1964b, p. 191).

$$F = (1000)QWg \qquad (19\text{–}21)$$

where:

F = total upward acting force applied to the spindle of the upper wheel, i.e., strain, pounds (minimum practical operating level)

W = width of blade (gullet to back), inches

g = thickness of blade, inches

Q = a constant; generally 10 for headsaws and 8 for resaws

For example, a 14-inch, 14-gauge headsaw requires a minimum of 11,620 pounds strain. Bandsaws carrying very much higher strains are in successful operation in Canada; as yet, however, none of these saws has seen service in the southern pine region. Since saws with high strain may cut a straight line even though thinner than normal, kerf can be reduced proportionally. It is likely, therefore, that high-strain bandsaws will be used to saw southern pine. Readers interested in further information on high-strain bandsaws will find Clark (1969), Cumming (1969), Foschi and Porter (1970), and Porter (1970, 1971) useful.

A saw speed of approximately 10,000 f.p.m. is common for southern

TABLE 19–25.—*Relationship of wheel diameter, saw gauge, saw width, and saw power for swage-set bandsaws cutting southern pine logs and timbers*

Wheel diameter (inches)	Saw thickness		Saw width[1]	Saw power
	BWG[2]	*Inch*	*Inches*	*Horsepower*
96	14(13)	0.083(.095)	12–14	200
84	15(14)	.072(.083)	12–13	150
72	16(14)	.065(.083)	12	125
66	16	.065	7–11	100
60	17	.058	5–9	75

[1] Saw width is normally 1 inch greater than wheel width.

[2] Birmingham wire gauge. First gauge given is that recommended by one saw manufacturer; gauge shown in parentheses is also in use.

◄

Figure 19–63.—Side clearance and shape of cut of bandsaw teeth. Width of kerf in inches = k; thickness of saw plate in inches = g; set or swage to each side of saw plate in inches = s; for swaged teeth, k is approximately equal to width of swage. (A) Swage set. (B) Spring set with no top bevel. (C) Spring set with top bevel. (D) Swaged tooth for wide bandsaw cutting southern pine. (E) Tooth contours for spring-set narrow bandsaws. (Drawing after Peter Koch 1964b, WOOD MACHINING PROCESSES, Copyright © 1964, The Ronald Press Company, New York.)

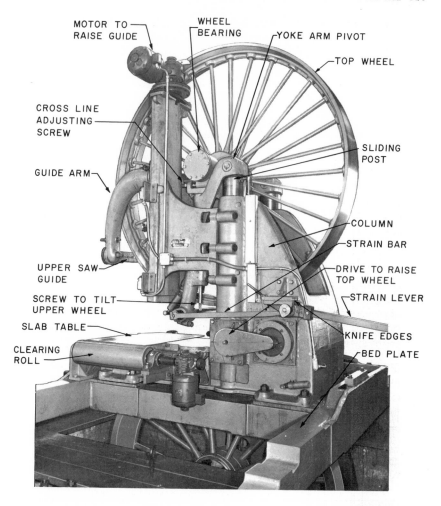

MOTOR TO RAISE GUIDE

WHEEL BEARING

YOKE ARM PIVOT

TOP WHEEL

CROSS LINE ADJUSTING SCREW

SLIDING POST

GUIDE ARM

COLUMN

STRAIN BAR

UPPER SAW GUIDE

DRIVE TO RAISE TOP WHEEL

SCREW TO TILT UPPER WHEEL

STRAIN LEVER

SLAB TABLE

KNIFE EDGES

CLEARING ROLL

BED PLATE

Figure 19–64.—Eight-foot band mill. (Photo from Filer and Stowell Company.)

pine. Assuming a bite per tooth of 0.25 to 0.60 of swage width, **feed** speed for a headrig cutting green southern pine is expressed (Koch 1964b):

$$f = \frac{Rkc}{p} \qquad (19\text{–}22)$$

f = feed speed, f.p.m.
k = width of kerf (approximately equal to swage width), inch
c = saw velocity, f.p.m.
p = pitch of teeth, inches
R = a constant based on sawing conditions:
    0.25, sometimes not enough; 0.50, good; 0.60, sometimes best.

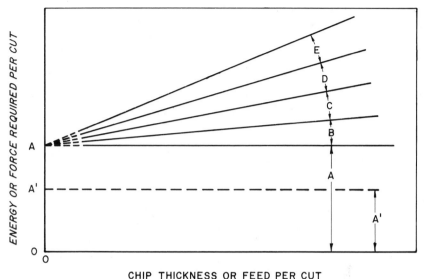

CHIP THICKNESS OR FEED PER CUT

Figure 19–65.—Graphical analysis of cutting resistance in the ripsawing process. A, fiber indentation and incision phase of cutting; A', lower indention and incision energy for sharper cutting edge; B, chip formation; C, chip breakage and associated friction; D, chip removal and associated friction; E, chip acceleration. (Drawing after Peter Koch 1964b, p. 186, **WOOD MACHINING PROCESSES**, Copyright © 1964, The Ronald Press Company, New York.)

For example, a 14-gauge saw swaged to 9 gauge, running at 10,000 f.p.m. with a tooth spacing of 2 inches, would cut well at feed speeds ranging from 178 to 444 f.p.m. Probably the saw would cut best at the higher feed speed. Saw performance is improved if feed speed is uniform.

Saws on a band headrig cutting bark-free southern pine can be expected to wear at a predictable rate, assuming good sharpening practice and no accidents (Koch 1964a, p. 192).

$$W = \frac{SY}{N} \qquad (19\text{–}23)$$

Where:
   W = wear per saw in inches
   S = shifts per day
   Y = months of service
   N = number of saws in set

For example, a set of eight 14-inch, 13-gauge saws on an 8-foot band mill running two shifts for 12 months might wear down to 11 inches in width, at which time the wheels would be trued and a new set of saws put in service. Ten-inch saws might be allowed to wear down to 8½ or 8 inches in width. **Double-cutting** bandsaws for southern pine are toothed on both edges and range in width from 10 to 14 inches; 1½ inches of wear on each edge might be allowable on wider saws under favorable conditions.

Power to drive a bandsaw is proportional to wheel diameter. The following values are typical for southern pine mills.

Wheel diameter	Power to drive saw
Inches	Horsepower
96	200
84	150
72	125
57	75

Power to drive a sawmill carriage can be applied by electric, hydraulic, or steam mechanisms. Average carriage speed on the cutting stroke can be calculated from equation 19–22; maximum speed when returning to pick up a new log may exceed 1,000 f.p.m. Power required is a function of the combined weight of log and carriage and the maximum acceleration required. Normally, the heaviest carriages are used in conjunction with the largest band mills cutting the heaviest logs. If the carriage is driven by a **steam gun,** the diameter of the gun (cylinder) is related to the carriage weight.

Gun diameter	Weight of carriage alone
Inches	Pounds
14	over 20,000
12	to 20,000
10	to 15,000
8	to 10,000

When hydraulic power is used to drive the bandsaw together with the carriage—or the carriage alone—the size of the electric motor required to turn the pump is related to carriage weight.

Carriage weight	Carriage drive alone	Carriage drive plus saw drive
Pounds	– – – – – – – – – Horsepower – – – – – – – – –	
28,000	400	———
18,000	150–200	250
10,000	100	200
6,000	60	150
3,000	25	75

In many southern pine mills, cants or heavy slabs cut with the headrig are resawn into lumber of thinner dimension on a smaller bandsaw called a linebar resaw (fig. 19–66). In an efficient installation, random-length slabs and cants flow nearly continuously through these heavy machines as a single board is ripped from each. The linebar, or guide, is equipped with setworks so that distance between guide and saw can be quickly and accurately set. Vertical press rolls, or horizontal spiral rolls, align the stock against the guide before the saw enters the cut. Since only one board is removed with each pass of a cant, each cant is repeatedly returned on a **merry-go-round** conveyor to the infeed side of the resaw until reduced to lumber of the desired size. A discussion of mill layouts for linebar resaws is available in Detjen (1961).

All bandsaws, including linebar-resaws, are sized according to wheel diameter. The illustrated 54-inch resaw (fig. 19–66), if cutting southern pine, might carry a 26-foot-long, 8-inch-wide, 17-gauge saw swaged to 11 gauge with 1¾-inch tooth spacing. The saw normally carries a "strain" of 4,640 pounds. The saw itself is driven by a 75-hp. motor. Saw speed is 7,400 f.p.m. The four 8-inch horizontal feed rolls and two 10-inch vertical rolls are driven by a 3- or 5-hp. electric variable-speed drive to give feed speeds infinitely variable between 100 and 300 lineal f.p.m. The maximum feed speed of 300 f.p.m. yields a bite per tooth of 0.072 inch. Normal high speed on a 12-inch-thick cant is 180 f.p.m., giving a bite per tooth of 0.043 inch. Maximum cant size that can be split in the center is 20 inches thick by 24 inches wide. The setworks on the linebar can be air or hydraulically operated and remotely controlled by the sawyer. While

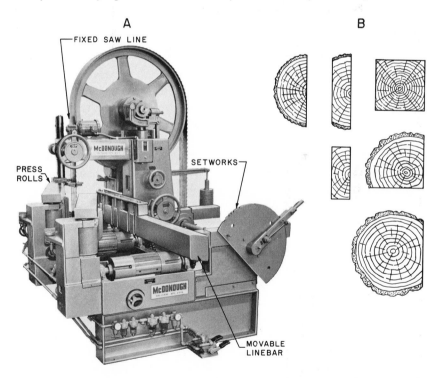

A   B

FIXED SAW LINE

McDONOUGH

PRESS ROLLS

SETWORKS

McDONOUGH

MOVABLE LINEBAR

Figure 19–66.—(A) Linebar resaw with 54-inch wheels and short frame. (B) Shapes of cants and slabs that can be resawn on the linebar resaw. Since only one board is removed with each pass of a cant, each cant is repeatedly returned on a merry-go-round conveyor to the infeed of the resaw until reduced to lumber of the desired size. The short frame permits lumber to approach the infeed from either saw or linebar side. (Photo and drawings from McDonough Manufacturing Company.)

one cant is being run, it is possible to preset the linebar for the next cant. Production per 8-hour shift on this machine is determined by stock size and cutting program but can reach 50,000 bd. ft. Automatic off-bearing is provided so that the operating crew consists of the sawyer only, unless the machine is used to salvage stock out of thin irregular slabs. Slab resawing usually requires a tail sawyer because the waste slab may break up into two or three pieces as it leaves the feedworks.

Sawmill resaws are also made so that the band runs horizontally between the wheels; this arrangement permits slabs to be fed face-down on the feed table. A split infeed table is sometimes provided so that two cants or slabs can be fed simultaneously and a different thickness board sawn from each.

Swaged-tooth band resaws for dry lumber.—Because remanufacturing plants commonly keep only a few thicknesses of dry lumber in inventory, they require resaws to convert these thicknesses to a multiplicity of thinner sizes. Since maximum lumber recovery is the objective when resawing dry boards, bandsaws for remanufacturing have much thinner kerf than primary bandsaws. Saw gauge varies according to wheel diameter (table 19–26). For southern pine, the tooth shapes illustrated in figure 19–62D and E are widely used with rake angle of 30° and sharpness angle of 44°.

Because efficient feeds per tooth are a function of swage width (and therefore saw gauge), gullet depths can be expressed as a function of blade thickness and tooth pitch. Thin saws take small bites per tooth and therefore need less gullet space (table 19–27). Tooth spacing on wide saws is greater than on narrow saws because they are capable of deeper cuts and need more gullet space.

Saw velocities of 7,000 to 9,000 f.p.m. are usual for cutting dry southern pine. Saw strain is given by equation 19–21. Practical feed speeds lie in the lower range defined by equation 19–22. Swage width for cutting dry southern pine should be 0.020 to 0.040 inch wider than saw thickness; for example, a 19-gauge blade is commonly swaged to 16 gauge.

Most band resaws for dry southern pine are vertical; they may be in

TABLE 19–26.—*Proportions of band resaws for dry southern pine*

Wheel diameter (inches)	Saw thickness[1]		Saw width	Saw power
	BWG	*Inch*	*Inches*	*Horsepower*
60_____	18–16	0.049–0.065	6–8	60–75
54_____	19–17	.042–.058	5–7	50–60
48_____	19–18	.042–.049	4–6	20–40
44_____	20–19	.035–.042	4–5	15–25
36_____	21–19	.032–.042	3–4	15–20

[1] Saw thickness should not exceed wheel diameter (in inches) divided by 1,000 plus 1 saw gauge.

TABLE 19–27.—*Tooth proportions for wide bandsaws ripping dry southern pine*[1]

Saw width (inches)	Saw gauge	Pitch	Gullet depth
	BWG	*Inches*	*Inch*
4	20 (18)	1¾ (1)	7/16 (¼)
5	19 (17)	1¾ (1½)	½ (7/16)
6	18 (16)	1¾	⅝
7	17 (15)	1¾	11/16
8	16 (14)	2 (1¾)	15/16 (¾)

[1] The first number in each entry is for pine of low and normal density; the second number, in parentheses, is for very dense pine.

single, twin, or tandem arrangement depending on the production required. Figure 19–67 shows a single vertical resaw on which the rolls tilt so that standard boards or cants, rectangular in cross section, can be center-resawn into two bevelled pieces of equal size and shape. Bevelled siding and much moulding stock is manufactured in this manner; as another example, triangular corner block for crates and pallet boxes can be readily cut on a resaw equipped with tilting rolls. When equipped to resaw dry southern pine moulding stock, this 36-inch band resaw might carry a 17-foot-long, 4-inch-wide, 20-gauge saw swaged to 15 gauge with a 1-inch tooth pitch and 9/32-inch gullet depth. Normal "strain" for this saw is 1,120 pounds. A 20-hp. motor drives the saw at 7,800 f.p.m. When splitting a 4-inch dry board, the saw would typically be fed at a bite per tooth of 0.02 inch, yielding a feed speed of 156 f.p.m. The four feed rolls are each 6 inches in diameter and 6 inches tall. They are driven by a pair of ½-hp. variable-speed motors that are mounted on, and tilt with, the feed roll mechanism. The feed speed is variable from 25 to 250 f.p.m. The rolls can be tilted up to 45°. The maximum-size workpiece that can be center-split on the saw is 8 inches wide and 8 inches thick.

Spring-set narrow bandsaws.—Saws more than ½-inch wide are primarily used to rip. Narrower saws can cut curves; for example, a ½-inch, 21-gauge saw can cut a curve of 2¼-inch radius, and a ⅛-inch, 25-gauge saw can cut a curve of ⅜-inch radius.

Proportions of narrow bandsaws are shown in figure 19–63E. Teeth on ¼-inch-wide saws are commonly set 0.005 inch to each side; those on saws 1 inch wide are set approximately 0.010 to each side, with other saw widths set proportionately. The thinnest and narrowest saws are run on the smallest wheels (table 19–28).

Wheels for saws less than 1 inch wide are commonly rubber covered, and the saw teeth do not project over the edge. For wide saws, easier-to-clean, hard-faced wheels are used; the spring-set teeth must project beyond the front rim of these wheels.

A   **B**

Figure 19–67.—(A) 36-inch band resaw with tilting rolls. (B) Typical cuts. (Photo from Tri-State Machinery Company.)

TABLE 19–28.—*Narrow bandsaw dimensions* (Koch 1964b, p. 200)

Wheel diameter (inches)	Saw gauge	Saw width	Saw speed	Points per inch[1]	Saw length
	BWG	*Inches*	*F.p.m.*		*Feet*
12–18..........	25	$\frac{3}{16}$–$\frac{1}{2}$	3000	7–5	6–10
20–30..........	22	$\frac{3}{16}$–$1\frac{1}{2}$	3500 (to 7500)[2]	7–4	10–15
36.............	21	$\frac{1}{4}$–2	4000–4500 (to 8500)[2]	6–3	18–20
42.............	20	1–$2\frac{1}{2}$	5000–5500 (to 9900)[2]	5–2	over 21

[1] Counts teeth in a 1-inch space, i.e., includes the tooth at each end of a measured inch; thus, if tooth points are spaced $\frac{1}{10}$ inch apart, there are considered to be 11 teeth per inch.

[2] On some current designs.

SASH GANGSAWING

The sash gangsaw carries several straight, short sawblades clamped in a reciprocating frame; the log (fig. 19–68A,B) or cant (fig. 19–68C) is fed continuously through this frame. The action is similar to that of a handsaw in the hands of a carpenter ripping a board. The saws cut on the downstroke only. For a detailed discussion of kinematics and power requirements see Koch (1964b, pp. 201–210).

Some important relationships can be seen from figure 19–68D. It is evident that saw velocity is maximum when the crank arm is horizontal, and zero when it is vertical.

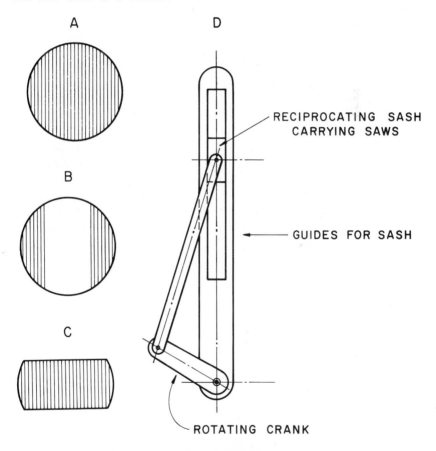

Figure 19–68.—Sawing patterns and kinematics for gangsaws.

(A) Log sawn into boards or dimension.

(B) Boards sawn from outer portion of log only, leaving central cant of desired dimension.

(C) Cant gangsawn into lumber.

(D) Diagram of sash motion on a reciprocating gangsaw; simplified to omit overhang or oscillation.

The workpiece feed per revolution of the crank, and the average chip thickness can be calculated:

$$x = \frac{12f}{n} \tag{19-24}$$

$$t_{avg} = \frac{12pf}{Sn} \tag{19-25}$$

where:

$x =$ workpiece feed per revolution of crank, inch
$f =$ feed speed of workpiece, feet per minute
$n =$ revolutions per minute of crank
$S =$ stroke of sash, inches $=$ twice length of crank arm
$t_{avg} =$ average chip thickness, inches
$p =$ pitch, inches

Saw overhang.—To cut southern pine, most gangsaws are equipped to feed the workpiece continuously at a uniform speed. To avoid interference between saw and workpiece, the saw must be moved out of the cut on the upstroke. **Overhang** (fig. 19–69), automatically adjusted in amount to correspond to the continuous feed speed, is a partial solution.

Oscillation.—Figure 19–70 shows an overhung saw cutting on the down-stroke. It is evident that, at the beginning of the upstroke, the point of each tooth will interfere with the surface it has just cut and cause sash power to be substantially increased; research by Kivimaa (1959) has confirmed this. Some European manufacturers have coped with this problem by incorporating overhang proportional to feed speed and in addition **oscillating** the sash, that is, swinging the bottom of the sash away from the workpiece at the instant of bottom reversal and then reposition-ing it at top reversal. No gangsaw manufactured in the United States, however, is designed with an oscillating ash.

Capacity and characteristics of gangsaws.—While whole-log gangs are much used in the world, most in the southern pine region are arranged to handle cants (figs. 19–68C, 19–71). Table 19–29 gives proportions of cant and log gangsaws suitable for use on southern pine. The horsepower figures shown in table 19–29 do not imply that these are the power demands at maximum feed rates on a workpiece occupying the full width and depth of opening. Horsepower demand is determined by saw velocity, bite per tooth, width of swage, depth of cut, and number of saws cutting. (See Koch 1964b, equations 6–40 and 6–43.)

If 75 hp. is required on a 12-inch-wide gangsaw to cut a 6- by 12-inch cant into 2-inch lumber at 20 feet per minute, a similar 6-inch-deep cant, but 18 inches wide, if cut into 2-inch lumber at 32 feet per minute on a 30-inch gangsaw, would require 150 to 225 hp. If feed speed is constant, power required to saw a cant is directly proportional to number of saws in the cant, e.g., if 100 hp. is required to saw a cant into 2-inch lumber, 200 hp. will be needed to reduce it to 1-inch boards. Horsepower demand is also directly proportional to depth of cut. Obviously, the amount of

of gangmills was 56 percent lumber, 31 percent chippable waste, and 13 percent sawdust; circle mills (of the two-saw scrag type) produced 52 percent lumber and 22 percent sawdust. (See table 19–23.)

Gangsaws, because they cut through-and-through, cannot remove high-grade lumber from all four sides of a log. This disadvantage can be partially overcome if the gangsaw is arranged to take cants from a circular or band headrig; the headrig removes any high-grade lumber available on two sides before the cants go to the gangsaw. Alternatively, two gangsaws can be arranged in tandem, the first slabbing two sides of the log and removing the sideboards, while the second reduces the cant to boards, including sideboards from the unslabbed sides.

If logs are gangsawn in diameter classes, a fixed saw spacing can be tailored to get highest value from each class. Gangsaws are not well suited for extremely rough logs; such logs should be prepared for the gangsaw by slabbing them on two sides on a preceding headrig.

CIRCULAR SAWING

The circular saw, in numerous variations, is used in all stages of pine manufacture. This text will discuss only a few of the most important applications. For discussions in greater depth, see Koch (1964b, pp. 217–273), Lubkin (1957), and Kollmann and Côté (1968, p. 490).

Nomenclature.—Figures 19–72, 19–73, and 19–74 illustrate nomenclature for circular saws.

Kinematics and fundamentals.—Depending on the direction of cut through the workpiece, circular saws may cut by **counter-sawing** or by **climb-sawing** (fig. 19–73). Counter-sawing, which resembles up-milling in that the cutting edge emerges from the workpiece more nearly at right angles to the direction of feed than where it entered, is sometimes called "'up-sawing." Similarly in climb-sawing, the cut is more nearly parallel to the feed where it leaves the workpiece; climb-sawing is sometimes called "down-sawing." Note that if the drawings in figure 19–73 were reversed top to bottom by turning them on their horizontal axes, their cutting directions relative to the workpiece would be similar to those for up-milling and down-milling respectively in figures 19–30A and 19–30B.

In order to rationally specify circular saws and matching drive motors, it is helpful to understand some basic relationships.

In planing, where the angle ω is small, the cumbersome expressions for the true trochoidal cutting path are necessary for accuracy. In circular sawing, however, the tooth traces can be closely approximated as arcs of circles. For counter-sawing (fig. 19–73):

$$\omega_1 = \text{arc cos} \left(\frac{d+h}{R} \right) \qquad (19\text{–}26)$$

$$\omega_2 = \text{arc cos} \frac{h}{R} \qquad (19\text{–}27)$$

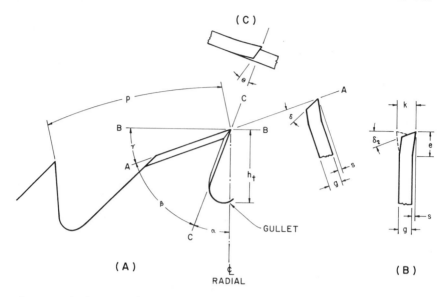

Figure 19–72.—Geometry of spring-set circular saw teeth. (A) Side view of tooth. (B) Front view of tooth. (C) Projection along rake plane.

α   Rake angle, degrees

γ   Clearance angle, degrees

β   Sharpness angle, degrees

δ   Top bevel angle, degrees (measured from clearance plane A–A, fig. 19–72A)

θ   Front bevel angle, degrees (measured from the rake plane, fig. 19–72A)

g   Thickness of saw blade, inch (may be variable from saw center to tooth extremity)

s   Amount of set (or swage) to each side of saw plate, inch

e   Length of tooth affected by set (measured from tooth extremity in a radial direction to the line of set, i.e., the line of set falls along a circle concentric with the cutting circle but of slightly smaller diameter)

k   Width of kerf, inch (nominally 2s + g; actual kerf may vary from nominal width because of vibration, runout, or other factors)

h_t Gullet depth measured radially, inches

N   Number of teeth in saw

p   Tooth pitch, inches

a   Area of tooth gullet, square inches.

(Drawing after Peter Koch 1964b, p. 219, WOOD MACHINING PROCESSES, Copyright © 1964, The Ronald Press Company, New York.)

For climb-sawing (fig. 19–73):

$$\omega_1 = \text{arc cos } \frac{h}{R} \tag{19–28}$$

$$\omega_2 = \text{arc cos } \left(\frac{d+h}{R}\right) \tag{19–29}$$

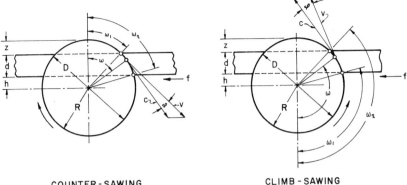

COUNTER-SAWING CLIMB-SAWING

Figure 19–73.—Angles, dimensions, and velocity vectors for circular saws.

- z Saw projection beyond the workpiece, inches
- d Depth of workpiece, inches
- h Distance between workpiece and axis of saw rotation, inches
- ω Instantaneous position angle of tooth under consideration
- ω_1 Angle through which tooth edge has rotated from reference line to entry in wood
- ω_2 Angle through which tooth edge has rotated from reference line to exit from wood
- f Feed speed, feet per minute
- n Saw blade, revolutions per minute
- c Cutting velocity, feet per minute (i.e., peripheral velocity of cutting edge)
- v Velocity of cutting edge relative to workpiece, feet per minute
- f_r Feed per revolution of saw blade, inches
- b Length of arc of tooth engagement with workpiece, inches
- R Blade radius, inches

(Drawing after Lubkin 1957.)

The angle at which instaneous chip thickness is the average chip thickness can be approximated as follows:

$$\omega_a \cong \text{arc cos} \frac{\left(h+\frac{d}{2}\right)}{R} \tag{19-30}$$

The length of path of tooth engagement for both counter-sawing and climb-sawing can be stated:

$$b = R(\omega_2 - \omega_1) \tag{19-31}$$

The tooth pitch for uniformly spaced teeth is:

$$p = \frac{2\pi R}{N} \tag{19-32}$$

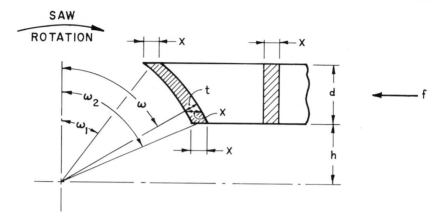

Figure 19–74.—Approximate chip geometry for circular saws.

t   Instantaneous chip thickness, inch (measured in a direction perpendicular to a
    tangent to the tooth trace, i.e., in an approximately radial direction)

t_a Average chip thickness, inch

x   Feed per tooth, or "bite" per tooth, inch

V   Volume of wood removed by a single tooth as it travels through the workpiece,
    cubic inches

E_s Specific cutting energy, kilowatthours per cubic inch kerf removed

(Drawing after Lubkin 1957.)

Feed per revolution of blade is:

$$f_r = \frac{f}{n} \qquad (19\text{--}33)$$

The feed per tooth is:

$$x = \frac{2\pi Rf}{Nc} = \frac{pf}{c} = \frac{12f}{nN} \qquad (19\text{--}34)$$

Chip thickness at any instant (fig. 19–74) can be approximately stated for swage-set teeth.

$$t = x \sin \omega = \frac{f \sin \omega}{nN} = \frac{pf}{c} \sin \omega \qquad (19\text{--}35)$$

For swage-set teeth the average chip thickness is:

$$t_a = \frac{xd}{b} = \frac{pfd}{bc} \qquad (19\text{--}36)$$

As shown in figures 19–63B and C, spring-set teeth penetrate to twice the depth that swage-set teeth penetrate for a given feed per tooth because the points of alternate teeth cut on opposite sides of the kerf; for spring-set teeth, the average chip thickness is:

$$t_{\text{avg spring-set}} = \frac{gt_a + (g + 2s - g)t_a}{g} = \frac{k}{g} t_a \qquad (19\text{--}37)$$

Rim speed, i.e., peripheral velocity of the saw teeth, can be expressed:

$$c = \frac{2\pi Rn}{12} = \frac{\pi Rn}{6} \qquad (19\text{-}38)$$

For both counter-sawing and climb-sawing, resultant tooth velocity (fig. 19-73) with respect to the workpiece is:

$$\nu = \sqrt{c^2 + f^2 + 2cf \cos \omega} \qquad (19\text{-}39)$$

The actual number of teeth engaged will alternate between the two integral numbers closest in value to the ratio b:p.

Obviously total cutting power required is positively correlated with width of kerf and with length of cutting path (thickness of workpiece). When evaluating the effect of feed per tooth on power required, it is convenient to use the concept of specific cutting energy, i.e., the energy to remove a unit volume of wood. From equations 19-1 and 19-2 it was observed that the parallel cutting force could be expressed in terms of chip thickness: curvilinearly (Kt^m) or linearly $(A + Bt)$. If the experimentally determined constants K and m (or A and B) are known, the specific cutting energy of a circular saw (E_s, kilowatt hours per cubic inch of kerf removed) can be calculated for any value of average chip thickness (t_a, equation 19-36 for swage-set saws, and 19-37 for spring-set saws); see Koch (1964b, p. 225) for development of the equations.

$$E_s = \frac{(0.377)(10^{-6})}{12} \left[\frac{K}{t_a^{1-m}} \right] \qquad (19\text{-}40)$$

$$E_s = \frac{(0.377)(10^{-6})}{12} \left(B + \frac{A}{t_a} \right) \qquad (19\text{-}41)$$

The shape of these curves is shown in figure 19-75. Normal rim speed for circular saws is approximately 10,000 f.p.m. It is, however, practical to increase the chip thickness and thereby reduce the power demand by reducing saw revolutions per minute, increasing tooth spacing, or increasing feed speed. Gullet capacity, tooth strength, plate strength, and surface quality (fig. 19-61) limit the feed per tooth to relatively low values, however—generally considerably less than 1/4-inch for log saws and much less for most other applications of circular saws. A detailed discussion of these limiting factors, the effects of size and orientation of the sawblade, and the effects of tooth angles, can be found in Koch (1964b, p. 226-271).

Insert-tooth ripsaws.—Circle headrigs and board edgers used in the southern pine region commonly are equipped with two-piece teeth having easily replaceable bits and shanks (fig. 19-76). The bit is drop-forged and has clearance angles factory-ground on top and sides. It is sharpened by grinding on the rake face only so that the cutting edge is perpendicular to the plane of the saw plate. The assembly, consisting of bit and shank,

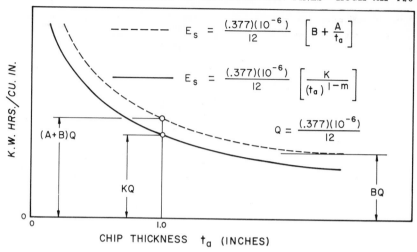

$$E_s = \frac{(.377)(10^{-6})}{12}\left[B + \frac{A}{t_a}\right]$$

$$E_s = \frac{(.377)(10^{-6})}{12}\left[\frac{K}{(t_a)^{1-m}}\right]$$

$$Q = \frac{(.377)(10^{-6})}{12}$$

Figure 19–75.—Forms of specific cutting energy curves. While most bandsaws cut a chip thinner than ¼-inch, chipping headrigs commonly feed ½-inch to 1 inch per knife. (Drawing after Lubkin 1957.)

rides in a grooved seat in the saw plate. The shank is slightly larger than the socket; thus, the entire assembly is securely spring locked in place. The inserted tooth is well designed to exhaust sawdust from the kerf; the gullet is capacious and rounded, and the shank is thickened (to chamber the sawdust) where it meets the bit (fig. 19–76).

Because the bits are replaceable when worn, the diameter of the saw remains constant regardless of the length of time the saw plate has been in service.

A rake angle of 30 to 40° is commonly employed for all insert-tooth ripsaws cutting southern pine. The maximum width of the forged bit is generally slightly less than twice the plate thickness, and may range from ⁷⁄₃₂- to ⅜-inch but is commonly ¼- to ⁵⁄₁₆-inch in width. Rim speed is usually approximately 10,000 f.p.m., but speeds of 8,000 to 12,000 f.p.m. are common. Feed per tooth on this type of saw is frequently about 0.08

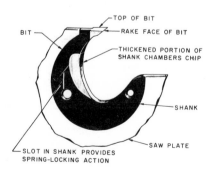

Figure 19–76.—Two-piece inserted tooth for a circular ripsaw.

inch, although many softwood mills operate at a bite per tooth of ⅛-inch. Figure 19–61 illustrates surfaces obtained with feeds per tooth of ⅛-, ¼-, and ⅓-inch.

Saw diameters on headrigs range from 40 to 60 inches, with plate thickness as thin as 9 by 10 gauge for 40-inch saws and as thick as 4 by 5 gauge for 60-inch saws. Saw plates are normally a gauge thicker in the center than at the rim. Tooth pitch is commonly 3 to 4 inches but may be as large as 6 inches.

Power data specific to southern pine have not been published; the requirement can be estimated, however, from a study made by Andrews (1955) on other species. A 38-tooth, 48-inch-diameter, 700-r.p.m., inserted-tooth saw cutting with a ⁹⁄₃₂-inch kerf and 0.077-inch feed per tooth might require the following saw power:

Depth of cut	Power required by saw only
Inches	*Horsepower*
2	14
4	29
6	44
8	59
10	73
12	88
14	102

A 54-inch circular saw, hydraulic log turner, and 6,000-pound carriage—if all hydraulically powered—require a 150-hp. electric motor to drive the pump. If the carriage weight is only 3,000 pounds, 100 hp. might be sufficient; a 10,000-pound carriage requires about 200 hp.

A typical small edger saw of insert-tooth design is 14 inches in diameter, 10 gauge, carries 14 teeth, cuts a ¼-inch kerf, and rotates at 2,725 r.p.m. Each saw in the cut requires from 10 to 30 hp. depending on thickness of stock and feed speed.

Tooth deflection and breakage are related to stress distribution in inserted-tooth circular saws; readers interested in studying the location and magnitude of these stresses will find the work by Malcolm and Koster (1970) useful.

Double-arbor gangsaws.—In an effort to boost productivity per man-hour in southern pine sawmills, the **double-arbor circular gangsaw** has been increasingly used. This machine carries two gangs of circular saws—one cutting from the top and the other from the bottom. Figure 19–57 illustrates such a machine built into the outfeed end of a chipping headrig. In some designs the top arbor carries climb-cutting saws.

Power demand is substantial—each arbor can carry as much as 250 hp. for 12-inch cuts (6 inches from top and 6 inches from the bottom) at a feed rate of 100 lineal feet per minute or more. Thin circular saws tend to be distorted by heat generated from friction between saw plate and kerf wall. Saws have recently been designed specifically for application to double-arbor gangsaws. Designs vary, but one reportedly successful saw has 16 carbide-tipped teeth cutting a ¼-inch kerf; the ³⁄₁₆-inch plate turns at 1,770 r.p.m. In addition to the normal gullets, the plate has two very deep gullets of constant width that run nearly to the saw collar but at a trailing angle; cutters the width of the kerf are attached to the face of each long gullet; these long knives cut themselves free whenever saw deflection occurs and eject the sawdust forcibly from the tops of the long gullets. A variation of this design has been described by Demsky (1967) and by DuClos (1967).

Water is sometimes used to cool and clean these saws. The saws may be clamped on the arbor, or they may float on a keyed arbor; in the latter case they are spaced as desired by babbitt-faced guides that bear against the rim on both sides of each saw plate.

Thin ripsaws.—The technique of high-speed ripping of thick cants with circular saws is developing rapidly; current efforts are concentrated on reducing kerf thickness. Readers desiring information on the state of the art are referred to Kintz (1969), Salemme (1969), Schliewe (1969), and Thrasher (1969). It is of substantial commercial interest that 6-inch-thick cants of some species can be ripped—at feeds approaching production speeds—with a kerf of less than ⅛-inch.

Salemme (1969) notes that thin-kerf, carbide-tipped, circular ripsaws require machines specially designed to provide the necessary precision of operation. He recommends use of the largest diameter, thickest, and flattest saw collar possible; the saw should be made of an excellent grade of steel and have the smallest eye possible.

General purpose swage-set ripsaws.—Expert saw filers who need circular saws for applications where change in diameter with wear is not a factor, may find swage-set ripsaws more economical than insert-tooth saws. As with bandsaws, swaging tools are designed for a limited range of tooth shapes. A rake angle of 30° with sharpness angle of 44° is common. Rim speeds are in the range from 8,000 to 14,000 f.p.m. Table 19–30 shows the proportions of small swage-set ripsaws. For thin material use the maximum number of teeth. Saws in the heavier gauges are suitable for power-fed machines or when cutting green or thick pine.

For saws 15 gauge and thicker the tooth height should be approximately (0.43)(pitch); for saws less than 15 gauge, tooth height can be somewhat less. Width of swage is commonly twice plate thickness.

Log cutoff saws.—The trend toward tree-length logging and diversion of each portion of the stem to its most appropriate use has stimulated new interest in log cutoff saws installed at central log decks. Circular log cutoff saws are generally arranged with the saw center above the workpiece. Figure 19–77A shows solid-tooth styles and bevels.

Typically, rake angle is negative (e.g., −20°), sharpness angle 45°, clearance angle 65°, and tooth height 0.76 times the pitch. Bevel is equally

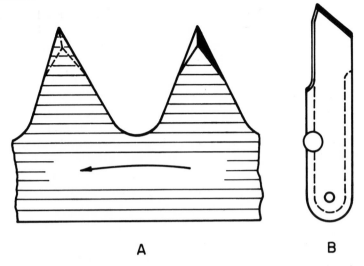

A   B

Figure 19–77.—Tooth styles commonly used for log cutoff saws. (A) Solid tooth. (B) Insterted tooth.

divided between front and back of the tooth, i.e., both front and top carry a 12 to 15° bevel. The point only is bevelled; the remainder of the tooth and gullet are ground straight across. The teeth are spring set about $\frac{3}{64}$-inch to each side of the saw plate.

The inserted tooth shown in figure 19–77B is a commonly used style for log cutoff saws ranging from 66 to 108 inches in diameter. It is spring set ($\frac{1}{8}$-inch to each side is common) and is riveted into a V-milled socket in the saw plate. The tooth illustrated is $4\frac{9}{32}$ inches long. It fits into a radially oriented socket in the saw plate that is $2\frac{13}{16}$ inches deep. Table 19–31 shows commonly used saw specifications.

TABLE 19–30.—*Proportions of general-purpose, solid-tooth swaged ripsaws* (Koch 1964b, p. 253)

Diameter (inches)	Gauge	Number of teeth	Diameter	Gauge	Number of teeth
	BWG		*Inches*	*BWG*	
6	18	36–40	22	8–12	30–36
7	18	36–40	24	7–11	30–36
8	18	36–40	26	7–11	30–36
9	16	36–38	28	10	36
10	12–16	24–36	30	10	36
12	10–14	24–36	32	10	36
14	10–14	24–44	34	9	36
16	10–14	24–40	36	9	36
18	9–13	24–40	38	8	36
20	8–13	24–36	40	8	36

UTILIZATION OF THE SOUTHERN PINES—KOCH AH 420

Figure 19–78 illustrates a 108-inch, 3-gauge, log cutoff saw with 164 inserted, spring-set teeth. Hydraulically operated jaws clamp the log on both sides of the cut. To give a rim speed of 10,000 f.p.m., the saw rotates at 354 r.p.m. and is driven by a 75-hp. motor. It is hydraulically fed and requires 2 seconds to cut through a 24-inch log at a feed per tooth of 0.012 inch. In the southern pine region, saw diameters of 60 to 96 inches are more common.

Cutoff saws for rough trimmers.—These crosscutting saws are used to trim green lumber to length. They may be mounted above or below the workpiece and arranged to either counter-saw or climb-saw. Typically the rake angle is 0° and the clearance angle 45°. Face bevel should not exceed top bevel and is commonly 12 to 15° (fig. 19–79). The face bevel should not extend into the gullet. Teeth are spring-set; a set of 2½ BWG gauges to each side of the saw is common. Table 19–32 shows common specifications.

A typical sawmill trimmer chain might travel at 70 f.p.m., which, with a 24-inch, 70-tooth saw rotating at 1,915 r.p.m., would produce a rim speed of 12,000 f.p.m. and a feed per tooth of 0.063 inch.

Smooth-trim saws.—Dry planed southern pine boards and dimension

Figure 19–78.—A 108-inch log cutoff saw. Hydraulic clamps hold log on each side of cut. Saw motor is 75 hp. For southern pine 60- to 96-inch saws are more common. (Photo from Sumner Iron Works, A Division of the Black Clawson Company.)

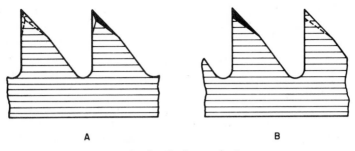

Figure 19–79.—Tooth styles for rough-trimmer saws.

lumber are ordinarily given an extremely smooth end-trim by a hollow-ground saw; this prepares the board end for printing of the mill mark and perhaps waxing to inhibit moisture pickup. Down-milling (climb-sawing) is commonly employed; rim speed is usually 20,000 f.p.m. or higher. On dry lumber, tooth pitch is approximately ⅝-inch and tooth height is

TABLE 19–31.—*Specifications for log cutoff saws*
(Koch 1964b, p. 261)

Diameter (inches)	Gauge	Number of teeth
	BWG	
60	6	96
62	6	100
64	6	104
66	5	108
96	4	158
108	3	164

TABLE 19–32.—*Specifications for rough-trimmer saws* (Koch 1964b, p. 263)

Diameter (inches)	Gauge	Number of teeth	Diameter	Gauge	Number of teeth
	BWG		*Inches*	*BWG*	
6	18	100	24	10–11	70
8	18	100	26	10	70
10	16	100–150	28	10	70
12	12–14	70–150	30	9–10	70
14	12–14	60–150	32	10	70
16	12–14	60–150	34	9	70
18	10–13	60–100	36	8–9	70–80
20	10–13	70–80	38	8	80
22	10–12	70	40	6–7	80

$\frac{7}{16}$-inch (fig. 19–80). Saws are hollow ground to reduce the plate thickness 4 to 5 gauges in an area concentric to the rim (table 19–33). The 45° face bevel, lack of set, high rim speed, and numerous teeth result in smoothly machined kerf walls.

Figure 19–81 illustrates a machine using smooth-trim saws to trim kiln-dry pine. The single operator at the control console in the foreground automatically loads the lugs, double-end trims each board to its longest possible even length (or trims back for grade, or permits the board to pass without trimming), imprints both ends of the random-length boards with one of two different brands, waxes the ends of the boards,

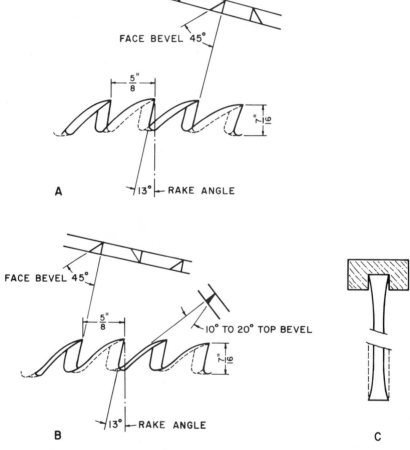

Figure 19–80.—Tooth styles for hollow-ground, smooth-trim saws. (A) Round-back tooth (approximately 45° top bevel). (B) Skew-back tooth (10° to 20° top bevel); this configuration gives more strength to the point of the tooth and is an exception to the rule of equally dividing face and top bevel. (C) Hollow-ground saw plate gives clearance to cutting corners. (Drawings after Peter Koch 1964b, pp. 247, 264, WOOD MACHINING PROCESSES, Copyright © 1964, The Ronald Press Company, New York.)

Figure 19–81.—Double-end smooth trim saw for random-length lumber. (Photo from Irving-ton Machine Works.)

and finally delivers them to one of two different levels for subsequent stacking. He can instantaneously control feed speeds from creeping to approximately 200 f.p.m. The automatic lug-loading device keeps pace with the feed chain, as do the double-end printing and takeaway devices behind the machine. One board per second is easily trimmed by this system.

Typically, the 5-hp. feed motor might drive the feed chains at 120 f.p.m. while trimming 1-inch, kiln-dry, planed pine boards. The saw arbors are individually driven by 7½-hp., arbor-mounted motors to give a spindle speed of 3,600 r.p.m. The 22-inch, 140-tooth, 6–11–6 gauge, hollow-ground saws operate at a rim speed of 20,700 f.p.m. The saw collars are 7 inches in diameter. At this feed speed, the trimmed end produced is smooth

TABLE 19–33.—*Hollow-ground smooth-trim saws for power trimming kiln-dried southern pine*

Diameter (inches)	Gauge	Number of teeth
	BWG	
18	8–12–8	100
20	8–12–8	120
22	6–11–6	140
24	6–10–6	140

enough to permit the longitudinal resin canals to be readily observed without magnification. In some installations of this type, the 0- and 16-foot saw are equipped with carbide-tipped teeth inasmuch as they are most frequently in the cut. Carbide saws for this purpose have the following specifications:

Diameter	20 or 22 inches
Number of teeth	120
Tooth style	25° alternate top bevel and 15° alternate face bevel
Saw gauge	9-gauge plate; 0.200-inch kerf

CHAINSAWING

While chainsaws are widely used to fell and crosscut southern pine trees, there are no published, quantitative cutting data specific to southern pine. In crosscutting applications, the cutting action most nearly approaches orthogonal cutting perpendicular to the grain with cutting edge parallel to the grain (90–0 direction); the cutting action is complicated because kerf boundaries are established by cutting (90–90 mode) in the planes of the kerf walls simultaneously with advance of the cutting edge (figs. 19–82, 19–83).

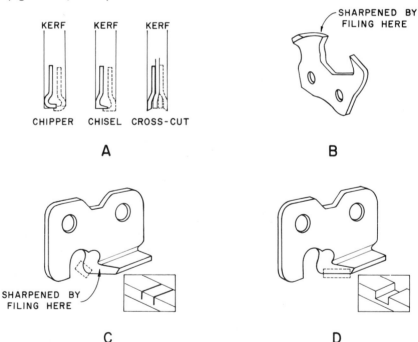

Figure 19–82.—Chain saw teeth. (A) Three types of chain saw teeth. (B) Saw tooth, intermediate between chipper and chisel type that can be sharpened on the back with a flat file. (C) Chipper-type chain; inset indicates that the corner cuts kerf boundary. (D) Chipper-type chain; inset indicates that the cutting edge lifts out the chip. (Drawings after Penberthy 1968.)

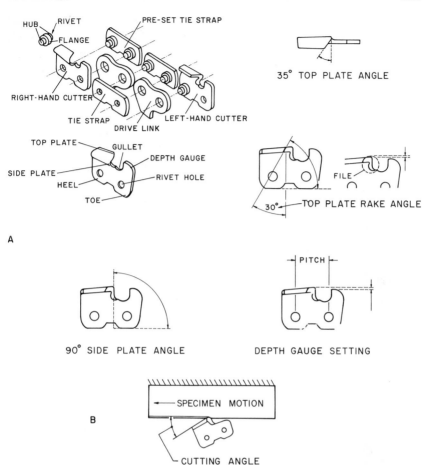

Gambrell and Byars (1966) reported data collected while chainsawing green red oak (*Quercus rubra* L.). In the range of cutting speeds from 500 to 3,640 f.p.m. in cuts from 0.010 to 0.060 inch deep, cutting forces in the three principal directions increased appreciably with increased depth of cut and decreased slightly with increased cutting speed; energy consumption was relatively independent of cutting angle (fig. 19–83B). Reynolds et al. (1970) developed relationships that predict power requirements of cutting chains; saw and engine designers should find the information useful.

Most southern pine is cut with one-man saws of less than 6 hp. that carry teeth similar to those illustrated in figure 19–82BCD. These one-man saws may have straight bars 14 to 16 inches long, or they may be equipped with curved rims or bows. The bowsaw is used primarily when bucking small roundwood on the ground. The bow enables the operator to make plunging cuts and thus avoid stooping unnecessarily; because of its narrow rim, it is pinched less in such cuts than a saw equipped with a straight bar. The trend is toward shorter bars and higher chain speeds. Factors determining chain selection include the following.

Saw chains are primarily classified according to the distance, or pitch, between articulations. Large-pitch chains $\frac{1}{2}$- to $\frac{7}{8}$-inch between articulations) are stronger because individual links, pins, and cutters are heavier. They carry longer, wider cutters that produce a wider kerf, take bigger chips, and require more power, but have a longer service life. Since there is more space between individual cutting edges they are less suited for removing small limbs or cutting small trees than chains of smaller pitch.

Small-pitch chains (less than $\frac{1}{2}$-inch between articulations) operate better on direct-drive saws because at their high chain speed (2,400 to 3,800 f.p.m.) the lighter links, smaller kerf, and lighter feed per tooth minimize shock load on the engine and pounding on bar entry, rails, and sprockets. Only small-pitch chains, whether direct-drive or gear-drive, are satisfactory on low-horsepower saws.

Medium- to large-pitch chains are more suitable for the slower chain speeds of gear-drive saws (800 to 2,000 f.p.m.), where the greater weight of the links has less adverse effects on the mechanism and power is adequate for heavier feeds per tooth. Specific cutting energy is lower with thick chips than with thin chips.

Tree-length logging of small trees is now common; equipment has been developed to cut whole truckloads of pine to shorter lengths suitable for the drum barker, i.e., 5 to 8 feet (fig. 19–84). The $1\frac{3}{16}$-inch-pitch chain of the saw illustrated is driven by a 25-hp. motor at 1,600 f.p.m. It cuts through loads up to 8.5 by 8.5 feet, controlled by a 10-hp. electric-hydraulic feed mechanism. Capacity is 30 to 45 cords per hour of 5-foot wood, and up to 60 cords per hour of 8-foot wood.

19–8 PLANING AND MOULDING

Peripheral-milling cutterheads (section 19–4) are used in jointers and shapers as well as in planers and moulders. Only planing and moulding will be described here. Readers desiring information on jointers and shapers will find it in chapter 7 of Koch (1964b).

PLANING

The peripheral milling of lumber to smooth one or more surfaces with simultaneous sizing to some predetermined thickness, width, or profile pattern is defined as **planing.** Normally, planing cutterheads, often called **cylinders,** cut in the up-milling direction (fig. 19–29).

Single surfacer.—This most elementary planer smooths one side of a

Figure 19–84.—Chain saw designed to reduce tree-length wood to lengths suitable for the drum barker. (Photo from Currie Chain Saw Company.)

board while removing enough wood to reduce it to a predetermined thickness (fig. 19–85). The depth of cut that must be removed to smoothly plane a flat board is determined by the roughness of the sawn surface. Malcolm et al. (1961), in studies of feed per tooth on southern pine, found that eliminating all tooth marks and tear-out required the cutter-head to remove $\frac{3}{32}$-inch if the lumber has been sawn with a feed per tooth of $\frac{1}{8}$-inch, $\frac{5}{32}$-inch if the feed per tooth is $\frac{1}{4}$-inch, and $\frac{8}{32}$-inch if feed per tooth is $\frac{1}{3}$-inch (fig. 19–61).

All industrial planers are power-fed to maintain uniformity of feed rate, reduce breakage, and avoid stoppages that cause burns from cutterheads and skidding rolls. Effectiveness of the feed is improved if both top and bottom rolls are power driven, and if the rolls are large in diameter, corrugated, and mounted in multiples—that is, two pairs of infeeding rolls are more effective than one pair. Ordinarily, the top and bottom rolls are both solid. If, however, the lumber is very uneven in thickness, or

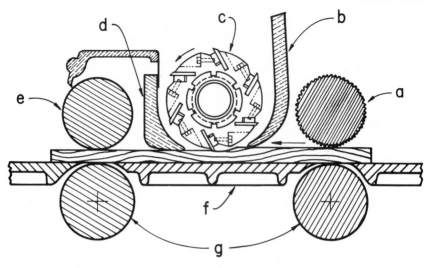

Figure 19–85.—Single surfacer. a, corrugated top infeed roll; b, chipbreaker; c, cutterhead; d, pressure bar; e, top outfeed roll; f, lower platen; g, bottom feed rolls.

if it is fed in multiples across the width of the machine, the top roll may carry independent narrow sections mounted on a common arbor but spring-supported on an internal arbor; in this way each section can yield as much as ¾-inch independently. To attain positive feed of rough or wet lumber, the bottom infeed roll should be corrugated and set a fraction of an inch above the platen; with dry, smooth, flat lumber the infeed roll should be smooth and raised barely above the platen.

In all planers a **chipbreaker** precedes the cutterhead (fig. 19–86). It holds the lumber firmly against the opposite **platen** limiting the cut to yield an accurate board thickness. Pressure of the tips of properly designed chipbreaker shoes helps reduce advance splitting (fig. 19–41A), permitting knives with higher rake angles and accompanying lower power consumption. The front face directs chips into the shavings collector pipe. Chipbreakers also minimize gouged ends or **snipes** when board-ends enter or leave the cutting zone out of control. In cruder designs the chipbreaker is simply a weighted bar resting on the lumber. In more sophisticated machines the bar is divided into counterbalanced hinged sections, permitting each chipbreaker tip to hug the cutting circle as it rises and falls with varying stock thickness; shoes also rock to follow the longitudinal undulations of the lumber. On very fast planers, pressure on the individual shoes may be regulated by air cylinders to suit lumber conditions. This arrangement also permits remote control of pressure and quick lifting of the chipbreaker assembly in the event of a breakup.

Rotating cutterheads in planing machines may be as short as 4 inches or as long as 48 inches (and even longer for timber sizers) depending on the work to be done. Usual width is 15 inches for southern pine lumber. Cutterhead diameter depends on the number of knives to be fitted into

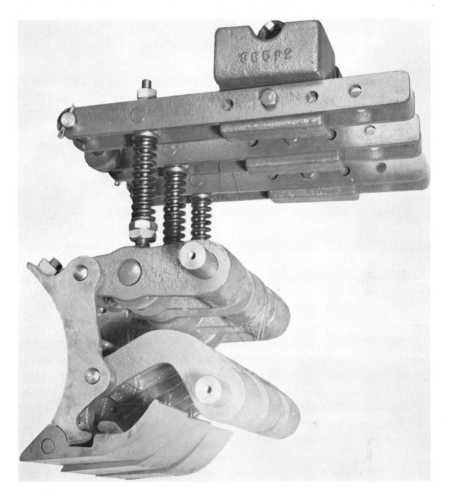

Figure 19–86.—Sectional rocking-nose chipbreaker. (Photo from Stetson-Ross.)

the cutting circle. The 8- to 16-knife planers commonly used on southern pine require cutting circles from 9 to 12 inches in diameter. As explained in section 19–4, the number of knife marks per inch substantially defines the quality of a planed surface (table 19–34 and equation 19–12). Large cutting circles improve surface quality (equation 19–13); however, the desirability of compact planer designs and inability to handle lumber flowing at speeds much above 1,000 f.p.m. have, so far, limited cutter-head diameters to about 12 inches.

A **pressure bar** behind the cutterhead is common to all planers (fig. 19–85). The lower surface of this bar is adjusted parallel to the opposite platen and tangent to the cutting circle. It holds the lumber down as it passes through and leaves the cutting zone. Some designs feature a quick-release mechanism to assist in clearing jams or breakups in the machine.

Depending on the machine design, the opening between cutterhead and lower platen is set to yield the desired board thickness by adjusting either the cutterhead or the lower platen.

Double surfacer.—A double surfacer smooths both sides of a board and simultaneously reduces it to a predetermined finished thickness. The arrangement shown in figure 19–87A is used on southern pine virtually to the exclusion of other systems in spite of its obvious shortcomings. The board is forced against the lower bed first, and the top cylinder removes the excess thickness, if any, to finish the top. The lower cylinder then takes a fixed cut from the lower side of the lumber regardless of whether the top has been surfaced or not. If the board is too thin to be surfaced on the top, it will be made still thinner by the cut from the lower cylinder. The top cylinder machines the top of the lumber while the lumber is still rough on the bottom. With this arrangement, boards are usually fed best-face-down.

The arrangement in figure 19–87B is used on facing planers, where it is desirable to plane off some degree of cup and twist. Because of the yielding hold-down device over the bottom cutterhead, however, it is not used on production planers where a good surface must be established in one pass through the machine; sudden excessive forces normal to the surface moving the board away from the cutterhead leave the surface uneven.

Although expensive, the arrangement in figure 19–87C has much to recommend it. Lumber is fed face up. The bottom cylinder cuts first, with the workpiece forced upward against the rigid top platen, cutting it to final thickness plus the thickness necessary for surfacing the top face. Thus, a varying cut is taken on the back of the workpiece by the bottom cylinder while it cuts against the solid overplate. Thus the board is, in effect, measured for thickness by the bottom head, and the excess is removed from the back or the low-grade side. If the stock is too thin to allow for planing fully on both sides, only a light cut, or no cut, will be removed from the back. After the lumber passes the bottom cylinder, it is flexed or pressed downward by the top chipbreakers and accurately thicknessed by the top cylinder. Thus a measured and predetermined cut is taken from the face of the board. The face surfacing is accomplished against a previously surfaced back. A rough board that is less than the desired thickness will emerge from this planer still rough on both sides.

The arrangement shown in figure 19–87C can, in some plants, be advantageously used to double-surface southern pine lumber at very high speeds before (or after) it is kiln-dried; the resulting smooth, uniformly-thick lumber can then be accurately planed to final pattern and width on conventional planers (fig. 19–87A). By this method mills need inventory only a few sizes of accurately-graded S4S boards; from these few, a multiplicity of patterns can be run quickly on order.

Conventional double surfacers (fig. 19–87A) for furniture plants and

TABLE 19–34.—*Relationship of planer feed rate and number of knives to knife cuts per inch; spindle speed 3,450 r.p.m.*

| Lineal feed rate (f.p.m.) | Number of knives in cutterhead[1] | | | | | | | | | |
	1	2	4	6	8	10	12	14	16	18	20
					Knife marks per inch						
10	28.8										
15	19.2										
20	14.4	28.8									
25	11.5	23.0									
30	9.6	19.2									
35	8.2	16.4									
40	7.2	14.4	28.8								
45	6.4	12.8	25.6								
50	5.8	11.5	23.0								
60	4.8	9.6	19.2	28.8							
70	4.1	8.2	16.4	24.6							
80		7.2	14.4	21.6	28.8						
90		6.4	12.8	19.2	25.6						
100		5.8	11.5	17.3	23.0	28.8					
110		5.2	10.5	15.7	20.9	26.1					
120		4.8	9.6	14.4	19.2	24.0	28.8				
130		4.4	8.8	13.3	17.7	22.1	26.5				
140		4.1	8.2	12.3	16.4	20.5	24.6	28.8			
150			7.7	11.5	15.3	19.2	23.0	26.8			
160			7.2	10.8	14.4	18.0	21.6	25.2	28.8		
170			6.8	10.1	13.5	16.9	20.3	23.7	27.1		
180			6.4	9.6	12.8	16.0	19.2	22.4	25.6	28.8	
190			6.1	9.1	12.1	15.1	18.2	21.2	24.2	27.2	
200			5.8	8.6	11.5	14.4	17.3	20.1	23.0	25.9	28.8
220			5.2	7.8	10.5	13.1	15.7	18.3	20.9	23.5	26.1
240			4.8	7.2	9.6	12.0	14.4	16.8	19.2	21.6	24.0
260			4.4	6.6	8.8	11.1	13.3	15.5	17.7	19.9	22.1
280			4.1	6.2	8.2	10.3	12.3	14.4	16.4	18.5	20.5
300				5.8	7.7	9.6	11.5	13.4	15.3	17.3	19.2
325				5.3	7.1	8.8	10.6	12.4	14.2	15.9	17.7
350				4.9	6.6	8.2	9.9	11.5	13.1	14.8	16.4
375				4.6	6.1	7.7	9.2	10.7	12.3	13.8	15.3
400				4.3	5.8	7.2	8.6	10.1	11.5	12.9	14.4
425				4.1	5.4	6.8	8.1	9.5	10.8	12.2	13.5
450					5.1	6.4	7.7	8.9	10.2	11.5	12.8
475					4.8	6.1	7.3	8.5	9.7	10.9	12.1
500					4.6	5.8	6.9	8.1	9.2	10.4	11.5
550					4.2	5.2	6.3	7.3	8.4	9.4	10.5
600						4.8	5.8	6.7	7.7	8.6	9.6
700						4.1	4.9	5.8	6.6	7.4	8.2
800							4.3	5.0	5.8	6.5	7.2
900								4.5	5.1	5.8	6.4
1,000								4.0	4.6	5.2	5.8
1,100									4.2	4.7	5.2
1,200										4.3	4.8
1,300										4.0	4.4
1,400											4.1

[1] Assumes knives are jointed.

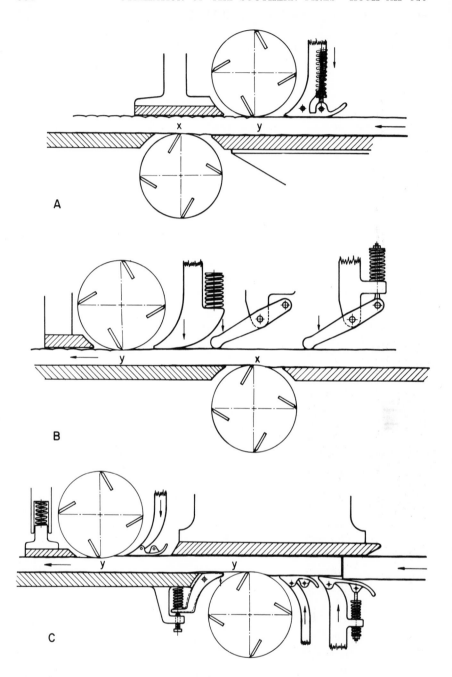

Figure 19–87.—Cutterhead arrangements for double surfacers; x indicates cuts of fixed depth, and y indicates cuts to controlled thickness. (A) Conventional double surfacer. (B) Facing head followed by thicknessing head. (C) Two-way thicknessing planer. If lumber has portions where thickness allowance for planing is scant, arrangements (A) and (B) will yield rough surfaces on upper side. (Drawings after Koch 1948.)

other woodworking plants are available in widths up to 50 inches and with feed roll diameters up to 6 inches. Feed and cutterhead horsepower are related to the number of knives in the head (seldom more than 6), class of work involved, width of machine and feed speed desired. Generally speaking, the top cylinder carries less than 40 hp., the bottom cylinder less than 20 hp., and the feed less than 15 hp. Feed speeds are generally below 125 f.p.m.

Figure 19–88 illustrates a specialized type of double surfacer that has been designed for the increasingly important timber laminating industry. The four-knife jointed cylinders are V-belt driven at 2,200 r.p.m. The machine has 50 hp. on the top and 50 hp. on the bottom cylinder. The two bottom infeed rolls and the single top infeed roll are all 12⅝ inches in diameter and are driven by a 15-hp. feed motor to yield a feed speed of approximately 50 to 75 f.p.m. The cutterhead arrangement on this design is that shown in figure 19–87B; the weight of the beam is sufficient to keep it from being thrust from the bottom head. The bottom platen preceding the lower cutterhead can be adjusted to permit removal of as much as ¾-inch from the lower surface of the beam.

Planer and matcher.—A planer and matcher is a double surfacer equipped with two opposed sideheads that can simultaneously machine both edges of a board. The machine usually has two additional horizontal spindles carrying **profile heads** to machine patterns on the top and/or bottom of the lumber. Profile heads may also be used to smoothly rip wide dimen-

Figure 19–88.—Outfeed end of three-roll 24- by 78-inch double surfacer to size laminated beams. (Photo from Stetson-Ross.)

sion lumber into planed 2 by 4's with eased edges; Macomber (1969) has given a description of the technique.

Figure 19–89 illustrates a six-head machine; each cutterhead carries 12 jointed knives. The cylinders (arrangement of 19–87A) are shown surfacing top and bottom, the opposed sideheads are cutting a shiplap pattern on both edges, and the top profile head is cutting a drop-siding pattern. The bottom profiler is idle and not visible. To mill southern pine, most planers and matchers have cylinders 15 inches long and can carry sideheads to machine timbers 6 or 8 inches thick. Proportions of machines suitable for southern pine are given in table 19–35.

Figure 19–90 shows a 16-knife planer and matcher with double profiler and an extra down-milling outside sidehead at the infeed end to remove excess lumber as pulp chips. Not shown, but widely used, is an inside sidehead at the infeed end that joints or planes the horns of incoming crooked lumber; the planed board emerges with much less crook. Some designs of these **crook reducers** have two cutterheads—both on the guide side and both down-milling—between feed table and planer proper.

For a discussion of handling equipment to get lumber into and away from the planer at high speed, the reader is referred to Koch (1951).

Timber sizers are similar to planers and matchers in having cylinders and sideheads (but not profilers) arranged as in figures 19–87A and 19–89. Normally they have one pair of infeeding and one pair of outfeeding rolls. Sizers are made to admit timbers 24 inches thick and 36 inches wide. Current motorized designs are fast and versatile; they can not only plane timbers (at slow speed) but can close down and run 2 by 4's at speeds to 500 f.p.m.

For descriptions of knife styles and sharpening techniques, see Koch (1964b, p. 303–318).

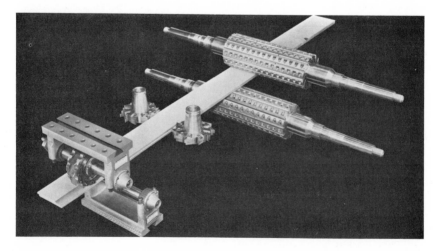

Figure 19–89.—Cutterhead arrangement of planer and matcher with double profilers. No cutterhead is mounted on lower profile spindle. (Photo from Stetson-Ross.)

Figure 19–90.—A 16-knife planer and matcher with double profiler. In addition to the six customary cutterheads, the machine has a seventh cutterhead—a down-milling outside sidehead at the infeed end to size overwidth boards by cutting pulp chips from the excess width. Not shown is an eighth cutterhead—an inside sidehead placed at the infeed end to straighten lumber by planing off the horns of boards with crook. (Photo from Stetson-Ross.)

TABLE 19–35.—*Typical proportions of six-head planers and matchers with double profilers* (Data from Koch 1964b, p. 301)[1 2 3]

	Number of jointed knives per cutterhead			
	8 or 10	12	14	16
Cutting-circle diameter, inches____	9	9⅜	10	11
Feed-roll diameter, inches_____	10	12	14	16
Maximum feed speed, f.p.m._____	350	500	750	1000
Horsepower:				
Feed table (variable speed)_____	15	20	25	30
Planer feed (variable speed)____	25	40	50	60
Top cylinder_____	50	80	130	150
Bottom cylinder_____	25	40	65	75
Outside sidehead_____	25	40	65	65
Inside sidehead_____	15	25	25	40
Top profile head_____	25	40	65	75
Bottom profile head_____	15	25	25	40

[1] The usual machine for southern pine will accept lumber 15 inches wide and 6 or 8 inches thick; 25-inch-wide machines are available.

[2] Planers and matchers usually have six powered rolls; i.e., two pair infeeding and one pair outfeeding.

[3] For southern pine, rake angles of 20 to 30° are commonly used; some profile knives for dry lumber have 15° rake angles.

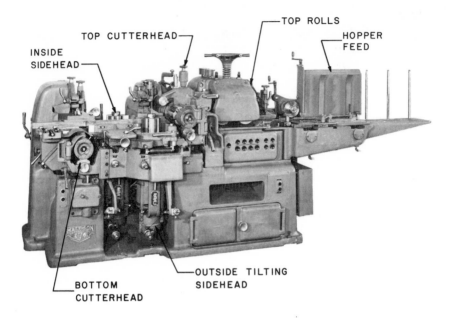

Figure 19–91.—A 6-inch, four-head moulder. Cutterheads can run jointed at 3,600 r.p.m. or unjointed at 6,000 or 7,200 r.p.m. Hopper feed is at infeed end. (Photo from Mattison Machine Works.)

MOULDING

The purpose of the moulder is to machine complex shapes on the surfaces or edges of long or short lumber. Moulding, like planing, is a peripheral milling process. A simple moulder has a top cutterhead followed by two sideheads followed by a bottom cutterhead (fig. 19–91). Instead of being directly opposed as in a planer and matcher, moulder sideheads are staggered to permit their spindle-mounted motors to clear each other when the spindles are tilted. Tilting sideheads permit angled saw cuts and varied bevels on the edges of the workpiece without changing knives. While the moulder can machine a very broad range of shapes, it cannot make tongue and groove flooring as accurately as a planer and matcher because the staggered sideheads do not rigidly control the workpiece width.

Productive capacity.—Characteristically moulders are designed for relatively short runs of any pattern. In some plants as many as 20 different shapes may be run in a day. In others the moulder setup may be unchanged for several days. The productivity of a moulder may be expressed by the following formula:

$$P = V(60T - CX)(Y)(K) \qquad (19\text{--}42)$$

where:

P = lineal footage of mouldings produced per shift

V = feed speed, feet per minute

T = length of shift, hours

C = idle machine time due to each pattern change, minutes

X = number of pattern changes per shift

Y = pattern multiples

K = continuity of feed, percent efficiency expressed as a decimal fraction. This factor must include all nonmachining time due to all causes other than pattern change.

From this expression it can be seen that quick pattern change is important. If, for example, eight different patterns were required during an 8-hour shift, and each pattern change took 60 minutes, the resulting production would be zero. Production is directly proportional to feed rate, which is in turn dictated by the desired surface quality as expressed in knife marks per inch.

There are two ways to increase the lineal rate of feed without reducing surface quality (16 to 30 knifemarks per inch for most mouldings):

- Increasing the cutterhead spindle speed
- Increasing the number of jointed knives in the cutterhead.

Of the several synchronous spindle speeds in common use, i.e., 3,600 r.p.m., 6,000 r.p.m., and 7,200 r.p.m., none but the 3600-r.p.m. speed can be consistently jointed. For this reason moulders with spindle speeds of 6,000 or 7,200 r.p.m. are limited to single-knife operation, that is, one cutting knife and one balancing knife per head. On the other hand, the feeding rate of moulders equipped with spindles operating at 3,600 r.p.m. may be increased in direct proportion to the number of jointed knives in each cutterhead. To maintain 20 knife marks per inch, a 7,200-r.p.m., one-knife machine must feed at 30 f.p.m., while a 3,600-r.p.m. machine with six jointed knives in each cutterhead can feed at 90 f.p.m.

Machine types.—The controls of many machines are so designed that synchronous spindle speeds can be selected at 3,600, 6,000, or 7,200 r.p.m. This arrangement permits one-knife operation at high spindle speed on short runs of nonstandard patterns as well as multiknife, 3,600-r.p.m. operation with jointed knives at high feed speeds on long runs of standard patterns.

In the cutterhead arrangement most frequently used on a four-head moulder, the top cutterhead cuts first and the bottom one last. Since the sides are machined while the bottom of the workpiece is still rough, pattern registration on the edges may not be accurate. Prior surfacing would, of course, eliminate this difficulty. The usual five-head arrangement places a second top head between the sideheads and the final bottom head. Designs are also available in which the fifth head cuts first and is on the bottom in order to smooth the bottom surface of the stock as an initial machining step. Six-head machines are available also.

Moulders are commonly equipped with two pairs of power-driven infeeding rolls, or with two top infeeding rolls over a lower endless bed. Figure 19–91 illustrates a machine with two 6-inch-diameter, corrugated, sectional, top infeed rolls and a bottom endless bed, all powered by a 5-hp., two-speed motor. Moulders do not have outfeed rolls. A hopper feeding device permits feeding short stock at speeds above 50 f.p.m. (fig. 19–91).

Moulders are made in 4-, 6-, 8-, 10-, and 12-inch widths and usually accept a workpiece up to 4 inches thick. Cutting circles range in diameter from 5 to 9 inches. Sideheads are provided with as much as 45° inward tilt and 15° outward. Cutterhead power depends entirely on the class of work to be done. The 6-inch moulder illustrated in figure 19–91 carries $7\frac{1}{2}$ hp. on the top and bottom heads, and 5 hp. on each sidehead.

19–9 MACHINING WITH COATED ABRASIVES

Wood panels are sanded to flatten and smooth their surfaces and, in some cases, to reduce their thickness to the desired dimension. While southern pine lumber is infrequently sanded, an important percentage of southern pine plywood—and virtually all particleboard—is smoothed and thicknessed on wide-belt sanders. A detailed discussion of machining with coated abrasives is available (Koch 1964b, chapter 11).

Panel sanding machines are usually double deck, that is, they simultaneously machine both top and bottom of the panel in one pass. Feed speeds range up to about 200 f.p.m. The coated abrasive belts are commonly 50 to 53, 63, or 67 inches wide. Belts 103 or 142 inches long are widely used. Most machines have four heads, and six heads are not uncommon; half the heads cut on the top and half on the bottom (fig. 19–92).

The **primary** heads, i.e., the first top and first bottom heads, do the major cutting job. Cuts of 0.03 inch per primary head on plywood and 0.04 inch on particleboard are common, but on neither should they exceed 0.1 inch. Belts are expected to last 50 to 60 hours, with 80 to 100 hours of machining not unusual (Stevens 1966). The steel **contact roll** (fig. 19–92) on each primary head has a diamond pattern of serrations. **Secondary** or finishing heads have steel contact rolls in which spiral serrations are milled.

Belt speeds of 5,000 to 6,750 f.p.m. are common. Belts are assembled with a skived splice $\frac{3}{8}$-inch wide made at an angle to the length of the belt. Cloth backing for the abrasive is the toughest possible x-weight drill, woven from long staple cotton and internally filled to increase wear resistance and stiffness. A thin film of urethane polymer on the inside of belts for primary heads may increase life of belts and rolls, but on secondary heads tends to strip the graphite covers from smoothing bars (Stevens 1966).

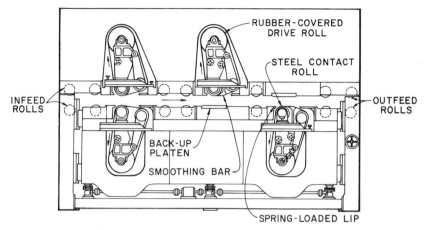

Figure 19–92.—Four-head panel sander for finishing plywood or particleboard. Abrasive belts travel counter to direction of panel feed. For maximum stock removal the first two heads are opposed; the next pair of top and bottom heads are staggered and provided with smoothing bars to yield a smooth surface. On a 53-inch-wide machine capable of feed speeds to 200 f.p.m. each sander head carries 125 hp. A total of 25 hp. drives the feed rolls; the top seven rolls are driven independently of the bottom. (Drawing from Tidland Machine Co.)

Silicon carbide, the hardest and sharpest of man-made abrasives, is most commonly used for primary heads on southern pine plywood and particleboard (Stevens 1966); Ferguson (1968), however, states that for rapid wood removal (deep cuts) aluminum oxide is best. Coarse grits (24, 36, or 40) are most effective. Secondary heads for either plywood or particleboard commonly use silicon carbide in grits from 80 through 120 (Stevens 1966).

The abrasive grains are bonded to primary belts with phenolic resin in both the underlying **make coat** and the later applied **size coat** (fig. 19–93). **Open-coat** construction—that is, with abrasive grains spaced apart—is preferred for sanding the somewhat resinous southern pines. The closed-coat belts are heavy and stiff and afford a maximum number of cutting points, but they have a tendency to load up.

R. Birkeland of the National Institute of Technology in Oslo, Norway has proposed (in a patent application) that abrasive grains should be placed in the "make coat" in such a manner that their cutting tips fall on a common plane; he would accomplish this either by classifying the abrasive particles by length as well as screen size, or by imbedding the particles at variable depths in the "make coat." By this means, he has found that coarse grits can be made to cut surfaces that are substantially smoother than surfaces made by commercial papers of the same grit (fig. 19–93 Bottom). For a greatly enlarged view of a conventionally sanded surface see fig. 25–7.

The performance of sanding heads can be measured in terms of the quality of the surface produced, the power required, and the amount of

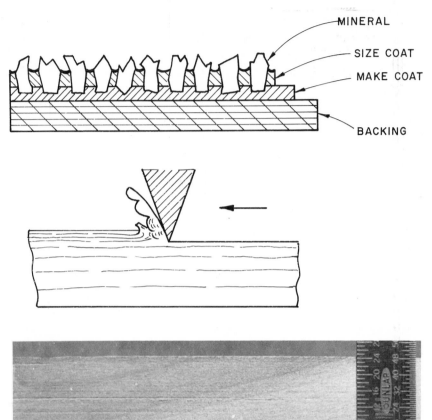

MINERAL

SIZE COAT

MAKE COAT

BACKING

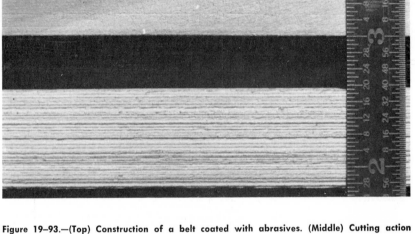

Figure 19–93.—(Top) Construction of a belt coated with abrasives. (Middle) Cutting action of an abrasive particle. (Bottom) Surfaces on dry (7-percent moisture content) yellow poplar produced with 36-grit, aluminum oxide, open-coat paper. The rougher of the two surfaces was made with commercial paper in which the mineral was imbedded on the backing without regard to the location of the cutting points; the smooth surface was made with the same grit carefully arranged so that the cutting points were all in a common plane. (Photo from R. Birkland.)

wood removed. All of these factors are time related—that is, as the belt wears, surface quality deteriorates, power rises, and wood removal slows. Factors affecting performance include grit size, belt pressure and velocity, depth of cut and feed speed, direction of feed, running time, and wood factors. To establish meaningful relationships specific to southern pine, a factorial experiment is required; to date no such comprehensive data are published. Available data are presented in the following paragraphs.

GRIT SIZE

Coarse grits (compared to fine) produce rougher surfaces, remove more wood per unit of time (Pahlitzsch and Dziobek 1959, 1961) and cause a greater temperature rise at the surface (Franz and Hinken 1954).

BELT PRESSURE AND VELOCITY

Increased pressure of the belt against the workpiece increases rate of wood removal (Franz and Hinken 1954; Hayashi and Hara 1964; Pahlitzsch and Dziobek 1959) and increases workpiece temperature (Franz and Hinken 1954; Pahlitzsch and Dziobek 1961). Power consumed by the belt is also proportional to the force applied by the contact roll to the machined surface (Nakamura 1966).

In a comparison of smooth and corrugated contact rolls, Holland (1966) found that rolls with narrow bands separated by open grooves gave the fastest wood removal, lowest belt temperature, and least belt clogging.

Belt velocity is positively correlated with rate of wood removal (Franz and Hinken 1954; Hayashi and Hara 1964; Nakamura 1966). According to Ward (1963) high belt speeds yield a smoother surface and consume less energy per unit volume of wood removed than low speeds. Belt velocity is, however, positively correlated with power consumed by the belt (Nakamura 1966). Temperature of the workpiece is positively correlated with belt velocity (Franz and Hinken 1954; Pahlitzsch and Dziobek 1961). According to Pahlitzsch and Dziobek (1959), the optimum belt speed—for maximum rate of wood removal on a modified stroke sander—is 5,850 f.p.m. for grit size 60 and slightly less for grit 120; there is some doubt that this conclusion is equally applicable to a wide-belt sander. Wear on the backing is one practical limit on the belt speed of a wide belt sander.

DEPTH OF CUT AND FEED SPEED

In a study probably applicable to southern pine, Stewart (1970) reported a positive linear correlation between depth of cut and power required for abrasive planing of hard maple (*Acer saccharum* Marsh) parallel to the grain (90–0 mode).

Power demand is positively correlated with feed rate (Ward 1963); Stewart (1970) found that the relationship was linear. According to Seto and Nozaki (1966) and Nakamura (1966), however, the amount of wood removed per unit of time is negatively correlated with feed speed; this appears anomalous, and additional study seems warranted.

DIRECTION OF FEED

According to Ward (1963) and Seto and Nozaki (1966), it is preferable to feed panels against the direction of belt travel.

In an experiment on hard maple—the results of which may be applicable to southern pine plywood—Stewart (1970) found that abrasive planing across the grain (0–90 mode) took 20- to 25-percent less power than parallel to the grain (90–0 mode); surface roughness was about the same for both modes. According to Pahlitzsch and Dziobek (1962), surface roughness is greatest when the angle between fiber axis and sanding direction is 0 to 30°.

The machined surface is smoother if the belt is oscillated (Pahlitzsch and Dziobek 1962). An oscillation of $3/8$-inch amplitude at 20 to 25 cycles per minute is common on wide belt sanders for southern pine. Optimum frequency of oscillation is positively correlated with feed speed.

RUNNING TIME

As the belt dulls with use, the rate of wood removal decreases. The energy consumed per unit volume removed increases as the abrasive gets very dull, even though the rate of power consumption is somewhat reduced (Pahlitzsch and Dziobek 1959, 1961, 1962). Abrasive belts fail not only from dulling but also from broken splices, lengthwise tears originating from punctures caused by debris riding on top of panels, and from edge damage caused when belt tracking controls fail.

WOOD FACTORS

At constant pressure between belt and panel, wood moisture content is positively correlated with rate of wood removal because the grit cuts moist wood more easily than dry wood. Wood is seldom sanded at a moisture content above 15 percent (Franz and Hinken 1954).

It has been reported that energy consumed per unit volume of wood removed is positively correlated with specific gravity (Seto and Nozaki 1966). Despite observable differences among species, no published data afford comparisons of sanding effectiveness between southern pine and other species.

POWER DATA

From the foregoing discussion it is evident that many factors affect the power required by each head on a wide belt sander. Unfortunately, there are no published data specific to southern pine.

From unpublished information on the sanding of particleboard with a belt speed of 6,688 f.p.m. and feed speed of 110 f.p.m. it appears that net belt power is linearly proportional to depth of cut in such a way that doubling the depth of cut more than doubles the power required.

Grit size	Depth of cut	
	0.015 inch	0.045 inch
	Net hp. per inch of belt width	
24	0.5	2.7
36	0.5	2.7
50	1.1	4.6

Unpublished data from another source gives the following information on power required to sand 4-foot-wide southern pine plywood at a feed speed of 80 f.p.m. with a 50-inch belt.

Belt grit	Depth cut	Approximate power on the sander head
	Inch	*Horsepower*
36	0.100	90
50	.050	70
60	.040	60
80	.025	42
100	.010	34
120	.006	23
280	.003	11
320	.002	7

19–10   VENEER CUTTING

The first southern pine plywood plant became operational in December 1963. Other mills soon followed, and by 1967 the annual capacity of the new industry reached 2.6 billion sq. ft., ⅜-inch basis (Guttenberg and Fasick 1968). By January 1, 1968 the 34 plants in operation (or under construction) in the southern pine region comprised about 18 percent of the softwood plywood plants in the United States with a capacity of about one-fifth of the total U.S. production of 13.0 billion sq. ft. (Bryan 1968; Anonymous 1968). The South's share of the plywood industry is still increasing.

This industry uses only rotary-peeled veneer. Although thin vertical-grain sliced southern pine veneer checks less and holds finishes better than rotary-cut veneer and has an attractive appearance, it is little used because it is costly to produce. It appears possible, however, that thick-sliced southern pine (**slicewood**) may become a limited competitor of sawn lumber (Lutz et al. 1962). If this happens, the technique of thick slicing will be of great commercial importance to the southern pine industry.

Veneer peeling and slicing closely approximate orthogonal cutting in the 0–90 mode (sec. 19–2) except that a **nosebar** is used to compress the wood ahead of the cutting edge (figs. 19–94, 19–95). Peeled or sliced veneer has a **loose** side (the side with tension checks—see figs. 19–14 and 19–94DE) and a **tight** side.

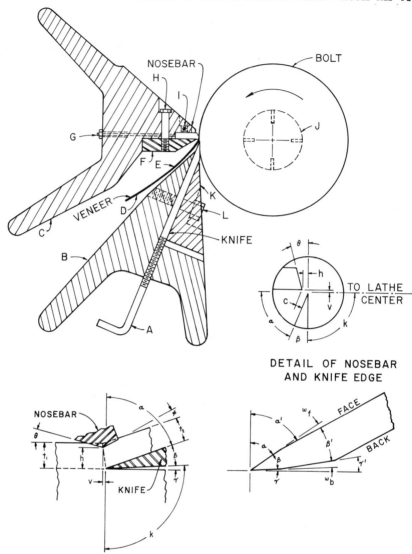

DETAIL OF NOSEBAR
AND KNIFE EDGE

Whether southern pine veneer is peeled or sliced, if the knife is sharp, the surface of latewood veneer differs from that of earlywood. In latewood, the surface is frequently formed by separation of the cells at the middle lamella; in earlywood, cell walls are usually severed cleanly at the cutting plane (fig. 19–96). For reasons not clear, this difference makes it difficult to achieve good latewood-to-latewood bonds (Hse 1968, fig. 4). See also figures 23–7 and 23–8.

NOMENCLATURE

Figure 19–94 illustrates peeling; figure 19–95 shows slicing. In figure 19–94 Bottom, veneer cutting geometry is drawn to correspond to the

←

Figure 19–94.—Nomenclature in veneer cutting. (Top) Cross section of rotary veneer lathe. A, knife adjusting screw; B, knife bar; C, pressure bar; D, loose side of veneer; E, tight side of veneer; F, nosebar cap; G, nosebar adjusting screw (horizontal); H, nosebar locking screw; I, nosebar adjusting screw (vertical); J, chuck; K, knife cap; L, knife cap bolt; Inset, detail of cutting edge and nosebar. (Bottom) Cross sections through cutting edge and solid nosebar arranged in convention of orthogonal cutting diagrams.

α Primary rake angle

α' Secondary rake angle

β Primary sharpness angle

β' Grinding angle, angle of ground bevel

γ Primary clearance angle

γ' Secondary clearance angle

ω_t Face honing angle

ω_b Back honing angle

θ Nosebar compression angle

ϕ Nosebar clearance angle

k Knife angle used in commercial practice ($90°$ plus the clearance angle)

t_1 Depth of cut; undeformed veneer thickness

t_2 Actual veneer thickness

h Horizontal nosebar opening

v Vertical nosebar opening

c Nosebar clearance

when v/h is equal to or less than $\tan(90 - \alpha)$

$$c = [h + v \tan(90 - \alpha)] \cos(90 - \alpha)$$

when v/h is more than $\tan(90 - \alpha)$

$$c = \sqrt{v^2 + h^2}$$

(Drawings after Peter Koch 1964b, pp. 439, 440, WOOD MACHINING PROCESSES, Copyright © 1964, The Ronald Press Company, New York.)

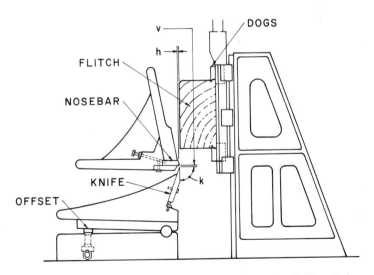

Figure 19–95. Cross section of veneer slicer. Knife is stationary; dogs holding flitch move up and down in vertical (or inclined) guides.

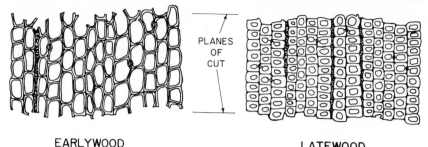

EARLYWOOD   LATEWOOD

Figure 19–96.—Cross sections through earlywood and latewood veneer peeled from southern pine.

terminology and diagrams of section 19–2 (fig. 19–2). Adjustment of the nosebar is sometimes stated in terms of percent nosebar compression:

$$\text{Percent nosebar compression} = \frac{(100)\ (t_1 - c)}{t_1} \qquad (19\text{–}43)$$

The **face** of the knife is the surface in contact with the veneer. (While this is not the terminology used by industry, it conforms to that used in fundamental machining studies.) The **back** of the knife is the ground bevel next to the bolt or flitch.

ROTARY PEELING

The cutting of rotary veneer is affected by the characteristics of the wood, pretreatments to soften the wood, knife angles, placement and shape of the nosebar, and cutting velocity. For a general discussion of veneer cutting, see Koch (1964b, chapter 12).

Wood factors.—Lutz (1956) has shown that in southern pine, with its prominent growth rings, eccentricity of the pith or off-center chucking of the bolt causes rough veneer. Surfaces are smoothest when the knife cuts in the mode shown in figure 19–97A. Veneer cut in the vicinity of knots or curly grain tends to be rough.

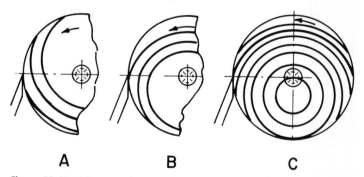

A   B   C

Figure 19–97.—Diagram of annual ring orientation in relation to cutting plane. (A) Favorable. (B) Unfavorable. (C) Combination of unfavorable and favorable. (Drawing after Lutz 1956.)

Fewer knife checks (fig. 19–14) occur in veneer peeled from slow-grown southern pine than from fast-grown. Lutz (1964) concluded that a growth rate that assures two annual rings or more in the thickness of the veneer will reduce warping, shelling, and depth of knife checks.

Moisture content of the wood when peeled affects veneer quality. Peeling southern pine at room temperature, high moisture content (about 110 percent), and high cutting speed (e.g., 300 f.p.m.) results in high loads on the nosebar, thin veneer, and veneer weak in tension perpendicular to the grain when compared to similar pine peeled at similar temperatures and speeds, but at 60-percent moisture content (Lutz et al. 1967).

Pretreatments.—Southern pine veneer bolts are generally heated in steam or hot water to reduce severity of knife checks (Koch 1965) and to soften knots. Veneer cut from heated pine has been reported to yield more uniform glue bonds (Bloomquist 1966). There is evidently a practical upper limit, however; H. H. Haskell (at a southern pine plywood seminar at Meridian, Miss., January 12–13, 1965) stated that bolts heated to temperatures above 180° F. may yield veneer having excessively pitchy surfaces. The pitch is detrimental to glue bond quality.

Knife deflection and nosebar loads decrease with increasing temperature of the wood (Lutz 1967). Temperature did not significantly affect thickness and roughness of veneer peeled from clear wood. Sound, pitchy knots that cut well at 140° F. turned the knife edge when temperature of the wood was dropped to 35° F. Veneer cut at 140° F. or higher had greater strength in tension perpendicular to the grain than that cut at 77° F. or lower. Usable veneer could not be cut from disks at 0° F.

If conditioned in water at 180° F., southern pine bolts, 12, 18, and 24 inches in diameter require heating times of approximately 8, 24, and 46 hours (USDA Forest Products Laboratory 1956).

Storage of southern pine veneer bolts in warm water or under water sprays in warm weather can lead to pronounced bacterial attack on the sapwood, removal of parenchyma, and increased permeability (Lutz et al. 1966); when disks stored for 6 months in warm water were rotary cut, loads on the nosebar were less than loads with matched disks stored at 35° F. Veneer from the disks stored in warm water was thicker and stronger in tension perpendicular to the grain than that cut from disks stored at 35° F.

Knife factors.—When rotary peeling southern pine, clearance angle γ is commonly 0°, i.e., k = 90° (fig. 19–94). Sharpness angle β is commonly 20 or 21°. A carefully sharpened knife requires only 50 to 75 percent of the cutting force of a knife dulled by use; the effect is less pronounced when cutting thick veneers (Leney 1960).

Veneer knives can cut effectively with minute negative clearance angles if the resulting interference is confined to the region immediately adjacent to the cutting edge by means of a **microbevel** (fig. 19–98). Microbevelled

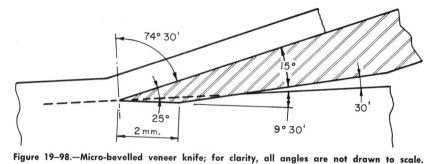

Figure 19–98.—Micro-bevelled veneer knife; for clarity, all angles are not drawn to scale. (Drawing after Peter Koch 1964b, p. 454, WOOD MACHINING PROCESSES, Copyright © 1964, The Ronald Press Company, New York.)

knives have been shown by Leney (1960) to have a number of advantages:

- An increased rake angle can be used thereby reducing the incidence of tension checks.
- A cutting edge with a 25° effective sharpness angle is more durable than one with a lesser angle (fig. 19–98).
- A tendency toward a "wire edge" at the cutting edge is eliminated.
- A short microbevel with $9\frac{1}{2}°$ negative clearance angle appears to depress the wood cells under the microbevel and thus increase the tension on the cells in front of the cutting edge. This effect tends to decrease the amount of compression tearing that would otherwise occur at the cutting edge.
- Force measurements indicate that microbevelling decreases the parallel cutting force, F_p, compared to a knife with the same geometry as figure 19–98 but not microbevelled.
- The normal force exerted on the workpiece by the negative clearance of the microbevel tends to counteract the normal force exerted on the forming chip by the face of the knife so that the net magnitude of the normal force, F_n, approaches zero or is at least reduced.

In the laboratory it has been shown that oscillation of the knife to give it the effect of inclined cutting (see sec. 19–2) reduces power demand and improves the surface of veneer. This feature has been incorporated into veneer lathes. No data specific to southern pine are published, but one firm is peeling Idaho white pine (*Pinus monticola* Dougl.) on an 8-foot lathe with an oscillating knife (1-inch amplitude and 180 cycles per minute) and ⅝-inch roller nosebar. The lathe, so equipped, can cut ⅙-inch veneer at 800 f.p.m.; less lathe power is required and spinouts are fewer than with a fixed knife. The oscillating knife evidently has had no effect on the number and depth of knife checks or on thickness variation in the veneer.

Nosebar.—Several manufacturers of southern pine veneer use lathes with solid nosebars; most of these have single bevels (fig. 19–94, inset), but others have a double bevel (fig. 19–94, Bottom). In more common use are ⅝-inch-diameter roller nosebars. While usually power driven, the roller bar may run idle. Ordinarily it is set to specific horizontal and vertical openings (fig. 19–99) and furnished with a quick-release mechanism so the lathe operator can draw it clear and remove jammed veneer. The roller bar is seated in a backup support along its entire length so that it does not deflect under load. Porter and Sanders (1970) have provided data on hydrostatic lubrication of roller nosebars that should be of interest to machine designers.

Table 19–36 presents optimum nosebar settings for peeling southern pine with a ⅝-inch diameter, idle nosebar in conjunction with a knife having zero clearance angle and 21° sharpness angle; cutting speed was about 20 f.p.m.

The horizontal forces (i.e., those normal to the workpiece) per inch of knife and bar were calculated for these settings (Lutz and Patzer 1966).

Nominal veneer thickness	Force per inch of knife		Force per inch of roller bar	
	Mean	Range	Mean	Range
Inch	– – – – – – – – – *Pounds* – – – – – – – – – –
0.094	45	0–70	105	10–170
.364	80	20–100	170	60–270

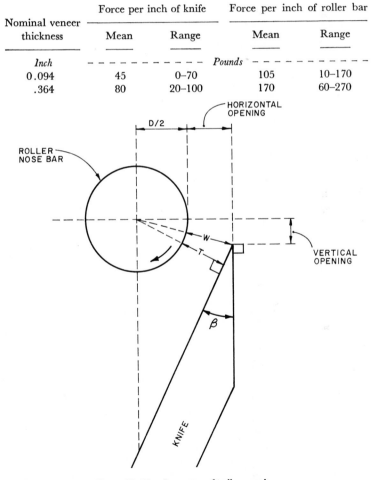

Figure 19–99.—Geometry of roller nosebar.

TABLE 19-36.—*Roller bar openings for southern pine* (after Lutz and Patzer 1966)[1]

Nominal veneer thickness (inch)	Horizontal opening (h)	Vertical opening (v)	W[2]	T[3]
	— — — — — — — — — — Inch — — — — — — — — — — —			
0.094_____	0.084	0.074	0.081	0.075
.364_____	.324	.062	.327	.304

[1] For southern pine of 0.51 specific gravity (green volume-ovendry weight basis) and 16 rings per inch.
[2] Clearance between roller and knife edge (see fig. 19-99).
[3] Clearance between roller and face of knife (see fig. 19-99).

In those mills where a solid nosebar with $15°$ angle (θ in fig. 19-94) is used, the following settings have been found satisfactory (USDA Forest Products Laboratory 1956).

Veneer thickness	Horizontal opening (h)	Vertical opening (v)
— — — — — — — Inch — — — — — — —		
$\frac{1}{8}$	0.110	0.028
$\frac{1}{16}$	.055	.016
$\frac{1}{32}$	.025	.008

On commercial lathes, the nosebar is set rigidly to prescribed vertical and horizontal openings. Following a suggestion by Lutz and Patzer (1966), Feihl and Carroll (1969) studied the practicality of veneer peeling with nosebar pressure applied hydraulically (elastically) instead of by fixing it rigidly in relation to the knife. They found that bolts peeled with an elastically-mounted solid nosebar (fig. 19-94) required about 30 to 40 pounds of force per lineal inch on the bar, with no indication that this force was strongly influenced by species or veneer thickness. When $\frac{1}{10}$- and $\frac{1}{6}$-inch veneer was peeled from red pine, *Pinus resinosa* Ait. (a species fairly comparable to the southern pines), with an elastically mounted, power-driven, roller nosebar, optimum veneer quality was achieved with a force of 50 to 60 pounds per lineal inch of bar. The elastically mounted bar yielded veneer whose thickness was not affected by wear and play in the horizontal adjustment mechanism of the bar—a frequent and serious defect in commercial lathes with rigid nosebars. Feihl and Carroll (1969) concluded that the direct reading of nosebar force (possible with the hydraulically actuated elastic nosebar) gave the operator better control than the fixed settings of a rigid bar.

Most lathes have some degree of play or looseness in the knife carriage mechanism. As shown by Lutz et al. (1969), forces between bolt and knife carriage reverse depending on whether or not the nosebar is in contact with the bolt (fig. 19-100). In the absence of a nosebar, carriage and bolt are pulled together; when the nosebar is pressed against the

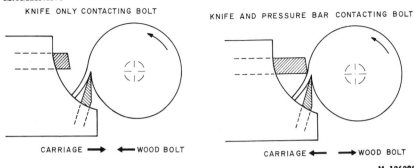

KNIFE ONLY CONTACTING BOLT

KNIFE AND PRESSURE BAR CONTACTING BOLT

CARRIAGE ➡ ⬅ WOOD BOLT

CARRIAGE ⬅ ➡ WOOD BOLT

M–136325

Figure 19–100.—Direction of forces acting on carriage and bolts when the knife only is contacting the bolt (left) and when both nosebar and knife are contacting the bolt (right). (Drawings after Lutz et al. 1969.)

bolt, carriage and bolt are forced apart. Normally veneer is peeled with the nosebar closed, but since many operators round up the log with nosebar open, and also at intervals clear jams by opening the nosebar, forces are frequently reversed and the play in the lathe carriage causes variations in veneer thickness. In brief, variation in veneer thickness is least if the nosebar can be kept in contact with the bolt at all times.

Cutting velocity.—Lutz et al. (1967) found that at very slow cutting speeds (0.2 f.p.m.) compression tearing of earlywood was more common than at 20 f.p.m. In the range from 20 to 300 f.p.m., cutting velocity was positively correlated with load on the roller bar and negatively correlated with veneer strength perpendicular to the grain; i.e., better southern pine veneer was cut in the laboratory at 20 f.p.m. than at 300 f.p.m. (Lutz et al. 1967). The large forces and accompanying veneer damage observed in southern pine peeled at high speed were attributed to wood ruptures caused by water pressure in the wet wood.

At a southern pine mill, Cade and Choong (1969) found that veneers from bolts heated in water to 106° F. were substantially weaker across the grain when cut at 500 f.p.m. than when cut at 100 f.p.m.

Commercial lathes.—An 8-foot lathe for peeling southern pine will normally accept a log $8\frac{1}{2}$ feet long and 30 inches in diameter. Most have retractable chucks to permit turning to a $5\frac{1}{4}$-inch core (fig. 19–101). Most use a power-driven, $\frac{5}{8}$-inch-diameter roller nosebar synchronized to the speed of the veneer. However, there is a trend toward use of a solid bar with a nosebar compression angle (θ in fig. 19–94) of 15°. Chuck rotation is variable up to 300 to 350 r.p.m. Power to rotate the bolt is commonly in the range from 125 to 175 hp. Automatic lathe chargers can maintain a charging rate in excess of two bolts per minute; some can charge as many as four or five bolts per minute over a short period. With good operating conditions, 900 to 1,200 bolts can be charged and peeled in 8 hours. Four-foot lathes are frequently used to cut core veneer from smaller bolts.

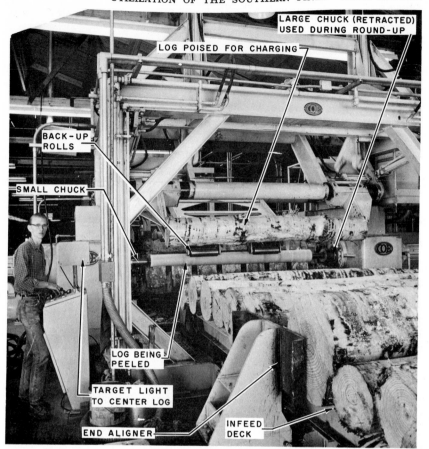

Figure 19–101.—Lathe charger with end aligner and log infeed conveyor. One log, gripped by small-diameter chucks, is being peeled; a second log, gripped near top of both ends, is poised for a quick swinging transfer to the chucks after the veneer core is dropped. (Photo from Coe Manufacturing Company.)

SLICING

Sliced veneer is usually cut to display vertical grain (fig. 19–1A, 0–90 mode), whereas peeled veneer has flat grain (fig. 19–1B, 0–90 mode). Commercial sliced veneer is cut by intermittent engagement of the knife (fig. 19–95) rather than by continuous peeling. In general, vertical-grain sliced veneer is smoother, has less shrinkage, is more attractive in appearance, and holds finishes better than rotary-peeled veneer.

Flitches are prepared for slicing to get the most favorable orientation of wood. Veneer is smoother if the cut proceeds from heartwood to sapwood. Quarter-cut (vertical-grain) veneer is usually smoother than flat-cut. Figure 19–102A shows favorable orientation of the flitch to minimize splits along planes of weakness caused by rays. In figure 19–103C, when the pith has been passed, the flitch should be turned end for end.

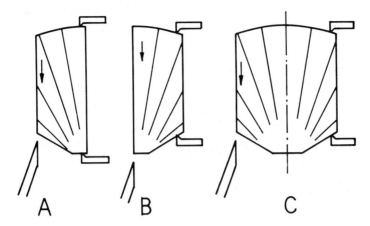

Figure 19–102.—Diagram of ray orientation in relation to the cutting plane for quarter-cut veneer. (A) Favorable. (B) Unfavorable. (C) Combination of favorable and unfavorable. (Drawings after Lutz 1956.)

Satisfactory thin veneer can be sliced with a knife having a sharpness angle of 22° and knife angle (k) of 90°15′ when used in conjunction with a solid nosebar ($\theta = 12°$) having the following settings (USDA Forest Products Laboratory 1956):

Veneer thickness	Horizontal opening (h)	Vertical opening (v)
– – – – – – –	Inch	– – – – – – –
¼	0.240	0.035
⅛	.115	.035

Of great promise to southern pine utilization is the developing technology of thick-sliced veneer, i.e., slicewood. Lutz et al. (1962) did early work on the process. He and his co-workers have recently constructed a heavy experimental slicer for cutting veneer as thick as 1 inch. Peters et al. (1969) have published data specific to southern pine. One-half- and 1-inch-thick slices were cut at 5, 50, 200, and 500 f.p.m. from flat-grain cants heated in water to 190° F. The cants had four or five rings per inch with specific gravity of about 0.52. The knife had a 20° sharpness angle and 0.5° clearance angle. The 15° solid nosebar was set to give a **restraint** (normal veneer thickness minus c in fig. 19–94) of 0.057 inch for the ½-inch slices and 0.154 inch for 1-inch slices.

Depth of knife checks was positively correlated with velocity as shown by the following tabulation of fracture depth expressed as a percent of veneer thickness.

Cutting velocity	½-inch thick	1 inch thick
F.p.m.	– – – – Percent – – – –	
5	46	59
50	64	68
200	66	73
500	76	82

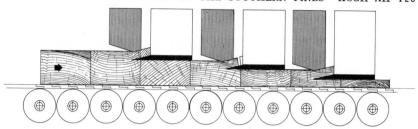

M–134597

Figure 19–103.—Concept of slicing multiple flitches. (Drawing after Peters 1968.)

Forces exerted on the knife and bar are shown in table 19–37.

In thick slicing, tearout is severe where the knife leaves the cant or **flitch.** This can be minimized by backing one cant with another (fig. 19–103). The multiple-flitch method would also afford good productivity at slower cutting speeds than conventional machines.

19–11 CHIPPING

To make chemical pulp or refiner groundwood, southern pine must first be reduced to chips of relatively uniform size.

CHIP DIMENSIONS

Optimum size and proportions of pulp chips vary according to pulping process and equipment. A study by Schmied (1964) of the effects of chip size and shape on the uniformity of wood delignification led to several conclusions. Size of the chips affects the cook when the cooking is rapid and if the chips have a high moisture content. Large chips are undercooked because their long diffusion paths delay penetration of the pulping chemicals to the chip centers. Hence, if large chips are used, the time of digester heating must be prolonged. A twofold increase of chip size requires a fourfold prolongation of the cooking time. Mixed sizes are detrimental; excessive absorption and side reactions in the small chips may

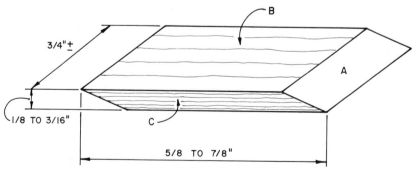

Figure 19–104.—Chip for kraft pulp. Surface A cut by chipping knife, surfaces B and C are split parallel to the grain.

TABLE 19–37.—*Summary of forces on knife and nosebar when southern pine is sliced into thick veneer* (Peters et al. 1969)

Feed thickness (inch)	Velocity	Forces[1] and horsepower per inch of bolt length					
		Knife		Bar		Combined	Net cutting power[4]
		Parallel	Perpendicular[2]	Parallel	Perpendicular	Parallel[3]	
	F.p.m.	– – – – – – – – –		*Pounds*	– – – – – – – – –		*Hp.*
½	5	123	171	45	283	168	0.03
	50	121	193	51	295	172	.26
	200	123	200	59	284	182	1.10
	500	191	246	84	339	275	4.17
1	5	195	279	79	438	274	.04
	50	186	295	74	319	260	.39
	200	239	420	140	623	379	2.30
	500	290	440	136	603	426	6.47

[1] Parallel and perpendicular to cutting direction.
[2] Perpendicular knife forces are in the opposite direction to perpendicular bar forces.
[3] Perpendicular forces as measured in this study cannot be combined.
[4] Horsepower calculated from combined parallel force and velocity.

deplete chemicals in the liquor penetrating the large chips. This is one reason for avoiding mixtures of chips with sawdust. Initially, the diffusion front of the chemicals follows the edges of the chips, but in later stages of cooking the front assumes a rounded form and the undercooked chips, depending on their initial shape, are either cylindrical or ellipsoidal. Schmied concluded that the effects of chip size and heterogeneity are considerably reduced when chips are dry because the lumens of dry wood can be filled more easily.

Specific recommendations concerning chip thickness were made by Wahlman (1967); in laboratory trials he found that maximum-strength alkaline pulps were made from chips 2 to 5 mm. (0.08 to 0.20 inch) thick and that screenings, i.e., particles of undigested wood, began to be excessive when chip thickness exceeded 5 mm. In the southern pine region, pulp chip dimensions shown in figure 19–104 are commonly used; there are, however, considerable differences in preferences at individual mills. For the interested reader, Borlew and Miller (1970) have reviewed the literature on the effect of chip thickness on the kraft pulping process.

CHIP SHREDDING

Miller and Rothrock (1963) and Nolan (1967) have shown that for the kraft pulping process there are some advantages to be gained from shredding southern pine chips prior to digestion.

In Nolan's experiments, conventionally cut slash pine chips at 40- to 45-percent moisture content were passed through a 28-inch Vertiflex attrition mill. The plates had teeth ¾-inch high in the inner zone and ⅜-inch high at the outer periphery. Plate clearance for shredding was 0.900 inch, corresponding to a clearance of 0.525 inch between the tips of the teeth on rotor and stator. Rotor speed was 1,800 r.p.m. Feed rate to the mill was 1.2 tons (air-dry) of chips per hour, which was less than 10 percent of the capacity of the 100-hp. unit.

Shredding increased the exposed surface of chips by splitting them along natural lines of cleavage without breakage across the grain and without crushing or otherwise damaging the fibers. The chief gains were: (1) high-yield pulps more easily produced; (2) chip screens eliminated; (3) knot breakers eliminated or operated lightly; (4) washing improved; (5) fiberizing power reduced; (6) pulp made cleaner; (7) cooking time reduced; and (8) digestion production increased.

CHIP FORMATION AND POWER REQUIRED

Pulp chips can be cut in any of three major modes (figs. 19–1, 19–54). Energy consumed per cubic inch of wood chipped is least if chips are long and thick rather than short and thin, if rake angles are high, if knives are sharp, and if 0–90 or 90–0 cutting mode is used rather than the 90–90 mode.

Conventional disk-type chippers (fig. 19–105) cut in a mode intermediate between 90–90 and 90–0. In these chippers, several straight knives are bolted in more or less radial disposition into a heavy disk that revolves in a vertical plane. Severed chips pass through a slot in the disk and may be discharged from top, bottom, or sides of the disk housing. Logs, slabs, or edgings are fed against the disk through the infeed spout (figs. 19–105 and 19–106). The angle between the face of the disk and the axis of the spout is usually 37½° (fig. 107, top); this angle may be attained by attaching the spout at a horizontal angle (ω in fig. 19–106) only, or in combination with a vertical angle (not illustrated). Chippers with a vertical spout angle are usually gravity fed; a powered conveyor delivers wood into horizontally fed chippers.

Erickson (1964) and Papworth and Erickson (1966) on tests of a three-knife disk chipper cutting 4- by 4-inch by 8-foot wood found that vertical spout angle had no effect on specific cutting energy; however, a 30° horizontal spout angle (ω in figure 19–106) decreased specific cutting energy slightly compared to a 0° angle; knife sharpness angle noticeably affected power consumption, with blunt knives requiring more power; long chips required less specific cutting energy than short chips.

On disk chippers, the angle θ (figure 19–107) appears to control the ratio of chip thickness to length, the chips becoming thicker as θ becomes larger; if θ is less than 90°, bristles are formed on the ends of the chips; if θ is more than 90°, the ends of the chips are compressed (Hartler

BEARINGS FOR SPINDLE
CARRYING DISK

HOUSING

DISK WITH
KNIVES

CHIP
DISCHARGE

INFEED
SPOUT

Figure 19–105.—Horizontal-feed, whole-log chipper designed for bottom discharge. (Photo
from Bush Manufacturing Company.)

1962). Helically-formed surfaces following each knife (fig. 19–107) keep
the workpiece in full contact with the face plate and help control chip
size. Swept-back knives (fig. 19–106) diminish knife impact and provide
an oblique cut that should reduce power and diminish bruising. Many
manufacturers place the knives radially, but place the spout so that the
bedknives and workpieces (see figs. 19–106 and 19–107B) are aligned to
prevent simultaneous impact of all parts of the knife edge across the full
width of a rectangular piece of wood to be chipped.

The power demand of a chipper is proportional to the volume of wood

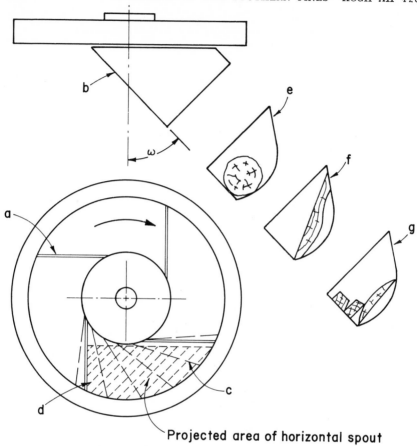

Projected area of horizontal spout

Figure 19–106.—Diagram of disk chipper. a, swept-back knives; b, spout position for horizontal feed; c, slicing action of knives across projected spout area; d, location of bedknife or anvil, against which the wood is pressed by the knives in passing. Infeed spout will admit wood in several forms; e, roundwood; f, wide slabs; g, slabs and edgings. ω = horizontal spout angle (commonly 90° − 37½° = 52½°).

it chips in a unit time. The number of cuts a machine makes per cubic foot of solid roundwood chipped is as follows:

$$X = 6912/L\pi D^2 \qquad (19\text{--}44)$$

where:

X = number of cuts per cubic foot of solid wood chipped
L = chip length, inches
D = diameter of bolt, inches

Thus, when cutting ⅝-inch-long chips, about 35 cuts per cubic foot are required for a 10-inch log, and 880 cuts per cubic foot are required for a pulp stick measuring 2 inches in diameter, or 3.5 and 88 revolutions, respectively, for a 10-knife disk.

The productiveness of a chipper is determined by the size of workpiece it will admit and the number of cuts it makes per minute. Therefore, the following relationship expresses the output of a chipper.

$$V = nN/X \qquad (19\text{--}45)$$

where:

V = cubic feet of solid wood chipped per minute
n = revolutions per minute of chipper disk
N = number of knives in the disk
X = number of cuts per cubic foot (from equation 19–44)

According to Rogers (1948) and Fobes (1959), specific cutting energy for disk-type chippers is proportional to wood specific gravity as follows:

Specific gravity	Horsepower-seconds per cubic foot of solid wood chipped
0.3	195
0.4	300
0.5	430
0.6	570

CHIPPER TYPES

Chippers are designed specifically for the wood to be chipped, e.g., pulpwood bolts, long logs, sawmill residues, or veneer residues. Spout shapes are tailored to the raw material and may be rectangular, square, V-shaped, round, or modified round. Rim speed on disk chippers is commonly 12,000 f.p.m.

For interested readers, McKenzie (1970) briefly reviewed the advantages and disadvantages of several types of chippers other than disk chippers.

Cordwood chippers at pulp mills.—The usual pulpwood chipper for southern pine receives wood in short lengths as it comes from the drum barker. These machines usually have vertically inclined spouts, are gravity-fed, will accommodate sticks up to 24 inches in diameter, and discharge from the bottom. A typical machine carries 10 to 12 knives in a 104-inch disk that rotates at 400 r.p.m. and is driven by a direct-connected 1,250-hp., wound-rotor (or synchronous) motor. When efficiently fed, output of the chipper is approximately 40 to 50 cords per hour.

Longwood chippers.—At many locations in the South, long-log chip mills have been installed in conjunction with a ring barker (commonly 26 to 30 inches). Disk chippers for these mills are chain fed horizontally; typically, the 75- or 84-inch disk carries eight knives and is rotated at 500 to 450 r.p.m. by a synchronous, 500- to 1,000-hp. motor (fig. 19–105). Assuming that operation is reasonably continuous, output should be about 30 cords per hour if wood averages 6 inches in diameter.

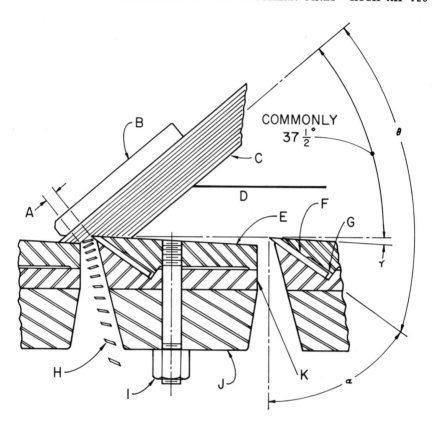

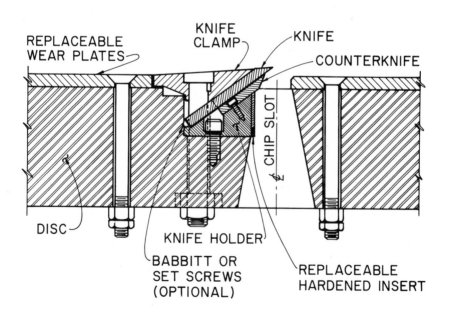

Chipping headrigs.—The development of the chipping headrig (sec. 19–6) is greatly changing chip procurement patterns in the South. Usually saw logs are more valuable than pulpwood, and veneer bolts are more valuable than saw logs. The chipping headrig can be the center of a wood conversion system that diverts each section of the tree to its most valuable use. Trees are logged in tree length; at the mill, tops are chipped as roundwood; 7- to 12-inch-diameter logs are converted on the chipping headrig to dimension lumber; 12-inch and larger sections are diverted to veneer mills. For each ton of green lumber manufactured, more than a ton of pulp chips is simultaneously produced.

Residue chippers.—Disk chippers for slabs and edgings usually carry three to six knives; smaller disks turn at higher rotational speed than larger disks to achieve comparable outputs. A mill equipped with saws and edgers (as contrasted to a mill with chipping headrig and chipping edger) that produces 10,000 bd. ft. of lumber per hour might chip all its residues in one chipper. Typically the 58-inch disk would carry six knives, turn at 720 r.p.m., and be driven by a 150-hp. squirrel-cage induction motor. Such a chipper would normally produce about 15 tons of green chips per hour of mill operation.

A veneer plant with two 8-foot lathes could have three chippers. Cores and lathe spinouts might be chipped on a horizontal-feed, top-discharge, 66-inch, eight-knife, 250-hp., 600-r.p.m. disk chipper. Waste veneer requires a special horizontal feed with crushing rolls; a typical installation would discharge from top or bottom, carry eight knives in an 84-inch disk driven at 500 r.p.m. by a 250-hp. motor. The trim ends of the veneer bolts (**lily pads**) require a special chipper that cuts chips in the 0–90 mode by an action somewhat similar to that illustrated in figure 19–54A. The 40- to 60-inch drum that carries the knives rotates at 205 to 100 r.p.m. and is driven by a 30- to 150-hp. motor. Productivity is in the range from 10 to 20 tons per hour.

Rechippers.—Oversize chips are objectionable to the pulpmills. They are screened out and either recycled through the chipper or rechipped on equipment specifically designed for this job.

Portable chippers.—Because it is becoming increasingly difficult to find labor to harvest southern pine pulpwood in the traditional cordwood lengths, much effort has been expended to improve the processing of tree-length material. Some mills do not have large consolidated timber

◂

Figure 19–107.—Cutting action of knives in disk chipper. (Top) Cross section through one type of disk. A, chip length; B, side bedknife; C, workpiece; D, bottom bedknife; E, helical face plate; F, knife; G, shim; H, chips; I, face plate stud and nut; J, chipper disk; k, knife carrier; α, rake angle (approximately 50°); γ, clearance angle (2° to 8°), θ, angle between rake face of knife and grain direction of workpiece. (Bottom) Cross section through disk in common use on southern pine. (Drawing at top from Sumner Iron Works; drawing at bottom from Bush Manufacturing Company.)

holdings, but must rely on small woodyards scattered throughout an area 200 or 300 miles in diameter. Such chip users may find it economically feasible to use mobile chip mills to process tree-length wood.

Several designs have been developed and are under test in the South, including some that are self-mobile with all the components on one chassis. A hydraulic loader places long logs in the infeed conveyor, which carries them at speeds up to 100 f.p.m. through an 18-inch ring barker and directly into a close-coupled chipper (disk or twin-cone—see fig. 19–59). The chipper is fan discharged to a chip truck. In locations where bark has high value, it may go to a pulverizer (bark hog)—also equipped with a fan discharge. Total power for the unit is commonly in the range from 300 to 600 hp. Production capacities vary, but 15 to 20 cords per hour on logs having an average diameter of 6 inches is considered attainable. The features, performance, and cost of seven different designs of mobile chip mills have been reviewed by Grant (1967).

19–12 BORING

Machine boring is a common operation whenever dowels, rungs, or screws are required in assembling wood components. Holes are also needed for bolted connections in poles, crossarms, trusses, and structural timbers. With appropriate selection of bit type and feed speed (chip thickness) it is possible to bore the required holes rapidly and smoothly in southern pine.

BIT TYPES AND NOMENCLATURE

Although there are many specialized bit designs, six types are most important. Figure 19–108A shows a double-spur, double-lip, single-twist, solid-center bit on which the spurs cut ahead of the lips. This bit may have a threaded or brad (plain) point.

Figure 19–108B illustrates a double-spur, double-lip, double-twist bit which may also have a threaded or brad point. The flat-cut, double-lip, double-twist bit (fig. 19–108C) is similar in design except that outlying spurs are not used. With the flat-cut bit, the side cutting spurs sever the end surface of the chip simultaneously with the cutting action of the lips.

Holes in excess of 6 inches deep are frequently bored with a ship auger (fig. 19–108D), a single-twist design with one cutting lip and one side cutting spur. The four types of bits described above are sharpened by filing on the rake face of the cutting lips and the inside surfaces of the spurs. The lips are commonly filed with a rake angle (α) of 30 to 35 degrees and a clearance angle (γ) of 10 to 15 degrees.

In contrast to the foregoing types, the spur machine bit illustrated in fig. 19–108E is sharpened by grinding on the clearance surface, or back side, of the lips. The rake angle therefore continuously varies along the cutting lip from about 0 degrees near the axis of rotation to about 45 degrees at the bit periphery.

The twist drill illustrated in figure 19–108F is also sharpened by grinding on the clearance surface of the lips. It has neither spurs nor point, and is most frequently used to drill in end grain and to bore dowel holes.

The symbols used in subsequent text of this section are defined as shown in figure 19–108 and the following tabulation.

α	Rake angle, degrees	P	Power required at the spindle, horsepower
β	Sharpness angle of lips, degrees		
β_1	Sharpness angle of spurs, degrees	T	Torque on spindle, inch-pounds
β_2	Sharpness angle of side cutting spurs, degrees	n	Spindle speed, revolutions per minute
γ	Clearance angle of lips, degrees	f	Feed speed, inches per minute
δ	Skew angle of lips, degrees	E	Energy, kilowatthours
ε	Angle of lead (spur to lip measured at circumference), degrees horsepower	E_s	Specific cutting energy, kilowatthours per cubic inch
		t	Chip thickness, inches
D	Diameter of bit, inches	N	Number of cutting lips
h_1	Height of point above lip, inches	v	Velocity of cutting edge of lip, feet per minute
h_2	Height of spur above lip, inches		
L	Length of spur at root, inches	d	Depth of hole, inches
r_1	Radius of bit, inches	V	Volume of hole, cubic inches
r_2	Effective radius of point, inches		

Table 19–38 lists typical geometrical specifications for all types except the twist drill.

FUNDAMENTAL ASPECTS

The velocity of the cutting edge varies with the spindle speed and the distance (r_i) from the axis of rotation.

$$v = 2\pi r_i n/12 = 0.5236 r_i n \qquad (19\text{--}46)$$

A 1-inch diameter bit rotating at 3,600 r.p.m. has a maximum cutting velocity of 942 f.p.m.

The thickness of the undeformed chip (t) is directly proportional to the feed speed and inversely proportional to the number of cutting lips and the spindle speed.

$$t = f/nN \qquad (19\text{--}47)$$

The tabulation below gives feed speeds required to yield 0.010, 0.020, and 0.030-inch thick chips at spindle speeds of 1,200, 2,400, and 3,600 r.p.m. for bits having two cutting lips. For bits having only one cutting lip, feed speeds are one-half those shown.

	Spindle speed		
Chip thickness	1,200 r.p.m.	2,400 r.p.m.	3,600 r.p.m.
Inches	– – – – – – *Inches/minute* – – – – – –		
0.010	24	48	72
.020	48	96	144
.030	72	144	216

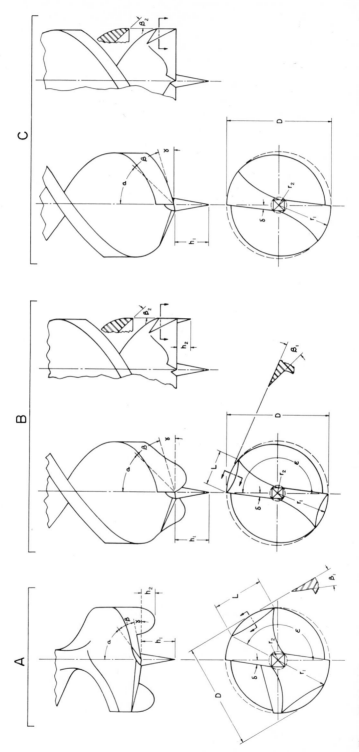

Figure 19–108ABC.—Bit types. (A) Double-spur, double-lip, single-twist, solid-center bit. (B) Double-spur, double-lip, double-twist bit. (C) Flat-cut, double-lip, double-twist bit. (Drawings after Woodson and McMillin.[5])

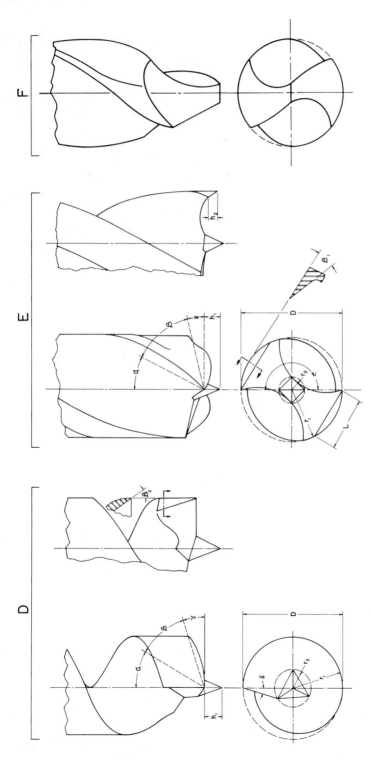

Figure 19–108DEF.—Bit types. (D) Ship auger. (E) Spur machine bit. (F) Twist drill. (Drawings after Woodson and McMillin.[5])

TABLE 19–38.—*Geometrical specifications for five bit types*

Bit type and diameter (inches)	α	β	β_1	β_2	γ	δ	ϵ	h_1	h_2	L	r_1	r_2
					Degrees					Inches		
Spur machine bit[1]												
0.50	20.2	54.4	37.3	------	15.4	------	------	0.10	0.03	0.21	0.250	0.07
1.00	19.3	60.6	35.1	------	10.1	------	------	.20	.10	.53	.500	.09
1.25	18.6	61.4	36.3	------	10.0	------	------	.20	.11	.62	.625	.11
Double-spur, double-twist												
0.50	30.6	44.9	31.9	33.2	14.6	18.2	161.8	.11	.05	.23	.250	.08
1.00	33.5	45.6	29.6	32.4	10.9	14.8	164.9	.21	.11	.45	.500	.14
1.25	31.8	47.7	29.7	35.9	10.4	12.1	167.9	.22	.12	.55	.625	.14
Flat-cut, double-twist												
0.50	29.6	45.1	------	31.1	15.3	17.8	------	.13	------	------	.250	.08
1.00	35.7	40.9	------	35.2	13.4	13.2	------	.23	------	------	.500	.11
1.25	33.3	42.7	------	33.7	14.1	10.9	------	.24	------	------	.625	.12
Double-spur, single-twist, solid-center												
0.50	30.0	47.8	29.8	------	12.2	15.5	151.5	.10	.04	.25	.250	.09
1.00	27.4	51.6	28.2	------	11.0	12.8	148.3	.22	.12	.46	.500	.13
1.25	31.8	46.1	27.8	------	12.1	11.7	152.3	.23	.12	.58	.625	.15
Ship auger, 12-inch twist												
1.00	37.5	45.2	------	35.0	7.3	15.1	------	.29	------	------	.500	.15

[1] For the spur machine bit, α, β, and γ were measured at the midpoint of the bit radius.

The net horsepower (P) requirement at the spindle is a positive linear function of the torque and the rotational speed of the spindle.

$$P = \frac{2\pi n T}{(33,000)\ (12)} = (1.587)\ (10^{-5})nT \qquad (19\text{--}48)$$

Since equation 19–48 neglects no-load idling losses of the motor and spindle assembly, actual power demand is somewhat higher than that indicated. Neither does the equation include power (normally only a fraction of a horsepower) to overcome thrust when advancing the bit.

Least energy is consumed boring a hole if bits cut thick chips. The net cutting energy (E), consumed in boring a hole can be calculated in kilowatthours from the following:

$$E = \frac{0.746Pd}{60f} = \frac{(12.43)(10^{-3})Pd}{tnN} \qquad (19\text{--}49)$$

Specific boring energy (E_s), an expression of efficiency of the cutting action, is defined as follows:

$$E_s = \frac{\text{Net cutting energy}}{\text{Volume removed}} = \frac{\text{Kilowatthours}}{\text{Cubic inches}} \qquad (19\text{--}50)$$

Since the volume of wood removed in boring a hole of depth d is

$$V = \frac{d\pi D^2}{4} \qquad (19\text{--}51)$$

then:
$$E_s = \frac{15.83(10^{-3})P}{fD^2} = \frac{(15.83)(10^{-3})P}{tnND^2} \qquad (19\text{--}52)$$

BORING DIRECTION AND CHIP FORMATION

Holes are usually bored in one of the three primary directions illustrated in figure 19–109. For southern pine, torque and thrust requirements do not differ significantly for holes bored in the tangential and radial directions; both directions may therefore be regarded as boring across the grain (Woodson and McMillin[5]). Generally, torque is greater and thrust is less when boring along the grain (longitudinal direction) than when boring across the grain. The tabulation below compares the effect of direction for a double-spur, double-lip, single-twist, solid-center

---

[5] Woodson, G. E., and McMillin, C. W. Machine boring of southern pine wood. III. Effect of six variables on torque, thrust, and hole quality. USDA Forest Service, Southern Forest Experiment Station, Alexandria, La., Final Report—Phase III FS–SO–3201–2.30 dated December 30, 1971.

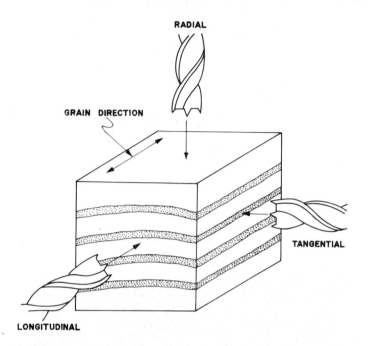

Figure 19–109.—Designation of the three main boring directions: feed longitudinal along the grain, and feed across the grain in radial or tangential direction.. (Drawing after Woodson and McMillin[5].)

bit boring dry southern pine (*Pinus* spp.) at 2,400 r.p.m. and removing 0.020-inch thick chips.

Bit diameter	Along the grain		Across the grain	
	Torque	Thrust	Torque	Thrust
Inches	*Inch-pounds*	*Pounds*	*Inch-Pounds*	*Pounds*
0.50	16.6	73.5	13.7	106.3
1.00	56.6	137.3	37.7	183.1
1.25	71.3	161.4	53.6	197.5

Woodson and McMillin[5] found that thrust is related to the force required to advance the spurs and brad into the work and, to a lesser extent, to the normal force component exerted by the cutting lips. When drilling across the grain, the spurs and brad stress fibers perpendicular to their long axes. When driling along the grain, fibers are separated parallel to their long axes. Since fibers are stronger when stressed in a direction perpendicular to their axes, greater thrust forces would be expected when drilling across the grain than when drilling along the grain.

Torque is primarily related to the parallel tool force component of the lips and the spurs and brad. When drilling along the grain, the lips sever tracheids perpendicular to their long axes. In contrast, tracheids are cut in a plane parallel to their axes when drilling across the grain. Since tracheids are stronger when stressed in the perpendicular direction, greater torque would be expected when boring along the grain than when boring across the grain.

When drilling in the longitudinal direction, the action of the lips (the cutting edges generating chips) approximates orthogonal cutting across the grain. For across the grain boring, cutting continuously alternates from the veneer cutting direction to the planing direction. (See sec. 19–2 for a discussion of the basic modes of chip formation in orthogonal cutting.)

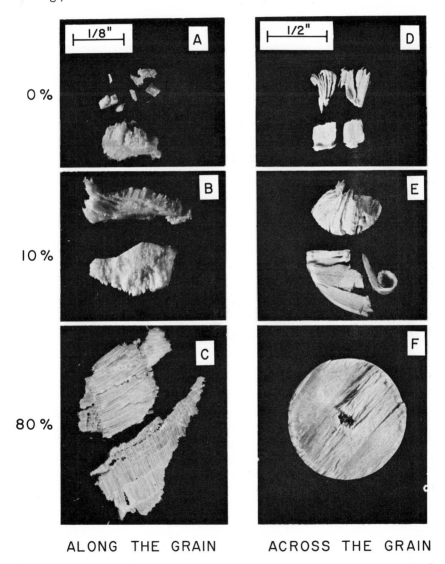

ALONG THE GRAIN   ACROSS THE GRAIN

F–520988

Figure 19–110.—Typical chips formed when boring in two directions at three moisture contents. The scale shown in A is applicable to B and C as well; the scale shown in D is applicable to E and F. (Photo from Woodson and McMillin[6].)

Woodson and McMillin[6] have described some general trends in chip formation with changes in wood moisture content when boring with a 1-inch diameter spur machine bit at 2,400 r.p.m. and removing 0.020-inch-thick chips. Typical chips are illustrated in fig. 19–110.

For along the grain boring, at 0- and 10-percent moisture content, chips similar to McKenzie Type II are generated (fig. 19–110A and 19–110B). Chips formed above the cutting plane (upper portions of the figures) were sheared into numerous, small subchips at 0-percent moisture; they were longer and more continuous at 10 percent. Chips formed below the cutting plane (lower portions of the figures) were somewhat smaller for holes bored at 0-percent moisture than for holes bored at 10 percent. At 80-percent moisture, typical McKenzie Type I chips were formed (fig. 19–110C). Although shear failures were present, most particles remained relatively intact. (For definition of McKenzie Type I and Type II chips see figures 19–16 and 19–17.)

For across the grain boring at 0- and 10-percent moisture content, Franz Type I chips were generally formed when the lips were cutting in the planing direction (lower portion of fig. 19–110D and 19–110E). The chips generated at 0-percent moisture were considerably shorter and less curled than those produced at 10 percent. At 80-percent moisture, chips similar to Franz Type II were most frequently formed (fig. 19–110F). (For definition of Franz Type I and Type II chips see figures 19–3 and 19–5.)

Cantilever beam type failures were generally observed when boring at 0- and 10-percent moisture content with lips cutting in the veneer direction (upper portion of fig. 19–110D and 19–110E). Failure occurred closer to the cutting edge for wood at 0-percent moisture than for wood at 10-percent moisture. At 80-percent moisture, chips appeared to form by failure in compression tearing (fig. 19–110F). (For definition of compression tearing see figure 19–12.)

FACTORS AFFECTING TORQUE AND THRUST

Woodson and McMillin[5] examined in detail the effects of seven variables on torque and thrust when boring 3½-inch deep holes in southern pine (*Pinus* spp). Variables in their factorial experimental design were:

Bit diameter—0.50-inch; 1.00-inch; 1.25-inch.
Spindle speed—1,200 r.p.m.; 2,400 r.p.m.; 3,600 r.p.m.
Chip thickness—0.010-inch; 0.020-inch; 0.030-inch.
Wood specific gravity (ovendry weight and volume at 10.4-percent moisture content)—Less than 0.52 (avg. 0.48); more than 0.55 (avg. 0.60).
Moisture content—Dry (avg. 10.4 percent); wet (avg. 73 percent).
Boring direction—Tangential; radial; longitudinal.
Depth of hole—1-inch; 2-inch; 3-inch.

---

[6] Woodson, G. E., and McMillin, C. W. Machine boring of southern pine wood. I. Effect of moisture content on tool forces and chip formation in machine boring. USDA Forest Service, Southern Forest Experiment Station, Alexandria, La., Final Report—Phase I FS-SO-3201-2.30 dated October 30, 1971.

TABLE 19–39.—*Torque demand for four bit types when boring along the grain*[1]

Bit type and diameter (inches)	Chip thickness (inches)		
	0.010	0.020	0.030
	- - - - - - - - - - Inch-pounds - - - - - - - - - -		
Spur machine bit			
0.50	9.1 (11.8)	14.1 (16.6)	19.1 (22.9)
1.00	27.9 (36.8)	40.5 (52.7)	50.8 (64.9)
1.25	47.5 (65.1)	64.3 (92.2)	81.8 (112.3)
Double-spur, double-twist			
0.50	9.2 (13.0)	11.8 (14.2)	14.2 (18.7)
1.00	35.1 (44.8)	44.0 (53.4)	52.7 (70.7)
1.25	44.1 (60.0)	67.5 (85.7)	73.6 (103.0)
Flat-cut, double-twist			
0.50	7.5 (10.4)	11.7 (14.6)	16.5 (21.0)
1.00	22.7 (31.2)	40.1 (45.7)	44.1 (57.2)
1.25	34.4 (46.4)	51.0 (66.7)	55.3 (75.1)
Double-spur, single-twist, solid-center			
0.50	9.2 (14.9)	13.2 (20.0)	20.3 (28.5)
1.00	31.6 (43.8)	45.2 (61.8)	54.5 (70.2)
1.25	45.6 (63.0)	63.0 (83.4)	79.6 (103.1)

[1] The first number in each entry is the torque for wood of low specific gravity (avg. 0.48); the number following in parentheses is the torque for wood of high specific gravity (avg. 0.60).

Four types of bits were evaluated: spur machine bit; double-spur, double-twist; flat-cut, double-twist; and double-spur, single-twist, solid-center. Schematic drawings are provided in fig. 19–108; geometrical specifications (based on a 33⅓-percent sample of the bits used) are given in table 19–38.

Boring along the grain.—When boring along the grain (longitudinal direction) torque was primarily correlated with bit diameter, wood specific gravity and chip thickness; it did not vary with spindle speed when the thickness of chips was held constant. Table 19–39 compares torque demand for each bit type when the data were averaged over all levels of depth, moisture content, and spindle speed. From the table, torque was a positive curvilinear function of diameter for all chip thicknesses and specific gravities. For a given bit diameter and wood density, torque increased with increasing chip thickness; the slope of the relationship between torque and chip thickness increased with increasing diameter. For a given diameter and chip thickness, torque was greater when boring wood of high density than when boring wood of low density. The magnitude of the difference increased with increasing diameter.

For 0.50-inch diameter bits, torques were essentially the same for all types. However, with 1.00- and 1.25-inch bits, the flat-cut, double-twist bit required less torque than did the other types.

With the exception of the double-spur, single-twist, solid-center bit, torque increased somewhat with increasing depth when holes were bored in wet wood with 0.50-inch diameter bits. Torque was unrelated to depth for the 1.00- and 1.25-inch diameter bits. Chips formed in dry wood are fragmented into small particles while those formed in wet wood remain relatively intact (fig. 19–110). When boring wet wood, it is probable that the increase in torque with increasing depth is associated with difficulty in exhausting such intact chips from deep holes.

In some cases, wet wood required less torque than did dry wood, although generally the effect of moisture content was slight for holes bored along the grain (Woodson and McMillin[5,6]).

Table 19–40 summarizes the results for thrust along the grain; the values shown are averages for all levels of depth, chip thickness and spindle speed. For most bits, the effect of chip thickness was small. Thrust was unrelated to spindle speed.

From the table, thrust increased rapidly with increasing diameter for all types except the flat-cut, double-twist bit. For a given diameter and moisture content, thrust was less when boring wood of low density than when boring wood of high density. For a given diameter and density, thrust was less for wet wood than for dry wood.

TABLE 19–40.—*Thrust requirements for four bit types when boring along the grain*[1]

Bit type and diameter (inches)	Specific gravity	
	Low (avg. 0.48)	High (avg. 0.60)
	– – – – – – – – – *Pounds* – – – – – – – – –	
Spur machine bit		
0.50	48.9(40.3)	67.8(49.8)
1.00	107.2(71.2)	149.1(79.0)
1.25	145.0(105.0)	224.6(133.5)
Double-spur, double-twist		
0.50	48.5(31.3)	62.3(44.6)
1.00	106.0(82.1)	148.7(108.8)
1.25	138.8(100.6)	199.7(133.6)
Flat-cut, double-twist		
0.50	28.5(24.7)	49.9(25.6)
1.00	44.0(38.8)	62.3(35.7)
1.25	43.0(30.2)	56.7(33.3)
Double-spur, single-twist, solid-center		
0.50	60.2(47.8)	91.9(70.9)
1.00	108.2(81.5)	150.2(105.3)
1.25	124.4(96.8)	179.5(128.6)

[1] The first number in each entry is the thrust for dry wood (avg. 10.4-percent moisture content); the number following in parentheses is the thrust for wet wood (avg. 72.5-percent moisture content).

With the flat-cut bit, thrust did not meaningfully differ with diameter; the average was 39.4 pounds. Thrust was less when boring wet wood (avg. 31.4 pounds) than when boring dry wood (avg. 47.4 pounds). It was also less for wood of low gravity (avg. 34.8 pounds) than for wood of high gravity (avg. 43.9 pounds).

In general, thrust also decreased with increasing depth of hole although the effect was slight. It is probable that frictional forces develop between the surface of the hole and the severed chips. These forces exert a component in a direction which lifts the workpiece. The lifting effect would be greater in deep holes since the total area in contact increases with increasing depth.

Of the four types of bits studied, the flat-cut bit required least thrust. Since this bit does not have outlining spurs, the result was expected.

Boring across the grain.—Woodson and McMillin's[5] factorial experiment revealed that torque and thrust requirements do not differ between the tangential and radial boring directions; therefore, their data for the two directions were pooled and regarded as boring across the grain. As when boring along the grain, they found that torque did not differ with spindle speed for chips of constant thickness. Torque demand did vary with bit diameter, chip thickness, moisture content and specific gravity. Their results are summarized in table 19–41.

From the table, torque increased with increasing diameter for all chip thicknesses, specific gravities, and moisture contents (except there was no significant difference in torque between the 1.00- and 1.25-inch diameter double-spur, double-twist bits when removing 0.010-inch-thick chips in wet wood). Torque increased with increasing chip thickness when boring wet or dry wood of all specific gravities. For a given diameter, chip thickness and moisture content, torque was greater when boring wood of high density than when boring wood of low density.

The variation in torque with changes in moisture content were less consistent. For the spur machine bit, torque was greater for wet than for dry wood when boring with the 0.50-inch diameter bit. It is probable that the intact chips formed when boring wet wood clogged the bit flutes. With the 1.00- and 1.25-inch bits, the trend reversed and torque was less for wet than for dry wood. For the double-spur, double-twist, and the double-spur, single-twist, solid-center bits, torque was less for wet than for dry wood. The effect of moisture was small and inconsistent when holes were bored with the flat-cut machine bit.

While not shown in table 19–41, torque also increased with increasing depth for all 0.50-inch diameter bits; the effect was greatest for holes bored in dense dry wood. For most combinations tested, torque was least when holes were bored with the flat-cut machine bit.

Values for thrust when boring across the grain are summarized in table 19–42. The values are arrayed by combinations of diameter, chip thickness, moisture content, and specific gravity.

TABLE 19–41.—*Torque demand for four bit types when boring across the grain*[1]

Bit type and diameter (inches)	Chip thickness (inches)					
	0.010		0.020		0.030	
	Dry	Wet	Dry	Wet	Dry	Wet
			Inch-pounds			
Spur machine bit						
0.50	8.0(10.6)	11.6(9.7)	11.3(15.0)	14.9(19.2)	15.1(19.8)	19.2(26.2)
1.00	22.3(28.7)	18.3(20.0)	30.3(38.1)	24.6(31.6)	38.3(45.8)	33.5(38.6)
1.25	34.7(41.5)	31.6(37.1)	52.4(64.0)	47.2(55.4)	62.4(78.8)	57.7(71.5)
Double-spur, double-twist						
0.50	12.4(20.6)	12.8(15.5)	19.1(26.2)	13.6(20.0)	21.7(30.0)	16.5(23.4)
1.00	28.7(34.0)	29.2(33.0)	34.0(41.0)	33.3(36.8)	41.9(54.2)	36.3(45.0)
1.25	34.7(42.2)	28.7(33.4)	45.7(56.1)	37.6(44.1)	56.3(68.4)	44.9(53.7)
Flat-cut, double-twist						
0.50	13.1(19.3)	13.0(14.8)	14.2(22.2)	18.6(19.1)	17.1(24.3)	21.0(24.3)
1.00	16.0(20.2)	21.6(24.6)	25.2(32.6)	28.0(34.4)	32.7(39.4)	34.7(42.2)
1.25	24.8(29.6)	25.9(29.0)	32.0(39.4)	33.8(40.6)	42.7(47.7)	42.8(48.5)
Double-spur, single-twist, solid-center						
0.50	9.5(12.9)	6.7(7.5)	12.8(15.8)	9.9(11.4)	14.5(19.1)	12.8(14.9)
1.00	22.3(29.8)	20.7(23.8)	32.8(42.5)	28.3(36.1)	40.1(49.7)	32.9(38.7)
1.25	36.7(41.3)	29.1(34.9)	48.0(59.2)	38.0(45.4)	56.5(70.5)	46.4(53.3)

[1] The first number in each entry is the torque for wood of low specific gravity (avg. 0.48); the number following in parentheses is the torque for wood of high specific gravity (avg. 0.60). The moisture content of dry wood was 10.4 percent; for wet wood moisture content averaged 72.5 percent.

TABLE 19-42.—*Thrust requirements when boring across the grain*[1]

Bit type and diameter (inches)	Chip thickness (inches)					
	.010		.020		.030	
	Dry	Wet	Dry	Wet	Dry	Wet
	Pounds					
Spur machine bit						
0.50	52.9 (78.4)	46.3 (50.2)	65.1 (100.1)	55.5 (82.2)	75.7 (112.7)	61.5 (96.4)
1.00	109.5 (175.1)	72.0 (88.7)	125.2 (183.0)	76.1 (111.9)	151.2 (206.6)	96.7 (132.5)
1.25	141.0 (193.0)	92.7 (125.3)	195.7 (274.4)	118.5 (164.6)	209.2 (297.3)	128.2 (194.0)
Double-spur, double-twist						
0.50	79.4 (118.8)	59.2 (76.2)	109.2 (150.7)	58.3 (102.0)	117.4 (169.2)	61.1 (105.7)
1.00	105.0 (163.0)	75.0 (94.7)	136.3 (211.8)	85.4 (128.8)	170.6 (249.7)	99.2 (149.5)
1.25	145.2 (205.6)	89.1 (122.3)	181.0 (261.9)	110.0 (154.6)	215.0 (307.2)	131.1 (174.8)
Flat-cut, double-twist						
0.50	56.4 (90.6)	30.3 (43.2)	53.2 (88.9)	34.6 (48.9)	50.9 (90.9)	32.3 (52.2)
1.00	41.3 (62.4)	33.1 (44.2)	67.9 (93.0)	33.0 (48.0)	83.0 (110.6)	41.5 (64.2)
1.25	43.5 (63.5)	26.7 (39.6)	59.6 (85.6)	38.3 (60.3)	74.1 (101.7)	39.5 (54.5)
Double-spur, single-twist, solid-center						
0.50	63.9 (87.0)	35.0 (45.9)	78.7 (113.1)	42.8 (62.2)	86.1 (129.3)	55.2 (77.9)
1.00	93.4 (143.8)	64.7 (90.9)	137.6 (217.9)	91.2 (137.2)	142.6 (216.7)	86.9 (131.7)
1.25	147.5 (185.6)	89.1 (120.4)	176.6 (244.5)	106.6 (144.6)	195.6 (282.9)	122.4 (162.9)

[1] The first number in each entry is the thrust for wood of low specific gravity (avg. 0.48); the number following in parentheses is the thrust for wood of high specific gravity (avg. 0.60). The average moisture content of dry wood was 10.4 percent; the average for wet wood was 72.5 percent.

For all types except the flat-cut machine bit, thrust increased with increasing diameter; the trend was curvilinear. For a given diameter, thrust increased with increasing chip thickness in wet and in dry wood of both densities. For a given diameter and chip thickness, thrust was less for holes bored in wet than in dry wood and was less for wood of low than for wood of high specific gravity.

Thrust was unrelated to diameter for holes bored with the flat-cut bit. For the 0.50-inch bit, thrust did not differ with chip thickness, but with the 1.00- and 1.25-inch bits, it increased with increasing thickness. For a given diameter and chip thickness, thrust was less for holes bored in wet than in dry wood and less for wood of low than for wood of high specific gravity.

While not shown in table 19–42, thrust increased slightly with increasing depth for holes bored with the 0.50-inch bits. The trend reversed with the 1.00- and 1.25-inch bits and thrust decreased with increasing depth.

Except for the flat-cut machine bit, Woodson and McMillin's results indicate that, for chips of constant thickness, thrust was somewhat greater when holes were bored at 3,600 r.p.m. than when bored at 1,200 r.p.m. To cut chips of a given thickness, the plunge rate must increase with increasing spindle speed. It is probable that thrust may be greater at high plunge speeds because the strength of wood increases with increasing rate of loading.

HOLE QUALITY

Woodson and McMillin[5] evaluated the smoothness of holes using a subjective rating scale of 1 to 3. Good quality holes were rated 1, fair quality rated 2, while poor quality holes were rated 3. Thus, holes of better quality had low numerical ratings. Figure 19–111 illustrates representative surfaces for wood bored wet and dry in each direction.

Table 19–43 tabulates the results in terms of smoothness units; the data are arrayed by bit types, boring direction, moisture content and diameter. In those cases where smoothness of the machined surface is of primary importance, the bit or bits having the lowest numerical ratings should be given preference.

Although not shown in table 19–43, Woodson and McMillin's data generally indicated that hole quality improved with decreasing chip thickness. Quality was unaffected by spindle speed (for chips of constant thickness) and wood specific gravity.

BORING DEEP HOLES

Thrust, torque, hole quality, and chip clogging were studied by Woodson and McMillin[7] when boring 10½-inch-deep holes in southern pine (*Pinus*

---

[7] Woodson, G. E., and McMillin, C. W. Machine boring of southern pine wood. II. Boring deep holes. USDA Forest Service, Southern Forest Experiment Station, Alexandria, La., Final Report—Phase II FS-SO-3201-2.30 dated February 26, 1971. (See also 1972 For. Prod. J. 22(4): 49–53.)

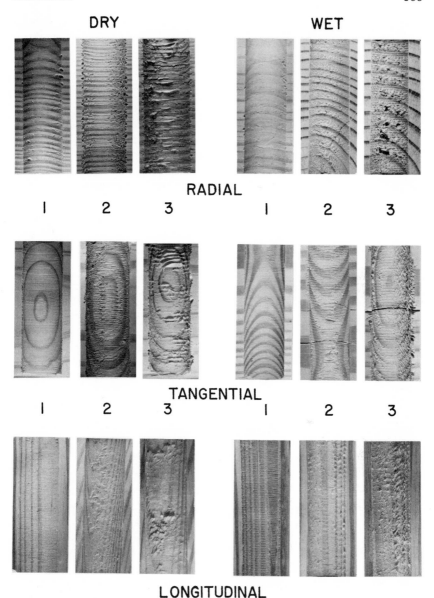

Figure 19–111.—Surface quality ratings (smoothness) for the three principal boring directions in dry (left) and wet (right) wood. (Photo from Woodson and McMillin[5].)

F–520989

spp.). They used a factorial experimental design with variables as follows:

Bit type—1-inch diameter double-spur, double-twist machine bit with two cutting lips. 1-inch diameter ship auger, with one cutting lip. (See table 19–38 for geometrical specifications and fig. 19–108 for schematic drawings.)

Spindle speed—1,200 r.p.m., 2,400 r.p.m.

Chip thickness—0.010-inch, 0.020-inch, 0.030-inch.

Wood specific gravity—Less than 0.52, More than 0.55 (ovendry weight and volume at 10.4-percent moisture content).

Moisture content—10.4 percent, Saturated.

Direction of boring—Along the grain, Across the grain.

Figure 19–112 illustrates typical clogged chips when boring deep holes with the ship auger (left) and double-spur, double-twist (right) bits. The maximum depth of hole attainable without evidence of chip clogging differed with boring direction—it was unaffected by other study factors. For both bits, clogging occurred at a shallower depth when boring across the grain (avg. 6.5 inches) than when boring along the grain (avg. 10.1 inches). There was no significant difference between bit types for a given boring direction.

When the data were averaged over all study variables for a given boring direction, thrust and torque (average values prior to evidence of

TABLE 19–43.—*Results of quality ratings for four bit types*[1]

Bit type and diameter (inches)	Boring direction		
	Longitudinal	Tangential	Radial
	– – – – – – – – *Smoothness units*[2] – – – – – – – –		
Spur machine bit			
0.50	1.6(2.5)	1.1(1.4)	1.0(1.6)
1.00	1.2(2.1)	1.0(1.0)	1.1(1.1)
1.25	1.4(2.2)	1.1(1.1)	1.3(1.2)
Double-spur, double-twist			
0.50	1.7(2.3)	1.1(1.4)	1.6(1.6)
1.00	1.6(2.6)	1.1(1.2)	1.1(1.3)
1.25	1.6(2.2)	1.1(1.1)	1.2(1.3)
Flat-cut, double-twist			
0.50	1.6(2.6)	1.5(2.7)	1.6(2.8)
1.00	1.7(2.2)	1.3(2.5)	1.5(2.5)
1.25	1.5(2.1)	1.3(2.3)	1.5(2.4)
Double-spur, single-twist, solid-center			
0.50	2.1(2.9)	1.0(1.1)	1.2(1.3)
1.00	1.6(2.6)	1.1(1.4)	1.3(1.4)
1.25	1.6(2.6)	1.3(1.4)	1.3(1.4)

[1] The first number in each entry is the quality rating for dry wood (avg. 10.4-percent moisture content); the number following in parentheses is the quality rating for wet wood (avg. 72.5-percent moisture content).

[2] A quality rating of 1 indicates a smooth hole; a rating of 3 indicates a very rough hole; 2 is intermediate.

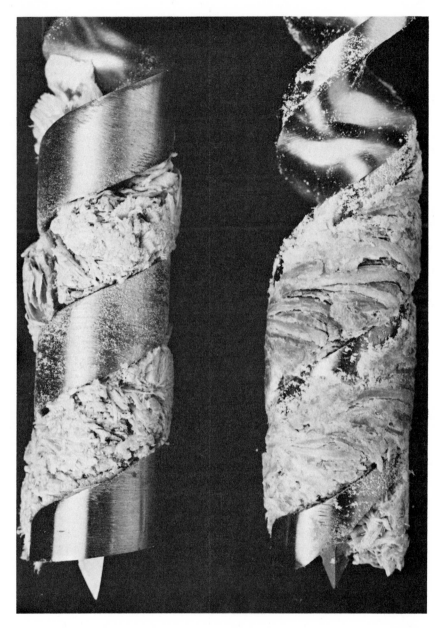

F–520990

Figure 19–112.—Typical clogged chips when boring deep holes with a ship auger (left) and a double-spur, double-twist bit (right). (Photo from Woodson and McMillin[7].)

chip clogging) were substantially lower when boring with the ship auger than when boring with the double-spur, double-twist machine bit. Under all conditions, plunge speed of the single-lip ship auger was half that of the double-lip machine bit.

	Along the grain		Across the grain	
Bit type	Torque	Thrust	Torque	Thrust
	Inch-pounds	*Pounds*	*Inch-pounds*	*Pounds*
Double-spur, double-twist bit_____	67.1	132.9	50.4	157.8
Ship auger_____	39.9	61.1	29.0	38.6

Generally, torque and thrust were positively correlated with chip thickness and specific gravity for both types of bits studied. Neither torque nor thrust differed with spindle speed when chip thickness was held constant. When boring in either direction with the double-spur, double-twist machine bit, wet wood required less thrust than did dry wood.

Although the ship auger required less horsepower than the machine bit, it was slightly less efficient; i.e., more energy was required to remove a unit volume of wood with the ship auger than with the machine bit.

For dry wood bored to $10\frac{1}{2}$-inch depth along the grain, quality was best when holes were drilled with the ship auger. There was no significant difference between bit types when boring wet wood. When boring across the grain, the double-spur, double-twist machine bit yielded holes of better quality in both wet wood and dry wood than did the ship auger.

19–13 MACHINING WITH HIGH-ENERGY JETS

Exploratory studies have been made (Bryan 1963a) on the cutting of wood with jets of water under a pressure of 35,000 pounds per square inch or more. At this time, the process is not competitive with conventional cutting methods for southern pine.

Development of continuous pumping systems, improved nozzle designs, and incorporation of additives that improve the cohesiveness of the water jet are all contributing to advancement of the technology, however. It is anticipated that in the near future water-jet cutting of certain products— e.g., corrugated board—will be practical and economically competitive with other methods (Franz 1970).

19–14 MACHINING WITH LASERS

Lasers (acronym for light amplification by stimulated emission of radiation) generate photon energy through an internal amplification process in which stimulated emission plays a dominant role. They emit a coherent beam of highly collimated monochromatic light that when focused to minimum diameter can produce power densities sufficient to vaporize most materials. Lasers offer a number of advantages over conventional machining processes, as follows:

- No residue (sawdust) is formed.
- Narrow kerf reduces waste.
- Ability to cut complicated profiles.
- No tool wear.
- Produces a smooth surface.
- Little noise.
- No reaction force exerted on the workpiece.

Bryan (1963b) investigated the feasibility of machining wood with a beam of highly collimated monochromatic light emitted from a pulsed ruby laser. Because of the low power output and single pulse nature of this type of laser, cutting was limited to 0.030-inch-diameter holes about $\frac{1}{16}$-inch deep.

A greater potential for laser cutting was realized with the development of the carbon-dioxide molecular gas laser. The collimated beam from this laser is continuous and output powers in excess of 1,000 watts are possible. The cutting action of the carbon dioxide laser can be further improved by using a co-axial jet of gas, usually air, to assist in removal of vapor and particles from the cut region and cool the top surface (Lunau and Paine 1969; Harry and Lunau 1971). With the gas jet, it is possible to produce deep, uniform cuts with square edges in a variety of materials.

Carbon-dioxide laser profile cutting machines have recently been developed for industrial use (Anonymous 1970ab; Doxey 1970; March 1970). These machines are used to prepare steel-rule die blocks of the type used for cutting and/or creasing paper cartons, gaskets and cloth. In this application, an intricate and accurate pattern of narrow slots is required in ¾-inch plywood (fig. 19–113); steel rules are inserted into the slots. At a cutting speed of 8 inches per minute, laser preparation of

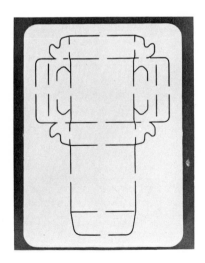

Figure 19–113.—Pattern of laser-cut kerf slots in steel-rule die block of ¾-inch birch plywood. With steel rules inserted in the kerf slots, the die is used to cut and crease stock for a cardboard box. The pattern measures about 7 inches in length; the kerf, which penetrates through the block, measures about 0.028 inch wide. (Photo from British Oxygen Co., Ltd., London, England.)

the die blocks is reported to be 10 times faster than conventional methods.

McMillin and Harry (1971) demonstrated that southern pine lumber can be cut with a carbon-dioxide laser and explored factors which affect the maximum rate of cutting. The laser used contained a mixture of carbon dioxide, nitrogen and helium and emitted radiation at a wavelength of 10.6 μm. The beam emerged horizontally from the laser tube and was deflected downwards by a 45 degree mirror (fig. 19–114). It was then focused by a lens which formed the upper sealing surface of an air-jet nozzle. The focused beam passed concentrically down the axis of the nozzle and was at minimum diameter about 2 mm. outside the nozzle. An air-hydraulic, variable speed feed system was used to traverse the workpiece past the focused beam. All cuts were made at 240 watts of output power.

The maximum feed speed at full penetration of the laser beam differed with workpiece thickness, wood specific gravity and moisture content. There was no significant difference in feed speed when cutting in a direction along the grain as compared to cutting across the grain.

As tabulated below, maximum feed speed at which southern pine wood could be cut decreased with increasing workpiece thickness in both wet and dry samples; the trend was curvilinear. For a given thickness, slower feed speeds were required for wet than for dry wood. The magnitude of the difference increased as the thickness of the workpiece decreased.

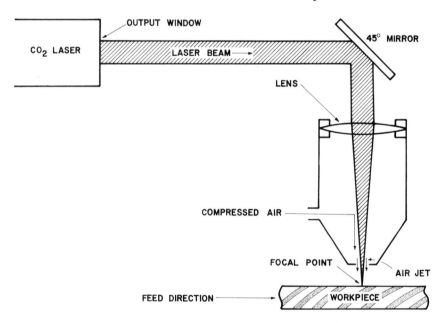

Figure 19–114.—Diagram of experimental air-jet-assisted, carbon-dioxide, laser-cutting device. (Drawing after McMillin and Harry 1971.)

Moisture content (percent)	Workpiece thickness (inches)		
	0.25	0.50	1.00
	– – – – Inches/minute – – – –		
Dry			
(avg. 12-percent)___	111.0	46.4	17.2
Wet			
(avg. 70-percent)___	87.1	36.1	12.0

When cutting wet wood, maximum feed speed was unrelated to specific gravity. For dry wood, slower speeds were required when cutting wood of high density than when cutting wood of low density. The difference was greatest for the 0.25-inch-thick samples.

Specific gravity (green volume and ovendry weight)	Workpiece thickness (inches)		
	0.25	0.50	1.00
	– – – – Inches/minute – – – –		
Low (avg. 0.45)_____	123.9	49.9	22.0
High (avg. 0.54)_____	98.2	42.9	12.5

The width of the kerf produced by the laser beam is extremely small (avg. 0.012 inch) compared to the kerfs produced by conventional saws. McMillin and Harry's data showed that kerf width was unrelated to cutting direction, moisture content and specific gravity but increased with increasing workpiece thickness. Kerf widths were 0.009, 0.012, and 0.015 inches for 0.25-, 0.50-, and 1.00-inch thick samples respectively.

Wood-based materials and paper products may also be cut with the carbon-dioxide laser. McMillin and Harry provided the following examples:

Material	Thickness	Power	Feed speed
	Inch	Watts	Inches/minute
Southern pine plywood_____	0.50	240	20
Southern pine particleboard_	.50	240	16
Tempered hardboard_____	.25	240	13
Hardboard_____	.25	180	12
Fiber insulation board_____	.50	180	14
Corrugated boxboard_____	.17	180	236
Illustration board_____	.10	180	91
Kraft linerboard_____	.02	180	207

Scanning electron micrographs prepared by McMillin and Harry (1971) show that laser-cut surfaces—while blackened—are far smoother than conventionally cut surfaces (fig. 19–115). On laser-cut surfaces, there is little evident damage to wood structure (fig. 19–116); some carbon deposits, however, are evident on cell walls and in lumen cavities.

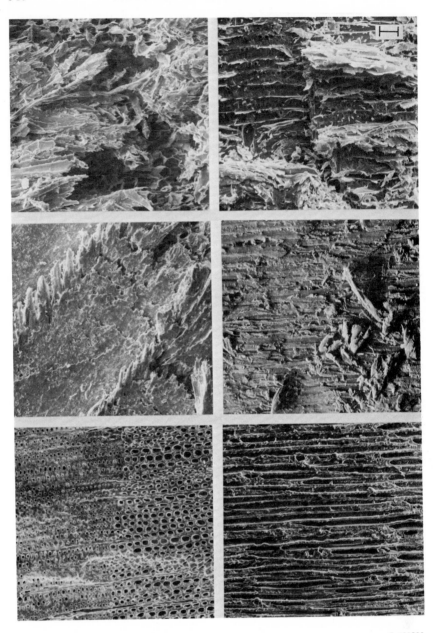

F-520991

Figure 19–115.—Scanning electron micrographs of southern pine surfaces cut across the grain (left column) and along the grain (right column) by (from top to bottom) bandsawing, circular sawing and laser cutting. Scale mark shows 0.1 inch. (Photos from McMillin and Harry 1971.)

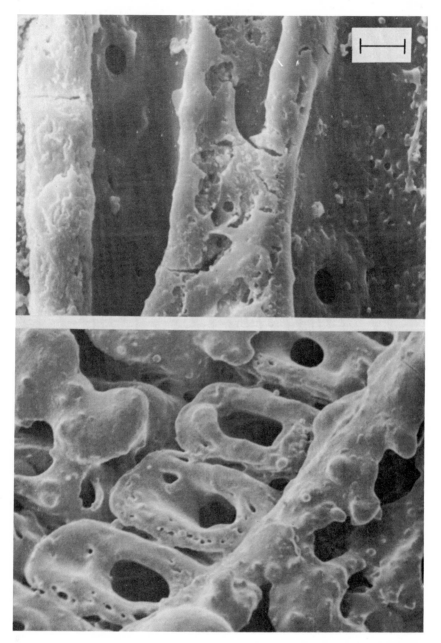

F-520992
Figure 19–116.—Scanning electron micrographs of southern pine surfaces cut with a carbon dioxide laser along the grain (top) and across the grain (bottom). Scale mark shows 10 μm. (Photos rfom McMillin and Harry 1971.)

19-15 LITERATURE CITED

Anonymous.
1968. Final tally records 1967 as another year of declining plywood production, but South's share still increasing. Forest Ind. 95(5): 13.

Anonymous.
1970a. Laser die-cutting. Part I. Paperboard Packag. 55(3): 29–31.

Anonymous.
1970b. Laser die-cutting. Part II. Paperboard Packag. 55(5): 38–41.

Anderson, W. C., and Kaiser, H. F.
1970. Economic implications of chipping headrigs for milling southern pine. Forest Prod. J. 20(3): 42–46.

Andrews, G. W.
1955. Sawing wood with circular headsaws. Forest Prod. J. 5: 186–192.

Aralo, R. A.
1971. Crosscut shearing of roundwood bolts. USDA Forest Serv. Res. Pap. NC–68, 21 pp. N. Cent. Forest Exp. Sta., St. Paul, Minn.

Blackford, J. M.
1961. Separating bark from wood chips. Forest Prod. J. 11: 515–519.

Blackford, J.
1965. Pulpwood harvesting now and twenty years from now. APA Quart., April 1965, pp. 4–6.

Bloomquist, P. R.
1966. Southern pine plywood adhesives technology. Forest Ind. 93(2): 39–41.

Borlew, P. B., and Miller, R. L.
1970. Chip thickness: A critical dimension in kraft pulping. TAPPI 53: 2107–2111.

Bridges, R. R.
1971. A quantitative study of some factors affecting the abrasiveness of particleboard. Forest Prod. J. 21(11): 39–41.

Bryan, E. L.
1963a. High energy jets as a new concept in wood machining. Forest Prod. J. 8: 305–312.

Bryan, E. L.
1963b. Machining wood with light. Forest Prod. J. 8: 14.

Bryan, R. W.
1968. Economic factors begin to mitigate pine plywood boom. Forest Ind. 95(1): 46–47.

Cade, J. C., and Choong, E. T.
1969. Influence of cutting velocity and log diameter on tensile strength of veneer across the grain. Forest Prod. J. 19(7): 52–53.

Clark, F.
1969. High strain band mills. In Proc. North. Calif. Sect. FPRS, pp. 2–5. Calpella, Calif.

Collins, E. H.
1965. Method of and apparatus for kerfless cutting of wood. (U.S. Pat. No. 3,327,747) U.S. Pat. Office, Wash., D.C.

Cumming, J. D.
1969. Stresses in band saws. In Proc. North. Calif. Sect. FPRS, pp. 21–23. Calpella, Calif.

Demsky, S.
1967. Merits of the Klear-Kut saw. Proc., 22nd Annu. Northwest Prod. Clin., pp. 33–35. Spokane, Wash.

Detjen, R. K.
1961. The linebar resaw in the southern pine and hardwood sawmill. Lumber J. 65(11): 12–13.

Dobie, J.
1970. Advantages of log sorting for chipper headrigs. Forest Prod. J. 20(1): 19–24.

Dobie, J., Sturgeon, W. J., and Wright, D. M.
1967. An analysis of the production characteristics of chipper headrigs, scrag mills and log-gang mills. Dep. Forest. and Rural Develop. Forest Prod. Lab. Inform. Rep. VP–X–21, 10 pp. Vancouver, Brit. Columbia.

Doxey, B. C.
1970. Line-following laser system for cutting die board. Boxboard Containers, Aug., pp. 50–55. BOC-Murex Welding Res. and Develop. Lab., London.

DuClos, A.
1967. Thin kerf sawing. Proc., 22nd Annu. Northwest Prod. Clin., pp. 37–42. Spokane, Wash.

Einspahr, D. W., Benson, M. K., and Peckham, J. R.
1969. Observations on a bark and wood chip separation procedure for aspen. Forest Prod. J. 19(7): 33–36.

Endersby, H. J.
1965. The cutting action of woodworking tools. IUFRO Congr. Proc. 1965, Vol. 3, Sect. 41, 7 pp. Melbourne.

Erickson, J. E.
1964. An investigation of power requirements for chipping hardwoods under various cutting conditions. Woodland Sect. Index, Can. Pulp and Pap. Assoc. 2301 (B–1) Append. B: 4–5.

Erickson, J. R.
1967. Crosscut shearing of wood. IUFRO Congr. Proc. 1967, Vol. 8, Sect. 31–32, pp. 324–337. Munich.

Fassnacht, D.
1966. Boards or chips? South. Lumberman 193(2417): 243–244.

Feihl, A. O., and Carroll, M. N.
1969. Rotary cutting veneer with a floating bar. Forest Prod. J. 19(10): 28–32.

Ferguson, J. S.
1968. What you should know about today's coated abrasives. Ind. Woodworking 20(6): 22–23, 28.

Fobes, E. W.
1959. Wood-chipping equipment and materials handling. USDA Forest Serv. Forest Prod. Lab. Rep. 2160, 25 pp.

Forest Products Research Society.
1959. Wood machining abstracts, 1957–1958. Forest Prod. Res. Soc. 20 pp.

Forest Products Research Society.
1960. Wood machining abstracts, 1958–1959. Forest Prod. Res. Soc. 19 pp.

Forest Products Research Society.
1961. Wood machining abstracts, 1959–1961. Forest Prod. Res. Soc. 18 pp.

Foschi, R. O., and Porter, A. W.
1970. Lateral and edge stability of high-strain band saws. Can. Dep. Fish. and Forest. Forest Prod. Lab. Inform. Rep. VP–X–68, 13 pp. Vancouver, B.C.

Franz, N.C.
1958. An analysis of the wood-cutting process. Ph.D. Thesis. Univ. Mich. Press. Ann Arbor. 152 pp.

Franz, N. C.
1970. High-energy liquid jet slitting of corrugated board. TAPPI 1111–1114.

Franz, N. C., and Hinken, E. W.
1954. Machining wood with coated abrasives. J. Forest Prod. Res. Soc. 4: 251–254.

Gambrell, S. C., and Byars, E. F.
1966. Cutting characteristics of chain saw teeth. Forest Prod. J. 16(1): 62–71.

Goodman, W. L.
1964. The history of woodworking tools. 208 pp. London: G. Bell and Sons, Ltd.

Grant, S. E.
1967. New developments in field manufacture and transportation of wood chips. TAPPI 50(5): 96A–98A.

Grondal, B. L.
1956. New process barks alder. Pulp and Pap. 30(3): 125–126.

Guttenberg, S., and Fasick, C.
1968. Economics of plywood production in the southern pine region. Forest Prod. J. 18(5): 43–47.

Hallock, H.
1965. Sawing to reduce warp of loblolly pine studs. USDA Forest Serv. Res. Pap. FPL–51, 52 pp. Forest Prod. Lab., Madison, Wis.

Hanchett, K. S., editor.
1946. The Hanchett saw and knife fitting manual. Ed. 6, 471 pp. Big Rapids, Mich.: Hanchett Manufacturing Co.

Harry, J. E., and Lunau, F. W.
1971. Electrothermal cutting processes using CO_2 laser. Inst. Elec. and Electron. Eng. Tech. Conf. on Elec. Process Heating in Ind. Proc., pp. 34–40. Milwaukee.

Hartler, N.
1962. The effect of spout angle as studied in an experimental chipper. Svensk Papperstidn. 65(9): 351–362.

Harvin, R. L., Nolan, W. J., and Brown, W. F.
1952. The barking of turkey oak. TAPPI 35(9): 164A–168A.

Hayashi, D., and Hara, O.
1964. Studies of surface sanding of lauan plywood. Wood Ind. 19(9): 16–21.

Hobbs, L. H., and Thomason, R. E.
1967. Lumber and chip production: A new approach. N. C. Agr. Ext. Serv. Misc. Pub. 22, 40 pp.

Holland, C. J.
1966. The changing face of wood sanding. Wood and Wood Prod. 71(4): 34, 36.

Holzhey, G.
1969. Modern debarkers—their technological and economical aspects. Holz als Roh- und Werkstoff 27: 81–102.

Hse, C. Y.
1968. Gluability of southern pine earlywood and latewood. Forest Prod. J. 18(12): 32–36.

Johnston, J. S.
1967. Investigation of some variables in the crosscutting of small logs by shear blades. IUFRO Congr. Proc. 1967, Vol. 8, Sect. 31–32, pp. 338–363. Munich.

Johnston, J. S.
1968a. An experiment in shear-blade cutting of small logs. Pulp and Pap. Mag. Can. 69(3): 77–82.

Johnston, J. S.
1968b. Crosscutting trees and logs by shear blades. Can. Forest Ind. 88(6): 34–37.

Johnston, J. S.
1968c. Experimental crosscut shearing of frozen wood. Proc., Forest Eng. Conf. Amer. Soc. Agr. Eng., ASAE Pub. PROC–368, pp. 47–49, 55. East Lansing, Mich.

Johnston, J. S.
1968d. Experiments in cross-cutting wood with shear blades. Forest Prod. J. 18(3): 85–89.

Kaiser, H. F., and Jones, C. A.
1969. Chipping head-rigs can help maintain profits in southern sawmills. South. Lumberman 219(2728): 141–142.

Kempe, C.
1967. [Forces and damage involved in the hydraulic shearing of wood.] Stud. Forest. Suecica 55, 38 pp.

Kintz, A. H.
1969. The role of the top arbor edger in precision thin sawing. In Proc. North. Calif. Sect. FPRS, pp. 6–10. Calpella, Calif.

Kivimaa, E.
1950. Cutting force in woodworking. State Inst. Tech. Res. Pub. 18, 101 pp. Helsinki, Finland.

Kivimaa, E.
1959. Cutting force in frame sawing. Pap. ja Puu 40(1): 3–6, 8–16.

Koch, P.
1948. Plane talk for better lumber. Two parts. I.—Wood 3(10): 26, 28, 30; II—3(11): 34, 36, 38, 53.

Koch, P.
1951. The ABC's of modern planing mill layout. A problem in tooling. Timberman 52(6): 56–58, 60, 62, 64, 68, 70–71.

Koch, P.
1954. An analysis of the lumber planing process. Ph.D. Thesis. Univ. Wash. Seattle. 339 pp. Available on microfilm from Univ. Mich. Ann Arbor.

Koch, P.
1955. An analysis of the lumber planing process: Part I. Forest Prod. J. 5: 255–264.

Koch, P.
1956. An analysis of the lumber planing process: Part II. Forest Prod. J. 6: 393–402.

Koch, P.
1964a. Square cants from round bolts without slabs or sawdust. Forest Prod. J. 14: 332–336.

Koch, P.
1964b. Wood machining processes. 530 pp. N.Y.: Ronald Press Co.

Koch, P.
1965. Effects of seven variables on properties of southern pine plywood. I. Maximizing wood failure. Forest Prod. J. 15: 355–361.

Koch, P.
1967a. Development of the chipping headrig. Rocky Mountain Forest Ind. Conf. Proc. 1967: 135–155. Fort Collins, Colo.

Koch, P.
1967b. History of wood machining. Wood Sci. and Technol. 1: 180–183.

Koch, P.
1967c. Too many crooked small logs? Consider a shaping-lathe head-rig! Southern Lumberman 215(2680): 147–149.

Koch, P.
1968a. Converting southern pine with chipping headrigs. Southern Lumberman 217(2704): 131–138.

Koch, P.
1968b. Wood machining abstracts, 1966 and 1967. USDA Forest Serv. Res. Pap. SO–34, 38 pp. Southern Forest Exp. Sta., New Orleans, La.

Koch, P.
1969. Sharing the tree. South. Lumberman 219(2718): 18.

Koch, P.
1970. New procurement approach increases pine utilization. Forest Ind. 97(3): 46.

Koch, P.
1971. Force and work to shear green southern pine logs at slow speed. Forest Prod. J. 21(3): 21–26.

Koch, P., and McMillin, C. W.
1966. Wood machining review, 1963 through 1965. Part I. Forest Prod. J. 16(9): 76–82, 107–115; Part II. 16(10): 43–48.

Kollmann, F. F. P., and Côté, W. A., Jr.
1968. Principles of wood science and technology. I. Solid wood. 592 pp. N.Y.: Springer-Verlag New York, Inc.

Kubler, H.
1960. [Cutting timber with vibrating knives.] Holz Zentralbl. 86: 1605–1606.

Leney, L.
1960. Mechanism of veneer formation at the cellular level. Mo. Agr. Exp. Sta. Res. Bull. 744, 111 pp.

Liiri, O.
1960. [Debarking of birch chips.] Paperi ja Puu 42: 293–298.

Liiri, O.
1961. [Investigations on the debarking of birch chips by the soaking method.] Paperi ja Puu 43: 711–715.

Lubkin, J. L.
1957. A status report on research in the circular sawing of wood. Cent. Res. Lab. Tech. Rep. CRL-T-12, 193 pp. Amer. Mach. and Foundry Co., Greenwich, Conn.

Lunau, F. W., and Paine, E. W.
1960. CO_2 laser cutting. Welding and Metal Fabr. 37(1): 9–14.

Lutz, J. F.
1956. Effect of wood-structure orientation on smoothness of knife-cut veneers. Forest Prod. J. 6: 464–468.

Lutz, J. F.
1964. How growth rate affects properties of softwood veneer. Forest Prod. J. 14: 97–102.

Lutz, J. F.
1967. Research at Forest Products Laboratory reveals that heating southern pine bolts improves veneer quality. Plywood and Panel Mag. 7(9): 20–28.

Lutz, J. F., Duncan, C. G., and Scheffer, T. C.
1966. Some effects of bacterial action on rotary-cut southern pine veneer. Forest Prod. J. 16(8): 23–28.

Lutz, J. F., Haskell, H. H., and McAlister, R.
1962. Slicewood—a promising new wood product. Forest Prod. J. 12: 218–227.

Lutz, J. F., Mergen, A., and Panzer, H.
1967. Effect of moisture content and speed of cut on quality of rotary-cut veneer. USDA Forest Serv. Res. Note FPL–0176, 13 pp. Forest Prod. Lab., Madison, Wis.

Lutz, J. F., Mergen, A. F., and Panzer, H. R.
1969. Control of veneer thickness during rotary cutting. Forest Prod. J. 19(12): 21–28.

Lutz, J. F., and Patzer, R. A.
1966. Effects of horizontal roller-bar openings on quality of rotary-cut southern pine and yellow-poplar veneer. Forest Prod. J. 16(10): 15–25.

McKenzie, W. M.
1961. Fundamental analysis of the wood-cutting process. Dep. Wood Technol. Sch. Natur. Resources. Univ. Mich., Ann Arbor. 151 pp.

McKenzie, W. M.
1970. Chipping for pulp production. Aust. Timber J. 36(4): 21–31.

McKenzie, W. M., and Cowling, R. L.
1971. A factorial experiment in transverse-plane (90/90) cutting of wood. Part I. Cutting force and edge wear. Wood Sci. 3: 204–213.

McKenzie, W. M., and Franz, N. C.
1964. Basic aspects of inclined or oblique wood cutting. Forest Prod. J. 14: 555–566.

McKenzie, W. M., and Hawkins, B. T.
1966. Quality of near longitudinal wood surfaces formed by inclined cutting. Forest Prod. J. 16(7): 35–38.

McIntosh, J. A., and Kerbes, E. L.
1969. Lumber losses in tree shear felling. Brit. Columbia Lumberman 53(10): 43–46.

McMillin, C. W.
1958. The relation of mechanical properties of wood and nosebar pressure in the production of veneer. Forest Prod. J. 8: 23–32.

McMillin, C. W.
1970a. Wood machining abstracts, 1968 and 1969. USDA Forest Serv. Res. Pap. SO–58, 35 pp. South. Forest Exp. Sta., New Orleans, La.

McMillin, C. W., and Harry, J. E.
1971. Laser machining of southern pine. Forest Prod. J. 21(10): 34–37.

Macomber, D.
1969. Smooth splitting. Paper presented at Brit. Columbia Planerman's Educ. Assoc. Annu. Meeting. 5 pp. Seattle: Stetson-Ross Machine Company.

Malcolm, F. B., and Koster, A. L.
1970. Locating maximum stresses in tooth assemblies of inserted-tooth saws. Forest Prod. J. 20(10): 34–38.

Malcolm, F. B., Reineke, L. H., and Hallock, H.
1961. Saw performance and lumber characteristics when producing pulpable southern pine sawdust. USDA Forest Serv. Forest Prod. Lab. Rep. 2210, 37 pp.

Mansfield, J. H.
1952. Woodworking machinery—history of development from 1852–1952. Mech. Eng. 74: 983–995.

March, B. W.
1970. Laser profiling machine gives high quality cuts in plywood. Furniture Industry Res. Assoc. Bull. 8(30): 34–35. Stevenage, Herts., England.

Miller, R. L., and Rothrock, C. W., Jr.
1963. A history of chip shredding. TAPPI 46(7): 174A–178A.

Nakamura, G.
1966. Studies on wood sanding by belt-sander. II. Industrial test of plywood sanding by wide belt-sander. Tokyo Univ. Agr. and Technol. Exp. Forest. Bull. 5, 17 pp.

Necesany, V.
1965. [Effect of heat and moisture on the properties of the middle lamella.] Drev. Vyskum 3: 149–154.

Nolan, W. J.
1967. Chip shredding—why not investigate further? Pulp and Pap. 41(44): 57–58.

Pahlitzsch, G., and Dziobek, K.
1959. [Investigation concerning belt polishing of wood using a straight-line cutting movement.] Holz als Roh- und Werkstoff 17: 121–134.

Pahlitzsch, G., and Dziobek, K.
1961. [On the blunting of sanding belts while sanding wood.] Holz als Roh- und Werkstoff 19: 136–149.

Pahlitzsch, G., and Dziobek, K.
1962. [Contribution to the determination of the surface quality of wood worked by chipping methods.] Holz als Roh- und Werkstoff 20: 125–137.

Papworth, R. L., and Erickson, J.R.
1966. Power requirements for producing wood chips. Forest Prod. J. 16(10): 31–36.

Penberthy, R. J.
1968. Engineering aspects of saw chain cutting. Proc., Forest Eng. Conf. Amer. Soc. Agr. Eng., ASAE Pub. PROC–368, pp. 44–46. East Lansing, Mich.

Peters, C. C.
1968. Multiple-flitch method for thick slicing. Forest Prod. J. 18(9): 82–83.

Peters, C. C., Mergen, A. F., and Panzer, H. R.
1969. Effect of cutting speed during thick slicing of wood. Forest Prod. J. 19(11): 37–42.

Plough, I. L.
1962. The use of a vibrated knife to machine superior wood surfaces. M.S. Thesis. Univ. Mich., Ann Arbor. 44 p.

Porter, A. W.
1970. Some engineering considerations of high-strain band saws. In Proc. Northwest Wood Prod. Clinic, pp. 13–32. Spokane, Wash.

Porter, A.W.
1971. Some engineering considerations of high-strain band saws. Forest Prod. J. 21(4): 25–32.

Porter, A.W., and Sanders, J.L.
1970. A hydrostatic roller bar for veneer lathes and thick slicing studies. Forest Prod. J. 20(10): 42–49.

Prokes, S.
1966. History of woodworking tools. Drevo 21(9): 318–320.

Reynolds, D.D., Soedel, W., and Eckelman, C.
1970. Cutting characteristics and power requirements of chain saws. Forest Prod. J. 20(10): 28–34.

Rogers, H. W.
1948. The wood chipper. Pap. Ind. and Pap. World 30: 883–888, 1042–1047.

Salemme, F. J.
1969. Thin carbide saws in the sawmills. In Proc. North, Calif. Sect. FPRS, pp. 10–13. Calpella, Calif.

Sampson, G. R., and Fasick, C. A.
1970. Operations research application in lumber production. Forest Prod. J. 20(5): 12–16.

St. Laurent, A.
1965. Effect of induced lateral vibration of a saw tooth on the cutting of wood. Forest Prod. J. 15: 113–116.

Schliewe, R.
1969. Thin kerf sawing considerations. In Proc. North. Calif. Sect. FPRS, pp. 14–18. Calpella, Calif.

Schmied, J.
1964. [The effect of the size, size nonuniformity, and the shape of chips on the cooking uniformity in pulping.] Pap. a Celulosa 19(4): 100–106.

Seto, K., and Nozaki, K.
1966. On the machining of plywood surface with coated abrasives; the performance of drum sander and drum type wide belt sander. Hokkaido Forest Prod. Res. Inst. Rep. 49, 27 pp. Japan.

Simons, E. N.
1966. The evolution of the saw. Part I. Wood 31(9): 33–36; Part II 31(11): 37–40.

Stevens, S. F.
1966. Care of belts and rolls— keys to good panel sanding. Ind. Woodworking 18(11): 24–25, 47.

Stewart, H. A.
1970. Abrasive vs. knife planing. Forest Prod. J. 20(7): 43–47.

Thrasher, A.
1969. Mill tour briefing. In Proc. North. Calif. Sect. FPRS, p. 21. Calpella, Calif.

Thunell, B.
1967. History of wood sawmilling. Wood Sci. and Technol. 1: 174–176.

USDA Forest Products Laboratory.
1955. Raised, loosened, torn, chipped and fuzzy grain in lumber. USDA Forest Serv. Forest Prod. Lab. Rep. 2044, 9 pp.

USDA Forest Products Laboratory.
1956. Veneer cutting and drying properties. Southern pine. USDA Forest Serv. Forest Prod. Lab. Rep. 1766–11, 5pp.

USDA Forest Products Laboratory.
    1964. Annual report of research
           at the Forest Products
           Laboratory. USDA Forest
           Serv. Forest Prod. Lab.,
           40 pp.
Wahlman, M.
    1967. Importance of chip thick-
           ness in alkaline pulping,
           and chip thickness analy-
           sis. Pap. ja Puu 49(3):
           107–110.
Ward, D.
    1963. Abrasive planing challenges
           your knife cutting tech-
           niques. Hitchcock's Wood
           Working Dig. 65(11):
           29–32.
Wesner, A. L.
    1962. Vac-sink for recovery of
           pulpwood chips from
           wood-bark waste. I. Pulp
           and Pap. 36(17): 61.

Wiklund, M.
    1967. Forces and damage in fell-
           ing and bucking with
           knife and shear type
           tools. Forsk. Skogsarbeten
           Rep. 9, 39 pp.

Wilkins, G. R.
    1966. History of circular saws.
           Timber Trades J. Annu.
           Spec. Issue: S/1–S/3, S/
           27, S/29.

Woodson, G. E., and Koch, P.
    1970. Tool forces and chip for-
           mation in orthogonal cut-
           ting of loblolly pine.
           USDA Forest Serv. Res.
           Pap. SO–52, 25 pp.
           South. Forest Exp. Sta.,
           New Orleans, La.

20

Drying

CONTENTS

20

Drying

For most uses, wood must first be dried. There are important reasons for drying wood prior to use:

- Because wood shrinks as it loses moisture, it should be dried to the moisture content it will have during use.
- Wood is dried to substantially reduce its shipping weight.
- Drying reduces the likelihood of stain or decay developing during transit, storage, or use.
- Dry wood is less susceptible to damage by insects than wet wood.
- Most strength properties of wood increase as it is dried below a moisture content of about 30 percent.
- Nailed and screwed joints are stronger in seasoned wood.
- Glued wood products perform better when assembled from dry wood.
- Prior drying usually makes treatment of wood with preservatives more successful.
- Dry wood takes finishes better than green wood.
- The electrical resistance of dry wood is much greater than that of wet wood.
- Dry wood is a better thermal insulating material than wet wood.

While it is possible to dry many southern pine products in "cook-book" fashion according to published schedules, some knowledge of wood-water relationships is helpful. A discussion of these relationships is contained in chapter 8 under section headings as follows: (8–1) MOISTURE CONTENT IN LIVING TREES; (8–2) FIBER SATURATION POINT; (8–3) EQUILIBRIUM MOISTURE CONTENT; (8–4) SHRINKING AND SWELLING; (8–5) HEAT OF SORPTION; (8–6) PERMEABILITY; (8–7) MECHANISM OF DRYING. References describing techniques for measuring and computing the moisture content of wood are listed in the opening pages of chapter 8.

Discussion in this chapter (chapter 20) is confined to the methods, schedules, and equipment required to dry various classes of southern pine products.

20–1 AIR-DRYING

Although most southern pine lumber is kiln-dried green from the saw, many timbers and poles, and sizeable amounts of lumber, are air-dried. The process depends upon air circulation within the pile, and is greatly affected by precipitation and the temperature and relative humidity of

951

outdoor air. Air entering a pile cools because it loses energy as water in the wood is moved and evaporated; vertical air movement—generally downward—is caused by increase in density of the air as it is cooled. Horizontal air movement is induced by this vertical flow. Of course, natural wind currents increase the velocity of horizontal airflow.

Drying conditions in the southern pine region are best from approximately April to October because of the high air temperatures (fig. 20–1). Equilibrium moisture content values are relatively constant at about 15 percent throughout the year. Because of seasonal and local variations in precipitation and climate, the time required to air-dry southern pine of a particular dimension can only be approximated.

Air-drying yards should be located on high, well-drained ground. Air near low ground, swamps, or bodies of water is likely to be damp. Nearby

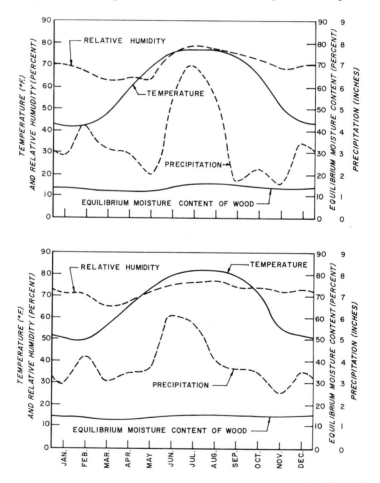

ZM–85755F, ZM–85752F

Figure 20–1.—Mean monthly temperatures, relative humidities, precipitation, and equilibrium moisture content of wood. (Top) In North Carolina, South Carolina, Virginia, and West Virginia. (Bottom) In eastern Texas, Louisiana, Mississippi, Georgia, northern Florida, and Arkansas. (Drawings after Peck 1961.)

trees, buildings, or hills are detrimental if they restrict air movement across the yard site.

A good yard surface is smooth, firm, well-drained, free from vegetation and debris, and preferably, paved. The yard layout for forklift operation includes main alleys, cross alleys, and rows of 6 to 12 piles having lateral spaces between piles and spaces between rows. Figure 20–2 illustrates this terminology (Peck 1961). The width of the main alley is determined by the length of the longest material to be stacked; 30 feet is suitable in yards designed for forklift handling of southern pine lumber. When main alleys are oriented north-south, the sun has best opportunity to dry up rainfall quickly. Alternatively, the main alleys can be lined up with the prevailing wind to stimulate airflow through the stickered packages. Lateral spaces and spaces between rows should be sufficient to permit air circulation. Wide cross alleys increase air circulation, reduce fire hazard, and permit quick identification of blocks of piles for inventory purposes.

The foundations for yard piles (pile bottoms) should be well designed and well placed. They must support the pile at least a foot clear of the yard surface without undue deflection, permit access by the handling equipment, and be durable.

Additional details on yard layout and operation have been given by Rietz (1970).

LUMBER

The yard layout in figure 20–2 is designed for use with package piles, whose essential features are shown in figure 20–3. While the outer two crossbeams on each end of the pile are fixed—at a spacing sufficient to permit the forklift to enter in the center—the center crossbeam is put into place when the pile is built, and removed when it is razed.

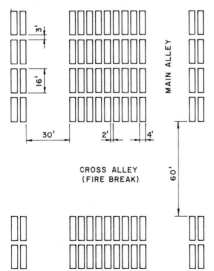

Figure 20–2.—Diagram showing a section of a yard with package piles for forklift handling. (Drawing after Peck 1961.)

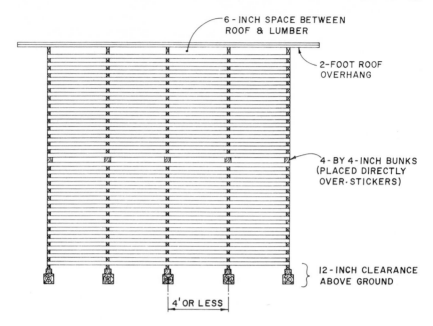

Figure 20–3.—Diagram of essential features of a package pile. Center crossbeam is removable after the pile is razed to permit forklift passage.

Stickers provide columns to support the pile, separate the courses of lumber, and restrain warping by holding the boards in a flat position. They should be perfectly aligned with the crossbeams and in good vertical alignment to prevent sagging of courses and warping of boards. Allowing end stickers to project slightly beyond the ends of the lumber reduces end checks and splits by retarding drying and sheltering the ends from sunshine and rain. Stickers for packages are commonly a uniform ¾-inch thick, approximately 1¾ inches wide, and of uniform length (a couple of inches longer than the width of the package); they should be straight. If lumber is thin or prone to warp, it needs more crossbeams and more stickers per course than lumber that is thick and less prone to warp.

The lower levels of a pile tend to dry more slowly than the upper levels. For this reason—and because extreme pile height places excessive weight on foundations and on stickers and boards in the lower part of the pile—package piles are generally limited to 16 or 20 feet in height.

A good pile roof shields the upper courses of lumber, and to a lesser extent the lower part of the pile, from precipitation and direct sunshine. Figure 20–3 illustrates roof construction. Boards may be nailed to a framework of 2x6's and securely covered with roofing paper or corrugated metal. The panel roofs are placed on the top package while it is still on the ground. While the roof for a package pile overhangs the pile at both ends, it can project only on one side—that furthest from the mast of the forklift. One successful operator uses precast concrete pile roofs to provide shelter and reduce warpage; they are put in place with a forklift. Used on southern pine, the weight of the roof must be sufficiently low to prevent compression of boards or stickers.

One-inch lumber.—Air-drying time for 1-inch southern pine boards varies with season and location. Mathewson[1] made limited observations of 1-inch No. 2 Common longleaf boards hand-stacked for air-drying at Fisher, La. Piles were 6 to 16 feet wide and generally 80 courses high. He tentatively concluded that, during the spring and summer, 2 months is ample drying time for 90 percent of the 1-inch boards to reach 19-percent moisture content or below, with the remaining pieces not exceeding 22 percent. Because of high relative humidities and rains during the late fall and winter, boards in piles razed during these periods may not meet the foregoing specification even though the stock was sufficiently dry during the preceding summer.

Peck[2] observed that in Malvern, Ark., a summer period longer than 2 months was required for 1-inch shortleaf pine boards to reach an average moisture content below 19 percent (fig. 20–4).

Page and Carter (1957, 1958) studied variations in moisture content of 1-inch southern pine air-dried in seven-package piles in Georgia during the summer of 1956. Among piles dried 31 to 104 days, average moisture content showed no relationship to length of drying time, but piles dried longest were most uniform in moisture content. At the end of the drying period, moisture content averaged 15.5 percent; one-fifth of the boards, however, exceeded 19 percent. Lumber in the top of the piles averaged slightly drier (14.3 percent) but varied more than lumber from the middle (15.8 percent) or from the bottom (16.6 percent).

In the study of Page and Carter (1957), stain was by far the most important degrading factor, accounting for 72 percent of the degrade in package piles. The cause and prevention of stain are discussed in chapter 16 and section 22–1. In brief, a suitable chemical dip within 24 hours of sawing, prompt piling for air-drying, and prevention of rewetting will control stain. Crook, bow, and cup made up the next most important class of defects. These defects can be reduced by sorted-length piling (or box piling so that packages have even ends if length sorting is not practical), by adhering to good piling practices, and by using pile roofs (fig. 20–3). Checking was not a serious problem in the 1-inch lumber. Pile roofs and placement of stickers overlapping board ends reduce degrade from checking.

Peck[2] summarized the degrade during air-drying of No. 2 Common mixed longleaf and shortleaf pine in hand-stacked flat piles as 1.8 percent of the green value. When this lumber was planed, the loss was an addi-

---

[1] Mathewson, J. S. 1936. Air seasoning periods for longleaf-pine lumber. Unpublished report, USDA Forest Serv., Forest Prod. Lab., Madison, Wis. Project L257. 9 pp.

[2] Peck, E. C. [1962]. Air drying of wood. Unpublished report, USDA Forest Serv., Forest Prod. Lab., Madison, Wis.

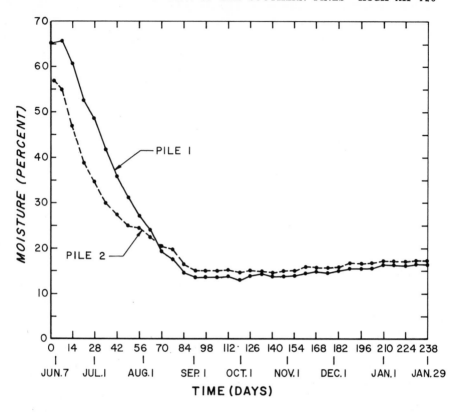

Figure 20–4.—Air-drying curves for 1-inch shortleaf pine in flat piles built by hand at Malvern, Ark. (Drawing after Peck[2].)

tional 4.6 percent. The loss from rough-green condition to dressed-dry condition was, therefore, equal to 6.4 percent of the rough green value.

Two-inch lumber.—A few data are available on the time required to air-dry 2-inch-thick southern pine. Mathewson[1] tabulated information taken in 1929 and 1930 at Fisher, La. on longleaf lumber hand stacked for air-drying in piles 6 to 16 feet wide and 24 to 42 courses high. Table 20–1 shows that in April, May, June, July and August of 1929, 8/4 lumber was dried to about 14-percent moisture content in 57 to 139 days. In 1929 the precipitation at Fisher, La. was 1.06 inches in July and 0.26 inch in August; e.m.c. during late August was about 10 percent.

In February, March, and April of 1930—when the rainfall was 3.56, 3.69, and 0.43 inches, and the e.m.c. was 16, 15, and 13 percent—8/4 lumber averaged about 19-percent moisture content after 41 to 46 days of drying.

TIMBERS

As with lumber—a well-drained yard location, a good yard surface, and well-elevated, durable pile foundations are required for a good timber drying operation. Some additional factors are also of importance to timber drying.

TABLE 20–1.—*Air-drying data for 2-inch longleaf pine at Fisher, La.*

Size (inches)	Average piling date	Air-seasoning period	Moisture content of pieces sampled		
			Maximum	Minimum	Average
	Month and Year	*Days*	– – – – – –	*Percent*	– – – – – –
2 by 4_____	April 1929	139	18.4	12.4	13.7
2 by 4_____	May 1929	103	15.4	12.4	13.5
2 by 4_____	June 1929	70	15.6	12.7	13.5
2 by 4_____	June 1929	74	18.4	13.2	14.5
2 by 6_____	April 1929	121	16.1	12.5	14.4
2 by 6_____	June 1929	57	15.2	12.9	13.6
2 by 8_____	May 1929	110	14.6	12.3	13.3
2 by 8_____	February 1929	203	15.5	12.4	14.3
2 by 4_____	February 1930	46	23.4	17.5	19.2
2 by 4_____	March 1930	41	20.7	17.3	18.9
2 by 6_____	February 1930	46	19.2	16.6	18.2
2 by 6_____	February 1930	45	22.5	15.9	18.5
2 by 8_____	February 1930	45	22.1	16.9	19.3
2 by 8_____	March 1930	42	22.6	15.0	20.2

Pile design.—Kempfer (1913) found that isolated piles of crossties permitted rapid seasoning regardless of spacing between ties in the stack, but if the piles were crowded together the influence of pile form became evident. The effect of pile form was demonstrated by air-drying crossarms. Ten-foot, 3¼- by 4¼-inch arms of loblolly pine sapwood were cut in July and piled openly with 20 arms in each tier; after 60 days' seasoning they reached 30-percent moisture content. Similar crossarms were stacked in the same size piles but with 28 arms per tier; after the same 60-day drying period they still contained 50-percent moisture content (fig. 20–5). Where the climate is especially favorable to rapid decay, a roof to provide protection against rainwetting may be desirable.

Sapwood vs. heartwood.—Figure 20–6 shows the average losses of moisture from crossarms cut in the spring months, of heartwood, sapwood, and heartwood mixed with sapwood. Because of initial differences in moisture content, the heartwood arms weighed 42.6 pounds per cubic foot, the mixed grade 50.3 pounds, and the sapwood 57.9 pounds. All had seasoned to the same weight in a little over a month's time. After further seasoning, the relative position of the sapwood and heartwood arms was reversed, the sapwood being considerably lighter than the heartwood.

Size of timbers.—The size of the piece influences the time required for seasoning because cross-sectional dimensions control the relation of the volume of a timber to its surface area, the total amount of water to be evaporated, and the distance which the moisture on the interior must travel to escape from the surface. This influence, according to Kempfer (1913), is not as great as might be expected. Shortleaf pine 5- by 8-inch

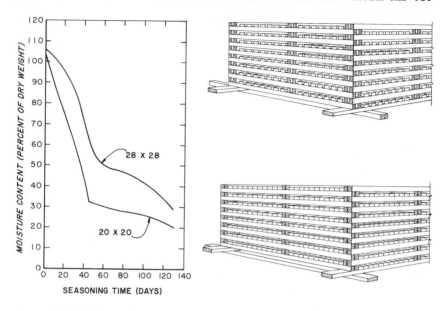

Figure 20–5.—Effect of pile form on drying rate of 10-foot-long, 3¼- by 4¼-inch, sapwood, loblolly pine crossarms air-dried in Norfolk, Va. Crossarms on ends turned on edge so that courses are separated by a 1-inch air gap. (Top right) Piled 20 to each course with all faces exposed to circulation. (Bottom right) Piled 28 to each course leaving no spaces for vertical ventilation. (Left) Comparison of time to dry. (Drawings after Kempfer 1913.)

beams attained only 3 percent lower moisture content after 15 months' seasoning than 8- by 12-inch timbers.

Air-drying curves for timbers.—Crossarms shipped in spring months from Montgomery County, N.C. were air-dried in Norfolk, Va. from an estimated initial moisture content of 80 percent to a final estimated moisture content of 26 percent as shown in figure 20–6 (Kempfer 1913). Arms in piles established in June, July, and August dried more slowly.

Figure 20–7 shows the weight-time relation for 16-foot shortleaf pine timbers measuring 5 by 8 and 8 by 12 inches. The curves show average data for 6 timbers at each size. Initial moisture content averaged 47 percent and final moisture content after 15 months averaged 13 percent (Kempfer 1913).

Air-seasoning rates for 8-foot-long, 6- by 8-inch southern pine crossties were reported by Kempfer (1913). Ties cut in January and February were fairly dry at the end of 4 or 5 months; weight loss was about 50 pounds per tie. Ties cut and piled from April to October seasoned so rapidly that there was little loss of weight after the first 2 or 3 months, even when the ties were held over to the following summer. The tests were conducted at Silsbee, Tex., and Ackerman, Miss.

Southern pine heartwood timbers 24 feet long and 12 inches square were air-seasoned to 20-percent moisture content in an open shed in Madison, Wis. in 12 to 15 months. The timbers were piled on 2- by 4-

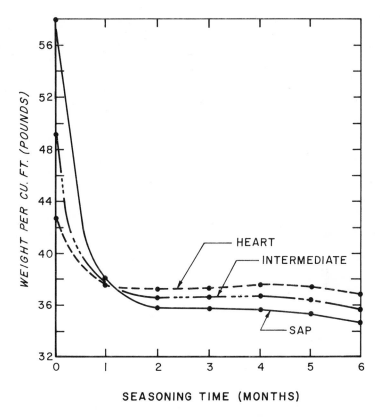

Figure 20–6.—Weight changes during seasoning of 10-foot-long, 3¼- by 4¼-
inch, loblolly pine crossarms air-dried in Norfolk, Va. Piles were established in spring months of 1906. (Drawing after Kempfer 1913.)

inch stickers and were spaced 2 to 3 inches apart. In two tests, relatively
little moisture was lost during winter months.

POLES

Poles are difficult to protect against fungus attack during air-drying.
There are indications that some early failures of treated poles in service
are indirectly caused by fungus; inadequate penetration of preservative
may result where permeability increases in infected wood and permits
excessive rainwater pickup prior to treatment. Section 16–7 (BARK-FREE
POLES AND TIMBERS) describes chemical treatment of poles to deter
attack by fungi. Later infection is possible, however, if checks provide
access to untreated wood still moist enough to sustain fungi. An alternative suggestion calls for brief pressure impregnation of the green material with a waterborne preservative prior to air-drying.

Figure 20–8 (Left) illustrates good piling practice in an air-drying yard

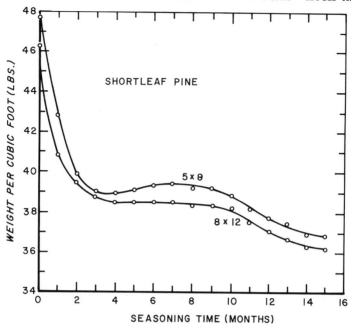

Figure 20–7.—Weight changes during seasoning of shortleaf pine timbers cut in Arkansas and air-dried (commencing July 15, 1907) in an enclosed shed in Lafayette, Ind. (Drawing after Kempfer 1913.)

for southern pine poles. The installation would be improved if the creosoted piers and beams supported the lowest layer of poles about 2 feet off the ground. Successive layers of poles are separated by treated stickers about 4 inches thick. Stickers should be accurately aligned over the piers

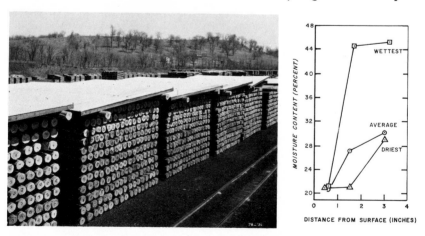

Figure 20–8.—(Left) Well-piled poles in an air-seasoning yard. (Right) Moisture distribution 6 feet from the butt end of the wettest, the driest, and the average of 12, Class 5, 40-foot southern pine poles after air-drying for 96 days. Moisture content at surface was approximately 11.3 percent. (Photo and drawings after Mathewson and Berger 1957.)

to prevent bending of lower poles. Pile height should be limited so that sticks are not crushed into poles of the lowest layer. A chimney 2 feet wide is left in the middle of the pile from top to bottom. Alternatively, poles can be stacked in a cross-hatch pile so that they act as their own pile stickers. According to Mathewson (1930), about 2 months in the summer or 4 months in the winter is the usual seasoning period prior to preservative treatment.

Mathewson and Berger (1957) made a study of moisture distribution in 12 class 5, 40-foot southern pine poles 96 days after they were shipped to an air-drying yard in Finney, Ohio. Their data showed that the moisture content at the surface (estimated at 11.3 percent) and ½-inch in from the surface (21 percent) were equal in the wettest and driest of the 12 poles, but 3 inches in from the surface, moisture content was 29 percent on the driest pole and 45 percent on the wettest. Measurements were taken approximately 6 feet from the butt of each pole (fig. 20–8 Right).

Burkhalter and Russell (1969) have proposed that air-drying of southern pine trees cut for poles and piling can be accomplished easily if the tops are not severed from the stem for a few weeks following felling. In a study of loblolly and slash pine they found that some trees left on the ground for a month and a half with crown intact lost as much as 30 percent of their green weight, whereas similar tree stems with crowns severed from stems lost only 3 percent of total weight during the same period on the ground (bark intact). More typically, 4 or 5 months was required for a felled tree with crown intact to lose 30 percent of its green weight (fig. 20–9). To make this drying system practical, a procedure to protect the stems against fungus attack would have to be developed.

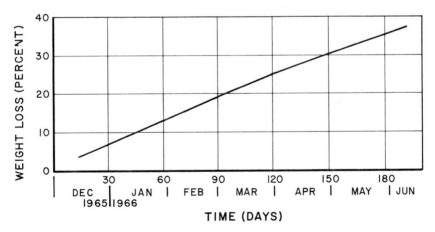

Figure 20–9.—Percent weight loss from the green condition of entire loblolly pine tree severed at ground level and left on the ground with crown intact for 6 months. Curve based on data from six trees. Slash pine trees cut under the same condition lost weight at virtually the same rate. (Drawing after Burkhalter and Russell 1969.)

CONTROL OF END CHECKS

End checking can degrade poles, piling, and heavy timbers during drying. In timbers, end checking can be reduced by prompt application of suitable coatings to freshly cut end surfaces. If applied after checking has begun, coatings rarely prevent deepening of the checks. Usually no attempt is made to control checking in piles, poles, and posts.

Studies have shown that single hot coatings are more effective than single coats of any of the cold coatings. McMillen (1961a) evaluated various hot coatings by completely covering small blocks of green shortleaf pine with the test coatings and exposing them to regulated conditions of temperature and humidity. In figure 20–10 the results are expressed in terms of the percentage of original evaporable moisture (above equilibrium moisture content) remaining in the wood.

Hot coatings must be heated above their melting point when applied. Among the hot coatings, paraffin, rosin and lampblack, coal tar pitches, and asphalt are highly effective when applied in a single coat $\frac{1}{20}$- to $\frac{1}{16}$-inch thick. Paraffin is generally suitable only for air-seasoning, rosin and lampblack are suitable for kiln temperatures up to 150° F., and pitches and asphalts can be selected for use at any ordinary kiln temperature. Blends of coal tar pitches and petroleum asphalts of suitable softening points form effective coatings that are tougher and more adhesive than the pitch alone. The coating with the lowest softening point that will safely withstand the drying temperatures used is recommended. Hot coatings can be applied by dipping the ends of the pieces in the molten coating, or more satisfactorily by means of a power-driven roller device.

Cold coatings may be of several types:

Type	Comment
White lead in linseed oil	Good moisture resistance
Aluminum particles in a phenolic-resin, tung-oil varnish (2 pounds aluminum per gallon of varnish)	Three brushed (or sprayed) coats gives best results
Unfilled resin varnish	Becomes brittle in final stages of kiln drying. Not abrasive to machine knives.
Asphaltic (in water emulsion or with petroleum solvent)	Water emulsion subject to breakdown on freezing or exposure to heavy rain.
Wax emulsions	Can be clear or colored. Economical. Subject to breakdown in heavy rain.

A list of manufacturers and distributors of both hot and cold proprietary coatings is available (USDA Forest Products Laboratory 1966).

Another approach to the reduction of end checking is application of mechanical restraint to the green wood. There are several forms of anti-checking irons (S and C shapes are popular) that can be driven into the ends of timbers and ties; they are most effective if placed to cross the

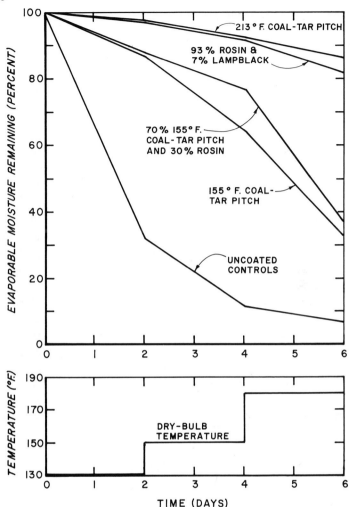

Figure 20–10.—(Top) Moisture content of small green shortleaf pine blocks, uncoated and completely coated with test materials, when subjected to accelerated drying conditions. Tested coal tar pitches are identified by melting point. Evaporable moisture remaining, percent =

$$(100) \left[\frac{\text{current moisture content} - \text{equilibrium moisture content}}{\text{original moisture content} - \text{equilibrium moisture content}} \right].$$

(Bottom) Dry-bulb temperatures during the 6-day drying period; wet-bulb temperatures were continuously adjusted to achieve a humidity appropriate for 11-percent equilibrium moisture content in uncoated controls. (Drawing after McMillen 1961a.)

greatest number of rays. Alternatively, crossties with end splits can be clamped on the ends so that the splits are closed, then drilled transversely across the split 3 inches from each end, and finally secured by driving headless spiral steel dowels into the holes. Data specific to southern pine on the necessity and relative efficiencies of these mechanical devices have not been published.

20–2 FORCED-AIR-DRYING

Shed-fan air-drying is the next step beyond conventional air-drying. In this system stickered package piles are placed in a building with fans on one side. The outdoor air is then pulled through the lumber in a single pass, without recirculation. While surface evaporation is speeded because of higher air velocity and because the air movement prevents buildup of high relative humidity between lumber courses, drying is still dependent on weather conditions.

LUMBER

Gaby (1959, 1961) dried 1-inch, rough, green, southern pine lumber in a wind tunnel simulating such an unheated drier. Fans were not reversible. During the winter (Athens, Ga.) when temperatures averaged 42° F., drying times from 85-percent moisture content to an average of 25-percent were 12, 10, and 7.5 days respectively for air velocities of 300, 500, and 800 feet per minute (f.p.m.) (fig. 20–11). The following spring when temperatures averaged 72° F., drying times from 91-percent moisture content to an average moisture content of 25 percent were 7.3, 5.6, and 4.0 days respectively, for similar velocities. Blue stain occurred when air velocity was low or when outside humidity was high; in the most severe case 44 percent of the boards had sufficient stain to cause degrade. Drying rate dropped substantially as load width was increased beyond 8 feet (fig. 20–12).

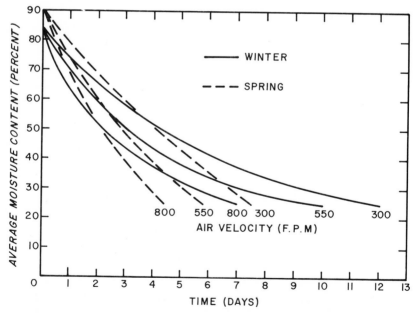

Figure 20–11.—Effect of air velocity and season on drying time of 1-inch southern pine in an unheated wind tunnel during spring and winter. (Drawing after Gaby 1961.)

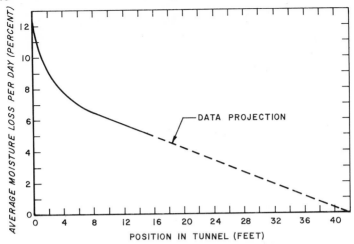

Figure 20–12.—Effect of length of air travel on drying rate of 1-inch southern pine. Drying time 8 days; air velocity 500 f.p.m.; no fan reversal; no
control of drying conditions. (Drawing after Gaby 1961.)

The forced-air dryer, or predryer, has two added features—a confining
structure to permit recirculation of the air, and a source of heat to raise
the temperature somewhat above ambient. These dryers generally operate
continuously at one relatively low temperature (120° F. or less) and do not
control humidity except by this slightly elevated air temperature.

With dryer temperature constant at 80° F and reversing the fans at
3-hour intervals Gaby (1959, 1961) found that 1-inch, rough, green
southern pine could be dried from green condition (110-percent moisture
content) to an average of 17 percent (with 95 percent of the boards at
20 percent or less) in 4 to 6 days (fig. 20–13). Two-inch pine required
about twice this time. Seasoning degrade was minor. Higher temperatures (up to 110° F.) can be expected to reduce drying time without
increasing degrade. Fan reversal reduced drying time compared to one-way
airflow. Length of air travel across the load should be limited to 8 feet
or less if possible.

POLES AND ROUND BOLTS

Gaby (1967) dried freshly cut, peeled slash and loblolly pine short logs
in a forced-air dryer after first storing them 1 week under water. Bolts
were 18 inches and 55 inches long. Air circulation was reversed every 6
hours. The mean air velocity was between 600 and 700 f.p.m. Bolts were
not end coated and were piled in bins without stickers so that circulating
air travelled the length of the bolts. A mean dry-bulb temperature of
120° F. was maintained. Wet-bulb temperature was not controlled, but
with vents open atmosphere in the dryer reached an e.m.c. condition of
3 to 4 percent early in the cycle.

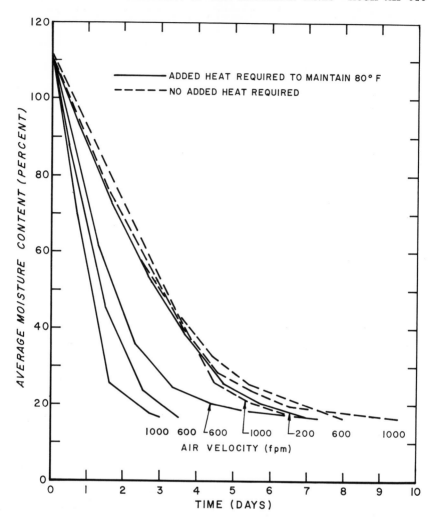

Figure 20–13.—Moisture content of 1-inch southern pine lumber dried at a constant 80° F. and at three air velocities. Addition of heat not required during warm months. (Drawing after Gaby 1961.)

Bolt diameter significantly affected drying rates. Time to dry 55-inch-long bolts from 115-percent initial moisture content to a target 25-percent was 4.8 days for 4- to 5-inch bolts, 10.2 days for 8- to 9-inch bolts, and 15.8 days for 12- to 13-inch bolts (fig. 20–14). Half-round bolts, originally 12 to 13 inches in diameter, dried in the same time as round bolts 8 to 9 inches in diameter.

Surprisingly, in diameter classes from 4 to 9 inches, 55-inch-long bolts dried 1 to 2 days sooner than 18-inch-long bolts. Drying rates were not affected by mixing large- and small-diameter bolts in the bins; bolts of comparable diameters dried at very similar rates.

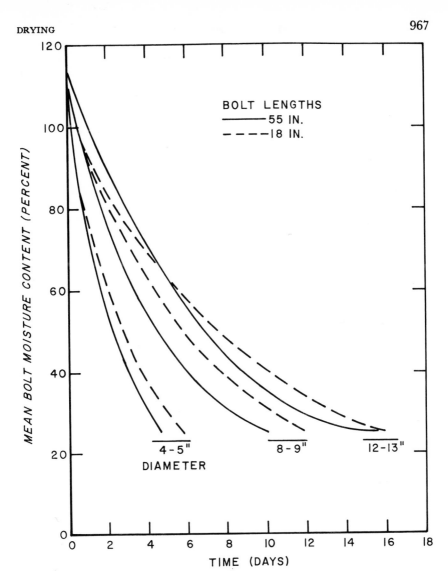

Figure 20–14.—Drying curves for two lengths of round, peeled southern pine bolts at 120° F., 17-percent relative humidity, and air velocity of 600 to 700 f.p.m. (Drawing after Gaby 1967.)

As would be expected, the outer shell of the bolts was substantially drier (15 percent) than the interior (30 to 40 percent) at the end of the drying cycle. Steam-equalization of these bolts (120° F. for 2 or 3 days) is discussed at the end of section 20–3.

20–3   KILN-DRYING

Dry kilns differ from forced-air dryers; they operate at dry-bulb temperatures generally in excess of 120° F. and with controlled wet-bulb temperatures. This is true of both indirectly heated (steam) and directly heated (gas-fired) kilns. The sensing elements for dry-bulb control are so located that regardless of direction of air circulation, the temperature of air entering the stack of lumber is controlled. The wet-bulb thermal element is conveniently located so that the wicks can be replaced readily. Wet-bulb instrumentation controls venting, fresh air intake, and moisture supply. When the wet-bulb temperature exceeds the set point, vents are opened; they close when the wet-bulb temperature drops to near the set point. The wet-bulb temperature has to drop somewhat below the setting before moisture is injected into the kiln (usually as steam). Venting in most southern pine kilns is accomplished through roof vents; differences in static air pressure on opposite sides of the fan baffle draw in fresh air and discharge kiln air to the atmosphere. Such venting wastes heat. Where the cost of fuel is high, the newly developed pressure-venting process should be considered (Dineen 1968).

Over the years, air circulation rates have been increased; research has shown that if lumber has moisture on the surface, high air velocity will increase the drying rate. Today, circulation rates in the range from 200 to 400 f.p.m. are usual; equipment manufacturers have infrequently used velocities in excess of 500 f.p.m. to dry lumber because of additional horsepower required to drive the fans.

Most southern pine is dried on the basis of manually adjusted time schedules for wet- and dry-bulb settings. The operator resets the recorder-controller according to time in the kiln. There are few program controllers in use that have precut cams or other devices for automatically adjusting settings as a function of time in the kiln.

It is probable that kiln controls will become increasingly automated. The USDA Forest Products Laboratory (1970) has developed a control system that monitors and records conditions within the kiln and automatically adjusts steam valves and air vents in response to moisture content of the charge so as to maintain programmed temperatures, airflow, and humidity for each stage of drying.

Most kilns in the South are steam heated and may be fired by gas, oil, or wood waste. Direct-fired kilns are also commercially available; those not equipped with auxiliary steam or water-spray humidification are less well adapted to equalization and conditioning treatments. Kilns may have single or double tracks to accommodate 8-foot-wide loads on rails, or they may be forklift loaded with smaller packages. Southern pine dries so readily and uniformly that large kilns can be used to advantage. Details of kiln construction can be found in chapter 2 of Rasmussen (1961).

LUMBER [3]

Through their cooperative efforts, the USDA Forest Products Laboratory and the Southern Pine Association (now the Southern Forest Products Association) have greatly stimulated good kiln-drying practices for lumber.

---

[3] The kiln schedules tabulated for lumber under this heading are taken from Rasmussen (1961).

Teesdale's (1930) USDA Technical Bulletin 165 was a landmark in this program. Today, the ventilated, forced-air-circulation dry kiln is the most economical equipment for drying lumber (Rietz 1965); its operation may be separated into three phases, i.e., drying, equalizing, and conditioning.

Drying.—Section 8–7 explained that while removal of moisture from the surface is the limiting factor, drying time is directly proportional to board thickness; it is inversely proportional to wet-bulb depression and approximately inversely proportional to air velocity over the surface. When moisture diffusion is the limiting factor, drying time is approximately proportional to board thickness squared; it is inversely proportional to the water vapor pressure at saturation.

While all of the southern pines are relatively easy to dry, natural variability within the tree complicates the process. For example, the green moisture content of sapwood is higher than that of heartwood (see sec. 8–1), but sapwood dries faster than heartwood. Because of this, either one may be overdried before the other reaches desired dryness. This may necessitate an equalizing treatment. Quarter-sawed boards generally dry more slowly than plain-sawed, but they are less susceptible to surface checking. Therefore, a faster drying schedule can be used on quarter-sawed boards to reduce drying time.

Over a period of time the USDA Forest Products Laboratory has developed a conservative group of schedules for drying various grades and thicknesses of a large number of commercial species. These schedules plus a wealth of additional information on the kiln-drying of lumber are available in handbook form (Rasmussen 1961). In general, the schedules are divided into two groups.

In **moisture content schedules,** sequential steps of dry- and wet-bulb temperatures are determined by observed moisture contents of sample boards in the kiln charge. Changes in wet-bulb depression between 15 and 35° F. are made gradually—not over 5° at a time, and depressions of 35° F. or more are avoided until the average moisture content of the wettest half of the kiln samples (**controlling samples**) reaches 25 percent. The initial temperature is maintained until the controlling kiln samples have an average moisture content of 30 percent. A disadvantage of this system is the difficulty in retrieving samples from a hot kiln, which should be cooled to a wet-bulb temperature of 130° F. or lower before it is entered to remove samples.

Moisture content schedules vary with lumber grade and thickness. Those in the accompanying tables are designed to dry southern pine lumber green from the saw without prior air-drying. Table 20–2 is for upper-grade 4/4, table 20–3 for lower-grade 4/4 and upper-grade 6/4 and 8/4, while table 20–4 is designed for 10/4 and 12/4 lumber.

Few southern pine lumber manufacturers use these kiln schedules based on change in moisture content, but instead use schedules based on time. With **time schedules** drying conditions are changed at convenient intervals,

TABLE 20–2.—*Moisture content kiln schedule for upper grades of 4/4 southern pine*[1]

Moisture content at start of step (percent)	Dry-bulb temperature	Wet-bulb depression	Wet-bulb temperature	Relative humidity	E.m.c.
	– – – – – °F. – – – – –			– – Percent – –	
Above 40_____	170	15	155	69	9.2
40_____	170	20	150	60	7.8
35_____	170	25	145	52	6.7
30_____	180	30	150	47	5.7
25_____	180	35	145	41	5.0
20_____	190	35	155	43	4.9
15_____	190	50	[2]	28	3.3

[1] Schedule T13–C6 from Rasmussen (1961).
[2] Close control of wet-bulb temperature not necessary. Steam spray shut off.

TABLE 20–3.—*Moisture content kiln schedule for upper grades of 6/4 and 8/4, and lower grades of 4/4, southern pine*[1]

Moisture content at start of step (percent)	Dry-bulb temperature	Wet-bulb depression	Wet-bulb temperature	Relative humidity	E.m.c.
	– – – – – °F. – – – – –			– – Percent – –	
Above 40_____	160	10	150	77	11.5
40_____	160	14	146	69	9.7
35_____	160	20	140	58	7.9
30_____	170	25	145	52	6.7
25_____	170	30	140	45	5.7
20_____	180	35	145	41	5.0
15_____	180	50	[2]	26	3.3

[1] Schedule T12–C5 from Rasmussen (1961).
[2] Close control of wet-bulb temperature not necessary. Steam spray shut off.

TABLE 20–4.—*Suggested moisture content kiln schedule for upper grades of 10/4 and 12/4 southern pine*[1]

Moisture content at start of step (percent)	Dry-bulb temperature	Wet-bulb depression	Wet-bulb temperature	Relative humidity	E.m.c.
	– – – – – °F. – – – – –			– – Percent – –	
Above 40_____	140	7	133	82	13.8
40_____	140	10	130	75	11.9
35_____	140	15	125	64	9.6
30_____	150	20	130	57	8.0
25_____	160	25	135	50	6.8
20_____	170	30	140	45	5.7
15_____	180	50	[2]	26	3.3

[1] Schedule T10–C4 from Rasmussen (1961).
[2] Close control of wet-bulb temperature not necessary. Steam spray shut off.

usually 12 or 24 hours. The schedules are guides developed from experimental work and mill experience. They are geared to performance of single-track (or booster-coil-equipped, double-track) internal fan kilns with air velocities from 200 to 400 f.p.m. through the loads. Individual mills may modify them to compensate for differences in lumber, kiln type, and kiln performance.

Time schedules in commercial use vary with lumber grade and thickness and are designed to dry lumber green from the saw without prior air-drying. Tables 20–5, 20–6, and 20–7 apply to upper grades of southern pine, and are for 4/4, 6/4, and 8/4 respectively. Tables 20–8 and 20–9 are for 4/4 and 8/4 lumber of the lower grades.

TABLE 20–5.—*Time-based kiln schedule for upper grades of 4/4 southern pine*[1]

Time (hours)	Dry-bulb temperature	Wet-bulb depression	Wet-bulb temperature	Relative humidity	E.m.c.
	– – – – – °F. – – – – – –			– – Percent – –	
20–12	165	15	150	68	9.3
1 –24	170	15	155	69	9.2
24–36	175	20	155	61	7.7
36–48	180	20	160	62	7.6
48–60	190	25	165	56	6.4
60–72	190	25	165	56	6.4
72–96[2]	200	30	170	57	6.2

[1] Schedule AS11–BK6 from Rasmussen (1961). Stock slightly air-dried on kiln trucks before entering the kiln probably will dry to 8-percent average (11-percent maximum) moisture content in approximately 96 hours.

[2] Conditioning may be desirable at conclusion of this schedule.

TABLE 20–6.—*Time-based kiln schedule for upper grades of 6/4 southern pine*[1]

Time (hours)	Dry-bulb temperature	Wet-bulb depression	Wet-bulb temperature	Relative humidity	E.m.c.
	– – – – – °F. – – – – – –			– – Percent – –	
0–12	160	7	153	83	13.4
12–24	165	10	155	78	11.4
24–36	170	15	155	69	9.2
36–48	180	20	160	62	7.6
48–60	180	25	155	54	6.5
60–72	190	30	160	49	5.5
72–96	190	35	155	43	4.9
96–120[2]	190	35	155	43	4.9

[1] Schedule AS10–AK4 from Rasmussen (1961). Stock slightly air-dried on kiln trucks before entering the kiln possibly will dry to 8-percent average (11-percent maximum) moisture content in approximately 120 hours. If the operator wishes to stop at a highre average moisture content, equalization and/or conditioning should be started earlier.

[2] Conditioning may be desirable at conclusion of this schedule.

TABLE 20–7.—*Time-based kiln schedule for upper grades of 8/4 southern pine[1]*

Time (hours)	Dry-bulb temperature	Wet-bulb depression	Wet-bulb temperature	Relative humidity	E.m.c.
	— — — — — °F. — — — — —			— — Percent — —	
0–12 _ _ _ _ _ _ _ _ _ _	160	7	153	83	13.4
12–24 _ _ _ _ _ _ _ _ _ _	165	10	155	78	11.4
24–36 _ _ _ _ _ _ _ _ _ _	170	15	155	69	9.2
36–48 _ _ _ _ _ _ _ _ _ _	180	20	160	62	7.6
48–60 _ _ _ _ _ _ _ _ _ _	180	25	155	54	6.5
60–72 _ _ _ _ _ _ _ _ _ _	190	30	160	49	5.5
72–96 _ _ _ _ _ _ _ _ _ _	190	35	155	43	4.9
96–120 _ _ _ _ _ _ _ _ _	190	35	155	43	4.9
120–144[2] _ _ _ _ _ _ _	190	35	155	43	4.9

[1] Schedule AS10–AK4 from Rasmussen (1961). Stock slightly air-dried on kiln trucks before entering the kiln possibly will dry to 9-percent average (12-percent maximum) moisture content in approximately 144 hours. If the operator wishes to stop at a higher average moisture content, equilization and/or conditioning should be started earlier.

[2] Conditioning may be desirable at conclusion of this schedule.

TABLE 20–8.—*Time-based kiln schedule for lower grades of 4/4 southern pine[1]*

Time (hours)	Dry-bulb temperature	Wet-bulb depression	Wet-bulb temperature	Relative humidity	E.m.c.
	— — — — — °F. — — — — —			— — Percent — —	
0–24 _ _ _ _ _ _ _ _ _ _	165	10	155	78	11.4
24–48 _ _ _ _ _ _ _ _ _ _	170	15	155	69	9.2
48–68 _ _ _ _ _ _ _ _ _ _	175	20	155	61	7.7

[1] Schedule BS11–BK5 from Rasmussen (1961). Stock slightly air-dried on kiln trucks before entering the kiln probably will dry to 15-percent average (19-percent maximum) moisture content in approximately 68 hours.

TABLE 20–9.—*Time-based kiln schedule for lower grades of 8/4 southern pine[1]*

Time (hours)	Dry-bulb temperature	Wet-bulb depression	Wet-bulb temperature	Relative humidity	E.m.c.
	— — — — — °F. — — — — —			— — Percent — —	
0–12 _ _ _ _ _ _ _ _ _ _	165	15	150	68	9.3
12–24 _ _ _ _ _ _ _ _ _ _	170	15	155	69	9.2
24–36 _ _ _ _ _ _ _ _ _ _	175	20	155	61	7.7
36–48 _ _ _ _ _ _ _ _ _ _	180	20	160	62	7.6
48–60 _ _ _ _ _ _ _ _ _ _	190	25	165	56	6.4
60–72 _ _ _ _ _ _ _ _ _ _	190	25	165	56	6.4
72–100 _ _ _ _ _ _ _ _ _	200	30	170	51	5.4

[1] Schedule AS11–BK6 from Rasmussen (1961). Stock slightly air-dried on kiln trucks before entering the kiln possibly will dry to 15-percent average (19-percent maximum) moisture content in approximately 100 hours.

While each table carries a footnote giving an approximate ending moisture content, it is recognized that results will differ according to the initial moisture content of the green lumber. It is usual practice to lengthen or shorten the final step to obtain the desired final average moisture content. At some mills, however, when the lumber is quite wet the initial step is prolonged or is preceded by a step with less wet-bulb depression; this practice sometimes reduces kiln degrade. In any event, final moisture content must be checked and the schedule lengthened or shortened accordingly.

It is sometimes necessary to kiln-dry lumber that has been previously air-dried. Rasmussen (1961, p. 132) outlines the procedure for southern pine.

- Sample representative slow- and fast-drying material and use the average moisture content of the wettest half of the samples.
- If the controlling moisture content is above 40 percent, dry the material as green stock.
- For moisture below 40 percent, use the suggested moisture-content schedule beginning at the temperature step corresponding to the moisture content as follows:

	Dry-bulb temperature step				
Grade and thickness	Above 30 percent	30 percent	25 percent	20 percent	15 percent
			°F.		
Upper grades of ⁴⁄₄	170	180	180	190	190
Upper grades of ⁶⁄₄ and ⁸⁄₄; lower grades of ⁴⁄₄	160	170	170	180	180
Upper grades of ¹⁰⁄₄ and ¹²⁄₄	140	150	160	170	180

- If the controlling moisture content is 40 percent or less, change the wet-bulb depression as follows:

  a. Use a depression of 10 to 15° F. for the initial 8 to 16 hours. (For stock over 8/4 thickness, use the 10° F. depression during the first 16- to 24-hour period and 15° F. for the second such period.)
  b. After this, if the controlling moisture content is between 15 and 25 percent, change the wet-bulb depression to 20° F.
  c. Use a depression of 30° F. or more after the stock reaches 15-percent moisture content.

Equalizing.—At the end of the drying schedule the moisture content may vary considerably among boards in a kiln charge. Such variation may cause serious trouble during storage, fabrication, or use. Too much variation also makes it difficult to relieve drying stresses (casehardening). Equalizing treatment near the end of drying is desirable to reduce variation in moisture content.

The procedure for equalizing a kiln charge of upper-grade lumber (in the range of 5- to 11-percent moisture content) is as follows:

- Start equalizing when the driest kiln sample in the charge has reached an average moisture content 2 percent below the desired final average. If, for example, the target moisture content is 8 percent, equalizing would start when the driest kiln sample reaches 6 percent.
- Establish kiln conditions for an equalizing e.m.c. 2 percent below target moisture content. In the example above, the equalizing e.m.c. would be 6 percent. During equalizing, use as high a dry-bulb temperature as the drying schedule permits.
- Continue equalizing until the wettest sample reaches the desired final average moisture content. In the example, the wettest sample would be dried to 8 percent. Samples on the outside of the load dry faster than those on the inside (Hallock 1965, fig. 11).

For construction lumber (or laminating lumber) limited to a 15-percent maximum moisture content, start equalizing when the driest material reaches 9 percent and use a 9-percent e.m.c.

For a 19-percent maximum, start equalizing when the driest material reaches 11 percent and use an 11-percent e.m.c.

If a conditioning treatment is to follow equalizing, it may be necessary to lower the temperature to obtain conditions for the desired conditioning e.m.c. When this is necessary, begin lowering the temperature 12 to 24 hours prior to the start of conditioning. Meanwhile, maintain the desired equalizing e.m.c. by lowering the wet-bulb temperature.

Conditioning.—If the boards are to be resawed, ripped into thin strips, or machined nonuniformly, a conditioning treatment is desirable. Such a treatment accomplishes two things—it relieves drying stresses, and it produces a more uniform moisture content throughout the thickness of the boards. Drying stresses and nonuniformity of moisture can result in serious deformation during fabrication and use.

The conditioning treatment, whether or not preceded by an equalizing treatment, should not be started until the average moisture content of the wettest sample reaches the desired final average moisture content.

The procedure for conditioning a kiln charge of lumber is as follows:

- The conditioning temperature is the same as the final step of the drying schedule or the highest temperature at which the conditioning e.m.c. can be controlled. Set the wet-bulb temperature so the conditioning e.m.c. will be 3 percent above the final average moisture content. (This procedure applies to moisture contents of 11 percent or less; conditioning is difficult at higher moisture contents; a 14-percent average moisture content can be approached in kilns which will maintain the correct high e.m.c. at temperatures of 140° F. or above.)
- Continue conditioning until satisfactory stress relief is attained.

The time required for conditioning varies considerably, depending upon thickness of the lumber, the type of kiln used, and kiln performance. One-inch pine can be conditioned in as little as 4 hours. The least time necessary to get stress relief is determined by prong tests (fig. 20–15). Reversing of air circulation during conditioning is desirable for uniform stress relief (Winkel 1956).

Average moisture content immediately after the conditioning treatment will be about 1 to 1½ percent above the desired value because of the surface moisture regain. After cooling, the average moisture content of the lumber should be close to that desired.

Curves showing moisture content vs. time in kiln.—The foregoing portion of section 20–3 has discussed and tabulated kiln schedules. Hopkins et al. (1969) have published data specific to 6-inch-wide, flat-grain, No. 2 Common and better southern pine that show the change in moisture content of ¾-inch, 1-inch, 1½-inch, and 2-inch lumber versus time in the kiln when dried under various time-based schedules taken from Rasmussen

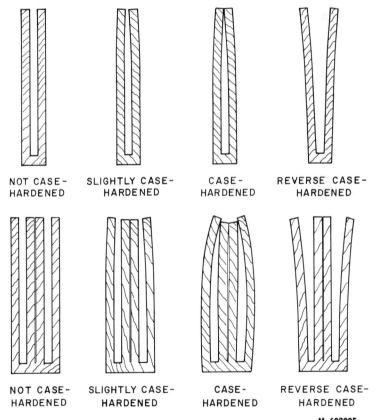

NOT CASE-HARDENED SLIGHTLY CASE-HARDENED CASE-HARDENED REVERSE CASE-HARDENED

NOT CASE-HARDENED SLIGHTLY CASE-HARDENED CASE-HARDENED REVERSE CASE-HARDENED

M–60300F

Figure 20–15.—Method of cutting specimens to determine degree of stress relief. Material that is less than 1½ inches thick is cut into three prongs, and the middle prong is removed; material that is 1½ inches thick or thicker is cut into six prongs, and the second and fifth prongs are removed.

(1961). In the kiln, air was cross-circulated at 450 f.p.m.; direction of airflow was reversed every 4 hours.

In figure 20–16 the top two drawings show an average commercial schedule for upper grades of 1-inch lumber; it ends with a wet-bulb depression of 30° F. at 200° F. and is designed to achieve rapid drying with a relatively mild initial temperature (165° F. with 15° depression). The middle two drawings show a moderate schedule with initial temperature of 170° F. and final wet-bulb depression of 50° F. at 200° F. achieved after 72 hours. The bottom drawings depict the most severe schedule; it starts at 170° F. with 20° F. depression and after 60 hours finishes at 200° F. with a 50° F. depression. Average ending moisture contents were as follows (Hopkins et al. 1969).

Schedule	¾-inch lumber		1-inch lumber	
	Moisture content	Time in kiln	Moisture content	Time in kiln
	Percent	Hours	Percent	Hours
Mild	7	84	3	84
Moderate	6	84	4	84
Severe	3	72	4	72

In figure 20–17, also from Hopkins et al. (1969), curves for 1½- and 2-inch-thick lumber are compared. Shown at the top is a mild schedule starting at 160° F. with 7° F. wet-bulb depression; in the final step, made after 72 hours, the ending temperature is 190° F. with depression of 35°. The middle drawings show a moderate schedule beginning at 165° F. with 15° F. depression; the final step—also reached after 72 hours—has a 50° F. depression from a dry-bulb temperature of 200° F. At the bottom is the most severe schedule; it begins at 170° F. with 20° F. depression and reaches the final step 60 hours later to end with a temperature of 200° F. and a 50° F. depression. Average ending moisture contents were as follows (Hopkins et al. 1969).

Schedule	1-½-inch lumber		2-inch lumber	
	Moisture content	Time in kiln	Moisture content	Time in kiln
	Percent	Hours	Percent	Hours
Mild	10	72	12	96
Moderate	11	60	13	84
Severe	13	48	10	84

Drying defects.—Residual drying stresses in lumber—in particular **case-hardening**—may be considered drying defects. Casehardened lumber cups when resawn, or when more is planed off one side than the other; cupped boards tend to suffer degrade from splits when planed. In addition, end checks frequently develop in freshly crosscut, casehardened boards that are exposed to dry air.

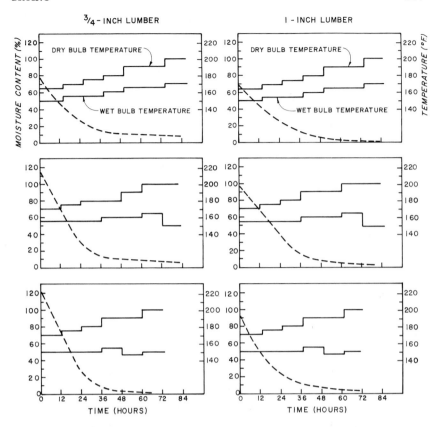

Figure 20–16.—Moisture content (dashed line) of ¾-inch by 6-inch (left) and 1-inch by 6-inch (right) southern pine lumber versus time in kiln when dried according to time-based schedules from Rasmussen (1961). (Top) Mild schedule AS11–BK6. (Middle) Moderate schedule AS11–AK6. (Bottom) Severe schedule AS12–AK8. (Drawings and data after Hopkins et al. 1969.)

The formation and effects of stresses in drying wood are influenced by several factors (McMillen and Youngs 1960):

- As any portion of a piece of wood loses moisture below the fiber-saturation point, it tends to shrink.
- If the normal shrinkage is restrained, a tensile stress is developed in that portion.
- Portions of the material that do the restraining tend to develop compressive stresses.
- The tendency of one portion of the wood to restrain the shrinkage of an adjacent portion produces shearing stress.
- When a material is stressed, it deforms or is strained. Stress that develops slowly and continues for long periods produces some in-elastic (or plastic) strain. Such strain remains after removal of stress. This permanent strain is known as plastic deformation, creep, or **set.**

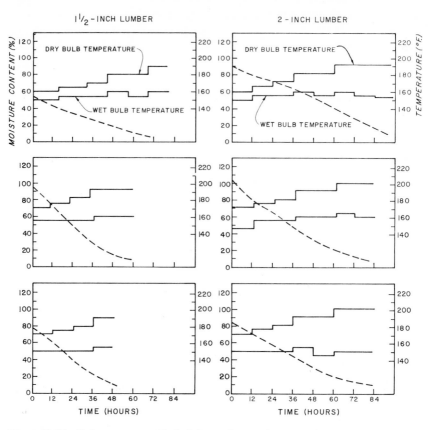

Figure 20–17.—Moisture content (dashed line) of 1½-inch by 6-inch (left) and 2-inch by 6-inch (right) southern pine lumber versus time in kiln when dried according to time-based schedules from Rasmussen (1961). (Top) Mild schedule AS10–AK4. (Middle) Moderate schedule AS11–AK6. (Bottom) Severe schedule AS12–AK8. (Drawings and data after Hopkins et al. 1969.)

Quantitative information on drying stresses and strains in southern pine is lacking. However, data on strains and sets for 2-inch ponderosa pine (*Pinus ponderosa* Laws.) give some clue to the probable behavior of southern pine during kiln-drying (McMillen 1968). When dried at 110° F., tension set in the outer portions of ponderosa pine planks built up to a moderately high value during the first half of drying. Compression set in the interior portion of the planks developed mainly during the middle third of drying and was generally small. Stress reversal (so that the wood near the surface ended up in compression and the interior wood was stressed in tension) occurred after average moisture content was at or below 20 percent. Residual stress and set were relieved by a 6-hour conditioning treatment.

Warp defects—twist, bow, crook, and cup—can be reduced most effectively by good kiln stacking practice. Lumber on each kiln truck should be of uniform thickness to reduce cupping of lumber and deformation of kiln stickers. Preferably, lumber of a single length should constitute each kiln pile. If this is not possible the lumber should be **box piled** (fig. 20–18 Left) with flush ends; a box pile is as long as the longest board, i.e., shorter boards are alternately pulled to opposite ends so that package ends have no projecting boards. A less desirable practice is **step-back** stacking (fig. 20–18 Right). Step-back koiln piles require extra baffling at the ends to maintain air velocity through the lumber courses. Kiln piles need strong foundation supports spaced not over 4 feet apart on the kiln trucks to prevent the lower courses from sagging. Stickers should be dry, straight, and of uniform thickness (usually about ¾-inch) and width (usually about 1¾ inches). Preferably, end stickers should be flush with board ends; a spacing of 2 to 4 feet between stickers is usual. Data from Teesdale (1930, p. 57) shows that 16-foot longleaf pine developed almost no crook when piled with 9 stickers per course, whereas, crook was very common in similar lumber stacked with 4 stickers per course. Stickers should be placed directly over pile supports and be in accurate vertical alignment.

Data from Hopkins et al. (1969) relate warp in 8-foot-long, 6-inch-wide No. 2 Common and better, southern pine lumber to the kiln schedules shown in figures 20–16 and 20–17 (see table 20–10). In Hopkins' study, no space was left between edges of the lumber; courses were separated by ¾-inch sticks placed on 2-foot centers. To reduce warping, especially in the upper courses, each 4-foot-wide load had weights placed on top to distribute a total weight of 4,000 pounds on the bottom layer. As Koch (1969, 1971) has shown, southern pine lumber dried under restraint warps less than unrestrained lumber.

The severe schedule (fig. 20–16 Bottom) caused greater bow and crook in ¾-inch and 1-inch lumber than the mild and moderate schedules; ¾-inch lumber had less twist and cup than 1-inch. Lumber dried by all three

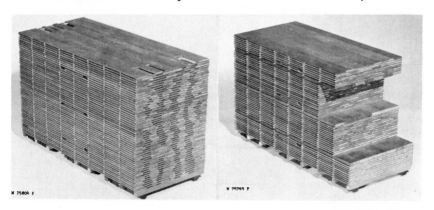

M–75804F, M–75793F

Figure 20–18.—Kiln piles with sample pockets and kiln samples shown. (Left) Box pile of random-length lumber. (Right) Step-back stacking in lower part of load and step-out stacking in upper part. Courses of thick dunnage, located as shown, minimize warp. (Photos from Rasmussen 1961.)

TABLE 20–10.—*Change in warp in No. 2 Common and better, 6-inch-wide, flat-sawn southern pine lumber when kiln dried on various schedules* (Hopkins et al. 1969)[1]

Schedule and thickness (inch)	Bow	Crook	Twist	Cup
			$\frac{1}{32}$-inch		
Mild[2]				
0.75	1.3(−7, +14)	2.6(−3, +19)	2.8(−3, +10)	1.4(0, +4)
1.00	.5(−19, +13)	2.4(−4, +20)	3.3(−6, +16)	1.7(0, +4)
Moderate[2]				
0.75	3.3(−3, +36)	2.6(−4, +29)	2.8(−3, +12)	1.1(0, +4)
1.00	1.1(−13, +13)	3.4(−2, +35)	3.2(−3, +23)	1.1(0, +3)
Severe[2]				
0.75	2.6(−13, +24)	6.3(−3, +40)	1.3(−2, +8)	1.4(0, +4)
1.00	3.5(−11, +23)	4.2(−2, +42)	3.2(−4, +14)	2.5(0, +5)
Mild[3]				
1.5	.6(−5, +11)	.7(−4, +10)	4.7(0, +28)	.6(0, +3)
2.0	.3(−6, +8)	.9(−4, +6)	2.1(0, +10)	.0(0, +1)
Moderate[3]				
1.5	1.1(−16, +23)	2.1(−5, +27)	3.1(−2, +32)	.6(0, +3)
2.0	1.1(−17, +9)	2.7(−4, +25)	2.6(−3, +21)	.0(0, +2)
Severe[3]				
1.5	.1(−6, +10)	1.2(−2, +21)	4.7(−2, +15)	.6(0, +2)
2.0	.1(−8, +9)	2.6(−3, +36)	4.5(−3, +20)	.0(0, +0)

[1] The first number in each entry is average warp; the numbers following in parentheses are minimum and maximum warp. A negative value indicates a decrease in warp during drying.
[2] See figure 20–16 for schedule.
[3] See figure 20–17 for schedule.

schedules had about the same amount of twist; cup was least in lumber dried on the moderate schedule.

When dried under the schedules shown in figure 20–17, lumber 1½ inches thick developed less crook than 2-inch lumber, and the mild schedule caused less crook than the moderate and severe schedules. The 1½-inch-thick lumber, however, twisted more than that 2 inches thick. The 1½-inch-thick lumber developed some cup, while the 2-inch lumber had virtually none.

More than half of the samples taken from the lumber dried by Hopkins et al. (1969) on the schedules shown in figures 20–16 and 20–17 were casehardened. This indicates that lumber dried according to these schedules should be conditioned before removal from the kiln.

Checks and splits that develop at board ends during drying usually stop at the first sticker they reach; therefore, stickers should be aligned as near the ends of the load as possible. Surface checks may develop during the kiln-drying of thick, wide, flat-sawn planks. These failures, usually occurring at wood rays and resin canals, are caused by transverse tensile stress in the relatively dry surface layer while it is restrained from shrinking by the relatively wet interior. Therefore, schedules that avoid extreme tensile stresses at the surface minimize surface checking. Knots check because of differences in shrinkage parallel to and across the annual rings within the knots. Knot checking, almost impossible to prevent, can be minimized by drying at high relative humidities and only to high moisture contents. Encased knots, held in place only by bark and pitch, loosen when the knot shrinks to a size smaller than the knothole. The drier the lumber, the more dead knots will fall out during machining (fig. 11–2).

Hopkins et al. (1969, p. 14) have provided data on surface checking observed in 6-inch-wide southern pine dried according to the schedules shown in figures 20–16 and 20–17. The ¾-inch and 1-inch lumber had very few surface checks when dried on the mild schedule; more checks developed during the moderate and severe schedules. The 1-inch lumber developed more checks than the ¾-inch lumber. In lumber 1½ and 2 inches thick, surface checking was most severe in the 1½-inch lumber; the severe schedule caused more checking than the moderate or mild schedules.

Shrinkage caused by drying is a defect only when it is sufficient to cause the lumber to be undersize after planing. The lumber manufacturer must obviously have some idea of the range of shrinkage commonly observed during kiln-drying if he is to avoid undersize lumber. Hopkins et al. (1969) have tabulated data applicable to 6-inch-wide, flat-grain, 8-foot-long, southern pine lumber dried on a variety of schedules (table 20–11). When thick and thin lumber were dried on the same schedule, shrinkage in length was generally greatest in the thickest lumber; in an 8-foot piece, longitudinal shrinkage was generally less than 0.1 inch but was sometimes as high as 0.7 inch. Width shrinkage of the ¾-inch and 1-inch lumber (dried to 4 or 5 percent moisture content) was commonly 0.27 to 0.37 inch, but was observed in some boards to be nearly ½-inch. In the 1½- and 2-inch-thick lumber, which was dried to about 12-percent moisture content, the width shrinkage was commonly 0.07 to 0.16 inch. Thickness shrinkage averaged 0.03 to 0.05 inch for ¾- and 1-inch lumber; for 1½- and 2-inch lumber it averaged 0.02 to 0.04 inch.

Pitch exudation is sometimes a defect in lumber. As southern pine dries, some of the volatiles from resin canals and pockets evaporate, causing the pitch to harden somewhat. Pitch can be thoroughly set (in boards for use at normal temperatures) by using a kiln temperature of 160° F. or higher (Rasmussen 1961). Teesdale (1930) observed that kiln temperatures in excess of 220° F. and low moisture content (2 to 4 percent) cause degrade in southern pine because of pitch exudation during the drying process. Koch (1971) found that pitch exudation caused by drying at 240° F. was readily removed by planing.

Degrade.—Carpenter and Schroeder (1968) measured the combined effects of drying, surfacing, and trimming on loss of grade and volume in

TABLE 20–11.—*Shrinkage during kiln-drying of 6-inch-wide, 8-foot-long, flat-grain, southern pine lumber dried on variety of schedules* (Hopkins et al. 1969)[1]

Schedule and thickness (inch)	Length	Width	Thickness
	— — — — — — — — — — *Inch* — — — — — — — — — —		
Mild[2]			
0.75	0.057 (0–.25)	0.270 (.13–.36)	0.025 (0–.07)
1.00	.072 (0–.25)	.284 (.15–.41)	.044 (0–.08)
Moderate[2]			
0.75	.062 (0–.38)	.356 (.17–.45)	.030 (0–.07)
1.00	.076 (0–.11)	.321 (.17–.42)	.047 (0–.10)
Severe[2]			
0.75	.151 (0–.53)	.345 (.19–.41)	.033 (0–.08)
1.00	.119 (0–.46)	.370 (.13–.40)	.047 (0–.10)
Mild[3]			
1.5	.046 (0–.28)	.153 (.03–.30)	.031 (0–.08)
2.0	.076 (0–.59)	.066 (0–.34)	.023 (0–.09)
Moderate[3]			
1.5	.059 (0–.62)	.164 (.06–.32)	.042 (0–.09)
2.0	.073 (0–.62)	.096 (0–.21)	.025 (0–.10)
Severe[3]			
1.5	.067 (0–.28)	.153 (.03–.22)	.028 (0–.07)
2.0	.078 (0–.69)	.146 (.06–.28)	.039 (0–.10)

[1] The first number in each entry is average shrinkage; the numbers following in parentheses are minimum and maximum shrinkage. Lumber 0.75 and 1.00 inches thick was dried to 4- or 5-percent moisture content; the 1.5- and 2.0-inch lumber was dried to about 12-percent moisture content.

[2] See figure 20–16 for schedule.

[3] See figure 20–17 for schedule.

southern pine lumber. Over 7,700 boards were graded and scaled when green, and again after drying and surfacing. Some of the substantial grade changes in tables 20–12 and 20–13 can be explained by remanufacturing —ripping or crosscutting to make two boards from one, end trimming to raise the grade of the board, and surfacing to remove minor defects. Also, a portion of the lumber grade change can be related to the difficulty of grading rough-green lumber.

The data reflect the practices of only one mill. No doubt the amount of grade change and volume loss from drying and processing varies from mill to mill.

TIMBERS

Although most timbers are not kiln-dried because of the long drying time required, a few products do call for kiln-drying. Roof decking, which may be machined from 4- by 6-inch timbers, needs to be dried prior to use. Industry practice for western species (no information is published

TABLE 20–12.—*Grade and volume change of 1-inch southern pine lumber from rough-green to dry-surfaced* (Carpenter and Schroeder 1968)

Rough-green		Dry-surfaced[1]							
Lumber grade	Volume	B & B	C	D & 1C	2C	3C	4C	Volume lost[2]	Total
	Bd. ft.	– – – – – – *Percent of rough-green volume* – – – – – –							
B & B	4,384	56	22	15	--	1	--	6	100
C	7,602	23	33	35	3	--	--	6	100
D & 1C	14,491	1	3	64	23	2	--	7	100
2C	19,207	------	1	5	73	15	--	6	100
3C	2,390	------	--	3	26	64	2	5	100
4C	267	------	--	8	21	29	19	23	100
Total	48,341								

[1] Dried to approximately 15-percent moisture content.

[2] Cull and remanufacturing.

TABLE 20–13.—*Grade and volume change of southern pine dimension lumber from rough-green to dry-surfaced* (Carpenter and Schroeder 1968)

Rough-green		Dry-surfaced[1]								
Lumber grade	Volume	1D	2D & Special	3D	4D	1 Dense	2 Dense	3 Dense	Volume lost[2]	Total
	Bd. ft.	– – – – – – *Percent of rough-green volume* – – – – – –								
1D	1,556	43	36	14	1	1	1	----	4	100
2D & Special	2,091	6	57	20	5	6	5	----	1	100
3D	354	2	------	76	17	----	----	----	5	100
4D	48	--	------	--	100	----	----	----	-----	100
1 Dense	13,666	--	------	--	---	71	24	2	3	100
2 Dense	2,052	--	------	--	---	8	67	22	3	100
3 Dense	313	--	------	--	---	13	25	56	6	100
Total	20,080									

[1] Dried to approximately 15-percent moisture content.

[2] Cull and remanufacturing.

for southern pine) is to dry the outer ½-inch to 15-percent moisture content or less in 7 to 10 days under a schedule that allows a small amount of surface checking (Rasmussen 1961).

Southern pine timbers measuring 3 by 6 and 4 by 8 inches are kiln-dried prior to conversion into treated flooring blocks. One manufacturer dries 8- and 10-foot lengths on a 10-day schedule.

Time in each step	Dry-bulb temperature	Wet-bulb temperature
Days	– – – – – °F. – – – – –	
2	140	125
2	150	130
2	160	135
2	170	138
2 (Approx.)	180	140

The timbers usually exceed 60-percent moisture content when charged; the 180° final step is prolonged if necessary to reduce the wettest samples to 18-percent moisture content.

Two commercial kiln schedules for partially air-dried crossarms are at hand. J. S. Mathewson in 1957 observed that 4½- by 5½-inch southern pine crossarms 8 feet long were being dried in a little over 100 hours by one Georgia firm, as follows:

Time in each step	Dry-bulb temperature	Wet-bulb temperature
Hours	– – – – – °F. – – – – –	
30	160	150
24	170	150
24	180	150
24	190	150
10–12	195	175

Final moisture content at 1-inch depth was 17 to 22 percent. Smaller crossarms took 10 to 12 hours less time.

Using somewhat lower temperatures, a Florida manufacturer took 137 hours to kiln-dry 3½- by 4½-inch, partially-air-dried crossarms, as follows:

Time in each step	Dry-bulb temperature	Wet-bulb temperature
Hours	– – – – – °F. – – – – –	
69	135	125
24	145	125
29	150	125
15	165	132

The foregoing schedules dry crossarms adequately for preservative treatment, i.e., to about 25-percent moisture content. If timbers are to be kiln-dried to 10 or 15 percent, longer schedules are required. Gerhards (1968) dried green 4- by 8-inch southern pine beams in a laboratory kiln with a mild schedule that started at 130° F. dry-bulb with 5° F. wet-bulb depression and ended 31 days later at 150° F. dry-bulb with 30° F. wet-bulb depression. This schedule was followed by 30 days of conditioning at 75° F. and 64-percent relative humidity. At the end of the 61-day period, moisture contents for shells of the beams ranged from 10 to 14 percent with an average of 11.5 percent. Core moisture contents ranged from 11 to 17 percent and averaged 13.4 percent.

POLES AND PILING

As is the case with heavy timbers, most poles and piles are not usually kiln-dried. Before they are given preservative treatment, they are conditioned by steam (sec. 20–4), vapor-dried (sec. 20–7), or air-dried (sec. 20–1). Materials of this size do not need to be completely free from seasoning checks.

A few firms do kiln-dry poles. Table 20–14 shows the 14 day schedule used by one Mississippi firm to dry poles to approximately 35-percent moisture content in gas-fired, track-type kilns with external blowers. Shorter schedules are more common, however.

A 7-day schedule has been used successfully to kiln-dry 10½-inch pile segments; the schedule was cited as typical of industrial practice (Wilkinson 1968, p. 22).

Time in each step	Dry-bulb temperature	Wet-bulb temperature
Hours	– – – – °F.	– – – –
24	134	120
47	144	120
47	153	120
46	165	120

Kiln-dried poles and piles are generally steamed 1 to 4 hours before starting preservative treatment.

Shorter and more severe schedules for drying southern poles prior to creosoting were tested around 1940 by Segelken (1941, 1942). To dry class 5 poles (25 and 40 feet in length) to 25-percent moisture content in 130 hours, the initial dry-bulb temperature of 140° F. was increased more or less linearly to 195° F. during the first 95 hours and then maintained at 195° F. for the final 35 hours; relative humidity was raised to 90 percent in the first 24 hours and then decreased more or less linearly to 30 percent by the end of the 130-hour run. During this time moisture content dropped from 66 percent to 25 percent. Weight per cubic foot

TABLE 20–14.—*Time-based kiln schedule for southern pine poles*[1]

Time in each step (days)	Dry-bulb temperature	Wet-bulb temperature	Relative humidity	E.m.c.
	– – – °F. – – –		– – *Percent* – –	
2_____	130	120	73	12.1
2_____	140	120	54	8.0
2_____	150	120	41	5.8
8_____	160	120	31	4.3

[1] Screpetis, G. Schedule for southern pine poles. Unpublished memorandum. USDA Forest Service. State and Private Forestry, Alexandria, La., 1967.

dropped from about 54 pounds to about 41 pounds, i.e., water loss per cubic foot was 0.10 pound per hour. In this particular test, 5 pounds of steam were required to evaporate 1 pound of water. The dry poles were a dark straw color and free of gummy deposits, and checking was uniform over the whole pole surface, individual checks averaging 0.10 to 0.15 inch in width and 12 to 36 inches in length.

The following year, Segelken (1942) used a different kiln to dry a mixture of shortleaf and longleaf pine poles of classes 1 to 7 in lengths varying from 20 to 45 feet. The poles were dried from about 83-percent moisture content to about 30-percent moisture content in 100 hours by holding the dry-bulb temperature constant at 232° F. and the wet bulb constant at 142° F. During the 100 hours, weight per cubic foot dropped from about 55 pounds to about 40 pounds, i.e., a weight loss per cubic foot of 0.15 pound per hour. In this well-insulated, cross-circulating kiln, only 2 to 2½ pounds of steam were required to evaporate 1 pound of water from the poles. Both stickered and unstickered charges were dried; evidence of faster drying rates in stickered loads was not conclusive. Checks in the dry poles averaged 30 inches long, 0.12 inch wide, and 1.75 inches deep. The poles were successfully treated with creosote. No evaluation of possible strength loss due to sustained exposure to high temperature (100 hours at 232° F.) was made; however, it is probable that pole temperature did not exceed 212° F. during most of the drying period. Section 15–2 discusses the weakening effect of long exposures to high temperatures.

A milder schedule, with time extended to bring poles near the moisture content they will reach in use, has been reported. Thompson (1969) found that 30-foot-long southern pine poles, 25 inches in circumference 6 feet from the butt, and with 40-percent or higher moisture content in the outer ½-inch of radius, could be kiln-dried to 13-percent moisture content (pole average) in 160 hours with dry-bulb temperatures of 170 to 180° F. and wet-bulb depressions of 50 to 65° F. He also dried similar poles to an average moisture content of 31.5 percent in 158 hours by using initial conditions of 140° F. dry-bulb with 20° F. wet-bulb depression and final conditions of 152° F. dry-bulb and 35° F. wet-bulb depression.

Thompson and Stevens (1972) reported on accelerated drying of green southern pine poles averaging 8 to 10 inches in diameter and about 60-percent moisture content. In air circulated at 300 feet per minute with dry-bulb temperatures of 225°, 212°, and 160° F. (with corresponding wet-bulb depressions of 50°, 42°, and 40° F.) poles required about 44, 66, and 90 hours, respectively, to reach 30-percent moisture content. These times were substantially less than the 177 hours required with the control— a conventional schedule, i.e., 120° F. wet-bulb temperature and initial and final dry-bulb temperatures of 130° and 160° F., with the latter reading attained in 10° increments over several days. Modulus of rupture

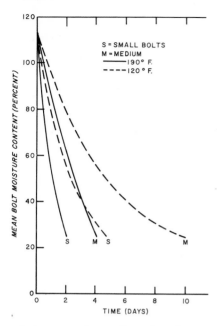

Figure 20–19.—Effect of temperature on drying time of round, peeled loblolly and slash pine bolts. Small bolts were 4 to 5 inches in diameter, medium bolts 8 to 9. (Drawing after Gaby 1967.)

of clear wood samples taken from poles dried at 225° F. was 14 percent lower than that of control samples. Strength of clear wood from poles dried at 212° F. was not significantly reduced. In commercial trials, checking patterns were similar in poles dried on accelerated and conventional schedules. When pressure treated, penetration and retention of creosote, pentachlorophenol, and CCA preservatives were adequate in the poles dried on the accelerated schedules.

Section 20–2 described forced-air drying of round, 18- and 55-inch-long, peeled bolts at 120° F. Gaby (1967) dried similar slash and loblolly pine bolts at 190° F. with an air velocity of 600 to 700 f.p.m. in a conventional dry kiln. Wet-bulb temperature was not controlled, but with vents open throughout the test, the e.m.c. reached a constant level of 3 to 4 percent early in the run. Figure 20–19 shows that a kiln temperature of 190° F. dried the bolts in only half the time required at 120° F. At the higher temperature, bolts 4 to 5 inches in diameter dried to approximately 25-percent moisture content in 2 days. Eight- to 9-inch bolts required approximately 5 days.

Figure 20–20 shows the radial and lengthwise distribution of moisture content after bolts were dried at 120° F. Two equalization treatments were tried. Soaking the bolts for 1 hour in cold water caused a moisture gain of 10 to 12 percent, compared to 3 to 5 percent during 2 to 5 days of steaming. With steaming, more moisture penetrated radially into the deeper parts of the bolt shell. Within-bolt variation in moisture content was controlled best by steaming at 120° F. (fig. 20–20); all parts of the bolts were brought within the range from 20- to 30-percent moisture content after 2 or 3 days of steaming.

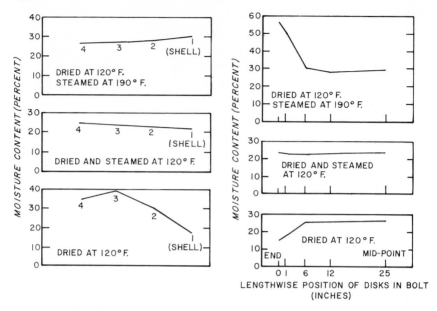

Figure 20–20.—Within-bolt moisture content distribution after drying and after steam equalizing. (Left) Radial distribution. Point 1 refers to the outer shell (one-fourth of radius in thickness); point 4 refers to the core (one-fourth of bolt diameter across); points 2 and 3 are intermediate between shell and core. (Right) Lengthwise distribution from end to midpoint of 55-inch-long bolts. (Drawings after Gaby 1967.)

At least one large surface check usually developed during the drying cycle. Steaming at temperatures of 120° F. or 190° F. caused a brown discoloration throughout the bolts.

20–4   HIGH-TEMPERATURE DRYING

Lowery et al. (1968) and Salamon (1969) have reviewed the history and technology of kiln-drying lumber at dry-bulb temperatures above 212° F. Following is a brief discussion of techniques and principles; some data specific to southern pine are presented.

There are two processes of high-temperature drying. The first uses superheated steam, i.e., steam above the boiling point of water. In this system, the steam occupies the kiln to the complete exclusion of air. The kiln, or retort, is completely sealed except for a single outlet which controls pressure buildup above atmospheric pressure. Heat is supplied primarily by coils within the kiln rather than by admitting steam under pressure. The steam can give up its superheat without condensing and thus acts as a drying agent. There is no air present and the process is controlled solely by manipulation of dry-bulb temperature. Superheated steam, like air, requires circulation to carry its heat to the lumber. Figure 8–12 shows the relationship of the e.m.c. of wood to the temperature of pure saturated steam at atmospheric pressure. During World War I, this process was used in the Pacific Northwest to dry 1-inch green soft-woods to 10-percent moisture content in as little as 24 hours. Since kilns deteriorated rapidly at these high temperatures, the process is not used currently for drying lumber in the United States.

The other process of high-temperature drying uses mixtures of air and steam. Air is brought into the kiln in the conventional manner; any steam present (apart from low-pressure steam injected for deliberate humidification) is moisture expelled from the lumber. The process is controlled by wet- and dry-bulb thermometers, as in a kiln with conventional temperatures. Table 8–3 shows wood e.m.c. values corresponding to various combinations of dry-bulb temperatures above 212° F. with wet-bulb temperature below 212° F. For example, at a dry-bulb temperature of 240° F., e.m.c. values corresponding to wet-bulb temperatures of 169, 189, 202, and 212° F. are 2, 3, 4, and 5 percent (Ladell 1957, p. 18). By 1954 over a hundred small kilns specifically designed for this process were in service (Mathewson 1954); their acceptance in Europe prompted research on high-temperature drying of softwoods at the Forest Products Laboratories of Canada (Ladell 1955, 1957; Guernsey 1957; Calvert 1958, 1965; Salamon and McBride 1966; Salamon and McIntyre 1970; Salamon 1970), in the United States (Kimball and Lowery 1967ab; Koch 1969, 1971), and in Australia (Christensen 1970).

There is not complete agreement on the manner in which moisture moves out of wood during high-temperature drying. Kollmann and Schneider (1961) classify three stages of drying. During the first stage—the constant-drying-rate period—which occurs only if the initial moisture content of the wood is above fiber saturation point, evaporation takes place at the wood surface. The second stage—the falling-rate period—occurs when free water is no longer present over all the surface and the surface temperature rises above the wet-bulb temperature. The third and final stage—also a falling-rate period—begins when the wettest portion of the wood falls below fiber saturation point and continues until all of the wood is in equilibrium with the drying conditions. Hann (1964) has also described stages two and three. A general description (after Hart 1965) of the mechanism of high-temperature drying is given in section 8–7.

LUMBER

There are no published data on the drying of southern pine lumber in superheated steam with air excluded. Data specific to southern pine are, however, available for the process of drying southern pine lumber at a dry-bulb temperature of 240° F. in a mixture of air and steam (Koch 1969, 1971; Koch[4]).

---

[4] Koch, P. Effects of wet-bulb depression, board thickness and specific gravity, and circulation velocity on time required to dry southern pine lumber at 240° F. USDA Forest Service, Southern Forest Experiment Station, Alexandria, La., Final Report FS-SO-3201-2.31 dated December 30, 1971.

In the first of two experiments, Koch (1971) compared 8-foot 2 by 4's (studs) conventionally stacked and kiln-dried on a mild schedule with temperatures not exceeding 180° F. (air velocity of 500 f.p.m.) with 2 by 4's dried on a high-temperature schedule; studs dried at high temperature were mechanically restrained against warp.

The 24-hour, high-temperature schedule was simple. The green lumber was clamped rigidly in aluminum frames, in almost total mechanical restraint against crook, bow, and twist (fig. 20–21). Still in frames, the studs were wheeled into the preheated kiln and dried for 21 hours at a dry-bulb temperature of 240° F. and a wet-bulb temperature of 160° F. Then, for the last 3 hours they were steamed at a dry-bulb temperature of 195° F. and a wet-bulb temperature of 185° F. Throughout the 24 hours, air was cross-circulated at 1,000 f.p.m.; direction of airflow was reversed every 75 minutes. Weight of charge together with energy consumption for heat, humidity control (steam spray), and fan were continuously charted against time. With the schedule completed, the studs were wheeled from the kiln and cooled under restraint for 48 hours in an atmosphere that ranged from 70 to 80° F. and 40- to 60-percent relative humidity.

To insure inclusion of juvenile wood in the kiln charges, half the lumber to be dried was cut from cores residual from steamed veneer logs and the remainder cut from very small logs. Lumber from these two sources was dried separately during the experiment. Prior to drying, the green studs were planed to uniform thickness (1⅞ inches) and width (4 inches).

Ending moisture content for the low-temperature charges averaged 11.8 percent, whereas the high-temperature charges averaged 9.1 percent at the finish (fig. 20–22).

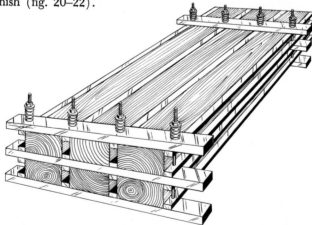

Figure 20–21.—Experimental setup provided restraint against warp during high-temperature drying. Longitudinal strips visible between 2 by 4's prevented excessive crook. Spring-loaded bolts running through the strips, from top to bottom of the pile, prevented excessive twist and bow. The studs were 8 feet long, 4 inches wide, and 1⅞ inches thick. Aluminum cross stickers were spaced 2 feet apart and measured ¾-inch thick and 1½ inches wide. (Drawing after Koch 1971.)

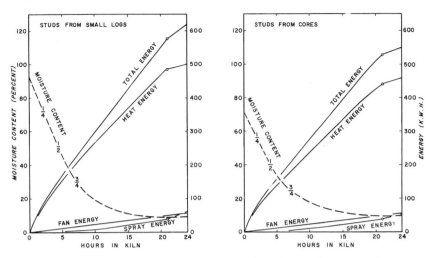

Figure 20–22.—Moisture content change and kilowatt-hour demand by 24-stud charge first dried 21 hours with dry- and wet-bulb temperatures of 240° and 160° F., and then steamed 3 hours with dry- and wet-bulb temperatures of 195° and 185° F. Air cross-circulated at 1,000 f.p.m. Lumber was 1⅞ inches thick. Moisture contents were calculated from the green and ovendry weights of each entire charge. Data from three charges were averaged to derive each curve. Numbers inset in moisture content curve indicate time to one-fourth, one-half, and three-fourths of total moisture loss. (Drawings after Koch 1971.)

Moisture content 48 hours after discharge from kiln

	High-temperature schedule	Low-temperature schedule
	Percent	
Studs from veneer cores		
Average	9.3	11.8
Standard deviation	3.3	2.4
Range	5.4–21.2	2.1–21.7
Studs from small logs		
Average	8.9	11.7
Standard deviation	3.2	2.7
Range	5.2–21.2	5.3–21.3

In general, the high-temperature schedule took less than one-fourth the time and about one-half the energy required for the low-temperature schedule (table 20–15).

While cheaper energy sources are available to most commercial kilns, the electric power used in the study for both heating and air circulation afforded valid and convenient comparisons of energy required. Largely because it took less time, requirements for the high-temperature schedule were lower. Thus power for fan motors in the high-temperature schedule, despite the 1,000-f.p.m. circulation rate, was only about half that for the low-temperature schedule. The longer, low-temperature schedule, with its high initial humidities, required five times as much energy for humidity

TABLE 20–15.—*Time and energy expended to kiln-dry each charge of 24 southern pine studs cut from veneer cores and small logs*[1] (Koch 1971)

Expenditure	High temperature		Low temperature[2]	
	From cores	From small logs	From cores	From small logs
Time, hours	24	24	102	113
Energy, k.w.h.				
Heat[3]	442	500	700	790
Humidity control[4]	54	61	295	290
Fan	55	57	107	119
Total	551	618	1102	1199

[1] Each figure is the average for three charges.
[2] Approximately the schedule shown in table 20–3.
[3] Supplied by electric resistance-type heating coils.
[4] Steam for humidification was provided by electric immersion heaters in a water bath.

control, and more than 1½ times as much for heat, as the high-temperature schedule.

Of course, results with this very small experimental kiln cannot be scaled directly to a commercial kiln, but the trends are evident. In experiments in Europe, Keyleworth (1952) found that a high-temperature kiln using air-steam mixtures required 1.2 to 1.5 kilowatt-hours per kilogram (2.2 pounds) of water evaporated; this compared with 2 to 4 kilowatt hours for low-temperature drying. The lower energy requirements were attributed to lower heat loss, lower heat capacity of the construction materials, and the shorter drying time in the high-temperature kiln.

Koch (1971) found that studs dried under restraint at high temperature warped significantly less than those conventionally stickered and dried at low temperature. Warp in the studs was measured 48 hours out of the kiln, just before planing, after planing, after a 20-day humid cycle (81° F. dry-bulb and 78° wet-bulb temperature) during which the studs were individually and freely suspended from hooks placed in one end, and after a 20-day dry cycle (130° F. dry-bulb and near 80° wet-bulb temperature). The differences charted in figure 20–23 were significant at all stages of manufacture.

Warp measured immediately after planing largely determines the mill grade and selling price of studs. Average values at this stage were:

Warp	High temperature, restrained	Low temperature, unrestrained
	– – – – – – *Inch* – – – – – –	
Crook	0.12	0.23
Bow	.21	.29
Twist	.09	.24

When studs are incorporated in buildings, they are frequently exposed

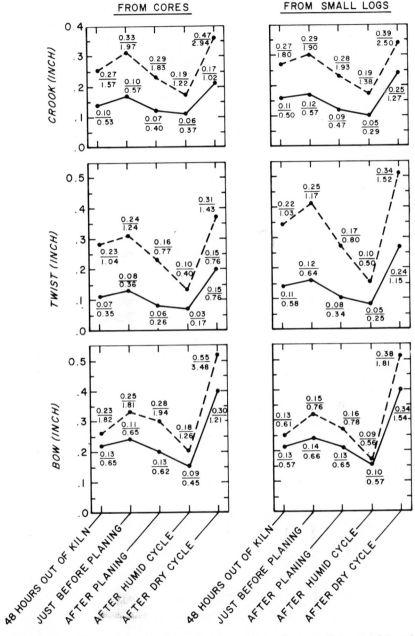

Figure 20–23.—Warp in 8-foot southern pine 2 by 4's cut from small logs (right) and steamed veneer cores (left), when kiln-dried at high temperature under restraint and at low temperature stacked conventionally. Each plotted point is the average for 72 studs; adjacent to each point, the standard deviation is printed just above the maximum value of warp observed at that point. (Drawing after Koch 1971.)

to high humidities until the roof is in place and the heating or air conditioning system activated. Exposing planed studs to high humidity for 20 days simulated this situation; average warp after exposure was least in wood dried at high temperature:

Warp	High temperature, restrained	Low temperature, unrestrained
	— — — — — — Inch — — — — — —	
Crook_____	0.10	0.17
Bow_____	.15	.18
Twist_____	.08	.14

Studs built into attic spaces may first go through a period of high humidity as described above, and then be subjected to extremely dry atmospheres when heat is turned on in winter. At the end of the 20-day dry cycle following the humid cycle, average warp was severe in all studs, but less extreme in the wood dried under restraint at high temperature:

Warp	High temperature, restrained	Low temperature, unrestrained
	— — — — — — Inch — — — — — —	
Crook_____	0.23	0.35
Bow_____	.42	.52
Twist_____	.23	.44

On average, studs cut from cores twisted significantly less than those cut from small logs when measured just after planing and after the dry cycle. When data from both schedules were pooled, average values were as follows:

Time of measurement	Twist in studs from veneer cores	Twist in studs from small logs
	— — — — — — Inch — — — — — —	
Just after planing_____	0.14	0.19
After dry cycle_____	.28	.39

With these exceptions warp in studs from cores did not significantly differ from that in studs from small logs.

In general, Koch (1971) found that studs dried under restraint at high temperature graded substantially higher after planing than those dried at low temperature (table 20–16). Because 8-foot 2 by 4's of Stud grade or better have approximately twice the value of studs in number 3 and 4 grades, a tabulation is of interest.

SPIB Grade	High temperature	Low temperature
	Percent	Percent
No. 1, No. 2, and Stud.....	91	59
No. 3 and No. 4..........	9	41
Total$...............	100	100

TABLE 20–16.—*Grade distribution of studs immediately following planing*
(Koch 1971)

Grade[1]	High temperature		Low temperature	
	From cores	From small logs	From cores	From small logs
	Number			
No. 1 Common_____	31	17	22	11
No. 2 Common_____	21	17	18	19
Stud Grade_____	17	28	6	9
No. 3 Common_____	1[2]	6[4]	20	23
No. 4 Common_____	2[3]	4[4]	6	10
Total_____	72	72	72	72

[1] Southern Pine Inspection Bureau (1968).

[2] Had crook of 0.38 inch.

[3] Warp was within Stud Grade limitations on both of these pieces, but both were downgraded to No. 4 because of readily identifiable compression wood.

[4] Three of the 10 studs in grades 3 and 4 were within Stud Grade limitations on warp.

With data from both schedules pooled, cores yielded more No. 1 Common and less No. 3 and 4 Common than small logs:

SPIB Grade	Studs from cores	Studs from small logs
	Percent	*Percent*
No. 1_____	37	19
No. 1, No. 2, and Stud_	80	70
No. 3 and No. 4_____	20	30

The higher grade yield in studs cut from cores was particularly evident with the high-temperature schedule; studs from cores yielded only 4 percent in grades 3 and 4, while studs from small logs yielded 14 percent in grades 3 and 4.

The 24-hour schedule brought considerable resin to the surface of the rough, dry 2 by 4's but planing removed all traces of resin and discoloration. All of the studs dried on the 24-hour schedule developed end checks that ranged from 1.5 to 2.1 inches in depth. In no case, however, were the checks a cause for degrade.

Koch (1971) compared the strength properties of southern pine studs cut from small logs or veneer cores when kiln-dried 24 hours at temperatures not exceeding 240° F. (see fig. 20–22 for schedule) with studs kiln-dried about 100 hours at temperatures not exceeding 180° F. Since studs cut from very small logs and veneer cores contain juvenile wood of low specific gravity, as well as defects such as knots and cross grain, they vary greatly in strength.

By analysis of variance, Koch found the edgewise bending properties of modulus of elasticity, proportional limit, and modulus of rupture did not differ significantly between the two drying treatments. In all three strength properties, however, the studs cut from veneer cores were significantly stronger than those from small logs (table 20–17).

Studs from small logs had the same specific gravity as those from cores (0.51, basis of ovendry volume and weight). It is likely, however, that knots in the wood from cores were smaller than those in wood cut from small logs. In the southern pines, the butt log (source of most veneer cores) tends to shed its limbs at an early age, whereas tops of mature southern pines (probably the source of most of the small logs) may have fairly large, live branches; large knots reduce the strength of studs containing them.

Toughness and specific gravity of clear wood cut from the studs did not differ significantly (0.05 level) between the two drying treatments. Each value in the following tabulation represents data from 72 studs (two replications per stud); average moisture content at test was 8.6 percent with standard deviation of 0.5 and range from 7.1 to 11.4 percent.

	High temperature		Low temperature	
Property	From cores	From small logs	From cores	From small logs
Toughness, inch-pounds				
Average	202	191	200	183
Standard deviation	71	75	77	63
Range	56–402	59–355	79–268	61–338
Specific gravity (basis of volume at test and ovendry weight)				
Average	0.52	0.52	0.52	0.52
Standard deviation	.06	.08	.08	.10
Range	.41–.70	.38–.72	.40–.85	.37–.89

Clear wood in studs from veneer cores was significantly tougher (201 inch-pounds) than clear wood in studs from small logs (187 inch-pounds). Since the specific gravities did not differ significantly, an explanation of this result is not readily seen.

In further experiments, Koch[4] obtained information about the effects of air velocity, lumber thickness, and wet-bulb depression. A total of 108 kilnloads (24 boards per load) of southern pine lumber was dried at 240° F. in an air-steam mixture. Boards were 8 feet long, 4 inches wide, and planed green to exact thicknesses of 1.9, 1.5, and 1.0 inches. Prior to drying, the lumber was stored in water, and therefore green moisture content was somewhat above normal—it averaged about 120 percent.

Air velocity.—Air velocities tested were 510 and 930 feet per minute. In the early stages of drying, moisture content was reduced more rapidly

TABLE 20-17.—*Comparison of edgewise-bending properties of southern pine studs cut from small logs or veneer cores when kiln-dried for 24 hours at temperatures not exceeding 240° F. or for about 100 hours at temperatures not exceeding 180° F.*[1][2]

(Koch 1971)

Property[3]	High temperature		Low temperature	
	From cores	From small logs	From cores	From small logs
	— — — — — — — — — — — P.s.i. — — — — — — — — — — —			
Modulus of elasticity				
Average	1,624,000	1,457,000	1,630,000	1,510,000
Standard deviation	393,000	433,000	498,000	496,000
Range	812,000–2,585,000	594,000–2,828,000	550,000–2,692,000	584,000–2,858,000
Proportional limit				
Average	5,050	4,650	5,390	4,740
Standard deviation	1,850	1,770	2,190	1,950
Range	1,490–9,130	1,090–9,600	1,180–10,000	1,100–10,220
Modulus of rupture				
Average	6,980	6,520	7,540	6,560
Standard deviation	3,330	3,020	3,620	3,290
Range	1,600–17,100	1,960–13,820	1,450–16,725	1,630–18,210

[1] Each average value shown represents data from 72 studs. Average moisture content at test was 7.6 percent with range from 6.1 to 9.6 percent.

[2] Studs cut from cores or small logs, dried at either high or low temperature; all averaged 0.51 specific gravity (basis of oven-dry volume and weight).

[3] For all three properties, values for studs from cores were significantly higher than values for studs from small logs; the kiln schedules, however, did not significantly (0.05 level) affect values. Interactions were not significant.

at the high velocity (fig. 20–24). For example, the 1.9-inch lumber (stud thickness) at 80° wet-bulb depression, was brought to about 60 percent moisture content after 5 hours in high-velocity air. In low-velocity air similar boards were near 80 percent after 5 hours. This early advantage is reflected in the number of hours required to reach 10 percent moisture

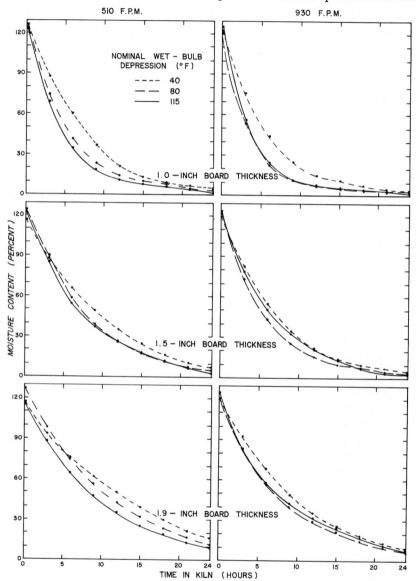

Figure 20–24.—Moisture content changes in 24-board charges of 4-inch-wide southern pine lumber dried at 240° F. in air-steam mixtures circulated at 510 f.p.m. (left) and 930 f.p.m. (right) as affected by board thickness and wet-bulb depression. Circulation velocities were measured at 70° F. Each curve is based on data from six kiln loads. (Drawing after Koch[4].)

content—that is, 21 hours at the high velocity and nearly 25 hours at the low velocity (fig. 20–25, bottom right and left).

Since Koch's[4] experiment had only two levels of circulation velocity (510 and 930 f.p.m.), it was not possible to establish the mathematical relationship between drying rate and circulation velocity. Kollmann and Schneider (1961), however, found that in the velocity range from 230 to 2,100 f.p.m., the drying rate during the first stage of drying increased as the 0.5 to 0.6 power of velocity. In the following stage of falling drying

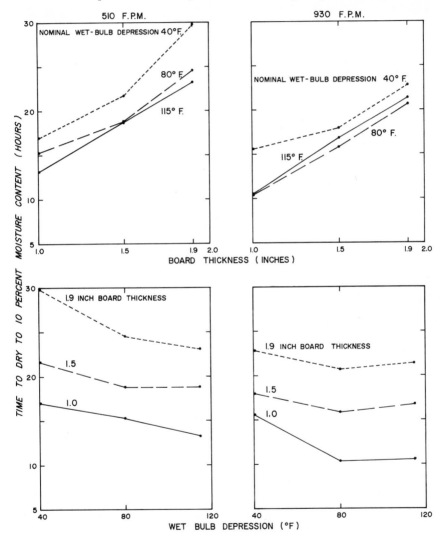

Figure 20–25.—Time required for 4-inch-wide southern pine lumber to dry at 240° F. from about 120-percent moisture content to 10-percent moisture content in an air-steam mixture circulated at 510 f.p.m. (left) and 930 f.p.m. (right) as affected by board thickness and wet-bulb depression. Circulation velocities of 510 and 930 f.p.m. were measured at 70° F. Each point is based on data from six kiln loads. (Drawing after Koch.[4])

rate, the effect of flow velocity became steadily smaller but was still discernible at 20-percent moisture content.

Board thickness.—Time to dry to 10-percent moisture content was approximately proportional to board thickness. With high air velocity and large wet-bulb depressions the relationship was nearly linear (fig. 20–25, top right).

Wet-bulb depression.—Three wet-bulb depressions were tested. A depression of 80° caused substantially faster water loss than a depression of 40° at both air velocities. A depression of 115° was slightly better than 80° in slow air, but in fast air it was no better than an 80° depression and may have been slightly inferior (fig. 20–25, bottom right).

For drying at 240°, then, the combination of 80° wet-bulb depression and the 930-foot air velocity proved faster than all other combinations tested. The times required to dry lumber to 10-percent moisture content were:

Lumber thickness	Time in kiln
Inches	*Hours*
1.0	10.4
1.5	15.8
1.9	20.7

Thus, wood of stud thickness was dry in 21 hours.

At the dry-bulb temperature of 240° F., time to dry to 10-percent moisture content could be expressed by regression fromulas in terms of air velocity, board thickness (inches), and wet-bulb depression (°F.):

For air velocity of 510 f.p.m.   (20–1)
Time in hours = 10.83
            + 11.69   (board thickness)
            − 0.1503   (wet-bulb depression)
            + 0.0005776 (wet-bulb depression)^2

This expression accounted for 84 percent of the observed variation, with standard error of the estimate (square root of the error mean square) of 2.14 hours.

For air velocity of 930 f.p.m.   (20–2)
Time in hours = 10.77
            + 10.56   (board thickness)
            − 0.2354   (wet-bulb depression)
            + 0.001283   (wet-bulb depression)^2

This expression accounted for 83 percent of the observed variation, with standard error of the estimate of 1.89 hours.

Initial moisture content and specific gravity of wood.—In Koch's[4] experiment neither initial moisture content of the loads (range 90 to 140 percent) nor load specific gravity was strongly correlated with drying time. The experimental design did not include moisture content as one of the main factors, and therefore data were insufficient to draw firm conclusions about the effect of moisture content and specific gravity as isolated factors. Average initial moisture contents of the loads in the three gravity classes were as follows:

Gravity class	Moisture content
	Percent
Low	140
Medium	124
High	105

Boards of low gravity had a greater percentage of moisture content than those of high gravity, and they lost water more rapidly during drying. This generalization was true for boards of all three thicknesses at the three humidities and two air velocities tested; pooled data were as follows:

Load specific gravity class	Initial water content per load	Average water loss per load after various times in the kiln		
		6 hours	12 hours	24 hours
		Pounds		
Low	284	156	224	271
Medium	275	148	213	260
High	258	143	201	243

Energy required to dry to 10-percent moisture content.—In the electrically powered and heated experimental kiln, energy was required for three purposes: heat, air circulation, and humidification by steam spray. For the three lumber thicknesses tested, total energy required per load was minimum with 80° F. depression; air circulation velocity did not significantly affect total energy to dry to 10 percent moisture content.

Shrinkage.—Since green lumber must be sawn sufficiently oversize to allow for later planing, the amount of shrinkage during high-temperature drying is of interest. Koch[4] observed the following shrinkage in 8-foot-long, 4-inch-wide southern pine boards dried for 24 hours at 240° F. with 80° F. wet-bulb depression and circulation velocity of 930 f.p.m.; each value is the average for 48 boards:

Specific gravity class (basis of ovendry weight and green volume) and dimension	Board thickness		
	1-inch	1.5-inch	1.9-inch
	– – – – – – Inch – – – – – –		
0.34–0.45			
Thickness	.04	.06	.07
Width	.15	.15	.11
Length	.14	.14	.16
0.45–0.48			
Thickness	.05	.06	.08
Width	.17	.16	.12
Length	.13	.12	.11
0.49–0.75			
Thickness	.05	.06	.08
Width	.18	.19	.15
Length	.10	.12	.10

In assessing the foregoing values, it should be noted that the thinner boards had substantially lower moisture content than the thicker boards (fig. 20–24) at the end of the 24-hour period. Boards of 1.0-, 1.5-, and 1.9-inch thicknesses were at 4.2-, 5.5-, and 10.3-percent moisture content when measured.

POLES AND TIMBERS

When southern pine poles and timbers are not air-dried or kiln-dried prior to preservative treatments, a steaming and vacuum process is frequently used to condition them under limitations stipulated by standards of the American Wood Preservers' Association. Southern pine timbers are steamed in a treating cylinder for a maximum of 17 hours; poles and piles are steamed for a maximum of 17 or 20 hours. Maximum permitted steaming temperature is 245° F. (about 12.5 p.s.i.) and the temperature must be reached in less than 1 hour. The wood is then subjected to a vacuum for an hour or more.

During the steaming period, usually 6 to 15 hours, water condenses on the surface of the poles and there is practically no loss in moisture content. When the steam pressure is released, moisture at temperatures above 212° F. (fig. 20–26) moves rapidly under slight steam pressure as a pressure flow of water vapor from the wet line to the wood surface.

Vacuum is applied to lower the boiling point and speed up the flow of water vapor to the surface. The wood is cooled rapidly by the evaporating moisture; most of the moisture loss takes place in the first hour after

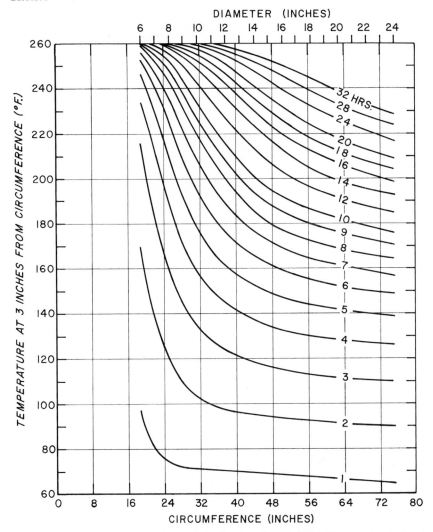

Figure 20-26.—Temperatures 3 inches in from the circumference of round, green longleaf and slash pine timbers of different dimensions, steamed at 260° F. (approximately 20 pounds gage pressure) for the times indicated on the curves. Initial temperature of wood taken as 60° F. (Drawing after MacLean 1934.) Note: Steaming at 260° F. is no longer permitted under the American Wood Preservers' Association standards. The temperatures attained in the wood at the 240° and 245° F. steaming temperatures now permitted would, of course, be lower than those shown in this figure. With MacLean's (1960) method they can be calculated from these curves.

application of vacuum. When steamed, green, round southern pine timbers are subjected to a 5- to 6-hour vacuum, 50 to 60 percent of the total moisture removed is taken out during the first hour and 70 to 80 percent during the first 2 hours (MacLean 1960). Approximately 5 to 6 pounds of water are removed per cubic foot of round, green, southern pine sapwood by the average steaming and vacuum treatment; smaller amounts are removed from timbers, particularly if they contain considerable heartwood. Little, if any water will be withdrawn from partially seasoned wood (MacLean 1960).

Section 15–2 describes the effects of steaming on the properties of wood. In brief, wood subjected to prolonged exposure in a steam atmosphere loses weight and strength, becomes discolored, and undergoes chemical degradation. It is for these reasons that limitations are placed on the severity of steam-drying schedules. (For air-steam drying see p. 986.)

VENEER

Southern pine veneers in the range of thicknesses commonly used in plywood ($\frac{1}{10}$- to $\frac{1}{4}$-inch) are fairly easily dried; checking and warping of veneer—sometimes a problem in older dryers—is not usually serious in modern impingement dryers. Rotary veneer, which shrinks considerably more than radially sliced veneer (see fig. 8–17), comprises the bulk of production; most of it goes into sheathing-grade plywood used in construction. Because southern pine veneer is rotary-cut from logs that average about 14 inches in diameter (leaving a 4- to 6-inch core), it is predominantly sapwood. Prior to peeling, most plants either steam the logs or soak them in hot water to improve cutting characteristics of the wood (see sec. 19–10). After the peeling operation, green southern pine veneer is customarily sorted by thickness, length, width and grade into solid piles without sticks; it remains in these solid piles for a period of hours, or days, until routed to the dryer. Moisture content of green veneers at the dryer commonly ranges from 40 to 180 percent; an average of nearly 120 percent is not unusual. (Sec. 8–1 contains a discussion of range in the moisture content of southern pine wood.) In one study of southern pine veneer cut in east Texas, an average moisture content of 114 percent was observed; sorting prior to drying according to weight of water per unit volume of green veneer was proposed for more uniform drying and increased dryer output (Walters 1970).

Dry veneers (for sheathing) are spread with phenol-formaldehyde glue, assembled into several-ply panels, and the glue cured in a hot press at about 285° F. Glue adds moisture to the veneer. Because panels that are too moist will suffer steam blows in the hot press, veneer must be quite dry before the glue is spread; moisture contents from 2 to 5 percent are common. Veneer dried to a slightly higher moisture content can be used with glues formulated with minimum water.

Jet dryers (fig. 20–27) are used by virtually all the plants. In this dryer design, the long (about 14 feet) top and bottom feed rolls are approximately 4 inches in diameter and the roll pairs are spaced about 1 foot apart along the length of the dryer. Between each roll pair, curtains of hot air impinge vertically on both the top and bottom surfaces of the

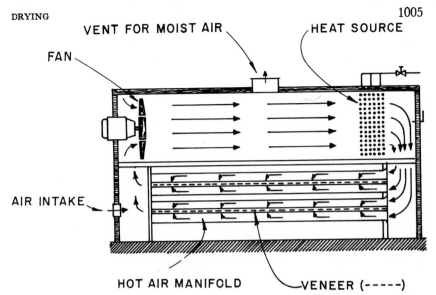

VENT FOR MOIST AIR   HEAT SOURCE

FAN

AIR INTAKE

HOT AIR MANIFOLD   VENEER (-----)

Figure 20–27.—Schematic cross section (transverse to veneer flow) through a two-deck, impingement-jet dryer. Heat can be applied by steam coils, but direct-gas-fired dryers are more common. Long slits in the hot-air manifolds cause curtains of hot air to impinge vertically at high velocity on both top and bottom surfaces of the moving veneer. (Drawing after Fessel 1964.)

veneer as it moves through the dryer. The air travels at very high velocity—usually 2,000 to 4,000 f.p.m. The dryers are arranged with multiple decks so that several layers of veneer flow simultaneously through the machine; four-deck dryers are in common use. The dryers are made in sections so that length is variable. A common arrangement incorporates four sections, each with conditions under separate control; the first three sections are used for drying and the final section for cooling. Cooling is needed where veneer goes directly to the glue spreaders. A better practice calls for dry, solid-piled veneer to be cooled and equalized for 48 hours prior to spreading.

The number of decks, width, length, and feed speed of the dryer depend on the production required and the operating temperatures. Table 20–18 shows drying temperatures and times (for impingement-jet dryers) in common use by the southern pine plywood industry.

Experience with Douglas-fir (*Pseudotsuga menziesii* (Mirb.) Franco) on the West Coast (Corder 1963) has shown that about 15 pounds of air are taken into a veneer dryer for each pound of water evaporated from the veneer. In theory the intake of air could be reduced to zero, since the e.m.c. of wood is 2 or 3 percent in pure, saturated, atmospheric steam at 300° F. (Kauman 1956). Reduced inflow of air lowers heat requirements, increases attainable temperatures and dryer capacity, and reduces likelihood of fires in the dryer. Minimizing the flow of air into the dryer is generally desirable.

TABLE 20-18.—Typical drying schedules for rotary-peeled southern pine veneer in direct-gas-fired jet dryers[1]

Kiln	Veneer thickness	Zone temperatures						Time in dryer	Final moisture content
		Entering Zone 1	Zone 2	Zone 3	Zone 4	Zone 5	Cooling zone		
	Inch	Degrees F.						Min.	Percent
A[3]	1/10	390	375	360	------	------	[2]	8.0	Below 6
	1/8	400	375	360	------	------	[2]	10.0	Below 6
	1/6	400	375	360	------	------	[2]	13.0	Below 6
	3/16	400	375	360	------	------	[2]	13.0	Below 6
	1/4	400	375	360	------	------	[2]	15.0	Below 6
B[4]	1/10	450	425	425	380	320	100–110	8.5	6
	1/8	450	425	425	380	320	100–110	10.5	6
B-1[4]	1/10	470	430	410	380	350	100–110	8.5	6
	1/8	470	430	410	380	350	100–110	10.5	6
C[5]	1/10	400	350	350	------	------	70–100	6.0	5
	1/8	500	400	350	------	------	70–100	8.0	5
	1/6	550	400	350	------	------	70–100	11.0	5
	3/16	550	400	350	------	------	70–100	13.0	5

[1] Based on industrial practice.
[2] Variable, but as cool as possible; in some cases cooling air is brought from outside the plant.
[3] Impingement velocity 2,800 to 3,000 f.p.m.
[4] Impingement velocity 3,700 f.p.m.
[5] Impingement velocity 3,500 f.p.m.

Drying rates.—Operators of veneer dryers should find the work of Fleischer (1958) useful in estimating veneer drying rates. Experimental data specific to southern pine veneer are not published for all thicknesses of veneer, but a few observations have provided some guidelines. Increases in dryer temperature accelerate the drying rate, but the surface temperature of the veneer must not go too high, or the veneer will be difficult to glue. Suchsland and Stevens (1968) found the acceptable momentary limit to be about 425° F. for unextracted southern pine veneer of relatively low specific gravity; extracted veneer tolerated a somewhat higher surface temperature before its gluability was impaired. It is probable that unextracted dense veneer will not tolerate surface temperatures above 400° F. without adverse effects on gluability. A study by Isaacs and Choong (1969) supports this conclusion.

Figure 20–28 shows the changes in moisture content and surface temperature of ⅛-inch, hot-peeled, sapwood, southern pine veneer when dried in an electrically heated, cross-circulation oven maintained at 500° F. Similar veneer, if subjected to vertical jet impingement of air at 500° F., could be expected to dry faster, and surface temperature would increase more rapidly.

The drying rate of ⅛-inch veneer subjected to jets of steam was studied by South (1968). The southern pine sapwood was dried using superheated steam over a range of temperatures, velocities, and angles of impingement. Parallel and 90° impingement (fig. 20–29) were found to yield similar drying curves, while 45° impingement was least effective. Although gluability of the steam-dried veneer was not studied, it would probably be impaired by momentarily attained surface temperatures above 400° F., as was unextracted ovendry veneer. Therefore, a dryer employing vertically impinging superheated steam would use a high initial temperature, followed by a lower temperature for the final drying. For example, it is estimated that at 50 feet per second impingement velocity, ⅛-inch southern pine veneer could be dried in about 6 minutes from an initial moisture content of 140 percent if steam at 600° and 350° F. were used in the first and second stages (fig. 20–29).

With the apparatus shown in figure 20–29, Laity (1970) found that at 350° F. jets of air dried more effectively than jets of steam; at 600° F. and above, however, steam was more effective than air. Laity further concluded that perpendicular impingement of the hot medium dries southern pine veneer more uniformly than parallel flow.

The drying of sawn southern pine veneers planed to ⁷⁄₁₆-inch thickness was studied by Koch (1964). The veneers ranged in moisture content from 45 to 180 percent and averaged about 117 percent. Four drying treatments were tried: a batch-type, cross-circulation kiln; a conventional roller-veneer dryer at 300° F.; an impingement jet dryer at 300° F.; and the same jet dryer at 350° F.

After 72 hours in a batch-type, cross-circulation kiln, the veneers reached

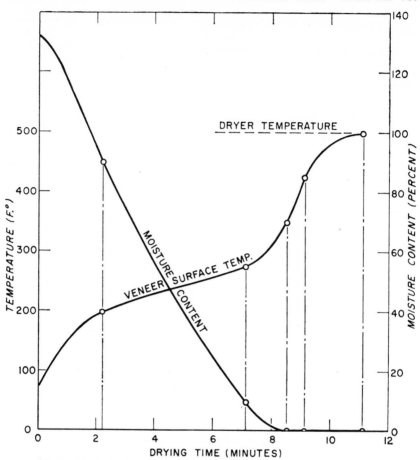

Figure 20–28.—Moisture content and veneer surface temperature for ⅛-inch southern pine veneer dried in a 500° F., cross-circulating, electrically heated oven until the surface temperature reached 500° F. (Drawing after Suchsland and Stevens 1968.)

an average moisture content of 4.7 percent with a range from 2.3 to 7.2 percent; the schedule called for 24 hours at 165° F. dry bulb and 150° F. wet bulb, plus 42 hours at 180° F. dry bulb and 156° F. wet bulb, and a final 6 hours at 186° F. dry bulb and 156° F. wet bulb. Resin exudation was spotty and light over 25 percent of each surface.

A 90-minute pass through a conventional roller veneer dryer at 300° F. brought the moisture content to an average of 4.4 percent with a range from 0 to 17.6 percent (fig. 20–30). The veneer was continuously fed longitudinally, as in a jet dryer, but the air was circulated in a counter-flowing horizontal direction instead of impinging vertically. Nominal air velocity was 600 f.p.m. Resin exudation was light but solid over a considerable portion of the veneers.

A 60-minute pass through an impingement jet-dryer at 300° F. with

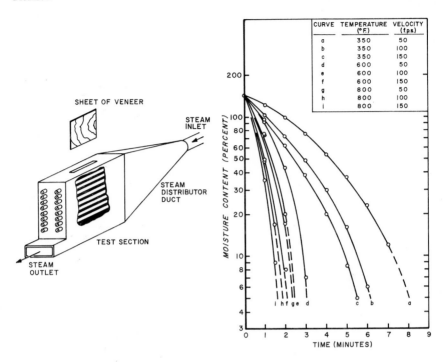

Figure 20–29.—Drying ⅛-inch, rotary-cut, southern pine sapwood veneer with superheated steam jets. (Left) Test apparatus for 45° and 90° impingement. (Right) Drying curves for 90° impingement. (Drawings after South 1968.)

air velocity of about 3,500 f.p.m. brought the ⁷⁄₁₆-inch veneers to an average moisture content of 5.1 percent with range from 0.2 to 14.3 percent (fig. 20–30).

When the temperature of the impingement-jet dryer was raised to 350° F., all of the veneers were dried to less than 10-percent moisture content in 40 minutes (fig. 20–30). In both of the jet dryer trials, resin exudation was heavy and solid over part of the surface of a good many of the veneers.

Kimball (1968) made a comparative evaluation of drying times for sawn and sliced loblolly pine veneers in the thickness range from ³⁄₁₆- to ⁹⁄₁₆-inch. Figure 20–31 shows that the sliced veneer dried somewhat faster than the sawn veneer in an impingement-jet dryer at 300° F. Impingement velocity was approximately 4,000 f.p.m. The ³⁄₁₆-inch veneer dried to 10-percent average moisture content in about 20 minutes, the ⅜-inch in about 40 minutes, and the ⁹⁄₁₆-inch in approximately 70 minutes. To have uniformity of final moisture content, either the original (green) moisture content must be uniform, or the dried veneer must be given an equalization treatment.

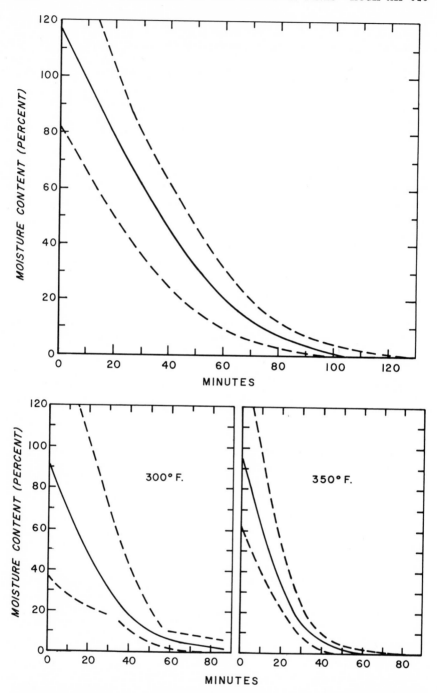

Figure 20–30.—Drying curves for S4S, 7/16-inch-thick southern pine veneers. Solid lines show average; dotted lines define envelope containing all veneers. (Top) Conventional roller veneer dryer at 300° F. (Bottom) Impingement-jet dryer at 300° and 350° F. (Drawings after Koch 1964.)

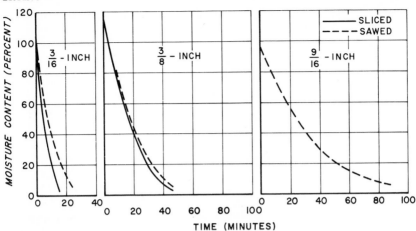

Figure 20–31.—Drying curves for S4S (sawn and planed) and sliced loblolly pine veneer in an impingement-jet dryer at 300° F. (Drawing after Kimball 1968.)

FLAKES, PARTICLES, AND FIBERS

Growing use of southern pine in flakeboards, particleboards, and fiberboards requires efficient equipment for bulk drying wood in finely divided form. Kollmann (1955) reviewed and diagrammed the characteristics of a variety of European machines designed to dry wood particles. Johnson (1956, pp. 145–153) edited an English-language handbook that included much of Kollmann's information. Maloney (1967, pp. 163–215) edited a compilation of papers that described current methods of drying wood particles.

The object of particle dryers is to reduce particle moisture content to a uniform low value of about 5 percent (ovendry basis) at a minimum drying cost. While travelling screen dryers and dryers that tumble the particles over heated elements are in use, most plants dry southern pine particles in a hot airstream (Stillinger 1967a). In these dryers, the furnish is introduced into a high-velocity, high-temperature airstream in a manner that exposes the maximum surface area of each particle to the drying atmosphere; drying time is very short.

Configuration of high-temperature flash dryers.—In the southern pine region, dryers are usually heated by natural gas. It is not uncommon to find primary gas burners with oil burners on standby in case of interrupted gas flow. Burners for finely ground wood residues may also be included in the design to reduce fuel costs and dispose of otherwise unusable residues.

Flash dryers may be classified as rotating horizontal (fig. 20–32), fixed horizontal (fig. 20–33), or vertical (fig. 20–34). In the rotating horizontal design, maximum inlet temperature is 1,200 to 1,400° F. and the entrance velocities for the inner, middle, and outer concentric drums (fig. 20–32 Top) are approximately 1,600, 640, and 320 f.p.m. The wet furnish enters

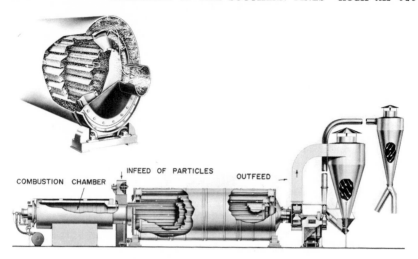

COMBUSTION CHAMBER   INFEED OF PARTICLES   OUTFEED

Figure 20–32.—Rotating, horizontal, high-temperature flash dryer. (Bottom) Major components. Infeed of furnish and hot air to inner drum on left; discharge from outer drum to hot cyclone (to separate hot gases from the dry particles) and final cyclone on right. (Top) Flow-path of furnish from hot inner drum to intermediate drum to cooler outer drum; baffles cause particles to tumble as they pass through the three drums. Outfeed end shown. (Drawings after Stillinger 1967b.)

the high-velocity, hot, central drum, and is discharged from the low-velocity, cooler, outer drum. Moisture content of the output is controlled by holding the outlet air temperature within narrow limits; the burner has a turn-down ratio of 10:1. With furnish having 400-percent moisture content (dry-weight basis), about 1,400 B.t.u. (British thermal units) are required to evaporate a pound of water; at 100- to 180-percent moisture content, 1,500 to 1,700 B.t.u. are required; and at 18- to 33-percent moisture content, about 1,800 to 1,900 B.t.u. (Stillinger 1967b). The dry output is normally separated from the hot gases through two cyclones before it is discharged into a storage bin.

In the fixed horizontal dryer shown in figure 20–33, wet material is fed into one end of a stationary drum; heated air is admitted through slots extending the entire length of the bottom of the drum. This heated air blows through the bed of material; the fluffing and forward movement of the bed is assisted by rotating raker arms. The slots are arranged so that the hot air enters tangentially and causes the material in the bed to rotate as it moves through the drum. The dried material is drawn out of the dryer drum, through a circulating fan, and is discharged from the drying system through a rotary air lock at the bottom of the cyclone collector. For maximum heat economy, spent air is recirculated, only enough being exhausted to equal the volume of moisture evaporated plus the makeup combustion gases from the heating unit. In this system the finer particles, which dry quickly, move faster through the drum than the coarser

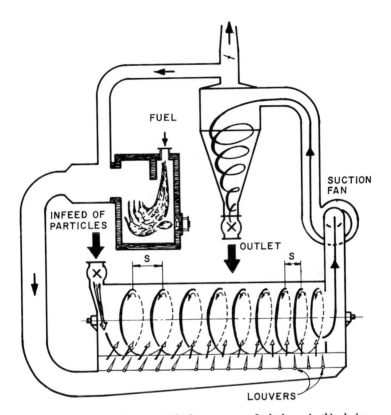

Figure 20–33.—Fixed, horizontal, high-temperature flash dryer. In this design gas (or oil) can be supplemented with sander dust from the particleboard sanders. Dimension "S," and hence retention time of particles in the dryer, is controlled by adjustment of vanes at bottom. (Drawing after Mottet 1967.)

material, which needs longer drying time. The drying process is controlled by: (1) adjusting firing rate of heating unit to regulate temperature of outlet air; (2) controlling proportion of recirculated exhaust air and fresh air; and (3) controlling vanes of entering-air slot to adjust dwell time in drum. These direct-heated dryers operate with inlet temperatures of 700 to 750° F. Energy consumption is in the range from 1,400 to 1,650 B.t.u. per pound of water evaporated, with average conditions in one West Coast plant requiring slightly under 1,650 B.t.u. per pound (Mottet 1967). A gas-fired dryer 8 feet in diameter and 26 feet long with heater capacity of 9 million B.t.u. per hour and drying capacity of 6,000 pounds of water per hour has 78½ connected horsepower driving the circulating fan, raker arms, air locks, and furnace.

In the vertical flash, or air-lift dryer, the furnish and the thoroughly mixed heated air are admitted to the bottom of a tower and discharged

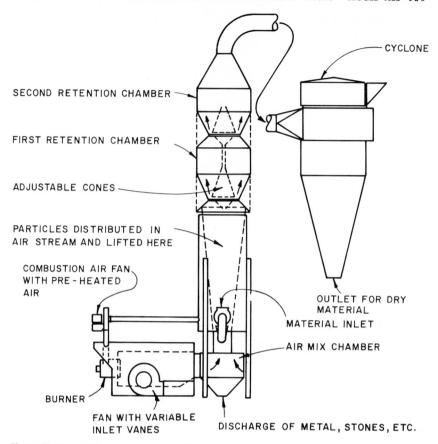

CYCLONE

SECOND RETENTION CHAMBER

FIRST RETENTION CHAMBER

ADJUSTABLE CONES

PARTICLES DISTRIBUTED IN
AIR STREAM AND LIFTED HERE

COMBUSTION AIR FAN
WITH PRE-HEATED
AIR

OUTLET FOR DRY
MATERIAL

MATERIAL INLET

AIR MIX CHAMBER

BURNER

FAN WITH VARIABLE
INLET VANES

DISCHARGE OF METAL, STONES, ETC.

Figure 20–34.—Positive-pressure vertical flash dryer with two retention chambers. (Drawing after Lengel 1967.)

from the top. Air circulation may be positive with the fan located at the bottom (fig. 20–34), or negative—with the fan located near the top discharge. The dryer in figure 20–34 has two retention chambers in a single tower. The geometry of these chambers is adjusted by internal cones when the plant initially starts up; thereafter the cones are adjusted infrequently. After the material passes the cones at high speed, it enters the large-diameter chambers. Placement of the cones influences the length of time that particles will dwell in each retention chamber. If the particles are heavy, they will tend to remain in each chamber longer and thus be exposed to the drying atmosphere for a longer time than light particles. The two chambers illustrated give longer dwell time than a single chamber. If, however, there is a large spread of particle size in the furnish, or if large particles are present, the relatively long retention times required may call for additional towers in series.

Either fibers or particles can be dried in a vertical dryer; one manufacturer successfully dried wood fiberized in an attrition mill under 50 to 90 pounds of steam pressure, the fibers being blown directly into the drying tower. The operation is difficult to start and requires a very uniform feed because the wet fibers tend to plaster inside the dryer. The manufacturer claims good efficiency for the system once it is started because the flashing off of the steam accomplishes part of the drying job (Lengel 1967).

Initial moisture content of furnish.—Drying of fine materials is complicated by wide variations in the moisture content of wood; some southern pine heartwood has less than 40-percent moisture, while sapwood may exceed 180 percent; an average of about 100 percent (ovendry basis) is common. The source of the furnish adds further variation. Dry planer shavings or dry veneer clippings will obviously need less drying capacity than furnish from green sawmill or veneer residues. Variation in the moisture content of the furnish is, however, more important than the average level of moisture content in determining the final quality of the drying operation. If surges of very wet and very dry material follow each other, the equipment must make rapid responses in fuel input (or retention time) to adjust for the changing heat requirements. The problem is minimized when changes in average moisture occur very slowly; preferably it is solved by uniformly mixing the moist and dry material to maintain a fairly constant average moisture content.

Size and shape of particles.—At a constant average moisture content, increasing the size of a particle of a given shape will tend to increase the cost of drying because more heat is required to remove a given weight of water from large particles. Small particles dry faster than large particles of the same general shape because they have a greater surface area per unit of volume. Variation in the size of particles causes varying final moisture content because the small particles get overdried. From a practical operating standpoint, this may not present a serious problem if the dried material is kept in in-process storage long enough to allow some moisture equalization.

Feed systems and ambient conditions.—Although most infeeding devices such as screw-feed or belt-feed equipment deliver a uniform volume of material, a better system would provide a constant rate of input based on weight. With a constant volume input, the load of the dryer changes with the bulk density of the furnish. Gradual changes cause no particular problem, but sudden changes cause the final moisture content of the output to fluctuate.

After leaving the dryer, the particles change moisture content in response to changing temperature and humidity in the board plant. A sudden rise in humidity can raise moisture content of the furnish 1 or 2 percent as it is conveyed through cyclones in the necessary handling operations prior to forming and pressing the board. These changes often call for minor adjustments in dryer outlet temperature.

Contaminations and discolorations.—If fuels, particularly oil, are not completely burned, they may contaminate particle surfaces. This contamination can impair adhesion when the particles are later bonded into a board. Excessively high inlet temperatures can char fine particles and scorch large particles. This scorching weakens glue bonds and may darken the color of the finished board.

FIBER MATS

Two different drying techniques are widely used, one for thick fiberboard mats and the other for thin mats or paper.

Thick mats.—Mechanical pressure will readily remove water from sawdust and pulps until moisture content approaches the fiber saturation point. To reduce the moisture content of groundwood to a point just below the fiber saturation point, however, requires greatly increased pressures—as high as 10,000 p.s.i. (McCarthy and Jahn 1936).

Commercially, wood fiberboard mats are mechanically prepressed to some degree and are then dried in tunnel dryers by air at temperatures from 250 to 500° F. As with veneer dryers these chambers may be steam heated or direct fired; they are commonly divided into three to five separate temperature zones. The boards move continuously through the zones on rollers (arranged in as many as eight decks or levels), and hot air is blown over the surfaces. Because of the rollers, the velocity of air over the bottom surface and the heat radiated to it, are less than for the top surface. Nominal air velocities are commonly 600 to 1,000 f.p.m. Total length of the dryer may vary from 300 to 550 feet; drying time is commonly 1½ to 3½ hours (Sinclair 1967).

Sinclair (1967) studied the drying process and described it in terms of exponential equations. Drying time depends on the thickness and density of the board, the initial moisture content, the temperature and humidity of the drying air, the temperature of the radiant heating coils, the velocity of the air over the surface of the board, and the thermal conductivity of the board. He observed that the initial constant-rate period—during which removal of water per unit of time is constant—occurred only when the dry board density was 11 pounds per cubic foot or less; for boards of greater density, the falling-rate period began immediately. Boards of high density have a low moisture content, since density is increased by increased pressing of the wet mat.

Figure 20–35 shows the drying curve for an 0.860-inch-thick fiberboard made from pine groundwood. The pilot-plant dryer was operated at 340° F. with air velocity of approximately 900 f.p.m. The board had an initial moisture content of 1.81 pounds of water per square foot of board and a dry density of 14.7 pounds per cubic foot. Drying time to 2-percent moisture content was 3.2 hours (Sinclair 1967).

In a three-zone dryer—420 feet long with average air temperature of over 300° F. (fig. 20–36 Left) and velocity of 850 f.p.m.—a ½-inch-thick

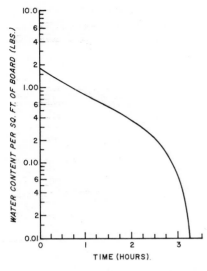

Figure 20–35.—Drying curve for 0.860-inch-thick pine fiberboard in tunnel dryer with air at 340° F. and about 900 f.p.m. velocity. (Drawing after Sinclair 1967.)

board was dried to 0.6-percent moisture content in about 90 minutes (fig. 20–36 Right); the board had a dry density of 16.7 pounds per cubic foot. Figure 20–36(Left) shows that the center of this board remained at 175° F. for an hour and then rose to a little over 200° F. during the last 30 minutes; the board surface finally approached close to air temperature (Sinclair 1967).

Thin mats.—As paper is formed on a moving wire screen by deposition of pulp fibers suspended in water, most of the water drains through the screen. The density of the fiber mat deposited on the screen varies locally

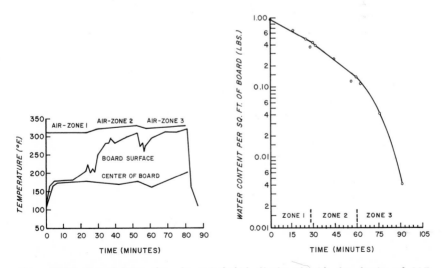

Figure 20–36.—Tunnel-drying data for ½-inch-thick fiberboard with dry density of 16.7 pounds per cubic foot. (Left) Board and zone temperatures. (Right) Drying curve. (Drawings after Sinclair 1967.)

to some degree, depending on the formation characteristics of the paper machine. The mat is further dewatered to near the fiber saturation point by its passage between pairs of nip rolls that mechanically press or wring out most of the free water. The dense spots in the sheet are compacted more than the surrounding fibers, but the sheet in these spots still remains somewhat thicker.

The sheet is then further dried by heat conduction as it passes over a series of large (e.g., 6 feet in diameter) drying rolls. Target final moisture content may be from 2 to 9 percent depending on product. The drying rolls or cylinders may have surface temperatures as low as 190° F. or as high as 290° F.; they are often in the range of 260 to 280° F. (Gardner 1967). The paper probably does not attain intimate contact with the dryer rolls; except where thick spots in the mat touch the rolls, a very small airgap generally separates the paper from the roll. The dense spots —because of closer contact with the hot surface and high rate of heat transfer due to density—may be overdried and further accentuate the variations resulting from poor mat formation.

The dryer rolls are mounted in multiples with the paper threading a passageway through them; felts or synthetic screens are commonly used to back up the paper sheet so that closer contact is maintained between the paper and the hot surface of the roll (fig. 20–37 Top).

The stacks or nests of rolls are all gear driven from one side (the back side); these gears with their housings often restrict airflow longitudinal to the roll axes, and hence the paper sheet across its width tends to be drier on the back side adjacent to the gears than on the front side. In addition, moist air is trapped in the pockets formed by the dryer rolls and the felt loops (fig. 20–37 Top). These traps hinder circulation of dry air to the center of the sheet with the result that the sheet typically has higher moisture content in the center than near the edges (fig. 20–37 Bottom). The problem is further aggravated by the extreme width of modern paper machines.

Metcalfe (1968) has described some remedies for this problem. For paperboard only, nozzles can be placed to blow dry air vertically against the full width of the surface of the moving sheet; air jet velocities range from 3,000 to 10,000 f.p.m. Another approach calls for jets of air to blow parallel to the roll axis in the areas where moisture is trapped; depending on nozzle design, air velocities may be as high, although with light sheets nozzles must be designed for lower velocities (4,000 to 8,000 f.p.m.) to avoid causing the sheet to flutter and wrinkle.

A current and effective solution is **pocket ventilation** whereby dry air is blown through the more or less permeable backup felts; moist air is exhausted laterally out the front and back sides of the machine (fig. 36A).

While variations as prominent as those shown in figure 20–37 (Bottom) are not uncommon, Metcalfe (1968) states that with proper attention to drying conditions, moisture differences across the sheet can be reduced

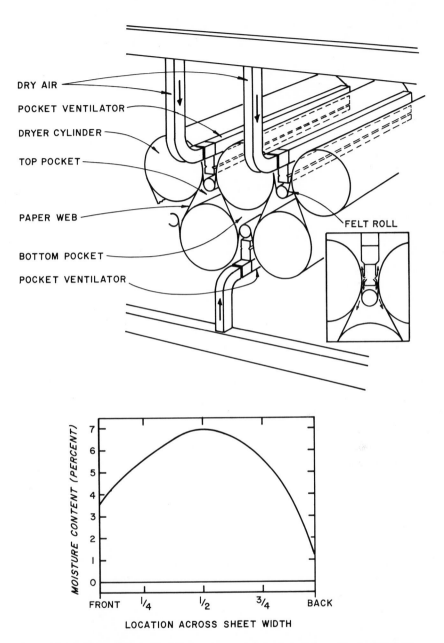

DRY AIR

POCKET VENTILATOR

DRYER CYLINDER

TOP POCKET

PAPER WEB

BOTTOM POCKET

POCKET VENTILATOR

FELT ROLL

MOISTURE CONTENT (PERCENT)

7

6

5

4

3

2

1

0

FRONT   ¼   ½   ¾   BACK

LOCATION ACROSS SHEET WIDTH

Figure 20–37.—Paper drying. (Top) Paper passes over heated drying rolls; backup felts on top and bottom hold paper in contact with rolls. Pocket ventilators even out variation in moisture content. (Bottom) Example of variation of moisture content across width of paper sheet emerging from dryer. (Top drawing after Gardner 1966; bottom drawing after Metcalfe 1968.)

to 0.3 percent. This degree of control is rare; knowledgeable people in the industry state that the best current practice when drying newsprint to 8-percent moisture content might give moisture differences across the sheet of ±¾-percent.

Dryers on modern paper machines are fast, large, and expensive. Newsprint running at 2,500 lineal f.p.m. might pass over 50 rolls each 5 feet in diameter and 25 feet long. Temperature of the first rolls is usually about 180° F., while the main group of rolls are heated to about 240° F. Passage through such a dryer would reduce the moisture content of newsprint from about 62 percent to about 9 percent.

The reader desiring a more fundamental discussion of fiber and mat drying phenomena is referred to Wrist (1966) and Han and Matters (1966). Other papers, that should be helpful to readers desiring additional information include: Gardner (1970), Han (1970), Hankin et al. (1970), Herdman (1970), Iannazzi and Strauss (1970), Janet (1970), Kennedy (1970), Khandelwal (1970), Race (1970), Rantala (1970), Wahlstrom (1970), Wieselman (1970), and Rhorer (1971).

PRESS DRYING

Press drying is high-temperature drying of sawn or sliced lumber and veneer; it is accomplished by applying a pair of heated platens (250 to 450° F.) to the board or veneer—one to each face. Good thermal contact between the heated platens and the board face is obtained by using a platen pressure of 25 to 85 p.s.i.

During drying, heat is transferred, mainly by conduction, from the platens to the wood, causing air in the wood to expand and water to vaporize. A mixture of vapor and liquid then moves to the surface of the board where it escapes. Ventilated cauls and wire screens have been interposed on top and bottom between the platens and the board to help vapor escape from the faces of the board (fig. 20–38 Top).

Heated platens as a heat source serve the useful purposes of holding the board flat during drying and of reducing width shrinkage; however, platen pressure and high temperatures generally lead to thickness shrinkage greater than that caused by conventional drying. Cyclic shrinking and swelling tests (Hittmeier et al. 1968) indicated that press-dried hardwood lumber was 30 to 60 percent more stable in width dimension than con-

→

Figure 20–38.—Hot-press drying of S4S southern pine veneers 7/16-inch thick. Temperature of platens 300° F. Specific pressure 82.6 pounds per square inch. (Top) System of ventilated cauls. The aluminum protector sheets are 0.064 inch thick. Top and bottom cauls are of aluminum and measure ¼ by 26 by 104 inches. Rectangular grooves 1/16-inch deep by 3/16-inch wide were milled on 1-inch centers on the back of each caul. One-eighth-inch holes were drilled at 1-inch intervals along each groove. A 75-mesh Fourdrinier wire screen was interposed between the veneer and each ventilated caul. (Bottom) Drying curves. Solid line is average; dotted lines define envelope containing all veneers. (Drawings after Koch 1964.)

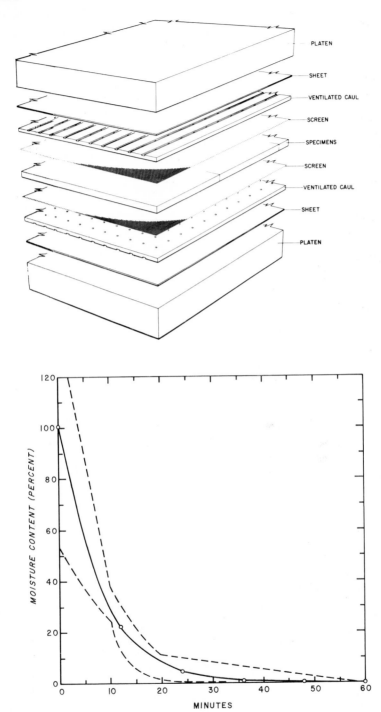

ventionally kiln-dried material but was, in general, 10 to 80 percent less stable in thickness dimension.

Drying rates.—The press-drying process for southern pine was evaluated by Koch (1964) on 8-foot-long, $\frac{7}{16}$-inch-thick, S4S, green veneers; the planed veneers were sawn (through and through) from heart-center cants measuring 4, 6, 8, 10, and 12 inches square. Veneers were dried in a 2- by 8½-foot, single-opening, hot-plate press (fig. 20–38 Top). Platen temperature was 300° F., and platen pressure was 82.6 p.s.i. Drying was accomplished in a single closed-press cycle of 23 minutes. Thermocouples placed in test boards indicated that the surface of the veneers reached 250° F. within ½-minute after press closure, and moved slowly up to a maximum of 280° F. during the remainder of the cycle. The center of these $\frac{7}{16}$-inch-thick S4S veneers reached 235° F. within 5 minutes after press closure and increased slowly to a maximum of 250° F. by the end of the cycle. Within 7 minutes from the time the press opened and the veneers were removed, surface temperature dropped to 175° F. and the center temperature to 145° F. The green test veneers had an average initial moisture content of 105 percent and ranged from 36 to 164 percent. The 23-minute drying procedure reduced the average to 3.4 percent, with a range of 0 to 15.1 percent (fig. 20–38 Bottom).

Figure 20–39 shows that if loblolly pine is submerged for 15 hours in hot water (180° F.) and then sliced to $\frac{3}{16}$- or $\frac{3}{8}$-inch thickness, the resulting veneer can be press dried at 300° F. slightly more rapidly than planed veneer of the same thickness sawn from the same logs (Kimball 1968). Results are summarized below:

Veneer thickness and description	Average green moisture content	Average dry moisture content	Drying time
	- - - Percent - - -		Minutes
$\frac{3}{16}$-inch			
Sliced	97.0	2.2	9
Sawn	110.6	8.1	9
$\frac{3}{8}$-inch			
Sliced	111.1	5.4	26
Sawn	99.5	6.9	26
$\frac{9}{16}$-inch			
Sawn	98.2	10.1	48

Warp and shrinkage.—The 8-foot-long, $\frac{7}{16}$-inch, press-dried, sawn veneers described by Koch (1964), when at the final moisture content of 3.4 percent, developed the following warp and shrinkage:

Shrinkage, percent
Width _____ 0.82
Length _____ .05
Thickness _____ 8.07
Warp, inch
Crook _____ .11
Cup _____ .04
Twist _____ .07
Bow _____ .21

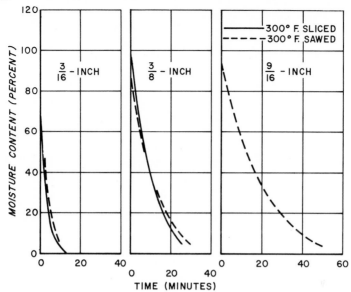

Figure 20-39.—Hot-press drying of sliced and sawn loblolly pine of three
thicknesses. Specific pressure, 75 pounds per square inch. (Drawing after
Kimball 1968.)

The 45-inch-long, press-dried, loblolly pine veneer evaluated by Kimball
(1968) had the following values of shrinkage and warp when conditioned
to a moisture content between 6 and 7 percent. Cup is expressed as the
reciprocal of the radius of curvature in inches.

Veneer thickness and description	Shrinkage		Warp	
	Width	Thickness	Cup	Crook
	---- Percent ----		1/rad.	Inch
³⁄₁₆-inch				
Sliced_____	0.46	11.93	0.007	0.00
Sawn_____	1.54	8.89	.010	.01
³⁄₈-inch				
Sliced_____	.56	10.78	.007	.02
Sawn_____	1.42	9.60	.010	.02
⁹⁄₁₆-inch				
Sawn_____	1.97	10.02	.015	.07

These data appear to indicate that sawn veneer develops more width
shrinkage and cup than sliced wood when press dried.

Resin exudation.—The southern pine veneer press dried by Koch
(1964) showed a varnishlike resin exudation over a substantial portion of
the surface. By contrast, the loblolly pine press dried by Kimball (1968)
showed no pitch exudation. The reason for this observable difference is
not yet clear.

DRYING WITH INFRARED ENERGY

Heat radiated from an infrared source (see fig. 15–4 for definition) penetrates wood slowly because wood is a good insulator and because wood is opaque to infrared. Continued heating to raise the interior temperature of lumber tends to cause excessive surface temperature (hence a steep moisture gradient) with accompanying surface checks and warpage (Keylwerth 1951). In contrast with normal kiln-drying practice, where hot air circulates through the pile, infrared radiation heats only the directly exposed surfaces.

While no information specific to southern pine is at hand, Narayanamurti and Prasad (1952) provided data on a number of species of rotary-cut, $1/16$- and $1/8$-inch-thick veneers dried under banks of 250-watt, tungsten-filament lamps. The lamps were placed to deliver 290 mW/cm² (mW = milliwatt = 10^{-3} watts) to each side of the veneer. With this irradiation, $1/16$-inch veneers required 15 to 50 minutes to dry from a green moisture content in the range from 67 to 101 percent to a dry moisture content in the range from 4.6 to 11.2 percent. In the same range of moisture contents, $1/8$-inch thick veneer required 55 to 65 minutes. Surface temperatures rose to approximately 190° C. after about 10 minutes of radiation and then remained constant. Narayanamurti and Prasad (1952) conclude that: (1) with proper equipment power consumption could be as low as 1 to 1½ kilowatt hours per kilogram (1,549 to 2,323 B.t.u. per pound) of water removed; (2) less power is consumed removing free water than bound water; and (3) efficiency is greatest with thin veneers. The green veneers were defect-free, and after drying they were in satisfactory condition.

Researchers in the United States believe that 1½ kilowatt hours per kilogram (a process efficiency of 60 percent) is a somewhat optimistic estimate. Even with this efficiency, assuming an electricity rate of 3¢/kilowatt hour and a water content of 1,800 pounds per thousand board feet (M b.f.) of lumber, electricity cost per M b.f. dried would be $36.

Kollmann et al. (1967) conducted detailed observations of spruce (*Picea* spp.) wood exposed to infrared. He concluded that far infrared was more effective than near in heating and drying wood.

If wood is exposed to radiation on both sides with natural air velocities of 0.2 to 0.3 m. per second, drying takes place more than twice as fast at high moisture content (during the constant-rate period) than if only one side is exposed. As drying proceeds into the range of decreasing drying rate (falling-rate period), the ratio between drying rates for two-sided and one-sided radiation increases progressively. If air is circulated past the specimen (2.6 m. per second) the drying rate is decreased considerably. It appears that natural air convection is adequate to take up and remove the moisture evaporated from the drying wood (Kollmann et al. 1967).

20–5 HIGH-FREQUENCY DIELECTRIC HEATING

It is technically possible to season southern pine by placing it in an electric field that oscillates at a high frequency (e.g., 1 million cycles per second) between condenser plates or electrodes. Such a field quickly heats the free water more than the wood because of the polarity of water molecules; the water is supplied energy sufficient to vaporize it and also heat the wood. In permeable woods, such as southern pine, the temperature tends to level off slightly above the boiling point as long as free water exists. When only bound water remains, the temperature rises. If these high temperatures are prolonged, they weaken the wood; local explosions or splits may result.

To date, this method of drying southern pine wood has not been of economic importance because of the high cost of high-frequency generators, power tubes, and electricity. McMillen and James (1961) estimated these costs to be at least $26 per M b.f. when drying green sapwood of ponderosa pine or western white pine (*Pinus monticola* Dougl.) to 8-percent moisture content.

20–6 CHEMICAL SEASONING [5]

Surface checking of wood occurs when the outer layers are dried below the fiber saturation point while the inside layers remain wet and swollen. As the outer layers shrink, they are subjected to large tension stresses across the grain because they remain attached to the still swollen wet core. Checks and splits develop to relieve these stresses; or in some cases, where the wet core has less strength to resist failure in compression than does the outer layer to resist failure in tension, internal collapse results.

Some organic chemicals and concentrated salt solutions depress the vapor pressure of water to a high degree (Stamm 1934). If these hygroscopic chemicals are applied to the surface of wood, they diffuse into the wood with diminished concentration at increasing depths from the surface. By this means, the moisture content in the surface layer is maintained above fiber saturation even though exposed to air of fairly low humidity. The inner layers, which contain no salt, continue to dry; because shrinkage is reduced in the wetter swollen shell, surface checking is reduced or eliminated (Loughborough 1948; McMillen 1960; Haygreen 1962).

Both inorganic and organic chemicals have been used as chemical seasoning agents. Among the inorganic are: sodium chloride (Colgrove 1956), calcium chloride, zinc chloride, borax, boric acid, ammonium sulfate, ammonium phosphate, magnesium sulfate, and sodium sulfate. Organic chemicals have included sucrose, dextrose, urea (Peck 1941), etc. Any low-cost hygroscopic chemical can be an effective chemical seasoning agent, but

---

[5] With some changes, secs. 20–6 and 20–7 are condensed from Hudson (1969) by permission of M. S. Hudson and the Forest Products Research Society.

practically, the method is greatly restricted because of undesirable side effects.

The lowest cost chemical found useful for this purpose has been ordinary salt (sodium chloride), but it is so corrosive to equipment in dry kilns, to woodworking machinery used to remove it, and to hardware applied to the wood in use if the salt layer is not planed off, that the process has severe limitations. Efforts to overcome this corrosive effect by the addition of corrosion inhibitors, such as sodium dichromate, have not been entirely successful.

Sodium chloride and in some cases urea have been the only chemicals used in commercial drying of southern pine. With sodium chloride, shrinkage will not take place at the surface until the prevailing relative humidity falls below 75 percent (Stamm 1934); with urea, shrinkage starts at a relative humidity of 90 percent (Stamm 1964, p. 453). Urea was used to some extent during World War II to dry Douglas-fir ponton stock; large Douglas-fir timbers have also been dried in arid climates by application of urea. No evaluation of urea as a drying agent for southern pine has been made.

Southern pine less than 4 inches thick dries so readily by ordinary methods that chemical seasoning pretreatment is not necessary. There may be some items of greater thickness that would benefit from such treatment, especially timbers in which heartwood is exposed on one face. No research has been done on this specific situation, however.

In the first of two studies (unpublished), the U.S. Forest Products Laboratory dried green 5- by 5-, 6- by 6-, and 7- by 7-inch timbers after soaking them in saturated sodium chloride solutions. These southern pine timbers were essentially sapwood, with heartwood small and almost centrally located. The most effective treatment reduced the average width of the large checks that formed in all specimens after air-drying to about one-third of the width of the checks in the untreated pieces. When treated wood was kiln-dried (initial drying condition about 150° F. and 50-percent relative humidity), check width was about one-half that observed in the untreated air-dried controls. The salt absorption was 13 percent of the ovendry weight after soaking the timbers in the saturated solution for 4 days at room temperature and 8 days at 150° F. When soaked 4 days cold and 2 days hot, absorption was 8 percent. At the end of treatment by the first method, salt concentration just under the surface was 45 percent; at 1 inch it was 11 percent; and at 2 inches it was less than 2 percent. During the early stages of drying there was further diffusion of salt toward the pith, but also some migration back towards the surface. In general, final salt concentration across the sapwood was 3 percent or higher. Very little salt entered the interior heartwood during the treating period, but some entered by diffusion during drying.

Results of chemical seasoning are best when the humidity during early drying is not too much below equilibrium with the saturated seasoning agent. In the case of salt, this is 75 percent. Perhaps an initial relative humidity of 65 or 60 percent would have dried the timbers essentially check-free. In a second experiment, dry salt was spread at the rate of 75 pounds per M b.f. on 3- and 4-inch by 6- and 8-inch southern pine timbers to be used in the production of end-block flooring. A relatively high temperature was used in the kiln schedule, and drying time was 8¾ days compared with 15 days being taken by the regular kiln schedule. The initial conditions were 180° F. with 55-percent relative humidity. The quality of drying was better than that of untreated material in the same kiln charge, but there was checking in the pieces containing boxed heart.

With relative humidity conditions above 75 percent, metal in contact with salt treated wood has corroded (even with corrosion-inhibiting chemicals present). Salt and similar chemicals also affect the electrical properties of the wood.

At the present time southern pine is not commercially dried by chemical seasoning. No estimate of the amount of southern pine dried in this way in the past is available.

20–7   DRYING IN CONDUCTIVE HEAT TRANSFER MEDIA[5]

Drying can be accelerated by heating wood in media that have greater heat conductivity than air. Several processes have been developed.

IMMERSION IN HOT ORGANIC LIQUIDS

The boiling-in-oil process, i.e., immersion of wood in an organic liquid and then heating the liquid above the boiling point of water, is probably the oldest method for evaporative drying of wood (McMillen 1961b; Maroney 1962). Like many other processes it has been promoted for a time, then forgotten, then rediscovered later and practiced on a little higher level using better chemicals and equipment. Barksdale (1949) revived interest in the boiling-in-oil process. He boiled southern pine lumber in number 2 fuel oil containing a small amount of paraffin. The lumber was heated in the oil to 260° F. in an open tank. It took about 16 hours to dry 4- by 8-inch southern pine timbers from 77-percent down to 22-percent moisture content. Severe casehardening occurred during drying. The wood absorbed about 4 percent of its weight of the drying oil (McMillen 1961b).

About 1958 a boiling-in-oil process using non-inflammable perchloroethylene as the drying agent was promoted by McDonald (1958). The method required very sophisticated equipment; the boiling operation was carried out in a closed vessel, and the drying agent that was steam distilled off with the water was recovered by condensation and gravity separation.

Neither of these processes was commercially successful because both methods badly discolored and severely casehardened the wood. Extractives from the wood contaminated the drying agent; prolónged heating darkened the contaminated liquid.

As a conditioning process prior to preservative treatment in pressure cylinders, the **Boulton** process of boiling green wood in oil under vacuum has the advantage of relative low temperature—and hence less damage to the strength of the wood—together with the capability of reducing the moisture content of sapwood in round green timbers below the fiber saturation point. With a creosote temperature of 200° F., temperature change in round southern pine specimens is about the same with or without vacuum (about 25 inches of mercury) until the wood reaches about 160° F. Under vacuum, the wood temperature then changes but little until a considerable amount of water has been removed from the sapwood. With the creosote at 200° F., green southern pine pole sections approximately 9 to 11 inches in diameter and 10 feet long lost 9 to 12 pounds of water per cubic foot of wood during 10 to 13 hours of boiling under a 25-inch vacuum (MacLean 1960).

When the empty-cell treatment is to be used following the Boulton process—as is commonly the case with southern pine—the hot oil must be drained from the cylinder and air admitted. Southern pine has a large preliminary absorption after the vacuum is discontinued and while the oil is being drained—particularly if air pressure is applied to hasten the draining. Because such preliminary absorption takes places under approximately full-cell conditions, the preservative does not penetrate as deeply as it should for the weight absorbed. Better penetrations can be obtained with 8- to 10-pound retentions if southern pine poles are conditioned by steaming and vacuum rather than boiled under vacuum (Hunt and Garratt 1967, p. 164). Steaming under vacuum is described in section 20–4 under the heading POLES AND TIMBERS.

VAPOR DRYING

Like the boiling-in-oil process, vapor drying is an improvement of older processes. The earliest reference to the method is a patent issued to Cresson in 1865 which disclosed a very crude process and apparatus for drying wood in vapors of organic chemicals.

The vapor-drying process as it is presently used was developed by Hudson (1947, 1948) in 1940. The process is carried out in the apparatus shown in figure 20–40. An organic liquid having a boiling point between 212 and 400° F. is used as the drying agent. This would include liquids like xylene, Stoddard solvent, and kerosene. Lower boiling liquids, e.g., hexane or benzene, that have boiling points below 212° F. could be used; being immiscible with water, they form azeotropes with the water, and the boiling points of the mixtures are below that of the lower boiling constituent. Maroney (1962) has reported on the azeotropic drying of hard-

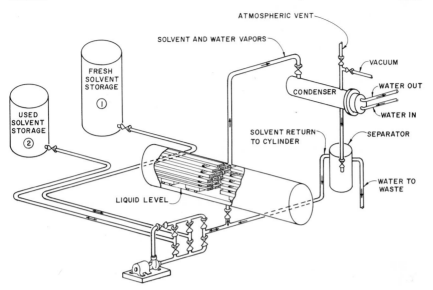

Figure 20–40.—Pressure-impregnating cylinder equipped for vapor drying and solvent recovery. (Drawing after Hudson 1969.)

woods with the solvent perchloroethylene. However, these liquids lengthen drying time, and they are hazardous because of low flash-point.

Wood to be dried is placed in a closed cylinder (fig. 20–40) and separated by stickers, as in air- or kiln-drying, to allow the vapor access to all surfaces. Drying agent sufficient to cover heating coils on the bottom of the cylinder is admitted and heated to its boiling point, usually about 260 to 280° F. Vapor from the boiling liquid condenses on the cold wood, delivering to the wood its latent heat of vaporization. This rapidly heats the wood up to the boiling point of its free water, which begins to boil off. Wherever there is free water in the wood, the temperature of the wood cannot rise above 212° F. despite vapor temperatures of 260 to 280° F., because the system is open to the atmosphere through the condenser and separator.

The water boiling from the wood is swept upward out of the cylinder by excess drying agent vapor. The vapor mixture is led to a condenser, where the temperature is lowered to about 150° F., condensing both the water that boiled from the wood and the drying agent to liquids. The drying agent is usually immiscible with water, so the two separate; the water in most cases is heavier and sinks to the bottom, where it leaves the separator. The drying agent returns to the cylinder, where it begins a new cycle.

After the wood has dried sufficiently—this point determined by reading a water meter on the separator discharge—heat is cut off, the cylinder is emptied of drying agent, and the hot wood is subjected to a vacuum applied through the separator. Under vacuum, the drying agent absorbed by the wood is rapidly evaporated and recovered at the condenser.

The approximate time required to vapor dry southern pine lumber from an initial moisture content of 100 percent down to 20 percent is as follows:

Thickness of lumber	Boiling point of drying agent	Time required to dry
Inches	*°F.*	*Hours*
1	240	9
3	240	11
1	260	5
3	260	8
1	280	4
3	280	7

Southern pine lumber can be dried to 20-percent moisture content with little or no degrade, but continuation of drying beyond that point can result in very severe casehardening. In addition, if relatively dry wood is held at these high temperatures for prolonged periods, some weakening can be expected.

The drying agent, whether it be xylene, kerosene, perchloroethylene, or other chemical, carries out its drying function merely as a heat transfer medium; the higher its boiling point, the faster the wood dries. However, if drying temperatures in excess of about 280° F. are used, there are increased troubles from excessive drying stresses. The drying agents, of course, must be inert with respect to the wood. The chemical properties of the drying agents seem to have no bearing on the rate of drying or on the quality of the dried wood unless they are polar chemicals like alcohols, aldehydes, ketones, esters and the like. These latter keep the wood swollen as it dries; therefore, with them it is possible to dry below 20 percent without casehardening. Because of their higher cost, however, these have not been used commercially.

Since a plant equipped for preservative impregnation of wood can be modified for vapor drying at moderate cost, the process combines well with wood preserving operations. It is used mainly to dry wood in preparation for treatment with preservatives, or to redry it after treatment with waterborne preservatives, or both. It is rarely used for drying only.

Figure 20–41 shows a typical schedule for predrying, preservative treatment, and redrying of 2- by 8-inch southern pine lumber using xylene as the drying agent. Green wood having an initial moisture content of about 75 percent is heated in xylene vapor for 6 hours. The average temperature of the vapor in the cylinder is 260° F., although the boiling point of xylene is 280° F. This is because water vapor in the mixture reduces the temperature. A vacuum of 25 inches of mercury is used to remove and recover drying agent absorbed by the wood. At this point the wood has a moisture content of about 35 percent. It is then impregnated with a water solution of a preservative salt for 3 hours. At the end of impregnation, the moisture content is about 110 percent. About 8 hours is required to redry the treated wood to 25-percent moisture content.

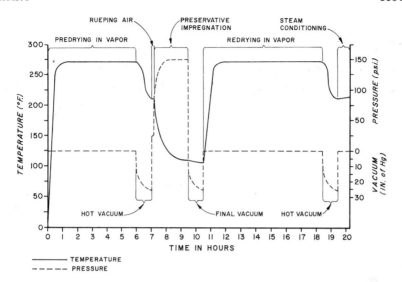

Figure 20–41.—Vapor drying schedule for processing lumber in salt treatment. Drying agent: Xylene. (Drawing after Hudson 1969.)

During drying of a charge containing 35,000 bd. ft. of pine lumber, the volume of drying agent condensing on the lumber amounts to about 10,000 gallons. This hot solvent pouring over the surface extracts large amounts of pine oleoresin. In the case of 1-inch lumber, the amount of extractives amounts to 16 to 20 pounds per M b.f. The used drying agent may be distilled to dryness to obtain the crude pine oleoresin.

Huffman (1955) found that most, if not all, of the extractives in the outer layers of southern pine lumber were removed by the vapor-drying process. It is probable that vapor-dried lumber, when painted, has less bleed-through and discoloration of the paint over knots and pitch streaks than does air- or kiln-dried southern pine.

Southern pine poles can be dried quickly by the vapor process. About 15 hours of heating in vapor is required to dry 12-inch-diameter poles from 90-percent moisture content to 35-percent with a drying agent temperature of 280° F. Hudson (1946) reported that vapor-dried southern pine poles were 20- to 25-percent stronger than poles dried by the steam (260° F. for 12 hours) and vacuum process. The strength tests were performed on 100 matched 25-foot sections cut from fifty 55-foot poles.

SOLVENT SEASONING

The solvent seasoning process developed by Anderson and Hermann (1950) uses liquid polar solvents, e.g., acetone or methanol, to dry wood. The heated, water-free solvent is passed over the wood, transferring heat to the wood and extracting water and other polar-solvent soluble constituents (McMillen 1961b; Anderson 1966). This process has not been used on the southern pines, but it should be as effective on these species as it is for western pines on which it has been used.

20-8 LITERATURE CITED

Anderson, A. B.
1966. Solvent drying pays dividends with ponderosa pine. Forest Prod. J. 16(12): 31–35.

Anderson, A. B., and Hermann, A.
1950. Process of treating wood. (U.S. Pat. No. 2,500,783) U.S. Pat. Office, Wash., D.C.

Barksdale, B. E., Sr.
1949. Apparatus for drying lumber. (U.S. Pat. No. 2,464,429) U.S. Pat. Office, Wash., D.C.

Burkhalter, H. D., and Russell, E. J.
1969. Tree harvesting method. (U.S. Pat. No. 3,460,288.) U.S. Pat. Office, Wash., D.C.

Calvert, W. W.
1958. High-temperature kiln-drying of lumber: A summary of Canadian progress. Forest Prod. J. 8:200–204.

Calvert, W. W.
1965. High-temperature kiln-drying of eastern Canadian species. Can. Wood Prod. Ind. 5(7): 34–39.

Carpenter, B. E., Jr., and Schroeder, J. G.
1968. Combined effects of drying, surfacing, and trimming on grade and volume of southern pine lumber. USDA Forest Serv. Res. Note SE–93, 3 pp. Southeast. Forest Exp. Sta., Asheville, N.C.

Christensen, F. J.
1970. Breakthrough in drying softwoods. CSIRO Forest Prod. Newslett. 377, pp. 3–5. Melbourne, Australia.

Colgrove, W. H.
1956. Chemical seasoning of lumber. Forest Prod. J. 6:417–419.

Corder, S. E.
1963. Ventilating veneer dryers. Forest Prod. J. 13: 449–453.

Dineen, N. J.
1968. Dry kiln pressure venting and lumber drying. Forest Prod. J. 18(5): 19–23.

Fessel, F.
1964. Continuous veneer drying with jet ventilation. Holz als Roh- und Werkstoff 22: 129–139.

Fleischer, H. O.
1958. A graphic method of estimating veneer drying rates. USDA Forest Prod. Lab. Rep. 2104, 8 pp.

Gaby, L. I.
1959. Operation predry . . . Variables in drying southern pine. Forest Prod. J. 9(5): 23A–27A.

Gaby, L. I.
1961. Forced air-drying of southern pine lumber. USDA Forest Serv. Southeast. Forest Exp. Sta., Sta. Pap. 121, 20 pp.

Gaby, L. I.
1967. Controlled drying of pine roundwood. Forest Prod. J. 17(1): 19–23.

Gardner, T. A.
1966. Pocket ventilator controls drying atmosphere. TAPPI 49(8): 113A–114A.

Gardner, T. A.
1967. Moisture profile variation on paper machines. TAPPI 50(7): 110A–114A.

Gardner, T. A.
1970. Realizing the best performance from a conventional dryer section. TAPPI 53: 990–992.

Gerhards, C. C.
1968. 4-inch southern pine lumber: Seasoning factors for modulus of elasticity and modulus of rupture. Forest Prod. J. 18(11): 27–35.

Guernsey, F. W.
1957. High temperature drying of British Columbia softwoods. Forest Prod. J. 7: 368–371.

Hallock, H.
1965. Sawing to reduce warp of loblolly pine studs. USDA Forest Serv. Res. Pap. FPL–51, 52 pp. Forest Prod. Lab., Madison, Wis.

Han, S. T.
1970. Drying of paper. TAPPI 53: 1034–1046.

Han, S. T., and Matters, J. F.
1966. Vapor transport in fiber mats during drying. TAPPI 49:1–4.

Hankin, J. W., Leidigh, W. J., and Stephansen, E. W.
1970. Microwave paper drying experience and analysis. TAPPI 53: 1063–1070.

Hann, R. A.
1964. Drying yellow-poplar at temperatures above 100° C. Forest Prod. J. 14: 215–220.

Hart, C. A.
1965. The drying of wood. N. C. State Univ. Sch. Forest. Tech. Rep. 27, 24 pp.

Haygreen, J. G.
1962. A study of the kiln-drying of chemically seasoned lumber. Forest Prod. J. 12: 11–16.

Herdman, R.
1970. Paper drying features of a modern computerized machine. TAPPI 53: 1007–1009.

Hittmeier, M. E., Comstock, G. L., and Hann, R. A.
1968. Press drying nine species of wood. Forest Prod. J. 18(9): 91–96.

Hopkins, W. C., Choong, E. T., and Fogg, P. J.
1969. Kiln-drying different thicknesses of southern pine lumber. La. State Univ. Bull. 636, 21 pp.

Hudson, M. S.
1946. Poles seasoned quickly in hydrocarbon atmosphere. I. Elec. World 126(11): 90–93; II. 126(13): 107–108.

Hudson, M. S.
1947. Vapor drying: The artificial seasoning of wood in vapor of organic chemicals. Forest Prod. Res. Soc. Proc. 1: 124–146.

Hudson, M. S.
1948. Apparatus and method for drying wood. (U.S. Pat. No. 2,435,218) U. S. Pat. Office, Wash., D.C.

Hudson, M. S.
1969. Chemical drying of southern pine wood . . . a review. Forest Prod. J. 19(3): 21–24.

Huffman, J. B.
1955. Distribution of resinous extractives after seasoning. Forest Prod. J. 5: 135–138.

Hunt, G. M., and Garratt, G. A.
1967. Wood preservation. Ed. 3, 433 pp. N.Y.: McGraw-Hill Book Co., Inc.

Iannazzi, F. D., and Strauss, R.
1970. Comparative manufacturing costs for wet-laid and dry-laid materials. TAPPI 53: 1026–1028.

Isaccs, C. P., and Choong, E. T.
1969. Effect of temperature during drying on surface properties of southern pine veneer. La. State Univ. LSU Wood Util. Notes 15, 5 pp.

Janett, L. G.
1970. Profile correction and economics in drying of paper. TAPPI 53:981–988.

Johnson, E. S., editor.
1956. Wood particle board handbook. 303 pp. Raleigh: N.C. State Coll.

Kauman, W. G.
1956. Equilibrium moisture content relations and drying control in superheated steam drying. Forest Prod. J. 6: 328–332.

Kempfer, W. H.
1913. The air-seasoning of timber. Amer. Railway Eng. Assoc. Bull. 15(161): 163–231.

Kennedy, W. H.
1970. Water removal by twin vertical wires. TAPPI 53: 974–975.

Keylwerth, R.
1951. [Infrared radiators in the wood industry.] Holz als Roh- und Werkstoff 9: 224–231.

Keylwerth, R.
1952. High-temperature drying installations. Holz als Roh- und Werkstoff 10: 134–138.

Khandelwal, K. K.
1970. Relatiinship between sheet formation and dryer section performance. TAPPI 53: 971–972.

Kimball, K. E.
1968. Accelerated methods of drying thick-sliced and thin-sawn loblolly pine. Forest Prod. J. 18(1): 31–38.

Kimball, K. E., and Lowery, D. P.
1967a. Methods for drying lodgepole pine and western larch studs. Forest Prod. J. 17(4): 32–40.

Kimball, K. E., and Lowery, D. P.
1967b. Quality of studs dried by high and conventional temperatures. Forest Prod. J. 17(9): 81–85.

Koch, P.
1964. Techniques for drying thick southern pine veneer. Forest Prod. J. 14: 382–386.

Koch, P.
1969. At 240° F. southern pine studs can be dried and steam-straightened in 24 hours. South. Lumberman 219(2723): 26, 28–29.

Koch, P.
1971. Process for straightening and drying southern pine 2 by 4's in 24 hours. Forest Prod. J. 21(5): 17–24.

Kollmann, F.
1955. Technology of wood and wood material. Ed. 2, 1183 pp. Berlin: Springer-Verlag.

Kollmann, F., and Schneider, A.
1961. [The influence of flow velocity on the kiln drying of timber in superheated steam.] Holz als Roh- und Werkstoff 19: 461–478.

Kollmann, F. F. P., Schneider, A., and Bohner, G.
1967. Investigations on the heating and drying of wood with infrared radiation. Wood Sci. and Technol. 1: 149–160.

Ladell, J. L.
1955. High temperature drying of lumber. Timber of Can. 15(11): 19, 22, 46.

Ladell, J. L.
1957. High-temperature kiln-drying of eastern Canadian softwoods, drying. guide and tentative schedules. Forest Prod. Lab. of Can. FPL Tech. Note 2, 18 pp. Ottawa.

Laity, W. D.
1970. Heat and mass transfer rates associated with the drying of southern pine and Douglas-fir veneer in air and steam at various temperatures and angles of impingement. M. S. Thesis. Ore. State Univ., Corvallis. 128 pp.

Lengel, D. L.
1967. The Reitz dryer. In Proc. of first symposium on particleboard, pp. 183–193. Pullman, Wash.: Wash. State Univ.

Loughborough, W. K.
1948. Chemical seasoning: its effectiveness and present status. USDA Forest Serv. Forest Prod. Lab. Rep. D1721, 13 pp.

Lowery, D. P., Krier, J. P., and Hann, R. A.
1968. High temperature drying of lumber—a review. USDA Forest Serv. Res. Pap. INT–48, 10 pp. Intermountain Forest and Range Exp. Sta., Ogden, Utah.

McCarthy, J. L., and Jahn, E. C.
1936. Measurement of gelatinization of wood and pulp by water retention under pressure. Pacific Pulp and Pap. Ind. 10(6): 9–11.

McDonald, D.
1958. Method of drying and impregnating wood. (U.S. Pat. No. 2,860,070) U.S. Pat. Office, Wash., D.C.

MacLean, J. D.
1934. Temperatures in green southern pine timbers after various steaming periods. Amer. Wood Preserv. Assoc. Proc. 30: 355–374.

MacLean, J. D.
1960. Preservative treatment of wood by pressure methods. USDA Agr. Handbook 40 rev., 160 pp.

McMillen, J. J.
1960. Special methods of seasoning wood: Chemical seasoning. USDA Forest Serv. Forest Prod. Lab. Rep. 1665–6 rev., 4 pp.

McMillen, J. M.
1961a. Coatings for the prevention of end checks in logs and lumber. USDA Forest Serv. Forest Prod. Lab. Rep. 1435, 20 pp.

McMillen, J. M.
1961b. Special methods of seasoning wood: Boiling in oily liquids. USDA Forest Serv. Forest Prod. Lab. Rep. 1665 rev., 4 pp.

McMillen, J. M.
1968. Transverse strains during drying of 2-inch ponderosa pine. USDA Forest Serv. Res. Pap. FPL 83, 26 pp. Forest Prod. Lab., Madison, Wis.

McMillen, J. M., and James, W. L.
1961. High-frequency dielectric heating. USDA Forest Serv. Forest Prod. Lab. Rep. 1665–7 rev., 4 pp.

McMillen, J. M., and Youngs, R. L.
1960. Stresses in drying lumber. Southern Lumberman 201(2513): 115–119.

Maloney, T. M., editor.
1967. Proceedings of first symposium on particleboard. 474 pp. Pullman, Wash.: Wash. State Univ.

Maroney, W. H.
1962. Azeotropic drying of hardwood lumber. Forest Prod. J. 12: 7–10.

Mathewson, J. S.
1930. The air seasoning of wood. USDA Tech. Bull. 174, 56 pp.

Mathewson, J. S.
1954. High-temperature drying: Its application to the drying of lumber. J. Forest Prod. Res. Soc. 4: 276–280.

Mathewson, J. S., and Berger, P. J.
1957. Comparison of three methods of determining whether southern pine poles are well air seasoned. Forest Prod. J. 7: 174–177.

Metcalfe, W. K.
1968. Paper machine air drying. TAPPI 51(4): 98A–102A.

Mottet, A. L.
1967. The Buettner jet dryer. In Proc. of first symposium on particleboard, pp. 175–181. Pullman, Wash.: Wash. State Univ.

Narayanamurti, D., and Prasad, B. N.
1952. Infrared-drying of veneers. Holz als Roh- und Werkstoff 10: 92–94.

Page, R. H., and Carter, R. M.
1957. Heavy losses in air seasoning Georgia pine and how to reduce them. USDA Forest Serv. Southeast. Forest Exp. Sta., Sta. Pap. 85, 20 pp.

Page, R. H., and Carter, R. M.
1958. Variations in moisture content of air-seasoned southern pine lumber in Georgia. Forest Prod. J. 8(6): 15A–18A.

Peck, E. C.
1941. Chemical seasoning of wood: Hygroscopic and antishrink values of chemicals. Ind. and Eng. Chem. 33: 653–655.

Bariska, M., Skaar, C., and Davidson, R. W.
1969. Studies of the wood-anhydrous ammonia system. Wood Sci. 2: 65–72.

Peck, E. C.
1961. Air drying of lumber. USDA Forest Serv. Forest Prod. Lab Rep. 1657, 21 pp.

Race, E.
1970. The economic value of paper machine clothing in water removal. TAPPI 53: 993–999.

Rantala, P. P.
1970. Modern press structures. TAPPI 53: 976–980.

Rasmussen, E. F.
1961. Dry kiln operator's manual. USDA Handbook 188, 197 pp.

Rietz, R. C.
1965. The kiln drying of wood. In Moisture in materials in relation to fire tests, pp. 38–51. Amer. Soc. for Testing and Mater. Spec. Tech. Bull. 385.

Reitz, R. C.
1970. Air drying lumber in a forklift yard. USDA Forest Serv. Res. Note FPL–0209, 16 pp. Forest Prod. Lab., Madison, Wis.

Rhorer, C. R.
1971. Diagnosis and correction of moisture profile problems on paper machines. TAPPI 54: 43–46.

Salamon, M.
1969. High-temperature drying and its effect on wood properties. Forest Prod. J. 19(3): 27–34.

Salamon, M.
1970. White spruce kiln schedule employs mixed air velocities. Can. Forest Ind. 90(9): 48–50.

Salamon, M., and McBride, C. F.
1966. High temperature drying: A comparison of western hemlock and balsam fir dried at high and conventional temperatures. Brit. Columbia Lumberman 50(11): 44, 46, 48–52.

Salamon, M., and McIntyre, S.
1970. Combination schedule improves drying of western white spruce lumber. Forest Prod. J. 20(7): 41–42.

Segelken, J. G.
1941. Kiln drying longleaf southern pine poles. Amer. Wood Preserv. Assoc. Proc. 37: 135–154.

Segelken, J. G.
1942. Kiln drying southern pine poles. Amer. Wood Preserv. Assoc. Proc. 38: 251–263.

Sinclair, D.
1967. Drying wood fiberboard. TAPPI 50: 424–432.

South, V.
1968. Heat and mass transfer rates associated with the drying of plywood veneer using superheated steam at various angles of impingement. M. S. Thesis. Ore. State Univ., Corvallis. 61 pp.

Southern Pine Inspection Bureau.
1968. Standard grading rules for southern pine lumber. 171 p. New Orleans, La.: Southern Pine Inspection Bureau.

Stamm, A. J.
1934. Effect of inorganic salts upon the swelling and shrinking of wood. J. Amer. Chem. Soc. 56: 1195–1205.

Stamm, A. J.
1964. Wood and cellulose science. 549 pp. N.Y.: Ronald Press Co.

Stillinger, J. R.
1967a. Drying principles and problems. In Proc. of first symposium on particleboard, pp. 163–173. Pullman, Wash.: Wash. State Univ.

Stillinger, J. R.
1967b. The Heil dryer. In Proc. of first symposium on particleboard, pp. 205–215. Pullman, Wash.: Wash. State Univ.

Suchsland, O., and Stevens, R. R.
1968. Gluability of southern pine veneer dried at high temperatures. Forest Prod. J. 18(1): 38–42.

Teesdale, L. V.
1930. The kiln drying of southern yellow pine lumber. USDA Tech. Bull. 165, 66 pp.

Thompson, W. S.
1969. Effect of steaming and kiln drying on the properties of southern pine poles. I. Mechanical properties. Forest Prod. J. 19(1): 21–28.

Thompson, W. S., and Stevens, R. R.
1972. Kiln drying of southern pine poles: results of laboratory and field studies. Forest Prod. J. 22(3): 17–24.

USDA Forest Products Laboratory.
1966. List of manufacturers and dealers for log and lumber end coatings. USDA Forest Serv. Forest Prod. Lab. Job 66–004 rev., 1 p.

USDA Forest Products Laboratory.
1970. Research news. USDA Forest Serv. Nat. Wood Res. Center, 4 pp. Madison.

Wahlstrom, P. B.
1970. Water removal on modern corrugating and kraft bag machines. TAPPI 53: 1011–1014.

Walters, E. O.
1970. Green southern yellow pine veneer—saturation principle of moisture measure to establish drying sorts. Forest Prod. J. 20(2): 25–28.

Wieselman, L.
1970. Survey of operating results of paper machines equipped with pocket air rolls. TAPPI 53: 1032–1033.

Wilkinson, T. L.
1968. Strength evaluations of round timber piles. USDA Forest Serv. Res. Pap. FPL–101, 44 pp. Forest Prod. Lab., Madison, Wis.

Winkel, L. D.
1956. Casehardening stress relief of ponderosa pine. Forest Prod. J. 6: 124–128.

Wrist, P. E.
1966. New concepts concerning paper structure and paper physics. TAPPI 49: 287–292.

21

Bending

CONTENTS

21

Bending

For many purposes, bending wood over a curved mold is preferable to machining it. Bending processes are quick and simple, require little power, and do not waste wood as chips or shavings. The resulting bent wood is generally stronger and stiffer than wood machined to the same contour. Major disadvantages are loss of wood by breakage and a tendency of the bent stock to lose some of its curvature when exposed to humid conditions.

The concave surface of a bent stick is shorter than the convex surface. Solid wood therefore can be permanently bent only when plastic enough to take and retain the proper amount of compressive deformation. Because wood is more plastic when hot and moist than when cool and dry, exposure to heat and moisture is an effective plasticizing treatment. Some chemicals, notably urea and ammonia, also plasticize wood.

21–1   STEAM BENDING [1]

The most complete discussion of the bending process appears to be that of Stevens and Turner (1948, 1970). Less extensive reviews include those by Wangaard (1952), Kubler (1957), Jorgensen (1965), and Kollmann and Côté (1968). Stress distributions during bending are discussed by Peck (1968, pp. 31–37). Peck also notes (p. 4) that hardwoods can be steam-bent more successfully than coniferous woods. He lists 25 hardwoods in descending order of bending quality; the top half of the list includes hackberry (*Celtis* spp.), white and red oaks (*Quercus* spp.), chestnut oak (*Quercus prinus* L.), magnolia (*Magnolia grandiflora* L.), pecan (*Carya illinoensis* (Wangenh.) K. Koch), black walnut (*Juglans nigra* L.), hickory (*Carya* spp.), beech (*Fagus grandifolia* Ehrh.), American elm (*Ulmus americana* L.), willow (*Salix* spp.), yellow birch. (*Betula alleghaniensis* Britton), and white ash (*Fraxinus americana* L.).

Stevens and Turner (1948, 1970) list the minimum radius of curvature to which various species can be formed without breaking more than 5 percent of the pieces. They give the radii listed below as applicable to air-dry,

---

[1] With some editorial changes, section 21–1 is condensed from Lemoine and Koch (1971) by permission of the Forest Products Research Society.

1-inch-thick wood of good bending quality—steamed at atmospheric pressure and bent with a tension strap:

	Minimum radius of curvature
	Inches
Hardwoods	
Dutch elm (*Ulmus hollandica* var. *major*) _____	0.4
White oak _____	1.0
Yellow birch _____	3.0
European beech (*Fagus sylvatica*) _____	4.0
American ash _____	4.5
Softwoods	
Caribbean pine (*Pinus caribaea* Morelet) _____	14.0
European spruce (*Picea abies*) _____	30.0

Lemoine and Koch (1971) have provided some information specific to southern pine. Their study was designed to determine the kind of southern pine wood that can be most successfully steam bent; some relationships affecting the percentage of specimens surviving the bending operation were observed, and changes in radius of unrestrained bent specimens were related to changes in service humidity conditions. Because knots, decay, shakes, and severe cross grain in wood cause excessive breakage during bending, only knot-free, sound, and straight-grained specimens were selected for the study.

Lemoine and Koch did not measure strength properties of steam-bent southern pine wood, but research on hardwoods has indicated that specimens steam bent to small radii have substantially less strength in flexure than matched straight specimens (Wangaard 1952), and less flexural strength and stiffness than wood laminated from thin strips into a bend of equal radius (Luxford and Krone 1962). According to Luxford and Krone (1962), however, steam-bent oak boat frames will absorb several times more impact energy before breaking than similar laminated frames.

TECHNIQUE

In preliminary tests with ½- and 1-inch stock, Lemoine and Koch (1971) found that the probability of a successful bend was greatest when specimens were conditioned to about 17-percent moisture content and then steamed for a short time. Steaming times of 10 minutes and 20 minutes per inch of thickness appeared to be sufficient. Longer steaming times generally resulted in an excess of both tension and compression failures.

Prebending treatments rejected as less desirable included water soaking the specimen until saturated (with or without subsequent steaming), and boiling in water (starting from a 10-percent moisture content or from a saturated condition). Steaming under pressure was not attempted since the literature indicates it is less effective than atmospheric steaming.

Preliminary trials showed that a bending jig incorporating a tension strap was essential for successful bending of southern pine (fig. 21–1). Steaming wood greatly increases its compressibility parallel to the grain but does not greatly affect its ability to elongate under tension. The tension strap, uniformly applying an end load during the bending operation, reduces breakage by decreasing tension stress in the convex side of the specimen.

A stratified random sample of 1½-inch-wide S4S southern pine wood was collected from sawmills and retail yards in central Louisiana. Most specimens were probably cut from loblolly pine, with some shortleaf, longleaf, and slash pine wood included. Study variables were:

- Thickness: ½-inch and 1 inch.
- Rings per inch: either less than 6 or more than 6.
- Specific gravity (ovendry volume and weight): either less than 0.58 or more than 0.58.
- Orientation of annual rings: flat grain or edge grain.
- Radius of curvature, inches: 12t—3 inches, 12t, and 12t + 3 inches; where t = specimen thickness in inches.
- Time steamed at atmospheric pressure before bending: 10 and 20 minutes per inch of specimen thickness.
- Replications of factors: two.
- Replications of specimens within each factor replication: 10.

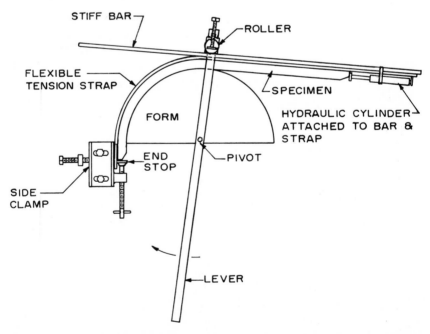

Figure 21–1.—End load applied through a flexible metal tension strap preloads the specimen in compression as it is being bent, thus reducing tensile stress on the convex side. (Drawing after Lemoine and Koch 1971.)

Thus, the experiment required 1,920 specimens.

While not a primary factor in the experiment, the maximum angle between resin canals exposed on the edge of each specimen and the face (resin canal angle) was observed as an indicator of cross grain. Both edges were measured and the largest angle recorded.

Bending direction (toward the pith or toward the bark) was at random, and was recorded after bending. While most readily determined on flat-grain pieces, it was also possible on those classified as edge grain because none had precisely vertical grain.

Specimens, equilibrated to 10-percent moisture content, were cut to length, end bevelled (fig. 21–2), and dipped in cool water until they picked up sufficient weight for 17-percent moisture content. They were then stored in polyethylene bags (at least 24 hours for ½-inch specimens and 48 hours for 1-inch specimens) to permit the moisture to diffuse into each piece.

Each was steamed over vigorously boiling water for the specified time in a vertical chamber vented through a fan at the top (fig. 21–3). The steady flow of steam produced appeared ample to prepare the wood for bending.

Following steaming, the bevelled-end specimen (fig. 21–2) was quickly transferred to the bending jig shown in figure 21–4. One end was firmly clamped with the screw shown on the lower left side of figure 21–4B, and the ball-bearing pressure point was made "finger-tight" with the screw shown in the upper left corner; then a steady end load was applied with a hydraulic cylinder (fig. 21–4C) so that the outside, or convex side, of the specimen was preloaded in compression. The ½-inch-thick pieces were given a 500-pound preload on a bearing surface of 0.375 sq. in., while a 1,000-pound load was applied to the 0.750-sq. in. bearing surface of the 1-inch-thick specimens. Woodclips visible in figures 21–4A, B, C prevented bowing in the specimen. Figure 21–4D shows the thin, flexible metal strap that was arranged on the convex side; the strap was anchored by a clamp at one end and to the hydraulic cylinder on the other. One end of a thicker bar was attached to the base of the hydraulic cylinder; its other end was

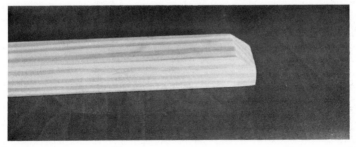

F–520993

Figure 21–2.—Specimens to be steam bent should have both ends bevelled to midthickness so that prestress compression force applies principally to the convex side. (Photo from Lemoine and Koch 1971.)

F–520994
Figure 21–3.—Vertical 10-chamber steamer; fan-vented duct leads steam out of building. Not visible are the immersion heaters in the water bath at the bottom. The hinged door of one chamber is partially open. For best control, each chamber should have its own water bath and heater. (Photo from Lemoine and Koch 1971.)

free. A pivoted lever rolled a ball-bearing pressure point over the surface of the bar, bending the strap and specimen into semicircular form (fig. 21–4D). A wire retaining rod was secured to the two sheet metal end clips shown in figures 21–4B, C; the bent specimen was then lifted from the jig, secured with glass filament tape so the retaining rod could be removed, and allowed to reach equilibrium in an atmosphere held at 72° F. and 50-percent relative humidity.

Twenty-four hours after removal from the bending jig, each specimen was rated on a scale ranging from 0 to 10; 0 indicated total failure and 10 complete success. In general, only specimens rated 8 or above would be serviceable for any purpose, and a rating of 10 would be required for most applications where appearance is a ruling factor (fig. 21–5).

AVERAGE RATING

Relationships influencing the average bending rating are evident in five two-factor interactions shown to be significant by analysis of variance (table 21–1). Steaming time was not a significant factor—alone or in combination with other factors. Specimen thickness entered into three interactions; growth rate, specific gravity, and thickness were each in-

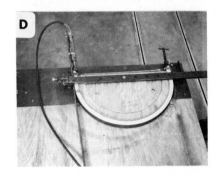

F–520995

Figure 21–4.—Bending jig with 1-inch-thick specimen in place. (A) As the lever bar is moved around its pivot, a constant end load is maintained by means of a hydraulic cylinder. Two removable plywood clips to prevent specimen bow are visible. (B) End clamp. The thin metal band running around convex side of specimen is attached to the hydraulic cylinder. Pivoted lever bar with ball-bearing pressure point is shown rolling over the thick steel bar also attached to the hydraulic cylinder. (C) Hydraulic pump, cylinder, and pressure controlled bypass valve for application of controlled force to reduce tension to convex side of specimen. (D) Specimen bent in full semicircle and ready for removal. Retaining rod is secured to metal end clips visible in figures 4B and C. (Photos from Lemoine and Koch 1971.)

volved in two of the interactions. Grain type interacted only with radius of curvature.

	Specimen thickness	
Factor	½-inch	1 inch
	– – – Rating – – –	
Rings per inch		
Less than 6 _____	7.1	6.5
More than 6 _____	6.8	4.9
Specific gravity		
Under 0.58 _____	7.1	6.4
More than 0.58 _____	6.9	5.1
Radius of curvature, inches		
12t — 3 _____	4.9	4.6
12t _____	7.2	5.7
12t + 3 _____	8.8	6.9

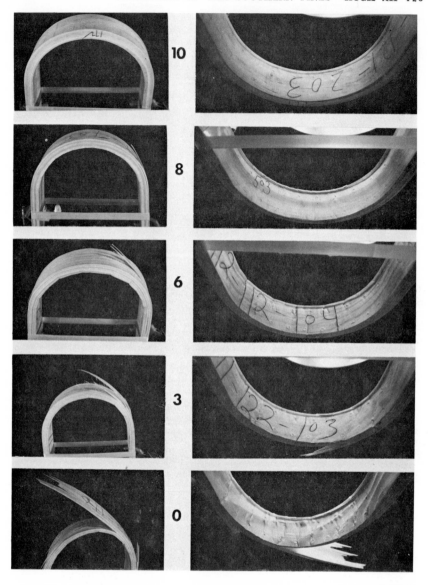

F–520996

Figure 21–5.—Rating system for steam-bent southern pine. Numerals show representative ratings from 0 (worst) to 10 (best). The ledge visible on the concave side of each specimen was caused by a too-narrow form, i.e., the form should have been wider than the specimen. (Photos from Lemoine and Koch 1971.)

	Specific gravity	
Rings per inch	Less than 0.58	More than 0.58
	– – – – – – Rating – – – – – –	
Less than 6 _____	7.0	6.7
More than 6 _____	6.5	5.3

TABLE 21-1.—*Effects of primary variables on bending ratings of southern pine wood*
(Lemoine and Koch 1971)[1]

Factor	Average rating	Percent of bent specimens with ratings of:		
		8, 9, 10	9, 10	10
		– – – – – *Percent* – – – – –		
A. Replication[2]				
B. Rings per inch				
Less than 6	6.8	57	47	33
More than 6	5.9	43	34	19
C. Specific gravity[3]				
Under 0.58	6.7	55	46	28
Over 0.58	6.0	44	36	24
D. Steaming time per inch thickness				
10 minutes	6.3	49	40	26
20 minutes	6.5	51	41	26
E. Radius of curvature, inches				
12t − 3	4.7	23	17	9
12t	6.5	53	42	24
12t + 3	7.9	74	63	44
F. Thickness				
½-inch	7.0	57	49	33
1 inch	5.7	43	33	19
G. Grain description				
Flat	5.9	42	32	17
Edge	6.9	58	50	36
Grand means	6.4	50	41	26
Significant interactions[4] (and significant factors where interactions did not involve them)			C	C
	BC	BC		
	BF	BF	BF	
	CF	CF		
	EF	EF	EF	
	EG	EG	EG	BDEFG

[1] Averages include data on all 1,920 observations; the only segregation is by the factors in column 1.

[2] Dummy factor.

[3] Basis of ovendry volume and weight.

[4] Significant at 0.01 level.

Radius of curvature	Grain description	
	Flat	Edge
Inches	– – – – *Rating* – – – –	
12t − 3	4.6	4.9
12t	5.6	7.4
12t + 3	7.4	8.3

These data indicate that southern pine bending stock yielded the highest ratings if edge grained, fast grown, and low in specific gravity. Highest ratings were achieved with thin stock bent to large radii. Thus, low-gravity, edge-grain, fast-grown specimens gave average ratings as follows when data from both steaming times were pooled.

Radius	Average rating for ½-inch thickness	Average rating for 1-inch thickness
Inches		
3	4.7	—
6	7.7	—
9	8.8	5.7
12	—	8.1
15	—	8.4

The interactions show that low ratings resulted when specimens were slow grown and thick, dense and thick, or slow grown and dense. When bent to small radii, flat-grain specimens—or thick specimens—had particularly low average ratings.

It was thought possible that bending ratings might be improved if the side of the specimen nearest the pith was always placed on the concave side of the bend; however, analysis of variance showed no significant effect. With all data pooled, average rating of specimens with the pith on the concave side was 6.5; with pith on the convex side, the average rating was 6.3.

Regression analyses, separate by each thickness, showed that no combination of factors was closely correlated with average bending rating. Only the following had an r value of 0.20 or greater.

	r value	
Factor correlated with bending rating	½-inch	1 inch
Radius of curvature _____	0.49	0.25
Radius of curvature ÷ grain angle _____	.34	
Resin canal angle _____	− .21	
Resin canal angle squared _____	− .20	
Rings per inch _____		− .20
(rings per inch) (specific gravity) _____		− .26

Had data been available on a spectrum of thicknesses, doubtless thickness would have proven significantly correlated with rating.

While success in explaining the total variability in bending ratings was not notable, a multiple regression expression was selected for each thickness through use of the Rex Program (Grosenbaugh 1967) as giving the best fit to the data; the equations provide considerable guidance to optimum selection of southern pine wood to be steam bent.

According to the equations, bending rating (average for ½- and 1-inch specimens was 7.0 and 5.7 respectively) can be predicted by summing the products of the coefficients and independent variables shown in table 21–2.

TABLE 21–2.—Coefficients and independent variables in regression equations for prediction of average bending ratings of ½- and 1-inch-thick southern pine (Lemoine and Koch 1971)

Coefficient[1]		Independent variable	Average values[1]		Range
½-inch	1 inch		½-inch	1 inch	
−3.007	1.650	(This coefficient is a constant.)			
−.2067	.0790	Rings per inch	7.130	6.980	1–32
−.00782	.0191	Rings per inch squared	63.38	61.28	
24.34	N.S.	Specific gravity, basis of ovendry volume and weight	.5774	N.S.	0.35–0.83
−23.77	N.S.	Specific gravity squared	.3381	N.S.	
N.S.	−1.185	(rings per inch) (specific gravity)	N.S.	4.06	10–20
N.S.	.0321	Steaming time, minutes per inch thickness	N.S.	15.0	$12t-3$ to $12t+3$[2]
.9341	.8439	Radius of curvature, inches	6.0	12.0	
−.0323	−.0183	Radius of curvature squared	42.0	150.0	
.0895	.0321	Grain angle (flat or edge), degrees	43.65	45.30	0–90
−.000870	−.000055	Grain angle squared	2813.8	2855.4	
.00239	N.S.	(radius of curvature) (grain angle)	262.47	N.S.	
.5016	−.6284	Resin canal angle, degrees	3.394	3.592	0–14.1
−.000650	.0166	Resin canal angle squared	15.17	16.36	
2.022	N.S.	Resin canal angle ÷ grain angle	.1525	N.S.	

[1] N.S. means not significant in the Rex Program.

[2] t = specimen thickness, inch.

The equation for ½-inch stock accounted for 32 percent of the variation in bending rating with standard error of the estimate of 2.8; comparable figures for the equation applicable to 1-inch specimens were 25 percent and 3.2.

Trends indicated by the equations are plotted in figures 21–6 and 21–7. For both thicknesses, the equations show that bending ratings were highest for specimens with specific gravity (ovendry volume and weight basis) of 0.4 to 0.5, 0° resin canal angle, and 1 to 5 growth rings per inch. While steaming time was not a significant factor for the ½-inch thickness, the 1-inch specimens yielded higher bending ratings when steamed 20 minutes per inch of thickness. With 1-inch specimens, high-gravity, slow-grown wood yielded very low ratings.

PROPORTION OF USABLE SPECIMENS

The factors and interactions that affected the proportion of specimens rated 8, 9 or 10 are indicated in table 21–1.

To yield a maximum proportion of pieces with ratings of 8, 9, and 10, or 9 and 10, southern pine bending stock should be edge grain, fast grown, and low in specific gravity. Obviously, greatest success in bending will be achieved with thin stock bent to a large radius. Steaming time—considered by itself or in interactions—proved to be not significant. Among specimens with the above characteristics, ratings after bending were as follows:

Specimen thickness and bending radius	Pieces rated 8, 9, and 10	Pieces rated 9 and 10
Inches	– – – – – *Percent* – – – – –	
½-inch		
3	20	20
6	80	70
9	88	85
1 inch		
9	45	38
12	75	63
15	80	68

Recovery of perfectly bent specimens, rated 10, was higher from low-gravity than from high-gravity wood (28 percent compared to 24 percent). There were interactions involving growth rate, steaming time, radius of curvature, thickness, and grain type which make further generalization difficult. Certain patterns, however, permitted description of the southern pine bending stock that yielded the highest percentage of 10-rated pieces (table 21–3). As the footnotes to table 21–3 indicate, high-gravity wood did not always perform badly in comparison to low-gravity wood.

In summation, the data of Lemoine and Koch (1971) suggest that fast-grown, edge-grain, low-gravity wood free of cross grain is probably the best selection for steam bending ½-inch and 1-inch southern pine. A steaming time of 20 minutes per inch of thickness appears to be adequate.

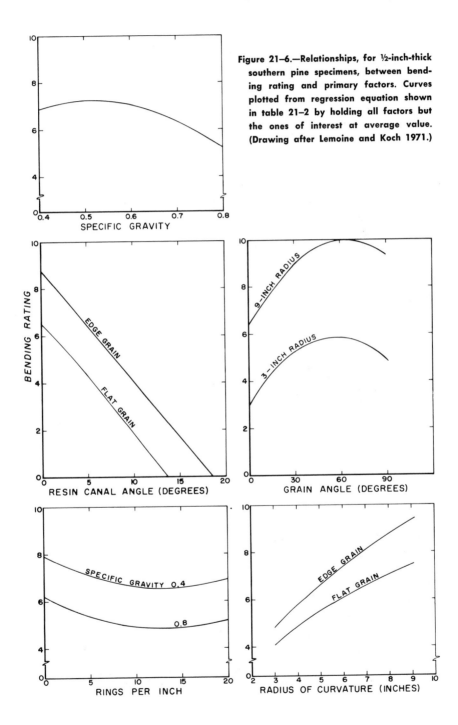

Figure 21–6.—Relationships, for ½-inch-thick southern pine specimens, between bending rating and primary factors. Curves plotted from regression equation shown in table 21–2 by holding all factors but the ones of interest at average value. (Drawing after Lemoine and Koch 1971.)

TABLE 21–3.—*Characteristics of southern pine wood and steaming time for maximum recovery of 10-rated pieces after bending* (Lemoine and Koch 1971)

Radius of bend (inches)	Optimum characteristics and steaming time	Portion bent with rating of 10
		Percent
	½-INCH-THICK SPECIMENS	
3	Fast grown, edge grain, low gravity, steamed 20 minutes per inch of thickness	25
6	Slow grown, edge grain, low gravity; steaming time not critical	48
9[1]	Slow grown, edge grain, low gravity; steaming time not critical	75
	1-INCH-THICK SPECIMENS	
9	Fast grown, edge grain, low gravity; steaming time not critical	30
12[2]	Fast grown, edge grain, low gravity, steamed 20 minutes per inch of thickness	40
15	Fast grown, edge grain, low gravity, steamed 20 minutes per inch of thickness	75

[1] When ½-inch stock was bent to a 9-inch radius, 85 percent of the edge-grain, high-gravity stock was rated 10; growth rate and steaming time were not critical. The reason for the good results with high-gravity wood at the 9-inch radius is not clear.

[2] When 1-inch stock was bent to a 12-inch radius, 55 percent of the fast-grown, edge-grain, high-gravity stock, which was steamed 20 minutes per inch of thickness, was rated 10. The reason for the relatively good performance of the high-gravity wood at this radius is not clear.

CHANGE IN CURVATURE WITH TIME AND EXPOSURE CONDITION

From the bent specimens in three categories (½-inch-thick bent to 12-inch diameter, ½-inch-thick bent to 18-inch diameter, and 1-inch-thick bent to 30-inch diameter), Lemoine and Koch (1971) found it possible to select six pieces in every factorial combination that rated 8 or better; these were studied for changes in formed diameter when the restraining tapes were cut. Then, two of each set of six were left in the laboratory at about 50-percent relative humidity; two were placed in a sealed polyethylene bag along with a water-soaked sponge, and two were sealed in a polyethylene bag together with a substantial quantity of desiccant; all were held at a dry-bulb temperature of 72° F. Diameter measurements were made weekly for 4 weeks. Finally, all specimens were ovendried and the diameter of each measured again.

The moisture content at the time the restraining tapes were cut averaged 8.7 percent with range from 7.5 to 10.9. After 4 weeks of exposure to the three conditions, moisture contents were as follows:

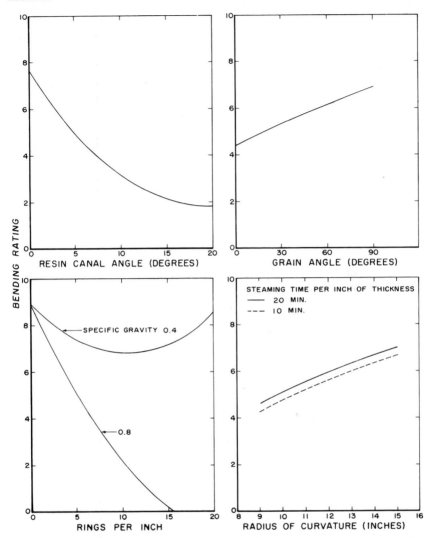

Figure 21–7.—Relationships, for 1-inch-thick southern pine specimens, between bending rating and primary factors. Curves plotted from regression equation shown in table 21–2 by holding all factors but the ones of interest at average value. (Drawing after Lemoine and Koch 1971.)

Condition	Average moisture content	Range in moisture content
	‒ ‒ ‒ ‒ *Percent* ‒ ‒ ‒ ‒	
In laboratory at about 50-percent relative humidity	8.2	7.1 to 9.0
In bags with desiccant _____	7.3	6.1 to 9.5
In bags with water-soaked sponge _____	13.6	11.3 to 15.7

When the restraining tapes were cut, diameter of the average specimen increased 0.50 inch. In general, diameter change on release was least in edge-grain wood that had been steamed 20 minutes per inch; also, diameter change on release was least in the ½-inch specimens bent to a 12-inch diameter (table 21–4). Specific gravity and growth rate of the wood did not significantly affect the change in diameter when the restraining tapes were cut.

After 4 weeks of exposure, the specimens in the humid atmosphere had increased in diameter most (from the restrained dimension), and those in the desiccators least; specimens held at about 50-percent relative humidity were intermediate. In general, change was least in edge-grain wood steamed 20 minutes per inch of thickness; the ½-inch-thick specimens bent to 12-inch diameter changed least; ½-inch specimens bent to 18-inch diameter changed most (table 21–4). Neither specific gravity nor growth rate of the wood had a significant effect on change in diameter. Figure 21–8 shows diameter changes for each of the three specimen categories as a function of time and exposure condition.

TABLE 21–4.—*Changes in formed diameter of ½- and 1-inch-thick, steam-bent southern pine specimens related to exposure conditions and experimental factors* (Lemoine and Koch 1971) [1] [2]

Factor and level	Increase in diameter when restraint removed	Change in diameter after 4 weeks of exposure	Change in diameter after then ovendrying
	— — — — — *Inches* — — — — —		
Post treatment		**	**
In laboratory at 50 percent relative humidity	——————	0.69	0.48
In bags with desiccant	——————	.31	.36
In bags with water-soaked sponge	——————	3.04	1.68
Growth rate, rings per inch			
Less than 6	0.49	1.35	.74
More than 6	.51	1.35	.94
Specific gravity (basis of ovendry volume and weight)			
Less than 0.58	.49	1.36	.94
More than 0.58	.50	1.34	.74
Grain angle	**	**	**
Flat grain	.54	1.45	.96
Edge grain	.45	1.24	.72
Pretreatment, steaming time	**	**	**
10 minutes per inch of thickness	.52	1.43	.96
20 minutes per inch of thickness	.48	1.26	.72
Thickness and bent diameter	**	**	**
½-inch thickness, 12-inch diameter	.24	.99	.43
½-inch thickness, 18-inch diameter	.64	1.65	1.28
1-inch thickness, 30-inch diameter	.61	1.40	.81

[1] Changes in diameter are increases from the restrained diameter. Each value listed is an average, with data on all factors pooled.

[2] Values tabulated below two asterisks differ significantly at the 0.01 level.

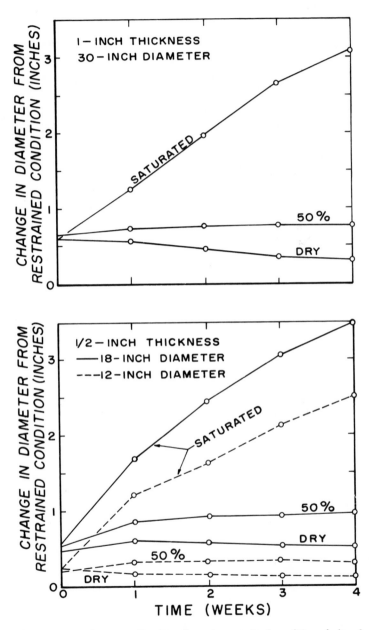

Figure 21-8.—Change in diameter, from the restrained condition, during 4 weeks of exposure to air which was saturated, at 50-percent relative humidity, or desiccated. The 0-week points show the changes in diameter that occurred when the restraining tapes were cut. Each curve based on data averaged from 32 specimens. (Drawings after Lemoine and Koch 1971.)

When the specimens were ovendried, all but the ones previously held in bags with desiccant were reduced somewhat in diameter; after ovendrying, all had diameters larger than the diameters measured when they were under restraint by the glass tape (table 21–4). Edge-grain specimens that had been steamed 20 minutes per inch of thickness most nearly contracted to their original restrained diameters when they were ovendried. Also, the ½-inch specimens bent to 12-inch diameter and stored in bags containing a desiccant, when subsequently ovendried, approached most closely to their original restrained diameter; the ½-inch specimens bent to 18-inch diameter and stored in water-saturated air contracted least when ovendried.

21–2 PLASTICIZING WOOD WITH UREA

Loughborough (1942) has shown that wood treated with urea alone or together with formaldehyde or dimethylolurea becomes thermoplastic and can be bent when hot even when the moisture content is low. When the treated wood cools, it retains its form.

No data specific to southern pine have been published. According to Peck (1968, p. 12), however, urea-treated wood does not bend as well as steamed wood and is weaker. His data show that white oak boiled in a urea solution for 20 minutes was bent successfully 28 times out of 40 attempts, but 14 of the successful bends failed in tension during drying; by contrast, steaming for 20 minutes yielded 37 successful bends out of 40 tries, and no tension failures occurred during drying. Urea-treated wood is more hygroscopic, and may be darker in color, than untreated wood.

21–3 PLASTICIZING WOOD WITH AMMONIA

The use of liquid (anhydrous) ammonia to plasticize wood was suggested by Stamm (1955) and given more comprehensive study by Schuerch (1963, 1964). Pentoney (1966) reported on some of the physical properties of wood treated with ammonia.

No data specific to southern pine have been published, but Schuerch (1964) reported that immersion in liquid ammonia plasticizes all species; he further observed that low-density species failed in compression when bent more frequently than high-density species.

From the limited data available, it appears that southern pine is somewhat more plastic when ammonia treated than when steamed, and when bent may retain its shape better than steam-bent pine (fig. 21–9).

Anhydrous ammonia is a commercial chemical sold as a liquid under pressure (about 150 p.s.i.) in tanks. At atmospheric pressure ammonia boils at −28° F. (−33° C.) and freezes at −108° F. (−78° C.).

Schuerch (1964) stated that wood samples, preferably precooled, can be directly immersed in an open vessel of chilled ammonia. The moisture content of the wood is not critical, but air-dried wood has been most used

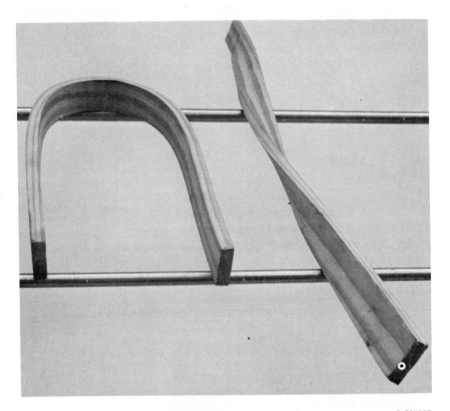

F–520997

Figure 21–9.—Ammonia-treated, ⅜-inch-thick by 1.1-inch-wide, southern pine, flat-grain strips. (Left) Bent to 2⅝-inch radius. (Right) Twisted 180° within a 20-inch length.

in experimental work. Time required to plasticize is dependent on specimen thickness and permeability. Veneer strips $\frac{1}{16}$-inch thick, 1 inch wide and 4 inches long have been softened in less than ½-hour. Hardwood slats ⅛-inch by 4 by 40 inches have required times in excess of 4 hours. Thicker stock should be evacuated before treating with the liquid ammonia or should be pressure treated.

Schuerch (1964) found that if sufficiently treated and then warmed toward room temperature, thin specimens become pliable and could be readily manipulated with gloved hands. Maximum plasticity is reported to last 8 to 30 minutes; wood will retain extreme bends after being hand-held or clamped in position for a few minutes.

GASEOUS AMMONIA

Wood will adsorb either gaseous or liquid ammonia; the amount of gaseous ammonia adsorbed is dependent on the relative vapor pressure of the ammonia atmosphere. Davidson (1968) reported that, when exposed to an ammonia atmosphere at 77° F. in which the relative vapor pressure of ammonia is about 1.0, hard maple adsorbed ammonia in an amount equal to 30 to 40 percent of its dry weight. Plasticization from the gaseous treatment was about equal to that obtained from immersion in liquid ammonia.

No data specific to southern pine are published, but Davidson (1968) reported general information on the process that is probably applicable to southern pine. He proposed that the treating system diagrammed in figure 21–10 has promise. With this system wood in the treating chamber is first subjected to a vacuum for 5 or 10 minutes before admitting the gaseous ammonia maintained at 77° F. and 145 p.s.i. pressure. Thick stock requires longer treating time than thin material; between zero- and 20-percent moisture content, optimum treating time is inversely proportional to moisture content. Davidson (1968) tentatively suggested the following times under pressure.

| | | Treating time | |
| | | 10-percent | 20-percent |
Thickness	Ovendry	moisture content	moisture content
Inch	– – – – – – – –	*Hours* – – – – – – – – – –	
⅛	8	1	½
¼	8	2	1

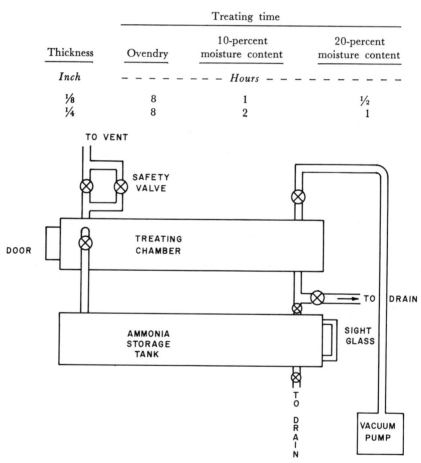

Figure 21–10.—Essential features of a treating plant for gaseous ammonia. Not shown are heaters required to maintain the treating temperature and pressure at about 77° F. and 145 p.s.i. (Drawing after Davidson 1968.)

At the end of the treating period, excess ammonia in the chamber is vented, and the wood is removed and formed immediately. Davidson (1968) reported that when room temperature is about 70° F., and wood is not exposed to intense sunlight, ⅛-inch-thick maple strips were formable for about ½-hour. If held on forms for about an hour, stresses in the wood relaxed and formed pieces could be released from clamps without danger of springback.

Further information on the properties of ammonia-treated wood has been published by Bariska et al. (1969) and Davidson and Baumgardt (1970). U.S. Patent 3,282,313 has been issued on the process.

21-4 COLD BENDING BY LAMINATING

If wood is very thin, it can be bent cold to a fairly small radius without breaking. When the bending force is removed, it will of course, return to original straight form. When thin strips, or laminae, are placed one on top of each other to build up a desired dimension, then the entire assembly can still be bent sharply—much in the manner of a deck of playing cards. If the laminae have been spread with adhesive prior to assembly, and if they are held in a bending form until the glue has cured, then the individual strips will no longer be free to move in relation to each other, and the bent shape will become permanent. By end joining individual strips into lengthy laminae, it is possible to fabricate long curved beams in this way.

Curved, laminated southern pine wood is both stiff and strong and is an important structural material. Because of stresses arising from forming the curved beam, however, strength of the assembled beam may be considerably less than that of a matched straight beam.

Woodson and Wangaard (1969) have published some basic information on the amount of strength reduction caused by various ratios of lamination thickness to radius of curvature (t/R). Their data were based on destructive tests of 120 small beams laminated from 0.2- to 0.5-inch-thick, vertical-grain laminae of clear loblolly pine; results can be conveniently expressed as **curvature stress factor,** i.e., the ratio of the strength of a curved beam to the strength of a matched straight beam. In the Woodson-Wangaard study, curved laminated beams loaded on the convex side had higher modulus of rupture values than matched straight beams. When loaded on the concave side, however, both modulus of rupture and fiber stress at proportional limit were substantially less than corresponding values for straight beams (fig. 21–11).

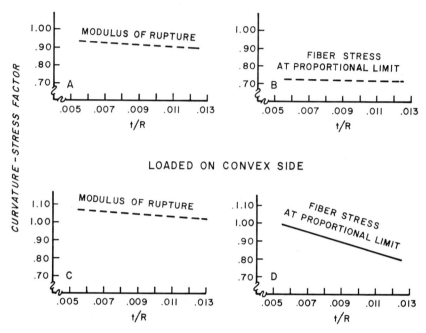

Figure 21–11.—Relationships between ratio of lamina thickness to radius of curvature and ratio of strength of curved beams to strength of straight beams when loaded on convex side and concave side. Only curve D showed a significant effect of t/R on curvature stress factor. (Drawings after Woodson and Wangaard 1969.)

21–5 LITERATURE CITED

Bariska, M., Skaar, C., and Davidson, R. W.
1969. Studies of the wood-anhydrous ammonia system. Wood Sci. 2:65–72.

Davidson, R. W.
1968. Plasticizing wood with anhydrous ammonia. State Univ. Coll. Forest., 4 pp. Syracuse.

Davidson, R. W., and Baumgardt, W. G.
1970. Plasticizing wood with ammonia—a progress report. Forest Prod. J. 20(3): 19–25.

Grosenbaugh, L. R.
1967. Rex—Fortran-4 system for combinatorial screening or conventional analysis of multivariate regressions. USDA Forest Serv. Res. Pap. PSW–44, 47 pp. Pacific Southwest Forest Exp. Sta., Berkeley, Calif.

Jorgensen, R. N.
1965. Furniture wood bending. I. Furniture Design and Manufacturing 37(12): 60, 62.

Kollmann, F. F. P., and Côté, W. A., Jr.
1968. Principles of wood science and technology. I. Solid wood. 592 pp. N.Y.: Springer - Verlag, New York, Inc.

Kübler, H.
1957. [On the persistancy and shape of bent and compressed wood.] Holz 11(10): 217–219. (English Transl. by W. C. Stevens as Transl. 58, Forest Prod. Res. Lab., Princes Risborough, Aylesbury, Bucks, England.)

Lemoine, T. J., and Koch, P.
1971. Steam-bending properties of southern pine. Forest Prod. J. 21(4): 34–42.

Loughborough, W. K.
1942. Impregnating and plasticizing wood. (U.S. Pat. No. 2,298,017) U.S. Pat. Off., Wash., D.C.

Luxford, R. F., and Krone, R. H.
1962. Laminated oak frames for a 50-foot Navy motor launch compared to steam-bent frames. USDA Forest Serv. Forest Prod. Lab. Rep. 1611, 52 pp.

Peck, E. C.
1968. Bending solid wood to form. USDA Agr. Handbook 125, 37 pp.

Pentoney, R. E.
1966. Liquid ammonia-solvent combinations in wood plasticization: Properties of treated wood. Ind. and Eng. Chem. Prod. Res. and Develop. 5: 105–110.

Schuerch, C.
1963. Plasticizing wood with liquid ammonia. Ind. and Eng. Chem. 55(10): 39.

Schuerch, C.
1964. Principles and potential of wood plasticization. Forest Prod. J. 14: 377–381.

Stamm, A. J.
1955. Swelling of wood and fiberboards in liquid ammonia. Forest Prod. J. 5: 413–416.

Stevens, W. C., and Turner, N.
1948. Solid and laminated wood bending. Dep. Sci. & Ind. Res., 71 pp. London: His Majesty's Stationery Office.

Stevens, W. C., and Turner, N.
1970. Wood bending handbook. Forest Prod. Res. Lab., 110 pp. London: Her Majesty's Stationery Office.

Wangaard, F. F.
1952. The steam-bending of beech. Beech Util. Ser. 3, 26 pp. USDA Forest Serv. Northeast. Forest Exp. Sta., Upper Darby, Pa.

Woodson, G. E., and Wangaard, F. F.
1969. Effect of forming stresses on the strength of curved laminated beams of loblolly pine. Forest Prod. J. 19(3)· 47–58.

22

Treating

CONTENTS

22

Treating[1]

22-1 TREATMENT FOR PRESERVATION [2]

Wood is given preservative treatment to make it durable. The resulting extended useful life reduces the annual cost of keeping wood in service. Preservative treatment also reduces the need for oversize design of structural members to compensate for anticipated deterioration.

The amount of wood treated with preservatives peaked in 1929 and 1947 (fig. 22–1). Trends for individual products have varied widely (Gill and Phelps 1968). In 1967, 23.4 million crossties were treated—much less than the 63.3 million treated in 1930; since 1962, however, the number of crossties treated has increased at least 10 percent per year. In 1930, 175.5 million bd. ft. of switch ties were treated; this compares to 97.3 million in 1967. The amount of lumber and construction timber treated has been increasing over the years to 801 million bd. ft. in 1967. In 1967, 5.9 million poles, 34.4 million fenceposts, 4.8 million crossarms, and 27.6 million lineal feet of piles were treated; consumption in all of these categories is increasing. In 1967, 1.1 million sq. yd. of wood blocks, 20.7 million bd. ft. of mine ties and timbers, and 19.1 million cu. ft. of miscellaneous products were treated. The amount of plywood treated in 1967 was 1.2 million cu. ft.—nearly double the 1966 volume. In all, 286.4 million cu. ft. of wood were treated (by 403 reporting plants) in

---

[1] Mention of a chemical in this chapter or elsewhere in this text does not constitute a recommendation; only those chemicals registered by the U.S. Environmental Protection Agency may be recommended, and then only for uses as prescribed in the registration—and in the manner and at the concentration prescribed. The list of registered chemicals varies from time to time; prospective users, therefore, should get current information on registration status from Pesticides Regulation Division, Environmental Protection Agency, Washington, D.C. This chapter contains frequent references to Federal (and other) specifications; since these specifications are changed from time to time, the reader is cautioned to get current information from the specifying agency.

[2] Sec. 22–1 is expanded from an outline: Blew, J. O., Jr. Preservations and preservative processes for southern pine wood—a review. Presented at a symposium, "Utilization of the Southern Pines," Alexandria, La., Nov. 6–8, 1968.

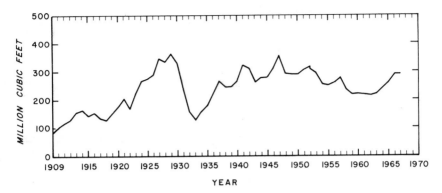

Figure 22–1.—Forest products treated with preservatives in the United States. (Drawing after Gill and Phelps 1968.)

1967; this compares to a total of 332.3 million cu. ft. treated by 204 plants in 1930.

In 1967, the total number of treating plants in the United States was 421 (fig. 22–2); of these, 57 percent, or 238, were in the Southeast or South-central States (Gill and Phelps 1968). Eighty-eight percent of the fenceposts, 77 percent of the poles and piling, and 58 percent of the lumber treated in the United States were southern pine. Other species predominated in marine piling, plywood, crossarms, switch ties, and crossties (table 22–1).

TABLE 22–1.—*Proportion of treated products made from southern pine in 1967* (Gill and Phelps 1968)

Product	Unit	Southern pine
		Percent of U.S. total
Fenceposts	Number	88
Poles (all)	Number	77
Poles (construction)	Number	71
Poles (utility)	Number	76
Piling (all)	Lineal feet	77
Piling (marine)	Lineal feet	41
Piling (foundation)	Lineal feet	86
Lumber	Board feet	58
Crossarms	Lumber	21
Plywood	Square feet	7
Crossties	Number	5
Switch ties	Board feet	4

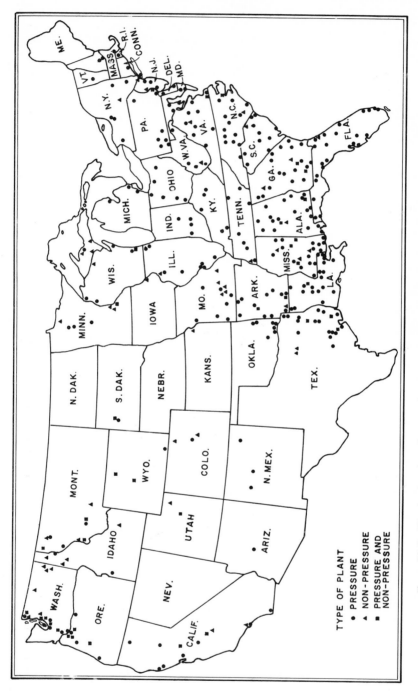

Figure 22–2.—Wood-preserving plants in the United States in 1967. (Drawing after Gill and Phelps 1968.)

WOOD PRESERVATIVES [1]

According to the American Wood Preservers Association (1951), chemical compounds (or mixtures of compounds) must satisfy seven requirements to be suitable for general use as wood preservatives. They must:

- Be toxic to wood-destroying organisms.
- Be supported by field and/or service data.
- Possess satisfactory physical and chemical properties relating to permanence under conditions recommended for use.
- Be free of objectionable qualities in handling and use.
- Be subject to satisfactory laboratory and plant control.
- Be available under provisions of current patents.
- Be in actual commercial use.

The preservatives in general use are described in readily available references (USDA Forest Products Laboratory 1955; Hunt and Garratt 1967). The principal preservatives are of two main types: oils and oilborne preservatives, and waterborne preservatives.

Oils and oilborne preservatives [1].—These include preservative oils in general use, e.g., the creosote formulations. The group also includes preservatives prepared by dissolving toxic chemicals such as pentachlorophenol in low-cost, light or heavy petroleum oils. The Federal specification number is in parentheses where applicable in the following list [1]:

By-product oils and oil mixtures	Oil solutions of toxic chemicals
coal tar creosote (TT–C–645)	pentachlorophenol (TT–W–570)
liquid coal tar creosote	other chlorinated phenols
anthracene oils	tetrachlorophenol
low-temperature coal tar creosotes	trichlorophenol
lignite-tar creosote	chloro-2-phenylphenol
coal tar	copper pentachlorophenate
creosote and coal tar solutions	zinc tetrachlorophenate
(TT–C–650)	copper naphthenate
petroleum oils	other naphthenic acids
creosote-petroleum solutions	zinc naphthenate
(TT–W–568)	mercuric naphthenate
water-gas tar	iron naphthenate
wood-tar creosote	solubilized copper-8-quinolinolate
creosote emulsions	phenyl mercury oleate
	water-repellent preservatives

Waterborne preservatives [1].—As a solvent for preservatives, water is cheap, available, incombustible, nontoxic, and it penetrates wood well. Treatments with waterborne chemicals are relatively cheap, add little to wood weight, and leave wood clean and free from solvent odor or added fire hazard; they are particularly suited for wood used in buildings. Because water swells wood, there may be shrinkage as wood is redried. Since water soluble chemicals tend to leach out of wood in wet situations, the newer waterborne preservatives are designed to form relatively insoluble compounds as the wood dries after treatment. Hager (1969) has provided data on the leaching of pine sawdust treated with copper-chromium-arsenic preservatives (type CCA), and Levi et al. (1970) discuss the role of a water-repellent additive used with such preservatives to lengthen service life.

Listed below are 10 low-solubility preservatives now in extensive commercial use for wood in contact with the ground or fresh water as well as for wood in interior use. Most of these mixed-salt preservatives increase the electrical conductivity of wood by leaving soluble chlorides, or sulfates of sodium or potassium in it. Since chemical changes are likely to occur in the mixed-salt preservatives if heated to high temperatures, standards of the American Wood Preservers Association (1969, C1–69) limit the maximum temperatures that may be used during the treating process or in use to 120, 140, or 150° F. depending on the preservative.

The following are standard waterborne preservatives whose designation and component chemicals can be listed (Federal specification number shown where applicable)[1]:

> Boliden salt (CZA): arsenic acid, sodium arsenate, sodium dichromate, and zinc sulfate.
>
> Boliden salt K-33 (CCA type B): arsenic acid, chromic acid, copper oxide, and water. TT–W–550, type II.
>
> chromated copper arsenate (CCA type C): arsenic acid, chromic acid, copper oxide, and water.
>
> Celcure (ACC): chromic acid, copper sulfate, and sodium (or potassium) dichromate. TT–W–546.
>
> Chemonite (ACA): acetic acid, arsenic trioxide, and copper hydroxide in ammonia and water. TT–W–549.
>
> chromated zinc chloride (CZC): sodium (or potassium) dichromate and zinc chloride. TT–W–551.
>
> copperized Boliden salt (CuCZA): arsenic acid, copper sulfate, sodium arsenate, sodium (or potassium) dichromate, and zinc sulfate.
>
> copperized chromated zinc chloride (CuCZC): cupric chloride, sodium (or potassium) dichromate, and zinc chloride.
>
> Erdalith Greensalt (CCA type A): arsenic pentoxide, copper sulfate, and potassium dichromate (or sodium dichromate, or chromic acid). TT–W–550.
>
> Osmose Osmosar (FCAP type B): dinitrophenol (or sodium pentachlorophenate), sodium arsenate, sodium (or potassium) dichromate and sodium fluoride. TT–W–535.
>
> Tanalith-Wolman salt (FCAP type A): dinitrophenol (or sodium pentachlorophenate), sodium arsenate, sodium chromate, and sodium fluoride. TT–W–535.

Hunt and Garratt (1967) list many other water soluble chemicals, some sold under proprietary names, most of which are little used in the United States today. An exception is sodium pentachlorophenate, a very satisfactory dip to control blue stain during air-seasoning of southern pine. Waterborne preservatives for which service life specific to southern pine posts is available (Blew and Davidson 1967) include: ACC, borax-boric acid, copper sulfate (with sodium arsenate applied by double diffusion), CZC, FCAP-A, FCAP-B, mercuric chloride, sodium chromate, sodium dichromate, zinc chloride, and zinc meta arsenite. Also, southern pine stakes treated with chromated copper arsenate (CCA types I and II) are under field test in Mississippi (Blew and Davidson 1969).

Effectiveness in ground or fresh water[1].—Laboratory tests for initial screening of toxicity and other characteristics of preservatives and standards applicable to them are described by Hunt and Garratt (1967, p. 79).

Ultimately, the effectiveness of preservatives must be proven in service tests on wood in commercial form, in actual use, and carrying the accustomed loads under a range of exposure conditions. Since controlled service tests are expensive and time consuming, accelerated field tests such as exposure of treated stakes are often used. Tests with full-sized fenceposts, while accelerated only in extreme soils and climates, are not considered service tests unless the wood is in use and carrying normal loads; resu lts are, however, comparable to those of service installations.

Southern pine has been exposed in stake tests at Saucier, Miss., Madison, Wis., Bogalusa, La., Jacksonville, Fla., and in the Panama Canal Zone. Installations began in 1938 and have been added to periodically. The stakes were all sapwood, 2 by 4 by 18 inches, and were set upright with half their length in the ground. Some smaller, untreated stakes were similarly installed. While no substitute for actual service trials, such tests are useful for screening out ineffective materials and exploring preservative properties of materials showing promise in the laboratory. Results with generally used preservatives at the Saucier, Miss. site are summarized in table 22–2 [1]. Details of these and other tests were reported by Blew and Davidson (1969).

Untreated stakes.—In these tests untreated 2- by 4-inch southern pine sapwood stakes had an average life of approximately 1 year in the Panama Canal Zone, 1.8 to 3.6 years at Saucier, Miss., Bogalusa, La., and Jacksonville, Fla., and 4 to 6 years at Madison, Wis. Untreated ¾-inch pine sapwood stakes in Mississippi have had an average life of 1.4 to 2.1 years.

Pressure-treated stakes.—Many pressure-treated stakes are still under observation, especially those in newer installations and those with more effective preservatives. While average life cannot be determined from such treatments, it has been estimated where failures have been sufficient to establish firm trends.

In the Canal Zone, stakes treated with **chromated zinc arsenate (Boliden salt)** and retaining 0.33 pound of the preservative per cubic foot have had an average life of 9 years, while those retaining 1.0 pound averaged 15.3 years. In Mississippi a failure was noted only with the low retention after 26 years, but failures have occurred in Wisconsin at both retentions. This is attributed to the presence of arsenic-tolerant fungi at the Wisconsin test area.

Stakes treated with retentions of from 0.5 to 1.0 pound of **chromated zinc chloride** per cubic foot have lasted, on an average, about 5 to 7 years in Panama, 14 to 20 years in Mississippi, and 15 to 18 years in Wisconsin. Stakes treated with **fluor chrome arsenate phenol (Wolman**

TABLE 22–2.—*Summary of Mississippi tests of 2- by 4-inch southern pine sapwood stakes pressure treated with wood preservatives in general use* (Blew and Davidson 1969)

Preservative	Average retention[1]	Average life	Remarks
	Pounds per cubic foot	*Years*	
Acid copper chromate (Fed. Spec. TT–W–546)	0.26	11.6	10 percent failed after 2 years
	.30		10 percent failed after 23 years
	.52		10 percent failed after 2 years
	.60		20 percent failed after 23 years
	.75		20 percent failed after 24 years
Ammoniacal copper arsenite (Fed. Spec. TT–W–549)	.28		No failures after 24 years
	.59, 1.12, 1.45		60 percent failed after 23 years
Chromated copper arsenate Type I (Fed. Spec. TT–W–550)	.26		No failures after 23 years
	.50, .78		
Type II (Fed. Spec. TT–W–550)	.26, .37, .52		No failure after 19 years
	.79, 1.04		
Chromated zinc arsenate (Former Fed. Spec. TT–W–538)	.42		10 percent failed after 26 years
	.55 to 1.34		No failure after 26 years
	.28		30 percent failed after 17 years
	.48, .97, 1.27		No failures after 17 years
Chromated zinc chloride (Fed. Spec. TT–W–551)	.49	14.2	
	.76	20.2	
	1.02	20.1	40 percent failed after 15 years
	1.5		No failures after 13 years
Copper naphthenate	2.91, 6.0		
0.11 percent copper in No. 2 fuel oil	10.3	15.9	
.29 percent copper in No. 2 fuel oil	10.2	21.8	
.57 percent copper in No. 2 fuel oil	10.6		50 perce: t fa led after 25 years
.86 percent copper in No. 2 fuel oil	9.6		20 perce t failed after 25 years

Creosote, coal tar	4.2	17.8	20 percent failed after 26 years
	8.0		No failures after 19 years
	8.3		No failures after 26 years
	11.8, 16.5		
	4.6	21.3	60 percent failed after 28 years
	10.0		No failures after 28 years
	14.5		
Low residue, straight run	4.1	14.2	
Medium residue, straight run	8.0	17.8	
High residue, straight run	8.0	18.8	
Medium residue, low in tar acids	7.8	20.3	
Medium residue, low in naphthalene	8.1	19.4	
Medium residue, low in tar acids and naphthalene	8.2	21.3	
Low residue, low in tar acids and naphthalene	8.0	18.9	
High residue, low in tar acids and naphthalene	8.0	19.2	
	8.2	20.0	
English, vertical retort	8.0	18.9	60 percent failed after 20 years
	5.3		20 percent failed after 20 years
	10.1		No failures after 20 years
	15.0		
English, coke oven	7.9	13.6	
	4.7	16.3	70 percent failed after 20 years
	10.1		60 percent failed after 20 years
	14.8		
Fluor chrome arsenate phenol	.2	10.2	
(Type A) (Fed. Spec. TT-W-535)	.3	18.0	
	.61	24.1	
	.35, .50, .75		No failures after 9 years

See footnote at end of table, page 1072.

TABLE 22–2.—(Blew and Davidson 1969)—Continued

Preservative	Average retention[1]	Average life	Remarks
	Pounds per cubic foot	*Years*	
Pentachlorophenol (various solvents)			
Liquefied petroleum gas	.14	-------	10 percent failed in 7–1/2 years
	.19	-------	10 percent failed in 7–1/2 years
	.34	-------	No failures in 7–1/2 years
	.34	-------	No failures in 5 years
	.49	-------	No failures in 5 years
	.58	-------	No failures in 7–1/2 years
	.65	-------	No failures in 5 years
Stoddard solvent (mineral spirits)	.14	-------	10 percent failed in 7–1/2 years
	.18	-------	10 percent failed in 7–1/2 years
	.38	-------	No failures in 7–1/2 years
	.67	-------	No failures in 7–1/2 years
	.2	13.7	-------
	.2	9.5	-------
	.4	13.5	-------
Heavy gas oil (Mid-United States)	.2	-------	22 percent failed in 20–1/2 years
	.4	-------	10 percent failed in 20–1/2 years
	.6	-------	10 percent failed in 20–1/2 years
No. 4 aromatic oil (West Coast)	.2	-------	60 percent failed in 17 years
	.4	-------	20 percent failed in 17 years
AWPA P9 (heavy petroleum)	.11	-------	No failures in 7–1/2 years
	.19	-------	No failures in 7–1/2 years
	.29	-------	No failures in 7–1/2 years
	.53	-------	No failures in 5 years
	.67	-------	No failures in 7–1/2 years
Untreated stakes	-------	1.8 to 3.6	-------

[1] Except for copper naphthenate and creosote (for which total preservative solution retained is indicated), values show retention of dry chemical.

FCAP) to retentions of 0.2 to 0.3 pound per cubic foot have had an average life in Panama of about 3 and 6 years, respectively, while those treated with 0.6 pound per cubic foot averaged 14 years. In Mississippi, stakes treated with 0.2, 0.3, and 0.6 pound of that preservative per cubic foot have had an average life of about 10, 18, and 20 years, respectively. In Wisconsin, average life for similar retentions was 14 to 16 years.

Of the waterborne preservatives under test, the formulations containing either copper and arsenic **(ammoniacal copper arsenite)** or copper, chromium, and arsenic **(chromated copper arsenate)** are the better performers, with no failures after 19 to 24 years when retentions were 0.5 pound per cubic foot or higher. **Acid copper chromate** with a retention of 0.26 pound per cubic foot has shown an average life of 11.6 years in Mississippi; there were failures after 23 years, with retentions of 0.52 and 0.75 pound per cubic foot and, after 2 years, with retentions of 0.3 and 0.6 pound per cubic foot.

Results thus far in tests of **pentachlorophenol** (approximately 0.2 pound per cubic foot) with different **hydrocarbon solvents** show better performance with heavy solvents such as heavy gas oil, lube oil extract, No. 4 aromatic oil, and AWPA–P9 (heavy petroleum solvent) than with volatile (LPG) or light oils such as Stoddard solvent (mineral spirits). Preservatives such as **rosin amine-D-pentachlorophenate, tributyltin oxide,** and **copper-8-quinolinolate** also show better performance with the heavy petroleum solvent than with the light Stoddard solvent (mineral spirits).

Ten **coal tar creosotes** installed in 1948 were less effective than those used in 1940–41, 8-pound treatments showing only a few serviceable stakes after 20 years, with average life estimated at 14 to 21 years. For comparable retentions, failures after 25½ to 28 years were 20 to 50 percent in the earlier installation.

Stakes pressure treated with a **fire-retarding formulation** containing ammonium phosphate and ammonium sulfate lasted, on an average, only 2 to 3 years in Mississippi. With these ammonium salts plus borax and boric acid average life was about 4 years. The fire-retarding formulation with borax and boric acid alone has provided protection against decay and termites for an average of about 6 years. The addition of zinc chloride and chromium compounds to combinations of boron and ammonium salts in fire retardants improves protection against decay fungi and termites.

In Mississippi, **copper naphthenate** is furnishing greater protection (average life 16, 22, and more years in four tests—see table 22–2) than zinc naphthenate with similar retentions.

Rosin amine D **pentachlorophenate** in Stoddard solvent is performing less satisfactorily than is pentachlorophenol with that solvent and similar retentions. Naval stores products such as rosin oil, oleoresin, and drop liquor concentrate in petroleum solvents appear to have limited value as preservatives but are improved by the addition of pentachlorophenol. Urea has also afforded limited protection, 5.8 pounds per cubic foot giving stakes average life of 9.1 years in Mississippi. Other products showing limited preservative value in the retentions used are acrylonitrile (cyanoethylation), ammonium hydroxide (thiamine destruction), amyl phenyl acetate, capric acid, copper-8-quinolinolate (in Stoddard solvent), diamyl phenol, DDT, dodecylamine, nickel stearate, and tribulyltin oxide (in Stoddard solvent).

Average life increases with **size of test stakes;** with coal tar creosote retention of 8 pounds per cubic foot, ½-inch-square stakes showed an average life of 17 years with 100-percent failure in 21½ years. After 27½ years, 1-inch-square stakes show 90-percent failures, 1½-inch-square stakes 80 percent, and 2- by 4-inch stakes 30-percent failures.

Stakes with nonpressure treatments.—Blew and Davidson (1969) also reported tests of southern pine stakes treated by nonpressure methods. Stakes given such treatments as brushing and brief dipping in coal tar creosote and solutions of pentachlorophenol, copper naphthenate, zinc naphthenate, and phenyl mercury oleate, have, in general, lasted 1 to 4 years longer than untreated controls. Stakes dipped for 15 minutes in coal tar creosote had a life of about 8 years in Mississippi. Stakes soaked 18 hours in solutions of pentachlorophenol or mixtures of chlorinated phenols have lasted 5 to 10 years in the Canal Zone and 8 to 16 years in the United States.

Pine stakes soaked in urea solution have lasted about 1 to 1½ years longer than control stakes in Mississippi, while those soaked in urea-formaldehyde solutions have outlasted controls by about 3 to 4 years. Stakes with higher retentions of copper chromate and with copper arsenate applied by **double diffusion** continue to perform well after 25 years in Mississippi. Failures thus far are attributed to poor penetration of the preservative.

Southern pine posts.—Blew and Davidson (1967) have reported on southern pine posts installed in exposure tests at the Harrison Experimental Forest, Saucier, Miss. in 1936, 1937, 1938, 1941, 1949, and 1964. The posts—round, bark-free, free of fungi, mostly sapwood, 6 to 7 feet long, and from 2½ to 7 inches in top diameter—were installed in dry, moist, and wet sites. Seventy preservative treatments were applied, including a few duplicates. Tables 22–3 and 22–4 summarize observations through January 1967 [1].

In the older tests, both treated and untreated posts have generally lasted longer on wet than on dry or moist sites. With few exceptions, this has been true for salts as well as oilborne preservatives.

Research indicates treatments[1] that should protect posts for an average life exceeding 40 years under southern Mississippi conditions include pressure treatments with coal tar creosote and used crankcase oil (50-50), pentachlorophenol (3 to 5 percent) in used crankcase oil, water-gas tar, and zinc meta arsenite, as well as double diffusion treatment wtih copper sulfate and sodium arsenate. Slightly less effective (25- to 40-year average life) are pressure treatments with acid copper chromate (Celcure), chromated zinc chloride, coal tar, coal tar creosote, fluor chrome arsenate phenol (Tanalith), lignite coal tar creosote, tetrachlorophenol (3 to 5 percent) in used crankcase oil, and zinc chloride; steeping in mercuric chloride and full-length Osmose (diffusion) treatments should also result in average lives of more than 25 years.

Results from the 1949 installation are still tentative, but only a few materials (relatively nontoxic ones) have so far proved ineffective. For the majority of treatments in the test, on which failures have been less than 10 percent in 18 years, average life should exceed 26 years. This is true of the treatments testing several petroleum oils as carriers for pentachlorophenol and diluent for creosote to replace used crankcase oils. The latter are unsuitable for pasture fencing because they may contain chemicals reported to be a cause of "X-disease" (hyperkeratosis) in cattle. Performance to date does not suggest any loss of effectiveness from the substitution[1].

While some waterborne treatments have proved quite effective at Saucier, these and other salt preservatives may be more effective where exposure to leaching is less severe.

Effectiveness in salt water.—Chief deteriorators of wood exposed to salt water are molluscan borers, called shipworms, of the genera *Bankia* and *Teredo,* and crustacean borers of the genus *Limnoria,* which are relatives of the common terrestial sowbugs. (See sec. 17–3.) The shipworms attack wood as free-swimming larvae, remaining as adults within a single burrow. They tolerate brackish water as dilute as 10 parts salts per million (by weight), and polluted water with dissolved oxygen as low as 2 parts per million. *Limnoria* adults are ant-size, mobile, limited to sea water (25 to 30 parts salt per million), and concentrate their attacks in the outer inch of submerged wood [3].

Creosote is the preservative most widely used to protect wood from marine organisms[1]. While adult shipworms tolerate this poison to some extent, larvae are more sensitive and rarely infect creosoted wood. Protection may fail, however, where untreated wood is exposed in, or in contact with a treated timber. One species of crustacean borer, *Limnoria tripuncta* Menzies, attacks creosoted wood (Beckman et al. 1957). Because copperbased paints and arsenicals have limited protective life in sea water, and it is virtually impossible to long maintain the essential complete coverage, heavy impregnations of creosote remain the best protection against *Limnoria.*

The American Wood Preservers Association (1969, C18–69) specification calls for creosote, or creosote-coal tar solution, applied with vacuum and pressure in the full-cell process to a retention of 20 or 25 pounds per

---

[3] Menzies, R. J. The nature of, and prevention of, marine borer attacks on southern pine wood—A review. Presented at a symposium, "Utilization of the Southern Pines," Alexandria, La. No. 6–8, 1968.

TABLE 22–3.—*Summary of observations on round southern pine posts installed at Saucier, Miss. 1936 to 1941, as of January 1967*
(after Blew and Davidson 1967)

Treatment[1]	Retention	Failures							Average life[1][2]	Remarks
		Site			Cause				
		Dry	Moist	Wet	Decay	Decay and termites	Termites		
	Pounds per cu. ft.	*Percent*						*Years*	
Untreated controls	0	100	100	100	13	84	3	3.3	2.6, 4.0, and 4.8 years average life on dry, moist, and wet sites, respectively
Acid copper chromate (Celcure)	.92[3]	33	7	12	21	4	-------	38	75 percent serviceable in January 1967
Beta-napthol, 5 percent, in oil	6.20	100	100	100	22	59	19	11.6	All posts had failed after 30 years
Borax-boric acid (50–50 mixture)	.92[3]	100	100	100	18	46	36	10.6	Average life—dry site 9.8, moist 11.0, and wet 13.2 years
Chromated zinc chloride	.87[3]	58	81	82	38	29	-------	28	
Coal tar	6.50	69	40	44	40	20	-------	30	
Coal tar creosote, grade 1	6.00	30	12	30	22	7	-------	37	71 percent serviceable in January 1967
Coal tar creosote and used crankcase oil, 50–50 mixture	5.40	12	2	1	15	-------	1	43	84 percent serviceable in January 1967

TABLE 22-3.—*Summary of observations on round southern pine posts installed at Saucier, Miss. 1936 to 1941, as of January 1967 (after Blew and Davidson 1967)*—Continued

Treatment[1]	Retention	Failures						Average life[2]	Remarks
		Site			Cause				
		Dry	Moist	Wet	Decay	Decay and termites	Termites		
	Pounds per cu. ft.	*Percent*			*Percent*			*Years*	
Coal tar creosote 10 percent, used crankcase oil 90 percent	7.10	91	82	65	75	9	1	11	Retention in failed posts—5.8
Crankcase oil (used)	7.60	100	87	88	92	4	------	8	
Fluor chrome arsenate phenol (Tanalith) (AWPA–P5)	.35[3]	57	71	60	34	19	7	30	Retention in failed posts—3.4
Lignite coal tar creosote	6.30	57	35	47	23	26	3	32	
Mercuric chloride	.09[3]	83	59	72	25	37	15	27	Treated by steeping process
No-D-K (hardwood-tar creosote)	6.60	97	63	45	31	48	4	21	
Osmosar	.30[3]	87	81	59	30	39	12	26	Treated by Osmose (diffusion) process
P.D.A. (Phenyldichlorasine) 0.84 percent in gas oil	5.90	95	81	72	22	53	13	21	
Pentachlorophenol, 4.82 percent in used crankcase oil	6.70	3	------	------	2	1	------	40+	97 percent serviceable in January 1967
Pentachlorophenol, 3.02 percent in used crankcase oil	6.40	18	------	------	13	4	1	42	Retention of failed posts—4.3
Sodium dichromate	.88[3]	95	100	89	8	40	47	18	
Sodium chromate	.93[3]	98	88	88	8	33	53	16	

TABLE 22–3.—*Summary of observations on round southern pine posts installed at Saucier, Miss. 1936 to 1941, as of January 1967 (after Blew and Davidson 1967)*—Continued

Treatment[1]	Retention	Failures						Average life[1][2]	Remarks
		Site			Cause				
		Dry	Moist	Wet	Decay	Decay and termites	Termites		
Tetrachlorophenol, 2.9 percent in used crankcase oil	7.10	42	7	6	29	1	----	37	70 percent serviceable in January 1967
Tetrachlorophenol, 4.83 percent in used crankcase oil	5.80	21	----	----	14	7	----	40	79 percent serviceable in January 1967
Water-gas tar	6.30	20	20	18	14	6	----	41	80 percent serviceable in January 1967; retention of failed posts—4.2
Zinc chloride	.94[3]	74	75	76	35	39	1	27	
Zinc meta arsenite	.42[3]	3	----	1	3	1	----	40+	96 percent serviceable in January 1967
Copper sulfate and sodium arsenate (installed 1941)	{ .35[3] .16	4	1	1	5	1	----	40+	Double diffusion treatment, 94 percent serviceable after 26

TABLE 22–3.—*Summary of observations on round southern pine posts installed at Saucier, Miss. 1936 to 1941, as of January 1967* (after Blew and Davidson 1967)—Continued

Treatment[1]	Retention	Failures						Average life[1][2]	Remarks
		Site			Cause				
		Dry	Moist	Wet	Decay	Decay and termites	Termites		
Osmoplastic groundline treatment (installed 1941)_____		100	100	100	32	55	13	11.2	0.34 pound per post applied to 15-inch band and top of post. All posts failed in 20 years

[1] All chemicals applied by pressure treatment, except as noted under remarks.
[2] Except where all posts have failed, tests are still in progress, and estimates of average life are based on projected curves.
[3] These numbers show retention of dry chemical, all others indicate total preservative solution retained.

TABLE 22–4.—*Summary of observations on longleaf pine sapwood posts exposed at Saucier, Miss. since 1949; as of January 1967 (after Blew and Davidson 1967)*

Treatment[1]	Form of preservative	Retention of preservative	Posts serviceable January 1967	Average life[2]
			Percent	Years
Ammoniacal copper arsenite (Chemonite) (AWPA–P5)	Dry salt	0.34	100	—
Boliden salt B (ZnO+H$_3$AsO$_4$+CrO$_3$)	--do--	.50	100	—
Carbosota (coal tar creosote)	Oil	6.0	100	—
Chromated zinc arsenate (Boliden salts) (AWPA–P5)	Dry salt	.70	96	23
Chromated zinc chloride, copperized (ZnCl$_2$+Na$_2$CrO$_7$·2H$_2$O+CuCl·(2H$_2$O))	--do--	.98	76	—
Chromated zinc chloride, FR (ZnCl$_2$+Na$_2$Cr$_2$O$_7$·2H$_2$O+H$_3$BO$_3$+(NH$_4$)$_2$SO$_4$)	--do--	3.25	96	—
Coal tar creosote:				
Straight run, low residue	Oil	5.9	100	—
Straight run, medium residue	--do--	5.6	96	—
Straight run, high residue	--do--	6.0	100	—
Medium residue, low in tar acids	--do--	5.7	100	—
Medium residue, low in naphthalene	--do--	6.1	96	—
Medium residue, low in tar acids and naphthalene	--do--	6.0	100	—
Low residue, low in tar acids and naphthalene	--do--	6.0	96	—
High residue, low in tar acids and naphthalene	--do--	6.1	100	—
Medium residue, low in fraction from 235° to 270° C., crystals removed	--do--	6.1	88	26
High residue, crystals removed	--do--	6.0	100	—
Low temperature	--do--	6.3	100	—
English, vertical retort	--do--	6.3	100	—
English, coke oven	--do--	6.0	100	—
English, vertical retort 50% and coke oven 50% (by volume)	Solution	6.0	100	—
Medium residue (low in tar acids and naphthalene) with 2-½% pentachlorophenol (by weight)	--do--	6.0	100	—
Coal-tar creosote 70%, and coal-tar 30% (by volume)	--do--	6.1	100	—
Coal-tar creosote (medium residue, low in tar acids and naphthalene) 50%, and petroleum oil (No. 2 distillate) 50% (by volume)	--do--	5.9	100	—

Coal-tar creosote (medium residue, low in tar acids and naphthalene) 50%, and petroleum oil (Wyoming residual) 50% (by volume)	---do---	6.0	100	—
Coal-tar creosote (medium residue, low in tar acids and naphthalene) 50%, and petroleum oil (Wyoming residual) 50% (by volume); fortified with 2-½% pentachlorophenol (by weight of total solution)	---do---	6.0	100	—
Copper naphthenate, 0.5% copper-metal equivalent (by weight) in petroleum oil (No. 4 aromatic residual)	---do---	6.0	96	—
Gasco (oil-tar creosote)	Solution	5.9	100	—
Gasco (oil-tar creosote) with 2% pentachlorophenol (by weight)	---do---	5.8	100	—
Lignite coal-tar creosote	Oil	6.3	88	26
Lignite coal-tar creosote, 50% and coal-tar creosote (medium residue, low in tar acids and naphthalene), 50% (by volume)	Solution	6.3	100	—
Lignite coal-tar creosote, 50% and petroleum oil (Wyoming residual), 50% (by volume)	---do---	6.4	88	26
Pentachlorophenol:[3]				
Five percent (by weight) in petroleum oil (No. 2 distillate)	---do---	6.3	100	—
Five percent (by weight) in petroleum oil (No. 4 aromatic residual)	---do---	5.9	100	—
Three percent (by weight) in petroleum oil (No. 4 aromatic residual)	---do---	6.0	100	—
Five percent (by weight) in petroleum oil (Wyoming residual)	---do---	6.0	96	—
Pentachlorophenol, 5% in petroleum oil (No. 4 aromatic residual), 50%; and copper naphthenate, 0.5% copper-metal equivalent, in petroleum oil (No. 4 aromatic residual), 50% (by volume)	---do---	6.2	100	—
Petroleum oil:				
Aromatic, high residue (S.W.)	Oil	6.1	100	—
Aromatic, low residue (S.W.)	---do---	6.1	100	—
Highly aromatic (S.O.)	---do---	6.0	84	25
Highly aromatic, high residue (S.O.)	---do---	6.1	80	24
No. 2 distillate (mid-United States)	---do---	5.9	—	6.2
No. 4 aromatic residual (California)	---do---	5.9	88	26
Wyoming residual	---do---	5.8	8	8
Termiteol (softwood-tar creosote)	---do---	6.1	76	23
Untreated control posts	—	—	—	2.3

[1] All treatments by pressure impregnation; 25 posts per treatment installed in April and May 1949.

[2] Estimated on basis of recorded failures. Where less than 10 percent of posts have failed in 18 years, average life is expected to be 26 years or more.

[3] Retention of pentachlorophenol stated in terms of solution weight.

cubic foot by assay of borings taken in the outer 3-inch shell. The 20-pound treatment will protect southern pine in salt water from Molluscan borers for a period of 10 to 20 years—or even longer under special ecological situations[3]. The 25-pound treatment is intended for application where *Limnoria* are active.

Baechler (1968) has reviewed causes for variable performance of creosoted marine piling. Many premature failures could be explained by low retentions, the use of unsuitable oil, or a combination of both. Baechler states that in producing a creosote for marine use, the type of tar selected is far more important than the manner in which it is distilled. Treatment of test panels with various high-temperature coal-tar oils was comparatively effective in combating *Limnoria* in tests at Aransas Pass, Texas.

The *Limoria* hazard may be aggravated by depletion of creosote or its toxic constituents from the outer layers of wood. Absorption of petroleum oils, common in most harbors from waste marine fuel, lowers toxicity of creosote; oil coatings probably hasten loss of creosote also (Baechler and Roth 1961).

Three approaches are underway to improve the service given by creosoted piling exposed to *Limnoria* in warmer harbors (Baechler 1968): (1) pretreatments with waterborne copper compounds; (2) additives to enhance permanence of creosote and toxicity to *Limnoria*; and (3) mechanical barriers in the form of coatings, plastic wrappings, or shields of some firm material. Readers desiring additional information on factors affecting performance of marine piling under attack by *Limnoria tripuncta* will find Colley (1969), Baechler et al. (1970ab), and Gjovik et al. (1970) of interest.

Effectiveness against ants, beetles, and woodpeckers.—Treatments specific to termites can be found in section 17–1. Preservatives effective against carpenter ants, powder post beetles, and other chewing insects are described in section 17–2. Section 17–4 describes progress in finding treatments that effectively protect southern pine wood from woodpeckers.

FACTORS AFFECTING PENETRATION AND ABSORPTION

While service life is the ultimate test of effectiveness of treatment, the immediate criteria are the amount of preservative retained, the depth of penetration, and the distribution of preservative within the zone of penetration. In creosoted southern pine poles, poor penetration of sapwood is the most important cause of decay. Inspection of over 3,000 poles in line 5 to 26 years showed that 95 percent of the failures were in poles with creosote penetration less than 1.8 inches and 60 percent of the sapwood thickness. No failures occurred in poles penetrated more than 2.1 inches and 75 percent of sapwood thickness (Colley and Amadon 1936). Inadequately penetrated wood fails early when checks extend beyond the treated zone or mechanical wear of the treated shell exposes untreated wood. Absorption of preservatives is affected by permeability of the wood, form of the timber to be treated, and the treating procedure.

Anatomy.—The anatomy and permeability of southern pine wood are described in chapter 5 and section 8–6. Southern pine sapwood is relatively permeable, i.e., it allows the passage of fluids under pressure. Tracheid lumens in southern pine are not occluded, and the pit membranes between sapwood cells contain relatively large openings. Pit aspiration is generally not sufficiently severe to cut off flow. Absorption and penetration obtained by dip treatment vary significantly within and between southern pine trees (Verrall 1965).

From a microscopic examination of southern pine wood pressure treated with pentachlorophenol in oil and with creosote, Behr et al. (1969) reported that there was little difference in distribution between the two preservatives. In heavily treated zones many lumens were full of preservative; in zones of lower retention the preservative was present as drops or "plugs" of liquid and in the tips of the cells. Preservative was present in both ray tracheids and ray parenchyma cells and in earlywood tracheids adjacent to the rays, but not in those at a distance. Resin canals and most epithelial cells contained preservative, as did many tracheids adjoining resin canals.

Resch and Arganbright (1971), in a study of Douglas-fir (*Pseudotsuga menziesii* (Mirb.) Franco) pressure impregnated with pentachlorophenol in liquefied petroleum gas, found evidence of the presence of pentachlorophenol not only on the lumen surfaces of cells, but also in the cell walls.

Specific gravity.—General experience with pressure treatment of the southern pines indicates that low-density samples often are the most difficult to penetrate, although density per se may not be the determining factor. When pressure treated to refusal, low-density material usually shows greater retentions than high-density wood.

Grain direction.—Penetration of preservative is greatest in the longitudinal grain direction. For southern pine heartwood under liquid pressure, Teesdale (1914) found the following ratios of tangential/radial/longitudinal penetration: longleaf 1/4/100, shortleaf 1/7/55, and loblolly 1/40/80. MacLean (1929) observed that in pressure-treated southern pine heartwood, coal tar creosote penetrated 12 times as far longitudinally as laterally, while zinc chloride penetrated 16 times as far. In dip treatments of heartwood and sapwood of southern pine in water and light oils, Verrall (1957) found the ratios of absorptions through radial, tangential, and transverse sections were 1/1.7/11.7, and the ratios of penetrations in tangential, radial, and longitudinal directions were 1/1.6/11.2; i.e., in dip treatments penetrations were proportional to absorptions.

Sapwood and heartwood.—While most southern pine trees are predominantly sapwood (sec. 5–1), every pole or pile contains some heartwood, and in some products, such as fenceposts cut from veneer cores, heartwood may predominate. Heartwood is less permeable than sapwood. In shortleaf pine, dips and cold soaks have been found to penetrate sapwood further than heartwood (Blew 1955). Verrall (1965) observed that during a 3-minute dip in oilborne preservatives southern pine sapwood absorbed about twice the amount absorbed by heartwood, although some heartwood specimens absorbed more than some sapwood specimens. Similarly, Teesdale (1914) found that some heartwood samples reacted like sapwood to pressure treatment. Differences between sapwood and heartwood are probably more pronounced with pressure treatments than with dips.

Earlywood and latewood.—In most species, latewood generally treats better under pressure than earlywood, or at least allows a greater lateral penetration (Blew 1955; Teesdale 1914). The earlywood of rapidly grown southern pine has particularly low lateral penetrability (Teesdale and MacLean 1918). In contrast, pressure-flow studies show that longitudinal flow through southern pine sapwood (Erickson et al. 1937) is greater in earlywood than in latewood. Earlywood has a greater void volume and can retain more preservative (Buckman 1936). In three dip tests (Verrall 1965), the penetration in latewood was usually double that in earlywood. This relation held for pentachlorophenol alone or with a water repellent, and for treatment with dyed water. Differences were marked in fast-grown wood but were small or absent in slow-grown, even-textured wood. Lateral penetration was greatest when latewood was exposed on the surface of the lumber. In samples heavily infected with *Trichoderma* or *Penicillium,* penetration of earlywood and latewood was equal.

Fungus infections.—Lindgren and Scheffer (1939) found that stain fungi increased creosote absorptions in pine sapwood 1.2 to 1.7 times with a 30-minute soak, and 2.1 to 2.5 times with hot-and-cold bath or pressure treatments.

Lindgren (1952) reported that *Trichoderma* mold greatly increased the permeability of southern pine posts to oilborne and waterborne preservatives and to rain water. Infected, end-sealed post sections soaked 5 minutes in pentachlorophenol in oil picked up 5 to 9 pounds per cubic foot, whereas uninfected sections absorbed only 1 pound per cubic foot. During 2 days of drizzling rain with intermittent showers, the infected posts picked up 28 to 30 pounds per cubic foot, and the uninfected only 7 to 8 pounds. Some early failures of poles may result from poor preservative penetration due to excessive rainwater in infected wood at the time of treatment.

Blew (1961) also showed that the degree of general fungus infection markedly affects absorption of preservative by southern pine posts treated by the cold-soaking process. Knuth and McCoy (1962) concluded that *Bacillus polymyxa* was the major organism producing porous sapwood in pond-stored pine logs. Verrall (1965) reported that infection of southern pine wood with various mold, stain, and decay fungi increased absorption of both oil and water.

Rough vs. dressed lumber.—In small laboratory tests with both water solutions of sap-stain-control chemical and pentachlorophenol in mineral spirits, rough samples removed 1.7 to 1.8 times as much solution from a dipping vat as did planed samples. Presumably, the roughened surface held more liquid on the surface, and some of this liquid later penetrated deeper, thus influencing the degree of stain control (Verrall and Mook 1951). This difference is probably of much less magnitude in pressure processes.

Treating procedures and preservatives.—Penetration and retention are of course, influenced by the treating procedure. (See subsection, PROCESSES.) Because southern pine sapwood is so permeable, some nonpressure methods give good penetration (but sometimes with excessive retention); these include diffusion of strong solutions of waterborne preservatives into green wood, hot-and-cold bath treating southern pine posts and poles with creosote or pentachlorophenol, and vacuum treating millwork with water-repellent preservative. In general, however, pressure treatments give better penetration and control of retention than nonpressure treatments; they are usually required where service conditions are severe.

With comparable treating procedures, waterborne salts usually give better penetration and retention than oilborne preservatives. Straight creosote penetrates deeper than creosote in coal tar or petroleum oil. In general, preservatives of low viscosity penetrate more readily than those of high viscosity. Under pressure, heated preservatives usually penetrate better than cool, and into hot wood more easily than into cool wood. MacLean (1960, p. 68) gives temperature-viscosity curves for zinc chloride and a number of creosote and oil preservatives.

In pressure treatment, penetration increases with pressure and time under pressure. Better penetrations usually result from moderate treating pressures and moderately long pressure periods than from very high pressures for very short periods (MacLean 1960).

Form of timber and effect of glue lines.—A round southern pine pile, pole, or fencepost in its natural form is readily penetrated because an unbroken layer of permeable sapwood surrounds the heartwood. In contrast, a fencepost made from a veneer core or a heart-center timber may have little if any sapwood exposed and therefore may be more difficult to penetrate. Four-inch-square southern pine posts treated with 0.35 pound of Tanalith per cubic foot, and those treated with 1.0 pound of chromated zinc chloride, showed an average life of 10 and 15 years in Mississippi (American Wood Preservers Association 1949); round southern pine posts with similar retentions of these preservations showed an average life of 26 and 25 years in the same area (Blew and Davidson 1967).

Large round or sawed timbers require less retention per gross cubic foot than smaller ones because they have less surface in proportion to their volume. Sawn timbers, however, often require heavier treatment to insure that exposed heartwood is adequately penetrated. Under these conditions, empty-cell processes give better penetration at a given retention than full-cell treatment.

The effect of glue lines on the absorption of preservatives in laminated timbers is not yet fully evaluated. Southern pine laminated bridge timbers creosoted after gluing have performed well for periods up to 20 years (Selbo et al. 1965). While most southern pine laminating stock today is sapwood, considerable heart-center 2-inch lumber is used in laminated beams. Probably most pressure-treated southern pine beams are penetrated to the first glue line at least; in most cases this provides a ¾- to 1¾-inch treated layer top and bottom. Deep, narrow laminated beams having much surface per unit of volume require relatively high retentions in severe service. Penetration from the sides of narrow beams should be readily achieved.

Plywood made from southern pine is virtually all sapwood. Most is made with three or less phenol-formaldehyde glue lines. The permeability of the veneer, the lathe checks present, and gaps in the core veneers should combine to make three-ply southern pine plywood relatively easy to treat; five-ply is more difficult to penetrate fully.

DETERMINATION OF PENETRATION AND RETENTION

Depth of penetration of the preservative is the best single measure of treatment adequacy. It is most accurately measured on sawn cross sections removed near midlength of treated timbers or poles. Because this destroys the products, it is usual practice to extract small cores from near midlength of the piece. An increment borer is used, and the resulting holes are filled with treated plugs. Many preservatives have a distinct color, and the depth of penetration can be accurately measured by prompt observation of the split surface of a full-length core split longitudinally. Penetration of preservatives without distinct coloration can be observed by the use of chemical indicators as described in Standard A3–63 of the American Wood Preservers Association (1969).

Retention of preservative is expressed in pounds per cubic foot, related either to gross volume or to a specified zone (usually an outer shell, 1 to 3 inches thick). Preservative entering wood as the treating cylinder is filled is called "initial absorption"; that retained at the end of the pressure period is "gross absorption"; that remaining in the wood after withdrawal of pressure and any post conditioning treatments is "net retention." "Kickback"—the difference between gross absorption and net retention—results primarily from expansion of air within the wood cells. In the empty-cell treatment of southern pine, "kickback" varies from 25 to 75 percent of gross absorption; with full-cell treatment, it is considerably below 25 percent (MacLean 1960, p. 95).

Average net retentions are usually determined from the volume of preservative in the working tanks before and after treatment. The volume at known temperature is converted into equivalent weight and divided by the volume of the charge to yield pounds per cubic foot retention.

Retention within specific zones is determined by analysis, or assay, of sample cores or groups of cores. Baechler et al. (1962, 1969) reported that, in southern pine timbers and 2-inch lumber, retentions in the outer ½- to ⅝-inch zone were similar to those calculated from gain in weight. In treatment of poles and timbers for severe conditions, adequate retention in an outer shell is critical because much of the central core is not reached by the preservative.

PRETREATMENT AND CONDITIONING

Prior to preservative treatment, southern pine usually requires preparatory measures such as debarking, machining, and seasoning. Such requirements vary with type of product and treating process.

Peeling.—Because bark is virtually impermeable to liquids, it must be removed from posts, poles, and pilings prior to treatment. It should also be removed from wany edges of timbers. Removal of bark accelerates seasoning and diminishes hazards from insects and decay. Since uniform treatment requires complete removal of bark, the mechanical ring barker commonly used in southern pine sawmills is not much used in post, pole, and piling plants. Mechanical pole shavers usually carry two rotating cutterheads; the first head removes the bark and some wood, while the second head smooths the surface of the rotating and slowly advancing pole (fig. 19–53). Skillful operation is required to avoid gouges and excessive diameter reduction with accompanying loss of strength and per-

Figure 22–3.—Chipping headrig designed to convert cordwood into fenceposts of uniform hexagonal shape. Surplus wood is converted to pulp chips. (Photo from Stetson-Ross.)

meable sapwood. Hand-peeled roundwood, from a strength standpoint, is superior to wood shaved mechanically.

Recently available for southern pine production is a chipping headrig, which machines conventionally peeled posts to uniform hexagonal size while converting surplus wood to pulp chips (fig. 22–3).

Machining.—Any machining operations required in the finished product should be accomplished prior to treating. Examples would include the adzing and boring of crossties, framing (or dapping) timbers, boring poles, and cutting gains in poles to seat crossarms. Holes that must be bored after treatment should be filled with hot preservative oil, preferably under pressure.

Seasoning.—Free water in the cell lumens of green wood prevents uniform penetration of the preservative (except in some diffusion processes and certain flow processes). The free water may be removed by air-drying (sec. 20–1), forced-air-drying (sec. 20–2), kiln-drying (secs. 20–3 and 20–4), drying in a heat-conductive media (sec. 20–7), steaming and then applying a vacuum (sec. 20–4), or by boiling in oil under vacuum (sec. 20–7).

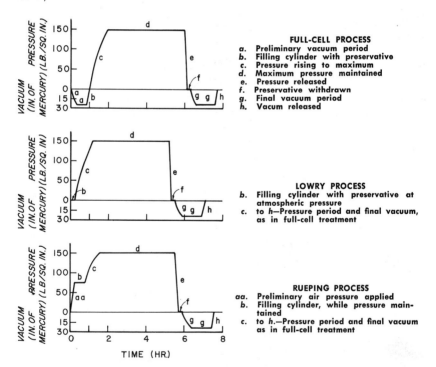

FULL-CELL PROCESS
a. Preliminary vacuum period
b. Filling cylinder with preservative
c. Pressure rising to maximum
d. Maximum pressure maintained
e. Pressure released
f. Preservative withdrawn
g. Final vacuum period
h. Vacum released

LOWRY PROCESS
b. Filling cylinder with preservative at atmospheric pressure
c. to h—Pressure period and final vacuum, as in full-cell treatment

RUEPING PROCESS
aa. Preliminary air pressure applied
b. Filling cylinder, while pressure maintained
c. to h.—Pressure period and final vacuum as in full-cell treatment

TIME (HR.)

Figure 22–4.—Typical pressure diagrams for full-cell, Lowry, and Rueping processes. When green wood is treated, a preliminary conditioning process precedes the steps shown in the diagrams. The duration of the different steps, as well as the intensity of vacuum, pressure, and preservative temperature, varies widely according to the character and condition of the wood and the judgment of the plant operator or timber purchaser. (Drawing from p. 200, Wood preservation, by G. M. Hunt and G. A. Garratt; © 1967 by McGraw-Hill, Inc.; used with permission of McGraw-Hill Book Co.)

Southern pine poles are commonly treated green after steam conditioning. Because prolonged high temperatures weaken wood, steaming time and temperatures as well as temperatures reached from boiling in oil must be limited, thus limiting the amount of moisture that can be removed. Longleaf pine poles with 85 percent sapwood have moisture contents from 60 to 85 percent after steam conditioning (Wood et al. 1960). Such poles may dry in service to an e.m.c. as low as 10 percent (Wood et al. 1960), causing objectionable checking and premature failure. Serviceability and penetration would be improved if the wood were closer to fiber saturation (25- to 30-percent moisture content) prior to treatment.

Figure 20–26 relates pole size and steaming time to interior temperatures of poles steamed at 260° F. MacLean (1960) explains (with examples) how to calculate time required to reach specified wood temperatures with steam at 260° F. and at the lower temperatures now specified.

For dip treatment, southern pine wood should be below 12-percent moisture content because penetration and absorption vary inversely with wood moisture content (Verrall 1965).

Post-treatments.—Southern pine may be subjected to an expansion bath of hot oil following the pressure cycle and before the vacuum is drawn. The purpose is to expand the remaining air in the cell lumens and drive out excess preservative. In general, expansion bath temperature is limited to 220° F. for southern pine.

Wood not destined for use in coastal waters is frequently steamed briefly following the vacuum. This steaming cleans the wood surface of excess preservative; it is generally limited to 240 to 245° F. with a duration dependent on product (American Wood Preservers Association 1969).

PROCESSES [1]

The objective of any treating process is to accomplish uniformly deep penetration into the wood. Methods are of two categories: pressure processes in closed retorts, and nonpressure processes. In general, better penetrations and retentions are obtained by pressure treatments than by nonpressure treatments (Blew 1955). In the United States most wood is treated by pressure processes, as shown by the following figures for 1967 (Gill and Phelps 1968).

Commodity	Pressure	Nonpressure
	– – – – – Percent – – – – –	
Piling	100.0	0
Crossties	100.0	0
Switch ties	100.0	0
Plywood	98.7	1.3
Lumber and timbers	98.6	1.4
Fenceposts	95.2	4.8
Poles	92.1	7.9
Crossarms	86.7	13.3
Other	77.1	22.9

The various treating processes are fully described in readily available references (MacLean 1960; Hunt and Garratt 1967). Salient points of each process are outlined below.

Pressure processes applied in closed cylinders.—There are two principal methods for injecting preservatives under pressure into wood—the full-cell and the empty-cell processes.

The objective in the **full-cell process** (fig. 22–4) is to retain as much liquid in the wood as possible, leaving the cell lumens full of the liquid preservative at the end of the treating cycle. Marine piling, for example, is treated with coal tar creosote by the full-cell method to attain the very high retentions specified. Also, the full-cell method is customarily used with waterborne preservatives; the usual retention of $\frac{1}{3}$ to $1\frac{1}{2}$ pounds of dry salt per cubic foot of wood is obtained by regulating the strength of the salt solution rather than by limiting the amount of liquid injected.

With seasoned southern pine in the cylinder, full-cell treatment with oil begins with a vacuum of at least 22 inches of mercury, which is held for 15 to 60 minutes. This removes much air from the cell lumens. Then, without admitting air, preservative oil at temperatures up to 210° F. is allowed to fill the cylinder to a pressure of 75 to 200 p.s.i. The pressure is maintained until the desired absorption is attained or until refusal. Pressure is then released, the preservative withdrawn, and a final vacuum of 22 inches of mercury is drawn for an hour or so to dry the surface of the timber.

Full-cell treatment with waterborne preservatives is very similar to the process used with oils, except the maximum solution temperature is kept below 120 to 150° F., depending on the mixed-salt used (American Wood Preservers Association 1969, C1–69). Treatment is generally to refusal.

The two **empty-cell processes** (Rueping and Lowry) are primarily used with preservative oils to impregnate crossties, poles, posts, and lumber. The American Wood Preservers Association (1969) specifies empty-cell treatment in preference to the full-cell process when the empty-cell process can accomplish the specified retention of oil.

In the **Rueping process** (fig. 22–4) conditoned southern pine is first subjected to an initial air pressure as high as 100 p.s.i. for as much as 30 minutes (rather than the vacuum used in the full-cell process). The cylinder is then filled with hot creosote (180 to 220° F.) so that the injected air is trapped in the wood and a pressure up to 100 p.s.i. more than the initial air pressure is maintained until the desired gross absorption is attained. Pressure is then released, the preservative drained, and a high vacuum is drawn for 30 minutes or more. During this final vacuum, the entrapped air expands and a portion of the preservative is ejected from the cell lumens. Net retention in southern pine poles varies from 25 to 75 percent of gross absorption.

The **Lowry process** differs from the Rueping process in that initial air is at atmospheric pressure (fig. 22–4). Maximum pressure on the preservative is limited to 250 p.s.i. For a given gross absorption, net retention in the Lowry process is intermediate between the full-cell process and the Rueping process.

The new **Cellon treatment** is distinguished by the fact that the preservative is pentachorophenol in solution in liquefied petroleum gas (Bescher 1965). Either full-cell or empty-cell processing may be used. If applied by the Rueping process, initial pressure is exerted by nitrogen (or other inert gas) since the solvent is highly inflammable. After the cylinder is drained, the solvent in the wood is evaporated under reduced pressure, recompressed, cooled, and stored under pressure. Solution viscosity is only about one-fifth that of water, and penetration is said to be good. Treating times and pressures are similar to those used with other preservatives. Because the treated wood retains no solvent, it is clear, paintable, not discolored, and offers no difficulty in gluing.

The **Slurry-seal** process of impregnating southern pine sapwood with waterborne preservatives in a pressure cylinder works best with green wood (Hudson 1968). In brief, unheated preservative under a pressure of about 200 p.s.i. is forced longitudinally into one end of the stick; the free water is displaced by the preservative, and treatment is complete when, within 1 to 4 hours, relatively undiluted preservative emerges from the low-pressure end.

The process uses a conventional treating cylinder modified as shown in figure 22–5. The wood to be treated is placed in the cylinder, on which the door adjacent to the dosing tank has been replaced by a perforated plate lined on the inside with a filter cloth. The end of each stick

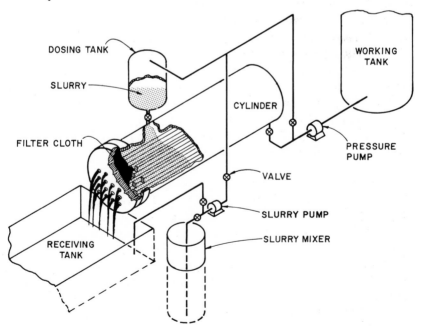

Figure 22–5.—Equipment for the slurry-seal preservative treatment of wood. (Drawing after Hudson 1968.)

to be treated is pressed firmly against the filter cloth. The cylinder is then filled with treating solution under sufficient pressure to cause it to flow out through the perforated door.

At this point, a slurry of finely ground sand and preservative solution is forced from the dosing tank into the cylinder, where it flows up against the filter and the perforated door, forming a seal around the end of each stick and permitting the preservative pressure in the cylinder to be raised to 200 p.s.i. According to the developer of the process, 2 by 4's 8 feet long can be treated in about 2 hours, and 16-foot lumber in 3 hours. With green round wood, peeling is not necessary, but retentions are higher in bark-free wood. A 20-foot peeled pole has been treated to retain 1.40 pounds per cubic foot of waterborne CCA at the butt and 1.16 pounds at the top. Retentions of solid chemical can be adjusted by varying the solution strength.

Advantages claimed for the system include low initial plant cost, elimination of drying prior to treatment, low temperature, and brevity of treatment. Disadvantages include lack of extensive information on uniformity and depth of penetration achievable, and the necessity of drying the wood after treatment to a moisture content approaching that achieved in use. Also, it is likely that the season in which poles are cut affects their treatability by this method.

Nonpressure processes.—If coal tar creosote is flooded over the surface of thoroughly air-seasoned southern pine posts or poles, service life may be extended 1 to 3 years; dipping for a few minutes may extend life 2 to 4 years. It is of little use to brush or spray preservatives over the sides of timbers already in service. **Brushing** and **spraying** are most effective when applied to end-grain surfaces such as pile heads (American Wood Preservers Association 1969, Standard M4–62), or unprotected wood exposed when bolt heads are drilled into treated timbers.

Dipping treatments are advantageous for some specialized purposes such as treating southern pine millwork, sash, doors, or products such as ammunition boxes (Browne 1958; Verrall 1965; Verrall and Scheffer 1969), and protecting green southern pine lumber against stain fungi during air drying (Verrall 1945; Verrall and Mook 1951).

In the **cold soak method,** wood is immersed in an unheated oil solution of the preservative—usually pentachlorophenol. Immersion periods of 2 days to a week or more are desirable to achieve retentions of 2 to 6 pounds of solution per cubic foot in well seasoned southern pine posts; more than half of this absorption takes place in the first 24 hours. Verrall (1965) has reported that the end absorption is about 10 times the lateral absorption; total absorption (for immersions longer than 5 seconds) is linearly correlated with the logarithm of immersion time. If the wood is infected by fungi, absorption may be excessive, i.e., up to 20 pounds per cubic foot.

The **hot and cold bath** (thermal) process has numerous variations. The wood is first heated (in or out of the preservative) to expand the air in the cell lumens and to evaporate surface water. The hot wood is then promptly submerged in cold preservative. Atmospheric pressure forces the preservative into the wood to fill the vacuum formed by contracting water vapor and air in the cold cavities. Salts that are water soluble at high temperatures are useable, but most operators use coal tar creosote and other oils because their slight evaporation does not modify solution strength. When coal tar creosote is used on southern pine, a hot-bath temperature of 220° F. is suitable. The cold bath should be between 150° F. and the temperature at which solids form in the preservative (American Wood Preservers Association 1969, Standard C7–58). Work done by the Texas Forest Service (Downey 1937) showed that small shortleaf and loblolly pine poles so treated had excellent penetrations averaging 2 inches, but the retentions of 18 to 20 pounds per cubic foot were excessive. Retention was reduced to 12.8 pounds per cubic foot with about the same penetration by a 1-hour bath at 220 to 225° F., followed by a 100° F. bath of just sufficient duration to accomplish 1-inch penetration, followed in turn by a 30-minute hot bath. The thermal process can be used for either full-length or butt treatment of poles and posts, as well as for treatment of lumber and timbers.

In the **vacuum processes,** which can accomplish much the same effect as the thermal method just described, the wood is placed in an empty air-tight tank, a vacuum is drawn, and then the preservative is admitted without allowing air to re-enter. Southern pine millwork can be well treated with pentachlorophenol in a volatile solvent by this method.

Blew et al. (1970) reported that retentions of acid copper chromate and pentachlorophenol in southern pine 2 by 6's vacuum treated at 12-percent moisture content were adequate to protect sapwood not in contact with the ground or water, but were marginal for heartwood. The lumber (54- to 57-percent heartwood) was first subjected to an initial vacuum of 27 inches of mercury for ½-hour; the preservative, at 90° F., was then introduced into the treating tank under vacuum. After the specimens were covered with preservative, they remained in the solution for 7½ hours at atmospheric pressure. A recovery, or final, vacuum was not used. The vacuum treatment for pentachlorophenol was similar, except that initial vacuum was only 20 inches, time in preservative was 6½ hours, and a recovery vacuum of 27 inches was held for 1 hour. The acid copper chromate penetrated 13 percent of the heartwood and 93 percent of the sapwood, while the pentachlorophenol penetrated 52 percent of the heartwood and 100 percent of the sapwood. Retentions were maximum in the outer shell and least in the heartwood, as follows[1]:

Chemical and assay zone	Heartwood	Sapwood	Entire cross section
	– – – – Pounds per cubic foot – – – –		
Acid copper chromate			
Entire cross section			0.68
Outer ⅛-inch	0.34	1.89	
⅛- to ⅜-inch	.06	1.16	
⅜- to ⅝-inch	.00	.54	
Core	.00	.18	

Chemical and assay zone	Heartwood	Sapwood	Entire cross section
	– – – – *Pounds per cubic foot* – – – –		
Five-percent pentachloro-phenol in heavy petroleum oil			
Entire cross section _____	_____	_____	.44
Outer ⅛-inch _____	.21	.46	
⅛- to ⅜-inch _____	.15	.36	
⅜- to ⅝-inch _____	.16	.33	
Core _____	.18	.38	

Blew et al. (1970), on the basis of comparative tests, concluded that penetration in vacuum treatment is significantly less than in pressure treatment.

There are a number of **diffusion processes.** In the steeping method green wood is submerged in a tank containing a strong (e.g., 10 percent) salt solution. Absorption takes places over a period of days or weeks by diffusion; the solution concentration in the tank decreases as the chemical diffuses into the green wood.

In a number of other diffusion processes the preservative is applied to the surface of green wood. In the **Osmose process** the preservative is applied in paste form, and the wood is stacked in covered solid piles; in the bandage method a bandage impregnated with salt preservative is wrapped tightly around the green timber; in one process the preservative is inserted in holes bored in green wood.

The **barrel method** of diffusion treatment of pine posts was developed by Clemson Agricultural College (Barker et al. 1950). Green, freshly trimmed posts, with or without bark, are placed butt end down in a waterborne preservative such as chromated zinc chloride. A gallon of solution containing 2 pounds of zinc chloride treats two average posts. About 1 pound of dry preservative per cubic foot is retained if posts stand in the preservative 4 days and then (after a 1-inch slice is cut from the top end) stand top down in the solution for 3 more days. After treating, posts are stored vertically, with tops down, for several weeks to further distribute the preservative.

In the **double diffusion method,** two soluble chemicals, which react to form preservative salts highly resistant to leaching, are separately diffused into the wood. Stake tests with southern pine in Mississippi (Blew and Davidson 1969) have shown good results from high retentions of copper chromate and copper arsenate; green wood is soaked in a solution of copper sulfate and then in a solution containing sodium chromate and sodium arsenate. Other chemicals can be used similarly. Baechler and Roth (1964) have reviewed results gained from 23 years of experiments with the double-diffusion method.

There are numerous treatments which, if well done, will prolong the life of standing poles 5 or 6 years. They have in common the steps of digging the earth away from the pole to a depth of 18 inches, inspection to see if remaining sound wood justifies the treatment, removal of dirt and decayed wood from the pole, and finally application of the preservative. In the **Osmoplastic process,** a thick coat of preservative is brushed over the cleaned surface and wrapped with a waterproof film before backfilling. The preservative is said to be 3.5 percent dinitrophenol, 2.2 percent pentachlorophenol, 2.5 percent bichromate, 45.8 percent sodium fluoride, and 46.0 percent oils, solvents, bodying agents, binding substances, or inerts (Hunt and Garratt 1967).

In the **Cobra process,** a hollow, tube-like needle is used to inject measured amounts of preservative paste at carefully spaced intervals around the pole, 1½ feet above and below the groundline. The preservative is said to be 23 percent arsenious anhydride, 23 percent dinitrophenol, 47 percent sodium fluoride, and 7 percent oils, solvents, bodying agents, binding substances, or inert (Hunt and Garratt 1967).

Only two of the many processes have been briefly described; others may be as effective.

PRESERVATION OF PARTICULAR PRODUCTS [1]

Some combinations of preservatives and treating processes are particularly suited for certain products. While other procedures may be equally effective, a number of preservative systems used widely for southern pine products are highlighted below. Applicable process standards are mentioned where appropriate. Where abbreviations for waterborne preservatives are used, the components can be found in section 22–1 under the paragraph heading: *Waterborne preservatives.*

Logs, bolts, cordwood, and pulp chips.—Water sprays afford temporary protection to logs and bolts (sec. 18–1) and cordwood (sec. 18–2) in storage. Section 16–6 briefly describes deterioration of pulp chips in outside storage; section 18–3 and figure 18–3 describe constructions details for chip piles and the conditions that prevail inside the pile after several months of storage.

Piling[1].—Checks that develop during air-seasoning make it difficult to devise an economical treatment to prevent fungi from reaching untreated wood in piles and poles stacked for air-drying. Panek (1963) found that a soak of at least 15 minutes in 30 percent ammonium bifluoride protected southern pine poles for 1 year during air-seasoning. Hunt and Garratt (1967) state that no convenient and inexpensive method of protecting poles and piles during air-seasoning is yet in general use; one plant has gone so far as to run green material into a treating cylinder for a brief pressure impregnation with waterborne preservative.

Piles for marine use are given full-cell pressure treatment. Federal Specification TT–W–571i requires deeper penetrations and heavier retention for severe exposure conditions. For use in coastal waters, 25-pound retention (measured by assay) of creosote-coal tar solutions (Fed. Spec. TT–C–650) in the outer 3 inches is required. Piles for land or fresh water use are required to have a 12-pound retention (in the outer 3 inches) of:

      1. Coal tar creosote (Fed. Spec. TT–C–645 or TT–C–655),
or 2. Creosote-coal tar solution (Fed. Spec. TT–C–650),
or 3. Creosote-petroleum solution (Fed. Spec. TT–W–568).

Piles for land or fresh water use under Federal Specification TT–W–571i may also be treated with a 4.5- to 5.5-percent solution of pentachlorophenol (Fed. Spec. 570) in heavy petroleum solvent (conforming to American Wood Preservers Association Standard P9) to an assayed retention in the outer 2 inches of 0.6 pound per cubic foot.

Commercial Standard CS250–62 for preservative-treated marine piles calls for a retention of not less than 25 pounds per cubic foot of creosote-coal tar solution in the outer 3 inches of each pile based on assay of borings. The preservative is required to penetrate at least the outer 4 inches and at least 90 percent of the sapwood of each pile.

The American Wood Preservers Association (1969, C3–69) calls for different treatments depending on the exposure. For all piling, however, initial steaming of the piles is limited to 20 hours at a temperature not to exceed 245° F.; the vacuum must be at least 22 inches of mercury, and the preservative temperature cannot exceed 220° F., with no time limit on immersion. Preservative pressure must be at least 125 p.s.i. but cannot exceed 200 p.s.i., and expansion-bath temperature cannot exceed 220° F. Final steaming is not permitted on marine piles and is limited to 3 hours at a maximum temperature of 245° F. for land and fresh-water piles.

For areas of extreme marine borer hazard, the American Wood Preservers Association (1969, C3–69) calls for two pressure treatments in sequence. In the first, a 1-inch penetration of certain waterborne salt mixtures, i.e., ACA or CCA, with retention (measured by assay) of 1.0 pound per cubic foot, is required. The second required treatment with creosote (American Wood Preservers Association Standard P1 or P13) or creosote-coal tar solution (Standard P2 or P12) calls for penetration of 4 inches or 90 percent of the sapwood and a retention of 20 pounds per cubic foot in the outer 1-inch zone as determined by assay.

For marine piles in areas of moderate and severe borer hazard AWPA Standard C3–68 calls for a single treatment with either creosote or creosote-coal tar solution to achieve penetration of 4 inches or 90 percent of the sapwood. Retention required in the outer 3 inches (measured by assay) is 25 pounds per cubic foot where borer hazard is severe and 20 pounds where hazard is moderate.

For land and fresh-water piles, AWPA Standard C3–68 calls for penetration of 3.5-inch depth or 90 percent of the sapwood. Retention in the outer 1 inch (measured by assay) is required to be 20 pounds per cubic foot with creosote or creosote-coal tar solution.

Poles[1].—Federal Specification TT–W–571i calls for retention of 10 pounds per cubic foot of coal tar creosote (Fed. Spec. TT–C–645 or TT–C–655) in the zone 0.5 to 2 inches from the surface. Alternatively, a 5-percent solution of pentachlorophenol can be used to give a retention of 0.38 or 0.45 pound of dry chemical per cubic foot in the same assay zone; the higher retention is required for poles over 37.5 inches in circumference, for poles in severe service, or for poles costly to replace.

Specification C4–69 (American Wood Preservers Association 1969) for pressure-treated southern pine poles limits initial steaming (245° F. maximum) to 17 hours for poles having a circumference 6 feet from the butt of less than 37.5 inches; if the circumference is more than 37.5 inches, 20 hours of steaming is the limit. A vacuum of at least 22 inches is specified. Maximum preservative temperature is 220° F. with no time limit on immersion. Pressure during treatment cannot exceed 200 p.s.i.; expansion-bath temperature cannot exceed 220° F., and final steaming must not exceed 2 hours at 245° F. or 3 hours at 240° F. Creosote-treated poles must have retentions of 6, 7.5, or 9 pounds per cubic foot measured by assay in the shell 0.5 to 2.0 inches from the surface; the higher retentions are for large poles or severe service conditions. Similarly, with pentachlorophenol in oil, retentions must be 0.30, 0.38, or 0.45 pound per cubic foot measured by assay. With either creosote or pentachlorophenol, the sapwood penetrations corresponding to the three levels of retention must be 2.5 inches or 85 percent, 3.0 inches or 90 percent, and 3.5 inches or 90 percent.

The American Wood Preservers Association (1969, C23–69) further provides a standard for poles in pole building construction. It cautions that where maximum service life is of primary importance, waterborne preservatives are not recommended for use under severe service conditions. Retentions are recommended:

Preservative	Retention
	Pounds per cubic foot
Creosote	8.00
Creosote-coal tar	8.00
Pentachlorophenol	0.40
ACA	0.40
CCA	0.40

In addition to the above, parallel standards include American Society for Testing and Materials, ASTM D1760–62T; and Rural Electrification Administration Specifications PE–9 (telephone) and DT5C (electric).

The foregoing specifications are for pressure processes. The hot-and-cold bath method also gives good results with southern pine poles. (See page 1092 for schedule.)

Posts[1].—The studies by Blew and Davidson (1967) and by Blew and Kulp (1964) provide data specific to the performance of southern pine posts. The results are summarized in section 22–1 (WOOD PRESERVATIVES, *Effectiveness in ground or fresh water*).

Federal Specification TT–W–571i lists preservatives, specification numbers, and retentions as shown in table 22–5. Retentions for the waterborne chemicals are for solid preservative.

The American Wood Preservers Association (1969, C5–69) standard for pressure treatment of southern pine posts limits initial steaming (245° F. maximum) to not over 10 hours. Vacuum must be not less than 22 inches of mercury. Preservative temperature must not exceed 220° F. at pressures between 75 and 200 p.s.i. Expansion-bath temperature must not exceed 220° F.; final steaming cannot exceed a temperature of 245° F. or a time of 3 hours. Penetration must be at least 2 inches or 85 percent of the sapwood. Retentions required by assay in the outer 1-inch shell or by gauge are as follows:

Preservative	Retention
	Pounds per cubic foot
Creosote and creosote solutions	
Creosote	6.00
Creosote-coal tar	6.00
Creosote-petroleum	7.00
Oilborne preservatives	
Pentachlorophenol	.30
Waterborne preservatives	
ACC	.50
ACA	.40
CCA	.40
CuCZA	.54
CZC	.62
FCAP	.32

Retentions required by Federal specification are listed in table 22–5. Commercial Standard CS235–61 applies to posts treated with creosote and creosote solutions and parallels the Federal specification.

While the empty-cell process is generally considered the most effective treating procedure for posts, double diffusion, hot-and-cold bath, and the barrel method developed by Clemson Agricultural College can also give good results (Blew and Champion 1967).

TABLE 22–5.—*Preservatives and minimum retentions listed for round posts in Federal Specification T T-W-571i*

Preservative and Federal specification		Retention
		Pounds per cubic foot[1]
Coal tar creosote	TT–6–645	6–15
Creosote-coal tar solutions	TT–C–650	6
Creosote-petroleum solution	TT–W–568	7
Pentachlorophenol equivalent to 5 percent in petroleum oil (AWPA Standard P9)	TT–W–570	0.3–0.75
Acid copper chromate	TT–W–546	1.00
Ammoniacal copper arsenite	TT–W–549	0.45–0.75
Chromated copper arsenate Type I	TT–W–550	0.75–1.2
Chromated copper arsenate Type II	TT–W–550	0.45–0.75

[1] First number applies to fenceposts; second to building posts.

Lumber and timbers[1].—Unless promptly kiln-dried, green southern pine needs **protection against stain** fungi until the wood is dry. Extensive tests on chemical control of fungi in green lumber during air-seasoning by Scheffer and Lindgren (1940) led to the general adoption by the lumber industry of certain organic mercurials and chlorinated phenolates for fungicidal treatment of green lumber. These are normally applied to southern pine by 5- to 10-second dips in water solutions. Table 22–6 lists principal chemicals used and concentrations considered "full strength" [1]. The information on mercurial fungicides, some of which may not be currently registered for use to control stain fungi, is included because of its importance in the record of research on the subject; also, some of the trade products mentioned may no longer be available, but research data pertinent to them are included for similar reasons[1].

Literature on control of fungi during air-seasoning was reviewed by Verrall (1945). Later Verrall and Mook (1951) appraised the effectiveness of chemicals and mixtures of chemicals for controlling fungi in green lumber and concluded (see table 22–6 for details of full-strength formulations) [1]:

- Among the commercial products available in 1951 (table 22–6), only those containing sodium pentachlorophenate, sodium tetrachlorophenate, or ethyl mercuric phosphate were effective in small-scale tests. All of the materials that have been thoroughly tested are known to have some disadvantages.

- Sodium pentachlorophenate is generally effective against all fungi, but at the usual lumber-dipping concentration it is irritating to the skin, especially at the concentrations needed for very moist situations or for timbers or surfaced lumber.

- Ethyl mercuric phosphate is effective against all fungi except the mold *Penicillium*. At recommended concentrations this product apparently has caused little skin irritation, but the dry powder can cause severe burns.

- Sodium pentachlorophenate ½ strength plus borax ³⁄₁₆ strength was almost as effective as full-strength sodium pentachlorophenate alone. It is much less irritating to the skin than the latter.

- Sodium pentachlorophenate ¼ strength plus ethyl mercuric phosphase ½ was highly effective in limited testing.

- Sodium pentachlorophenate ¼ strength plus borax ⅐ plus soda ¹⁄₂₀ has low skin-irritating tendencies and has given good mold control. In stain control it was less effective on pine under severe conditions, probably because of the low phenolate content. Use of increased concentrations during the warm, wet months should overcome this difficulty.

● Sodium tetrachlorophenate is effective on southern hardwoods and certain west coast coniferous woods, but not on southern pine. It is less irritating to the skin than the pentachlorophenate. Unless planed subsequent to treatment, wood treated with tetrachlorophenate and used for food containers is more likely to impart objectionable odor and taste to certain foods than wood treated with other chemicals.

With the exception of the commercial product containing ethyl mercuric phosphate plus sodium pentachlorophenate, all the commercial products occasionally failed to prevent mold or stain under severe conditions.

The frequency of such prevention failures can be reduced, along with the skin irritation of the phenolates and the mold hazard of the mercurials, by using mixtures of sodium pentachlorophenate with ethyl mercuric phosphate or borax, or with both of these. Performance of the mixtures was as follows:

● Mixtures of ethyl mercuric phosphate and borax appeared to retain the mold hazard of the mercurial alone and showed little or no promise of superior stain control.

● Mixtures of sodium pentachlorophenate and borax at the higher concentrations of sodium pentachlorophenate ¼ or ½, plus borax ⅜, or higher strengths, prevented objectionable stain. When both effectiveness and bulk are considered, the commercial product containing sodium pentachlorophenate ½ plus borax ³⁄₁₆ appeared to be the most efficient mixture of this type. Its advantage was was that it reduced skin irritation even though it was not superior in controlling stain.

TABLE 22–6.—*Chemicals used in dip treatments to control fungi in green lumber* (after Verrall and Mook 1951, p. 8)

Chemical	Trade name	Composition of commercial product[1]	Full strength, amount per 50 gallons
Mercurials:			
Ethyl mercuric phosphate.	Lignasan_____	6.25 percent ethyl mercuric phosphate plus 93.75 percent inerts (metallic mercury 4.79 percent).	1 pound (.015 percent mercurial).
Other organic mercurials.	_____	_____	.015 percent mercurial.

Table 22–6.—*Chemicals used in dip treatments to control fungi in green lumber* (after Verrall and Mook 1951, p. 8)—Continued

Chemical	Trade name	Composition of commercial product[1]	Full strength, amount per 50 gallons
Chlorinated phenolates:			
Sodium pentachlorophenate.	Dowicide G or Santobrite.	75 percent sodium pentachlorophenate plus 13 percent of other chlorophenates, and excess alkali.	4 pounds[2]
Other chlorophenolates.	Various Dowicides_	------------------	----Do[3]-------
Adjuvants:			
Borax_____	_____	Technical powdered borax.	16 pounds
Soda_____	_____	Mixture of technical sodium carbonate and sodium bicarbonate.	29 pounds
Commercial products__ {	Permatox 10s_____	Technical sodium pentachlorophenate 40 percent, plus borax 60 percent.[4]	5 pounds
	Noxtane_____	Technical sodium pentachlorophenate 20 percent, borax 48 percent, and soda 29 percent.[5]	----Do-------
	Melsan_____	Technical sodium pentachlorophenate 50 percent, ethyl mercuric phosphate 1.56 percent, inerts 48.44 percent.	2 pounds.

[1] Composition based mainly on data from container labels. In some instances these data were modified by further information received from the manufacturers.

[2] Dowicide G and Santobrite are ordinarily used at the rate of 3.5 pounds per 50 gallons. In most of the tests 3.5 pounds were used in reference treatments, but in some early tests 4 pounds were used. Because there was very little difference in the effectiveness of the two concentrations, both were included as "full strength." All reduced concentrations in mixtures are expressed as fractions of 4 pounds.

[3] In commercial practice the various chlorophenolates are used at rates of 3 to 4 pounds per 50 gallons. However, for these tests full strength was considered 4 pounds in all cases, so that all would be comparable to sodium pentachlorophenate.

[4] After these tests were started, the composition of Permatox 10s was changed to technical sodium pentachlorophenate 35 percent, plus borax 65 percent.

[5] The manufacturers stated that the proportions of the ingredients are being changed.

- Mixtures of sodium pentachlorophenate and ethyl mercuric phosphate are superior stain-control treatments, give good mold control, are low in bulk, and have low skin-irritating properties. Stain control might be better if relatively higher mercurial content was used in the winter and higher phenolate content in the summer, but the advantage probably would not be great. Mixtures containing equal relative proportions of the two seem best.

Mixtures containing ¼ strengths of each component were about equal in effectiveness to full-strength sodium pentachlorophenate, while those containing ⅜ or ½ strengths of each component were superior. The latter two never allowed objectionable amounts of stain in any open-piled test. The commercial mixture (ethyl mercuric phosphate ½ plus sodium pentachlorophenate ¼) was about equal in effectiveness to the ⅜ plus ⅜ mixture, but it did not show the high degree of superiority that the ½ plus ½ mixture did.

- Mixtures containing sodium pentachlorophenate, ethyl mercuric phosphate, and borax also showed considerable promise. The ⅛ plus ⅛ plus ⅜ was equal to full-strength sodium pentachlorophenate in average effectiveness and in the percentage of tests with objectionable stain. The ³⁄₁₆ plus ³⁄₁₆ plus ³⁄₁₆ and the ¼ plus ¼ plus ³⁄₁₆ mixtures averaged more effective than the full-strength sodium pentachlorophenate and only slightly exceeded the latter in bulk (3.9 pounds and 4.2 pounds, respectively, per 50 gallons compared to 3.5 pounds recommended by manufacturers for the pentachlorophenate alone). The ¼ plus ¼ plus ³⁄₁₆ mixture never allowed objectionable stain in any open-piled test; the ³⁄₁₆ plus ³⁄₁₆ plus ³⁄₁₆ mixture in this respect was equal to the ⅛ plus ⅛ plus ⅜ mixture. There was no indication in the test data that increasing the borax concentrations beyond ³⁄₁₆ strength added to the effectiveness of the ³⁄₁₆ plus ³⁄₁₆ plus borax or the ¼ plus ¼ plus borax mixtures. The triplex mixtures afford a high degree of fungus control at very low concentrations of phenolate, with resultant low skin-irritation hazard.

When seasoning conditions are abnormally severe for short periods, any of the commercially available treatments are less likely to fail if concentrations are increased. Under such conditions the use of commercial mixtures seems preferable to the use of increased concentrations of phenolates or mercurials alone. With mixtures, superior effectiveness can be attained without increasing skin irritation or mold hazard.

As far as could be determined from the few tests made and from observations at mills, the chemical protection of large, sawed timbers presents no special problem. With good handling practices and treating solutions 1.5 to 2 times as strong as used on 1-inch lumber, satisfactory protection should result for the periods timbers are usually held at mills.

All the treatments tested lost some effectiveness when the treated wood was subjected to leaching immediately after dipping. If washing was delayed until an hour after treating, the effect of leaching was remarkably small. Protection of treated lumber from rainwash is most needed immediately after dipping at the green chain.

Preservative treatments for lumber and timbers in use, as required by Federal Specification TT–W–571i, are listed, with minimum retentions, in table 22–7 [1]. With pentachlorophenol (Fed. Spec. TT–W–570) retention of 0.3 pound of solid preservative per cubic foot is required for lumber or timbers not in contact with ground or water; 0.5 retention is specified for use in fresh water or in ground contact.

The American Wood Preservers Association (1969, C2–69) standard for lumber, timber, and ties treated by pressure processes limits initial steaming (245° F. maximum) to not over 17 hours. Vacuum must not be less than 22 inches of mercury. Preservative and expansion-bath temperature cannot exceed 220° F., with no limitation on duration of immersion. If the wood is to be exposed in coastal waters, no final steaming is permitted; otherwise, up to 2 hours at not over 240° F. is allowed.

Retentions measured by assay, gauge, or weight are specified for creosote, creosote-coal tar solutions, and creosote-petroleum solutions.

Use	Retention
	Pounds per cubic foot
Coastal waters	20 (full cell with creosote or creosote-coal tar; creosote-petroleum not recommended)
Soil contact	8
Above ground	6

Pentachlorophenol in oil is not suitable for coastal waters; specifications of the American Wood Preservers Association call for dry-chemical retention of 0.4 pound per cubic foot when in soil contact and 0.3 pound when above ground.

Retentions of waterborne preservatives (measured by assay, gauge, or weight) are specified as follows:

Preservative	Above ground	Soil contact
	Pounds of solid chemical per cubic foot	
ACC	0.25	not recommended
ACA	.23	0.40
CCA	.23	.40
CuCZA	.27	not recommended
CZC	.46	not recommended
FCAP	.22	not recommended

In this specification for lumber and timbers, the preservative must penetrate 2.5 inches or 85 percent of the sapwood.

Crossties [1].—In 1967, 5 percent of the 23.4 million crossties and 4 percent of the 97.3 million bd. ft. of switch ties treated in the United States were southern pine.

TABLE 22–7.—*Preservatives and minimum retentions listed for lumber and timbers in Federal Specification TT-W-571i*

Preservative and Federal specification		In coastal waters	In fresh water, in contact with the ground, or for important structural members not in contact with ground or water	Not in contact with ground or water[1]
		— — — — Pounds per cubic foot — — — —		
Coal tar creosote	TT–6–645 or TT–6–655	22	10	6
Creosote-coal tar solutions	TT–C–650	22	10	6
Creosote-petroleum solution	TT–W–568	------	12	7
Pentachlorophenol equivalent to 5 percent in petroleum oil (AWPA Standard P9)	TT–W–570	------	0.5	0.3
Pentachlorophenol in solution with light petroleum solvent (AWPA Standard P9)	TT–W–570	------	------------	0.3
Pentachlorophenol in solution with volatile petroleum solvent (AWPA Standard P9)	TT–W–570	------	------------	0.3
Acid copper chromate	TT–W–546	------	------------	0.50–1.00
Ammoniacal copper arsenite	TT–W–549	------	------------	0.25–0.45
Chromated copper arsenate type I	TT–W–550	------	------------	0.40–0.75
Chromated copper arsenate type II	TT–W–550	------	------------	0.25–.045
Chromated zinc chloride	TT–W–551	------	------------	0.75–1.00
Fluor-chrome arsenate phenol mixture	TT–W–535	------	------------	0.35–0.50

[1] Where two figures are given, the second applies to exposure to occasional rain-wetting but not to contact with the ground (except for items of low replacement cost).

Federal Specification MM–T–371d for ties calls for treatment as outlined in TT–W–571i and AWPA Standard C6–67.

Preservative	Federal specification	Minimum retention
		Pounds per cubic foot
Coal tar creosote	TT–C–645 or TT–C–655	8
Creosote-coal tar solutions	TT–C–650	8
Creosote-petroleum solution	TT–W–568	8

An American Wood Preservers Association (1969, C2–69) Standard covers bridge ties and mine ties; these specifications are the same as their standards just cited for *Lumber and timbers.*

An American Wood Preservers Association (1969, C6–67) Standard applies to crossties and switch ties. Crossties under this Standard may be air-dried, kiln-dried, dried by boiling in oil at a temperature from 170 to 210° F. at a vacuum of not less than 22 inches of mercury, or by vapor drying (see sec. 20–7) with a suitable organic solvent having a boiling point between 270 and 340° F. In the vapor-drying process the temperature of the effluent vapor and water-vapor mixture coming from the cylinder should be in the range from 240 to 260° F.; drying should not be continued below 25-percent moisture content, and after drying, a vacuum of at least 22 inches of mercury should be pulled on the retort (through the condenser) for not less than an hour.

Under this standard of the American Wood Preservers Association (1969, C6–67), southern pine crossties and switch ties can be steam conditioned at a temperature not to exceed 245° F. for not more than 18 hours. If the full-cell process is used, vacuum must exceed 22 inches of mercury. Preservative temperature during the pressure period must average 180° F. but not exceed 210° F., and pressure must be between 50 and 200 p.s.i. Retentions of 8 pounds per cubic foot are in general use for creosote, creosote-coal tar solutions, and creosote-petroleum solutions. For 5-percent pentachlorophenol solutions in oil, a retention of 0.4 pound of solid chemical per cubic foot is in general use. The preservative must penetrate 2.5 inches or 85 percent of the sapwood.

Laminated wood [1].—Federal Specification TT–W–572i specifies that laminated timbers and laminates prior to gluing can be treated with coal tar creosote, creosote-coal tar solution, or creosote-petroleum solution; retention by assay in the 0- to ⅝-inch zone to be 6 pounds per cubic foot if a minor member not in contact with ground or water, and 12 pounds if in contact with fresh water or ground or if an important structural member not in contact with the ground or water. If pentachlorophenol is used, retentions of dry chemical under comparable conditions are set at 0.3 and 0.6 pound. Retentions specified for waterborne preservatives are the same as those stated for lumber.

An American Wood Preservers Association (1969, C28–69) Standard covers preservative treatment of glued laminated wood, as well as the laminations prior to treatment. Pressure during treatment of glued wood must not exceed 150 p.s.i., and final steaming is permitted for a total of 3 hours at a temperature not to exceed 240° F. With southern pine, a retention (in a zone 0 to 3 inches from the edge of interior laminates) of 6 pounds per cubic foot for service above ground and 12 pounds for ground contact is required for creosote or creosote-coal tar solutions; creosote-petroleum solutions are not recommended. Retention in pounds of dry pentachlorophenol per cubic foot is specified at 0.3 (above ground) or

0.6 (ground contact). The preservative must penetrate 3 inches or 90 percent of the beam.

Individual laminations treated before gluing should be made oversize so that after treatment (including drying) they can be surfaced to the desired dimension. The full-cell process is recommended for waterborne preservatives; preservative oils should be applied by the process that assures the most uniform penetration with the retention specified. Treating pressure cannot exceed 150 p.s.i.; final steaming is permitted for a total of 3 hours at a temperature not to exceed 240° F. Specified retentions (by assay) in a zone 0.5 to 1.0 inch from the edge of laminates are:

Preservative	Above ground	Ground contact
	— — — — *Pounds per cubic foot* — — — —	
Creosote	6	12
Creosote-coal tar	6	12
Creosote petroleum	not recommended	not recommended
Pentachlorophenol	0.30	0.60
ACA	.23	.40
ACC	.25	not recommended
CCA	.23	.40
CZC	.46	not recommended
FCAP	.22	not recommended

The preservative is required to penetrate 3 inches or 90 percent of the volume of the lamination.

Plywood [1].—Federal Specification TT–W–571i specifies treatment of plywood with coal tar creosote at 10 pounds per cubic foot if in contact with the ground, and 6 pounds if not in contact with ground or water. If pentachlorophenol is used under similar conditions, retentions of dry chemical at 0.5 and 0.3 pound per cubic foot are specified. Retentions of waterborne salts identical with those for lumber are required.

An American Wood Preservers Association (1969, C9–69) Standard covers the preservative treatment (by pressure processes) of southern pine plywood glued with waterproof adhesives. Full-cell treatment is recommended with waterborne preservatives, but preservative oils should be applied by the process that assures the most uniform penetration with the retention specified. Pressure during treatment must not exceed 150 p.s.i. Final moisture content of the plywood should approximate that which the product will attain in use.

Retentions, as determined by assay taken 12 inches from any edge, are specified:

Preservative	Above ground	Soil or water contact
	− − − − *Pounds per cubic foot* − − − −	
Preservative oils		
Creosote_____	6.00	10.00
Pentachlorophenol_____	.30	.50
Waterborne preservatives		
ACA_____	.23	.40
ACC_____	.25	not recommended
CCA_____	.23	.40
CZC_____	.46	not recommended
FCAP_____	.22	not recommended

The Standard requires that each veneer be penetrated as observed in borings taken 12 inches from panel edge.

For use in coastal waters, creosote is required (at a retention of 25 pounds per cubic foot).

Crossarms.—An American Wood Preservers Association (1969, C25–65) Standard covers southern pine crossarms treated by pressure processes. The empty-cell method is required. With creosote, retentions of 6, 8, or 10 pounds per cubic foot are required depending on severity of service. Similarly, the levels of dry pentachlorophenol retention are 0.3, 0.4, and 0.5 pound per cubic foot.

Millwork and other wood requiring clean treatment.—The preservative treatment of millwork such as sash, doors, siding, bleacher seats, and exposed decking should leave the surface clean and paintable. Blew and Panek (1964) reviewed the problems encountered in the production of clean pressure-treated wood and defined the objectives of a clean treatment as follows:

> Specifically, where the treated wood is to be finished with a paint or varnish, the preservative should not interfere with these coatings. Where treated lumber or veneer is to be used in manufacturing laminated timber or plywood, the preservative should not interfere with the gluing operation. Where treated lumber is used in buildings, the preservative should not cause an objectionable odor, contribute to staining of adjacent materials such as flooring, plaster, and wallpaper, or should not cause softening and dripping of asphalt in roofing materials. For treating outdoor decks, boardwalks, seating, and tables, there should not be an objectionable powdery surface residue, and wood surfaces should not be too sticky or oily to paint over or for people to walk or sit on.

So-called clean, nonswelling, paintable, water-repellent preservatives containing principally pentachlorophenol, have been used successfully since 1938 for the treatment of window sash and related millwork (Lance 1958). For such treatment, the preservative and water-repellent components are dissolved in solvents of the mineral-spirits type, often with limited amounts of supplementary solvents such as naphtha, kerosene, light fuel oil, or diesel oil. Small amounts of waxes are added to provide increased water repellency or to prevent recrystallization of pentachlorophenol on the surface of the treated wood after drying. Federal Specification TT–W–572 describes this class of preservative, which usually contains not less than 5-percent pentachlorophenol by weight.

Preservative is applied by brief immersion (3-minute dip or light vacuum), resulting in retentions of approximately 10 gallons of solution per M b.f. or less than 1 pound (dry) per cubic foot. No oil-treating solution will always yield paintable treated wood. Wood with normal absorptions from short-period dips can be painted safely after 24 to 48 hours of drying, but an occasional board will absorb excessive oil, which will bleed through subsequently applied paint unless unusually long drying time is provided (Verrall 1965). Commercial Standard CS 262–63 describes the treatment required in terms of National Woodwork Manufacturers Association test method NWMA–M–2.

Millwork treatments are not adequate for uses that require a high degree of protection against decay fungi and subterranean termites (Blew 1967).

A specification of the Vacuum Wood Preservers Institute covering treatments of wood for use in buildings has been published (Wier 1958, p. 95). Under this specification the dry wood is placed in an initial vacuum; the vacuum is then released and the wood soaked in preservative at atmospheric pressure. Finally, the preservative is drained and a final vacuum applied to remove excess preservative. Retention of water-repellent preservative (Federal Specification TT–W–572) is specified:

Desired properties	Retention of liquid
	Pounds per cubic foot
High preservative value and paintable 14 days after treatment	2
Lower preservative value but paintable 24 to 48 hours after treatment	1

Vacuum treating (of products not damaged by bleeding) with pentachlorophenol (Federal Specification TT–W–570) dissolved in heavy petroleum oil is also covered by this Specification; it calls for a retention of 6 pounds per cubic foot and penetration of 2½ inches or 85 percent of sapwood depth.

Pressure treatments of southern pine with pentachlorophenol and water repellents in light petroleum distillates have been used overseas with some success by the Department of Defense for protection from fungi and termites. Domestic users have had difficulty evaporating excess solvent to make pressure-treated wood clean and paintable. The problem of achieving cleanliness with a high degree of protection is not yet entirely solved. In southern pine pressure treated by the empty-cell process, Panek (1968) found best paintability from post-treatment conditioning by solvent recovery followed by an emulsion paint. The wood was conditioned by three solvent recovery cycles in light aromatic solvent vapor at 280° F.—reached in 30 minutes and held for 30 minutes—followed by a 1-hour vacuum.

The Cellon process of applying pentachlorophenol dissolved in liquefied petroleum gas, and evaporating the gas after pressure impregnation, is a major contribution toward achievement of clean treated wood; time and service tests are needed to fully evaluate its effectiveness.

Treatment with waterborne solutions of salts can result in serviceable, paintable, clean southern pine if certain precautionary steps are taken (Blew and Panek 1964).

- Warp should be controlled by rejecting warp-prone boards prior to treatment, by using quarter-sawed lumber, by placing stickers with precision during redrying, and by restraining the wood during redrying with spring takeup devices or weights on top of the stack.
- Checking of lumber treated with waterborne solutions should be controlled by using proper kiln schedules during redrying.
- Adequate penetration (that will permit surfacing prior to lamination) requires that southern pine wood be kiln-dried or thoroughly air-dried prior to treatment. Kiln-drying of poles greatly improves penetration of ammoniacal copper arsenite and chromated copper arsenate—both effective in contact with the ground.
- Dimensional changes can be avoided if wood is dried before, as well as after, treatment to the moisture content anticipated in use.
- Surface deposits or **bloom** of preservative can be removed by sanding after the deposits harden; bloom can be controlled or prevented by setting pitch in kiln-dried wood prior to treatment, by reducing treating temperatures (e.g., to 100° F.), and by stacking lumber or plywood on edge during treatment to avoid accumulation of surface deposits of sludge. To achieve clean treatment, equipment should be used only for waterborne preservatives and not alternated with oil treatments.
- Discoloration to paint and masonry work under wet conditions is understood to be controlled by omission of dinitrophenol from preservative formulations.

Particleboard [1].—Particleboard is not ordinarily used under conditions where decay hazard is high. Research indicates that if preservative treatment is necessary, 1 to 2 percent of pentachlorophenol (based on the dry weight of particles) added to the resin before blending affords satisfactory protection, without impairing board properties (Stolley 1958).

Fiberboard [1].—It is not usual to install fiberboard in contact with ground or water. Under certain local conditions, however, hazards from decay and insects may be high.

Pentachlorophenol is used as a preservative. Sodium pentachlorophenate is added at the stock chest—usually before sizing—and is precipitated as pentachlorophenol by alum during sizing. Based on ovendry weight of fiber, 0.50 to 0.75 percent of pentachlorophenol provides adequate protection against decay in most exposures where fiberboard is used. Copper pentachlorophenate can also be used; fiberboard for roof construction should have at least 0.25 percent for effective protection (Meyer and Spalding 1958).

Meyer and Spalding (1958) further state that arsenical compounds are cheaper and perhaps a little more effective against termites than pentachlorophenol. When added at the headbox, a retention of 0.60 percent of arsenic trioxide is considered adequate for tropical conditions.

Insulating boards coated with materials containing starch develop spots caused by growth of the fungus *Aspergillus restrictus*. This spotting can be prevented by addition of 0.5 percent pentachlorophenol to the coating (French and Christensen 1969).

Further information on preservation of fiberboard is available in French and Christensen (1958), Merrill and French (1963, 1964, 1965, 1966ab), and Merrill et al. (1965).

22–2 TREATMENT FOR FIRE RETARDATION [1] [4]

Building fire losses in the United States in 1967 totalled 1.7 billion dollars, and almost 12,000 people lost their lives in fires. On a per capita basis, this loss of life is twice that of Canada, four times that of the United Kingdom, and 6½ times that of Japan. Continued high loss of life and property in building fires has resulted in increased interest in fire research and safety, as evidenced by the Fire Research and Safety Act of 1968. Passage of more restrictive building codes is additional evidence of increased concern.

Untreated wood is a relatively fire-safe material for frame and heavy-timber types of construction. Fire safety in the ordinary frame building—with its open interior arrangement—can best be obtained by limitation of flammable contents, care in smoking, proper installation and use of electrical, heating, and cooking equipment, and by installation of adequate exits. Heavy-timber or mill-type construction provides greater endurance to fire than is obtainable with unprotected metal construction. It is possible, however, to expand the uses of wood in building construction by application of fire-retardant treatments which limit surface flammability, rate of heat release, and smoke.

FIRE PERFORMANCE

Related subjects are discussed elsewhere in the text: burning in chapter 26, heat of combustion in section 9–4, thermal degradation in section 15–2, and destructive distillation in section 28–1. In brief, burning of southern pine is accelerated if the wood is dry, of small particle size surrounded by

[4] Sec. 22–2 is expanded from a paper: Eickner, H. W. Fire retardant treatments for southern pine wood. Presented at a Symposium "Utilization of the Southern Pines," Alexandria, La., November 6–8, 1968.

adequate oxygen, of high extractive content, low in density, rough in surface texture, and exposed to high temperature from a sustained exterior heat source in the presence of an ignition flame.

Although fire-retardant treatments have little effect on the rate at which wood chars, they reduce its surface flammability and the amount of heat it contributes during the initial phase of fires. When treated with properly formulated fire-retardant chemicals, southern pine is self extinguishing, i.e., it promptly ceases to flame or glow when the primary source of heat is removed or exhausted.

REASON FOR EFFECTIVENESS OF FIRE RETARDANTS

Among the tentative explanations of how fire-retardant-chemical treatments reduce the flammability of wood are theories that they: (1) decompose to release gases which extinguish the flame; (2) form impervious or insulative layers to prevent pyrolysis and release of flammable gases; (3) improve the thermal conductivity or consume heat to undergo physical and chemical change during pyrolysis which retard the ignition of the wood; or (4) that certain chemical decomposition products restrict the flammability range for the combustible gas-air mixture released above the wood surface. Several of these effects may be involved for some of the retardant systems.

The theory most widely accepted, based on recent basic studies, is that the chemicals decompose just below the normal charring temperatures for wood and release a strong acid or base. These chemical products then react with the wood components, particularly the celllulose and hemicellulose, to dehydrate them during pyrolysis to form carbon and water rather than the normal levoglucosan-tar products which are responsible for the flaming of wood.

METHODS FOR EVALUATION OF FIRE RETARDANTS

A number of standardized methods have been devised for testing performance of materials exposed to fire. Tests, for which data are presented in this section, are described below.

Large-tunnel test ASTM E84.—Surface flammability, the factor chiefly reduced by fire-retardant treatment of southern pine is measured for code-rating purposes by the 25-foot-tunnel method. Details of the test equipment and procedures are given in American Society for Testing and Materials Standard E84. This large-tunnel test exposes a test panel 25 feet long and 20 inches wide to a standard gas flame placed at one end of a box-like tunnel. The test panel forms the ceiling of the otherwise noncombustible chamber so that the impinging flames and hot gases maintain contact with the panel as they move toward the outlet. Rate of flame spread is visually observed through viewing ports along the tunnel. Smoke density is measured in the vent pipe with a photoelectric cell. Temperatures in the panel and in the chamber can also be measured. The performance of the test panel is compared with that of a similar panel made from untreated red oak flooring.

Under this test, untreated southern pine lumber has flame-spread values ranging from 130 to 195 on a scale which rates untreated red oak at 100 and asbestos-cement board at 0 (Underwriters' Laboratories, Inc. 1968, 1969). While treated lumber with a rating below 70 is eligible for listing by Underwriters' Laboratories, Inc., treated southern pine lumber produced by a number of manufacturers is rated at 25 or less in flame spread, heat index, and smoke index. Most of these products also qualify as having rated 25 or less in flame spread in a 30-minute test, and showing "no evidence of significant progressive combustion."

USDA Forest Products Laboratory fire-tube test.—The fire-tube test was developed (Truax and Harrison 1929) as a research tool to screen and evaluate chemicals for effectiveness in retarding fire in wood. The 40-inch-long specimen measures 3/8- by 3/4-inch in cross section and is suspended in a perforated tube from a weight-sensing device at the top (fig. 22–6). A Bunsen burner is placed with the top of the burner 1 inch or less below the specimen so that an 11-inch-high, 1,000° C. flame envelops the lower end of the specimen for 4 minutes. During the test, loss in weight of the specimen and temperature rise at the top of the tube are indicators of the efficiency of the fire retardant. The test procedure is described by the American Society for Testing and Materials Standard E 69. Untreated wood samples generally lose 80 to 90 percent of their weight while temperatures rise to 700 or 800° C. at the top of the tube. In well-treated specimens, weight loss is only 15 to 20 percent, and tube-top temperature seldom exceeds 200° C. (Hunt and Garratt 1967).

Eight-foot tunnel furnace test.—This test, developed by the USDA Forest Products Laboratory, Madison, Wis., is described in detail in American Society for Testing and Materials Method E 286–65T. The test panel (14 inches wide by 8 feet long) is placed face-down within the angle-iron frame of the furnace (fig. 22–7). This positions the specimen to slope lengthwise at 6° from the horizontal, and to slope at 30° across its short dimension. An asbestos-faced cover is then placed over the back of the specimen. Radiant heat is applied to the face of the panel from a stainless-steel partitioning plate within the furnace, which is heated by a gas burner producing 3,400 B.t.u.'s of heat per minute. A small pilot flame at the lower end of the furnace near the panel surface starts the initial flaming.

The test is conducted for 18.4 minutes, the time normally required for the flames to spread from the pilot to the farthest observation port (87 inches) on a standard red oak lumber specimen (density, 39 pounds per cubic foot). The progress of the flame along the face of the specimen is measured, and expressed as a flame-spread index value, I_s, relative to the

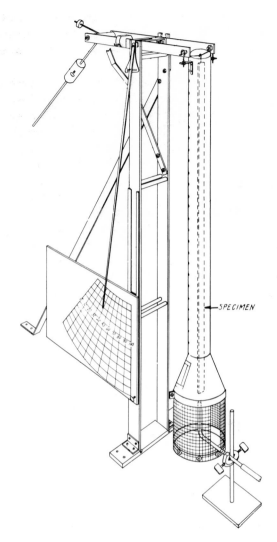

SPECIMEN

2M–26719F

Figure 22–6.—The USDA Forest Products Laboratory fire-tube apparatus developed by M. E. Dunlap. The percentage of loss in specimen weight is indicated by the needle and scale.

flame-spread index for red oak lumber, which is arbitrarily assigned 100 by the relationship:

(1) For flame spread faster than on red oak,

$$I_s = \frac{T_o}{T_s} \times 100 \qquad (22\text{--}1)$$

where T_o is the standard time of 18.4 minutes for the flame to spread the length of a red oak specimen and T_s is the time for flames to spread the same distance on the test specimen.

Figure 22–7.—Specimen side of USDA Forest Products Laboratory 8-foot tunnel furnace. 1, tunnel burner in firebox; 2, ignition burner flow meter; 3, ignition burner; 4, sand to seal cover; 5, angle iron specimen holder; 6, holes in hot plate inset with Meker burner tops; 7, hot plate over firebox; 8, flame progress observation ports; 9, natural draft air inlets; 10, specimen cover; 11, collecting hood for combustion gases and smoke; 12, photoelectric equipment for smoke density measurements; 13, thermocouple for stack temperature measurement. Ports for observation of flame spread are on the back side.

(2) For flame spread slower than on red oak,

$$I_s = \frac{D_s}{D_o} \times 100 \qquad (22\text{--}2)$$

where D_s equals the distance reached by flames on the test specimen in the standard test period of 18.4 minutes, and D_o equals the distance (87 inches) reached by flame on a red oak specimen in the same standard test period.

Smoke density and heat-contribution measurements are also taken throughout the test with a light source and photoelectric smoke meter and with thermocouples embedded in copper rods within the stack of the furnace. Smoke density and heat-contributed index values, I_d and I_c, are computed relative to the red oak standard by comparison with an asbestos millboard specimen:

$$I_d = \frac{A_{ds} - A_{da}}{A_{do} - A_{da}} \times 100 \qquad (22\text{--}3)$$

where A_{ds} equals under the specimen smoke density curve, A_{da} equals area under the asbestos smoke density curve, and A_{do} equals area under red oak smoke density curve; and

$$I_c = \frac{A_{cs} - A_{ca}}{A_{co} - A_{ca}} \times 100 \qquad (22\text{--}4)$$

where A_{cs} equals area under the specimen heat-contributed curve, A_{ca} equals area under the asbestos heat-contributed curve, and A_{co} equals area under the red oak heat-contributed curve.

Schlyter panel test.—In this test two panels ($11\frac{7}{8}$ inches by 31 inches) are supported 2 inches apart, vertically, as shown in figure 22–8, with the bottom of the one panel 4 inches above the other. For the severe test, fire exposure is supplied by a modified No. 4 Meker burner, consuming

Figure 22–8.—The Schlyter-panel apparatus for the severe fire test. (Photo from Eickner and Schaffer 1967.)

natural gas at 18,000 B.t.u.'s per hour. The burner is inserted between the panels, near their lower ends and midway between the panel edges. The vertical height of flames is recorded at 15-second intervals during 3 minutes of exposure. The burner is then removed and the time for flaming and glowing to cease is recorded. An average flame height is calculated, based on the differences between the original height of flaming and subsequent observations during the 3-minute period. An average flame height of 12 inches or less in this test usually indicates an effective chemical treatment.

Comparability.—Each of the four tests measures somewhat different aspects of flammability than the others; generally, results of one test cannot be accurately estimated in terms of the others. Relationships between flame-spread index determined by the FPL 8-foot tunnel furnace and severe Schlyter test values vary with chemicals; they are not well defined for the most effective treatments. Relations between fire-tube weight losses and flame-spread indices are not well defined in the lower range of flammability (Eickner and Schaffer 1967). Data from the large-tunnel test are required by most agencies as a basis for code ratings. The other, less expensive, tests are widely used in research on the effectiveness of fire retardants.

Test procedures for measurement of amount of smoke from wood products under controlled fire exposure are still under development. Readers interested in optical measurement techniques will find Brenden's (1970) discussion useful.

IMPREGNATION WITH FIRE RETARDANTS

Two methods are available for treating wood with fire retardants. One method calls for impregnating the wood with waterborne chemicals. In the second method, fire-retardant coatings are painted on the surface. Of the two, impregnation is usually more effective and lasting. Impregnation is used, therefore, when treating materials prior to construction. For wood in existing structures, surface application of fire-retardant paint is the principal process.

In the impregnation treatment, a waterborne chemical is pressure injected into the wood using full-cell methods and equipment similar to those for pressure preservative treatments. Retentions of fire-retardant chemicals must be fairly high to be effective, ranging from 2.5 to 5.0 pounds of dry chemical per cubic foot of wood near the surface. For wood to be recognized as equal to "noncombustible" materials, the fire retardant must completely penetrate all sections.

As southern pine is easily treated, it is very suitable for fire-retardant treatments requiring deep penetration. It is not normally necessary to incise the surface to improve penetration; but pieces containing high-density heartwood should be excluded, as they are difficult to treat.

Southern pine lumber to be pressure treated is seasoned or kiln-dried, and then subjected to a vacuum applied for 30 minutes to 1 hour. The fire-retardant solution, usually at a concentration of 12 to 18 percent, is then introduced to completely immerse the charge of wood, and pressure is applied to reach 150 p.s.i. within 30 minutes. This pressure is maintained until solution refusal; from 1.5 to 3.0 hours is required, depending on the dimensions of the lumber.

The charge is then removed, drained of the excess solution, and air- or kiln-dried after treatment to the anticipated moisture content the product will reach in service. In kiln-drying, the maximum drying temperature must not exceed 160° F. Higher temperatures may result in a thermal-chemical degradation reaction. Because of the hygroscopicity of fire-retardant chemicals, it is possible to lower the relative humidity more rapidly for treated wood than for untreated wood during the early part of the drying cycle. This partially compensates for the longer time required at the final drying temperature. Treated wood darkens somewhat during drying.

If the lumber must be resurfaced after treating, a minimum amount of wood should be removed, as retention—hence protection—is greatest in the outermost zone.

Southern pine plywood can be adequately treated with the same schedule used for southern pine lumber. Retention of treating solution in plywood should exceed 25 pounds, and retention of dry chemical should be 3.0 or more pounds per cubic foot. Plywood to be treated must be bonded with an adhesive which can resist delamination during the pressure impregnation and drying cycle. Warping during redrying of plywood can be reduced if kiln sticks are closely spaced and carefully aligned over pile supports. Graham and Erickson (1969) have observed that cross-grooved stickers can greatly reduce the incidence and severity of discoloration under stickers during drying; with certain fire retardants, low initial temperatures may be necessary to prevent the formation of crystals on the surface.

On the basis of tests on Douglas-fir, particleboard can be adequately treated if the fire-retardant solution is applied to the particles before they are dried; tests indicated that modulus of rupture of treated boards was about 75 percent that of untreated boards and gluing was made more difficult, as evidenced by reduced tensile strength perpendicular to the surface (Syska 1969).

Effectiveness of various chemicals[1].—Truax and Harrison (1930) used the fire-tube test (fig. 22–6) to evaluate a large number of chemicals. The progression of weight loss (in treated and untreated specimens) and the rise and fall of tube-top temperature during this test are shown in figure 22–9. Each curve records data taken on a single southern pine specimen. Test sticks had been surfaced following treatment and drying. Figure 22–10, in which each point is the average for 16 to 20 southern pine specimens, shows that approximately 9 pounds of dry diammonium phosphate per 100 pounds of air-dry wood (about 3 pounds per cubic foot)

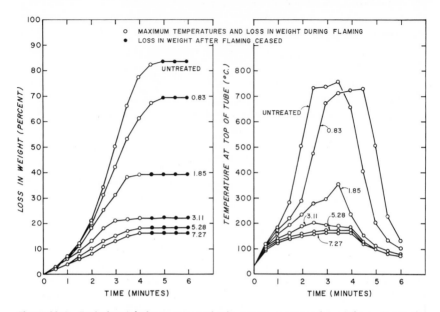

Figure 22–9.—Typical weight-loss curves and tube-top temperatures for southern pine in the fire-tube test. Heat source removed at end of 4 minutes. Numbers on curves indicate absorption of diammonium phosphate, pounds per cubic foot. (Drawing after Truax and Harrison 1930.)

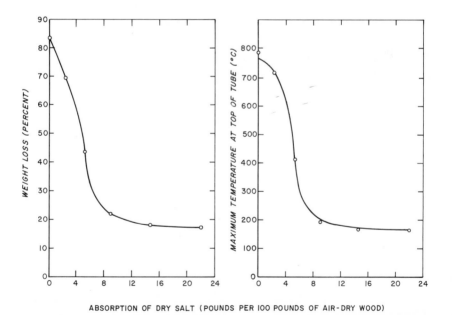

ABSORPTION OF DRY SALT (POUNDS PER 100 POUNDS OF AIR-DRY WOOD)

Figure 22–10.—Final weight-loss and maximum tube-top temperatures sustained by southern pine during fire-tube tests. Retentions of diammonium phosphate were varied. Each circle represents the average of 16 to 20 samples. (Drawing after Truax and Harrison 1930.)

are required to substantially reduce total weight loss and maximum temperatures at the top of the tube.

Table 22–8 is a summary of results for selected chemicals evaluated by Truax et al. (1935) with the fire-tube test. Only a few chemicals used singly stopped both flaming and glowing. In addition to ammonium phosphate and monobasic magnesium phosphate (table 22–8), earlier tests showed that phosphoric acid, aluminum sulphate, and ammonium bromide at retentions of 5 to 7 pounds of dry chemical per cubic foot of wood kept weight loss below 20 percent and stopped glowing[1].

Eickner and Schaffer (1967) evaluated the effects of a number of individual salts (table 22–9) on fire performance characteristics of 3/8-inch, Douglas-fir, dry plywood, using the 8-foot tunnel furnace test, the Schlyter panel test, and the fire tube test. While the tests were not specific to southern pine, the results are indicative of the relationships to be expected [1].

Of the individual chemicals evaluated, monoammonium phosphate was the most effective in reducing the **flame-spread index** by the 8-foot tunnel method (fig. 22–11). Flame-spread values were reduced from 115 for the untreated plywood to approximately 55 at a retention of 2.0 pounds per cubic foot, 35 at 3.0 pounds, 20 at 4.0 pounds, and leveled off at about 15 for retentions of 4.5 pounds and higher. The zinc chloride was generally next in effectiveness, but required a retention of about 5.5 pounds per cubic foot to reach the effectiveness of a 3.0-pound retention of monoammonium phosphate. At 7.0 pounds per cubic foot, zinc chloride reduced the flame-spread index to 25.

Ammonium sulfate was as effective as zinc chloride at the lower retentions, but tended to level off at an index value of about 40 at a retention of 6.0 pounds per cubic foot. The borates showed similar performance at the lower retentions, but leveled off between 50 and 45 at retentions of 4.0 pounds per cubic foot and higher.

Boric acid was partially effective as a flame retardant but required a retention of 6.0 pounds per cubic foot to reduce the flame-spread index to 60. The sodium chloride and sodium dichromate slightly reduced flammability at high retentions.

Of the two fertilizer formulations (not plotted in figure 22–11), the 11–37–0 produced flame-spread indices almost identical to monoammonium phosphate, while indices for the 18–46–0 formulation were only 5 to 10 units higher.

Two of the chemicals most effective in reducing flame spread, monoammonium phosphate and zinc chloride, greatly increased **smoke-density index** values (8-foot tunnel furnace) for the plywood at retentions above 2.0 pounds per cubic foot (fig. 22–11). Except for boric acid, the other individual chemicals generally decreased the smoke development. The sodium borates and sodium dichromate notably reduced the smoke-index values for the plywood but either promoted **afterglow reactions** or did not inhibit them.

TABLE 22-8.—*Effectiveness of various chemicals and mixtures of chemicals in preventing glow and controlling weight loss, as evaluated by the USDA Forest Products Laboratory fire-tube test* (after Truax et al. 1935)

Chemical	Retention of anhydrous chemical/ cu. ft. of wood	Loss in weight[1]	Tendency to glow[2]
	Pounds	*Percent*	
None (untreated wood)_____	—	83.5	Moderate
Ammonium chloride_____	1.50	66.5	Slight
	2.10	53.8	Slight
	3.14	23.2	Slight
	5.36	24.2	Slight
	7.54	19.7	Very slight
Ammonium phosphate (dibasic)_____	0.90	69.4	None
	1.84	43.4	None
	3.23	21.8	None
	5.15	17.9	None
	7.25	17.1	None
Ammonium phosphate (monobasic)_____	0.91	67.4	None
	1.84	56.9	None
	2.60	26.5	None
	4.99	19.0	None
	7.29	15.7	None
Ammonium sulfate_____	1.35	70.4	Slight
	1.86	64.3	Slight
	3.17	31.6	Slight
	4.96	25.9	Slight
	6.70	20.1	Slight
Sodium tetraborate (borax)_____	1.02	54.4	Moderate
	1.76	36.0	Moderate
	3.08	25.0	Moderate
	5.36	21.8	Moderate
	6.02	20.0	Moderate
Boric acid, 60 percent; sodium tetraborate (borax), 40 percent_____	1.18	69.5	Slight
	2.08	64.6	Slight
	3.11	60.3	Slight
	5.32	28.3	Slight
	7.14	19.1	None
Borax, 67 percent, ammonium phosphate (monobasic), 33 percent_____	1.09	68.6	Very slight
	2.20	52.9	Very slight
	3.41	27.2	None
	5.69	16.5	None
	8.49	14.6	None

See footnotes at end of table.

TABLE 22–8.—*Effectiveness of various chemicals and mixtures of chemicals in preventing glow and controlling weight loss, as evaluated by the USDA Forest Products Laboratory fire-tube test* (after Truax et al. 1935)—Continued

Chemical	Retention of anhydrous chemical/ cu. ft. of wood	Loss in weight[1]	Tendency to glow[2]
Boric acid	1.00	78.2	None
	2.04	75.1	None
	3.32	72.2	None
	5.42	66.8	None
	6.83	58.4	None
	8.74	29.9	None
Magnesium chloride, 45 percent; ammonium phosphate (monobasic), 55 percent	1.09	77.1	None
	2.19	72.0	None
	3.19	67.8	None
	5.85	21.1	None
	8.39	17.4	None
Magnesium chloride, 39 percent; ammonium phosphate (monobasic), 47 percent; ammonia gas, 14 percent	1.24	71.4	Very slight
	2.61	52.5	None
	3.88	22.5	None
	6.63	16.6	None
	9.66	15.6	None
Magnesium chloride, 44 percent; sodium phosphate (monobasic), 56 percent	1.14	76.9	Moderate
	2.34	73.3	Moderate
	3.57	70.2	Slight
	5.78	54.2	Very slight
	8.83	33.2	Very slight
Magnesium chloride, 38 percent; sodium phosphate (monobasic), 48 percent; ammonia gas, 14 percent	1.32	66.4	Slight
	2.64	54.9	None
	4.01	27.4	None
	6.85	19.4	None
	10.09	16.2	None
Magnesium phosphate (monobasic)	1.06	75.7	None
	2.18	70.0	None
	3.10	67.4	None
	5.45	54.5	None
	7.44	18.4	None
Magnesium phosphate (monobasic), 81 percent; ammonia gas, 19 percent	1.31	70.0	None
	2.68	49.8	None
	3.85	21.6	None
	6.66	16.1	None
	9.38	14.0	None

See footnotes at end of table.

TABLE 22–8.—*Effectiveness of various chemicals and mixtures of chemicals in preventing glow and controlling weight loss, as evaluated by the USDA Forest Products Laboratory fire-tube test* (after Truax et al. 1935)—Continued

Chemical	Retention of anhydrous chemical/ cu. ft. of wood	Loss in weight[1]	Tendency to glow[2]
Zinc chloride_____	1.13	73.8	Moderate
	1.88	63.5	Moderate
	2.77	47.7	Moderate
	5.08	20.7	Moderate
	8.28	18.3	Moderate
Zinc chloride, 54 percent; ammonium phosphate (monobasic), 46 percent	1.04	75.8	None
	2.09	69.8	None
	3.24	65.8	None
	5.40	22.9	None
	7.60	18.4	None
Zinc chloride, 48 percent; ammonium phosphate (monobasic), 40 percent; ammonia gas, 12 percent	1.19	72.6	None
	2.27	67.9	None
	3.74	37.8	None
	6.15	18.1	None
	8.55	16.3	None

[1] When flaming stopped.
[2] Based on untreated wood as "moderate".

TABLE 22–9.—*Chemicals evaluated by Eickner and Schaffer (1967) for fire-retardant characteristics*

Name	Formula
Sodium chloride_____	NaCl
Sodium dichromate_____	$Na_2CR_2O_7 \cdot 2H_2O$
Sodium tetraborate_____	$Na_2O \cdot 2B_2O_3 \cdot 10H_2O$
Sodium 1:4 borate_____	$Na_2O \cdot 4B_2O_3 \cdot 4H_2O$
Sodium 1:5 borate_____	$Na_2O \cdot 5B_2O_3 \cdot 10H_2O$
Boric acid_____	H_3BO_3
Monoammonium phosphate_____	$NH_4H_2PO_4$
Ammonium sulfate_____	$(NH_4)_2SO_4$
Zinc chloride_____	$ZnCl_2$
Ammonium polyphosphate fertilizer 11–37–0	
High-phosphate fertilizer 18–46–0	

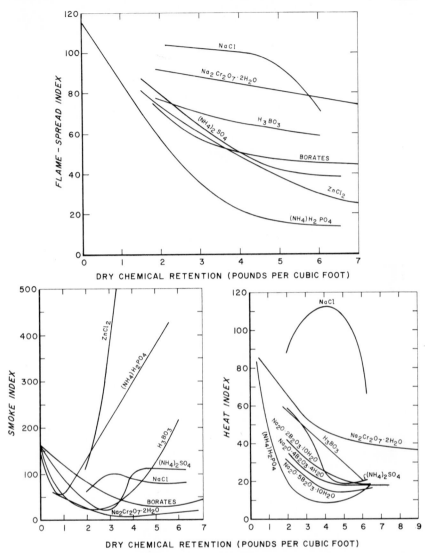

Figure 22–11.—Effect of various chemicals and retentions on fire performance of ⅜-inch Douglas-fir plywood, as evaluated by the USDA Forest Products Laboratory 8-foot tunnel furnace method. (Top) Flame-spread index. (Bottom, left) Smoke index. (Bottom, right) Heat index. (Drawings after Eickner and Schaffer 1967.)

Generally, the commercial fire-retardant formulations for wood (based either on ammonium phosphate or zinc chloride) are listed (Underwriters' Laboratories, Inc. 1969) as having low smoke density values when evaluated by the 25-foot tunnel furnace. The high smoke densities found by Eickner and Schaffer (1967) probably reflect the burning conditions in the 8-foot tunnel furnace, which was designed for high sensitivity in smoke measurements. Their numerical values are not directly comparable to code requirements by other test methods. Several laboratories are at work on techniques for obtaining more widely acceptable data on smoke density.

All of the fire-retardant chemicals (table 22–9) decreased the amount of **heat evolved** in the tunnel test as chemical retention increased. Their individual effectiveness in reducing this evolved heat was positively correlated with their effectiveness in reducing flame spread. Figure 22–11 includes all of the chemicals evaluated except the two phosphate fertilizers and zinc chloride; data for the fertilizers parallel the monoammonium phosphate curve, and the effectiveness of zinc chloride closely parallels that of ammonium sulfate.

For additional information on the use of ammonium polyphosphate liquid fertilizers as fire retardants, see Eickner et al. (1969).

The chemicals in current commercial use as fire retardants include monoammonium and diammonium phosphate, ammonium sulfate, zinc chloride, borax, and boric acid. These are usually combined in formulations intended to give improved overall performance not obtainable with a single chemical.

For example, ammonium phosphate (relatively expensive) and zinc chloride are the most effective flame retardants but do produce considerable smoke under certain conditions. These salts used alone can corrode metals; they also cause premature charring of products when exposed to relatively high temperatures during processing. Ammonium sulfate, a relatively inexpensive chemical, can be combined to reduce flammability without increasing smoke density. Borax is an alkaline salt which reduces flammability without causing premature charring. Borax, ammonium sulfate, and zinc chloride are not particularly effective in reducing afterglow; the incorporation of boric acid or active phosphates in formulations will reduce afterglow. To reduce corrosion, sodium dichromate or other corrosion inhibitors are frequently added to the formulations, but an excess of these inhibitors may promote afterglow.

Standards for formulation, penetration, and retention[1].—An American Wood Preservers Association (1969, P10–68) Standard specifies formulations and tolerances in composition of four commercial fire retardants. Type A (chromated zinc chloride) is used as a preservative treatment; if fire retardance is required, specified retentions are higher than when used as a preservative only. Formulations are:

Type and component	Composition
Type A *Chromated zinc chloride*	*Percent*
Zinc chloride ($ZnCl_2$)	81.5
Sodium dichromate ($Na_2Cr_2O_7 \cdot 2H_2O$)	18.5
Type B *Chromated zinc chloride (FR)*	
Chromated zinc chloride	80
Ammonium sulfate [$(NH_4)_2SO_4$]	10
Boric acid (H_3BO_3)	10
Type C *Minalith*	
Diammonium phosphate [$(NH_4)_2HPO_4$]	10
Ammonium sulfate [$(NH_4)_2SO_4$]	60
Sodium tetraborate (anhydrous) ($Na_2B_4O_7$)	10
Boric acid (H_3BO_3)	20

Type and component	Composition
Type D *Pyresote*	*Percent*
Zinc chloride (ZnCl$_2$)	35
Ammonium sulfate (NH$_4$)$_2$SO$_4$	35
Boric acid (H$_3$BO$_3$)	25
Sodium dichromate (Na$_2$Cr$_2$O$_7 \cdot$2H$_2$O)	5

While not included in AWPA Standards because its formulation has not been disclosed, the fire retardant sold under the registered name of "Nom Com" is used in considerable quantities and has been approved for the label of the Underwriters' Laboratories, Inc. as effective in fire retardance (Hunt and Garratt 1967). There are also fire-retardant additives, such as triaryl phosphate compounds, which can be used in combination with oilborne preservatives to increase the fire retardancy of treated wood; emulsifying of borax-boric acid or sodium calcium borate with the oilborne preservative is another method of combining fire retardants with preservatives.

The American Wood Preservers Association (1969, C20–69) Standard for structural southern pine lumber specifies that subsequent to treatment, material 2 inches and less in thickness shall be air-dried or kiln-dried to an average moisture content of 19 percent or less; when tested in the large tunnel (American Society for Testing and Materials Standard E84), the material shall have no greater flame spread than 25, and when the test is extended to 30 minutes' duration, it shall have no greater flame spread than equivalent of 25 and no evidence of progressive combustion.

The requirements for military use are set forth in Military Specification MIL–L–19140B, Lumber and Plywood, Fire-Retardant-Treated, 1963.

Permanence.—Most of the fire-retardant formulations are based on inorganic salts, which are not subject to decomposition at normal or slightly elevated temperatures. Treatments are considered permanent in interior applications. Practically all of the salts are water soluble, however, and can be easily leached from the wood by running water; current treatments are not recommended for exterior exposure unless adequately protected. Some progress is evident, however; Underwriters' Laboratories, Inc. have tested one proprietary product that provided fire retardancy undiminished by 12 weeks of leaching (Bescher 1967). (See also St. Clair 1969.)

Bromination of wood, through a process developed by Lewin (1964) of the Israel Institute for Fibres and Forest Products Research, is said to result in a water-resistant, fire-retardant treatment.

Corrosive effects.—Some of the individual chemicals used in the fire-retardant formulations are corrosive to certain metals (Van Kleek 1942). Corrosiveness is reduced by combining chemicals in the recognized standard formulations, and by adding sodium dichromate or commercial corrosion inhibitors.

Moisture absorption.—Many of the fire-retardant formulations are hygroscopic (McKnight 1962). Wood treated with these formulations usually has a higher equilibrium moisture content than untreated wood at 65-percent relative humidity and higher (Deery 1941). Prolonged exposure to relative humidities above 80 percent may cause these salts to migrate to the surface, become damp, and drip. Wood impregnated with conventional fire retardants should not be applied where it will be subjected to such exposure.

Strength.—Some of the chemicals used in the fire-retardant formulations have a marked effect on the strength properties of wood. Combinations specified in the standard formulations minimize any weakening effect of individual chemicals. Tests (unpublished) on closely matched pine specimens treated by current fire-retardant methods showed that modulus of elasticity values were decreased by 8 percent and modulus of rupture values by 10 to 14 percent, as compared to untreated controls. The greatest decrease—32 percent—was in the work-to-maximum load values, a measure of resistance to impact loading not generally considered in structural design, but important for energy absorption. In these tests, the test material was conditioned at the same relative humidity as the controls; it therefore had a slightly higher moisture content and volume and a slightly lower density. There is no direct evidence that wood treated with fire-retardant chemicals will undergo further deterioration on aging under normal exposure conditions.

Percival and Suddarth (1971) found that trusses made from southern pine lumber treated with fire retardants, and assembled with metal plate connectors or nail-glued plywood plates, had slightly lower ultimate strength than trusses made from untreated controls.

The National Lumber Manufacturers Association (National design specification for stress-grade lumber and its fastenings, AIA file 19–B–1, 1962) reduces allowable unit stresses by 10 percent compared to untreated wood. Based on a summary of available test data, Gerhards (1970) concluded that observed reductions in bending strength of fire-retardant-treated wood are consistent with the 10-percent reduction in design stresses recommended for fire-retardant-treated wood.

Machinability.—Wood treated with fire-retardant salts has a dulling effect on conventional cutting tools. Tungsten-carbide knives and saws are recommended for machining large volumes of fire-retardant-treated wood.

Gluability.—For doors and decorative panels, fire-retardant-treated wood can be bonded quite successfully with conventional adhesives. However, for structural assemblies such as glued trusses and beams, present glues and gluing techniques do not generally give as good bonds with treated as with untreated wood. Bonds adequate for interior structural members laminated from treated southern pine can be obtained by lightly surfacing the wood and then bonding it with a specially formulated resorcinol adhesive cured at slightly elevated temperautre (Selbo 1965; Schaeffer 1966, 1967, 1969).

Paintability.—The fire-retardant treatment of wood generally has not interfered with the adhesion of paints for interior use except at high equilibrium moisture contents. Preferably, the moisture content of treated wood should be 12 percent or less at the time of painting. Prolonged exposure to high relative humidity may cause salt crystals to appear on the surface of paint coatings over wood having high salt retentions. Natural finishes generally are not practical for wood treated with fire retardants; the chemicals frequently cause darkening and irregular staining.

Use and acceptance.—Consumption of wood impregnated with fire-retardant chemicals has greatly increased in recent years. The production was 4.7 million cu. ft. in 1967 (Gill and Phelps 1968), more than 10 times the amount produced in 1957, and an increase of 32 percent over 1966. Much credit for the expanded use must be given to the wood-preserving industry, which has worked closely with the insurance and code authorities to gain this acceptance. Fire-retardant-treated wood has become recognized, listed, and labelled as a standard product by organizations such as the Underwriters' Laboratories, Inc. The wood-preserving industry has been active in performance evaluation, and in developing the standards and process controls upon which this recognition is based.

Retardant-treated wood is used for frames of wood fire doors, cores for decorative paneling in areas requiring low flammability, and for interior trim products. New uses include treated pine studs in combination with gypsum board facings for nonloadbearing partitions (Degenkolb 1965), and treated roof framing and decking in certain types of noncombustible buildings. Some codes permit a 50-percent increase in floor area when treated structural members are used in combustible construction. Fire-retardant-treated wood is also accepted by some codes for construction for exhibition areas, warehouses, and educational and institutional buildings formerly limited to noncombustible materials.

FIRE-RETARDANT COATINGS

Fire retardance for southern pine wood in existing constructions can be obtained by the application of fire-retardant coatings. The degree of protection depends upon the composition, amount, and thoroughness of the application, and the severity of the fire exposure.

Many of the coatings that limit flame spread owe their effectiveness to water soluble compounds such as ammonium phosphate, borax, and sodium silicate. Oil-base fire-retardant paints, depending on zinc borate, antimony trioxide, and chlorinated paraffin, and elastomers to give them fire retardance, are also available.

In addition to these fire-retardant chemicals, many of the fire-retardant coatings have **intumescent** characteristics; the coating foams and expands when exposed to fire, thus insulating and protecting the wood surfaces from thermal decomposition. This intumescent characteristic is obtained by combining certain carbonates, vinyl acetates, starches, acid phosphates, amine aldehydes, tung, or isano oils as a part of the paint formulation.

Flame-spread, heat, and smoke indices, as determined on Douglas-fir plywood panels in the USDA Forest Products Laboratory 8-foot tunnel furnace for 19 fire-retardant paints, were reported by Eickner and Peters (1963).

To be effective, these fire-retardant paints must be applied in fairly thick films. The recommended coverages are usually 125 to 175 sq. ft. per gallon. This is about three times the amount of paint normally applied. Thus, although the per-gallon cost of fire-retardant paints is only slightly higher, the larger amounts required and the labor to apply the additional coats increase the cost much above that for ordinary decorative paint. Difficulty in brushing out adds further to labor costs.

Properly applied, many of the current commercial fire-retardant paints intumesce, insulate, and protect wood surfaces during moderate fire exposure and have low surface flammability. The Underwriters' Laboratories, Inc. (1969) list a number of formulations with index values less than 25; these index values for flame spread, smoke developed, and fuel contribution are measured according to American Society for Testing Materials Standard E–84. Wood coated with these products may be used as interior finish for such critical applications as the lobbies and corridors of assembly and institutional buildings. To be effective, coatings must be of the required thickness throughout the area, and the surface must be maintained; because inspection is difficult, many code authorities approve such coatings reluctantly. Acceptance is often limited to existing constructions where there is little alternative to treatment in place.

The primary use of these paints should be for interior protection. Some are said to resist weathering, but in general they do not have the durability of conventional exterior paints nor do they maintain their fire-retardant properties after weathering. Because the most effective fire-retardant additives are water soluble, it is difficult to formulate coatings that can resist washings and still maintain fire retardance. In fact, many of the fire-retardant paints lose some of their effectiveness on exposure to high humidity conditions; for these, a sealer topcoat often improves durability. A list of suppliers of fire-retarding coatings is available (USDA Forest Products Laboratory 1968).

22–3 TREATMENT FOR MODIFICATION OF PROPERTIES [15]

The objective of treatment to modify properties may be dimensional stabilization or improvement of physical and mechanical characteristics. More or less successful have been applications of heat and pressure, impregnation with plastics or chemical reagents, and exposure to radiation. Two excellent reviews of these processes have been published, each with a large number of references (Seborg et al. 1962; Tarkow 1966). Little

---

[5] With minor additions and editorial changes, sec. 22–3 is taken from Meyer and Loos (1969) by permission of J. A. Meyer, W. E. Loos, and the Forest Products Research Society.

of this research used southern pine as a substrate, but some review of all processes is desirable to cover the possibilities available.

HEAT-STABILIZED WOOD (Staybwood)

In this process kiln-dried lumber is held at 150 to 300° C. for various lengths of time ranging from minutes to hours. In comparison with moisture-related instability of untreated wood, staybwood has **antishrink efficiencies** (ASE's) up to 60 percent

$$\left(ASE = \frac{\text{swelling of untreated blank} - \text{swelling of treated sample}}{\text{swelling of untreated blank}} \right)$$

However, this dimensional stabilization is accompanied by a serious loss in strength, toughness, and abrasion resistance. (Seborg et al. 1953; Stamm and Seborg 1955; Stamm 1964, p. 317). There is no commercial application for staybwood.

HEAT-STABILIZED COMPRESSED WOOD (Staypak)

Pressures of 400 to 4,000 p.s.i. are applied to the wood after it has been heated. Both heat and pressure plasticize wood. At 320° F. and 12-percent moisture content, the maximum plastic yield per increment of pressure occurs at 1,100 p.s.i. Pressures of 1,500 to 2,500 p.s.i. are generally required to yield a specific gravity of 1.3. Highly densified wood must be cooled in the press. Strength properties are increased in direct proportion to the density; impact strength and hardness are substantially increased. Staypak finds limited application for handles and desk legs (Seborg et al. 1962; Stamm 1964, p. 344).

Haygreen and Daniels (1969) have described experiments with 1-inch green loblolly pine sapwood in which platen drying to 1-percent moisture content at 290 to 340° F. is combined with densification to a specific gravity of 0.7 to 1.0. The process calls for heating green sapwood in a platen press until the core temperature reaches 212° F.; the board is then compressed abruptly to the desired thickness and confined in the hot press until an average moisture content of 1 percent is attained. With a platen temperature of 340° F., 65 minutes were required to dry and densify 0.75-inch loblolly pine to 0.5-inch thickness; 110 minutes were required to dry and reduce 1-inch boards to 0.75-inch thickness.

The product has a slightly lower coefficient of shrinkage (i.e., percent dimensional change per percent of moisture content change) across the wood (and is reverse in direction) than normal wood, but in the thickness direction the coefficient is several times as great as normal wood. Thickness springback due to two humidity cycles from 43-percent to 95-percent relative humidity amounts to 1 or 2 percent; a soaking treatment causes 10- to 15-percent springback in thickness accompanied by a slight negative springback in width.

Steeping treatment to a retention of 8 g. of phenolic resin per 100 g.

of dry wood, followed by a several-day storage period prior to pressing, reduced springback from water soaking by about 90 percent.

Densified (but unsteeped) material had 1- to 2-percent lower e.m.c. than normal sapwood. Bending strength and modulus of elasticity were about proportional to density; hardness increased more rapidly with increases in density than did bending strength.

WOOD-PHENOL-FORMALDEHYDE COMPOSITE (Impreg)

Green or kiln-dried veneer is impregnated with a water solution of a phenol-formaldehyde prepolymer whose molecules are small enough to penetrate the cell wall along with the water. The prepolymer swells the cell wall up to 25 percent beyond the swelling in water; after curing, the composite has a final volume about equal to that of water-swollen wood (Seborg and Vallier 1954; Stamm 1964, p. 326). Following impregnation in a vacuum or pressure system, the veneer is dried, but the phenol-formaldehyde is not polymerized. The desired thickness is then asembled from layers of veneer and, under heat and pressure, the impregnant is polymerized to yield a cohesive composite. At a loading of 35 percent by weight of the dry wood there is no visible deposition of the polymer in the voids of the wood, and the composite has an antishrink efficiency of 70 to 75 percent.

Impreg is in commercial use, primarily for die models and patterns in the automobile industry.

COMPRESSED WOOD-PHENOL-FORMALDEHYDE COMPOSITE (Compreg)

This material is similar to impreg in that the veneer, whether green or dried, is soaked in a water or alcohol solution of low-molecular-weight phenol-formaldehyde and dried at a temperature low enough to prevent precure. A stack of treated veneer sheets is then placed in a press with heated platens and, as the composite material is heated, pressure up to 1,000 p.s.i. is applied to compress the wood and collapse the cell structure (Stamm and Seborg 1955; Stamm 1964, p. 346). The density of the final cured composite approaches that of the cell wall (solid wall substance) with a specific gravity of 1.3 to 1.4. Incorporation of the resin prevents springback in the presence of high relative humidities and imparts high dimensional stability. Optimum stability requires retention of resin solids equal to about 30 percent of dry wood weight. Compreg will absorb less than 1 percent of moisture when immersed in water for 24 hours. Strength (particularly in compression), hardness, and abrasion resistance are all increased, and the composite is quite resistant to decay and termites. Impact strength, however, is impaired by the process.

Many specialty items, knife and cutlery handles in particular, are made from compreg. It is also used for electrical insulators requiring high tensile strength. Compreg can be precisely machined, and the natural surface finish can be renewed by sanding and buffing because the treatment penetrates throughout the composite.

POLYETHYLENE GLYCOL (PEG)

The polymers of dihydric alcohols are polyethers with an oxygen atom separating the hydrocarbon groups and with reactive hydroxyl groups only on the ends; up to molecular weights of 6,000, they are highly soluble in water (Stamm 1956, 1964, p. 333). Because of the low vapor pressure of the PEG, it remains in the cell walls when the wood is dried; this bulking action prevents the wood from shrinking. According to Stamm (1964, p. 333), as water evaporates and increases the concentration of PEG in the solution, the rate of diffusion into the cell wall increases. This is evident by the swelling of the treated wood as it dries. Green cross sectional disks of southern pine sapwood 1¼ inches thick, treated with polyethylene glycol, have bulked sufficiently to prevent checking during air-drying. Treatment consisted of an overnight, or longer, soak in a 30-percent solution of polyethylene glycol-1000, or two surface coats of molten PEG, a day apart. For thicker disks, soak time should be increased in proportion to the square of the thickness. Heartwood requires more soaking time or more coats than sapwood (Stamm 1959b).

Green loblolly pine 5 inches long, 3 inches wide, and ⅜-inch thick can be dried in 10 to 40 minutes by immersion in molten polyethylene glycol-1000 at 135° C.; drying time is shorter than in air. Sufficient PEG diffuses into the samples during the immersion to give about 35-percent antishrink efficiency (Stamm 1967).

The PEG-bulked wood feels moist when relative humidity is above 70 percent because of its hygroscopicity, but certain polyurethane finishes tend to reduce this. The treated wood is highly stable to changes in humidity, but in water the PEG is leached out with time. Treatment causes a slight loss in abrasion resistance and bending strength, but the toughness is essentially unaffected when the wood contains about 45-percent PEG. The antishrink efficiency is approximately 80 percent. PEG treatment is used where wood must have dimensional stability to prevent cracking and checking. Valuable art carvings have been preserved in this manner, and PEG treatment has permitted marine archeologists to preserve waterlogged wooden ships brought up from lakes and oceans.

ACETYLATION

Since the cellulose molecule has many reactive hydroxyl groups available for hydrogen bonding attempts have been made to chemically alter its composition.

One of the most successful approaches was by Stamm (1964, p. 329) and Stamm and Seborg (1955) at the USDA Forest Products Laboratory, where they reacted the OH groups with acetic anhydride and pyridine in the gas phase. The pyridine acts as a swelling agent (Tarkow et al. 1950; Clermont and Bender 1957) for penetration of the cell wall and as a catalyst for the ester formation. Other anhydrides such as crotonic and butyric have been used but did not show any advantage over acetic (Risi and Arseneau 1957ab; Goldstein et al. 1961). Antishrink efficiencies of 70 percent were obtained with an acetyl content of about 25 percent, and this did not change after 4 months at a relative humidity of 97 percent. The external appearance of the acetylated wood is unaltered, although the ovendry volume is greater than that of untreated wood. Higher acetyl content is required in softwoods than in hardwoods for comparable stabilization. Since the rate of diffusion of a gas into a porous solid is inversely proportional to the square of the thickness, acetylation is usually used on thin stock, such as $\frac{1}{8}$-inch veneers. Most mechanical properties are improved slightly. Goldstein has extended this process so that lumber 2 x 6 x 48 inches can be acetylated in 8 to 16 hours (Goldstein et al. 1961).

ETHYLENE OXIDE TREATMENT

An attempt has been made, with some success, to modify the cell wall chemical structure by exposing wood to ethylene oxide gas (McMillin 1963). Samples are placed in a pressure chamber, the air is pumped out, the wood is exposed to the catalyst trimethylamine, and ethylene oxide under high pressure is then admitted. Antishrink effiicencies up to 65 percent have been obtained with a weight increase of 11 percent; there was no deposition of polymer in the capillaries. Maple becomes a distinct brown at high treatment levels. Limited mechanical tests indicate no change in strength due to treatment. There is no known commercial application of this process.

CROSSLINKING WITH FORMALDEHYDE

When wood containing about 2 percent of zinc chloride as a catalyst is exposed to paraformaldehyde for 20 minutes at 120° C., bound formaldehyde content reaches approximately 4 percent of the wood weight. The treatment gives an antishrink efficiency of about 85 percent (Tarkow and Stamm 1953; Stamm 1959a, 1964, p. 328). Dry dimensions of the treated wood are the same as those of untreated controls, but the wet swollen treated samples have a smaller volume. This is just the reverse of impreg and is an indication of crosslinking. Unfortunately mechanical properties such as toughness and abrasion resistance are reduced drastically. Other crosslinking reagents and catalysts have been tried (Sadoh et al. 1960), many of which formed no stable crosslinks (Weaver et al. 1960). There is no commercial use of this process at present.

β-PROPIOLACTONE TREATMENT AND CYANOETHYLATION

Goldstein et al. (1959) treated shortleaf pine with β-propiolactone by the full- and empty-cell methods. The lactone was diluted with acetone to prevent excessive swelling and splitting, the wood was loaded with the solution, and the reaction carried out by heating. The extent of the reaction was measured by the gain in weight. About one-third of the weight increase was attributed to self-polymerization of the lactone. Excellent stabilization was observed when the treated wood was exposed in water and in moist atmospheres because the cellulose was kept in the swollen condition by polyester side chains grafted to the cellulose backbone. The compression strength was increased considerably with no decrease in toughness for moderate treatments. Higher lactone treatments, which cause excessive swelling, decrease toughness.

Attack by fungi was decreased as the gain in weight due to treatment was increased. The polyester chains resulting from treatment contain carboxyl end groups which are capable of reacting with copper and zinc salts in solution. These metallic elements are toxic to fungi. When the ρ-propiolactone-treated pine blocks (25 percent weight gain level) were reacted with copper acetate solution, tests showed essentially no decay after weathering.

Cyanoethylation is the process of reacting cellulose with acrylonitrile. Goldstein et al. (1959) used the empty-cell process to place a 5-percent sodium hydroxide catalyst solution in southern yellow pine samples. This was followed by a full-cell impregnation with acrylonitrile and heating to 70 to 100° C. The amount of reacted acryonitrile was determined by the percent nitrogen in the wood sample. For treated wood exposed to 100-percent relative humidity, the decrease in equilibrium moisture content was linear with the net weight gain until a minimum of 4.5 percent was reached at 30-percent increase in weight. The inability to completely stabilize the wood indicates that certain regions of the wood structure are accessible to water but not to acrylonitrile. A higher equilibrium moisture content was found for β-propiolactone; the acrylonitrile thus reaches more of the cellulosic hydroxyl groups than the lactone. As the substitution of the hydroxyls increases, the impact strength falls off. At a weight gain of 25 percent, the cyanoethylated wood was not attacked by fungi even under weathering conditions.

OZONE GAS-PHASE TREATMENT

This process holds little promise for solid wood treatment because both the cellulose and lignin are degraded. Lantican et al. (1965) and Schuerch (1963a) describe the effect of ozone on small wood samples, ground wood, and chips.

AMMONIUM LIQUID AND VAPOR TREATMENT

Application of this process shows promise as an alternative to steam bending (see chapter 21). Some of the disadvantages of steam bending include recovery of the original shape if exposed to high relative humidity, necessity of holding the part in a form until the wood is set and partially dried, and high breakage. The use of anhydrous ammonia (in the liquid or vapor phase) for bending many woods into much more complicated shapes is now in the development stage (Schuerch 1963b, 1964; Pentoney 1966; Davidson and Baumgardt 1970). Complicated shapes can be formed without clamping because there is no springback. The evacuated wood is exposed to ammonia vapor at a pressure of 150 p.s.i. at room temperature. The time of exposure is determined by the thickness of the wood and its moisture content and ranges from minutes to hours. One-hundred-and-eighty-degree bends have been made with wood $1\frac{1}{2}$ inches thick. Loblolly pine has been used experimentally and is typical of the softwoods in requiring longer exposure to the ammonia vapor than the hardwoods. After treatment the color of the bent wood is much darker and in many cases streaked. The ammonia vapor reacts with some of the wood components to form a liquid which drains from the wood when the pressure is released. This process is not in commercial use at present, but an active research program is underway at the State University College of Forestry in Syracuse, New York.

GAMMA AND BETA IRRADIATION

Since wood is essentially a mixture of high-molecular-weight polymers, the effect of high radiation doses is to depolymerize the cellulose; lignin is more resistant to radiation. Some slight increase in the mechanical properties and a decrease in hygroscopicity were noted with radiation exposures up to 10^6 rads (Kenaga and Cowling 1959). Exposures above this level degraded the cellulose and impaired the mechanical properties; the wood was entirely soluble above 3×10^8 rads exposure (Mater 1957; Siau et al. 1965).

WOOD-VINYL-POLYMER COMPOSITES (WPC) AND OTHER WOOD-PLASTIC COMBINATIONS

Vinyl monomers have been used in recent years to stabilize wood dimensionally and improve its mechanical properties without impairing desirable aesthetic qualities. Unlike deep-colored, phenol-based, thermosetting polymers, the vinyl polymers are clear, colorless, hard thermoplastic materials. Polymerizing the vinyl monomers in the void spaces of the wood does not discolor the wood or alter in any way its eye-appealing nature. The feel of the surface of a wood-vinyl-plastic object is like wood—in textile terminology, it has a good hand.

Vinyl monomers can be polymerized or cured in the wood by radiation or by heating with free radical catalysts. Kenaga et al. (1962) at Dow Chemical Company did some of the original research with irradiation and have received many patents covering its application. They used solvent-monomer mixtures to swell the wood prior to the irradiation, which fixes it in its expanded shape to achieve high antishrink efficiencies. A comprehensive research program sponsored and supported by the Atomic Energy Commission during the period 1961 to 1968 at West Virginia University used radiation to produce wood-plastic composites. Gamma radiation, usually from a cobalt-60 source, is used for in-depth polymerization in wood, while beta radiation is used for polymerization of surface coatings[6].

The catalyst-heat system for making wood-plastic was first mentioned in a paper by DuPont on methacrylate resins (Anonymous 1936). This system for polymerizing vinyl monomers in wood was further developed at the State University College of Forestry in Syracuse, N.Y. (Meyer 1965).

Surface densification and coating of veneers, plywood, solid wood, or particleboard with cured polymers was made possible by the development of a continuous belt press by Lam-N-Hard in Ann Arbor, Mich.[7] The very hard surface of this composite is scratch and mar resistant, and forms a vapor barrier for the unaltered interior wood. Southern pine has been treated on this press and has characteristics similar to other woods; excess natural resin is forced, along with the polymer, deep into the wood. The heat and pressure required for densification make the final product relatively dark in color; with proper conditions most woods can be made to resemble walnut. Of all the wood-plastic processes in use today, the Lam-N-Hard system appears to offer the most promise for volume production of wall panels, table tops, and other large flat wood surfaces.

Comprehensive work on wood-plastic composites using southern pines was carried out at West Virginia University during the past 8 years and is now being continued at the School of Forestry, Louisiana State University. The results from research sponsored by the Atomic Energy Commission have been published and are available from the Superintendent of Documents in Washington, D.C.

Loos et al. (1967) had no difficulty in filling the cell lumens of loblolly pine with a number of vinyl monomers. The process called for an initial vacuum on the wood of 0.3 inch of mercury; the monomer was then admitted to cover the wood without loss of vacuum, and finally 125-p.s.i. hydrostatic pressure was applied for 18 hours. In other work, Loos found that pressure periods as short as 5 hours may be satisfactory.

---

[6] Swanholm, C. E., and Spencer, P. Commercialization of prefinishing by electron radiation. Paper presented at Annual Meeting Forest Products Research Society, Vancouver, B.C., Canada. July 2–7, 1967.

[7] Wahl, B. D. High-density plastic impregnated wood surfaces. Paper presented at annual meeting Forest Products Research Society, Minneapolis, Minn. July 17–22, 1966.

A wide variety of treating cycles were examined by Loos et al. (1967) in an attempt to find one that would give uniform partial loading in loblolly pine. The Lowry process gave relatively uniform partial loadings, but the average overall polymer loading was always high. The Rueping process gave shell-type loading (fig. 22–12).

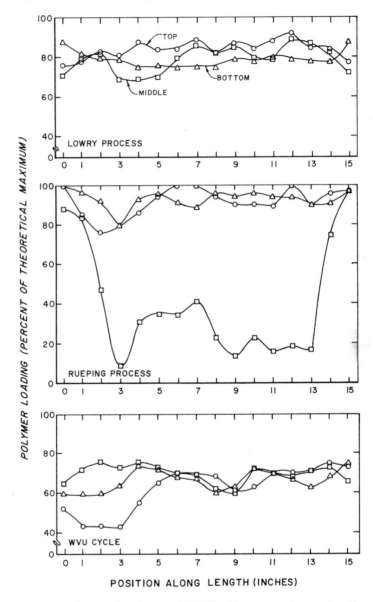

Figure 22–12.—Distribution of polymer in loblolly pine sapwood treated with methyl methacrylate by three processes. Samples were 1¾ inches square and 15¾ inches long. In the WVU cycle, soak-time objective was 67-percent loading. (Drawing after Loos et al. 1967.)

Good control of the overall polymer loading and distribution was obtained with a procedure called the WVU cycle; the wood was subjected to a partial vacuum, covered with monomer, and then soaked for a specific time depending on the loading desired and the species of wood used. The monomer was then drained away and a super atmospheric pressure of nitrogen applied to distribute the monomer uniformly throughout the wood (fig. 22–12). In a study of the WVU cycle, Loos and Boyle[8] impregnated four sizes of loblolly pine specimens at two target loading levels (one-third and two-thirds theoretical maximum) with four monomer systems: methyl methacrylate, methyl methacrylate + Phosgard (a fireproofing agent), styrene + acrylonitrile, and ethyl acrylate + acrylonitrile. Size had no significant effect on the ability to attain the desired percent of theoretical maximum loading or uniformity of load. At one-third loading there was a tendency toward concentration of polymer in the outer shell, while at two-thirds loading some surface depletion was observed.

Another approach to uniform partial loading is impregnation of wood with a chemical in its vapor phase. Barnes et al. (1969) treated the four major species of southern pine with vinyl chloride vapors and then polymerized the monomer by radiation. With this technique insufficient quantities of vinyl chloride were absorbed in the wood to change any of the properties measured. In another trial, Barnes et al. (1969) preimpregnated the wood with trimethyl amine catalyst and then vapor-phase impregnated the wood with ethylene oxide; he was able to get approximately 11 percent retention of the chemical in the wood; despite this relatively low retention, antishrink efficiency was comparatively high.

Diffusion is another method by which an impregnant may be put into either the lumen or the cell wall of wood. Choong and Barnes (1969) used two diffusion processes as well as vacuum pressure impregnation to treat the four major species of southern pine with polyethylene glycol, three commercially available phenolic resins, methyl methacrylate, styrene, and styrene-acrylonitrile. The vacuum-pressure treating method was used with all the impregnants; the two diffusion processes (capillary uptake and solvent exchange) were also used on all these impregnants except the phenolic resins. Results of these treatments are shown in table 22–10.

Kent et al. (1967) found that loblolly pine followed the same radiation kinetics as most other species of wood tested, such as sugar maple (*Acer saccharum* Marsh.), birch (*Betula alleghaniensis* Britton), yellow-poplar (*Liriodendron tulipifera* L.), white spruce (*Picea glauca* var. *glauca*), etc., even though it has a high resin content. This is fortunate; eastern white pine (*Pinus strobus* L.), which also has a high resin content, cannot be successfully treated with vinyl acetate to produce a wood-polymer combi-

---

[8] Loos, W. E., and Boyle, W. B. Analysis of the WVU treating cycle for uniformity of polymer loading. Unpublished Report U.S. AEC, ORO–2945–10. 1968.

TABLE 22–10.—*Effect of chemicals and impregnation methods on dimensional stability of loblolly pine* (Choong and Barnes 1969)

Impregnation method and chemical or solvent	Polymer loading (Pct. of ovendry weight of wood)	Average volumetric swelling		Antishrink efficiency ovendry to water soaked
		(15– to 75–pct. R.H.)	(0– to 100–pct. R.H.)	
– – – – – – – – – –		*Percent*	– – – – – – – – –	
		POLYETHYLENE GLYCOL		
Capillary uptake_____	62	0.73	1.65	87.8
Solvent exchange_____	63	1.10	1.28	90.5
Vacuum-pressure_____	53	1.07	1.66	87.7
		PHENOLIC RESINS		
Vacuum-pressure_____				
Resinox 468_____	78	1.48	2.82	79.2
Compregnite_____	67	2.08	3.11	77.0
Synco 352_____	78	2.09	3.34	75.3
		METHYL METHACRYLATE		
Capillary uptake_____	102	4.47	11.44	15.5
Solvent exchange (acetone)_____	93	2.37	7.25	46.5
Vacuum-pressure_____	94	3.19	7.98	41.1
		STYRENE		
Capillary uptake_____	25	4.76	14.68	8.5
Solvent exchange (ethanol)_____	69	2.00	3.57	73.6
Solvent exchange (dioxane)_____	49	3.24	6.95	48.7
Vacuum-pressure_____	56	1.93	4.26	68.5
		STYRENE-ACRYLONITRILE		
Capillary uptake_____	100	2.97	7.32	45.9
Solvent exchange (ethanol)_____	106	2.56	4.03	70.2
Vaccum-pressure_____	98	2.11	3.52	74.0
		CONTROL (UNTREATED)		
		4.92	13.54	—

nation. Apparently, certain of the resins present in white pine inhibit polymerization of vinyl acetate so greatly that it will not completely cure with gamma radiation.

Dimensional stability.—Loos (1968) treated loblolly pine with polymethyl methacrylate P(MMA) and a copolymer of poly(styrene + acrylonitrile) P(ST + ACN) by the full-cell process and at one-third and two-thirds of theoretical maximum loading by the WVU treating cycle. The maximum antishrink efficiency of about 20 percent was found to occur at approximately 50-percent maximum loading when wood was treated with polymethyl methacrylate. About 50-percent antishrink efficiency was obtained with the P(ST + ACN) and was relatively independent of polymer loading.

The higher dimensional stability measured by Loos (1968) in wood-plastic combinations made with P(ST + ACN) than in those made with polymethyl methacrylate is attributed to entry of the former into the cell walls of the wood (Loos and Robinson 1968). In the latter study, loblolly pine wafers were soaked in the two vinyl monomer systems. Swelling of the wafers soaked in the methyl methacrylate monomer was caused primarily by migration from the monomer to the wood. With styrene + acrylonitrile (60:40 solution), swelling was much greater, and virtually all was due to the acrylonitrile, which by itself swells wood much more than can be attributed to the residual water swelling. From his dimension-stability studies Loos (1968) concluded that the dimensional stability results in part from coating action of the polymer in the wood capillaries and in part from a bulking action due to polymer entering the cell wall itself.

The effect of five chemicals on the dimensional stability of loblolly pine impregnated by three different systems is shown in table 22–10. Table 22–11 indicates the antishrink efficiency of specimens of all four major southern pines when treated with four of these chemicals by the method found most effective. Polyethylene glycol gave best results. Treated wood of low specific gravity was more stable than wood of high specific gravity. Stability of treated corewood and treated mature wood did not differ significantly. Additional sampling is required to establish valid species differences (Choong and Barnes 1969).

When the four major southern pines were impregnated with ethylene oxide in vapor phase (Barnes et al. 1969), the treated wood had relatively good dimensional stability for the amount of polymer placed in the wood. The overall average was 42-percent antishrink efficiency for an 11.4-percent polymer loading. This is more than could be obtained if bulking alone had occurred, so some of the hydroxyl groups on the cellulose must have been removed from hygroscopic reactivity.

Strength.—A cooperative research project [9] was conducted at North Carolina State University and West Virginia University on the production and mechanical testing of radiation produced wood-plastic composites made from four species of wood, including loblolly pine, and with four vinyl monomer systems. The monomer systems were: methyl methacrylate, methyl methacrylate with Phosgard, styrene + acrylonitrile (60:40), and ethyl acrylate + acrylonitrile (80:20). The latter forms a rubbery type

---

[9] Atomic Energy Commission. Mechanical properties of radiation-produced wood-plastic combinations. Research Triangle Institute and North Carolina State University. To be published by U.S. Atomic Energy Commission, Division of Isotope Development.

TABLE 22–11.—*Antishrink efficiency[1] of southern pine wood impregnated with selected chemicals by the most favorable process* (Choong and Barnes 1969)

Chemical, and treatment process; age of wood	Pine species				Specific gravity		Group average
	Loblolly	Slash	Longleaf	Shortleaf	Low	High	
	– – – – – – – – – – – *Percent* – – – – – – – – – – – –						
Polyethylene glycol (solvent exchange)_____	82.2	75.9	76.2	81.9	81.0	77.1	79.1
Phenolic resin (vacuum-pressure)_____	77.4	80.0	76.5	76.4	79.7	75.4	77.6
Methyl methacrylate[2] (solvent exchange)_____	69.8	68.8	69.3	71.1	72.4	67.1	69.8
Styrene-acrylonitrile (vacuum-pressure)_____	69.1	62.7	63.6	71.4	71.0	62.4	66.7
Corewood_____	76.8	70.9	69.4	75.7	75.5	70.9	73.2
Mature wood_____	72.5	72.8	73.4	74.4	76.6	70.1	73.3
Group average____	74.6	71.9	71.4	75.3	76.0	70.7	_____

[1] Antishrink efficiency $= \dfrac{\text{swelling of untreated blank} - \text{swelling of treated sample}}{\text{swelling of untreated blank}}$.

[2] Methanol was used as the swelling agent.

polymer when polymerized in bulk. The wood was conditioned to 12-percent moisture content, and the polymer loadings used were one-third, two-thirds, and three-thirds of theoretical maximum loading.

Static bending strength, toughness, and tensile strength perpendicular to the grain were 20 to 50 percent greater in treated than in untreated pine. Strength in compression perpendicular to the grain, hardness, and abrasion resistance were increased several times over untreated pine values.

Adams et al. (1970) have reported on the bending strength of loblolly pine wood impregnated with methyl methacrylate and then subjected to gamma radiation. The 16-inch-long samples were 1 inch square, had six to eight rings per inch, and were about 50-percent latewood. The 21 specimens treated were conditioned to 12-percent moisture content, submerged in the monomer for 12 days at atmospheric pressure, then subjected to a vacuum (26 inches of mercury) for 20 minutes, and finally pressure treated with the monomer for 3 hours at 80 to 90 p.s.i. gauge pressure. Polymerization was accomplished with a cobalt-60 source at a dose rate of 2,000 rads per minute applied for 8 to 30 hours at 40° C. Resulting polymer loading averaged 0.75 grams per gram of ovendry wood and had a negative linear correlation with wood specific gravity, i.e., highest loadings were obtained in the wood of least density. The treatment did not affect fiber stress at proportional limit. Modulus of rupture and modulus of elasticity, however, were 27 to 17 percent greater in the treated specimens than in the untreated controls; this improvement was evident for wood of every specific gravity (fig. 22–13) in the range from 0.55 to 0.75 (basis of ovendry weight and volume at 12-percent moisture content). Modulus of rupture and modulus of elasticity were maximum at a polymer loading of 0.45 gram per gram of ovendry wood.

Weathering.—Boyle et al.[10] studied the weathering resistance of 4/4, flat-sawn, clear, 6-inch-wide by 12-inch-long, treated southern pine boards.

Treatment	Loading
Control	
Polymethyl methacrylate (PMMA) _____	Full
Polymethyl methacrylate _____	Half
Polymethyl methacrylate plus plasticizer _____	Full
Polymethyl methacrylate plus plasticizer _____	Half

When given 4 months of 45° south exposure in Miami, Fla., none of the treatments was satisfactory as a natural finish. The general appearance deteriorated very rapidly in the first 2 months, then tended to level off. The order of general appearance from highest to lowest was full loaded PMMA, full-loaded PMMA + plasticizer, half-loaded PMMA, half-loaded PMMA + plasticizer, and control. The fully loaded PMMA went from an initial rating of 10 (best) to 3, while the controls attained ratings of less than 1. Checks were not a cause of degradation.

[10] Boyle, W., Winston, A., Loos, W. E., and Taylor, G. B. Preparation of wood-plastic combinations using gamma radiation. Unpublished Final Report U.S. AEC, ORO–2045. 1969.

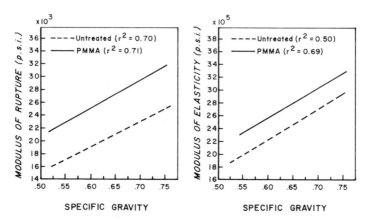

Figure 22–13.—Effect of treatment with methyl methacrylate (PMMA) on relationships between specific gravity of untreated wood (basis of volume at 12-percent moisture content and ovendry weight), modulus of rupture, and modulus of elasticity of clear loblolly pine wood tested in bending at 12-percent moisture content. All relationships significant at the 0.01 level. (Drawings after Adams et al. 1970.)

High-polymer loading gives the best weatherability, but the composite is still unsatisfactory as a natural finish; if gloss and little discoloration are required, a hard polymer should be used. If protection from checking, cracking, mildew and dirt is more important, then a more plastic polymer should be used.

Biological attack.—Field tests (Boyle et al.[10]) indicate that wood-vinyl-polymer composites have good resistance to termite and fungus attack. Additional field evaluations of the composite, with varying amounts of pentachlorophenol dissolved in the monomer, are in process.

FUTURE PROSPECTS

Penetration of the cell wall structure is the key to chemical modification of wood. In an extensive and thought-provoking paper Schuerch (1968) explains that the distribution of any compound in the wood substance will be determined by the hydrogen bonding character of the functional groups on the molecule, "since a high hydrogen bonding capacity is required for any substance to penetrate cellulose or lignin." Penetration depends also upon molecular weight, viscosity, volatility, and other properties.

A question asked by most wood products producers about wood-plastic composites is, "Can I impregiate the finished wood product, complete the polymerization, and simply buff the surface and pack for shipment?" This question can be answered quite simply, but the solution to the problem is far from simple. If the impregnant does not penetrate the cell wall and does not change the moisture content of the wood, then there will be no change in dimension and the finished part can be treated and shipped. On the other hand, if any of the impregnant enters the cell wall, then there will be swelling and a change in dimensions. This swelling is not consistently uniform because of the heterogeneous nature of the wood. Compression wood, earlywood, latewood, heartwood, sapwood, tangential/radial anisotropy, and other physical and chemical properties determine how much impregnant will enter the cell wall. Two parts made from the same tree will seldom react identically to a given treatment.

Extractives can be leached from the solid wood by the liquid monomers and other chemicals during impregnation. This extraction varies with species and treatment. Generally, if treatment removes water from wood at a high equilibrium moisture content or adds water to wood at a low equilibrium moisture content, dimensional changes will take place. Polyethylene glycol exchange is one of the few treatments where water is replaced with little dimensional change.

At the present time, wood-plastic composites containing more than 10-percent polymer probably should be treated in the semifinished form with the final machining done after polymerization.

Vapor phase treatment of wood is obviously the best approach from the standpoint of cell wall penetration. If bulking takes place in the cell walls only, then the void spaces in the wood remain empty. This in turn means that less chemical is required, the weight of the final composite is much less, and possibly the composite can be nailed like untreated wood. Schuerch (1968) discussed the vapor phase treatment and suggested the use of some new organic compounds, such as butadiene dioxide, propylene oxide, chlorinated poly-p-xylene (which, as coherent film formers, could coat the cells walls and make them less permeable to moisture), methyl borate tin, and lead alkyls, and alkyl hydrides which form solids. Choong and his group at Louisiana State University appear to be making progress in the gas phase treatment of wood with ethylene oxide and vinyl chloride.

The ideal treatment for stabilization would be a gas or vapor that would penetrate the wood structure along the capillaries of the fibers, condense on the cell wall surface, diffuse into the cell wall, swell the cell wall to the same extent saturated water vapor does, and finally polymerize, crosslink, and graft to the cellulose without any byproducts or excessive heat. With such a reagent the wood composite would be only 30 percent heavier than untreated wood, stable, and nailable. Abrasion resistance, hardness, and compressive strength might also be increased. If decay and fire resistant, the wood composite would last indefinitely; it would be an excellent material. Attainment of this ideal wood composite seems remote today, but not impossible.

22–4 LITERATURE CITED

Anonymous.
1936. Methacrylate resins. Ind. and Eng. Chem. 28: 1160–1163.

Adams, D. G., Choong, E. T., and McIlhenny, R. C.
1970. Bending strength of radiation-produced southern pine wood-plastic combinations. Forest Prod. J. 20(4): 25–28.

American Wood Preservers' Association.
1948. Report of committee 6–5 —Seasoning practice. Amer. Wood Preserv. Assoc. Proc. 44: 313–320.

American Wood-Preservers' Association.
1951. Report of committee P–4, new preservatives. Amer. Wood Preserv. Assoc. Proc. 47: 32–33.

American Wood Preservers Association.
1969. AWPA standards (loose leaf and currently revised). Amer. Wood Preserv. Assoc., Wash., D.C.

Baechler, R. H.
1968. Further thoughts regarding variable performance of creosoted marine piling. Amer. Wood Preserv. Assoc. Proc. 64: 117–126.

Baechler, R. H., Blew, J. O., Jr., and Roth, H. G.
1962. Studies on the assay of pressure-treated lumber. Amer. Wood Preserv. Assoc. Proc. 58: 21–34.

Baechler, R. H., Gjovik, L. R., and Roth, H. G.
1969. Assay zones for specifying preservative-treated Douglas-fir and southern pine timbers. Amer. Wood Preserv. Assoc. Proc. 1969: 114–121.

Baechler, R. H., Gjovik, L. R., and Roth, H. G.
1970a. Marine tests on combination-treated round and sawed specimens. Amer. Wood Preserv. Assoc. Proc. 66: 249–256.

Baechler, R. H., Richards, B. R., Richards, A. P., and Roth, H. G.
1970b. Effectiveness and permanence of several preservatives in wood coupons exposed to sea water. Amer. Wood Preserv. Assoc. Proc. 66: 47–62.

Baechler, R. H., and Roth, H. G.
1961. Further data on the extraction of creosote from marine piles. Amer. Wood Preserv. Assoc. Proc. 57: 120–132.

Baechler, R. H., and Roth, H. G.
1964. The double-diffusion method of treating wood: A review of studies. Forest Prod. J. 14: 171–178.

Barker, W. J., Stewart, G. H., Nettles, W. C., and Dunkelberg, G. H.
1950. Longer life for fence posts. Clemson Agr. Coll. Ext. Circ. 262 rev., 15 pp.

Barnes, H. M., Choong, E. T., and McIlhenny, R. C.
1969. An evaluation of several vapor phase chemical treatments for dimensional stabilization of wood. Forest Prod. J. 19(3): 35–39.

Beckman, C., Menzies, R. J., and Wakeman, C. M.
1957. The biological aspects of attack on creosoted wood by *Limnoria*. Corrosion 13: 32–34.

Behr, E. A., Sachs, I. B., Kukachka, B. F., and Blew, J. O.
1969. Microscopic examination of pressure-treated wood. Forest Prod. J. 19(8): 31–40.

Bescher, R. H.
1965. Process for impregnating wood with pentachlorophenol and composition therefor. (U.S. Pat. No. 3,200,003) U.S. Pat. Office, Wash., D.C.

Bescher, R. H.
1967. A new class C treatment for wooden shingles and shakes. Fire J. 61(5): 52–56.

Blew, J. O., Jr.
1955. Study of the preservative treatment of lumber. USDA Forest Serv. Forest Prod. Lab. Rep. 2043, 39 pp.

Blew, J. O., Jr.
1961. Treating wood by the cold-soaking method. USDA Forest Serv. Forest Prod. Lab. Rep. 1445 rev., 20 pp.

Blew, J. O., Jr.
1967. Comparison of wood preservatives in stake tests (1967 progress report). USDA Forest Serv. Res. Note FPL–02, 86 pp. Forest Prod. Lab., Madison, Wis.

Blew, J. O., Jr., and Champion, F. J.
1967. Preservative treatment of fence posts and farm timbers. USDA Farmers' Bull. 2049 rev., 33 pp.

Blew, J. O., Jr., and Davidson, H. L.
1967. Comparison of wood preservatives in Mississippi post study (1967 progress report). USDA Forest Serv. Res. Note FPL–01, 24 pp. Forest Prod. Lab., Madison, Wis.

Blew, J. O., and Davidson, H. L.
1969. Comparison of wood preservatives in stake tests. USDA Forest Serv. Res. Note FPL–02, 90 pp. Forest Prod. Lab., Madison, Wis.

Blew, J. O., Jr., and Kulp, J. W.
1964. Service records on treated and untreated fence posts. USDA Forest Serv. Res. Note FPL–068, 52 pp. Forest Prod. Lab., Madison, Wis.

Blew, J. O., Jr., and Panek, E.
1964. Problems in the production of clean treated wood. Amer. Wood Preserv. Assoc. Proc. 60: 89–97.

Blew, J. O., Panek, E., and Roth, H. G.
1970. Vacuum treatment of lumber. Forest Prod. J. 20(2): 40–47.

Brenden, J. J.
1970. Determining the utility of a new optical test procedure for measuring smoke from various wood products. USDA Forest Serv. Res. Pap. FPL–137, 20 pp. Forest Prod. Lab., Madison, Wis.

Browne, F. L.
1958. Preservative treatment of window sash and other millwork. USDA Forest Serv. Forest Prod. Lab. Rep. 919, 12 pp.

Buckman, S. J.
1936. Creosote distribution in treated wood. Distribution of creosote in the sapwood of freshly creosoted southern yellow pine poles with special references to the bleeding of treated poles. Ind. and Eng. Chem. 28: 474–480.

Choong, E. T., and Barnes, H. M.
1969. Effect of several wood factors on dimensional stabilization of the southern pines. Forest Prod. J. 19(6): 55–60.

Clermont, L. P., and Bender, F.
1957. The effect of swelling agents and catalysts on acetylation of wood. Forest Prod. J. 5: 167–170.

Colley, R. H.
1969. Treating marine piling for areas of extreme borer hazard. Wood Preserv. 47(6): 4–18.

Colley, R. H., and Amadon, C. H.
1936. Relation of penetration and decay in creosoted southern pine poles. Bell Telephone Syst. Monogr. B–937, 17 pp.

Davidson, R. W., and Baumgardt, W. G.
1970. Plasticizing wood with ammonia—a progress report. Forest Prod. J. 20(3):19–25.

Deery, H. L.
1941. Equilibrium moisture content of salt-treated wood. N.Y. State Coll. Forest. Tech. Pub. 58, 15 pp.

Degenkolb, J. G.
1965. FRTW framing—24 in. centers. Non-bearing partition passes ASTM 1-hr fire test. Wood Preserv. News 42(12): 14–17.

Downey, E. J.
1937. Open tank creosote treatment of shortleaf and loblolly pine poles. J. Forest. 35: 349–352.

Eickner, H. W., and Peters, C. C.
1963. Surface flammability of various decorative and fire-retardant coatings for wood as evaluated in FPL 8-foot tunnel furnace. Offic. Dig. 35: 800–813.

Eickner, H. W., and Schaffer, E. L.
1967. Fire-retardant effects of individual chemicals on Douglas fir plywood. Fire Technol. 3: 90–104.

Eickner, H. W., Stinson, J. M., and Jordan, J. E.
1969. Ammonium polyphosphate liquid fertilizer as fire retardant for wood. Amer. Wood Preserv. Assoc. Proc. 65: 260–271.

Erickson, H. D., Schmitz, H., and Gortner, R. A.
1937. The permeability of woods to liquids and factors affecting the rate of flow. Minn. Agr. Exp. Sta. Tech. Bull. 122, 42 pp.

French, D. W., and Christensen, C. M.
1958. Nature and cause of spots on coated insulating boards. TAPPI 41: 309–312.

French, D. W., and Christensen, C. M.
1969. Coated insulating board: influence of coating additives and relative humidity upon spotting by fungi. Forest Prod. J. 19(9): 108–110.

Gerhards, C. C.
1970. Effect of fire-retardant treatment on bending strength of wood. USDA Forest Serv. Res. Pap. FPL–145, 8 pp. Forest Prod. Lab., Madison, Wis.

Gill, T. C., and Phelps, R. B.
1968. Wood preservation statistics 1967. Amer. Wood Preserv. Assoc. Proc. 64: 241–261.

Gjovik, L. R., Roth, H. G., and Lorenz, L. F.
1970. Quantitative differences in preservative penetration and retention in summerwood and springwood of longleaf pine. Amer. Wood Preserv. Assoc. Proc. 66: 260–262.

Goldstein, I. S., Dreher, W. A., Jeroski, E. B., and others.
1959. Wood processing—inhibiting against swelling and decay. Ind. and Eng. Chem 51: 1313–1317.

Goldstein, I. S., Jeroski, E. B., Lund, A. E., and others.
1961. Acetylation of wood in lumber thickness. Forest Prod. J. 8: 363–370.

Graham, R. D., and Erickson, H. D.
1969. Cross-grooved stickers reduce marking on FRT plywood. Forest Prod. J. 19(1): 42–43.

Hager, B.
1969. Leaching tests on copper-chromium-arsenic preservatives. Forest Prod. J. 19(10): 21–26.

Haygreen, J. G., and Daniels, D. H.
1969. The simultaneous drying and densification of sapwood. Wood and Fiber 1:38–53.

Hudson, M. S.
1968. New process for longitudinal treatment of wood. Forest Prod. J. 18(3): 31–35.

Hunt, G. M., and Garratt, G. A.
1967. Wood preservation. Ed. 3, 433 pp. N.Y.: McGraw-Hill Book Co., Inc.

Kenaga, D. L., and Cowling, E. B.
1959. Effect of gamma radiation on ponderosa pine: Hygroscopicity, swelling and decay susceptibility. Forest Prod. J. 9:112–116.

Kenaga, D. L., Fennessey, J. P., and Stannett, V. T.
1962. Radiation grafting of vinyl monomers to wood. Forest Prod. J. 12: 161–168.

Kent, J. A., Winston, A., Boyle, W. R., and Taylor, G. B.
1967. Preparation of wood-plastic combinations using gamma radiation to induce polymerization. U.S. At. Energy Comm. AEC Res. and Develop. Rep. ORO–2945–7, 53 pp.

Knuth, D. T., and McCoy, E.
1962. Bacterial deterioration of pine logs in pond storage. Forest Prod. J. 12: 437–442.

Lance, O. C.
1958. History and development of wood preservation for millwork. Forest Prod. J. 8(10): 61A–65A.

Lantican, D. M., Côtè, W. A., Jr., and Skaar, C.
1965. Effect of ozone treatment on the hygroscopicity, permeability and ultrastructure of the heartwood of western red cedar. Ind. and Eng. Chem. Prod. Res. and Develop. 4: 66–70.

Levi, M. P., Coupe, C., and Nicholson, J.
1970. Distribution and effectiveness in Pinus sp. of a water-repellent additive for water-borne wood preservatives. Forest Prod J. 20(11): 32–37.

Lewin, M.
1964. Fire-proofing lignocellulosic structures with bromine and chlorine compositions. (U.S. Pat. No. 3,150,919.) U.S. Pat. Office, Wash., D.C

Lindgren, R. M.
1952. Permeability of southern pine as affected by mold and other fungus infection. Amer. Wood Preserv. Assoc. Proc. 48: 158–168.

Lindgren, R. M., and Scheffer, T. C.
1939. Effect of blue stain on the penetration of liquids into air-dry southern pine wood. Amer. Wood Preserv. Assoc. Proc. 35: 325–336.

Loos, W. E.
1968. Dimensional stability of certain wood-plastic combinations to moisture changes. Wood Sci. and Technol. 2: 308–312.

Loos, W. E., and Robinson, G L.
1968. Rates of swelling of wood in vinyl monomers. Forest Prod. J. 18(9): 109–112.

Loos, W. E., Kent, J. A., and Walters, R. E.
1967. Impregnation of wood with vinyl monomers. Forest Prod J. 17(5): 40–49.

MacLean, J. D.
1929. Absorption of wood preservatives should be based on the dimensions of the timber. Amer. Wood Preserv. Assoc. Proc. 25: 129–141.

McKnight, T. S.
1962. The hygroscopicity of wood treated with fire-retardant compounds. Can. Dep. Forest Rep. 190, 12 pp.

MacLean, J. D.
1960. Preservative treatment of wood by pressure methods. USDA Agr. Handbook 40 rev., 160 pp.

McMillin, C. W.
1963. Dimensional stabilization with polymerizable vapor of ethylene oxide. Forest Prod. J. 13: 56–61.

Mater, J.
1957. Chemical effects of high energy irradiation of wood. Forest Prod. J. 7: 208–209.

Merrill, W., and French, D. W.
1963. Evaluating preservative treatment of rigid insulating materials. TAPPI 46: 449–452.

Merrill, W., and French, D W.
1964. Wood fiberboard studies. I. A nailhead pull-through method to determine the effects of fungi on strength. TAPPI 47: 449–451.

Merrill, W., and French, D. W.
1965. Wood fiberboard studies. III. Effects of common molds on the cell wall structure of the wood fibers. TAPPI 48: 653–654.

Merrill, W., and French, D W.
1966a. Decay in wood and wood fiber products by *Sporotrichum pruinosum*. Mycologia 58: 592–596.

Merrill, W., and French, D. W.
1966b. Wood fiberboard studies. IV. Effects of decay on lateral nail resistance and correlation of lateral nail resistance with nailhead pull - through resistance. TAPPI 49: 33–34.

Merrill, W., French, D. W., and Hossfeld, R L.
1965. Wood fiberboard studies. II. Effects of common molds on physical and chemical properties of wood fiberboard. TAPPI 48: 470–474.

Meyer, F. J., and Spalding, D. H.
1958. Anti-termite and anti-fungal treatment for fiberboard, hardboard and particle board. *In* Fibreboard and particle board, Vol. 3, Pap. 5.24, 10 pp. Rome: Food and Agr. Organ. of the UN.

Meyer, J. A.
1965. Treatment of wood-polymer systems using catalyst-heat techniques. Forest Prod. J. 15: 362–364.

Meyer, J. A., and Loos, W. E.
1969. Processes of, and products from, treating southern pine wood for modification of properties. Forest Prod J. 19(12): 32–38.

Panek, E.
1963. Pretreatments for the protection of southern yellow pine poles during air-seasoning. Amer. Wood Preserv. Assoc. Proc. 59: 189–195.

Panek, E.
1968. Study of paintability and cleanliness of wood pressure treated with water-repellent preservative. Amer. Wood Preserv. Assoc. Proc. 64: 178–193.

Pentoney, R. E.
1966. Liquid ammonia-solvent combinations in wood plasticization: Properties of treated wood. Ind. and Eng. Chem. Prod. Res. and Develop. 5: 105–110.

Percival, D. H., and Suddarth, S K.
1971. An investigation of the mechanical characteristics of truss plates on fire-retardant treated wood. Forest Prod. J. 21(1): 17–22.

Resch, H., and Arganbright, D. G.
1971. Location of pentachlorophenol by electron microprobe and other techniques in cellon treated Douglas-fir. Forest Prod. J. 21(1): 38–43.

Risi, J, and Arseneau, D. F.
1957a. Dimensional stabilization of wood. Forest Prod. J. 7: 210–213.

Risi, J., and Arseneau, D. F.
1957b. Dimensional stabilization of wood. II. Crotonylation and Crotylation. Forest Prod. J. 7: 245–246.

Sadoh, T, Araki, M., and Teruo, G.
1960. Studies on the dimensional stabilization of wood. VIII. Hygroscopicities of formaldehyde-treated wood. J. Jap. Wood Res. Soc. 6(6): 242–246. (Abstr. Forest Prod. J. 11: 328. 1961.)

St. Clair, W. E.
1969. Leach resistant fire-retardant treated wood for outdoor exposure. Amer. Wood Preserv. Assoc. Proc. 65: 250–259.

Schaeffer, R. E.
1966. Preliminary study of the gluing of ammonium salt-treated wood with resorcinol-resin glues. USDA Forest Serv. Res. Note FPL–0112, 9 pp. Forest Prod Lab., Madison, Wis.

Schaeffer, R. E.
1967. Gluing ammonium-salt-treated southern pine with resorcinol-resin adhesives. USDA Forest Serv. Res. Note FPL–0151, 16 pp. Forest Prod. Lab., Madison, Wis.

Schaeffer, R. E.
1969. Cure rate of resorcinol and phenolresorcinol adhesives in joints of ammonium salt-treated southern pine. USDA Forest Serv. Res. Pap. FPL–121, 12 pp. Forest Prod. Lab., Madison, Wis.

Scheffer, T. C., and Lindgren, R. M.
1940. Stains of sapwood and sap-
        wood products and their
        control. USDA Tech.
        Bull. 714, 124 pp.

Schuerch, C.
1963a. Ozonization of cellulose
        and wood. J. Polymer
        Sci. (Part C, Polymer
        Symp.) 2: 79–95.

Schuerch, C.
1963b. Plasticizing wood with liq-
        uid ammonia. Ind. and
        Eng. Chem. 55(10): 39.

Schuerch, C.
1964.   Principles and potential of
        wood plasticization. For-
        est Prod. J. 14: 377–381.

Schuerch, C.
1968.   Treatment of wood with
        gaseous reagents. Forest
        Prod. J. 18(3): 47–53.

Seborg, R. M., Millett, M. A., and
    Stamm, A. J.
1962.   Heat-stabilized compressed
        wood (Staypak). USDA
        Forest Serv. Forest Prod.
        Lab. Rep. 1580 rev., 22
        pp.

Seborg, R. M., Tarkow, H., and
    Stamm, A. J.
1953.   Effect of heat upon the di-
        mensional stabilization of
        wood. J. Forest Prod.
        Res. Soc 3(3): 59–67.

Seborg, R. M., and Vallier, A. E.
1954.   Application of impreg for
        patterns and die models.
        J. Forest Prod. Res. Soc.
        4: 305–312.

Selbo, M. L.
1965.   Summary of information on
        gluing of treated wood.
        USDA Forest Serv. For-
        est Prod. Lab. Rep. 1789,
        21 pp.

Selbo, M. L., Knauss, A. C., and
    Worth, H. E.
1965.   After two decades of serv-
        ice . . . Glulam timbers
        show good performance.
        Forest Prod. J. 11:
        466–472.

Siau, J. F., Meyer, J. A., and Skaar, C.
1965.   A review of developments
        in dimensional stabiliza-
        tion of wood using radia-
        tion techniques. Forest
        Prod. J. 15: 162–166

Stamm, A. J.
1956.   Dimensional stabilization of
        wood with carbowaxes.
        Forest Prod. J. 6:
        201–204.

Stamm, A. J.
1959a. Dimensional stabilization
        of wood by thermal reac-
        tions and formaldehyde
        cross-linking. TAPPI 42:
        39–44.

Stamm, A. J.
1959b. Effect of polyethylene
        glycol on the dimensional
        stability of wood. Forest
        Prod. J. 9: 375–381.

Stamm, A. J.
1964.   Wood and cellulose science.
        549 pp. N.Y.: Ronald
        Press Co.

Stamm, A. J.
1967.   Heating dry wood and
        drying green wood in
        molten polyethylene
        glycol. Forest Prod. J.
        17(9): 91–96.

Stamm, A. J., and Seborg, R. M.
1955.   Forest Products Laboratory
        resin-treated laminated,
        compressed wood (Com-
        preg). USDA Forest
        Serv. Forest Prod. Lab.
        Rep. 1381, 19 pp.

Stolley, I.
1958   Some methods of treating
        particle boards to in-
        crease their resistance
        against fungi and ter-
        mites. In Fibreboard and
        particle board, Vol. 4,
        Pap. 5.38, 7 pp. Rome:
        Food and Agr. Organ. of
        the UN.

Syska, A. D.
1969.   Exploratory investigation of
        fire-retardant treatments
        for particleboard. USDA
        Forest Serv. Res. Note
        FPL–0201, 20 pp. Forest
        Prod. Lab., Madison, Wis.

Tarkow, H.
1966.   Dimensional stability. In
        Encycl. Polymer Sci. and
        Technol. 5: 98–121.

Tarkow, H., Stamm, A. J., and Erick-
    son, E. C. O.
1950.   Acetylated wood. USDA
        Forest Serv. Forest Prod.
        Lab. Rep. 1593 rev., 29
        pp.

Tarkow, H., and Stamm, A. J.
1953.   Effect of formaldehyde
        treatments upon the di-
        mensional stabilization of
        wood. J. Forest Prod.
        Res. Soc. 3(2): 33–37.

Teesdale, C. H.
1914.   Relative resistance of var-
        ious conifers to injection
        with creosote. USDA
        Bull. 101, 43 pp.

Teesdale, C. H., and MacLean, J. D.
　1918. Tests of the absorption and penetration of coal tar and creosote in longleaf pine. USDA Bull. 607, 43 pp.

Truax, T R., and Harrison, C. A.
　1929. A new test for measuring the fire resistance of wood. Amer. Soc. Testing Mater, Proc. 29, Part II, pp. 973–988.

Truax, T. R., and Harrison, C. A.
　1930. Measuring fire resistance of wood. Trans. Amer. Soc Mech. Eng. 52(17): 33–43.

Truax, T. R., Harrison, C. A., and Baechler, R. H.
　1935. Experiments in fireproofing wood—fifth progress report. Amer. Wood Preserv. Assoc. Proc. 31: 231–245.

Underwriters' Laboratories, Inc.
　1968. Wood—fire hazard classification. Card Data Serv. C60. Serial Number UL527.

Underwriters' Laboratories, Inc.
　1969. Building materials list. 673 pp. Chicago: Underwriters' Lab., Inc.

USDA Forest Products Laboratory.
　1955. Wood handbook. USDA Agr. Handbook 72, 528 pp.

USDA Forest Products Laboratory.
　1968. Partial list of suppliers of fire retarding-coatings for wood. USDA Forest Serv. Forest Prod. Lab. Job 65–034, rev., 2 pp.

Van Kleeck, A.
　1942. Corrosion studies with certain fire-retardant chemicals. Amer. Wood Preserv. Assoc. Proc. 38: 160–171.

Verrall, A. F.
　1945. The control of fungi in lumber during air-seasoning. Bot. Rev. 11: 398–415.

Verrall, A. F.
　1957. Absorption and penetration of preservatives applied to southern pine wood by dips or short-period soaks. USDA Forest Serv. Southern Forest Exp. Sta. Occas. Pap. 157, 31 pp.

Verrall, A. F.
　1965. Preserving wood by brush, dip, and short-soak methods. USDA Tech. Bull. 1334, 50 pp.

Verrall, A. F., and Mook, P. V.
　1951. Research on chemical control of fungi in green lumber, 1940–51. USDA Tech. Bull. 1046, 60 pp.

Verrall, A. F., and Scheffer, T. C.
　1969. Preservative treatments for protecting wood boxes. USDA Forest Serv. Res. Pap. FPL–106, 8 p. Forest Prod. Lab., Madison, Wis.

Weaver, J. W., Nielson, J. F., and Goldstein, I. S.
　1960. Dimensional stabilization of wood with aldehydes and related compounds. Forest Prod. J. 10: 306–310.

Wier, T. P., Jr.
　1958. Lumber treatment by the vacuum process. Forest Prod. J. 8: 91–95.

Wood, L. W., Erickson, E. C. O., and Dohr, A. W.
　1960. Strength and related properties of wood poles. Amer. Soc. for Testing Mater. Wood Pole Res. Program Final Rep., 83 pp.

23

Gluing and bonding

CONTENTS

23

Gluing and bonding

Some knowledge of gluing technology is required to manufacture virtually all southern pine solid wood products except lumber and poles; even lumber is sometimes end- or edge-glued and poles are sometimes laminated. In all wood fiber products, strength is dependent on the integrity of fiber-to-fiber bonds. As the southern pine industry more nearly achieves whole-tree utilization, gluing and bonding techniques will become increasingly important; this is so because whole-tree utilization will likely be accomplished through reduction of tops, limbs, bark, roots, and needles into particles or fibers for reconstitution into products.

The text in this chapter is organized to describe published gluing and bonding research specific to major southern pine products. The principal adhesives are briefly described in the initial section. Readers desiring an introduction to the theory of adhesion are referred to Reinhart (1954), Clark et al. (1954, pp. 9–73), Bikerman (1961, pp. 1143), Weiss (1962, pp. 1–45), Voiutskii (1963, pp. 5–178 and 197–233), and Stamm (1964, pp. 488–540).

23–1 GLUES

Adhesives for southern pine are polymers; some are natural, but most are synthetic. Ideally, wood and glue should have similar hygroscopicity and swelling characteristics, coefficients of thermal expansion, and moduli of elasticity. If thus matched, stress concentrations at the glueline are minimized; if hygroscopicity and expansion coefficients differ, the adhesive must be sufficiently plastic to relieve stresses of swelling and shrinking and those built up during cooling of hot-pressed joints. Glues should set with a minimum of volume change. For most purposes they should be thermosetting. They should be quite viscous at the temperature applied to avoid excessive squeezeout from the joint or absorption into the wood—both of which cause poor joints.

NONRESIN GLUES

Natural glues not much used on southern pine because of their lack of resistance to heat and moisture cycling include animal glue from hides, sinews, and bone marrow of cattle, starch glue made chiefly from the cassava root, blood glue from a slaughter-house byproduct, and soybean glue.

Casein.—Because it cures at room temperature, has a long storage life, is cheap, easily applied, light in color, and moderately resistant to moisture and temperature cycling, casein glue is much used to laminate southern pine for interior use. It is made of protein from soured milk reacted with alkali (Brunauer et al. 1938; Browne and Brouse 1939; USDA Forest Products Laboratory 1939).

Brouse (1956) described two typical formulations that cure at room temperature: (A) 1 part of dry casein, 3.3 parts of water, 0.28 part of hydrated lime, and 0.70 part of sodium silicate; (B) 1 part of dry casein, 2.4 parts of water, 0.5 part of hydrated lime, and 0.12 part of sodium hydroxide. Plywood panels (not southern pine) assembled with these glues showed no delamination during 160 weeks of cycling between 30- and 80-percent relative humidity; when cycled between 30- and 90-percent relative humidity, however, they began to delaminate after 80 weeks.

If required, casein glues can also be formulated for use in a hot press.

SYNTHETIC RESIN GLUES

Synthetic resins are man-made polymers resembling natural resins in physical characteristics, but having special properties that can be tailored to meet specific requirements (USDA Forest Products Laboratory 1948). With the exception of polyvinyl emulsions, the synthetic resin glues used in the wood industry—all developed since 1930—are thermosetting and depend on a condensation type of polymerization reaction in which water is eliminated; the water formed in the reaction migrates into the wood. Polyvinyl-acetate emulsions are thermoplastic, entirely prepolymerized, and set by a loss of dispersing solvent. Modern synthetic resin glues are formulated from the corresponding synthetic polymers of the plastics industry. Readers interested in the chemistry of these resins should find the following references useful: Carswell (1947), Delmonte (1947), Mark and Tobolsky (1950), Meyer (1950), Burnett (1954), Schildknecht (1955), Redfarn and Bedford (1960), Sorenson and Campbell (1961), Billmeyer (1957), and Stille (1962).

Phenol formaldehyde.—These dark-colored glues are used, to the virtual exclusion of all other adhesives, in the hot pressing of southern pine plywood. They are relatively cheap and are highly durable in joints subjected to temperature and moisture cycling, and to severe weather exposure.

For use at hot-press temperatures near 275° F., they are manufactured in an alkaline-catalyzed, resin-forming condensation reaction of formaldehyde with phenol or phenol-cresol mixtures. Southern pine plywood plants usually purchase a partially prepolymerized resin (containing the catalyst) in solution in water.

Acid catalyzed resins formulated to set at temperatures as low as 75° F. are also available, but with certain of such resins there is a possibility that the acid catalyst may damage the wood. Phenol-formaldehyde glue is also available as a partially prepolymerized powder ready for dispersion in water or water-alcohol mixtures. For certain applications where bleed-through of glue must be avoided, e.g., in the attachment of very thin hardwood veneers, or for convenience, it is possible to obtain phenol-formaldehyde resin impregnated into a thin tissue paper; this dry sheet, which is inserted between surfaces to be joined in a hot press, replaces the wet glueline.

Urea formaldehyde.—In the southern pine industry, the light-colored urea resins are primarily used to make hot-pressed, interior grades of particleboard. Formulations designed to set at room temperature (70° F.) are used in some nonstructural laminated products and in some end- and edge-glued products. Urea-formaldehyde glues may also be cured rapidly and easily by radio frequency energy. Because of their light color, low cost, and ability to cure quickly at temperatures below 260° F., urea-formaldehyde glues are much used for interior applications; they should not be used, however, where the product will undergo severe temperature and moisture cycling or exterior service. Urea-formaldehyde glue joints resist cycling and weathering poorly in comparison with those made with phenol-formaldehyde glues (Brouse 1939; USDA Forest Products Laboratory 1956; Blomquist and Olson 1957).

Urea-formaldehyde resins are made in a condensation reaction. The resins are partially prepolymerized and are available in aqueous solution, with a separate acid catalyst to be added just before use; they are also available in powdered form, including the catalyst, to be mixed with water for use. As is the case with phenol-formaldehyde glues, urea-formaldehyde glues can be extended with wheat flour or other extender to reduce glueline cost.

Melamine formaldehyde.—These light-colored glues are more weather resistant than urea-formaldehyde glues (Brouse 1939, 1957); in plywood their resistance to weather is approximately equivalent to that of phenol-formaldehyde or resorcinol-formaldehyde glues. The melamine glues are substantially more expensive than urea-formaldehyde glues, and require curing at 240° F. or higher for most applications.

Resorcinol formaldehyde.—Assemblies made with the dark-colored resorcinol glues are extremely resistant to delamination when exposed to temperature and humidity cycling. Their resistance to weathering and ability to cure at a temperature of 70° F. or slightly above cause resorcinol-formaldehyde glues to be much used in southern pine laminated products designed for exterior exposure. They are, however, several times more costly than phenol-formaldehyde glues. To reduce glue cost, resorcinol formaldehyde and phenol formaldehyde can be copolymerized together to produce phenol-resorcinol resin glues.

In phenol-formaldehyde resins, condensation of the phenol and formaldehyde is usually complete with all formaldehyde reacted during resin manufacture. Resorcinol-formaldehyde resins are only partly reacted, however, and the additional required formaldehyde is added just prior to use as paraformaldehyde hardener or curing agent.

Polyvinyl emulsion.—Because these white glues set rapidly, need no heating in the pot, have a long working life, cure at room temperature, are cheap, and form colorless gluelines, they are much used in place of animal glue in certain furniture joints.

Uses for polyvinyl-acetate emulsion glues are limited because they are thermoplastic; that is, they undergo repeated liquefication and solidification as temperature is increased and decreased. Hence, at high temperature they tend to soften and yield when continuously stressed. They also soften and yield at high moisture content. Moreover, these glues have little resistance to weathering. Under normal indoor temperature and humidity conditions, however, dowelled or mortised joints assembled with polyvinyl-acetate glues give good service.

The newest class of modified vinyl emulsions—said to have some cross-linking properties—have intermediate weather resistance, outlasting polyvinyl-acetate emulsions but inferior to phenol-formaldehyde and resorcinol-formaldehyde glues. Gluelines in laminated beams assembled with modified vinyl glues cured at room temperature failed in 2 to 3 years of exposure in Ottawa, Canada climate (Canada Department of Fisheries and Forestry 1970).

23–2   LAMINATED WOOD [1]

The wood laminating industry produces thick lumber and timbers by gluing together boards, usually more than ½-inch in thickness. Freas (1953) and Selbo and Knauss (1954) traced the growth of the industry and the research that accompanied its early development in this country; they noted that laminated, straight and curved structural beams of southern pine have been manufactured in the United States since the mid-1930's and that use of these products has been steadily increasing.

In 1958, the Census of Manufacturers reported that about 48 million bd. ft. of lumber of all species was used for glued laminated timbers; by 1968, three times this volume (148 million bd. ft.) was converted to laminated timbers valued at more than $39 million. These figures do not include glued laminated lumber used in combination with sawn lumber for manufactured components, nor do they include laminated decking (Sampson 1970).

PRODUCTION TRENDS

While accurate statistics on the southern pine laminators' share of the total market for glued laminated timber are not available, Sampson (1970) estimated that the volume of southern pine lumber used for laminated arches, beams, and timber decking doubled between 1961 and 1964; in 1969 volume was over 2½ times that in 1961. In 1969, about 30 percent

---

[1] The text under this heading is expanded from Blomquist (1969) by permission of R. F. Blomquist and the Forest Products Research Society.

of this volume was used in church construction, 30 percent in industrial and commercial construction, 13 percent in school buildings, 12 percent in community buildings, and the remaining 15 percent in residential and other construction. He also noted that there is a possibility of developing a major market in laminated wood transmission towers.

GLUING UNTREATED WOOD

According to the USDA Forest Products Laboratory (1955), wood of the 10 southern pines is moderately easy to glue; that is, it glues well with different adhesives under a moderately wide range of gluing conditions. This rating is based on wood failure in gluelines of natural non-resin glues (Truax 1929). Among 40 softwoods and hardwoods tested, southern pine ranked between 10 and 20 when the species were arranged in order of glueline quality. In later, unpublished studies by W. Z. Olson and R. F. Blomquist, in which synthetic resin glues were used, southern pine was similarly rated.

In tests of southern pine lumber glued with urea-formaldehyde glue and cured at room temperature, Eickner (1942) reported dry block shear strengths of 1,719 p.s.i. with 97 percent wood failure; with casein glue he observed a shear shrength of 1,950 p.s.i. and 86 percent wood failure. These results were comparable to those recorded by Truax (1929) and Olson and Blomquist.

Glues for interior applications.—Because it takes a substantial amount of time to lay up and clamp a large laminated beam, adhesives for structural laminated timbers must tolerate a long assembly time; moreover, due to the size and heat conductivity properties of large structural beams, glues for such beams must generally be cured at room temperature.

Of the two major, room-temperature-setting, interior, structural glues (urea formaldehyde and casein), casein will tolerate the longer assembly time. Primarily for this reason, but also because of their low cost, water-resistant casein glues are the principal adhesives used to laminate southern pine structural beams for interior use. On southern pine, the casein glues are normally spread at about 60 to 90 pounds per M sq. ft. of single glueline when single spread and cured at ambient shop temperature. The spread should be 75 to 110 pounds when glue is applied to both mating surfaces; such double spreading is the usual industrial practice.

For the foregoing reasons, and because of their limited durability at elevated temperatures, urea-formaldehyde glues are not used in the United States for interior laminated structural timbers. They are, however, much used for nonstructural, interior, small, laminated or edge-glued southern pine products that can be spread and layed up with a minimum of delay in assembly time and cured quickly with radio frequency or conventional heat energy. Melamine-formaldehyde glues are also used for this purpose.

Glues for exterior applications.—Since straight phenol-formaldehyde glues are substantially cheaper than resorcinol-formaldehyde glues, some efforts have been made to use them in the lamination of southern pine; because of the higher cure temperature required by these glues and slow heat transfer to gluelines in large members, however, they are today little used by themselves to make heavy timbers. Currently, resorcinol and blends of phenol and resorcinol glues are used on virtually all structural glued laminated wood designed for exterior exposure.

In early work, heating of the resorcinol and phenol-resorcinol gluelines to 110° and 140° F. respectively was considered necessary to achieve a high resistance to delamination in high-density southern pine. Although resorcinol and phenol-resorcinol glues cured at normal room temperatures usually gave good joint strengths and high percentages of wood failure in dry block shear tests, resistance to delamination from moisture changes and shrinkage stresses usually was considerably higher when some heat curing was used.[2]

In current practice, however, southern pine is commonly laminated with resorcinol and phenol-resorcinol glues without heating above a minimum ambient temperature of 70° F. This change in practice is attributable to better glues and improved control over the gluing process. The glues are spread at about 50 to 75 pounds per M sq. ft. of single glueline when conventional double spreading (on both mating surfaces) is used.

Some years ago in Texas, southern pine 2 by 4 studs were laminated from 1 by 4's on a commercial basis; the studs were glued with acid-catalyzed phenol-formaldehyde and phenol-resorcinol-formaldehyde glues cured in clamp carriers in a chamber heated to 115° to 120° F. for a minimum of 3 hours (Musselwhite 1953). Discontinuance of the operation was probably attributable more to the price and supply situation for 1 by 4's and 2 by 4's rather than to any inadequacy of the glueline.

GLUING PRESERVATIVE-TREATED WOOD

Use of laminated southern pine in exterior exposure may cause decay of the wood as well as delamination at the glueline. It is therefore necessary to protect the wood with suitable preservative treatment either before or after gluing. Since a clean, flat wood surface is required to obtain a good glue joint, it is necesary to resurface treated wood before it is glue-laminated.

Oilborne preservatives, such as creosote or pentachlorophenol, do not cause significant gluing problems in southern pine if the oil does not bleed appreciably when lumber is surfaced after treatment (Freas and Selbo 1954; Selbo 1961). Any oil present on the wood surface should be drained and wiped off cleanly before glue application. As preservative-treated wood

---

[2] Selbo, M. L. Durability of glue joints in beams laminated of high-density longleaf pine. Unpublished file report. USDA Forest Products Laboratory, Madison, Wis. 1949.

is designed for exterior exposure, glues used are principally resorcinol or phenol resorcinol.

Southern pine lumber treated with waterborne preservatives can also be satisfactorily laminated with resorcinol and phenol-resorcinol glues; the wood must be redried after treatment, however, before resurfacing and gluing. Since some preservatives appear to retard curing of some glues, it is generally considered desirable to use a somewhat higher cure temperature in gluing treated than untreated wood. Selbo (1965) has summarized information on gluing of treated wood, including experience with southern pine.

Henry and Gardner (1954) also studied the gluing of preservative-treated southern pine lumber with resorcinol-type glues. Preservatives included both oilborne and waterborne. Tests were limited to accelerated vacuum-pressure soaking and drying cycles. They reported that wood treated with nine of the tested preservative systems could be glued satisfactorily when the resorcinol and phenol-resorcinol glues were cured at 150° F. glueline temperatures for 2 hours. With some treatments, such as ammoniacal copper arsenite and acid cupric chromate, curing at 150° F. for a longer period was necessary to achieve adequate bonding. Others have reported similar results.

Durability of preservative-treated laminated beams.—Hanna (1955) reported on southern pine crossarms for utility poles, laminated with phenol-resorcinol glues and treated with various preservatives including creosote and pentachlorophenol. Performance, evaluated from outdoor exposure in New Jersey and Colorado, was promising.

The most convincing demonstration of the permanence of glued joints in laminated southern pine is obtained from actual service. Selbo (1967) and Selbo et al. (1965), summarizing 20 years of service experience, cited good performance of shortleaf pine laminated stringers in two railroad trestles. On one in Texas, stringers were glued with phenol-resorcinol resin, cured at 180° F., and pressure treated after gluing with distillate creosote; in the other at Alexandria, Va., laminates pressure treated with creosote-coal tar are still giving good service more than 20 years after installation. Sections from both sets of timbers had been tested initially in block shear tests and cyclic delamination and showed good quality joints. Sections were also exposed outdoors in Madison, Wis. During service in the trestles, very little delamination has been observed, although checking of the wood has sometimes been a problem.

In another installation, a number of laminated stringers of southern pine were glued from lumber that had been treated with a fluor-chrome-arsenate-phenol process (FCAP). These were installed in a bridge in Florida in 1949. Some additional stringers were glued with creosote-treated pine, and some were glued from untreated pine and then treated with the FCAP process. The bridge was rebuilt in 1956 and some of the stringers reused in another open-deck trestle in Florida.

GLUING FIRE-RETARDANT-TREATED WOOD

Southern pine lumber can also be treated with fire-retardant salt solutions, redried, resurfaced, and then glued. It is desirable to assemble such laminations with resorcinol or phenol-resorcinol glues in order to provide resistance to heat. Laboratory tests and experience have shown that typical ammonium salt fire-retardant systems do reduce the quality of bonds made with these glues. The exact mechanism is not completely understood, but there are probably some side reactions between the ammonium ions and the resorcinol resin (Selbo 1965; Schaeffer 1966, 1967). The percentages of wood failure in block shear tests are often considerably more erratic and lower than with untreated wood, and resistance to delamination in cyclic vacuum-pressure delamination tests is considerably lower. The use of higher curing temperatures in laminating such treated woods is only partially effective, and special resorcinol-type resin systems have been proposed. Because the effects of preservatives and fire retardants on gluing are due primarily to the chemicals involved, they apply equally to other species as well as to southern pine.

TECHNIQUES TO ACHIEVE A GOOD GLUEBOND

Good gluebonds result from close control of many factors, including moisture content of the wood, preparation of the surface, glue selection, mixing and spreading, assembly technique, pressure application, and temperature and time of cure. Adherends must mate with the adhesive. Because of surface irregularities and warp in lumber to be laminated, a substantial amount of pressure is required to accomplish the desired mating of surfaces. For 1- and 2-inch southern pine lumber, experience indicates that a specific pressure of about 100 to 200 p.s.i. is required (Freas and Selbo 1954).

Since research has shown that most beams glue-laminated from southern pine eventually come to equilibrium at a moisture content close to 9 percent (Hann et al. 1970), it is reasonable to adjust lumber moisture content and water content in the gluespread so that the finished beam contains about 9-percent moisture content. Such precautions should minimize unnecessary strains on gluelines caused by shrinkage of the laminae and insure good dimensional stability and performance.

Glue, regardless of formulation, should be spread only on a clean lumber surface. Best bond quality is obtained if the laminae are planed with sharp knives just prior to glue application.

TECHNIQUE OF FABRICATING LAMINATED TIMBERS

It is beyond the scope of this text to describe fabrication procedures; the interested reader should find the comprehensive work by Freas and Selbo (1954) useful. Steps in fabrication include organization of laminae, spreading, layup, curing under pressure, and finishing.

The introduction of nondestructive testing techniques to evaluate the strength of individual laminae has led to several publications describing systems to position southern pine laminae efficiently in beams (Koch 1964ab, 1967ac, 1971; Koch and Bohannan 1965; Koch and Woodson 1968; Bohannan and Moody 1969; Moody and Bohannan 1970). It is likely that the industry will, to some degree, adopt the principle of placing laminae having the highest moduli of elasticity in the outer, most highly stressed region of each beam.

Techniques for applying glue to laminae with roll spreaders are simple and well developed. For structural laminated beams, double spreading of glue on both mating surfaces is the usual practice because of the long assembly periods required to lay up big beams. Application of glue to both mating surfaces permits longer assembly times—both open and closed, but particularly closed—than application of glue to only one surface.

As an alternative to the roll-spreading technique, Webb (1970) reported that a thixotropic phenol-resorcinol glue of high viscosity could be advantageously extruded in a ribbon pattern on southern pine laminae. Advantages claimed for the ribbon spread—which was accomplished by pumping glue through orifices as the lumber passed below—included cleanliness of operation, accurate control of spread rate, little waste of glue, and little solvent evaporation; by this system glue is spread only on one surface.

Following glue application and beam layup, pressure is uniformly applied for a time appropriate for both glue and press temperature. Most heavy laminated beams and arches are pressed several hours (or overnight) in massive clamps temporarily arranged to manufacture only a few of each structure.

Descriptions of presses utilizing the stored-heat principle to laminate small beams and decking have been provided by Marra (1956) and Malarkey (1963). Mann (1954), Syme (1960), and Anonymous (1962) reviewed fast-cycling batch equipment designed to edge-glue and laminate with radio frequency heating, and Carruthers (1965) described a continuous laminating machine for beams that uses radio frequency energy to cure the gluelines. Miller and Cole (1957), Clark (1959), Carruthers (1963), and Miller and George (1965) have reviewed gluing problems associated with the use of radio frequency energy to cure gluelines.

STANDARDS FOR STRUCTURAL GLUE LAMINATED TIMBER

U.S. Commercial Standard CS 253–63 for structural glued laminated timber is a voluntary standard originated by the industry; it—or its current revision—is available from U.S. Superintendent of Documents, Washington, D.C.

AITC 117–71, standard specifications for structural glued laminated timber of Douglas-fir, western larch, southern pine, and California redwood, is available from the American Institute of Timber Construction, Englewood, Colo. From time to time this standard, also, is revised.

23–3 END-GLUED LUMBER [1]

Well-made edge-glued or face-to-face-glued laminated joints in southern pine have been proven equal in strength to solid wood. Glued end joints equal in strength to solid wood, however, have not yet been developed.

End-jointing is important to the southern pine industry since virtually all long laminated beams are comprised of end-glued lumber. Also, because long southern pine millwork and structural lumber has more value to builders than short, improvement of end-glued joints is a major objective of manufacturers.

Mainly, end-glued joints in lumber take two forms: scarf joints and fingerjoints; butt joints have generally not provided sufficient strength for commercial use.

SCARF JOINTS

Glued joints carefully made by overlapping smoothly machined bevelled ends of boards, i.e., scarf joints, are the strongest end joints in common use. Their strength, both absolute and as a fraction of the strength of solid wood, is negatively correlated with the angle of scarf—i.e., the lower slope, the better the joint; for this reason, structural scarf joints are usually bevelled on a slope of $\frac{1}{8}$ or flatter.

Richards and Goodrick (1959) provided data on strength of 1/6, 1/9, 1/12, and 1/15 scarf joints in southern pine of a variety of densities. Urea-formaldehyde and resorcinol-formaldehyde glues were used to make the joints; glue was cured at room temperature. Absolute joint strength increased only slightly with increases in wood specific gravity, but increased markedly as slope of scarf was decreased (fig. 23–1). Joint strengths, expressed as a percentage of matched solid wood strengths, were related to wood specific gravity (basis of ovendry weight and volume) as follows:

Slope of scarf	Wood specific gravity		
	0.47	0.55	0.62
	– – – – – Percent – – – – –		
1/6 ____	56	54	52
1/9 ____	73	68	64
1/12 ____	81	72	67
1/15 ____	87	81	77

Tensile strength of the solid wood controls increased with increased specific gravity as shown in figure 23–1.

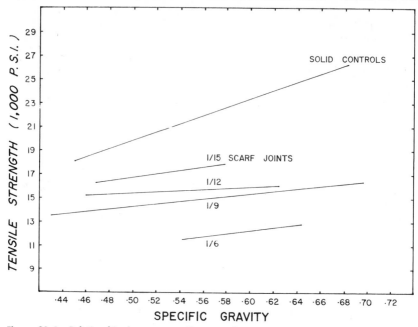

Figure 23–1.—Relationship between tensile strength, at 8.5-percent moisture content, and specific gravity (basis of ovendry weight and volume) in scarf-jointed southern pine. Top line shows strength of solid wood controls with no joints. (Drawing after Richards and Goodrick 1959.)

Fengel and Kumar (1970) have provided electron micrographs illustrating the penetration of phenol-formaldehyde glue into scarf joints in Scotch pine (*Pinus sylvestris* L.). They observed that the glue did not penetrate very deeply, but generally the adhesion between glue and cell wall was very good; they concluded that the glue grafted onto the inner layer of the cell wall. Locally poor adhesion between glue and cell wall appeared to occur where the warty layer (fig. 5–9) adhered poorly to the S_3 layer; the explanation for this lack of adhesion was not entirely clear.

From tests on a number of softwoods (not including southern pine) Marion et al. (1958) concluded that the real problem in obtaining very high strength ratios in scarfed end joints is the strength reduction caused by contact between earlywood and latewood, and the difficulty in transmitting stresses between these two cell types. Research specific to southern pine (Hse 1968) indicates that adequate latewood-to-latewood bonds are the most difficult to achieve.

FINGERJOINTS

A $\frac{1}{12}$ scarf joint in 2-inch lumber calls for an overlap of 24 inches—a footage loss of 12.5 percent if boards average 16 feet in length; moreover, scarf joints are difficult to align and press on a production basis. The footage loss inherent in scarf joints can be substantially reduced by machining scarfs of about the same slope but in folded multiples to form a fingerjoint (fig. 23–2). Fingerjoints also help keep short pieces aligned as they are rapidly assembled into endless lumber. For high-strength joints, fingertips should have feathered ends and should match perfectly with seats, but such closely matching joints are difficult to machine. Manufacturing problems are substantially lessened, but joint strength is reduced if fingertips and seats are blunt (Selbo 1963). For this reason two major types of fingerjointed lumber have evolved: nonstructural for use in millwork, and structural for use in high-strength products.

Nonstructural fingerjoints.—Numerous designs of fingerjoints are used in the manufacture of pine millwork, but in general they resemble that shown in figure 23–2. Tip thickness commonly measures $\frac{1}{32}$-inch or more, finger length may be approximately 1 inch, and slope is generally steeper than $\frac{1}{12}$.

In general, the millwork manufacturer desires short joint length to conserve wood and a fingertip thickness that can be cut without undue cutter maintenance. Tip and seat must make a closed butt joint on both top and bottom surfaces so that the resulting straight, even, inconspicuous joint will not detract from surface appearance. On wide, long, heavy lumber it is particularly difficult to fabricate joints that show no openings when assembled. To minimize cutterhead investment and setup time, the pattern selected should be applicable to a range of lumber thicknesses. Oberg (1961) described some of the considerations involved in the selection of a fingerjoint pattern.

In millwork plants, joints are usually cut by conveying the lumber—one

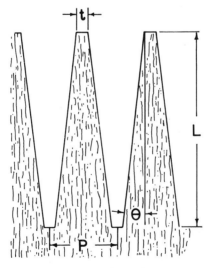

Figure 23–2.—Nomenclature for geometry of fingerjoints. P is pitch, t is tip thickness, L is finger length, and tangent θ is the slope. (Drawing after Selbo 1963.)

piece at a time—past a rotating cutterhead so that the fingers are cut parallel to board faces. A formed roll applicator (or a spray injector) then coats the fingers with 60 to 80 pounds of glue per M sq. ft. of glueline.

In most plants, the glued joint—assembled under end pressure—locks together sufficiently to permit immediate offbearing and stacking so that glue curing is completed at room temperature in the stack. In some plants, however, glue joints made with thermosetting resin glues are cured by application of radio frequency energy as the joint is made. Syme (1960) has provided a description of lumber end-gluing operations in such a mill-work plant.

In millwork plants, pieces to be fingerjointed are commonly 2 inches or less in thickness, 12 inches or less in width, and not less than 6 inches long. Completely conveyorized equipment commonly processes 60 pieces per minute; from this it can be computed that production (with no lost time) approaches 3,600 bd. ft. per hour if lumber to be jointed averages 1 inch thick, 6 inches wide, and 2 feet long. Because fingerjointed stock is run from previously planed lumber, finished thickness is less than the usual standard, e.g., 4/4 fingerjointed boards commonly measure only $11/_{16}$-inch instead of the standard $3/_4$-inch thickness.

Principal glues used, listed in order of increasing water resistance, are polyvinyl acetate and copolymers, urea formaldehyde, and mixtures of melamine-formaldehyde resins with urea-formaldehyde resins. None of these glues are sufficiently waterproof to permit use in products given extended unprotected exterior exposure. Melamine-urea resins require heat for curing—usually supplied by radio frequency energy. Still in the ex-primental stage is the use of gap-filling adhesives in southern pine finger-joints. Schaeffer (1970) found that by pretreating southern pine with resorcinol solution and heating mating surfaces or using hot-melt adhesives on untreated cool surfaces, joints comparable in strength to commercial fingerjoints could be made even though the fingers were warped and loose fitting; glues evaluated included three epoxy formulations and one poly-urethane hot-melt adhesive. These experimental adhesive formulations were used to improve performance in gap filling, rather than to achieve a high level of durability.

Appearance rather than strength is the governing factor in the manu-facture of fingerjointed millwork. Virtually all is made in clear grades. When cutting common and shop grades of lumber into clears for finger-jointing, 30 to 45 percent of the wood is commonly wasted as trim.

The advent of factory-finished millwork in which joints are hidden, stim-ulated production and consumer acceptance of fingerjointed wood. Ac-cording to one producer, the prefinished moulding market in 1970 totaled $100 million in the United States and represented 25 percent of the total moulding footage produced.

Recently, the development of a process to finish certain millwork items with a vinyl wrap has again increased the demand for nonstructural fingerjointed wood. Moreover, builders and fabricators in the United States increasingly request millwork cut to precise lengths—a demand that is most easily met with fingerjointed wood.

Structural fingerjoints.—Structural fingerjoints differ from those used in millwork because they must unfailingly have high strength; most must be designed for exterior exposure to fluctuating temperature and moisture conditions. For this reason fingertip thicknesses are the minimum achievable and glues used are commonly resorcinol or phenol-resorcinol types. These glues, which cure slowly at room temperatures, call for rigorous control of the cure cycle to maintain joint quality on a production basis.

Fingerjoint designs for southern pine has been greatly influenced by the work of D. B. Richards and his associates (Richards and Cool 1953; Richards 1958ab, 1962, 1963, 1968; Pincus et al. 1966). This work showed that truncated tips should not be located at or near board surfaces, i.e., the surface scarfs of the finished member should run out in a well-glued feather edge. Thick square tips, wherever located, are damaging to strength; rounded tips and seats yield higher strength ratios than square tips and seats.

Selbo (1963) briefly reviewed the literature on structural fingerjoints; based on his tests of fingerjointed Sitka spruce (*Picea sitchensis* (Bong.) Carr.), Douglas-fir (*Pseudotsuga menziesii* (Mirb.) Franco), and white oak (*Quercus alba* L.), he observed that with thick tips, strength increased significantly with increase in pitch (distance between tips), but with very thin tips the effect of pitch became practically nil. He found that tensile strength of fingerjoints was negatively correlated with slope of scarfs, but the loss in strength was small as slope was increased from 1/16 to 1/12; a slope of 1/14 appeared most efficient for joint strength. With slope and tip thickness held constant, joint strength generally increased with increase in pitch. Joint strength was positively correlated with effective (sloping) glue joint area. Joints with thin tips were stronger than those with thick tips. The joints were made with resorcinol-resin glues and fabricated under close control.

From his data on Sitka spruce, Selbo (1963) summarized the effect of joint geometry (fig. 23–2) on tensile strength of fingerjoints as follows:

"The stress developed in the net section of a fingerjoint (total section minus area of fingertips) is not greatly dependent on slope of fingers in the range 1/10 to 1/16 but is dependent on sloping joint area or ratio of finger length to pitch (L/P), reaching a maximum for L/P greater than about 4. This maximum stress in Sitka spruce was approximately 17 percent less than the strength of the material (probably due to stress concentrations at the tips). Thus the strength of a fingerjoint is dependent on the area of the net section:

$$A_s = 1 - \frac{t}{P} \tag{23–1}$$

and the strength of the scarf joints in the net section."

Richards (1963), stimulated by experiments of Strickler (1962), demonstated that very high joint strengths in southern pine could be obtained with feather-edged fingers and seats having virtually zero tip thickness. He modified previously standardized fingers (Auburn B, fig. 23–3 top) so that the male tips were feather edged (fig. 23–3 middle) and then impressed a steel wedge in the female tip, to achieve a matching seat (fig. 23–3 bottom). Tensile strengths for southern pine joined by this system were as follows:

Density of southern pine wood	Unmodified Auburn B fingers	Modified fingers and seats with feather-edge tips
	– – – – – – P.s.i. – – – – – –	
Medium _____	7,167	13,288
Dense _____	10,744	15,023

The joints were in dry wood assembled with urea-formaldehyde glue cured under a top pressure of 150 p.s.i.

The system that Stricker (1962, 1966, 1967, 1970) invented employs fingerjoints of greatly reduced length (0.380 inch) and relies on a heated (500° F.) steel die to diminish male and female tip thickness after the rough outlines of the fingers have been machine cut (fig. 23–4). For

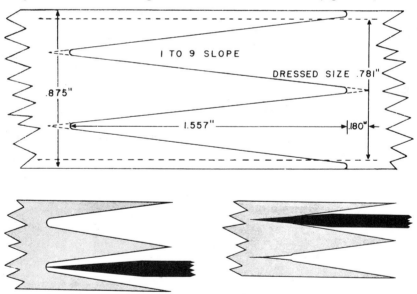

Figure 23–3.—(Top) Solid lines show edge view of Auburn B joint; dotted lines show modification to reduce tip thickness, and lumber thickness as tested. Completed joint measures 1.917 inches long. (Bottom left) Edge view of one member of a fingered scarf joint; the male tips have been machined to a feather edge by a cutterhead. The steel wedge (dark) is in position to wedge open one of the blunt female tips. (Bottom right) Steel wedge in position after cold forming and the resulting feather-edge female tip. (Drawing after Richards 1963.)

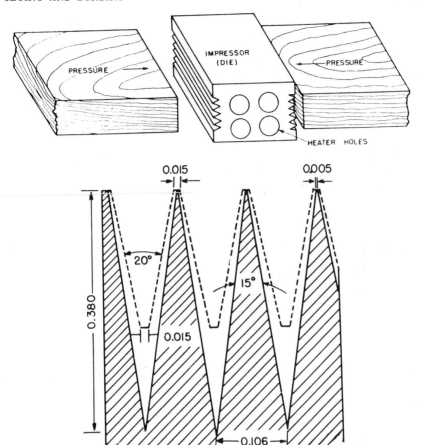

Figure 23–4.—(Top) Technique of forming impression fingerjoints with hot steel die. (Bottom) Dimensions of structural fingerjoint, inches. The dotted lines outline the preshaped machined joint end, and the coss-hatched portion the impressed joint end. (Drawings after Strickler 1967.)

southern pine, a force on the impressor die sufficient to yield about 1,900 p.s.i. pressure on the board cross section is required. Glue is spread subsequent to finger formation, and the heat stored at the surface of the newly formed fingers is used to cure the glueline. No data on joints formed in dry southern pine are published. With dry Douglas-fir, however, Strickler (1967) obtained strengths of about 9,500 p.s.i.

Strickler's process is applicable to green wood as well as dry. Southern pine, under the combined effect of high die temperature and some moisture, softens very quickly, permitting the die to cleave and compress the wood fibers with minimum grain disturbance. The softening effect persists fleetingly during impression, and because moisture migrates rapidly away from the heat source along the wood grain, glue dilution by wood moisture is reduced. Moreover, the combination of heat and pressure densifies the fingers and closes cell lumens, thus reducing excessive glue penetration.

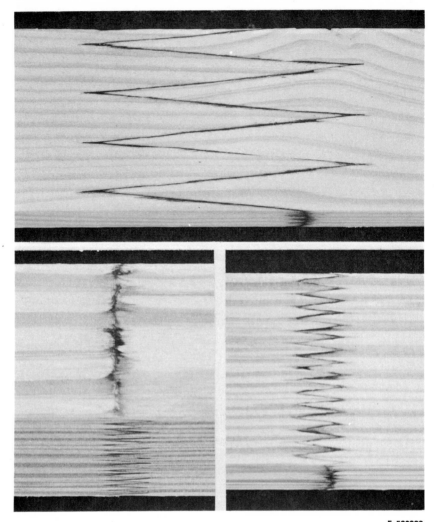

F-520999

Figure 23–5.—(Top) Slice removed from edge of structural, commercial, sawn fingerjoint in 6/4 southern pine. Fingers run parallel to board face, are 2⅛ inches long, and have tip thickness near zero. (Bottom) 0.38-inch-long impression fingerjoints in southern pine made with the process and dimensions shown in figure 23–4; fingers may be parallel to the face (left) or perpendicular (right).

With Strickler's process (figs. 23–4, 23–5 bottom) 29 fingerjoints were made in green southern pine 2 by 4's with average moisture content of 107 percent. Specific gravity of the 2 by 4's ranged from about 0.38 to 0.52 (basis of green volume and ovendry weight) with average of about 0.44. When test specimens cut from the 2 by 4's were broken in bending and tension at 15-percent moisture content, modulus of rupture and ultimate tensile strength were as follows (data previously unpublished):

Statistic	MOR	Tensile strength
	– – – – – – *P.s.i.* – – – – – –	
Average	7,076	6,307
Range	4,100—10,000	3,040—8,420
Standard deviation	1,379	1,140

Wood failure in the tension specimens averaged 88.4 percent. Many of the failures were in pith-associated wood and not in the joint. High-density pieces bonded to high-density pieces had about 2,100 p.s.i. higher MOR and 1,380 p.s.i. more strength in tension than low-density pieces bonded to low-density pieces. Strengths of bonds between high- and low-density pieces were intermediate. All joints were glued with a resorcinol-formaldehyde resin (fig. 23–5 bottom).

Strickler's process is not without disadvantages. The wet strength of small specimens having impression joints is considerably less than the wet strength of machined joints, having the same geometry, an effect apparently due to surface swelling of the wood fingers densified by die formation. In larger specimens, however, swelling is restrained, and the effect of surface swelling on strength is negligible. Cyclic delamination tests (on species other than southern pine) indicate an acceptable level of durability for impression joints formed in green lumber and assembled with resorcinol-resin glues (Strickler 1970).

A fully machined short fingerjoint similar in appearance to that shown in figure 23–5 (bottom) has been developed and patented (Marian 1968, 1969), and highly mechanized equipment is available that will cut and assemble three to four joints per minute. The joint is 7.5 mm. long with pitch of 2.5 mm. and tip thickness near zero. After the joint is machined by a cutterhead revolving at 6,000 r.p.m., glue is spread and the joint is assembled with a brief end pressure of 1,800 to 2,000 p.s.i. No further pressing is required. Polyvinyl-acetate, urea-formaldehyde, and resorcinol-formaldehyde glues are all used without addition of heat to cure the glueline. The machine will accept pieces up to 12 inches wide and 6 inches thick; minimum acceptable length is 20 inches. The cutup, machining, assembling, and off-bearing equipment cost approximately $100,000 in 1970. No test data on southern pine end-jointed by the process have been published.

Neither of the short joints (Strickler 1966; Marian 1969) is used by southern pine laminators. At least one producer of southern pine laminated beams, however, has devised a method of cutting, assembling, and curing structural fingerjoints with near zero tip thickness and $\frac{7}{16}$-inch pitch; the joint is $2\frac{1}{8}$ inches long (fig. 23–5 top). By use of substantial skill in saw filing and maintenance, the joints are sawn on a production basis. While each joint is assembled under end pressure, a portable hot metal clamp is tightened on the joint; the clamp remains in place when the end pressure is released and the lumber—in a long continuous ribbon—

moves toward the distant cutoff saw where it is cut to length for laminated beams. The portable clamps are then removed and returned to the assembly station. Resorcinol and phenol-resorcinol glues are used.

Structural fingerjoints may be cut so that the fingers are parallel to the face, or they may be perpendicular (fig. 23–5 bottom). Evidence available at this time suggests that the two arrangements can yield bonds of comparable strength. Gluebonds are usually poorest in the outermost fingers, however; members may have reduced strength, therefore, if flexed in such manner that the outermost fingers must carry the highest stresses.

Fingerjoints, more than scarf joints, are weakened by local defects in the wood; strong fingerjoints in southern pine can be consistently manufactured only if wood adjacent to and in the joint is free of knots, cross grain, checks, and pith-associated or juvenile wood.

Moody (1970) evaluated the weakening effect of pith-associated wood on structural fingerjoints commercially fabricated in 2- by 6-inch southern pine lumber selected to meet or exceed the American Institute of Timber Construction (1967) tension lamination grade. The lumber was divided into two classes (fig. 23–6 top), with pith-associated wood (PA) and that with no pith-associated wood (NPA). Specific gravity of the NPA lumber averaged about 0.55 based on ovendry weight and volume at time of test (13-percent moisture content); the PA lumber averaged about 0.52 in gravity.

Fingers in the joints were 1.11 inches long with 0.03-inch tip thickness and pitch of 0.25 inch. Entire fingerjointed boards and matching solid control boards were tested in tension. Moody's (1970) results are summarized in figure 23–6 (bottom) and as follows:

- Pith-associated material greatly affects the tensile strength of both fingerjointed lumber and lumber without joints.
- For the nonjointed lumber used as controls, the tensile strength of the pith-associated (PA) specimens averaged 34 percent less than that of specimens free of pith-associated material (NPA). About one-half of this difference was attributed to grade and specific gravity effects and the other half to lower strength pith-associated material.
- The average tensile strength of fingerjointed lumber containing PA wood was 22 percent less than that of fingerjointed NPA lumber.
- The tensile strength of fingerjointed NPA lumber averaged 66 percent of the tensile strength of similar control lumber. For the PA lumber, the fingerjointed lumber averaged 79 percent of similar control lumber.
- Fingerjointed lumber consisting of one NPA and one PA board had an average tensile strength about equal to that of fingerjointed lumber made entirely of PA boards.

Durability, test procedures, and standards.—Discussion of the durability of structural fingerjoints and their strength retention under repetitive

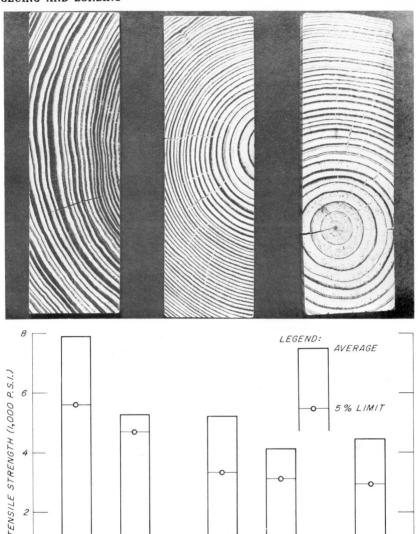

M–137074, M–136860

Figure 23–6.—(Top) Examples of end sections from specimens containing a significant amount of pith-associated material (PA) shown on the right and in the center. Non-pith-associated material (NPA) is shown on the left. The PA specimen shown on the right contains the pith and has wide-ringed nondense material over about one-half of the section. The PA specimen in the center has wide-ringed nondense material over the first inch from the pith. All PA specimens contained as much or more nondense pith-associated wood as the one shown in the center. The NPA specimen on the left is narrow-ringed and dense throughout the cross section. (Bottom) Summary of tension tests parallel to grain on southern pine lumber showing averages and 5 percent exclusion limits. (Photo and drawing from Moody 1970.)

load is beyond the scope of this text. The interested reader, however, should find the following references useful: Dorn and Egner (1961), Egner and Jagfield (1964), Richards (1968), and Bohannan and Kanvik (1969).

Readers interested in methodology for evaluating strength of finger-joints are referred to Markwardt and Youngquist (1956), Richards (1958b), Bolger and Rasmussen (1962), Selbo (1962), Dawe (1964), Bohannan and Selbo (1965), and Strickler et al. (1970).

Standards applicable to glued fingerjoints include: U.S. Department of Commerce (1963), Southern Pine Inspection Bureau (1965), Federal Housing Administration (1969), American Institute of Timber Construction (1969, 1970), and Western Wood Products Association (1969).

BUTT JOINTS

Most simple of all end joints is the butt joint; it requires a minimum of machining (a square end cut), and therefore wastes least wood. The glue in a butt joint is primarily stressed in tension, whereas that in a scarf joint or fingerjoint is primarily stressed in shear. To date, there is no gluing procedure for butt-joining southern pine that approaches the full strength of either adherend or adhesive in tension.

In studies of balsa wood (*Ochroma lagopus* Sw.), a weak wood, Bassett (1960) was generally unable to develop butt-joint strengths higher than 55 percent of the strength of clear wood.

Quirk et al. (1967abc, 1968) reported on extensive studies of transverse bonding of slash pine wood in which carefully machined butt joints in small sections of earlywood and latewood were assembled and tested in tension. Strengths achievable in the butt joints were low, mainly falling in the range from 1,000 to 5,000 p.s.i.; most joints had strengths less than 3,000 p.s.i. Joints were assembled with two forms of an epoxy-resin adhesive. Changing the nature of a basic epoxy resin from a rigid to a ductile form by adding an elastomer resulted in increased strength, efficiency, and quality of bonded joints. Increasing age (and viscosity) of both forms of mixed adhesive significantly reduced joint strength. With a stress-relieving ductile adhesive, joints fabricated from earlywood and from latewood differed significantly in strength; joints in earlywood were stronger. There was no significant correlation between joint strength and average depth of adhesive penetration. A combination of the two materials with the lowest intrinsic tensile strengths (earlywood 8,465 p.s.i. and ductile adhesive 5,900 p.s.i.) produced the strongest joints (4,230 p.s.i.).

In an effort to achieve stronger joints, Schaeffer and Gillespie (1970) later studied butt joints in eastern white pine (*Pinus strobus* L.). By heating and pretreating mating surfaces, they were able to achieve tensile strengths in butt joints with experimental epoxy adhesives that approached the strength of clear eastern white pine wood; however, the toughness of the butt joints under dynamic loading was only about one-third that of the clear wood. Gluelines 15 and 30 mils in thickness gave stronger and more uniform joints than 5-mil gluelines. In the most generally used pre-treatment, mating smooth-sawn surfaces were dipped for 5 seconds in a 10-percent aqueous solution of resorcinol, dried for 30 minutes, dipped a second time for 5 seconds, and air-dried for 4 hours. Then mating surfaces were exposed for 5 minutes at a distance of 1 inch from a 250-watt infrared lamp; this exposure resulted in wood surface temperatures of about 350° F. The adhesive (modified epoxy resin) was then spread on the hot mating surfaces and the joint was end pressed for 20 hours at 1.3 p.s.i.

Data on southern pine butt joints made by this procedure have not been published.

23–4   PLYWOOD [1]

Since events leading to establishment of the southern pine plywood industry have been extensively reported (Anonymous 1963; Fassnacht 1964; Norman 1964ab; Locke[3]; Orth 1968), they will not be again reviewed here, except to note that early plywood studies of the USDA Forest Products Laboratory, Madison, Wis. (Fleischer and Lutz 1963), played an important part in developing the necessary technology.

The first commercial plant opened in 1963. In 1966 total production of 23 operating plants in the South was 1.3 billion sq. ft. of plywood on a ⅜-inch basis (Sherman 1967). By the end of 1967, 29 plants were operating, with a total capacity of 2.3 billion sq. ft. (Bryan 1968).

In 1968, about 15 percent of the softwood plywood used in the United States was southern pine (Hair and Ulrich 1969, p. 25). This share of the market will likely increase; Guttenberg (1970) predicted that the South's output of plywood will reach 6 billion sq. ft. by the middle 1970's, possibly rising to 8 billion sq. ft. later in the decade. Holley (1969) predicted that by 1975 the South will be supplying 30 percent of the Nation's softwood plywood while maintaining its current proportion of lumber output.

SPECIFICATIONS AND TESTING PROCEDURES

U.S. Product Standard PS 1–66 (U.S. Department of Commerce 1966b) covers southern pine plywood of both interior and exterior types. Procedures for measuring wet shear strength and wood failure in shear specimens—the major test criteria for adequacy of exterior gluelines—are specified in this standard. In brief, exterior southern pine plywood must average 85 percent or more wood failure in gluelines evaluated after the specified wetting cycle.

---

[3] Locke, E. G. Southern pine plywood: Research to reality. Unpublished. 1965.

EXTERIOR AND INTERIOR GLUES

For a number of reasons, one of which is its ready permeability to water, most southern pine plywood is hot pressed with phenol-formaldehyde-resin glues so formulated that the plywood will satisfy the criteria for exterior gluelines as specified by Standard PS 1–66. In understanding this development it is useful to review the work of Blomquist and Olson (1964).

Their principal purpose was to determine whether glues typical of those used by the West Coast Douglas-fir plywood industry could also be used to produce acceptable southern pine plywood. They found that conventional cold-press soybean glue failed to meet acceptable interior-type glueline requirements by a wide margin. With southern pine, a hot-press, blood-phenol resin glue, and an interior-type phenol resin extended with ligno-cellulosic material widely used on the West Coast, met the requirements for interior-type gluelines; these glues would be logical candidates for interior-type plywood. A hot-press protein blend glue was marginal in quality for joints in interior-type plywood of southern pine. One of the phenol-formaldehyde glues tested was considered suitable, with some modification, for making southern pine exterior plywood.

In short, Blomquist and Olson (1964) concluded that exterior southern pine plywood should be feasible with modified, but conventional, phenol-formaldehyde glues; interior southern pine plywood could be made with some of the better interior-type glues, but the protein glues used at the time in the Douglas-fir industry were not adequate for southern pine.

Weakley and Mehltretter (1965) incorporated dialdehyde starch, a polymeric crosslinking or fortifying agent for proteins, in a low-cost, moderately alkaline, soybean-blood glue for hot pressing interior-type southern pine plywood. Although this fortified glue is a definite improvement over unfortified protein glues for interior applications, it is not commercially used since little interior-grade southern pine plywood is manufactured.

Phenol-formaldehyde, hot-pressed exterior glues have emerged as the dominant adhesives in the southern pine plywood industry. Gluebonds attained with these glues, and their quality as affected by veneers, glue formulations, spread, and pressing and curing techniques are discussed in the following pages. Also discussed are the gluing of hardwood core veneer to southern pine faces and backs, and the durability of southern pine in exterior exposure.

VENEER

From chapters 5 and 7 it is evident that veneer rotary cut from southern pine must show substantial variations in growth rings per inch and specific gravity. These variables, together with roughness of the veneer, its moisture and pitch content, and its degree of surface contamination all affect gluebond quality in southern pine plywood.

Specific gravity and growth rate.—Koch (1965ab) explored the effects of wood specific gravity and rate of tree growth on the properties of exterior plywood made from loblolly pine, together with the interacting effects of tightness of peel, resin content of glue, type of secondary extender, gluespread, and assembly time. Glueline quality, as measured by wood failure in thoroughly soaked shear specimens, was best in veneer of low specific gravity cut from slow-growing trees. Maximum wet and dry shear strengths were obtained by using veneer of high specific gravity, but high specific gravity veneers showed low wood failure and tended to delaminate more rapidly on exterior exposure; tree growth rate was not significantly correlated with either wet or dry shear strength of plywood gluelines (Koch 1965b, 1967b, 1970; Koch and Jenkinson 1965).

Earlywood and latewood.—Southern pine has wider bands of latewood than most other softwood species used for plywood (fig. 25–1). Differences in roughness and other properties between earlywood and latewood veneer surfaces (figs. 23–7, 23–8) thus greatly affect the gluability of southern pine veneers.

From an assumed tracheid model, Hse[4] derived equations for determining the roughness; with data measured on southern pine veneers, the

---

[4] Hse, C.-Y. Characterization of phenol-formaldehyde-resin adhesives as related to effectiveness in gluing southern pine veneer. USDA Forest Service, Southern Forest Experiment Station, Alexandria, La., Final Report FS–SO–3201–2.23 dated May 1, 1972.

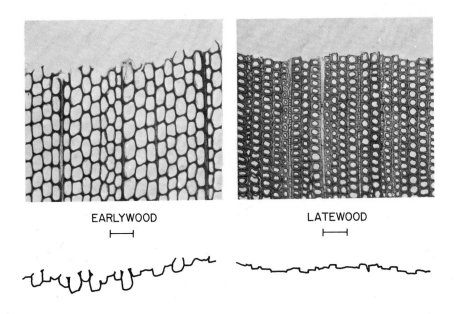

EARLYWOOD   LATEWOOD

F–521000

Figure 23–7.—(Top) Transverse sections showing tight side of rotary-cut southern pine veneer. (Bottom) Surface profiles. Scale mark shows 100 μm. (Photos from Hse[4].)

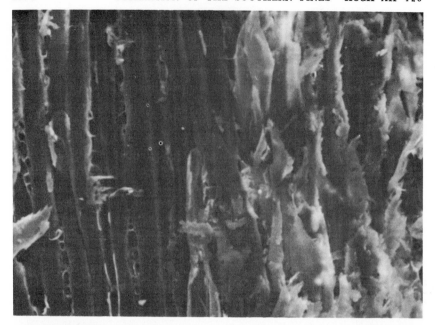

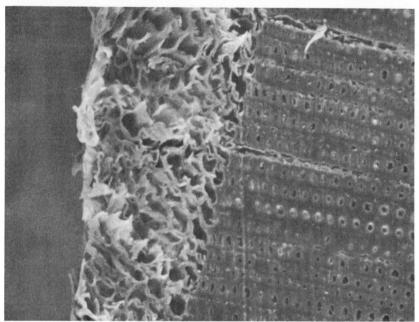

Figure 23–8.—Scanning electron micrographs of southern pine rotary-cut veneer. (Top) Surface, relatively smooth over the latewood tracheids at left; rough earlywood surface at right. 140X. (Bottom) Transverse section, with earlywood veneer surface at left; tracheids at and near the surface are much distorted. 100X. (Photos from Part III of Zicherman, J. B. The localization of coating components within the ultrastructure of wood by use of a micro-incineration technique. USDA Forest Service, Southern Forest Experiment Station, Alexandria, La., Final Report FS-SO-3201-2.22 dated March 3, 1971.)

equations indicated that the roughness factor of latewood was near unity, whereas that of earlywood was about 2 (fig. 23–7). Roughness factor may be defined as follows:

$$\text{Roughness factor} = \frac{\text{True surface area}}{\text{Apparent surface area}} \qquad (23\text{--}2)$$

where the true surface area is the total exposed (or daylit) surface including all irregularities, and the apparent surface area is the area of the cut surface projected to the cutting plane.

Hse (1968) also investigated gluebond quality and durability of southern pine earlywood and latewood by studying two-ply, cross-laminated, ½-inch-square specimens comprised entirely of earlywood or latewood. He used a commercial exterior phenolic resin.

Gluebond quality, as tested wet and dry in tension, was best with earlywood to earlywood and poorest with latewood to latewood; earlywood to latewood was intermediate. Optimum closed assembly time (glue application to closing of hot press) for latewood to latewood was 0 minutes, while the optimum for earlywood to earlywood was 15 minutes; the range tested was 0 to 120 minutes. When these optima were exceeded by 30 minutes, bond strength and percentage of wood failure decreased 90 percent in latewood-to-latewood bonds but less than 3 percent in earlywood-to-earlywood. Moreover, latewood-to-latewood bonds showed a sharp increase in percentage of delamination (after exterior exposure) with increase in assembly time.

Earlywood cells in the vicinity of the glueline were compressed and impregnated with resin. These cells formed a transition layer between glueline and undeformed wood substrate. The dense, thick-walled latewood showed no such cell deformation, and resin impregnation was confined to the cells immediately adjacent to the glueline (fig. 23–9).

At any given percentage of wood failure, bond strength was proportional to wood density. Percentage of delamination during exterior

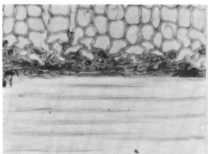 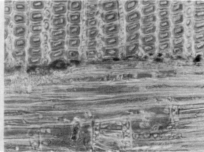

F–521001

Figure 23–9.—Photomicrographs of gluelines in southern pine plywood. (Left) Earlywood to earlywood bond. Earlywood cells were deformed near the interface, and resin penetrated deeply. (Right) Latewood to latewood bond. Penetration into latewood was less evident, and cells near the interface were not deformed. (Photos from Hse 1968.)

exposure was not correlated with bond strength or percentage of wood failure.

Quality of peel.—At present, output of southern pine plywood is primarily in the sheathing grades. Sheathing plywood is produced in huge volumes at maximum rates, and from variably dense small logs; as a result, veneer is sometimes excessively rough, its surface uneven, and its thickness variable. Because it is difficult to get a uniform gluespread on such veneer, because its moisture content may be variable, and because uniform pressure distribution on plywood made from it is hard to achieve, rough and uneven veneer makes poorly bonded plywood (Haskell [5]; Freeman 1970). The technique of peeling smooth southern pine veneer of uniform thickness is described in section 19–10.

A greater percentage of wood failure in gluelines may sometimes be obtained with a veneer peeled from unheated logs, and thus with deep lathe checks, than with smoother veneer peeled hot (Koch 1965a) ; wet and dry shear strength, however, are both highest in plywood made from veneer smoothly peeled from heated logs (Koch 1965b; Koch and Jenkinson 1965). Frequency and depth of lathe checks did not significantly affect the rate of delamination in exterior exposure (Koch 1967b, 1970). Koch's data did suggest, however, that plywood made of dense veneer delaminates more slowly if tight peeled from heated veneer bolts rather than loose peeled from cold bolts. None of the veneer used in Koch's studies was extremely rough, and all was of fairly uniform thickness.

Drying method and moisture content.—With commonly used phenol-formaldehyde glues, optimum moisture content of southern pine veneers to be glued is near 4 percent; if moisture content is excessive, steam formed during hot pressing causes localized blowups when the press is opened. Overdried veneer yields very poor gluebonds as measured by percentage of wood failure in wet shear specimens, as follows:

Reference and veneer moisture content	Wood failure
	Percent
Bloomquist (1966)	36
Ovendry	36
Near 4 percent	86
Haskell et al. (1966)	
Ovendry	59
Near 4 percent	94

Similar results have been observed by others working with southern pine veneers.

Because commercial dryers do not perfectly control veneer surface temperatures throughout veneer passage, hot spots (and overdried veneer) may result from very high dryer temperatures. Fairly low temperatures in the dryer may lessen the amount of overdried veneer. Haskell [5] noted that

---

[5] Haskell, H. H. The triangle: Veneer, adhesives, and production conditions. Unpublished paper presented at Borden Chemical Co. Symposium, Meridian, Miss. Jan. 12–13, 1965.

most consistent joints were obtained when kiln temperature was 350° to 375° F., and that higher temperatures caused excessive flow of pitch and glazed veneer surfaces, which impaired glueline quality.

If the kiln is under good control, however, higher temperatures are practical and time in the dryer can be reduced substantially. Suchsland and Stevens (1968) found that veneers could be safely dried at a dryer temperature of 500° F., if drying was terminated before the veneer reached the temperature of the drying air (fig. 20–27); the gluability of unextracted veneers deteriorated if surface temperatures were allowed to exceed about 400° F. If veneers were solvent extracted prior to drying, however, acceptable joints could be glued even when veneer surface temperatures were allowed to reach 500° F.

From research at Oregon State University, Kozlik [6] concluded that in the initial stages of drying, southern pine veneer could tolerate even higher kiln temperatures without loss of strength or gluebond quality. His research indicated that, if circulation velocity of the heating medium did not exceed 25 feet per second, initial dryer stages could operate at 800° F. (with steam or air atmosphere); Kozlik further concluded, however, that dryer temperature should not exceed about 350° F. in those stages where veneer moisture content is reduced below the fiber saturation point.

Mold.—Where green core veneers are stored for several days preparatory to drying, molds growing on surfaces to be glued can cause poor gluelines (see sec. 16–9). Haskell et al. (1966) observed that moldy veneer yielded only 63 percent wood failure compared to 97 percent in matched clear southern pine veneer. The obvious solution is elimination of mold by prompt drying of all veneer as it comes from the lathe.

Extractives and pitch.—Gluebonds may be adversely affected if wood surfaces are contaminated with extractives or pitch before glue is spread. When southern pine wood is dried at high temperature, the extractives tend to concentrate on the surface; the effect is more noticeable on thick veneer than on thin. Heavy depositions of extractives may adulterate glue and reduce its cohesive strength. Moreover, extractives may block reaction sites on wood surfaces and prevent wetting by the adhesive. Oxidation of some extractives may increase acidity of wood, promote degradation, and weaken cohesive forces between wood fibers.

In spite of these effects, pitch in southern pine veneers causes relatively few production problems. Haskell et al. (1966) found that pitch-soaked southern pine veneer made slightly poorer gluelines than normal veneer; wood failures in their tests averaged 86 and 90 percent respectively. They attributed the poorer bonds not only to presence of the pitch, but also to the roughness often associated with pitch-soaked veneer.

---

[6] Kozlik, C. J. Gluability and strength of Douglas-fir and southern pine rotary-peeled veneer dried in air and steam at temperatures to 800° F. USDA Forest Service, Southern Forest Experiment Station, Alexandria, La., Progress Report FS–SO–3201–2.26, dated April 23, 1971.

Chemical treatment.—Data on gluability of southern pine veneers treated with preservatives, fire retardants, and stabilizing chemicals is meager. Choong and Attarzadeh (1970) found that dipping green southern pine veneers for 5 minutes in ammonium salts fire retardant, Wolman salts preservative, and polyethelene glycol—or dry veneers for 5 minutes in copper naphthenate and methyl methacrylate—did not seriously diminish their gluability with a phenol-formaldehyde, hot-press glue. A 24-hour soak in the same chemicals, however, caused all treated veneers to fall below the acceptable limit for percent wood failure (85 percent) in plywood.

PHENOL-FORMALDEHYDE-RESIN GLUES

Gluebond quality in southern pine plywood is strongly affected by the properties of the resin, the resin formulation variables, and by the extenders.

Resin properties related to bond quality.—Hse (1971) reported on the relationships between the quality of gluebonds in southern pine plywood and the physical and chemical properties of resins incorporated in the glues. His conclusions, based on experimental plywood panels assembled with 36 glues mixed to incorporate 36 different phenol-formaldehyde resins plus water, furafil, wheat flour, and caustic are summarized as follows.

In the range tested, contact angle (fig. 23–10) between resin and veneer (57° to 105°), heat of resin curing reaction (95 to 235 calories per gram), and glueline thickness (8 to 21 μm.) were linearly and positively correlated with wet shear strength and percentage of wood failure. Resin shrinkage (11 to 21 percent) during cure also was linearly correlated with shear strength and percentage of wood failure, but the relationship was negative, i.e., resins with the most shrinkage yielded glues with the poorest bonds.

Surface tension, time to cure, and pH of resins were in general negatively correlated with wet shear strength and wood failure; the regression relationships were parabolic with maxima.

The most effective bonding occurred when the resin wetted—but did not overpenetrate—the veneer surfaces. For the formulations tested, this condition resulted when the resin had a high contact angle and a surface tension of approximately 68.4 dynes per centimeter.

The optimum gluebonds were from resins with high chemical reactivities. Such resins appeared to produce a high degree of crosslinking when cured and required short cure times.

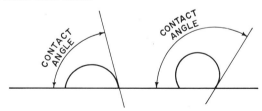

Figure 23–10.—Definition of contact angle between glue droplet and veneer surface. (Drawing after Hse 1971.)

Koch (1965ab, 1967b, 1970) and others have observed that glueline quality in southern pine plywood—as measured by percentage of wood failure, wet shear strength, and durability in exterior exposure—is improved if percentage of resin solids in the mixed glue is 26 percent rather than 21 percent.

Resin formulation related to bond quality.—Hse[4] studied bond quality in southern pine plywood by measuring shear strength and percentage wood failure in thoroughly wetted shear specimens, and percentage delamination of duplicate small exposure specimens (all earlywood or all latewood) assembled with 36 phenolic glues. Resins for the glues were factorially prepared with three formulation variables: mole ratio of sodium hydroxide to phenol (0.4, 0.7, and 1.0), level of resin solids content (37, 40, and 43 percent), and mole ratio of formaldehyde to phenol (1.6, 1.9, 2.2, and 2.5)—all replicated.

Gluebond quality decreased substantially with a change of NaOH/phenol ratio from 0.4 to 0.7, but was not significantly affected by a change in ratio from 0.7 to 1.0. On average, bond quality increased as percent solids content increased. Changes in formaldehyde/phenol ratio affected only percentage delamination; the lower ratios yielded gluelines that delaminated least.

Extenders.—Published evaluations of extenders for phenol-formaldehyde glues are limited in number and not comprehensive in coverage.

Koch (1965ab) studied performance of extenders in glues comprised of water (19.7 to 27.4 percent), furafil primary extender (9.0 to 13.7 percent), soluble blood secondary extender (0 to 1.9 percent), wheat flour secondary extender (0 to 2.6 percent), 50 percent caustic soda solution (2.8 to 4.6 percent), soda ash (1.1 to 1.7 percent), and phenol-formaldehyde resin (52.6 to 64.8 percent). He concluded that percentage of wood failure was highest and gluebonds best when wheat flour only was used as a secondary extender. Wet shear strength was greatest with no secondary extender, but glue extended only with wheat flour made bonds nearly as strong. Extension with blood reduced gluebond quality as measured by wood failure, wet shear strength, and durability in exterior exposure. The glues were spread at 65 and 75 pounds per M sq. ft. of core, equally divided on the two sides of the core. The three-ply southern pine plywood was ⅜-inch thick.

Fischer and Bensend (1969) reported acceptable wet shear strengths and percentages of wood failure in southern pine plywood glued with 90-pound spreads of exterior phenolic glues containing 5 percent soluble beef blood. The plywood was glued with no closed assembly time prior to prepress, 4.5 minutes prepress time, and 5.5 minutes in a hot press at 285° F.

SPREADING

The quality of a gluebond is substantially affected by the uniformity with which the glue is spread, the amount spread, the manner in which it wets the wood, and the temperature of glue and wood at time of spreading.

Wettability of veneer and surface tension of resin.—Hse[4] judged the wettability of the veneers by measuring contact angles (fig. 23–10) made between southern pine veneers at about 5-percent moisture content and 36 phenol-formaldehyde resins. Resins were factorially prepared by mole ratio of sodium hydroxide to phenol (0.4, 0.7, and 1.0), level of resin solids content in the reaction mixture (37, 40, and 43 percent), and mole ratio of formaldehyde to phenol (1.6, 1.9, 2.2, and 2.5). All resins were mixed with furafil and wheat flour to achieve 26 percent resin solids in the final glue mix.

He found that the mole ratio of sodium hydroxide to phenol was the dominant factor affecting contact angle; mole ratio of formaldehyde to phenol was second in importance. As mole ratios of sodium hydroxide to phenol increased and ratios of formaldehyde to phenol decreased, the contact angle decreased. Contact angle was not related to solids content. Contact angle on earlywood was less than that on latewood, apparently because earlywood surfaces were rougher.

Hse[4] observed that contact angle (in range 57° to 105°) was positivey correlated with gluebond quality. High contact angle of the resin—and low wetting of the veneer—may prevent excess glue penetration, which often causes poor bonds in southern pine plywood.

With the same 36 resins and glues described above, Hse[4] found that the relationship between surface tension of the resin (not the mixed glue) and bond quality in southern pine plywood was curvilinear. The optimum gluebond was obtained with a resin having a surface tension of 68.4 dynes per centimeter; higher surface tensions caused poor spreading, and lower ones caused excess penetration of the glue. Glues made from resins with high surface tensions tended to form impervious skins; contraction (of the spread glue) accompanying condensation during curing took place inside the skin so that voids were produced and adhesive bonds weakened.

Methods and spread rate.—In most southern pine plywood mills, roll spreaders are used to apply the glue. The design of these machines is fairly well standardized, and their construction features will not be discussed here. Readers concerned with roll design will find descriptions by Barnes (1970) and Lambuth (1970) of interest.

Two alternative methods of spreading glue on veneer have been developed. In one (Cone 1969), the glue is first foamed to about five times its original volume and then extruded onto the veneer top surface in the form of flexible coherent rods about $\frac{1}{10}$-inch in diameter deposited in straight parallel lines. In this system there are areas of bare wood between the rods; less than half the veneer surface is directly covered with glue. Advantages claimed for the system included improved bond quality and less waste of glue. As yet, the system has not been applied in southern pine plywood plants.

In a second method now being evaluated in southern pine plywood mills, liquid glue is sprayed rather than rolled onto the top surface of the moving veneer. Impetus for adoption of the spray and extrusion methods comes from mill managers who desire more complete mechanization of gluespreading and layup operations. Manual feeding and offbearing of a roll spreader is hard, dirty work, and expensive in terms of manpower.

Efforts are also being made to find methods for reducing the amount of glue required to bond each M sq. ft. of exterior-type plywood. On a ⅜-inch basis, Douglas-fir requires only about 57 pounds per M sq. ft. Data from Koch (1965ab, 1967b, 1970) and others indicate that southern pine generally requires a gluespread in excess of 65 pounds per M sq. ft. to obtain acceptable gluelines; if assembly time is long, even heavier spreads are required.

Glueline thickness.—Hse[4] correlated glueline thickness with bond quality in southern pine plywood glued with the 36 phenolic resins previously described. Glueline thickness ranged from 8 to 21 μm. and was negatively correlated with NaOH/P ratio; i.e., high NaOH/P ratios yielded relatively thin gluelines. Resin solid content and F/P ratio had little effect on the glueline thickness.

Of the resin properties, surface tension, contact angle, and time to cure were found related to the glueline thickness. Because panel preparation and gluing conditions were the same for all resins, differences in glueline thickness presumbaly reflected the combined effects of flow, transfer, penetration, wetting, and hardening of the resin in the process of bond formation.

Hse[4] concluded that, within the range of his data, wet shear strength and percentage of wood failure increased as glueline thickness increased. Since thin gluelines were likely to develop discontinuities or defective spots, they yielded weak gluebonds.

Veneer and mill temperatures.—Glues for southern pine plywood are frequently formulated to match the season of the year because mill temperatures may range from as low as 50° F. in winter to 100° or 120° F. in summer. Resins for use in summer are generally in a less polymerized state, whereas in winter a more advanced resin can be used (Haskell et al. 1966). Control of both resin and water temperature is desirable so that glue temperature remains uniform.

Veneers moved too quickly from kiln to spreader may be warm (85° to 115° F.) or even hot (over 115° F.). Glue spread on hot veneers warms immediately, and its water content migrates into the wood; the resulting dried-out glueline yields a poor bond. Freeman (1970) found that mill temperatures up to 108° F. did not adversely affect gluebonds as long as there was no appreciable delay between spreading and layup.

PRESSING AND CURING

The curing of plywood glue is a complex reaction involving properties of the resin and the wood, assembly times, prepressing procedures, and hot pressing technique.

Readers interested in the mechanism of cure of thermosetting phenolic plywood adhesives will find Hse's[4] discussion of interest. In brief, he observed that crosslinking of such resins (formulations previously described) is achieved mainly through methylene linkages. In these resins, an exothermic cure reaction took place rapidly at about 148° C.

Assembly time.—Gluebound quality in southern pine exterior-type plywood is sensitive to assembly time, i.e., the elapsed time between the moment glue is spread and the moment the hot press is closed. For earlywood-to-earlywood bonds, optimum time may be near 15 or 20 minutes with tolerable time as much as 30 minutes; for latewood-to-latewood bonds, however, zero assembly time (at 70° F.) is optimum with conventional phenol-formaldehyde glues (Hse 1968).

Koch (1965ab, 1967b, 1970) has shown that gluebond quality in high-density southern pine plywood—as measured by wood failure, wet shear strength, and durability in exterior exposure—decreases as assembly time is lengthened beyond about 13 minutes (at 70° F.). With low-density veneers, a 24-minute assembly time was tolerable. Long assembly times were more tolerable if glue was spread liberally.

If mill temperatures are high, permissible assembly times are even shorter than those indicated above.

One glue manufacturer now offers a series of new phenol resins for pine veneering which can be allowed to dry to a dust-dry film before pressing. Flow and transfer from the coated veneers to the adjacent uncoated veneers is provided by melting under heat and pressure. These glues are said to avoid the "dryout" problem of longer assembly periods encountered in some plants processes, since they tolerate assembly times up to 30 or 40 minutes. Such glue formulations would seem to be similar to the early bag-molding phenol-resin glues used during World War II, where the glue films were dried essentially to a tackfree condition during open assembly and yet had the necessary flow under hot-pressing conditions for transfer and flow for good adhesion. This same firm now provides a series of phenol resins in five stepwise levels of reactivity versus flow to meet various mill conditions for pine plywood production. Adoption of these new resin systems has apparently been limited to date, however.

Prepressing.—Prepressing of panels—i.e., cold-pressing before placement in the hot press—is practiced in many southern pine plywood plants, but not in all. Compacting panels by prepressing speeds mechanical loading into the hot press; those using prepresses believe the extra step reduces manufacturing defects.

Many plants in which the hot press is loaded manually prefer not to prepress since the operation may add 4 to 8 minutes to total assembly time unless carefully scheduled. Lengthened assembly time, particularly in warm weather when veneers are warm, can cause poor gluebonds.

Hot-pressing.—Southern pine plywood made with phenol-formaldehyde glues is pressed between hot platens in multiple-opening hydraulic presses. Panels produced may have from three to 11 plys, but usually have three or five. Panel thickness may be as much as 2 inches, but is usually 1 inch or less. Specific pressures used may range from 100 to 300 p.s.i., but are usually 175 to 225 p.s.i. Freeman (1970) found that pressures in this range gave better bonds than lower pressures. Temperatures are usually 275° to 315° F. but may range up to 325° F. Time in the press is dependent on panel thickness and glue formulation; ⅜-inch, three-ply panels pressed two to the opening at 285° F. may require about 6½ minutes of closed press time. Press times for phenol-formaldehyde glues have been decreased substantially in recent years (Shelton 1969).

With the increasingly large presses used—up to 36 openings—precure of gluelines in the first panels loaded in the press is likely; increasing the gluespread by 5 to 10 pounds per M sq. ft. of double glueline may alleviate problems caused by this precure (Haskell et al. 1966).

All southern pine plants stack the plywood as it is discharged from the press and leave the stacks undisturbed for at least 4 hours so that the heat stored in the wood completes the glueline cure.

HARDWOOD CORES

Product Standard PS 1–66 allows hardwood inner plys to be incorporated with southern pine faces and backs. Limited studies by Blomquist and Olson (1964) showed that when hickory (*Carya* sp.) was glued to southern pine veneers with conventional phenol-formaldehyde exterior glues, percentages of wood failure were inconsistent and sometimes low, particularly in the hickory plys. Similar observations were made by Haskell[5] on white and red oaks (*Quercus* spp.) veneers glued to southern pine. Hursey and Fogg (1970), however, obtained acceptable bonds in three- and five-ply panels with oak and sweetgum (*Liquidamber styraciflua* L.) cores and southern pine faces. They used a phenol-formaldehyde-resin glue extended with blood and spread at 85 to 90 pounds per M sq. ft. of double glueline. Even after these panels were pressure treated with FCAP (type B) preservative salt to a retention of 0.35 pound per cubic foot, they had acceptable shear strength and percentage of wood failure.

Because hardwood trees suitable for core veneer bolts are available at lower stumpage prices than pine, it is likely that research will accelerate until a glue can be formulated that will make an acceptable gluebond under production conditions.

DURABILITY IN EXTERIOR EXPOSURE

Tests specified in U.S. Product Standard PS 1–66 are designed to control the quality of southern pine plywood at the time it is manufactured; it is assumed that a glue of established durability (such as a conventional phenol-formaldehyde type) is used. While the major criterion, percent wood failure in thoroughly soaked shear specimens after a soak-dry cycle, is positively correlated with durability in exterior exposure, final proof of durability can be established only by observing plywood in service. Since the southern pine plywood industry dates from 1963, little service information is available, and much of what is available came from accelerated tests that used small samples rather than conventional 4- by 8-foot panels. All available evidence indicates, however, that southern pine plywood, properly hot-pressed with phenol-formaldehyde glues, is an excellent and durable structural material.

Small specimens.—Hse (1968) investigated the durability of gluebonds in two-ply, cross-laminated, ½-inch-square specimens comprised entirely of southern pine earlywood or latewood glued with a commercial exterior phenolic resin. He found that the latewood-to-latewood bonds delaminated far more rapidly on exterior exposure than the earlywood-to-earlywood bonds; earlywood-to-latewood bonds were intermediate in durability. Explanation of his data lies in the fact that latewood is denser than earlywood and it shrinks and swells more with changes in moisture content; the resulting glueline stresses accelerate delamination. Increased assembly time in manufacture, in the range from 0 to 120 minutes, sharply increased percentage of delamination after exterior exposure in latewood-to-latewood bonds.

Koch (1967b, 1970) reported on delamination observed over a 3-year period in 1,152 pieces of southern pine plywood asesmbled in 576 different ways. The plywood was made from eight loblolly pine trees selected to exhibit a range of specific gravity and growth rate and glued with exterior-type phenol-formaldehyde resins. The ⅜-inch-thick, three-ply specimens (1 by 3¼ inches) were exposed outdoors in Pineville, La. on a 45°, south-facing deck. Percentage of delamination was measured annually.

Rings per inch and tightness of peel had minor effects. A low glue-spread resulted in rapid delamination, particularly with high-density veneer or long assembly time. Of glues having a low percentage of resin solids, those extended solely with wheat flour resisted delamination best. Glues extended with blood suffered more severe delamination, even when percentage of resin solids was high. High specific gravity wood delaminated more rapidly than low specific gravity wood, particularly if gluespread was low or assembly time long. All plywood given a long assembly time tended to delaminate, and dense veneer or light gluespread accelerated the effect. Rate of delamination decreased after the first year, but general conclusions about the primary variables were the same after 3 years as after 6 months (fig. 23-11).

An 11-factor equation explained 35 percent of the variation in terms of wood properties and results of a standard shear test (fig. 23-12).

Large panels.—Selbo (1969) found that 18- by 18-inch laboratory-made southern pine plywood panels painted and exposed to the weather near Madison, Wis. and Gulfport, Miss. showed no glue joint separation after

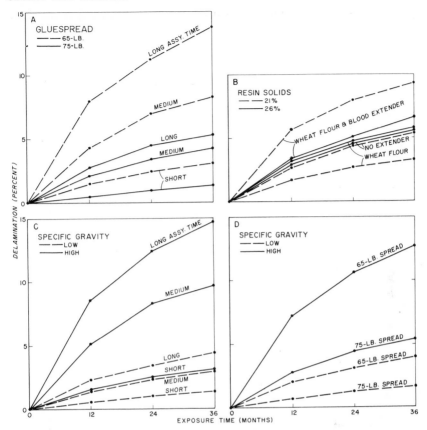

Figure 23–11.—Delamination of small specimens of ⅛-inch three-ply, southern pine plywood during 45°, south-facing, exterior exposure in Pineville, La.

   (A) Interaction of gluespread per M sq. ft. of double glueline and assembly times of 13, 24, and 32 minutes including 5 minutes of prepress time.

   (B) Effect of three types of secondary extender and percentage of resin solids in the final glue mix.

   (C) Interaction of specific gravity of peelable portion of log (0.45 and 0.55 on basis of ovendry weight and green volume) and assembly time.

   (D) Interaction of specific gravity and gluespread.

   (Drawing after Koch 1970.)

5 years; face checking and some mold growth occurred on all panels.

    The three-ply, ⅜-inch panels were assembled from loblolly and long-leaf pine veneer, of less than 5-percent moisture content, hot-pressed for 8 minutes at 175 p.s.i. and 275° F. The glue was a commercial phenol-formaldehyde mix spread at about 85 pounds per M sq. ft. of double glueline; closed assembly time was 15 minutes. Wood failure and wet shear strength averaged 77 percent and 192 p.s.i.

    Similar southern plywood panels overlaid with medium-density, phenolic-resin-impregnated overlay, and painted with two coats of an acrylic-emulsion paint, were in excellent condition after 5 years of weathering at both

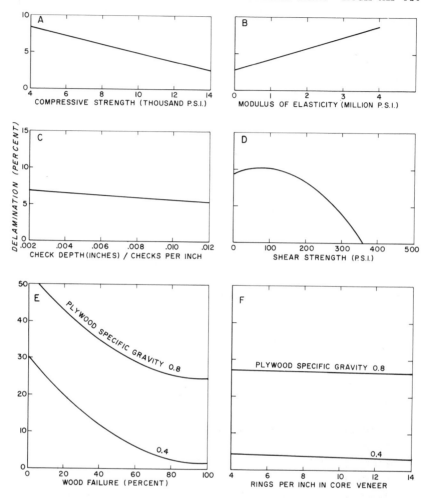

Figure 23–12.—Delamination of small specimens of southern pine plywood after 36 months of exterior exposure, as related to wood properties and to percent of wood failure and wet shear strength in standard American Plywood Association vacuum-pressure-soak test. (Drawing after Koch 1970.)

the northern and southern exposure sites. Mold growth occurred on the overlaid panels at both sites (Selbo 1969).

While not directly causing delamination, severe face checks in plywood may contribute to delamination over a long period of exterior exposure; for this reason, control measures are of interest. Koch (1965c) studied face checks in 10.5-inch-square, three-ply, 3/8-inch-thick exterior plywood hot-pressed from loblolly pine veneer. As is customary, the tight side of face and back veneer was placed outermost. Using Batey's (1955) index, panels were quantitatively evaluated for severity of face checking after several cycles of wetting and drying.

Face checking was minimized by: (1) Reducing the hygroscopicity of the plywood by dipping the panels for 10 seconds in a water repellent. Checking index was 4.4 for treated panels and 12.8 for untreated. (2) Peeling veneer hot and tight rather than cold and loose. Checking index was 5.5 for tight-peeled face veneers and 11.7 for loose-peeled. (3) Using veneer of low specific gravity rather than high. Checking index was 6.9 for low-density faces and 10.4 for high-density faces.

With all the above factors favorable, the average checking index was minimum at 2.4; if all were unfavorable, the checking index was 20.4.

Factors that did not significantly affect severity of face checking were: rate of growth (rings per inch in the veneer); moisture content of the veneer before gluespreading; and proximity of plywood face to hot platen when pressing two panels per opening.

23–5 OVERLAYS

Since southern pine plywood tends to check severely on exterior exposure, overlays of various types are sometimes applied. A short discussion of factors involved in the selection and gluing of these overlays can be found in sections 25–5 and 25–6.

23–6 PARTICLEBOARD

In the South, as in the Nation, production of particleboard has increased substantially since the end of World War II. Between 1956 and 1966 average annual increase in particleboard production capacity (national) was 24 percent (Dougherty 1968). A high rate of increase has been maintained through 1970, and is expected to continue (fig. 23–13). There is an accelerating trend toward larger plants; 75 percent of capacity in 1972 will be in plants producing more than 60 million sq. ft. annually. The proportion of the output used in construction has increased in recent years. One-third of the nation's particleboard capacity in 1967 was in the South; by 1972 the South's proportion will be 46.5 percent (Vajda[7]).

THE INDUSTRY [8]

Of the 26 particleboard mills operating in the South in 1968, the six pioneer plants built mostly in the 1950's to make extruded board (fig. 23–14) accounted for less than 10 percent of southern production. Only two of the six used southern pine; 25 percent of the output of all six was captive, i.e., it went into products made by the firm manufacturing the particleboard.

Of the 20 plants making flat-pressed boards, 13 used predominantly southern pine (fig. 23–15), and their combined 1968 capacity was rated

---

[7] Vajda, P. The economics of particleboard manufacture revisited or an assessment of the industry in 1970. Presentation at a symposium, "Fourth Particle Board Symposium," Washington State University, Pullman, Wash., March 1970.

[8] The text under this heading is taken, with minor editorial changes, from Suchsland (1968) by permission of O. Suchsland and the *Southern Lumberman*.

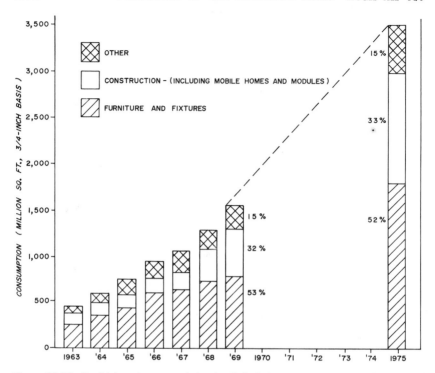

Figure 23–13.—Particleboard consumed in the United States, 1963–1969, and estimated consumption in 1975. (Drawing after Vajda[7].)

at 550 million sq. ft. of ¾-inch board annually. The 1967 production of these 13 plants was approximately 260 million sq. ft., or about 23 percent of total U.S. output of 1,120 million sq. ft. (Dougherty 1968; Suchsland 1968).

Nine of the 13 mills had 90 percent of the southern pine capacity in 1968; these mills all produce three-layer or multi-layer boards. The four

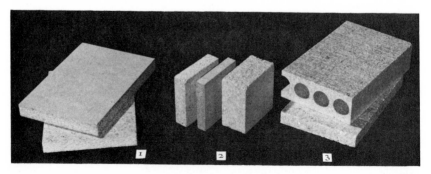

Figure 23–14.—Samples of commercial particleboard made from southern pine. (1) Three-layer. (2) Single-layer. (3) Extruded. (Photo from Suchsland 1968.)

ANNUAL CAPACITY
(MILLION SQUARE FEET, 3/4 – INCH BASIS)

* 0 – 9
o 10 – 49
● 50 OR MORE

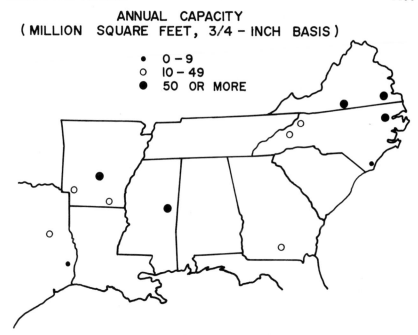

Figure 23–15.—Location and capacity of 13 particleboard plants using southern pine as a primary raw material source in 1968. (Drawing after Suchsland 1968.)

smaller mills had 10 percent of the capacity and make single-layer boards (fig. 23–14).

Since 1968, a number of new, large, southern-pine-using plants have been built or announced; included in the expansion are three plants in Louisiana with combined annual capacity of about 200 million sq. ft., ¾-inch basis (Anonymous 1970; Louisiana Forestry Association 1971), and one in Mississippi with capacity of 100 million sq. ft. (Bryan 1970). Continued further expansion is anticipated.

In 1968, underlayment was the primary product of the 13 southern pine plants and accounted for 54 percent of the total production. Boards— primarily core stock—for the furniture and cabinet industries accounted for 37 percent of the output. Industrial markets took 6 percent, and the balance of 3 percent was sold in miscellaneous markets.

The industry anticipates major expansion into product lines other than core stock and underlayment. Since 1968, for example, the mobile home industry has accepted particleboard as its preferred product for floors. In this application, the product is designed to be intermediate in strength between the present relatively weak underlayment and the present relatively strong furniture core stock.

In 1968, 52 percent of the wood raw material for the 13 previously mentioned plants was in the form of planer shavings. Only 24 percent was in the form of cordwood; the remaining 24 percent was waste wood, primarily from plywood plants and sawmills. There is some evidence of a trend away from manufactured flakes produced from roundwood. Although there is good equipment available for generating flakes, the economics of starting with roundwood and ending with dry flakes at the forming station results in an additional cost of approximately $25 per 1,000 sq. ft. (¾-inch basis) for producing flakeboard vs. board made from planer shavings. Consumers have recently appeared unwilling to pay a premium price for flakeboard since several other particle-type board products are now available with strength properties approaching that of flakeboard. A major Arkansas flakeboard plant now uses planer shavings rather than flakes manufactured from roundwood.

Incoming material, whatever its form, is milled and screened (fig. 23–16) and dried (see sec. 20–4 and figs. 20–32, 20–33, and 20–34) before use. Glue is sprayed on the milled and screened particles, which are then formed into a mat and hot-pressed into flat boards by a variety of processes; notable are the Novoply, Behr, and Bahre-Bison processes.

Figure 23–17 illustrates the material flow chart for the Bahre-Bison process for making three-layer, flat-pressed board; the air classification system used in the board-forming process (fig. 23–18) results in a graduated dispersion of particle size with the finest material concentrated on top and bottom of board surfaces (Anonymous 1968). Boards made by this and

Figure 23–16.—Raw materials for southern pine particleboard. (1) Plywood trim. (2,3) Planer shavings, unmilled. (4,5,6,7) Milled and screened particles. (Photo from Suchsland 1968.)

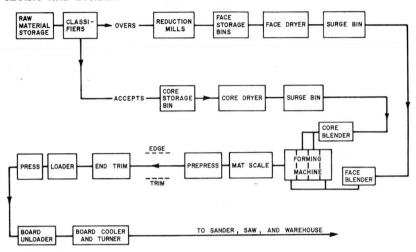

Figure 23–17.—Typical flow chart for Bahre-Bison particleboard process. Sized, dry particles are coated with glue in the blenders before the mat is formed. (Drawing after Suchsland 1968.)

similar processes combine smooth surfaces with high bending strength at moderate board densities. Forming by wind separation (fig. 23–18) does not preclude the possibility of applying extra faces to the core thus formed. These faces can be made of very fine particles, or even fibers, for special surface smoothness or hardness. These surface layers can also be graduated by using one-half of the forming device for each face layer, one preceding the core forming machine and one following it.

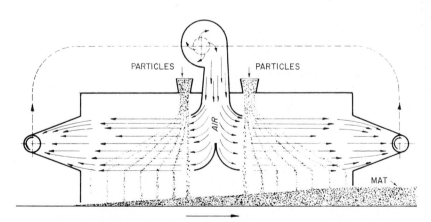

Figure 23–18.—Air classification of particle size in the Bahre-Bison mat-forming machine places finest particles on top and bottom surfaces and coarser particles in the core. (Drawing after Greten 1965.)

PARTICLE LENGTH-THICKNESSES AND DENSIFICATION RATIOS [8]

Particle geometry and **densification ratio,** i.e., the quotient of board specific gravity divided by species specific gravity, have long been recognized for their effects on mechanical properties of particleboard (Post 1958, 1961; Keylwerth 1959; Suchsland 1959, 1960; Plath 1963; Rackwitz 1963).

Particle length-thickness ratio.—Gluelines in plywood, due to continuity of the laminae, contribute relatively little to most of the elastic and mechanical properties of plywood (fig. 23–19 top). The laminae in particleboard, however, are discontinuous; and the gluelines must transmit stresses from one particle to the next.

A simplified model (fig. 23–19 bottom) indicates that the tensile strength of particleboard is determined either by the tensile strength of the individual particles or by the shear strength of the glue joints. The tensile strength of the particle will be limiting when the glue joints are able to transmit forces equivalent to the particle strength. If, however, the glueline fails in shear before the ultimate tensile strength of the particle has been reached, then particle strength is of secondary importance. It is clear from figure 23–19 (bottom) that the balance can be shifted in the direction of shear failure or tension failure by varying the particle geometry. Increasing

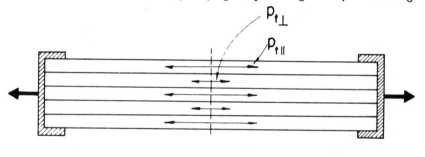

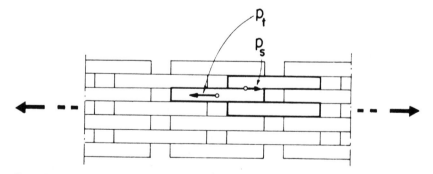

Figure 23–19.—Forces in members under tensile load P. (Top) Plywood; $P_{t\parallel}$ is tensile force parallel to grain, and $P_{t\perp}$ is force perpendicular to grain in cross bands. (Bottom) Particleboard; P_t is tensile force within a particle, and P_s is shear force in the glueline. (Drawing after Rackwitz 1963.)

the length of overlap of particles results in larger forces transmitted by the glue joints and consequently in higher tensile strength of the board until a point is reached where the shear forces equal the ultimate tensile strength of the particle. Beyond this point, longer overlap will not increase tensile strength of the board (fig. 23–20).

If particle thickness is held constant, the average length of overlap can be increased by increasing the ratio of particle length to particle thickness; i.e., long particles overlap more than short particles. Figure 23–21 suggests that over a wide range of particle length-to-thickness ratios the glueline is the weakest link in the composite, and that the leveling-off point is outside the practical range of particle dimension.

Densification ratio.—If the density of plywood is changed by using veneers of a different density, the elastic and mechanical properties of the plywood will change according to the well-established relationship between elastic and mechanical properties of solid wood and its density.

The density of a particleboard can be changed in two ways—by using wood of different specific gravity, and by varying the densification of the mat (fig. 23–22). A particleboard of a given density, if made from a heavier and therefore often stronger wood, has a lower bending strength than a board made from a lighter wood. This is true because there are fewer particles per pound and per cubic inch in the board made from the heavier wood. Consequently, there are fewer bonds per unit volume and probably less overlap between particles in this board. To make boards of equal bending strength from particles of a given geometry, higher density wood requires higher board densities.

In brief, the strength of particleboard is largely dependent on the strength of the gluelines; the spacers—or particles—which contribute bulk

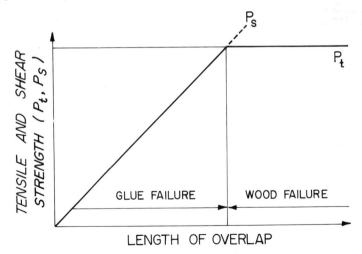

Figure 23–20.—Tensile and shear strengths of glued particles as a function of length of overlap. P_t is tensile force in particle; P_s is shear force in glueline. (Drawing after Rackwitz 1963.)

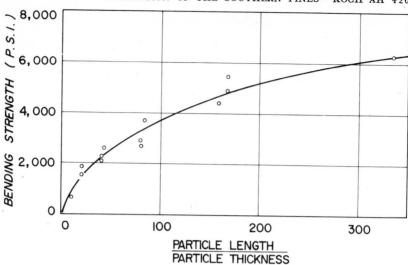

Figure 23–21.—Bending strength of particleboard as affected by ratio of particle length to thickness. Board density, gluespread, and manufacturing conditions constant. (Drawing after Keylworth 1959 from data by Post 1958.)

and mass should preferably be low in density and have a high ratio of particle length to particle thickness.

The quality of particleboard is not judged by strength alone, of course; light color, surface smoothness, dimensional stability, machinability, and screw-holding capacity are also desirable properties for most purposes.

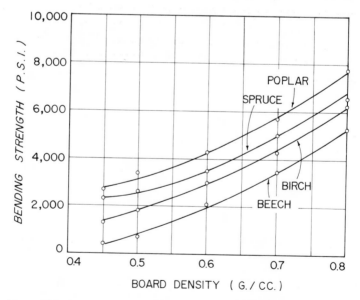

Figure 23–22.—Relationship between board density and bending strength of particleboard made from four species. (Drawing after Klauditz and Stegmann 1957.)

STANDARDS AND TEST METHODS

Major standards for particleboard include Commercial Standard CS 236–66 (U.S. Department of Commerce 1966a) and ASTM Designation D 1037–64 (American Society for Testing and Materials 1964). Due to the youth and rapid growth of the industry, standards and test procedures are still in the process of development. A few references on developing test procedures are listed as follows.

Subject	Reference
Accelerated aging	West Coast Adhesive Manufacturers Association (1966, 1970)
Dimensional stability	Heebink (1967b)
Effect of fire retardants on strength	Syska (1969)
Internal bond strength	Shen (1970)
Showthrough of particleboard cores	Heebink (1960)
Standard for particleboard decking for factory built housing	National Particleboard Association Standard 2–70 dated June 1970

SUITABILITY OF SOUTHERN PINE FOR PARTICLEBOARD [8]

The specific gravity of southern pine wood is somewhat higher than that of most other softwoods and considerably higher than that of aspen (*Populus grandidenta* Michx.) and yellow-popular (*Liriodendron tulipifera* L.). Southern pine particleboards therefore must be pressed to slightly higher densities if mechanical properties comparable to those of boards made from lighter species are required.

The pH of southern pine particles is within the range of other commonly used species, so usually glues need not be specially formulated for southern pine particleboard. Southern pine wood has substantially higher pitch content than some other species in common use. Pitch, while it may cause some problems in gluing (Suchsland and Stevens 1968), causes most difficulty by accumulating on surfaces of dryers and conveyors and by loading abrasive belts used to sand the finished board to thickness.

SOME FACTORS AFFECTING BOARD PROPERTIES

In addition to particle length-thickness ratio and densification ratio, numerous factors affect the properties of particleboard in a complex interaction among wood properties, surface texture of particles, particle-drying technique, particle size distribution, glue formulation and application, method of mat formation, prepressing procedure, and hot-pressing technique.

While particleboards can be fabricated with phenol-formaldehyde resin, allowing more severe exterior exposure (Deppe and Ernst 1966; Gatchell et al. 1966; Heebink 1967a; Deppe 1969), most southern pine particleboard is designed for interior use and is assembled with urea-formaldehyde glues. Information specific to southern pine particleboard assembled with urea-formaldehyde glues is presented in the two following subsections.

For the reader wishing to study in greater depth, the 99 references in Halligan's (1969) review of the literature on gluing of particleboard, and Mitlin's (1968) 222-page text on the manufacture and application of particleboard, should prove helpful. Proceedings from the series of symposia on particleboard that have been held periodically since 1967 by the College of Engineering, Washington State University, Pullman, Wash., and which are available from the Wood Technology Section of that institution, provide a useful and up-to-date compendium of information related to the manufacture of particleboard.

Effect of particle geometry, adhesive spread, and wood properties[9].— McMillin studied the effect of wood specific gravity, flake thickness, and adhesive spread on the properties of boards made from loblolly pine. Variables in his factorial experimental design were:

Specific gravity of unextracted wood (ovendry weight and green volume)
> Less than 0.49
> More than 0.49

Flake thickness (width constant at ⅜-inch, length constant at 1½ inches)
> 0.035 inch
> .025 inch
> .015 inch

Adhesive spread (based on weight of adhesive solids per unit area of surface)
> 6 g./m.²
> 12 g./m.²

Because adhesive was applied on a surface area basis, content in terms of percent of ovendry wood weight (range 5 to 12 percent) differed depending on the flake thickness and wood specific gravity.

Board consolidation factors were held constant as follows:
> Board density—45 pounds/cu. ft. ovendry.
> Mat moisture content at pressing—10 percent.
> Adhesive—Liquid urea-formaldehyde, uncatalyzed.
> Press temperature—325° F.
> Press closing time (time to stops)—1 minute.
> Total press time—7 minutes.

Flakes having the desired geometry were obtained from ribbons produced on a metal-working lathe in a manner similar to rotary veneer cutting. The cutting geometry reasonably simulated that of the shaping-lathe chipping headrig (fig. 19–54A). With this type of headrig, the

---

[9] The text under this heading is condensed from: McMillin, C. W. Aspects of wood and particle characteristics affecting the properties of aggregates from southern pine flakes. USDA Forest Serv., Southern Forest Exp. Sta., Alexandria, La., Final Report FS–SO–3201–3.10, dated November 23, 1971.

entire volume outside the cant is machined into flakes which are suitable for certain types of board products. Because the resulting cant has high value, a substantial portion of the cost of producing such flakes can be absorbed by the solid wood product produced from the cant.

Adhesive was applied to dried ribbons by feeding them between two spray guns. After brief reconditioning, the ribbons were clipped into ⅜-inch-wide flakes, hand felted, and consolidated into boards. In general, properties were evaluated in accordance with ASTM Designation D 1037–64.

By analysis of variance, modulus of rupture in bending (MOR) differed with flake thickness and wood specific gravity, as follows; it was unrelated to resin coverage:

	Wood specific gravity	
Flake thickness	Low (avg. 0.45)	High (avg. 0.53)
Inches	– – – – – – *P.s.i.* – – – – – –	
0.015 _____	5,300	5,000
.025 _____	4,300	3,400
.035 _____	3,200	2,300

As expected, MOR increased with decreasing flake thickness for both wood of low and high specific gravity; the trend was curvilinear. For a given flake thickness, MOR was greater for boards made from wood having low specific gravity.

Modulus of elasticity differed with only one study variable—flake thickness. Values were 487,000, 645,000 and 825,000 p.s.i. for thicknesses of 0.035, 0.025, and 0.015 inch, respectively.

Internal bond strength differed with resin coverage and wood specific gravity; it was unrelated to flake thickness. From the following tabulation, internal bond strength was greatest for boards made from wood of low specific gravity; it was also improved by using the higher adhesive coverage:

	Wood specific gravity	
Resin coverage	Low (avg. 0.45)	High (avg. 0.53)
g./m.²	– – – – – – *P.s.i.* – – – – – –	
6 _____	73	58
12 _____	107	63

Holding capacity of screws inserted into board faces was somewhat greater in boards made from wood of low specific gravity (avg. 344 pounds) than in those made from wood of high specific gravity (avg. 303 pounds). It was unaffected by flake thickness and adhesive content.

Linear expansion (percent change in dimension between equilibrium moisture content at 0- and 90-percent relative humidity) averaged 0.47

percent. Between 0- and 60-percent relative humidity, the average value was 0.19 percent.

Effects of specific surface[9].—Although in McMillin's experiment the length-to-thickness ratio differed with the thickness of flakes, the average length of particle overlap was unaffected because both length and width of flakes were held constant. It can be shown that the nominal surface area per unit weight of flakes (specific surface) is a function of particle geometry and specific gravity. Flakes of high specific surface form boards having a greater number of adhesive bonds per unit of volume and hence, are stronger.

Consider a particle of width W, length L, and thickness T. If smooth plane surfaces are assumed, its surface area (a) will be:

$$a = 2(TL + WL + TW) \qquad (23\text{--}3)$$

Its weight (w) will be:

$$w = WTL(\text{weight per unit volume}) \qquad (23\text{--}4)$$

The specific surface (S) will be:

$$S = \frac{a}{w} = \frac{2(TL + WL + TW)}{WTL(\text{weight per unit volume})} \qquad (23\text{--}5)$$

If all dimensions are in centimeters and the weight is in grams, the weight per unit volume is equal to specific gravity (G) and

$$S = \frac{2}{G}\left[\frac{TL + WL + TW}{WTL}\right] = \frac{2}{G}\left[\frac{1}{W} + \frac{1}{T} + \frac{1}{L}\right] \qquad (23\text{--}6)$$

In McMillin's study, particle length and width were held constant at $1\frac{1}{2}$ inches and $\frac{3}{8}$-inch respectively, and specific surface in square meters per kilogram was therefore:

$$S = \frac{0.2}{G}\left[3.3325 + \frac{1}{T}\right] \qquad (23\text{--}7)$$

where T is in inches.

From equation 23–7 and from McMillin's measurements of log specific gravity and flake thickness, specific surface increased with decreasing flake thickness. For a given thickness, specific surface was greater for wood of low specific gravity than it was for wood of high gravity, as follows:

Flake thickness	Wood specific gravity	
	Low (avg. 0.45)	High (avg. 0.53)
Inches	- - - - m.²/kg.	- - - -
0.015	12.6	11.1
.025	7.4	6.3
.035	5.4	4.5

Specific surface (computed from equation 23–7) was positively correlated with modulus of rupture and modulus of elasticity. Since there were small between-board variations in density, density (D) in pounds per cubic foot was considered first to account for its effect before that of specific surface (S). The equations are applicable only to boards of 45 pounds/cu. ft. density having resin spreads of 6 to 12 g./m.^{2} and flakes having specific surfaces ranging from 4 to 13 m.^{2}/kg.

$$MOR = 31,045.1 - 1,562.2(D) + 19.0(D)^2 + 853.2(S) - 30.6(S)^2 \qquad (23\text{--}8)$$

$$MOE = 8,265,217.7 - 403,272.2(D) + 4,928.4(D)^2 + 101,347.5(S) \qquad (23\text{--}9)$$
$$- 3,562.7(S)^2$$

Equation 23–8 accounted for 81 percent of the total variation in MOR; standard error of the estimate was 560 p.s.i. Corresponding values for MOE (equation 23–9) were 88 and 60,400. Linear regressions of specific surface alone accounted for 73 percent of the variation in MOR and 71 percent of the variation in MOE.

The assumption that a flake has a smooth plane surface is admittedly an oversimplification. Surface roughness can increase true areas substantially (equation 23–2). Moreover, within a group of flakes there is great variation in specific surface because of differences in wood specific gravity. For example, one flake may consist entirely of earlywood, while another flake may be totally latewood.

McMillin experimentally measured the specific surface and the distribution of specific surface by introducing flakes into a horizontal airstream of constant velocity (fig. 23–23). By this method, flakes blown a further distance down the airstream have higher specific surface than those blown only a short distance. The apparatus was divided into a series of six equally spaced compartments and calibrated with paper flakes having known specific surfaces. By fixing the weight of incoming flakes and measuring the weight of flakes in each compartment, it was possible to compute a weight average specific surface and the distribution of specific surface in percent by weight for each sample. The mean specific surface for each compartment was as follows:

Compartment number (fig. 23–23)	Specific surface
	m.^{2}/kg.
1	2.96
2	6.54
3	10.53
4	14.92
5	18.72
6	21.61

The weight of flakes passing compartments 6 (normally small) was considered to fall in compartment 7, having a specific surface in excess of 21.61 m.^{2}/kg.

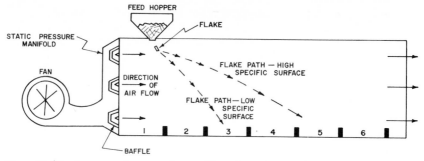

Figure 23–23.—Apparatus for measuring specific surface of flakes. (Drawing after McMillin.[9])

The mean weight average specific surface from wind tunnel measurements are tabulated below for three flake thicknsses and two specific gravities. They are in good agreement with those calculated from equation 23–7.

Flake thickness	Wood specific gravity	
	Low (avg. 0.45)	High (avg. 0.53)
Inches	– – – – *m.²/kg.* – – – –	
0.015	11.9	10.6
.025	7.8	6.6
.035	5.5	4.3

The correlation between the wind-tunnel-determined weight average specific surface and strength in bending was good.

$$MOR = 24,832.7 - 1,329.8(D) + 16.5(D)^2 + 1,102.5(S) - 45.6(S)^2 \quad (23\text{--}10)$$

$$MOE = 8,551,625.5 - 417,754.1(D) + 5,102.9(D)^2 \quad (23\text{--}11)$$
$$+ 103,666.2(S) - 3,667.3(S)^2$$

The equation for MOR accounted for 82 percent of the total variation with a standard error of the estimate of 554 p.s.i. Corresponding values for MOE were 88 percent and 59,978 p.s.i.

The distribution of specific surface in percent by weight differed with flake thickness as shown in figure 23–24. McMillin[9] observed that the forms of these distribution patterns accounted for virtually all of the variation in bending properties of boards fabricated under his test conditions. In brief, flakes having distribution curves similar to that shown for 0.015-inch-thick flakes yielded boards of highest bending strength.

BOARD PROPERTIES VS. GLUE PROPERTIES [10]

Hse[10] studied urea-formaldehyde resin synthesis to determine the relationships between southern pine particleboard properties and the physical and chemical properties of the resins. His results follow.

---

[10] The text under this heading is condensed from Hse, C.-Y. Urea-formaldehyde resin formulation factors and their effect on properties of southern pine particleboard. USDA Forest Service, Southern Forest Experiment Station, Alexandria, La., Final Report FS–SO–3201–2.33 dated May 1, 1972.

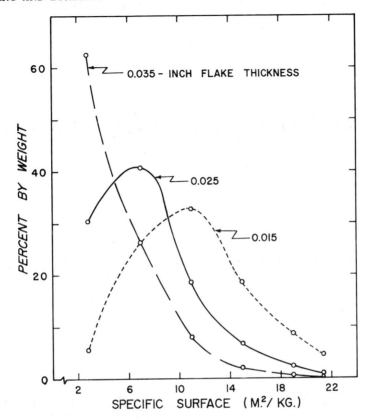

Figure 23–24.—Distribution of specific surface, in percent by weight, for flakes of three thicknesses. (Drawing after McMillin[9].)

Resin formulation variables vs. board properties.—Forty-five urea resins were formulated and replicated by factorial arrangement of three formulation variables: molar ratio of formaldehyde to urea (1.5, 1.7, 1.9, 2.1 and 2.3), reactant concentration (35, 42.5, and 50 percent), and reaction temperature (75°, 85°, and 95° C.). Board quality was determined by measuring internal bond strength (IB), modulus of rupture (MOR), modulus of elasticity (MOE), and screw withdrawal forces (SW).

Board quality increased substantially with a change in molar ratio of formaldehyde to urea from 1.5 to 1.7; higher ratios yielded only minor improvements in properties. On average, all strength properties of the particleboard increased as the reactant concentration increased. Change in the reaction temperature affected only MOR and SW; i.e., resins formulated at the higher reaction temperatures yielded boards with the highest MOR and SW.

Resin shrinkage, surface tension, and formaldehyde and methylol content vs. board properties.—In the range of the 90 urea resins previously described (45 resins with replication), free formaldehyde content (1.3 to 6.7 percent) was linearly and positively correlated with IB and MOR. The methylol content (3.2 to 10.3 percent) was also positively correlated with IB but was not significantly related to MOR. Resin shrinkage (24 to 36 percent) during cure was, in general, negatively correlated with IB and MOR; i.e., resins with most shrinkage yielded the poorest bonds. No significant correlation was found between surface tension and bond strength.

pH during resin reaction vs. board properties.—The simplest reaction products of formaldehyde and urea are methylol compounds; they are produced under neutral or weakly alkaline conditions. The methylol ureas are not resinous materials; therefore, at an appropriate time after their formation, the reaction mixture is made weakly acid to promote a condensation reaction leading to resin formation. Results of an experiment designed to optimize board properties through control of pH follow.

Twelve resins were prepared with factorial combinations of alkaline and acidic reaction pH; i.e., the reaction mixture was adjusted to pH 7, 8, 9, or 10 for the first hour of reaction and then made weakly acid to pH 5.8, 4.8, or 3.8. Resin adhesion properties were determined by measuring internal bond and modulus of rupture of boards assembled with these resins.

On average, the resins formulated at pH 8 resulted in higher IB and MOR than those at pH 7, 9, or 10. Change in acidic pH had little effect on adhesion strength of the resins when the initial pH was 8 or 9. If initial pH was 7 or 10, the adhesion strength of the resins increased or decreased as the acidic pH increased. This pH effect was especially important in the weakly acid range of 5.8, i.e., pH 5.8 in combination with initial pH of 7 yielded the resin with the best adhesion strength.

Catalysts vs. board properties.—As has been shown, pH of the reaction mixture during resin formulation affects resin bonding properties. Catalysts used during resin formulation also affect resin bonding properties. In an effort to optimize catalyst selection, Hse[10] formulated 12 urea resins with factorial combinations of three alkaline catalysts (i.e., sodium hydroxide, hexamethylenetetramine, and triethanolamine) and four acidic catalysts (i.e., acetic acid, hydrochloric acid, ammonium chloride, and phosphoric acid). The resins were replicated. Resin adhesion properties were determined by measuring internal bond and modulus of rupture of boards fabricated with the resins.

The resins catalyzed with sodium hydroxide in general had higher IB and MOR than resins prepared with hexamethylenetetramine or triethanolamine. All acidic catalysts in combination with sodium hydroxide as alkaline catalyst yielded IB and MOR values in excess of those called for by Commercial Standard CS 236–66 (U.S. Department of Commerce 1966a). Only two out of the four acidic catalysts (i.e., hydrochloric acid and phosphoric acid) in combination with hexamethylenetetramine as alkaline catalyst yielded resins that met this standard. With triethanol-amine as the alkaline catalyst, only acetic acid among the acidic catalysts yielded resin bond strengths comparable to those of resins catalyzed with sodium hydroxide. These results are summarized as follows:

Alkaline and acidic catalysts	Internal bond	Modulus of rupture
	– – – – – P.s.i. – – – – –	
Sodium hydroxide		
Ammonium chloride	119	2,056
Phosphoric acid	110	1,828
Acetic acid	109	1,818
Hydrochloric acid	108	1,721
Hexamethylenetetramine		
Hydrochloric acid	123	1,836
Phosphoric acid	97	1,659
Acetic acid	94	1,591
Ammonium chloride	47	1,323
Triethanolamine		
Acetic acid	121	1,931
Hydrochloric acid	66	1,413
Ammonium chloride	63	1,383
Phosphoric acid	51	1,207

23–7 MOLDED PRODUCTS

Mixtures of powdered resin glues termed **binders,** usually phenolic, and southern pine particles (usually milled to pass an 8-mesh-per-inch or finer screen) can be hot pressed or molded into simple shapes. Complexity of the shape is primarily limited by the poor flow characteristics of woody mixtures containing less than 20 percent binder (Patterson and Snodgrass 1959; Watson 1959). No data on the molding properties of southern pine particles are published, but information provided by Gatchell and Heebink (1964, 1965) on Douglas-fir should generally apply.

They found that Douglas-fir flakes (without binder) milled to pass a 20-mesh screen and be retained on a 40-mesh screen (20–40), when piled into a cone 8.5 inches in diameter and hot pressed at 1,000 p.s.i. specific pressure into disks of the same diameter, compressed to substantially different specific gravities depending on the press temperature and the initial moisture content of the particles, as follows:

Press temperatures and moisture content (percent)	Specific gravity (ovendry weight and volume at test)
75° F.	
5	0.64
13	.73
335° F.	
5	.85
13	1.07

With Douglas-fir blends (20–40 screen fraction at 5-percent moisture content) containing 12-percent phenolic resin and molded at 335° F., Gatchell and Heebink observed that the best flow was obtained in those containing the greatest percentage of cubical material, e.g., those from rip-cut sawdust. Poorest flow was in blends made from planer shavings. Linear stability during moisture cycling, and modulus of rupture of the molded disks were negatively correlated with flow index, i.e., the cube-cut particles made weaker disks with less linear stability than the particles derived from planer shavings.

Parent particle shape	Flow index	Modulus of rupture	Linear movement index
		P.s.i.	Percent
Shavings, flakes, and slivers _____	52	5,700	0.80
Rip-cut sawdust _____	66	3,600	1.67

Thickness swelling of humidified or soaked disks pressed from shaving-derived material, however, averaged about 17 percent—substantially more than the 11 percent observed in material derived from rip-cut sawdust.

Blends of Douglas-fir with 6-, 12-, and 18-percent resin content did not exhibit greatly different flow indices, nor was there substantial difference in flow index between 20–40 and 40–80 screen fractions. As would be expected, disks molded with the highest resin content had the greatest specific gravity, modulus of rupture, and stability. When resin content was sufficient to establish somewhat continuous gluelines between particles, however, addition of more resin did not proportionately improve strength.

23–8 FIBERBOARD

A discussion of the theory of fiber-to-fiber bonds in fiber networks is beyond the scope of this text. The reader may become introduced to the large, and rapidly expanding, body of literature on the subject through study of the following references: Bolam (1961, 1966), Simmonds and Chidester (1963), Fowkes (1967), Nissan (1967), Stannett (1967), McMillin (1969a), Van den Akker (1969), Page (1969, 1970, 1971), and Dillon (1970).

THE INDUSTRY [11]

The first fiberboard plant in the South, Masonite Corp., began operations in 1926; it utilized residues from sawmills cutting southern pine.

---

[11] Text under this heading is condensed from Turner, H. D. Fiberboard, hardboard, and moulded fiber from southern pine wood—processes and products. Presentation at a symposium, "Utilization of the Southern Pines," Alexandria, La., November 6–8, 1968.

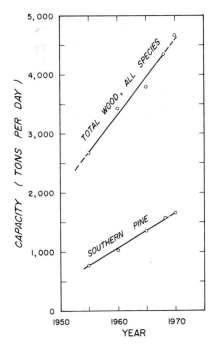

Figure 23–25.—Production capacity of fiberboard plants in the United States and the
contribution of southern pine wood to
the total requirement. (Drawing after
Turner.[11])

Productive capacity of this plant, now the largest of its kind in the world, has been several times expanded, and roundwood of numerous species is used as well as residue from sawmills.

Industry capacity in the United States shows steady growth, and utilization of southern pine in fiberboard also increases steadily but not in direct proportion (fig. 23–25). In the decade from 1958 to 1968 plant capacity increased approximately 50 percent, i.e., from 3,000 tons per day to 4,400.

In 11 States of the southern pine region, there were 13 companies manufacturing fiberboard in 1968. By 1970, a 14th plant was in operation and several had expanded. The industry makes two general classes of product: insulation and low-density fiberboards, and hardboard.

Insulation and low-density fiberboards.—In the manufacture of low-density boards, high-yield mechanical pulp is made with stone grinders or disk refiners (see sec. 27–1); a water suspension of the pulp is formed into a continuous thick mat on a moving wire screen. The formed mat is cut to length and dried in multideck tunnel dryers (see sec. 20–4 and figs. 20–35 and 20–36). A broad range of board properties can be obtained through adjustment of forming operations, incorporation of additives in the pulp, and by post-forming operations and addition of coatings. Readers desiring an introduction to the manufacturing technology are referred to Rydholm (1965, ch. 7, pp. 368–400).

The process is highly mechanized, automatically controlled, and requires a multi-million-dollar plant investment and large volume production to achieve low unit costs. Although yields are high compared to the pulp industry—generally 75 percent or more—wood costs are vitally important. In 1968 commodity grades of fiberboard sold for about $100 per ton.

Hardboard.—In contrast to insulation board, which is formed in low-density mats and dried in tunnel dryers, hardboard is hot-pressed to much higher density. Fibers for hardboard may be produced by the steam gun explosion technique developed by W. H. Mason in 1924, or by revolving-disk mills. Brief descriptions of these processes can be found in Koch (1964c, pp. 510–518).

The fibers may be wet-formed in mats and then consolidated and dried in the hot press. When pressed in this manner, one side of the board rests on a screen so that steam can escape from the heated mass of wet fiber; consequently the board as it comes from the press is smooth on one side only and has a screen pattern on the other.

Alternatively, the fibers can be dried first and then air-formed into a mat. Refined fiber treated with resins can be dried extremely rapidly without thermal damage to the fiber or appreciable polymerization of the resin. Mats of dry fibers can be pressed without screens; hence they emerge from the hot press smooth on both sides.

Board properties are affected by complex interactions among many factors including degree of fiber refining, content of resin glues, waxes, and other additives mixed with the fibers, mat-forming procedure, hot press conditions, and board density. In general, strength properties are positively correlated with resin content and board specific gravity. Resin content of hardboard is usually less than 3 percent based on dry weight of wood fiber, and in some boards no resin is added.

EFFECTS OF GROSS WOOD CHARACTERISTICS ON FIBERBOARD PROPERTIES

In a large study of wet-formed fiberboard from disk-refined loblolly pine chips, McMillin (1968) found that most strength properties of the fiberboards were increased when the fiber was refined from wood of high specific gravity but containing relatively little latewood.

McMillin concluded that dense veneer cores should be a desirable raw material for fiberboards; fiber refined from slabs and edgings of low density should yield boards of lesser strength.

EFFECTS OF FIBER MORPHOLOGY ON FIBERBOARD PROPERTIES

From data obtained in the experiment mentioned under the foregoing heading, McMillin (1969b) also was able to relate strength properties of loblolly pine fiberboards to dimensions of the fibers from which the boards were formed.

Most board properties were improved by using fiber refined from wood having short, slender tracheids with thin walls. A theoretical analysis suggested that the fibers fail in bending while under stress induced by the pressing operation. Such bending failures, because they promote intimate fiber-to-fiber contact, improve conditions for hydrogen bonding—thus improving board properties. Tracheids having narrow diameters and thin walls flex easily and collapse readily, further promoting good fiber-to-fiber contact. Short, flexible tracheids are more desirable than long, because short tracheids result in a greater number of fiber crossings per unit weight in the pulp mat; most strength properties increase with increased numbers of crossings.

STANDARDS AND TEST PROCEDURES

Major standards and test procedures for the various classes of fiberboard include the following (published by the American Society for Testing and Materials, Philadelphia, Pa.):

Product and subject	Reference
Insulation board and sheathing	ASTM C–208–60 (1966)
Interior hardboard	ASTM D1037–64A and B
Definition of terms	ASTM D1554–67

23–9 LITERATURE CITED

Anonymous.
  1962. How to upgrade lumber for today's markets. Wood & Wood Prod. 67(8): 30–31, 70, 73.
Anonymous.
  1963. Big plywood from little logs. Bus. Week, Sept. 14, pp. 92, 94.
Anonymous.
  1968. Southern pine residuals converted into panels. Forest Ind. 95(2): 83–85.
Anonymous.
  1970. Board producers 1970. Forest Ind. 97(8): 86–97.
American Institute of Timber Construction.
  1967. Tension laminations in structural glued laminated timber members in bending. Amer. Inst. Timber Constr. AITC 301–67, 1 p.
American Institute of Timber Construction.
  1969. Structural glued laminated timber. U.S. Commercial Stand. CS 253–63, 22 pp. Amer. Inst. Timber Constr. Englewood, Colo.

American Institute of Timber Construction.
  1970. Standard specifications for structural glued laminated timber of Douglas-fir, western larch, southern pine, and California redwood. Amer. Inst. Timber Constr. 203–70, 16 pp. Englewood, Colo.
America Society for Testing and Materials.
  1964. Evaluating the properties of wood-base fiber and particle panel materials. ASTM Des. D1037–64, 31 pp. Amer. Soc. Testing and Mater., Philadelphia.
Barnes, D.
  1970. Glue spreading efficiency of roll spreaders. Forest Prod. J. 20(1): 24–29.
Bassett, K. H.
  1960. Effect of certain variables on strength of glued end joints. Forest Prod. J. 10: 579–585.
Batey, T. E.
  1955. Minimizing face checking of plywood. Forest Prod. J. 5: 277–285.

Bikerman, J. J.
1961. The science of adhesive joints. 258 pp. N.Y.: Academic Press.

Billmeyer, F. W.
1957. Textbook of polymer science. 518 pp. N.Y.: Interscience Publ.

Blomquist, R. F.
1969. Gluing of southern pine. Forest Prod. J. 19(4): 36–44.

Blomquist, R. F., and Olson, W. Z.
1957. Durability of urea-resin glues at elevated temperatures. Forest Prod. J. 7: 266–272.

Blomquist, R. F., and Olson, W. Z.
1964. Experiments in gluing southern pine veneer. USDA Forest Serv. Res. Note FPL–032, 33 pp. Forest Prod. Lab., Madison, Wis.

Bloomquist, P. R.
1966. Southern pine plywood adhesives technology. Forest Ind. 93(2): 39–41.

Bohannan, B., and Kanvik, K.
1969. Fatigue strength of finger joints. USDA Forest Serv. Res. Pap. FPL–114, 8 pp. Forest Prod. Lab., Madison, Wis.

Bohannan, B., and Moody, R. C.
1969. Large glued-laminated timber beams with two grades of tension laminations. USDA Forest Serv. Res. Pap. FPL–113, 44 pp. Forest Prod. Lab., Madison, Wis.

Bohannan, B., and Selbo, M. L.
1965. Evaluation of commercially made end joints in lumber by three test methods. USDA Forest Serv. Res. Pap. FPL–41, 40 pp. Forest Prod. Lab., Madison, Wis.

Bolam, F. (Ed.)
1961. Fundamentals of paper-making fibres. 497 pp. London: Tech. Sect. of the Brit. Pap. and Board Makers' Assoc.

Bolam, F. (Ed.)
1966. Consolidation of the paper web. Vol. 1 & 2, 1115 pp. London: Tech. Sect. of the Brit. Pap. and Board Makers' Assoc.

Bolger, R. J., and Rasmussen, C. A.
1962. A rapid, continuous method of testing glued end joints. Forest Prod. J. 12: 422–425.

Brouse, D.
1939. Contribution of synthetic resins to improvement of plywood properties. USDA Forest Serv. Forest Prod. Lab. Rep. R1212, 16 pp.

Brouse, D.
1956. Serviceability of glue joints. USDA Forest Serv. Forest Prod. Lab. Rep. R1172, 7 pp. Also in Mechanical Engineering 60: 306–308. 1938.

Brouse, D.
1957. The ideal glue—how close are we? Forest Prod. J. 7: 163–167.

Browne, F. L., and Brouse, D.
1939. Casein glues. In Casein and its industrial applications, pp. 233–292. Ed. 2, E. Sutermeister and F. L. Browne, eds. N.Y.: Reinhold Publishing Corp.

Brunauer, E., Emmett, P. H., and Teller, E.
1938. Adsorption of gases in multimolecular layers. J. Amer. Chem. Soc. 60: 309–319.

Bryan, R. W.
1968. In the South economic factors begin to mitigate pine plywood boom. Forest Ind. 95(1): 46–47.

Bryan, R. W.
1970. Giant board plant uses pine, hardwood. Forest Ind. 97(8): 46–48.

Burnett, G. M.
1954. Mechanism of polymer reactions. High polymers, vol. III, 493 pp. N.Y.: Interscience Publ.

Canada Department of Fisheries and Forestry.
1970. Weather resistance of wood adhesives. Res. News 13(5): 9. Can. Dep. Fish. and Forest.

Carruthers, J. F. S.
1963. A new method for selecting glues for RF heating. Forest Prod. J. 13: 190–194.

Carruthers, J. F. S.
1965. The Risborough continuous laminating machine. Wood 30(10): 51–54.

Carswell, T. S.
1947. Phenoplasts, their structure, properties and chemical technology. High polymers, vol. VII, 267 pp. N.Y.: Interscience Publ.

Choong, E. T., and Attarzadeh, H.
1970. Gluability of non-pressure treated southern pine veneer. La. State Univ. LSU Wood Util. Note 18, 4 pp.

Cone, C. N.
1969. Foam extrusion—a new way of applying glue. Forest Prod. J. 19(11): 14–16.

Clark, L. E.
1959. Urea resins for RF and heated-platen edge gluing. Forest Prod. J. 9(6): 15A–16A.

Clark, F., Rutzler, J. E., and Savage, R. L., editors.
1954. Adhesion and adhesives—fundamentals and practice. 229 pp. N.Y.: John Wiley and Sons.

Dawe, P. S.
1964. Standard tests for finger joints. Wood 29(12): 45–47.

Delmonte, J.
1947. The technology of adhesives. 516 pp. N.Y.: Reinhold Publ. Corp.

Deppe, H. J.
1969. Developments in the production of multi-layer foamed wood particleboards. Forest Prod. J. 19(7): 27–33.

Deppe, H. J., and Ernst, K.
1966. [Durability of urea and phenolic resins in particle boards.] Holz als Roh- und Werkstoff 24: 285–290.

Dillon, J. H.
1970. The physics of fiber contact. Third Edward R. Schwarz Memorial Lect., Amer. Soc. Mech. Eng. Textile Conf. 1969, 37 pp. Raleigh, N.C.

Dorn, H., and Egner, K.
1961. Investigations on finger joints in bearing wooden structural parts after long years in use. Holz als Roh- und Werkstoff 19(3): 100–112.

Dougherty, R. E.
1968. Particle-board industry forges ahead toward new production record. South. Lumberman 217(2704): 145.

Egner, K., and Jagfeld, P.
1964. Investigations on finger-jointed planks after many years of use—behavior under pulsating tensile stress. Holz als Roh- und Werkstoff 22(3): 107–113.

Eickner, H. W.
1942. The gluing characteristics of 15 species of wood with cold-setting, urea-resin glues. USDA Forest Serv. Forest Prod. Lab. Rep. 1342, 10 pp.

Fassnacht, D. L.
1964. The story behind the new southern pine plywood industry. Forest Prod. J. 14: 21–22.

Federal Housing Administration.
1969. Structural end-jointed lumber. Dep. Housing and Urban Develop., Fed. Housing Admin., Use of Mater. Bull. UM–51, 4 pp.

Fengel, D., and Kumar, R. N.
1970. Electron microscopic studies of glued wood joints. Holzforschung 24: 177–181.

Fischer, C., and Bensend, D. W.
1969. Gluing of southern pine veneer with blood modified phenolic resin glues. Forest Prod. J. 19(5): 32–37.

Fleischer, H. O., and Lutz, J. F.
1963. Technical considerations for manufacturing southern pine plywood. Forest Prod. J. 13: 39–42.

Fowkes, F. M.
1967. Molecular forces at interfaces. In Surfaces and coating related to paper and wood, pp. 99–125. (R. H. Marchessault and C. Skaar, eds.). N.Y.: Syracuse Univ. Press.

Freas, A. D.
1953. Laminated southern pine. South. Lumberman 187 (2345): 168–169.

Freas, A. D., and Selbo, M. L.
1954. Fabrication and design of glued laminated wood structural members. US DA Tech Bull. 1069, 220 pp.

Freeman, H. G.
1970. Influence of production variables on quality of southern pine plywood. Forest Prod. J. 20(12): 28–31.

Gatchell, C. J., and Heebink, B. G.
1964. Effect of particle geometry on properties of molded wood-resin blends. Forest Prod. J. 14: 501–506.

Gatchell, C. J., and Heebink, B. G.
1965. Free-close molding versus molding to stops in wood-resin blend processing. USDA Forest Serv. Res. Note FPL–0103, 15 pp. Forest Prod. Lab., Madison, Wis.

Gatchell, C. J., Heebink, B. G., and Hefty, F. V.
1966. Influence of component variables on properties of particleboard for exterior use. Forest Prod. J. 16(4): 45–59.

Greten, E.
1966. Bison-verfahren. In Holzspanwerkstoffe, pp. 441–445. (F. Kollmann, ed.) N.Y.: Springer-Verlag.

Guttenberg, S.
1970. Prospects for the southern pine plywood industry. Forest Prod. J. 20(10): 12–14.

Hair, D., and Ulrich, A. H.
1969. The demand and price situation for forest products 1968–69. USDA Misc. Pub. 1086, 74 pp.

Halligan, A. F.
1969. Recent glues and gluing research applied to particleboard. Forest Prod. J. 19(1): 44–51.

Hann, R. A., Oviatt, A. E., Markstrom, D. M., and Duff, J. E.
1970. Moisture content of laminated timbers. USDA Forest Serv. Res. Pap. FPL–149, 6 pp. Forest Prod. Lab., Madison, Wis.

Hanna, O. A.
1955. Laminated crossarms. Forest Prod. J. 5: 127–130.

Haskell, H. H., Bair, W. M., and Donaldson, W.
1966. Progress and problems in the southern pine plywood industry. Forest Prod. J. 16(4): 19–24.

Heebink, B. G.
1960. A new technology for evaluating show-through of particle board cores. Forest Prod. J. 10: 379–388.

Heebink, B. G.
1967a. A look at degradation in particleboards for exterior use. Forest Prod. J. 17(1): 59–66.

Heebink, B. G.
1967b. A procedure for quickly evaluating dimensional stability of particleboard. Forest Prod. J. 17(9): 77–80.

Henry, W. T., and Gardner, R. E.
1954. Gluing pressure treated wood with resorcinol type adhesives. Forest Prod. J. 4: 300–303.

Holley, D. L.
1969. Potential growth of the southern pine plywood industry. USDA Forest Serv. Res. Pap. SO–41, 22 pp. South. Forest Exp. Sta., New Orleans, La.

Hse, C. Y.
1968. Gluability of southern pine earlywood and latewood. Forest Prod. J. 18(12): 32–36.

Hse, C. Y.
1971. Properties of phenolic adhesives as related to bond quality in southern pine plywood. Forest Prod. J. 21(1): 44–52.

Hursey, P. B., and Fogg, P. J.
1970. Bond strength in southern pine plywood with hardwood inner plies as affected by preservative treatment. La. State Univ. LSU Wood Util. Note 19, 2 pp.

Keylwerth, R.
1959. [Actual and possible reduction of anisotrophy in wood-based boards.] Holz als Roh -und Werkstoff 17: 234–238.

Klauditz, W., and Stegmann, G.
1958. Über die Eignung von Pappelholz zur Herstellung von Holzspanplatten. Holzforschung 11: 174–179.

Koch, P.
1964a. Beams from boltwood: a feasibility study. Forest Prod. J. 14: 497–500.

Koch, P.
1964b. Strength of beams with laminae located according to stiffness. Forest Prod. J. 14: 456–460.

Koch, P.
1964c. Wood machining processes. 530 pp. N.Y.: Ronald Press Co.

Koch, P.
1965g. Effects of seven variables on properties of southern pine plywood. I. Maximizing wood failure. Forest Prod. J. 15: 355–361.

Koch, P.
  1965b. Effects of seven variables on properties of southern pine plywood. II. Maximizing wet shear strength. Forest Prod. J. 15: 463–465.

Koch, P.
  1965c. Effects of seven variables on properties of southern pine plywood. IV. Minimizing face checking. Forest Prod. J. 15: 495–499.

Koch, P.
  1967a. Location of laminae by elastic modulus may permit manufacture of very strong beams from rotary-cut southern pine veneers. USDA Forest Serv. Res. Pap. SO–30, 12 pp. South. Forest Exp. Sta., New Orleans, La.

Koch, P.
  1967b. Minimizing and predicting delamination of southern plywood in exterior exposure. Forest Prod. J. 17 (2): 41–47.

Koch, P.
  1967c. Super-strength beams laminated from rotary-cut southern pine veneer. Forest Prod. J. 17(6): 42–48.

Koch, P.
  1970. Delamination of southern pine plywood during three years of exterior exposure. Forest Prod. J. 20(11): 28–31.

Koch, P.
  1971. Process of making laminated wood product utilizing modulus of elasticity measurement. (U.S. Pat. No. 3,580,760) U.S. Pat. Off., Wash., D.C.

Koch, P., and Bohannan, B.
  1965. Beam strength as affected by placement of laminae. Forest Prod. J. 15: 289–295.

Koch, P., and Jenkinson, P.
  1965. Effects of seven variables on properties of southern pine plywood. III. Maximizing dry strength. Forest Prod. J. 15: 488–494.

Koch, P., and Woodson, G. E.
  1968. Laminating butt-jointed, log-run, southern pine veneers into long beams of uniform high strength. Forest Prod. J. 18(10): 45–51.

Lambuth, A. L.
  1970. Progress report on soft spreader rolls. Forest Prod. J. 20(1): 42.

Louisiana Forestry Association.
  1971. $7 million particleboard plant announced by Willamette. La. Forest. Assoc. Newsletter 13(1): 3.

McMillin, C. W.
  1968. Fiberboards from loblolly pine refiner groundwood: effects of gross wood characteristics and board density. Forest Prod. J. 18(8): 51–59.

McMillin, C. W.
  1969a. Aspects of fiber morphology affecting properties of handsheets made from loblolly pine refiner groundwood. Wood Sci. and Technol. 3: 139–149.

McMillin, C. W.
  1969b. Fiberboards from loblolly pine refiner groundwood: aspects of fiber morphology. Forest Prod. J. 19(7): 56–61.

Malarkey, N.
  1963. Continuous lamination of lumber. Forest Prod. J. 13: 68–69.

Mann, J. W.
  1954. Some fundamentals of high frequency gluing. Forest Prod. J. 4(6): 16A–18A.

Mark, H. F., and Tobolsky, A. V.
  1950. Physical chemistry of high polymeric systems. Ed. 2, 506 pp. High Polymers, vol. II. N.Y.: Interscience Publ.

Markwardt, L. J., and Youngquist, W. G.
  1956. Tension test methods for wood, wood-based materials, and sandwich constructions. USDA Forest Serv. Forest Prod. Lab. Rep. 2055, 25 pp.

Marian, J. E.
  1968. Wood finger jointing. I. A new procedure for wood finger-jointing and its principles. Holz als Roh- und Werkstoff 26(2): 41–45.

Marian, J. E.
  1969. Method of forming finger joints. (U.S. Pat. No. 3,480,054.) U.S. Pat. Office, Wash., D.C.

Marian, J. E., Stumbo, D. A., and Maxey, C. W.
1958. Surface texture of wood as related to glue-joint strength. Forest Prod. J. 8: 345–351.

Marra, G. G.
1956. Development of a method for rapid laminating of lumber without the use of high-frequency heat. Forest Prod. J. 6: 97–104.

Meyer, K. H.
1950. Natural and synthetic high polymers. Ed. 2, 912 pp. High Polymers, vol. IV. N.Y.: Interscience Publ.

Miller, D. G., and Cole, T. J. S.
1957. The dielectric properties of resin glues for wood. Forest Prod. J. 7: 345–352.

Miller, D. G., and George P.
1965. Causes of radio frequency burns in edge glued joints. Forest Prod. J. 15(1): 33–36.

Mitlin, L., (Ed.).
1968. Particleboard manufacture and application. 222 pp. Great Britain: Pressmedia Ltd.

Moody, R. C.
1970. Tensile strength of finger joints in pith-associated and non-pith-associated southern pine 2x6's. USDA Forest Serv. Res. Pap. FPL–138, 20 pp. Forest Prod. Lab., Madison, Wis.

Moody, R. C., and Bohannan, B.
1970. Flexural properties of glued-laminated southern pine beams with laminations positioned by visual-stiffness criteria. USDA Forest Serv. Res. Pap. FPL–127, 20 pp. Forest Prod. Lab., Madison, Wis.

Musselwhite, R. C., Jr.
1953. Laminating small timbers and dimension lumber from southern yellow pine. Forest Prod. J. 3(2): 20–21, 86.

Nissan, A. H.
1967. The significance of hydrogen bonding at the surfaces of cellulose network structure. In Surfaces and coating related to paper and wood, pp. 221–265. (R. H. Marchessault and C. Skaar, eds.) N.Y.: Syracuse Univ. Press.

Norman, W. C.
1964a. A look at the future of the southern pine plywood industry. Wood & Wood Prod. 69(1): 39–40, 42.

Norman, W. C.
1964b. The future of the new southern pine plywood industry. Forest Prod. J. 14: 23–24.

Oberg, J. C.
1961. The new vs. the old in finger joints. Wood & Wood Prod. 66(5): 35–36, 74.

Orth, T. M.
1968. Southern pine plywood— five years old and still growing! Wood & Wood Prod. 73(5): 28–29, 40, 42.

Page, D. H.
1969. The structure and properties of paper. Part I. The structure of paper. Trend 15: 7–12.

Page, D. H. (Ed.)
1970. The physics and chemistry of wood pulp fibers. Spec. Tech. Assoc. Pub. 8, TAPPI. 348 pp.

Page, D. H.
1971. The structure and properties of paper. Part II. Shrinkage, dimensional stability and stretch. Trend 18: 6–11.

Patterson, T. J., and Snodgrass, J. D.
1959. Effect of formation variables on properties of wood particle moldings. Forest Prod. J. 9: 330–336.

Pincus, G., Cottrell, E. F., and Richards, D. B.
1966. Rigid roof trusses with glued-finger corners. Forest Prod. J. 16(2): 37–42.

Plath, E.
1963. [Effect of wood density on the properties of wood-based materials.] Holz als Roh- und Werkstoff 21: 104–108.

Post, P. W.
1958. Effect of particle geometry and resin content on bending strength of oak flake board. Forest Prod. J. 8: 317–322.

Post, P. W.
   1961.   Relationship of flake size and resin content to mechanical and dimensional properties of flake board. Forest Prod. J. 11: 34–37.

Quirk, J. T., Blomquist, R. F., and Kozlowski, T. T.
   1967a.   Transverse bonding of slash pine joints. Forest Prod. J. 17(12): 40–42.

Quirk, J. T., Kozlowski, T. T., and Blomquist, R. F.
   1967b.   Effects of adhesive formulation and age on strength of bonded butt joints. USDA Forest Serv. Res. Note FPL–0178, 16 pp. Forest Prod. Lab., Madison, Wis.

Quirk, J. T., Kozlowski, T. T., and Blomquist, R. F.
   1967c.   Location of failure in adhesive-bonded butt joints. USDA Forest Serv. Res. Note FPL–0177, 16 pp. Forest Prod. Lab., Madison, Wis.

Quirk, J. T., Kozlowski, T. T., and Blomquist, R. F.
   1968.   Contributions of end-wall and lumen bonding to strength of butt joints. USDA Forest Serv. Res. Note FPL–0179, 12 pp. Forest Prod. Lab., Madison, Wis.

Rackwitz, G.
   1963.   [The effect of chip dimensions on some properties of wood particle boards.] Holz als Roh- und Werkstoff 21: 200–209.

Redfarn, C. A., and Bedford, J.
   1960.   Experimental plastics; a practical course for students. Ed. 2, 140 pp. N.Y.: Interscience Publ.

Reinhart, F. W.
   1954.   Nature of adhesion. J. Chem. Educ. 31: 128–132.

Richards, D. B.
   1958a.   End gluing lumber. Forest Prod. J. 8: 99–104.

Richards, D. B.
   1958b.   Simplified tension test for wood. Forest Prod. J. 8: 14–17.

Richards, D. B.
   1962.   High-strength corner joints for wood. Forest Prod. J. 12: 413–418.

Richards, D. B.
   1963.   Improved tips for finger joints. Forest Prod. J. 13: 250–251.

Richards, D. B.
   1968.   Glue durability in finger-jointed southern pine. Forest Prod. J. 18(10): 54–56.

Richards, D. B., and Cool, B. M.
   1953.   End joints for southern pine. Ala. Polytech. Inst. Agr. Exp. Sta. Leafl. 39, 4 pp.

Richards, D. B., and Goodrick, F. E.
   1959.   Tensile strength of scarf joints in southern pine. Forest Prod. J. 9: 177–179.

Rydholm, S.
   1965.   Pulping processes. 1269 pp. N.Y.: John Wiley and Sons.

Sampson, G. R.
   1970.   Market outlook for the southern pine glue-laminating industry. Forest Prod. J. 20(11): 7–10.

Schaeffer, R. E.
   1966.   Preliminary study of the gluing of ammonium salt-treated wood with resorcinol-resin glues. USDA Forest Serv. Res. Note FPL–0112, 9 pp. Forest Prod. Lab., Madison, Wis.

Schaeffer, R. E.
   1967.   Gluing ammonium-salt-treated southern pine with resorcinol-resin adhesives. USDA Forest Serv. Res. Note FPL–0151, 16 pp. Forest Prod. Lab., Madison, Wis.

Schaeffer, R. E.
   1970.   Gap-filling adhesives in finger joints. USDA Forest Serv. Res. Pap. FPL–140, 7 pp. Forest Prod. Lab., Madison, Wis.

Schaeffer, R. E., and Gillespie, R. H.
   1970.   Improving end-to-end grain butt joint gluing of white pine. Forest Prod. J. 20(6): 39–43.

Schildknecht, C. E., (Ed.).
   1955.   Polymer processes; chemical technology of plastics, resins, rubbers, adhesives and fibers. High Polymers, vol. X. 934 pp. N.Y.: Interscience Publ.

Selbo, M. L.
    1961.   Effect of solvent on gluing preservative-treated red oak, Douglas-fir and southern pine. Amer. Wood Preserv. Assoc. Proc. 57: 152–163.

Selbo, M. L.
    1962.   Test for quality of glue bonds in end-jointed lumber. USDA Forest Serv. Forest Prod. Lab. Rep. 2258, 18 pp.

Selbo, M. L.
    1963.   Effect of joint geometry on tensile strength of finger joints. Forest Prod. J. 13: 390–400.

Selbo, M. L.
    1965.   Summary of information on gluing of treated wood. USDA Forest Serv. Forest Prod. Lab. Rep. 1789, 21 pp.

Selbo, M. L.
    1967.   Long term effect of preservatives on gluelines in laminated beams. Forest Prod. J. 17(5): 23–32.

Selbo, M. L.
    1969.   Performance of southern pine plywood during five years exposure to weather. Forest Prod. J. 19(8): 56–60.

Selbo, M. L., and Knauss, A. C.
    1954.   Wood laminating comes of age. Forest Prod. J. 4: 69–76.

Selbo, M. L., Knauss, A. C., and Worth, H. E.
    1965.   After two decades of service . . . Glulam timbers show good performance. Forest Prod. J. 11: 466–472.

Shelton, F. J.
    1969.   Plywood adhesives—developments and trends. Forest Prod. J. 19(1): 9–12.

Shen, K. C.
    1970.   Correlation between internal bond and the shear strength measured by twisting thin plates of particleboard. Forest Prod. J. 20(11): 16–20.

Sherman, D. F.
    1967.   Plywood weathers rough '66, yet scores notable gains. Forest Ind. 94(1): 42–45.

Simmonds, F. A., and Chidester, G. H.
    1963.   Elements of wood fiber structure and fiber bonding. USDA Forest Serv. Res. Pap. FPL–5, 9 pp. Forest Prod. Lab., Madison, Wis.

Sorenson, W. R., and Campbell, T. W.
    1961.   Preparative methods of polymer chemistry. 337 pp. N.Y.: Interscience Publ.

Southern Pine Inspection Bureau.
    1965.   Glued-lumber standards. South. Pine Insp. Bur., 16 pp. New Orleans, La.

Stamm, A. J.
    1964.   Wood and cellulose science. 549 pp. N.Y.: Ronald Press Co.

Stannett, V. T.
    1967.   Mechanisms of wet-strength development in paper. *In* Surfaces and coating related to paper and wood, pp. 269–299. (R. H. Marchessault and C. Skaar, eds.) N.Y.: Syracuse Univ. Press.

Stille, J. K.
    1962.   Introduction to polymer chemistry. 248 pp. N.Y.: John Wiley and Sons.

Strickler, M. D.
    1962.   Impression finger jointing of lumber. Wash. State Univ. Res. Rep. 62, pp. 15–104. *Also in* Forest Prod. J. 17(10): 23–28. 1967.

Strickler, M. D.
    1966.   Finger jointing of lumber. (U.S. Pat. No. 3,262,723.) U.S. Pat. Office, Wash., D.C.

Strickler, M. D.
    1967.   Impression finger jointing of lumber. Forest Prod. J. 17(10): 23–28.

Strickler, M. D.
    1970.   End gluing of green lumber. Forest Prod. J. 20(9): 47–51.

Strickler, M. D., Pellerin, R. F., and Talbott, J. W.
    1970.   Experiments in proof loading structural end-jointed lumber. Forest Prod. J. 20(2): 29–35.

Suchsland, O.
    1959.   An analysis of the particle board process. Mich. Agr. Exp. Sta. Quar. Bull. 42: 350–372.

Suchscland, O.
    1960.   An analysis of a two-species three-layer wood flakeboard. Mich. Agr. Exp. Sta. Quar. Bull. 43: 375–393.

Suchsland, O.
1968. Particle-board from southern pine. South. Lumberman 217(2704): 139–144.

Suchsland, O., and Stevens, R. R.
1968. Gluability of southern pine veneer dried at high temperatures. Forest Prod. J. 18(1): 38–42.

Syme, J. H.
1960. Factors for efficiency in lumber end and edge-gluing operations. Forest Prod. J. 10: 228–233.

Syska, A. D.
1969. Exploratory investigation of fire-retardant treatments for particleboard. USDA Forest Serv. Res. Note FPL–0201, 20 pp. Forest Prod. Lab., Madison, Wis.

Truax, T. R.
1929. The gluing of wood. USDA Bull. 1500, 78 pp.

USDA Forest Products Laboratory.
1948. Synthetic-resin glues. USDA Forest Serv. Forest Prod. Lab. Rep. 1336 (rev.), 21 pp. Madison, Wis.

USDA Forest Products Laboratory.
1955. Wood handbook. USDA Agr. Handbook 72, 528 pp.

USDA Forest Products Laboratory.
1939. Casein glues: their manufacture, preparation, and application. USDA Forest Serv. Forest Prod. Lab. Rep. 280, 11 pp. Madison, Wis.

USDA Forest Products Laboratory.
1956. Durability of water-resistant woodworking glues. USDA Forest Serv. Forest Prod. Lab. Rep. 1530 (rev.), 40 pp.

U.S. Department of Commerce.
1963. Structural glued laminated timber. Commercial Standard CS 253–63. U.S. Dep. Comm., Wash., D.C.

U.S. Department of commerce.
1966a. Mat-formed wood particle board. Commercial Standard CS 236–66. U.S. Dep. Comm., Wash., D.C.

U.S. Department of Commerce.
1966b. Softwood plywood—construction and industrial. U.S. Product Standard PS 1–66. U.S. Dep. Comm., Wash., D.C.

Van den Akker, J. A.
1969. An analysis of the Nordman "bonding strength." TAPPI 52: 2386–2389.

Voiutskiĭ S. S.
1963. Autohesion and adhesion of high polymers. 272 pp. N.Y.: John Wiley and Sons.

Watson, D. A.
1959. Low cost wood-particle moldings. Mater. in Design Eng. 49(5): 103–105.

Weakley, F. B., and Mehltretter, C. L.
1965. Low cost protein glue for southern pine plywood. Forest Prod. J. 15: 8–12.

Webb, D. A.
1970. Wood laminating adhesive system for ribbon spreading. Forest Prod. J. 20(4): 19–23.

Weiss, P., editor.
1962. Adhesion and cohesion. 272 pp. N.Y.: Elsevier Publ. Co.

West Coast Adhesive Manufacturers Association.
1966. A proposed new test for accelerated aging of phenolic resin-bonded particleboard. Forest Prod. J. 16(6): 19–23.

West Coast Adhesive Manufacturers Association.
1970. Accelerated aging of phenolic resin bonded particleboard. Forest Prod. J. 20(10): 26–27.

Western Wood Products Association.
1969. WWPA certification and quality control program for end jointed light framing, joists and planks and decking. Western Wood Products, 4 pp. Portland, Oreg.

24

Mechanical fastening

CONTENTS

24

Mechanical fastening[1]

Southern hurricanes have shown conclusively that the strength and storm resistance of structures built from southern pine depend on good anchorage (Stern 1970a) and strong fastenings at all crucial points. Stated simply, good fasteners develop the full strength of the materials which they join. Observations of damage have resulted in general recommendations on structural fastenings in buildings (Smith 1961; Anderson and Smith 1965; McDonald 1967; Patterson 1969; Southern Pine Association 1969; Stern 1969a; Zornig and Sherwood 1969; American Plywood Association 1967; Dikkers and Thom 1970).

The text in this chapter does not treat structures in their entirety, but instead discusses a few of the most important devices used for fastening timbers, poles, lumber, plywood, particleboard, and fiberboard to each other and to other materials. Included are nails of numerous designs, spikes, drift bolts, screws, bolts, connector rings and plates, sheet-metal hangers, and explosive-driven pins and studs.

Values for the allowable loads tabulated in this chapter have come from three sources: USDA Forest Products Laboratory (1955), Southern Pine Association (1964), and the National Design Specification (National Forest Products Association 1968). Because the standards for lumber dimensions and specific gravity change occasionally, designers of mechanically fastened joints for southern pine should maintain a current version of the National Design Specification.

Two measures of fastener efficiency are in common use. **Withdrawal resistance** is a measure of the force, applied parallel to the fastener axis, required to pull a fastened member away from the member holding the fastener's point; if a nail, screw, or bolt is improperly designed, joint failure may result from head pullthrough, in which case the head is drawn through the member adjacent to the head before the shank can be withdrawn from the member holding the point. **Lateral resistance** is a measure of the load required to cause failure when a joint is loaded so that adjacent faces of mating members define a shear plane (fig. 24–17).

The strength of certain mechanically fastened joints is a function of fractional powers of specific gravity (G) of the wood. As shown in chapter 7, specific gravity varies greatly between species, within species, and within trees. The tabulation following should be useful when calculat-

---

[1] Chapter 24 has been condensed from Stern (1969c) by permission of E. George Stern and Virginia Polytechnic Institute.

ing allowable loads for southern pine throughout a range of specific gravities.

G	$G^{3/2}$	G^2	$G^{5/2}$
0.40	0.253	0.160	0.101
.45	.302	.203	.136
.50	.354	.250	.177
.55	.408	.303	.224
.59	.453	.348	.267
.60	.465	.360	.279
.65	.524	.423	.341
.70	.586	.490	.410
.75	.649	.563	.487

24–1 DURATION OF LOAD

Since wood can sustain higher stresses for short periods of time than for long periods, allowable loads transmitted by mechanical fasteners into wood are influenced by the duration of load application. In recognition of this, duration-of-load adjustment factors have been incorporated in the National Design Specification (National Forest Products Association 1968) for seasoned lumber used in dry locations. The tabulated allowable design values are **normal** loads, for application continuously or cumulatively for a duration of approximately 10 years.

If the design load is applied **continuously** throughout the remaining life of the structure, the allowable load values are reduced 10 percent. If the design load is applied for only a **2-month duration,** as in the case of snow loads, the allowable load values can be increased 15 percent. If the design load is applied for **1-week duration,** the allowable load values can be increased 25 percent. For **wind** and **earthquake** loads, the allowable load values can be increased 33-1/3 percent; and for **impact** loads, the allowable loads can be increased 100 percent. These decreases and increases, not to be applied cumulatively, are applicable to loads transmitted by mechanical fasteners into wood, provided the wood surrounding the fastener, and not the strength of the fastener, determines the load-transmission capability.

24–2 NAILS AND SPIKES

According to Percival (1965), there are about 75,000 fasteners—mostly nails—in a 1,500-square-foot rectangular frame house. The effectiveness of these nailed joints depends on the properties of the wood, the dimensions and shape of the nail, the manner in which the nail is driven, and the conditions of use.

The term "penny (d)", originally the price per hundred, is used to specify sizes of nails and spikes; twopenny, tenpenny, etc. nails have approximately the dimensions shown in table 24–1. American Society for Testing and Materials Standard D2478–69 contains a glossary of terms

TABLE 24–1.—*Sizes of common wire nails and spikes*

Size	Gage (W&M)[1]	Length	Diameter D	$D^{3/2}$
		– – –	*Inches*	– – –
		NAILS		
2d	15	1	0.072	0.0193
4d	12½	1½	.098	.0307
6d	11½	2	.113	.0380
8d	10¼	2½	.131	.0474
10d	9	3	.148	.0570
12d	9	3¼	.148	.0570
16d	8	3½	.162	.0652
20d	6	4	.192	.0841
30d	5	4½	.207	.0942
40d	4	5	.225	.1067
50d	3	5½	.244	.1205
60d	2	6	.263	.1349
		SPIKES		
10d	6	3	.192	.0841
12d	6	3¼	.192	.0841
16d	5	3½	.207	.0942
20d	4	4	.225	.1067
30d	3	4½	.244	.1205
40d	2	5	.263	.1349
50d	1	5½	.283	.1505
60d	1	6	.283	.1505
5⁄16-inch		7	.312	.1743
		8	.312	.1743
⅜-inch		8	.375	.2296
		9	.375	.2296
		10	.375	.2296
		12	.375	.2296

[1] Washburn and Moen wire gage.

descriptive of types of nails, together with illustrations of various nail heads and points. Federal Specification FF–N–105a (General Services Administration 1963) specifies sizes, finishes, shank design, and metals for nails and staples. Stern (1967a) has published a handbook that contains definitions of nail types and sizes.

EFFECT OF WOOD FACTORS ON WITHDRAWAL RESISTANCE

The principal variables in wood that affect withdrawal resistance of nails are specific gravity, penetration into the wood, grain direction, moisture content at time the nail is driven, change in moisture content with time in use, and content of preservatives or other impregnants in the wood.

Specific gravity.—According to the National Design Specification (National Forest Products Association 1968), withdrawal resistance from side grain is proportional to $G^{5/2}$, where G equals the specific gravity based on ovendry volume and weight; i.e., withdrawal resistance of a nail driven in wood of 0.7 specific gravity is approximately four times that of the same nail in wood of 0.4 specific gravity. Compared with most other softwoods in common use, southern pine has a high specific gravity and its strength at nailed joints is exceptionally high.

Grain direction.—Nails driven perpendicular to the grain have 25 to 50 percent greater withdrawal resistance than those driven parallel to the wood fibers into the end of the piece; the difference is less pronounced in dense woods than in lighter woods. After a time interval, or after moisture content changes, the ratio between end-grain and side-grain withdrawal resistance is generally higher than that observed immediately after driving (USDA Forest Products Laboratory 1955, p. 171).

Stern (1950c) has provided some data specific to southern pine for nails pulled immediately after driving. His results were stated as a ratio between withdrawal resistance in end-grain southern pine at about 12-percent moisture content and side-grain southern pine at about 20-percent moisture content.

Type of nail shank	Ratio of end- to side-grain withdrawal resistance
Plain	0.93
Helically threaded	.84
Annularly threaded	.54

When data from Stern (1950c) for side-grain southern pine at 10- to 11-percent moisture content were compared with those for end-grain southern pine at 12-percent moisture content, the ratios were 0.75 for helically threaded shanks and 0.48 for annularly threaded shanks.

Stern (1969c, p. 40) published additional data comparing withdrawal resistance of five types of 3-1/4- and 3-1/2-inch-long nails driven into side and end grain of green southern pine; these data showed that the ratio between end-grain and side-grain withdrawal resistance was a function of time and manner of withdrawal, as well as nail type (table 24–2). A delay of several weeks prior to pulling resulted in an increased ratio of withdrawal resistance between end-grain and side-grain southern pine; coated nails had higher ratios than uncoated nails. The ratios were lower for impact withdrawal than for withdrawal at 0.1 inch per minute.

Moisture content and time elapsed after driving.—In general, nails driven into green wood and pulled before any seasoning takes place offer about the same withdrawal resistance as nails driven into seasoned wood and pulled soon after driving. If, however, smooth-shank common wire nails are driven into green wood that is allowed to season, or into seasoned wood that is subjected to cycles of wetting and drying before the nails are pulled, approximately 75 percent of the initial withdrawal resistance may be lost (USDA Forest Products Laboratory 1955, p. 169).

When nails of the types shown in figure 24–1 were driven into green southern pine and then pulled at intervals during 26 weeks of air-drying, common wire nails lost about three-fourths of their withdrawal resistance;

Figure 24–1.—Steel nails used to fasten floor underlayment. From left to right:
   2½- x 0.129-inch, plain-shank, common wire nail; 101 per pound.
   2½- x 0.132-inch, diagonally barbed square-wire nail; 115 per pound.
   2½- x 0.130-inch, helically threaded nail; 95 per pound.
   2½- x 0.135-inch, annularly threaded nail; 96 per pound.
   2⅜- x 0.113-inch, helically threaded sinker; 140 per pound.
   2⅜- x 0.118-inch, annularly threaded sinker; 140 per pound.
   2¼- x 0.099-inch, helically threaded sinker; 213 per pound.
   2¼- x 0.101-inch, annularly threaded sinker; 210 per pound.
(Photo from Stern 1957c.)

TABLE 24–2.—*Withdrawal resistance ratios for coated and uncoated smooth nails driven into end grain and side grain of green southern pine* (adapted from Stern 1969c, p. 40)

Nail description	Ratio of end-grain to side-grain withdrawal resistance			
	Static[1] immediate	Static[1] delayed[2]	Impact immediate	Impact delayed[2]
3½- by 0.162-inch common wire _____	0.49	0.99	0.49	0.66
3½- by 0.136-inch smooth box _____	.53	1.23	.44	.45
3¼- by 0.150-inch cement coated _____	.65	1.53	.46	.70
3½- by 0.127-inch plastic coated _____	.74	1.65	.24	.86
Average _____._____	.60	1.35	.41	.67

[1] Withdrawn at 0.1 inch per minute.
[2] Several weeks.

helically and annularly threaded nails, however, gained substantially in withdrawal resistance. Diagonally barbed, square-wire nails were intermediate with a slight loss in withdrawal resistance (fig. 24–2).

Elapsed time causes little loss in withdrawal resistance of smooth nails driven into dry southern pine; this holds true for coated and uncoated nails (table 24–3). Smooth nails—whether uncoated or coated—driven into green southern pine lose considerably more than half of their initial withdrawal resistance if pulled after a delay of 6 weeks (table 24–3).

TABLE 24–3.—*Effect of time since driving on withdrawal resistance of smooth, uncoated and coated nails driven into edge-grain dry and green southern pine* (adapted from Stern 1969c, pp. 16–17)

Type nail	Diameter	Penetration	Withdrawal resistance	
			Immediate	After delay[1]
	– – – *Inches* – – –		– – – – *Pounds* – – – –	
	DRY			
Common wire_____	0.162	1.75	453	431
Smooth box_____	.136	1.75	352	308
Cement coated_____	.150	1.50	411	387
Uncoated plain shank_____	.127	1.75	384	331
Plastic coated_____	.127	1.75	589	536
	GREEN			
Common wire_____	.162	2.50	700	273
Smooth box_____	.136	2.50	519	206
Cement coated_____	.150	2.25	550	162
Uncoated plain shank_____	.127	2.50	409	112
Plastic coated_____	.127	2.50	596	210

[1] Pulled 3 weeks after driving into dry wood and 6 weeks after driving into green wood.

Impregnants in wood.—Since nails are lubricated by oilborne preservatives, driving forces and withdrawal resistance of smooth nails may be less in treated than in untreated southern pine. As in untreated wood, withdrawal resistance of smooth nails diminishes with time after driving in freshly creosoted wood. Helically threaded and annularly threaded nails of hardened, medium-carbon steel, however, not only have high initial withdrawal resistance in pressure creosoted southern pine, but withdrawal

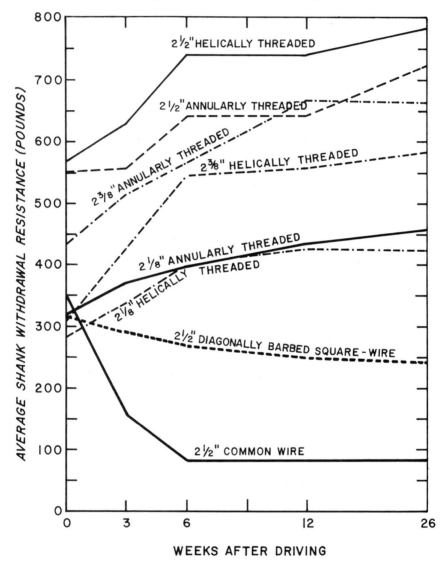

Figure 24–2.—Relationship between elapsed time after driving and withdrawal resistance of variously shaped nails 0.099 to .135 inch in diameter driven through green, ⅞-inch subflooring into green (119-percent moisture content) southern pine of 0.54 ovendry specific gravity. See figure 24–1 for description of nails. (Drawing after Stern 1957c.)

resistance has been shown by Stern (1956c) to increase over a 6-1/2-week period (fig. 24–3).

The effects of 18 different preservative treatments (salts and pentachlorophenol) on withdrawal resistance were studied by Scholten (1965a). He used ponderosa pine (*Pinus ponderosa* Laws.) boxes exposed outdoors for 5 years in Madison, Wis., and then equilibrated to about 12-percent moisture content; specific gravity was 0.42 based on volume at test and ovendry weight (approximately equivalent to 0.44 ovendry specific gravity. Sixpenny, cement-coated box nails, 1-7/8 inches long, 0.0865 inch in diameter, were driven to a penetration of about 1.1 inches into side grain. The average withdrawal resistance after exposure did not vary appreciably for different types of treatments except that those preservatives containing a water repellent gave substantially lower values; for the 13 treatments without a water repellent it was 133 pounds, whereas the four treatments with water repellent averaged 73 pounds. Exposed

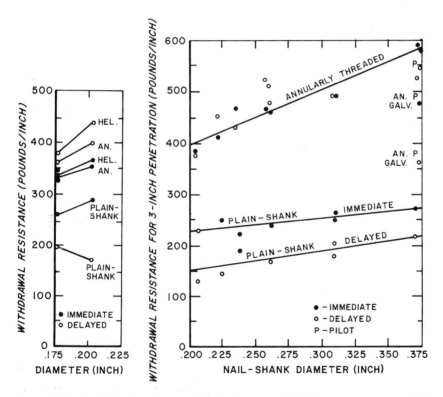

Figure 24–3.—Withdrawal resistance of nails driven radially into a pressure-creosoted southern pine pole (0.66 ovendry specific gravity) at 30-percent moisture content; moisture content at time of delayed withdrawal (6½ weeks after driving) was 22 percent. (Left) Hardened, medium-carbon-steel nails with plain, annularly threaded, and helically threaded shanks. (Right) Plain-shank and annularly threaded, bright, low-carbon-steel nails; also galvanized, annularly threaded nails driven into pilot holes. (Drawing after Stern 1956a.)

treated boxes had higher withdrawal resistance (40 pounds) than untreated boxes stored inside for the same period. The higher value in the treated wood was attributed to roughening of the nails from corrosion.

While no data on the withdrawal resistance of nails in southern pine treated with fire retardants have been published, such treatments, which slightly diminish strength properties of wood, probably diminish withdrawal resistance of nails also. Variations in degree of fire-retardant-caused corrosion make generalization difficult.

EFFECT OF MANNER OF DRIVING ON WITHDRAWAL RESISTANCE

Nails are usually driven at right angles to wood surfaces without prebored pilot holes and without clinching nail points. Preboring and clinching increase withdrawal resistance of nails driven into southern pine. The effect of slant driving is not entirely clear, but withdrawal resistance (normal to mating surfaces) appears to be diminished by slant driving.

Slant driving.—According to Scholten (1965b), the withdrawal load per nail in toenailed stud joints (fig. 24–4A), for all conditions of seasoning, is about two-thirds that for nails straight driven through the sill into the end grain of the stud (fig. 24–4B).

Scholten and Molander (1950) measured the maximum tensile force required to pull Douglas-fir (*Pseudotsuga menziesii* (Mirb.) Franco) studs away from a sill when studs were toenailed to the sill with four common wire nails; this force was compared to that required when two nails of the same size were driven straight through the sill into the end grain of the stud (fig. 24–4). In this experiment, nails slant driven in toenailed joints probably had greater penetration into the side grain of the sill than the straight-driven nails had into the end grain of the stud. For this reason it is not surprising that the four-nail toenailed joints were more than twice as strong as the two-nail joints; see data following on maximum tensile force to separate the joints shown in figure 24–4.

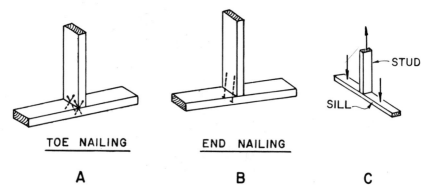

Figure 24–4.—Nailed joints between studs and sills. (A) Stud toenailed onto sill; four nails. (B) Sill straight nailed onto stud; two nails. (C) Mode of tension test.

Moisture content at fabrication and at test; nail size	Studs toenailed to sill with four nails	Two nails driven straight through sills into end grain of studs
	— — — — — — — Pounds — — — — — — —	
Fabricated dry and tested dry		
10d_____	816	310
16d_____	871	211
Fabricated green and tested green		
10d_____	795	224
16d_____	1,032	346
Fabricated green and tested dry_____		
10d_____	865	128
16d_____	1,028	163

Stern (1951b) compared the effectiveness of 3-inch nails straight driven and cross-slant driven into side grain of southern pine (fig. 24–5). He found that in no case did the pair of cross-slant-driven nails have twice the

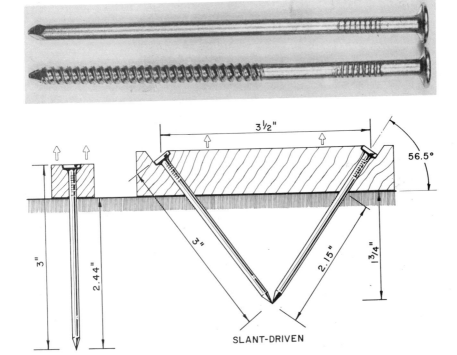

Figure 24–5.—Comparison of nails slant driven and straight driven into side grain of southern pine. (Top) Low-carbon-steel, plain-shank and helically threaded nails both 3 inches long and 0.124 inch in diameter. (Bottom) Test setup for single straight nail and two slant-driven nails. Withdrawal resistance was measured perpendicular to the joint interface (arrows) at a withdrawal rate of 0.06 inch per minute. Lateral resistance of slant nails was measured perpendicular to the plane formed by the two nails. (Drawings and photo from Stern 1951b.)

withdrawal resistance of a single straight-driven nail (table 24–4) ; contributing to this result is the lesser pentration of the slant-driven nails. Results were generally similar for both smooth and helically threaded nails. Stern did not compare slant nailing with nails driven through a sill into end grain of a stud as shown in figure 24–4B. The results of Stern's test were somewhat confounded by the fact that the specific gravity of the wood into which the slant-driven nails were set was 6 percent less than the wood into which the straight-driven nails were set.

Clinching.—A nail driven through the southern pine lumber and then **clinched** by bending the emergent point along or across the grain has greater withdrawal resistance than an unclinched nail of the same size and type. The percentage gain in withdrawal resistance depends on nail type, size, and penetration. Data from Stern (1950a, 1967b, 1968c) indicate that if nails 0.135 inch in diameter are driven through dry (11-percent moisture content) southern pine 7/8-inch thick, clinched about 1/4-inch, and pulled immediately, the ratio between clinched and unclinched withdrawal strength is approximately as follows:

	Direction of clinch	
Nail type	Along grain	Across grain
Annularly threaded	1.24	1.35
Cement coated	1.48	1.45
Plain shank	1.45	1.65
Helically threaded	1.90	2.00
Average	1.52	1.61

TABLE 24–4.—*Withdrawal resistance[1] of a pair of nails cross-slant-driven into side grain of southern pine, expressed as a percentage of the value for a single nail of the same size and type straight driven into side-grain southern pine* (adapted from Stern 1951b)

Moisture content at fabrication and at test	Nail type	
	Plain shank	Helically threaded
	– – – – – *Percent* – – – – –	
Fabricated and tested green	96	96
Fabricated green, tested at 12 to 14 percent	126	112
Fabricated green, tested at 10 to 11 percent	-----	119
Fabricated and tested at 19 percent	80	121
Fabricated at 19 percent, tested at 11 to 12 percent	146	142
Fabricated and tested at 11 percent	90	148

[1] See figure 24–5 for test mode.

Stern's (1950a) data indicate that a plain-shank nail given a 3/4-inch length of clinch across the grain did not have greater withdrawal resistance than one given a 1/4-inch clinch across the grain.

Clinching nails is most advantageous when plain-shank nails are driven into moist wood and pulling is delayed until the lumber has dried. When nails 0.120 inch in diameter were driven through 3/4-inch southern pine at 21-percent moisture content, clinched 1/4-inch across the grain, and pulled after the lumber had dried to 12 percent, the ratio of clinched to unclinched withdrawal resistance was as follows (Stern 1967b):

Type nail	Ratio, clinched to unclinched
Plain shank_____	5.45
Helically threaded_____	2.03

Low-carbon-steel nails can be automatically clinched by driving them at a slight angle against a steel back-up plate (fig. 24–6). Automatically clinched nails driven at 15° (or slightly more) from perpendicular to the lumber surface offer highest withdrawal resistance values (Stern 1968c). The following tabulation shows withdrawal resistance (perpendicular to board surface) of 0.120-inch nails driven through 3/4-inch southern pine of 0.62 ovendry specific gravity and about 19-percent moisture content so that 1/4-inch extended beyond the board and was clinched; for the nails driven perpendicularly, however, projection was only 1/8-inch.

Time tested and nail type	Angle from perpendicular					
	0°	10°	15°	20°	25°	30°
	- - - - -			*Pounds*	- - - - -		
Immediate withdrawal						
Plain shank_____	116	138	148	131	179	168
Helically threaded_____	256	275	284	298	---	---
Delayed (4 weeks) withdrawal						
Plain shank_____	54	100	186	156	159	172
Helically threaded_____	240	341	324	372	---	---

A soft nail can be **bradded,** that is, blunted on the end, by driving it through a board against a steel back-up plate. Tests with 0.120-inch-diameter, low- and medium-carbon-steel nails driven through 3/4-inch southern pine of 0.56 ovendry specific gravity and 20-percent moisture content, showed that withdrawal resistance of bradded nails was a few percent less than unclinched and unbradded nails (Stern 1967b).

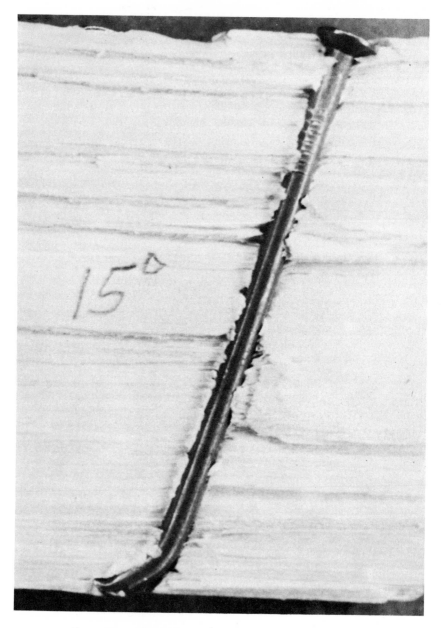

Figure 24–6.—Plain-shank, low-carbon-steel, 2⅞- by 0.120-inch sinker nail driven at 15° angle into southern pine, with its diamond point automatically clinched by driving it against a steel plate. (Photo from Stern 1968c.)

Time tested and nail type	Ratio of bradded to unclinched withdrawal resistance
Immediate withdrawal	
Plain shank _____	1.00
Helically threaded _____	.97
Delayed 4 weeks	
Plain shank _____	.93
Helically threaded _____	.93

Preboring.—Nails driven into lead holes with a diameter slightly smaller than that of the nail are less prone to cause splits, and have somewhat higher withdrawal resistance than nails driven without lead holes (USDA Forest Products Laboratory 1955).

Withdrawal tests by Stern (1957b) indicate that pilot holes in dry southern pine should be prebored with a drill about two-thirds the diameter of the nail shank (fig. 24–7).

EFFECT OF NAIL DIMENSIONS ON WITHDRAWAL RESISTANCE

Withdrawal resistance of a nail is determined not only by wood factors and manner of driving, but also by its diameter, length, and penetration and the shape of its point.

Diameter.—The USDA Forest Products Laboratory (1955) has published a formula, generally applicable to all wood species, for allowable withdrawal load of common wire nails driven into the side grain of seasoned wood that remains seasoned, or unseasoned wood that will remain wet; this allowable load is calculated to be one-sixth of the ultimate load.

$$p = 1{,}150 \ G^{5/2}D \qquad (24\text{–}1)$$

where:

p = allowable withdrawal load, pounds per inch of penetration into the piece retaining the point.

G = wood specific gravity, based on ovendry volume and weight.

D = nail diameter, inches.

Values of $G^{5/2}$ for selected specific gravities are listed in the introduction to this chapter.

Tests specific to southern pine (Stern 1957b) indicated that equation 24–1, when multiplied by 6 to give ultimate load, accurately predicts withdrawal loads of plain-shank wire nails in diameters from 0.20 to 0.24 (most nails used in framing measure less than 0.24 inch in diameter); for larger diameters, however, it overestimated immediate withdrawal resistance of plain-shank spikes driven into side grain of southern pine of 0.50 specific gravity (ovendry volume and weight) and 10-percent moisture content (fig. 24–8).

Penetration.—In general, withdrawal resistance has a positive linear correlation with depth of shank penetration into the piece retaining the point;

as indicated by the definition of p in equation 24–1, a nail with penetration of 4 inches is generally considered to have twice the withdrawal resistance of the same nail given only 2 inches of penetration. Figure 24–9 confirms this straight-line relationship in southern pine for penetrations of 1 to 3 inches.

Point.—The common wire nail usually has a diamond point (fig. 24–1,

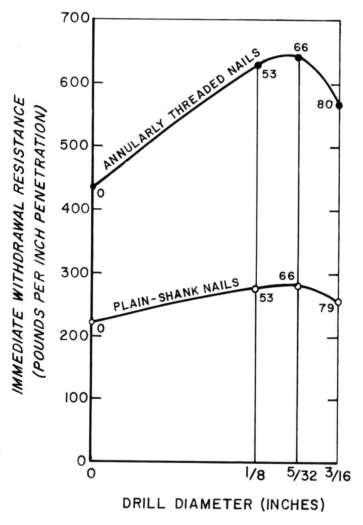

Figure 24–7.—Influence of pilot hole diameter on immediate withdrawal resistance of annularly threaded nails 0.235 inch in diameter and plain-shank nails 0.238 inch in diameter when driven 3 inches into side grain of southern pine of 0.50 ovendry specific gravity and 10-percent moisture content. The pilot holes were drilled 2¾ inches deep. Numbers adjacent to each point indicate the size of the drill diameter as a percent of shank diameter. (Drawing after Stern 1957b.)

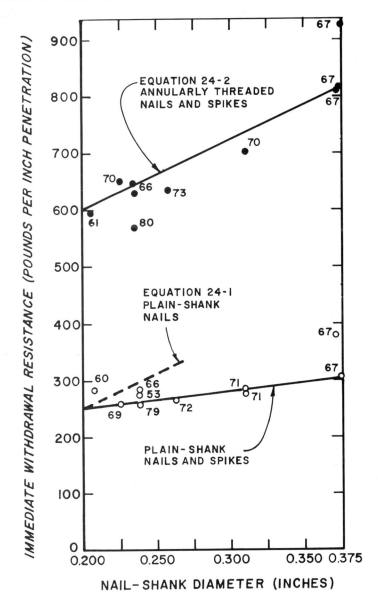

Figure 24–8.—Influence of nail shank diameter on immediate withdrawal resistance of plain-shank and annularly threaded nails driven into side grain of southern pine of 0.50 ovendry specific gravity and 10-percent moisture content. Nails were driven to 3-inch penetration in pilot holes 2¾ inches deep and about 0.7 the shank diameter. Numbers beside each point indicate pilot hole diameter as a percentage of nail diameter. Equations 24–1 and 24–2 (both multiplied by 6 to show ultimate withdrawal resistance) are plotted for comparison. (Drawing after Stern 1957b.)

left). Scholten (1962) reported the effect of point geometry on immediate withdrawal resistance of plain-shank nails 0.098 inch in diameter driven in side grain of southern pine of 0.51 specific gravity (based on volume at the test moisture content of about 11 percent and on ovendry weight).

Description and length of point (inch)	Penetration	Withdrawal resistance
	Inches	*Pounds*
Sharp conical, ⅜----------	1⁷⁄₁₆	158
Truncated conical, ⅜------	1⁵⁄₁₆	150
Diamond, ⅛--------------	1⅜	116
Completely blunt, 0--------	1⁵⁄₁₆	68

Long points decrease driving resistance and increase withdrawal resistance, but tend to split southern pine. Short or blunt points increase driving resistance, decrease withdrawal resistance, and decrease the tendency to split. Where lumber splitting should be minimized, truncated blunt points are preferable. Completely blunt points cause considerable distortion of fibers as they penerate (fig. 24–10).

EFFECT OF SHANK CHARACTERISTICS ON WITHDRAWAL RESISTANCE

Withdrawal resistance of nails is affected by the roughness, coating, and shape of the shank.

Plain-shank nails.—Allowable withdrawal resistance of plain-shank nails is stated for all species by equation 24–1 in terms of wood specific gravity and nail diameter and penetration. For southern pine, some modification of the general formula is indicated by figures 24–8 and 24–9, i.e., the equation may overestimate the allowable withdrawal resistance of large nails with low penetrations, and it may overestimate the allowable immediate withdrawal resistances of plain-shank nails with diameters larger than 0.24 inch. Withdrawal resistances for 16d common wire nails driven into southern pine are compared with those for other smooth-shank nails in table 24–5.

Cement-coated nails.—If properly applied, a cement coating on nails may double immediate withdrawal resistance in the softer woods; in harder woods the coating may be scraped off during driving and therefore be ineffective. Any increase in withdrawal resistance of cement-coated nails is not permanent, but diminishes after a month or so (USDA Forest Products Laboratory 1955, p. 169). Table 24–5 shows data specific to southern pine.

Etched nails.—Nails, chemically etched with a 2-percent solution of ferric chloride in wa'er in the presence of mercuric chloride or salts or other metals, give somewhat higher withdrawal resistance than cement-coated nails and retain much of their superiority under varying moisture conditions (Martin and Van Kleeck 1941; Gahagan and Beglinger 1956). Under impact loading, however, the withdrawal resistance of the etched nails is little different from that of plain or cement-coated nails. Sand-blasted

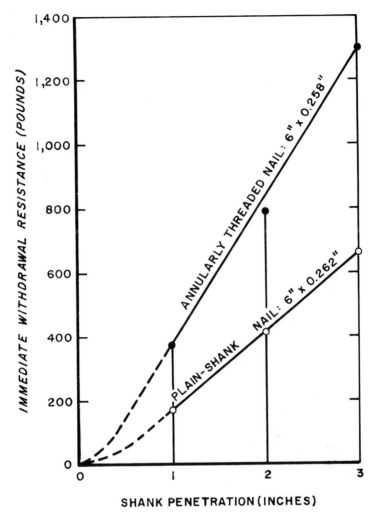

Figure 24–9.—Influence of shank penetration on withdrawal resistance of plain-shank and annularly threaded nails driven into side grain of southern pine of 0.50 ovendry specific gravity and 10-percent moisture content. (Drawing after Stern 1957b.)

nails have approximately the same withdrawal resistance as chemically etched nails (USDA Forest Products Laboratory 1955, p. 169).

Zinc-coated (galvanized) nails.—These nails are intended primarily for applications where corrosion and staining need to be reduced. If the coating is evenly applied, withdrawal resistance may be increased; extreme irregularities in the coating, however, may reduce withdrawal resistance. Repeated cycles of wetting and drying of wood penetrated by nails uniformly coated with zinc cause their withdrawal resistance to approximate that of uncoated nails with plain shanks (USDA Forest Products Laboratory 1955, p. 169).

Plastic-coated nails.—Plastic coated nails are a relatively recent development. Stern (1968b) observed that the type of plastic applied strongly affected ease of driving, immediate and delayed withdrawal resistance, and corrosion resistance of plain-shank and helically threaded nails (2-1/2

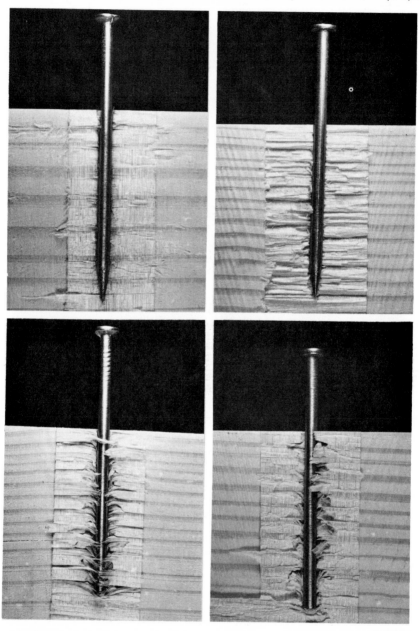

F-521002

Figure 24-10.—Fiber distortion in medium-density southern pine caused by nails with sharp (top) and blunt (bottom) points, driven into green (left) and dry (right) wood. Before the blocks of wood were split, they were equilibrated to 10-percent moisture content.

TABLE 24-5.—*Withdrawal resistance of 0.127- to 0.162-inch-diameter nails driven into side and end grain of green and dry southern pine[1]* (adapted from Stern 1969c, pp. 16-17)

Nail type[1] and grain direction	Driven 2 inches into green wood[2]				Driven 2½ inches into green wood[3]; static separation[4]		Driven 2 inches into dry wood[2]; static separation[4]	
	Static separation[4]		Impact separation					
	Immediate	Delayed 6 weeks	Immediate	Delayed 6 weeks	Immediate	Delayed 6 weeks	Immediate	Delayed 3 weeks
	- - Pounds - -		- - Inch-pounds - -		- - - - - - Pounds - - - - -		- - - - - Pounds - - - - -	
Common wire								
Side	557	163	540	242	700	273	453	431
End	273	162	264	159	—	—	—	—
Smooth box								
Side	438	125	455	268	519	206	352	308
End	230	154	199	120	—	—	—	—
Cement-coated sinker								
Side	392	97	300	125	550	162	411	387
End	253	148	139	88	—	—	—	—
Uncoated step-head								
Side	328	74	510+	115	409	112	384	331
End	232	116	144	81	—	—	—	—
Plastic-coated step-head								
Side	443	212	670	130	596	210	589	536
End	326	349	158	112	—	—	—	—

[1] See figure 24-11 for description of nails.
[2] Except that the cement-coated sinker nails penetrated only 1¾ inches.
[3] Except that the cement-coated sinker nails penetrated only 2¼ inches.
[4] Withdrawn at 0.1 inch per minute.

by 0.120 inches) driven into southern pine of 0.56 ovendry specific gravity and 19- and 26-percent moisture content. In general, driving resistance was reduced 38 percent Immediate withdrawal resistance of plain-shank nails increased as much as 125 percent, and that of helically threaded nails as much as 67 percent. The delayed withdrawal resistance of plain-shank steel and aluminum nails was increased as much as 312 and 725 percent respectively, and that of helically threaded steel nails as much as 103 percent.

In a factorial experiment, Stern (1969c, p. 15) compared plastic-polymer-coated nails (two-step head, coating unidentified), 16d common wire nails, smooth box nails, cement-coated sinker nails, and smooth un-

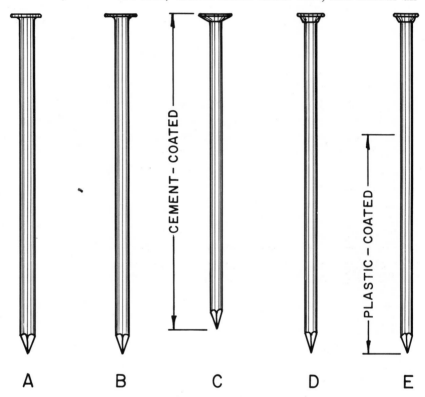

A   B   C   D   E

Figure 24–11.—Five types of uncoated and coated steel nails evaluated for withdrawal resistance in southern pine.

	Shank diameter	Nails per pound
	Inch	Number
(A) Common wire nail	0.162	45
(B) Smooth box nail	.136	64
(C) Cement-coated sinker nail	.150	61
(D) Uncoated step-head nail	.127	75
(E) Plastic-coated, step-head nail	.127	74

Nails were 3½ inches long except for (C), which was 3¼ inches in length. Nails (A, B, C) had heads 11/32-inch in diameter; diameter of nail heads (D, E) was 9/32-inch. (Drawing after Stern 1969c, p. 15.)

coated nails with a two-step head found useful in collating nails for power drivers (fig. 24–11).

These nails were driven into green and dry side grain and end grain of southern pine lumber of 0.43 to 0.61 ovendry specific gravity; immediate and delayed withdrawal resistance was measured at a withdrawal rate of 0.1 inch per minute and under impact load (table 24–5).

The plastic-coated, step-head nails had substantially higher static and impact withdrawal resistance in both side grain and end grain at all moisture contents than uncoated step-head nails or the cement-coated nails; the latter were 11 percent larger in diameter than the step-head nails but had 11 to 13 percent less penetration.

Static withdrawal resistances of common wire and box nails driven into green wood were comparable to the 12-percent smaller (in diameter) plastic-coated, step-head nails; under impact load or when driven into dry wood, however, the plastic-coated nails had the highest withdrawal resistance.

Withdrawal resistance of all nails driven into side grain of green wood was diminished by more than half if the wood was allowed to dry before the nails were pulled. Withdrawal resistance of nails driven into green end-grain wood was not so greatly diminished after the wood dried.

In Stern (1970g, pp. 18 and 19) the interested reader can find additional information on withdrawal resistance of four sizes of common and step-head nails (coated and uncoated) driven through 3/4-inch dry southern pine lumber or 3/4-inch Douglas-fir plywood into seasoned southern pine 2 by 4s.

Diagonally barbed square-wire nails.—Figure 24–2 shows that 2½-inch-long, barbed, square-wire nails driven into side grain of green southern pine had about the same immediate withdrawal resistance as common wire nails and helically threaded nails of roughly comparable size (fig. 24–1); if pulled after a delay of several weeks, the barbed nails had withdrawal resistance higher than that of common wire nails but substantially below that of threaded nails (Stern 1957c).

Twisted square-wire nails.—Stern (1964a) compared the withdrawal resistance of cement-coated, twisted square-wire nails with that of cement-coated plain-shank nails and helically threaded nails. The nails were driven through a 31/32-inch-thick longleaf pine board into side grain of longleaf pine having 0.60 ovendry specific gravity and 10-percent moisture content. Penetration in the member holding the point equalled nail length less 31/32-inch. Half the nails were pulled immediately at 0.1 inch per minute, and the remanider after 2 days' exposure to 100-percent relative humidity followed by 19-day exposure to 50-percent relative humidity.

The 18-percent heavier square wire nails offered 5 percent lower immediate withdrawal resistance but 502 percent higher delayed withdrawal resistance than the plain-shank nails tested. The helically threaded nails (uncoated) had the greatest withdrawal resistance regardless of time of pulling.

Nail type and size (inches)	Weight per nail	Withdrawal resistance	
		Immediate	Delayed 3 weeks
	Grams	Pounds	
Cement-coated, twisted square-wire 2½ by 0.107 (measured over the diagonal)_____	3.915	307	239
Cement-coated, plain-shank cooler 2⅜ by 0.113_____	3.305	324	48
Hardened helically threaded 2½ by 0.120_____	3.881	424	448

Helically fluted nails.—Data from Stern (1956d) indicate that helically fluted nails made of medium-carbon-steel wire, when driven into southern pine, have about the same immediate withdrawal resistance as plain-shank nails of the same weight and length; delayed withdrawal resistance of helically fluted nails is higher than that of plain-shank nails but lower than that of helically or annularly threaded nails of the same weight and length.

Data from Stern (1964a) and Dove (1955) permit comparison of the withdrawal resistance of helically fluted nails with that of plain-shank and threaded types (fig. 24–12); test data on nails driven to a depth of 1-1/8 inches in green southern pine of 0.51 ovendry specific gravity and 27-percent moisture content follow:

Nail type and size (inches)	Weight per nail	Withdrawal resistance per inch of penetration	
		Immediate	Delayed
	Grams	– – – – Pounds – – – –	
Helically fluted 1½ by 0.086_____	1.118	57.5	58.1
Plain shank 1½ by 0.091_____	1.383	69.3	23.7
Helically threaded 1½ by 0.076_____	.953	90.7	157.3
1½ by 0.078_____	.986	109.3	118.7
Annularly threaded 1½ by 0.085_____	1.072	112.7	108.7

Helically fluted auto nails.—These nails are ¼ to 5¼ inches in length and are sheared with a bevel or straight across from helically fluted, medium-carbon-steel wire 0.032 to 0.162 inch in diameter. The nails are sheared to length and driven at rates up to one per second by a machine that forms a brad or rivet head on each nail and, if driven against a steel back-up plate, clinches the point into brad or rivet form (fig. 24–13). General applications and performance of these nails have been described by Johnston (1964), Stern (1962b, 1965a), Wilkerson et al. (1968)

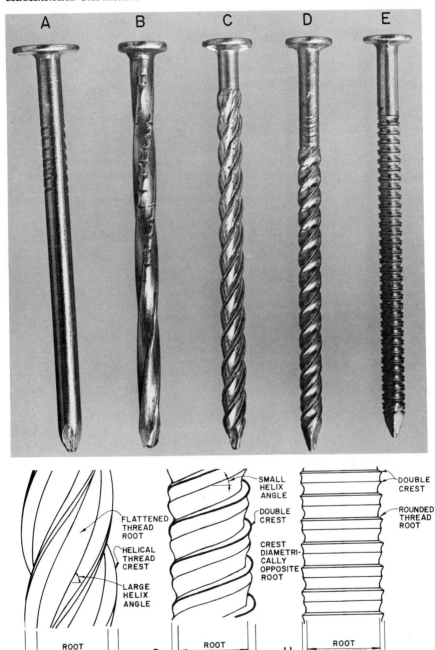

Figure 24–12.—Helically fluted nail compared to plain-shank and threaded nails; all are 1½ inches long and of low-carbon steel except for the fluted nail, which is of medium-carbon steel or stiff stock. Diameter of a threaded nail is measured on the plain portion of the shank between head and threads. (A) Plain-shank nail; 0.091 inch. (B) Helically fluted nail; 0.086 inch. (C,D) Helically threaded nails; 0.076 and 0.078 inch. (E) Annularly threaded nail; 0.083 inch. (F) Standard (60°)-lead helical thread. (G) Short-lead helical thread. (H) Annular thread. (Photo from Stern 1964a; drawings after Stern 1951c, p. 7.)

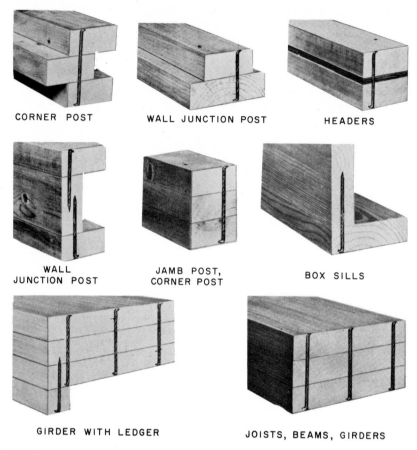

CORNER POST   WALL JUNCTION POST   HEADERS

WALL JUNCTION POST   JAMB POST, CORNER POST   BOX SILLS

GIRDER WITH LEDGER   JOISTS, BEAMS, GIRDERS

Figure 24–13.—Built-up framing members fastened with helically fluted auto nails. (Photos from Stern 1969c, p. 27.)

and Wilkerson (1969, 1970). Superior performance of auto-nailed southern pine pallets was reported by Stern (1968b, 1970c).

Stern (1970f) found that for attaching Douglas-fir plywood to southern pine cleats, average energy to failure for clinched 15-gauge auto nails was 77 percent of that for clinched cement-coated sinker nails. He confirmed the recommendation of the USDA Forest Products Laboratory that three auto nails can be substituted for two conventional nails in attaching plywood.

Threaded nails.—Threaded nails (fig. 24–12CDE) have helical or annular, symmetrical or non-symmetrical, flat-bottom or round-bottom deformations; they may have single- or double-crest shoulders with rounded or flat flanks. The shank is formed by roll-threading dies after the nail is headed. Threaded nails can be made from copper and aluminum as well as ferrous metals; most are of low-carbon steel or medium-carbon steel (stiff stock). They may or may not be hardened after forming (Stern 1967a).

Diameter of a threaded nail is measured on the plain portion of the shank between head and threads.

Since withdrawal resistance is dependent on thread angle and depth, low-density southern pine fastened with well-threaded nails can have greater joint strength than high-density pine fastened with poorly threaded nails. According to Stern (1950b, 1951cd, 1952, 1956abcd, 1957abc, 1959abc, 1966, 1968a, 1969bc), properly threaded nails have greater withdrawal resistance than any other type of nail of comparable size. In general, optimum threads for nails to be driven into southern pine have four, helical, non-symmetrical, buttress-type, flat-bottom threads with double-crest shoulders and a distinct leading flank on the point side of the crest and a following flank on the head side of the crest; there should be a plain-shanked section between the head of the nail and the start of the threads. Figure 24–12F, G, H shows details of three types of threaded nails.

Allowable withdrawal resistance of annularly threaded, large-diameter (0.2 inch and over), bright nails and spikes of low-carbon steel driven into predrilled dry southern pine can be approximated by the following equation proposed by Stern (1957b).

$$p = 350 + 1{,}150G^{5/2}D \qquad\qquad (24\text{--}2)$$

where:

$p =$ allowable withdrawal load, pounds per inch of penetration into the piece retaining the point.

$G =$ wood specific gravity, based on ovendry volume and weight.

$D =$ nail diameter, inches.

Values of $G^{5/2}$ for selected specific gravities are listed in the introduction to this chapter.

Slender, hardened-steel, threaded nails, because of their great withdrawal resistance, can replace common wire nails of larger diameter. Driving resistance of the two nails may be similar, but because the buckling resistance of the hardened nail is greater, it can be driven with fewer, more powerful, hammer blows. The immediate static withdrawal resistance of the more slender helically threaded nail may be twice that of the common wire nail; delayed withdrawal resistance in seasoned southern pine is generally several times as high. Also, slender, threaded nails are less likely to split southern pine than the thicker, common wire nails required for equivalent withdrawal resistance. On the basis of many tests, Stern (1969c, p. 28) has proposed the nail sizes shown in table 24–6 as equivalent and appropriate for fastening 1-1/2-inch-thick southern pine framing lumber.

Selected data on nails 0.120 to 0.203 inch in diameter are illustrative of immediate and delayed withdrawal resistance of plain-shank, and threaded nails of low-carbon steel and hardened, medium-carbon steel. Nails 2, 2-1/2, 3, 3-1/2, and 4 inches long were driven to two-thirds of their length

TABLE 24–6.—*Common wire nails, and hardened, helically-threaded nails of equivalent withdrawal resistance in southern pine*[1] (adapted from Stern 1969c, p. 28)

Length (inches)	Common wire nails			Equivalent, hardened threaded nails	
	Diameter	Size	Nails per pound	Diameter[2]	Nails per pound
	Inch			*Inch*	
3	0.148	10 l	68	0.135	78
3¼	.148	12d	63	.135	73
3½	.162	16d	49	.148	57
4	.192	20d	31	.177	36

[1] As threaded nails nominally 30d through 60d are all manufactured from wire 0.177 inch in diameter, they have the same allowable withdrawal load per inch of penetration as the values shown in table 24–7 (and the same allowable lateral load as shown in table 24–9) for 20d common wire nails (Southern Pine Association 1964; National Forest Products Association 1968).

[2] Wire diameter of the plain-shanked portion of the nail.

in partially seasoned side grain of southern pine and withdrawn at 0.060 inch per minute (Stern 1951c). Average withdrawal resistance (fig. 24–14) expressed as a percentage of values for plain-shank nails is summarized as follows:

Nail type	Immediate	Delayed
	– – – *Percent* – – –	
Plain shank	100	100
Annularly threaded	199	617
Helically threaded	139	494

Small-diameter, plain-shank nails (e.g., 7d) also have substantially less immediate and delayed static withdrawal resistance in side grain of southern pine than threaded nails of the same wire size; in general, impact withdrawal resistance is also improved if nails of this size have shanks helically threaded with standard lead angle (fig. 24–15).

Cut nails and toothed nails.—Figure 24–16 illustrates nails used to attach finish flooring to underlayment boards. Cut nails, once widely used, have diminished in importance in recent years (Stern 1964a). Toothed nails of L-shape, with the short arm serving as the head, are known as cleats; they are machine driven with ease and speed.

Stern (1964a) compared immediate and delayed static withdrawal resistance (perpendicular to joined surfaces) of these nails driven at a 45° angle up to 11/16 inch from the top of the head through dry white oak (*Quercus alba* L.) into side grain of southern pine at 25-percent moisture content (0.65 ovendry specific gravity); delayed measurements were taken after 2 weeks, by which time the pine was at 16-percent moisture content.

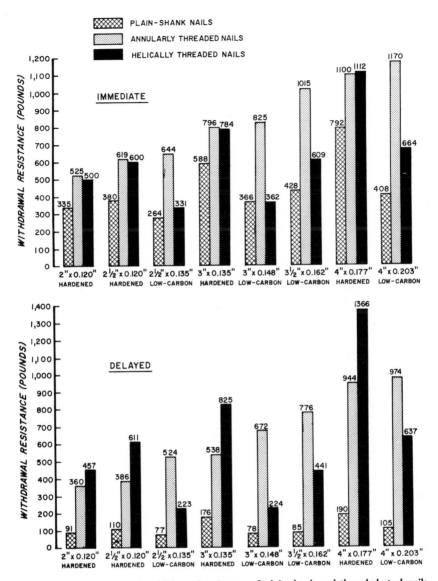

Figure 24–14.—Average static withdrawal resistance of plain-shank and threaded steel nails of various lengths, diameters, alloys, and treatments driven to two-thirds shank penetration into side grain of southern pine at 20-percent moisture content. Delayed withdrawal was made at 10- to 11-percent moisture content 5 to 7 months after the nails were driven. (Drawing after Stern 1969c, p. 30.)

Also, nails driven into southern pine at 9-percent moisture content and 0.52 ovendry specific gravity were evaluated; here, delayed measurements were made after 2 days of water soaking the nailed assembly followed by 12 days of drying at 12-percent moisture content.

The 1-11/16-inch toothed cleat averaged about half the withdrawal

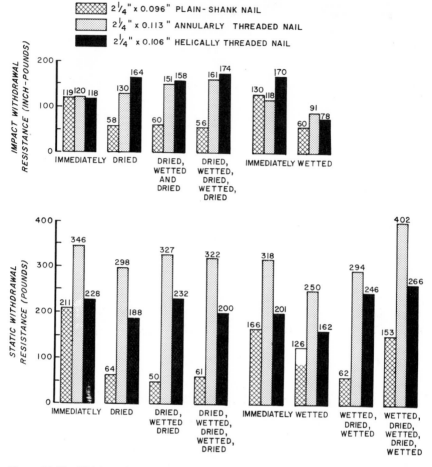

Figure 24–15.—Withdrawal resistance of plain-shank and threaded, 2¼-inch-long, low-car-bon-steel nails driven 1½ inches into side grain of southern pine and pulled under the conditions noted. (Left) Driven into wood above fiber saturation point. (Right) Driven into wood of about 12-percent moisture content. Static withdrawal was at 0.07 inch perminute. (Drawing after Stern 1969c, p. 29, based on unpublished data of 1950 from E. H. Borkenhagen and O. C. Heyer.)

resistance of the 2-1/2-inch, plain-shank brad, about one-fourth that of the cut nail, and about one-fifth that of the 2-1/4- and 2-1/2-inch threaded nails (fig. 24–16).

ALLOWABLE WITHDRAWAL LOADS

The National Design Specification (National Forest Products Associa-tion 1968, table 16) and Southern Pine Architects' Bulletin No. 7 (South-ern Pine Association 1964) contain tables of allowable withdrawal resist-ance for plain-shank nails and spikes; both tables are based on equation 24–1. The National Design Specification uses an ovendry specific gravity

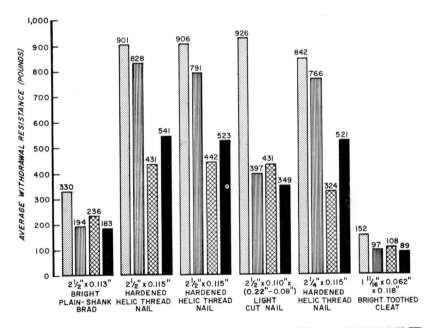

Figure 24–16.—Fasteners used in the laying of tongue-and-groove flooring. (Top) From top to bottom: bright, low-carbon-steel, plain-shank flooring brad; two hardened medium-carbon-steel, helically threaded flooring nails; light, New York Pattern, cut flooring nail; hardened, medium-carbon-steel, helically threaded flooring nail; toothed cleat. (Bottom) Immediate and delayed static (0.1 inch per minute) withdrawal resistance. Nails were driven at 45° angle to penetrate southern pine 2 by 4's by to 11/16-inch from top of head. (Photo and drawing after Stern 1964a.)

of 0.55 for southern pine; the Southern Pine Association, however, bases its tables on an ovendry specific gravity of 0.59. Obviously, use of the 0.55 value results in lower allowable withdrawal loads (table 24–7)

The allowable withdrawal load in toenailed joints is two-thirds that given in table 24–7 for 0.55 specific gravity (National Forest Products Association 1968, para. 800–H).

Section 24–1 outlines duration-of-load adjustment factors applicable to values given for normal loading in table 24–7.

LATERAL LOAD-CARRYING CAPACITY OF NAILS

The lateral resistance provided by nailed joints (fig. 24–17) is less affected by wood and nail varaibles than withdrawal resistance. In general, lateral resistance of nails driven into side grain varies approximately as the 5/4 power of ovendry specific gravity; on this basis, an increase in specific gravity of 25 percent (e.g., from 0.48 to 0.60) is accompanied by an increase of somewhat more than 30 percent in lateral resistance (Scholten 1965b).

TABLE 24–7.—*Allowable withdrawal loads per inch of penetration of common wire nails and spikes driven into the side grain of southern pine*[1] [2] (adapted from Southern Pine Association 1964; National Forest Products Association 1968)

Assumed specific gravity[3]	Size										Diameter	
	6d	8d	10d	12d	16d	20d	30d	40d	50d	60d	5/16-inch	3/8-inch
	- - - - - - - - - - *Pounds* - - - - - - - - - - - -											
				NAILS								
0.55	35	41	46	46	50	59	64	70	76	81		
.59	42	48	55	55	60	71	76	83	90	97		
				SPIKES								
.55		59	59	64	70	76	81	88	88		97	116
.59		71	71	76	83	90	97	104	104		115	138

[1] Applicable to nails driven into seasoned wood or unseasoned wood that will remain wet. If common wire nails or spikes are driven into unseasoned wood which will subsequently season under load, the allowable load is one-fourth the tabular value; for hardened, threaded nails (see table 24–6 for equivalent sizes), however, use full allowable loads. For wood pressure-impregnated with fire-retardant chemicals, use one-fourth the tabular values; if kiln-dried after treatment, use 90 percent of the tabular values. For hardened, threaded nails, use full allowable load even if treated with fire retardants.

[2] Nails and spikes should not be loaded in withdrawal from end grain.

[3] Based on ovendry volume and weight. The values corresponding to 0.55 specific gravity are from the National Design Specification (National Forest Products Association 1968); those for 0.59 specific gravity are from the Southern Pine Association (1964).

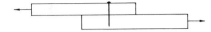

Figure 24–17.—Lateral load applied to nailed joint.

Depth of penetration of plain-shank nails into structural species such as southern pine should be about 11 times nail diameter to develop maximum lateral resistance; since maximum lateral resistance is associated with nail withdrawal, depth of penetration required for maximum lateral resistance varies inversely with withdrawal resistance of nails (Scholten 1965b).

There is also an optimum member thickness for the nailhead side of the joint; the relationship $T = 50D^2$ has been suggested by Brock (1954) where:

    T = thickness of member on nailhead side of joint, inches
    D = nail diameter in inches

Plain-shank nails.—According to the USDA Forest Products Laboratory (1955, p. 173), the lateral load-carrying capacity of a common wire nail driven into side grain of seasoned southern pine to a depth of at least 10 (for dense wood) to 14 (for lightweight woods) times the diameter of the nail is approximately as follows:

$$\text{Allowable load} = 1375D^{3/2} \tag{24–3}$$

$$\text{Proportional limit} = (1.6)(1375)D^{3/2} \tag{24–4}$$

$$\text{Ultimate load} = (6)(1375)D^{3/2} \tag{24–5}$$

where D = nail diameter, inches. Table 24–1 lists values of diameters raised to the 3/2 power. These equations apply to lateral loads either parallel or perpendicular to the grain of the joined pieces.

For a common wire nail driven into end grain (parallel to fibers) of seasoned southern pine, the following approximate relationships apply (USDA Forest Products Laboratory 1955, p. 174):

$$\text{Allowable load} = (2/3)(1375)D^{3/2} \tag{24–6}$$

$$\text{Proportional limit} = (1.6)(1375)D^{3/2} \tag{24–7}$$

$$\text{Ultimate load} = (4)(1375)D^{3/2} \tag{24–8}$$

Ultimate lateral resistance of nails driven into side grain of unseasoned wood is approximately equal to that in seasoned wood, but the proportional limit is somewhat less in green than in dry wood. Nails have lower proportional limits for lateral resistance when driven into green wood that subsequently dries than in seasoned wood. Therefore, allowable lateral loads for nails and spikes driven into unseasoned southern pine should be about 25 percent lower than those for nails and spikes driven into seasoned wood (USDA Forest Products Laboratory 1955, p. 174).

Lateral loads for aluminum alloy nails are slightly lower at small distortions in the joint than they are for common wire nails, but are somewhat higher at greater distortions; an aluminum nail with shank diameter 3 to

10 percent larger than that of a steel nail, however, sustains lateral loads at small distortions that are comparable to those for a steel nail. In general, nails helically threaded with standard lead angle have higher ultimate lateral resistance than common wire nails, but both types sustain similar lateral loads at small distortions in the joint (USDA Forest Products Laboratory 1955, p. 174).

Coated nails.—In tests of lateral load resistance of $3\frac{1}{2}$-inch nails in green southern pine, Stern (1970d) found plastic-coated step-head nails to be 23 percent less effective than the 28-percent stouter common wire nails.

Twisted square-wire nails.—Stern (1964a) compared the ultimate lateral resistance of cement-coated, twisted-square-wire nails with that of cement-coated, plain-shanked nails and hardened, helically threaded nails all driven through a 31/32-inch-thick longleaf pine board of 0.60 ovendry specific gravity and 10-percent moisture content into a similar dry substrate with depth of penetration in excess of 11 times nail diameter.

Nail type and size (inches)	Weight per nail	Delayed lateral resistance
	Grams	*Pounds*
Cement coated, twisted square wire $2\frac{1}{2}$ by 0.107	3.915	634
Cement coated, plain-shank cooler $2\frac{3}{8}$ by 0.113	3.305	408
Hardened, helically threaded $2\frac{1}{2}$ by 0.120	3.881	767

The twisted square-wire nail was 18 percent heavier than the plain-shanked nail and provided 55 percent greater lateral resistance; the threaded nail had 88 percent more lateral resistance. A smaller helically threaded nail (2.25 inches by 0.110 inch) in the same test series had 55 percent more lateral resistance than the plain-shanked cooler nail.

Helically fluted auto nails.—Properly applied helically fluted auto nails transmit shear loads effectively in built-up building components (fig. 24–13); they also make joints in southern pine pallets that are more rigid and have more lateral load-carrying capacity than plain-shank nails of the same diameter and length (Stern 1953, 1965b, 1968d, 1969c, pp. 46–50).

Threaded nails.—Annularly threaded nails are not recommended for lateral transmission of loads because they are weakened by reduced cross section at thread roots (Stern 1969c, p. 46). Helically threaded nails; however, have more shock resistance than annularly threaded nails, and greater lateral resistance to static loading than plain-shank nails. There are numerous publications to support this conclusion; data from a single test by Stern (1951c) are illustrative (fig. 24–18). In this test, nails 0.120 to 0.203 inch in diameter were driven into partially seasoned side grain of southern pine. Average lateral resistance expressed as a percentage of values for plain-shank nails were summarized as follows:

Nail type	Immediate	Delayed
	— — — — Percent — — — —	
Plain shank _____	100	100
Annularly threaded _____	127	128
Helically threaded _____	141	170

Static lateral resistance of threaded nails in pressure creosoted southern pine poles at 30-percent moisture content has been evaluated immediately after driving the nails to one-half their length (Stern 1956c).

Nail type and size (inches)	Lateral resistance
	Pounds
Plain shank	
5 by 0.177_____	1,189
7 by 0.203_____	1,716
Annularly threaded	
5 by 0.177_____	1,224
7 by 0.203_____	1,446
Helically threaded	
5 by 0.177_____	1,376
7 by 0.203_____	2,009

Values for annularly threaded nails were little different from those for plain-shank nails; however, the helically threaded nails had values about 16 percent higher than those for plain-shank nails.

Joints fastened with hardened steel nails deform less under impact load than joints secured with unhardened nails. After drop tests of southern pine pallets assembled with seasoned deck boards and green stringers, pallet distortion was about 63 percent less if assembled with 2-1/2- by 0.120-inch, hardened, medium-carbon-steel, helically threaded nails than if fastened with unhardened, medium-carbon-steel (stiff stock), helically threaded nails of the same dimension (Stern 1969b).

Short, stout (1-1/2 by 0.135 inch), helically threaded nails effectively transmit shear loads between plywood roof sheathing and rafters (Stern 1965c). Such nails also are effective in transmitting shear loads between gusset plates and joined members (Stern 1958, 1961bc, 1964bc).

Selection of nails for use in double shear in three-member joints (similar to fig. 24–24) is described by Stern (1964c), Stern and Stoneburner (1952), and Stern and Pletta (1967).

Slant-driven nails.—Figure 24–5 illustrates nails driven into side grain of southern pine to test the effect of cross-slant-driving on lateral resistance to a load applied perpendicular to the plane formed between the two nails. Only in one case, that of plain-shank nails driven into wood at 19-percent moisture content and pulled at 11 percent, did the pair of cross-slant-driven nails have twice the lateral resistance of a single nail

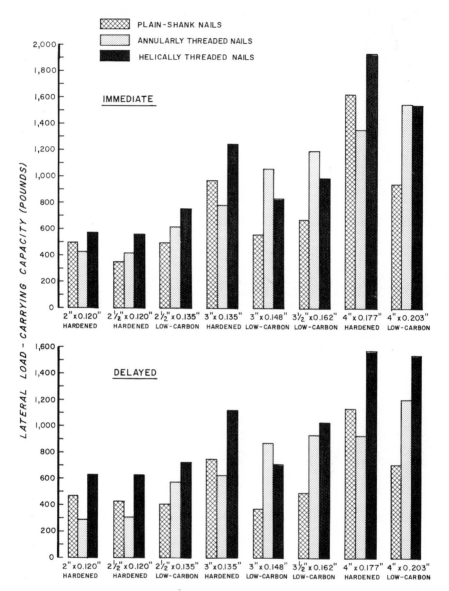

Figure 24–18.—Average static lateral load-carrying capacity of plain-shank and threaded steel nails driven through a removable gage block to two-thirds shank penetration into side grain of southern pine at 20-percent moisture content. Delayed tests were made at 10- to 11-percent moisture content 5 to 7 weeks after the nails were driven. (Drawing after Stern 1969c, pp. 51, 52.)

driven perpendicular to the grain (table 24–8). Stern (1951b) concluded that in comparison with straight driving, slant driving at an angle of 56.5° to the joint plane decreases lateral resistance to a load applied perpendicular to the plane of the cross-slant-driven nails.

According to Scholten and Molander (1950), maximum strength of toe-nailed joints (fig. 24–4A) under lateral and uplift loads is obtained by: (1) using the largest nail that will not cause excessive splitting; (2) starting the nail one-third the length of the nail from the end of the member entered; (3) driving the nail at an angle of 30° to the member first entered by the nail; and (4) burying the full shank of the nail but avoiding excessive mutilation of the wood by hammer blows.

Clinched nails.—In a review of the literature, Leach (1964) concluded that increased lateral resistance in nailed joints probably cannot be safely attained by clinching nails randomly parallel and perpendicular to the grain; data from Brock (1956) indicate that nails clinched perpendicular to the grain have about 50 percent greater ultimate lateral resistance than unclinched nails.

Multi-nail joints.—The literature indicates that if wood is not split during the driving process, and if the number of nails in a line is 10 or less, there is an approximately linear relationship between the number of nails used in a joint and the lateral resistance of the joint (Leach 1964).

Some nail sizes and spacings to minimize splitting are suggested in a later paragraph of this section.

ALLOWABLE LATERAL LOADS

Lateral load resistance in nailed joints is linearly proportional to deformation or slip in the joint only at small deformations; as lateral loads approach the ultimate, deformations increase more than proportionately.

TABLE 24–8.—*Lateral resistance*[1] *of a pair of nails cross-slant-driven into side grain of southern pine, expressed as a percentage of the value for a straight-driven, single nail of the same size and type* (Stern 1951b)

Moisture content at fabrication and at test	Nail type	
	Plain shank	Helically threaded
	– – – – – *Percent* – – – – –	
Fabricated and tested green_____	139	141
Fabricated green and tested at 12 to 14 percent_____	153	161
Fabricated green and tested at 10 to 11 percent_____	---	158
Fabricated and tested at 19 percent_____	153	166
Fabricated at 19 percent and tested at 11 percent_____	233	148
Fabricated and tested at 10 percent_____	186	182

[1] See figure 24–5 for details of nails. Load applied perpendicular to the plane formed by the two cross-slant-driven nails.

The allowable lateral load applied to a nailed joint, therefore, is a function not only of the ultimate lateral resistance but also of the amount of deformation. Allowable values, as now established, are based primarily on a limiting amount of slip; for nailed joints used in construction, a load sufficient to cause a slip of 0.015 inch is not accompanied by a sizeable amount of "creep" in service. In many joints, the ultimate lateral load is three to four times the load required to cause this amount of slip. Selection of a specific limit of slip as a design criterion is not entirely satisfactory, however, because slip in a joint varies with size and type of nail, nail composition and hardness, and specific gravity, moisture content and size of members joined (Scholten 1965b).

The National Design Specification (National Forest Products Association 1968, table 17) and Southern Pine Architects' Bulletin No. 7 (Southern Pine Association 1964) contain tables of allowable lateral loads for plain-shank nails and spikes; both are based on the following equation and are applicable where penetration into the member receiving the point is not less than 11 times the nail diameter.

$$p = KD^{3/2} \qquad (24\text{--}9)$$

where:

p = allowable lateral load per nail, pounds.
K = a constant = 1,650 for southern pine.
D = nail diameter, inches (see table 24–1).

Values of p for a range of nail and spike sizes are shown in table 24–9.

For nails and spikes driven into side grain of unseasoned wood which will remain wet or will be loaded before seasoning, or in wood pressure impregnated with fire-retardant chemicals, the allowable lateral load is three-fourths that given in table 24–9, except that for threaded, hardened-steel nails the full load may be used (National Forest Products Association 1968). Table 24–6 gives the sizes of helically threaded nails equivalent to common wire nail sizes.

For nails and spikes in double shear and fully penetrating all members in a three-member joint, the allowable load may be increased one-third when each side member is not less than one-third the thickness of the center member, and may be increased two-thirds when each side member is equal in thickness to the center member. For intermediate thicknesses of side members, the increase in allowable load is determined by straight-line interpolation (Southern Pine Association 1964; National Forest Products Association 1968).

For nails or spikes in double shear with side members at least 3/8-inch thick, the allowable load given in table 24–9 may be doubled for nails not exceeding 12d in size when the nail extends at least three diameters beyond the side member and is clinched (National Forest Products Association 1968).

Where properly designed metal side plates are used, the allowable loads in table 24–9 can be increased 25 percent. The allowable lateral load for a nail or spike driven into end grain (parallel to fibers) is two-thirds

TABLE 24–9.—*Allowable lateral loads (normal duration) for common wire nails and spikes, driven into the side grain of seasoned southern pine*[1] (adapted from Southern Pine Association 1964; National Forest Products Association 1968)

Size										Diameter	
6d	8d	10d	12d	16d	20d	30d	40d	50d	60d	$\frac{5}{16}$-inch	$\frac{3}{8}$-inch
						Pounds					
				COMMON WIRE NAILS							
63	78	94	94	107	139	154	176	202	223	--	--
				SPIKES							
--	--	139	139	155	176	202	223	248	248	289	380

[1] Load applied in any lateral direction (fig. 24–17) if penetration is not less than 11 diameters; for penetration from 11/3-diameters to 11 diameters, the allowable value is linear between 0 load at 0 penetration and the tabulated value.

that given in table 24–9. The allowable lateral load in a toenailed joint (fig. 24–4A) is five-sixths that shown in table 24–9 (Southern Pine Association 1964; National Forest Products Association 1968).

Section 24–1 outlines duration-of-load adjustment factors applicable to values given in table 24–9.

DEFECTS IN NAILED JOINTS

Common defects in nailed joints include splits in the wood, nails that back out of the joint, and wood stains caused by nails reacting with wood and air.

Splits.—Southern pine, especially when dry, splits fairly readily even when carefully nailed. Drilled pilot holes are probably the most effective deterrent to splits. Slim, helically threaded, hardened steel nails can equal the holding power of larger plain-shank nails, with less splitting. Nails with flattened or bradded points reduce splitting, but have less withdrawal resistance than nails with sharp points. Splitting is reduced by driving nails as far from board ends as possible and by placing warped boards to obtain maximum bearing where a nail is driven.

In multinail joints, proper nail spacing and nail selection can reduce splitting. While no recommendations specific to southern pine have been published, Scholten (1965b) has suggested some guidelines for Douglas-fir. He proposed that nail diameter should be about one-sixth or one-seventh the thickness of the attached member (nailhead side); for example, an 8d common nail with diameter of 0.131 inch could be used with an 0.8-inch-thick board.

Ramos (1960) suggested the following minimum lateral spacings applicable to 6d and 8d common wire nails in Douglas-fir multi-nail joints.

Dimension	Multiple of nail diameter	Approximate spacing for 8d nail
	– – – *Inches* – – –	
Parallel to grain_____	17	2.3
Perpendicular to grain_____	7	.9
Unstressed end distance_____	12	1.6
Edge distance_____	10	1.3
Stressed end distance_____	15	2.0

According to German Government Specifications, the spacings can be 50 to 75 percent of these values when nails in a row are staggered by 1D, i.e., by one nail diameter.

The Southern Pine Association (1964) suggests a minimum distance from the loaded end of 13 to 20D, and a minimum spacing of 12 to 15D in the direction of load and 5D perpendicular to load.

Nail popping.—Nailheads driven flush with the surface of gypsum board attached to green studs may lift from the surface as time goes by; this phenomenon, called pop, is generally associated with drying of the wood into which the nails are driven. Two extreme cases illustrate the problem and suggest a partial solution.

Consider the behavior of a long, plain-shank nail driven through the 3-5/8-inch dimension of a green southern pine 2 by 4 so that the head is flush; assume that the emergent point is welded to a metal plate glued securely to the back side of the 2 by 4. Under these conditions, when the 2 by 4 is dried and shrinks, the head of the nail must lift (or pop) from the 2 by 4 because the nail length remains unchanged while the wood shrinks.

Now consider the behavior of a nail driven in the same manner, but with the head welded to a metal plate securely glued to the side entered by the nail. Under this condition, the nailhead cannot lift from the surface, and the point must further emerge from the back side as the stud dries and shrinks.

From these illustrations, it is concluded that nail pop will be diminished if the nail is fixed in the wood as closely as possible to the stud surface adjacent to the gypsum board; obviously the shortest possible nail that has the necessary withdrawal resistance is required. Uncoated, threaded nails have greater withdrawal resistance per inch of length than cement-coated, plain-shank nails; therefore, a short, threaded nail would appear to be a reasonable choice to minimize nail popping. Stern (1956a) has published data specific to southern pine that support this conclusion.

Stains and corrosion.—Where corrosion of the nail or staining of the wood must be minimized, nails of stainless steel or alloys of copper or aluminum are used. Galvanized nails, while less corrosion resistant than the alloyed nails, are frequently used where corrosion is a factor. Cadmium-plated nails have very limited corrosion resistance, are used for indoor exposure, and should not be used outdoors or exposed to chemicals fostering corrosion.

NAILHEAD DESIGN

Most nailheads are designed with sufficient strength for withdrawal with a claw hammer. Except for certain finish nails and brads designed to be countersunk, nailheads are large enough to prevent them from pulling through boards attached to thicker substrates.

Figure 24–11 illustrates five 16d nails, three of which have heads 11/32-inch in diameter; two have smaller heads measuring 9/32-inch. Stern (1969c, p. 18) showed that when these nails were driven through the 1-1/2-inch dimension of southern pine 2 by 4's into side grain and end grain of southern pine lumber of 0.43 to 0.61 ovendry specific gravity, the head pull-through resistance in the nailed member was in all cases greater than the withdrawal resistance from the member retaining the point (fig. 24–19).

NAILING OF PARTICULAR PRODUCTS

Additional information on the nailing of specific southern pine products can be found in the following references. Most are by E. G. Stern, who has done much research on nailed joints in southern pine; few other researchers have studied these species.

Product	Reference
Subflooring to joists	Stern (1954a, 1957c, 1961c)
Finish flooring to subflooring	Stern (1951a, 1954b)
Plywood sheathing	Stern (1958, 1961c); Anderson (1965)
Lumber sheathing	Anderson (1965)
Pallets and skids	Stern (1953, 1965ab, 1966, 1968d, 1969b, 1970c, 1971)
Sheet metal to rafters and studs	Stern (1961a)
Trusses	Stern (1957a, 1961c, 1965d); Stern and Pletta (1967)
Building components	Stern (1956e, 1964a)
Gypsum board to studs	Stern (1956ab)
Creosoted wood	Stern (1956c)
Containers	USDA Forest Products Laboratory (1953a)
Hardboard	Stern (1959d); Anderson (1965)
Fiberboard sheathing	Stern (1955); Anderson (1965); Merrill and French (1966)

24–3 STAPLES

Although U. S. Government specifications listing steel staples for given applications are available (Federal Housing Administration 1961; General Services Administration 1963), there are no published design criteria for allowable loads on staples fastening southern pine components.

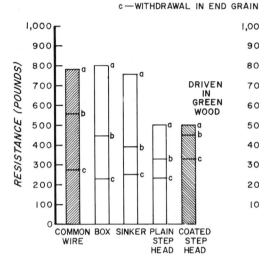

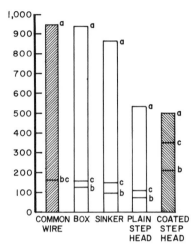

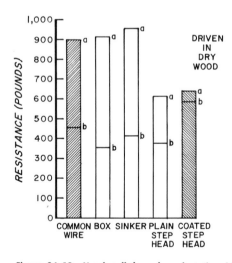

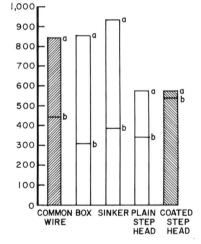

Figure 24–19.—Head pull-through and static withdrawal resistance of 16d nails (described by fig. 24–11) driven through the 1½-inch dimension of southern pine 2 by 4's into side and end grain of southern pine wood. (Top) Driven through green pine into green pine. (Bottom) Driven through dry pine into dry pine. (Left) Immediate withdrawal. (Right) Withdrawal after delay of 6 weeks in green wood and 3 weeks in dry wood. (Drawing after Stern 1969c, pp. 18, 19.)

EXPERIMENTAL DATA

Equipment to rapidly power drive staples has been developed relatively recently; since wide use of staples did not occur until this equipment became available, experimental data on the holding power of staples in southern pine is scarce.

Tests with other species suggest the following conclusions, which are probably applicable to southern pine as well: (1) withdrawal resistance of staples varies almost directly with the diameter and depth of penetration of the legs; (2) lateral resistance varies as the 3/2 power of the wire diameter; (3) seasoned lumber joints assembled with coated galvanized steel fasteners are stronger than green lumber joints similarly fastened; (4) nylon-coated staples have shown exceptional resistance to withdrawal for at least a year after driving; (5) strength of dry-lumber joints, particularly, are increased by use of some coatings on staples; (6) pull-through withdrawal resistance is proportional to width of staple crown; (7) staples with divergent points probably offer less withdrawal resistance than staples with symmetrical points (Countryman and Colbenson 1955; Stern 1962a; Kurtenacker 1965, p. 18; Scholten 1965b; Albert and Johnson 1967).

Since static loads are of most importance in building construction, while impact stresses are more critical to containers and pallets, available data on resistance of staples in southern pine to these two types of loading are presented separately.

Static withdrawal resistance.—Stern (1970b) compared the withdrawal resistance of uncoated, 2-1/2-inch-long, galvanized steel staples with identical staples coated with an unidentified plastic polymer. They had symmetrical points, a 7/16-inch crown, and were made from 15-gage wire [2] (0.067 by 0.072 inch); they were power driven through 3/4-inch southern pine boards (0.47 ovendry specific gravity and 21-percent moisture content) into side grain of southern pine 2 by 4's (0.52 ovendry specific gravity and 22-percent moisture content). Withdrawal resistance was tested at intervals during 24 weeks of exposure to 70° F. at 50-percent relative humidity. Moisture content of the wood after 3, 6, 12, and 24 weeks of exposure was 12.2, 10.9, 10.3, and 11.5 percent respectively. Staples were withdrawn at 0.1 inch per minute.

The withdrawal resistance of the coated staples was substantially higher than that of the uncoated staples at all times during the 24-week test period; the curvilinear form of the graph in the 3- to 24-week interval is evidently a response to the varying wood moisture content (fig. 24–20).

Effects of penetration and time of pulling on withdrawal resistance and crown pull-through resistance were also evaluated by Stern (1969b, p. 63). Plastic-coated, galvanized-steel, 16-gage staples with 3/8-inch crown and symmetrical points were driven through 1/2-inch Douglas-fir ply-

---

[2] Many, if not all, staples are rectangular in cross section, although formed from round wire; gage given is Washburn and Moen.

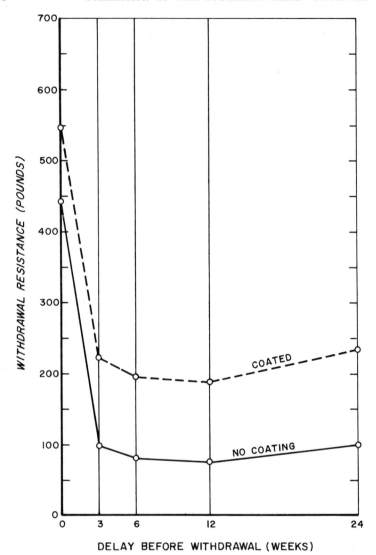

Figure 24–20.—Immediate and delayed static withdrawal resistance of coated and uncoated, 15-gage staples driven 1¾ inches into the side grain of partly dried southern pine. Test details are in text. (Drawing after Stern 1969c, p. 64.)

wood (0.46 ovendry specific gravity and 6.8-percent moisture content) into side grain of southern pine (0.53 ovendry specific gravity and 27.8-percent moisture content); staples were pulled at 0.1 inch per minute immediately after driving and after a 2-week delay, which was sufficient to reduce moisture content of the lumber to 14.4 percent.

Immediate withdrawal resistance appeared to be linearly related to penetration; delayed withdrawal resistance, however, was approximately the same at all penetrations from 15/16-inch to 1-5/16-inches (fig. 24–21

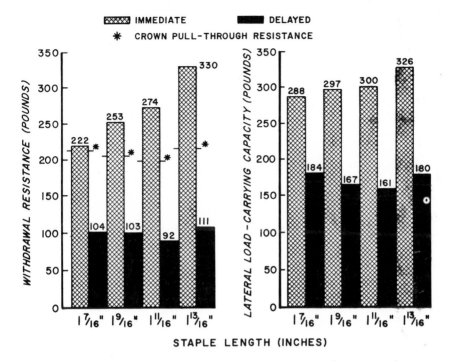

Figure 24–21.—Immediate and delayed static withdrawal and lateral resistance of various lengths of 16-gage, plastic-coated staples driven through ½-inch-thick plywood into side grain of partly dry southern pine. See text for test details. (Drawing after Stern 1969c, p. 63.)

left). Crown pull-through resistance in the Douglas-fir plywood was less than the shank withdrawal resistance offered by the southern pine.

Stern (1969c, p. 63) observed results very similar to those shown in figure 24–21 when the assembly just described was cycled through a series of exposures to dry and humid air.

Static lateral resistance.—Stern (1970e) tested lateral load resistance of the 15 gage staples and configuration described in connection with figure 24–20. He found that at 0.015- and 0.030-inch joint deformation, immediate lateral load resistances of joints formed by coated staples exceed that of joints with uncoated staples by 21 and 12 percent; delayed (6 weeks) lateral load resistance, however, was only 10 and 8 percent higher than for uncoated staples. The same joint described in connection with figure 24–21 (left) was also used for static lateral resistance by Stern (1969c, p. 63); immediate lateral resistance increased somewhat with increased staple length, but delayed lateral resistance showed no relationship to staple length (fig. 24–21, right).

Kurtenacker (1962) determined the static lateral resistance of two sizes of staples driven through 1/4-inch Douglas-fir plywood and 25/32-inch white pine (*Pinus strobus* L.) into southern pine at 12-percent moisture content and loaded at 0.25 inch per minute. These values (each the average of five replications) were compared to lateral resistance of clinched common wire nails (table 24–10) ; in no case did lateral resistance of the staples exceed that for the clinched common wire nails. Static lateral resistance of the staples in southern pine varied greatly with staple orientation. If the plane through the legs of the staple was perpendicular to the annual rings of the southern pine, the crown of the staple pulled through the plywood or white pine; if parallel to the rings, however, the legs tended to pull from the southern pine.

Impact lateral resistance.—The impact lateral resistance of clinched common wire nails was compared with that of unclinched 16-gage staples driven into the side grain of southern pine at 12-percent moisture content (table 24–11). The staple wire was only 0.065 inch in diameter compared to 0.113 and 0.131 inch for the nails, and the penetration of the staples into the southern pine was always at least 1/4-inch less than that of the nails. In general, the impact lateral resistance of the staples was less than that of the nails (Kurtenacker 1962).

In another test, 2-inch-long, clinched, 14-gage, uncoated staples with 7/16-inch crown width, however, gave about the same impact lateral resistance as 11-1/2-gage, clinched, uncoated, common wire nails when used to fasten 1/4-inch plywood to southern pine.

Results not shown in table 24–11 caused Kurtenacker (1962) to conclude

TABLE 24–10.—*Static lateral resistance of single, 16-gage staples with $\frac{7}{16}$-inch crown width and divergent chisel points compared to that of hammer-clinched, common wire nails driven into dry southern pine* (Kurtenacker 1962)

Fastener	Length of shank	Coating	Clinch[1]	Maximum load[2]	Work to maximum load[2]
	Inches			*Pounds*	*In.-lbs.*
		DRIVEN THROUGH $\frac{1}{4}$-INCH GROUP III[3] CONTAINER-GRADE PLYWOOD INTO $1\frac{5}{8}$-INCH SOUTHERN PINE			
Nail (11½ gage)_____	2	Plain	H	485	197.0
Staple_____	1⅝	Cement or rosin	N	391	99.5*
Staple_____	2	Galvanized	P	341*	78.8*
		DRIVEN THROUGH 25/32-INCH WHITE PINE INTO $1\frac{5}{8}$-INCH SOUTHERN PINE			
Nail (10¼ gage)_____	2½	Plain	H	392	117.4
Staple_____	2	Galvanized	N	261	77.5

[1] N—no clinch; H—clinched by hand with a hammer; P—clinched by driving through specimen against a steel backup plate.

[2] Values followed by an asterisk are significantly lower than values for common nails.

[3] Lower in specific gravity than southern pine.

TABLE 24–11.—*Impact lateral resistance of unclinched, single, 16-gage staples with $7/16$-inch crown width and divergent chisel points compared with that of hammer-clinched, plain wire nails driven into dry southern pine* (Kurtenacker 1962)

Fastener, coating, and length (inches)	Maximum load[1]	Energy expended[1]
	Pounds	*In.-lbs.*
DRIVEN THROUGH $1/4$-INCH GROUP III[2] CONTAINER-GRADE PLYWOOD INTO $1 5/8$-INCH SOUTHERN PINE		
$11 1/2$-gage nail, uncoated		
2	432	228
Uncoated staple		
$1 5/8$	338*	201
Galvanized staple		
1	273*	101*
$1 1/4$	342*	154*
$1 1/2$	379*	216
Cement- or rosin-coated staple		
1	293*	108*
$1 1/4$	324*	145*
$1 1/2$	351*	202
$1 5/8$	393*	211
DRIVEN THROUGH $25/32$-INCH WHITE PINE INTO $1 5/8$-INCH SOUTHERN PINE		
$10 1/4$-gage nail, uncoated		
$2 1/2$	397	190
Uncoated staple		
2	351*	241* (higher)
Cement- or rosin-coated staple		
2	324*	244* (higher)

[1] Values followed by an asterisk are significantly lower (unless indicated higher) than values for common nails.

[2] Lower in specific gravity than southern pine.

that clinched staples generally outperformed unclinched staples and that the optimum length of clinch was somewhat over 3/32-inch but less than 7/32-inch.

STAPLE SIZE AND SPACING FOR CONSTRUCTION APPLICATIONS

Because of the large variety of staple designs made by numerous suppliers, broadly accepted tables of recommended staple sizes and spacings have not been published. Some guidelines for stapling a variety of wall sheathing, roof sheathing, gypsum board, and underlayment materials were, however, reproduced by Stern (1969c, p. 62) from a report of the

Southern Building Code Congress (1968); the information is applicable only to staples coated with an unidentified plastic polymer (tables 24–12 and 24–13).

24–4 WOOD SCREWS

Figure 24–22 illustrates common types of wood screws. Dimensional data for these and similar screws with recessed heads have been published by American Society of Mechanical Engineers (1962); nominal size, threads per inch, diameters, and lengths are listed in table 24–14.

ALLOWABLE WITHDRAWAL LOADS

The USDA Forest Products Laboraotry (1955, p. 176) gives the allowable withdrawal load (one-sixth of the ultimate withdrawal load) of wood screws inserted in side grain of seasoned wood as follows.

$$p = 2,370G^2D \qquad (24\text{--}10)$$

where:

$p =$ allowable withdrawal load per inch of penetration of the threaded portion, pounds.

$G =$ specific gravity based on ovendry weight and volume.

$D =$ shank diameter of screw, inches.

The equation is applicable to the size ranges indicated below if screws are inserted in softwoods predrilled with pilot holes of a diameter equal to seven-tenths the root diameter of the threads; the root diameter for most

TABLE 24–12.—*Sizes and spacings for 16-gage, galvanized, plastic-coated staples for wall sheathing* (after Southern Building Code Congress 1968)

Type and thickness of sheathing (inches)	Minimum crown of staple	With diagonal bracing		Without diagonal bracing	
		Spacing at edges of sheet[1]	Minimum leg length of staple	Spacing at edges of sheet[1]	Minimum leg length of staple
		– – – – – – – – – – *Inches* – – – – – – – – – –			
Fiberboard					
½-----------	$\frac{7}{16}$	4	1⅛	3	1½
25⁄32 ---------	$\frac{7}{16}$	4	1½	3	1½
Plywood					
5⁄16 ----------	⅜	4	1⅛	3	1¼
⅜-----------	⅜	4	1¼	3	1⅜
½-----------	⅜	4	1⅜	3	1½
⅝-----------	$\frac{7}{16}$	3	1⅝	3	1⅝
¾-----------	$\frac{7}{16}$	3	1¾	3	1¾
Gypsum board					
½-----------	$\frac{7}{16}$	6	1½		

[1] In intermediate members, staples can be spaced 6 inches apart.

TABLE 24–13.—*Sizes and spacings for 16-gage[1], galvanized, plastic-polymer-coated staples for roof sheathing, subflooring, lath, and underlayment* (after Southern Building Code Congress 1968)

Type and thickness of material (inches)	Minimum crown of staple	Spacing of staples in intermediate members	Spacing at edges of sheet	Minimum leg length of staples
		− − − − − − − − − Inches − − − − − −		
Plywood roof sheathing				
$\frac{5}{16}$ ----------	$\frac{3}{8}$	6	3	$1\frac{1}{4}$
$\frac{3}{8}$ ----------	$\frac{3}{8}$	6	3	$1\frac{3}{8}$
$\frac{1}{2}$ ----------	$\frac{3}{8}$	6	3	$1\frac{1}{2}$
$\frac{5}{8}$ ----------	$\frac{3}{8}$	6	3	$1\frac{5}{8}$
$\frac{3}{4}$ ----------	$\frac{3}{8}$	6	3	$1\frac{3}{4}$
Plywood subflooring				
$\frac{1}{2}$ ----------	$\frac{3}{8}$	6	3	$1\frac{1}{2}$
$\frac{5}{8}$ ----------	$\frac{3}{8}$	6	3	$1\frac{5}{8}$
$\frac{3}{4}$ ----------	$\frac{3}{8}$	6	3	$1\frac{3}{4}$
Gypsum lath				
$\frac{3}{8}$ ----------	$\frac{7}{16}$	5	5	$\frac{7}{8}$
$\frac{1}{2}$ ----------	$\frac{7}{16}$	5	5	1
Plywood, hardboard, particleboard floor underlayment				
$\frac{3}{16}$[2] --------	$\frac{3}{16}$	6	3	$\frac{7}{8}$
$\frac{1}{4}$[2] ----------	$\frac{3}{16}$	6	3	$\frac{7}{8}$
$\frac{5}{16}$[2] --------	$\frac{3}{16}$	6	3	1
$\frac{3}{8}$ ----------	$\frac{3}{8}$	6	3	$1\frac{1}{8}$
$\frac{1}{2}$ ----------	$\frac{3}{8}$	6	3	$1\frac{5}{8}$
$\frac{5}{8}$ ----------	$\frac{3}{8}$	6	3	$1\frac{5}{8}$

[1] Except as noted.
[2] For these thicknesses, staples may be 18 gage.

screws is about two-thirds the shank diameter. Values of G^2 for selected specific gravities are listed in the introduction to this chapter.

Screw length	Limits of screw number or gage
Inches	
$\frac{1}{2}$	1–6
$\frac{3}{4}$	2–11
1	3–12
$1\frac{1}{2}$	5–14
2	7–16
$2\frac{1}{2}$	9–18
3	12–20

The National Design Specification (National Forest Products Association 1968, table 18) and the Southern Pine Association (1964) give allowable withdrawal loads for wood screws based on the equation:

$$p = 2,850G^2D \qquad (24\text{–}11)$$

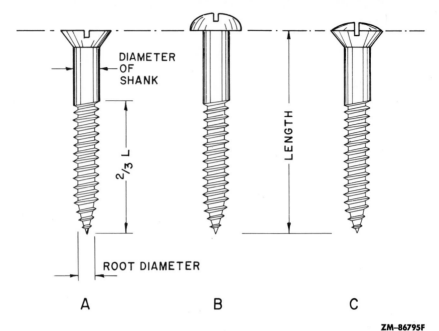

Figure 24–22.—Types of slotted-head wood screws. (A) Flathead. (B) Roundhead. (C) Ovalhead. Recessed-head screws with these three head shapes are also commonly available, as are screws with shanks fully threaded.

TABLE 24–14.—*Dimensions of common wood screws*

Nominal size (number)	Threads per inch	Diameter (D) of screw shank	D^2	Root diameter ($\frac{2}{3}$ D)	Lengths (L)[1]
		Inch		– – – – *Inch* – – – –	
0	32	0.060	0.0036	0.040	$\frac{1}{4}$–$\frac{3}{8}$
1	28	.073	.0053	.049	$\frac{1}{4}$–$\frac{1}{2}$
2	26	.086	.0074	.057	$\frac{1}{4}$–$\frac{3}{4}$
3	24	.099	.0098	.066	$\frac{1}{4}$–1
4	22	.112	.0125	.075	$\frac{1}{4}$–1$\frac{1}{2}$
5	20	.125	.0156	.083	$\frac{3}{8}$–1$\frac{1}{2}$
6	18	.138	.0190	.092	$\frac{3}{8}$–2$\frac{1}{2}$
7	16	.151	.0228	.101	$\frac{3}{8}$–2$\frac{1}{2}$
8	15	.164	.0269	.109	$\frac{3}{8}$–3
9	14	.177	.0313	.118	$\frac{1}{2}$–3
10	13	.190	.0361	.127	$\frac{1}{2}$–3$\frac{1}{2}$
12	11	.216	.0467	.144	$\frac{5}{8}$–4
14	10	.242	.0586	.161	$\frac{3}{4}$–5
16	9	.268	.0718	.179	1–5
18	8	.294	.0864	.196	1$\frac{1}{4}$–5
20	8	.320	.1024	.213	1$\frac{1}{2}$–5
24	7	.372	.1384	.248	3–5

[1] Screw lengths are available in $\frac{1}{8}$-inch intervals up to 1 inch, $\frac{1}{4}$-inch intervals from 1$\frac{1}{4}$ to 3 inches, and $\frac{1}{2}$-inch intervals from 3$\frac{1}{2}$ to 5 inches.

Values of G^2 for selected specific gravities are listed in the introduction of this chapter.

The National Design Specification assumes 0.55 as the ovendry specific gravity of southern pine, whereas the Southern Pine Association values are based on 0.59. Table 24–15 lists allowable withdrawal values for equation 24–11 appropriate for each of these specific gravities. Adjustments for duration of load are given in text section 24–1.

ALLOWABLE LATERAL LOADS

The USDA Forest Products Laboratory (1955, p. 177) gives the allowable lateral load of wood screws inserted in side grain of southern pine wood at 15-percent moisture content as follows:

$$p = 3,300D^2 \qquad (24\text{–}12)$$

where:

$p =$ allowable lateral load, pounds.
$D =$ diameter of screw shank, inches.

The equation yields loads reduced by a factor of 1.6 from the proportional limit and by a factor of 6 from the ultimate load; at the computed load, slip in the joint will be 0.007 to 0.01 inch. The equation applies when the depth of penetration of the screw into the piece receiving the point is not less than seven times the shank diameter. For penetration less than seven times shank diameter, ultimate load is reduced about in proportion to the reduction in penetration; load at proportional limit is reduced somewhat less rapidly. In tests of southern pine leading to development of equation 24–12, the lead hole receiving the shank was about seven-eighths of the root diameter of the shank and that for the threaded portion was about seven-eighths of the root diameter of the screw. To develop maximum wihtdrawal and lateral resistance, screws should always be turned in, i.e., not started with a hammer (USDA Forest Products Laboratory 1955, pp. 177, 178).

The National Design Specification (National Forest Products Association 1968) and the Southern Pine Association (1964) give allowable lateral loads for wood screws based on the equation:

$$p = 3,960D^2 \qquad (24\text{–}13)$$

Values for various screw sizes as computed from equation 24–13 are given in table 24–16.

In addition to conditions stated in the footnotes of table 24–16, the Southern Pine Association (1964) specifies that for lumber pressure impregnated with fire-retardant chemicals, tabular values should be reduced by 25 percent; if kiln-dried after treatment, however, the reduction need be only 10 percent.

Adjustments for duration of load are given in text section 24–1.

TABLE 24–15.—*Allowable withdrawal loads per inch of penetration of threaded portion of wood screw in side grain of seasoned southern pine—normal duration*[1] [2] (adapted from Southern Pine Association 1964; National Forest Products Association 1968)

Screw number or gage	0.55[3] specific gravity	0.59[3] specific gravity
	− − − *Pounds* − − −	
6	119	137
7	130	150
8	141	163
9	153	176
10	164	189
12	186	214
14	209	240
16	231	266
18	253	292
20	276	317
24	321	369

[1] Applicable if lead hole diameter is 70 percent of the root diameter of the wood screw and the allowable tensile load of the net (root) section of the screw is not exceeded.

[2] Wood screws should not be loaded in withdrawal from end grain of wood.

[3] Based on ovendry volume and weight. The values corresponding to 0.55 specific gravity are from the National Design Specification (National Forest Products Association 1968); those for 0.59 specific gravity are from the Southern Pine Association (1964).

SCREW SIZE AND SPACING FOR ATTACHMENT OF PLYWOOD

Data specific to southern pine plywood have not been published. Based on spacings applicable to other species (USDA Forest Products Laboratory 1953b) the following is suggested as a guideline for attachment of 3/8-inch southern pine plywood panels to frames of structural softwoods.

Gage of screws	11 or 12
Screw length, inches	1¼ to 1½
Minimum edge distance, inch	¾
Optimum spacing between screws in a single row, inch	¾ to ⅞

These gages and lengths are the smallest that can be used if the screws are not to break or pull out when the full strength of the plywood is developed. Flathead screws without washers give results about equal to roundhead screws with washers; roundhead screws without washers are inferior in holding power. Staggering of screws is preferable to linear arrangement (USDA Forest Products Laboratory 1953b). Based on tests of Douglas-fir plywood, withdrawal resistance is linearly correlated with

TABLE 24–16.—*Allowable lateral loads for wood screws in side grain of seasoned southern pine—normal duration* [1][2][3][4] (after Southern Pine Association 1964; National Forest Products Association 1968)

Screw number or gage	Allowable lateral load
	Pounds
6	75
7	90
8	106
9	124
10	143
12	185
14	232
16	284
18	342
20	406
24	548

[1] Tabulated values are for loads applied in any direction.

[2] For screws inserted in end grain (parallel to fibers), reduce tabulated values by one-third.

[3] For screws securing metal side plates to wood, tabulated values may be increased 25 percent.

[4] The tabulated values are for screws embedded at least seven times the shank diameter into the member holding the point; for less penetration, reduce values in proportion. Penetration should not be less than four times the shank diameter.

penetration and is not affected by veneer thickness (Douglas-fir Plywood Association 1964). According to Johnson (1967), screw withdrawal resistance in Douglas-fir plywood is less than that in Douglas-fir lumber.

SCREW WITHDRAWAL RESISTANCE IN PARTICLEBOARD

Data specific to southern pine particleboard have not been published; since particleboard is pressed to certain densities regardless of species, however, data from other species provides guidelines probably applicable to southern pine particleboard.

In studies of Douglas-fir particleboard, Johnson (1967) concluded that maximum withdrawal resistance usually, but not always, was proportional to screw diameter. Little difference in withdrawal resistance was observed between wood screws and sheet-metal screws inserted in lead holes and self-drilling screws that required no lead holes. Withdrawal resistances of wood screws in particleboard were not significantly different with lead-hole diameters 50, 70 and 90 percent of the root diameter of the screw. Among particleboards, greatest resistance to withdrawal was observed in flakeboards, and least resistance in boards made of planer shavings. Among particleboards made of hammer-milled veneer, withdrawal resistance was greatest in boards with a density of 48 pounds per cubic foot, but little difference was observed between boards of 40- and 44-pound densities. Screws in Douglas-fir lumber generally had greater withdrawal resistance than in Douglas-fir particleboard.

Overdriving of screws tends to reduce their withdrawal resistance in particleboard. To achieve maximum withdrawal force from screws inserted in the face of particleboard they should be turned one turn or less beyond flush; screws inserted in the edge of particleboard should be turned less than three-eighths of a turn past flush. Power driving of screws in particleboard requires care because threads strip out with only a little more torque than is needed for flush setting (Carroll 1970).

24–5 LAG SCREWS

Lag screws (lag bolts) have bolt heads; their threads are similar to those of wood screws but larger; (fig. 24–23). They are used in applications where fastening with a bolt is not practical because of inaccessibility of one side of the joint, or where the presence of a nut on the surface is objectionable. Diameters of lag screws range from 3/16-inch to 1-1/4-inches and lengths from 1 to 16 inches (table 24–17). Lag screw lengths increase by 1/2-inch increments to 8 inches and by 1-inch increments in lengths over 8 inches. Thread length (T in fig. 24–23) depends on nominal length (L) as follows:

Length of lag screw (L)	Length of thread (T)
– – – – – – – – – – *Inches* – – – – – – – – – –	
1 _____	¾
1½ _____	1⅛
2 _____	1½
2½ _____	For ¼-inch lag screws, T = 1½ inches; for ⁵⁄₁₆- and ⅜-inch, T = 1⅝ inches; for ⁷⁄₁₆-, ½-, and ⅝-inch, T = 1¾ inches.
3 _____	2
4 _____	2½
5 _____	3
6 _____	3½
7 _____	4
8 _____	4½
9 _____	5
10 _____	5¼
11 _____	5½
12 _____	6
13 _____	6½
14 _____	7
15 _____	7½
16 _____	8

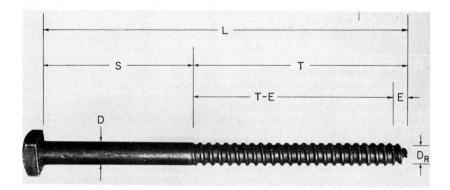

F–521003

Figure 24–23.—Nomenclature for standard lag screws.

L = nominal length of lag screw
D = nominal diameter
S = length of shank
T = length of thread
E = length of tapered tip

T-E = effective length of thread to be used in calculating penetration of threaded portion
D_R = diameter of root section.

For intermediate lengths, length of thread is that of the next shorter length listed (Southern Pine Association 1964).

The allowable withdrawal and lateral loads given in following paragraphs and tables should be adjusted for duration of loading as specified in section 24–1. The listed allowable loads apply to common lag screws inserted in lead holes in dry lumber to be continually dry in service. The lead hole for the shank must be bored the same diameter and length as the shank, and the lead hole for the threaded portion must have a diameter of 60 percent of the shank diameter for the smallest screws and

TABLE 24–17.—*Dimensions of standard lag screws*
(Southern Pine Association 1964)

Nominal size (inches)	Shank diameter (D)	($D^{3/4}$)	Diameter of root of threads (D_R)	Length (L)	Length of tapered tip (E)
			– – – – – – – – – – *Inches*- – – – – – – – – – –		
1/4	0.250	0.354	0.173	1–10	3/16
5/16	.313	.418	.227	1–10	1/4
3/8	.375	.479	.265	1–12	1/4
7/16	.438	.538	.328	1–12	9/32
1/2	.500	.595	.371	1–12	5/16
5/8	.625	.703	.471	2–16	3/8
3/4	.750	.806	.579	2–16	7/16
7/8	.875	.905	.683	3–16	1/2
1	1.000	1.000	.780	3–16	9/16
1 1/8	1.125	1.092	.887	4–16	5/8
1 1/4	1.250	1.182	1.010	4–16	3/4

75 percent for the largest. Slightly larger lead holes should be used for very long lag screws. Lag screws should be lubricated (soap is commonly used) and inserted by turning with a wrench, not by driving with a hammer. The threaded portion of the screw should penetrate the piece retaining the point to about 7 times the shank diameter; allowable withdrawal resistance should not, however, exceed the allowable tensile strength of the lag screw at its net or root section (USDA Forest Products Laboratory 1955; Southern Pine Association 1964; National Forest Products Association 1968).

Essentially comparable adjustments in allowable loads have been published by the Southern Pine Association (1964) and the National Forest Products Association (1968). For lumber which is installed unseasoned and becomes seasoned in place, the full allowable loads may be used for a joint having a single lag screw loaded parallel or perpendicular to the grain, or for a joint having a single row of lag screws loaded parallel to the grain, or for a joint with multiple rows of law screws loaded parallel to the grain with separate splice plates for each row. For other types of joints in unseasoned lumber, the allowable lag screw loads are 40 percent of the tabulated loads; for lumber partially seasoned when fabricated, proportional intermediate loads may be used. Where joints are to be exposed to the weather, allowable loads are 75 percent of tabulated values; where always wet, allowable loads are 67 percent of the tabulated values. For lumber pressure impregnated with fire-retardant chemicals and kiln-dried after treatment, 90 percent of the tabulated values shall apply; for lumber so treated but not kiln-dried after treatment, the 90-percent value shall be further reduced as described in the third sentence of this paragraph.

ALLOWABLE WITHDRAWAL LOADS

Based on one-fifth the ultimate loads observed by Newlin and Gahagan (1938), the USDA Forest Products Laboratory (1955, p. 178) gives allowable withdrawal loads for lag screws as follows:

$$p = 1,500G^{3/2}D^{3/4} \qquad (24\text{--}14)$$

where:

  $p =$ allowable withdrawal load from side grain, pounds.
  $G =$ specific gravity, basis of ovendry volume and weight.
  $D =$ diameter of shank, inches.

Values of $G^{3/2}$ for selected specific gravities are listed in the introduction to this chapter.

The Southern Pine Association (1964) and the National Design Specification (National Forest Products Association 1968, table 14) employ the same relationship given in equation 24–14 to calculate allowable withdrawal loads from side grain, except that the constant used is 1,800 instead of 1,500 (table 24–18).

TABLE 24–18.—*Allowable withdrawal loads[1] for single lag screws in side grain of southern pine—normal load duration*

Size	Specific gravity 0.55[2][3]	Specific gravity 0.59[2][4]
Inch	– – – *Pounds* – – –	
¼	260	290
⁵⁄₁₆	305	340
⅜	350	390
⁷⁄₁₆	395	440
½	435	485
⅝	515	575
¾	590	655
⅞	665	740
1	735	815
1⅛	800	890
1¼	870	965

[1] Per inch of penetration of the threaded portion into the member holding the point; axis of the lag screw perpendicular to the fibers.

[2] Basis of ovendry volume and weight.

[3] Values from National Design Specification (National Forest Products Association 1968); rounded to nearest 5 pounds.

[4] Values from Southern Pine Association (1964); rounded to nearest 5 pounds.

Lag screws should not be loaded in withdrawal from end grain, but when this condition cannot be avoided, the allowable load is three-fourths that given in table 24–18.

ALLOWABLE LATERAL LOAD

The USDA Forest Products Laboratory (1955, p. 179) gives the allowable lateral load for lag screws inserted in side grain of seasoned southern pine (0.59 ovendry specific gravity) and loaded parallel to the grain:

$$p = 1,900D^2 \qquad (24\text{–}15)$$

where:

p = allowable lateral load parallel to grain, pounds.
D = shank diameter of lag screw, inches.

The values calculated from this formula are applicable when the thickness of the attached member is 3.5 times the shank diameter of the lag screw and the depth of penetration in the member holding the point is seven times shank diameter. For other thicknesses of side members, values calculated from equation 24–15 should be adjusted by an appropriate factor, e.g., 0.62 for side members twice shank diameter and 1.22 for side members six times shank diameter.

Values for allowable lateral load applied perpendicular to the grain can be calculated from equation 24–15 by further multiplying by a suitable reduction factor as follows:

Shank diameter	Factor
Inch	
¼	0.97
½	.65
¾	.55
1	.50

For other angles of lateral loading intermediate between parallel and perpendicular to the grain, allowable loads may be calculated from the Hankinson formula:

$$N = \frac{pQ}{p \sin^2\theta + Q \cos^2\theta} \qquad (24\text{–}16)$$

where:

p = allowable load parallel to the grain, pounds.

Q = allowable load perpendicular to the grain, pounds.

N = allowable load applied at angle θ to the grain, pounds.

θ = angle between grain direction and direction of load application, degrees.

A nomograph that provides a readily solved approximation of equation 24–16 is available (USDA Forest Products Laboratory 1955, p. 181; 1956; National Forest Products Association 1968, p. A–4).

If the shank of the lag screw penetrates through the side member and into the member holding the point, values calculated from equation 24–15 can be increased substantially as follows (USDA Forest Products Laboratory 1955, p. 180):

Ratio of shank penetration (into member holding the point) to shank diameter	Increase in allowable load
	Percent
1	8
3	26
5	36
7	39

When lag screws are used to attach metal side plates, allowable loads parallel to the grain may be increased 25 percent, but allowable lateral loads applied perpendicular to the grain should not be increased (USDA Forest Products Laboratory 1955, p. 182).

The National Design Specification (National Forest Products Association 1968) and the Southern Pine Association (1964) provide identical tables for allowable loads applied laterally to lag bolts inserted in side grain of dry southern pine; in contrast to equation 24–15, these values are arranged to show the effect of depth of penetration as well as shank diameter (table 24–19).

The allowable lateral load for a lag screw inserted parallel to the fibers (i.e., in the end grain of the member holding the point) is two-thirds the tabulated value for a lag screw inserted into side grain and loaded perpendicular to the grain.

The spacings, end distances, edge distances, and net section for lag screw joints should be the same as for joints with bolts of a diameter equal to the shank diameter of the lag screw used (National Forest Products Association 1968). See section 24–6.

HEAD EMBEDMENT

Based on unpublished information from J. A. Scholten, Stern (1969c, p. 75) has observed that steel lag screws with square heads and washers may pull through southern pine framing members at loads below those required to withdraw the screws; the data presented indicate, however, that allowable withdrawal loads (table 24–18) should cause bolt heads (with or without washers) to be embedded less than 0.1 inch in side grain of southern pine.

24–6 BOLTS

Allowable lateral loads for bolted joints in southern pine are calculated from basic stress values of 1,450 p.s.i. parallel to the grain and 320 p.s.i. perpendicular to the grain (USDA Forest Products Laboratory 1955, p. 168). These values are for seasoned lumber used in an inside dry location. For loads applied parallel to the grain, the basic stress of 1,450 p.s.i. is reduced as the ratio of bolt length (L) to bolt diameter (D) increases. For the situation depicted in figure 24–24, the allowable lateral load parallel to the grain is given as:

$$p = (1,450)(k)(r)(L)(D) \qquad (24-17)$$

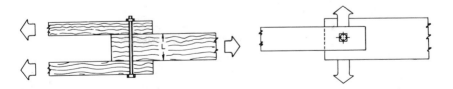

Figure 24–24.—Three-member bolted joint with wood side plates each half the thickness (L) of the middle member. Arrows show direction of forces in lateral loading, parallel to grain (left) and perpendicular to grain (right).

where:

    p = allowable lateral load parallel to grain (per bolt), pounds

    k = 0.8 for three-member joints with wood splice plates, each of which is half the thickness of the middle member.

    r = a multiplier dependent on the ratio L/D; representative values for various L/D ratios follow:

L/D	r
1	1.00
3	.99
6	.67
9	.45
12	.34

    L = length of bolt in bearing, inches. (See fig. 24–24.)

    D = bolt diameter, inches.

The USDA Forest Products Laboratory (1955, p. 184) gives the allowable lateral load acting in a three-member joint perpendicular to the grain of the wood and through metal side plates or wood side plates, each of which is half the thickness of the middle member.

$$p = (320)(r)(v)(L)(D) \qquad (24\text{--}18)$$

where:

    p = allowable lateral load perpendicular to grain (per bolt), pounds

    r, L and D are the same as for equation 24–17.

    v = a multiplier dependent on bolt diameter; representative values follow:

D	v
Inches	
¼	2.50
½	1.68
¾	1.41
1	1.27
1½	1.14
2	1.07
3 or more	1

Allowable lateral loads applied at intermediate angles to the grain may be calculated from the Hankinson formula (equation 24–16). Kojis and Postweiler (1953) published information on deformations of bolted joints in southern pine as a function of the angle between direction of lateral load application and grain direction (fig. 24–25). In these tests, 1-inch common steel bolts inserted in side grain of 4-inch-thick, dry southern pine were assembled into a three-member joint in which the side plates were 1-inch-thick steel with hardened bushings to accommodate the bolt; deformations were observed by recording the movement of the side plates in relation to the central wood member. Kojis and Postweiler (1953) concluded that, for 1-inch bolts loaded at angles to the grain of

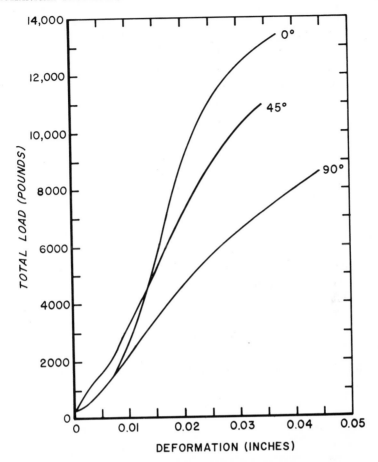

Figure 24–25.—Relationship between load and deformation of 1-inch steel bolt in central member of 3-member joint as affected by angle between load and grain direction. Central member was 4-inch-thick southern pine of higher than average specific gravity and 12.5-percent moisture content; bolts were inserted through bushed holes in 1-inch-thick steel side plates, and the central member was predrilled with a 1-inch bit. Load was applied at 0.006 inch per minute. (Drawing after Kojis and Postweiller 1953.)

20 to 60°, the values computed from the Hankinson formula should be reduced about 10 percent.

The National Forest Products Association (1968) and the Southern Pine Association (1964) have published virtually identical design data for bolted joints in southern pine. In the following four subsections, the text of the Southern Pine Association (1964) is followed almost verbatim.

ALLOWABLE LOADS PARALLEL TO GRAIN

The allowable loads for bolts in southern pine are shown in table 24–20. The values are based on one bolt in double shear when the thickness of wood side members is equal to or greater than one-half the thick-

TABLE 24–19.—*Allowable lateral loads for single lag screws in side grain of seasoned southern pine—normal load duration* (Southern Pine Association 1964; National Forest Products Association 1968)

Side member, load direction in wood, and lag screw length (inches)	Diameter of lag screw shank, inches										
	$\frac{1}{4}$	$\frac{5}{16}$	$\frac{3}{8}$	$\frac{7}{16}$	$\frac{1}{2}$	$\frac{5}{8}$	$\frac{3}{4}$	$\frac{7}{8}$	1	$1\frac{1}{8}$	$1\frac{1}{4}$
					Pounds						
1⅝-inch-thick wood											
Parallel to grain											
4	170	210	240	270	300	360					
5	190	280	360	400	450	540					
6	220	320	410	520	610	710					
7	240	350	450	560	670	810					
Perpendicular to grain											
4	170	170	180	190	190	210					
5	180	240	270	280	290	320					
6	210	270	320	360	390	430					
7	230	300	340	390	440	490					
2⅝-inch-thick wood											
Parallel to grain											
6			370	430	480	560	630	730	800		
7			410	550	650	750	860	970	1,080		
8			460	610	770	970	1,110	1,220	1,380		
9			500	670	830	1,120	1,350	1,480	1,670		
Perpendicular to grain											
6			280	300	310	340	350	380	400		
7			310	390	420	450	470	500	540		
8			360	430	500	580	610	630	690		
9			380	470	540	670	740	770	830		

TABLE 24–19.—Allowable lateral loads for single lag screws in side grain of seasoned southern pine—normal load duration (Southern Pine Association 1964; National Forest Products Association 1968)—Continued

Side member, load direction in wood, and lag screw length (inches)	Diameter of lag screw shank, inches										
	1/4	5/16	3/8	7/16	1/2	5/8	3/4	7/8	1	1 1/8	1 1/4
					Pounds						
1/2-inch-thick metal											
Parallel to grain											
3	210	265	320	370	415	490					
4	235[1]	355	480	575	625	740					
5		375	535	710	850	1,005	1,190				
6		400[1]	545	735	945	1,250	1,480				
7			555[1]	750	970	1,460	2,030	2,720			
8				760[1]	985	1,500	2,130	2,880			
9					990[1]	1,510	2,160	2,960			
10						1,540[1]	2,190	2,990	3,710		
11							2,220[1]	3,000	3,880		
12								3,030[1]	3,900	4,900	
13									3,930	4,920	
14									3,950	4,950	6,060
15									3,960	4,980	6,110
16									3,960[1]	5,000[1]	6,150[1]

TABLE 24–19.—*Allowable lateral loads for single lag screws in side grain of seasoned southern pine—normal load duration* (Southern Pine Association 1964; National Forest Products Association 1968)—Continued

Side member, load direction in wood, and lag screw length (inches)	Diameter of lag screw shank, inches										
	1/4	5/16	3/8	7/16	1/2	5/8	3/4	7/8	1	1 1/8	1 1/4
1/2-inch-thick metal											
Perpendicular to grain											
3	160	180	245	210	215	235					
4	185¹	240	290	320	325	355	525				
5		255	325	405	440	480	650				
6		270¹	330	415	490	600	890				
7			340¹	425	505	700	935				
8				430¹	510	720	950	1,130			
9					515¹	725	965	1,200			
10						740¹	970¹	1,230	1,485		
11								1,240	1,550		
12								1,250	1,560	1,960	
13								1,260¹	1,570	1,970	
14									1,570	1,980	2,420
15									1,580	1,990	2,450
16									1,580¹	2,000¹	2,460¹

¹ Greater lengths do not permit higher allowable loads.

ness of the middle member, and with the load parallel to the grain (fig.
24–24). When the side members are thinner than one-half the thickness
of the middle member, a value is selected by using an L equal to twice
the thickness of the thinner member (fig. 24–26A). Adjustments for duration of load are given in text section 24–1.

When the joint consists of two members (bolt in single shear), use
one-half the value obtained by using an L equal to twice the thickness of
the thinner member (fig. 24–26B).

For joints of more than three members, whose pieces are of equal
thickness (fig. 24–26C), the allowable load is equal to the summation of
the loads for the individual shear planes involved; the allowable load
for each shear plane shall be equal to one-half the tabulated load for a
piece the thickness of the member involved. Thus, when a joint consists
of four members of equal thickness, 1-1/2 times the load obtained by
using an L equal to the thickness of one of the members shall apply.
When metal side plates are used, the parallel to grain values may be increased 25 percent, but perpendicular to grain values discussed below
shall not be increased. The metal plates shall be of ample strength to
support the load.

ALLOWABLE LOADS PERPENDICULAR TO GRAIN

When the load on the bolt acts perpendicular to the grain of the
middle member and is applied through wood or steel side plates, use an
L equal to the thickness of the main member in obtaining a value from
table 24–20. Adjustments of tabulated values for duration of load are
stated in text section 24–1. Where wood side plates are used, the joint
capacity should not exceed the capacity of the side plates loaded parallel
to the grain.

ALLOWABLE LOAD AT AN ANGLE TO THE GRAIN

When the bolt load acts at an angle between 0 and 90° to the grain
of the middle member, use a value for L equal to the thickness of the
middle member for determining parallel and perpendicular loads from
table 24–20; the allowable load is then determined from the Hankinson
formula (equation 24–16).

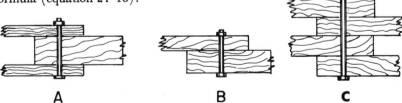

A   B   C

Figure 24–26.—Bolted joints. (A) Three-member joints with side pieces thinner than middle
member. (B) Single shear with one member thinner than the other. (C) Four members of
equal thickness assembled to provide three shear planes.

TABLE 24–20.—*Allowable load on three-member bolted joint in southern pine with wood side plates each half the thickness of the middle member—normal duration* [12] (Southern Pine Association 1964; National Forest Products Association 1968)

Length of bolt in middle member L (inches)	Diameter of bolt D	L/D	Projected area of bolt A = L×D	Load parallel to grain P	Load perpendicular to grain Q
	Inches		*Sq. In.*	*Pounds*	*Pounds*
	½	3.3	0.8125	1,010	480
	⅝	2.6	1.0156	1,290	540
1⅝----------	¾	2.2	1.2188	1,550	600
	⅞	1.9	1.4219	1,810	670
	1	1.6	1.6250	2,070	730
	½	4.0	1.0000	1,180	590
	⅝	3.2	1.2500	1,560	670
2------------	¾	2.7	1.5000	1,910	740
	⅞	2.3	1.7500	2,230	820
	1	2.0	2.0000	2,550	890
	½	5.3	1.3125	1,280	780
	⅝	4.2	1.6406	1,890	880
2⅝----------	¾	3.5	1.9688	2,430	980
	⅞	3.0	2.2969	2,900	1,080
	1	2.6	2.6250	3,340	1,170
	½	6.0	1.5000	1,290	890
	⅝	4.8	1.8750	1,980	1,000
3------------	¾	4.0	2.2500	2,660	1,120
	⅞	3.4	2.6250	3,250	1,230
	1	3.0	3.0000	3,790	1,340
	½	7.3	1.8125	1,290	1,020
	⅝	5.8	2.2656	2,010	1,210
3⅝----------	¾	4.8	2.7188	2,860	1.350
	⅞	4.1	3.1719	3,680	1,490
	1	3.6	3.6250	4,430	1,620
	½	8.0	2.0000	1,290	1,040
	⅝	6.4	2.5000	2,010	1,330
4------------	¾	5.3	3.0000	2,890	1,490
	⅞	4.6	3.5000	3,830	1,640
	1	4.0	4.0000	4,720	1,790

If wood side plates are used, the allowable load should not exceed the capacity of the side plates loaded parallel to the grain.

Values in table 24–20 are for loads acting perpendicular to the axis of

TABLE 24–20.—*Allowable load on three-member bolted joint in southern pine with wood side plates each half the thickness of the middle member—normal duration*[1,2] (Southern Pine Association 1964; National Forest Products Association 1968)—Continued

Length of bolt in middle member L (inches)	Diameter of bolt D	L/D	Projected area of bolt A=L×D	Load parallel to grain P	Load perpendicular to grain Q
	Inches		*Sq. In.*	*Pounds*	*Pounds*
	½	9.0	2.2500	1,290	1,020
	⅝	7.2	2.8125	2,010	1,440
4½	¾	6.0	3.3750	2,890	1,680
	⅞	5.1	3.9375	3,920	1,840
	1	4.5	4.5000	4,980	2,010
	1⅛	4.0	5.0625	5,980	2,190
	⅝	8.8	3.4375	2,010	1,450
	¾	7.3	4.1250	2,890	1,940
5½	⅞	6.3	4.8125	3,940	2,250
	1	5.5	5.5000	5,120	2,460
	1⅛	4.9	6.1875	6,440	2,680
	⅝	10.4	4.0625	2,010	1,390
	¾	8.7	4.8750	2,890	1,940
6½	⅞	7.4	5.6875	3,940	2,510
	1	6.5	6.5000	5,140	2,880
	1⅛	5.8	7.3125	6,500	3,170
	⅝	12.0	4.6875	2,010	1,300
	¾	10.0	5.6250	2,890	1,880
7½	⅞	8.6	6.5625	3,940	2,500
	1	7.5	7.5000	5,140	3,130
	1⅛	6.7	8.4375	6,500	3,610
	¾	12.7	7.1250	2,890	1,690
	⅞	10.9	8.3125	3,940	2,350
9½	1	9.5	9.5000	5,140	3,050
	1⅛	8.4	10.6875	6,500	3,830
	1¼	7.6	11.8750	8,040	4,590
	1	11.5	11.5000	5,140	2,850
11½	1⅛	10.2	12.9375	6,500	3,660
	1¼	9.2	14.3750	8,040	4,490

[1] See figure 24–24.

[2] Tabulated loads are for one bolt. For more than one bolt, use the sum of the loads permitted for each. Loosening of nuts, due to shrinkage, has been allowed for in the table. Bolt holes should be drilled 1/32- to 1/16-inch larger than the bolt, and well aligned. Tight fits requiring driving are not recommended. A standard cut washer or steel strap or plate should be used under both bolt head and nut.

the bolt. If the load in a two-member joint acts at an angle with the axis of the bolt (fig. 24–27), the allowable load component acting at 90° with the bolt axis shall be equal to one-half the tabulated load for an L twice the length of the bolt in the thinner piece. Ample bearing area under washers or plates shall be provided to resist the load component acting parallel to the axis of the bolt.

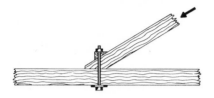

Figure 24–27.—Load applied at angle to axis of bolt.

EFFECT OF CONDITION OF LUMBER AND SERVICE

The values given in table 24–20 are for bolts in lumber seasoned to a moisture content approximately equal to that to which it will eventually come in service. For lumber installed at or above the fiber saturation point and which becomes seasoned in place, the full allowable bolt loads may be used for a bolted joint with wood side members having a single bolt and loaded parallel or perpendicular to the grain, or a single row of bolts loaded parallel to the grain, or multiple rows of bolts loaded parallel to the grain with a separate splice plate for each row. The last recommendations make provision for shrinkage stresses across the grain.

The full allowable bolt loads may also be used for a bolted joint with metal gusset plates having a single row of bolts parallel to the grain in each member at the joint and loaded parallel or perpendicular to the grain. For other arrangements of bolted joints, the allowable bolt loads shall be 40 percent of the tabulated load values.

The values given in table 24–20, adjusted for the condition of the lumber, apply to bolted joints used in a continuously dry location as in most covered structures. For lumber which is occasionally wet but quickly dried, use 75 percent of the tabulated values; if continuously wet, use 67 percent. For lumber pressure impregnated with fire-retardant chemicals and kiln-dried after treatment, use 90 percent of the tabulated values.

HOLE SIZE AND QUALITY

Bolts should fit neatly so that they can be inserted by tapping lightly with a wood mallet. An oversize hole causes nonuniform bearing of the bolt; an undersize hole causes a member to split when the bolt is driven.

In general, smooth holes have higher bearing strengths than rough holes. Section 19–12 describes procedures required to bore smooth holes in green and dry southern pine. (See figure 19–111.)

BOLT SPACING AND NET SECTION

Minimum spacing, end distance, and edge distance are shown in figure 24–28. The spacing between rows for parallel to grain loading is generally determined by dividing the width of the member by the number of rows of bolts; however, this should be reduced if edge distance requirements are not met. If this spacing exceeds 5 inches, separate splice plates must be used. The number of bolts and number of rows are usually limited by the net area of the critical section which in seasoned lumber must equal at least 80 percent of the total area in bearing under all the bolts in the member. For unseasoned wood that will season in place, the net area of the critical section should be at least 33 percent. Staggered bolts should be avoided wherever possible. Where they are used, the net area is determined by considering the adjacent staggered bolts as being at the critical section unless spaced at a minimum of 8D. For loads at an angle to the grain, the axis of the members shall pass through the center of the bolt group.

LOAD DISTRIBUTION IN MULTIPLE-BOLT TENSION JOINTS

The National Design Specification (National Forest Products Association 1968) and the Southern Pine Association (1964) stipulate that multiple-bolt joints have an allowable load equal to the sum of the allowable loads for each bolt as determined from table 24–20. Cramer (1968) has shown by analysis and by tests on Douglas-fir that joints containing six or more bolts in a row have an uneven distribution of bolt loads. His conclusions were as follows.

The two end bolts together usually carry over 50 percent of the load. The addition of more than six bolts in a row does not substantially

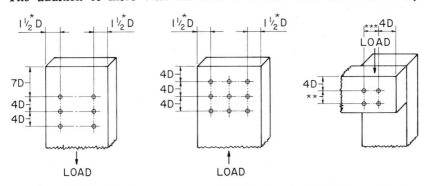

Figure 24–28.—Minimum bolt spacing. L is thickness of middle member (fig. 24–24). *, for L/D more than 6 use one-half of the distance between rows of bolts; a row is a number of bolts placed in a line parallel to the direction of load; **, 4D when design load is equal to bolt-bearing capacity of side members; if not, the spacing may be reduced proportionately; ***, 2.5D for L/D of 2; 5D for L/D of 6 or more. Use straight line interpolation for values between 2 and 6. (Drawing after Southern Pine Association 1964, p. 8.)

increase the elastic strength of the joint, in that the additional bolts tend to reduce only the load on the less heavily loaded interior bolts.

A small misalignment of bolt holes may cause large shifts in bolt loads. Therefore, in field-fabricated joints, the distribution of bolt loads is difficult to predict. The most even distribution of bolt loads occurs in a butt joint in which the tensile stiffness of the main member is equal to that of both splice plates.

Ultimate strength tests show some slight redistribution of load from the more heavily loaded end bolts to the less heavily loaded interior bolts when bolt bearing is the mode of failure. A partial specimen failure occurs before substantial redistribution takes place if final failure is in shear.

BOLTED JOINTS IN PLYWOOD

No data specific to southern pine are published; however, two reports applicable to Douglas-fir—while not summarized here—are available for the guidance of the interested reader (Douglas-fir Plywood Association 1951; American Plywood Association 1968, p. 67).

24–7 DRIFT BOLTS

Plain, round drift bolts (or drift pins), usually driven into predrilled holes 1/8-inch smaller in diameter than the drift-bolt diameter, offer relatively small withdrawal resistance but high lateral resistance in southern pine. Hammer-driven, twisted, square-wire rods offer greater withdrawal resistance than plain, round drift bolts and are often used in their place.

Beams and girders with pin-connected joints between steel-pipe diagonals with flattened ends and slotted lumber chords provide a good example of successfully applied drift bolts (fig. 24–29).

The USDA Forest Products Laboratory (1955, p. 175) gives the ulti-

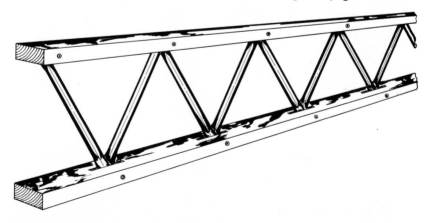

Figure 24–29.—Drift bolts transmit forces from steel-pipe diagonals to lumber chords of beams and girders spanning up to 60 feet.

mate withdrawal load of a round drift bolt in the side of seasoned wood as follows:

$$p = 6{,}000 \ G^2 D \qquad (24\text{--}19)$$

where:

p = ultimate withdrawal load per inch of penetration into the member holding the point, pounds

G = wood specific gravity based on ovendry volume and weight

D = diameter of the drift bolts, inches

Values of G^2 for selected specific gravities are listed in the introduction to this chapter.

ALLOWABLE WITHDRAWAL LOAD

The National Design Specification (National Forest Products Association 1968) and the Southern Pine Association (1964) have published allowable loads for drift bolts in southern pine based on one-fifth the ultimate load computed from equation 24–19, they assume ovendry specific gravities of 0.55 and 0.59 respectively. Following are allowable withdrawal loads per inch of penetration based on **normal** load duration:

Diameter	Specific gravity 0.55	Specific gravity 0.59
Inch	– – – – – – *Pounds* – – – – – –	
¼ ------	91	104
⅜ ------	136	157
½ ------	182	209
⅝ ------	227	261
¾ ------	272	313
⅞ ------	318	365
1 ------	363	418

Adjustments for duration of loading are specified in section 24–1.

ALLOWABLE LATERAL LOAD

The allowable lateral load for a drift bolt driven in the side grain of southern pine does not exceed, and ordinarily is considered less than, that for a common bolt of the same diameter; when possible, additional penetration of a drift bolt into members is desirable to compensate for its lack of head, nut, and washers (National Forest Products Association 1968).

24–8 TIMBER CONNECTORS

Timber connectors are made in a variety of designs and sizes but may be categorized as split rings, toothed rings, shear plates, and spike grids (fig. 24–30).

Design information on timber connectors is based on work done by the Timber Engineering Company, Stern (1941), Scholten (1944), the USDA Forest Products Laboratory (1955), Longworth (1967), Powell (1968), and others.

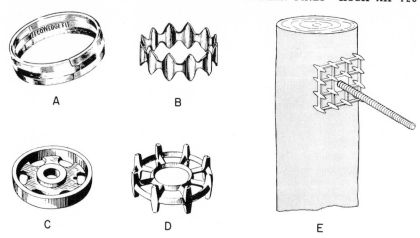

Figure 24–30.—Timber connectors. (A) Beveled split ring. (B) Toothed ring. (C) Shear plate; the reverse side has a flush surface. (D) Circular spike grid. (E) Square spike grid with single curvature.

SPLIT RINGS

Early split rings were of flat steel with uniform cross section (fig. 24–31) ; current designs are beveled (fig. 24–30A) and provide very efficient transmission of loads in timber joints. The effectiveness of a split-ring connector can be attributed to friction between mating surfaces, the bearing resistance of the bolt, the shear resistance of the core within the ring, and the bearing resistance of the wood surrounding the ring (fig. 24–32).

Available in 2-1/2- and 4-inch diameters, they are inserted in grooves pre-cut into mating surfaces of joined timbers, with half the depth of the ring embedded in each member; a bolt holds them in place (fig. 24–31). The 2-1/2-inch rings are widely used in trussed rafters and in 2-inch wood framing. The 4-inch rings are used in heavier beam and girder construction, towers, bridges, and moderate- to long-span trusses.

TOOTHED RINGS

Available in diameters of 2, 2-5/8, or 3-3/8 inches, toothed rings are commonly applied to transfer lateral forces between timbers used in light construction. The toothed rings are embedded with pressure, and no grooves need to be cut (fig. 24–33).

SHEAR PLATES

These connectors are designed primarily for wood-to-steel connections, or—when used in pairs—for wood-to-wood connections in demountable structures (fig. 24–34). Examples of use cited by the Southern Pine Association (1964, p. 10) include attachment of columns to footings with steel

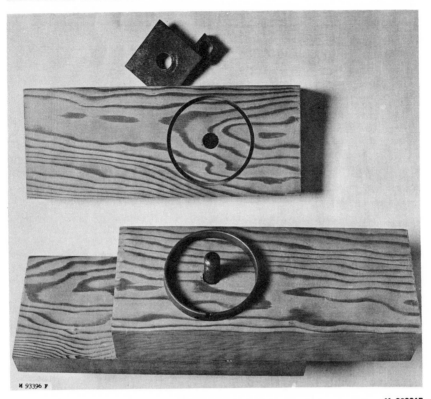

M–93396F

Figure 24–31.—Split-ring connector assembly—connector, precut groove, bolt, washer, and nut. Ring illustrated is an early design; beveled ring shown in fig. 24–30A is currently used. (Photo from USDA Forest Products Laboratory 1955.)

straps, connection of timber members to steel gusset plates, attachment of steel heel straps in bowstring trusses, and other steel-to-wood connections in timber structures. In demountable structures, shear plates can be installed directly after fabrication and held in place with nails; the lack of projecting surfaces allows the members to slide by one another without interference. Shear plates are available in diameters of 2-5/8 and 4 inches.

SPIKE GRIDS

Spike grids are available as 3-3/16-inch-diameter round connectors (fig. 24–30D), or as 4-1/8-inch squares with two flat faces, with one curved face (fig. 24–30E), or with two curved faces. They are designed for use with piles and poles in trestle construction, wharves, transmission lines, and other heavy construction. They are installed by application of pressure.

In southern pine, the load-carrying capacity of 4-1/8-inch-square spike grids (with two flat faces) considerably exceeds that of the smaller round spike grids (fig. 24–35).

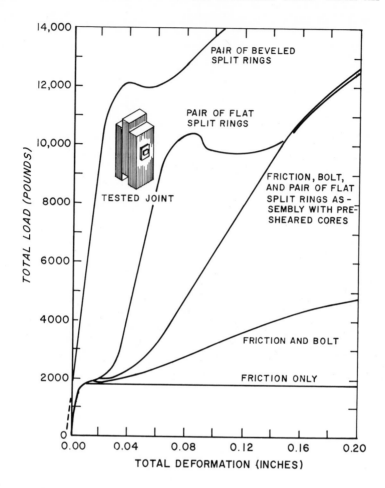

Figure 24–32.—Contribution of friction, bolt bearing, and split-ring (2½-inch) bearing to the load-carrying capacity of a southern pine joint loaded in compression parallel to the grain. (Drawing after Stern 1941.)

ALLOWABLE LONG-CONTINUED LOAD

Allowable **long-continued** loads for southern pine, as advanced by the USDA Forest Products Laboratory (1955), are shown in table 24–21. For split rings and shear plates, these values are one-fourth the ultimate loads parallel to the grain of seasoned wood and do not exceed five-eighths the proportional limit. For toothed rings, allowable loads were calculated by dividing ultimate loads by 4.5.

Conditions of use and direction of load application.—Since the tabulated allowable loads apply to seasoned southern pine which will remain dry, they should be reduced 33 percent if the wood is green during fabrication or will be wet or damp in use. If the load is applied at an angle to the grain, the Hankinson formula (equation 24–16) is applicable,

M–32890F

Figure 24–33.—Assembly of toothed-ring connector. (Photo from USDA Forest Products Laboratory 1955.)

except in the instance of the toothed rings where the allowable load perpendicular to the grain is applicable for loads in the direction from 45 to 90° to the grain.

Member width.—If the minimum member width given in table 24–21 is increased, the allowable perpendicular-to-grain load may be increased one-tenth for each 1-inch increase in width up to a board width twice the connector diameter. When the connector is placed off center and the load applied perpendicular to the grain in one direction only, the proper allowable load can be determined by considering the width of member as equal to twice the edge distance (the distance between the center of the connector and the edge of the member toward which the load is acting), but the distance between the center of the connector and the opposite edge should not be less than one-half the permissable minimum width of the member.

Spacing.—Since the allowable loads are influenced by the parallel-to-grain end distance and the center-to-center spacing between connectors, the strength ratios given in table 24–22 are to be given consideration when arriving at design load values for given joints. A straight-line interpolation for intermediate end distances and spacings is appropriate.

M 92355 F

M–92355F

Figure 24–34.—Shear-plate connector assemblies. (A) Installed back to wood with wood side members. (B) Assembled with steel side members. (Photo from USDA Forest Products Laboratory 1955.)

The clear distance in the direction perpendicular to the grain between connectors loaded parallel to the grain shall not be less than 1/2-inch. The clear distance in the direction parallel to the grain between connectors loaded perpendicular to the grain shall be at least equal to the clear distance from the loaded edge of the member. In the latter instance, the connectors shall be staggered along the grain if feasible.

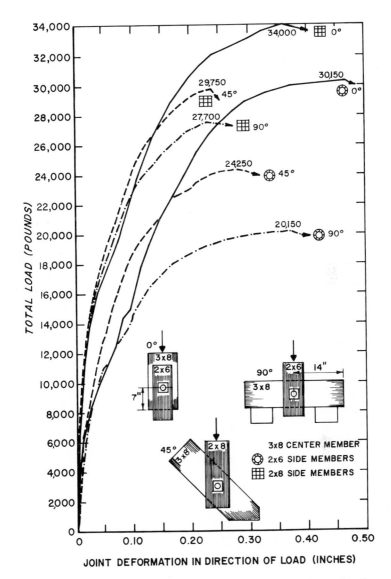

Figure 24–35.—Effectiveness of one pair of 3–3/16-inch round and one pair of 4⅛-inch-square spike grids with single 1-inch bolt in three-member compression joint assembled from southern pine of 0.57 to 0.97 ovendry specific gravity and 14- to 19-percent moisture content. Bolts were inserted in holes drilled 1-1/16 inches in diameter. Joints were loaded at 0.03 inch per minute. (Drawing after Stern 1969c, p. 86.)

The use of cross-bolts at the ends of tension members or at intermediate panel points can be advantageous in reinforcing the members. They may also be used to reinforce members that have, through change of moisture content in service, developed checks to an undesirable degree.

TABLE 24–21.—*Allowable long-continued loads for a single split ring, toothed ring, or shear plates in seasoned southern pine members*[1 2] (USDA Forest Products Laboratory 1955, pp. 190, 191, 192)

Timber connector size (inches)	Diameter of bolt	Minimum member thickness: One connector	Minimum member thickness: Two connectors[3]	Minimum member width	Loading parallel to grain: Dense southern pine	Loading parallel to grain: Southern pine	Loading perpendicular to grain: Dense southern pine	Loading perpendicular to grain: Southern pine
	Inches				*Pounds*			
				SPLIT RING				
2½	½	1	1⅝	3⅝	2,395	2,065	1,435	1,230
		1⅛	2	3⅝	2,875	2,480	1,725	1,475
4	¾	1⅛	1⅝	5½	3,915	3,355	2,270	1,945
		1¼	2	5½	4,500	3,860	2,610	2,240
		1½	2⅝	5½	5,480	4,695	3,175	2,725
		1⅝	3	5½	5,580	4,780	3,235	2,775
				TOOTHED RING				
2	½	1	1⅝	2⅝	1,100	1,000	735	665
		1⅝	2	2⅝	1,210	1,100	805	735
2⅝	⅝	1	1⅝	3⅝	1,650	1,500	1,100	1,000
		1⅛	2	3⅝	1,825	1,660	1,220	1,105
		1⅜	2½	3⅝	2,060	1,875	1,375	1,250
3⅜	¾	1	1⅝	4⅝	2,145	1,950	1,430	1,300
		1⅛	2	4⅝	2,350	2,135	1,565	1,425
		1½	2⅝	4⅝	2,690	2,445	1,795	1,630
		1⅝	3	4⅝	2,895	2,630	1,930	1,755
4	¾	1	1⅝	5½	2,585	2,350	1,725	1,565
		1⅛	2	5½	2,795	2,540	1,865	1,695
		1½	2⅝	5½	3,150	2,865	2,100	1,910
		1⅝	3	5½	3,360	3,055	2,240	2,035

See footnotes at end of table.

TABLE 24-21.—Allowable long-continued loads for a single split ring, toothed ring, or shear plates in seasoned southern pine members[1][2] (USDA Forest Products Laboratory 1955, pp. 190, 191, 192)—Continued

Timber connector size (inches)	Diameter of bolt	Minimum member thickness		Minimum member width	Loading parallel to grain		Loading perpendicular to grain	
		One connector	Two connectors[3]		Dense southern pine	Southern pine	Dense southern pine	Southern pine
		--- Inches ---			--- Pounds ---			
				SHEAR PLATE				
2⅝	¾	---	1⅝	3½	2,386	2,045	1,384	1,186
		---	2	3½	2,667	2,483	1,680	1,440
		1⅝	2⅝	3½	2,667	2,629	1,779	1,525
4	¾	---	1¾	5½	3,086	2,645	1,789	1,533
		---	2	5½	3,442	2,950	1,996	1,711
		---	2⅝	5½	4,035	3,458	2,340	2,006
		1⅝	---	5½	4,320	3,700	2,510	2,150
		---	3	5½	4,391	3,763	2,547	2,182
		1¾	3⅝	5½	4,625	3,967	2,684	2,301
	⅞	---	1¾	5½	3,086	2,645	1,787	1,533
		---	2	5½	3,442	2,950	1,996	1,711
		---	2⅝	5½	4,035	3,458	2,340	2,006
		---	2¾	5½	4,320	3,700	2,510	2,150
		---	3	5½	4,391	3,763	2,547	2,182
		1¾	3⅝	5½	4,625	3,967	2,684	2,301

[1] Connector with one bolt, two washers, and a tight nut.
[2] Use twice the tabulated load value for three-member joint with one connector in each of opposite faces of center member.
[3] One connector in each of opposite faces of center member.

In no instance (tension or compression) is it permissable to exceed the safe stress of clear wood in compression parallel to the grain at the critical cross section, which is the area remaining after deducting the combined projected areas of connectors and bolt from the actual cross-sectional area of the member.

Side members on shear-plate connectors.—The tabulated allowable loads for shear plate connectors apply for metal and wood side members except that, for 4-inch shear plates with metal side members, the parallel-to-grain loads may be increased 11 percent for southern pine and 18 percent for dense southern pine. The allowable loads for all loading conditions, except wind, shall not exceed 2,900 pounds for 2-5/8-inch shear plates or 4,970 pounds and 6,760 pounds for 4-inch shear plates with 3/4- and 7/8-inch bolts, respectively. For wind loads, the corresponding allowable loads shall not exceed 3,870 pounds, 6,630 pounds, and 9,020 pounds.

TABLE 24–22.—*Strength ratios related to parallel-to-grain spacings and end distances for split rings, toothed rings, and shear plates*[1] (USDA Forest Products Laboratory 1955, p. 198)

Connector and diameter (inches)	Spacing[2]	Strength ratio	End distance[3]		Strength ratio
			Tension member	Compression member	
Split-ring	*Inches*	*Percent*	*Inches*	*Inches*	*Percent*
2½	6¾+	100	5½+	4+	100
2½	3⅜	50	2¾	2½	62
4	9+	100	7+	5½+	100
4	4⅞	50	3½	3¼	62
Shear-plate					
2⅝	6¾+	100	5½+	4+	100
2⅝	3⅜	50	2¾	2½	62
4	9+	100	7+	5½+	100
4	4½	50	3½	3¼	62
Toothed-ring					
2	4+	100	3½+	2+	100
2	2	50	2	--------	67
2⅝	5¼+	100	4⅝+	2⅝+	100
2⅝	2⅝	50	2⅝	--------	67
3⅜	6¾+	100	5⅞+	3⅜+	100
3⅜	3⅜	50	3⅜	--------	67
4	8+	100	7+	4+	100
4	4	50	4	--------	67

[1] Strength ratios for spacing and end distances intermediate to those listed may be obtained by interpolation; design loads are then obtained by multiplying the ratio times the appropriate allowable load in table 24–21. Spacings and end distances should not be less than the minimum shown.

[2] Spacing is measured from center to center of connectors.

[3] End distance is measured from center of connector to end of member.

Wind and earthquake loads.—When designing for wind and earthquake forces, the allowable loads may be increased 25 to 50 percent.

Connector	Increase
	Percent
Split-ring connector, any size, bearing in any direction _____	50
Shear-plate connector, any size, bearing parallel to grain _____	33⅓
Shear-plate connector, any size, bearing perpendicular to grain _____	50
Toothed-ring connector, 2-inch, bearing in any direction _____	50
Toothed-ring connector, 4-inch, bearing in any direction _____	25

Percentages for shear-plate connectors bearing at intermediate angles and for toothed-ring connectors of other sizes can be obtained by interpolation.

Impact loads.—Impact loads may be disregarded up to the following percentage of the static effect of the live load producing the impact:

Connector	Impact allowance
	Percent
Split-ring connector, any size, bearing in any direction _____	100
Shear-plate connector, any size, bearing parallel to grain _____	66⅔
Shear-plate connector, any size, bearing perpendicular to grain _____	100
Toothed-ring connector, 2-inch, bearing in any direction _____	100
Toothed-ring connector, 4-inch, bearing in any direction _____	50

Percentages for shear-plate connectors bearing at intermediate angles and for toothed-ring connectors of other sizes may be obtained by interpolation.

One-half of any impact load that remains after disregarding the percentages indicated should be included with the other dead and live loads in obtaining the total force to be considered in designing the joint.

ALLOWABLE NORMAL-DURATION LOAD

The National Design Specification (National Forest Products Association 1968) presents allowable loads for **normal** loading conditions for split rings, toothed rings, and shear plates in southern pine seasoned to approximately 15-percent moisture content to a depth of 3/4-inch from the surface prior to fabrication. These loads, as given in table 24–23, are subject to adjustments for duration of load (see section 24–1) except in the case of the toothed rings, for which an increase of only 20 percent is permitted for wind, earthquake, or impact loads. If the lumber is fabricated prior to having reached the above specified seasoning and later will season further, the adjusted load values shall be reduced 20 percent. If the lumber is fabricated in seasoned or unseasoned condition and will be wet while in service, the adjusted load values shall be reduced 33 percent.

Edge and end distances as well as spacings between connectors govern the allowable loads as is indicated in tables 24–23, 24–24, and 24–25; straight-line interpolation is applicable for intermediate distances except in certain special instances (National Forest Products Association 1968).

The total allowable load shall be the sum of the allowable loads for

TABLE 24–23.—*Allowable load for one split ring, toothed ring, or shear-plate unit (single shear) in seasoned southern pine members under normal loading[1] [2]* (National Forest Products Association 1968)

Minimum member thickness		Loading parallel to grain			Loading perpendicular to grain			
One connector (inches)	Two connectors[3] (inches)	Minimum edge distance	Dense southern pine	Southern pine	Minimum edge distance Unloaded	Minimum edge distance Loaded[4]	Dense southern pine	Southern pine
		Inches	— — — Pounds — — —		— — Inches — —		— — — Pounds — — —	
SPLIT RING (2½-INCH SIZE WITH ½-INCH BOLT)								
1 --------	1⅝	1¾	2,630	2,270	1¾	1¾	1,580	1,350
						2¾	1,900	1,620
1⅝ -------	2	1¾	3,160	2,730	1¾	1¾	1,900	1,620
						2¾	2,280	1,940
SPLIT RING (4-INCH SIZE, E WITH ¾-INCH BOLT)								
1 --------	---	2¾	4,090	3,510	2¾	2¾	2,370	2,030
						3¾	2,840	2,440
1⅝ -------	3	2¾	6,140	5,260	2¾	2¾	3,560	3,050
						3¾	4,270	3,660
	1⅝	2¾	4,310	3,690	2¾	2¾	2,490	2,140
						3¾	3,000	2,570
	2	2¾	4,950	4,250	2¾	2¾	2,870	2,470
						3¾	3,440	2,960
	2⅝	2¾	6,030	5,160	2¾	2¾	3,490	3,000
						3¾	4,180	3,600
TOOTHED RING (2-INCH SIZE WITH ½-INCH BOLT)								
1 --------	1⅝	1¼	1,210	1,100	1¼	1¼	810	730
						2	930	840
1⅝ -------	2	1¼	1,330	1,210	1¼	1¼	890	810
						2	1,020	930

TABLE 24–23.—*Allowable load for one split ring, toothed ring, or shear-plate unit (single shear) in seasoned southern pine members under normal loading*[1] [2] (National Forest Products Association 1968)—Continued

Minimum member thickness		Loading parallel to grain			Loading perpendicular to grain			
One connector (inches)	Two connectors[3] (inches)	Minimum edge distance	Dense southern pine	Southern pine	Minimum edge distance		Dense southern pine	Southern pine
					Unloaded	Loaded[4]		
		Inches	Pounds	Pounds	Inches	Inches	Pounds	Pounds
TOOTHED RING (2⅝-INCH SIZE WITH ⅝-INCH BOLT)								
1 --------	1⅝	1¾	1,820	1,650	1¾	1¾	1,210	1,100
						2½	1,390	1,260
1⅝ --------	2⅝	1¾	2,270	2,030	1¾	1¾	1,510	1,370
						2½	1,730	1,570
	2	1¾	2,010	1,830	1¾	1¾	1,340	1,220
						2½	1,540	1,400
TOOTHED RING (3⅜-INCH SIZE WITH ¾-INCH BOLT)								
1 --------	1⅝	2¼	2,360	2,150	2¼	2¼	1,570	1,430
						3¼	1,880	1,720
1⅝ --------	3	2¼	3,180	2,890	2¼	2¼	2,120	1,930
						3¼	2,540	2,320
	2	2¼	2,590	2,350	2¼	2¼	1,720	1,570
						3¼	2,060	1,880
	2⅝	2¼	2,960	2,690	2¼	2¼	1,970	1,790
						3¼	2,370	2,150

See footnotes at end of table.

TABLE 24–23.—*Allowable load for one split ring, toothed ring, or shear-plate unit (single shear) in seasoned southern pine members under normal loading*[1][2] (National Forest Products Association 1968)—Continued

Minimum member thickness		Loading parallel to grain			Loading perpendicular to grain			
One connector (inches)	Two connectors[3] (inches)	Minimum edge distance	Dense southern pine	Southern pine	Minimum edge distance Unloaded	Minimum edge distance Loaded[4]	Dense southern pine	Southern pine
		Inches	*Pounds*	*Pounds*	*Inches*	*Inches*	*Pounds*	*Pounds*
TOOTHED RING (4-INCH SIZE WITH ¾-INCH BOLT)								
1--------	1⅝	2¾	2,840	2,590	2¾	2¾	1,900	1,720
						3¾	2,280	2,060
1⅝-------	3	2¾	3,700	3,360	2¾	2¾	2,460	2,240
						3¾	2,960	2,690
	2	2¾	3,070	2,790	2¾	2¾	2,050	1,860
						3¾	2,460	2,240
	2⅝	2¾	3,470	3,150	2¾	2¾	2,310	2,100
						3¾	2,770	2,520
SHEAR PLATES (2⅝-INCH SIZE WITH ¾-INCH BOLT)[5]								
1⅝-------	2⅝	1¾	3,370[5]	2,890	1¾	1¾	1,960	1,680
						2¾	2,350	2,020
	1⅝	1¾	2,620	2,250	1¾	1¾	1,520	1,300
						2¾	1,820	1,560
	2	1¾	3,190[5]	2,730	1¾	1¾	1,850	1,590
						2¾	2,220	1,910

TABLE 24–23.—*Allowable load for one split ring, toothed ring, or shear-plate unit (single shear) in seasoned southern pine members under normal loading*[1] [2] (National Forest Products Association 1968)—Continued

SHEAR PLATES (4-INCH SIZE WITH 3/4-INCH BOLT)[5]

Minimum member thickness		Loading parallel to grain			Loading perpendicular to grain			
One connector (inches)	Two connectors[3] (inches)	Minimum edge distance	Dense southern pine	Southern pine	Minimum edge distance Unloaded	Loaded[4]	Dense southern pine	Southern pine
		Inches	*Pounds*	*Pounds*	*Inches*	*Inches*	*Pounds*	*Pounds*
1⅝	------	2¾	4,750	4,070	2¾	2¾	2,760	2,360
						3¾	3,310	2,830
1¾	3⅝	2¾	5,090[5]	4,360	2¾	2¾	2,950	2,530
						3¾	3,540	3,040
	1¾	2¾	3,390	2,910	2¾	2¾	1,970	1,680
						3¾	2,360	2,020
	2	2¾	3,790	3,240	2¾	2¾	2,200	1,880
						3¾	2,640	2,260
	2⅝	2¾	4,440	3,800	2¾	2¾	2,580	2,210
						3¾	3,100	2,650
	3	2¾	4,830	4,140	2¾	2¾	2,800	2,400
						3¾	3,360	2,880

See footnotes at end of table.

TABLE 24–23.—*Allowable load for one split ring, toothed ring, or shear-plate unit (single shear) in seasoned southern pine members under normal loading*[1][2] (National Forest Products Association 1968)—Continued

Minimum member thickness		Loading parallel to grain			Loading perpendicular to grain			
One connector (inches)	Two connectors[3] (inches)	Minimum edge distance	Dense southern pine	Southern pine	Minimum edge distance		Dense southern pine	Southern pine
					Unloaded	Loaded[4]		
		Inches	- - - - *Pounds* - - - -		- - - *Inches* - - -		- - - *Pounds* - - -	
			SHEAR PLATES (4-INCH SIZE WITH ⅞-INCH BOLT)[5]					
1⅝ ------	------	2¾	4,750	4,070	2¾	2¾	2,760	2,360
						3¾	3,310	2,830
1¾ ------	3⅝	2¾	5,090	4,360	2¾	2¾	2,950	2,530
						3¾	3,540	3,040
	1¾	2¾	3,390	2,910	2¾	2¾	1,970	1,680
						3¾	2,360	2,020
	2	2¾	3,780	3,240	2¾	2¾	2,200	1,880
						3¾	2,640	2,260
	2⅝	2¾	4,440	3,800	2¾	2¾	2,580	2,210
						3¾	3,100	2,650
	3	2¾	4,830	4,140	2¾	2¾	2,800	2,400
						3¾	3,360	2,880

[1] Assembled with one bolt, two washers, and tight nut.

[2] For three-member joint with one connector in each of opposite faces of center member, use twice the tabulated load value.

[3] One connector in each of opposite faces of center member.

[4] The **loaded edge** is the edge toward which the load is acting.

[5] The allowable loads for shear plates apply for metal and wood side plates except that, for 4-inch shear plates with metal side plates, the parallel-to-grain loads may be increased 11 percent for southern pine and 18 percent for dense southern pine. The allowable loads for all loading conditions, except wind, shall not exceed 2,900 pounds for 2⅝-inch shear plates or 4,970 pounds and 6,760 pounds for 4-inch shear plates with ¾-inch and ⅞-inch bolts, respectively. For wind loads, the corresponding allowable loads shall not exceed 3,870 pounds, 6,630 pounds, and 9,020 pounds. If bolt threads are in bearing on the shear plate (in the case of unavailability of larger bolt which would prevent the bolt threads from bearing on the shear plate as a result of the inclusion of a washer or of several washers), the preceding values shall be reduced by one-ninth.

TABLE 24-24.—*Connector spacings and end distances for parallel-to-grain loading with corresponding percentages of tabulated loads* (National Forest Products Association 1968)

Connector and diameter (inches)	Spacing parallel to grain		Spacing perpendicular to grain		End distance		
	Spacing	Percentage of tabulated load	Minimum	Percentage of tabulated load[1]	Tension member	Compression member	Percentage of tabulated load[1]
	Inches	*Percent*	*Inches*	*Percent*	*- - - - Inches - - - -*		*Percent*
Split ring							
2½	6¾	100	3½	100	5½	4	100
2½	3½	75	3½	100	2¾	2½	62.5
4	9	100	5	100	7	5½	100
4	5	75	5	100	3½	3¼	62.5
Toothed ring							
2	4	100	2½	100	3½	2[2]	100
2	2½	75	2½	100	2	---	66.7
2⅝	5¼	100	3⅛	100	4⅝	2⅝[2]	100
2⅝	3⅛	75	3⅛	100	2⅝	---	66.7
3⅜	6¾	100	3⅞	100	5⅞	3⅜[2]	100
3⅜	3⅞	75	3⅞	100	3⅞	---	66.7
4	8	100	4½	100	7	4[2]	100
4	4½	75	4½	100	4	---	66.7
Shear plate							
2⅝	6¾	100	3½	100	5½	4	100
2⅝	3½	75	3½	100	2¾	2½	62.5
4	9	100	5	100	7	5½	100
4	5	75	5	100	3½	3¼	62.5

[1] To obtain loads, multiply these percentages by allowable loads from table 24–23.

[2] No reduction in end distance permitted for compression members loaded parallel to grain.

TABLE 24–25.—*Connector spacings and end distances for perpendicular-to-grain loading with corresponding percentages of tabulated loads* (National Forest Products Association 1968)

Connector and diameter (inches)	Spacing parallel to grain		Spacing perpendicular to grain		End distance	
	Minimum	Percentage of tabulated load[1]	Spacing	Percentage of tabulated load[1]	Distance[2]	Percentage of tabulated load[1]
	Inches	*Percent*	*Inches*	*Percent*	*Inches*	*Percent*
Split ring						
2½ --------	3½	100	4¼	100	5½	100
2½ --------	3½	100	3½	75	2¾	62.5
4 ---------	5	100	6	100	7	100
4 ---------	5	100	5	75	3½	62.5
Toothed ring						
2 ---------	2½	100	3	100	3½	100
2 ---------	2½	100	2½	75	2	66.7
2⅝ --------	3⅛	100	3¾	100	4⅝	100
2⅝ --------	3⅛	100	3⅛	75	2⅝	66.7
3⅜ --------	3⅞	100	5	100	5⅞	100
3⅜ --------	3⅞	100	3⅞	75	3⅜	66.7
4 ---------	4½	100	5¾	100	7	100
4 ---------	4½	100	4½	75	4	66.7
Shear plate						
2⅝ --------	3½	100	4¼	100	5½	100
2⅝ --------	3½	100	3½	75	2¾	62.5
4 ---------	5	100	6	100	7	100
4 ---------	5	100	5	75	3½	62.5

[1] To obtain design loads, multiply these percentages times allowable loads from table 24–23.
[2] Tension or compression members.

each of the connectors in a joint, except in the following instances. If grooves for two sizes of split rings are cut concentrically in the same timber surfaces, rings shall be installed in both grooves and the total allowable load shall be only the allowable load for the larger ring. In contrast, if two toothed rings (2- and 3-3/8-inch, 2- and 4-inch, or 2-5/8- and 4-inch) are placed concentrically in the same timber surfaces, the total allowable load shall be the allowable load for the larger ring plus 25 percent of the allowable load for the smaller ring.

Considerable additional design information and assistance can be found in the National Design Specification (National Forest Products Association 1968) and TECO Design Manual (Timber Engineering Company 1962).

The allowable connector loads advanced by the Southern Pine Association (1964) are the same as those recommended by the National Forest Products Association (1968).

ALLOWABLE LOAD FOR SQUARE SPIKE GRIDS

The TECO Design Manual (Timber Engineering Company 1962, p. 25) presents allowable normal loads for 4-1/8-inch-square flat and curved spike grids; these loads are subject to adjustment for duration of load as indicated in section 24–1. These loads—tabulated below—are in pounds for one spike grid with one bolt, two washers, and a tight nut in southern pine.

Connector type and bolt diameter (inches)	Edge distance	End distance	Dense southern pine	Southern pine
	– – – Inches – – –		– – – Pounds – – –	
Flat				
¾				
	3¾	7	3,900	3,500
	2¾	5	3,315	2,975
1				
	3¾	7	4,200	3,800
	2¾	5	3,570	3,230
Single curve				
¾				
	3¾	7	4,200	3,800
	2¾	5	3,570	3,230
1				
	3¾	7	4,500	4,100
	2¾	5	3,825	3,485

For intermediate edge and end distances, straight-line interpolation is appropriate. The allowable loads apply if the width of the lumber is at least 5-1/2 inches and its thickness is at least 1-5/8 inches with the flat connector in a single face or 2-5/8 inches if flat connectors are in both opposite faces. The minimum diameter of a pole or pile with curved grids shall be 10 inches. The minimum center-to-center spacing of all spike grids parallel to the grain with the load applied at an angle to the grain of 0 to 30° shall be 7 inches and in all other instances 5-1/2 inches. The allowable loads can be increased 30 percent for wind and/or earthquake loads in combination with dead and/or live loads. The allowable loads for combined static and impact loads can be increased 15 percent.

24–9 PLATE CONNECTORS

Light-gage, punched, galvanized plate connectors are used primarily in the fabrication of trusses (fig. 24–36). They may be flat and attached with nails or with deformed short prongs (barbs) or longer teeth (plugs) integral with the plate (fig. 24–37). Stern (1969c, pp. 82, 83) has illustrated a variety of available plates and shown performance curves for eight of them. These curves indicate that in general, when applied to butt joints of seasoned 1-5/8-inch-thick southern pine, a pair of 18- to 20-gage, 3- to 3-1/2-inch-wide connectors measuring 3 to 9 inches long will carry an ultimate tensile load of 6,000 to 10,000 pounds; at a joint deformation of 0.03 inch, tensile load may be in the range from 4,000 to 6,000 pounds. Trusses assembled with plate connectors have been built to span as much as 100 feet (Anonymous 1966).

Design information for assemblies involving metal plate connectors with barbs and plugs can be found in Design Specification for Light Metal-Plate Connected Wood Trusses (Truss Plate Institute 1970). According to the National Design Specification (National Forest Products Association 1968), the allowable design load for normal loading shall be determined by dividing the test load value at wood-to-wood slip of 0.03 inch by 1.6, or by dividing the ultimate load by 3.0; the smaller of these two values shall be the design load. Adjustment for duration of load should be made according to text section 24–1. Load evaluation tests must be made on seasoned lumber according to ASTM Designation D 1761–68 (American Society for Testing and Materials 1968).

For metal plate connectors installed in unseasoned lumber, the allowable loads should be reduced 20 percent. If installed in lumber pressure impregnated with fire-retardant chemicals and kiln-dried after treatment, the allowable loads should be reduced 10 percent; if not kiln-dried after treatment, the allowable loads should be reduced 20 percent.

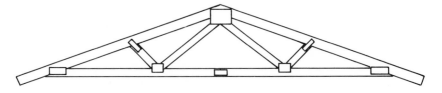

Figure 24–36.—Roof truss assembled with plate connectors.

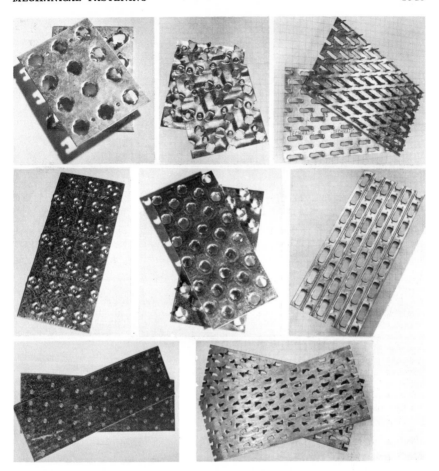

Figure 24–37.—Preformed plate connectors for use in assembling trusses. The plates are of galvanized 18- to 20-gage (W&M) steel and measure 3 to 3½ inches in width and 4 to 9 inches in length. Only the plates shown at middle left and lower left rely on nails for load transmission. None of the others require nails for attachment; integral barbs, prongs, and teeth are impressed into truss members by hydraulic or roll presses. (Photo from Stern 1969c, p. 82.)

Because of connection flexibility, mechanically fastened wood trusses are difficult to analyze for stresses and displacements. Efforts to devise suitable analytical methods have been reviewed by Suddarth (1969).

Sliker (1969), in an analysis of factors affecting creep in plate-connected tension joints, concluded that creep was reduced if nails were of high-strength steel, if plates were relatively thick, and if nail shanks were bonded to the wood they penetrated.

24–10   SHEET METAL AND ANGLE IRON ANCHORS

Anchorage of lightweight buildings at all important joints from roof to foundation is an important aspect of good construction.

Sheet metal anchors include a variety of steel straps, framing anchors, clips, and grips; they have sufficient cross-sectional area for the metal-to-wood fasteners—usually nails—to govern their effectiveness. The allowable lateral loads of the fasteners, therefore, are the limiting factors in load transmittal. Timber Engineering Company, while not the only manufacturer of sheet metal anchors, makes a variety of anchors for which allowable loads are published. Brief descriptions of these anchors, plus one made by Panel Clip Company, follow.

TRIP-L-GRIP FRAMING ANCHORS

Figure 24–38 shows TECO anchors made from 18-gage,[3] galvanized-steel sheet. They measure 4-7/8 inches high; the rectangular flange is 1-5/8 inches wide, the triangular flange is 2-3/8 inches wide, and the bent portion on the A and B types is 1-5/8 inches long. The allowable short- and long-duration loads transmitted by one of these anchors applied to southern pine is as follows (Southern Pine Association 1964).

	Direction of load (see fig. 24–38)					
Condition	A	B	C	D	E	F
	—	—	—	—	—	—
	— — — — — — — — *Pounds* — — — — — — — — —
Short-term loading— wind or earthquake	450	825	420	300	450	675
Long-term loading— live loads and dead loads	300	530	290	200	300	450

Special short nails, approximately equal in strength to 8d common nails are used with these anchors.

---

[3] Thickness of sheet metal anchors specified by Washburn and Moen gage.

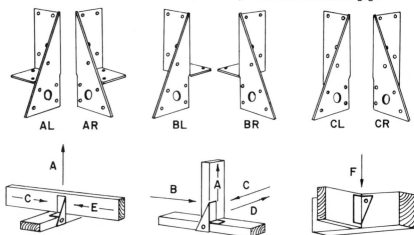

Figure 24–38.—Three types of Trip-L-Grip framing anchors; arrows indicate principal directions of applied loads.

DU-AL-CLIP

Figure 24–39 shows another type of anchor formed of 18-gage galvanized-steel sheet. These are 5-1/2 inches high with flanges 1-5/8 inches wide. They are secured by special 1-1/2- by 0.120-inch nails. Timber Engineering Company (1970) gives allowable long-duration live and dead loads per anchor as follows:

Direction (see fig. 24–39)	Load
	Pounds
A ----------------	400
B ----------------	300
C ----------------	120
D ----------------	400

Allowable short-duration loads imposed by wind or earthquake may be one-third to one-half higher.

U-GRIP JOIST AND BEAM ANCHORS

Figure 24–40 illustrates joist and beam anchors of 16- and 18-gage galvanized-steel sheet for fastening southern pine members ranging in size from 2 by 6 to 4 by 14 inches. Barbed nails 1-1/2 inches by 0.148 inch

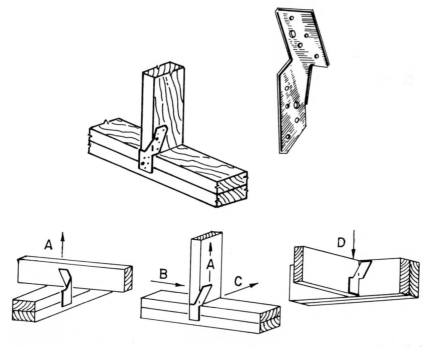

Figure 24–39.—Du-Al-Clip framing anchors; arrows indicate principal directions of applied loads.

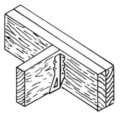

Figure 24–40.—U-Grip joist and beam anchor.

are used for the 2-inch member; the 4-inch members call for barbed nails 2-1/8 inches by 0.192 inch. According to Timber Engineering Company (1970), the allowable **long-duration** load—equal to one-fourth the ultimate load—for a single anchor applied to southern pine is as follows:

Beam thickness and depth (inches)	Steel gage	Anchor height	Seat width	Seat depth	Load
	W & M	– – – – –	*Inches*	– – – – –	*Pounds*
2 inches					
6 to 10	18	5	1⅝	2	900
10 to 14	18	8½	1⅝	2	1,200
3 inches					
6 to 10	16	5¼	2⅝	2¾	1,700
10 to 14	16	8½	2⅝	2¾	2,800
4 inches					
6 to 10	16	5¼	3⅝	2¾	1,700
10 to 14	16	8½	3⅝	2¾	2,800
4 inches (a pair of 2-inch joists)					
6 to 10	16	5¼	3¼	2¾	1,700
10 to 14	16	8½	3¼	2¾	2,800

TY-DOWN RAFTER ANCHORS

These 18-gage, galvanized, 1-9/16-inch-wide, steel anchors are designed to fasten rafters to plates or to studs below the plates (fig. 24–41A, B). In the former case they are 5-1/4 inches long with an allowable uplift load of 312 pounds per anchor; in the latter case the allowable uplift load is 780 pounds per anchor (Timber Engineering Company 1970). In both cases, 1-1/2- by 0.135-inch threaded nails are used to secure the anchors to the wood.

ANGLE CLIPS

The Panel Clip Company manufactures an angle clip formed of 20-gage, galvanized-steel sheet; it is designed to fasten framing members at right angles to each other. The punched-out teeth are hammer-driven into the wood members and take the place of nails (fig. 24–42). According to the manufacturer, a pair of clips at the end of a 2- by 10-inch or smaller southern pine joist transmits an allowable load of 514 pounds.

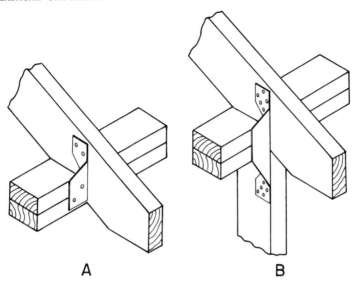

A   B

Figure 24—41.—Ty-Down rafter anchors. (A) To secure rafter to plate. (B) To secure rafter to stud.

TEN-CON CONNECTORS

The anchor shown in figure 24–43 is designed to secure concrete pile caps to foundation piles. It is fabricated in 15-inch lengths from 1/4-inch-thick, 4- by 7-1/2-inch, hot-rolled steel angles. Tapered circular holes are punched in the 7-1/2-inch leg; special 3-1/2- by 0.126- by 0.250-inch,

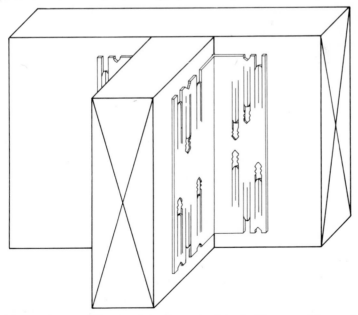

Figure 24—42.—Joist attached to header with a pair of Angle Clips secured by punched-out, hammer-driven prongs.

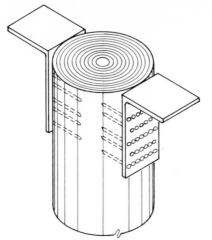

Figure 24–43.—Ten-Con connector designed to fasten concrete pile caps to foundation piles (Drawing after Timber Engineering Co. 1970.)

hardened-steel rivets are hammer driven through these holes to form a wedge fit and thus provide a nail rigidly cantilevered from the connector and piercing the wood. According to McGowan (1966), the allowable wind uplift load for a minimum of two connectors fastened to a southern pine pile is 20,000 pounds, and that of each additional connector is 10,000 pounds.

24–11 EXPLOSIVE-DRIVEN PINS AND STUDS

Explosive-driven steel pins and studs (fig. 24–44) can be used to fasten southern pine in thicknesses up to 3-5/8 inches to concrete and steel. This type of fastener is especially useful if the side away from the wood is inaccessible as is the case when framing members and components are secured to walls and foundations.

Stern (1969c, p. 96) observed that withdrawal resistance of pins driven into concrete or steel can be higher than the pull-through resistance of the washer (1-7/16-inch and smaller) sometimes used between wood and head. For this reason, the number of explosive-driven pins required may depend on the size and type of washers through which the pins can be effectively driven. If no washer is used, depth of penetration may be uncertain.

Explosive-driven studs, however, can be provided with the standard washers normally used for anchor bolts (fig. 24–44). Standard washers are listed below:

Washer type	Diameter
	Inches
Round cast iron and round malleable iron	2, 2⅝, 3, 3½
Round wrought iron	1⅜, 2, 2¼
Square steel	2, 2½, 3, 3½

These larger washers provide adequate resistance against pullthrough.

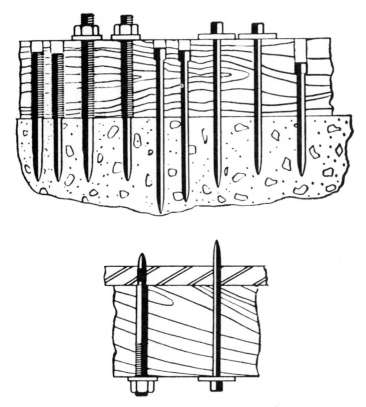

Figure 24–44.—Explosive-driven pins (right) and studs (left), with and without washers between fastener head and wood. (Top) Anchoring wood to concrete. (Bottom) Anchoring wood to steel. (Drawing from Remington Arms Co.)

24–12 LITERATURE CITED

Anonymous.
> 1966. Would you believe—a 100 ft. wooden truss? Pract. Builder 31(11): 53, 55.

Albert, T. J., and Johnson, J. W.
> 1967. Lateral holding capacity of power-driven fasteners. Forest Prod. J. 17(9): 59–67.

American Plywood Association.
> 1967. When the wind blows. Amer. Plywood Assoc., 15 pp. Tacoma, Wash.

American Plywood Association.
> 1968. Design data on plywood for transportation equipment. Amer. Plywood Assoc. Lab. Rep. 114, 86 pp. Tacoma, Wash.

American Society of Mechanical Engineers.
> 1962. Slotted and recessed head wood screws. ASA B18.6.1–1961, 15 pp.

American Society for Testing and Materials.
> 1968. Standard methods of testing metal fasteners in wood. ASTM Des. D 1761–68. Amer. Soc. for Testing and Mater., Philadelphia, Pa.

Anderson, L. O.
> 1965. Guides to improved framed walls for houses. USDA Forest Serv. Res. Pap. FPL–31, 28 pp. Forest Prod. Lab., Madison, Wis.

Anderson, L. O., and Smith, W. R.
1965. Houses can resist hurricanes. USDA Forest Serv. Res. Pap. FPL–33, 48 pp. Forest Prod. Lab., Madison, Wis.

Brock, G. R.
1954. The strength of nailed timber joints. Timber Technol. 62: 283–286, 333–335, 407–408.

Brock, G. R.
1956. The strength of nailed timber joints. Timber Technol. 64: 19–21, 74–77.

Carroll, M. N.
1970. Relationship between driving torque and screw-holding strength in particleboard and plywood. Forest Prod. J. 20(3): 24–29.

Countryman, D., and Colbenson, P.
1955. Strength of stapled plywood-lumber joints. Douglas Fir Plywood Assoc. Lab. Rep. 68, 12 pp.

Cramer, C. O.
1968. Load distribution in multiple-bolt tension joints. J. Struct. Div. Amer. Soc. Civil Eng. 94(ST5): 1101–1117.

Dikkers, R. D., Thom, H. C. S., and Marshall, R. D.
1969. Hurricane Camille—August 1969. U.S. Nat. Bur. Stand. Rep. 10393, 67 pp.

Douglas Fir Plywood Association.
1951. Tentative summary of tests on bolted plywood joints. Douglas Fir Plywood Assoc., 2 pp. Tacoma, Wash.

Douglas Fir Plywood Association.
1964. The screw-pulling strength of plywood. Douglas Fir Plywood Assoc. Lab. Bull. 47–B, 3 pp. Tacoma, Wash.

Dove, A. B.
1955. The influence of nail design and manufacturing practices on joint strength. Wire and Wire Prod. 30: 657–666, 724–725.

Federal Housing Administration.
1961. Power-driven wire staples. Use Mater. Bull. UM–25a, 7 pp.

Gahagan, J. M., and Beglinger, E.
1956. New nail treating process increases holding power. USDA Forest Serv. Forest Prod. Lab. Rep. R970, 3 pp.

General Services Administration.
1963. Federal specification: Nails, wire, brads, and staples. Fed. Specif. FF–N–105a and Interim Amend.–2. Gen. Serv. Admin.

Johnson, J. W.
1967. Screw-holding ability of particle board and plywood. Oreg. State Univ. Sch. Forest., Forest Res. Lab. Rep. T–22, 23 pp.

Johnston, E. A.
1964. The fluted auto nail. Wire and Wire Prod. 39: 727, 730–731, 767–769.

Kojis, D. D., and Postweiler, R. H.
1953. Allowable loads for common bolts at various angles to the grain for southern yellow pine. J. Forest Prod. Res. Soc. 3(3): 21–26.

Kurtenacker, R. W.
1962. Lateral loading evaluation of staples and T-nails. In Mechanical fasteners for wood, pp. 54–72. Building Res. Inst. Pub. 1003.

Kurtenacker, R. S.
1965. Performance of container fasteners subjected to static and dynamic withdrawal. USDA Forest Serv. Res. Pap. FPL–29, 20 pp. Forest Prod. Lab., Madison, Wis.

Leach, K. E.
1964. A survey of literature on the lateral resistance of nails. Can. Dep. Forest. Pub. 1085, 12 pp.

Longworth, J.
1967. Behavior of shear plate connections in sloping grain surfaces. Forest Prod. J. 17(7): 49–53.

McDonald, J. K.
1967. Homes for hurricane country. Forests and People 17(3): 22–23, 29, 31.

McGowan, W. M.
1966. A nailed plate connector for glue-laminated timbers. J. Mater. 1: 509–535.

Martin, T. J., and Van Kleeck, A.
1941. Fastening. (U.S. Pat. No. 2,268,323.) U.S. Pat. Office, Offic. Gaz. 533: 1226.

Merrill, W., and French, D. W.
1966. Wood fiberboard studies. IV. Effects of decay on lateral nail resistance and correlation of lateral nail resistance with nailhead pull-through resistance. TAPPI 49: 33–34.

National Forest Products Association.
1968. National design specification for stress-grade lumber and its fastenings. A.I.A. File 19–B–1, 63 pp. Nat. Forest Prod. Assoc.

Newlin, J. A., and Gahagan, J. M.
1938. Lag-screw joints: their behavior and design. USDA Tech. Bull. 597, 27 pp.

Patterson, D.
1969. Pole building design. Amer. Wood Preserv. Inst., 48 pp. Wash., D.C.

Percival, D. H.
1965. Present status of mechanical fasteners. Forest Prod. J. 15: 42–45.

Powell, A. E.
1968. Notching and timber connection combination in joints between wood members. Amer. Soc. Agr. Eng. Trans. 11: 146–148.

Ramos, A. N.
1960. Spacing of sixpenny and eightpenny wire nails in Douglas-fir multi-nail joints. USDA Forest Serv. Forest Prod. Lab. Rep. 2155, 13 pp.

Scholten, J.A.
1944. Timber-connector joints: their strength and design. USDA Forest Serv. Tech. Bull. 865, 106 pp.

Scholten, J. A.
1962. Effect of nail points on the withdrawal resistance of plain nails. USDA Forest Serv. Forest Prod. Lab. Rep. 1226, 3 pp.

Scholten, J. A.
1965a. Effects of various preservative treatments of field boxes on nail holding. USDA Forest Serv. Res. Pap. FPL–42, 8 pp. Forest Prod. Lab., Madison, Wis.

Scholten, J. A.
1965b. Strength of wood joints made with nails, staples, or screws. USDA Forest Serv. Res. Note FPL–0100, 16 pp. Forest Prod. Lab., Madison, Wis.

Scholten, J. A., and Molander, E. G.
1950. Strength of nailed joints in frame walls. Agr. Eng. 31: 551–555.

Sliker, A.
1969. Creep in nailed wood-metal tension joints. Wood Sci. 3: 23–30.

Smith, W. R.
1961. Building homes to withstand hurricane damage. Forest Prod. J. 11: 176–177.

Southern Building Code Congress.
1968. Senco staples and sen-nails. Comm. Compliance Approval Rep. 6853, 2 pp. Senco Prod., Inc., Cincinnati, Ohio.

Southern Pine Association.
1964. Fastenings for lumber—technical data on southern pine. South. Pine Assoc. Architects Bull. 7, 11 pp.

Southern Pine Association.
1969. How to build storm resistant structures. South. Pine Assoc., 23 pp. New Orleans, La.

Stern, E. G.
1941. Tests on wood joints with metal connectors. Civil Eng. 11: 298–301.

Stern, E. G.
1950a. Holding power of clinched nails. Contract. Dig. (November), 5 pp.

Stern, E. G.
1950b. Improved nails, their driving resistance, withdrawal resistance, and lateral load - carrying capacity. Amer. Soc. Mech. Eng. Pap. 49–A–115, 14 pp.

Stern, E. G.
1950c. Nails in end-grain lumber. Timber News 58(2138): 490–492.

Stern, E. G.
1951a. Efficiency of flooring nails. Va. Polytech. Inst. Bull. 44(4), Part B, 8 pp.

Stern, E. G.
1951b. Nail tests show effectiveness of straight over slant driving. Wooden Box and Crate 13(4): 14–17, 29–30.

Stern, E. G.
1951c. Nails and screws in wood assembly and construction. Va. Polytech. Inst. Wood Res. Lab. Bull. 3, 30 pp.

Stern, E. G.
1951d. The nail, an indispensable fastener. Va. Polytech. Inst. Wood Res. Lab. Bull. 4, 16 pp.

Stern, E. G.
1952. Immediate vs. delayed holding power of nails. Va. Polytech. Inst. Wood Res. Lab. Bull. 8, 12 pp.

Stern, E. G.
1953.   Strength of auto-nailer assembled skids of green and dry lumber. Va. Polytech. Inst. Wood Res. Lab. Bull. 12, 23 pp.

Stern, E. G.
1954a. Effectiveness of flooring nails versus toothed fastener. Va. Polytech. Inst. Wood Res. Lab. Bull. 16, 8 pp.

Stern, E. G.
1954b. Effectiveness of nails versus staples for fastening underlayment. Va. Polytech. Inst. Wood Res. Lab. Bull. 13, 5 pp.

Stern, E. G.
1955.   Effectiveness of nails versus staples for fastening insulating sheathing. Va. Polytech. Inst. Wood Res. Lab. Bull. 19, 6 pp.

Stern, E. G.
1956a. Nail popping, its causes and prevention. Va. Polytech. Inst. Wood Res. Lab. Bull. 24, 12 pp.

Stern, E. G.
1956b. Better construction with threaded nails. Va. Polytech. Inst. Wood Res. Lab. Bull. 25, 16 pp.

Stern, E. G.
1956c. Nails and spikes in creosote-pressure-treated southern pine poles and timbers. Va. Polytech. Inst. Wood Res. Lab. Bull. 26, 19 pp.

Stern, E. G.
1956d. Plain-shank vs. fluted vs. threaded nails. Va. Polytech. Inst. Wood Res. Lab. Bull. 27, 23 pp.

Stern, E. G.
1965b. Nailing of jamb assemblies of wood window frames: casing, blind stop, and jamb. Va. Polytech. Inst. Wood Res. Lab. Bull. 28, 19 pp.

Stern, E. G.
1957a. Wood, plywood or steel gusset plates for nailed trussed rafters. Va. Polytech. Inst. Wood Res. Lab. Bull. 29, 11 pp.

Stern, E. G.
1957b. Holding power of large nails and spikes in dry southern pine. Va. Polytech. Inst. Wood Res. Lab. Bull. 30, 11 pp.

Stern, E. G.
1957c. Nailing of subflooring with supplement on effectiveness of square barbed versus threaded bronze nails in redwood. Va. Polytech. Inst. Wood Res. Lab. Bull. 31, 11 pp.

Stern, E. G.
1958.   Nailing of plywood sheathing with "Hi-load" nails. Va. Polytech. Inst. Wood Res. Lab. Bull. 35, 15 pp.

Stern, E. G.
1959a. Fasteners for better buildings and storm-proofing methods that save lives. 67 pp. Chicago: Practical Builder.

Stern, E. G.
1959b. What's new in pallet fasteners. Va. Polytech. Inst. Wood Res. Lab. Bull. 37, 3 pp.

Stern, E. G.
1959c. Better utilization of wood through assembly with improved fasteners. Va. Polytech. Inst. Wood Res. Lab. Bull. 38 rev., 41 pp.

Stern, E. G.
1959d. Nailed trussed rafters with hardboard gusset plates. Va. Polytech. Inst. Wood Res. Lab. Bull. 40, 15 pp.

Stern, E. G.
1961a. Nailing of sheet metal roofing and siding with washered roofing nails. Va. Polytech. Inst. Wood Res. Lab. Bull. 42, 36 pp.

Stern, E. G.
1961b. Fastening of truss plates with "screwtite hi-load" nails. Va. Polytech. Inst. Wood Res. Lab. Bull. 43, 12 pp.

Stern, E. G.
1961c. Fastening of plywood with "Screwtite hi-load" nails. Va. Polytech. Inst. Wood Res. Lab. Bull. 44, 23 pp.

Stern, E. G.
1962a. Effectiveness of 16-gauge staples vs. helically threaded pallet nails in the fastening of pallet deckboard to pallet stringer. Va. Polytech. Inst. Wood Res. Lab. Bull. 47, 7 pp.

Stern, E. G.
1962b. Building component assembly with 5¼" helically fluted auto nails. Va. Polytech. Inst. Wood Res. Lab. Bull. 48, 16 pp.

Stern, E. G.
1964a. Significance of the special nail in residential frame construction. Wire and Wire Prod. 39: 384–399, 429–431.

Stern, E. G.
1964b. Fastening of steel truss plates with threaded nails. Va. Polytech. Inst. Wood Res. Lab. Bull. 54, 16 pp.

Stern, E. G.
1964c. Load transmission by nails in double shear. Va. Polytech. Inst. Wood Res. Lab. Bull. 55, 11 pp.

Stern, E. G.
1965a. Pallets assembled with 10-gauge automatic nails. Forest Prod. J. 15: 242–246.

Stern, E. G.
1965b. The new concept of furniture skids. Va. Polytech. Inst. Wood Res. Lab. Bull. 56, 11 pp.

Stern, E. G.
1965c. Effectiveness of T-beams. Va. Polytech. Inst. Wood Res. Lab. Bull. 57, 15 pp.

Stern, E. G.
1966. Pallet nails in 1965. Va. Polytech. Inst. Wood Res. Lab. Bull. 58, 7 pp.

Stern, E. G.
1967a. Nails—definitions and sizes, a handbook for nail users. Va. Polytech. Inst. Wood Res. Lab. Bull. 61, 51 pp.

Stern, E. G.
1967b. Effects of bradding and clinching of points of plain-shank and helically threaded nails. Va. Polytech. Inst. Wood Res. Lab. Bull. 64, 6 pp.

Stern, E. G.
1968a. Slender nails are the answer. Automation in Housing 5(2): 32.

Stern, E. G.
1968b. Plastic-coated nails, a study of their effectiveness. Va. Polytech Inst. Wood Res. Lab. Bull. 65, 20 pp.

Stern, E. G.
1968c. Effects of angular driving of nails on automatic clinching of diamond points. Va. Polytech. Inst. Wood Res. Lab. Bull. 66, 15 pp.

Stern, E. G.
1968d. Auto-nailed southern-pine pallets. Va. Polytech. Inst. Wood Res. Lab. Bull. 77, 23 pp.

Stern, E. G.
1969a. Hurricane Camille—a furious monitor to builders and rebuilders. Forest Prod. J. 19(12): 18–20.

Stern, E. G.
1969b. Up-grading of pallets by assembly with hardened-steel nails. Va. Polytech. Inst. Wood Res. Lab. Bull. 83, 31 pp.

Stern, E. G.
1969c. Mechanical fastening of southern pine—a review. Va. Polytech. Inst. Wood Res. Lab. Bull. 87, 98 pp.

Stern, E. G.
1970a. Importance of light-building anchorage. The Constr. Specifier 23(2): 29–33.

Stern, E. G.
1970b. Quality control for 2½" 15-gage Senco staples. Va. Polytech. Inst. Wood Res. and Wood Constr. Lab. Bull. 86, 26 pp.

Stern, E. G.
1970c. Low-profile versus conventional single-face pallets. Va. Polytech. Inst. Wood Res. Lab. Bull. 88, 15 pp.

Stern, E. G.
1970d. Effectiveness of Senco nails. Va. Polytech. Inst. Wood Res. Lab. Bull. 91, 43 pp.

Stern, E. G.
1970e. Lateral load transmission by 4½" 15-gage Senco nails. Va. Polytech. Inst. Wood Res. Lab. Bull. 92, 10 pp.

Stern, E. G.
1970f. Effectiveness of certain auto-nailed cleated-plywood container panels. Va. Polytech. Inst. Wood Res. Lab. Bull. 95, 10 pp.

Stern, E. G.
1970g. Effectiveness of 2½", 3", 3¼", and 3½" Senco nails. Va. Polytech. Inst. Wood Res. Lab. Bull. 96, 19 pp.

Stern, E. G.
1971. Effectiveness of 2½" fasteners in deckboard-stringer joints for permanent warehouse pallets. Va. Polytech. Inst. Wood Res. Lab. Bull. 99, 11 pp.

Stern, E. G., and Pletta, D. H.
1967. All-nailed lumber truss of 60 to 80-ft. span. Va. Polytech. Inst. Wood Res. Lab. Bull. 63, 43 pp.

Stern, E. G., and Stoneburner, P. W.
1952. Design of nailed structures. Va. Polytech. Inst. Eng. Exp. Sta. Ser. 81, 67 pp.

Suddarth, S. K.
1969. The engineering design of mechanically fastened trusses—a review. Wood Sci. 1: 193–199.

Timber Engineering Company.
1962. TECO design manual for TECO timber connector construction. TECO Pub. 109, 27 pp. Timber Eng. Co., Wash., D.C.

Timber Engineering Company.
1970. Structural wood fasteners. TECO Pub. 101, 15 pp. Timber Eng. Co., Wash., D.C.

Truss Plate Institute.
1970. Design specifications for light metal plate connected wood trusses. TPI–70, 44 pp. Wash., D.C.: Truss Plate Inst.

USDA Forest Products Laboratory.
1953a. The nailing of wood boxes. USDA Forest Serv. Forest Prod. Lab. Tech. Note B–10 rev., 4 pp.

USDA Forest Products Laboratory.
1953b. Strength of screw fastenings in plywood. USDA Forest Serv. Forest Prod. Lab. Tech. Note 149, 2 pp.

USDA Forest Products Laboratory.
1955. Wood handbook. USDA Agr. Handbook 72, 528 pp.

USDA Forest Products Laboratory.
1956. Bearing strength of wood at angle to the grain. USDA Forest Serv. Forest Prod. Lab. Rep. 1203 rev., 2 pp.

Wilkerson, W. H.
1969. Low-profile pallets. Paper presented at 22nd Annu. Meeting Nat. Wooden Pallet and Container Assoc. 9 pp.

Wilkerson, W. H.
1970. The world is ready for low-profile pallets. Auto-Nailer Co., 29 pp. Atlanta, Ga.

Wilkerson, W. H., Sheppard, D. W., and Stern, E. G.
1968. Auto-nailed pallets. Paper presented at Meeting of Fasteners Comm. Nat. Wooden Pallet and Container Assoc. 25 pp.

Zornig, H. F., and Sherwood, G. E.
1969. Wood structures survive hurricane Camille's winds. USDA Forest Serv. Res. Pap. FPL–123, 16 pp. Forest Prod. Lab., Madison, Wis.

25

Finishing

CONTENTS

25

Finishing

Southern pine wood readily accepts a wide variety of finishes designed for interior use. A few of them are briefly described in the concluding section of this chapter (sec. 25–7).

If unprotected by coatings, southern pine wood, like other woods, is degraded by exposure to light—particularly the ultraviolet component of sunlight (sec. 15–3); and it is susceptible to decay, stain, mildew, and warp. Southern pine wood has unique characteristics, also, which make durable exterior finishes difficult to achieve.

In contrast with the soft pines (e.g., *Pinus strobus* L.) and those western species most favored for exterior siding—notably redwood (*Sequoia sempervirens* (D. Don) Endl.) and western redcedar (*Thuja plicata* Donn)—southern pine has broad bands of dense latewood (fig. 25–1). Coatings tend to adhere poorly to these latewood bands. In addition, since latewood and earlywood shrink at different rates with moisture content changes, checks (fig. 25–2) and raised grain (figs. 19–34, 25–3) may develop.

Also, because southern pine has a higher resin content than many woods, and contains some pitch pockets (fig. 11–7), an occasional piece of lumber may exude sufficient pitch to locally discolor finishes. Because of these problems, this chapter emphasizes exterior finishes.

25–1 NATURALLY WEATHERED SURFACES

It is possible, with appropriate precautions, to circumvent the difficulty of durably coating exposed southern pine by leaving it uncoated to weather naturally. Uncoated southern pine exposed outdoors changes first to a brownish-orange color and ultimately to rather dark gray with little or no sheen, as described in section 15–3.

Checking, which may be severe in flat-grain wood (fig. 25–2), can be minimized by using vertical-grain boards—preferably slow grown and of low density. Because weathered boards cup, warp, and pull at their fastenings, secure nailing is required on unpainted wood (see sec. 24–2). Butt joints in vertical siding should be avoided.

1327

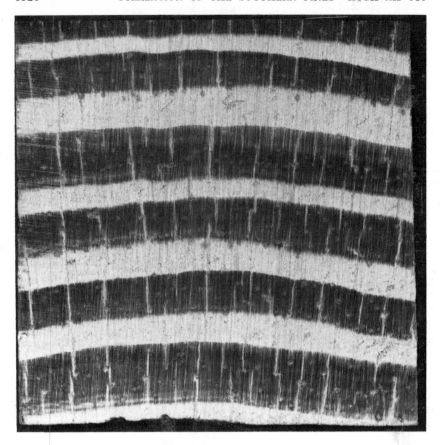

F–521004

Figure 25–1.—One-inch-square transverse section of loblolly pine wood showing broad
bands of dense latewood characteristic of much southern pine lumber.

Chemical changes in the gray layers add to the surface roughness and make it soft and erodable; board thickness may be reduced by as much as 1/4-inch over a period of 100 years. Other problems with naturally weathered southern pine exteriors are concerned with uniformity of color.

To avoid stains from fasteners, nails should be of stainless steel or aluminum. Resin exudation presents a problem in some southern pine. Kiln-drying probably reduces exudation, but occasionally some pieces (perhaps 1 percent) will exude resin in service; objectionable exudation can be minimized by avoiding use of pitchy boards in critical positions.

In the South, and in other warm, humid climates, the color and appearance of weathered southern pine is frequently made blotchy and unsightly by dark-colored spores and mycelia of fungi growing on the surface. In very dry climates and in coastal regions with salt atmospheres, the growth of micro-organisms is inhibited, and wood is more likely to develop an attractive, clean, silvery-gray appearance.

F–521005

Figure 25–2.—Checks in uncoated southern pine wood after extreme exposure in central Louisiana; if coated and given less severe exposure, checks will be less prominent. (Top) Flat-grain, 2- by 6-inch board after 3 months of exterior exposure. (Bottom) Three-ply, ⅜-inch southern pine plywood of rotary-peeled veneer after 6½ years on a 45°, south-facing exposure fence. Specimen is 1 inch wide and 3¼ inches long.

Mold and mildew fungi can be killed and cleaned temporarily from large wood surfaces with the following solution [1] (National Paint, Varnish, and Lacquer Association 1960):

> 3 ounces trisodium phosphate (e.g., Soilax)
> 1 ounce detergent (e.g., Tide)
> 1 quart 5 percent sodium hypochlorite (e.g., Chlorox)
> 3 quarts warm water

---

[1] Mention of a chemical in this chapter or elsewhere in this text does not constitute a recommendation; only those chemicals registered by the U.S. Environmental Protection Agency may be recommended, and then only for uses as prescribed in the registration—and in the manner and at the concentration prescribed. The list of registered chemicals varies from time to time; prospective users, therefore, should get current information on registration status from Pesticides Regulation Division, Environmental Protection Agency, Washington, D.C.

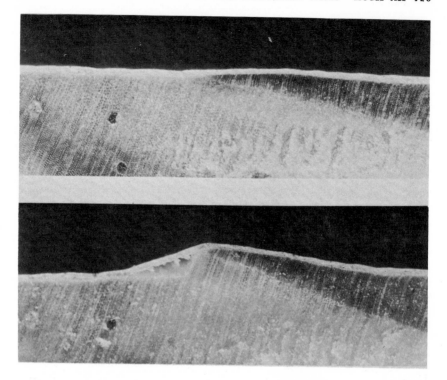

M–121550
Figure 25–3.—(Top) End grain near the pith side of a dry, flat-grain board of southern pine machined with dull planer knives and then coated with one thick coat of TT-P-25 primer, an oil-base paint. (Bottom) Board after wetting; paint film is separated from substrate; surface discontinuity was caused by swelling of crushed earlywood cells underlying the latewood. (Photos from Miniutti 1964.)

The solution should be applied undiluted, and the surface scrubbed with a soft brush. When the surface is clean, it should be rinsed thoroughly with fresh water. Smaller surfaces can be cleaned with a powdered abrasive household cleanser. Subsequent growth of fungi can be controlled by periodic application of a fungicide.

As with other woods, much time is required for new southern pine lumber to achieve the silvery appearance of weathered wood, and the change seldom takes place evenly over an entire wall; boards receiving most exposure to rain and sun weather first. Usually the lowest courses of siding on a south wall become fully grayed sooner than the top courses under eaves or overhangs.

To avoid delay in attaining a weathered appearance, Browne (1952) suggested using rough-sawn rather than planed lumber and initially applying a gray stain—for example, one made from raw umber in oil, white lead in oil, boiled linseed oil, and mineral spirits. The stain need only be applied once; by the time it deteriorates, the wood will have developed its natural gray color.

Alternatively, planed lumber can be used and a bleaching oil applied, i.e., a natural finish of the sealer type containing some pigments to give a gray color. This finish may be renewed occasionally or allowed to wear away, leaving the wood in its natural weathered condition.

The USDA Forest Products Laboratory (1968) suggests that an application of water-repellent preservative (WRP) to otherwise unfinished wood will promote even coloration and will reduce warping, cracking, and water staining. The first application of WRP is usually short lived. A second liberal brush application—made after removal of fungal and mold stains—should last much longer. The treatment is more durable on rough surfaces than on smooth.

WRP solutions are available in most paint and lumber stores; for readers who wish to make their own formulation, however, the USDA Forest Products Laboratory (1968) provided the following formula that will serve effectively as a natural exterior finish for wood or as a pretreatment before painting.

Ingredients	Quantity to make approximately 1 gallon
Penta concentrate 10:1 [1]	1¾ cups
Boiled linseed oil	1½ cups
Paraffin wax	⅟₁₆-pound
Solvent (turpentine, mineral spirits, or paint thinner)	3 quarts

The paraffin wax, melted in the top unit of a double boiler, should be slowly poured into vigorously stirred, room-temperature (60° to 80° F.) solvent. After the paraffin wax and solvent are mixed, add—in order— the linseed oil and penta concentrate and stir until the mixture is uniform. At low or freezing temperatures ingredients in the mixture will separate but can be redissolved if reheated and stirred.

Also, workers at the USDA Forest Products Laboratory found that substantial protection against degradation was provided by certain chromate salts, especially copper and lead chromate, and chromate compounds combined with pentachlorophenate and potassium ferricyanide.[1] These inorganic treatments not only provided excellent resistance to photodegradation but also were effective fungicides. The chromate finishes are still in the experimental stage.

Initial field tests in Wisconsin of two chromate-type formulations indicate that they are not only cheap, but may provide a natural-looking finish that could last 4 years or more (Anonymous 1969). Formulation details have been provided by Black (1969):

Ingredients	Formula A	Formula B
Chromic acid (chromium trioxide), pounds	2.5	2.5
Concentrated ammonium hydroxide (30 percent ammonia), pounds	5.0	5.0
Copper hydroxide or copper oxide, pounds	.25	None
Water, gallons	5.0	5.0

The copper hydroxide in Formula A enhances the fungicidal properties of the treatment. Sodium chromate (approximately 6 pounds) can be substituted for the chromic acid and 1/2 to 1 pound of copper sulfate can be used instead of copper hydroxide.

Mixing may be done in plastic containers or in metal containers with heavy polyethylene bag liners. Covers on the containers will prevent excessive loss of ammonia from the solution and unnecessary exposure to ammonia vapors. To mix the solution, dissolve the chromic acid in the water; then add the ammonium hydroxide slowly while stirring. Add the copper hydroxide and continue periodic stirring for several hours until complete solution is achieved. Skin contact with the chromic acid or mixed solution should be avoided; if contact occurs, wash promptly with soap and water.

A gallon of solution should be applied (by dipping, brushing, or spraying) to each 200 sq. ft. of surface. Since its effectiveness depends on penetration, the solution should not be applied to previously painted or sealed surfaces. Rough-sawn and weathered surfaces, which are highly absorptive, are ideal for treating. Wetting the wood surface with water 1/2 to 2 hours before application will improve penetration of the chemicals (Black 1969).

25–2 STAINS

A properly formulated stain for southern pine has low cost of initial application, good color retention, and good durability on both rough and smooth exterior surfaces. Applied to smooth surfaces, service life should be about 3 years, and on rough surfaces up to 8 or 10 years. A stain finish, when eroded away with time, is easily renewed.

Because stain penetrates and does not form a coating that can fail by cracking and peeling, it is effective on surfaces where moisture problems cause early paint failures. Generally, stain finishes have less hiding power than paints, i.e., less pigment content, so that some of the wood grain shows through—an effect particularly pleasing to the eye on rough-sawn and stained southern pine.

USDA FOREST PRODUCTS LABORATORY STAIN

The USDA Forest Products Laboratory (1970a) has developed a modified semitransparent oil-base penetrating stain formulated particularly for use on southern pine used in climates where protection against discoloration by mildew is an important requirement.

Ingredients.—The ingredients to make approximately 5 gallons of this stain are as follows:

Material (and usual source)	Quantity
Paraffin wax (grocery store)	1/2-pound
Zinc stearate (drug store)	2 ounces
Turpentine, mineral spirits or paint thinner (paint store)	2½ to 3 gallons
Boiled linseed oil (paint store)	1 gallon
Penta concentrate 10:1 (mail order houses)	1 gallon
Tinting colors (paint store)	1 to 2 quarts

Zinc stearate, which helps keep pigments in suspension during use and prevents them from caking during storage, can be deleted if the stain is stirred frequently and used soon after mixing. "Penta," an abbreviation for pentachlorophenol, is added to protect from mildew; when used in the amount specified, a 5-gallon batch of finish contains about 3.8 pounds of pentachlorophenol.[1]

Tinting colors.—By varying ratios of tinting colors in the above formulation, various hues can be obtained. Colors of high-quality, iron-oxide pigments are known to possess good durability; other colors may prove less durable. Color durability is also related to the amount of pigment applied to the surface; doubling the amount of pigment in the formula will improve the durability but will make the finish less transparent and the color more intense. Tinting colors (also termed colors-in-oil at artist supply stores), obtainable at paint stores, will give stain colorations as follows:

Stain color	Tinting colors required
Cedar	1 pint burnt sienna, 1 pint raw umber
Light redwood	2 pints burnt sienna
Green gold	1 pint chromium oxide, 1pint raw sienna
Tan (burnished gold)	1 quart raw sienna, 3 fluid ounces burnt umber
Chocolate brown	1 quart burnt umber
Forest green	1 quart medium chrome green
Fruit wood brown	1 pint raw sienna, 1 pint raw umber, 0.5 pint burnt sienna
Smoky gray	1 quart white oil-base house paint, 6 fluid ounces raw umber, 3 fluid ounces lampblack

Mixing.—To mix the stain, the paraffin wax is first melted in a container heated by hot water, i.e., a double boiler. The melted paraffin is then slowly poured into the paint thinner (or other solvent) while the mixture is stirred vigorously to insure complete solution. Because the mixture is volatile and flammable, it is safest to prepare it outdoors where the solution or its vapors will not be exposed to flame or sparks.

After the paraffin and paint thinner are mixed, the zinc stearate, boiled linseed oil, penta concentrate, and tinting colors are added and the mixture stirred until uniform. Preferred temperature for mixing is 70° to 80° F.; at lower temperatures, the ingredients are less soluble.

Application.—This finish may be applied by brush or spray. In brush applications, lap marks can be avoided if the stain is brushed with the grain for the full length of each board or course without stopping. Uneven penetration of the stain can be minimized if stain is applied to walls while they are shaded rather than sunlit; best success results from following the sun around the structure to be painted. The stain should not come into excessive contact with the skin or be inhaled while spraying. It may also injure shrubbery and other vegetation.

Smoothly planed surfaces will absorb only one coat.

Absorptive rough-sawn or weathered surfaces can be finished with a two-coat system. The second coat must be applied soon after the first and before the first has dried. Stain which has not penetrated after 1 hour should be wiped from the surface with a rough cloth. Failure to do so will result in a shiny or glossy area which will be unsightly. To reduce fire hazard, the wiping rags should be disposed of promptly.

Refinishing.—After a previous application of the USDA Forest Products Laboratory stain has eroded away, it is advisable, before refinishing, to remove dirt by sanding the surface lightly with abrasive paper or steel wool. When refinishing, the stain may penetrate better if thinned with not more than 1 quart of mineral spirits per gallon of stain.

Limitations.—The USDA Forest Products Laboratory stain finish dries rather slowly; a day of good drying weather is generally required. The wax in the finish may interfere with subsequent painting, although tests have demonstrated that it can be painted over with house paints after as little exposure to the weather as 1 year. Where the stain finish has been protected from the weather, as under an overhang, it should be wiped well with a paint thinner or some other wax solvent before painting.

Availability.—For the convenience of those users not desiring to formulate their own stain, the USDA Forest Products Laboratory in Madison, Wis., maintains a list of manufacturers who make and sell this stain.

DESIGN CONSIDERATIONS FOR STAINED SIDING

Southern pine with stained finish is rather widely used as siding for dwellings and other buildings. While sometimes used dressed, as horizontal siding, or as vertical boards and battens, in its most common applications rough-sawn surfaces are exposed. Its success in all such outdoor exposures requires suitable design and attachment of the siding.

Patterns.—Arrangement of board and batten, and board on board vertical siding, usually installed with rough surface exposed, is shown in figure 25–4AB. Vertical siding, if applied over wood sheathing backed up by horizontal nailing girts on 24-inch centers, will have good anchorage for nails. Adequate overlap and secure nailing of battens or outside boards are essential.

Siding patterns suitable for either vertical or horizontal installation (25–4CD) may be dressed on all sides or the exposed face may be left rough.

For vertical arrangements, tongue and groove patterns can also be employed if suitably designed. McMillin (1969) obtained good results with southern pine vertical siding manufactured in lengths from 10 to 24 feet for application without butt joints and specified as follows (fig. 25–5):

"One- by 6-inch, bandsawn, B and better, kiln-dried southern pine with rough face and edge-V on bark side and 3/8-inch center match tongue and groove. Face width 5-1/8 inches; thicknessed on back only (hit and miss) to 7/8-inch. Back side with two grooves 1/4-inch deep by 1/4-inch wide on third points."

These specifications differ slightly from those for standard tongue and

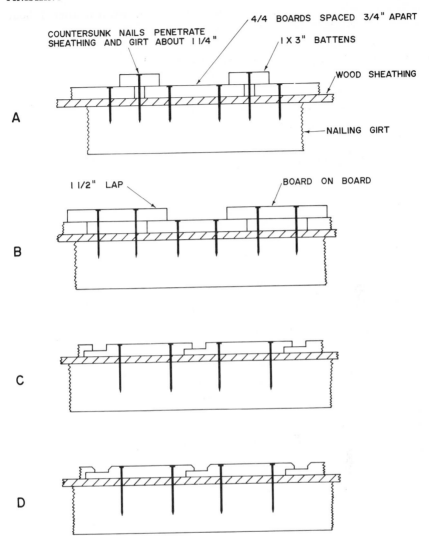

Figure 25-4.—Patterns for stained southern pine siding. (A) Board and batten vertical siding. (B) Board on board vertical siding. (C,D) Lap patterns, usually installed horizontally.

groove siding. Of particular importance is the longer tongue and groove, the 7/8-inch thickness, and the grooves in the back to minimize cupping. The 6-inch width is sufficiently narrow to reduce width shrinkage to acceptable limits. Boards should be milled so that the rough surface for exposure is that which was nearest the bark in the tree; the pith side should carry the anti-cupping grooves.

Moisture content.—Tongue and groove or lap-jointed siding should be applied at a moisture content equal to that which it will attain in service; this will insure that the joint will not be overly exposed through shrinkage.

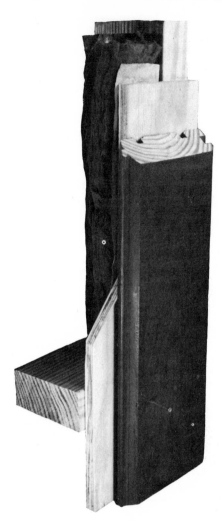

F–521006
Figure 25–5.—Application system and pattern found suitable for stained, tongue-and-groove, vertical southern pine siding. Boards are ⅞-inch thick, rough sawn on exposed surface, and 6 inches in nominal width with ⅜-inch-long, center-match tongue. Grooves machined in back minimize cupping. Color-matched, stainless steel, helically threaded nails are 2⅛ inches long. (Photo after description by McMillin 1969.)

Experience in central Louisiana indicates that moisture content at application should be close to 10 percent. The stained, rough-sawn southern pine cut to the tongue and groove pattern described by McMillin (1969) was equilibrated to 9-percent moisture content before application. The average gap between boards never exceeded 0.04 inch during the driest months (widest gaps were nearly 0.2 inch), nor did buckling occur during humid periods.

Application of heavily pigmented stains.—Formulations and application methods other than those developed by the USDA Forest Products Laboratory, as previously described, may also give acceptable service. McMillin (1969) observed good performance of a stain system applied as follows. Boards milled to the pattern previously described and equilibrated to 9-

percent moisture content were first dipped for 3 minutes in a water-repellent solution containing pentachlorophenol [1] (Woodlife) and allowed to dry for about 24 hours. They were then dipped in a dark russet-colored, oil-base stain that was heavily pigmented and contained a fungicide. (The stain was manufactured by Olympic Stained Products Company.) After dipping, the boards were placed on edge and allowed to dry for 24 hours. They were then placed on stickers and again equilibrated to 9-percent moisture content before installation. A second coat was brushed on after installation.

After 5 years of severe exposure in central Louisiana, these rough-sawn, stained boards suffered some loss in color but were still attractive in appearance. Surface checking was moderate, but not objectionable. There was no evidence of mold, stain, or decay. Where rain-splashed, the lower couple of feet of the 22-foot-high walls were faded somewhat more than the upper portions. Occasional resin exudation was evident, but not unsightly.

Fastening.—To be successful, stained, rough-sawn, southern pine siding must not only be of the proper pattern, at the right moisture content when applied, and finished with a durable stain correctly applied—it must also be securely fastened.

In the successful system described by McMillin (1969), the siding was applied vertically over 3/8-inch southern pine plywood sheathing. It was used full length, i.e., without butt joints. It was fastened (fig. 25–5) to horizontal girts placed on 2-foot centers, each board being fixed to each girt with three nails. Nails were of stainless steel, 2-1/8-inches long, annularly grooved, and with blunt points. With this attachment system there was no evidence of nail withdrawal after 5 years, no unsightly distortion of boards, no open joints, and no stains caused by fastener corrosion.

Other nailing patterns are shown in figure 25–4. For use in the South, nails should be extremely corrosion resistant; stainless steel and aluminum nails serve well. If first coated to match the siding color, nails will be inconspicuous when flush-driven. Stainless steel nails, if not coated, can be countersunk and filled with matching pigmented putty.

25–3 PAINTS

Southern pine, notable for its many excellent properties as a building material, has notoriously poor exterior performance when painted. New systems developed by the paint industry, which are better suited to wood of the southern pines, combined with good design and some care in lumber selection, can go far toward solution of painting problems with these species. Durability of paint depends on a complex interaction involving wood surface, paint formulation, application technique, and service conditions. Some of these interactions are briefly discussed in the following text.

TOPOGRAPHY OF WOOD SURFACES

Surfaced southern pine, even if knot free, displays considerable variation in surface topography. The variations, which are mostly attributable to method of surfacing, cell type, and duration of exposure, have been illustrated by Zicherman.[2] Microtomed surfaces proved to be smoother than planed surfaces (fig. 25–6); pine sanded after planing had a smooth but cluttered surface (fig. 25–7). Transwall (i.e., across-wall) severance in earlywood and intrawall (i.e., within-wall) failure in latewood is evident in figures 25–6 and 25–7, and is further apparent from the pits shown in figure 25–8.

Earlywood topography promotes formation of a deep wood-coating interface; in earlywood, lumens are typically open, and U-shaped surfaces are usually exposed. In latewood, however, smooth surfaces resulting from intrawall failures are typical; on such topography a deep wood-coating interface is not readily attainable.

Surface topography is also modified by exposure to the weather (see sec. 15–3). Data specific to southern pine has been provided by Zicherman,[2] who illustrated surface degradation of uncoated loblolly pine exposed to ultraviolet radiation. Such degradation probably diminishes the likelihood of obtaining a good paint-to-wood bond. In Zicherman's experiment, he cycled specimens under an ultraviolet source for 20 hours at 170° F., followed by a 4-hour soak at room temperature in tap water. Some specimens were also exposed continuously to the ultraviolet source without cyclic wetting.

After 58 hours of ultraviolet treatment, diagonal checks developed in the cell walls of soaked specimens. In unsoaked specimens, however, about 500 hours of exposure to ultraviolet treatment were required to develop visible checks in earlywood cell walls, and little deterioration was visible in latewood at that time. After 1,250 hours of dry ultraviolet exposure, pit structures were deteriorated (fig. 25–9 Top); 1,500 hours of ultraviolet exposure combined with water soaking caused substantial degradation and wall checks became clearly visible (fig. 29–9 Bottom). Zicherman concluded that changes in surface topography caused by exposure to ultraviolet radiation are accelerated if wood is wetted at intervals.

BASIC COATING TECHNOLOGY [3]

Paints for application on wood consist of pigment particles in a binder. The binder may itself serve as a carrier for the pigment, or it may be dissolved or dispersed in a separate volatile carrier. Paint coatings should

---

[2] Zicherman, J. B. The localization of coating components within the ultrastructure of wood by use of a micro-incineration technique. Final Report FS–SO–3201–2.22. USDA Forest Serv. Southern Forest Exp. Sta., dated March 3, 1971.

[3] The text under this heading is condensed, with some revisions, from Zicherman (1969) by permission of J. B. Zicherman and the Forest Products Research Society.

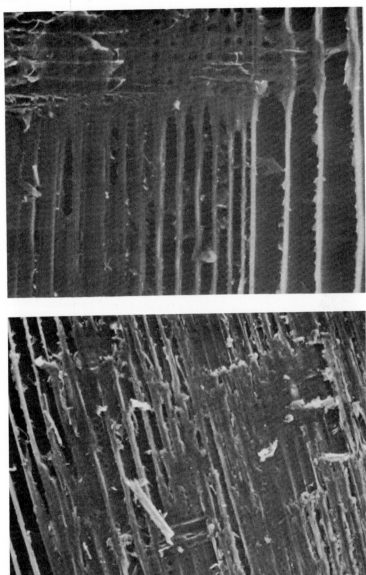

Figure 25–6.—Radial sections cut on loblolly pine. (Top) Microtomed surface. At right is earlywood with transwall failures. Latewood, mostly with intrawall failures, is evident at left. Ray cells are seen in upper portion of figure. 160X. (Bottom) Planed surface. Latewood at right shows intrawall failures and occasional fractures at right angles to grain. Earlywood at left shows transwall failures. 100X. (Photos from Zicherman[2].)

limit passage of water in and out of wood, thus avoiding the high moisture gradients which cause rapid dimensional changes. Pigments provide color and opacity to painted surfaces and a measure of protection from both

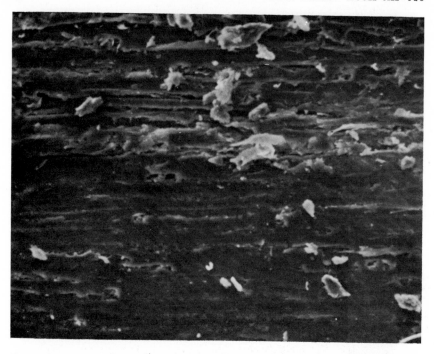

Figure 25–7.—Sanded tangential surface of loblolly pine. In upper portion of figure, earlywood with transwall failures is evident. Lower half shows smoother latewood surface. 120X. (Photo from Zicherman[2].)

mechanical and chemical deterioration. They also absorb ultraviolet radiation, which, if unimpeded, deteriorates wood surfaces. Pigments for coatings may be classified into three types: reactive, extending, and inactive.

Reactive pigments such as leaded zinc oxide and zinc oxide are effective ultraviolet absorbers and offer good mildew protection. Zinc oxide, however, yields a hard surface which may become brittle, resulting in flaking, and/or cracking, of the coating. Leaded pigments form softer films, which are subject to chalking, cracking, and checking. Reactive pigments also may combine with hydrogen sulfide in the air, causing the coating to yellow or darken. Both leaded zinc and zinc oxides will react with organic acids that may be present in the binder or that may develop in curing or film aging. In oil-based paints containing reactive pigments, excess acid groups may form and cause rapid breakdown of the paint film (Nylén and Sunderland 1965). The compatibility of these pigment types with modern emulsion formulations is not yet fully proven. Zinc pigment types are especially important in the South because of their good tint retention and mildew resistance (Werthan 1963).

The **extending pigments** are typified by magnesium silicate and the calcium carbonates. These pigments have a different size distribution than

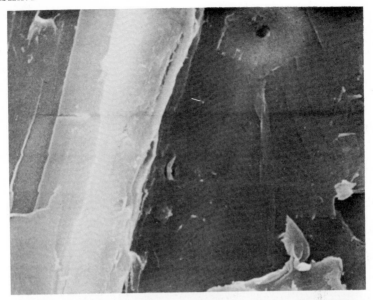

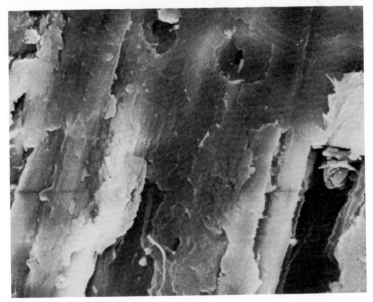

Figure 25-8.—Planed radial surfaces of loblolly pine. (Top) Earlywood showing cut tangential wall of tracheid, at left, and open lumen with pit exposed and border intact. 1,000X. (Bottom) Latewood with intrawall failure evident in upper portion of photo; the pits, with membrane and one border removed, lead through the remaining border into the lumen beyond. 1,000X. (Photos from Zicherman[2].)

the reactive pigments, which may lead to better pigment packing and lower resin requirements.

The **inactive, hiding pigments** come from a variety of materials. Tita-

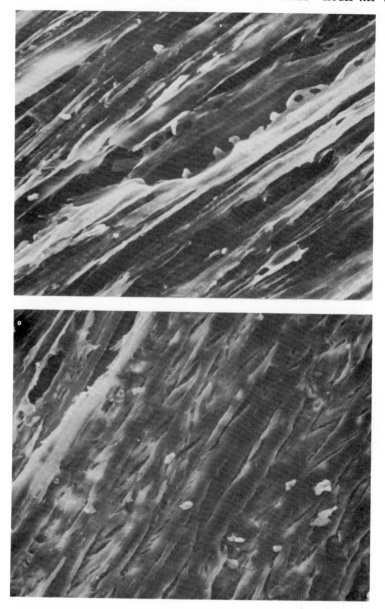

Figure 25–9.—Sanded loblolly pine surfaces after exposure to ultraviolet radiation. (Top) Pit structures deteriorated after 1,250 hours of exposure without water soak. 250X. (Bottom) After 1,500 hours of exposure with intermittent water soak, cell wall checks were clearly visible. 200X. (Photos from Zicherman[2].)

nium dioxide is a member of this group, and is in common use as the prime, white, hiding pigment. Rutile titanium dioxide (nonchalking) and anatase (chalking) can be mixed to give a controlled pigment breakdown, and to yield a good surface for repainting (Nylén and Sunderland 1965).

In a study of southern pine paints in which Rutile titanium dioxide was extended with a variety of extender pigments, Bohlen (1963) concluded that the type of extender pigment is of minor importance in preventing paint problems on southern pine.

With the exception of pigments, the components of the older types of coatings (drying-oil-based solutions and dispersions) and the new types (latex systems, also termed emulsion systems) are quite different. The older paints utilize drying oils (usually modified with alkyd resins) as the binder into which pigment particles are dispersed and most other components are dissolved. Latex paints are emulsions of pigments and polymer resins, usually in water; also alkyd-oil emulsion systems are used.

One of the fundamental problems encountered in the use of **drying-oil-based formulations** is embrittlement of the film. Drying-oil binders are subject to an oxidative embrittlement on aging, yielding limited durability on substrates subject to dimensional change. The drying reaction proceeds with solvent evaporation to a cross-linking stage, which continues and eventually creates an inelastic and brittle film, which may be unable to tolerate the shrinking and swelling typical of southern pine. Aging of drying-oil binders is a photochemical process, variously affected by inclusion of different pigments.

A **latex paint** consists basically of a dispersing medium and nonaqueous droplets, composed of resin. The pigments, thickeners, and wetting agents are found in both phases. Wetting agents or emulsifiers are of great importance because, although present in small concentration, they create a balanced system in which the droplets are evenly and readily dispersed. They also allow the resin to adequately wet the pigment particles, so that they will be tightly held in the film upon drying. To these ingredients, others such as preservatives, antifoamers, and viscosity controlling agents are added (Martens 1964).

In addition to the original **styrene butadiene latex,** the **polyvinyl acetate** and **acrylic** based resins form the bulk of the emulsions presently used in coating applications. **Alkyd-oil** resins are also widely used.

Being prepolymerized, the water-based latexes do not undergo extensive chemical reactions on aging, eliminating this source of deterioration. New formulations of the latexes retain more plasticity than drying-oil-based coatings, making them more compatible with southern pine. In addition, they dry rapidly and eliminate the dangers of flammability and air pollution which result from the use of organic solvents (important factors in their factory use), and are clean and easy to apply (Martens 1966).

Figure 25–10 shows surface and cross section views of a water-based acrylic emulsion applied in a single coat to sanded loblolly pine. In the surface view, pigment particles can be seen. In cross section, the porous nature of the film is evident. Zicherman [2] reported that 1,500 hours of exposure to ultraviolet radiation with intermittent water soak did not cause macroscopic film failures. When coating failures did occur, they

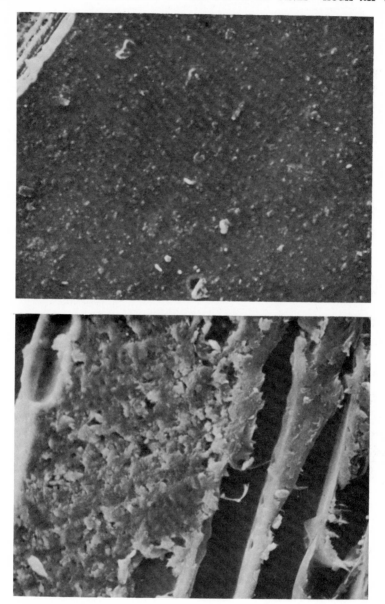

Figure 25–10.—Water-based acrylic emulsion (latex) paint on sanded surface of loblolly pine. (Top) Surface; pigment particles are visible, as is a pinhole, near lower edge. 140X. (Bottom) Latex coating in cross section photographed after 118 hours of exposure to ultraviolet-soak cycle. Porosity of coating is evident. 340X. (Photos from Zicherman[2].)

appeared near the junction of earlywood and latewood. Bonds with latewood failed before bonds with earlywood.

Disadvantages of latex paints include a generally lower solids content than oil-based systems (meaning more coats must be applied to yield a given film thickness), poor adhesion to weathered or chalky surfaces, and poorer penetration of the coating into wood due to the comparatively large size of the emulsion particles (Browne 1959; Allyn 1961; Werthan 1961).

Primers strongly affect paint durability. Certain systems perform poorly when self-primed but satisfactorily when used with a proper primer (Bohlen 1967). Older opinions held that an oil-type primer should be heavily absorbed by the substrate in order to reinforce the surface. This implied the use of a low viscosity system consisting of 60 to 70 percent oil. Newer primers are nonpenetrating and apparently perform best when formulated like the topcoat but with lower solids content (Nylén and Sunderland 1965).

Because water-based primers do not adhere tightly to weathered or chalky painted surfaces, however, penetrating oil-based primers still find wide use. They seem to stabilize a deteriorated surface and create a good base for topcoating (Werthan 1961). Readers desiring additional information on oil- and water-based primers will find the reviews of Pierce and Holsworth (1966) and Bilek et al. (1967) useful.

SELECTION, PREPARATION, AND INSTALLATION OF WOOD

Builders can preclude many—perhaps most—early paint failures by first properly selecting the southern pine wood to be painted and then installing it in such a manner that its moisture content does not vary excessively.

Wood selection and preparation.—Paint failures on southern pine normally begin sooner and proceed more rapidly on flat-sawn than on quarter-sawn (vertical-grain) lumber (Thompson 1968, p. 26). If flat-sawn boards cannot be avoided, loosened grain (fig. 19–34) and resulting paint failures can be reduced if the side that, in the tree, was nearest the bark is exposed to the weather. Most paint technologists agree that slow-grown wood of low specific gravity holds paint better than fast-grown wood of high density. Best results are obtained if the lumber is well manufactured so that machining defects of raised, chipped, and fuzzy grain are absent (fig. 19–34).

Prior to application, siding should be kept clean, and bundled face to face to avoid unnecessary exposure of surfaces to air and sunlight. Bonds between wood and the initial coat of a paint system are strongest if the coat is applied soon after wood is machined.

Moisture content.—Since latewood of southern pine shrinks and swells more than earlywood, the paint-wood bond and the film may be overstressed if moisture content of the wood changes after the paint is applied. Therefore, siding should be installed and painted at a moisture content near that which it will attain in service—generally close to 10 percent. When paint is applied to wood at a moisture content slightly higher than that which it will attain in service, it has been suggested that shrinkage of the wood in service will induce compression stresses in the coating that will reduce subsequent cracking failures should the wood temporarily re-swell.

Following is a highly condensed discussion of the complex moisture-caused problems of blistering, peeling, and cracking; readers desiring additional details are referred to the source publication (USDA Forest Products Laboratory 1970b).

If, subsequent to painting, moisture enters and excessively wets wood behind paint films, water-filled blisters may occur that later dry out and collapse; in this type of paint failure, the film separates at the wood-paint interface.

Peeling is also a moisture-related type of paint failure. It is particularly prevalent with porous paint systems so installed that water is held on the surface for a sufficient time to penetrate into the layers of paint to cause separation at the wood interface or in a plane of weakness between layers of paint. Some peeling failures—such as those observed in gable ends of heated buildings—may be caused by moisture coming from within the building.

Cracking failure, followed by peeling at the ends of boards and on the lower courses of horizontal siding indicates that rain and dew may be penetrating through the paint.

To combat moisture-related paint failures, it is desirable to minimize the amount of water coming into contact with the paint film from the outside. Wide roof overhangs limit rain splash against outside walls—and equally important—limit the amount of sunlight impinging on walls. If leaks in the roof, gutters, flashings, or casements allow outside water to enter walls, early paint failure will result.

Water from inside the building is equally damaging. It may come from leaks in plumbing, overflow of sinks and bathtubs, or shower spray on improperly sealed bathroom walls. Frequently it comes from high humidity within buildings. If construction is such that humid air condenses on the interior surface of siding boards, the boards become wet and the paint may blister. In addition to moisture admitted to the air by respiration of occupants, common sources of humidity in houses include water vapor from cooking, dishwashing, laundering, and bathing. Other sources are humidifiers and unvented gas heaters and clothes dryers. Crawl spaces also contribute moisture that moves in through floors and out through walls.

Assuming that siding temperatures are generally lower than interior temperatures and that humidity in the interior is high, then condensation problems can be reduced by placing a vapor barrier in the warm interior walls, by increasing insulation and ventilation in the attic, and by reducing interior humidity by shutting off humidifiers, and venting gas heaters, clothes dryers, and kitchen and bath exhaust fans to the outside. A vapor-proof ground cover applied in crawl spaces will also cut down on moisture moving to the interior.

PAINT SYSTEMS

While it would be convenient to recommend a specific formulation as best, knowledge is insufficient at this time; moreover, paint technology is changing rapidly. The paragraphs that follow, therefore, are in the nature of general observations, with findings of a few responsible sources given some emphasis. Readers desiring a more complete review of paint technology for southern pine will find the citations in this chapter and in Zicherman (1969) useful in obtaining an introduction to the subject.

The first step in painting southern pine for exterior exposure should be application of a water-repellent preservative to the bare wood as a protection against entrance of rain and heavy dew (USDA Forest Products Laboratory 1966c, 1968). The solutions are available from most paint and building supply dealers. (See sec. 25–1 for a formulation.[1]) For new construction, pretreated lumber can be purchased from the manufacturer; cut ends should be re-treated by brush application of the solution. It is especially important that window and sash trim be treated. If not factory treated, the lumber can be brush treated on the job. The solution should be brushed thoroughly into butt and lap joints. At least two warm, sunny days are required for adequate drying of the water repellent before application of a prime coat of paint.

Paint technologists agree that a three-coat system (prime coat of paint followed by two additional coats of paint) is substantially superior to a prime coat followed by a single topcoat (USDA Forest Products Laboratory 1966c; Thompson 1968, p. 20).

The USDA Forest Products Laboratory (1966c) recommends that the prime coat be a linseed oil-base paint with pigments that do not contain zinc oxide; Federal Specification TTP–25a describes such a primer. The prime coat should not permit capillary flow of dew and rain through the film. The Laboratory recommends that primer coat thickness be 1.5 to 2 mils; a gallon of primer, if at least 85 percent solids by weight, should cover 400 to 450 sq. ft. per gallon.

For finish coats over primer, the USDA Forest Products Laboratory (1966c) recommends use of high-quality paint; the paint can contain zinc oxide pigment and can be of the linseed oil, alkyd, or latex type. A total of three coats (primer and two topcoats) should result in a thickness of 4-1/2 to 5 mils. Topcoats should be applied within 2 weeks after the primer. Wood should not be primed in the fall with topcoats delayed until spring; it is better to treat with water-repellent preservative and delay all painting until spring. Incidence of temperature blisters in oil-base paint films can be reduced if paint is never applied to a cool surface that will be heated by the sun in a few hours. Wrinkling and flatting of oil-base paint and watermarks on latex paints can be reduced if paint is not applied in the evenings of cool spring and fall days when heavy dews frequently form. Best procedure calls for following the sun around the house.

Thompson (1968) evaluated several paint systems for southern pine and observed that reasonably good appearance after 2 years of exposure was obtained with a few of them. His publication gives details on each system.

Readers interested in paint formulation details will find publications by

Bohlen (1963, 1967) useful. He concluded from more than 5 years of exterior exposure testing that latex paints, either self-primed or applied over a primer, can be formulated to perform better on southern pine than conventional oil-based systems. Primers significantly affected coating durability; acrylic, polyvinyl acetate, and oil types were satisfactory. In general, however, latex systems without an oil-base primer gave best results and showed greatest mildew resistance. The final report includes a sample formulation, based on an acrylic latex, which should perform well (Bohlen 1967).

Another self-priming latex system (all acrylic) has been extensively tested on southern pine in the South and has demonstrated superior adhesion, crack and blister resistance, and film flexibility (Allyn 1966). The Southern Wood Products Association has also reported good results with a self-primed latex (acrylic) system.

Additional systems evaluated on southern pine have been reported by Antlfinger (1967), who provided formulations and test data on vinyl-chloride-acrylic polymers, and Beardsley and Kennedy (1967) who gave formulations and performance data on exterior paints based on a vinyl-acetate-ethylene emulsion vehicle.

REPAINTING

A repaint job is only as good as the old paint beneath it. Glossy and unweathered surfaces should be washed or roughened well with steel wool to remove contaminants. Failure to do this is a common cause of intercoat peeling. Repainting should be delayed until the old paint has weathered so that it no longer protects the wood. Excessive chalk and old paint should be removed with steel wool. Where paint is peeling and wood surfaces are exposed, loose paint should be removed from adjacent areas and the exposed spot treated with water-repellent preservative and primed. On chalky surfaces, certain latex paints reportedly give best durability when applied over an oil-base primer (Bohlen 1963, 1967).

25–4 CLEAR FINISHES

In spite of substantial research efforts to improve performance, clear film-forming exterior finishes are not recommended for southern pine. The deleterious effect of sunlight, water, and atmosphere causes their early failure.

Readers desiring information pertinent to clear exterior finishes will find the following references useful: Browne and Simonson (1957); Browne (1960); California Redwood Association (1962); Miniutti (1964, 1967, 1969); Kalnins et al. (1966); Tarkow et al. (1966); USDA Forest Products Laboratory (1966ab); Ashton (1967); Golden Gate Society for Coatings Technology (1967); Philadelphia Society for Paint Technology (1967); Rothstein (1967); Schneider and Côté (1967); Côté and Robinson (1968); Heebink (1970); Zicherman.[2]

Clear finishes for interior exposure are discussed in section 25–7.

25–5 PAINTABLE OVERLAYS FOR LUMBER

Because many of the difficulties in painting southern pine stem from differential shrinkage in earlywood and latewood and from poor paint adhesion to latewood, it seems a reasonable approach to overlay boards with a sheet designed to provide a uniform, stable substrate for paint. Heebink (1961) and Fleischer and Heebink (1964) summarized the results of many years of research at the USDA Forest Products Laboratory to determine which overlays are best adapted for use on lumber, how best to attach the overlays, and paintability of overlaid lumber.

OVERLAY MATERIAL

They found that southern pine overlaid on one side would cup as the wood changed moisture content unless the overlay material closely matched the shrinkage properties of wood (fig. 25–11). Among many sheet materials studied, two appeared to satisfy this requirement.

One was **vulcanized fiber,** an unsized, unloaded paper that has been run through a solution of zinc chloride and then washed. They found that a 0.005-inch-thick sheet of this material made from rag furnish had a dimensional movement across the machine direction (i.e., direction the

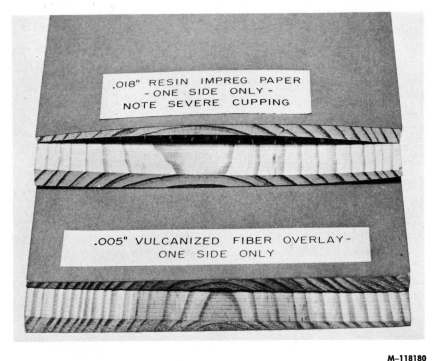

M–118180

Figure 25–11.—Cupping in southern pine bevel siding overlaid on one side only with resin-impregnated paper compared to similar siding overlaid with vulcanized fiber. (Photo from Heebink 1961.)

paper flowed through the paper forming machine) of about 10 percent when moistened from ovendry to soaked.

Another suitable material was **parchmentized paper,** i.e., paper treated in a sulfuric acid bath to give it toughness and water, weather, and abrasion resistance. Parchmentized paper shrinks even more than vulcanized fiber in the cross machine direction. Both materials made successful overlays if applied so that the machine direction of the overlay sheet paralleled grain direction of the board.

Neither vulcanized fiber nor parchmentized paper has proven entirely satisfactory as a paintable overlay for southern pine lumber, however. Another overlay material—a **resin-impregnated cellulose-fiber sheet—** continues to show promise. Cooper and Barham (1971) have reported favorably on use of such a kraft paper sheet 0.015 to 0.020 inch thick; the sheet contained about 20 percent of water-dispersible phenolic resin added at the beater and fully cured before bonding to the lumber.

From accelerated weathering tests of various resin-impregnated paper overlays applied to Douglas-fir (*Pseudotsuga menziesii* (Mirb.) Franco) plywood, Fahey and Pierce (1971) concluded that phenolic-impregnated paper overlays resist weathering better than overlays impregnated with urea or melamine. Treatments of 30 percent phenolic resin were noticeably more effective than treatments of 20 and 10 percent. Phenolic paper overlays tended to crumble gradually during accelerated weathering. Urea and melamine paper overlays developed fractures and checks which ultimately resulted in delamination or peeling of the paper. Performance was comparable for overlay papers made from spruce (*Picea* sp.) kraft and spruce sulfite pulps. Ammonimum chromate, an ultraviolet absorber, applied to the surface of the paper overlays greatly improved resistance to accelerated weathering (Fahey and Pierce 1971).

BOND BETWEEN OVERLAY AND WOOD

In Heebink's (1961) work with overlaid southern pine siding, he bonded vulcanized fiber to boards by cold pressing them for a minimum period of 4 hours at 200 p.s.i., after first spreading the wood surface only with an acid-catalyzed phenol-resin adhesive. He described the spread as "normal." Advantages of this adhesive include exterior durability, attractive light amber color, relatively low cost, and ability to cure at room temperature in a simple press. Cooper and Barham (1971) used a similar cold-setting adhesive to glue vulcanized fiber and resin-impregnated paper overlays to solid wood siding; they used about 33 pounds of glue per thousand square feet of single glueline and a press time of at least 7 hours at 150 p.s.i.

The several-hour press time required is a major deterrent to commercial application of the process. Since 4/4 southern pine lumber frequently exudes pitch—particularly in the vicinity of resin-soaked knots—when pressed into contact with a hot plate, it has not been possible to use hot-press equipment and the cheap, fast-setting glues generally in use in the southern pine plywood industry. If resin or pitch moves to the interface between board and overlay, the resulting stain mars the appearance of the overlay. It is likely that wide-scale commercial application of paintable overlays to southern pine lumber will be delayed until a rapid and continuous roll laminating process can be developed that transmits no significant amount of heat to board surfaces; the system must be designed, of course, for adhesives with exterior durability. Many of the problems inherent in making and selling overlaid lumber are discussed by Mueller et al. (1970) based on pilot plant experience with ponderosa pine (*Pinus ponderosa* Laws.).

PERFORMANCE OF OVERLAID LUMBER

Heebink (1961) reported on No. 2 Common southern pine siding overlaid with 0.005-inch-thick vulcanized fiber and installed on a building in Alabama. Before installation the siding was dipped in a clear, paintable, water-repellant preservative with the intention of inhibiting decay and mold growth. The dip resulted in a waxy and oily deposit on the overlay that made it appear unpaintable, and the siding was washed with turpentine before commercial white lead and oil house paint was applied. Three and one-half years after installation, the paint was in excellent condition, although in some locations mildew growth was heavy.

Cooper and Barham (1971) reported that a resin-impregnated paper overlay outperformed a vulcanized fiber overlay in a 6-year exposure test of eastern cottonwood (*Populus deltoides* Bartr.) siding painted with titanized pure white lead house paint. They noted that almost all the paint flaked from the vulcanized fiber surface, whereas the paint on the kraft overlay remained in a continuous, though eroded, film. In this test, the lumber was dipped for 10 seconds in a 5-percent solution of water-repellent pentachlorophenol [1], stored for two weeks, primed, and given two additional coats of paint.

On the basis of these and other related studies, it is concluded that the paint retention characteristics of flat-grain southern pine siding are improved remarkably by the use of certain paper overlays. In the South, mildewcides should be incorporated in paints designed for application to overlays.

DESIGN OF OVERLAID SIDING

To avoid breaks in the sheet, overlays on lumber siding should be applied to flat, rather than sharply contoured surfaces. For successful application of overlays, lumber must be sound and have virtually no openings in the surface; rough spots will show through, and large knots that check in service will crack the overlay. Economics usually dictate that the overlay be applied on one side only. Figure 25–12 illustrates one system for manufacturing an overlaid, bevel, horizontal siding. The tongue and groove pattern on board ends is designed to reduce distortion at end joints.

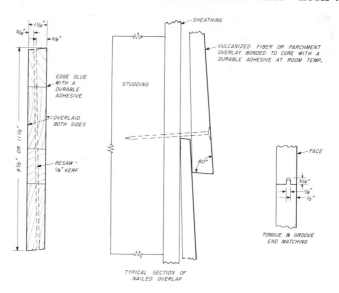

Figure 25–12.—Details of manufacture and installation of overlaid resawn bevel siding. For a paintable overlay, resin impregnated paper has tested superior to both vulcanized fiber and parchmentized paper. (Drawing after Fleischer and Heebink 1964.)

PRECAST COLORED FILMS

The application of colored, precast, flexible, plastic films to lumber and millwork items is a rapidly developing technology, but beyond the scope of this text. Most of the films, which require no painting, are for interior application—but a few have exterior durability.

25–6   PRODUCTS OTHER THAN LUMBER

Various reconstituted or laminated products such as plywood, hardboard, particleboard, signs, and laminated beams present special problems and require special finishes.

PLYWOOD

Successful finishing systems for southern pine plywood begin with protection of the uncoated surface. Plywood should be kept clean and stored prior to use in a cool, dry place protected from windblown rain, exposure to heaters, and direct sunlight. If tarps or plastic covers are used to protect stacked plywood, they should be open at the bottom to permit air circulation and prevent condensation or mold growth.

Finishes are most successful if applied to clean, freshly manufactured plywood; for this reason panel exposure time after erection and before finishing should be minimized. Extended exposure of unfinished panels not only ages surfaces and reduces likelihood of obtaining a successful coating-wood bond, but it also promotes checking; even in dry climates, variation between day and night humidities can cause sufficient shrinking and swelling to initiate surface checks in plywood.

Veneer for virtually all southern pine plywood is rotary peeled and therefore has flat-grain surfaces with broad bands of latewood. These surfaces do not hold paint as well as edge-grain wood. Moreover, exterior exposure causes more checks in plywood than in lumber because of the lathe checks present on the loose side of face veneers (fig. 19–14); the checks (fig. 25–2) frequently cause paint coatings applied directly on southern pine plywood to deteriorate fairly rapidly when exposed outside.

Face Checking.—Koch (1965) rated face checking in southern pine by Batey's (1955) index, which expresses severity as the product of check frequency per inch and the average check width in inches multiplied by 1,000.

Three-ply, 3/8-inch-thick exterior plywood was hot-press-bonded from veneer cut from eight loblolly pine trees selected to exhibit a range of specific gravity and growth rate. As is customary, the panels were assembled so that the tight side of each face veneer was outermost. Panels were quantitatively evaluated for severity of face checking after several cycles of wetting and drying.

Face checking was minimized by: (1) Reducing the hygroscopicity of the plywood by dipping the panels for 10 seconds in a water repellent. Checking index was 4.4 for treated panels and 12.8 for untreated. (2) Peeling veneer hot and tight rather than cold and loose. Checking index was 5.5 for tight-peeled face veneers and 11.7 for loose-peeled. (3) Using veneer of low specific gravity rather than high. Checking index was 6.9 for low-density faces and 10.4 for high-density faces.

With all the above factors favorable, the average checking index was minimum at 2.4; if all were unfavorable, the checking index was 20.4.

Factors that did not significantly affect severity of face checking were: rate of growth (rings per inch in the veneer); moisture content of the veneer before glue spreading; and proximity of plywood face to hot platen when pressing two panels per opening.

Checking severity in southern pine plywood can be reduced if any changes in panel moisture content are made slowly rather than abruptly. Application of certain **latex emulsion sealers** under conventional paint systems are reported by the American Plywood Association to substantially reduce checking in southern pine plywood.

Because of face checking, southern pine plywood to be painted for exterior exposure serves best if it is first overlaid with stabilized resin-treated paper. Southern pine plywood can also be left to weather naturally, or be stained. Some paint coatings applied directly to the plywood have a short, but perhaps acceptable service life. No clear film-forming finishes are available that perform satisfactorily in exterior exposure on southern pine plywood.

Natural and semiannual finishes.—The USDA Forest Products Laboratory (1966b) suggests three methods for finishing exterior southern pine plywood to show the grain. The first method is a dip (30 seconds or longer) or liberal brush treatment with a water-repellent preservative; plywood treated in this manner may require a second application within a year, but need for subsequent applications should be less frequent.

In a second method, color is added to the finish by inclusion of 1 to 2 ounces of pigment (colors-in-oil) per gallon of water-repellant preservative. The third method calls for finishing the plywood with the stain described in the opening paragraphs of section 25–2.

These finishes, applied in one-coat treatments, penetrate the wood and do not form a continuous film that may crack, peel, or blister. As with lumber, plywood given a natural or seminatural finish should be fastened with aluminum or stainless steel nails. With these finishing systems, visible checks will develop in southern pine plywood exposed outside.

In the three foregoing finishing systems, the first step should be liberal application of a water-repellent preservative to panel edges; if panels are to be stained, the repellent should be allowed to dry 72 hours before stain application.

Paint finish on nonoverlaid plywood.—The USDA Forest Products Laboratory (1966b) suggests the following procedure for painting southern pine plywood.

Before painting, all edges and joints of plywood siding should be brushed with a solution of paintable water-repellent preservative. The treated areas should dry for about 72 hours with good air circulation before painting.

The plywood surface and all edges should then be primed with a nonporous linseed-oil-base paint pigmented with only titanium and lead. This prime coat should not contain zinc oxide pigment, and the film should be thick enough to totally obscure the wood grain pattern. The moisture-repelling properties of aluminum paint also make this an excellent primer for plywood. It is important that the aluminum paint be specifically formulated for use on wood and not for general purposes or metals.

Two additional coats of high-quality house paint should then be applied over the prime coat; they may be of oil, alkyd, or a latex type, but must be compatible with the prime coat. Two days to 2 weeks of drying should be allowed between coats of paint.

Low-luster and porous-type paint systems which permit the capillary flow of water through the film are not recommended for plywood. Frequent wetting and drying of the plywood surface leads to abnormally early checking of the plywood and paint flaking from latewood.

The American Plywood Association recommends application of acrylic latex topcoats (over a compatible nonstaining primer) in preference to oil or alkyd topcoats. Their experience indicates that brush application of paint—particularly the prime coat—yields substantially better results than spray application.

The American Plywood Association employs a 7-month test series to evaluate very-high-performance coatings that can be certified on southern pine plywood. Since the evaluation program began in 1960, only one brush-applied paint for bare plywood has been certified for exterior use. Best suited for factory application, it is a highly modified urethane system composed of a vinyl-chloride vinyl-acetate vinyl-alcohol copolymer, a castor oil-derived polyol, and a castor oil-derived urethane prepolymer (Legue 1966). The certification specifies a film thickness of 8 mils.

Paint finish for plywood overlaid with resin-treated paper.—Southern pine plywood can be purchased with a resin-impregnated cellulose-fiber sheet overlaid on the surface. The **medium-density overlay** of this type is defined by U. S. Product Standard PS 1–66 (paragraph 3.5.2) as containing not less than 17 percent resin solids for a beater loaded sheet or 22 percent for an impregnated sheet; the resin must be a thermo-setting phenol or melamine type. After application, the sheet must measure not less than 0.012 inch thick. Additional adhesive is required to bond these overlay sheets to plywood. Some manufacturers precoat one side of the overlay sheet with phenolic adhesive; for other overlays, however, it is necessary to spread glue on the plywood prior to hot-pressing the assembly for 5 or 6 minutes.

The USDA Forest Products Laboratory (1966b) suggests that paper-overlaid plywood be painted in the same manner as nonoverlaid plywood, but notes that it can be self-primed successfully in a three-coat system with latex paint without using an oil-base primer. It is not uncommon for a good three-coat paint system to last 10 years on overlaid plywood; this is at least twice the durability of paint applied to nonoverlaid southern pine plywood. For application in the South, a mildewcide should be incorporated in the paint.

Selbo (1969) reported on the durability of southern pine plywood overlaid wtih a medium-density paper, edge treated with water-repellent preservative, and given a total of two coats of acrylic emulsion paint (self-primed). During 5 years of exposure at Madison, Wis. and Gulfport, Miss., the paint held up well; no face checking or paint flaking occurred. Mold growth, however, darkened the panels somewhat—particularly at the southern site.

Additional information on recommended finishes for overlaid southern pine plywood is available from the American Plywood Association, Tacoma, Wash.

Other coatings for plywood.—There are a variety of dense overlays, precast films, and thick coatings that can be applied to southern pine plywood and that do not require additional painting. The **high-density cellulose fiber sheet** defined by U. S. Product Standard PS 1–66 (paragraph 3.5.1) contains at least 45 percent resin solids; it is the same thickness, and is bonded to plywood in the same manner as the medium-density overlay previously described. It is translucent to opaque and on Douglas-fir plywood is generally used unpainted on industrial panels or concrete forms. As yet, it has been little used on southern pine.

Further information on precast films and thick coatings for plywood may be obtained from the American Plywood Association, Tacoma, Wash.

HARDBOARD [4]

Horizontal lap siding is the major hardboard product designed for exterior exposure. Most is sold factory primed for field application of topcoats, but some is completely prefinished in the factory. Because coatings are applied before shipment from the factory, hardboard finishes are judged not only by their durability in exterior exposure, but also by their scuff resistance and resistance to self adherence (**blocking**) when packed face to face in bundles.

Since finishes for hardboard develop failures of a somewhat different nature than those of lumber or plywood on exterior exposure, special test procedures may be used for evaluation. The drip-edge of hardboard siding —that is, the lower edge of horizontally applied siding—is evaluated for water resistance by a water soak and air-dry cycle. **Chalking, color change, fiber popping** (caused by fibers that on exposure rise sufficiently above the board surface to show through the paint film), and **edge cracking** may be evaluated by a 4-hour boil in water followed by 20 hours in a weatherometer; thirty 24-hour cycles are usually sufficient to produce a high degree of the foregoing failures; data from this severe test, while useful, have given only fair correlation with exterior weathering data.

Forty-five-degree, south-facing exterior exposure tests in south Florida can provide a fairly quick (6 to 12 months) estimate of comparative performance of prime coats, even though failure of the paint film by cracking normally takes 12 to 24 months. **Holdout** of the prime coat is measured by observing the degree to which a semigloss linseed oil house paint penetrates the primer; areas of low gloss visible 4 to 8 hours after topcoat application indicate poor holdout.

Substrate.—Hardboards to be coated for exterior exposure should be dimensionally stable, with good internal bond, and with a smooth exterior surface. Boards composed of fine fibers are generally less porous, easier to coat, and less subject to fiber popping than boards of coarse fibers. Good coatings will not protect poor boards from failure on exposure.

Typically, the remanufacture of hardboard lap siding begins by ripping large sheets in'o strips 1 foot wide and 16 feet long. The strips are then brush cleaned of surface dust and loose fibers. If the cut edges are rough, they may be burnished by heat or mechanical action in preparation for the prime coat. Hardboards prone to edge failure may receive one or more edge coats of sealer applied by spray, flowcoater, brush, or roller before they are primed.

Methods of applying prime coat.—Factory-applied prime coats are

[4] The information under this heading is condensed from Gluck (1971) by permission of D. G. Gluck and the Forest Products Research Society.

usually 1-1/4 to 1-1/2 mils thick. If two coats of house paint are field applied, the resultant dry film thickness will be close to 4 mils—the minimum requirement of Federal Housing Authority standards.

Two methods of applying prime coats to board surfaces are widely used. **Roll coaters** are simple to operate, and do a good job of smoothing excess sealer from a prior edge-priming step, but cannot lay down thick films. They also tend to impart an undesirable texture to the film. To build up the required film thickness and minimize texturing, roll coaters may be used in series. For rough, porous boards, a roll turning in opposition to board flow forces paint into irregularities and produces a smooth surface; such a reverse coater must be followed by additional coaters to build up required film thickness.

Curtain coaters, in which boards pass through a continuous curtain of primer that falls from a narrow slot, are used to apply a thick, smooth film. Because film thickness is controlled primarily by the speed with which the board passes through the curtain, speed-up and slow-down conveyors are needed upstream and downstream of the coater—a disadvantage because of the space required. Also, curtain coaters cannot apply paint films much thinner than about 3 mils.

Spray and brush applications are possible, but coating stations tend to be untidy and film thickness is difficult to control.

Following application of the prime coat, boards pass into an oven. Typically the oven has an initial section in which hot air circulates to evaporate most of the solvents; a second section with infrared heaters dries or cures the coating. The siding is then cooled and packaged—sometimes with a protective sheet between boards to minimize board-to-board adherence, pressure marking, scuffing, and burnishing during shipment.

Primers.—Oil-modified alkyd resins are the principal primers used because they adhere well to hardboard and are reasonably durable in exterior exposure. They are also cheap and easily handled in coating equipment. Moreover, most common house paints adhere well to alkyd primers, and holdout is usually good.

Oil-modified alkyds do not thermoset to any significant degree during an oven bake, but are only freed of solvent; oven temperature is therefore not critical. Since chemical cross-linking takes place in the days and weeks following application, however, the coating film may be somewhat thermoplastic when the siding is packaged—a condition favorable to self adhesion, i.e., blocking.

Formulations with low oil content and alkyd resins of high molecular weight (i.e., harder resins) and high pigmentation levels aid in reducing tendency to block. Some primers contain small amounts of heat-reactive urea or melamine resins to increase initial hardness. Unfortunately, these formulation changes aggravate a basic deficiency of alkyd primers—mediocre performance in tests of drip-edge durability. Moreover, formulations modified to make primers harder result in a coating with diminished flexibility to accomodate board expansion and contraction with change in moisture content.

Not in wide use, but under evaluation, are **acrylic** and **polyvinyl acetate emulsions**; these coatings have good film integrity during exterior exposure and also give excellent protection to the drip edge. In contrast to oil-modified alkyd resin primers, which require low-molecular-weight polymers for ease of solubility, water-based primers can use tough, high-molecular-weight polymers in the form of emulsions. The latex paints are flexible and do not crack at the drip edge. Except for rapid chalking, they equal or better the exterior performance of alkyds.

These water-based primers are simple to handle in the factory due to elimination of solvents. Once partially dried on equipment, however, the high-molecular-weight polymers are difficult to remove. Moreover, emulsion primers are usually not roll coated because of texturing, so that application is largely limited to curtain coaters.

In contrast to the alkyds, water-based primers are fully cross-linked in the oven and no further reaction takes place after packaging. If not fully cured in the oven, emulsion paints tend to block severely; oven temperatures are therefore critical and must be monitored constantly.

Topcoats for factory-primed siding.—Hardboard siding that has been prime coated in the factory should be topcoated soon after the siding is erected. Two coats of topcoat are preferable to one. Paints used can be the same as those for lumber or plywood. Because of buckling caused by longitudinal swelling, it is important that hardboard siding be equilibrated at service humidity and temperature before attachment to walls.

Prefinished siding.—Factory-prefinished hardboard siding is being manufactured with 5- to 10-year guarantees against certain types of paint and substrate failures. Dry film thicknesses on these factory-finished boards are less than those customary with ordinary house paints; they range from 1-½ to 3 mils. The formulator of field-applied house paints has relatively few resins or oils with which to work because the coating must dry by water evaporation or oxidation under ambient conditions. In the factory, where finishes can be ovendried, and film thickness and drying conditions controlled, resins can be used which have inherently better durability. The relatively slow acceptance of prefinished hardboard siding can be partially attributed to difficulty in developing a satisfactory total system including substrate, coating, installation technique, and the accessory coated nails, corners, joint covers, touchup paint, and caulking compound.

Prefinishes under test for hardboard siding include alkyds, acrylics, polyvinyl chlorides, polyesters, and silicone copolymers. **Alkyd** prefinishes are similar to the primers previously described, with minor formulation changes to gain better durability. They are easy to handle in the factory and cheap, but tend to pick up dirt and change color. At this time the alkyd coatings appear the best candidates for economical prefinishes.

Most thermoset **acrylic emulsion** prefinishes have given exceptionally good performance; some formulations, however, have shown significant chalking or edge cracking after limited tests (1½ years) on an exposure fence. **Polyvinyl chloride** solvent coatings offer easy application and low-temperature drying, but have shown substantial chalking and color changes on exposure panels. A **polyester** coating, after 2 years of exposure, has shown no sign of chalking, edge cracking, or color change; in other tests, however, some formulations have chalked badly. In short, test data are still too limited to reach definitive conclusions.

Silicone copolymers have been proposed as 20-year finishes; their test-fence performance has been outstanding in every respect except that edge cracking appears worse than that of other prefinishes. This weakness, unless rectified, would appear to preclude their further consideration.

The diversity of prefinishes under test is an indication of the unsettled state of the art. Development of new precast films, hot melt coatings, and extruded coatings, plus new methods of radiation, microwave, and ultraviolet curing will likely alter present finishing techniques.

Readers desiring additional information can write the American Hardboard Association, Chicago, Ill., who, in cooperation with the National Paint, Varnish, and Lacquer Association, are working to improve the performance of exterior finishes for hardboard.

PARTICLEBOARD

While particleboards can be fabricated with phenol formaldehyde resin, allowing more severe exterior exposure, most southern pine particleboard is designed for interior use and is assembled with urea-formaldehyde glues. (See sec. 23-6.)

Published data on finishes for particleboards designed for some degree of exterior exposure are meager. Since the technology for such coatings is developing rapidly, readers should consult the National Particleboard Association, Washington, D. C. for current recommendations.

For those readers interested in interior coatings, Rundle and Cheo (1969) point out that hot melt coatings on particleboard have the advantages of low fire hazard during application, rapid setting, excellent moisture barrier properties, ability to fill large defects, and low cost. Coker (1968) described systems for painting and lacquering particleboard, and Enzenberger (1968) discussed the problem of overlaying particleboard with resin-impregnated paper. Additional information on particleboard finishes for interior exposure can be obtained from the National Particleboard Association, Washington, D.C.

SIGNS

Southern pine exterior plywood provided with a medium- density overlay is satisfactory for signs for exterior exposure.
Signs should be primed and given one—preferably two—coats of topcoat

paint as described under the heading PLYWOOD in this section. (A brown background paint reported to give good results with a single coat applied to medium-density overlay is Rustoleum No. 792 brown enamel.) For rustic appearance and durability, letters can be routed into the coated plywood and letters smoothed by light sanding. The letters can then be painted with a high-gloss alkyd enamel. (A yellow alkyd enamel reported to give good results is that manufactured by Cosden Chemical Coatings Corp. of Berkeley, N.J.; for use, it was thinned 10 percent with synthetic enamel thinner. Edges of signs should be liberally brushed with a paintable water-repellent preservative, dried for 72 hours, primed, and given two coats of topcoat paint.

LAMINATED BEAMS

Southern pine laminated beams, if made from lumber pressure treated with appropriate preservatives (see sec. 22–1), can be safely exposed outdoors in all climates.

The USDA Forest Products Laboratory (1966c) has recommended procedures for painting outside wood surfaces, including laminated southern pine beams; an abstract of these recommendations can be found in section 25–3 under the subhead PAINT SYSTEMS.

25–7 INTERIOR FINISHES

Southern pine lumber and millwork readily accept a wide variety of finishes designed for interior use. Information on opaque paints for interior walls, ceilings, and floors is available from numerous paint manufacturers. Readers desiring knowledge of characteristics and properties necessary for good durability and low maintenance of interior finishes should find Leary's (1970) review useful. The discussion following is limited to semitransparent finishes for pine wall paneling and clear finishes for southern pine floors.

SEMITRANSPARENT FINISH FOR WALL PANELING

Southern pine has an attractive, warm, natural golden color. Because it tends to darken on exposure to light, however, a finish lighter than natural is frequently desired for interior wall paneling. Such a finish can be obtained by first applying a white or light-colored paint of very thin consistency made by mixing enamel undercoater, flat wall paint, or even ordinary house paint with about twice its volume of a mixture of equal parts of boiled linseed oil and turpentine or mineral spirits. Another suitable mixture is wood sealer with enough added color-in-oil or color-in-japan to give the required color and opacity. For a fast-drying material, lacquer enamel may be mixed with twice its volume of a clear lacquer. The paint-based coloring materials should be spread on the wood surface with a mop, brush, or spray gun, allowed to stand 5 to 10 minutes, and then wiped with clean rags, burlap, or cotton waste to remove excess material and leave only what sinks into the grain of the wood. Lacquer must be wiped immediately after applying, before it has time to harden. In wiping, the first strokes should be across the grain of the wood and the last strokes parallel to the grain. After the coloring material has had time to dry, further protective finish, such as clear wood sealer, varnish, or lacquer, may be applied according to the type of finish desired (USDA Forest Products Laboratory 1967, p. 7).

CLEAR FLOOR FINISH

Many years ago interior wood floors were commonly finished with repeated applications of hot linseed oil; each application was buffed by hand. The finish is durable, does not show scratches, and is readily patched at places of maximum wear without refinishing the floor. In time, the finish darkens; since the finish penetrates a substantial layer of wood, the darkening effect is less readily remedied than darkening of a superficial finish. For this reason, and because of the labor of application, the old oil finish has largely been replaced by shellac, varnish, and floor-seal finishes (Browne 1953).

Regardless of the finish selected for a new structure, floors should be protected by heavy paper from the time they are laid until all other interior work has been completed. Vertical grain southern pine flooring accepts and holds finish better—and also wears longer and more evenly— than flat-grain. Finishing of southern pine floors commences with preparation of the floor by sanding.

Sanding.—The sanding of a floor prior to its finishing is best performed by a skilled specialist operating a well-maintained power sander of rugged design. In sanding, the floor should be gone over several times—first across the grain and then in the direction of the grain. On the first traverse, No. 2 sandpaper is generally used, with No. $\frac{1}{2}$ paper used on the second pass; on southern pine floors it may or may not be practical to use No. 0 paper on a third pass. After the last sanding, the floor may be buffed with No. 3 steel wool. After the floor has been sanded, it should be swept clean and carefully inspected by looking across the floor toward light from a window; any blemishes will appear greatly accentuated when the finish is applied (Browne 1953).

Shellac.—Shellac is used chiefly because it dries so rapidly that a floor may be finished or refinished and put back in service within 24 hours. Shellac has less resistance to wear and water than varnish, and should be cleaned and renewed before traffic has worn through to bare wood. Where wax is used over shellac to improve durability and cleanability, the shellac is often limited to one or two coats, which are sanded or buffed so that the shellac acts more as a seal to support the wax than as a coating (Browne 1953).

Shellac for floors should be purchased in the form of 5-pound cut shellac and should be pure shellac unadulterated with cheaper resins. It should either be freshly manufactured or put up in glass containers. Shellac that has stood long in contact with metal may contain iron or salts that discolor southern pine by reacting with its tannins. The correct thinner for shellac is 188-proof No. 1 denatured alcohol. For application, 5-pound cut shellac should be thinned with 1 quart of thinner per gallon. It should be applied with a wide brush that will cover three boards of strip flooring at one stroke and should be put on with long, even strokes, taking care to join the laps smoothly. The first coat on bare wood requires 15 to 20 minutes to dry. It should then be rubbed lightly with steel wool or sandpaper and the floor swept clean. A second coat should be applied, allowed to dry 2 or 3 hours, then gone over with steel wool or sandpaper, swept, and a third coat applied. The floor should not be put back in service until next morning if possible but may be walked upon in about 3 hours after finishing, if necessary. If wax is to be used, it should not be applied less than 8 hours after the last coat of shellac and should be a paste wax, not a water-emulsion wax, since water may turn the shellac white (Browne 1953).

Varnish.—Varnish, which may be based on phenolic, alkyd, epoxy, or polyurethane resins, gives a highly lustrous floor finish that is more re-sistant to water spotting than shellac. Like shellac, it is easily kept clean by sweeping and dry mopping.

Methods of applying floor varnish are usually described on the labels of the containers. Only floor varnishes should be used for floor finishing; varnishes made for other purposes and the so-called all-purpose varnishes are not as durable. At least two coats are needed over paste filler or over a first coat of shellac, and at least three coats where the varnish is applied directly to the bare wood. The floor should be clean when varnish is applied, and the brush must be clean to avoid leaving grains and lumps in the coating. The room should be kept at 70° F. or warmer, and plenty of fresh air should be provided, since oxygen is taken from the air when varnish dries. Low temperature and high relative humidity greatly retard the drying of varnish.

Varnish, even the quick-drying kind, requires longer intervals between coats then shellac and remains tender for some time; floors newly coated should be kept out of service for several days. As with shellac, varnish floor finishes should be renewed before they wear through to bare wood. Failure to do so will necessitate complete removal before refinishing if uniform color is to be achieved (Browne 1953).

Floor seals.—Specially compounded floor seals, the most widely used fin-ish for residential wood floors, are being used to achieve—with less labor—finishes somewhat comparable to the old linseed oil finish. They may be regarded as thin varnishes or bodied drying oils prepared so that they penetrate less deeply into the wood than unbodied drying oils. Floor-seal finishes require more maintenance, but are more readily refinished, than varnish finishes.

Manufacturers' directions for applying floor seals vary widely and in some cases are very inadequate. In general, floor seals may be brushed on with a wide brush or mopped on with a squeegee or lamb's wool applicator, working first across the grain of the wood and then smoothing out in the direction of the grain. After an interval of 15 minutes to 2 hours, depending upon the characteristics of the seal, the excess is wiped off with clean rags or a rubber squeegee. For best results the floor should then be buffed with No. 2 steel wool; those willing to sacrifice something in appearance and service to save labor omit the buffing. If possible, the buffing should be done by a rugged power-driven machine designed specifically for buffing with steel wool. The next best procedure is buffing with steel wool pads attached to the bottom of a sanding machine. The buffing may be done by hand if a machine is not available. One application of seal may be sufficient, but a second application is recommended for new floors or floors that have just been sanded. The floor should be swept clean before making the second application. A coat of wax completes the finishing system (Browne 1953).

Floor maintenance.—Wood floors with fine finishes should never be scrubbed with water or unnecessarily brought in contact with water. Sweeping or dry mopping should be all that is necessary for routine cleaning. A soft cotton floor mop kept barely dampened with a mixture of 3 parts of kerosene and 1 part of paraffin oil is excellent for dry mopping. When the mop becomes dirty, it should be washed in hot soapy water, dried, and again dampened with the mixture of kerosene and paraffin oil. Exceptional patches of dirt that cannot be removed in this way may be removed by rubbing lightly with fine steel wool moistened with turpentine. Where the finish is a floor seal, badly soiled spots, such as gray spots where water has been allowed to stand on the floor for a time, can be sanded by hand, patched with seal, and buffed with a pad of steel wool (Browne 1953).

For the interested reader, the USDA Forest Products Laboratory (1961) has published a Handbook further describing wood floors for dwellings.

25–8 LITERATURE CITED

Anonymous.
1969. New finish for rough sawn lumber tested. Forest Prod. J. 19(11): 8B.

Allyn, G.
1961. Acrylic emulsion house paint. Off. Dig. 33: 1615–1617.

Allyn, G.
1966. Acrylic primer for yellow southern pine. Paint and Varn. Prod. 56(7): 35–37, 39.

Antlfinger, G. J.
1967. Vinyl chloride-acrylic polymers as exterior coatings. J. Paint Technol. 39: 300–309.

Ashton, H. E.
1967. Clear finishes for exterior wood. J. Paint Technol. 39(507): 212–224.

Batey, T. E.
1955. Minimizing face checking of plywood. Forest Prod. J. 5: 277–285.

Beardsley, H. P., and Kennedy, R. J.
1967. Performance of exterior paints based on a vinyl acetate-ethylene emulsion vehicle. J. Paint Technol. 39: 88–98.

Bilek, G., Hughes, H. J., and Stephenson, H. B.
1967. Study of lead pigments in water thinned prime coats for wood. J. Paint Technol. 39: 329–333.

Black, J. M.
1969. Wood finishing: experimental chromate finish. USDA Forest Serv. Res. Note FPL–0134, 2 pp. Forest Prod. Lab., Madison, Wis.

Bohlen, J. A.
1963. Latex paints on southern yellow pine. Off. Dig. 35(466): 1176–1187.

Bohlen, J. A.
1967. Latex paints on southern yellow pine. J. Paint Technol. 39: 693–699.

Browne, F. L.
1952. Wood siding left to weather naturally. Architect. Rec. pp. 197–199. (November)

Browne, F. L.
1953. Finishing of wood floors. USDA Forest Serv. Forest Prod. Lab. Rep. 1962, 8 pp.

Browne, F. L.
1959. Understanding the mechanisms of deterioration of house paint. Forest Prod. J. 9: 417–426.

Browne, F. L.
1960. Wood siding left to weather naturally. South. Lumberman 201(2513): 141–143.

Browne, F. L., and Simonson, H. C.
1957. The penetration of light into wood. Forest Prod. J. 7: 308–314.

California Redwood Association.
1962. Wood and wood finishes in exterior use: an annotated bibliography of significant studies of coatings, treatments, and substrate modification. Calif. Redwood Assoc., 90 pp. San Francisco.

Coker, E. E.
1968. Painting and lacquering of particleboard. In Particleboard manufacture and application, pp. 148–155. (Leo Mitlin, ed.) Ivy Hatch, Sevenoaks, Kent, U.K.: Pressmedia Books Ltd.

Cooper, G. A., and Barham, S. H.
1971. The performance of a house paint on two overlays on cottonwood siding. Forest Prod. J. 21(3): 53–56.

Côté, W. A., and Robinson, R. G.
1968. A comparative study of wood. Wood coating interaction using incident fluorescence and transmitted fluorescence microscopy. J. Paint Technol. 40(525): 427–432.

Enzensberger, W.
1968. Finishing chipboard with resin impregnated paper. In Particleboard manufacture and application, pp. 138–145. (Leo Mitlin, ed.) Ivy Hatch, Sevenoaks, Kent, U.K.: Pressmedia Books Ltd.

Fahey, D. J., and Pierce, D. S.
1971. Resistance of resin-impregnated paper overlays to accelerated weathering. Forest Prod. J. 21(11): 30–38.

Fleischer, H. O., and Heebink, B. G.
1964. Overlays for lumber—an old product in a new dress. USDA Forest Serv. Res. Note FPL–035, 11 pp. Forest Prod. Lab., Madison, Wis.

Gluck, D. G.
1971. Selection and field testing of coatings for exterior hardboard products. Forest Prod. J. 21(11): 24–29.

Golden Gate Society for Coatings Technology.
1967. Exterior durability of catalyzed clear coatings on redwood. J. Paint Technol. 39(514): 655–662.

Heebink, B. G.
1961. Paper overlaid lumber. Forest Prod. J. 11(4): 167–175.

Heebink, T. B.
   1970. Performance of exterior natural wood finishes in the Pacific Northwest. Forest Prod. J. 20(3): 31–34.

Kalnins, M. A., Stellink, C., and Tarkow, H.
   1966. Light-induced free radicals in wood. USDA Forest Serv. Res. Pap. FPL–58, 8 pp. Forest Prod. Lab., Madison, Wis.

Koch, P.
   1965. Minimizing face checking. Forest Prod. J. 15(12): 495–499.

Leary, P. E.
   1970. Interior coatings—maintainability and durability. Forest Prod. J. 20(12): 36–39.

Legue, N.
   1966. Thermosetting vinyl reaction product for use on exterior wood products. J. Paint Technol. 38(501): 620–626.

McMillin, C. W.
   1969. Performance evaluation of stained, rough-sawn southern pine siding. Forest Prod. J. 19(2): 51–52.

Martens, C. R.
   1964. Emulsion and water-soluble paints and coatings. 160 pp. N.Y.: Reinhold Publ. Corp.

Martens, C. R.
   1966. Review of latex and water-soluble coatings. J. Paint Technol. 38: 46A–49A.

Miniutti, V. P.
   1964. Preliminary observations—microscale changes in cell structure at softwood surfaces during weathering. Forest Prod. J. 14(12): 571–576.

Miniutti, V. P.
   1967. Microscopic observations of ultraviolet irradiated and weathered softwood surfaces and clear coatings. USDA Forest Serv. Res. Pap. FPL–74, 32 pp. Forest Prod. Lab., Madison, Wis.

Miniutti, V. P.
   1969. Reflected-light and scanning electron microscopy of ultraviolet irradiated redwood surfaces. *In* Proc. Engis Stereoscan Colloquium, pp. 135–147.

Mueller, L. A., Barger, R. L., and Bourke, A.
   1970. Roll laminating fiber overlays on low-grade ponderosa pine: a progress report. Forest Prod. J. 20(9): 75–80.

National Paint, Varnish, and Lacquer Association.
   1960. Mildew. Nat. Paint, Varn., and Lacquer Assoc., Inc., Circ. 786, 6 pp. Wash., D.C.

Nylén, P., and Sunderland, E.
   1965. Modern surface coatings. 750 pp. N.Y.: Interscience Publ.

Philadelphia Society for Paint Technology.
   1967. Ultraviolet light absorbers in clear coatings for wood. J. Paint Technol. 39(515): 736–751.

Pierce, P. E., and Holsworth, R. M.
   1966. The mechanical properties and performance of wood primers. J. Paint Technol. 38: 584–590.

Rothstein, E. C.
   1967. Compatibility and reactivity of UV absorbers in clear wood coatings. J. Paint Technol. 39(513): 621–628.

Rundle, V. A., and Cheo, Y. C.
   1969. Hot melt coatings for wood products. Forest Prod. J. 19(9): 73–79.

Schneider, M. H., and Côté, W. A.
   1967. Studies of wood and coating interactions using fluorescence microscopy and pyrolysis gas-liquid chromatography. J. Paint Technol. 39(511): 465–471.

Selbo, M. L.
   1969. Performance of southern pine plywood during five years exposure to weather. Forest Prod. J. 19(8): 56–60.

Tarkow, H., Feist, W. C., and Southerland, C. F.
   1966. Interaction of wood with polymeric materials, penetration versus molecular size. Forest Prod. J. 16(10): 61–65.

Thompson, W. S.
   1968. Permeability and weathering properties of film-forming materials used in wood finishing. Forest Prod. Util. Lab. Res. Rep. 4, 32 pp. Miss. State Univ., State College.

USDA Forest Products Laboratory.
1961. Wood floors for dwellings. USDA Agr. Handbook 204, 44 pp.

USDA Forest Products Laboratory.
1966a. Surface characteristics of wood as they affect durability of finishes. USDA Forest Serv. Res. Pap. FPL–57, 60 pp. Forest Prod. Lab., Madison, Wis.

USDA Forest Products Laboratory.
1966b. Wood finishing: finishing exterior plywood. USDA Forest Serv. Res. Note FPL–0133, 3 pp. Forest Prod. Lab., Madison, Wis.

USDA Forest Products Laboratory.
1966c. Wood finishing: painting outside wood surfaces. USDA Forest Serv. Res. Note FPL–0123, 3 pp. Forest Prod. Lab., Madison, Wis.

USDA Forest Products Laboratory.
1967. Bleaching wood. USDA Forest Serv. Res. Note FPL–0165, 9 pp. Forest Prod. Lab., Madison, Wis.

USDA Forest Products Laboratory.
1968. Wood finishing: water-repellent preservatives. USDA Forest Serv. Res. Note FPL–0124, 7 pp. Forest Prod. Lab., Madison, Wis.

USDA Forest Products Laboratory.
1970a. Forest Products Laboratory natural finish. USDA Forest Serv. Res. Note FPL–046 rev., 7 pp. Forest Prod. Lab., Madison, Wis.

USDA Forest Products Laboratory.
1970b. Wood finishing: blistering, peeling, and cracking of house paints from moisture. USDA Forest Serv. Res. Note FPL–0125, 7 pp. Forest Prod. Lab., Madison, Wis.

Werthan, S.
1961. Exterior latex paints for wood substrates. Off. Dig. 33: 1053–1072.

Werthan, S.
1963. A current look at exterior house paints. Off. Dig. 35: 671–690.

Zicherman, J. B.
1969. Painting of southern pine —a review. Forest Prod. J. 19(4): 44–51.

26
Burning

CONTENTS

26

Burning[1]

The United States is on the threshold of the most rapid growth of electrical energy consumption in its history. One authority (Gambs 1970b) predicts that during the next 30 years it must build more than 10 times the generating capacity acquired since the first commercial electrical power became available in 1903. By 1990, according to this prediction, the country will have about five times the generating capacity in existence in 1970. Total consumption of fuels for power generation will therefore also rise sharply (fig. 26-1), and the industry probably will vigorously seek additional sources of fuel.

Both wood and bark from southern pine trees are good fuels and have been much used to generate heat, steam, and electrical power in the pine mills of the South. In the years 1950–1970, however, most waste wood became more valuable for pulp and other products than for fuel. Chipped wood could be sold for more than $6/ton at the mill, chipping headrigs (see sec. 19–6) reduced sawdust production, and the use of sawdust for fiber products increased. It became economical for mills requiring moderate power (up to about 1,500 hp.) to sell their wood residue, shut down their steam boilers, and purchase electrical power from larger and more efficient oil- gas-, or coal-fired utility plants; steam required for dry kilns was then either produced in small, gas-fired boilers or eliminated in favor of direct-gas-fired kilns.

Bark from southern pine trees, however, has less economic value; in the years prior to 1970 huge quantities were burned in waste incinerators without thought of energy recovery. As noted in section 2–1, annual consumption of southern pine wood is expected to rise to about 7 billion cu. ft. by the year 2000; accompanying this quantity of wood will be about 0.7 billion cu. ft. of bark, i.e., at least 20 million tons if the bark is half water by weight (10 million tons ovendry). Because of national concern over air pollution, it is likely that the practice of incinerating bark in waste burners will be curtailed or discontinued.

Bark finds its way into a number of industrial products. These uses will increase, but probably not very fast. By present lights, the most promising way of disposing of large volumes of bark is to make fuel of it. Some wood-using plants currently burn bark in order to generate their

---

[1] Secs. 26–2, 26–3, 26–4, and 26–5 are taken with some modification from Koch and Mullen (1971) and from: Mullen, J. F. Controlled burning of southern pine wood and bark for steam generation. USDA Forest Service, Southern Forest Experiment Station, Alexandria, La., Final Report FS–SO–3201–5.143 dated October 9, 1970.

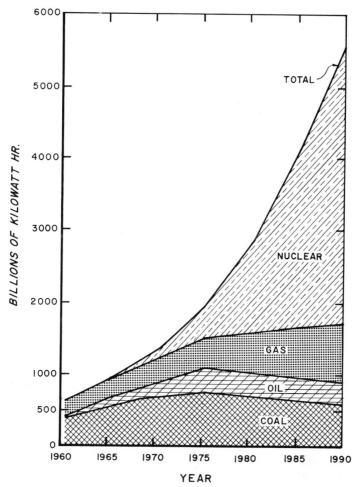

Figure 26–1.—The top or total line of this chart represents the forecasted generation of electricity in thermal plants of the United States; the total is based on preliminary data of the 1970 National Power Survey by the Federal Power Commission. The shaded portions represent Gambs' forecast of electrical power generation according to type of fuel. Some authorities do not envision such early and massive development of nuclear plants. (Drawing after Gambs 1970b.)

own electricity, but the investment in equipment is so heavy that all but the biggest firms find it cheaper to purchase power. Large electrical generating plants, with their huge and reasonably constant demands for fuel, may be able to burn bark economically.

Other fuels derived from woody materials include charcoal, producer gas, and methyl and ethyl alcohol; they are discussed briefly in chapter 28. Lignin, a byproduct of the kraft pulping industry, is also a fuel of industrial importance, and its combustion is briefly described in section 26–4.

26-1 IGNITION OF WOOD

The voluminous literature on thermal degradation of wood and its components has been reviewed by Beall and Eickner (1970); literature on the mechanism of thermal degradation of cellulose has been reviewed by MacKay (1967). Only a few citations pertinent to the ignition of southern pine wood will be mentioned here as an introduction to a discussion of combustion.

In brief, the literature contains three distinct definitions of ignition temperature:

- The exothermic reaction point—the temperature at which the rate of heat dissipation exceeds the rate of heat absorption—resulting in eventual flaming or glowing if in an atmosphere that will support combustion; when wood is analyzed on a differential scanning calorimeter, this point is observable as an endothermic peak.
- The temperature at which a glowing wire or pilot light will cause flaming ignition of the combustible gases evolving from heated wood.
- The auto-ignition point, at which the test specimen ignites and burns. Auto-ignition takes place at temperatures above either the flame point or the exothermic reaction point.

General texts, such as Stamm (1964, p. 291) report the exothermic reaction point for spruce (green or ovendried) as 273° ± 2.5° C. Kollmann and Côté (1968, p. 151) report flaming ignition of evolved gases at 225° to 260° C. and a burning point for wood at 260° to 290° C. Much wider ranges in the temperatures of these thermal transitions have been reported by other researchers.

Browne (1958) defined the general course of thermal degradation and decribed four reaction zones that develop parallel to the heated surface when wood is heated in air.

Zone A, to 200° C.: water vapor, formic acid, acetic acid, and possibly carbon dioxide are evolved. Charring may eventually occur at temperatures as low as 95° C.

Zone B, 200° to 280° C.: the reaction becomes exothermic between 150° and 260° C. With sufficient time—and under favorable conditions—ignition is possible.

Zone C, 280° to 500° C.: ignitable gases are evolved and block oxygen from the wood surface, thereby preventing ignition. The forming charcoal has lower thermal conductivity than wood; thus heat conduction to the center of the wood—and therefore attainment of the exothermic reaction point—is delayed. Surface temperatures high enough for spontaneous combustion have been reported over the entire range of Zone C.

Zone D, above 500° C.: charcoal glows.

Beall (1968) observed weight losses when 50-mg. samples of ground southern pine wood were heated at 5.5° C. per minute in oxygen flowing at 500 ml./min. In contrast with other softwoods tested, extraction of southern pine changed degradation behavior very little; the following data show the temperatures by which weight losses of 10, 50, and 90 percent had occurred in southern pine.

Weight loss	Unextracted	Extracted
Percent	– – – – – °C. – – – – –	
10	277	276
50	313	314
90	430	430

Beall observed that unextracted southern pine reached a maximum decomposition rate of 5.2 mg./min. at 300° C.; maximum rate for extracted wood was 4.9 mg./min. at 290° C.

Fons (1950) analyzed the effects of initial temperature, moisture content, and size of wood on time to ignition. He heated small cylinders (5-1/8 inches in length and of various diameters less than 1/2-inch) of ponderosa pine (*Pinus ponderosa* Laws.) at constant temperatures in the range 443° to 704° C. According to Fons, flame may appear in a mass of material at a furnace temperature of 427° C. (800° F.) or higher. Differences in the initial temperature of the sample (from 10° to 66° C.) did not affect results, but moisture content significantly increased time to ignition. At ignition, the surface temperature was 343° C. (650° F.) for a 3/8-inch-diameter specimen heated at 621° C. (1,150° F.).

Matson et al. (1959) surveyed information on ignition temperatures below 300° C. They observed that solid wood itself does not burn directly; thermal decomposition products and flammable vapors react with the oxygen in air to burn. After these volatiles are driven off, the residual charcoal reacts with the air to produce heat by glowing combustion; little flame is generated. They reviewed a study in which ovendry specimens of wood (1-1/4 by 1-1/4 by 4 inches) were heated at a constant temperature in a furnace; the time delay until a pilot light 1/2-inch above the specimens ignited the evolving gases was measured. For longleaf pine, the results were as follows.

Temperature	Time delay to ignition
°C.	Min.
157	No ignition within 40 min.
180	14.3
200	11.8
300	2.3
400	.5

As reported by Matson et al. (1959), the National Bureau of Standards observed ignition temperatures of shortleaf and longleaf pine to be

228° to 230° C. respectively; in their test, shavings were heated in a glass test tube in the presence of a measured flow of heated air.

Graf (1949) heated both hardwoods and softwoods (not including southern pine) in the form of 2-1/4-inch matchsticks bundled together to a total weight of 7 to 13 g. Specimens were at 7-percent moisture content or less. In an electric oven with air flowing at 0.05 or 0.2 cu. ft./min., they were heated at a rate between 4° and 30° F./hour; ignition temperatures between 423° and 570° F. (217° and 299° C.) were observed. The interdependence of sample weight, air flow, and heating rate on ignition temperature was discussed on page 42: ". . . samples of smaller mass, tested at slow heating rates and high air flow rates, permitted an excessive amount of combustible material to escape into the air with the result that instead of ignition, a slow gasification and carbonization took place. The faster heating rate gave less time for combustible vapors and gases to escape while lower air flow rates carried less away. When the larger samples were used, there was enough material present to cause ignition even at low heating rates and high air flow rates".

Using ponderosa pine sapwood (0.16 by 46 by 77 mm.) in thermogravimetric analysis (TGA), and 5 g. of 0.25-mm. ground particles for differential thermal analysis (DTA), Browne and Tang (1962) studied pyrolysis, i.e., chemical decomposition by heat in the absence of air. Cellulose was completely pyrolyzed at 400° C., while at the same temperature, lignin was 70 percent unvaporized. This they explained as due in part to the less complex polymeric structure of cellulose. From DTA, lignin showed an exotherm at 415° C.; cellulose had a sharp endotherm at 350° C. and a large exotherm at 470° C. For wood, there was a valley between exotherms at 340° and 440° C. due to the cellulose endotherm at 350° C. Most of the weight loss in wood occurred in the exothermic region between the two peaks (β_1 and β_2 of fig. 26–2).

In tests of loblolly pine (saturated and at 10-percent moisture content), Johnson and Koch (1972) placed cubes of extracted and unextracted earlywood and latewood measuring 1, 2, and 3 mm.—end grain down—on the sample pan of a differential scanning calorimeter (DSC)[2], and then heated the pan at constant rates (10° and 20° C./min.) from 150° to 513° C.; the cubes were confined under a glass cover with room-temperature atmospheric air circulated at 40 ml./min. to purge decomposition products and maintain a uniform atmosphere. By this means, only one face of the cube was heated directly. Recorded temperatures were those of the sample holder; these temperatures were not necessarily equal to average cube temperature. Endothermic and exothermic reaction points, temperatures at which glowing ignition occurred, and duration of glow were observed. Time to glow and duration of glow were also measured

---

[2] Descriptions of the manner in which the DSC functions can be found in O'Neil (1964), Watson et al. (1964), and Koch (1969).

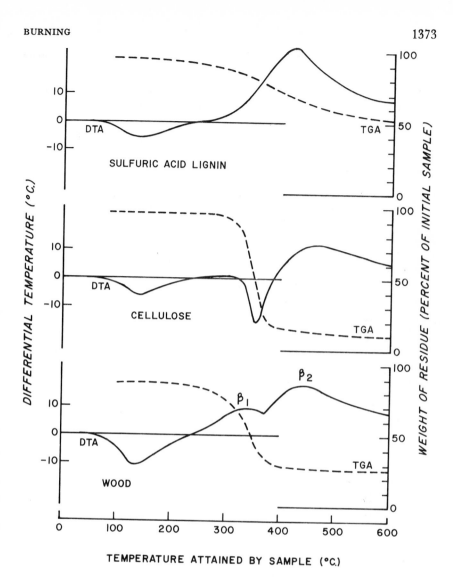

Figure 26–2.—Solid lines (scale at left) show curves for differential thermal analysis (DTA) of the pyrolysis of sulfuric acid lignin, cellulose, and wood; the reference material was aluminum oxide. The broken lines (scale at right) show weight of residue determined by thermogravimetric analysis (TGA). (Drawing after Browne and Tang 1962.)

in static tests with the cubes placed on a calorimeter pan maintained at 513° C. The results, specific to loblolly pine, follow. They are of interest because they quantitatively show that elapsed time to ignition is shortest during static heating if particles are small, initially dry, and of low specific gravity. Also, the length of time the particles glow before they are consumed is shortest if they are small.

No particles showed visible flame at ignition; instead, they either exhibited **glowing ignition** or decomposed without igniting. After the first endothermic peak (all-specimen average 345° C.), an exothermic trend continued in 54 of the 72 latewood specimens until glowing ignition started (fig. 26–3BC); in all of the earlywood and the remaining latewood specimens, however, the trend reversed (fig. 26–3A) and led to a second endothermic peak (480° C. for earlywood). The literature indicates that the temporary interruption of the exotherm might be caused by absorption of gases by the charcoal or because evolving gases block oxygen from the charcoal surface. Table 26–1 compares the thermal transition temperatures of earlywood and latewood cubes and shows the proportion of specimens exhibiting second endothermic peaks and glowing ignition.

Gases first became visible at the first endothermic peak (345° C.), and the cubes began to char; the gases did not ignite. Evolution of visible gases ceased when the exothermic reaction yielded to the second endotherm (average temperature 434° C. for earlywood—see fig. 26–3A for typical plot). In these cases, the ensuing endotherm progressed until sufficient heat was absorbed to initiate a second and final exotherm.

The fact that 48 of the 144 specimens heated dynamically degraded to ash without glowing combustion supports Graf's (1949) finding that a minimum sample mass is required for ignition of wood subjected to slow heating. However, because even the small earlywood specimens did display two endothermic peaks and one exothermic peak, a minimum mass was evidently not required for thermal transitions below glowing ignition.

A 20° C./min. rate of temperature rise (compared to a 10° rate)

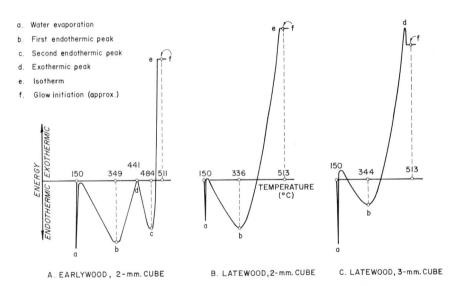

a. Water evaporation
b. First endothermic peak
c. Second endothermic peak
d. Exothermic peak
e. Isotherm
f. Glow initiation (approx.)

A. EARLYWOOD, 2-mm. CUBE   B. LATEWOOD, 2-mm. CUBE   C. LATEWOOD, 3-mm. CUBE

Figure 26–3.—Typical differential scanning calorimeter plots of loblolly pine wood heated from 150° to 513° C. at 20° C./min. in a dynamic air flow of 40 ml./min. Cubes were heated on one face only. Full-scale chart deflection on ordinate: 16 millicalories for A and B, and 32 millicalories for C. (Drawing after Johnson and Koch 1972.)

Table 26–1.—*Range of thermal transition temperatures and frequency of occurrence for loblolly pine earlywood and latewood cubes heated in air*[1] (Johnson and Koch 1972)

Transition	Earlywood		Latewood	
	Frequency	Range	Frequency	Range
		°C.		°C.
First endothermic peak	72/72	313–380	72/72	320–382
Exotherm change to second endotherm	72/72	391–486	39/72	394–512
Second endothermic peak	72/72	436–513	18/72	460–511
Glowing ignition				
1-mm. cube	1/24	506	17/24	507–513[2]
2-mm. cube	9/24	508–513[2]	24/24	501–513[2]
3-mm. cube	21/24	490–513	24/24	498–513[2]

[1] Includes values for extracted and unextracted specimens at both rates of temperature increase.

[2] Ignition of some cubes took place only after a time delay at 513° C.

delayed endothermic and exothermic peaks from 14° to 19° C.; saturation of cubes further delayed these peak temperatures 5° to 15° C. Since specimens lost all residual moisture during testing and became ovendried before reaching 200° C., the increase in peak temperatures may mean that saturation removed some water-soluble substances that contribute to early thermal degradation.

Extraction was not a significant factor in all cases. It did increase the temperature of the first endotherm (by 4° C.) and the temperature of the second endotherm for earlywood (by 6° C.). This result corresponds to Beall's (1968) finding that extraction of southern pine did not significantly change thermal degradation reaction.

The average temperature at the first endothermic peak was not a strong function of cube size (range 342° to 349° C., see table 26–2) or of cell type. It seems, therefore, that the temperature at which gases started to evolve was not clearly related to sample size or density.

The first exothermic peak temperature for earlywood, however, was strongly correlated with cube size. (See table 26–2.) Therefore, it appeared that the temperature at which gas evolution ceased in earlywood was a function of sample mass.

Temperatures reported for glowing ignition (490° to 513° C.) were higher than many reported in the literature (260° to 300° C.). Others have heated wood specimens in a furnace, thus bringing heated air into contact with all surfaces. The scanning calorimeter, employed in the Johnson and Koch study, applied heat to a single cube face; the surrounding air remained near room temperature. Internal temperature of

TABLE 26–2.—*Effect of primary variables on transition temperatures of earlywood when heated dynamically*[1] (Johnson and Koch 1972)

Factor	First endothermic peak[2]	First exothermic peak	Second endothermic peak
	— — — — — — — — °C. — — — — — — — —		
Cube size, mm.	*	*	*
1	344	408	475
2	349	435	482
3	340	458	481
Moisture content	*	*	*
10 percent	337	431	475
Saturated	351	436	484
Extractive content	*		*
Unextracted	342	433	476
Extractive-free	346	434	483
Rate of temperature increase, °C./min.	*	*	*
10	335	424	470
20	353	443	489

[1] Values tabulated below an asterisk differ significantly (0.05 level). Refer to figure 26–3A for plot of typical data.

[2] For latewood the first endothermic peak occurred at 346° C., a value not significantly different from the 344° C. temperature observed for earlywood; other values in this column were similar to those observed for latewood.

the cube was thus partially determined by the thermal conductivity of the wood and rate of dissipation into the cooler air. All 72 specimens heated statically ignited and glowed; in contrast, only 96 out of 144 cubes subjected to dynamic heating ignited and glowed. This would support the belief that slow heating causes gradual dissipation of heat and mass.

Because many specimens decomposed without glowing, valid conclusions about glow initiation temperatures and glow duration during dynamic tests are hard to frame. Some comments, however, seem in order. Ignition temperature was lowest in 3-mm., initially dry earlywood cubes (e.g., 494° C. for extracted and unextracted specimens heated at 10° C./min.). In dynamic tests, glow duration was shortest in 1-mm cubes (e.g., 6 sec.); generally speaking, small earlywood cubes failed to ignite at all. Glow duration was longest for 3-mm. latewood cubes (e.g., 106 sec.).

In static tests at 513° C. (table 26–3), elapsed time before glow initiation was shortest with 1-mm., initially dry, extractive-free earlywood cubes (average 6 sec.); elapsed time was longest with 3-mm., initially saturated, unextracted latewood cubes (average 189 sec.). Glow time was maximum for 3-mm., initially dry, extractive-free latewood cubes (average 112 sec.);

TABLE 26–3.—*Effect of primary variables on time lapse before ignition and duration of glow for cubes of loblolly pine earlywood and latewood heated statically at 513°C. in air*[1] (Johnson and Koch 1972)

Factor	Time to glow	Glow duration
	— — — — — Sec. — — — — —	
Cell type	*	*
Earlywood_____	30	20
Latewood_____	80	54
Cube size, mm.	*	*
1_____	15	7
2_____	37	36
3_____	113	68
Moisture content	*	*
10-percent_____	44	40
Saturated_____	66	34
Extractive content	*	*
Unextracted_____	57	35
Extractive-free_____	53	39

[1] Values tabulated below an asterisk differ significantly (0.05 level).

it was minimum for 1-mm., initially saturated earlywood cubes (average 3.5 sec.). The interaction of cube size and type of wood on time to ignition and length of glow when statically heated at 513° C. was as follows:

	Earlywood		Latewood	
Cube size	Time lapse	Length of glow	Time lapse	Length of glow
Mm.	— — — — — — — — Sec. — — — — — — — —			
1	5–15	2–5	11–44	7–13
2	12–39	12–24	32–64	47–62
3	20–110	31–52	146–196	77–128

Effects of primary variables can be seen from table 26–3.

Charring occurred first at the cube face in contact with the heat source, then progressed to the opposite face. Glowing followed the opposite direction, starting at the face exposed to the air, then progressing to the center of the cube, and finally burning very brightly at the center just before ceasing. Cubes either burned completely or left a minute amount of ash in the sample pan.

26–2 COMBUSTION REACTIONS

From section 26–1 it is evident that combustion of wood is a complex phenomenon; it can be described simply, however, as the rapid oxidation of wood accompanied by release of energy and increase in temperature.

COMBUSTION EQUATIONS

Only three elements of common fuels have heat value—carbon, hydrogen, and sulfur. Wood and bark, in contrast with the more common industrial fuels (gas, oil, coal), have little or no sulfur content.

Although the chemical reactions are often complex, the combustion process can be represented as a simple combination of oxygen and the combustible element. The combustion of hydrogen in oxygen is shown by the following reaction.

$$2H_2 + O_2 \rightarrow 2H_2O \qquad (26-1)$$

The atomic weight of oxygen is 16 and that of hydrogen approximately 1; it may therefore be calculated from equation 26–1 that 8 lb. of oxygen are required to completely burn 1 lb. of hydrogen and that this reaction results in the formation of 9 lb. of water.

Other common combustion equations are as follows:

$$C + O_2 \rightarrow CO_2 \qquad (26-2)$$

$$2C + O_2 \rightarrow 2CO \qquad (26-3)$$

$$S + O_2 \rightarrow SO_2 \qquad (26-4)$$

$$CH_4 + 2O_2 \rightarrow CO_2 + 2H_2O \qquad (26-5)$$

$$2C_8H_{18} + 25O_2 \rightarrow 18H_2O + 16CO_2 \qquad (26-6)$$

As noted previously, equation 26–4 is not usually applicable to ordinary solid wood or bark fuels because they have little or no sulfur content.

FUEL ANALYSIS

The amount of each constituent in a fuel, expressed as a percentage of the total weight, is determined by **ultimate analysis.** The elements normally reported are carbon, hydrogen, oxygen, nitrogen, and sulfur. In addition, the water and ash content are usually given along with the heating value of 1 lb. of the fuel.

The amount of water, volatile material, and ash present in a fuel are determined through a **proximate analysis** according to procedures defined in American Society for Testing and Materials (ASTM) Designation D–271–58. The residue that remains after extraction of the water, volatile material, and ash is defined as **fixed carbon,** a term not synonymous with **carbon** as determined by ultimate analysis.

Ultimate and proximate analyses of a limited sample of southern pine bark are given in table 26–4. No analysis has been published for southern pine wood. Data from other pines indicate, however, that by ultimate analysis the ash content of southern pine wood is probably closer to 0.4 percent than 0.6 percent. Also, the carbon content of southern pine wood (about 52 percent) may be a few percent lower, and the oxygen content (about 41 percent) a few percent higher than that of bark. Informa-

TABLE 26-4.—*Ultimate and proximate analyses of southern pine bark from single trees of four species; composition expressed as percentage by weight*[1] *(data from Mullen, see text footnote 1)*

Type of analysis and components	Loblolly		Longleaf		Shortleaf		Slash		Average	
	Partly dry	Ovendry	Partly dry	Ovendry	Partly dry	Ovendry	Partly dry	Ovendry	Partly dry	Ovendry
	Percent									
Ultimate										
Hydrogen	3.8	5.6	3.8	5.5	4.1	5.6	3.8	5.4	3.9	5.5
Carbon	38.1	56.3	39.0	56.4	41.5	57.2	39.4	56.2	39.5	56.5
Sulfur	nil	nil	nil	nil	nil	nil	nil	nil	nil	nil
Nitrogen	Included	with O_2	Included	with O_2	.3	.4	.3	.4	.3	.4
Oxygen	25.4	37.7	25.8	37.4	26.2	36.1	26.2	37.3	25.8	37.0
Ash	.3	.4	.5	.7	.5	.7	.5	.7	.5	.6
Total[2]	67.6	100.0	69.1	100.0	72.6	100.0	70.2	100.0	70.0	100.0
Proximate										
Water	32.4	.0	30.9	.0	27.4	.0	29.8	.0	30.0	.0
Volatile matter	44.4	65.7	46.3	67.0	47.5	65.5	46.3	65.9	46.2	66.0
Fixed carbon	22.9	33.9	22.3	32.3	24.6	33.8	23.4	33.4	23.3	33.4
Ash	.3	.4	.5	.7	.5	.7	.5	.7	.5	.6
Total	100.0	100.0	100.0	100.0	100.0	100.0	100.0	100.0	100.0	100.0
Heat of combustion, B.t.u./lb.	6,363	9,400	6,300	9,130	6,940	9,550	6,600	9,380	6,551	9,365

[1] At moisture content received and ovendry; analyses performed according to American Society for Testing and Materials Designation D-271-58. Trees were 30 to 45 years old.

[2] Equal to 100 percent when totalled with percentage of water content noted immediately below.

tion derived from proximate analysis of wood of other pine species indicates that volatile matter content may be higher (75 to 79 percent of ovendry weight) and fixed carbon content lower (near 20 percent) in southern pine wood than in southern pine bark. Some modification of ASTM procedures, and results obtained on eight western woods, are advanced by Mingle and Boubel (1968).

Obviously the moisture content of either wood or bark reflects treatment of the fuel prior to combustion. The natural moisture content of wood in standing pine trees is close to 100 percent of the ovendry weight (see sec. 8–1). Weldon (1967) found that moisture content of southern pine sawdust in east Texas averaged about 108 percent of ovendry weight. A pound of green sawdust therefore contains about half a pound of water and half a pound of dry wood.

As noted in section 12–3, inner bark of living southern pines has a much higher moisture content than outer bark, and whole bark from upper stem portions contains more moisture than that at breast height. In living southern pines of 6-inch d.b.h. and larger, it is likely that whole stem bark (breast height to 4-inch top) averages somewhat less than half water by weight. (See sec. 12–3.)

Weldon (1966), in his study of southern pine bark in east Texas, found that stored bark residues contained 53 to 76 percent moisture content (dry basis). Southern pine logs and pulpwood are commonly stored under water sprays, however, and pulpwood is frequently conveyed by flume to drum barkers; furthermore, bark storage piles in the South are frequently wetted by heavy downpours of rain. Because of these factors, bark fuel frequently has 100 percent moisture content, i.e., a pound of wet bark may be comprised of half a pound of water and half a pound of dry matter.

AIR REQUIREMENT

In power plants, oxygen for the combustion reactions described by equations 26–1 through 26–6 normally comes from the atmosphere, which also contains a large amount of nitrogen plus traces of water vapor, carbon dioxide, and other gases. For the purpose of calculating the amount of air required for combustion, it is sufficiently accurate to describe air as comprised only of oxygen and nitrogen.

| | Approximate composition of air | |
Element	By volume	By weight
	Percent	
Oxygen	20.9	23.1
Nitrogen	79.1	76.9

Thus, in air there are 3.78 cu. ft. of nitrogen for each cubic foot of oxygen and 3.32 lb. of nitrogen for each pound of oxygen.

As carbon has an atomic weight of 12, it is seen from equation 26–2 that 2.66 lb. of oxygen are required to burn 1 lb. of carbon; to supply this amount of oxygen, (4.32)(2.66) or 11.49 lb. of air are required. By similar calculation it can be shown from equation 26–1 that 34.56 lb. of air are required to burn 1 lb. of hydrogen.

The amount of air required to completely burn a fuel is determined from its ultimate analysis. Southern pine bark of 30-percent moisture content (green basis) contains about 39.5 percent carbon, 3.9 percent hydrogen, and 25.8 percent oxygen (table 26–4, second column from right). The amount of oxygen required from the air to burn a fuel is diminished by the amount of oxygen in the fuel. The air required to burn a pound of southern pine bark containing 30-percent moisture content (green basis) is therefore calculated as follows:

$$\begin{aligned}
\text{Pounds of air to burn the carbon} &= (0.395)(11.49) = 4.54 \\
\text{Pounds of air to burn the hydrogen} &= (0.039)(34.56) = +1.35 \\
\text{Less the pounds of air equivalent} & \\
\text{to the oxygen in the bark} &= (0.258)(4.32) = -1.11 \\
\hline
\text{Pounds of air required per pound of fuel} & \quad\quad\quad 4.78
\end{aligned}$$

This is the amount of air theoretically required. To insure sufficient oxygen for the burning process, it is common practice to supply additional or **excess air,** in an amount dependent on the fuel and the burning equipment, but usually equalling about one-quarter the theoretical amount. In industry terminology, 25 percent excess air, or 125 percent total air, means that air totalling 1.25 times the theoretical requirement is supplied. Too great an excess of air reduces the amount of heat recoverable from a fuel because heat is lost in raising the temperature of the excess air to flue temperature.

STAGES IN THE COMBUSTION OF WOOD AND BARK

Because of the high water and volatile contents of hogged (coarsely pulverized) southern pine wood and bark, the process of combustion takes place in three consecutive overlapping stages. In the first stage heat is absorbed by the fuel, and its water content is evaporated as steam; the fuel temperature does not much exceed 212° F. until its moisture content approaches zero. The duration of the first stage depends on the rate of heat supply and transfer into the fuel particles.

To accelerate evaporation of moisture, particles of wood and bark fuels should be reduced to the smallest size practical and economical. Reduction of particle size increases surface area and reduces the distance heat must penetrate to drive out moisture and other volatiles.

The second stage is one of liberation and burning of the volatile matter other than water. After the moisture evaporates, the temperature rises as heat is added until the volatile matter is removed. The rate of liberation of volatiles depends on the rate at which heat is supplied. At about 1,000°

to 1,100° F. (538° to 593° C.) the volatiles ignite, burn, and give off heat.

The third stage in the combustion process occurs when most of the volatile matter has been removed and the surface of the remaining residue reaches a glowing temperture and burns as oxygen from the air is brought in contact with it. This combustion exposes additional surface until the entire mass is consumed. Temperature of the burning gases above the fuel bed may exceed the temperature within the fuel bed.

Burning of the volatile matter and much of the fixed carbon takes place above and on top of the fuel bed. Since volatiles comprise 65 to 80 percent of the combustible material in southern pine bark and wood, a large proportion of the air required for combustion should be applied above the surface of the fuel bed rather than through it. As carbon reacts with oxygen, carbon dioxide is formed (equation 26–2) and forms a barrier to the admittance of more oxygen to the fuel surface. To speed combustion by rapid diffusion of oxygen through this layer of carbon dioxide, overfire air is supplied in a manner that causes turbulence above the fuel bed.

26–3 HEATING VALUE

Section 9–4 contains data on the heat of combustion of fuels derived from various portions of southern pine trees. (See subsection headed HEAT OF COMBUSTION and table 9–8.)

From these data it appears likely that southern pine wood has an average heat of combustion of about 8,600 B.t.u. per ovendry pound. The average value for southern pine bark is somewhat higher, probably 8,900 B.t.u. per ovendry pound or higher.

USABLE HEAT CONTENT

Reineke (1947) described the calculation of usable heat content in wood fuel as follows. Moisture in the fuel does not reduce the total heat produced during combustion, but its presence in the flue gases together with the water formed during burning of the hydrogen in the fuel reduces recoverable heat by carrying heat up the stack. Since flue gas temperature may be approximately 400° F., any water present is in the form of steam. Because vaporization of water to steam requires about 970 B.t.u./lb., and additional heat is required to raise the water temperature from ambient (65° F., for example) to 212° F. and to raise the steam temperature from 212° F. to a flue temperature of about 400° F., each pound of steam carries with it up the flue 1,210 B.t.u. Typically, green sapwood of the southern pines contains 1 lb. of water for each pound of wood. Since there is ½-lb. of dry wood and ½-lb. of water in each pound of freshly cut sapwood, to calculate its useable heat one must reduce the dry-wood heat of combustion by half, and also deduct about 600 B.t.u.

Approximately 0.55 lb. of water is formed in burning the hydrogen in 1 lb. of dry wood, causing a loss of about 660 B.t.u. A further small loss is attributable to the water (approximately 0.1 lb.) contained in the combustion air required to burn 1 lb. of dry wood. An additional 690 B.t.u. may be lost up the stack in other hot flue gases (carbon dioxide, nitrogen, and excess air); if excess air is limited to 30 percent, this loss may be reduced by one-third.

Therefore, the net usable heat from 2 lb. of green southern pine sapwood (assuming that this fuel contains equal weights of wood and water) is approximately as follows (ignoring humidity in the combustion air):

Heat of combustion of 1 lb. of dry wood	8,600 B.t.u.
Less	
Heat loss associated with water content	−1,210
Heat loss associated with hydrogen combustion	− 660
Heat loss in other flue gases	− 690
Net usable heat	6,040 B.t.u.

The usable heat from 1 lb. of this wet fuel is therefore only 6,040/2 or 3,020 B.t.u., i.e., about 70 percent of the 4,300-B.t.u. input.

26–4 STEAM GENERATORS

Steam is generated by passing hot combustion gas through water-carrying heat exchangers. Industrial boilers fed with fuel derived from southern pine trees are designed to produce a predicted steam flow (50,000 to 1 million lb./hr.), at a specified gage pressure and temperature (150 p.s.i.g. at 520° F. for the smaller units, to 1,335 p.s.i.g. at 958° F. or higher for the biggest units), with a specified rate of fuel consumption (as high as 200 tons of wet bark per hour for the largest units). If properly designed, these steam generators require little manpower for operation and do not contaminate atmosphere, land, or water.

The discussion that follows applies particularly to the burning of southern pine bark, but combustion principles and basic equipment are the same for hogged wood, sawdust, or other pulverized cellulosic fuels.

EFFICIENCY

Efficiency of a steam generator is expressed as the percentage of input heat that is utilized.

$$\text{Percent efficiency} = \left(\frac{Q_1 - Q_2}{Q_1}\right) 100 \qquad (26\text{–}7)$$

where Q_1 = total heat input
Q_2 = sum of heat losses

The major factor affecting heat loss is the temperature of the flue gas when it is discharged into the atmosphere. As the gas flows from the combustion chamber through the heat exchangers, it continually drops in temperature as heat is transferred. The rate at which heat is transferred is dependent on the temperature difference between the gas and the fluid in the heat exchanger. For a steam temperature of 750° F., obviously the gas temperature must be somewhat higher. The smaller the temperature differential, the greater the amount of heat transfer surface required; it follows that an extremely efficient unit is more costly than a less efficient one, since it contains a large amount of heat transfer surface to reduce the major loss—that due to energy lost in hot exhaust gas.

To salvage heat from the exhaust gas after it has passed through heat exchangers designed to produce steam, additional heat exchangers are employed. These include **economizers** to preheat the intake water, and air heaters to preheat air before it is introduced to the combustion chamber. It is possible to utilize some of the heat still remaining in flue gas to predry the incoming fuel; for example, finely divided wet bark or sawdust can be partially dried—and therefore improved as a fuel—in a **fuel suspension dryer.** Corder (1958) calculated that a wood-fueled boiler with a capacity of 50,000 lb. of steam per hour would hourly emit about 95,000 lb. of exhaust gas at 600° F.; potential heat of the gas above 200° F. would be about 10 million B.t.u./hour—sufficient to evaporate about 3 tons of water per hour from wet sawdust or bark. (Sec. 26–5 contains an example illustrating calculation of weight of exhaust gas emitted for any level of fuel consumption.)

Steam at 165 p.s.i. absolute (150.3 p.s.i.g.) and 550° F. contains heat energy of 1,118 B.t.u./lb. more than feedwater at 212° F. To convert 50,000 lb. of this water per hour to such steam in a boiler fired with wet bark (half water) at an efficiency of 66.5 percent, therefore requires $(50,000)(1,118) \div (8,900/2)(0.665)$, or 18,890 lb. of wet bark per hour. If 3 tons of water were driven out of this 9.4 tons of wet bark before it was fired, efficiency would be increased to over 75 percent; because moisture content of the bark would be reduced from 100 percent to 36.5 percent (dry basis) each pound of fuel would contain $8,900/1.365$ B.t.u. To produce 50,000 lb. of steam per hour, therefore, only $(50,000)(1,118) \div (8,900/1.365)(0.75)$, or 11,431 lb. of the drier fuel would be required.

While these potential gains appear attractive, use of flue gas to dry fuel is not generally practiced because of the expense of additional fuel handling, the practical necessity of maintaining flue gas temperature substantially higher than fuel temperature in heat-exchanger-type dryers, and the limited ability of the flue gas to carry off evaporated water; in short, it is apparently more economical to dry southern pine fuels in the combustion chamber than in external dryers.

Efficiency of a boiler to burn black liquor from a kraft pulpmill (half water and half solids) is typically less—about 60 percent—and a pound of liquor containing $6,000/2$, or 3,000 B.t.u. might usefully give up $(0.60)(3,000)$, or 1,800 B.t.u. to generate steam.

ECONOMICS OF BARK-FIRED POWER PLANTS

In most mills using southern pine, bark is an expensive nuisance that does not have uses sufficient to provide income equal to the costs of its growth, harvest, transport, remanufacture, or even removal from the site. Although these same plants are also major consumers of electrical energy and heat, only the very largest mills—primarily pulpmills—have been able to justify operation of bark-fed boilers. The reasons for this limited use of bark as fuel are largely economic; i.e., only mills with very great demands for power and steam can afford to amortize and operate the large boilers required to produce energy competitive with public utility plants. Also, because mill power demands are fairly constant, while bark supplies are variable, most bark-burning boilers must be designed for alternative firing of one or more fossil fuels.

The larger mills and also public utility plants can, however, consider bark as an economically practical fuel if it is priced competitively, supplied continuously, and produced in sufficient quantities. Fossil fuels, with which bark must compete, can be burned more efficiently than bark and have higher heats of combustion, but cost more per ton (table 26–5). To determine the delivered price at which bark is competitive with the fossil fuels, the fuel cost to generate 1,000 lb. of steam can be calculated from the data in table 26–5 by assuming that 1,100 B.t.u. (usable) are required to generate 1 lb. of steam and that water is converted to steam with 66.5-percent efficiency. A delivered price of about $2 per green ton of bark (half water) appears to be competitive. To be directly equivalent in price to coal, green bark would have to sell for $1.96 per green ton. The equivalent to oil would be $2.18, and to gas $2.45.

TABLE 26–5.—*Comparison of fuel values of fossil fuels and southern pine bark*

Fuel	Efficiency	Heat of combustion as fired		Delivered cost[1]		Input to generate 1,000 lb. of steam	
				Per ton[2]	Per million B.t.u.	Heat	Fuel cost
	Percent	*B.t.u./ lb.*	*Million B.t.u./ ton*	– *Dollars* –		*Million B.t.u.*	*Dollars*
Bituminous coal__	85.0	13,500	27.0	7.56	0.28	1.29	0.36
No. 6 oil_____	82.5	18,000	36.0	10.80	.30	1.33	.40
Natural gas_____	77.8	18,550	37.1	11.87	.32	1.41	.45
Wet bark (half water)____	66.5	4,450	8.9	1.96	.22	1.65	.36

[1] As of spring 1970; subject to variation according to location.

[2] Values for oil and gas converted from price per barrel and price per cubic foot.

Because amortization and interest costs are a substantial portion (one-third to one-half) of total cost to produce 1,000 lb. of steam, fuel cost alone does not provide a complete index to economic feasibility. Since bark-burning furnaces are larger than oil- or gas-fired units, they are more expensive; because of material-handling equipment, coal-fired boilers cost more than oil-fired units. The approximate relative costs (installed) that follow are subject to considerable variation according to steam generating capacity and manner of assembly, i.e., whether shop-assembled or field-erected.

Primary fuels	Relative cost of steam generator
Gas only _____	1.0
Oil only _____	1.2
Coal only _____	1.8
Coal and oil _____	2.0
Bark only _____	2.2
Oil and bark _____	2.4

In a study of Montana sawmills and plywood plants, Host and Lowry (1970) concluded that shifting from natural gas to bark-burning boilers would result in annual savings of about $44,000 for a 25,000-lb./hour boiler and about $95,000 for a 50,000-lb./hour boiler. Comparable savings should be achievable in large mills processing southern pine. Elimination of air pollution caused by the present practice of disposing of bark in waste burners or inefficient **Dutch ovens** (a type of furnace that burns woody fuels in a deep pile rather than in suspension; see fig. 26–4) is a further incentive to use efficient bark-fired boilers.

BARK SUPPLY AND TRANSPORT

As noted earlier, the harvest of green southern pine bark will likely exceed 20 million tons annually by the year 2000. This is sufficient to fuel 12 generating plants, each with a capacity of 1 million lb. of steam per hour (1,000° F.). In total, these 12 plants could supply the present electrical demands of the cities of Savannah, Mobile, and Pensacola.

A bark price of $2 per green ton (delivered into the fuel pile) permits only minimal transportation charges. Therefore, potential users of bark require knowledge of its location. The immediate sources are the sawmills, plywood plants, pulpmills, and other pine conversion plants that have bark in excess of their requirements. These sources are widely distributed throughout the Southern States. There have been few regional studies of residue location; notable are the Texas surveys of bark and sawdust volume (Weldon 1966, 1967). A basic approach to source identification can be made through analysis of the location of standing pine trees in the South; for this purpose the maps prepared by Sternitzke and Nelson (1970) are an excellent reference. (See ch. 3 and figs. 3–1, 3–3, 3–5, 3–7, 3–9, 3–11, 3–13, 3–15, 3–17, and 3–19).

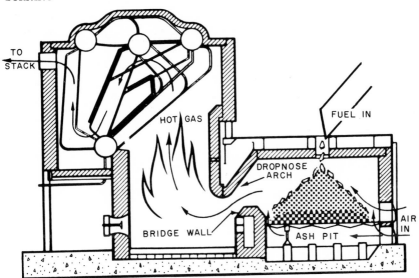

Figure 26–4.—Dutch oven boiler. Most of the fuel is destructively distilled. Combustible gas emerging from the fuel pile mixes with air entering through overfire ports and the fuel-charging chute. The air-gas mixture burns in the combustion chamber; hot flue gases, en route to the stack, pass through water-carrying heat exchangers and generate steam. (Drawing after McKenzie 1968.)

To minimize transportation costs, bark from pine-using mills would probably be conveyed into open-top freight cars or motor vans and delivered to power generating plants for bulk discharge into outdoor fuel piles; the delivery system would be closely comparable to that now used to convey pulpchips from sawmills to pulpmills. Haul distances would necessarily be short.

EQUIPMENT

Infeeding equipment for bark- or wood-burning boilers should include surge bins from which fuel can be metered in response to demand. The fuel should be homogeneous in moisture content if possible; for suspension burning, particles should be of uniform small size (¼- to ¾-inch maximum dimension and preferably smaller). Bark is generally admitted to a furnace in several streams, each carrying the correct proportion to obtain good fuel distribution in the furnace (Roberson 1967).

In new construction, the traditional Dutch oven furnace (fig. 26–4) has been almost completely supplanted; the concept of water-cooled furnaces and **suspension burning** of bark and wood (Ellwanger 1952) has resulted in more efficient steam generators fired with bark alone and also with bark (or wood) in combination with coal, oil, and gas.

Suspension firing of bark is analogous to the firing of pulverized coal; a large percentage of the fuel is burned before it reaches a small grate at the bottom of the furnace where the larger bark particles are burned.

Examples of steam-generating units, consecutively numbered according to capacity, are shown in figures 26–5 through 26–12. In boilers depicted by figure 26–5 and 26–9, fuel is distributed mechanically; in the other furnaces bark is injected and spread pneumatically.

Steam generators are normally guaranteed to produce a specified amount of steam on one fuel only—usually coal, gas, or oil. For woody fuels—which may vary in moisture and heat content—steaming rates are predicted but not usually guaranteed. Figures 26–5 through 26–12 show bark-

1. Coal Feeder	5. Ash Pit	9. Steam Out	13. Air Heater
2. Bark Feeder	6. Ash Hopper	10. Water Inlet	14. Char Hopper
3. Fuel Spreader	7. Water Tubes	11. Cold Air In	15. Gas Outlet
4. Ash Pit Door	8. Superheater	12. Hot Air	16. Safety Valve
			17. Dump Grate

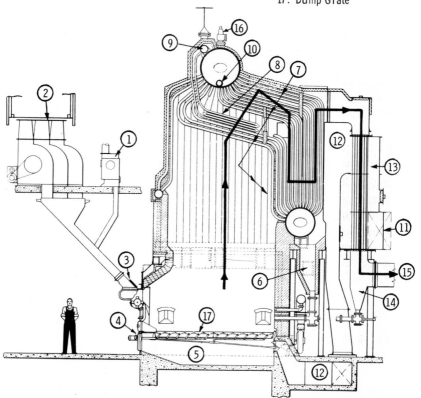

Figure 26–5.—Steam generator with capacity of 55,000 lb. of steam per hour.
Fuel: ....10,000 lb. of bark per hour if bark is only fuel; also burns bark at lesser rates in combination with coal, or burns coal alone.
Steam pressure: ....150 p.s.i.g. (pounds per square inch gage).
Steam temperature:...520° F.
Firing equipment: .....Mechanical distributors with dump grate.
(Drawing from Combustion Engineering, Inc.)

1. Coal Inlet
2. Coal Spreader
3. Bark Inlet
4. Steam Outlet
5. Water Inlet
6. Main Air In
7. Over-Fire Air Fan
8. Ash Hopper
9. Ash Removal Door
10. Dust Collector
11. Gas to Stack
12. Air Heater
13. Char Hopper
14. Continuous Ash Discharge Stoker
15. Boiler Tubes
16. Superheater
17. Economizer
18. Furnace Wall Tubes
19. Safety Valve
20. Gas Path

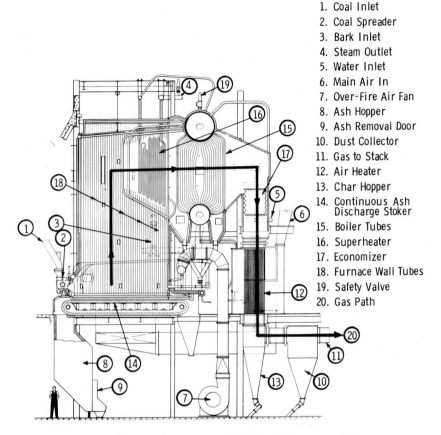

Figure 26–6.—Steam generator with capacity of 120,000 lb. of steam per hour.

Fuel: .... 20,000 lb./hour of bark if fired alone, also burns bark at lesser rates in combination with coal, or burns coal alone.

Steam pressure: .... 615 p.s.i.g.

Steam temperature:...750° F.

Firing equipment: ..... Barked fired pneumatically through side wall; coal spread mechanically. Travelling grate discharges ash continuously.

(Drawing from Combustion Engineering, Inc.)

fueled furnaces; some, however, are designed primarily for gas or oil (e.g., fig. 26–8) or coal (fig. 26–6). The boiler shown in figure 26–7 is designed for bark alone, and its fuel consumption is typical.

If moist bark (half water by weight) has a heat of combustion of $8,900/2 = 4,450$ B.t.u./lb., and if the boiler is designed to add 1,200 B.t.u./lb. to the water and convert it to high-pressure, high-temperature steam, then the efficiency should be about 70 percent. Under these conditions, about 2.60 lb. of steam can be generated from each pound of moist bark, i.e., $(4,450)(0.70) \div 1,200$. About 10,000 kw. of electrical power can be generated from 100,000 lb./hr. of such steam. From these data bark consumption and power output can be tabulated.

Steam capacity	Moist bark required	Electrical power output
Lb./hr.	*Tons/hr.*	*Kw.*
100,000	19.3	10,000
200,000	38.5	20,000
500,000	96.3	50,000
1,000,000	192.5	100,000

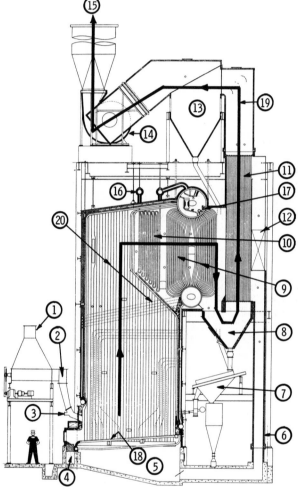

1. Bark Bin
2. Bark Feedchute
3. Bark Air Spreader
4. Ash Pit
5. Air Chamber
6. Hot Air Duct
7. Sand Separator
8. Char and Sand Collecting Hopper
9. Boiler Tubes
10. Superheater
11. Air Heater
12. Air Inlet
13. Dust Collector
14. Induced Draft Fan
15. Gas to Stack
16. Steam Out
17. Water In
18. Grate Surface
19. Gas Path
20. Furnace Wall Tubes

Figure 26–7.—Steam generator with capacity of 150,000 lb. of steam per hour.

Fuel: ....50,000 to 60,000 lb. of bark per hour.

Steam pressure: ....475 p.s.i.g.

Steam temperature: ..725° F.

Firing equipment: ......Bark fired and spread pneumatically at controllable rate; travelling grate discharges ash continuously.

(Drawing from Erie City.)

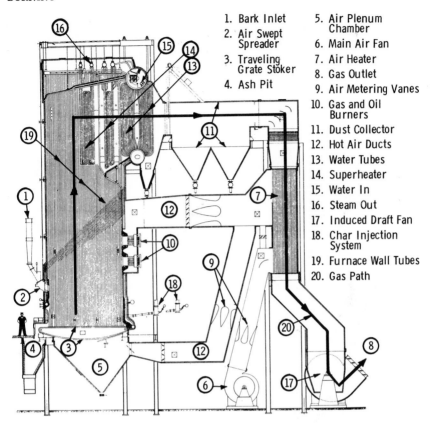

1. Bark Inlet
2. Air Swept Spreader
3. Traveling Grate Stoker
4. Ash Pit
5. Air Plenum Chamber
6. Main Air Fan
7. Air Heater
8. Gas Outlet
9. Air Metering Vanes
10. Gas and Oil Burners
11. Dust Collector
12. Hot Air Ducts
13. Water Tubes
14. Superheater
15. Water In
16. Steam Out
17. Induced Draft Fan
18. Char Injection System
19. Furnace Wall Tubes
20. Gas Path

Figure 26–8.—Steam generator with capacity of 350,000 lb. of steam per hour.

Fuel: ....50,000 lb./hour of bark in combination with either gas or oil.

Steam pressure: ....990 p.s.i.g.

Steam temperature:....900° F.

Firing equipment: ......Bark fired and spread pneumatically at controlled rate for use simultaneously with burners for gas or oil. Travelling grate discharges ash continuously.

(Drawing from Erie City.)

It is practical to transport bark by pneumatic conveyor to combustion chambers from surge piles up to 5,000 feet distant from the furnace. The air/fuel ratio (by weight) in the transport pipe should be about 0.25 at rated capacity.

There are a number of alternative ways to meter bark into a furnace. In one arrangement (fig. 26–12), bark is fed at a controlled rate into a cyclone and then discharged to a virbrating distributor which diverts it to each burner nozzle via pneumatic conveyor. Another system has been described by Mullen (1968). In this arrangement the bark is introduced by a metering feeder to each pneumatic system leading to a burner; excess bark is conveyed back to the storage area (fig. 26–13). Details of the bark-

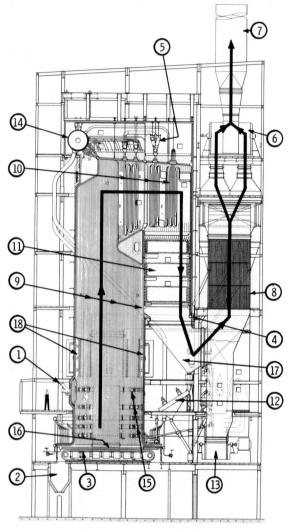

1. Bark Spreader
2. Ash Pit
3. Traveling Grate Stoker
4. Water Inlet
5. Steam Outlet
6. Induced Draft Fan
7. Gas Outlet Duct
8. Air Heater
9. Furnace Water Walls
10. Superheaters
11. Economizer
12. Char-Sand Separator
13. Main Air Fan
14. Steam Drum
15. Over-Fire Air Nozzles
16. Grate Surface
17. Char Collecting Hopper
18. Gas Burners

Figure 26–9.—Steam generator with capacity of 600,000 lb. of steam per hour.

Fuel: .... Designed for 140,000 lb. of bark per hour if fired with bark alone, but actually will burn 202,000 lb./hour of bark as fired; bark can be burned in combination with gas, or unit can be fired with gas alone.

Steam pressure: ....1,335 p.s.i.g.

Steam temperature: ..958° F.

Firing equipment: ....High-set mechanical bark spreaders; travelling grate discharges ash continuously.

(Drawing from Combustion Engineering, Inc.)

metering device are shown in figure 26–14. Fuel is usually fed into the furnace through four injection nozzles (fig. 26–15), located one at each furnace corner. The major portion of the bark is burned in suspension,

1. Steam Outlet   3. Superheater   5. Boiler Tubes   7. Dust   8. Hot Air
2. Water Inlet   4. Air Heater   6. Furnace   Collector   9. Gas Path

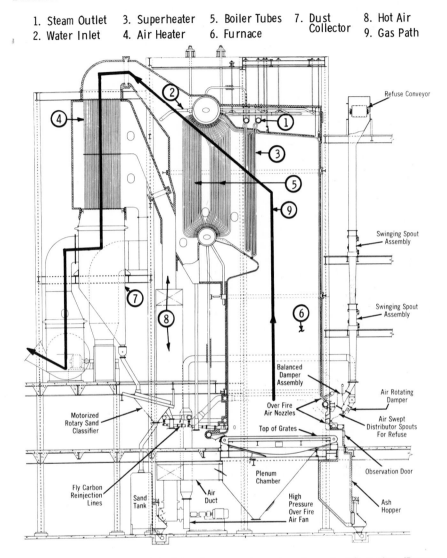

Figure 26–10.—Components of bark-burning steam generator; shown in side section. (Drawing from Detroit Stoker Company.)

combustion patterns being controlled by vertically tilting the fuel injection nozzles.

Preferably, a bark-burning furnace should be designed with bark injection nozzles about 16 feet above the grate; the **high set** promotes more complete burning of bark particles before they fall to the grate (fig. 26–9). Furnaces with **low set** fuel injectors (8 feet or less above the grate) are more economical to construct but less efficient.

Residual material not burned in suspension is retained on a small grate,

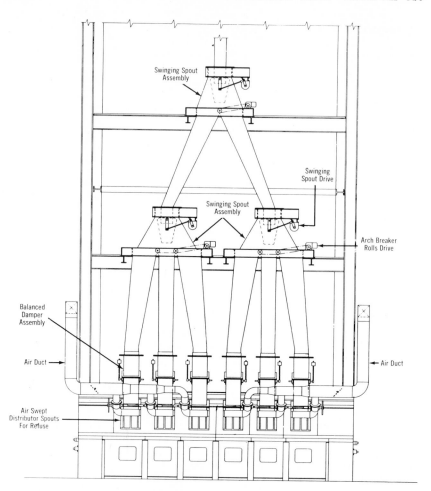

Figure 26–11.—Detail of bark-distributing system (front view of unit shown in fig. 26–10) that insures equal distribution of fuel to each injection nozzle. (Drawing from Detroit Stoker Company.)

where hot air from above and below completes combustion. **Dump grates** deposit ash at intervals directly into ash pits (figs. 26–5, 26–12, 26–13); **traveling grates** continuously discharge ash to collection pits (figs. 26–6, 26–7, 26–8, 26–9, 26–10).

CONTROL OF EMISSIONS OF CHAR

Fly ash, the fine particles of ash carried out of the stack by flue gases, may contain highly visible particulate charcoal or **char** in addition to less visible mineral ash. This char contaminates not only residential properties adjacent to the boiler (swimming pools and laundry areas, for example), but also pulp chips, paper, planed lumber, and plywood in transit to and

1. Bark Distributor
2. Bark Nozzle
   (1) Each Corner
3. Grate Surface
4. Main Air Fan
5. Ljungstrom
   Air Heater
6. Dust Collector
7. Gas Outlet
8. Superheater
9. Water In
10. Steam Out

11. Rectangular Furnace
12. Ash Pit

13. Air Blowers (4)
14. Air Lock Feeders (4)

See Fig. 26-15
for Further
Details

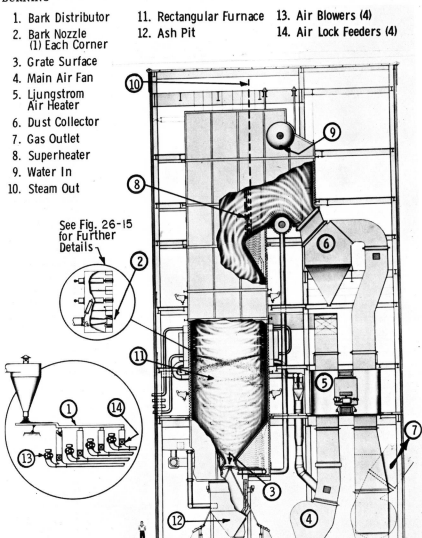

Figure 26–12.—Steam generator showing method of pneumatically transporting, feeding, and burning hogged cellulosic fuels alone or in combination with other fuels. Bark is fed at a controlled rate to the cyclone, then drops to a vibrating distributor, and finally proceeds to each burner nozzle via pneumatic conveyor. Four sets of fuel nozzles (one in each corner) may be manually or automatically tilted up or down to distribute the fuel. This boiler can be designed to produce up to 1 million lb. of steam per hour with a maximum consumption of 70 tons per hour of wet bark (half water by weight) alone or in combination with coal, oil, or gas. (Drawing from Combustion Engineeing, Inc.)

from the mill serviced by the steam generator. This charcoal results from incomplete combustion. Because southern pine bark has about 10 to 13 percent less volatile matter by proximate analysis than wood, it also tends

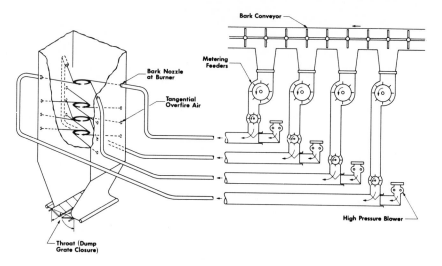

Figure 26–13.—Metering device, pneumatic feeders, overfire air nozzles, and dump grates for steam generator. In this system, the bark is metered to each nozzle individually; excess fuel is returned to storage. (Drawing from Combustion Engineering, Inc.)

to have a correspondingly greater fixed carbon content; the term "fixed carbon" is not synonymous with char, but fuels with a high fixed carbon content tend to produce more char than those lower in fixed carbon.

Emissions of char are controlled by burning all of the charcoal in the combustion chamber; long fuel retention time in the furnace promotes this complete combustion. Time required to consume all of the charcoal is short if furnace temperatures are high, fuel particles are small, oxygen supply is ample, and the combustion atmosphere is turbulent.

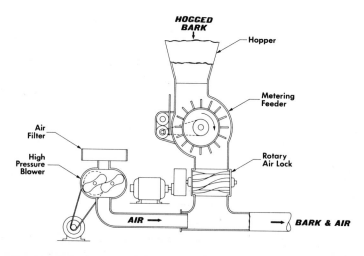

Figure 26–14.—Device to meter bark into pneumatic fuel injection nozzle. (Drawing from Combustion Engineering, Inc.)

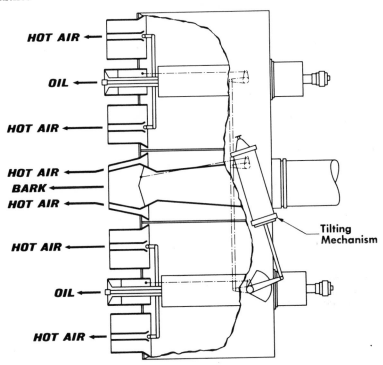

HOT AIR ←

OIL ←

HOT AIR ←

HOT AIR ←
BARK ←
HOT AIR ←

HOT AIR ←

OIL ←

HOT AIR ←

Tilting
Mechanism

Figure 26–15.—Burner assembly for simultaneous or solo injection of bark and oil (or gas). Hot air is introduced in a jet around each fuel jet. Fuel nozzles (with accompanying air jets) can be tilted vertically to alter trajectory for desired distribution of fuel in the furnace. Normally, one burner assembly is located at each of four corners of rectangular furnace. (Drawing from Combustion Engineering, Inc.)

Furnaces designed to burn wood or bark supply oxygen in overfire air to combine with methane, carbon monoxide, hydrogen, and formaldehyde from wood pyrolysis to form carbon dioxide and water vapor. The overfire air system not only supplies oxygen above the fuel bed to burn the volatile matter, but also increases turbulence and extends retention time of char in the furnace, thus promoting more complete consumption and reducing char carryover to the gas-cleaning equipment.

A typical sieve analysis of char entering the dust collector from a bark-fired boiler is listed in table 26–6.

Flue gas-cleaning equipment.—Flue gas from bark-burning boilers can be cleaned by cyclone mechanical collectors in single or multiple arrangements. The **multicyclone mechanical dust collector** (fig. 26–16) is assembled from many units, each comprised of a pair of tubes mounted together. The clean-gas outlet is partially inserted into the larger dirty-gas inlet tube; curved vanes at the top of the inlet tubes impart a swirling action to the incoming dirty gas, and the dirt is separated by centrifugal force

TABLE 26–6.—*Typical sieve analysis of char carried by flue gas entering the dust collector of a bark-fired boiler* (Booth 1966)

Size of mesh in sieve (openings per lineal inch)	Retention on sieve	Cumulative retention
	– – – – – *Percent* – – – – –	
20	43.8	43.8
30	6.2	50.0
40	3.9	53.9
80	11.3	65.2
100	2.8	68.0
200	7.7	75.7
325	9.3	85.0
325	15.0 (through)	100.0

(fig. 26–17). Mechanical cyclone collectors are usually guaranteed on the basis of the percentage of solids above 10 μm (a micrometer is 10^{-6} m.) in size that will be separated from the gas stream at a given pressure drop through the cyclone; a large pressure drop will yield a cleaner gas than a small drop.

As air pollution regulations become enforced more stringently, **electrostatic precipitators** are likely to be more frequently used in bark-fired boilers to clean flue gases. In these devices, dust particles in the gas flow to electrically charged collecting plates (fig. 20–18, point 6) and are then vibrated off the plates into a hopper below.

If properly installed and maintained, either the mechanical or electrostatic devices will do a good job of cleaning flue gas; a combination of the two types is most effective—though most costly.

According to Mullen (1964) and Barron (1970), char accumulated in the dust collector should not be reinjected into the furnace for further burning; the practice lowers the efficiency of the dust collector, increases air pollution, and causes added erosion of boiler parts exposed to the flue gas.

WOOD BASED FUELS OTHER THAN BARK

All wood-based fuels can be burned in suspension if they are finely divided and are not more than half water by weight. While combustion systems other than suspension burners are in use, newer installations burn woody fuels in suspension because the method is efficient and, if properly controlled, causes little air pollution.

Hog fuel, sawdust, and shavings.—Because most southern pine veneer bolts, saw logs, and pulpwood are stored under water sprinklers—and in the case of pulpwood, may be flume conveyed to a drum barker—the bark

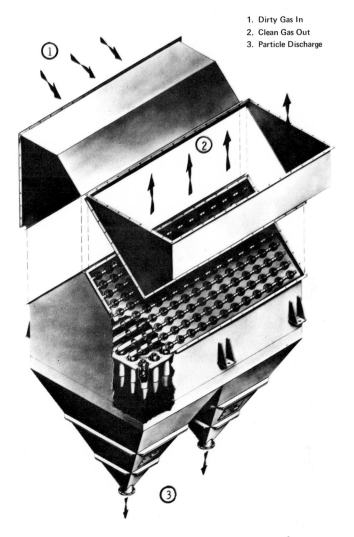

1. Dirty Gas In
2. Clean Gas Out
3. Particle Discharge

Figure 26–16.—Multicyclone mechanical cleaner for flue gas from steam generators burning southern pine bark. Each small cyclone measures about 10 inches in outside diameter. (Drawing from Research Cottrell, Inc.)

is likely to be uniformly wet. Wood waste, however, is variable in moisture content because a portion of it comes from sawdust, trimmings, and shavings cut from kiln-dried or air-dried lumber. Variations in moisture content —which call for variations in fuel/air ratios and cause fluctuations in burning rates and temperatures—can be reduced if the fuel is first distributed into large storage bins or piles prior to admission to the fuel-metering mechanism. Southern pine wood has a slightly lower heat of combustion than southern pine bark (see sec. 9–4, HEAT OF COMBUSTION, and

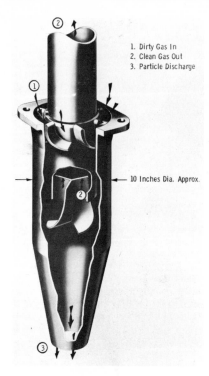

1. Dirty Gas In
2. Clean Gas Out
3. Particle Discharge

10 Inches Dia. Approx.

Figure 26–17.—Detail of individual cyclone from multicyclone mechanical cleaner shown in figure 26–16. (Drawing from Research Cottrell, Inc.)

table 9–8) and can seldom compete with fossil fuels on a price basis because of its high value as furnish for pulp and board products.

Sander dust.—Reineke (1947) has described the hazards entailed in burning sander dust. A combustible dust will burn with explosive force if the particles are surrounded by sufficient air for combustion and are spaced sufficiently close to permit propagation of flame from one particle to the next so that all particles are simultaneously heated to the ignition point. Greater or lesser concentrations are not explosive.

Explosion hazards can be eliminated in closed pneumatic systems by using any inert atmosphere (nitrogen, carbon dioxide, flue gas) in which the oxygen content is relatively low (under 12 percent). If the fine sander dust is mixed with bark, sawdust, or shavings, and fed to the fire so that the dust does not separate, explosion risks will be eliminated. Another alternative is concentration of the dust, in suspension, to a density above the explodable concentration before it is introduced into the furnace. In one Wisconsin installation, sander dust is accumulated in a separate cyclone where it is stored in suspension. An electronic "eye" measures the dust concentration, and when the desired concentration is reached, it actuates a valve permitting the dust to pass to a special dust burner opening into the combustion chamber of the main furnace. As the fuel is used up and the concentration of dust diminishes to a value somewhat above the explodable level, the control stops the flow of dust to the burners (Rieneke 1947).

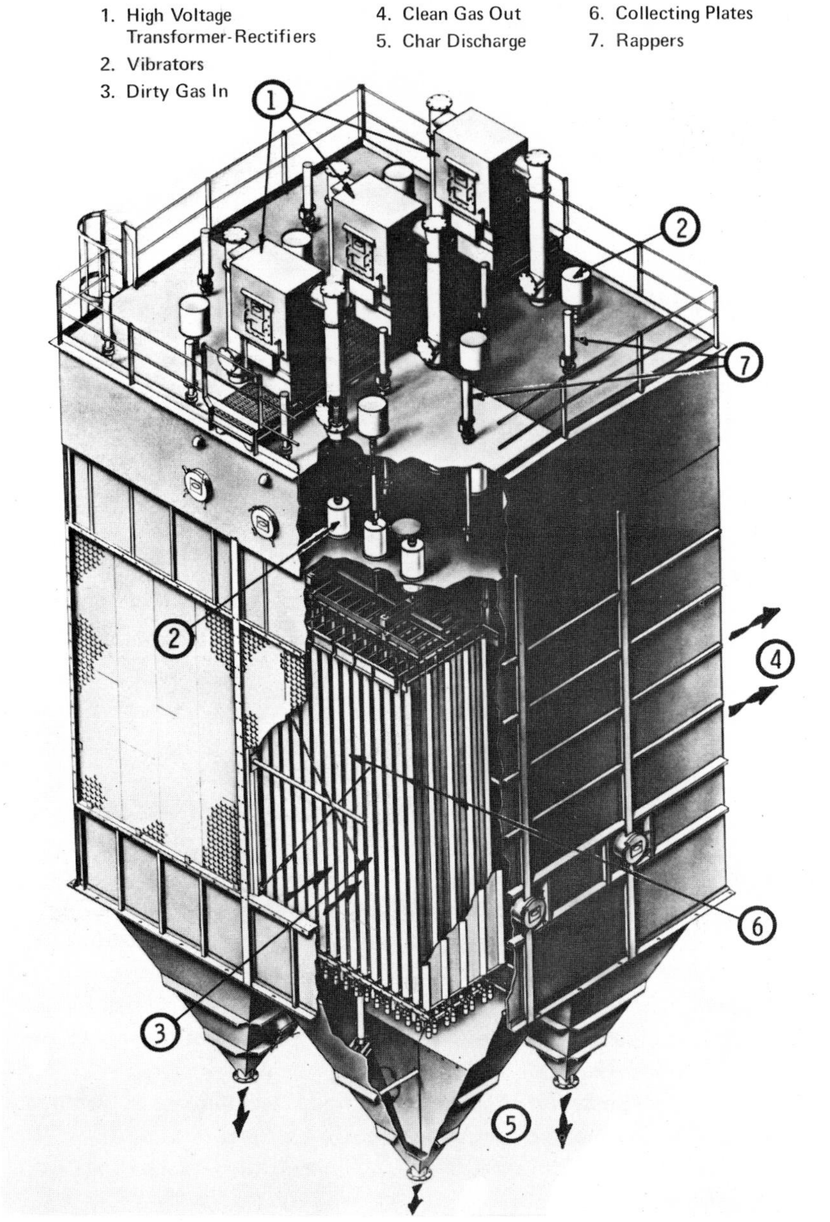

1. High Voltage
   Transformer-Rectifiers
2. Vibrators
3. Dirty Gas In

4. Clean Gas Out
5. Char Discharge

6. Collecting Plates
7. Rappers

Figure 26–18.—Electrostatic precipitator for flue gas from bark-fired steam generators. (Drawing from Research Cottrell, Inc.)

In more recent designs, dust concentration is not measured, and the sander dust is blown directly into the furnace. In this system the sander dust is treated as though it were a combustible gas, and necessary precautions are taken to insure flame stability; this entails close control of

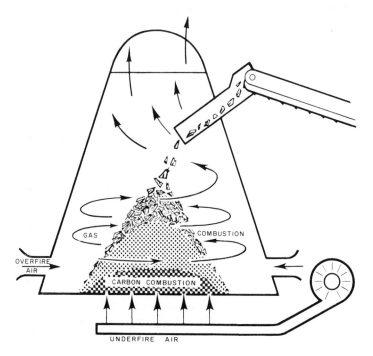

Figure 26–19.—Wigwam waste burner. (Drawing from McKenzie 1968.)

furnace temperature and use of flame monitors to cut off fuel if the burner is extinguished.

Lignin.—Kennedy (1954) has reviewed the combustion of **black liquor,** the lignin and chemical residue from the kraft pulping process. Chemical recovery is part of the technique; in the process, makeup chemicals are added to the black liquor after it is discharged from the digesters and tall oil has been recovered from it, but before it is burned in the furnace. Because of these complicating aspects, the burning of black liquor will not be discussed at length in this text.

Canovali and Suda (1970) have described techniques to incinerate malodorous gaseous compounds from the kraft process.

When black liquor is evaporated to a concentration of one-half water (by weight), it can be suspension fired with an efficiency of about 60 percent. As 1,000 lb. of steam contains about 1,100,000 B.t.u., it follows that 1,100,000/0.60, or 1,835,000 B.t.u. of black liquor must be supplied to produce 1,000 lb. of steam. Ovendry residue of black liquor (after tall oil extraction but before makeup chemicals are added) has a heat of combustion of about 6,000 B.t.u./lb. From these data and the data in table 26–5, it can be calculated that black liquor (concentrated to half water by weight) must be delivered to the steam generator at the following prices to be competitive in heating value with fossil fuels:

Fuel and cost (dollars/ton)		Equivalent cost of black liquor
		Dollars per ton
Coal	7.56	1.18
Oil	10.80	1.31
Gas	11.87	1.47

26–5 BYPRODUCTS FROM BARK COMBUSTION

Since the average heat of combustion of ovendry southern pine bark is about 8,900 B.t.u./lb. (sec. 9–4), then the total heat input for each pound of moist bark (half water by weight) fired is 8,900/2, of 4,450 B.t.u. It follows that about 225 lb. of moist bark are required for an input of 1 million B.t.u. of heat energy.

Southern pine bark—moistened until half water by weight—contains about 2.8 percent hydrogen, 28.3 percent carbon, 18.5 percent oxygen, and 0.3 percent ash (derived from table 26–4, right-hand column). From these data it can be calculated that theoretically about 770 lb. of air are required to burn 225 lb. of moist bark; i.e., $[(0.283)(11.49) + (0.028)(34.56) - (0.185)(4.32)]\,225 = 769.7$ lb. The resulting flue gas will be comprised of nitrogen, carbon dioxide, and water vapor as shown by the following calculations.

Product	Source	Computation	Weight
			Lb.
Dry products			
Nitrogen	In 730 lb. of air	(770)(0.769)	= 592.1
Carbon	In 225 lb. of fuel	(225)(0.283) = 63.7	
Oxygen	To burn 63.7 lb. of carbon	(63.7)(2.66) =169.4	
Carbon dioxide	Carbon plus oxygen	63.7+169.4	= 233.1
Water vapor			
Water	From hydrogen in 225 lb. of fuel	(225)(0.028)(9)	= 56.7
Water	From moisture in 225 lb. of fuel	(225)(0.5)	= 112.5
Water	From humidity of 770 lb. of theoretical air	(770)(0.013)	= 10.0

In addition to the exhaust gas, about 0.7 lb. of ash will be formed, i.e., 0.3 percent of 225 lb. of fuel.

In summary, if the input (no excess air) comprises 225 lb. of fuel, 770 lb. of dry air, and 9.5 lb. of water vapor in the combustion air for a total of about 1,005 lb. the output should be heat plus 592 lb. of nitrogen, 233 lb. of carbon dioxide, 179 lb. of water vapor, and 0.7 lb. of ash for a total of about 1,005 lb. of byproducts. Excess air is heated as it passes through the system but is discharged into the atmosphere without taking part in the combustion reactions.

With very few exceptions, the nitrogen and carbon dioxide in flue gases are not utilized, although it is technically possible to salvage and purify them for industrial use.

Similarly, ash from southern pine bark burned in steam generators is little utilized. When analyzed according to Designation D271–58 of the American Society for Testing and Materials, a limited sample of southern pine bark ash was found to contain about 27 percent CaO, 21 percent Al_2O_3, 19 percent sand (SiO_2), 9 percent K_2O, 6 percent SO_3, 5 percent MgO, 4 percent P_2O_5, 3 percent Na_2O, 1 percent Fe_2O_3, and 5 percent other material. (See table 26–7.)

No comparable data on ash from southern pine wood are published, but tests of several western woods indicate that the content of Al_2O_3 (6 percent or less) may be lower and CaO content (50 to 60 percent) higher in wood than in bark (Mingle and Boubel 1968). SiO_2 content in bark can be considerably higher than that of wood because of sand imbedded in the bark during logging operations.

If wood (or bark) ash is treated with water, the potassium compounds present dissolve and can be separated from the remaining solids; on evaporation of the solution, potash is recovered.

Large steam-generating plants need to market the ash they create, not only for economic reasons, but because in many areas there are regulations against dumping it. Ash from coal-fired plants is increasingly utilized in mixes yielding high-strength concrete for highways and high-rise buildings; a light-weight fraction of the ash (floatable on water) has been shown suitable for the manufacture of high-grade refractories (Gambs 1970a). It is likely that ash from bark or wood can be similarly marketed.

TABLE 26–7.—*Analysis of ash from southern pine bark taken from single trees of four species; composition expressed as percentage of dry weight*[1]

Compound	Loblolly	Longleaf	Shortleaf	Slash	Average
			Percent		
SiO_2	16.4	17.2	17.0	24.5	18.8
Al_2O_3	20.8	23.0	21.5	17.5	20.7
Fe_2O_3	1.3	1.2	1.3	1.6	1.3
CaO	25.4	21.6	33.0	26.3	26.6
MgO	6.0	4.9	4.6	5.0	5.1
Na_2O	1.8	4.5	1.0	4.5	2.9
K_2O	10.6	10.3	6.8	8.6	9.1
TiO_2	.3	.5	.2	.3	.3
P_2O_5	5.5	4.8	4.0	3.2	4.4
SO_3	7.6	7.1	4.5	4.6	6.0
Unaccounted	4.3	4.9	6.1	3.9	4.8
TOTAL	100.0	100.0	100.0	100.0	100.0

[1] Data from same trees described by the proximate and ultimate analyses in table 26–4; analysis according to ASTM Designation D271–58.

26–6   WASTE INCINERATORS

For years, unutilized residues of wood and bark have been incinerated in **wigwam burners** that combine the features of a gas producer (retort to destructively distill wood and bark in the absence of oxygen) and a gas combustion chamber (fig. 26–19). These incinerators, if improperly operated, pollute the air with smoke; installation of new units has therefore been sharply regulated.

McKenzie (1968) has published recommendations for improving the performance of existing wigwam burners to reduce pollution; they are summarized as follows.

Fuel must be uniformly fed to the burner at a rate commensurate with the size of the burner; the diameter of the fuel pile should be about two-thirds the base diameter of the burner.

For efficient destructive distillation in the burner, fuel should be admitted in neither excessively large chunks nor extremely fine particles; these fuel sizes require special burning techniques.

Underfire air (figure 26–19) must be adjustable to provide the correct carbon combustion rate and must distribute air uniformly at the correct rate to all portions of the base of the fuel pile.

The supply of overfire air must also be readily adjustable and must introduce air in a way that assures thorough mixing with the combustible gases in an optimum air/fuel ratio; the overfire air should induce circumferential flow to cause turbulence and maximum fuel retention time in the burner. To properly control overfire air and to insure high ignition temperatures, the burner shell must be reasonably air tight. A pyrometer to measure the temperature of exit gases, which should exceed 640° F. to burn carbon particles and 1,000° F. to burn the gas produced by distillation, is helpful in attaining optimum adjustment of overfire air. If gas exit temperature is maintained in excess of 800° F., burner operation will tend to be smokeless. Automatic control of air improves combustion.

It is good practice to remove clinker ash from the underfire outlets daily and all ash and clinker from the burner weekly.

Even well-designed burners may smoke periodically, particularly during start-up operations or when extremely wet fuel is deposited on the burning pile. Stoddard (1970) found that under such conditions, operation of three natural gas torches spaced around the burner perimeter substantially lessened smoke emission; the torches were horizontally mounted in short sections of 18-inch pipe that penetrated the burner wall near ground level.

In a 1967 survey of sawmill waste burners on the West Coast, Boubel (1968) found that particulate emissions from wigwam burners varied from a low of 0.004 grain/cu. ft. of flue gas (corresponding to 0.17 lb./ ton of fuel burned) to a high of 0.607 grain/cu. ft. of gas (26.94 lb./ton of fuel). Percent of ash in emissions was negatively correlated with gas temperature at emission; in the range from 90 to 1,500° F., high emission temperatures corresponded with low particulate emissions.

Further information on wigwam burners and incinerators of various kinds can be found in the following publications (chronologically arranged); all but four report work done at Oregon State University; the design described by Lausmann (1970) has considerable acceptance on the West Coast.

Boubel et al. (1958, 1965)	Atherton and Corder (1969)
Boubel (1965, 1968)	Cowan (1969)
Kreichelt (1966)	Franklin (1969)
Boubel and Wise (1968)	Corder et al. (1970)
Corder et al. (1968)	Lausmann (1970)
McKenzie (1968)	Stoddard (1970)

26–7 DOMESTIC FIREPLACES, STOVES, AND FURNACES

Farms in the rural South have long used dry split pine to fire cooking stoves, and virtually all people in the southern pine region have used lightwood (resin-rich southern pine wood—usually stumpwood) to start fireplace fires. Because natural gas, oil, and coal have largely replaced wood as a domestic fuel in the South, discussion will be limited to listing a few pertinent references.

Subject and reference

Fireplace wood
  Simmons 1951)
  Nagle and Manthy (1966)
Stoves and furnaces
  Jenkins and Guernsey (1937)
  Winters (1939)
  Harris (1942)
  Reineke (1947, 1965)
  Northeastern Wood Utilization Council (1949abc)
Frost protection in orchards and citrus groves
  Corder (1961)

26–8 LITERATURE CITED

Atherton, G. H., and Corder, S. E.
  1969. A study of wood and bark residue disposal in the forest products industries. Oreg. State Univ. Forest Res. Lab., 60 pp.

Barron, A., Jr.
  1970. Studies on the collection of bark char throughout the industry. TAPPI 53: 1441–1448.

Beall, F. C.
  1968. Thermal degradation analysis of wood and wood components. Ph.D. Thesis. N.Y. State Coll. Forest. at Syracuse. 312 p.
Beall, F. C., and Eickner, H. W.
  1970. Thermal degradation of wood components: a review of the literature. USDA Forest Serv. Res. Pap. FPL–130, 26 pp. Forest Prod. Lab., Madison, Wis.

Booth, J. B.
1966. Some guidelines to aid in the selection of collectors for hogged fuel applications. Pulp and Pap. 40(27): 32–33.

Boubel, R. W.
1965. Wood residue incineration in tepee burners. Oreg. State Univ. Eng. Exp. Sta. Circ. 34, 30 pp.

Boubel, R. W.
1968. Particulate emissions for sawmill waste burners. Oreg. State Univ. Eng. Exp. Sta. Bull. 42, 12 pp.

Boubel, R. W., Northcraft, M., Van Vliet, A., and Popovich, M.
1958. Wood waste disposal and utilization. Oreg. State Coll. Eng. Exp. Sta. Bull. 39, 96 pp.

Boubel, R. W., Thornburgh, G. E., and Pavelka, B. R.
1965. A study of wood waste disposal by combustion and its effect on air quality in the Medford area. Oreg. State Univ. Eng. Exp. Sta. Proj. 307, 60 pp.

Boubel, R. W., and Wise, K. R.
1968. An emission sampling probe installed, operated, and retrieved from ground level. J. Air Pollut. Contr. Assoc. 18(2): 84–85.

Browne, F. L.
1958. Theories of the combustion of wood and its control. A survey of the literature. USDA Forest Serv. Forest Prod. Lab. Rep. 2136, 59 pp.

Browne, F. L., and Tang, W. K.
1962. Thermogravimetric and differential thermal analysis of wood and of wood treated with inorganic salts during pyrolysis. Fire Res. Abstr. and Rev. 4(1&2): 76–91.

Canovali, L. L., and Suda, S.
1970. Case history of selection and installation of a kraft recovery odor-reduction system. TAPPI 53: 1488–1493.

Corder, S. E.
1958. Suspension drying of sawdust. Forest Prod. J. 8: 5–10.

Corder, S. E.
1961. Wood fuel for protecting crops from frost. Oreg. Forest Res. Center, Forest Prod. Res. Inform. Circ. 16, 28 pp.

Corder, S. E., Atherton, G. H., Hyde, P. E., and Bonlie, R. W.
1970. Wood and bark residue disposal in wigwam burners. Ore. State Univ. Forest Res. Lab. Bull. 11, 68 pp.

Corder, S. E., Atherton, G. H., and Murray, M. L.
1968. A bibliography of selected references from the study "Disposal of wood and bark wastes by incineration or alternative means." Oreg. State Univ. Sch. Forest. and Public Health Serv. 48 pp.

Cowan, W. C.
1969. Conical refuse burners—principles of efficiency. In Wood utilization, 21–26. Proc. Annu. Meeting Mid-South Sect. Forest Prod. Res. Soc.

Ellwanger, R.
1952. Suspension burning of bark refuse. TAPPI 35: 108–111.

Fons, W. L.
1950. Heating and ignition of small wood cylinders. Ind. and Eng. Chem. 42: 2130–2133.

Franklin, D. M.
1969. Waste disposal by burning. In Wood utilization, pp. 9–12. Proc. Annu. Meeting Mid-South Sect. Forest Prod. Res. Soc.

Gambs, G. C.
1970a. Expanding the market for fly ash. Mech. Eng. 92(1): 26–28.

Gambs, G. C.
1970b. The electric utility industry: future fuel requirements 1970–1990. Mech. Eng. 92(4): 42–48.

Graf, S. H.
1949. Ignition temperatures of various papers, woods, and fabrics. Oreg. State Coll. Eng. Exp. Sta. Bull. 26, 69 pp.

Harris, P.
1942. Burning sawdust. Wood 7(3): 70–72.

Host, J. R., and Lowery, D. P.
1970. Potentialities for using bark to generate steam power in western Montana. Forest Prod. J. 20(2): 35–36.

Jenkins, J. H., and Guernsey, F. W.
1937. The utilization of sawmill waste and sawdust for fuel. Can. Dep. Mines and Resources Vancouver Forest Serv. Forest Prod. Lab. Circ. 48, 15 pp.

Johnson, E. J., and Koch, P.
1972. Thermal reactions of small loblolly pine cubes heated on one face in an air atmosphere. Wood Sci. 4: 154–162.

Kennedy, E. H.
1954. The burning of sulfate, soda and sulfite waste liquors. Combustion 26(5): 52–59.

Koch, P.
1969. Specific heat of ovendry spruce pine wood and bark. Wood Sci. 1: 203–214.

Koch, P., and Mullen, J. F.
1971. Bark from southern pine may find use as fuel. Forest Ind. 98(4): 36–37.

Kollmann, F. F. P., and Côté, W. A., Jr.
1968. Principles of wood science and technology. I. Solid wood. 592 pp. N.Y.: Springer-Verlag New York, Inc.

Kreichelt, T. E.
1966. Air pollution aspects of tepee burners. U.S. Dep. Health, Educ., and Welfare, Div. Air Pollut. Public Health Serv. Pub. 999–AP–28, 35 pp.

Lausmann, J.
1970. Lausmann modification to teepee burners. Twenty-fifth Northwest Wood Prod. Clin. Proc., pp. 51–55.

MacKay, G. D. M.
1967. Mechanism of thermal degradation of cellulose: a review of the literature. Can. Dep. Forest. Dep. Pub. 1201, 20 pp.

McKenzie, H. W.
1968. Wigwam waste burner guide and data book. Oreg. State Sanit. Authority, 24 pp. Portland.

Matson, A. F., Dufour, R. E., and Breen, J. F.
1959. Survey of available information on ignition of wood exposed to moderately elevated temperatures. In Performance of type B gas events for gas-fired appliances, p. 269–279. Underwrit. Lab., Inc. Bull. Res. 51

Mingle, J. G., and Boubel, R. W.
1968. Proximate fuel analysis of some western wood and bark. Wood Sci. 1: 29–36.

Mullen, J. F.
1964. A method for determining combustible loss, dust emission, and recirculated refuse for a solid fuel burning system. Amer. Soc. Mech. Eng. Pap. 64–WA–FU–4, 13 pp. Windsor, Conn.

Mullen, J. F.
1968. System for pneumatically transporting high-moisture fuels such as bagasse and bark and an included furnace for drying and burning those fuels in suspension under high turbulence. (U.S. Pat. No. 3,387,574.) U.S. Pat. Office, Wash., D.C.

Nagle, G. S., and Manthy, R. S.
1966. The market for fireplace wood in an urban area of Connecticut. USDA Forest Serv. Res. Pap. NE–51, 16 pp. Northeast. Forest Exp. Sta., Upper Darby, Penn.

Northeastern Wood Utilization Council.
1949a. A home made wood burning furnace. Northeast. Wood Util. Counc. Bull. 26, 11 pp. New Haven.

Northeastern Wood Utilization Council.
1949b. How to burn wood. Northeast. Wood Util. Counc. Bull. 28, 18 pp. New Haven.

Northeastern Wood Utilization Council.
1949c. The woodomat furnace. Northeast. Wood Util. Counc. Bull. 27, 15 pp. New Haven.

O'Neill, M. J.
1964. An analysis of a temperature-controlled scanning calorimeter. Anal. Chem. 36: 1238–1245.

27

Pulping

CONTENTS

27

Pulping

Southern pines grown in the United States supply 45 percent of the kraft pulp manufactured in the world (Kleppe 1970). They also supply 41 percent of the mechanical pulp (Trevelyan 1969) and almost 40 percent of the market dissolving pulp (Durso 1969) produced in the United States.

In 1962, annual harvest from the 105 million acres of southern pine commercial forest totalled 2.5 billion cu. ft. Of this total pine volume, more than 50 percent (1.3 billion cu. ft.) was converted into pulp products (USDA Forest Service 1965, pp. 195-197, 205). It is evident that the pulp industry is a major factor in southern pine utilization. Readers interested in industry statistics will find Welch's (1970) summary of southern pulpwood production useful.

One of the objectives of wood scientists everywhere is complete utilization of all the substance in every tree. Research on pulping processes has made particularly significant progress toward this objective. The southern pulp industry has taken giant strides in recovery of pulpable chips from sawmill and plywood mill residues. Even sawdust is being increasingly utilized by the industry (Cumbie 1969). Extensive reclamation of waste paper, currently under intensive study (Anonymous 1970), shows promise of further stretching the wood resource. These programs will continue to significantly improve utilization of wood harvested throughout the South.

Continuous research is conducted by numerous private and public laboratories to improve the efficiency of equipment and pulping processes. Of the three major methods by which pine is pulped, the kraft and sulfite processes are chemical and separate cellulose from the other wood constituents. Since southern pine wood is less than half alpha-cellulose (see ch. 6), these processes inherently give pulp yields from 40 to 55 percent of the ovendry weight of wood pulped.

The chemical processes (kraft or sulfite) can be stopped short of a full chemical cook so that chips discharged from the digester are only softened for subsequent conversion into fibers by mechanical means. By such a **semichemical** process, pulp yields for some purposes can be increased substantially (range 60 to over 80 percent).

Fully mechanical processes, which produce pulp for newsprint, coated papers, and insulating board, by physically separating wood fibers without greatly changing their chemistry—and hence have nearly 100-percent yield—offer the greatest possibilities for improvement. One approach has been suggested by McMillin's (1968, 1969abc) work with experimental refiner pulps from loblolly pine. His findings point to the possibility that

1413

further research may make a larger fraction of wood usable through a mechanical process whereby thick-walled, stiff, tubular southern pine cells can be unwound into flat, fibrillated, relatively conformable, ribbon-like elements. Strong, versatile pulps from improved high-yield mechanical processes—if they could be developed—would likely find expanded markets in competition with lower yield chemical pulps, thus meeting increased demands with less raw material.

27-1 MECHANICAL PULPING [1]

Growing demand for newsprint after 1920 directed the industry's attention toward the large reserves of pine in the United States, Canada, Western Europe, and Russia. Before 1940, experimental work was done in all these countries or regions. Commercial production of pine groundwood for newsprint seems to have been achieved during this period in Canada from jack pine, *Pinus banksiana* Lamb., (Paterson 1937); in France from maritime pine, *Pinus pinaster* Ait., (Porphyre 1929); and in Russia (Martynoff and Weiss 1937). Large-scale commercial production of groundwood in the South began in January 1940 when the Southland Paper Mills, Inc. went into the production of newsprint at Lufkin, Tex. (McHale 1948). Succeeding years saw steady, if not spectacular growth of groundwood production for newsprint in locations widely distributed throughout the South.

Substantial demands also developed for pine groundwood in coated publication papers, insulating board, and asphalt-impregnated sheathing. It is interesting to note that Bedford Pulp and Paper Co. produced pine groundwood for wrapping paper in the early 1930's, well before commercial production of newsprint began at the Southland mill (Foster 1932.)

Figure 27-1 shows the location of the current producers of southern pine newsprint and those projected to be producing by the end of 1970. Forty-one percent of the U.S. groundwood capacity is now in the South (table 27-1). Nearly three-quarters of the 1966-1969 expansion in the newsprint industry of the United States took place in this region.

The establishment of a newsprint industry in the South owes much to to the enthusiastic research of Dr. C. H. Herty and his co-workers at the laboratory he helped found in Savannah, Ga. (Herty 1933). Concurrent with Herty's work were studies by many others in industrial laboratories and institutions. Schafer, of the USDA Forest Products Laboratory, Madison, Wis., and Brecht in Germany were particularly active in publishing research results on pine species. Despite the size of the pine groundwood industry in the South today, however, the literature on it is not extensive and contains few descriptions of modern operating practices.

---

[1] With minor editorial changes, sec. 27-1 is taken from Trevelyan (1969) by permission of Benjamin J. Trevelyan and the Forest Products Research Society.

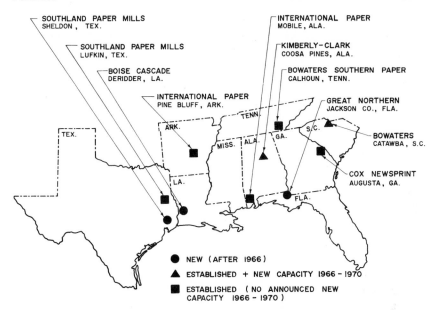

Figure 27–1.—Location of current producers of newsprint in the South and those projected to be producing by the end of 1970. (Drawing after Trevelyan 1969.)

A number of textbooks (Klemm 1958; Johnson 1960; Gavelin 1966) and numerous papers are available on the general subjects of groundwood manufacture and groundwood properties. The following discussion is concentrated on the factors and problems associated with, and peculiar to, the production of mechanical pulp from pines.

TABLE 27–1.—*Groundwood pulp capacity in the United States*
(American Paper Institute 1968)

	1966		1969	
	Number of mills	Capacity	Number of mills	Capacity
		Tons/year		*Tons/year*
South Atlantic[1]_ _ _ _ _ _ _ _	3	271,000	4	411,000
East south central[2]_ _ _ _ _	6	814,000	6	936,000
West south central[3]_ _ _ _	3	444,000	4	658,000
Total United States (exclusive of above three regions)	_ _ _ _	2,701,000	_ _ _ _	2,882,000

[1] South Atlantic—Delaware, Maryland, District of Columbia, Virginia, West Virginia, North Carolina, South Carolina, Georgia, and Florida.
[2] East south central—Kentucky, Tennessee, Alabama, and Mississippi.
[3] West south central—Arkansas, Louisiana, Oklahoma, and Texas.

Currently all mills producing mechanical pulp in the South rely on **stone grinders** to effect the reduction of boltwood to fibers. **Disk refiners** (in which chips or fiber bundles are further reduced between counter-rotating plates fixed in close proximity) are used only in the processing of rejects from the screening and cleaning operations.

Most of the experimental work reported in the literature was done with loblolly pine; references were also made to shortleaf, longleaf, slash, and occasionally other pines.

MANUFACTURE OF STONE GROUNDWOOD

The characteristics of southern pines which gave rise to major problems in the manufacture of groundwood are:

- The presence of thick-walled, stiff, latewood fibers, and the high ratio of these latewood fibers to earlywood fibers.

- The high resin content of pines compared with northern species such as the spruces (*Picea* spp.) and balsam fir (*Abies balsamea* (L.) Mill.).

- The susceptibility of the pines to attack by blue-stain and other fungi under the hot, humid climatic conditions of the South.

Eventually, methods were developed to cope with the problems arising from all three characteristics.

Effects of gross wood properties and fiber morphology.—The predominance of latewood in southern pine proved the most difficult problem in groundwood production. The subject has been much discussed in the literature, most recently by Chidester (1966). Figure 27–2 illustrates the fact that shortleaf, in common with the other pines, has more latewood than northern black spruce (*Picea mariana* (Mill.) B.S.P.). Table 27–2 illustrates other important differences between southern pine and the northern pulp species. The earlywood fibers of southern pine are thin walled, flexible (see ch. 5), and quite comparable to northern spruce in papermaking properties. The latewood fibers, however, are thick walled, inflexible, and tend to be nonconforming when incorporated into a paper sheet. Because of the high proportion of latewood fibers, groundwood pulp from southern pine tends to yield rough, porous, low-density paper. To overcome this problem and to obtain the proper balance of fines and larger fractions for papermaking, the latewood fibers must therefore be thoroughly disintegrated (Bishop 1959). The many fewer fibers per unit weight of pulp from latewood of southern pines support these observations (table 27–2).

An important consequence of the presence of latewood is its influence on wood density (see ch. 7 and fig. 27–11). One of the few benefits of high latewood content is its influence on wood cost (Chidester 1966). The thick-walled fibers yield wood of high density at a relatively rapid rate of growth. Klemm (1950) noted that wood purchased on a volume basis

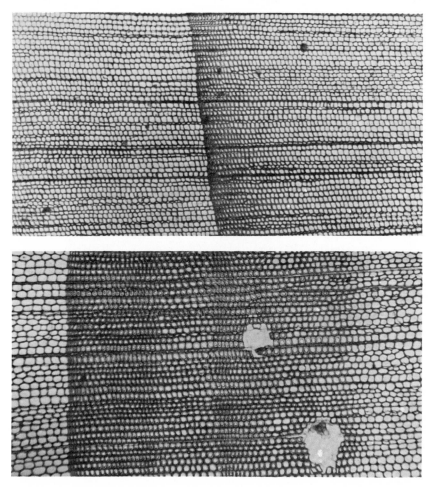

Figure 27–2.—Photomicrographs of northern black spruce (top) and shortleaf pine (bottom), showing the distinct differences in percentages of latewood between these species. (Photo from Trevelyan 1969.)

costs least per ton if it has a high latewood content; he further observed, however, that the best quality paper is made from wood with a high earlywood content.

The amount of latewood—and hence the density—of southern pine is influenced by a variety of factors including age, location of the wood in the stem, growth rate, and geographical location (see secs. 4–3, 7–5, and 7–6). Loblolly pine wood formed during the fifth year of growth has been reported as 75 percent earlywood, that formed in the 10th year as 66 percent, and during the 15th year as 60 percent [2]. Chidester (1966)

---

[2] Ciriacks, J. A., and Knight, V. J. Juvenile and mature wood trials in newsprint. Kimberly-Clark Corp., Neenah, Wis. Unpublished. 1968.

TABLE 27–2.—*Measurements of latewood tracheids in kraft fiber from several northern and southern softwood species*[1]

	Fiber length	Fiber diameter	3 mm. fibers[2] per gram
	Mm.	*μm.*	*Number × 10⁻⁶*
Spruce_____	3.26	30	2.84
Balsam fir_____	3.15	32	2.82
Jack pine_____	3.10	29	2.84
Loblolly pine_____	3.67	36	1.87
Longleaf pine_____	3.59	34	1.77
Shortleaf pine_____	4.23	36	1.71
Virginia pine_____	3.56	30	2.32

[1] Braun, R. V. 1961. Unpublished data.
[2] A Kimberly-Clark test used to express fiber coarseness. Note that the numbers bear an inverse relation to those determined by TAPPI Suggested Method T234 Su67.

found that wall thickness of latewood cells and percentage of latewood increase considerably up to the 10th year and beyond; the progressively less mature wood up the tree stem shows a progressively decreasing density. Since rapid growth may reduce density (Bray and Curran 1938; see also text p. 244), the use of young and rapidly grown wood was recommended over 30 years ago by Schafer et al. (1938) for production of high-quality groundwood. These factors, together with environmental effects (sec. 4–3), cause variability in the wood supply, which is reflected in pulp quality. Variability in the specific gravity of southern pine wood is discussed in chapter 7; chapter 5 has quantitative information on variability of tracheid dimensions.

The presence of latewood in varying proportions presented very real operating problems to the groundwood manufacturer. High quality groundwood contains a rather delicate balance of fiber size distribution and of fiber characteristics within each fraction. The surface and composition of a stone are carefully chosen to yield the quality of groundwood demanded. For southern pine, the choice of stone is not easy since the high-density latewood fibers present an entirely different wood surface to the grinding stone than do the earlywood fibers. Unfortunately, they have to be ground together. Compared to southern pine, the northern softwoods present a relatively uniform raw material.

The steps finally taken to resolve the problems caused by latewood and wood density variations are only sketchily reported in the literature. In discussing the effect of wood density, Fuller and Carpenter (1938) noted that at the same **mullen strength** dense wood gave consistently lower **freeness** pulp than less dense wood. (Mullen strength is defined as the hydrostatic pressure required to rupture a 1.2-inch-diameter circular paper sheet. Freeness is the quality of pulp related to the rate at which it parts with water when formed into a sheet or mat on a wire screen; the index number is positively correlated with this rate.) After much research by the Herty Foundation and others, Carpenter (1939) agreed essentially with Walker (1937) that coarse stones were best for southern pine and recommended that they be dull.

In a report written many years after the startup of the Southland mill, McHale and Porter (1954) discussed rather candidly the problems encountered with pulp quality. Reading between the lines, one can only guess at the many technical crises this mill must have faced in its early days. As suggested by Walker, Southland initially used relatively coarse stones of high hardness. This approach was abandoned, however, because heat release from the high power input necessary on pine caused breakage of segments and spalling of stone faces. There followed 18 to 24 months of development in cooperation with stone manufacturers. The solution was to use stones which produced a pulp much lower in freeness with considerably more fines fraction than that typical of spruce. The high specific surface of these fibers and the high specific filtration resistance gave the sheet properties necessary to make southern newsprint competitive with Canadian.

This solution is being pursued by all other manufacturers of newsprint in the South. An effort is made to maximize the energy input (as usually expressed by horsepower-days per ton) at lower freeness levels in accordance with the well-known positive relationship between energy consumption and pulp quality; as in other machining processes, more specific machining energy is required to produce small pieces than large (e.g., see fig. 19–75). Thoroughly defibrated southern pine yields strong pulp of low freeness. Grinder conditions are therefore chosen with this intention, and experimental work is still continuing to effect further improvements. Table 27–3 compares typical southern pine groundwood with northern black spruce groundwood. Differences in freeness, strength levels, and other properties are apparent. The differences in fractionation are concentrated mostly in the +28 and −200 fractions. While some of the differences noted in table 27–3 may be partly due to the systems involved and not due to wood species alone, it is felt these data tend to be typical for the two woods.

The literature contains few comparisons of groundwood made from the different southern pine species, although some unreported studies may have been made. Density variations within a species may be more significant in determining groundwood quality than differences between species (Fuller and Carpenter 1938). Currently a number of companies exclude longleaf and slash pine wood because of the coarseness of their fibers and their high resin content. Virginia pine, with its finer fiber structure, seems to be a particularly favorable species. It has more 3-mm.

TABLE 27–3.—*Comparison of northern and southern stone groundwoods for newsprint*[1]

Factor[2]	Northern black spruce	Southern pine
Freeness_____	72.0	48.0
Burst factor_____	17.6	11.6
Tear factor_____	36.0	25.0
Tensile_____	4009	2712
Percent stretch_____	1.6	1.3
Brightness_____	64.0	61.9
Opacity_____	94.2	92.9
Fractionation (percent retained on each screen in sequence)[3]		
28_____	11.0	3.3
48_____	18.7	12.2
100_____	20.3	21.1
200_____	13.4	14.7
−200_____	36.6	48.7
Drainage time_____	27.6	51.8

[1] Kimberly-Clark unpublished data.
[2] TAPPI standards.
[3] According to the USDA Forest Products Laboratory (correspondence), some southern pine newsprint mills make fewer coarse fibers and more fines than tabulated here.

fibers per gram than the other southern pines (table 27–2). The immediate effect on the pulp in changing from a wood mix which is predominantly loblolly to pure longleaf or pure Virginia pine is a rise or drop in pulp freeness, respectively. This suggests a reason for variations in freeness and pulp quality when using a wood supply uncontrolled in proportion of wood species. Where one or two species predominate, such as loblolly or shortleaf, this factor would be minor.

Currently, commercial mills put little emphasis on selecting by species. What selection is being practiced is somewhat dependent on geography. Groundwood mills that have predominantly loblolly and shortleaf pines in their mix can tolerate small quantities of less desirable species. Mills in Alabama that occasionally receive sizable quantities of longleaf are quite conscious of the coarse fiber and high pitch problems to which this species gives rise. They try to keep longleaf separate and prefer to consign it to the kraft mills. Slash pine in large quantities is similarly avoided, largely because of its resin content.

A number of mills are aware of the potential advantage of Virginia pine, but each has also had some problems due to the limbiness of this tree. Knots give rise to many fines in the groundwood, absorb much energy, and can damage the stones. No mill at present is purposely selecting Virginia pine for groundwood, but a number of mills are attempting to grow Virginia pine of better form.

Resin content.—The problems that could arise from the high resin content of southern pines were well recognized in the early experimental work on groundwood. Early researchers were hopeful they could be avoided by using only wood from young stems, free of heartwood (Herty 1933; Schafer et al. 1938; Brecht et al. 1940). Brecht et al. (1938) showed that high water temperatures in the pit (see fig. 27–3g) increased the proportion of the resin entering the water phase. Kirmreuther (1938) recommended 65° to 70° C.; Wetmore and Dunphy (1949) recommended 93° C.

More effective were chemical approaches to the problem. Martynoff and Weiss (1937) recommended grinding at 80° C. with the addition of 2 percent Na_2CO_3. Paterson (1937) found that control of pH with alum allowed the use of a good proportion of jack pine fed to grinders; he recommended an acid condition. Freeman (1947) recommended the use of phosphates at the grinder. However, the judicious use of alum and sodium hydroxide proved finally to be more effective.

McHale and Porter (1954) described the solution to the pitch problem at Southland. As recommended by Herty, the mill was initially supplied with young wood having a minimum of heartwood. Hot water soaking of the pulpwood was also thought to be of some benefit. Alum was not used at the grinders, but was applied at later stages; much of the wash water was not recycled. Nevertheless, pitch caused serious problems that

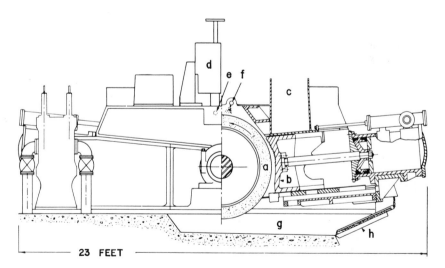

Figure 27–3.—Sectional view of two-pocket Great Northern-Waterous grinder. a, pulp stone; b, hydraulically operated pressure foot retracts automatically to admit a new charge of wood as required; c, hopper for incoming bolts of wood; d, hydraulically operated dressing and trueing lathe; e, position of burr; f, top shower; g, pit; h, adjustable dam. (Drawing from Montague Machine Company.)

were eventually remedied by adding alum at controlled rates to the fresh water of the grinder showers (fig. 27–3f). This not only controlled the pitch problem, but permitted recycling wash water for additional dilution, and obviated the need for hot soaking and careful selection of the wood. A Canadian patent was granted to Carpenter et al. (1949) on alum addition in this manner.

A modification of the Southland process was patented by Craig and Hackbert (1958) who generated an unstable, nascent hydrosol of aluminum hydroxide by the addition of caustic to alum in the shower water at a controlled pH in the range 4 to 6. The hydrosol considerably increases stability of the pitch.

According to Jenkins (1966), pitch problems with groundwood for publication grade papers were not fully solved at Bowaters' Carolina plant by regulation of pH, temperature, and age of the wood supply, nor by avoidance of shocks to the system.

In current practice, all southern newsprint manufacturers are adding alum to the showers on the stone at a pH sufficient (4.8 to 6.0) to precipitate colloidal aluminum hydroxide. All mills except one add caustic to the shower water to control pH. All mills except the same one keep their **white water** (waters of a pulp or paper mill which have been sepa-' rated from the pulp suspension at the grinder, accessory equipment, or paper machine) systems as closed as possible and therefore use mainly white water at the showers. The one exception uses fresh water only at the showers. This water is received at such high pH that caustic is not required. The quantity of alum added at the showers varies from 25 to 40 lb. per ton of finished product. Additional alum is used at the paper machine.

Fungus attack.—In the warm climate of the South, stain fungi seriously attack stored pulpwood, the most common being those causing blue stain (ch. 16) ; badly infected wood produces a gray, unattractive groundwood. Decay fungi develop and cause deterioration with further storage. Herty (1933), who sometimes peeled and ground experimental bolts the same day they were cut, recommended a low inventory of wood at the mill, a common practice at the then existing kraft mills in the South.

Later, studies determined the limits of damage to pulp by the blue-stain fungus. Brecht et al. (1940) concluded that loss of **brightness** was the sole effect (brightness, measured under standardized conditions, is an index of pulp or paper reflectively of a specified light) ; strength properties and power consumption were unaffected. Schafer et al. (1938) came to a similar conclusion in experiments with *Ceratostomella pilifera,* one of the most common blue-stain organisms. He found that up to 10 percent stained wood caused a masking of the natural orange without loss of **whiteness;** an excess of 20 percent stained wood, however, caused a distinct loss of whiteness. (Whiteness is an index of the degree to which pulp or paper approaches ideal white.)

Storage of wood in ponds (Moon 1954) or under water sprays prevents blue stain and decay by keeping wood moisture too high for the fungi to flourish (sec. 16–5). In an unpublished study[3], wood fresh cut, peeled, and ground, was compared with similar wood stored 25 days under water sprays and with wood stored dry. The wood aged wet discolored only on the surface with a slimy growth. Upon grinding, the brightness dropped only 0.5 point compared to the control. The wood aged dry was markedly blue stained, yielding groundwood with brightness 7.5 points lower than the control. Aging the wood either wet or dry substantially increased freeness, especially in the wood aged wet. Mason et al. (1963) studied wood similarly stored for 6 months at Bowaters. Pulp from the wet-aged wood dropped significantly in brightness but not nearly so much as the pulp from dry-aged wood.

Most mills make every effort to keep the time period between cutting and grinding the wood as short as possible; therefore all mills maintain very small inventories of wood for groundwood. Where it is necessary to store wood, every effort is made to turn it over as rapidly as possible. The general reaction of mill personnel is, "The fresher the wood, the better." Such wood not only yields maximum-brightness pulp but also is more responsive to bleach chemicals such as zinc hydrosulfite.

Grinding practices.—There are few published descriptions of modern operating practices and equipment used in groundwood operations in the South. Groundwood used at paper machines is a product of a total system and not just of the grinders. Much attention has been given to screening, cleaning, and rejects handling to meet requirements for such properties as the optical characteristics, strength, formation properties, and freedom from shivy material (bundles of fibers).

In order to more clearly define current practices, a survey was made of all the major newsprint and publication grade producers consuming pine groundwood in the South.

All mills except one use Great-Northern-type grinders (fig. 27–3) exclusively. The one exception was originally equipped with ring-type grinders which are still in use. However, this mill also has installed Great Northerns in its expansion since 1958. The southern newsprint industry, since its beginning in 1940, has tended to use increasingly larger grinders with larger stones, higher connected horsepower, higher grinding pressures, and increased rotational speed. The most recent stones are 67 inches in diameter with a 69-inch face. The original mills did not have over 2,500 attached hp. per grinder. Much of the current expansion has been made with 6,000 and 8,000 hp. per grinder, and grinders with 10,000 hp. are in sight. Grinding pressures are increasing; line pressures of 400 to 500 p.s.i. are common now, with considerable interest being shown in pressures up to 850 or more. In past practice, grinding pressures have

---

[3] Cottle, B. J. Groundwood physical qualities of fresh-cut, aged-dry, and aged-wet pine. Kimberly-Clark Corp., Neenah, Wis. Unpublished. 1956.

been in the range from 15 to 35 lb./sq. in. of wood in contact with the stone; currently, grinding pressures on the wood may be as high as 100 p.s.i. Rotational speeds and peripheral velocities are increasing. Some of the original stones operated at 200 r.p.m. The most recent are geared as high as 360 r.p.m.

A two-pocket machine with 8,000 hp. driving a 67-inch stone with 69-inch face at 360 r.p.m. might turn out 100 tons of air-dry southern pine pulp for newsprint per 24-hour day.

Stone composition (fig. 27–4) and conditioning are much debated. All mills, with one exception, are presently using both alumina and silicon carbide stones. The consensus seems to be that the silicon carbide stones preferred by the majority, produce a high quality pulp at a higher freeness with increased energy consumption per ton and somewhat lower production rate. The fused alumina stones give a lower +28 fraction and a much higher 100-200 fraction. The lowest energy consumption per ton occurs at the mill using predominantly fused alumina stones, that is, 65 to 70 hp.-days versus 80 to 85 hp.-days/ton for a mill using nearly all silicon carbide stones (at roughly the same freeness level). However, it is cautioned again that other subtle differences may also account for this difference in energy consumption. Where both types of stones are being used, generally the best properties of each are desired. Most stones have 60 grit and 0 hardness.

All grinders are equipped with a lathe-type device that permits a dressing tool or **burr** (fig. 27–3e) to be traversed across the face of the rotating stone. It is the purpose of the burr to maintain concentricity of the stone, to expose new abrasive, and to establish a pattern on the face of the stone that will assist in separating the fiber from the workpiece. The quality of pulp produced is related to this pattern. Stone conditioning practices vary considerably from mill to mill; most run their stones slightly dull.

Process conditions at grinders in five southern mills are described in table 27–4. Some mills are attempting to achieve lower freenesses in order to improve strength and sheet characteristics; this practice, however, leads to drainage problems on the paper machine. Several mills have tried **pitless grinding** (i.e., without reservoir shown in fig. 27–3g) and in general the reactions are favorable, although no mill is currently practicing this production method. Most mills attempt to keep their stones fully loaded. All mills except one are cooling white water for the showers on the stones.

Nearly all groundwood mills have given much attention to screening, cleaning, and rejects handling systems in recent years. The major trends are toward a double fine screening of the groundwood after coarse screening, and toward high consistency refining of screen rejects (see footnote to table 27–4 for definition of **consistency**). All mills are currently using rotary screens, although one mill is planning to install pressurized screens.

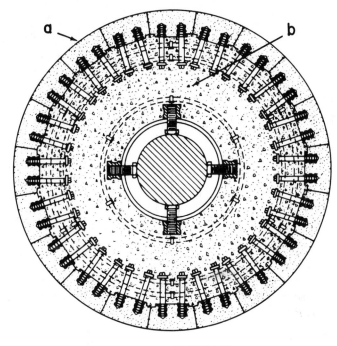

CROSS SECTION

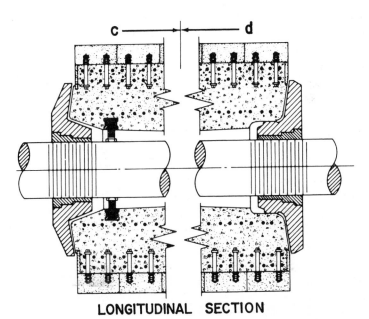

LONGITUDINAL SECTION

Figure 27–4.—Pulp stone. a, abrasive sections (replaceable); b, reinforced concrete center; c, older style flange and centering screws; d, inverted flange wih centering hub. (Drawing from Norton Company.)

TABLE 27–4.—*Summary of process conditions and pulp brightness at five groundwood mills processing southern pine*[1]

Mill number	Pit temperature	Pit consistency[2]	pH in pit	Shower temperature	Shower pressure	Alum added at showers	Canadian Standard Freeness at decker	Energy, grinders only	Brightness
	°F.	Percent		°F.	P.s.i.	Lb./ton finished product		Hp.-days/ton	
1-----------	155[3]	-----	5.5	100	25	30	45–50	70	60
	165	-----	-----	108	80	-----	-----	-----	-----
2-----------	175	2–4	5.2	125	80–125	40	50	80–85	-----
3-----------	170	2.5–3	6.0 (shower water)	100 (or below)	80	24	70→52[4]	80	-----
4-----------	175–180	1.5–2	6.0	135	80	30	40→30[4]	70–75 →90–95[4]	61–64
5-----------	175–180	3.5–4	4.6	94 (fresh water only)	90	20	50–55	84	56

[1] Each mill represents a different company.

[2] Percent consistency = $\dfrac{\text{moisture-free weight of pulp sample}}{\text{weight of water and pulp}}$ (100).

[3] Equipped with ring-type grinder; all other data are for Great-Northern-type grinders.

[4] First number is freeness at time of survey; second number represents future objective.

The coarse-screen rejects are processed with the fine-screen rejects after first being reduced in size with disk refiners. The refined rejects are then commonly passed through rotary or pressure-type screens and centrifugal cleaners. In some cases the only pulp sewered from the system is from the third stage of the centrifugal cleaners. The pulp obtained from the rejects system is claimed to be the best of the groundwood fibers. With high consistency refining, the rejects pulp is long fibered and has considerably more strength than the bulk of the groundwood. One mill using two stages of high consistency refining (20 percent or above) experiences a mullen increase of 1.5 points in the pulp. While screening and cleaning equipment vary considerably, common patterns are emerging as groundwood quality is improved to achieve paper machine speeds of 3,000 f.p.m. without sacrificing paper quality.

A number of mills are bleaching groundwood with zinc hydrosulfite. Southern pine responds well to this treatment; a 10-point increase in brightness can be expected from use of normal quantities of the chemical.

Pulp testing procedures are of considerable interest to each mill. Most mills are dissatisfied with the present tests, and in particular the freeness test. Below 70 Canadian Standard Freeness, the freeness test is of doubtful significance. A drainage test that could be rapidly performed would be much preferred. Fractionation tests and the usual strength tests are commonly used. At least one mill uses microscopic projection of pulp samples to observe fiber characteristics.

MANUFACTURE OF REFINER GROUNDWOOD

Equipment used to reduce chips to fiber consists of at least two stages of single- or double-disk refiners (fig. 27–5) in series. High consistencies (18 percent and above) promote reduction of chips to individual fibers with less production of fines, and are required to achieve the strength characteristics expected of this type groundwood. Various mechanical or chemical pretreatments have been tried to improve the fiber characteristics and reduce power costs. The system is completed with facilities for screening, cleaning, and reject handling.

Strength and printability.—Morkved and Larson (1969) have reported superior tear, burst, tensile, and folding strengths, and excellent runnability on paper machines and printing presses for refiner pulp manufactured in Oregon and Washington. These advantages of refiner groundwood over stone groundwood can perhaps be realized with southern pine wood.

A number of studies have been made to produce refiner groundwood from southern pine; some results have been published. Swartz (1963) summarized the work done at Bowaters Southern Corp. Results of work at Kimberly-Clark by Braun and Davis (1969) are summarized in table 27–5. All strength data were similarly affected. The strength levels attained were, in fact, very close to those of the mixtures of standard stone groundwood with semibleached pine kraft pulp currently used in southern pine newsprint.

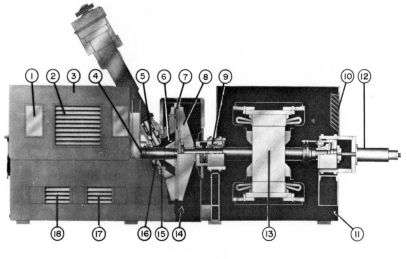

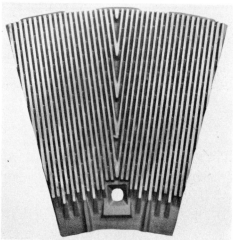

Figure 27–5.—(Top) Cross section through double-disk refiner. 1, inspection port in motor enclosure; 2, 17, 18, air outlets; 3, removable motor enclosure; 4, shafts supported near their centerlines; 5, twin-screw feeder gives positive displacement at variable rates; 6, area from which chips enter the refining zone between plates; 7, refiner plates furnished in balanced sets; 8, one of the two counter-rotating stainless steel disks; 9, tapered roller bearings for radial and thrust loads; 10 and 11, air inlets; 12, housing for hydraulic controls that position the movable disk; 13, one of the two induction or synchronous motors; 14, discharge outlet for refined stock; 15, dilution connection for entry of liquids to control consistency of stock in infeed and refining zones; 16, alloy steel shaft protected from refining chamber by renewable stainless steel sleeves. (Bottom) Segment of removable plate typical of disk refiners for direct fiberization of southern pine chips for mechanical pulp. Six segments are required for each disk. (Drawing and photo from the Bauer Bros. Co.)

Results from a laboratory study at the USDA Forest Service, Southern Forest Experiment Station (McMillin, 1968, 1969abc) indicated that additional research is needed to develop a better mechanical process whereby the thick-walled, tubular latewood tracheids of southern pine can be unwrapped into more nearly ribbon-like shapes.

The major problem with refiner groundwood is its poor printability. Braun and Davis (1969) compared the printing characteristic of refiner groundwood with stone groundwood for a number of species by the Kimberly-Clark printability tests, in which larger numbers indicate poorer printing quality. Stone groundwood was more printable than refiner groundwood even at comparable freeness levels (table 27–5). These results were confirmed by mill trial [4] using 100 percent refiner groundwood in place of stone groundwood. Blends of refiner groundwood with standard stone groundwood and pine kraft, however, possess printability equivalent to the standard sheet with somewhat superior strength.

There is considerable evidence that the printability problems with groundwood can be related to the quantity of $+28$ fraction of the pulp (Braun and Davis 1969). The exact nature of this relaiton is not known; whether it is a symptom or the disease is open to speculation. In refiner groundwood this $+28$ fraction is generally much larger than in stone groundwood unless special attention is paid to reducing it. In southern pine the portion of the $+28$ fraction derived from latewood is large and difficult to reduce by high consistency refining. Some supplementary mechanical action is necessary, such as appropriate low consistency refining or some combination of screening and refining.

Pretreatments effect negligible improvement in pulp quality (Swartz 1963). Experience in the Kimberly-Clark experiments confirm this observation. Of the many chemical and mechanical pretreatments tried at this company, the most effective was a crushing action in a screw press, although other types of crushing action, as in the nip of two press rolls, have a similar effect. Whether the improved strength quality observed (1.5 to 2.0 points in burst factor) is due to the removal of wood resins or to some unique mechanical action on the fiber is not known. The effect of chip crushing on printing properties was negligible. Pretreatments with chemicals such as soluble sulfite salts at various pH's had little effect, nor did heat pretreatments within the time limits imposed by the equipment. Obviously, extended chemical and heat treatment must ultimately have some effect, perhaps not always desirable.

Descriptions of groundwood production for products other than newsprint are rare in the literature. One of the more thorough describes grinders for insulating board manufacture (Fields 1960), and another (Belova and Konovalova 1967) discusses the applicability of refiner groundwood to the manufacture of boxboard. In such products and others where

---

[4] Hurston, M. S. Evaluation of mechanical pulp from pine chips in the mill furnish. Kimberly-Clark Corp., Neenah, Wis. Unpublished. 1964.

TABLE 27–5.—*Comparison of stone and refiner groundwood[1] from southern pine* (Braun and Davis 1969)

Pulp type[2]	Canadian Standard Freeness	Burst[3] factor	Tear[3] factor	Letterpress printability		Bauer McNett fractionation				
				Half tones	Solids	+28	+48	+100	+200	−200
Refiner groundwood___	102	14.0	71	9.0–10.0	9.0–10.0	32.0	18.0	13.0	5.0	32.0
Refiner groundwood___	56	20.0	70	7.5–8.5	7.5–8.5	23.0	18.0	12.0	7.0	40.0
Stone groundwood_____	48	11.6	25	6.4–7.5	6.9–7.7	3.3	12.2	21.1	14.7	48.7

[1] 100 percent groundwood handsheets.
[2] Listed according to freeness.
[3] TAPPI standard.

strength is of primary concern, the printing properties can be ignored; it would therefore seem that refiner groundwood offers opportunities to improve these products.

Energy required.—The energy consumed in producing the high-strength groundwood described by Braun and Davis (1969) was in excess of 100 hp.-days/ton. A refiner pulp of strength comparable to stone groundwood would be expected to require far less energy. The positive correlation between energy consumption and pulp quality—particularly strength— seems to hold for refiner groundwood as well as stone groundwood (McMillin 1968). For reasons not entirely clear, specific refining energy is inversely related to connected horsepower, i.e., refiners with the most horsepower yield pulp requiring the least horsepower-days per ton.

GENERAL

The wood of southern pines still presents a real challenge to the maker of groundwood. Better means of mechanically working the latewood fibers would seem to be basic to further improving the mechanical pulp processes. Forgacs (1963), in his microscope studies of groundwood fractions, has pointed out the difficulty in unraveling the thick-walled tracheids of southern pine, an effect which, if accomplished, could considerably enhance the strength properties of the pulp. The grinder stone presents somewhat limited possibilities in dealing with the problem; disk refining, however, would seem to offer some opportunities (McMillin 1969a). An extensive study of alternative means of reducing the latewood to useful fiber would be well warranted. Evaluation of the results could include the Forgacs L and S factors (McMillin 1969b), which originally were intended to predict strength properties but could be extended also to printability.

An alternative to mechanical processing of the latewood fibers may be the elimination or reduction of these fibers through tree breeding. Virginia pine offers opportunities, provided the limbiness of this tree can be overcome. Virginia pine, however, is not adaptable to all soils and other species must also be considered.

27–2   KRAFT PULPING [5]

Since 1940, the southern section of the United States has become the kraft pulping center of the world. By the end of 1968 the kraft mills of the South produced approximately 25 percent of the total pulps and approximately 45 percent of the kraft pulps required in the world. The basic reasons for the tremendous growth of kraft pulping in the South are the vast renewable supply of southern pine trees and an abundance of

---

[5] With minor editorial changes, section 27–2 is taken from Kleppe (1970) by permission of Peder J. Kleppe and the Forest Products Research Society.

TABLE 27-6.—*Kraft pulping capacity and pine species used in the South* (Kleppe 1970; Welch 1970)

State	Estimated total production capacity of kraft pulp at the end of 1970	No. of pulp mills	Size of the mills	Species of southern pines used for pulpwood (ranked according to frequency)
	Tons per 24 hours		*Tons per 24 hours*	
Alabama	9,580	13	400–1,400	Loblolly, shortleaf, longleaf, slash, Virginia, spruce pines
Arkansas	3,785	6	150–1,300	Shortleaf, loblolly pines
Florida	8,675	9	625–1,700	Slash, longleaf, loblolly, pond, sand, shortleaf, spruce pines
Georgia	12,190	11	500–2,600	Slash, loblolly, longleaf, shortleaf, pond, Virginia, spruce pines
Kentucky	800	2	200–600	Shortleaf, Virginia pines
Louisiana	8,750	10	240–1,630	Loblolly, shortleaf, longleaf, slash, spruce pines
Maryland	800	1	800	Virginia, loblolly, pitch pine, Table-Mountain pines
Mississippi	4,500	4	725–1,700	Loblolly, shortleaf, longleaf, slash, spruce pines
North Carolina	5,080	5	600–1,290	Loblolly, shortleaf, pond, Virginia, longleaf, pitch pines
Oklahoma	0	4	0	Shortleaf, loblolly pines
South Carolina	4,850	4	600–2,000	Loblolly, shortleaf, longleaf, slash, pond, Virginia, spruce pines
Tennessee	1,200	2	500–700	Shortleaf, Virginia, loblolly, pitch pine, Table-Mountain pines
Texas	3,950	5	400–1,200	Loblolly, shortleaf, longleaf, slash pines
Virginia	3,850	4	850–1,060	Loblolly, Virginia, shortleaf, pond, pitch, Table-Mountain pines
TOTAL South	67,960	76	150–2,600	Loblolly, shortleaf, longleaf, slash, pond, Virginia, spruce, sand, pitch, Table-Mountain pines

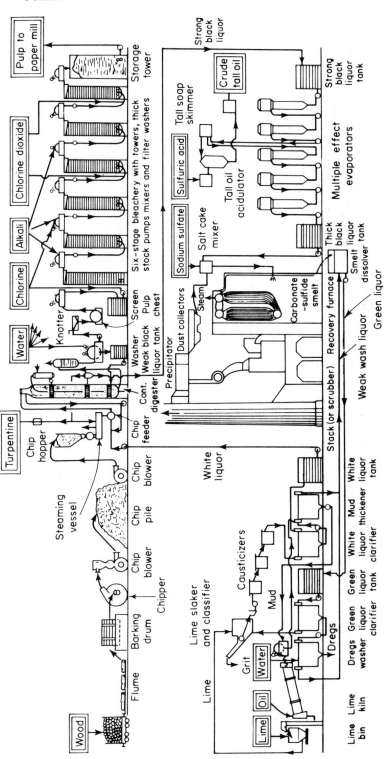

Figure 27-6.—The kraft process. (Top) Conversion of wood to pulp. (Bottom) Cooking liquor cycle and tall oil recovery. (Drawing from Rydholm © 1961, by permission of John Wiley and Sons.)

fresh water. Technological developments in kraft pulping, in chemical recovery, and in bleaching have also been important contributing factors.

In 1970 Georgia, Alabama, Florida, and Louisiana led the Southern States in kraft pulping capacity (table 27–6); the entire South had a capacity of about 68,000 short tons per day in 76 pulpmills (Kleppe 1970). Softwood yielded approximately 77 percent of the output (Christopher and Nelson 1963; Slatin 1967). Since about 1.6 cords of wood are required for each ton of pulp (Hair 1967), approximately 84,000 cords of southern pine pulpwood were required daily in 1970. During the period 1962-1968, the kraft pulping capacity (per 24 hours) in the South increased 20,000 tons (Thuemmes 1962; Sanford 1968); of this increase at least 17,400 tons were in 31 units of continuous digesters (Kamyr Incorporated 1970).

Of the 10 southern pines, loblolly ranks first in kraft production and is likely to continue to do so. Shortleaf, longleaf, and slash pines, followed by pond, Virginia, and spruce pines are also important raw materials for kraft pulp, whereas sand, pitch, and Table-Mountain pines are used only to a small extent. The range and volume of the 10 species are reported in chapter 3.

THE PROCESS

Of the South's pulpwood requirements in 1967, 45 percent was delivered to mill sites as rail roundwood, 33 percent as truck roundwood, 13 percent as rail chips, and 9 percent as truck chips (Bromley 1968). Chips delivered to the mills were primarily residue from sawmills. The roundwood came mostly in the form of 5- or 5¼-foot bolts with bark in place. Some mills received a minor part of their wood in whole-tree lengths. The pulpwood is debarked by tumbling in huge rotating horizontal cylinders (fig. 19–50) provided with coarse slots to allow bark to pass out. Long logs—up to tree length—are usually debarked individually by advancing them through mechanical ring barkers (fig. 19–51). The loss of good pulpwood fibers during debarking is about 0.5 to 2.0 percent. Bark content of southern pine logs is approximately 10 to 24 percent of stem volume. (See sec. 12–2 and table 29–55.)

The debarked logs are converted into chips 15 to 25 mm. long and 2 to 4 mm. thick by multiple-knife chippers having capacities of 50 to 250 tons/hour (figs. 19–104 through 19–107). During the chipping operation 1 to 3 percent of the wood is turned into fine sawdust, which is partially or completely removed through screening. The chips are temporarily stored (figs. 18–3 and 18–4) or directly transported pneumatically or by belt conveyors to the digesters. Batch digesters in southern mills usually have a loading capacity from 20 to 40 tons of pine chips (ovendry basis). The corresponding pulping capacity is approximately 60 to 140 tons of air-dried pulp per day. Continuous digesters have pulping capacities of 150 to 1,000 tons/day.

The chips are cooked with a kraft liquor initially containing sodium hydroxide and sodium sulfide in a molar ratio of approximately 4:1 to 2.5:1, both expressed as equivalent Na_2O. The liquor-to-wood ratio can be from approximately 3.3:1 to 5.0:1. The chemical charge (expressed as a percentage of the ovendry weight of wood) may be from about 15 to about 23 percent NaOH as effective alkali (NaOH + ½ Na_2S); the exact percentage depends on whether the pulp will be used for linerboard, unbleached paper, or bleached grades. The batch digesters are usually heated indirectly with steam in 30 to 60 minutes and attain a maximum temperature of 170° to 175° C. Forced circulation of the cooking liquor is practiced in some of the mills. The cooking time at maximum temperature varies from 50 to 100 minutes. The batch digesters are then emptied, or blown, from full pressure into a **blow tank.**

Figure 27–6 diagrams a kraft pulpmill built around a continuous, rather than batch, digester. Cooking is less severe in continuous digesters. After steaming, chips are heated in cooking liquor to approximately 170° C. in 90 to 100 minutes, and held at maximum temperature about the same time. The cooking is usually interrupted by dilute black liquor (spent liquor) which is forced countercurrent to the downflowing "delignified" chips. Pre-washing for a period of 90 to 120 minutes (or longer) is often practiced in continuous digesters before the wood residues (i.e., the cooked mass of chips) is discharged to a blow tank at a low temperature (100° to 110° C.).

The force of blowing is usually sufficient to fiberize the cooked chips to a reject level of 1 to 3 percent, if the **kappa number** of the pulp is below approximately 30 to 45. Kappa number is a rapid, empirical measure of lignin content of pulp, estimated by observing the consumption of potassium permanganate by the pulp during a standard time interval. According to TAPPI Standard Method T 236 m–60, it is the number of milliliters of 0.1N $KMnO_4$ solution reduced by 1 g. of pulp at standard conditions. Tasman and Berzins (1957) and Kleppe (1970) state the following relationship is valid for kraft pulps:

$$\text{Percent of lignin in pulps} = (0.15)(\text{kappa number}) \qquad (27\text{–}1)$$

Digested wood with a kappa number above 55 (lignin content of 8.5 percent or higher) is generally further fiberized by passing it through mechanical defibrators. The pulp is then screened and washed. Rejects are often returned to the digesters if the pulp is to be bleached; for un-bleached grades, rejects are usually fiberized in disk or conical refiners and then mixed with the screened pulp. Pulp from batch digesters is washed in stages on a three- or four-drum rotary washer. Prewashed pulps from continuous digesters are washed in one or two stages. Figure 27–7 illustrates a high-yield (high-kappa-number) pulping system with a continuous digester; figure 27–8 diagrams the elements of a continuous digester.

Pulps for products requiring moderate to high brightness are bleached in three to seven sequences. The bleaching chemicals are chlorine (C), sodium hydroxide (E), sodium or calcium hypochlorite (H), chlorine dioxide (D), and in some cases hydrogen peroxide (P). For production of

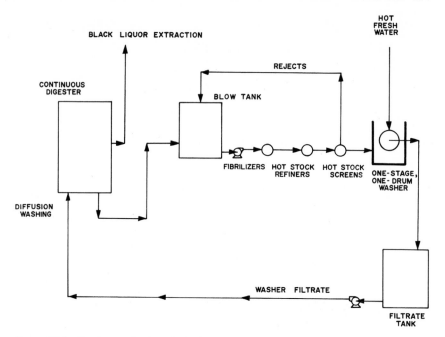

Figure 27–7.—Continuous-digester, high-yield, kraft pulping system at the Union-Camp mill in Savannah, Ga. (Drawing after Bristow et al. 1967.)

semibleached pulps, a CEH schedule is most frequent. High brightness pulps are commonly processed through a CEHD, CEDED, or CEHDED sequence. The yield loss from bleaching is generally 5 to 8 percent of dry pulp weight(Valeur 1951; Virkola and Vartiainen 1964).

FACTORS INFLUENCING PULP YIELD

Yield of pulp per ton of wood is generally the major economic factor in the kraft process. Wood quality and preparation, as well as variables in the pulping processes, strongly affect yield.

Kappa number.—The literature indicates that a 10-unit increase in kappa number generally causes pulp yield from softwoods to increase about 1.4 percent (of the weight of ovendry wood) in the kappa number range 30 to 90, and by 1.8 percent in the kappa number range 90 to 140. This relationship is valid only at constant sulfidity and alkali charge. Pulping experiments by Kleppe[6] confirmned this relationship between kappa number and total pulp yield (percent of ovendry wood) for southern pine wood as follows (see fig. 27–9):

in kappa number range 30-90
    total pulp yield = A + 0.14 kappa number   (27–2)
in kappa number range 90-140
    total pulp yield = A − 3.5 + 0.18 kappa number   (27–3)

---

[6] Kleppe, P. J. Unpublished work. 1968.

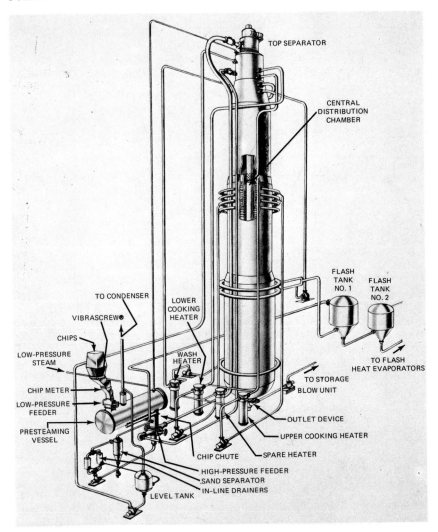

TOP SEPARATOR

CENTRAL
DISTRIBUTION
CHAMBER

FLASH
TANK
NO. 1

FLASH
TANK
NO. 2

TO CONDENSER

VIBRASCREW®

CHIPS

LOWER
COOKING
HEATER

LOW-PRESSURE
STEAM

WASH
HEATER

TO FLASH
HEAT EVAPORATORS

CHIP METER

TO STORAGE
BLOW UNIT

LOW-PRESSURE
FEEDER

OUTLET DEVICE

PRESTEAMING
VESSEL

UPPER COOKING HEATER

CHIP CHUTE

SPARE HEATER

HIGH-PRESSURE FEEDER

SAND SEPARATOR

IN-LINE DRAINERS

LEVEL TANK

Figure 27–8.—Continuous-digester system for kraft pulp. Units capable of producing 1,000 tons of pulp per day measure about 20 feet in diameter and nearly 300 feet above the ground. (Drawing from Kamyr, Inc.)

The constant A, which can be used to characterize a chip source for estimation of yield, is mainly dependent on wood specific gravity (fig. 27–10) but is also somewhat influenced by effective alkali charge, sulfidity of the cooking liquor, and chip size.

Reduction in kappa number below 26 to 28 decreases the total pulp yield by more than 0.14 percent (based on ovendry weight of wood, i.e., "on wood") per kappa number unit.

Alkali charge.—Effective alkali (NaOH + ½ Na₂S) varies from about 15 to about 23 percent of the ovendry weight of the chips charged. Data from Legg and Hart (1960) and Aurell and Hartler (1965) indicate that

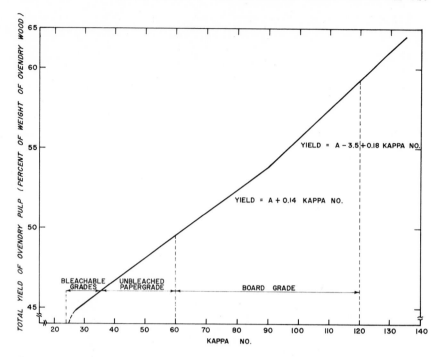

Figure 27–9.—Relationship between kappa number and kraft pulp yield from southern pine wood. See figure 27–10 for definition of constant A. (Drawing after Kleppe 1970.)

an increase in the effective alkali charge of 1 percent NaOH (on wood) will decrease A by 0.1 to 0.15 percent (on wood). The effective alkali charge in industrial pulping is usually kept at a level which will give an excess of 5 to 10 g. of sodium hydroxide per liter of liquor at the end of the cooking period.

Sulfidity.—Percent sulfidy, i.e., $[Na_2S \div (Na_2S + NaOH, \text{ as } Na_2O)]$ (100), influences pulp yield. The scant data available in the literature (Hägglund 1945; Legg and Hart 1960; Aurell 1963) indicate that an absolute sulfidity increase of 10 percent in the sulfidity range of 15 to 50 percent will give 0.3 to 0.5 higher yield (on wood). The influence of sulfidity seems to be greatest at low effective alkali charges (Legg and Hart 1960).

Chip size.—Reduction in chip size improves the uniformity of pulping and increases the screened pulp yield at a given kappa number (Nolan 1957; Hartler and Onisko (1962). There are also strong indications that reduction in chip size by shredding (Nolan 1967) can lead to 0.5 to 1 percent (on wood) higher total yield at a given number (Vethe 1967).

Carbohydrate stabilization.—It has been demonstrated (Sanyer and Laundrie 1964) that addition of elementary sulfur to the cooking liquor can improve the total pulp yield up to 12 percent (on wood). Practical gains are, however, of the magnitude of 1.5 to 4 percent (on wood); they are obtained by addition of 1 to 2 percent (on wood) of elementary sulfur (Kleppe 1964; Venemark 1964; Landmark et al. 1965).

Wood quality.—The most practical and common way of characterizing wood quality is by specific gravity. An increase in specific gravity from 0.37 to 0.57 is accompanied by an increase in pulp yield of 10 percentage points (fig. 27–10). The positive correlation between pulp yield and specific gravity is probably caused by the higher yield (2 to 7 percent of wood weight) from latewood compared to earlywood (Watson and Dadswell 1962; Gladstone et al. 1970). Because of the wide variation in lignin and extractive contents of southern pine wood (see secs. 6–2 and 6–3), the good correlation shown in figure 27–10 may not always be observable.

EFFECT OF WOOD QUALITY ON PAPER PROPERTIES

Kraft pulps from earlywood generally give much denser papers with higher bursting and tensile strengths than papers made from latewood (Cross and Bevan 1920; Nilson 1926; Holzer and Lewis 1950; Watson and Hodder 1954; Watson and Dadswell 1962). The differences in properties have been attributed to the thicker walls of the latewood fibers. Bray and Curran (1937) concluded from tests made on handsheets from longleaf, shortleaf, slash, and loblolly pine pulps that the most important factor influencing the papermaking properties is the ratio of latewood to earlywood fibers, and that greater differences in papermaking properties can be noticed in pulps from different parts of the same tree than in pulps from wood of different species and growth rates.

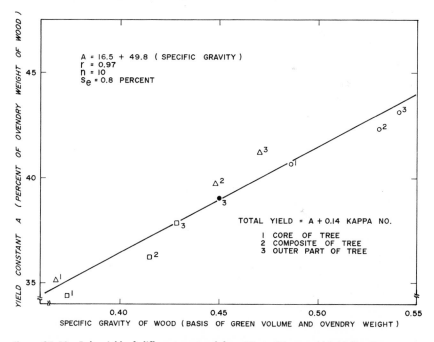

Figure 27–10.—Pulp yield of different parts of four 35- to 37-year-old loblolly pine trees as a function of specific gravity. (Drawing after Kleppe 1970 based on data from Barefoot et al. 1964.)

Barefoot et al. (1964, 1966) concluded that in general those fiber characteristics associated with wood density are predominant in determining papermaking properties of kraft pulps. Similar results were reported by Wangaard et al. (1966, 1967). These results are in good agreement with earlier findings that wood density is highly correlated with the latewood/earlywood ratio. Theoretically, the specific gravity of a wood sample can be expressed by the formula:

specific gravity =
(specific gravity of latewood) (fraction of latewood   (27–4)
by volume) + (specific gravity of earlywood)
(1 — fraction of latewood)

Figure 27–11 relates percentage of earlywood to specific gravity of longleaf, shortleaf, slash, and loblolly pines (Bray and Curran 1937). The observed variation in density at a given earlywood content is caused by variation in latewood and earlywood densities (Wangaard et al. 1966). See chapter 7 for a discussion of the variability of specific gravity between species, within species, and within trees.

The work of Mühlsteph (1941) and Runkel (1949) initiated a quantitative approach for establishing the relationship between fiber morphology and kraft paper properties; and work by Barefoot et al. (1964, 1966, 1970) on loblolly pine and by Wangaard et al. (1966) on slash pine have strongly indicated that multiple regression analyses can be used to predict

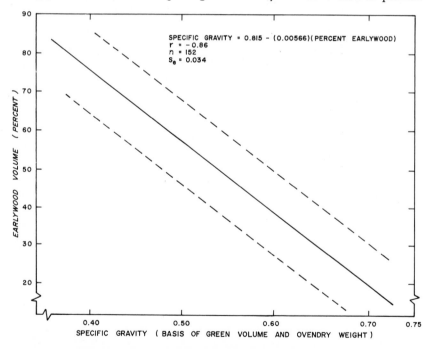

Figure 27–11.—Relationship between specific gravity and percentage of earlywood volume in loblolly, longleaf, shortleaf, and slash pines. Dashed lines show 95-percent confidence limits. (Drawing after Kleppe 1970 based on data from Bray and Curran 1937.)

paper properties from the morphological and physical characteristics of the wood.

In a test of the effects of wood selection on kraft paper properties, Fahey and Laundrie (1968) found that pulps from slash pine and loblolly pine thinnings and core wood (pith to 8- or 10-year growth ring) had burst and tensile strengths equal to pulps from mature pulpwood logs, but their tear resistance and pulp yield were lower. Pulps from the thinnings and the core wood had comparable strength characteristics. The outer wood of both pines gave pulps that were comparable in burst and tensile strengths to pulps from mature pulpwood logs, but their tear resistance was greater. Paper and linerboard made with the pulp from the loblolly pine thinnings generally were better formed, had higher tensile and burst strengths, but had lower tear resistance than papers made with pulp from the mature wood. The thinnings pulp gave softer and more absorbent tissue paper, smoother and more closed printing papers, and linerboard with greater compressive resistance.

Properties of southern pine pulpwood are summarized in table 27–7. A more detailed discussion of the morphological variations in southern pine wood can be found in chapter 5.

In the following four paragraphs, established correlations are listed for individual paper properties; they are indicated as either positive ($+$) or negative ($-$). Figures 27–12 and 27–13 illustrate the relationships.

Sheet density.—Specific gravity of the wood ($-$) and especially that of the latewood ($-$) seems to be the most influential factor affecting sheet density (Dadswell and Watson 1962; Barefoot et al. 1964; Wangaard et al. 1966, 1967). Other factors making significant contributions are fiber length ($-$) (Dadswell and Watson 1962; Dinwoodie 1966; Wangaard et al. 1966) and amount of compression wood ($+$) (Barefoot et al. 1964). Figure 27–12A shows sheet density as a function of wood specific gravity for pulps from slash pine.

TABLE 27–7.—*Properties of southern pine pulpwood*[1]

	Range	Most frequent
Whole wood specific gravity[2]_____	0.38–0.75	0.42–0.55
Latewood specific gravity[2]_____	.40– .85	.60– .75
Earlywood specific gravity[2]_____	.26– .40	.28– .32
Lignin content, percent_____	24–30	26–29
Extractive content (benzene alcohol), percent__	2–10	2.5–4.5
Fiber length, mm._____	2.0 –5.5	2.5 –4.5

[1] Estimated from literature given in table 27–8 and Isenberg (1951, pp. 11–12, 16–31), Watson and Hodder (1954), Mitchell (1958, 1964), Perry and Wang (1958), Zobel and McElwee (1958), Goddard and Strickland (1962), and Watson and Dadswell (1962).

[2] Basis of green volume and ovendry weight.

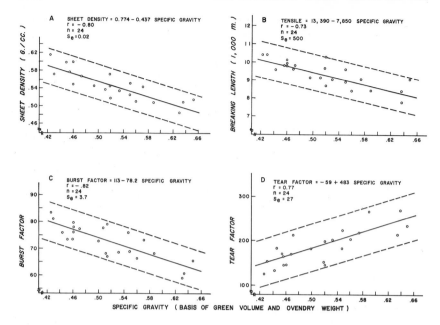

Figure 27–12.—Relationship of wood specific gravity to sheet density and strength properties of handsheets from slash pine kraft pulps at 500 Canadian Standard Freeness. (A) Sheet density. (B) Breaking length. (C) Burst strength. (D) Tear strength. Dashed lines show 95-percent confidence limits. S_e means standard error of the estimate; r is simple correlation coefficient. (Drawings after Kleppe 1970 based on data from Wangaard et al. 1966.)

Breaking length.—Fiber density expressed by wood specific gravity $(-)$, wall thickness $(-)$, or the ratio of wall thickness/fiber diameter $(-)$ appears to account for the greatest amount of variance in breaking length— a measure of tensile strength of paper expressed in meters of paper supported before failure (fig. 27–12B). There are strong indications that fiber length is of secondary importance $(+)$ (Barefoot et al. 1964, 1966, 1970; Einspahr 1964; Dinwoodie 1966; Wangaard et al. 1966, 1967). Dimensions of the latewood cells seem to exert a special influence (Barefoot et al. 1966).

Burst factor.—The relationships reported for burst (fig. 27–12C, 27–13 top) are quite similar to those for breaking length (Barefoot et al. 1964, 1966, 1970; Einspahr 1964; Dinwoodie 1966; Wangaard et al. 1966, 1967).

Tear factor.—The best property for predicting tear seems to be wood specific gravity $(+)$, and especially specific gravity of the latewood $(+)$ (Barefoot et al. 1964, 1966, 1970; Wangaard et al. 1966, 1967). Fiber length is also frequently reported to be positively correlated with tearing strength (Dadswell and Watson 1962; Wangaard et al. 1966). Figures 27–12D and 27–13 bottom show tear factor as a function of wood specific gravity.

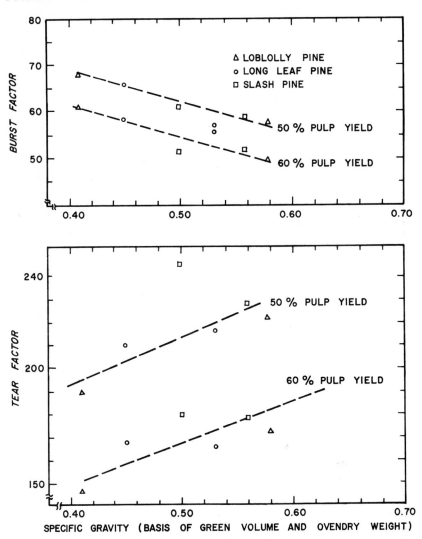

Figure 27–13.—Relationship of wood specific gravity to burst and tear strengths of hand-sheets from loblolly, longleaf, and slash pine kraft pulps at 600 Canadian Standard Freeness. (Drawing after Kleppe 1970 based on data from Cole et al. 1966.)

EFFECT OF SPECIES AND PULPING CONDITIONS ON PAPER PROPERTIES

Figure 27–13 shows burst and tear strengths of handsheets from kraft pulps of slash, loblolly, and longleaf pines grown in a mixed natural stand (Cole et al. 1966). There were no significant differences in the strength properties of the pulps from the different species, if compared at the same wood density. Increasing the yield from 50 to 60 percent (on wood) decreased strength of the pulp.

Pulping literature applicable to the various species is given in table 27–8.

Pulping conditions have some influence on the strength of pulps. Increasing the alkali charge gives pulps a slightly higher tear strength but reduces the breaking length and burst strength somewhat (Aurell and Hartler 1965). Higher sulfidity generally increases the strength properties of the pulp (Christiansen et al. 1957), and should be kept above approximately 15 percent in the kraft pulping of pine. In the South, continuous kraft pulping seems to give pulps with 10 to 15 percent higher strength properties than batch-cooked pulps (Bristow et al. 1967; Kleppe[6]).

TABLE 27–8.—*Literature on kraft pulping and papermaking properties of particular species of southern pine*

Pine species	Literature reference
Loblolly	Wells and Rue (1927); Curran and Bray (1931); Bray and Curran (1937); Chidester et al. (1938); Pillow et al. (1941); Holzer and Booth (1950); Browning and Baker (1950); Graff and Isenberg (1950); Lewis et al. (1950); Simmonds et al. (1956); Van Buijtenen et al. (1961a); Ahlm and Leopold (1963); McIntosh (1963); Sanyer and Laundrie (1964); McIntosh (1967); Gladstone et al. (1970); Barefoot et al. (1964, 1966, 1970).
Longleaf	Surface and Cooper (1914); Wells and Rue (1927); Bray and Curran (1933, 1937); Bray et al. (1937); USDA Forest Products Laboratory (1962).
Pitch	Wells and Rue (1927).
Pond	Wells and Rue (1927); Reis and Libby (1960).
Sand	Wells and Rue (1927); Bray and Martin (1942); USDA Forest Products Laboratory (1962).
Shortleaf	Wells and Rue (1927); Bray and Paul (1934); Bray and Curran (1937); Chidester et al. (1938); Martin and Brown (1952).
Slash	Wells and Rue (1927); Bray and Curran (1937); Schwartz and Bray (1941); Nolan et al. (1951); Nolan and Brown (1952); Nolan (1953); McKee (1960); Thornberg (1963); Van Buijtenen (1964); Wangaard et al. (1966, 1967).
Spruce	Wells and Rue (1927); Martin (1943); Koch et al. (1958).
Table Mountain	---
Virginia	Wells and Rue (1927); Hill (1944).
Southern (*Pinus* spp.)	Curran (1938); Suttle (1944); Murto and Itkonen (1950); Dickerscheid (1958); Cann and Robertson (1960); Somsen (1962); Mason et al. (1963); Einspahr (1964); Cole et al. (1966); Leopold (1966); Van Buijtenen et al. (1961b); Kleppe (1970).

PRACTICAL ASPECTS

Properties of pine pulps from southern kraft mills are mainly dependent on the age of the wood, the climate where the wood has grown, the heritage of the wood, and the lignin content of the pulps. Wood species seem to have minor influence. But as the different pine species are limited to, or concentrated in, specific climatic zones, they appear to give pulps with difinite papermaking characteristics.

The solid content of the wood is of great economic importance for the pulpmill which buys wood on a weight basis. Figure 27–14 shows the high positive correlation between specific gravity and the nonvolatile (i.e., ovendry) solid content of green wood (Bray and Curran 1937).

The desired properties of a pulp vary according to the product to be made from it. For linerboard, where a burst factor of only 39 to 40 is required, high density wood can be used which will also be favorable for

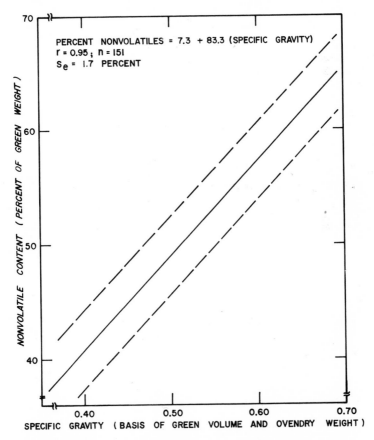

Figure 27–14.—Relationship between wood specific gravity and percentage of nonvolatile solid content (i.e., ovendry weight as a percentage of green weight) in green loblolly, longleaf, shortleaf, and slash pine wood. Dashed lines show 95-percent confidence limits. (Drawing after Kleppe 1970 based on data from Bray and Curran 1937.)

producing high stiffness and good runnability on the paper machine (Jones et al. 1966). Wrapping, bag, and sack paper requires moderate to high tensile, tear, and bursting strengths (high toughness). Wood of moderate density (0.45 to 0.55) should therefore be best suited for these products. The same applies to bleached board, magazine, book, printing, writing, tissue, and sanitary paper, where the southern pine kraft pulps are added in an amount of approximately 20 to 60 percent in order to improve strength. For newsprint, where kraft pulp is added (15 to 30 percent) to improve tensile strength, low density wood is best.

It should be possible for mills producing pulps requiring different paper-making properties to select wood according to density. For example, purchased sawmill chips, which are predominantly from the outer parts of the tree (slabs), are best suited for linerboard pulps; wood of small diameter that has a high content of juvenile wood can be pulped for products requiring especially high tensile and burst strengths.

27–3   SULFITE PULPING [7]

There is only one sulfite mill in the South (Rayonier Corp. at Fernandina Beach, Fla.) pulping southern pine; it produces dissolving grades of pulp by the acid sulfite process. In the early 1960's, Hammermill Paper Co. pulped Virginia pine by the sodium bisulfite process at Erie, Pa.; the bisulfite pulp has been replaced by bleached sulfate (kraft) pulp from the company's Selma, Ala. mill.

In all sulfite processes sulfur is burned to form SO_2 gas, which is dissolved in an alkaline solution to form sulfurous acid in the cooking solution. The base ion used in combination with the acid, listed in ascending order of solubility of their salts, may be magnesium, sodium, or ammonia. Magnesium base may be used only at a pH lower than 6 because of its limited solubility.

The three sulfite processes differ primarily in the acidity (pH) of the cooking liquor charged to the digester. They are:

Acid sulfite. Initial pH range, 1 to 2; chemical agent, H_2SO_3 + bisulfite salt of Ca, Mg, Na, or NH_3.

Bisulfite. Initial pH range, 3 to 6; final pH, 2 to 5; chemical agent $Mg(HSO_3)_2$, $NaHSO_3$, or NH_4HSO_3. Excess of either HSO_3. or base ion over the stoichiometric proportions for bisulfite determines the initial pH. Calcium base cannot be used because of limited solubility.

Neutral sulfite. Initial pH range, 6 to 10; final pH, 6 to 9; principal chemical agent Na_2SO_3 with or without Na_2CO_3, $(NH_4)_2SO_3$, or $MgSO_3$. Magnesium base may be used only in the lower pH range because of limited solubility.

---

[7] Condensed from Nolan (1969) by permission of W. J. Nolan and the Forest Products Research Society.

Any of these processes may be further defined as full chemical or **semichemical,** depending on whether the cooking agents convert the wood chips to individual fibers or only soften the chips before mechanical conversion to fiber. Combinations of any two of the above listed processes may be used successively in the digester.

In the 1920's and early 1930's, when the paper industry began moving into the South on a large scale, the only three chemical pulping processes in common use were calcium or magnesium base sulfite, kraft (pulping chemical, a mixture of NaOH and Na₂S) and soda (pulping agent, NaOH). It was known that acid sulfite agents would not satisfactorily delignify the heartwood of the southern pines. This was attributed to the high pitch (resin acids and fatty acids) content of the heartwood. The highly alkaline kraft and soda processes converted the pitch to soluble sodium soaps, and yielded a resin-free pulp. Since the kraft processes produced higher strength pulps at higher yield than the soda process, they became the predominant pulping methods. Efficient recovery of alkali—practical after 1930—made them competitive with northern sulfite processes, especially for linerboard, bag, wrapping, and other high-strength papers.

Since 1935, researchers have learned much about the reasons for incompatibility of pine heartwood with acid sulfite liquors, and processes for bisulfite and neutral sulfite pulping of conifers have been developed. These and other research developments have opened up possibilities for pulping the southern pines that are particularly attractive because these processes eliminate the sulfide ion, which is responsible for the objectionable odors of the kraft process. It is the opinion of one knowledgeable scientist that by 1980 the kraft pulping process will be seriously challenged in the South by some form of sulfite pulping in the neutral or slightly alkaline range.

ACID SULFITE PULPING

Prior to 1950, commercial sulfite pulping was carried out almost exclusively by the acid sulfite process, using calcium or magnesium as the base. As pressures began to build against air and water pollution, and markets expanded for high-yield linerboard pulps, much research was conducted on recovery of chemicals previously discharged into streams, and on sulfite systems to handle southern pines. By the early 1940's sulfite recovery systems, including the Mead, the Institute of Paper Chemistry, and the Western Precipitation systems (Shaffer 1958) enabled sulfite processes to be competitive with kraft from both the air and water pollution standpoints. Progress was also made toward pulping pine by the acid sulfite and other sulfite processes.

Early researchers felt that the poor response of pine heartwood to acid sulfite pulping was due to its high resin content. Hägglund (1951) credited C. G. Schwalbe with disproving this theory by showing that heartwood, which had been extracted with benzene and ether would still not respond to acid sulfite pulping. Work at Hägglund's laboratory showed that if further extracted with alcohol or acetone, pine heartwood responded as readily to sulfite pulping as did pine sapwood or spruce. H. Erdtman, at the Hägglund laboratory, identified the alcohol and acetone extractives as 3, 5- dihydroxystilbine and its monomethyl ether, and called them pinosylvin and pinosylvin monomethyl ether. These phenolic compounds, in highly acid solution, react with lignin to form a condensation (polymerization) product that prevents delignification by acid sulfite liquor.

Hägglund had earlier observed, however, that pine heartwood could be readily pulped by sodium or magnesium bisulfite solutions at a pH of 4.5. As a consequence of these facts it was found that if pine heartwood is first pulped at moderate acidity, as with $NaHSO_3$, the lignin becomes sulfonated but does not react with the phenols. After this sulfonation, pulping proceeds quite normally, even when highly acid sulfite cooking liquor is subsequently used.

Erdtman (1944) found inhibiting phenols in the heartwood of Scotch pine (*Pinus sylvestris* L.) and six additional pine species, among them longleaf pine. He later (Erdtman 1949b) reviewed their structural formulas and pointed out their highly beneficial properties as fungicides and insect repellents. He also (Erdtman 1949a) described a probable mechanism of the inhibiting action of these phenolic compounds with a schematic presentation in which he likened the condensation of lignin by phenols to the formation of penolic plastics. In the lignin condensation, the phenol plays a part similar to formaldehyde in the phenolic plastic polymerization.

During the 1930's and early 1940's, most of the domestic research reported on pulping of southern and similar pine species by the acid sulfite process was carried out at the USDA Forest Products Laboratory in Madison, Wis. Curran (1936), recognizing that most pines were second growth and low in heartwood, considered them pulpable by the lime-base acid sulfite process. He found that fast-grown pines afforded a higher pulp yield, took less cooking time, and produced pulp with higher burst strength; tear strength, however, was lower in acid sulfite pulp made from fast-grown trees.

McGovern (1936) found that unusually high concentrations of SO_2 in the calcium-base cooking acid (15 percent total SO_2, 1.1 percent combined SO_2) greatly improved the pulping of loblolly and three other resinous pines. Screenings were fewer in pulps from these high concentration cooks than in those from cooks of conventional concentration (5.0 percent total SO_2, 0.9 percent combined SO_2) ; the pulps were equal or superior in strength properties. Chidester et al. (1938) cooked loblolly, shortleaf, longleaf, and slash pine wood successfully with lime-base acid sulfite liquors of conventional SO_2 concentrations. All four species cooked to good yield with low screenings and satisfactory strength properties; since all pulpwood tested had less than 0.4 percent heartwood, however, the condensation problems created by the phenols in heartwood were avoided, rather than solved. (See figs. 5–4 and 5–5 for information on percentage heartwood commonly found in the southern pines 20 years of age and older.)

Chidester and McGovern (1940) pulped jack pine, Douglas-fir (*Pseudotsuga menziesii* (Mirb.) Franco) and slash pine with lime-base acid bisulfite liquors. (Douglas-fir heartwood resists pulping much as southern pine heartwood does.) Results agreed with the previous work of Mc-Govern (1936), in that high concentrations of SO_2 (7.3 percent) were necessary to pulp the heartwood of all three species to satisfactory yield with low screenings. For acid sulfite pulping of Douglas-fir containing 60 to 75 percent heartwood, Chidester and McGovern (1941) found sodium-base liquors superior to magnesium, and lime-base least satisfactory. They also found that sodium bisulfite liquors pulped the Douglas-fir to a high screened yield of 55 percent, but 160° C. had to be used instead of the normal 130° to 140° C. Sodium sulfite liquors required 181° C. for satisfactory pulping.

Subsequently, McGovern and Chidester (1941) cooked seasoned (6 months) loblolly pine heartwood with lime-, magnesium-, and sodium-base acid bisulfite liquors. Screenings amounted to 10 percent of lime-base pulps, 3.8 percent of those with magnesium base, and only 0.4 percent of those from sodium-base liquors. When wood was seasoned for 9½ months after it was chipped, screenings in pulps made with all three liquors were reduced to about one-third the above values.

BISULFITE PULPING

Early in the 1950's the Pulp and Paper Research Institute of Canada developed the Va-purge process for rapid impregnation of cooking liquor into chips before cooking (Hart 1954). In this technique, steaming the chips in the digester before liquor is admitted drives off air from the chips, and fills the fiber lumens with water vapor. When cooking liquor, at a somewhat lower temperature, is admitted, condensation sucks the liquor into the chips. After impregnation, excess liquor is drawn off before the cook is started by direct steaming. This procedure permits much more rapid cooking cycles than were previously realized.

During the 1950's much research was done on systems using Va-purge impregnation and mechanical fiberizing to produce high-yield pulps. Hart et al. (1954) using black spruce, produced yields of 53 to 62 percent after a short-period, vapor-phase cooking. At highest yield, tensile and burst strengths were good, but tear strength was somewhat reduced. Hart and Woods (1955), with somewhat different temperatures and pH, obtained 64.5 percent yield from western hemlock (*Tsuga heterophylla* (Raf.) Sarg.), spruce, and balsam fir. Despite a lignin content of 19.5 percent, tensile and bursting strength compared well with that of southern pine kraft. Bolviken and Giertz (1956) added SO_2 gas to Na_2SO_3 liquor in a 4- to 5-hour cook to produce from Scotch pine a good-quality pulp of 65-percent yield.

Tomlinson et al. (1958) and Tomlinson and Tomlinson (1958) described the Magnifite process for the pulping of conifers, and the Magnefite chemical recovery system (see also Darmstadt and Tomlinson 1960). By this process chips were impregnated before cooking with $Mg(HSO_3)_2$ liquors containing 2.0 percent combined SO_2, with a weight ratio of liquor to wood of 4.2:1. Initial pH of liquor was 3.6. After 30 minutes to reach maximum temperature, 3 hours at 166° C. produced fully cooked pulps of 47- to 52-percent yield, while 1.5 hours at 166° C. resulted in 65.5-percent total yield (54.2-percent screened yield). It was claimed that pines whose heartwood contains minor quantities of objectionable phenols can be pulped successfully by this process.

Dorland et al. (1958) described and patented (Dorland and McKinney 1959) the Arbiso pulping process, which has 16 to 20 percent $NaHSO_3$ as the active pulping agent, and produced from spruce, pulp yields of 47 to 70 percent at maximum temperatures of 155° to 180° C. with liquor-wood ratios of 4 or 5:1. Although not in use in the South, the process is applicable to wood of the southern pines.

Stockman (1960) stated that increased pH of the cooking liquor requires increased temperatures for removal of sulfonated lignin by hydrolysis. Higher temperatures tend to reduce the viscosity (chain length of cellulose molecule) of the pulp with consequent loss in strength. He found that pulping in single stage at initial pH of 4.0 (bisulfite) and a temperature of 160° C. permits pulping of pines containing phenols, and results in a strong pulp with yields of 58 to 60 percent, without the need for mechanical fibration. Such pulps had strength characteristics approaching those produced by kraft pulping, except in tear strength, which was low. A single-stage cook at pH 6.0 required 180° C. for delignification, resulting in pulps of very low strength properties.

A U.S. patent granted to Rasch et al. (1962) disclosed a procedure for $NaHSO_3$ semichemical pulping that was used commercially for several years to pulp Virginia pine. Chips were pulped with bisulfite liquor with an initial pH between 3.0 and 5.0 (9 to 12 percent SO_2, based on weight of dry wood) at a temperature in the range of 155° to 170° C. Yield, after knot removal, was 50 to 62 percent. Cooked chips were mechanically fiberized, and hemicellulose and wood resins were then removed from the pulp by alkali digestion. Final pulp yield was in the range of 40 to 50 percent.

Keller and Fahey (1968) pulped a loblolly-slash pine mixture by the Magnefite, $Mg(HSO_3)_2$, process. Pulp yield ranged from 49.2 to 70.9 percent; pulps were very light in color, i.e., 41 to 51 on the G.E. brightness scale. The very-high-yield pulps were fiberized in a disk refiner. All pulps, whether fully cooked or fiberized, were about 55 percent as strong in tear as fully cooked kraft of the same species. In tensile strength, fully cooked pulps were almost as strong as kraft, while the fiberized pulps were 75 percent as strong. Bursting strengths were low, the fully cooked pulps being 70 percent as strong and the fiberized pulp about 50 percent as strong as kraft. Pulps presented no pitch (wood resin) problems, perhaps because the wood had been stored 6 months before chipping.

MULTISTAGE SULFITE PULPING

Because adjustment of pH of the liquors in the various stages permits control of hemicellulose content of the pulp and insures efficient removal of wood resins, multistage pulping of some conifers has increased recently. Most of these processes involve either sodium- or magnesium-base liquors for which chemical recovery systems have been developed to meet the increasingly stringent controls on stream pollution.

Long before multistage pulping became popular, however, Meunier (1931) described the Rosen process for manufacturing sulfite pulps from resinous woods; it consisted of a first-stage treatment in the digester with dilute alkali at temperatures up to 110° C. for 2 to 5 hours, followed by washing with salt solution. The chips were then treated with SO_2 gas and subjected to the usual low-temperature acid sulfite cook. Very pure pulps containing 92.4 percent alpha-cellulose were produced.

Sivola (1955) was granted a U. S. patent for multistage pulping. His method of cooking consists of a first stage involving sodium acid sulfite liquor in the pH range of 1 to 2. At the end of the first stage, SO_2 gas is relieved for recovery. In the second stage alkali is injected into the digester without draining or reductions in pressure. The composition of injection liquor may vary from Na_2CO_3 alone, to mixtures of carbonate, bicarbonate, and sulfide. In the third stage the cook is completed in the pH range of 7 to 10 at temperatures of 150° to 180° C. Sivola (1956) was granted another U.S. patent, in which a complex recovery system is described for the multistage processing covered in the earlier patent (see also Kennedy 1960). Pascoe et al. (1959) described a variant Sivola process (wherein the first stage calls for treatment with $NaHSO_3$ at a starting pH of 4.0, instead of the acid bisulfite stage described in the Sivola patent), by which jack pine pulps were produced that were as strong as those yielded by the kraft process. This process is said to have a much higher tolerance to thiosulfate than conventional acid sulfite pulping.

Lagergren and Lunden (1959) described the Stora Kopparburg process used for pine in a mill in Skutskar, Sweden. The first stage liquor is comprised of a mixture of Na_2SO_3 and $NaHSO_3$ at a starting pH of 5 to 7. This stage brings about penetration of the liquor into the chips and sulfonation of the lignin without lignin condensation. The second (delignification) stage uses acid sulfite liquor made by adding liquid SO_2 to part of the first stage liquor. The cook requires 10 hours pulping time. A wide variety of pulp grades is obtained, depending on variations in pH and time in each stage and variations in the five-stage bleaching cycle. Cederquist et al. (1960) and Scholander (1960) described the Stora liquor recovery process.

Dyer (1961) described the first American commercial installation of highly flexible, two-stage, magnesium-base pulping at the Weyerhaeuser mill at Cosmopolis, Wash. By modifying schedules and liquor composition, premium pulps are produced with a wide range of qualities, including dissolving grades.

Bryce and Tomlinson (1962) described the two-stage Magnifite process, in which $Mg(HSO_3)_2$ liquor was at a pH of about 4 in the first stage and about 6.0 to 6.5 in the second. Pulps from spruce of 51 to 54 percent yield were stronger than those from single-stage Magnifite and were much stronger than those from conventional acid sulfite pulping.

Sanyer et al. (1962) studied multistage, sodium-base sulfite pulping with two- and three-stage combinations of acid sulfite, bisulfite, and neutral sulfite. For jack pine, neutral sulfite followed by acid sulfite gave the highest yields, while bisulfite-neutral sulfite produced lowest yield for the same lignin content. In strength, however, the combination of bisulfite-neutral sulfite was most satisfactory, being slightly better in tensile strength, equal in tear, and not quite as strong in bursting strength as kraft pulp from the same species.

Croon (1963) found that a pretreatment of coniferous wood chips with dilute caustic (5.5 g. NaOH per liter) at 70° C., followed by acid sulfite pulping, resulted in pulp yields as high as 68 to 70 percent before mechanical fibration was necessary. For Norwegian spruce (*Picea abies* (L.) Karst) and Scotch pine, both containing extractive-rich heartwood, a 60-minute first stage treatment at pH 7, followed by 120-minute treatment with sodium-base acid sulfite improved yield over a pH 6 first stage (Croon 1965). Glucomannan, the principal hemicellulose component in the conifers, is deacetylated in the nearly neutral first stage and thereby stabilized against acid hydrolysis and dissolution in the second, highly acid stage of cooking.

NEUTRAL SULFITE PULPING (SINGLE STAGE)

In neutral sulfite pulping, Na_2SO_3 or $(NH_4)_2SO_3$, or a combination of Na_2SO_3 and Na_2CO_3 delignify wood slowly and require very long cooking cycles to produce fully cooked pulps. Commercially the process has been confined to the hardwoods.

Chidester and McGovern (1939) pulped shortleaf pine with concentrated Na_2SO_3 liquor (138 g. Na_2SO_3 per liter at a pH of 8.1). Weight ratio of liquor to wood was about 7:1. Cooking time of 9.5 hours (3.0 hours to the maximum temperature of 180° C.) produced a fully cooked pulp yield of 42.8 percent. Strength of the pulp was comparable to kraft. Additions of NaOH, Na_2CO_3, and Na_2S to the Na_2SO_3 liquor had little effect on yield; the Na_2S addition improved strength characteristics and reduced bleach requirements.

Nolan (1970) presented the results of neutral sulfite (mixtures of Na_2SO_3 and Na_2CO_3) pulping of slash pine. Ratios of sulfite to carbonate varied between 3:1 and 6:1. The higher ratios of sulfite resulted in higher yields for the same lignin content. Semichemical pulps of 53 percent yield were as strong in all categories as, and 10 points brighter on the G.E. scale than, fully cooked kraft from the same species. Total cooking time of 2.66 hours (1.0 hour to maximum temperature of 190° C.) was required. Fibration of pulp at 20 percent consistency (percent dry fiber) in an attrition mill equipped with toothed plates required less than 5.0 hp. day/ton of dry pulp. Tear strength of these pulps was as high as for fully cooked neutral sulfite pulp, indicating no fiber damage during fibration. The alkalinity of the cooking liquor, pH 8.5, saponified and dissolved the wood resins as satisfactorily as highly alkaline kraft liquors. Further increases in the ratio of sulfite to carbonate should result in higher yields of brighter pulps without loss in strength.

Shick (1970) found that southern pine pulped with an alkaline sulfite system, which combined sulfide or hydrosulfide-carbonate and sulfite, gave pulps with properties desirable for linerboard manufacture, at yields 6 to 10 percent higher than those obtained by conventional kraft pulping. Such an alkaline sulfite pulp, at a yield of 61.7 percent, had a burst of 105 p.s.i., a tear of 171 g., a ring crush of 62 lb., and a brightness of 22.1 percent. The corresponding kraft pulp at a yield of only 51.8 percent had a burst of 103 p. s. i., a tear of 186 g., a ring crush of 56 lb., and a brightness of 19.2 percent. A high concentration of active chemicals was found to be desirable in such alkaline sulfite cooks, and it was observed that total cooking time could be reduced to the commercial kraft range, without loss in strength, by increasing the cooking temperature.

Another process that may have application to southern pine is that patented by Ingruber and Allard (1970); it calls for pulping with Na_2SO_3 and controlled amounts of NaOH to maintain pH in the range of 8 to 11.

FUTURE POSSIBILITIES FOR SULFITE PULPING OF THE SOUTHERN PINES

The thick-walled, stiff fibers of the southern pines suit them to the production of rather coarse, high-strength grades such as linerboard, bag, and wrapping papers. These grades constitute the highest proportion of total U.S. paper production. Any successful sulfite or combinations of sulfite processes, therefore should yield pulp with high-strength properties.

It would seem, at the present state of the art, that neutral sulfite semichemical pulps show prospects of successful competition with kraft. It may be possible to produce pulps of 60 percent (ovendry basis) or higher yield, as strong as kraft and considerably brighter in color. Processes are available for chemical recovery, and elimination of the sulfide ion in the cooking liquor should simplify air pollution problems. Future research may prove the applicability of two-stage pulping, in which the first stage stabilizes glucomannans and the second stage delignifies the fibers. However, such multistage pulping must preserve the high-strength properties of the southern pines to be commercially competitive with the huge southern kraft industry.

27–4   DISSOLVING PULP [8]

The art of converting native cellulose fibers into solutions from which other cellulose forms are regenerated has been known for about 100 years (Haynes 1953). Large scale use of wood cellulose for manufacture of manmade fibers began in 1916, 1919, and 1921 by application of the **acetate, cuprammonium, and viscose** processes respectively.

From these beginnings, uses for **dissolving pulp,** the dry, loosely matted sheets of refined fibers used for chemical processing (also termed chemical cellulose), have grown along with other uses for wood fiber. In 1966 world production of all types of pulp was 95,646,000 tons (Wilson 1967a). Approximately 20 percent, or 20 million tons, represents an item of commerce known as **market pulp,** that is, pulp manufactured by one organization and used by another. In 1966 market pulp shipments of dissolving plus special alpha pulps totalled 2,663,000 tons, all of which originated in in North American and Scandinavia (Wilson 1967b).

Since 1951, mills for dissolving pulp have been built in five locations in North America—two in the far Northwest and three in the Southeast. These three southern mills plus an existing mill (1939 construction) in Florida—all operating on southern pine—produce almost 40 percent of North American market dissolving pulp.

Regenerated cellulose fiber made by the viscose process, cellophane (made by extruding viscose through a slit to produce a clear film), and cellulose acetate in the form of film, fiber, and tow (for cigarette filters) accounted for more than 80 percent of the 1966 dissolving pulp consump-

---

[8] With minor editorial changes taken from Durso (1969) by permission of Donald F. Durso and the Forest Products Research Society.

TABLE 27–9.—*North American consumption of dissolving pulp in 1966* (Vincent 1967)

Type	Quantity
	Thousands of short tons
Viscose fibers—filament, staple, tow_	602
Cellophane_ _ _ _ _ _ _ _ _ _ _ _ _ _ _ _ _ _ _ _	205
Acetate fibers—filament, staple, tow_	267
All other[1]_ _ _ _ _ _ _ _ _ _ _ _ _ _ _ _ _ _ _	188

---

[1] Other: Acetate plastics, acetate film, nitrate lacquers, cuprammonium fibers, ethers, sponges, caps and bands, and special papers.

tion in North America (table 27-9). The product showing greatest recent sales growth is viscose fiber with high modulus of elasticity and tensile strength when wet. In certain applications these fibers can replace cotton and be blended with other synthetic fibers. Use of regular viscose staple fiber in nonwoven fabrics for the medical-surgical and hygienic fields is growing (Anonymous 1968a). Charles (1963) and Wilson (1959) provide additional details on the many uses of dissolving pulps.

The high molecular weight of cellulose and its long chain molecules account for the desirable strength properties of derived fibers and films. The complex nature of cellulose solutions requires knowledge of sophisticated theoretical chemistry for understanding (Elmgren 1965), but with advanced technology allows the manufacture of products having a wide range of controllable hydrophilic properties, which provide the comfort factor so necessary in many fiber applications.

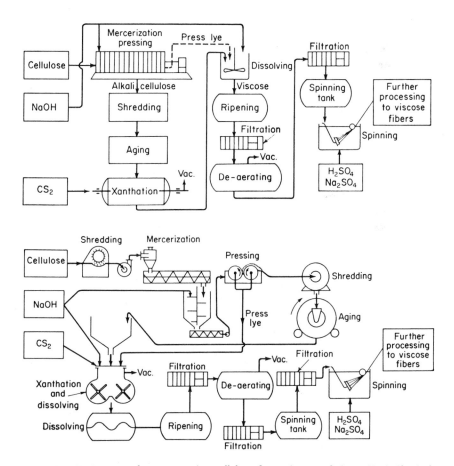

Figure 27-15.—Processes for regenerating cellulose from viscose solutions. (Top) Classical. (Bottom) Continuous or semicontinuous. (Drawing after Rydholm © 1965, reprinted by permission of John Wiley and Sons.)

ACETYLATION FLOW DIAGRAM

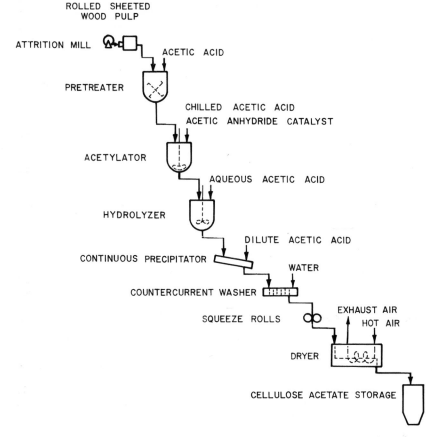

Figure 27–16.—Process for cellulose acetate, an ester of cellulose. (Drawing after Durso 1969.)

Figures 27–15 and 27–16 summarize the steps of the viscose and acetate processes, respectively (Rydholm 1965; Williams[9]). The fine details of the major dissolving pulp processes are the subject of frequent publications (e.g., Mitchell 1949; Treiber 1967); summaries of the conversion process are found in Gotze (1967) and Rydholm (1965). Durso et al. (1967) reported efforts to improve filtration to remove undissolved particles before spinning. Bartunek (1967) reviewed technology and described standard laboratory methods for analysis of pulp, viscose, and fibers made from viscose.

Publications related to dissolving pulp and specific to southern pine have described morphological properties of the native fibers (Jurbergs 1960ab) and detailed technical evaluation of how they react in the viscose process (Dean et al. 1960). The latter attempts to explain the difference in "reactivity" of sulfate pine pulp versus sulfite pine pulp in the viscose process. In recent years, research with statistical designs and computer analysis has been directed toward attaining process conditions designed to extract all of the potential value from the pulp (Wyatt 1966). Williams[9] showed that NaOH treatment, freeze-drying, and other structure-changing procedures have large effects on the rates of reaction and degradation during acetylation of pine sulfate pulp.

PROCESSES

Of the three major methods of preparing dissolving pulps, two, the sulfite and the sulfate processes, are applied to the southern pines. The soda process is applied primarily to make pulps from cotton linters, historically the chief alternate source of chemical cellulose.

Soda (linters).—Although the sulfite process for making woodpulps was developed in 1865, and the sulfate process in 1885, these pulps were not convertible to cellulose derivatives before World War I. Early dissolving pulps were made exclusively from cotton linters, the short fibers which are removed from cottonseed before it is crushed to extract the oil (Jurbergs 1960c; Jurbergs and Dowling 1964).

"Reactive" unbleached pulp from linters was used to prepare cellulose nitrate for gunpowder before 1905. This required only a mild cook, about 2 hours at 170° C. in 1 percent NaOH (solution basis), to remove dense foreign matter such as stems and seed hulls. Viscose and acetate required a more refined cellulose, obtained by a soda cook in the presence of additives which removed fats, waxes, and proteins. By 1930 special types of cotton pulps were designed for viscose, acetate, cuprammonium, and ether production, and were quoted at different prices related to their degree of purification (Anonymous 1955).

Despite increasing use of refined woodpulps in recent decades, linter pulps continued until about 1955 to be a major raw material for high-tenacity viscose fibers, and other cellulose derivatives. Recent increased costs of raw linters, due to declining cotton production, have restricted uses of linter pulps to those demanding high purity, heat stability, and high DP (degree of polymerization, i.e., number of glucose units per cellulose molecule).

Sulfite (general).—Dissolving woodpulps approach the chemical concept of pure cellulose and thus they must be substantially free of lignin, resin, minerals, and hemicelluloses. Figure 27–17 shows yield for dissolving pulps compared to that for other sulfite pulps. Dissolving pulp has the lowest yield, i.e., about 40 percent before bleaching. Great difficulty was encountered by an experienced sulfite paper pulp producer in his first efforts in 1924 to make a dissolving grade of pulp (Schur 1963). Digesting was no problem, but the later stages of purification, required for preparing a pulp with high alpha-cellulose content along with high brightness and appropriate DP, presented some very challenging problems. The most

---

[9] Williams, J. C. 1968. The influence of pulp properties on acetylation reactivity. Presented at the 2nd TAPPI Dissolving Pulps Conference, New Orleans, La., June 4-6.

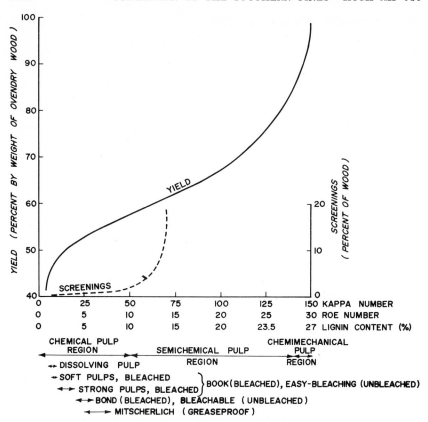

Figure 27–17.—Yield of spruce sulfite pulps of various grades. (Drawing after Rydholm ©
1965 by permission of John Wiley and Sons.)

important step was a hot caustic extraction stage placed between acid
chlorination and alkaline hypochlorite stages. This hot caustic stage used
NaOH solution at about 1 percent concentration and a temperature up
to about 96° to 98° C. It removed hemicellulose material and led to
products having alpha-cellulose contents of about 90 to 94 percent, compared to 85 to 86 percent alpha in paper pulps from the same wood species.

Multistage sulfite processes for chemical cellulose are designed to yield
dissolving pulps with alpha-cellulose contents as high as 96.0 percent. Some
North American producers now offer sulfite pulps with alpha-cellulose
contents up to 97.0 percent; the production processes for these pulps have
not been revealed.

Cooking solutions used for dissolving pulp are much the same as those
used for the manufacture of paper pulp, but cooking temperatures and
times are carefully programmed (Rydholm 1965, p. 576). For dissolving
pulp, maximum temperatures are usually about 145° C., with the major
portion of the cooking cycle time required to obtain penetration of the
wood chips without burning (Rydholm 1965, pp. 338 and 653). Very

little pulping action (lignin solution) occurs below 120° C. The total time from raw wood chips through digester unloading ranges from about 6 to about 12 hours, with the longer times required for the multistage processes.

Sulfite (southern pine).—The sulfite process was rather easily adapted to many species of softwoods and hardwoods, but as noted in section 27–3, it did not at first satisfactorily pulp southern pines because of their extractive content. In 1938 there appeared the first reference to successful preparation of a pine dissolving pulp which could replace the "standard" spruce pulp in the preparation of cellulose derivatives (Bunger et al. 1938). In 1939 Rayonier, Inc. constructed a pulpmill at Fernandina, Fla. to produce sulfite pine pulp, using a new (unidentified) principle of purification (Anonymous 1940) to increase alpha-cellulose content and decrease resin content. The Fernandina plant has been successful from the time of its dedication. In 1940 its capacity was given as 64,000/tons per year (Anonymous 1940); in 1953 it was over 300 tons/day, or about 100,000 tons/year of pulps for acetate, tire yarn, and viscose textile fibers (Anonymous 1953). Very recently additional capacity was installed for a premium grade acetate pulp (Anonymous 1967). The Fernandina plant is not only unique in its use of southern pine but also has the distinction of being upgraded while many other sulfite mills are being retired (Anonymous 1958).

Sulfate (southern pine).—Since the first demonstration in 1885 that wood could be delignified by the action of sodium hydroxide and sodium sulfide, use of the kraft process has grown until it is now the dominant pulping procedure. (See sec. 27–2.) Unlike the sulfite, the kraft process needs more than minor modification of cooking conditions to produce a dissolving grade of pulp. Impurities which become alkali stable during the kraft cook can be removed by a combination of acid and alkaline stages *after* the cook, but the pulp will not have the required reactivity even though desired chemical analyses can be achieved (Rydholm 1965, p. 657). In 1931 Richter discovered that an acid hydrolysis *prior* to the sulfate cook would provide the necessary purity and reactivity in the pulp (Ott et al. 1954, p. 616). This finding was used in Germany during World War II to make dissolving pulp from hardwoods (Ott et al. 1954, p. 546). The pulping procedure was further developed by Industrial Cellulose Research Ltd. in North America and became a considerable factor in the dissolving pulp industry by early 1951 (Anonymous 1950, 1968c).

Simmonds et al. (1956) detail the range of prehydrolysis conditions which must be used to break down and remove the hemicellulose from loblolly pine while leaving the lignin in a form which responds to pulping reactions. In another study of loblolly pine, Simmonds and Chidester (1960) reported on one of the rare systematic comparisons of sulfate pulp preparation with and without prehydrolysis.

It was learned rather early in the use of the prehydrolysis sulfate process that the usual purification procedures would not raise the alpha-cellulose level beyond about 95 percent. Based on previous broad experience with high-purity dissolving pulps from linters, the Buckeye-Cellulose Corp. in 1959 patented a process for purification of woodpulp to much higher alpha levels (Rogers et al. 1959). The process uses a cold, concentrated alkali extraction step which can be incorporated into a bleaching procedure as indicated by Rydholm (1965, p. 1074, Type 25, also pp. 996-997). This first high-alpha wood pulp, called "V-5" pulp, has been on the market since 1955 (Schenker and Heath 1959). Through suitable combinations of prehydrolysis-pulping-purification procedures, a wide range of sulfate pine dissolving pulps thus became available.

The construction of pulpmills by Rayonier in Jesup, Ga. (Anonymous 1954b) and by Buckeye at Foley, Fla. (Anonymous 1954a) marked the beginning of sulfate dissolving pulp manufacture from southern pine. Because of the range of pulp types which they could produce (table 27–10), demand rapidly exceeded initial capacity of these mills, and both carried out a series of expansions (Waters and Waters 1958; Anonymous 1959, 1960, 1962ab, 1964a). There are now two essentially independent pulpmills on each site, and current capacities are about 300 percent of the initial.

Sulfite-sulfate comparisons.—The success of the sulfate southern pine ventures in the face of well-entrenched and highly useful sulfite pulps is not due alone to lower wood and processing costs. Tippetts (1950) stated that even though the rayon manufacturer uses the same process for both

TABLE 27–10.—*Typical characteristics of dissolving pulps from southern pine*

	Sulfate	Sulfite
Alpha-cellulose, percent _____	93.6–98.3	91.8–97.0
Pentosans, percent _____	.4– 2.3	.5– 2.2
[1]Viscosity, 0.5 percent in		
CED, cp. _____	3.9–11.8	5.5–21.3
[2]S–10, percent__ _____	1.9–11.3	4.3–11.3
S–18, percent _____	1.1– 4.7	1.7– 6.0
S–21.5, percent_____	.9– 4.0	1.4– 5.4
Brightness, GE. _____	83.4–92.7	88.4–91.4

[1] Viscosity of a solution of cellulose (0.5 percent by weight) in cupri-ethylene diamine is directly proportional to the molecular weight of cellulose. See TAPPI Standard T 230–su–66. Cp. means centipoise.

[2] The percentage of a pulp that will dissolve in an NaOH solution is inversely correlated with pulp purity; different components dissolve in various concentrations. Values opposite S–10, for example, give the weight percentage that will dissolve in a 10-percent solution of NaOH. See TAPPI Standard T 235–m–60.

linters and woodpulp, some unknown intrinsic property of the linters cellulose carries through to the final product and significantly affects its functional behavior. Similarly, he observed that tire rayons made from prehydrolysis sulfate pulp have better properties than those obtainable from the best sulfite pulps; properties of the sulfate tire rayons closely approach those from cotton linters. Since the standard cellulose characterization tests do not detect the reasons for the improved performance, it appears that other—perhaps more sophisticated—analyses will be required to understand these differences so that better pulps can be developed.

Among other differences, it is known that sulfite chemicals attack the structure of cellulose fibers more severely, affecting their strength, porosity, and other gross properties (Rydholm 1965, p. 319; Stone and Scallan 1968). Parks (1959) has also shown by X-ray diffraction that sulfate southern pine pulp has a structure more closely approaching that of cotton linters than either sulfite southern pine or sulfate hardwood pulps. Furthermore, he found that the similarity persisted when the supermolecular structure was exposed to treatments with strong NaOH. Sulfate processing of southern pine leads to cellulose in which the molecules are arranged into ordered regions which in size and/or degree of perfection rival those found in linters. The combination of pine wood and prehydrolysis sulfate pulping produces a unique chemical cellulose.

Much research has been directed toward answering the question: Does the structural difference noted in woodpulp fibers carry over into the regenerated cellulose? Ranby et al. (1956), through electron microscopy, found that regenerated viscose cellulose contains fibrillar structures resembling those in the starting pulp. Comparing cotton linters with sulfite and sulfate wood pulps, they concluded that differences among the structures in the end products were depedent on the starting material. However, this work establishes neither the presence nor the absence of "original structures" in the end product.

A different avenue for speculation was opened through the discovery that order and crystallinity in manmade polymers arises from the phenomenon of chain folding. Tonnesen and Ellefsen (1960), Dolmetsch (1961), and Manley (1964) have proposed that similar chain folding leads to the ordered structure found in both native and regenerated cellulose. If this be true, then the findings of Hess et al (1951), Elmgren (1965), and Brown (1966) could provide a bridge for relating structure in the end product with structure in the original chemical cellulose. Hess et al. (1951) demonstrated that in viscose preparation both the alkali steeping and the CS_2 reaction take place through a permutoid reaction; that is, the basic structure is swollen to accommodate the reagents but the structure is not destroyed. The others have established that cellulose molecules approach the shape of random coils in solution, and that both derivative preparation and solution cause only slight changes in the degree of coil expansion while "structure" is maintained. Therefore, one can visualize that during the dissolving process the ordered structure in the native fiber is "destroyed" by loosening a cellulose molecule from its neighbors without disturbing its intramolecular organization. When the molecule is regenerated, only its association with neighboring molecules is reestablished.

This grossly oversimplified picture is postulated to rationalize observed results, but there is no body of data to prove it [10]; however, the concept of structure "memory" has been found useful for understanding the performance of sulfate pine pulps in either the viscose or the acetate process. A high degree of order is a hindrance during conversion, but once solution is achieved and the cellulose recovered as a new form, then inherent benefits are attainable from the same inherent higher degree of order.

The sulfate process has a 2 to 1 time advantage over the traditional sulfite process in terms of digester cycle (Rydholm 1965, p. 653), plus advantages in pollution control and chemical recovery. The result has been increased sulfate dissolving pulp capacity and pulp types (Anonymous 1962b, 1964b, 1968b), while sulfite mills are being phased out (Anonymous 1963). At the end of 1968, only 14 years after introduction, sulfate southern pine pulps represent one-third of the North American market dissolving pulp production. These pulps, selling at a higher price than many domestic sulfite pulps, also comprise a large percentage of North American pulp exports to Europe and Japan because they fulfill specialized technical demands of conversion processes.

SPECIES

The effect of species on the dissolving pulp process has not been clearly established. Of the 10 southern pine species, seven are probably used in the manufacture of dissolving pulp; this is primarily because the mills (at Fernandina, Fla.; Foley, Fla.; and Jesup, Ga.) are within—or close to—their natural ranges (See ch. 3.)

Both sulfite and sulfate pine dissolving pulps are now derived mainly from slash pine; appreciable quantities of longleaf pine are also used. Loblolly, shortleaf, pond, spruce, and Virginia pines are probably utilized as they may be encountered in natural stands; it is probable, however, that pitch and Table-Mountain pines rarely occur in furnish for dissolving pulp. Although the range of sand pine is not distant from the sulfite mill at Fernandina, Fla., sand pine is not accepted there—presumably because of its relatively high heartwood content (table 5–1) and consequent lack of response to acid bisulfite pulping liquors.

As shown in chapters 5, 6, and 7, the four major species plus spruce pine are characterized in a rather extensive body of literature. Data are less complete for the other five species. Studies have emphasized wood

---

[10] Since this section was written, Manjunath and Peacock (1969) have obtained X-ray evidence for the transfer of native cellulose structure from pulp to viscose fibers.

specific gravity and dimensions of tracheids, especially their length. Critical and extensive studies within single species show rather remarkable ranges of properties from tree to tree and within a tree (Jurbergs 1963). There is a great deal of overlap in fiber properties among southern pines, resulting from both environmental and genetic factors. (See ch. 4.)

Section 27–2 described the effects of fiber dimensions on the strength of paper made from sulfate pulps. While variations in fiber dimensions and fiber structure would logically have rather gross effects during the dissolving of cellulose fibers, no studies comparable to those for paper have been published. If differences do exist, they cannot be established with data now in hand because of limitations in laboratory evaluation procedures. Until more sensitive evaluations are available, it must be concluded that any southern pine can be converted into useful dissolving pulp because the capabilities of the pulp-converting processes far overshadow the possible differences among the pulps made from the different species.

Faced with the practical problem of selecting a dominant species for their woodlands, the dissolving pulp manufacturers have concentrated their efforts on those species which grow best in their locality while providing acceptable performance during pulping and bleaching (Wyatt and Beers 1964).

27–5 LITERATURE CITED

Anonymous.
1940. Rayonier Incorporated, Fernandina, Fla. Pap. Trade J. 110(12): 27–32.

Anonymous.
1950. International Paper's new Natchez mill. Pap. Trade J. 131(14): 18–20, 22–24.

Anonymous.
1953. Progress made at all divisions of Rayonier. Pap. Trade J. 136(20): 38–43.

Anonymous.
1954a. New plants of Buckeye Cellulose Corporation, Foley, Ala. South. Pulp and Pap. J. 17(10–A): 20, 22, 24, 26, 30–32, 34, 36.

Anonymous.
1954b. Rayonier's 5th plant opens at Jesup, Ga. Pap. Trade J. 138(28): 16–20.

Anonymous.
1955. Buckeye. TAPPI 38(3): 121A–123A.

Anonymous.
1958. More cellulose arrives. Chem. and Eng. News 36(4), Part 1, p. 24.

Anonymous.
1959. New pulp mill of Buckeye at Foley has many unusual features. Pap. Trade J. 143(20): 38–39.

Anonymous.
1960. New Buckeye cellulose expansion to increase Florida Mill capacity by 33,000 tons. South. Pulp and Pap. Manufacturer 23(7): 39–40.

Anonymous.
1962a. New Rayonier pulp nears cellulose ultimate. South. Pulp and Pap. Manufacturer 25(5): 50.

Anonymous.
1962b. The history of Buckeye. J. Amer. Oil Chem. Soc. 39(7): 4–5.

Anonymous.
1963. Rayonier to dispose of Shelton Pulp Mill. Pap. Trade J. 147(15): 29.

Anonymous.
1964a. Buckeye announces 20 per cent expansion for Foley Mill. Pap. Trade J. 148(5): 25.

Anonymous.
1964b. Sulfite vs. sulfate pulping. Pap. Ind. 45: 657–659.

Anonymous.
1967. Rayonier announces additions to Florida and Washington Mills. Pap. Trade J. 151(17): 39.

Anonymous.
1968a. Cotton markets facing assault from rayon. Chem. and Eng. News 46(29): 18–20.

Anonymous.
1968b. Kraft pulper takes on new challenge. Chem. Week 102(6): 62–63.

Anonymous.
1968c. The new look at ICR: Pilot plant continuous digester simulates mill-scale conditions. Pulp and Pap. Mag. Can. 69(8): 42–47.

Anonymous.
1970. FPL recycles municipal trash for fiber products. Forest Prod. J. 20(8): 11.

Ahlm, C. E., and Leopold, B.
1963. Chemical composition and physical properties of wood fibers. IV. Changes in chemical composition of loblolly pine fibers during the kraft cook. TAPPI 46: 102–104.

American Paper Institute.
1968. Monthly statistical summary. Amer. Pap. Inst. 46(5): 1–22.

Aurell, R.
1963. The effect of lowered pH at the end of birch kraft cooks. Svensk Papperstidn. 66: 437–442.

Aurell, R., and Hartler, N.
1965. Kraft pulping of pine. II. The influence of the charge of alkali on the yield, carbohydrate composition, and properties of the pulp. Svensk Papperstidn. 68: 97–102.

Barefoot, A. C., Hitchings, R. G., and Ellwood, E. L.
1964. Wood characteristics and kraft paper properties of four selected loblolly pines. I. Effect of fiber morphology under identical cooking conditions. TAPPI 47: 343–356.

Barefoot, A. C., Hitchings. R. G., and Ellwood, E. L.
1966. Wood characteristics and kraft paper properties of four selected loblolly pines. III. Effect of fiber morphology in pulps examined at a constant permanganate number. TAPPI 49: 137–147.

Barefoot, A. C., Hitchings, R. G., Ellwood, E. L., and Wilson, E. H.
1970. The relationship between loblolly pine fiber morphology and kraft paper properties. N.C. Agr. Exp. Sta. Tech. Bull. 202, 88 pp.

Bartunek, R.
1967. Die Untersuchung der Zellstoffe. In Chemiefasern nach dem Viskoseverfahren. Vol. II, Part VI, ed. 3, pp. 992–1266. Berlin: Springer.

Belova, S. I., and Konovalova, A. A.
1967. The use of refiner groundwood in the composition of boxboard. Khim. Pererab. Drev., Ref. Inform. 15: 8–9.

Bishop, F. W.
1959. Newsprint quality groundwood from southern pines. Pap. Trade J. 143(24): 62–64.

Bolviken, A., and Giertz, H. W.
1956. High yield sulfite pulping. Norsk Skogindustri 10: 344–348.

Braun, R. V., and Davis, J. W.
1969. Printability and strength qualities of refiner groundwood as related to wood species. TAPPI 52: 282–288.

Bray, M. W., and Curran, C. E.
1933. White papers from southern pines. III. Pulping longleaf pine for strong, easy-bleaching pulp. Pap. Trade J. 96(6): 30–34.

Bray, M. W., and Curran, C. E.
1937. Sulphate pulping of southern yellow pines: Effect of growth variables on yield and pulp quality. Pap. Trade J. 105(20): 39–46.

Bray, M. W., and Curran, E. C.
1938. Sulfate pulping of southern yellow pines. Effect of growth variables on yield and pulp quality. Tech. Assoc. Pap. Ser. 21, 458–465.

Bray, M. W., Martin, J. S., and Schwartz, S. L.
1937. Sulphate pulping of long-leaf pine: Effect of chemical wood ratio on yield and quality of pulp. Pap. Trade J. 105(24): 39–44.

Bray, M. W., and Martin, J. S.
1942. Pulping Florida sand pine (*Pinus clausa*) for kraft, high-grade papers, and newsprint. Southern Pulp and Pap. J. 5(1): 7–14.

Bray, M. W., and Paul, B. H.
1934. Evaluation of southern pines for pulp production. III. Shortleaf pine (*Pinus echinata*). Pap. Trade J. 99(5): 38–41.

Brecht, W., Schröter, H., and Süttinger, R.
1938. [Influence of grinding temperature on the resin content of waste waters in the grinding of white pine.] Papier-Fabrikant 36(41): 425–428.

Brecht, W., Schröter, H., and Süttinger, R.
1940. [The influence of age on the wood on the mechanical pulping of Scots pine.] Papierfabr. 38(13/14): 77–94.

Bristow, O. J., Kelly, R. J., and Smith, W. L.
1967. High-yield kraft for linerboard—batch vs. continuous pulping. Pap. Trade J. 151(44): 39–40.

Bromley, W. S.
1968. Pulpwood pressures persist in South. Pulpwood Prod. and Saw Mill Logging 16(5): 14, 16, 18, 20.

Brown, W. J.
1966. The configuration of cellulose and derivatives in solution. TAPPI 49: 367–373.

Browning, B. L., and Baker, P. S.
1950. The characteristics of unbleached kraft pulps from western hemlock, Douglas fir, western red cedar, loblolly pine, and black spruce. TAPPI 33: 99–101.

Bryce, J. G. R., and Tomlinson, G. H.
1962. Modified magnefite pulping: the two-stage neutral process. Pulp and Pap. Mag. Can. 63(7): T355–T361.

Bunger, H., Doud, E., and Sugarman, N.
1938. Studies in the viscose rayon process. I. The suitability of Georgia pine pulp for the production of viscose rayon. Ga. State Eng. Exp. Sta. Bull. 3, Vol. 1(4): 3–8.

Cann, E. D., and Roberson, W. B.
1960. The effects of the active alkali charge upon unbleached pulp yields and quality in the kraft cooking of southern pinewood. TAPPI 43: 97–104.

Carpenter, C.
1939. Experimental demonstration work of the Herty Foundation Laboratory. Mon. Rev., Amer. Pap. and Pulp Assoc. 6(5–6): 20–23.

Carpenter, C., Porter, C. C., Fox, J. S., and others.
1949. Means and method of controlling pitch in groundwood and paper products. (Can. Pat. No. 454,036) Can. Pat. Office, Ottawa, Can.

Cederquist, K. N., Ahlborg, N. K. G., Lunden, B., and Wentworth, T. O.
1960. Stora sodium-base chemical recovery process. TAPPI 43: 702–706.

Charles, F. R.
1963. Dissolving pulp and its expanding use. Pulp and Pap. Mag. Can. 62(6): 73–77.

Chidester, G. H.
1966. Fiber characteristics and paper quality from southern pine. Amer. Pulpwood Assoc. Tech. Pap. 66–7: (5.613) 22–24.

Chidester, G. H., McGovern, J. N., and McNaughton, G. C.
1938. Comparison of sulfite pulps from fast-growth loblolly, shortleaf, longleaf and slash pines. Pap. Trade J. 107(4): 36–39.

Chidester, G. H., and McGovern, J. N.
1939. Effect of the addition of sodium salts in pulping shortleaf pine neutral sodium sulphite liquor. Pap. Trade J. 108(6): 31–32.

Chidester, G. H., and McGovern, J. N.
1940. Effect of acid concentration and temperature schedule in pulping resinous woods. Pap. Trade J. 110(10): 39–42.

Chidester, G. H., and McGovern, J. N.
1941. Sulphite pulp from Douglas fir. Pap. Trade J.
113(9): 34–38.
Christiansen, C. B., Hart, J. S., and Ross, J. H.
1957. Sulphidity as a variable in the pulping of western red cedar: The effect of the Na₂S/wood ratio on pulp properties. TAPPI 40: 355–361.
Christopher, J. F., and Nelson, M. E.
1963. Southern pulpwood production, 1962. USDA Forest Serv. Resource Bull. SO–1, 24 pp. Southern Forest Exp. Sta., New Orleans, La.
Cole, D. E., Zobel, B. J., and Roberds, J. H.
1966. Slash, loblolly, and longleaf pine in a mixed natural stand; a comparison of their wood properties, pulp yields, and paper properties. TAPPI 49: 161–166.
Craig, K. A., and Hackbert, C. R.
1958. Preparation of groundwood pulp. (Can. Pat. No. 565,955) Can. Pat. Office, Ottawa, Can.
Croon, I.
1963. Softwood sulfite pulps in increased yield by the alkali-sulphite (A–S) method. Svensk Papperstidn. 66(1): 1–5.
Croon, I.
1965. The flexibility of sodium-base two-stage neutral-acid sulfite pulping. Pulp and Pap. Mag. Can. 66(2): T71–T76.
Cross, C. F., and Bevan, E. J.
1920. A text-book of paper-making. Ed. 5, 527 pp. N.Y.: Spon and Chamberlain.
Cumbie, J.
1969. Sawdust utilization in the pulp and paper industry. In Wood residue utilization, pp. 2–8. Third Tex. Ind. Wood Seminar, Tex. Forest Prod. Lab. Lufkin.
Curran, C. E.
1936. Some relations between growth conditions, wood structure and pulping quality. Pap. Trade J. 103(11): 36–40.
Curran, C. E.
1938. Relation of growth characteristics of southern pine to its use in pulping. Pap. Trade J. 106(23): 40–43.

Curran, C. E., and Bray, M. W.
1931. White papers from southern pines. I. Pulping loblolly pine for strong, easy-bleaching sulphate pulp. Pap. Trade J. 92(1): 47–52.
Dadswell, H. E., and Watson, A. J.
1962. Influence of the morphology of woodpulp fibres on paper properties. In The formation and structure of paper, pp. 537–564. London: Tech. Sect. Brit. Pap. and Board Makers' Assoc.
Darmstadt, W. J., and Tomlinson, G. H., II.
1960. Magnesia-base pulping and recovery. TAPPI 43: 674–676.
Dean, W. L., Wyatt, W. R., and Parks, L. R.
1960. Nature and site of surfactant action in viscose preparation. Svensk Papperstidn. 63: 570–576.
Dickerscheid, J. L.
1958. Varying sulphidity in southern pine sulphate pulping: A comparison of the active and effective alkali basis for applying alkali. TAPPI 41: 526–529.
Dinwoodie, J. M.
1966. The influence of anatomical and chemical characteristics of softwood fibers on the properties of sulfate pulp. TAPPI 49: 57–67.
Dolmetsch, H.
1961. [Existence of chain folding for cellulose.] Kolloid-Z. 176(1): 63–64.
Dorland, R. M., Leask, R. A., and McKinney, J. W.
1958. Pulp production with sodium bisulfite. I. The cooking of spruce. Pulp and Pap. Mag. Can. 59(C): 236–246.
Dorland, R. M., and McKinney, J. W.
1959. High yields bisulphite pulping process. (U.S. Pat. No. 2,906,659.) U.S. Pat. Office, Wash., D.C.
Durso, D. F.
1969. Dissolving pulp from southern pine wood. Forest Prod. J. 19(8): 49–56.
Durso, D. F., Benning, T. C., and Goode, J. R.
1967. The filterability problem. III. Development of a screen filter. Svensk Papperstidn. 70: 837–845.

Dyer, H.
1961. The first two-stage premium sulfite pulps in North America. Pap. Trade J. 145(44): 20–25.

Einspahr, D. W.
1964. Correlations between fiber dimensions and fiber and handsheet strength properties. TAPPI 47: 180–183.

Elmgren, H.
1965. The macromolecular properties of sodium cellulose xanthate in dilute solution. Arkiv för Kem. 24: 237–282.

Erdtman, H.
1944. [The phenolic constituents of pine heartwood. VII. The heartwood of *Pinus nigra* Arn., *Pinus montana* Mill., *Pinus banksiana* Lamb., and *Pinus palustris* Mill.] Svensk Kem. Tidskr. 56: 95–101.

Erdtman, H.
1949a. Compounds inhibiting the sulphite cook. TAPPI 32: 303–305.

Erdtman, H.
1949b. Heartwood extractives of conifers. TAPPI 32: 305–310.

Fahey, D. J., and Laundrie, J. F.
1968. Kraft pulps, papers, and linerboard from southern pine thinnings. USDA Forest Serv. Res. Note FPL–0182, 8 pp. Forest Prod. Lab., Madison, Wis.

Fields, W. F.
1960. Recent improvements in pulpwood grinders for insulating fiberboard manufacture. TAPPI 43(4): 202A–205A.

Forgacs, O. L.
1963. The characterization of mechanical pulps. Part II: A microscopic examination of mechanical pulps. Pulp and Pap. Mag. Can. 64: T92–T100.

Foster, S. C.
1932. Strong groundwood from pine. Pap. Mill 55(51): 10.

Freeman, H.
1947. A new method of pitch control in newsprint manufacture. Pulp and Pap. Mag. Can. 48(8): 73–75.

Fuller, A. C., and Carpenter, C.
1938. Newsprint from pine mechanical and chemical pulps. Grinding experiments with a coarse grit synthetic stone. Tech. Assoc. Pap. Ser. 21, pp. 438–440.

Gavelin, N. G.
1966. Science and technology of mechanical pulp manufacture. 250 pp. N.Y.: Lockwood Publishing Co., Inc.

Gladstone, W. T., Barefoot, A. C., and Zobel, B. J.
1970. Kraft pulping of earlywood and latewood from loblolly pine. Forest Prod. J. 20(2): 17–24.

Gaddard, R. E., and Strickland, R. K.
1962. Geographic variation in wood specific gravity of slash pine. TAPPI 45: 606–608.

Götze, K.
1967. Chemiefasern nach dem Viskoseverfahren. Ed. 3, 2 vols., 1322 pp. Berlin: Springer-Verlag.

Graff, J. H., and Isenberg, I. H.
1950. The characteristics of unbleached kraft pulps from western hemlock, Douglas fir, western red cedar, loblolly pine, and black spruce. II. The morphological characteristics of the pulp fibers. TAPPI 33: 94–95.

Hägglund, A. E.
1945. Undersökningar över sulfatkokningsprocessen. Svensk Papperstidn. 48(8): 195–199.

Hägglund, E.
1951. Chemistry of wood. 631 pp. N.Y.: Academic Press.

Hair, D.
1967. Use of regression equations for projecting trends in demand for paper and board. USDA Forest Resource Rep. 18, 178 pp. Wash., D.C.

Hart, J. S.
1954. The Va-Purge process in chemical pulping. TAPPI 37: 331–335.

Hart, J. S., Strapp, R. K., and Ross, J. H.
1954. High-yield sulphite pulping. I. High-yield sulphite pulping with a soluble base. Pulp and Pap. Mag. Can. 55(10): 114–123.

Hart, J. S., and Woods, J. M.
1955. High-yield sulphite pulping. II-III. The influence of yield on pulp qualities; eastern spruce-balsam and western hemlock. Pulp and Pap. Mag. Can. 56(9): 95–101.

Hartler, N., and Onisko, W.
1962. The interdependence of chip thickness, cooking temperature and screenings in kraft cooking of pine. Svensk Papperstidn. 65: 905–910.

Haynes, W.
1953. Cellulose—the chemical that grows. 386 pp. N.Y.: Doubleday.

Herty, C. H.
1933. White paper from young southern pines. Tech. Assoc. Papers 16(1): 298–302.

Hess, K., Kiessig, H., and Koblitz, W.
1951. The permutoid character of xanthation of fiber cellulose. Z. Für Elektrochem. 55: 697–708.

Hill, E. H.
1944. Substitutes for round pine wood in making alkaline pulps. Pap. Trade J. 119(19): 27–29.

Holzer, W. F., and Booth, K. G.
1950. The characteristics of unbleached kraft pulps from western hemlock, Douglas fir, western red cedar, loblolly pine, and black spruce. III. The comparative pulping of the woods. TAPPI 33: 95–98.

Holzer, W. F., and Lewis, H. F.
1950. The characteristics of unbleached kraft pulps from western hemlock, Douglas fir, western red cedar, loblolly pine, and black spruce. VII. Comparison of springwood and summerwood fibers of Douglas fir. TAPPI 33: 110–112.

Ingruber, O. V., and Allard, G. A.
1970. Alkaline sulfite pulping. (Can. Pat. No. 847,218) U.S. Pat. Off., Wash., D.C.

Isenberg, I. H.
1951. Pulpwoods of United States and Canada. Ed. 2, 187 pp. Appleton, Wis.: Institute of Paper Chemistry.

Jenkins, D. F.
1966. How Bowaters Carolina blade coats southern publication grades. Amer. Pap. Ind. 48(11): 54–57.

Johnson, E. H., (Ed.).
1960. Mechanical pulping manual. TAPPI Monogr. Ser. 21, 183 pp.

Jones, E. D., Campbell, R. T., and Nelson, G. G., Jr.
1966. Springwood - summerwood separation of southern pine pulp to improve paper qualities. TAPPI 49: 410–414.

Jurbergs, K. A.
1960a. An electron microscope study: Slash pine and sweetgum fibers. TAPPI 43: 865–871.

Jurbergs, K. A.
1960b. Morphological properties of cotton and wood fibers. I. Cotton linters. TAPPI 43: 554–560.

Jurbergs, K. A.
1960c. Morphological properties of cotton and wood fibers. II. Slash pine. TAPPI 43: 561–568.

Jurbergs, K. A.
1963. Determining fiber length, fibrillar angle, and springwood - summerwood ratio in slash pine. Forest Sci. 9: 181–187.

Jurbergs, K. A., and Dowling, D. J., Jr.
1964. Determination of foreign materials of plant origin in cotton linters. J. Amer. Oil Chem. Soc. 41: 545–547.

Kamyr Incorporated.
1970. Continuous cooking installations. Kamyr Bull. 200E, 28 pp. Glens Falls, N.Y.

Keller, E. L., and Fahey, D. J.
1968. Magnesium bisulfite pulping and paper making with southern pine. TAPPI 51: 98–103.

Kennedy, E. H.
1960. The Sivola sodium-base pulping and chemical recovery process. TAPPI 43: 683–687.

Kirmreuther, Dr.
1938. [Pine groundwood pulp.] Wochenbl. Papierfabr. 69: 563–568.

Klemm, K. H.
  1950. [Recent ideas in the field
        of the manufacture of
        white groundwood pulp.]
        Wochenbl. Papierfabr.
        78: 567–571, 595–598,
        727–730.
Klemm, K. H.
  1958. Modern method of me-
        chanical pulp manufac-
        ture. 241 pp. Chicago:
        Lockwood Trade Journal
        Co., Inc.
Kleppe, P. J.
  1964. Discussion. [Emil Vene-
        mark's "Some ideas on
        polysulfide pulping."]
        Svensk Papperstidn.
        67(5): 165–166.
Kleppe, P. J.
  1970. The process of, and prod-
        ucts from, kraft pulping
        of southern pine. Forest
        Prod. J. 20(5): 50–59.
Koch, R. O., Sapp, J. E., and McCray,
  R. L.
  1958. Kraft pulping of spruce
        pine. TAPPI 41:
        349–353.
Lagergren, S., and Lunden, B.
  1959. Some recent developments
        in sulphite pulp making.
        Pulp and Pap. Mag. Can.
        60(11): T338–T341,
        T345.
Landmark, P. A., Kleppe, P. J., and
  Johnsen, K.
  1965. Cooking liquor oxidation
        and improved cooking
        techniques in polysulfide
        pulping. TAPPI 48(5):
        56A–58A.
Legg, G. W., and Hart, J. S.
  1960. Alkaline pulping of jack-
        pine and Douglas fir. The
        influence of sulphide and
        effective alkali charge on
        pulping rate and pulp
        properties. Pulp and Pap.
        Mag. Can. 61:
        T299–T304.
Leopold, B.
  1966. Effect of pulp processing
        on individual fiber
        strength. TAPPI 49:
        315–318.
Lewis, H. F., Wise, L. E., and Browning, B. L.
  1950. The characteristics of un-
        bleached kraft pulps from
        western hemlock, Doug-
        las-fir, western red cedar,
        loblolly pine, and black
        spruce. I. The chemical
        constituents of the un-
        bleached kraft pulps.
        TAPPI 33: 92–94.

McGovern, J. N.
  1936. Effect of high sulphur
        dioxide concentrations
        and high pressures in sul-
        phite pulping. Pap.
        Trade J. 103(20):
        29–42.
McGovern, J. N., and Chidester, G. H.
  1941. Pulping loblolly pine heart-
        wood with calcium-, mag-
        nesium-, and sodium-base
        sulphite liquors. Pap.
        Trade J. 113(16):
        32–35.
McHale, W. L.
  1948. History and growth of
        newsprint industry in the
        South. Pap. Trade J.
        127(27): 25–27.
McHale, W. L., and Porter, C. C.
  1954. The paper industry and the
        Southland mill. Southern
        Pulp and Pap. Manufac-
        turer 17(7): 84, 86.
McIntosh, D. C.
  1963. Tensile and bonding
        strengths of loblolly pine
        kraft fibers cooked to dif-
        ferent yields. TAPPI 46:
        273–277.
McIntosh, D. C.
  1967. The effect of refining on
        the structure of the fiber
        wall. TAPPI 50:
        482–488.
McKee, J. C.
  1960. The kraft pulping of small
        diameter slash pines.
        TAPPI 43(6):
        202A–204A.
McMillin, C. W.
  1968. Gross wood characteristics
        affecting properties of
        handsheets made from
        loblolly pine refiner
        groundwood. TAPPI 51:
        51–56.
McMillin, C. W.
  1969a. Aspects of fiber morphol-
        ogy affecting properties
        of handsheets made from
        loblolly pine refiner
        groundwood. Wood Sci.
        and Technol. 3: 139–149.
McMillin, C. W.
  1969b. Quality of refiner ground-
        wood pulp as related to
        handsheet properties and
        gross wood characteris-
        tics. Wood Sci. and
        Technol. 3: 287–300.
McMillin, C. W.
  1969c. Wood chemical composition
        as related to properties
        of handsheets made from
        loblolly pine refiner
        groundwood. Wood Sci.
        and Technol. 3: 232–238.

Manley, R. St. J.
1964. Chain folding in amylose crystals. J. Polymer Sci. 2A(10): 4503–4515.

Manjunath, B. R., and Peacock, N.
1969. Recrystallization of the cellulose I lattice in mercerized and regenerated cellulose fibers. Textile Res. J. 39(1): 70–77.

Martin, J. S.
1943. Sulfate pulping of mixtures of selected southern hardwoods, southern yellow pine. Southern Pulp and Pap. J. 6(7): 13–18.

Martin, J. S., and Brown, K. J.
1952. Effect of bark on yield and quality of sulphate pulp from southern pine. TAPPI 35: 7–10.

Martynoff, M., and Weiss, J. D.
1937. [Wood pulp from pine.] Zellst und Pap. 17: 102–103.

Mason, R. R., Muhonen, J. M., and Swartz, J. N.
1963. Water sprayed storage of southern pine pulpwood. TAPPI 46: 233–240.

Meunier, E.
1931. The Rosen method for the manufacture of sulphite pulp from resinous woods. Papeterie 53(4): 214, 217–218.

Mitchell, R. L.
1949. Vicose processing of cellulose: Changes in basic properties. Ind. and Eng. Chem. 41: 2197–2201.

Mitchell, H. L.
1958. Wood quality evaluation from increment cores. TAPPI 41: 150–156.

Mitchell, H. L.
1964. Patterns of variation in specific gravity of southern pines and other coniferous species. TAPPI 47: 276–283.

Moon, D. G., (Ed.).
1954. New Bowaters Southern mill in operation. Pap. Mill News 77(35): 14, 16, 18, 20, 22, 24–34.

Morkved, L., and Larson, P.
1969. Refiner groundwood. TAPPI 53: 1465–1467.

Mühlsteph, V. W.
1941. [Significance of fiber shapes for properties of pulp. IV. Anatomical consideration of pulp woods and fibers.] Wochenbl. Papierfabr. 72(14): 201–204, 219–224.

Murto, J., and Itkonen, J.
1950. [Southern pine and its use as raw material in the sulphate pulp industry.] Pap. ja Puu B 32(4): 108–123.

Nolan, W. J.
1953. Studies in continuous alkaline pulping. III. The pulping of slash pine. TAPPI 36: 406–417.

Nolan, W. J.
1957. Studies in continuous alkaline pulping. V. The effects of chip size and preimpregnation on quality and yield. TAPPI 40: 170–190.

Nolan, W. J.
1967. Chip shredding—why not investigate further? Pulp and Pap. 41(44): 57–58.

Nolan, W. J.
1969. Sulfite pulping of southern pines. Forest Prod. J. 19(9): 97–102.

Nolan, W. J.
1970. Pulping of slash pine with sodium sulfite and sulfite-bisulfite liquors. TAPPI 53: 1309–1315.

Nolan, W. J., and Brown, W. G.
1952. Experimental development of high-speed continuous alkaline pulping. Pulp and Pap. Mag. Can. 53(9): 98–110.

Nolan, W. J., Harvin, R. L., Reeder, L. M., and Rothrock, C. W., Jr.
1951. Studies in continuous alkaline pulping. I. Evaluation of variables for rapid pulping. TAPPI 34: 529–538.

Ott, E., Spurlin, H. M., and Grafflin, M. W., (Ed.).
1954. High polymers. Vol. V. Cellulose and cellulose derivatives. Ed. 2, 3 parts, 1601 pp. N.Y.: Interscience, Publ.

Parks, L. R.
1959. Classification of pulps according to supermolecular structure of cellulose. TAPPI 42: 317–319.

Pascoe, T. A., Buchanan, J. S., Kennedy, E. H., and Sivola, G.
1959. The Sivola sulphite cooking and recovery process. TAPPI 42: 265–281.

Paterson, H. A.
1937. The grinding of jack pine for newsprint manufacture. Pulp and Pap. Mag. Can. 38(2): 146–147.

Perry, T. O., and Wang, C. W.
1958. Variation in the specific gravity of slash pinewood and its genetic and silvicultural implications. TAPPI 41: 178–180.

Pillow, M. Y., Chidester, G. H., and Bray, M. W.
1941. Effect of wood structure on properties of sulphate and sulphite pulps from loblolly pine. Southern Pulp and Pap. J. 4(7): 6–12.

Porphyre, J. A.
1929. Pine wood in the paper industry. Inst. du Pin Bull. 57, pp. 82–84.

Ranby, B. G., Giertz, H. W., and Treiber, E.
1956. An electron microscopic investigation of the viscose process. Parts I and II. Svensk Papperstidn. 59: 117–127; 205–217.

Rasch, R. H., Leemhuis, P. L., and Sutton, H.
1962. Semichemical pulping process for soft woods. (U.S. Pat. No. 3,069,310.) U.S. Pat. Office, Wash., D.C.

Reis, C. J., and Libby, C. E.
1960. An experimental study of the effect of Fomes pini (Thore) Loyd on the pulping qualities of pond pine Pinus serotina (Michx) cooked by the sulfate process. TAPPI 43: 489–499.

Rogers, L. N., Heath, M. A., Gutliph, E. W., and Hiett, L. A.
1959. Purified cellulose fiber and process for producing same. (U.S. Pat. No. 2,878,118). U.S. Pat. Office, Wash., D.C.

Runkel, R. O. H.
1949. Making of pulp from wood of the species Eucalyptus and experiments with two different Eucalypt species. Das Pap. 3: 476–490.

Rydholm, S.
1965. Pulping processes. 1269 pp. N.Y.: John Wiley and Sons.

Sanford, R., (Ed.).
1968. Lockwood's directory of the paper, and allied trades. Ed. 93, 1704 pp. N.Y.: Lockwood Publishing Co., Inc.

Sanyer, N., Keller, E. L., and Chidester, G. H.
1962. Multistage sulfite pulping of jack pine, balsam fir, spruce, oak, and sweetgum. TAPPI 45: 90–104.

Sanyer, N., and Laundrie, J. F.
1964. Factors affecting yield increase and fiber quality in polysulfide pulping of loblolly pine, other softwoods, and red oak. TAPPI 47: 640–652.

Schafer, E. R., Pew, J. C., and Curran, C. E.
1938. Grinding of loblolly pine. Relation of wood properties and grinding conditions to pulp and paper quality. Tech. Assoc. Pap. Ser. 21, 449–456.

Schenker, C., and Heath, M. A.
1959. Development of high purity dissolving wood pulp for tire cord production. TAPPI 42: 709–712.

Scholander, A.
1960. The Stora Kopparberg recovery process in the Mo and Domsjö AB Domsjö sulfite mill. TAPPI 43: 706–708.

Schur, M. O.
1963. Dissolving pulps—in retrospect. TAPPI 46(8): 16A–24A.

Schwartz, S. L., and Bray, M. W.
1941. Suitability of high-density, high-summerwood slash pine for kraft and high-grade papers. Pap. Trade J. 113(10): 33–39.

Shaffer, M. R.
1958. Three commercial processes for NSSC recovery. South. Pulp and Pap. Manufacturer 21(2): 40, 42, 44, 48, 50.

Shick, P. E.
1970. High-yield pulping process for coniferous woods. TAPPI 53: 1451–1457.

Simmonds, F. A., and Chidester, G. H.
1960. Sulfate and prehydrolysis-sulfate pulp for nitration relation of pulp characteristics to certain preparation variables. USDA Forest Serv. Forest Prod. Lab. Rep. 2189, 42 pp.

Simmonds, F. A., Kingsbury, R. M., Martin, J. S., and Mitchell, R. L.
1956. Loblolly pine high alpha prehydrolysis-sulphate pulps. TAPPI 39: 641–647.

Sivola, G.
1955.   Process of manufacturing pulp from cellulosic fibrous materials. (U.S. Pat. No. 2,701,763.) U.S. Pat. Office, Wash., D.C.

Sivola, G.
1956.   Integrated lignocellulose digestion and recovery process (U.S. Pat. No. 2,730,445). U.S. Pat. Office, Wash., D.C.

Slatin, B.
1967.   The paper industry in the south: New directions in new mills. Southern Pulp and Pap. Manufacturer 30(10): 32–34, 36, 38, 40.

Somsen, R. A.
1962.   Outside storage of southern pine chips. TAPPI 45: 623–628.

Stockman, L. G.
1960.   Some developments in Swedish sulfite pulping research. TAPPI 43: 112–120.

Stone, J. E., and Scallan, A. M.
1968.   The effect of component removal upon the porous structure of the cell wall of wood. III. A comparison between the sulphite and kraft processes. Pulp and Pap. Mag. Can. 69(12): 69–74.

Surface, H. E., and Cooper, R. E.
1914.   Longleaf pine. Pap. Mill 37(24): 16, 20; (25): 14, 44; (26): 14, 35, 36; (27): 14, 32, 34, 35; (28): 13, 14, 32, 35.

Suttle, B.
1944.   Length of chips in cooking southern pine. Pap. Mill News 67(9): 22.

Swartz, J. N.
1963.   [Contribution to Symposium on refiner groundwood.] Can. Pulp and Pap. Assoc. Tech. Sect. Proc. 49: D–12–D–14.

Tasman, J. E., and Berzins, V.
1957.   The permanganate consumption of pulp materials. III. The relationship of the KAPPA number to the lignin content of pulp materials. TAPPI 40: 699–704.

Thornburg, W. L.
1963.   Effect of roundwood or chip storage on tall oil and turpentine fractions of slash pine. TAPPI 46: 453–455.

Thuemmes, R. E., (Ed.).
1962.   Lockwood's directory of the paper, and allied trades. Ed. 87, 1572 pp. N.Y.: Lockwood Publishing Co., Inc.

Tippetts, E. A.
1950.   The position of cellulose as a chemical raw material. TAPPI 33(2): 32A–34A.

Tomlinson, G. H., and Tomlinson, G. H., II.
1958.   Method and apparatus for recovering heat and chemicals from the residual liquor resulting from the digestion of cellulosic fibrous material in an alkaline liquor. (U.S. Pat. No. 2,840,454.) U.S. Pat. Office, Wash., D.C.

Tomlinson, G. H., Tomlinson, G. H., II, Bryce, J. R. G., and Tuck, N. G. M.
1958.   The magnefite process—a new pulping method. Pulp and Pap. Mag. Can. 59(C): 247–252.

Tonnesen, B. A., and Ellefsen, O.
1960.   Chain folding—a possibility to be considered in connection with the cellulose molecule? Norsk Skogindustri 14(7): 266–269.

Treiber, E.
1967.   Viscosereyon und viscosespinnfaser. In Ullmanns encyklopädie der technischen chemie, pp. 131–175. Ed. 3, vol. 18. Urban & Schwarzenberg, Munchen.

Trevelyan, B. J.
1969.   Mechanical pulping of southern pine wood. Forest Prod. J. 19(1): 29–38.

USDA Forest Products Laboratory.
1962.   Kraft pulping of west Florida and sand pine and longleaf pine. USDA Forest Serv. Forest Prod. Lab. Rep. 2248, 12 pp.

USDA Forest Service.
1965.   Timber trends in the United States. USDA Forest Resource Rep. 17, 235 pp.

Valeur, C.
1951.   Cooking of bleachable kraft pulp. Svensk Papperstidn. 54: 613–620.

Van Buijtenen, J. P., Joranson, P. N., and MacLaurin, D. J.
1961a. Pulping southern pine increment cores by means of a small scale kraft procedure. TAPPI 44: 166–169.

Van Buijtenen, J. P., Zobel, B. J., and Joranson, P. N.
1961b. Variation of some wood and pulp properties in an even-aged loblolly pine stand. TAPPI 44: 141–144.

Van Buijtenen, J. P.
1964. Anatomical factors influencing wood specific gravity of slash pines and the implications for the development of a high-quality pulpwood. TAPPI 47: 401–404.

Venemark, E.
1964. Some ideas on polysulfide pulping. Svensk Papperstidn. 67: 157–165.

Vethe, A. A.
1967. Bruk av "shredded" flis ved cellulosekoking. Norsk Skogindustri 21: 180–187.

Vincent, R.
1967. Chemical cellulose—big shifts in markets. Pulp and Pap. 41(29): 46, 48.

Virkola, N., and Vartiainen, V.
1964. Criteria of successful bleaching. TAPPI 47: 765–773.

Walker, W. J.
1937. Grinding southern pine under semi-commercial conditions. Pap. Trade J. 105(12): 44–54.

Wangaard, F. F., Kellogg, R. M., and Brinkley, A. W.
1966. Variation of wood and fiber characteristics and pulp-sheet properties of slash pine. TAPPI 49: 263–277.

Wangaard, F. F., Kellogg, R. M., and Djerf, A.
1967. Prediction of whole-tree pulp properties for slash pine. TAPPI 50: 109–114.

Waters, J. W., and Waters, V. F.
1958. Rayonier's newest Georgia pulp mill in operation. South. Pulp and Pap. Manufacturer 21(7): 32, 34, 36, 66–68.

Watson, A. J., and Dadswell, H. E.
1962. Influence of fibre morphology on paper properties. II. Early and late wood. APPITA 15(6): 116–128.

Watson, A. J., and Hodder, I. G.
1954. Relationship between fibre structure and handsheet properties in Pinus taeda. APPITA 8: 290–310.

Welch, R. L.
1970. Southern pulpwood production, 1969. USDA Forest Serv. Resour. Bull. SE–18, 20 pp. Southeast. Forest Exp. Sta., Asheville, N.C.

Wells, S. D., and Rue, J. D.
1927. The suitability of American woods for paper pulp. USDA Dep. Bull. 1485, 102 pp.

Wetmore, R. T., and Dunphy, L. W.
1949. Groundwood for newsprint. TAPPI 32: 150–154.

Wilson, A. W.
1967a. Paper and pulp again set world records. Pulp and Pap. 41(29): 8–13.

Wilson, A. W.
1967b. World market pulp near 20 million tons; 26 nations export various grades. Pulp and Pap. 41(29): 31–33, 36–39, 42–45.

Wilson, J. W.
1959. High alpha pulps and their utilization. Can. Pulp and Pap. Ind. 12(8): 25–26, 30, 32, 34, 36, 38.

Wyatt, W. R.
1966. Optimum viscose process studies. I. Steeping and pressing. TAPPI 49: 464–468.

Wyatt, W. R., and Beers, W. L., Jr.
1964. A growth chamber study of plus tree progeny. TAPPI 47: 305–309.

Zobel, B. J., and McElwee, R. L.
1958. Natural variation in wood specific gravity of loblolly pine, and an analysis of contributing factors. TAPPI 41: 158–161.

28

Chemical processing

CONTENTS

28
Chemical processing

Southern pine wood is comprised of polysaccharides, lignin, extractives, and inorganic components (see ch. 6). From these constituents, most consumer products originating in the organic chemical industry could be produced, though only a few competitively (Harris et al. 1963). Except for cellulose (basis of the pulp and cellulose plastics industries; see ch. 27), extractives are the major southern pine constituent on which wood-using, chemical processing industries are based. Southern pine forests in the United States are the source of about one-half the naval stores and three-fourths the crude tall oil produced outside the Sino-Soviet bloc; nearly 100 percent of the U.S. requirement for turpentine and rosin comes from southern pine trees (King et al. 1962).

The polysaccharides in southern pine residues can be converted to sugars—a procedure that could possibly alleviate some of the food shortages in the world; at present, however, the process is economically viable only in certain circumstances, and at very few locations.

Sulfate lignin, a byproduct of the kraft pulping process, has limited, but increasing, uses other than for fuel. These uses, however, account for only a fraction of the tonnage produced; most is now burned.

At this time, virtually no economic use is made of the inorganic constituents of wood. Organic carbon in the form of charcoal, however, is commercially produced from southern pine residues in considerable quantity.

Soil amendments made from southern pine residues of wood and bark provide a kind of chemical processing of these materials; research results pertinent to southern pine are discussed in chapter 12.

28-1 NAVAL STORES [1]

Pine gum products, pitch, tar, spirits of turpentine, and rosin—the naval stores of wooden sailing ships—have historically been a cash crop from southern pine trees. Oils, resins, and tars obtained from pine trees are still termed **naval stores.** If obtained from pine **oleoresin** (commonly referred to as pine **gum**) collected from wounded living trees, they are known as **gum naval stores.** Only two species of southern pine, longleaf and slash pine, have ever been important for gum production. The oleoresins of the other southern pines tend to crystallize rapidly upon exposure to air and moisture and do not flow freely following regular wounding.

---

[1] The text in the subsection on producing oleoresin from living trees has been taken from Harrington (1969) by permission of T. A. Harrington and the Forest Products Research Society. The balance of sec. 28-1 is condensed from Lawrence (1969) by permission of R. V. Lawrence and the Forest Product Research Society.

Wood naval stores, as the term indicates, are from wood rather than gum; those extracted by solvents and steam from pitch-soaked stumps are termed steam distilled, while those obtained by heating pine wood in the absence of air are called destructively distilled. Naval stores collected as a byproduct of the kraft paper process are known as tall oil rosin and sulfate turpentine.

Further definitions of terms relating to naval stores can be found in ASTM (American Society for Testing and Materials) Standard Designation D 804–863.

GUM NAVAL STORES

Less than half a dozen plants in the South produce destructively distilled wood naval stores; these plants are a major source of pine tar in the United States. The other three processes provide practically all of the turpentine, pine oil, and rosin; also, a number of pine tar products, distinct from those obtained by destructive distillation of wood, are now made from tall oil pitch. The annual production of these raw materials from all sources in the United States has not varied greatly over the past 70 years, averaging close to 1 billion pounds of rosin and 30 million gallons of turpentine; pine oil production in 1969, part of which was derived from turpentine, was about 13.9 million gallons.

Initially, all of this production came from pine gum. Although steam distillation of longleaf and slash pine stumps began in 1910, and recovery of turpentine from sulfate pulping about 1928, gum naval stores still accounted for 85 percent of the total production in 1930. When tall oil rosin entered the picture after World War II, production shifted rapidly away from gum. In 1950, gum furnished 40 percent of the turpentine and rosin. Production dropped to 20 percent in 1960 and to 10 percent in 1967. At the present time, steam-distilled wood supplies 50 percent of the rosin and 20 percent of the turpentine. Tall oil rosin represents the final 40 percent of our rosin supply, and 70 percent of our turpentine comes from sulfate pulping (King et al. 1962; Hair and Ulrich 1967).

This shift of source is due mainly to economic factors. Under present conditions, more than 60 percent of gum production costs are for labor and supervision. Semiskilled labor cannot produce naval stores products as efficiently as highly mechanized operations and quality-controlled chemical processes. Consequently, gum rosin and gum turpentine are priced higher than similar materials from other sources.

Early production methods.—Gum farmers have been slow to seek or to accept changes in production methods. In fact, for the first 300 years, turpentining was carried out in the Southeast with no changes in techniques. Nearly all the timber worked was virgin longleaf pine. New crops were started during the winter months by cutting one or more cavities, called boxes, in the base of each tree. Varying with the size of the timber, boxes were from 10 to 14 inches wide, 5 to 7 inches deep, and

2½ to 3½ inches front to back. The gum flowed from the worked faces into these cavities.

Weekly from March through October, a fresh streak of 10 to 14 inches long was chipped across the upper edge of each face, penetrating into the wood above the face about 1 inch. Each weekly streak was more distant from the box; the 32 to 34 streaks chipped during a full season produced an annual face height of 20 to 30 inches.

Gum was gathered, or dipped, from the boxes every 3 to 4 weeks with a dip iron, and delivered in barrels to the distillery. By the end of each season, a large amount of oleoresin had hardened on the face. This "scrape" was also removed and collected in barrels for distillation (Pridgen 1921).

Although damaging to timber, wasteful of oleoresin, and inefficient in use of labor, the gum naval stores industry produced an excellent cash crop for 300 years (1600-1900) from trees that had little or no market value. Even though early research by Fernow (1892) proved that turpentining mature trees did not adversely affect the strength of the lumber, the butt cut was generally wasted or used as fuel wood. Frequently, the worked-out trees were not even harvested.

Herty (1903) revolutionized the industry when he introduced cups and gutters to replace the cut boxes. In Herty's system, two strips of 2-inch-wide galvanized iron (fig. 28–1) were placed in broadax incisions below the face to divert the gum flow into a clay pot. It caused less injury to the tree, and the cup and gutters could be moved up the face each year as the chipping surface advanced. An undesirable outgrowth of this technique was the working of small trees for gum, often as small as 6 inches in diameter.

Beginning in 1910, the staff of the National Forests in Florida had demonstrated that high gum yields, a longer working life, and less mortality resulted from shallow and low chipping (Ostrom 1945). Gerry (1922) of the USDA Forest Products Laboratory furnished the scientific proof of this fact by showing that wounding stimulated the production of resin ducts above the worked face, and chipping unnecessarily high streaks wasted this gum-producing tissue.

Further investigations by Dr. Gerry, Austin Cary, Lenthall Wyman, and other Forest Service researchers resulted in guidelines for the optimum size of streaks and chipping frequency, the tree sizes best suited to gum production, the optimum number of faces per tree, the effects of turpentining on tree growth, improved methods of cup and gutter installation, and other practical techniques for conservative gum production. This information, combined with forest management recommendations, was published as a Naval Stores Handbook (USDA Forest Service 1935).

Starting in 1936 the Forest Service's Naval Stores Conservation Program, in cooperation with the Agricultural Stabilization and Conservation Service, distributed small incentive payments to gum producers for the

F-521007
Figure 28–1.—The Herty system, developed in 1903, revolutionized the naval stores industry. Metal gutters were placed in incisions made with a mallet-driven broadax. Clay pots replaced the cut boxes. Although an improvement over the ancient practices, the deep chipping—about an inch into the xylem—and the broadax wounds reduced the tree's vigor. Because the heavy metal gutters were frequently left in the face, trees were generally jump-butted when harvested. (Photo from Harrington 1969.)

adoption of good management practices. N.S.C.P. foresters gave on-the-ground assistance to timberland owners and gum producers. The program played a major role in teaching producers to work only trees 9 inches d.b.h. and larger, to adopt other conservation practices, and to manage their timber stands for the production of both gum and wood.

Development of modern methods.—Research on chemical gum flow stimulants by Russian and German scientists precipitated similar investigations by the Forest Service at Olustee, Fla. in 1936. At that time rosin and turpentine were in surplus supply, and no one was interested in new techniques for increasing production. However, war demands for naval stores soon exceeded supply, and research on chemical stimulation was increased in 1942.

For longleaf and slash pine, a 50-percent water solution of sulfuric acid, applied to fresh wounds every 2 weeks, proved to be the most suitable treatment (Snow 1944, 1948ab). The acid did not increase the production of oleoresin, but facilitated its outflow by keeping the resin ducts open longer after wounding (Ostrom et al. 1958). Snow (1944) found, too, that with sulfuric acid only a narrow strip of bark need be removed across the face. He devised a new hack that would cut only through the bark and phloem, an easier task than deep wood chipping. Faces were chipped only at 2-week intervals, and production per man-day of chipping was virtually doubled.

Many people worked on techniques for applying the acid to the fresh wound. At first, cloth swabs and insect sprayers of the "flit gun" type were used. Next, a glass or lead "lung-powered" spray gun was developed by Bourke and Dorman (1946). From this research, the presently used plastic squeeze bottle evolved (Schopmeyer 1947; Ryberg and Burney 1949).

Figure 28–2 shows the system used after World War II. Spiral gutters and curved aprons, attached to the round faces with double-headed nails, were easily removed from the worked-out trees, and had virtually no adverse influence on tree vigor (Ryberg et al. 1949). Larger turpentine cups reduced dipping expenses without affecting gum yield or grade (Clements and Collins 1950). To assist the producers, manuals were prepared that described currently accepted methods (Clements 1960; Dyer 1963). With bark chipping, acid treatment, and removable gutters, the face is not severely damaged by the wounding. The worked-out butt section can be readily freed of metal and used for pulpwood, poles, ties, or lumber (Snow 1948b; Anonymous 1950; Gruschow 1950; Schopmeyer 1955).

Management practices.—Although not seriously reducing tree vigor, current turpentining slows growth like the old technique (Cary 1928; Harper 1937; Schopmeyer 1955). As a rule, annual volume growth is reduced about 25 percent per face each year the tree is worked, but the value of gum produced more than compensates for this growth loss if the worked-out trees are cut promptly at the end of the naval stores cycle (table 28–1).

Production of gum and wood makes a more profitable operation than the production of either product alone (Bennett and Clutter 1968). Even-aged management is best because adequate numbers of trees of suitable size are available at several periods during the life of the stand, and a cycle of regular rough-reduction burning is possible (Clements and Harrington 1965.)

Because crown development and tree diameter greatly affect gum yield (table 28–2), stocking should be regulated during the life of the stand to keep the length of live crown at least 0.30 of tree height, and trees to be worked should be at least 9 inches in diameter. Trees to be worked should be selected a naval stores cycle in advance of projected thinnings or the final harvest and worked for gum, 4, 6, or 8 years, depending on whether they are worked 2, 3, or 4 years on front and back faces. A minimum of 20 faces per acre, capable of yielding 200 standard barrels of gum per crop (10,000 faces) per year is required for an operable naval stores chance.

In the absence of wildfire or bark beetle epidemics, mortality in naval

TABLE 28–1.—*Amount and value of gum yield and reduced growth, per tree, produced by working single faces on slash pine* (Harrington 1969)

Volume and value variables	D.b.h. of tree at start of gum production, inches		
	10	12	14
Total height, feet_____	66	72	74
Merchantable volume[1], cords_____	0.198	0.318	0.437
Expected annual volume increment of an unworked tree[1], cords_____	0.0132	0.0149	0.0185
Annual volume deficit of a turpentined tree,[1][2] cords _____	0.0033	0.0037	0.0046
Annual gum yield per tree,[3] pounds____	9.9	13.1	16.3
Value of annual volume deficit,[4] dollars_____	0.04	0.04	0.06
Net value of annual gum yields per tree[4], dollars_____	0.13	0.18	0.22

[1] Based on local volume tables for Olustee Experimental Forest, Baker County, Fla., using 90 as factor to convert cubic feet to cords.

[2] Deficit computed as 25 percent of expected annual volume increment.

[3] Data are from Bengtson and Schopmeyer (1959), and values are based on a 30-percent crown ratio.

[4] Based on pulpwood at $12 per cord, stumpage, and gum at $30 per barrel (435 lb.). Trees are normally leased for gum production at a lease rate of 20 percent of the gross value of the gum produced.

TABLE 28–2.—*First-year gum yields from a crop of 10,000 faces on slash pines[1]* (Bengston and Schopmeyer 1959)

D.b.h. (inches)	Gum yields by crown ratios of—		
	0.20	0.40	0.60
	— — — — — — — Barrels — — — — — — —		
9_____	172	208	244
10_____	209	245	281
11_____	246	282	318
12_____	283	319	355
13_____	320	356	392
14_____	357	393	429
15_____	394	430	466

[1] Trees were single faced and treated with 16 biweekly streaks. Gum yields are given in standard barrels of 435 lb. each.

Figure 28–2.—Following World War II, spiral gutters, double-headed nails, bark chipping, and acid treatment replaced deep wood chipping and inserted gutters. (Photo from Harrington 1969.)

stores stands under current practices is not significantly different than in unworked timber. Logging in or near stands being worked should be restricted to avoid beetle buildup. Extra fire protection should be provided. A hot wildfire, defoliating the trees and causing severe stem burn, can put the gum producer out of business, since fire-injured trees yield little gum (Harper 1944).

Conversion process.—All of the pine gum produced in this country is converted into turpentine and rosin by the Olustee process (Smith et al.

1941; Lawrence 1942, 1946; Patton and Feagan 1943; McConnell 1963). The crude gum is diluted with about 20 percent by weight of turpentine, heated in a melter to about 180° to 190° F., and filtered to remove the chips and trash. To remove iron contamination, 2 to 4 ounces of oxalic acid per barrel of gum may be added in the melter, forming iron oxylate, which filters out. The filtered gum is washed with water to remove water-soluble impurities, including any excess oxalic acid, and allowed to settle for at least 4 hours and usually overnight.

The diluted, filtered, washed, and settled gum is pumped into a still and gradually heated by steam coils to 320°-340° F. to distill off the turpentine. When the turpentine has been stripped off, the rosin is discharged from the still and packaged in drums, paper bags, or tank cars. These products are known as **gum turpentine** and **gum rosin.**

Natural oleoresin exudate from the resin ducts of southern pine contains about 66 percent resin acids, 25 percent turpentine, 7 percent nonvolatiles, and 2 percent water (Wise and Jahn 1952, p. 591). A barrel (435 lb.) of gum converted by the Olustee process will yield products as follows:

Product	Yield per barrel of gum
Turpentine, gallons _____	10 to 11
Rosin, pounds _____	300
Pine oil _____	nil

Future of the industry.—Although easily integrated into multiple product management and important to rural economy, the gum naval stores industry appears to be failing rapidly. Low-grade gum is being produced because of sloppy woods work and iron contamination from old cups. High costs and labor shortage make the business rather unattractive. Currently, 2 man-days of hard work and 10 miles of walking are required for each barrel of crude gum, and laborers are finding easier ways to make a living. A practical system of mechanization is badly needed if the industry is to survive (Harrington 1966a, 1968).

In 1966, sulfuric acid paste was introduced as a relatively safe chemical stimulant for prolonging gum flow up to 28 days (Clements 1967). Producing good gum yields with monthly chipping, the paste again doubles the man-day productiveness of chipping labor. Easier to apply correctly and more readily checked, the paste gives more uniform stimulation and is safer than the acid water spray (Harrington 1966b).

Because the acid paste stays in place on the face, ordinary materials can be used to collect the gum. At this time, 1-gallon disposable paper gum bags are being evaluated on commercial operations (fig. 28–3). The containers are larger than metal cups, more efficient to handle, and four collections during the season replace the usual eight or nine dippings.

The bags are stapled to the face, just below the fresh streak, eliminating cups and gutters and reducing low-grade scrape; they are torn from the face when collected. Light, compact, and inexpensive, they can be used

F–521009
Figure 28–3.—Acid paste is safer to use, and it stimulates gum flow for longer periods than does the acid-water solution. Chipping and streaking can be done on a monthly basis, rather than every 2 weeks. When paste is used, nonmetallic materials—such as this disposable paper bag—can be used to collect the gum. (Photo from Harrington 1969.)

with acid paste to produce high-grade gum at half present labor costs. The light, soft staples should be no hazard to saws or knives when trees are harvested.

Other possibilities for making the woods work easier and more attractive involve powered tools and a self-propelled power source. The USDA Forest Service is presently investigating the possibilities of using pneumatic tools, powered by a Scuba tank carried on the workman's back. Pneumatic bark hacks capable of cutting a chip 2 inches wide, and pneumatic staple guns for fastening the disposable gum bags to the trees are currently being evaluated. The ultimate objective is to design or modify a woods vehicle to carry the man and the powered tools from tree to tree (Taylor 1968).

Harrington (1969) concluded that the goal of marketing gum rosin and gum turpentine at a competitive price is achievable within 5 years; the current problem is to keep the gum naval stores industry alive long enough to get it mechanized.

DESTRUCTIVE DISTILLATION

When southern pine wood is heated in the absence of air, i.e., **destructively distilled,** the hydrogen, oxygen, and some of the carbon are converted into volatile compounds containing these elements. Pine tar—distinctive of the process—is possibly the most important product obtained; in the days of sailing ships, pine tar was used in large quantities for the manufacture of oakum and the preservation of cordage, fish nets, and tarpaulins; today it finds use in the manufacture of rubber and soaps.

While once of great economic importance in the manufacture of naval stores, destructive distillation of southern pine wood has declined since development of the more effective solvent-steam distillation process and the near depletion of highly resinous old-growth stumpwood; by 1969 less than half a dozen southern pine distillation plants were operating.

Yield of naval stores (designated **D.D.**) from destructively distilled pine varies considerably; one chemist knowledgeable in the subject estimated the yield from a cord (4,000 lb.) of resinous stumpwood as follows:

Product	Yield per cord
	Gallons
Turpentine	6 to 12
Pine oil	1 to 2
Tar oils	30 to 50
Tar	30 to 60

In addition, each cord should yield 750 to 900 lb. of charcoal.

Brief descriptions of the process can be found in Beglinger (1958), and Panshin et al. (1962, p. 415). Goos (1952, pp. 845-851) concluded a 26-page discussion on the thermal decomposition of wood with a lengthy tabulation of all the products in gaseous, solid, and liquid components resulting from destructive distillation of wood.

STEAM DISTILLATION

The term **steam distillation,** while appropriate for the older process of first steaming resinous pine wood to recover turpentine and other volatile oils before solvent extraction of rosin, is today something of a misnomer.

The procedure currently used, primarily a solvent extraction process, has been described by Palmer (1930) and more recently by Enos et al. (1968). In brief, old-growth longleaf pine stumps, after 25 years or more in the ground has rotted away their sapwood, are removed with power equipment and ground into particles about the size of a paper match. Resin is extracted from this ground wood in vertical cylindrical extractors with a hydrocarbon solvent. Extractors are arranged in series so that each charge of new chips is extracted by several portions of solvent in succession; extraction is counter-current, i.e., spent solvent is used for the initial extraction and fresh solvent is used for the final one.

After the wood is steamed to remove any remaining solvent, the extract containing resin and solvent is fractionally distilled to separate three primary products—terpenes (yielding refined turpentine and dipentene), pine oil, and rosin of rather dark color. The solvent must have a narrow boiling range and be completely distilled at a temperaure low enough to permit easy separation from the terpenes. Benzene, V. M. and P. naphtha, lactol, toluene, methyl isobutyl keytone, and plant-prepared mixtures of these chemicals have all been used.

Yield of naval stores (designated **S.D.**) from a ton of steam-distilled stumpwood containing an average of 22 percent resin by weight is approximately as follows (Beglinger 1958); some smaller plants do not achieve this recovery:

Product	Yield per ton of stumpwood
Turpentine, gallons	6
Pine oil, gallons	4
Dipentene (a mixture of terpenes with a higher boiling point than turpentine), gallons	1¼
Rosin, pounds	385

The extracted wood chips (about 1,100 ovendry pounds per ton of stumpwood) are primarily utilized as fuel, but it is likely that they will be increasingly needed for fiber products; one company has announced that spent chips will be used to manufacture linerboard. Because chips are mainly rootwood, fibers are longer, larger in diameter, and have thinner walls than those from stemwood near ground level (see sec. 13–3 and fig. 13–22).

As the source of old-growth longleaf pine stumps becomes depleted, volume of steam-distilled naval stores must diminish because stumps from young (less than 100 years of age) longleaf and slash pine trees contain insufficient resin for economical extraction.

BYPRODUCTS OF KRAFT PULPING PROCESS

When southern pine wood is digested to convert it into kraft pulp, turpentine is vaporized. The steam, turpentine vapor, and other gases from the pulping digester are passed hrough a condenser to collect the crude **sufate turpentine.** The pulping liquors are alkaline, and the resin acids and fatty acids present in the wood are converted to their sodium salts in the digester. When the digester liquor (black liquor) is concentrated by evaporation, these sodium soaps (known as black liquor soaps) separate as a brown curdy mass; they are then skimmed off and acidified to yield crude **tall oil** (Weiner 1959; Sanderman 1960; Weiner and Byrne 1968; Zachary et al. (1965).

Crude tall oil contains about 40 to 60 percent fatty acids, 40 to 60 percent resin acids, and 12 to 15 percent non-acidic materials. This mixture can be fractionally distilled to give acids containing only a trace of resin acids, a center cut containing a mixture of fatty acids and resin acids, and a tall oil rosin fraction that contains less than 4 percent fatty acids (Barnes and Taylor 1958; Agnello and Barnes 1960). In 1949, tall oil rosin became available on a commercial scale in this country. Although it differed somewhat from other rosins, its quality was improved during the next 20 years; it is now a very important source of rosin.

Yield of naval stores from southern pine pulped by the kraft process is approximately as follows:

Product	Yield
Crude sulfate turpentine, gallons per cord of wood _____	0.50 to 1.75
Crude tall oil, pounds per cord of wood _____	56 (range 31 to 62)

From these crude materials, 0.4 to 1.5 gallons of refined sulfate turpentine and 6 to 22 lb. of rosin can be recovered.

TURPENTINE AND TURPENTINE DERIVATIVES

Turpentine, once almost exclusively a paint thinner, is now used almost entirely as a chemical raw material (Goldblatt 1951). For the season 1967-1968, the reported consumption of all turpentine in this country was 571,350 barrels (U.S. Department of Agriculture 1969). Of this only 4,320 barrels were reported used in paint and varnish and 563,550 barrels were used in chemicals and rubber.

American gum turpentine contains about 60 to 65 percent alpha-pinene and 25 to 35 percent beta-pinene, with 1 or 2 percent each of limonene, camphene, beta-phellandrene, and myrcene (Goldblatt 1951; Mirov 1961).

Crude sulfate turpentine contains mercaptans and related bad-smelling materials, some of which are removed by oxidation and fractional distillation in the refining process (Drew and Pylant 1966). Recovery of refined sulfate turpentine is usually about 80 percent of the crude product. The major components of the refined sulfate turpentine are also alpha- and beta-pinene, but its composition varies depending on mill location and the species of pine used.

The terpene fraction from steam-distilled wood naval stores contains a variety of hydrocarbons (Stonecipher 1955). A turpentine fraction containing a high concentration of alpha-pinene with some limonene—but only 1 to 2 percent beta-pinence—can be separated by fractional distillation. These and other fractions are more suitable for most chemical uses when separately concentrated. In the past, turpentine was sold as a mixture of alpha- and beta-pinene; currently it is more profitable to separate them.

The beta-pinene will bring a higher price when polymerized to a high molecular weight polyterpene resin or when passed through a hot tube at about 400° to 600° C. to isomerize it to myrcene (Goldblatt and Palkin 1941, 1947). High molecular weight polyterpene resins prepared from alpha-pinene and limonene are less desirable than those from beta-pinene. Alpha-pinene can be isomerized to a mixture of limonene and alloocimene by passing it through a hot tube. Alpha-pinene is also isomerized to camphene, which can be used as a starting material for camphor, or chlorinated to give a very important insecticide that is especially effective on the cotton boll weevil (Goldblatt 1951). A wide variety of perfumes, odorants, and flavors are prepared by further reaction of these terpenes (Derfer 1963, 1966).

Insufficient natural pine oil is steam distilled from pitch-soaked stumps to meet present demands. Synthetic pine oil is prepared by treating alpha-pinene or a mixture of alpha- and beta-pinene with 25 percent sulfuric acid or other strong acid, which converts it to a mixture of terpene alcohols, the major component of which is alpha-terpineol (Pickett and Schantz 1934; Sellers and Doyle 1968). Terpin hydrate (used as a pharmaceutical) can be separated from either natural or synthetic pine oil. Pine oil is used in cleaners, disinfectants, textile chemicals, and ore flotation processes.

The monocyclic hydrocarbons are hydrogenated to para-menthane, and alpha-pinene can be hydrogenated to pinane. Either of these products, when oxidized by blowing with air or oxygen, can be converted to the corresponding hydroperoxide. The para-menthane hydroperoxide is widely used in this country as a catalyst in the production of synthetic rubber. Pinane hydroperoxide has been used in this country and in Europe for the same purpose.

Several terpenes react with maleic anhydride to form the anhydride of a dibasic acid that can be used in alkyd and polyester resins.

ROSIN

Rosin makes up about 80 percent by weight of the products obtained by the gum and steam-distillation industries (Lawrence 1951; Enos et al. 1968). The pulp industry is now producing about twice as much tonnage of rosin as turpentine. American rosin production is approximately 1 billion pounds per year. This is about one-half of the world production. The United States exported 365 million pounds, or about 38 percent of domestic production in the 1967-1968 crop year. Other countries important in the production of naval stores are Russia, Portugal, Greece, Spain, France, India, China, and Mexico.

Rosin is graded and sold on the basis of color, the paler colors bringing the higher prices. Color grades range from pale yellow, graded X, to dark red (almost black), graded D. Three new rosin grades paler than X have been added—XA, XB, and XC. The colors between these extremes increase progressively through the grades—WW, WG, N, M, K, I, H, G, F, and E. Because of improved modern methods, about 80 percent of the gum rosin produced is Grade M or better, and a great deal of the tall oil rosin is paler than X. Unrefined wood rosin, as produced directly from the extracting solvent, is ruby red, color Grade FF. The high-colored material obtained in refining wood rosin is no longer classifiable as rosin. It is sold as B resin or under various trade names. (Resin is a general term that refers to a wide variety of natural and synthetic products. Rosin is a specific kind of resin that is obtained only from pine trees.)

Oleoresin as it comes from the tree yields practically colorless rosin; off colors in gum rosin come almost entirely from iron contamination and oxidation products (Lawrence 1942). Since good woods practices avoid most contaminants, gum rosins are rarely clarified.

Wood rosin is highly colored by oxidized resin acids and other organic compounds extracted from the wood with the resin. These are commonly removed by selective solvents such as furfural, or solid adsorbents such as fuller's earth.

When a 15-percent solution of dark rosin in a low-solvency hydrocarbon such as heptane or isooctane is thoroughly mixed with furfural, most of the color remains in the furfural layer.

A similar solution of dark rosin, when pumped through fuller's earth, is freed of most dark products (Lawrence 1951; Mirov 1961). The dark material recovered from the fuller's earth by working with alcohol, though not classified as rosin, is saleable as B resin.

Rosin consists of about 90 percent resin acids and 10 percent neutral matter. Of the resin acids, about 80 to 90 percent are isomeric with abietic acid, whose composition is $C_{20}H_{30}O_2$. The other 10 to 20 percent is dehydroabietic acid $(C_{20}H_{28}O_2)$ and various oxygenated derivatives. The relative amounts of these depend on the type of rosin and processing conditions used to prepare it (Joye and Lawrence 1967). About half the total resin acids in rosin can be converted to abietic acid by acid or heat isomerization (Loeblich et al. 1955). Eight of these resin acids—pimaric, isopimaric, levopimaric, palustric, abietic, neoabietic, and dehydroabietic—make up about 85 percent of the acid portion (Joye and Lawrence 1967) of commercial pine gum and rosins. The relative amount of these acids present may vary from 5 percent to more than 50 percent for different rosins. Levopimaric acid makes up more than 25 percent of the acids in most commercial pine gum but is almost completely converted into palustric, abietic, and neoabietic acids on processing to rosin.

Elliotinoic, sandaracopimaric, and Δ^8-isopimaric acids are present in quantities of less than 5 percent each, and there are also small amounts of hydroxy and other oxygenated acids present in some rosins. The difference in properties of commercial rosins depends to a great extent on the relative amounts of these acids as well as on the composition of the neutral fraction. Although not thoroughly investigated, gum rosin neutrals have been shown to contain methyl chavicol, stilbene derivatives, terpene dimers, aldehydes, alcohols, and a mixture of hydrophenanthrene hydrocarbons, which serve as plasticizers for the resin acids. The diterpene alcohol elliotinol is the major component of the neutral portion of gum rosin from slash pine.

Rosin for export is packaged in drums holding about 500 or 520 lb. each; for domestic consumption it is usually packaged in 520-lb. drums or 100-lb. paper bags. For many large consumers, however, rosin is shipped in the molten state in railroad tank cars.

Paper size.—The most important use for rosin is for sizing to reduce the penetrability of paper by liquids (Weiner and Byrne 1968). Rosin is the most important sizing agent for paper; practically all papers except those designed for high absorbency contain some rosin. It is the only internal size used to any appreciable extent; most of the other sizing agents, e.g., starch and casein, are surface sizes. There are some other internal sizes, but they are more expensive than rosin.

To make the size, rosin is usually cooked with a sodium carbonate or sodium hydroxide solution. The rosin may be completely neutralized and converted to its water-soluble salt (sodium resinate), or about a third of it may be converted to its sodium soap and this used to keep the other two-thirds emulsified. Some special paper sizes are made by neutralizing only 10 to 15 percent of the rosin and using a protective colloid such as casein to keep the finished size emulsified.

Fortified rosin size, a more effective product, is prepared from maleic or fumaric-modified rosin. About 4 percent by weight of maleic anhydride (or a mixture of maleic anhydride and fumaric acid) is added to the rosin at 200° to 220° C. After heating at this temperature for an hour or two, the product is converted to its sodium salt to give the fortified rosin size. Size made from rosin that has a high abietic acid content may crystallize. This is avoided by heating the rosin with a small amount of formaldehyde.

Rosin size is usually sold as a paste containing about 30 percent water and 70 percent solids. It is usually added to the paper pulp in the beater, where it is precipitated onto the paper fibers by adding 1 to 2 parts of alum (aluminum sulfate) for each part of rosin. The amount of rosin required for sizing varies from as little as 0.2 to 2 percent on regular grades of paper up to 8 percent on special types.

Soaps.—Rosin is used in a variety of soaps which are much more soluble in water than are the ordinary soaps from fatty acids. Rosin improves the sudsing, the detergency, and the wetting rate of the soap, as well as its germicidal activity. At one time, almost a third of all rosin produced went into soap, much of which was the old yellow-bar laundry soap. Currently, however, lower-cost, more effective, synthetic detergents have almost completely replaced rosin in household soaps.

Soaps composed entirely of sodium or potassium rosinate find specialized uses. A stabilized rosin soap, for example, serves in the manufacture of synthetic rubber as an emulsifying agent in the polymerization of butadiene and styrene and as a softener and tackifier. Because of its good solubility in water, this soap is especially effective in the preparation of low-temperature-rubber. Rosin used for this soap should contain less than 1 percent abietic-type acids and should be free of inhibitors that retard the rate of polymerization. Rosin soap serves a purpose in addition to emulsification, i.e., the polymer is coagulated by the addition of salt and acid, the acid decomposes the soap, and practically all of the rosin used remains in the rubber to act as a softener and tackifier.

Softening agent in rubber.—Rosin is used as a softening agent or plasticizer in both natural and synthetic rubber; it is added when the compounding ingredients, such as carbon black, sulfur, zinc oxide, and accelerators, are being mixed with the raw rubber on the mixing rolls. Frequently, a small amount of terpene solvent is added to rosin used for this purpose. Both the rosin and the terpenes impart tack to the finished product.

Surface coatings.—Numerous rosin derivatives are used in the preparation of paints, varnishes, lacquers, and printing inks.

Varnish is usually prepared by heating a drying oil and a resin together until the desired amount of polymerization, or combining of the molecules, of the drying oil has taken place. When the mixture has reached the proper consistency, it is thinned to a satisfactory viscosity with a volatile solvent. A wide variety of resins may be used, including numerous rosin derivatives. For use in varnish, rosin is usually converted to one of its derivatives to raise its melting point and lower its acidity. Most commonly used are the esters, including the maleic-modified esters, rosin phenol-formaldehyde resins, limed rosins, zinc resinates, and various combinations of these derivatives. Rosin may also be hydrogenated, dehydrogenated, disproportionated, or polymerized to obtain derivatives for use in varnish.

The rosin esters most commonly used in varnish are the glycerol and the pentaerythritol esters. The glycerol ester (Pohle and Smith 1942) has the better solubility characteristics; the pentaerythritol has the higher melting point. If maleic anhydride is reacted with the rosin before esterification, the modified rosin will have a higher melting point. While rosin will react with 25 percent of its weight of maleic anhydride, 10 to 15 percent is much more commonly used.

Rosin is combined with a heat-reactive, phenol-formaldehyde resin to give widely used varnish resins having much more desirable properties than either material alone. Their properties vary with the ratio of phenol and formaldehyde to rosin and with the type of phenol derivative used. They are usually esterified with glycerol to give varnish resins with a low pH and high melting point.

By combining rosin with a small amount of lime, a derivative suitable for use in varnish is produced whose melting point and pH can be controlled (within certain limits) by varying the amount of lime used. The rosin may be limed in the presence of drying oil, so that the varnish is prepared in a single step.

Zinc resinate resembles limed rosin in that the rosin has reacted with a metal oxide or salt to reduce the acidity and raise the melting point. Zinc resinates are more difficult to prepare, but they have several advantages, including greater resistance to water (Palmer and Edelstein 1944; St. Clair and Lawrence 1951, 1952).

Some rosin derivatives have uses in paints and varnishes other than serving as a resin. Certain metal resinates are used as dryers, which act as catalysts. For a drying-oil film to harden within a reasonable time, a small amount of dryer has to be present. The most commonly used dryers are the oil-soluble salts of cobalt, lead, and manganese, generally the resinate, naphthenate, or tallate. "Fused" resinates are prepared by the addition of the metal oxide, hydroxide, or acetate to molten rosin, "precipitated" resinates by the precipitation of the metal resinate from an aqueous solution of sodium resinate with a water-soluble salt of the desired metal. The fused resinates contain less metal but are more soluble in the varnish solvents. The precipitated resinates, being in a fine state of subdivision, are more difficult to store since they are readily damaged by oxidation.

Unmodified rosin is preferred for other uses. Because of its excellent solubility, it may be mixed with less soluble resins to improve their solubility in formulations in which they would not otherwise be satisfactory.

Another use for rosin in varnish is to retard gelation of certain highly reactive drying oils. Thus rosin facilitates processing of tung oil varnish and improves its quality by greatly retarding the polymerization of the oil into an insoluble gel. If the tung oil has already gelled, rosin may also serve as a peptizing, or solubilizing, agent.

The use of rosin and many of its derivatives in printing ink closely parallels their use in ordinary varnish, since a printing ink is essentially a varnish having a high resin and a high pigment content with little or no thinner.

Present-day lacquers consist largely of cellulose derivatives, resins, plasticizers, and solvents. The cellulose derivatives, usually cellulose nitrate or acetate, are the film-forming materials, but they lack adhesion, gloss, and workable viscosity.

Various natural and synthetic resins, rosin esters, rosin-modified phenolics, and maleic-modified rosin esters improve viscosity characteristics. A 20-percent solution of ester gum has a very low viscosity in lacquer solvents and when mixed with a like concentration of nitrocellulose in similar solvents, it gives satisfactory viscosity. Because both the nitrocellulose and the resin are usually too brittle to form satisfactory films, a plasticizer is required. The methyl ester of rosin and other low-melting rosin esters are often used for that purpose.

Floor coverings.—Because of its peptizing or solubilizing action on gelled oils, rosin finds use in the preparation of linoleum or linoleum-type floor coverings. Since color is not usually critical, the darker grades of rosin are commonly used. A mixture consisting of about 20 percent rosin and 80 percent drying oils, with a small amount of oil-soluble salts of cobalt, manganese, and lead, is blown with air for about 15 hours. The mixture is thus converted into a rubbery plastic substance known as cement, and used as a binder for the linoleum sheet. Mixed with pigments and ground cork or wood flour, it is passed between heavy rolls to form a plastic surface on a woven or felted fabric base.

Trends of price and demand for rosin.—In 1938, the average price for all grades of gum rosin on the Savannah Market reached a low of approximately 1 cent per pound. During 1968 prices of the paler grades of gum rosin were fairly steady at 10 to 11 cents per pound. Since 1938, many of the competing products have decreased in price. In spite of these changes, the demand for rosin as grown slowly over this period, though its markets have changed greatly through development of new uses and new derivatives. It should be possible to find new markets to replace those that are lost, so long as adequate research programs are maintained.

28–2 HYDROLYSIS [2]

The polysaccharides or carbohydrates of wood, principally cellulose and hemicelluloses, may be converted into simple sugars by acid catalyzed hydrolytic cleavage of their glycosidic bonds. This conversion, known as wood **hydrolysis** or wood **saccharification**, is potentially one of the best methods of utilizing bark-free wood residues from mills processing southern pine. Difficulties in hydrolyzing the cellulose constituent of the woody cell wall and the decomposition of simple sugars concomitant with the hydrolysis reaction make present processes uneconomical, however.

Carbohydrates make up 65 to 70 percent of the southern pine cell wall. (See table 6–1.) Approximately 64 percent of this carbohydrate content is cellulose, and the remainder is comprised of hemicelluloses, predominantly hexosans. (See table 6–2.) The crystalline structure of cellulose makes it very resistant to acid hydrolysis. Hemicelluloses, on the other hand, are amorphous in structure and are more readily hydrolyzed to their constituent sugars by the action of dilute acids. Efficient production of simple sugars from wood must take into account this differential ease of hydrolysis.

Hydrolysis of wood and other ligno-cellulosic substances has been reviewed by Harris (1949, ch. 4), Hägglund (1951), Wise and Jahn (1952), FAO (1954), Pearl and Gregory (1959), Savard (1962), and Bubl [3]. The processes developed thus far use either concentrated or dilute acids as the hydrolyzing agent.

DILUTE ACID PROCESS

Hydrolysis with dilute acid uses either multiple step batch processes or continuous percolation. The batch processes react the wood chips in pressure cookers at high temperatures, after which the hydrolyzate is drained off and the sugar solution concentrated. The yield is low (20 to 30 percent) due to decomposition of the simple sugars. A report by Cederquist (1952), however, describes a multiple batch process, affording yields as high as 50 percent of the dry wood weight.

---

[2] Sec. 28–2 is adapted from an unpublished review of the subject by L. F. Burkart, Stephen F. Austin State College, Nacogdoches, Tex.

[3] Bubl, J. L. The hydrolysis of cellulose and wood. Abstracts from Chemical Abstracts, 1918-1943. USDA Forest Service, Forest Products Laboratory, FPL DP–37. Unpublished.

Of the percolation processes, only that developed by Scholler and his associates in Germany prior to World War II has been used commercially (Schaal 1935; Scholler 1939; Locke et al. 1945). A metered quantity of preheated dilute acid is percolated through wood chips or sawdust and promptly pressed out through the bottom of the digester by steam pressure. The short time between the formation and withdrawal of the simple sugars allows less decomposition than in the batch processes. As many as 20 cycles are used before the hydrolysis is complete. Because the sugar solutions are dilute and would otherwise require costly concentration, these processes are particularly adapted to direct fermentation to alcohol.

The Madison Wood Sugar Process (Harris et al. 1945; Wise and Jahn, 1952, pp. 908-909; Stamm and Harris 1954, ch. 16), an adaptation of the Scholler process, continuously admits hot dilute acid under pressure at the top of the digester with simultaneous withdrawal of the hydrolyzate from the bottom. This process has been thoroughly tested in the pilot plant stage but is not in commercial use.

CONCENTRATED ACID PROCESS

A number of processes have been developed using concentrated hydrochloric or sulfuric acid (at about 70° F.) as the hydrolyzing agent. Hemicelluloses are first removed by a dilute acid prehydrolysis. The strong acid is then introduced to swell the crystalline structure of the cellulose with accompanying partial hydrolysis. This action is stopped by dilution with water, and the process is completed as a dilute acid hydrolysis. The concentrated acid processes provide higher yields and more concentrated sugar solutions than the dilute acid processes; installations for handling the concentrated acids are costly, however.

The only concentrated acid process which has had any degree of economic success is the Rheinau or Bergius method using fuming hydrochloric acid (Bergius 1937; Locke et al. 1945). More recently the Japanese have developed several advanced processes using concentrated sulfuric acid, concentrated hydrochloric acid, or gaseous hydrogen chloride as the hydrolyzing agent (Oshima et al. 1959; FAO 1960; Kobayashi et al. 1960; Locke and Garnum 1961). All of these processes have been developed to the pilot plant stage but not to large-scale commercial operations. Wood hydrolysis plants are known to be in commercial operation in the Soviet Union, but little information on their economics is available (Locke and Garnum 1961; Harris et al. 1963, ch. 11).

OTHER POSSIBILITIES

New ways of disrupting the crystalline structure of cellulose need to be found and adapted to our present hydrolysis technology. Irradiation with cathode rays has been found to increase the accessibility of cellulose and thus to increase the rate of hydrolysis; also amines and other organic reagents affect the crystal structure of the cellulose by disrupting the hydrogen bonds holding the molecules together (Harris et al. 1963, pp. 552-560).

A process currently in the research stage removes lignin and much of the hemicellulose fraction in an initial step using triethylene glycol with a suitable acid catalyst as the solvent (Burkart 1969, 1970). The lignin and hemicelluloses are easily precipitated from the liquor and separated in forms that are suitable for further processing. The residual cellulose is available for use as fiber, or by further treatment with triethelene glycol at higher temperatures may be dissolved for chemical uses. The glycol is reclaimed for reuse. The reactions take place at atmospheric pressures, so expensive high-pressure digesters are not required.

Utilization of lignin, which constitutes 20 to 30 percent of pine wood, will no doubt be the deciding factor in the possible establishment of a stable wood hydrolysis industry. The usefulness of this potentially valuable by-product may be greatly enhanced by a separation process in which it acquires different characteristics than those resulting from kraft or sulfite pulping.

In the production of dissolving pulp by the kraft process, if chips are first treated (prehydrolyzed) with hot dilute mineral acids or hot water, a substantial portion of the noncellulosic carbohydrate fraction (pectins, arabinans, arabinogalactans, glucomannans, etc.) can be removed before alkaline pulping.

In studying the mechanism of prehydrolysis, Casebier et al. (1969) found that room temperature and hot (100° C.) water extraction removed only small amounts of the arabinogalactan type carbohydrate; when temperature was increased to 170° C. or higher, all hemicelluloses of this type plus significant amounts containing mannose and xylose were removed. At the higher temperatures much of the arabinogalactan polymer is hydrolyzed to free sugars. If held more than 90 minutes at 170° C., these may be lost as volatile compounds such as furfural or as insoluble condensation products.

Prehydrolysis removes 4 to 13 percent of the weight (ovendry basis) of southern pine chips, depending on the time and temperature of the reaction. Technology is available to concentrate the dissolved carbohydrate material for livestock feed.

Masonite Corporation, in "exploding" pine and hardwood chips into fibers for hardboard production, uses a high-pressure steam treatment which is essentially a prehydrolysis (Leker 1969). Free sugars and soluble polysaccharides are removed in a wash water containing about 4 percent soluble material, which is concentrated in multiple evaporators and sold for livestock feed as wood hydrolyzate molasses or in powder form.

PRODUCTS OF HYDROLYSIS

End products of wood hydrolysis can be grouped into three categories: crystalline sugars and wood molasses, biologically derived products, and chemically derived products.

Crystalline sugar and wood molasses.—The concentrated acid processes produce hydrolyzates with high sugar concentration. These hydrolzates can be further concentrated and refined to produce crystalline glucose and xylose suitable for human and animal consumption, and for the chemical sugar markets (Locke and Garnum 1961; Harris et al. 1963, ch. 11). Concentration to approximately 50 percent solids by weight produces a wood molasses which extensive tests have shown to be comparable in food value to blackstrap molasses as a livestock feed (Harris 1950; Lloyd and Harris 1955). Improved multiple evaporators available to industry now make it technically feasible to concentrate the dilute hydrolyzates produced by the dilute acid processes. The production of sugars and molasses is one of the most attractive possible uses for wood hydrolysis, especially in areas where other sources of sugar are limited.

Limited hydrolysis accomplished by exposure of southern pine wood to steam (Leker 1969) or hot water (Casebier et al. 1969), yields some simple sugars plus soluble polysaccharide precursors of simple sugars.

Low cost of sugars from other sources makes widespread production of wood sugars uneconomical in the United States under present conditions. More stringent antipollution legislation, however, should stimulate interest in recovery of polysaccharides and sugars from process effluents (Leker 1969).

Biologically derived products.—Early interest in wood hydrolysis was primarily focused on the production of industrial ethyl alcohol by fermentation; while hexosans are readily converted in this manner, pentosans were largely wasted in early processes. The first commercial plants in the United States were built about 1914 in Fullerton, La. and Georgetown, S. C.; these plants converted southern pine sawmill waste into more than 6 million gallons of ethyl alcohol during World War I (Harris 1945). During the 1920's however, both plants ceased operations. Today, industrial ethyl alcohol is synthesized from petroleum-derived products.

Fermentation processes have been developed, however, for large-scale production of products from both hexose and pentose sugars. The largest users of sugar for industrial purposes (and consequently the largest potential users of wood sugars) are the producers of yeast, citric acid, and vinegar (Harris et al. 1963). Other fermentation products are butanol, lactic acid, butyric acid, 2- and 3-butylene glycol, and glycerine (Harris et al. 1963). Since these products usually bring higher prices than ethyl alcohol and since both pentoses and hexoses can be used, they promise greater economic feasibility.

Chemically derived products.—Both pentose and hexose sugars can be readily converted into useful products by chemical processes. Locke and Garnum (1961), reporting on the chemical wood conversion industry in Japan, state, "Intensive research is done there on the utilization of chemicals derived from wood. This may lead to the further development of the new industry into relatively large units producing a variety of chemical compounds and end products now mainly derived from the petro-chemical industry."

Chemicals that possibly could be produced competitively from southern pine, and which have a large industrial demand, include: furfural, hydroxy-methyl furfural, levulinic acid, lactic acid, acetic acid, formic acid, xylitol, and sorbitol (Harris 1949; Lloyd and Harris 1955; Harris et al. 1963).

WOOD RESIDUES AS ANIMAL FOOD

In addition to the animal food potential of molasses from mill effluents, there exists the possibility of hydrolysis of wood and cellulose by cellulotic enzymes present in the digestive system of ruminant animals. Wood residues of a number of hardwood, and a few softwood, species have been shown to have value both as a non-nutritive roughage and, with modification, as an energy-containing food (Durham 1969; Scott et al. 1969; Feist et al. 1970; Heaney and Bender 1970). While not extensively evaluated, it is probable that southern pine—in common with some other softwoods—will be more difficult for ruminants to utilize than most hardwoods because its terpenes and other volatile resinous compounds are likely toxic or inhibiting to micro-organisms of the ruminant.

In an unpublished paper[4], Cody et al. reported results from feeding screened shortleaf pine sawdust to bulls and heifers; grain intake was controlled by a ration of grain mixed with sawdust (35 percent wood). A 15-percent level of wood was insufficient for maintaining normal rumen mucosa. Neither slaughtered carcass nor feeding habits of the live animal appeared to suffer harmful effects from the wood-containing rations.

In 1968, R. W. Scott of the USDA Forest Products Laboratory abstracted the world literature relating to the use of wood and other lignocellulosic materials as feed for livestock; several references described experiments with pine species. König (1919) reported on attempts to use sulfite pine pulping liquor as animal food. Nehring and Schramn (1949) fed pine sulfite cellulose to ruminant animals; Ellenberger and Waentig (1918) made similar experiments with nonruminant animals, i.e., horses.

Honcamp (1929) reported that pine needles were 39 percent digestible; the animals were unidentified, but it is likely he worked with sheep. Eichmeyer (1943) found that pine needles and pine wood were respectively 43 percent and 46 percent digestible by sheep.

Dahlberg and Guettinger (1956) discussed jack pine (*Pinus banksiana* Lamb.) as a food for deer. Fermentation of pine wood and pine pulps was described by Olson et al. (1937), Fontaine (1941), and Virtanen and Nikkilä (1946).

---

[4] Cody, R. E., Morrill, J. L., and Hibbs, C. M. Evaluation of health and performance of dairy animals fed wood fiber as a roughage source or intake regulator. Presented at the 63rd Annual Meeting of the American Dairy Association, Columbus, Ohio. 1968.

28–3 KRAFT LIGNIN PRODUCTS [5]

As noted in section 6–2, dissolved lignin (fig. 6–4) produced in kraft pulp manufacture, constituting 20 to 30 percent of the ovendry weight of wood pulped, is modified from native pine lignin by the aqueous alkaline cooking liquors.

In spite of the enormous tonnages produced daily in the kraft mills of the South, kraft lignin has proven difficult to utilize at a profit. The West Virginia Pulp and Paper Company, Charleston, S. C., first made available to other industries a reproducible and inexpensive kraft lignin. This phenolic polymer had a wide solubility range and was readily reactive with, and modified by, various other chemical compounds. A series of lignin-derived products formulated to the requirements of different users are described by technical bulletins published by the company.

Where lignin is used in combination with phenolic resins to bond together pine and hardwood fibers in the core of decorative laminates, it is necessary to properly tailor both the lignin and the phenolic resin to optimize processing characteristics, properties, and economics (Schulerud and Doughty 1961). Similarly, a properly formulated combination of lignin products, urea, and a minor portion of special phenolic resins is an economic and effective binder to spray on the forming fibers in rock wool insulation (Ball 1962; Sarjeant 1966).

In the manufacture of cement and concrete, various lignin products fulfill specific economic and technical needs. Proprietary grinding aids containing pine lignin derivatives are widely added to cement clinker at 0.01- to 0.05-percent level to speed up grinding by 15 to 25 percent. Other pine lignin products retard setting time of Portland cement and are water-reducing and plasticizing agents for masonry and block cement.

Pine lignin products with varying degrees of sulfonation are extensively used as versatile dispersants for wettable pesticide and herbicide powders. Similar approaches have produced a dozen efficient and economical surface active agents for acetate, polyester, and vat dyes. Required dispersing characteristics can be obtained through changes in molecular weight, sulfonate content, and cation content.

Specific pine lignin amines are now quite effectively used as cationic asphalt stabilizers (Borgfeldt 1964), while other pine lignin derivatives foster plant growth through their ability to chelate with and maintain availability of plant micronutrients which are added with fertilizers to deficient soils (Schneider et al. 1968).

Despite these economic uses, however, the great preponderance of kraft lignin is still utilized as low-value fuel; heat of combustion of kraft liquor

---

[5] With some editorial changes, sec. 28–3 is taken from Ball, F. G. Lignin in the cellular structure of southern pine wood and lignin products from southern pine. Presentation at a symposium, "Utilization of the Southern Pines", Alexandria, La., November 6-8, 1968.

is about 6,000 B.t.u. per ovendry pound (see table 9–8), which gives it a fuel value of less than $1.50 per ton when concentrated to half water by weight.

28–4 CHARCOAL

Wood destructively distilled yields a solid carbonaceous residue termed charcoal, a product much used in the early 1900's in the iron and chemical industries as well as for cooking and heating, but now used primarily for charcoal briquets—a consumer fuel for outdoor grills. Charcoal production in 1961 was considerably above the levels prevailing in the 1950's, but substantially below output in the early 1900's (fig. 28–4). Virtually all charcoal consumed in the United States is from domestic production; net imports in 1961 were only 5,342 tons. Production is concentrated in the Eastern States; in both 1956 and 1961 this section accounted for 98 percent of all the charcoal manufactured. The Southern States produced 29 per-cent of the total. In 1961 thirteen large producers (out of about 2,000 total) accounted for 56 percent of total production. In the South and Southeast the selling price of bulk unscreened charcoal averaged $32 per ton in 1961, lowest of any region in the country; the highest prices (average $64 per ton) were obtained by producers in the Northeastern States. In 1961, 50 plants produced 235,640 tons of charcoal briquets; 44 of the plants (97 percent of the production) were in the East, with the greatest tonnage (94,600 tons) produced in Southern and Southeastern States. Only 21,000 tons of briquets were produced from nonwood sources (e.g., lignite and agricultural residues) in 1961. The foregoing data are all from USDA Forest Service (1963).

Since 1961, briquet manufacturing capacity has increased, but the num-ber of briqueting plants has decreased; in 1968, plants numbered 32, with a combined capacity of 94 tons per hour (fig. 28–5). In 1970 it was esti-

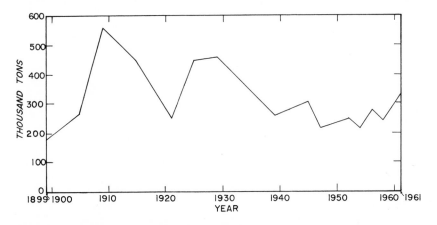

Figure 28–4.—Charcoal production in the United States from 1899 to 1961. (Drawing from USDA Forest Service 1963.)

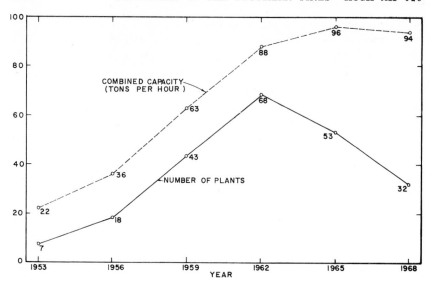

Figure 28–5.—Charcoal briquet production capacity in the United States. (Drawing from Aeroglide Corp.)

mated that 35 plants (owned by 25 firms) had a total capacity of 103 tons per hour.

For the guidance of charcoal purchasers and prospective manufacturers, a list of charcoal producers active in the South during 1961 was published by the Southern Forest Experiment Station (USDA Forest Service 1962). In 1970, there were about 22 briqueting plants in the Southern States.

Charcoal can be manufactured from any woody waste; yields are commonly about 1 ton of charcoal from 3 to 4 tons (ovendry basis) of wood. Southern pine roundwood and chips have a high value for fiber products, and dry residues are valuable for wood flour and particleboard; therefore, only a few types of southern pine residues are economical candidates as raw material for charcoal. Green southern pine sawdust and particularly southern pine bark, appear to offer possibilities for charcoal manufacture.

EQUIPMENT

There is a wide variety of equipment available to convert wood to charcoal. Descriptions of equipment and procedures for coaling roundwood, slabs, and edgings are widely available (e.g., USDA Forest Products Laboratory 1961). Because the few types of southern pine residues economically available as possible raw material for charcoal are in particulate form, only certain types of equipment like the multiple-hearth furnace are suitable.

Multiple-hearth furnace.—In June of 1969 seven Herreshoff multiple-

---

[6] This description of the multiple-hearth furnace is adapted from Gallagher (1969).

hearth furnaces for the continuous production of charcoal were operating in the United States, with three more under construction. The furnaces are designed for three-shift production, preferably operating 7 days per week. Production rates are in the range from 1 to 2 tons of charcoal per hour. Four tons of ovendry wood or bark will yield about 1 ton of charcoal. Gases produced during carbonization are substantial, and preferably are captured and burned to generate steam; alterntively the gases can be incinerated and scrubbed to comply with antipollution codes. The furnace can be operated by one man per shift and will accept bark, planer shavings, sawdust, pulverized wood, or a mixture of these fuels. Little external fuel is required, as part of the wood gases generated in the furnace are burned as needed to maintain carbonization.

The Herreshoff multiple-hearth furnace consists of several hearths or burning chambers stacked one on top of the other, the number depending on the capacity. The hearths are contained in a cylindrical, refractory-lined, steel shell and are constructed in arched form to serve simultaneously as the floor of one hearth and the roof of the hearth below.

Passing up through the center of the furnace is a shaft to which are attached two to four toothed arms for every hearth. As the shaft turns slowly (usually 1 to 2 r.p.m.), the teeth constantly plough through and turn over the fuel resting on the hearth floors, thus constantly exposing fresh material to the hot gases. The teeth also move material through the furnace; i.e., on every other hearth the teeth are canted to spiral the material from the shaft toward the outside wall of the furnace, and on alternate hearths the material is moved from the outside wall toward the center shaft. Around the center shaft is an annular space through which material drops on alternate hearths, while on the remaining hearths material drops through holes in the outer periphery of the hearth floor. In this way, material fed in at the top furnaces moves alternatively across the hearth floors until it is discharged from the floor of the bottom hearth.

The initial heat for startup is provided by gas- or oil-fired burners mounted in the sides of the hearths. When the proper furnace temperature has been attained, the auxiliary fuel can be turned off. Combustion air admitted through the cold burners is then used to ignite the evolving wood gases; air entry is regulated to maintain furnace temperatures at 900° to 1,200° F. The hot gases flow upward and across each hearth countercurrent to the flow of solid material.

Where air pollution is not a problem, the effluent gases, or **off-gases,** can be burned in stacks and vented to the atmosphere. Adjustable doors in the base of the stacks admit the proper amount of air for burning. Under this condition the stacks emit a lick of flame and light smoke of intensity approximating a ringelmann number of 2. There is also a trace of fly ash emitted. Where pollution codes are strict, the gases are induced by a fan through a chamber for afterburning, water scrubbed to remove particulate matter, and vented to a stack.

Where there are requirements for steam, the pollution problem can be solved and requirements for other fuels reduced by means of a waste heat boiler. Approximately 20,000 to 25,000 lb. of steam per hour can be generated for every ton of charcoal produced. The boiler need not depend entirely on the off-gases. An automatic control system can be installed that will burn oil or gas to compensate for a diminishing or complete shut-off of the waste gas flow.

Charcoal exiting from the furnace at about 1,000° F. is cooled in a paddle cooler by water sprays and the water jacketing on the cooler. These sprays are controlled automatically by a temperature regulator set for a given charcoal temperature. Charcoal to be briqueted is usually hammer-milled. A charcoal storage tank with a holding capacity adequate for 2 or 3 days is usually provided.

Multiple-hearth furnaces are made in several standard sizes. Small units have four hearths about 21 feet in diameter and have a capacity of 1 ton of charcoal per hour. The larger units have six hearths about 26 feet in diameter and will produce 2 to 2½ tons of charcoal per hour. These capacities assume that the particulate fuel as fired has a moisture content of 45 percent of the green weight (82-percent moisture content on a dry weight basis). If the water content of the fuel is 60 percent of the green weight (150-percent moisture content on a dry weight basis), these productive capacities will be halved to about ½ and 1¼ tons of charcoal per hour respectively.

The furnace can operate on any wood waste or combination of wood waste if the material is hogged to uniform size to promote even carbonization. As the furnace must operate without interruption, fuel storage adequate for several days' operation should be maintained; fuel can be conveyed automatically from storage to furnace. About 100 tons (ovendry basis) of fuel per day is required for the smallest economical operation.

Schubert's (1969) description of studies leading to installation of a Herreshoff multiple-hearth furnace to manufacture charcoal (plus off-gases for boiler fuel) from southern pine particulate residues should be helpful to anyone considering such an installation.

Briqueting equipment.—Because charcoal from particulate southern pine residues is not in lump form, it is briqueted for sale on the consumer market. Briqueting equipment is available for production rates from about 1 to 10 tons per hour. According to one manufacturer, the investment required (1970) for a briqueting plant with a capacity of 1 ton per hour is $500,000; such a plant requires eight men on the fi.st shift, two on the second, and two on the third. Briquets are made 24 hours per day, but packaging, warehousing, and shipping are performed only during the day shift.

The charcoal is first hammermilled or crushed to pass a ⅛-inch or smaller screen aperture, and then moved to a surge bin for metered flow to a paddle mixer in which 9 to 10 percent (by weight) of corn-, milo-, or wheat-starch binder is added before transfer to the forming press.

The wet-formed briquets (30- to 35-percent moisture content) are then passed through a continuous tunnel dryer. Retention time in the dryer varies from 4.5 hours in a small unit to 2.5 hours in the larger plants; about 25 percent of this time is devoted to cooling the briquets. The dry (5-percent moisture content) briquets are then bagged and stored for shipment.

Assuming a charcoal cost of $33 per ton, total costs per ton of bagged briquets has been computed by one equipment manufacturer to vary from $80 per ton for a 1-ton-per-hour plant, to $64 per ton for a 6-ton-per-hour operation.

CHARCOAL ANALYSIS

The USDA Forest Products Laboratory (1961, p. 116) has published a recommended procedure for analyzing charcoal from wood; typical results from unbriqueted charcoal (not from southern pine) by this method were as follows:

Component	Portion by weight
	Percent
Moisture	1.8— 2.8
Volatile	12.0—27.0
Ash	1.9— 4.5
Fixed Carbon	70.7—83.6

A limited sample of charcoal briquets manufactured from southern pine residues was found to have heat of combustion of about 12,335 B.t.u. per ovendry pound when evaluated in an oxygen bomb calorimeter. (See table 9–8.)

ACTIVATED CARBON

Not all charcoal is sold on the consumer market. An industrial product of considerable importance is **activated carbon,** an amorphous form of carbon which is treated to give it a very large specific surface area (300 to 2,000 m.^{2}/g.). To achieve this large surface area, the internal pore structure in the particles is highly developed; it is this structure that gives activated carbon the ability to adsorb gases, vapors from gases, and dissolved or dispersed substances from liquids. Two types of activated carbon are manufactured. Liquid phase (decolorizing) carbons are generally light, fluffy powders; gas phase (vapor adsorbent) carbons are hard, dense granules or pellets (Doying 1964, p. 149).

The details covering the manufacture and applications of activated carbon are beyond the scope of this text. For a review of the subject, see Doying (1964, pp. 149-158). To assist prospective manufacturers in locating technical information, a few additional citations are listed.

Manufacture of activated carbon from lignocellulosic materials	Applications of activated carbon
Hirota et al. (1944)	Beebe and Stevens (1967)
Schumacher and Heise (1944)	Koppe (1967)
Adler (1945)	Lee (1964)
Heller (1946)	Eliason and Tchobanoglous (1968)
Hormats (1946)	Kuzin (1968)
Stoneman (1946)	Mattia and Weiss (1969)
Yoshimura and Murakami (1953)	Slack (1969)
Kishimoto and Kono (1954)	
Puri et al. (1954)	
Tanaka and Tachi (1954)	
Hanzawa and Satonaka (1955, p. 439-463)	
Singh et al. (1958)	
Seth (1965)	
Ketov and Shenfel'd (1968)	
Moores (1969)	
Siedlewski and Majewski (1969)	

28–5 STEROIDS AND PROTEINS

It is possible that commercial systems may one day more fully utilize southern pine chemical and protein extracts (Stanley 1969). Prior to World War II the isolation of steroids from southern pine was merely of academic interest (Hall and Gisvold 1936); in 1968, however, Russia erected the first industrial plant producing steroids as a pulp byproduct (Nekrasova et al. 1968).

Proteins (enzymes) isolated from the living wood of slash pine have been applied to synthesize microlevels of cellulose and polyglucan-like polymers in a test tube (Stanley 1966; Stanley and Thomas 1968). While of academic interest today, the idea may be of wider interest in the future.

28–6 LITERATURE CITED

Anonymous.
1950. Bark-chipped, acid-treated turpentine butts found suitable for pulpwood. J. Forest. 48: 99.

Adler, R.
1945. Activated carbon and method of producing same. (U.S. Pat. No. 2,377,063.) U.S. Pat. Office, Wash., D.C.

Agnello, L. A., and Barnes, E. O.
1960. Tall oil. Ind. and Eng. Chem. 52: 726–732.

Ball, F. J.
1962. Mineral fiber mat formation. (U.S. Pat. No. 3,056,708) U.S. Pat. Office, Wash., D.C.

Barnes, E. O., and Taylor, M. L.
1958. The naval stores and tall oil industries. TAPPI 41(8): 16A, 18A, 20A, 22A.

Beebe, R. L., and Stevens, J. I.
1967. Activated carbon system for wastewater renovation. Water & Wastes Eng. 4(1): 43–45.

Beglinger, E.
1958. Distillation of resinous wood. USDA Forest Serv. Forest Prod. Lab. Rep. 496 rev., 8 pp.

Bengtson, G. W., and Schopmeyer, C. S.
1959. A gum yield table for ¾-inch, acid-treated streaks on slash pine. USDA Forest Serv. Southeast. Forest Exp. Sta. Res. Note 138, 2 pp.

Bennett, F. A., and Clutter, J. L.
1968. Multiple-product yield estimates for unthinned slash pine plantations—pulpwood, sawtimber, and gum. USDA Forest Serv. Res. Pap. SE–35, 21 pp. Southeast. Forest Exp. Sta., Asheville, N.C.

Berguis, F.
1937. Conversion of wood to carbohydrates and problems in the industrial use of concentrated hydrochloric acid. Ind. and Eng. Chem. 29: 247–253.

Borgfeldt, M. J.
1964. Cationic bituminous emulsions. (U.S. Pat. No. 3,126,350) U.S. Pat. Office, Wash., D.C.

Bourke, N., and Dorman, K. W.
1946. Florida spray gun for pine tree gum flow stimulation. Fla. Eng. and Ind. Exp. Sta. Bull. 10, 36 pp.

Burkart, L. F.
1969. Pulping of lignocellulosic material with a reaction product of triethyleneglycol and organic acid. (U.S. Pat. No. 3,442,753) U.S. Pat. Office, Wash., D.C.

Burkart, L. F.
1970. Process for separating lignin from vegetable material using a mixture of triethyleneglycol and arylsulfonic acids. (U.S. Pat. No. 3,522,230) U.S. Pat. Off., Wash., D.C.

Cary, A.
1928. How the growth of trees in height and diameter is affected by working for naval stores. Nav. Stores Rev. and J. Trade 38(27): A–G.

Casebier, R. L., Hamilton, J. K., and Hergert, H. L.
1969. Chemistry and mechanism of water prehydrolysis on southern pine wood. TAPPI 52: 2369–2377.

Cederquist, K. N.
1952. Some remarks on wood hydrolyzation. In The production and use of power alcohol in Asia and the Far East, pp. 193–198. Tech. Assistance Admin. and Econ. Comm. for Asia and the Far East. N.Y.: United Nations.

Clements, R. W.
1960. Manual, modern gum naval stores methods. USDA Forest Serv. Southeast. Forest Exp. Sta., 29 pp.

Clements, R. W.
1967. Composition and method for stimulating flow of pine gum. (U.S. Pat. No. 3,359,681.) U.S. Pat. Office, Wash., D.C.

Clements, R. W., and Collins, D. N.
1950. Larger turpentine cups prove more efficient without effect on product yields or grade. Nav. Stores Rev. 60(13): 16–18.

Clements, R. W., and Harrington, T. A.
1965. Gum naval stores from plantations. In A guide to loblolly and slash pine plantation management in Southeastern USA, pp. 199–210. Ga. Forest Res. Counc. Rep. 14.

Dahlberg, B. L., and Guettinger, R. C.
1956. The white-tailed deer in Wisconsin. Wis. Conserv. Dep. Tech. Wildlife Bull. 14, 282 pp.

Derfer, J. M.
1963. Flavor and perfume chemicals from sulfate turpentine. TAPPI 46: 513–517.

Derfer, J. M.
1966. Flavor oils from turpentine. TAPPI 49(10): 117A–120A.

Doying, E. G.
1964. Carbon (activated carbon). In Kirk-Othmer Encycl. Chem. Technol. Ed. 2, Vol. 4, 937 p.

Drew, J., and Pylant, G. D.
1966. Turpentine from the pulpwoods of the United States and Canada. TAPPI 49: 430–438.

Durham, R. M.
1969. Feeding mesquite wood as a maintenance ration for beef cattle. In Wood utilization, pp. 36–41. Proc. Annu. Meeting Mid-South Sect. Forest Prod. Res. Soc.

Dyer, C. D.
1963. Naval stores production for extra forest income. Univ. Ga. Agr. Ext. Serv. Bull. 593 rev., 28 pp.

Eichmeyer.
1943.   [Experiences with the use of fir needles as fodder in Norway.] Mitt. Landwirt. 58: 382.

Eliassen, R., and Tchobanoglous, G.
1968.   Advanced treatment processes. Chem. Eng. 75(22): 95–99.

Ellenberger, W., and Waentig, P.
1918.   [The digestibility of the crude fiber of wood.] Dtsch.   Landwirthsch. Presse 45(31): 195–196.

Enos, H. I., Jr., Harris, G. C., and Hedrick, G. W.
1968.   Rosin and rosin derivatives. In Kirk-Othmer Encyclopedia of chemical technology. Ed. 2, Vol. 17, pp. 475–508.

FAO.
1954.   Proceedings of the Sixth Meeting of the FAO Technical Panel on Wood Chemistry. 169 pp. Rome.

FAO.
1960.   Working party on wood hydrolysis. Final Rep. 2nd Meeting. FAO. Rome.

Feist, W. C., Baker, A. J., and Tarkow, H.
1970.   Alkali requirements for improving digestibility of hardwoods by rumen micro-organisms. J. Anim. Sci. 30: 832–835.

Fernow, B. E.
1892.   Strength of "boxed" or "turpentine"   timber. USDA Forest. Div. Circ. 8, 3 pp.

Fontaine, F. E.
1941.   The fermentation of cellulose and glucose by thermophilic bacteria. PhD. Thesis. Univ. Wisconsin. Madison. 55 pp.

Gallagher, F.
1969.   Use of the multiple hearth furnace in the production of charcoal from wood waste. In Wood residue utilization, pp. 13–20. Third Tex. Ind. Wood Seminar.

Gerry, E.
1922.   Oleoresin production: a microscopic study of the effects produced on the woody tissues of southern pines by different methods of turpentining. USDA Bull. 1064, 46 pp.

Goldblatt, L. A.
1951.   Chemicals we get from turpentine. In Crops in peace and war, pp. 815–821. USDA Yearbook Agr. 1950–51.

Goldblatt, L. A., and Palkin, S.
1941.   Vapor phase thermal isopinene. J. Amer. Chem. Soc. 63: 3517–3522. merization of α- and β-

Goldblatt, L. A., and Palkin, S.
1947.   Process for converting nopinene to myrcene. (U.S. Pat. No. 2,420,131.) U.S. Pat. Office, Wash., D.C.

Goos, A. W.
1952.   The thermal decomposition of wood. Wood Chem. 2: 826–851.

Gruschow, G. F.
1950.   Acid-treated   turpentine butts yield quality saw timber. South. Lumber J. 54(7): 84–85.

Hägglund, E.
1951.   Chemistry of wood. 631 pp. N.Y.: Academic Press.

Hair, D., and Ulrich, A. H.
1969.   The demand and price situation for forest products, 1968–1969. USDA Misc. Pub. 1086, 74 pp.

Hall, J. A., and Gisvold, O.
1936.   Chemistry of slash-pine (Pinus caribaea, Morelet). II. Fats, waxes, and resins of the growing tips. J. Biol. Chem. 113: 487–496.

Hanzawa, M., and Satonaka, S.
1955.   Carbonization of wood by dehydrating agent. I. On the preparation and the decolorizing power of the hydrated active charcoal from wood. Hokkaido Univ. Res. Bull. 17, 997 pp.

Harper, V. L.
1937.   The effect of turpentining on the growth of longleaf and slash pine. USDA Forest Serv. South. Forest Exp. Sta. Occas. Pap. 64, 4 pp.

Harper, V. L.
1944.   Effects of fire on gum yields of longleaf and slash pines. USDA Circ. 710, 42 pp.

Harrington, T. A.
1966a.   The future of gum naval stores. Nav. Stores Rev. 25[75]11: 4–6, 18.

Harrington, T. A.
1966b. Using acid paste—a new gum production technique. AT–FA J. 28(8): 9–11.

Harrington, T. A.
1968. Mechanized gum naval stores. Nav. Stores Rev. 78(3): 6–7, 11.

Harrington, T. A.
1969. Production of oleoresin from southern pine trees —a review. Forest Prod. J. 19(6): 31–36.

Harris, E. E.
1945. Industrial alcohol from wood waste. S. Lumberman 171(2153): 244–247.

Harris, E. E.
1949. Wood saccharification. In Advances in carbohydrate chemistry. Vol. 4, pp. 153–188. N.Y.: Academic Press.

Harris, E. E.
1950. Hydrolysis of wood for stock feed. USDA Forest Serv. Forest Prod. Lab. Rep. R1731 rev., 6 pp.

Harris, E. E., Beglinger, E., Hajny, G. J., and Sherrard, E. C.
1945. Hydrolysis of wood: treatment with sulfuric acid in a stationary digester. Ind. Eng. Chem. 37(1): 12–23.

Harris, J. F., Saeman, J. F., and Locke, E. G.
1963. Wood as a chemical raw material. In The chemistry of wood, pp. 535–585. B. L. Browning, ed. N.Y.: Interscience Publ.

Heaney, D. P., and Bender, F.
1970. The feeding value of steamed aspen for sheep. Forest Prod. J. 20(9): 98–102.

Heller, O.
1946. Activated carbon. (Brit. Pat. No. 583,113.)

Herty, C. H.
1903. A new method of turpentine orcharding. USDA Bur. Forest. Bull. 40, 43 pp.

Hirota, K., Takano, T., Taniguichi, K., and Iguchi, K.
1944. [Utilization of the bark of Manchurian white birch.] J. Soc. Chem. Ind. 47: 922–929. Kokyo, Japan.

Honcamp, F.
1929. Die naturalichen pflanzlichen Futtermittel. In Handbuch der Ernährung und des Stoffwechsels der Landwirtschaftlichen Nutztiere, pp. 266–347. Vol. 1, E. Mangold, ed. Verlag Von Julius Springer, Berlin.

Hormats, S.
1946. German process for manufacture activated charcoal. Chem. and Met. Eng. 53(6): 112–114.

Joye, N. M., Jr., and Lawrence, R. V.
1967. Resin acid composition of pine oleoresins. J. Chem. and Eng. Data 12: 279–282.

Ketov, A. N., and Shenfel'd, B. E.
1968. Electron paramagnetic resonance of birch activated charcoal. Zh. Khim. 42: 2104–2105.

King, D. B., Wagner, H. B., and Goldsborough, G. H.
1962. The outlook for naval stores. 89 pp. USDA.

Kishimoto, S., and Kono, K.
1954. Studies on charcoal. VII. On charcoal materials for carbon. J. Jap. Forest. Soc. 36: 228–231.

Kobayashi, T., Sakai, Y., and Iizuka, K.
1960. Hydrolysis of cellulose in a small amount of concentrated sulfuric acid. Bull. Agr. Chem. Soc. Jap. 24: 443–449.

König, I.
1919. [Ingredients of wood and their economic utilization.] Fühlings Landwirthsch. Ztg. 68(19/20): 361–369.

Koppe, P.
1967. [Investigations concerning the competitive adsorption on activated charcoal in drinking water treatment.] Gesundheits-Ingenieur 88(10): 312–317.

Kuzin, I. A.
1968. [Use of activated charcoals for purifying inorganic compounds.] Zh. Vses Khim. Obshchest. 13(5): 551–557.

Lawrence, R. V.
1942. Removal of metallic contaminants from pine oleoresin. Ind. and Eng. Chem. 34: 984–987.

Lawrence, R. V.
  1946. Process for refining oleore-
      sin. (U.S. Pat. No.
      2,411,925.) U.S. Pat.
      Office, Wash., D.C.

Lawrence, R. V.
  1951. The industrial utilization of
      rosin. *In* Crops in peace
      and war, p. 822–826.
      USDA Yearbook Agr.
      1950–51.

Lawrence, R. V.
  1969. Naval stores products from
      southern pines. Forest
      Prod. J. 19(9) : 87–92.

Lee, D.
  1964. Elimination of gaseous sur-
      face contamination. Sur-
      face   Contamination
      Symp.   Proc.   1964:
      251–255.   Gatlinburg,
      Tenn.

Leker, J. E.
  1969. Utilization of hardboard
      residues. *In* Wood utiliza-
      tion, pp. 50–54. Proc.
      Annu.   Meeting   Mid-
      South Sect. Forest Prod.
      Res. Soc.

Lloyd, R. A., and Harris, J. F.
  1955. Wood hydrolysis for sugar
      production. USDA Forest
      Serv. Forest Prod. Lab.
      Rep. R2029, 13 pp.

Locke, E. G., and Garnum, E.
  1961. FAO technical panel on
      wood chemistry: working
      party on wood hydrolysis.
      Forest   Prod.   J.   11:
      380–382.

Locke, E. G., Saeman, J. F., and Dick-
    erman, G. K.
  1945. Production of wood sugar
      in Germany and its con-
      version to yeast and alco-
      hol. U.S. Dep. Com.
      Offic. Pub. Board Rep.
      7736. 119 pp.

Loeblich, V. M., Baldwin, D. E.,
    O'Connor, R. T., and Lawrence,
    R. V.
  1955. Thermal isomerization of
      levopimaric   acid.   J.
      Amer. Chem. Soc. 77:
      6311–6313.

McConnell, N.C.
  1963. Operating instructions for
      cleaning and distillation
      of pine gum. USDA Agr.
      Res. Serv. Publ. 687, 3 p.
      S. Util. Res. & Develop.
      Div. Nav. Stores Lab.,
      Olustee, Fla.

Mattia, M. M., and Weiss, B. M.
  1969. Process for concentrating
      organic material from an
      equeous stream. (U.S.
      Pat. No. 3,448,042.) U.S.
      Pat. Office, Wash., D.C.

Mirov, N. T.
  1961. Composition of gum tur-
      pentine of pines. USDA
      Tech. Bull. 1239, 158 pp.

Moores, G. T.
  1969. Improvements in or relat-
      ing to the manufacture of
      carbonised   materials.
      (Brit.   Pat.   No.
      1,162,141) The Pat. Off.,
      London.

Nehring, K., and Schramm, W.
  1949. Digestibility   of   various
      kinds of cellulose by rum-
      inants. Tierzucht 1: 11.

Nekrasova, V. B., Agranat, A. L., and
    Solodkii, F. T.
  1968. [Some results of the opera-
      tion of an experimental-
      industrial   arrangement
      for   phytosterol   collec-
      tion.] Les. Zh. 11(2):
      124–126.

Olson, F. R., Peterson, W. H., and
    Sherrard, E. C.
  1937. Effect of lignin on fermen-
      tation of cellulosic mate-
      rials. Ind. and Eng.
      Chem. 29: 1026–1029.

Oshima, M., Kusama, J., and Ishii, T.
  1959. Process for saccharification
      of   cellulose-containing
      material. (U.S. Pat. No.
      2,900,284.) U.S. Pat.
      Office, Wash., D.C.

Ostrom, C. E.
  1945. History of the gum naval
      stores industry. Chemurg.
      Dig.   4(13):   217,
      219–223.

Ostrom, C. E., True, R. P., and Schop-
    meyer, C. S.
  1958. Role of chemical treatment
      in stimulating resin flow.
      Forest Sci. 4: 296–306.

Palmer, R. C.
  1930. Producing   naval   stores
      from waste wood. Chem.
      and Met. Eng. 37:
      289–292.

Palmer, R. C., and Edelstein, E.
  1944. Resinlike   product   and
      method of preparing
      same. (U.S. Pat. No.
      2,346,994.) U.S. Pat.
      Office, Wash., D.C.

Panshin, A. J., Harrar, E. S., Bethel, J.
    S., and Baker, W. J.
  1962. Forest   products—their
      sources, production, and
      utilization. Ed. 2, 538 pp.
      N.Y.: McGraw-Hill Book
      Co., Inc.

Patton, E. L., and Feagan, R. A., Jr.
1943. Operation of the Olustee Naval Stores Station process of gum refining. Nav. Stores Rev. 52(41): 12.

Pearl, I. A., and Gregory, A. S.
1959. Review of chemical utilization. Forest Prod. J. 9: 85–99.

Pickett, O. A., and Schantz, J. M.
1934. New uses for naval stores products. Ind. and Eng. Chem. 26: 707–710.

Pohle, W. D., and Smith, W. C.
1942. Ester gums from rosin and modified rosins. Ind. and Eng. Chem. 34: 849–852.

Pridgen, A.
1921. Turpentining in the south Atlantic country. *In* Naval stores: history, production, distribution and consumption, pp. 101, 103–104. (Thomas Gamble, ed.) Savannah, Ga.: Review Publishing & Printing Company.

Puri, B. R., Laklanpal, M. L., and Gupta, P. C.
1954. Preparation of activated charcoal by phosphoric acid treatment. J. Indian Chem. Soc., Ind. & News Ed. 17(1): 35–38.

Ryberg, M. E., and Burney, H. W.
1949. Research in equipment for the production of gum naval stores. Fla. Eng. and Ind. Exp. Sta. Tech. Pap. 32, 20 pp.

Ryberg, M. E., Burney, H. W., and Clements, R.
1949. A new type of gutter for bark-chipped trees. Nav. Stores Rev. 58(52): 14, 27.

St. Clair, W. E., and Lawrence, R. V.
1951. Metal resinates and method of preparation. (U.S. Pat. No. 2,572,071.) U.S. Pat. Office, Wash., D.C.

St. Clair, W. E., and Lawrence, R. V.
1952. Fused zinc resinates from aldehyde-modified rosin. Ind. and Eng. Chem. 44: 349–351.

Sanderman, W.
1960. Naturharze - terpentinol - tallöl. Chemie und technologie. 483 pp. Berlin: Springer Verlag.

Sarjeant, P. T.
1966. Lignin-containing resin binder. (U.S. Pat. No. 3,285,801) U.S. Pat. Office, Wash., D.C.

Savard, J.
1962. [Wood hydrolysis.] Drevarsky Vyskum 3: 205–222.

Schaal, O.
1935. Present status of the Scholler-Tornesch procedure for saccharification of cellulose. Cellulosechemie 16: 7–10.

Schneider, E. O., Chesnin, L., and Jones, R. M.
1968. Micronutrients—the "fertilizer shoe-nails." IV. The elusive nutrient-iron. Fert. Solutions 12(4): 18–20, 22, 24.

Schöller, H.
1939. Saccharification of wood with dilute acid under pressure. Chim. Ind. Agr. Biol. 15: 195–202.

Schopmeyer, C. S.
1947. New acid sprayer. Nav. Stores Rev. 57(29): 14, 28.

Schopmeyer, C. S.
1955. Effects of turpentining on growth of slash pine: first-year results. Forest Sci. 1: 83–87.

Schubert, S.
1969. From pipe dream to on stream. *In* Wood utilization, pp. 1–9. Proc. Annu. Meeting Mid-South Sect. Forest Prod. Res. Soc.

Schulerud, C. F., and Doughty, J. B.
1961. Reactive lignin-derived products in phenolic, high-pressure laminates. TAPPI 44: 823–830.

Schunacher, E. A., and Heise, G. W.
1944. Activated carbon catalyst bodies and their preparation and use. (U.S. Pat. No. 2,365,729.) U.S. Pat. Office, Wash., D.C.

Scott, R. W., Millett, M. A., and Hajny, G. J.
1969. Wood wastes for animal feeding. Forest Prod. J. 19(4): 14–18.

Sellers, H. G., and Doyle, W. C.
1968. Production of synthetic pine oil. (U.S. Pat. No. 3,415,893.) U.S. Pat. Office, Wash., D.C.

Seth, G. K.
1965. Application of activated carbon in water treatment processes. Environ. Health 7(1): 44–48. India.

Siedlewski, J., and Majewski, R.
  1969. Studies on the preparation
        of activiated carbons of
        various porous structure.
        Przem.   Chem.   48:
        360–363.
Singh, D. D., Parkash, S., and Puri, B.
  R.
  1958. Steam activation of char-
        coal in relation to its sur-
        face oxygen complexes
        and surface behavior. In-
        dian J. Appl. Chem. 21:
        187–192.
Slack, J. G.
  1969. Sewage effluent treatment
        for water recovery. Ef-
        fluent & Water Treat. J.
        9(5): 257–261.
Smith, W. C., Reed, J. O., Vietch, F.
  P., and Shingler, G. P.
  1941. Process for gum refining.
        (U.S.   Pat.   No.
        2,254,785.) U.S. Pat.
        Office, Wash., D.C.
Snow, A. G., Jr.
  1944. The use of chemical stimu-
        lants to increase gum
        yields in slash and lon-
        gleaf pines. USDA Forest
        Serv. South. Forest Exp.
        Sta. Occas. Pap. 106, 36
        pp.
Snow, A. G., Jr.
  1948a. Effect of sulfuric acid on
        gum yields from slash
        and   longleaf   pines.
        USDA   Forest   Serv.
        Southeast. Forest Exp.
        Sta. Tech. Note 68, 35
        pp.
Snow, A. G., Jr.
  1948b. Turpentining and poles.
        South. Lumberman 177
        (2225): 276, 278–279.
Stamm, A. J., and Harris, E. E.
  1954. Chemical processing of
        wood. 595 pp. N.Y.:
        Chemical   Publishing
        Company, Inc.
Stanley, R. G.
  1966. Biosynthesis of cellulose
        outside of living tree.
        Forest Prod. J. 16(11):
        61–68.
Stanley, R. G.
  1969. Extractives of wood, bark
        and needles of the south-
        ern pines—a review. For-
        est Prod. J. 19(11):
        50–56.
Stanley, R. G., and Thomas, D. des S.
  1968. Cellulose biosynthesis in a
        pine cambium extract.
        Abstr. Amer. Chem. Soc.
        A–92.
Stonecipher, W. D.
  1955. Turpentine. Encycl. Chem.
        Technol. 14: 381–397.
Stoneman, A. C.
  1946. Manufacture of activated
        carbon. (U.S. Pat. No.
        2,402,304.)   U.S.   Pat.
        Office. Wash., D.C.

Tanaka, K., and Tachi, I.
  1954. Studies on active charcoal.
        II. Preparation of active
        carbon by steam process,
        and in a furnace with ad-
        mission of air. Wood Res.
        12: 1–8. Kyoto, Japan.
Taylor, H. T., Jr.
  1968. Engineered system for col-
        lecting gum naval stores.
        Proc., Forest Eng. Conf.
        ASAE Pub. PROC–368,
        pp. 52–53.
U.S. Department of Agriculture
  1969. Naval stores annual reports
        1968–1969. USDA Sta-
        tistical Reporting Serv.,
        Crop. Reporting Board,
        Washington, D.C. 10 pp.
USDA Forest Products Laboratory.
  1961. Charcoal production, mar-
        keting, and use. USDA
        Forest Serv. Forest Prod.
        Lab. Rep. 2213, 137 pp.
USDA Forest Service.
  1935. A naval stores handbook
        dealing with the produc-
        tion of pine gum or oleo-
        resin. USDA Misc. Pub.
        209, 201 pp.
USDA Forest Service.
  1962. Wood charcoal and bri-
        quetting producers in the
        Midsouth. USDA Forest
        Serv. South. Forest Exp.
        Sta. South. Forest Surv.
        Progr. Rep. 8, 7 pp.
USDA Forest Service.
  1963. Charcoal and charcoal bri-
        quette production in the
        United   States,   1961.
        USDA Forest Serv. Div.
        Forest Econ. and Market-
        ing Res., 33 pp.
Virtanen, A. I., and Nikkilä, O. E.
  1946. Cellulose fermentation in
        wood-dust. Suomen Kem-
        istil. 19B(½): 3–4.
Weiner, J.
  1959. Tall oil. Bibliogr. Ser.
        133–135. Ed. 3, 450 pp.
        Appleton, Wis.: Inst.
        Pap. Chem.
Weiner, J., and Byrne, J.
  1968. Sizing of paper. Bibliogr.
        Ser. 165. Ed. 2, Suppl. 2,
        131 pp. Appleton, Wis.:
        Inst. Pap. Chem.
Wise, L. E., and Jahn, E. C., (Ed.).
  1952. Wood chemistry. Vol. 1,
        ed. 2, 688 pp. N.Y.:
        Reinhold Publishing Cor-
        poration.
Yoshimura, F., and Murakami, M.
  1953. Active charcoal. II. Car-
        bonization of cellulose
        with certain chemicals. J.
        Chem. Soc. Jap., Ind.
        Chem. Sect. 56: 97–98.
Zachary, L. G., (Ed.).
  1965. Tall oil and its uses. 136
        pp. N.Y.: Training Serv-
        ices Division, Dodge.

29
Measures and yields of products and residues

CONTENTS

29

Measures and yields of products and residues[1][2]

29–1 UNIT OF MEASURE

Wood-using industries employ a variety of units to measure southern pine trees and logs. Pulpwood dealers have historically used stacked measure—the cord or related unit; lumber manufacturers have preferred the board foot. As the industry has moved toward whole-tree utilization, however, measures of total or bark-free volume (cubic feet) and of weight (pounds) have become increasingly popular; this trend is likely to continue

Since wood is a variable material, and much of it is produced in irregular shapes, all units provide more or less imperfect approximations of intrinsic value. Applicability of measuring systems to specific situations must often be determined by experience. Even more variable are estimates of wood yield, which are additionally affected by factors specific to individual sites, stands, and processes. The data on product and byproduct yields are presented as best available approximations—yields in specific situations can be determined accurately only by local studies.

THE CORD

A **standard rough cord** occupies 128 gross cubic feet and is ordinarily comprised of 4-foot-long **rough** (bark in place) roundwood stacked into a pile or rick 4 feet high, 4 feet wide, and 8 feet long; a rick of any dimension that contains 128 cu. ft. of wood, bark, and airspace, however, is considered a standard cord. The word cord, if it appears unmodified in this text, refers to the standard rough cord of 128 cu. ft.

Because southern pine pulpwood is commonly cut about 5 feet in length, numerous wood procurement programs in the South are based on nonstandard units. The most prevalent of these are defined as follows:

---

[1] Acknowledgment is due David L. Williams and William C. Hopkins whose publication (Williams and Hopkins 1969) included most of the information contained in this chapter. For convenient reference, all tables are grouped at the end of the chapter.

[2] Some abbreviations are used throughout the chapter as follows:

M b.f.—Thousand board feet.

D.b.h.—Tree diameter at breast height, i.e., 4.5 feet above ground outside bark

D.o.b.—Diameter outside bark.

D.i.b.—Diameter inside bark.

Scaling diameter—Log diameter inside bark at small end.

1. The 160-cu. ft. **long cord** comprised of 5-foot rough bolts stacked in a rick 4 feet high and 8 feet long.

2. The **168-cu. ft. unit** of 5-foot 3-inch rough bolts stacked in a rick 4 feet high and 8 feet long. According to Forest Farmers Association (1966), one of these units is equivalent in volume to 1.315 standard cords.

3. The **200-cu. ft. unit** of straw-piled rough bolts 5 feet 3 inches long.

Volume of solid wood in a cord.—The volume of solid bark-free wood in a standard rough cord is most if the wood is compactly piled, thin barked, short, well trimmed, straight, and of large diameter (figs. 29–1, 29–2; tables 29–1, 29–2). Airspace in a cord of southern pine may range from 14 to 40 percent; 25 percent is about average. Bark may occupy 13 to 16 percent of the gross space. Solid wood content ranges from 56 to 94 cu. ft. per cord. The average for loblolly pine is about 76 cu. ft.; longleaf, which has less tendency to be crooked and rough, averages about 85. Measure-

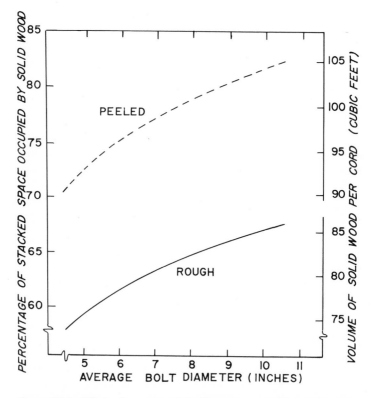

Figure 29–1.—Effect of average bolt diameter on solid wood content (exclusive of bark) of stacked, 4-foot, rough and peeled, loblolly pine pulpwood. The diameter indicated on the abscissa was measured inside bark on the peeled wood and outside bark on the rough wood. (Drawing after MacKinney and Chaiken 1946, p. 19.)

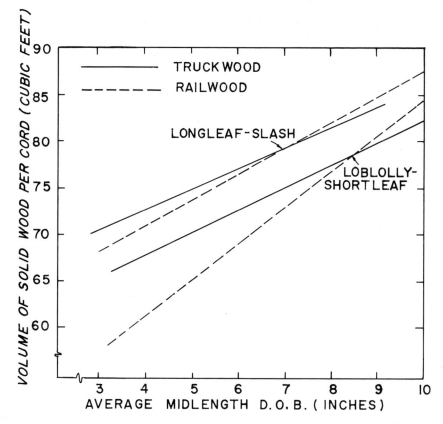

Figure 29–2.—Effect of transport method, species, and average bolt diameter on solid wood content of standard rough cords of southern pine pulpwood scaled at the receiving point. (Drawing after Williams and Hopkins 1969, p. 10.)

ments of 50,000 cords of southern pine by one mill averaged 76.7 cu. ft. of wood, 16.2 cu. ft. of bark, and 35.1 cu. ft. of airspace.

In 1964-1965 larger timber went into southern pine pulpwood in the Midsouth than in 1950, resulting in increased wood content per cord (81 compared to 75 cu. ft.) ; the west Gulf region averaged 82 cu. ft. per cord in 1965 compared to 80 cu. ft. in the east Gulf region in 1964 (Van Sickle 1966).

The usual minimum diameter at the small end of pulpwood sticks is 3.5 inches inside bark; the average maximum diameter for southern pine pulpwood is about 22 inches, although some mills frequently process bolts up to 30 inches. Increasing demand for plywood bolts and widespread adoption of the chipping headrig are likely to divert material of these maximum diameters to other uses.

A cord of large bolts contains more solid wood than a cord of small bolts. Large bolts tend to come from lower bole positions and are straighter and more nearly free of trimmed branches and protruding knots than small bolts;

the smooth surface of bolts from butt logs more than offsets the thick bark associated with lower bole positions (fig. 29–1).

A cord of wood cut from open-grown, limby trees has less solid wood content than wood from well-pruned trees, and a cord of tops and branches has less solid content than one of stemwood; cords of loblolly pine from thinnings have been reported to contain 82 cu. ft. of solid wood, whereas cords from mixed tops and thinnings had only 74 (Forbes 1961).

Data from different tests on the relationship of diameter and form to solid wood content are difficult to reconcile. Table 29–1, while comparing reasonably well with figure 29–2 (both based on midlength d.o.b.), shows considerably more solid wood content in cords of longleaf pine pulpwood than does table 29–2 (based on midlength d.i.b.).

A stacked cord of long sticks has less solid wood than one of short sticks, e.g., piled 5-foot pulpwood contains about 1.5 percent less solid wood per cord than the same timber cut to 4-foot lengths and piled (Williams and Hopkins 1969, p. 7). Kraft mills in the Southeast generally specify 63-inch lengths, whereas Appalachian mills and mills west of the Mississippi call for 60-inch wood because of more limited railroad clearances. In general, groundwood mills request 48-inch lengths. As the move toward tree-length logging progresses, these patterns are likely to change.

Hand-stacked wood is compact and usually has a higher solid wood content than mechanically stacked wood. Cordwood in transit may settle to yield increased solid wood content when rescaled at the receiving point; railwood, especially in small sizes, reportedly settles more than wood shipped by truck (fig. 29–2).

Number of pieces per cord.—The number of pieces in a standard rough cord is obviously a function of bolt diameter and length, irregularities in the bolts, and compactness of the pile. Table 29–2 indicates that only 14 longleaf pine bolts 4 feet long and 16 inches in diameter (inside bark) are required to make a cord, whereas 128 pieces 5 inches in diameter are needed.

For pulpwood of better than average straightness and surface smoothness, table 29–3 shows the number of rough bolts required to make a standard cord, as a function of both bolt length and midlength d.i.b.; e.g., 152 4-foot-long, 5-inch bolts are required, whereas only twenty 6-foot-long, 12-inch bolts are needed.

Veneer cores approach the ultimate in straightness and surface smoothness; the number of 4-foot veneer cores required to make a cord is of interest because this number should represent the upper limit for extremely straight and smooth, bark-free pulpwood (table 29–4).

A cord of peeled southern pine wood contains 7 to 18 percent more solid wood than a rough cord (Williams and Hopkins 1969, p. 9). Information on bark volumes can be found in section 29–3 (see equation 29–27).

Number of trees required per cord.—The number of southern pine trees required to yield a standard rough cord depends on tree diameter, height, and form. For rough approximations, the *Service Foresters Handbook* (USDA Forest Service 1970) gives the following tabulation.

D.b.h.	Trees per cord
Inches	*Number*
5	46
6	21
7	15
8	10
9	8
10	6
11	5
12	4

Table 29–5 relates the number of southern pine trees required per standard rough cord to the number of bolts per tree (a measure of tree height) and to tree diameter; table 29–6 provides an estimate of the number of merchantable bolts contained in loblolly pine trees of various diameters and total heights.

Table 29–7, in addition to tree height and diameter effects, includes the effect of stem taper, i.e., **form class,** on tree volume.

$$\text{Form class} = (100) \left[\frac{\text{D.i.b. at top of 16-foot butt log}}{\text{D.b.h.}} \right] \qquad (29\text{–}1)$$

According to Mesavage and Girard (1956, p. 5), second-growth southern pines have an average form class of 78, ranging from about 65 for small, branchy, old-field pines to about 83 for older trees growing in dense stands.

Readers interested in the 168-cu. ft. unit rather than the standard cord will find table 29–8 useful.

Cords of topwood per tree after removal of saw logs.—Substantial volumes of pulpwood can be cut from the tops residual after southern pine saw logs are removed. The pulpwood yield per tree may be as little as 0.01 cord from large trees (whose tops are too rough for pulpwood) to as much as 0.06 cord from 9-inch trees on which several usable bolts are available above the point where diameter is too small for saw logs (table 29–9).

Cords per acre.—When entire stands are converted to pulpwood, the yield is proportional to basal area and total tree heights as follows (Minor 1943a):

Average tree height	Volume per square foot of basal area
Feet	*Cords*
30	0.14
40	.18
50	.24
60	.30
70	.34
80	.37

Alternately, cordwood volume per acre can be computed from knowledge of the number of trees per acre and the height of the tallest trees. An acre with but 400 trees of 25-foot maximum height contains only 0.3 cord, whereas an acre with 1,000 trees of 50-foot maximum height has about 34 standard rough cords (table 29–10).

THE BOARD FOOT—LUMBER SCALE

Traditionally, southern pine lumber was sawn to correspond to nominal thickness in inches and designated by thickness in quarter-inches, e.g., 4/4, 6/4, and 8/4 corresponded to 1-, 1.5- and 2-inch-thick rough green boards. Rough green boards were also sawn to even widths of 4, 6, 8, 10, and 12 inches. A **board foot (lumber scale)** is the volume of wood in a 1-foot length of a 12-inch, 4/4 board; alternatively, it could be defined as a 1-foot length of a 6-inch, 8/4 board or any other combination that would yield a similar volume.

Boards retain their green board foot measure, regardless of reductions in width and thickness during drying and planing. If resawn to yield two pieces of equal thickness, however, each resulting piece is tallied at half the board foot measure of the original piece.

In 1970, U.S. Department of Commerce Standard (PS 20–70) stipulated that manufacturers must produce green framing lumber to one schedule of sizes and dry lumber to another schedule of slightly smaller sizes. The two schedules are based on average shrinkage of commercial lumber as established by the USDA Forest Products Laboratory. The schedules follow:

Nominal thickness	Actual dressed thickness		Nominal width	Actual dressed width	
	Sold dry	Sold green		Sold dry	Sold green
	— — — — — Inches — — — — — — — — — — — —			Inches — — — — — — —	
4/4	3/4	25/32	2	1½	1 9/16
5/4	1	1 1/32	3	2½	2 9/16
6/4	1¼	1 9/32	4	3½	3 9/16
8/4	1½	1 9/16	5	4½	4 5/8
10/4	2	2 1/16	6	5½	5 5/8
12/4	2½	2 9/16	8	7¼	7½
14/4	3	3 1/16	10	9¼	9½
16/4	3½	3 9/16	12	11¼	11½

As virtually all southern pine lumber 8/4 and thinner is sold dry, the new smaller sizes apply; as a result, 8/4 lumber is now sawn a scant 1⅞ inches thick, and 4/4 lumber is sawn approximately ⅞-inch thick. Obviously, reductions in green board thickness increase the yield from each log. In this chapter, however, information on yield of sawn lumber (tables 29–39, 29–40, and 29–50), is all based on the original concept of the board foot, i.e., a 1-foot length of rough green board, 1 full inch thick, and a full 12 inches wide.

THE BOARD FOOT–LOG SCALE

Numerous scaling procedures, i.e., **log scales,** have been developed to estimate the board foot (lumber scale) yield of logs. Application of log scales can only approximate lumber yield from logs because individual scalers differ in precision of measurement and because sawmills vary widely in efficiency of lumber recovery. Schumacher and Jones (1940) discussed general development of empirical log rules applicable to particular mills; in the paragraphs that follow, specific formulae are presented.

Most widely used in the South are the Doyle, Scribner Decimal C, and International ¼-inch log scales. Log diameter, usually measured inside bark at the small end, and log length are the primary determinants of log content.

Doyle log scale.—The Doyle log scale is defined as follows:

$$V = \frac{L(D - 4)^2}{16} \tag{29-2}$$

To facilitate linear programming studies, Grosenbaugh (1952, p. 12) expressed the Doyle log scale as a regression equation:

$$V = 0.0625D^2L - 0.500DL + 1.000L \tag{29-3}$$

where:

$V =$ volume, board feet
$D =$ scaling diameter, inches
$L =$ scaling length, feet

Gross board foot volumes in logs as computed by the Doyle scale (equation 29–2) are shown in tables 29–11 and 29–12. For a given scaling diameter, volumes of 8-foot logs are half those shown in table 29–12.

Gross log scale may be reduced because of defects in logs. The reductions (board feet) are calculated by selecting the diameter-related factor tabulated below (Forbes 1961, p. 1.62), and multiplying it by the appropriate value from table 29–15.

Scaling diameter	Factor
Inches	
8 to 11	0.6
12 to 13	.8
14 to 20	.9
21 to 31	1.0
32 to 40	1.1

Actual scaling practices differ widely from textbook scales. Some deviations occurring in the application of log rules are: giving logs 8 inches or less in diameter their length in feet as the board foot value; rounding scaling diameters to the nearest inch; and including various bark thicknesses in the diameter measurement. A modification of the Doyle rule, to include one bark thickness in the diameter, gives upward bias of:

Scaling diameter	Upward bias
Inches	*Percent*
6	20.0
9	10.7
12	9.2
15	8.4
18	1.8

Errors may be introduced by scaling to even inches. If measurements are always rounded downward—i.e., logs 12.0 to 12.9 inches tallied as exactly 12 inches—the average downward bias for the Doyle rule is (Row and Guttenberg 1966):

Scaling diameter	Downward bias
Inches	*Percent*
6	35.9
9	17.3
12	11.5
15	8.6
18	6.8

Scribner Decimal C log scale.—Scribner did not base his log scale on a formula; instead he drew circles of different diameters and plotted the ends or cross sections of boards which might be sawn within each circle, computed the board cross sectional area in square inches, divided this value by 12 to get board feet per foot of log length, and finally, multiplied by the log length. As a result of this method of computation, values for successive inch classes increase in an irregular manner. In the Scribner Decimal C rule, the last figure in the scale of a log is rounded to the nearest 10 (e.g., a log scale of 114 bd. ft. is rounded to 110). Log contents according to the Scribner Decimal C log scale are shown in table 29–13.

Grosenbaugh (1952, p. 12) expressed the Scribner scale in a regression equation as follows:

$$V = 0.0494D^2L - 0.124DL + 0.269L \qquad (29\text{–}4)$$

To compute the contents of 16-foot logs (table 29–14) according to the Scribner scale, the following equation is useful:

$$V = 0.79D^2 - 2D - 4 \qquad (29\text{–}5)$$

In these equations,

V = volume, board feet
D = scaling diameter, inches
L = scaling length, feet

Gross log scale may be reduced because of defects. Appropriate deductions (board feet) can be read from table 29–15 if the length and cross sectional area of the defects are known.

International ¼-inch log scale.—This formula-based scale accounts for taper in logs by evaluating them in 4-foot lengths. Content of a log is computed by summing the contents of the 4-foot lengths comprising it and assuming that taper increases diameter ½-inch in each 4 feet of log length. Saw kerf is assumed to be ¼-inch. The formula for each 4-foot length of log is as follows:

$$V = 0.905 \ (0.22D^2 - 0.71D) \qquad\qquad (29\text{–}6)$$

Log contents computed from this formula are usually rounded to the nearest 5 bd. ft. as shown in table 29–16.

Row and Guttenberg (1966) expressed the International ¼-inch log scale as a regression expression containing both scaling diameter and length, as follows:

$$V = 0.0498D^2L - 0.185DL + 0.0422L + \qquad (29\text{–}7)$$
$$0.00622DL^2 + 0.000259L^3 - 0.0116L^2$$

To compute the contents of 16-foot logs by scaling diameter in tenths of an inch (table 29–17), the following equation for the International ¼-inch log scale is useful:

$$V = 0.796D^2 - 1.375D - 1.230 \qquad\qquad (29\text{–}8)$$

For 8-foot logs (table 29–17):

$$V = 0.905 \ (.44D^2 - 1.20D - 0.3) \qquad\qquad (29\text{–}9)$$

In these equations:

V = volume, board feet
D = scaling diameter, inches
L = scaling length, feet

Gross log scale may be reduced by deductions (board feet) computed by selecting the diameter-related factor tabulated below (Forbes 1961, p. 1.62), and multiplying it by the appropriate value from table 29–15.

Scaling diameter	Factor
Inches	
8 to 14	1.2
15 to 19	1.1
20 to 36	1.05

Gross volume in trees.—At least one-third—and in less than three-log trees more than half—the board foot volume in southern pine trees, as measured by the International ¼-inch log scale, is in the butt log; for form class 78, which is typical of southern pine trees, the volume distribution is as follows (Rothacher 1948) :

	Number of 16-foot logs								
Log position	1	1.5	2	2.5	3	3.5	4	4.5	5
	– – – – *Percent of total tree volume* – – – –								
Butt_____	100	74	59	52	47	41	39	34	33
Second_____		26	41	36	33	30	29	27	26
Third_____				12	20	21	20	20	19
Fourth_____						8	13	14	14
Fifth_____								5	8

Mesavage and Girard (1956) have reported the amount of taper typical of 16-foot logs taken above the butt log (Table 29–18) ; in general, taper is minimum in the second log of tall trees (about 1 inch) and maximum in the sixth log (4 to 5 inches).

Tables 29–19, 29–20, and 29–21 give board foot volumes of southern pine trees of form class 78 as measured by the three major log scales. Merchantable height, applicable to these three tables, includes that portion of a tree from stump height to a point on the stem at which merchantability for sawtimber is limited by branches, deformity, or minimum diameter. For smooth stems this minimum diameter is usually not less than 60 percent of tree diameter breast high in the case of the smallest (10-inch) saw log trees, or 40 percent for large trees 30 to 40 inches in diameter. If height measurements include small tops of old-field southern pines, the tables will overscale. Tree volumes for form classes other than 78—considered average for southern pine—can be found in Mesavage and Girard (1956).

Table 29–22 relates crown diameter and total height visible in aerial photographs to board foot volume per tree (International ¼-inch scale).

THE CUBIC FOOT

While the cord and board foot (log scale) are convenient units of volume, they are indirect and only approximate measures of actual cubic volume.

Cubic feet in logs.—Many cubic foot scales are based on formulae that mathematically transform logs and bolts into equivalent true cylinders. Volumes, therefore, are computed by multiplying log length by cross-sectional area. The principal variation among cubic foot scales is in the method of computing cross-sectional areas of logs and trees.

Row and Guttenberg (1966) have provided a regression equation for cubic volume of wood in southern pine logs based on the assumption that logs are segments of cones tapering 1 inch in diameter for every 8 feet of log length, and that there is no allowance for trim. The equation follows:

$$V = kD^2L + \frac{kDL^2}{8} + \frac{kL^3}{192} \qquad (29\text{–}10)$$

where:

V = volume, cubic feet

D = scaling diameter, inches

L = log length, feet

$$k = (4)\,\frac{\pi}{12^2} = 0.005454 = \text{constant for converting } D^2 \text{ to cross-sectional area in square feet}$$

Equation 29–10 more closely estimates volume of solid wood (table 29–23) than do simpler methods of computing cubic volume.

Gross scale may be reduced if defects are visible; defect-associated cubic footage can be computed from the cross-sectional area and length of defects and deducted from the tabulated values.

Cubic feet in individual trees.—Gross cubic foot volumes (inside bark) based on length and form class (equation 29–1) of merchantable stems have been published by Mesavage (1947); table 29–24, applicable to form class 78, gives values typical of southern pine trees.

Burns (1965) and MacKinney and Chaiken (1946) have published tabulations of merchantable cubic volume (inside bark) based on total tree height of southern pines (tables 29–25, 29–26). Table 29–25 is a condensation of Minor's (1950) form class volume table. For timber estimates it is often convenient to measure enough trees to establish a curve relating diameter to average height. Average volumes by diameter classes are then interpolated from the table for the appropriate form class to prepare a local volume table. Merrifield and Foil (1967) confirmed that Minor's tables were accurate for use with southern pine.

Minor (1953b) developed a cubic foot volume table for use in interpreting aerial photographs of southern pine saw log timber (except longleaf pine); it provides a rough estimate of tree volume inside bark for low-density, even-aged stands or for all-aged stands (table 29–27).

Since southern pine stands with trees of small diameter are marketable, volume tables for bark-free wood, with error estimates, have been developed for small loblolly, shortleaf, and Virginia pines in upland areas and for small loblolly, slash, and longleaf on the southern Coastal Plain. The equations following are generally applicable to trees 8 inches or less in diameter. For young pines in the southern Coastal Plain (Schmitt and Bower 1970):

Pine species	Equation	Standard error	
Slash	$V = 0.02408 + 0.0021058(D^2H)$	0.10633	(29–11)
Loblolly	$V = .03789 + .0020911(D^2H)$	.10693	(29–12)
Longleaf	$V = .02855 + .0020404(D^2H)$	.03192	(29–13)

For young pines in the upper South Carolina Piedmont (Goebel and Warner 1962):

| | | Correlation |
| Pine species | Equation | coefficient |

Loblolly $V = 0.03371 + 0.0196128 \left(\dfrac{D^2H}{10} \right)$ 0.9882   (29-14)

Shortleaf $V = -.00489 + .0206058 \left(\dfrac{D^2H}{10} \right)$ .9891   (29-15)

Virginia $V = .02056 + .0218664 \left(\dfrac{D^2H}{10} \right)$ .9932   (29-16)

In the equations:

V = volume without bark, cubic feet
D = d.b.h., inches
H = total tree height, feet

For young shortleaf and loblolly pines in Tennessee, Potts (1952) developed data on volume without bark (table 29-28).

Hawes (1940), USDA Forest Service (1969), and Romancier (1961) have provided information on cubic volumes of merchantable stems including bark (tables 29-29, 29-30, and 29-31).

Cubic feet in tops.—Tops of sawtimber are utilized for pulpwood; Mesavage (1947) has provided information to estimate their cubic volume (table 29-32) as a function of **top form index**—defined in the table. High, medium, and low values for this index in southern pine are 85, 75, and 67 respectively.

THE POUND

While the weight of a cubic foot of southern pine wood varies with its moisture content (sec. 8-1), ovendry extractive-free specific gravity (ch. 7), and extractive content (sec. 6-3), gross weight is for loggers and many wood users a convenient and equitable measure of value. Conversion of weights to conventional volume measurement is difficult both because of this variation and because the irregularity of tree sections makes volume calculation difficult.

Weight of a standard rough cord.—Table 7-1 shows the weight of a cubic foot of southern pine wood as a function of specific gravity and moisture content. Table 8-1 gives an estimate of tree moisture contents by species, and table 7-4 unextracted tree specific gravity by species. With this knowledge, plus an estimate of the cubic foot content of solid wood (tables 29-1, 29-2, figures 29-1 and 29-2) and bark (table 29-2, col. 4) in a cord, it should be possible to compute an approximate weight for cordwood of any species. The specific gravity of bark is given in chapter 12.

Williams and Hopkins (1969, p. 46) give the following average values for a 128-cu. ft. cord; these are not computed values, but are weights reportedly in use by industry.

Pine species and region	Green weight per standard rough cord
	Lb.
Loblolly-shortleaf	
Texas and west Louisiana _____	4,700
Central Louisiana and throughout the Southeast ___	5,200
Longleaf-slash	
Throughout range _____	5,200

Figure 29–3 shows regional variation in the weight of cordwood; weights and locations shown were selected because they state purchasing practice or the results of weight studies.

Weight of saw logs.—The weight of saw logs can be computed from general knowledge of unextracted specific gravity and moisture content together with bark volume and specific gravity as previously noted for cordwood. The variable form of logs makes such computations difficult, however. Schumacher (1946) was among the first to explore volume-weight ratios. Row and Guttenberg (1966) reviewed the effects of log taper, log shape, trim allowance, bark volume and specific gravity, and wood moisture content and specific gravity; they concluded that total log weight was best expressed by an equation of the following form:

$$W = a_1 D^2 L + a_2 D L^2 + a_3 L^3 \qquad (29\text{–}17)$$

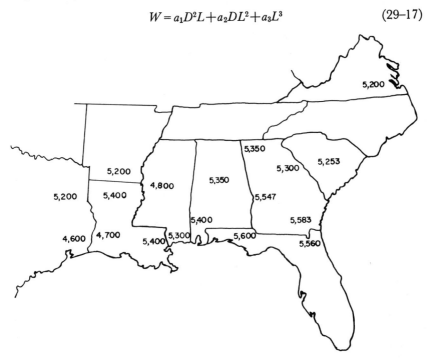

Figure 29–3.—Regional variation in the weight (pounds) of a green standard rough cord of southern pine pulpwood. (Drawing after Williams and Hopkins 1969, p. 48.)

where

W = log weight, pounds

D = scaling diameter, inches

L = scaling length, feet

a_1, a_2, and a_3 = constants determined by regression analysis of weights of sample logs.

Southern pine log weights determined by direct measurements (table 29–33) have been published by Page and Bois (1961) and Barton (1966). A nomograph devised by Davis (1963) also facilitates quick estimation of the weights of various-length logs in the diameter range from 6 to 19 inches (fig. 29–4).

Weight by merchantable stems.—Relatively few studies have been made of total stem weights. Curtis (1966) sampled over 900 trees in north Florida along the Gulf of Mexico about 55 miles south of Tallahassee; while longleaf, loblolly, sand, slash, and spruce pines were studied, only the

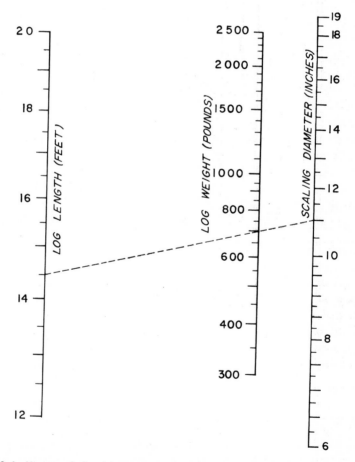

Figure 29–4.—Nomograph for determination of southern pine log weights. (Drawing after Davis 1963 based on data provided by Siegel and Row 1960.)

equations for slash pine were published, as follows:

Equation	R^2	
$Y_1 = 0.145X_1 + 2.501X_2 - 60.3$	0.985	(29–18)
$Y_2 = 0.012X_1 + 0.619X_2 + 15.7$	.908	(29–19)
$Y_3 = -1.788X_3 - 0.099X_4 + 0.777$	.461	(29–20)
$Y_4 = (Y_1 - Y_2)(Y_3)$	—	(29–21)

where:

Y_1 = weight of rough green limbed tree stem to 2-inch top outside bark, pounds

Y_2 = weight of green bark to 2-inch top, pounds

Y_3 = weight of ovendry peeled tree stem ÷ weight of peeled green stem

Y_4 = weight of ovendry wood in tree stem, pounds

X_1 = (d.b.h., inches)^2(total tree height, feet)

X_2 = tree age, years

X_3 = reciprocal of X_2

X_4 = reciprocal of specific gravity of breast-height increment core, ovendry weight and green volume basis

Weights of merchantable stems of slash pine planted in the Carolina Sandhills are given in table 29–34. From this table it is seen that, including bark, a green slash pine stem of 10-inch d.b.h. to a 2-inch top outside bark weighs 997 lb. if the tree is 70 feet in total height. This compares to a value of 1,055 lb. computed from equation 29–18 for a north Florida tree of the same dimensions (assuming a tree age of 40 years).

Loblolly and shortleaf pine stems from north Louisiana and Arkansas have green weights (including bark) to a 6-inch top inside bark as shown in table 29–35. Data relating total tree height and d.b.h. to weight of wood and bark have been published by Romancier (1961) for plantation-grown loblolly pine in Georgia (table 29–36).

Weight of lumber.—Estimated lumber weights for all standard items are included in grade books for southern pine, e.g., Southern Pine Inspection Bureau (1970, pp. 198-199). The tabulated values are not actual weights, however, but are used in computing delivered prices per M b.f. of lumber in freight movements. Railroads base their transportation charges to the shipper on actual lumber weights, which are generally less than the estimated weights tabulated in grade books.

Accurate weights per M b.f. lumber scale can be computed by multiplying the appropriate weight per cubic foot (from table 7–1) by the actual cubic foot content of 1,000 bd. ft. of lumber.

PRIMARY UNITS—A NEW MEASUREMENT CONCEPT

Access to electronic computers and dendrometers has enabled foresters to avoid many of the difficulties associated with traditional units of measure. Grosenbaugh (1954) found that the products derivable from trees or logs can be closely approximated in terms of aggregate cubic volume, surface area and length, or less accurately in terms of aggregate weight and length. He proposed and developed computer programs (Grosenbaugh 1967ab, 1968), for systems in which felled or standing tree inventory data are sampled with varying probability and measured in terms of these primary units. Essentially, such timber estimates require physical or optical segmenting of tree stems into sections of irregular length but each reasonably homogeneous as to quality and defect, and the measurement, by calipers, diameter tape, or precision dendrometer, of sectional diameters and lengths. Volumes and surface areas, along with lengths, are computer-accumulated by species, quality, and defect classes.

Local product-yield studies can relate these aggregates of primary units to actual outturn and value for a specific operation, and can provide estimates of costs and residues at any desired stage of the manufacturing process. At the same time, estimates can be cheaply made in terms of outmoded traditional units for accounting or other purposes.

Although not yet widely employed, this concept could greatly improve the accuracy of product estimation wherever a wide range of size, defect, or value classes is involved.

CONVERSION TABLES

The foregoing paragraphs describe the content of logs and trees in terms of cords, board feet, cubic feet, and pounds. Since all of these units of measure are in widespread use, conversion data are useful; some tables for this purpose follow.

Cords to cubic feet.—Tables 29–1 and 29–2 with figures 29–1 and 29–2 provide data to convert cords to cubic feet.

Cords to board feet log scale.—Cordwood volume should not be expressed in terms of board foot log scale unless the cordwood is comprised of bolts large enough for lumber manufacture, i.e., more than 6 inches in diameter. According to the *Service Foresters Handbook* (USDA Forest Service 1970, p. 6), the following conversion factors permit cords to be approximately expressed in terms of board foot log scale.

Cords per Mb.f. log scale

Tree d.b.h.	Int'l ¼	Scribner	Doyle
Inches			
8	4.0	4.4	6.8
9	3.7	4.1	6.8
10	3.4	3.8	6.8
11	3.2	3.6	6.3
12	2.9	3.4	6.2
13	2.7	3.2	5.2
14	2.5	3.0	4.5

Cords to board feet lumber scale.—To make this conversion, it is first necessary to convert cord volume to cubic foot volume as previously explained. Then, according to Bruce and Schumacher (1935, p. 160), 5 to 7 bd. ft. can be cut from each cubic foot of cordwood; the ratio depends on the cordwood diameter as follows:

Diameter at small end	Bd. ft. (Int'l ¼ log scale) per cu. ft.
Inches	
6	4.9
7	5.5
8	6.0
9	6.4
10	6.7

In many mills, lumber yield closely approaches International ¼-inch log scale.

Cords to weight.—The weight of a cord of southern pine pulpwood is discussed in a previous subsection, THE POUND, and summarized in figure 29–3.

Log volume in board feet by various log scales.—Log volumes in terms of one scale can be converted to another by use of previously tabulated board foot scales, values in table 29–37, and the following procedures by Lane and Schnur (1948).

To convert International volume to Doyle or Scribner, multiply the International volume by the percentage (from table 29–37) for the desired scale, log diameter, and length. Example: Given 1,000 bd. ft., International volume, in 14-inch logs 12 feet long, what is the Doyle volume?

$$1,000 \ (0.77) \ = \ 770 \text{ bd. ft., Doyle volume}$$

To convert Doyle or Scribner volume to International, divide the Doyle or Scribner volume by the percentages for the given scale, log diameter, and length. Example: Given 1,000 bd. ft., Doyle volume, in 16-inch logs 10 feet long, what is the International volume?

$$1,000 \ \div \ 0.83 \ = \ 1,205 \text{ bd. ft. International}$$

Doyle volume can be converted to Scribner, or vice versa, by first changing to International and then to the desired scale, using the above procedures.

Dollar values per unit volume in terms of one scale can be converted to another scale by substituting dollar values for log volumes in the above procedures and by dividing where multiplying is indicated and vice versa. Example: Given a number of logs 16 inches in diameter and 12 feet long, worth $100.00 per M b.f. International scale, what is an equal value by the Doyle scale per M b.f.?

$$\$100.00 \ \div \ 0.82 \ = \ \$121.95$$

Tree volume in board feet by various log scales.—Tree volumes in terms of one log scale can be converted to another log scale by application of the conversion factors given in table 29–38.

Board feet log scale to board feet lumber scale.—The amount of lumber actually sawn from a log in excess of the log scale is expressed as **overrun.**

$$\text{Percent overrun} = (100)\left[\frac{\text{Bd. ft. lumber yield} - \text{Bd. ft. log scale}}{\text{Bd. ft. log scale}}\right]$$

$$(29\text{–}22)$$

Overrun is greatly influenced by width and thickness of the product, accuracy of manufacture, thickness of saw kerfs, and ability of the sawyers and edgermen. Data in table 29–39, from "better-than-average" mills producing a specific product mix, are an indication of the approximate overrun that can be expected when sawing a mixture of full thickness (1 inch for 4/4 and 2 inches for 8/4) boards and dimension pine lumber.

It is difficult for many mills, particularly those using wide-kerf saws, to saw full thickness lumber equivalent to log scale as measured by the International ¼-inch log scale.

The Doyle scale, however, yields substantial overruns, particularly on small logs. The Scribner scale yields overruns intermediate to the other two log scales.

Overrun data reflecting the new lumber size standards of 1970 (U.S. Department of Commerce Standard PS20–70), and accompanying changes in mill cutting practices, were not available when this manual was prepared.

In a study of overruns in six mills cutting the four major southern pine species plus pond pine, Yandle (1968) tabulated lumber overrun per tree scale as a function of tree diameter (table 29–40). The tree overrun (or underrun) was expressed as the percentage difference between the total lumber volume tallied per tree and the sum of the individually scaled logs from each tree (see equation 29–22). Headsaws in the mills studied generally had ¼-inch saw kerf; some mills had band resaws with thinner kerfs.

Board feet log scale to cubic feet.—Table 29–41 presents cubic foot volume per M b.f. by log scale for 8- and 16-foot logs. The Doyle scale disregards taper, and requires more wood volume per M b.f. for the longer logs.

The first four columns of table 29–38 relate tree diameter to cubic foot content and board foot content as measured by the three principle log scales. Table 29–42 shows the number of cubic feet of wood volume per M b.f. of log scale as a function of tree diameter.

Cubic feet to board feet lumber scale.—The number of cubic feet required to yield 1,000 bd. ft. of lumber varies widely; if pieces are sawn in large sizes from large logs and if saw kerf is small, fewer than 125 cu. ft. will yield 1,000 bd. ft. of timbers; if, however, 4/4 boards are inaccurately sawn from small logs with saws taking a large kerf, more than 250 cu. ft. of logs are required to yield 1,000 bd. ft. of lumber. Table 29–41 shows the cubic footage of wood required to yield 1,000 bd. ft. International ¼-inch log scale according to log diameter and length; these values could also be used for lumber yield, as the International ¼-inch log scale yields close to zero overrun on a mill equipped with bandsaws.

In brief, from logs 8 to 10 inches in diameter, approximately 6 bd. ft. of lumber can be cut from each cubic foot of log volume; with logs 16 inches in diameter, the ratio increases to about 7 bd. ft. lumber scale per cubic foot.

Cubic feet to log weight.—Data are available on the cubic foot content of southern pine cordwood (tables 29–1, 29–2), logs (table 29–23), trees (tables 29–8, 29–24 through 27), and tops (table 29–32). Weight per cubic foot of green southern pine wood is extremely variable, however, because of variations in specific gravity (see ch. 7) and moisture content (see sec. 8–1). If it is assumed that most wood in living southern pines is near 100-percent moisture content and that most southern pine wood has a specific gravity (basis of ovendry weight and green volume) in the range 0.40 to 0.55, then from table 7–1:

Specific gravity O.D. wt., green vol.	Weight of green wood per cu. ft.
	Lb.
0.40	49.9
.45	56.2
.50	62.4
.55	68.7

Obviously a delay in bucking after the tree is felled will cause the wood to drop below 100-percent moisture content (fig. 20–9), as will a delay in getting wood to the weight scaling station. Also, typically, wood percentage of moisture content is inversely correlated with wood specific gravity (fig. 27–14).

To make a reasonable estimate of rough log weight based on cubic foot content of wood, one must first pick the appropriate volume inside bark from the tables, then multiply by an appropriate green density in pounds per cubic foot based on knowledge of the log source; to this product, approximately 10 percent (see equation 29–26) should be added to account for weight of the bark.

Log weight to board feet log scale.—Weights of single logs or whole truckloads can be accurately and quickly determined; less readily determined is the weight per M b.f. log scale. This is so because of species and regional variability in wood moisture content and specific gravity, and also because cubic foot content per M b.f., the primary determinant of weight varies with diameter and length of log, and with the various log scales.

Tables 29–43 and 29–44 give an indication of variability between species, log scales, and sets of test data. For example, these two tables give quite different values for the weight of a thousand board feet of loblolly pine as measured by the Scribner Decimal C scale (12, 801 and 14,900 lb.).

Bower (1961) measured 243 16-foot loblolly pine logs harvested in southern Virginia and related scaling diameter to pounds required for 1,000 bd. ft. log scale, as follows:

Scaling diameter	Log scale		
	Doyle	Scribner	Int'l ¼
Inches	– – – – – – –	*Lb./M b.f.*	– – – – – – –
8	28,000	14,900	11,500
9	22,000	13,100	10,800
10	18,600	12,200	10,300
11	16,500	11,600	10,100
12	15,000	11,100	9,900
13	13,500	10,600	9,500
14	12,100	9,900	8,900

From these data it is apparent that conversion factors between weight and Doyle scale are strongly related to diameter.

The literature, as well as logic, indicates that log weight to log scale conversion factors must be adjusted to fit particular localities. For example, Freeman (1962), in measuring shortleaf and loblolly pine saw logs cut in southeast Arkansas and northeast Louisiana, found that 1,000 bd. ft., Doyle log scale, weighed 14,038 lb. Bair (1965), however, measuring mixed southern pine saw logs in east Texas, found that log weight per M b.f., Doyle-Scribner scale, was substantially higher, as follows:

East Texas location	Log scale	
	Doyle-Scribner	Int'l ¼
	– – – *Lb./M b.f. log scale* – – –	
Sabine County (mostly bottomland)__	15,280	10,140
Angelina County (mostly upland)____	19,032	10,745

In diameters typical of southern pine saw logs there is no practical difference between the Doyle scale used by Freeman and the Doyle-Scribner scale used by Bair.

Siegel and Row (1960) provided data (table 29–45) relating log weight and diameter to the board foot (log scale) content per ton of green loblolly and shortleaf pine saw logs; the logs were cut in north Louisiana and south Arkansas in lengths from 12 to 20 feet, and about one-third were butt cuts. Barton (1966) provided similar information for mixed southern pine saw logs cut in Alabama (table 29–46); surprisingly, Barton obtained more board feet (Doyle log scale) per 1,000 lb. of long logs than per 1,000 lb. of short logs.

Table 29–33 (bottom) and 29–46 published by Barton (1966) illustrate how truckloads of logs can be weight scaled in a manner that takes into account both log length and diameter class. Obviously, tables appropriate for local conditions must be used. The steps are as follows:

1. Determine the weight of the load of logs.
2. Count the number of logs on the load.
3. Determine the length class under which the load is to be categorized.
4. Divide the number of logs into the net weight and obtain the average weight per log.
5. With the average length and weight, refer to table 29–33 (bottom) to determine the average diameter class.
6. With the average diameter and average length, refer to table 29–46 and obtain the number of board feet per 1,000 lb. for this specific average diameter and length.
7. Multiply the number of 1,000 lb. on the load by the conversion factor and obtain the board foot volume for the load of logs.

Bair (1965) and Freeman (1962) have published diameter-weight relationships that facilitate truckload scaling procedures for southern pines in east Texas and in the Louisiana-Arkansas area (tables 29–47 and 29–48).

Row and Guttenberg (1966) concluded that log length was not a major factor in the relationship between log weight and board feet log scale. The results of their analyses are summarized in the equations of table 29–49.

To facilitate widespread application of weight scaling, Row and Fasick (1966) described development of a computer program for fitting weight and scale information for single logs on loads to a proven equation form, testing of the results, and preparation of tables for practical application.

Log weight to board feet lumber scale.—This conversion can be accomplished indirectly by first converting log weight to log scale as described in the foregoing paragraphs and then computing the overrun from table 29–39.

Some data are also available to obtain lumber yield directly from log weight. Log species, diameter, and moisture content, however, strongly affect the conversion factors. The weight of saw logs required to yield 1,000 bd. ft. of lumber has been reported, according to species, as follows:

Pine species	Weight of logs to yield 1,000 bd. ft. of lumber	Citation
	Lb.	
Loblolly_____	10,890	Page and Bois (1961)
Longleaf_____	13,087	Page and Bois (1961)
Shortleaf_____	10,796	Page and Bois (1961)
Slash_____	14,191	Page and Bois (1961)
Loblolly-shortleaf_____	10,300	Guttenberg et al. (1960)

The effect of log diameter on conversion factors is substantial. Table 29–50 shows that a ton of 16-inch logs yields about twice the lumber (182 bd. ft. for slash pine) that a ton of 5-inch logs (85 bd. ft. for slash pine) yields.

Guttenberg et al. (1960) developed an equation to predict lumber yield from the weight of a truckload of loblolly and shortleaf pine saw logs 12 to 20 feet long and 6 to 20 inches in diameter, as follows (r = 0.971):

$$\text{Lumber yield, board feet} = \frac{\text{load weight in pounds}}{10.17} - 13.44 \qquad (29\text{--}23)$$

The logs were cut in southern Arkansas and northern Louisiana.

29–2 PRODUCT YIELDS AND MEASURES

Most wood products are sold by measures distinctive to the product. The paragraphs and tables in this section contain conversion information that has been found useful.

POLES

Classes of poles are described in section 11–5 and in tables 11–15 and 11–16. Board foot content of poles is given in figure 29–5 (International ¼-inch log scale) and in table 29–51 (Scribner log scale). If the values shown in table 29–51 prove inconsistent with local measurements, a volume table for local use may be constructed using the method of Hawes (USDA Forest Service 1959, p. 42) as follows:

1. Arrange poles by pole classes according to table 29–52; for each class and length determine the average pole circumference at the large end.
2. Convert each average circumference value to d.b.h.
3. Convert each d.b.h. to d.i.b. at top of first 16-foot log by assuming a suitable form class (Hawes used form class 89.)
4. From table 29–18, determine the d.i.b. for each 16-foot log (or fraction thereof) contained in the pole.
5. From table 29–14 determine the Scribner volume of each pole by summing the volumes of the logs contained in the pole. This step completes construction of the pole volume table.

The same procedure can be followed to construct similar tables based on the International or Doyle volumes, using appropriate tables from the board foot volume section.

Table 29–52 gives the weight, volume, and dimensions of the nine classes of southern pine poles.

LUMBER

The subsection, THE BOARD FOOT—LUMBER SCALE, defines the unit of measure for lumber. Data on lumber yields, by volume, are given in this chapter in paragraphs headed: *Cords to board feet lumber scale,* page 1528; *Board feet log scale to board feet lumber scale,* page 1530, (see also tables 29–39 and 29–40); *Cubic feet to board feet lumber scale,* page 1530; *Log weight to board feet lumber scale,* page 1533, (see also table

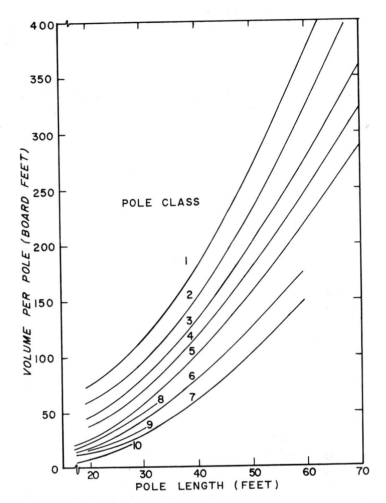

Figure 29–5.—Board foot volume of southern pine poles, International ¼-inch scale, by length and pole class. (Drawing after Williston 1957.)

29–50). Mills cutting to the new standards for lumber sizes made effective in 1970 by adoption of U.S. Department of Commerce Standard PS20–70 will obtain greater lumber yield per cord, M b.f. log scale, and ton of logs than indicated by these paragraphs.

Lumber yields, by grade, from southern pine trees and logs are described in sections 11–2 and 11–3 (see tables 11–1 through 11–13).

The weight of 1,000 bd. ft. of lumber is discussed in this chapter under the paragraph heading *Weight of lumber.*

VENEER AND PLYWOOD

Although southern pine plywood is manufactured in a variety of thicknesses from a range of thicknesses of veneer, the mensurational common denominator of the industry is 1,000 sq. ft. of ⅜-inch-thick plywood. Surface measure (square feet) of other thicknesses can be converted to ⅜-inch basis if multiplied by the following factors:

Panel thickness

Not sanded	Sanded	Factor
– – – – Inch – – – –		
⁵⁄₁₆	¼	0.8333
⅜		1.0000
⁷⁄₁₆	⅜	1.1667
½		1.3333
⁹⁄₁₆	½	1.5000
⅝		1.6667
¹¹⁄₁₆	⅝	1.8333
¾		2.0000
¹³⁄₁₆	¾	2.1667

Because log scales have been devised primarily for logs in lengths different from the 53-inch and 103-inch lengths (termed bolts or blocks) common to the plywood industry, and because veneer is cut without kerf and thin (compared to boards), the usual yield and overrun tables are not directly applicable for veneer yield computation.

Yield of veneer for ⅜-inch plywood per board foot log scale.—Guttenberg (1967) measured the amount of $1/10$-inch veneer cut from 103-inch-long southern pine bolts and related this volume to the Doyle scale of the bolts as computed by the formula $0.53125(D - 4)^2$, where $D =$ scaling diameter in inches and the constant represents bolts 8½ feet long. Bolts were peeled to a core diameter of 5.2 inches. Veneer volume from Grade 1 and 2 bolts, converted to its equivalent volume in ⅜-inch panels, was as follows:

Bolt diameter	Yield, ⅜-inch basis, per M b.f. Doyle log scale
Inches	*M sq. ft.*
10 _____	2.61
12 _____	2.75
14 _____	2.74
16 _____	2.64
18 _____	2.59
20 _____	2.54
22 _____	2.46
24 _____	2.43

Grade 3 bolts, as evaluated by the Forest Service standard grading system for southern pine yard lumber logs, had conversion ratios ranging from 3.26 M sq. ft. of panels (⅜-inch basis) per M b.f. Doyle scale for 8-inch bolts to 1.83 for 20-inch bolts.

In a study of 8-foot loblolly and shortleaf pine bolts averaging 14.8

inches in diameter, veneer yield and losses were as follows (Williams and Hopkins 1969, p. 60):

Source and class of yield	Yield
	Percent of volume
From bolts peeled on lathe	
Total veneer _____	87.1
Loss from spurs and core _____	12.9
From veneer fed into green clipper	
Usable cuts _____	57.6
Loss from clipping _____	42.4

In this study, bolts were mostly graded 2 and 3 by USDA Forest Service grades for southern pine logs; cores were 5.5 inches in diameter, and veneer was cut ⅛-inch thick.

Yield of ⅜-inch plywood per bolt.—Williams and Hopkins (1969, p. 62) assumed a 40-percent loss of veneer, including the following: 20-percent clipping loss green; 15-percent loss during drying, dry clipping, and spreading; a 5-percent loss during panel trimming. On this basis, they estimated the bolts needed for 1,000 sq. ft. of ⅜-inch plywood as follows:

	Core diameter, inches		
Bolt diameter	3	4	5
Inches		*Number of bolts*	
8	22	25	31
10	13	14	16
12	9	9	10
14	6	7	7
16	5	5	5
18	4	4	4
20	3	3	3

Lathe productivity.—Hourly output of veneer is a function of bolt revolutions per minute in the lathe, loading time, bolt diameter, core diameter, and delay time. At one plant where cores averaged 5.2 inches in diameter and delay time was about 11 minutes per hour, Guttenberg (1967) estimated hourly lathe capacity as follows:

Bolt diameter	Capacity per hour
Inches	*M b.f. Doyle scale*
8 _____	1.62
10 _____	3.13
12 _____	4.77
14 _____	6.37
16 _____	7.87
18 _____	9.21
20 _____	10.40
22 _____	11.45
24 _____	12.37

Bolts were scaled as 8.5 feet in length.

Theoretical veneer yield per bolt.—If bolts were perfect cylinders, the lineal footage of veneer produced from each would be a function only of bolt and core diameters and veneer thickness (table 29–53).

Veneer yields by grade and width.—Grade yields of veneer rotary cut from southern pine peeler bolts are described in section 11–4 and table 11–14.

Veneer is normally clipped to standard widths of 54 or 27 inches when possible; narrower veneer is clipped to random widths. **Fishtails** are pieces of veneer that are not constant width full length; they are either salvaged as 4-foot-long veneers for center plys or chipped for pulp. According to one southern pine mill, percentage of veneer volume in each width class is related to bolt diameter as follows (Williams and Hopkins 1969, p. 59):

	Veneer width			
Bolt diameter	54 inches	27 inches	Random	Fishtails
Inches	– – – – – –	*Percent*	– – – – – –	
8	0	39	35	26
9	0	36	51	13
10	5	56	25	14
11	53	19	18	10
12	42	37	15	6
13	59	13	23	5
14	50	11	28	11

Williams and Hopkins (1969, p. 60) reported that another mill peeling 8-foot loblolly and shortleaf pine bolts averaging 14.8 inches in diameter (mostly USDA Forest Service southern pine log Grades 2 and 3) obtained 29.4, 22.7, and 47.9 percent yield in 54-inch, 27-inch, and random widths of green $\frac{1}{8}$-inch veneer.

Volume in stacks of veneer.—Stacked veneer sometimes accumulates in mills and must be inventoried in terms of equivalent $\frac{3}{8}$-inch plywood. According to one mill, a 103-inch-long stack of 54-inch-wide, $\frac{1}{8}$- or $\frac{1}{10}$-inch-thick dry veneer contains enough veneer per inch of stack height to make 55.9 sq. ft. of $\frac{3}{8}$-inch plywood; a comparable figure for random-width dry veneers is 44.1.

At the same mill, stacked green veneers were equivalent to the following square footage of $\frac{3}{8}$-inch plywood per inch of stack (Williams and Hopkins 1969, p. 60):

	Veneer thickness in inches	
Veneer width	$\frac{1}{10}$	$\frac{1}{8}$
Inches	– – *Sq. ft.* – –	
54 _____	56.9	58.5
27 _____	56.9	58.5
Random _____	54.9	56.4
Fishtails _____	27.4	28.2

The foregoing conversion factors allow for normal losses during manufacture.

KRAFT PULP

According to one manufacturer, a standard rough cord of southern pine (mostly loblolly), when processed into unbleached kraft pulp, yields only 39 percent of its volume as finished pulp, as follows (Williams and Hopkins 1969, p. 64):

Product	Volume
	Percent
Bark removal_____	11
Fiber lost during debarking_____	2
Chips lost_____	1
Cooking rejects_____	7
Lignin and hemicelluloses in spent liquor_____	40
Unbleached kraft pulp_____	39
	100

Pulp yields vary with the pulp process and grade, among mills, and according to the species, specific gravity, and age of trees from which the pulpwood is cut. Not reproduced here, but of interest to some readers, is an alignment chart developed by Perry and Wang (1958) for estimating yield of dry kraft pulp from single slash pine trees. Williams and Hopkins (1969, p. 64), in a survey of the southern pine kraft industry, noted that average loss of pulp volume attributable to bleaching is 6 percent; ovendry chips or cordwood required to make 1 ton of pulp at 6-percent moisture content were estimated as follows:

Product	Requirements per ton of pulp	
	Cordwood	Ovendry chips
	Standard rough cords	*Tons*
Unbleached kraft pulp _____	1.63	1.76
Unbleached kraft dissolving pulp _____	1.72	1.89
Bleached kraft pulp _____	1.85	2.04

In response to the survey by Williams and Hopkins (1969, p. 65), one manufacturer expressed dry pulp yields as a percentage of the ovendry weight of chips pulped, as follows:

Product	Midsouth	Southeast
	– – – *Percent*	– – –
Bleached kraft pulp_____	41	45
Unbleached kraft dissolving pulp_____	43	46
Unbleached kraft pulp_____	48	49
Linerboard base stock_____	52	54

No explanation of variation by region was noted.

The amount of tall oil recovered per cord of southern pine pulped varies greatly among mills. According to Williams and Hopkins (1969, p. 65), the average in 1966 was 5.5 lb. of tall oil per cord pulped.

FIBERBOARD

One manufacturer of southern pine fiberboard roofing, who makes a 0.5-inch-thick board weighing 665 lb. per M sq. ft., and a 1-inch-thick board weighing 1,116 lb. per M sq. ft., states that 1 ton of green chips is required to make 1.26 M sq. ft. of the 1-inch board (Williams and Hopkins 1969, p. 87).

EXCELSIOR

One standard cord of southern pine pulpwood yields about 1 ton of excelsior (8-percent moisture content) with a range from 1,800 to 2,200 lb. (Williams and Hopkins 1969, p. 87).

SQUARES

According to Williams and Hopkins (1969, p. 87), 1,000 bd. ft. (Doyle scale) of southern pine logs sawn on a circle mill will provide sufficient slabs and edgings for 120 1-inch by 1-inch squares measuring 8 feet long.

29–3 RESIDUE YIELDS AND MEASURES

The southern pine industry is moving toward the goal of whole-tree utilization. Because this trend began fairly recently, reliable mensurational data on tree portions other than the stem are meager; volumetric data on manufacturing residuals are also incomplete. Changing manufacturing methods (e.g., adoption of tree shears and chipping headrigs) and changing manufacturing standards (e.g., adoption of new lumber standards calling for thinner boards) have substantially changed amounts of residuals from those reported in the older literature.

While no data specific to southern pine have been published, it is estimated that southern pine loggers leave about one-third of the total tree weight (ovendry basis) in the woods; this woods residue is comprised of tops generally smaller than 4 inches d.o.b., needles, branches, stumpwood, and rootwood.

E. T. Howard (table 13–4) provided data on weight distribution of above- and below-ground parts of three 22-year-old, 7.7-inch, unthinned, plantation-grown slash pine trees cut in central Louisiana. A summary of her data, all on an ovendry basis, follows. Root weight includes only those roots within a 3-foot radius of the stump. Total tree weight, including all above- and below-ground portions, averaged 317 pounds per tree, ovendry. Above-ground tree parts averaged 264 pounds, and weight of the bark-free stem to a 4-inch top d.o.b. averaged 186 pounds.

Fraction of weight

Portion of tree	Of total tree	Of above-ground parts	Of bark-free stem to 4-inch top d.o.b.
	– – – – – –	Percent	– – – – –
Bark-free stem_____	58 .5	70 .2	100 .0
Roots and stump_____	16 .5	19 .8	28 .2
Stem bark to 4-inch top_____	12 .5	15 .0	21 .4
Top (with bark)_____	5 .0	6 .0	8 .5
Needles_____	4 .0	4 .7	6 .7
Branches (with bark)_____	3 .5	4 .2	5 .9
Total_____	100 .0		

From these data it is seen that tree portions not currently used averaged about 41 percent of total tree weight, and about 71 percent of bark-free stem weight to a 4-inch top.

Metz and Wells (1965) have shown that the percentage of total ovendry tree weight above ground contributed by needles, stemwood, stembark, and branches of loblolly pines is a function of tree age (table 15–54). For a single 21-year-old, 46.4-foot-high loblolly pine 9.6 inches in diameter, percentages by weight were as follows:

Portion of tree above ground	Ovendry	Green
	– – – – Percent – – – –	
Needles_____	4.7	4.7
Branches_____	15.3	12.7
Stembark_____	10.0	8.0
Stemwood_____	70.0	74.6
Total _____	100.0	100.0

For 10-inch and larger loblolly pines cut in Arkansas, T. C. Carlson and D. J. Henckel (unpublished) found that needles, branches, and tops smaller than 4 inches d.i.b. comprised only 10 percent of the total ovendry weight of above-ground parts; 90 percent of the weight was in the stembark and stemwood to a 4-inch top d.i.b.

Utilization of the stem varies greatly among sawmills because of sawing equipment and practices, product mix, drying procedures, and planing mill practice. The trend toward increased production of 8/4 lumber—and diminished 4/4 board production—plus widespread adoption of chipping headrigs (see sec. 19–6)—has reduced sawdust production in some mills from as much as 22 percent of log volume to as little as 5 percent (see table 19–23).

One pulp and paper company integrated with a sawmill cutting loblolly and shortleaf pines reported the following distribution of log volume at the sawmill (Williams and Hopkins 1969, p. 77):

Utilization channel	Portion of cubic log volume
	Percent
Bark _____	5.0
Sawdust and end trim _____	16.2
Planer shavings _____	12.8
Shrinkage _____	4.6
Slabs and edgings (chippable) _____	23.0
Finished lumber _____	38.4
	100.0

Kerbes and McIntosh (1969), in a study of 138 spruce (*Picea* spp.) trees in British Columbia, Canada, measured the residues at each step of lumber manufacture. The trees ranged from 9 to 25 inches in diameter; logs were taken to a 6-inch top. Residues from this portion of the merchantable stem were expressed as percentages of the solid wood volume in the merchantable stem, as follows:

Fraction and source	Portion of bark-free merchantable stem volume
	Percent
Residue	
Logging, stem losses only _____	7.8
Sawmill, chippable _____	18.1
Sawmill, sawdust _____	17.2
Planing mill, shavings _____	14.3
Planing mill, trim ends _____	1.9
Shrinkage in kiln _____	3.9
Dry, surfaced lumber _____	36.8
	100.0

NEEDLES

As discussed in section 14–2 and shown in table 29–54, the needles of loblolly pine seedlings account for as much as 43 percent of total ovendry weight; by age 21, however, needles account for only about 5 percent of total weight of above-ground tree parts.

E. T. Howard's data on three 22-year-old slash pines (table 13–4) showed that, on an ovendry basis, needles accounted for 4.0 percent of total tree weight; they were 4.7 percent of the weight of above-ground tree parts and 6.7 percent of the weight of the bark-free stem to a 4-inch top outside bark.

TOPS AND BRANCHES

Cordwood volume to a 4-inch top (outside bark) remaining in southern pine trees after saw logs are removed varies substantially with tree size and species. Table 29–9 shows that 9-inch, two-log slash pine trees have about 0.07 cord of topwood per tree, whereas 18-inch, two- to four-log longleaf yield only 0.01 cord. Table 29–32 gives topwood volume for southern pines as a function of length of merchantable top, top form index, and scaling diameter of the top log.

Table 29–54 shows that branches of young loblolly pines comprise 12 to 24 percent of the total ovendry weight of above-ground tree parts; the two 21-year-old trees measured by Metz and Wells (1965) had branches that averaged 13.4 percent of total ovendry weight.

Loomis et al. (1966) found that the ovendry weight of branchwood (of all diameters and including bark) on shortleaf pine in southeast Missouri could be accurately estimated from tree diameter at breast height outside bark and the ratio of the live crown length to total tree height. Their values—computed from an equation that accounted for 99 percent of the variation—are tabulated as follows:

Breast height diameter	Crown ratio, percent		
	30	50	70
Inches	– – – – – – –	Lb.	– – – – – –
3	1	3	4
6	8	17	27
9	24	51	83
12	55	116	189
15	106	224	364

For 22-year-old slash pine cut in central Louisiana, E. T. Howard's data (table 13–4) showed that tops smaller than 4 inches (d.o.b.) and branches (ovendry basis and not including needles) accounted for 8.5 percent of total tree weight; they were 10.2 percent of the weight of above-ground tree parts and 14.4 percent of the weight of the bark-free stem to a 4-inch top outside bark.

STUMPS AND ROOTS

The same data from Howard (table 13–4) showed that the taproot with laterals to a 3-foot radius and stump to 6-inch height accounted for 16.5 percent of total tree weight (ovendry basis); root and stump were 19.8 percent of the weight of all above-ground tree parts and 28.2 percent of the weight of the bark-free stem to a 4-inch top outside bark.

Other than this meager information, there are no published data on the tonnage or volume of stumpwood and rootwood in 20- to 60-year-old southern pines of the various species.

BARK

By the year 2000, the cut of southern pine is expected to produce an annual harvest of over 20 million tons of green bark. In devising uses for this tonnage, it is helpful to know something of the quantities available per tree, cord, M b.f. log scale, and M b.f. lumber scale.

Bark weight and volume per tree or log.—Because bark thickness varies with species, size and age of trees, density of stand, and site conditions (see sec. 12–2), percentage of stem volume in bark varies considerably among trees. For southern pines of pulpwood size, bark volumes usually range between 12 and 24 percent and are negatively correlated with tree diameter (table 29–55).

Snow (1949), in a sample of 4 to 8 trees of each of three species, also noted that bark comprised a greater percentage of stem volume in small trees than in large.

Pine species and tree size	D.b.h.	Merchantable height	Bark portion merchantable Bark portion of total merchansable stem volume including bark	Weight of green bark per tree
	Inches	*Feet*	*Percent*	*Lb.*
Loblolly				
Saw log size_ _ _ _ _	16.3	44	18.6	306
Pulpwood size_ _ _ _	9.4	37	23.3	135
Shortleaf				
Saw log size_ _ _ _ _	15.8	54	18.4	328
Pulpwood size_ _ _ _	9.8	40	24.1	101
Virginia				
Saw log size_ _ _ _ _	14.4	50	12.0	186
Pulpwood size_ _ _ _	915	38	13.9	103

The Virginia pines sampled had less volume (about 13 percent) and weight of bark per tree than either shortleaf or loblolly. This agrees with data from Chamberlain and Meyer (1950), who found that bark comprised about 11.4 percent of the gross merchantable stem volume of Virginia pine pulpwood.

The weight and in-place green volume of stembark of spruce pine trees (to a 4-inch top outside bark) have been given by Manwiller[3] in terms of diameter outside bark at breast height (D, inches) and total tree height (h, feet), as follows (see fig. 29–6):

Volume per tree, cubic feet $= 0.0038Dh - 0.616$ (29–24)

Ovendry weight per tree, pounds $= 0.091Dh - 15.0$ (29–25)

Equation 29–24 accounted for 94 percent of the observed variation in volume, with standard error of the estimate of 0.45 cu. ft. Equation 29–25 also accounted for 94 percent of the observed variation, with standard error of the estimate of 10.6 lb.

For trees of all ages, Manwiller[3] found that spruce pine bark comprises about 10.7 percent of stem volume including bark (to a 4-inch top outside bark) and about 9.8 percent of the ovendry stem weight (including bark) as follows:

Tree age and growth rate at stump height (rings per inch)	Volume	Weight
	- - - Percent - - -	
15 years		
More than 6_____	14.1	12.2
Less than 6_____	10.8	9.7
30 years		
More than 6_____	11.2	10.1
Less than 6_____	10.0	9.5
45 years		
More than 6_____	10.0	9.5
Less than 6_____	8.2	7.9

Bark volume and weight—as a percentage of stem volume and weight—were least in fast-grown older trees; the percentages were greatest in slow-grown young trees.

Green bark weights for loblolly and shortleaf pine saw logs from southern Arkansas and northern Louisiana are given in table 29–56, based on data accumulated by Guttenberg et al. (1960) and developed in the form of a regression equation ($R^2 = 0.897$), as follows by Row et al. (1965):

W = weight of green bark, pounds

where:

$$W = 0.0639DL + 0.0176D^2L \qquad (29\text{–}26)$$
$$D = \text{log diameter inside bark at small end, inches}$$
$$L = \text{log length, feet}$$

Nine to 10-percent of the gross green weight of shortleaf and loblolly pine saw logs is bark, as follows (Row and Guttenberg 1966):

D.i.b. at small end	Log length, feet		
	12	16	23
Inches	*- - - - - - Percent - - - - - -*		
6	9.8	10.2	10.5
9	9.4	9.7	10.0
12	9.1	9.4	9.6
15	8.9	9.1	9.4
18	8.8	9.0	9.2

Metz and Wells (1965) found that in loblolly pines 7 and 21 years old, stembark comprised about 18 and 11 percent of the total ovendry weight of above-ground tree parts (table 29–54).

Unpublished data from T. C. Carlson and D. J. Henckel on Arkansas

---

[3] Manwiller, F. G. Characterization of spruce pine. USDA Forest Service, Southern Forest Experiment Station, Alexandria, La., Final Report FS–SO–3201–1.1 dated May 1, 1972.

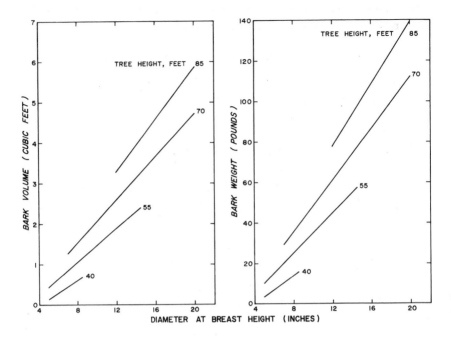

Figure 29–6.—Green volume and ovendry weight of bark on spruce pine stems to a 4-inch top (outside bark) as related to stem diameter outside bark at breast height and tree height. (Drawing after Manwiller[3].)

loblolly pine indicated that bark (ovendry) comprised 17, 14, and 11 percent of the ovendry weight of stemwood plus stembark (to a 4-inch top d.i.b.) in trees 5 inches and less, 6 to 10 inches, and 12 to 20 inches in diameter breast height outside bark.

For longleaf and slash pine saw logs cut in Georgia, Page and Bois (1961) reported that green bark averaged 9.8 and 9.9 percent, respectively, of total log weight, as follows:

D.i.b. at small end	Longleaf	Slash
	— — — *Percent* — — —	
5	10.10	------
6	10.00	11.10
7	9.90	10.65
8	9.80	10.25
9	9.75	9.80
10	9.65	9.40
11	9.60	8.95

According to Cole et al. (1966), the green weight of bark (expressed as a percentage of weight of wood and bark combined) is greater in trees of high density than low; for the two lower 5-foot bolts cut from 16- to 21-year-old trees of three species, results were as follows:

Pine species	Low-density bolts	High-density bolts
	----- Percent -----	
Loblolly_____	6.9	8.6
Longleaf_____	9.8	13.5
Slash_____	10.8	16.6

For slash pine in north Florida, the weight of green stembark (to a 2-inch top) is given by equation 29–19.

Howard (table 13–4) provided data on weight of bark from the merchantable stem (to a 4-inch top, d.o.b.) of 7.7-inch, 22-year-old slash pine cut in central Louisiana. On an ovendry basis, stembark accounted for 12.5 percent of total tree weight, 15.0 percent of weight of above-ground tree parts, and 21.4 percent of the weight of the bark-free merchantable stem.

Bark weight and volume per standard rough cord.—According to Williams and Hopkins (1969, pp. 5, 9), bark comprises about 17 percent of the solid volume including bark and about 11 percent of the gross stacked volume in southern pine cordwood. Chamberlain and Meyer (1950) developed a regression equation for stacked cordwood to predict bark volume (V) as a percent of solid volume including bark in terms of a constant (k) equal to the average ratio of d.i.b. to d.o.b. The equation follows:

$$V = 80(1 - k^2) \qquad (29\text{–}27)$$

This equation indicates that bark volume percentages are 7.8 and 22.2 for k values of 0.95 and 0.85.

Williams and Hopkins (1969, p. 83) state that weight of southern pine bark per standard rough cord is approximately 448 lb. when green and 357 lb. if ovendry. Taras (1956, p. 5) tabulated data for green bark weight per cord and per cubic foot of bark-free solid wood, by species, as follows:

Species	Green bark weight per rough cord of wood	Green bark weight per cu. ft. of solid wood
	--------- Lb. ---------	
Loblolly_____	497	6.2
Longleaf_____	716	9.0
Sand_____	450	5.2
Shortleaf_____	680	8.7
Slash_____	880	12.5

Unpublished data from T. C. Carlson and D. J. Henckel indicated that loblolly pine cut in Arkansas averaged 3.8 lb. of ovendry bark per cubic foot of bark-free, solid, green wood.

Bark weight per M b.f. log scale.—Small shortleaf and loblolly pine saw logs contain nearly ½-ton of bark (green) per M b.f. International ¼-inch log scale; large logs of the same species, however, have less than ¼-ton per M b.f. (table 29–57).

King (1952, p. 49) found that green and ovendry weights of bark per M b.f. log scale of southern pine logs cut in east Texas were as follows:

Scaling diameter of log and moisture content	Per M b.f. Doyle-Scribner log scale	Per M b.f. Int'l ¼ log scale
	– – – – – – – Lb. – – – – – – –	
7.6 to 10.5 inches		
Green_____	1,820	940
Ovendry_____	1,240	640
10.6 to 13.5 inches		
Green_____	1,200	880
Ovendry_____	800	600
13.6 to 16.5 inches		
Green_____	960	940
Ovendry_____	660	640
16.6 to 19.5 inches		
Green_____	660	660
Ovendry_____	440	440

The logs in King's study were from 8 to 20 feet in length, but were mostly 14 and 16 feet long.

Bark weight per M b.f. lumber scale.—Sixteen-foot longleaf and slash pine saw logs cut in Georgia yielded about 1 ton of bark for each M b.f. of lumber sawn from 5-inch logs compared to about ½-ton for 11-inch logs, as follows (Page and Bois 1961):

Log d.i.b. at small end	Longleaf	Slash
Inches	– – – – Lb. – – – –	
5	2,010	_____
6	1,630	1,800
7	1,400	1,660
8	1,230	1,530
9	1,120	1,390
10	1,040	1,260
11	990	1,120
Weighted average_____	1,281	1,400

Figure 29–7 relates bark tonnage per M b.f. of lumber scale, to southern pine saw log diameter as observed by Page and Saucier (1958) in Georgia.

Data comparable to that shown in figure 29–7 was published by Applefield (1958). He showed that less than 30 percent of the gross weight of a 6-inch log is converted into green rough lumber; the rest is bark, sawdust, and chippable residue; for 15-inch logs, however, nearly 50 percent of the gross weight is converted to green lumber (table 29–58).

King (1952, p. 49) found that green and ovendry weights of bark per M b. f. of green lumber sawn from southern pine logs cut in east Texas were as follows:

Scaling diameter of log	Green bark weight	Ovendry bark weight
Inches	– – – – – – *Lb.* – – – – – –	
7.6 to 10.5_____	920	620
10.6 to 13.5_____	840	580
13.6 to 16.5_____	820	560
16.6 to 19.5_____	620	420

Bark weight and volume in slabwood.—Slabwood from southern pine mills has a much higher proportion of bark (about 35 percent by volume

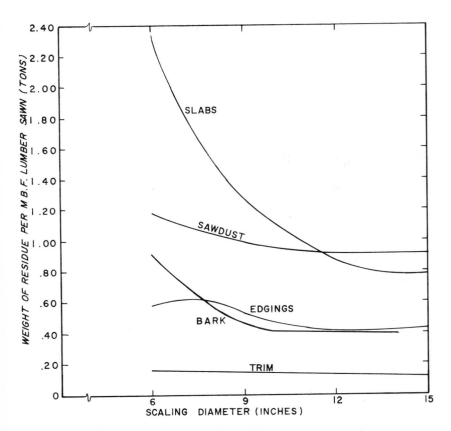

Figure 29–7.—Green weight of slabs, sawdust, edgings, bark, and trimmed board ends produced by Georgia sawmills for each M b.f. of lumber sawn. (Drawing after Page and Saucier 1958.)

and 21 percent by weight) than round pulpwood of the same species (table 29–59).

Density of bark in piles.—In piles, smooth topwood bark has greater density than rough bark from butt cuts. One study of loblolly pine bark (removed by a mechanical barker) showed that 100 lb. of green bark occupied 3.8 cu. ft.; conversely, 1 cu. ft. of green bark weighed 26.3 lb. Bark run through a hog and reduced to smaller particles (of unspecified size) weighed about 20 lb. per cubic foot when moisture content was 39 percent of the green weight (Williams and Hopkins 1969, p. 83).

Bark from drum and mechanical ring barkers has relatively little wood attached—usually less than 10 percent by weight. Bark from pole shavers (fig. 19–53), however, may contain 50 percent wood by weight.

SLABS AND EDGINGS

While virtually all sawmills in the South now remove bark from logs before sawing them, much of the published yield data on slabs and edgings reflect weights and volumes of slabs and edgings with bark attached. The newest mills equipped with both chipping headrigs and chipping edgers make neither slabs nor edgings, but instead convert their equivalent volumes directly into pulp chips (see sec. 19–6). The information under the following three paragraph headings is applicable only to sawmills with conventional headrigs and edgers, primarily those carrying circular saws.

Slab yield per M b.f. log scale.—One study at a southern pine sawmill (Williams and Hopkins 1969, p. 74) showed that yield of green bark-free slabs and edgings averaged 1.73 tons per M b.f. of logs (Doyle scale) sawn, virtually all of which could be converted into acceptable pulp chips. Each ton of rough green slabs and edgings (weighed with bark attached) yielded about 1,350 lb. of acceptable pulp chips after bark was removed.

Lehman (1958) reported that tonnage yield of green slabs, edgings, and trim from 1,000 bd. ft. of small logs sawn on a headrig with circular saw was two to five times greater than the tonnage from 12-inch logs, depending on the log scale used, as follows:

	Log scale	
Log d.i.b. at small end	Int'l ¼	Doyle
Inches	*Tons per M b.f. of logs sawn*	
7	2.2	7.2
8	1.8	4.9
9	1.6	3.3
10	1.3	2.3
11	1.1	1.7
12	1.0	1.5

Slab yield per M b.f. lumber scale.—Lehman (1958) also related tonnage of green slabs, edgings, and trim ends to the lumber tallied out of a mill equipped with a circular saw on the headrig; yields for 7-, 8-, 9-, 10-, 11- and 12-inch logs were 2.4, 2.1, 1.8, 1.6, 1.3, and 1.2 tons respectively per M b.f. of lumber sawn.

Data from Page and Saucier (1958) indicate somewhat higher tonnages; e.g., from figure 29–7, 12-inch logs yielded nearly 1.5 tons of slabs, edgings, and trim per M b.f. of lumber sawn. Sawmill equipment and sawing practice, as well as wood specific gravity and moisture content, strongly affect the tonnage yield of these residues.

Applefield (1960) compared yields of chippable residues under three systems of bark removal, i.e., debarking the whole log, debarking both slabs and edgings after removal from the log, and debarking only the slabs and not the edgings. His data showed that maximum recovery of bark-free wood (and acceptable pulp chips) resulted from debarking the entire log prior to sawing (table 29–60).

Solid wood content of slabs and edgings.—In a study of shortleaf pine residues at mills in the South Carolina Piedmont, Todd and Anderson (1955) found that an average of 1,570 lb. of green wood (728 lb. ovendry) was contained in a ton of green slabs with bark attached; a ton of green edgings with bark attached averaged 1,674 lb. of green wood (776 lb. ovendry). These yields did not vary significantly between sawmills, and only slightly with diameter of logs sawed.

Applefield (1956) observed that a standard cord of slabs (bark attached) contained 65 cu. ft. of bark-free wood, whereas a cord of edgings contained only 40 cu. ft. of wood.

Todd (1955) concluded that a standard cord of southern pine slabs averaged 79 cu. ft. of solid wood and bark and about 50 cu. ft. of bark-free wood; slabs from small logs stacked into cords contained up to twice as much wood as cords from large-log slabwood, and cords of slash pine slabs contained less wood than slabs cut from the other three major species (table 29–61).

PULP CHIPS

Yield of acceptable pulp chips per ton of green wood fed into the chipper varies with type of wood, chipper design and operation, and screen design. Data compiled by a southern kraft mill over a period of 3 months showed that about 94.5 percent of the chips received from 19 southern pine saw-mills was acceptable, as follows (Williams and Hopkins 1969, p. 80):

Chip size	Volume	Acceptability
	Percent of total	
Retained on 1-inch screen _____	3.16	Oversize
Through 1-inch screen, on ¾-inch screen _____	10.60	Acceptable
Through ¾-inch screen, on ½-inch screen _____	28.75	Acceptable
Through ½-inch screen, on ⅛-inch screen _____	55.16	Acceptable
Dust (fines and sawdust) _____	2.20	Undersize

Average bark content of these chips was 0.8 percent of total volume; chip moisture content averaged 51.9 percent of gross weight as received.

Chip yield per cord of wood.—According to Williams and Hopkins (1967, p. 78), a standard rough cord of southern pine wood yields an average of 1.2 tons of air-dry chips. A locally applicable conversion factor can be computed from knowledge of the wood cubic foot content of cordwood, weight per cubic foot of wood at various moisture contents (table 7–1), and screening losses after the wood is chipped. Screening losses should be well under 10 percent of total weight.

Chippable residue per M b.f. (log scale) sawn.—Chippable residue varies with log diameter, length, and sawing practice. An overall average for southern pine sawmills is about 1.6 tons of green chips per M b.f. (Doyle scale) of logs sawn. In a study of east Texas sawmills, Kramer (1957) observed that small logs yielded substantially more chips per board foot log scale than did large logs, as follows:

Scaling diameter	Log scale		
	Doyle	Scribner	Int'l-¼
Inches	– – – – – – – *Lb.* – – – – – – –		
7	- - -	4.8	4.3
8	9.8	4.3	3.7
9	6.6	3.7	3.1
10	4.6	3.2	2.6
11	3.5	2.8	2.2
12	2.9	2.5	1.9
13	2.5	2.2	1.7
14	2.2	1.9	1.6
15	2.1	1.7	1.5

Row and Guttenberg (1966) studied residual chip yields for loblolly and shortleaf pine saw logs from northern Louisiana and southern Arkansas. Chip yield varied with log diameter, length, and position in the tree as expressed by the following two regression equations. For butt logs:

$$W = 2.12DL - 9.75L \qquad (29\text{--}28)$$

For upper logs:

$$W = 1.63DL - 4.47L \qquad (29\text{--}29)$$

where W = weight of green chips in pounds; L = length in feet; D = log d.i.b. at small end.

Tables 29–62 and 29–63 were constructed from these equations to show chip yield per log and per M.b.f. log scale sawn.

Chip yield from plywood mills.—Guttenberg (1967) constructed a series of regression equations to predict the tonnage of green pulp chips from veneer clippings that could be expected from conversion of bolts of various grades and sizes into plywood; product yields per M.b.f. Doyle log scale for bolts graded 1 and 2 by the USDA Forest Service standard grading system for southern pine logs were as follows:

Bolt diameter	Veneer ⅜-inch basis	Pulp chips	Veneer cores
Inches	*M sq. ft.*	– – – *M lb.* – – –	
10	2.61	5.26	3.03
12	2.75	3.48	1.70
14	2.74	2.62	1.09
16	2.64	2.12	.76
18	2.59	1.82	.56
20	2.54	1.62	.43
22	2.46	1.46	.34
24	2.43	1.36	.27

The foregoing data are based on a core diameter of 5.2 inches. The green cores weighed 32 to 64 lb. per cubic foot and averaged about 46 lb. per cubic foot.

In a study of southern pine veneer cores residual from steamed veneer bolts cut in northern Louisiana, Koch (1971) observed that they averaged 0.51 in specific gravity (ovendry weight and green volume basis), and that their moisture content was 75 percent of their ovendry weight.

Weight and volume of chips in piles.—According to Williams and Hopkins (1969, p. 78), green chips from southern pine sawmill residue weigh about 24 lb. per cubic foot of gross space occupied; green chips from southern pine plywood clippings pile less compactly and weigh about 20 lb. per cubic foot.

According to Forbes (1961, p. 14.71), a standard rough cord of southern pine pulpwood yields about 232 cu. ft. of pulp chips as piled into a freight car.

SAWDUST

As much as 25 percent of saw log volume may be converted into sawdust if saw kerf is wide and logs are cut into 4/4 lumber; if primary manufacture is done with a chipping headrig, however, and breakdown into 8/4 lumber is accomplished with thin-kerf bandsaws and chipping edgers, as little as 5 percent of the log volume will end up as green sawdust. The data presented in the next few paragraphs describe sawdust yield in mills not equipped with chipping headrigs or chipping edgers.

Sawdust residue per M b.f. (log scale) sawn.—Row et al. (1965) developed a regression equation to express the weight of sawdust produced by sawing loblolly and shortleaf pine logs of various diameters and lengths, as follows:

$$W = 0.068D^2L \qquad (29\text{--}30)$$

where W = weight of green sawdust, pounds; D = log d.i.b. at small end, inches; and L = log length, feet.

Obviously, on a per log basis, the most sawdust is made from the largest logs (table 29–64); on a per M b.f. basis, however, small logs yield the greatest tonnage of sawdust, as follows:

Log scaling diameter	Weight of green sawdust per M b.f. (Doyle scale) of logs sawn
Inches	Tons
8	2.18
10	1.51
12	1.22
14	1.07
16	.97
18	.90

Values in the foregoing tabulation are computed from equation 29–30. Log length (8 to 16 feet) had virtually no effect on amount of sawdust produced per M b.f. log scale.

King (1952, p. 51) found that green and ovendry weights of sawdust per M b.f. of southern pine logs sawn in east Texas were as follows:

Scaling diameter of log and moisture content	Per M b.f. Doyle-Scribner log scale	Per M b.f. Int'l-¼ log scale
	– – – – – – Tons – – – – –	
7.6 to 10.5 inches		
Green_____	1.62	0.96
Ovendry_____	.80	.47
10.6 to 13.5 inches		
Green_____	1.12	.74
Ovendry_____	.56	.40
13.6 to 16.5 inches		
Green_____	.94	.74
Ovendry_____	.47	.37
16.6 to 19.5 inches		
Green_____	.76	.67
Ovendry_____	.38	.33

These data apply to logs—mostly 14 and 16 feet long—cut in mills with band headsaws; mills with circular headsaws made about 10 percent more sawdust on the smaller logs and about 40 percent more on the larger logs.

Sawdust residue per M b.f. (lumber scale) sawn.—Figure 29–7, based on southern pine logs sawn in Georgia, shows that 1.0 to 1.2 tons of green sawdust were produced per M b.f. of lumber sawn in the Page and Saucier (1958) study.

For southern pine logs cut in east Texas, King (1952, p. 51) observed that green and dry weights of sawdust per M b.f. of green lumber tally were as follows:

Scaling diameter of log and moisture content	In mills with circular headsaws	In mills with band headsaws
	----- *Tons* -----	
7.6 to 10.5 inches		
Green_____	0.98	0.90
Ovendry_____	.48	.45
10.6 to 13.5 inches		
Green_____	.92	.76
Ovendry_____	.45	.38
13.6 to 16.5 inches		
Green_____	1.00	.71
Ovendry_____	.49	.35
16.6 to 19.5 inches		
Green_____	.91	.64
Ovendry_____	.45	.32

Sawdust weight per unit volume.—Sawdust weight per unit volume varies according to the particle size, moisture content, and degree of compaction. Williams and Hopkins (1969, p. 81) reported that one manufacturer observed the following weights for southern pine sawdust at 8-percent moisture content:

Sawdust size	Weight per gross cubic foot
	Lb.
Through ¼-inch screen unsifted _____	16
Through 10-mesh screen _____	15
Through 20-mesh screen _____	18

Bois (1968) related the weight of shortleaf pine sawdust, cut with an inserted tooth saw (fig. 19–76) having a $\frac{9}{32}$-inch kerf, to moisture content and degree of compaction. In his tabulation (following), **light** compaction is the condition that might arise from filling a railcar or truck from an overhead conveyor; **shaken** compaction stimulates the densification caused by vibration of a car or truck in transit; and **packed** compaction represents the highest degree of packing possible.

TRIM

Trim ends of green lumber, according to figure 29–7, amount to 0.1 to 0.2 ton per M b.f. of southern pine lumber sawn. According to Carpenter and Schroeder (1968) about 6 percent of total lumber footage is lost as cull or trim when converting green rough 4/4 boards to kiln-dry planed boards; for 8/4 boards, they measured a board foot loss of about 3 percent.

| Moisture | Degree of compaction | | |
content	Light	Shaken	Packed
Percent	– – – –	*Lb./cu. ft.*	– – – –
0	9.3	12.3	15.5
5	9.8	12.9	15.8
10	10.2	13.5	16.3
15	10.7	14.1	16.8
20	11.2	14.8	17.3
25	11.6	15.4	17.8
30	12.1	16.0	18.3
50	13.9	18.4	20.5
75	16.3	21.5	23.8
100	18.6	24.6	27.2
125	20.9	27.7	31.9
140	22.3	29.5	34.7

SHAVINGS

In the opening paragraphs of section 29–3, it was noted that one southern pine sawmill operator observed that 12.8 percent of gross sawlog volume is converted to planer shavings.

Obviously the tonnage of planer shavings made is closely correlated with sawing accuracy, rough lumber size, planed lumber dimensions, and wood specific gravity and moisture content. It is quite evident that a mill making a high proportion of knotty pine panelling with deep patterns and long tongues will make more shavings per M b.f. of lumber planed than a mill specializing in kiln-dried S4S 2 by 4's.

From table 7–1 and from shrinkage data given in section 20–4, it is possible to compute the weight of shavings produced by planing. If it is asumed that the mill is manufacturing 8-foot 2 by 4's sawn green 1.9 inches thick, 4.0 inches wide, and 96 inches long, and that these studs are dried to 10-percent moisture content and planed to 1.5- by 3.5-inch dimension, then about 715 lb. of shavings will be produced per M b.f. of lumber planed. The foregoing computation assumes that the lumber has a specific gravity of 0.50 on a green volume, ovendry weight basis.

If lumber is sawn oversize, or milled with deep patterns, however, it is not unusual for a ton of shavings to be produced from each M b.f. of lumber planed at 10-percent moisture content.

TABLE 29–1.—*Volume of solid wood in standard rough cords of 4-foot longleaf and loblolly pine bolts as related to average midlength diameter and character of the bolts* (Williams and Hopkins 1969, p. 5[1])

Character of bolts	Midlength d.o.b., inches					
	Less than 6		6 to 12		Greater than 12	
	LL[2]	Lob[3]	LL	Lob	LL	Lob
	— — — — — — — — — — — Cu. ft. — — — — — — — — — — —					
Straight						
Smooth_____	84	76	89	80	94	84
Slightly rough_____	81	74	87	78	92	83
Slightly rough						
and knotty_____	79	71	85[4]	76[4]	90	81
Not Straight						
Slightly crooked						
and rough_____	75	67	83	74	87	78
Very crooked_____	71	64	80	71	84	76
Crooked, rough						
and knotty_____	66	58	74	66	78	70
Tops and branches_____	63	56	—	—	—	—

[1] Data adapted from USDA Forest Service (1935). Original data, based on spruce, were reduced by Williams and Hopkins for the southern pine species, which have less uniform bolt characteristics.

[2] Longleaf pine.

[3] Loblolly pine.

[4] Working averages for longleaf and loblolly pines.

TABLE 29–2.—*Number of bolts, solid wood volume, bark volume, and weight per standard rough cord of longleaf pine 4-foot pulpwood as related to bolt diameter* (Williams and Hopkins 1969, p. 7)[1]

Average bolt diameter (inches)[2]	Bolts	Solid wood	Bark	Average green weight[3]
	Number	— — — — — Cu. ft. — — — — —		Lb.
5_____	128.0	56.2	23.1	4,837
6_____	97.0	63.2	23.1	5,264
7_____	64.0	67.2	22.0	5,441
8_____	51.2	69.8	21.2	5,551
9_____	41.3	70.9	20.7	5,588
10_____	33.7	73.9	20.7	5,771
11_____	28.5	74.2	20.3	5,765
12_____	24.1	75.3	19.5	5,783
13_____	20.6	77.0	19.6	5,893
14_____	17.8	78.2	20.0	5,990
15_____	15.6	80.0	20.0	6,100
16_____	13.7	83.2	20.5	6,326

[1] Based on measurements of 133 pine stems, scaled at one pulpmill in the Southeast.

[2] D.i.b. at midlength.

[3] Based on a green weight of 61 lb./cu. ft. of solid wood and bark.

TABLE 29–3.—*Number of pulpwood bolts[1] of various lengths and diameters to make a standard rough cord* (Hawes 1940)

Bolt diameter[2] (inches)	Bolt length in feet				
	4	5	5.25	5.66	6
			Number		
5	152	122	116	108	102
6	109	87	84	78	73
7	82	66	62	58	55
8	64	51	49	45	43
9	51	41	39	36	34
10	42	33	32	30	28
11	35	28	27	25	23
12	30	24	23	21	20

[1] Bolts of better than average straightness and surface smoothness.
[2] D.i.b. at midlength.

TABLE 29–4.—*Number of veneer cores per nominal cord[1]* (Williams and Hopkins 1969, p. 9)

Core diameter (inches)	Core length in inches	
	102[2]	54[3]
	Number	
3.5	191	402
4.0	148	312
4.5	117	245
5.0	93	196
5.5	78	163
6.0	64	135
6.5	55	116

[1] Calculations based on volumes of true cylinders.
[2] This cord measures 48 by 48 by 102 inches (136 cu. ft. gross).
[3] This cord measures 48 by 96 by 54 inches (144 cu. ft. gross).

TABLE 29–5.—*Number of southern pine trees per standard rough cord* (Forest Farmers Association 1966, p. 143[1])

D.b.h. (inches)	Tree height in number of 5-foot 3-inch bolts[2]										
	2	3	4	5	6	7	8	9	10	11	12
					Trees per cord						
5	69.4	49.3	38.3								
6	48.8	36.1	28.7	23.8							
7	36.9	27.9	22.4	18.7	16.1	14.1					
8		22.2	18.0	15.1	13.0	11.4	10.2	9.16	8.34		
9		18.2	14.7	12.4	10.7	9.40	8.38	7.56	6.89	6.33	5.85
10			12.3	10.4	8.95	7.87	7.02	6.34	5.77	5.30	4.90
11			10.5	8.82	7.60	6.68	5.96	5.38	4.90	4.50	4.16
12			9.03	7.58	6.53	5.74	5.12	4.61	4.21	3.86	3.57
13			7.86	6.59	5.67	4.98	4.44	4.00	3.64	3.35	3.09
14			6.90	5.78	4.97	4.36	3.88	3.50	3.19	2.92	2.70
15						3.85	3.43	3.09	2.81	2.58	2.38
16						3.42	3.04	2.74	2.49	2.29	2.11

[1] Derived from Forbes (1961, p. 2.10).
[2] To 4-inch merchantable top (outside bark).

TABLE 29–6.—*Number of 5-foot bolts per tree*[1] *in loblolly pines of various diameters and heights* (MacKinney and Chaiken 1946)

D.b.h. (inches)	Total tree height in feet								
	20	30	40	50	60	70	80	90	100
					Number of bolts				
5	1.5	2.1	2.9	3.5	4.2	4.9	5.8		
6	2.0	2.9	3.9	4.6	5.6	6.6	7.5		
7	2.2	3.4	4.5	5.6	6.9	8.5	9.4	10.3	
8	2.3	3.8	5.0	6.4	7.7	9.6	10.7	11.6	
9	2.3	4.1	5.3	6.9	8.3	10.4	11.6	12.3	
10		4.3	5.5	7.2	8.8	10.9	12.3	12.8	
11		4.4	5.7	7.4	9.2	11.3	12.6	13.2	14.4
12		4.5	5.9	7.6	9.5	11.6	12.9	13.5	14.7
13		4.5	6.0	7.6	9.7	11.8	13.1	13.8	15.0
14		4.5	6.1	7.7	9.8	11.9	13.3	14.0	15.3
15			6.2	7.7	9.9	12.0	13.4	14.2	15.5
16			6.2	7.8	9.9	12.0	13.5	14.4	15.6
17			6.3	7.8	10.0	12.1	13.6	14.5	15.6
18				7.8	10.0	12.1	13.7	14.6	15.7
19				7.9	10.0	12.2	13.8	14.6	15.7
20				7.9	10.1	12.2	13.8	14.7	15.7

[1] Average number of bolts that can be cut above an 0.7-foot stump to a merchantable top of 4.0 inches outside bark.

TABLE 29–7.—*Merchantable volume per southern pine tree in standard rough cords* (Burns 1965[1])

Form class[2] and d.b.h. (inches)	Total tree height in feet							
	30	40	50	60	70	80	90	100
	— — — — — — — — — — — Cords — — — — — — — — — — —							
65–69								
6	0.029	0.035	0.040	0.045	0.052			
8	.055	.063	.074	.084	.094	0.104		
10		.097	.115	.132	.148	.165	0.179	
12		.136	.160	.182	.207	.226	.250	0.272
14			.221	.250	.280	.309	.343	.372
16			.277	.313	.350	.391	.433	.469
75–79								
6	.036	.045	.052	.058	.068			
8	.069	.081	.096	.109	.122	.136		
10		.124	.148	.170	.192	.213	.232	
12		.174	.207	.236	.269	.295	.328	.357
14			.282	.321	.360	.399	.443	.482
16			.357	.407	.455	.511	.566	.627
85–89								
6	.044	.055	.064	.072	.084			
8	.087	.101	.120	.136	.153	.169		
10		.154	.185	.213	.240	.268	.292	
12		.216	.258	.295	.336	.368	.410	.447
14			.351	.401	.451	.501	.557	.607
16			.444	.506	.568	.638	.708	.770

[1] Compiled from Minor (1950).   [2] See equation 29–1.

TABLE 29–8.—*Volume and weight of loblolly pine trees and number of trees required per 168–cu. ft. unit* (Wahlenberg 1960, p. 501)

Dimensions of average pine tree			Weight per tree[3]	Trees per unit[4]	Volume of wood plus bark per unit[4]
D.b.h. (inches)	Height[1]	Volume[2]			
	Feet	*Cu. ft.*	*Lb.*	*Number*	*Cu. f.*
4	30	0.6	40	162	97
	38	1.2	79	83	99
6	45	2.5	164	41	101
	51	4.3	281	24	103
8	56	6.5	422	16	105
	62	9.4	607	11	107
10	67	12.8	824	8	108
	71	16.7	1,074	7	110
12	75	21.1	1,355	5	111
	78	26.1	1,673	4	112
14	82	31.8	2,035	4	113

[1] Merchantable height to 4-inch top (outside bark).   [3] Includes bark.

[2] Wood only, to merchantable top.   [4] 168-cu. ft. unit of 5¼-foot rough wood.

TABLE 29–9.—*Standard rough cords of topwood[1] volume remaining per tree after removal of saw logs* (Bennett 1953)

Species and d.b.h. (inches)	Number of 16-foot logs removed					
	1	1½	2	2½	3	3½
	— — — — — — — — — Cords — — — — — — — — —					
Slash pine						
9	0.062	0.064	0.066			
10	.050	.052	.054	0.054		
11	.041	.043	.044	.045	0.045	
12	.034	.036	.037	.038	.038	0.038
13	.029	.031	.032	.032	.032	.033
14	.025	.027	.027	.028	.028	.028
15	.022	.023	.024	.024	.024	.024
16	.019	.020	.021	.021	.021	.021
17	.017	.018	.019	.019	.019	.019
18	.015	.016	.017	.017	.017	.017
Longleaf pine						
9	.054	.046				
10	.046	.039	.035	.033		
11	.039	.033	.029	.027	.025	
12	.032	.027	.024	.023	.022	.021
13	.026	.023	.021	.019	.018	.018
14	.023	.020	.018	.017	.016	.015
15	.020	.017	.015	.014	.014	.013
16	.017	.015	.014	.013	.012	.012
17	.015	.014	.012	.012	.011	.011
18	.014	.012	.011	.010	.010	.009

[1] Volume to merchantable top of 4 inches outside bark after removal of specified number of saw logs.

TABLE 29–10.—*Merchantable volume per acre of 9- to 16-year-old slash pine plantations* (Goggans and Schultz 1958)

Trees per acre	Total height of tallest trees in feet					
	25	30	35	40	45	50
	— — — — — — — — — Cords — — — — — — — — —					
400	0.30	5.39	10.49	15.59	20.69	25.78
500	1.62	6.71	11.81	16.91	22.01	27.11
600	2.94	8.04	13.13	18.23	23.33	28.43
700	4.26	9.36	14.46	19.55	24.65	29.75
800	5.58	10.68	15.78	20.87	25.97	31.07
900	6.90	12.00	17.10	22.20	27.29	32.39
1,000	8.22	13.32	18.42	23.52	28.62	33.71

TABLE 29–11.—*Doyle log scale, contents of logs in board feet*

Scaling diameter (inches)	Log length in feet					
	6	8	10	12	14	16
	- - - - - - - - *Bd. ft.* - - - - - - -					
6	2	2	3	3	4	4
7	3	5	6	7	8	9
8	6	8	10	12	14	16
9	9	13	16	19	22	25
10	14	18	23	27	32	36
11	18	25	31	37	43	49
12	24	32	40	48	56	64
13	30	41	51	61	71	81
14	38	50	63	75	88	100
15	45	61	76	91	106	121
16	54	72	90	108	126	144
17	63	85	106	127	148	169
18	74	98	123	147	172	196
19	84	113	141	169	197	225
20	96	128	160	192	224	256
21	108	145	181	217	253	289
22	122	162	203	243	284	324
23	135	181	226	271	316	361
24	150	200	250	300	350	400
25	165	221	276	331	386	441
26	182	242	303	363	424	484
27	198	265	331	397	463	529
28	216	288	360	432	504	576
29	234	313	391	469	547	625
30	254	338	423	507	592	676

Table 29–12.—*Volume of 16-foot logs to nearest board foot by the Doyle log scale* (Mesavage and Girard 1956)

Scaling diameter (inches)	Scaling diameter in tenths of inches									
	.0	.1	.2	.3	.4	.5	.6	.7	.8	.9
					Bd. ft.					
5	1	1	1	2	2	2	3	3	3	4
6	4	4	5	5	6	6	7	7	8	8
7	9	10	10	11	12	12	13	14	14	15
8	16	17	18	18	19	20	21	22	23	24
9	25	26	27	28	29	30	31	32	34	35
10	36	37	38	40	41	42	44	45	46	48
11	49	50	52	53	55	56	58	59	61	62
12	64	66	67	69	71	72	74	76	77	79
13	81	83	85	86	88	90	92	94	96	98
14	100	102	104	106	108	110	112	114	117	119
15	121	123	125	128	130	132	135	137	139	142
16	144	146	149	151	154	156	159	161	164	166
17	169	172	174	177	180	182	185	188	190	193
18	196	199	202	204	207	210	213	216	219	222
19	225	228	231	234	237	240	243	246	250	253
20	256	259	262	266	269	272	276	279	282	286
21	289	292	296	299	303	306	310	313	317	320
22	324	328	331	335	339	342	346	350	353	357
23	361	365	369	372	376	380	384	388	392	396
24	400	404	408	412	416	420	424	428	433	437
25	441	445	449	454	458	462	467	471	475	480
26	484	488	493	497	502	506	511	515	520	524
27	529	534	538	543	548	552	557	562	566	571
28	576	581	586	590	595	600	605	610	615	620
29	625	630	635	640	645	650	655	660	666	671
30	676	681	686	692	697	702	708	713	718	724
31	729	734	740	745	751	756	762	767	773	778
32	784	790	795	801	807	812	818	824	829	835
33	841	847	853	858	864	870	876	882	888	894
34	900	906	912	918	924	930	936	942	949	955

TABLE 29–13.—*Scribner Decimal C log scale, contents of logs in board feet*

Scaling diameter (inches)	Log length in feet					
	6	8	10	12	14	16
	– – – – – – – Bd. ft. – – – – – – –					
6	5	5	10	10	10	20
7	5	10	10	20	20	30
8	10	10	20	20	20	30
9	10	20	30	30	30	40
10	20	30	30	30	40	60
11	20	30	40	40	50	70
12	30	40	50	60	70	80
13	40	50	60	70	80	100
14	40	60	70	90	100	110
15	50	70	90	110	120	140
16	60	80	100	120	140	160
17	70	90	120	140	160	180
18	80	110	130	160	190	210
19	90	120	150	180	210	240
20	110	140	170	210	240	280
21	120	150	190	230	270	300
22	130	170	210	250	290	330
23	140	190	230	280	330	380
24	150	210	250	300	350	400
25	170	230	290	340	400	460
26	190	250	310	370	440	500
27	210	270	340	410	480	550
28	220	290	360	440	510	580
29	230	310	380	460	530	610
30	250	330	410	490	570	660

TABLE 29–14.—*Volume of 16-foot logs to the nearest board foot by the Scribner log scale*[1] (Mesavage and Girard 1956)

Scaling diameter (inches)	Scaling diameter in tenths of inches									
	.0	.1	.2	.3	.4	.5	.6	.7	.8	.9
	— — — — — — — — — *Bd. ft.* — — — — — — — — — —									
6	12	13	14	15	16	16	17	18	19	20
7	21	22	23	24	24	25	26	27	28	29
8	30	31	32	33	34	36	37	38	39	41
9	42	43	45	46	47	48	50	51	52	54
10	55	56	58	60	61	63	64	66	67	69
11	70	72	74	75	77	78	80	81	83	84
12	86	88	90	91	93	95	97	99	101	102
13	104	106	108	110	111	113	115	117	119	121
14	123	125	127	129	131	133	135	137	140	142
15	144	146	148	150	153	155	157	159	161	164
16	166	168	171	173	175	177	180	182	185	187
17	189	191	194	196	199	202	204	207	210	213
18	216	218	221	224	227	229	231	234	237	240
19	243	245	248	251	254	257	260	263	266	269
20	272	275	278	281	284	287	290	293	296	299
21	302	305	308	311	314	317	320	323	327	330
22	334	337	340	344	348	351	354	358	361	365
23	368	372	375	379	382	386	390	394	397	400
24	403	406	410	414	418	422	426	429	432	436
25	440	444	448	452	456	460	464	468	472	475
26	478	482	486	490	494	498	502	506	510	514
27	518	522	526	530	534	538	542	546	550	554
28	559	563	567	571	575	579	583	587	592	597
29	602	606	611	615	620	624	629	633	638	642
30	647	651	656	660	665	669	674	678	683	688
31	693	698	703	708	712	717	722	726	731	736
32	741	746	751	756	761	766	770	775	780	785
33	790	795	800	805	810	815	820	825	830	835
34	841	846	851	856	862	867	872	877	883	888
35	894	900	905	910	915	921	926	931	937	942

[1] Computed from equation 29–5.

TABLE 29–15.—*Deductions for defect[1] from Scribner Decimal C log scale* (USDA Forest Service 1965)

Defect length (feet)	Deduction in board feet																			
	Cross-sectional area of defect in square inches																			
	10	20	30	40	50	60	70	80	90	100	110	120	130	140	150	160	170	180	190	200
2	38	113	188	263	338	413	488	563	638	—	—	—	—	—	—	—	—	—	—	—
4	19	57	94	132	169	207	244	282	319	357	394	432	469	507	544	582	619	657	—	—
6	13	38		88	113	138	163	188	213	238	263	288	313	338	363	388	413	438	463	488
8	10	29	47	66	85	104	122	141	160	179	197	216	235	254	272	291	310	329	347	366
10	8	23	38	53	68	83	98	113	128	143	158	173	188	203	218	233	248	263	278	293
12	7	19	32	44	57	69	82	94	107	119	132	144	157	169	182	194	207	219	232	244
14	6	17	27	38	49	59	70	81	92	102	113	124	134	145	156	167	177	188	199	209
16	5	15	24	33	43	52	61	71	80	90	99	108	118	127	136	146	155	165	174	183
18	5	13	21	30	38	46	55	63	71	80	88	96	105	113	121	130	138	146	155	163
20	4	12	19	27	34	42	49	57	64	72	79	87	94	102	109	117	124	132	139	147

[1] Example: If the end of the defect measures 9 by 11 inches (99 sq. in.), and the length is 12 feet, read horizontally from defect length of 12 feet to 99 sq. in. or next lower number found (in this case 94); read up to find the deduction of 80 bd. ft. at column head.

TABLE 29–16.—*International ¼-inch log scale, contents of logs in board feet*

Scaling diameter (inches)	Log length in feet					
	6	8	10	12	14	16
				Bd. ft.		
6	5	10	10	15	15	20
7	10	10	15	20	25	30
8	10	15	20	25	35	40
9	15	20	30	35	45	50
10	20	30	35	45	55	65
11	25	35	45	55	70	80
12	30	45	55	70	85	95
13	40	55	70	85	100	115
14	45	65	80	100	115	135
15	55	75	95	115	135	160
16	60	85	110	130	155	180
17	70	95	125	150	180	205
18	80	110	140	170	200	230
19	90	125	155	190	225	260
20	100	135	175	210	250	290
21	115	155	195	235	280	320
22	125	170	215	260	305	355
23	140	185	235	285	335	390
24	150	205	255	310	370	425
25	165	220	280	340	400	460
26	180	240	305	370	435	500
27	195	260	330	400	470	540
28	210	280	355	430	510	585
29	225	305	385	465	545	630
30	245	325	410	495	585	675

TABLE 29–17.—*Volumes of 8- and 16-foot logs to the nearest board foot by the International ¼-inch log scale*

Scaling length (feet) and diameter (inches)	Scaling diameter in tenths of inches									
	.0	.1	.2	.3	.4	.5	.6	.7	.8	.9
						Bd. ft.					
8 foot[1]										
6	8	8	9	9	9	10	10	10	11	11
7	12	12	13	13	13	14	14	15	16	16
8	17	17	18	18	19	19	20	20	21	22
9	22	23	23	24	25	25	26	27	27	28
10	29	29	30	31	31	31	32	33	34	35
11	36	37	38	38	39	40	41	42	42	43
12	44	45	46	47	47	48	49	50	51	52
13	53	54	55	56	57	58	59	60	61	62
14	63	66	65	66	67	68	69	70	71	72
15	73	74	75	76	77	79	80	81	82	83
16	84	85	87	88	88	90	91	93	94	95
17	96	98	99	100	101	103	104	105	107	108
18	109	110	112	113	115	116	117	119	120	121
19	123	124	126	127	129	130	131	133	134	136
20	137	139	140	142	143	145	146	148	149	151
21	152	154	156	157	159	160	162	164	165	167
22	169	170	172	174	175	179	179	180	182	184
23	185	187	189	191	192	194	196	198	200	201
24	203	205	207	208	210	212	214	216	217	220
25	221	224	225	227	229	231	233	235	237	239
26	241	243	245	247	249	251	253	255	257	259
27	262	264	265	266	269	271	273	275	277	279
28	282	284	286	288	290	292	294	296	299	301
29	303	305	307	310	312	314	316	319	321	323
30	325	329	330	332	334	337	339	342	343	346

See footnotes at end of table.

TABLE 29–17.—*Volumes of 8- and 16-foot logs to the nearest board foot by the International ¼-inch log scale*—Continued

Scaling length (feet) and diameter (inches)	Scaling diameter in tenths of inches									
	.0	.1	.2	.3	.4	.5	.6	.7	.8	.9
16 foot[2]										
6_____	19	20	21	22	23	23	24	25	26	27
7_____	28	29	30	31	32	33	34	35	36	38
8_____	39	40	41	42	43	45	46	47	48	50
9_____	51	52	54	55	56	58	59	60	62	63
10_____	65	66	68	69	71	72	74	75	77	78
11_____	80	82	83	85	87	88	90	92	93	95
12_____	97	99	100	102	104	106	108	110	112	114
13_____	115	117	119	121	123	125	127	129	131	133
14_____	136	138	140	142	144	146	148	151	153	155
15_____	157	160	162	164	166	169	171	173	176	178
16_____	181	183	185	188	190	193	195	198	200	203
17_____	205	208	211	213	216	219	221	224	227	229
18_____	232	235	237	240	243	246	249	251	254	257
19_____	260	263	266	269	272	275	278	281	284	287
20_____	290	293	296	299	302	305	308	311	315	318
21_____	321	324	327	331	334	337	341	344	347	351
22_____	354	357	361	364	367	371	374	378	381	385
23_____	388	392	395	399	403	406	410	413	417	421
24_____	424	428	432	435	439	443	447	451	454	458
25_____	462	466	470	474	478	481	485	489	493	497
26_____	501	505	509	513	517	521	526	530	534	538
27_____	542	546	550	555	559	563	567	572	576	580
28_____	584	589	593	598	602	606	611	615	620	624
29_____	628	633	637	642	647	651	656	660	665	669
30_____	674	679	683	688	693	697	702	707	712	716
31_____	721	726	731	736	741	745	750	755	760	765
32_____	770	775	780	785	790	795	800	805	810	815
33_____	820	826	831	836	841	846	851	857	862	867
34_____	872	878	883	888	894	899	904	910	915	921
35_____	926	931	937	942	948	953	959	964	970	976

[1] Computed from equation 29–9.
[2] Computed from equation 29–8.

TABLE 29–18.—*Average upper-log taper in southern pine trees containing two, three, four, five, or six 16-foot logs (Mesavage and Girard 1956)*

D.b.h. (inches)	Two-log	Three-log		Four-log			Five-log				Six-log				
	2nd[1]	2nd	3rd	2nd	3rd	4th	2nd	3rd	4th	5th	2nd	3rd	4th	5th	6th
								Inches							
10	1.4	1.2	1.4	—	—	—	—	—	—	—	—	—	—	—	—
12	1.6	1.3	1.5	1.1	1.4	1.9	—	—	—	—	—	—	—	—	—
14	1.7	1.4	1.6	1.2	1.5	2.0	—	—	—	—	—	—	—	—	—
16	1.9	1.5	1.7	1.2	1.6	2.1	—	—	—	—	—	—	—	—	—
18	2.0	1.6	1.8	1.3	1.7	2.2	—	—	—	—	—	—	—	—	—
20	2.1	1.7	1.9	1.4	1.8	2.4	1.1	1.6	2.2	2.9	—	—	—	—	—
22	2.2	1.8	2.0	1.4	2.0	2.5	1.1	1.7	2.3	2.9	—	—	—	—	—
24	2.3	1.8	2.2	1.5	2.2	2.6	1.1	1.8	2.4	3.1	—	—	—	—	—
26	2.4	1.9	2.3	1.5	2.3	2.7	1.1	1.9	2.5	3.2	—	—	—	—	—
28	2.5	1.9	2.5	1.6	2.4	2.8	1.2	1.9	2.6	3.3	0.9	1.4	2.1	3.2	4.4
30	2.6	2.0	2.6	1.7	2.5	3.0	1.2	2.0	2.7	3.5	.9	1.4	2.1	3.2	4.5
32	2.7	2.0	2.7	1.7	2.5	3.1	1.2	2.1	2.9	3.7	1.0	1.4	2.1	3.2	4.6
34	2.8	2.1	2.7	1.8	2.5	3.3	1.3	2.1	3.0	3.8	1.0	1.4	2.2	3.3	4.7
36	2.8	2.1	2.8	1.8	2.6	3.4	1.3	2.2	3.0	3.9	1.1	1.5	2.2	3.3	4.9
38	2.9	2.1	2.8	1.9	2.6	3.4	1.3	2.2	3.1	3.9	1.1	1.5	2.3	3.4	5.1
40	2.9	2.2	2.8	1.9	2.7	3.4	1.4	2.3	3.2	4.0	1.2	1.5	2.4	3.5	5.3

Position of each log within the tree

[1] In a two-log tree; similarly, the other columns show values for three-, four-, five-, and six-log trees.

TABLE 29–19.—*Gross volume of southern pine trees in form class[1] 78, Doyle log scale* (Mesavage and Girard 1956)

D.b.h. (inches)	Merchantable height in number of 16-foot logs										
	1	1½	2	2½	3	3½	4	4½	5	5½	6
						Bd. ft.					
10	14	17	20	21	22	–	–	–	–	–	–
11	22	27	32	35	38	–	–	–	–	–	–
12	29	36	43	48	53	54	56	–	–	–	–
13	38	48	59	66	73	76	80	–	–	–	–
14	48	62	75	84	93	98	103	–	–	–	–
15	60	78	96	108	121	128	136	–	–	–	–
16	72	94	116	132	149	160	170	–	–	–	–
17	86	113	140	161	182	196	209	–	–	–	–
18	100	132	164	190	215	232	248	–	–	–	–
19	118	156	195	225	256	276	297	–	–	–	–
20	135	180	225	261	297	322	346	364	383	–	–
21	154	207	260	302	344	374	404	428	452	–	–
22	174	234	295	344	392	427	462	492	521	–	–
23	195	264	332	388	444	483	522	558	594	–	–
24	216	293	370	433	496	539	582	625	668	–	–
25	241	328	414	486	558	609	660	709	758	–	–
26	266	362	459	539	619	678	737	793	849	–	–

27	292	398	505	594	684	749	814	877	940	-	-
28	317	434	551	651	750	820	890	961	1,032	1,096	1,161
29	346	475	604	714	824	902	980	1,061	1,142	1,218	1,294
30	376	517	658	778	898	984	1,069	1,160	1,251	1,339	1,427
31	408	562	717	850	983	1,080	1,176	1,273	1,370	1,470	1,570
32	441	608	776	922	1,068	1,176	1,283	1,386	1,488	1,600	1,712
33	474	654	835	994	1,152	1,268	1,385	1,497	1,609	1,734	1,858
34	506	700	894	1,064	1,235	1,361	1,487	1,608	1,730	1,866	2,003
35	544	754	964	1,149	1,334	1,472	1,610	1,743	1,876	2,020	2,163
36	581	808	1,035	1,234	1,434	1,583	1,732	1,878	2,023	2,173	2,323
37	618	860	1,102	1,318	1,534	1,694	1,854	2,013	2,172	2,332	2,492
38	655	912	1,170	1,402	1,635	1,805	1,975	2,148	2,322	2,491	2,660
39	698	974	1,250	1,498	1,746	1,932	2,118	2,298	2,479	2,662	2,844
40	740	1,035	1,330	1,594	1,858	2,059	2,260	2,448	2,636	2,832	3,027

[1] Defined by equation 29-1.

TABLE 29–20.—*Gross volume of southern pine trees in form class[1] 78 Scribner log scale* (Mesavage and Girard 1956)

D.b.h. (inches)	Merchantable height in number of 16-foot logs										
	1	1½	2	2½	3	3½	4	4½	5	5½	6
						Bd. ft.					
10	28	36	44	48	52	---	---	---	---	---	---
11	38	49	60	67	74	---	---	---	---	---	---
12	47	61	75	85	95	100	106	---	---	---	---
13	58	76	94	107	120	128	136	---	---	---	---
14	69	92	114	130	146	156	166	---	---	---	---
15	82	109	136	157	178	192	206	---	---	---	---
16	95	127	159	185	211	229	247	---	---	---	---
17	109	146	184	215	246	268	289	---	---	---	---
18	123	166	209	244	280	306	331	---	---	---	---
19	140	190	240	281	322	352	382	---	---	---	---
20	157	214	270	317	364	398	432	459	486	---	---
21	176	240	304	358	411	450	490	523	556	---	---
22	194	266	338	398	458	504	549	588	626	---	---
23	214	294	374	441	508	558	607	652	698	---	---
24	234	322	409	484	558	611	665	718	770	---	---
25	258	355	452	534	617	678	740	799	858	---	---

26	281	388	494	585	676	745	814	880	945	---	---
27	304	420	536	636	736	811	886	959	1,032	---	---
28	327	452	578	686	795	877	959	1,040	1,120	1,190	1,261
29	354	491	628	746	864	953	1,042	1,132	1,222	1,306	1,389
30	382	530	678	806	933	1,028	1,124	1,224	1,325	1,421	1,517
31	411	571	731	871	1,011	1,117	1,223	1,328	1,434	1,541	1,648
32	440	612	784	936	1,089	1,206	1,322	1,432	1,543	1,661	1,779
33	469	654	838	1,001	1,164	1,280	1,414	1,534	1,654	1,783	1,912
34	498	695	892	1,066	1,239	1,373	1,507	1,636	1,766	1,906	2,046
35	530	742	954	1,141	1,328	1,473	1,618	1,757	1,896	2,044	2,192
36	563	789	1,015	1,216	1,416	1,572	1,728	1,877	2,026	2,182	2,338
37	596	836	1,075	1,290	1,506	1,670	1,835	1,998	2,160	2,324	2,488
38	629	882	1,135	1,366	1,596	1,769	1,942	2,118	2,295	2,466	2,637
39	666	935	1,204	1,449	1,694	1,881	2,068	2,251	2,434	2,616	2,799
40	703	988	1,274	1,532	1,791	1,993	2,195	2,384	2,574	2,768	2,961

[1] Defined by equation 29-1.

TABLE 29–21.—*Gross volume of southern pine trees in form class*[1] *78 International ¼-inch log scale* (Mesavage and Girard 1956)

D.b.h. (inches)	Merchantable height in number of 16-foot logs										
	1	1½	2	2½	3	3½	4	4½	5	5½	6
						Bd. ft.					
10	36	48	59	66	73						
11	46	61	76	86	96						
12	56	74	92	106	120	128	137				
13	67	90	112	130	147	158	168				
14	78	105	132	153	174	187	200				
15	92	124	156	182	208	225	242				
16	106	143	180	210	241	263	285				
17	121	164	206	242	278	304	330				
18	136	184	233	274	314	344	374				
19	154	209	264	311	358	392	427				
20	171	234	296	348	401	440	480	511	542		
21	191	262	332	391	450	496	542	579	616		
22	211	290	368	434	500	552	603	647	691		
23	231	318	404	478	552	608	663	714	766		
24	251	346	441	523	605	664	723	782	840		

25	275	380	484	574	665	732	800	865	930	--	--
26	299	414	528	626	725	801	877	949	1,021	--	--
27	323	448	572	680	788	870	952	1,032	1,111	--	--
28	347	482	616	733	850	938	1,027	1,114	1,201	1,280	1,358
29	375	521	667	794	920	1,016	1,112	1,210	1,308	1,398	1,488
30	403	560	718	854	991	1,094	1,198	1,306	1,415	1,517	1,619
31	432	602	772	921	1,070	1,184	1,299	1,412	1,526	1,640	1,754
32	462	644	826	988	1,149	1,274	1,400	1,518	1,637	1,762	1,888
33	492	686	880	1,053	1,226	1,360	1,495	1,622	1,750	1,888	2,026
34	521	728	934	1,119	1,304	1,447	1,590	1,727	1,864	2,014	2,163
35	555	776	998	1,196	1,394	1,548	1,702	1,851	2,000	2,156	2,312
36	589	826	1,063	1,274	1,485	1,650	1,814	1,974	2,135	2,298	2,461
37	622	873	1,124	1,351	1,578	1,752	1,926	2,099	2,272	2,444	2,616
38	656	921	1,186	1,428	1,670	1,854	2,038	2,224	2,410	2,590	2,771
39	694	976	1,258	1,514	1,769	1,968	2,166	2,359	2,552	2,744	2,937
40	731	1,030	1,329	1,598	1,868	2,081	2,294	2,494	2,693	2,898	3,103

[1] Defined by equation 29–1.

TABLE 29–22.—*Gross volume in southern pine trees in form class[1] 80 for use with aerial photographs, International ¼-inch log scale[2]*
(Minor 1953b)

Crown diameter (feet)	Total visible height in feet						
	50	60	70	80	90	100	110
	– – – – – – – – – – Bd. ft. – – – – – – – – – –						
10_____	64	77	90	103	115		
12_____	80	103	120	128	146	161	
14_____	101	122	140	161	182	203	223
16_____		144	166	190	215	239	263
18_____		170	198	227	256	285	313
20_____		198	231	264	297	330	363
22_____		231	270	308	348	386	424
24_____			311	355	400	445	490
26_____			344	394	443	493	542
28_____			386	441	497	552	607
30_____			429	491	552	613	675

[1] Defined by equation 29–1.

[2] For rough estimates of volume in all-aged, or low-density even-aged stands of saw logs of all southern pine species except longleaf.

TABLE 29–23.—*Bark-free cubic foot volume of southern pine saw logs*[1] (Row and Guttenberg 1966)

Scaling diameter (inches)	Log length in feet														
	4	8	12	16	20	24	28	32	36	40	44	48	52	56	60
								Cu. ft.							
6	0.85	1.85	2.99	4.30	5.79	7.56	9.33	11.40	13.70	16.22	18.98	21.99	25.26	28.81	32.64
7	1.15	2.49	3.94	5.61	7.48	9.56	11.85	14.37	17.13	20.14	23.42	26.96	30.80	34.92	39.35
8	1.48	3.16	5.02	7.10	9.39	11.91	14.67	17.68	20.96	24.51	28.34	32.46	36.89	41.64	46.71
9	1.87	3.94	6.23	8.76	11.52	14.53	17.81	21.36	24.30	29.31	33.74	38.48	43.56	48.97	54.73
10	2.29	4.81	7.58	10.59	13.86	17.41	21.24	25.37	29.80	34.54	39.62	45.03	50.79	56.91	63.40
11	2.76	5.77	9.05	12.60	16.43	20.55	24.98	29.73	34.80	40.21	45.98	52.10	58.59	65.46	72.73
12	3.28	6.82	10.65	14.78	19.21	23.95	29.03	34.44	40.20	46.35	52.80	59.69	66.96	74.62	82.71
13	3.83	7.96	12.39	17.13	22.20	27.62	33.38	39.50	45.99	52.87	60.14	67.80	75.89	84.40	93.35
14	4.43	9.18	14.25	19.66	25.42	31.54	38.03	44.91	52.18	59.85	67.93	76.45	85.39	94.78	104.64
15	5.07	10.49	16.25	22.37	29.86	35.73	43.00	50.66	58.76	67.27	76.21	85.61	95.46	105.78	116.58
16	5.76	11.88	18.38	25.25	32.52	40.42	48.27	56.78	65.73	75.12	84.97	95.29	106.10	117.38	129.18
17	6.49	13.37	20.63	28.30	36.39	44.90	53.84	63.24	73.09	83.41	94.21	105.50	117.30	129.60	142.43
18	7.27	14.94	23.02	31.53	40.48	49.87	59.72	70.04	80.84	92.13	103.93	116.24	127.07	142.43	156.34
19	8.08	16.60	25.54	34.93	44.78	55.11	65.92	77.20	88.99	101.30	114.13	127.49	141.41	155.87	170.90
20	8.95	18.34	28.19	38.51	49.31	60.60	72.39	84.70	97.54	110.90	124.81	139.87	154.31	169.92	186.12
21	9.85	20.17	30.97	42.26	54.06	66.37	79.20	92.56	106.47	120.94	135.97	151.58	167.78	184.58	201.99
22	10.80	22.09	33.88	46.19	59.02	72.38	86.29	100.75	115.79	131.41	147.60	164.41	181.82	199.85	218.52
23	11.79	24.10	36.93	50.29	64.20	78.67	93.70	109.31	125.51	142.32	159.72	177.76	196.42	215.73	235.70
24	12.83	26.19	40.10	54.57	69.60	83.21	101.41	118.21	135.62	153.66	172.32	191.63	211.60	232.22	253.53
25	13.91	28.38	43.41	59.02	75.22	92.02	109.43	127.46	146.13	165.44	185.40	206.03	227.34	249.33	272.02
26	15.03	30.64	46.84	63.64	81.05	99.09	117.75	137.06	156.99	177.66	198.96	220.95	243.65	267.02	291.18
27	16.20	33.00	50.41	68.44	87.11	106.42	126.38	147.01	168.32	190.31	213.00	236.40	260.52	285.37	310.96
28	17.41	35.44	54.11	73.42	93.38	114.01	135.32	157.31	180.00	203.40	227.52	252.37	277.96	304.31	331.42
29	18.66	37.97	57.94	78.57	99.87	121.86	144.50	167.95	192.07	216.93	242.52	268.86	295.97	323.85	352.52
30	19.96	40.59	61.90	83.89	106.58	129.98	154.10	178.95	204.54	230.89	257.99	285.88	314.55	344.01	374.28

[1] Based on equation 29-10.

TABLE 29–24.—*Gross bark-free cubic foot volume*[1], *form class*[2] *78* (Mesavage 1947)

D.b.h. (inches)	Length of merchantable stem in feet												
	12	16	20	24	28	32	36	40	44	48	52	56	60
								Cu. ft.					
5	1.3	1.7	2.0	2.3	2.6	2.9	3.2	3.5	3.8	4.1	4.4	4.7	5.0
6	1.8	2.4	2.8	3.2	3.6	3.9	4.3	4.7	5.1	5.5	5.9	6.2	6.6
7	2.4	3.1	3.6	4.1	4.6	5.1	5.6	6.1	6.6	7.1	7.6	8.1	8.6
8	3.0	3.9	4.5	5.1	5.7	6.3	7.0	7.6	8.2	8.8	9.4	10.0	10.6
9	3.8	4.9	5.6	6.4	7.1	7.8	8.6	9.3	10.0	10.8	11.5	12.2	13.0
10	4.6	6.0	6.8	7.7	8.5	9.4	10.2	11.0	11.9	12.7	13.6	14.4	15.2

D.b.h. (inches)	Number of 16-foot logs										
	1	1½	2	2½	3	3½	4	4½	5	5½	6
						Cu. ft.					
10	6.0	8.2	10.4	12.0	13.6						
11	7.4	10.1	12.8	14.8	16.9						
12	8.7	12.0	15.2	17.7	20.2	22.0					
13	10.2	14.0	17.9	20.8	23.8	26.0	28.2				
14	11.7	16.2	20.6	24.0	27.5	30.0	32.6				
15	13.6	18.7	23.8	27.9	32.0	35.2	38.4				
16	15.4	21.2	27.1	31.8	36.6	40.4	44.1				
17	17.4	24.0	30.6	36.0	41.4	45.7	50.0				
18	19.4	26.8	34.2	40.2	46.3	51.2	56.0				
19	21.7	30.0	38.4	45.2	52.0	57.5	63.0	75.0			
20	24.0	33.3	42.6	50.2	57.8	63.9	70.0		80.1		

TABLE 29–24.—*Gross bark-free cubic foot volume*[1], *form class*[2] *78 (Mesavage 1947) (continued)*

21------	26.8	37.1	47.4	55.9	64.4	71.3	78.2	84.0	89.9		
22------	29.6	41.0	52.3	61.6	71.0	78.8	86.5	93.1	99.7		
23------	32.4	44.8	57.3	67.6	78.0	86.3	94.6	102.2	109.7		
24------	35.3	48.8	62.3	73.6	84.9	93.8	102.7	111.2	119.7		
25------	38.6	53.4	68.1	80.4	92.8	102.8	112.8	122.1	131.4		
26------	41.9	57.9	73.9	87.3	100.7	111.8	122.8	133.0	143.2		
27------	45.2	62.5	79.8	94.4	108.9	120.8	132.6	143.8	155.0		
28------	48.6	67.1	85.6	101.4	117.1	129.8	142.4	154.6	166.7	177.8	188.8
29------	52.7	72.6	92.6	109.6	126.6	140.2	153.9	167.2	180.6	193.2	205.7
30------	56.8	78.2	99.6	117.8	136.1	150.8	165.4	180.0	194.6	208.6	222.6
31------	61.2	84.1	107.0	126.8	146.5	162.5	178.5	194.0	209.4	224.7	240.0
32------	65.5	90.0	114.5	135.7	156.9	174.2	191.6	207.8	224.1	240.8	257.4
33------	70.0	96.0	122.0	144.6	167.2	185.7	204.2	221.6	239.0	257.1	275.2
34------	74.4	102.0	129.6	153.6	177.5	197.2	216.9	235.4	253.9	273.4	293.0
35------	79.4	108.8	138.2	163.8	189.4	210.5	231.6	251.4	271.3	291.8	312.2

[1] In merchantable stem to variable top diameter, but generally not less than 6 inches outside bark.
[2] Defined by equation 29–1.

TABLE 29–25.—*Merchantable bark-free cubic foot volume of southern pine trees based on form class and total tree height* (Burns 1965[1])

Form class[2] and d.b.h. (inches)	Total tree height							
	30	40	50	60	70	80	90	100
	Cu. ft.							
65–69								
6	2.1	2.5	2.9	3.2	3.7			
8	4.1	4.7	5.6	6.3	7.1	7.8		
10		7.5	8.9	10.2	11.5	12.7	13.8	
12		10.8	12.7	14.5	16.4	17.9	19.9	21.6
14			17.8	20.2	22.6	25.0	27.7	30.1
16			22.7	25.7	28.7	32.1	35.5	38.5
70–74								
6	2.3	2.8	3.3	3.7	4.3			
8	4.7	5.5	6.5	7.4	8.2	9.1		
10		8.6	10.2	11.7	13.1	14.6	15.9	
12		12.2	14.5	16.5	18.8	20.6	22.8	24.8
14			20.3	23.1	25.9	28.7	31.8	34.6
16			26.0	29.5	33.1	37.1	41.0	44.6
75–79								
6	2.6	3.2	3.8	4.2	4.9			
8	5.2	6.0	7.2	8.2	9.2	10.2		
10		9.6	11.5	13.2	14.8	16.5	18.0	
12		13.8	16.4	18.7	21.4	23.4	26.0	28.4
14			22.8	25.9	29.1	32.2	35.8	38.9
16			29.3	33.3	37.3	41.9	46.4	50.4
80–84								
6	2.8	3.5	4.1	4.6	5.3			
8	5.8	6.8	8.1	9.2	10.3	11.4		
10		10.8	12.9	14.8	16.8	18.6	20.3	
12		15.2	18.2	20.7	23.6	25.9	28.8	31.4
14			25.6	29.3	32.9	36.5	40.6	44.2
16			32.7	37.3	41.8	46.9	52.0	56.6
85–89								
6	3.2	4.0	4.6	5.2	6.0			
8	6.5	7.6	9.0	10.2	11.5	12.7		
10		11.9	14.3	16.5	18.6	20.7	22.6	
12		17.2	20.5	23.4	26.7	29.3	32.6	35.5
14			28.4	32.4	36.4	40.5	45.0	49.0
16			36.4	41.5	46.6	52.3	58.0	63.1

[1] Compiled from Minor's (1950) form class tables.
[2] Defined by equation 29–1.

TABLE 29–26.—*Bark-free cubic foot volume of merchantable stem of loblolly pine trees*[1] (MacKinney and Chaiken 1946)

D.b.h. (inches)	Total tree height in feet								
	20	30	40	50	60	70	80	90	100
					Cu. ft.				
5	0.46	0.80	1.28	1.77	2.36	3.01	3.59		
6	.74	1.32	2.08	2.96	3.76	4.55	5.37		
7	1.07	2.06	3.17	4.22	5.29	6.37	7.48	8.63	
8	1.57	2.96	4.30	5.66	7.06	8.48	9.94	11.40	
9	2.20	3.91	5.56	7.30	9.07	10.86	12.71	14.53	
10		4.92	6.99	9.12	11.29	13.51	15.73	17.96	
11		6.07	8.56	11.13	13.76	16.42	19.07	21.80	24.54
12		7.32	10.41	13.33	16.42	19.55	22.70	25.94	29.25
13		8.66	12.15	15.71	19.28	22.98	26.70	30.47	34.20
14		10.12	14.16	18.21	22.39	26.65	30.95	35.23	39.55
15			16.28	20.93	25.74	30.60	35.42	40.86	45.87
16			18.51	23.88	29.32	34.71	40.72	46.36	52.96
17			20.93	26.97	33.00	39.18	45.87	53.10	59.62
18				30.21	36.90	44.30	52.18	59.38	66.66
19				33.58	41.56	49.43	58.01	65.99	74.09
20				37.13	45.96	55.39	64.13	72.97	81.91

[1] From 0.7-foot stump height to top diameter of 4 inches outside bark. Trees selected from 32 stands in the Coastal Plain of the Carolinas.

TABLE 29–27.—*Bark-free cubic foot volume related to crown diameter and height of southern pine trees*[1] (Minor 1953b)

Crown diameter (feet)	Total visible height in feet						
	50	60	70	80	90	100	110
				Cu. ft.			
10	10.9	13.0	15.2	17.4	19.6		
12	13.3	17.0	18.5	21.1	24.1	26.7	
14	16.3	19.7	22.7	26.0	29.3	32.7	36.0
16		22.6	26.2	30.0	33.8	37.6	41.5
18		26.2	30.5	34.9	39.5	43.8	48.1
20		30.0	35.0	40.0	45.0	50.0	55.0
22		34.5	40.2	46.0	51.9	57.6	63.3
24			45.7	52.3	58.9	65.4	72.0
26			50.2	57.4	64.7	71.9	79.2
28			55.9	63.9	72.0	80.0	88.0
30			61.8	70.6	79.4	88.2	97.1

[1] For use with aerial photographs; data applies to trees of form class 80. The table is not applicable to longleaf pine.

TABLE 29–28.—*Bark-free cubic foot volume of small-diameter loblolly and shortleaf pine trees in Tennessee* (Potts 1952)

D.b.h. (inches)	Tree height in feet						
	20	30	40	50	60	70	80

- - - - - - - - - - - - Cu. ft. - - - - - - - - - - - - -

TO TOP DIAMETER OF 2 INCHES INSIDE BARK							
3	0.2	0.4	0.5				
4	.5	.7	1.0	1.4			
5	1.0	1.2	1.6	2.3			
6		1.9	2.4	3.4	4.3	5.5	
7		3.0	3.7	4.7	5.9	7.6	
8		3.8	4.9	6.2	7.9	10.1	12.1
9		4.7	6.1	8.4	10.3	13.1	15.8
TO TOP DIAMETER OF 3 INCHES INSIDE BARK							
4	.4	.4	.6	.8			
5	.8	1.0	1.3	1.8			
6		1.6	2.1	3.1	4.0	5.3	
7		2.7	3.4	4.5	5.8	7.4	
8		3.6	4.6	6.2	7.8	9.9	11.6
9		4.6	6.0	8.0	10.1	12.6	15.2
TO TOP DIAMETER OF 4 INCHES INSIDE BARK							
5	.7	.6	.5	.8			
6		1.4	1.5	2.3	3.1	5.1	
7		2.6	3.0	3.9	5.2	7.1	
8		3.6	4.3	5.7	7.3	9.3	11.1
9		4.6	5.8	7.7	9.6	12.1	14.6

TABLE 29–29.—*Cubic foot volume, including bark, of southern pine trees[1] (after Hawes 1940[2])*

Form and form point[3] (percent)	D.b.h. (Inches)	12	16	20	24	28	32	36	40	44	48	52	56	60	64
								Cu. ft.							
Above average form															
85	6	1.7	2.3	2.8	3.4	4.0	4.5	5.1							
83	8		3.8	4.8	5.8	6.7	7.7	8.7	9.6	10.6	11.6				
81	10			7.2	8.6	10.0	11.4	12.9	14.3	15.7	17.2	18.6	20.0	21.5	
79	12				11.8	13.7	15.7	17.6	19.6	21.6	23.5	25.5	27.4	29.4	31.4
77	14					17.7	20.3	22.8	25.3	27.9	30.4	32.9	35.5	38.0	40.5
75	16						25.1	28.3	31.4	34.5	37.7	40.8	43.9	47.1	50.2
Average form															
83	6	1.6	2.2	2.7	3.2	3.8	4.3	4.8							
81	8		3.6	4.6	5.5	6.4	7.3	8.3	9.1	10.1	11.0				
79	10			6.8	8.2	9.5	10.8	12.3	13.6	14.9	16.3	17.7	19.0	20.4	
77	12				11.2	13.0	14.9	16.7	18.6	20.5	22.3	24.2	26.0	27.9	29.8
75	14					16.8	19.3	21.7	24.0	26.5	28.9	31.3	33.7	36.1	38.5
73	16						23.8	26.9	29.8	32.8	35.8	38.8	41.7	44.7	47.7
Below average form															
81	6	1.6	2.1	2.6	3.1	3.7	4.2	4.7							
79	8		3.5	4.3	5.2	6.0	6.9	7.8	8.6	9.5	10.4				
77	10			6.5	7.8	9.0	10.3	11.6	12.9	14.2	15.5	16.8	18.1	19.4	
75	12				10.6	12.4	14.1	15.9	17.7	19.4	21.2	23.0	24.8	26.5	28.3
73	14					15.9	18.1	20.4	22.7	24.9	27.2	29.5	31.8	24.0	36.3
71	16						22.7	25.5	28.4	31.2	34.0	36.9	39.7	42.5	45.4

[1] To a top diameter of 3.8 inches outside bark on the smaller trees and 6.0 inches on the largest.

[2] Adapted by Williams and Hopkins (1969, p. 39).

[3] Form point $= (100)\dfrac{\text{D.o.b. at midpoint of merchantable length}}{\text{D.b.h.}}$

TABLE 29–30.—*Cubic volume, including bark, of southern pine trees*[1] (USDA Forest Service 1969[2])

D.b.h. (inches)	Merchantable height in feet								
	10	20	30	40	50	60	70	80	90
					Cu. ft.				
5	.7								
6	1.1	2.1	3.2						
7	1.4	2.9	4.3						
8	1.9	3.7	5.6	7.5					
9	2.4	4.7	7.1	9.5	11.4				
10	2.9	5.8	8.8	11.7	14.6				
11	3.5	7.1	10.6	14.1	17.7	21.2	24.7		
12	4.2	8.4	12.6	16.8	21.0	25.2	29.4		
13	4.9	9.9	14.8	19.7	24.6	29.6	34.5	39.5	
14	5.7	11.5	17.2	22.9	28.6	34.3	40.1	45.8	51.5
15	6.6	13.1	19.7	26.3	32.8	39.4	46.0	52.6	59.1
16	7.5	15.0	22.4	29.9	37.4	44.8	52.3	59.8	67.3
17	8.4	16.9	25.3	33.8	42.2	50.6	59.1	67.5	75.9
18	9.5	18.9	28.4	37.8	47.3	56.8	66.2	75.7	85.1
19	10.5	21.1	31.6	42.2	52.7	63.2	73.8	84.3	94.8
20	11.7	23.4	35.0	46.7	58.4	70.1	81.7	93.4	105.1
21	12.9	23.8	38.6	51.5	64.4	77.2	90.1	103.0	115.9
22	14.1	28.3	42.4	56.5	70.6	84.8	98.9	113.0	127.2
23	15.5	30.9	46.3	61.8	77.2	92.7	108.1	123.5	139.0
24	16.8	33.6	50.4	67.3	84.1	101.0	117.7	134.5	151.3
25	18.3	36.5	54.7	73.0	91.2	109.3	127.7	146.0	164.2
26	19.7	39.5	59.2	78.9	98.7	118.4	138.1	157.9	177.6
27	21.3	42.6	63.8	85.1	106.4	127.7	149.0	170.2	191.5
28	22.9	45.8	68.7	91.5	114.4	137.3	160.2	183.1	206.0
29	24.6	49.1	73.7	98.2	122.7	147.3	171.8	196.4	220.9
30	26.3	52.5	78.8	105.1	131.4	157.6	183.9	210.2	236.4
31	28.1	56.1	84.2	112.2	140.3	168.3	196.3	224.4	252.5
32	29.9	59.8	89.7	119.6	149.7	179.3	209.2	239.1	269.0
33	31.8	63.6	95.4	127.2	158.9	190.7	222.5	254.3	286.1
34	33.7	67.5	101.2	135.0	168.7	202.5	236.2	269.9	303.7

[1] To a top diameter, outside bark, of 4 inches.
[2] Data from James H. Bamping, School of Forestry, University of Georgia, Athens, Ga.

TABLE 29–31.—*Cubic volume, including bark, of plantation-grown loblolly pine stems*[1] (Romancier 1961)

D.b.h. (inches)	Total tree height in feet								
	30	35	40	45	50	55	60	65	70
	– – – – – – – – Cu. ft. – – – – – – – – – –								
TO TOP DIAMETER OF 3.6 INCHES INSIDE BARK									
5	0.9	1.4	1.8	2.2	2.6	3.0	----	----	----
6	2.1	2.6	3.1	3.6	4.1	4.6	5.0	----	----
7	----	4.1	4.6	5.2	5.8	6.4	6.9	7.5	----
8	----	----	6.4	7.1	7.8	8.4	9.1	9.8	10.4
9	----	----	----	9.3	10.0	10.8	11.6	12.3	13.1
10	----	----	----	----	12.6	13.4	14.3	15.2	16.1
11	----	----	----	----	15.3	16.4	17.4	18.4	19.4
12	----	----	----	----	----	19.5	20.7	21.9	23.0
TO TOP DIAMETER OF 2.0 INCHES INSIDE BARK									
5	1.8	2.2	2.6	3.0	3.4	3.8	----	----	----
6	2.8	3.3	3.8	4.3	4.8	5.3	5.8	----	----
7	----	4.6	5.2	5.8	6.4	7.0	7.6	8.2	----
8	----	----	6.8	7.6	8.3	9.0	9.7	10.5	11.2
9	----	----	----	9.6	10.4	11.3	12.1	13.0	13.9
10	----	----	----	----	12.8	13.8	14.8	15.8	16.9
11	----	---	---	---	15.4	16.6	17.8	19.0	20.1
12	----	---	---	---	----	19.6	21.0	22.4	23.8

[1] Data based on 116 trees cut in the lower Piedmont of middle Georgia.

TABLE 29-32.—*Cubic foot bark-free volume, in merchantable top wood remaining per tree after removal of saw logs from southern pines* (Mesavage 1947)

Top form index[1] and scaling diameter of top log (inches)	Length of merchantable top in feet										
	4	8	12	16	20	24	28	32	36	40	44
	– – – – – – – – – – – – *Cu. ft.* – – – – – – – – – – – –										
Index 85											
5____	0.4	0.8	1.2	1.5	1.9	2.3	2.7	3.1	3.5	3.8	4.2
6____	.6	1.1	1.7	2.3	2.8	3.4	4.0	4.5	5.1	5.7	6.2
7____	.8	1.6	2.4	3.1	3.9	4.7	5.5	6.5	7.1	7.9	8.6
8____	1.0	2.0	3.0	4.0	5.0	6.1	7.1	8.1	9.1	10.1	11.1
9____	1.3	2.5	3.8	5.0	6.5	7.6	8.8	10.1	11.3	12.6	13.9
10____	1.6	3.2	4.7	6.3	7.9	9.5	11.0	12.6	14.2	15.8	17.3
11____	1.9	3.9	5.8	7.7	9.6	11.6	13.5	15.4	17.3	19.3	21.2
12____	2.3	4.5	6.8	9.1	11.4	13.6	15.9	18.2	20.4	22.7	25.0
13____	2.6	5.3	7.9	10.6	13.2	15.8	18.5	21.1	23.8	26.4	29.0
14____	3.1	6.2	9.3	12.4	15.4	18.5	21.6	24.7	27.8	30.9	34.0
15____	3.6	7.1	10.7	14.3	17.9	21.4	25.0	28.6	32.2	35.7	39.3
16____	4.0	8.1	12.1	16.1	20.2	24.2	28.2	32.3	56.3	40.4	44.4
17____	4.5	9.0	13.6	18.1	22.6	27.1	31.7	36.2	40.7	45.2	49.8
18____	5.1	10.2	15.3	20.4	25.5	30.6	35.8	40.9	46.0	51.1	56.2
19____	5.7	11.5	17.2	22.9	28.6	34.4	40.1	45.8	51.5	57.3	63.0
20____	6.3	12.6	18.9	25.2	31.5	37.8	44.1	50.4	56.7	63.1	69.4
Index 75											
8____	0.8	1.6	2.4	3.1	3.9	4.7	5.5	6.3	7.1	7.9	8.6
9____	1.0	2.0	3.0	4.0	5.0	6.1	7.1	8.1	9.1	10.1	11.1
10____	1.2	2.5	3.7	4.9	6.1	7.4	8.6	9.8	11.0	12.3	13.5
11____	1.5	3.0	4.5	6.0	7.5	9.0	10.5	12.0	13.5	15.0	16.5
12____	1.8	3.5	5.3	7.1	8.8	10.6	12.4	14.1	15.9	17.7	19.4
13____	2.1	4.2	6.3	8.4	10.5	12.6	14.7	16.8	18.9	21.0	23.0
14____	2.4	4.8	7.2	9.6	12.0	14.4	16.8	19.2	21.6	24.1	26.5
15____	2.8	5.6	8.4	11.1	13.9	16.7	19.5	22.3	25.1	27.9	26.3
16____	3.1	6.3	9.4	12.6	15.7	18.8	22.0	25.1	28.3	31.4	34.6
17____	3.6	7.1	10.7	14.3	17.9	21.4	25.0	28.6	32.2	35.7	39.3
18____	4.0	8.0	11.9	15.9	19.9	23.9	27.8	31.8	35.8	39.8	43.7
19____	4.5	8.9	13.4	17.8	22.3	26.8	31.2	35.7	40.2	44.6	49.1
20____	4.9	9.8	14.7	19.6	24.5	29.5	34.4	39.3	44.2	49.1	54.0
Index 67											
11____	1.2	2.4	3.6	4.8	6.0	7.2	8.4	9.6	10.8	12.0	13.2
12____	1.4	2.8	4.2	5.6	7.0	8.4	9.8	11.2	12.6	14.0	15.4
13____	1.7	3.3	5.0	6.6	8.3	9.9	11.6	13.2	14.9	16.5	18.2
14____	1.9	3.9	5.8	7.7	9.6	11.6	13.5	15.4	17.4	19.3	21.2
15____	2.2	4.4	6.5	8.7	10.9	13.1	15.3	17.4	19.6	21.8	24.0
16____	2.5	5.0	7.5	10.0	12.5	15.0	17.5	20.0	22.5	25.0	27.5
17____	2.8	5.7	8.5	11.3	14.2	17.0	19.9	22.7	25.5	28.4	31.2
18____	3.2	6.4	9.6	12.8	16.0	19.2	22.4	25.6	28.8	32.0	35.2
19____	3.5	7.0	10.6	14.1	17.6	21.1	24.6	28.2	31.7	35.2	38.7
20____	3.9	7.8	11.7	15.7	19.6	23.5	27.4	31.3	35.2	39.2	45.1

[1] Top form index = $(100)\dfrac{\text{D.i.b. at midpoint of usable top}}{\text{Scaling diameter of the top saw log.}}$

TABLE 29–33.—*Weight per log for southern pine*

Pine species and scaling diameter (inches)	Log length in feet		
	12	14	16
	Lb.		
Loblolly and shortleaf[1]			
5	120	145	175
6	180	215	250
7	240	290	340
8	320	380	445
9	400	480	560
10	500	600	700
11	600	720	840
12	715	860	1,000
13	840	1,005	1,175
14	970	1,165	1,360
15	1,110	1,340	1,560
16	1,260	1,520	1,770
Longleaf[1]			
5	140	160	180
6	205	235	260
7	280	320	360
8	360	415	465
9	460	520	595
10	560	645	730
11	680	780	880
12	805	925	1,045
13	945	1,095	1,225
14	1,090	1,260	1,420
15	1,250	1,450	1,625
16	1,420	1,645	1,845

Pine species and scaling diameter (inches)	Log length in feet		
	12	14	16
	Lb.		
Slash[1]			
5	150	175	195
6	210	245	280
7	285	335	375
8	375	435	490
9	480	550	620
10	580	680	765
11	700	820	925
12	835	955	1,100
13	980	1,145	1,285
14	1,130	1,350	1,490
15	1,295	1,515	1,705
16	1,465	1,715	1,940
Southern pine[2]			
7½	261–300	313–358	365–418
8	301–340	359–405	419–474
8½	341–380	406–455	475–531
9	381–450	456–540	532–630
10	451–550	541–660	631–770
11	551–658	661–790	771–920
12	659–778	791–933	921–1,088
13	779–905	934–1,085	1,089–1,268
14	906–1,040	1,089–1,253	1,269–1,460
15	1,041–1,185	1,254–1,430	1,461–1,665
16	1,186–1,335	1,431–1,610	1,666–1,875
17	1,336–1,565	1,611–1,800	1,876–2,085

[1] Data on logs cut in Georgia (Page and Bois 1961).

[2] Data from Barton (1966) as adapted from Martin (1965).

TABLE 29–34.—*Merchantable green weight, including bark, of slash pine stems from trees planted on old fields in the Carolina Sandhills* (McGee 1959)

Top diameter outside bark and d.b.h. (inches)		Total tree height in feet											
		20	25	30	35	40	45	50	55	60	65	70	75
								Lb.					
4 inches	5	--	32	45	64	82	100	119	137	155			
	6	42	67	94	120	146	173	199	226	252	279		
	7		115	151	187	223	259	295	331	367	403	439	
	8			217	264	311	358	405	452	499	546	593	640
	9				351	411	470	530	589	649	708	768	827
	10					522	596	669	743	816	890	963	1,037
	11					646	734	824	913	1,001	1,090	1,179	1,268
	12					781	887	992	1,098	1,204	1,310	1,416	1,521
3 inches	5	49	67	84	102	120	138	156	174	192			
	6	81	106	131	158	183	209	235	261	287	313		
	7		153	188	223	258	293	328	364	399	434	469	
	8			252	298	344	390	436	482	528	574	620	666
	9				384	443	502	560	619	678	737	795	854
	10					552	624	696	767	839	911	983	1,054
	11						758	845	932	1,019	1,106	1,193	1,279
	12							1,012	1,116	1,220	1,325	1,429	1,533
2 inches	5	71	89	107	124	142	160	177	195	213			
	6	102	128	154	179	205	231	256	281	307	333		
	7		174	209	244	279	314	349	384	418	453	488	
	8			273	319	364	410	455	501	547	592	638	683
	9				403	461	519	576	634	692	749	807	865
	10					569	640	712	783	854	925	997	1,068
	11						775	861	947	1,034	1,120	1,206	1,292
	12							1,025	1,125	1,230	1,332	1,435	1,537

TABLE 29–35.—*Merchantable green weight, including bark, of loblolly and shortleaf pine stems*[1] (Seigel and Row 1960)

D.b.h. (inches)	One-log tree Form class 66	Two-log tree Form class 77	Three-log tree Form class 79	Four-log tree Form class 81
			Tons	
10_____	0.16	0.35	0.48	--
12_____	.21	.48	.69	--
14_____	.28	.65	.93	1.15
16_____	--	.83	1.19	1.54
18_____	--	1.05	1.51	1.95
20_____	--	1.30	1.78	2.38

[1] Trees were cut in north Louisiana and south Arkansas. Minimum top diameter was about 6 inches inside bark.

TABLE 29–36.—*Green weight, including bark, of plantation-grown loblolly pine stems*[1] (Romancier 1961)

D.b.h. (inches)	Total tree height in feet								
	30	35	40	45	50	55	60	65	70
					Lb.				
TO TOP DIAMETER OF 3.6 INCHES INSIDE BARK									
5_____	34	56	79	101	124	146	-----	-----	-----
6_____	77	109	141	172	204	236	268	-----	-----
7_____	---	171	214	257	299	342	385	428	-----
8_____	---	---	298	354	409	465	520	576	631
9_____	---	---	---	464	534	604	674	744	814
10_____	---	---	---	---	673	759	845	931	1,017
11_____	---	---	---	---	827	931	1,035	1,139	1,242
12_____	---	---	---	---	---	1,119	1,242	1,366	1,489
TO TOP DIAMETER OF 2.0 INCHES INSIDE BARK									
5_____	72	97	121	146	170	195	-----	-----	-----
6_____	107	142	176	211	246	281	315	-----	-----
7_____	---	194	241	288	335	382	429	476	-----
8_____	---	---	316	377	438	499	560	620	681
9_____	---	---	---	478	555	631	708	785	861
10_____	---	---	---	---	685	779	874	968	1,063
11_____	---	---	---	---	829	943	1,057	1,171	1,285
12_____	---	---	---	---	---	1,122	1,258	1,393	1,528

[1] Data based on 116 trees cut throughout the year in the lower Piedmont of middle Georgia.

TABLE 29–37.—*Comparison of Doyle and Scribner volumes with International ¼-inch scale—values given in percentages of International ¼-inch log scale volume* (Lane and Schnur 1948)

Scaling diameter (inches)	Log length in feet									
	8		10		12		14		16	
	Doyle	Scribner	Doyle	Scribner	Doyle	Scribner	Doyle	Scribner	Doyle	Scribner
	Percent									
8	47	88	45	84	44	81	42	79	41	77
10	62	96	60	90	59	88	57	86	55	85
12	73	98	71	96	69	93	67	90	66	89
14	79	98	78	96	77	94	75	92	74	90
16	86	99	83	97	82	95	81	93	80	92
18	90	99	88	97	87	96	86	94	84	93
20	93	99	92	98	91	97	90	95	88	94
22	96	99	95	98	94	97	93	95	92	94
24	99	99	97	98	96	97	95	96	94	95
26	100	99	99	98	99	97	98	96	97	95
28	102	99	101	98	100	97	99	96	99	96
30	104	99	103	98	102	98	101	97	100	96
32	105	99	104	99	104	98	103	97	102	96
34	106	99	105	99	105	98	104	97	103	96
36	107	99	107	99	106	98	105	97	104	97
38	108	99	107	99	107	98	106	97	105	97
40	109	99	108	99	107	98	106	97	106	97

TABLE 29–38.—*Tree volume conversions among log scales for southern pine sawtimber*[1] (USDA Forest Service 1941)

D.b.h. (inches)	Cu. ft. to bd. ft.			Doyle to Int'l	Int'l to Doyle	Scribner to Int'l	Int'l to Scribner	Doyle to Scribner	Scribner to Doyle
	Doyle	Scribner	Int'l						
					Ratios				
10	2.30	4.45	5.90	2.56	0.39	1.325	0.755	1.93	0.52
11	2.70	4.85	6.05	2.24	.45	1.250	.800	1.80	.56
12	3.00	5.10	6.20	2.07	.48	1.210	.825	1.70	.59
13	3.40	5.35	6.35	1.87	.54	1.185	.845	1.57	.64
14	3.70	5.55	6.50	1.76	.57	1.170	.855	1.50	.67
15	4.00	5.70	6.60	1.65	.61	1.155	.865	1.43	.70
16	4.20	5.85	6.70	1.60	.63	1.140	.875	1.39	.72
17	4.40	6.00	6.80	1.54	.65	1.130	.885	1.36	.73
18	4.70	6.15	6.85	1.46	.69	1.115	.895	1.31	.76
19	4.90	6.25	6.90	1.41	.71	1.105	.905	1.28	.78
20	5.10	6.35	6.95	1.36	.73	1.095	.915	1.25	.80
21	5.30	6.45	7.00	1.32	.76	1.085	.920	1.22	.82
22	5.50	6.50	7.00	1.27	.79	1.080	.925	1.18	.85
23	5.70	6.60	7.05	1.24	.81	1.075	.935	1.16	.86
24	5.90	6.65	7.10	1.20	.83	1.070	.940	1.13	.89
25	6.10	6.70	7.15	1.17	.85	1.065	.940	1.10	.91

[1] Log scales are Doyle, Scribner Decimal C, and International 1/4-inch.

TABLE 29–39.—*Percent overrun, by scaling diameter and log scale, from manufacture of logs into lumber*

Data source and log d.i.b. (inches)	Log scale			Logs
	Doyle	Scribner	Int'l $\frac{1}{4}$	
	– – – – – Percent – – – – –			Number
Campbell (1962)[1]				
6	+400	+28	−2	89
7	200	26	−2	102
8	130	23	−3	134
9	90	21	−3	162
10	70	19	−4	155
11	50	17	−4	132
12	42	14	−5	167
13	32	12	−5	119
14	26	10	−6	128
15	20	8	−6	85
16	16	5	−7	74
17	12	3	−8	43
18	8	1	−8	42
19	4	−2	−9	22
20	0	−4	−9	16
21	−2	−6	−10	8
22	−4	−8	−11	8
23	−6	−10	−11	3
24	−8	−13	−12	2
				1,491
Rodenbach (1966)[2]				
6	+172	+21	−3	70
7	124	20	−4	94
8	95	19	−4	106
9	74	17	−4	108
10	59	16	−5	115
11	48	15	−5	96
12	39	14	−5	82
13	31	13	−6	73
14	25	11	−6	59
15	20	10	−6	51
16	16	9	−6	27
17	12	8	−7	16
18	8	6	−7	11
19	5	5	−7	8
20	2	4	−8	4
21	00	3	−8	1
				921

[1] Sound logs, collected Southwide, sawn on circle mills.

[2] Prediction equation for Doyle overrun $= \dfrac{100}{-0.5411 + 1.1684 \log_{10} D} - 100$.

Prediction equation for Scribner overrun $= 28.6082 - 1.237D$.

Prediction equation for International overrun $= -1.5028 - 0.3086D$.

TABLE 29–40.—*Tree overrun by diameter class*[1] (Yandle 1968)

Tree d.b.h. (inches)	Trees measured	Log scale		
		Doyle	Scribner	Int'l ¼
	Number	– – – –	*Percent overrun*	– – – –
8	21	296	9	−11
9	22	214	11	−10
10	46	160	12	−9
11	49	123	13	−8
12	55	97	13	−7
13	66	78	14	−6
14	91	63	14	−5
15	73	52	14	−5
16	67	44	14	−4
17	77	37	13	−4
18	54	32	13	−4
19	62	27	12	−4
20	41	24	11	−4
21	33	21	9	−4
22	25	18	8	−4
23	17	16	6	−5
24	10	14	4	−5
25	7	13	2	−6
26	5	11	−1	−6
27	4	10	−3	−7
Total	825			

[1] The prediction equations are:

Doyle overrun $(\%) = 10^{4.96305-2.7588 \log_{10} \text{(d.b.h.)}}$

Scribner overrun $(\%) = -9.4687 + 3.2548(\text{d.b.h.}) - 0.11217(\text{d.b.h.})^2$

International overrun $(\%) = -25.566 + 2.2969(\text{d.b.h.}) - 0.060164(\text{d.b.h.})^2$

TABLE 29–41.—*Cubic feet of peeled wood per M b.f. log scale of southern pine saw logs*

Scaling diameter (inches)	8-foot saw logs[1]		16-foot saw logs[2]		
	Int'l-¼	Doyle	Int'l-¼	Doyle	Scribner
	— — — — — — —	—	Cu. ft./M b.f. log scale	— — — — — —	—
6.0	246.7	925.0	210.5	1,000.0	333.3
6.5	225.3	690.3	191.3	733.3	275.0
7.0	214.6	553.3	178.6	555.6	238.1
7.5	200.7	457.3	169.7	466.7	224.0
8.0	191.5	395.0	161.5	393.8	203.2
8.5	184.4	350.5	157.8	355.0	197.2
9.0	177.9	315.2	154.9	316.0	188.1
9.5	172.3	288.7	151.7	293.3	183.3
10.0	167.6	267.2	150.8	272.2	178.2
10.5	163.9	250.2	150.0	257.1	174.2
11.0	160.3	235.5	147.5	240.8	168.6
11.5	157.4	223.4	146.6	230.4	165.4
12.0	155.0	213.1	146.4	221.9	165.1
12.5	152.5	204.4	145.3	213.9	163.8
13.0	150.5	196.5	145.2	206.2	160.6
13.5	148.4	189.6	143.2	198.9	158.4
14.0	146.6	183.6	141.2	192.0	156.1
14.5	145.0	178.2	140.4	186.4	154.1
15.0	143.7	173.3	140.1	181.8	152.8
15.5	142.1	168.9	139.0	178.0	151.6
16.0	140.9	165.0	138.1	173.6	150.6
16.5	139.8	161.4	138.3	171.2	150.0
17.0	138.8	158.2	138.5	168.0	149.5
17.5	137.7	155.2	137.9	165.9	148.8
18.0	136.8	152.4	137.9	163.3	148.1
18.5	135.9	149.8	137.8	161.4	148.0
19.0	135.1	147.6	137.7	159.1	147.3
19.5	134.3	145.3	137.4	157.5	147.1
20.0	133.6	143.3	137.2	155.5	146.3
20.5	132.9	141.4	137.0	153.7	145.6
21.0	132.3	139.6	136.4	151.6	145.0
21.5	131.7	137.4	135.9	149.7	144.0
22.0	131.0	136.4	135.0	147.5	143.1
22.5	130.5	134.9			
23.0	129.9	133.5			
23.5	129.5	132.2			
24.0	129.0	130.9			
24.5	128.6	129.5			
25.0	128.2	128.7			
25.5	128.3	127.6			
26.0	127.3	126.6			
26.5	126.9	125.7			
27.0	126.6	124.8			
27.5	126.2	123.9			
28.0	125.9	123.0			
28.5	125.6	122.3			
29.0	125.3	121.5			
29.5	125.0	120.8			
30.0	124.7	120.1			

[1] After Williams and Hopkins (1969, p. 29).   [2] Adapted from Reynolds (1937).

TABLE 29–42.—*Cubic feet of peeled volume per M b.f. log scale in merchantable lengths of loblolly and shortleaf pine trees in southeast Arkansas* (Reynolds 1937)

D.b.h. (inches)	Int'l-¼	Doyle	Scribner
	– – – –	*Cu. ft./M b.f. log scale*	– – – –
10	247.2	655.0	409.4
11	186.1	386.8	262.5
12	158.9	293.1	207.3
13	146.7	248.1	177.9
14	143.5	223.1	165.1
15	145.0	207.8	161.0
16	146.0	198.3	159.4
17	146.4	192.5	159.5
18	146.8	188.5	160.1
19	146.9	185.5	161.1
20	145.5	182.3	159.9
21	143.9	177.0	157.7
22	141.4	170.5	154.6
23	139.6	162.8	150.6
24	137.4	156.2	146.5
25	134.9	150.2	142.5
26	132.5	145.4	138.9
27	130.5	141.6	135.8
28	128.8	138.1	133.0
29	127.2	135.2	130.3
30	125.8	132.5	127.7

TABLE 29–43.—*Weight of green southern pine saw logs, bark included, per M b.f. log scale according to species and scale* (Page and Bois 1961)[1]

Pine species	Log scale		
	Doyle	Scribner Decimal C	Int'l-¼
	– – – – –	*Lb./M b.f.*	– – – – –
Loblolly	17,754	12,801	11,013
Longleaf	24,227	14,350	12,240
Shortleaf	17,917	12,655	10,866
Slash	23,856	14,989	12,729

[1] Logs were of the four major species, cut in Georgia, and weighed at the stump immediately after they were cut.

TABLE 29–44.—*Weight of green southern pine saw logs, bark included, per M b.f. log scale (Scribner Decimal C) by species*[1] (Williams and Hopkins 1969, p. 50)

Pine species	Average	Range
	– – – – – –	*Lb.* – – – – – –
Loblolly	14,900	--------------
Longleaf	15,500	14,215 to 18,150
Longleaf-loblolly	15,000	--------------
Pond	13,770	--------------
Shortleaf	14,700	--------------
Slash	15,100	12,984 to 16,336
Slash, pond, loblolly, longleaf	15,400	14,017 to 15,953
Slash-loblolly	14,900	14,097 to 16,090
Slash-longleaf	15,100	13,136 to 16,564

[1] Average and range values were derived from many sales made on weight basis, and have been used for weight scaling in southeastern Georgia.

TABLE 29–45.—*Board feet, log scale, per ton of loblolly and shortleaf pine saw logs as related to diameter and log scale*[1] (Siegel and Row 1960)

Average scaling diameter (inches)	Average log weight	Log scale		
		Doyle[2]	Scribner	Int'l $\frac{1}{4}$
	Lb.	– – – – – – – *Bd. ft./ton* – – – – – – –		
8	440	78(95)	141	180
9	540	100(109)	158	190
10	660	121(126)	171	200
11	780	138(142)	182	208
12	920	154(158)	191	215

[1] Logs were cut in north Louisiana and south Arkansas; they were 12 to 20 feet long, and about one-third were butt cuts.

[2] Of the two sets of figures under the Doyle scale, those in parentheses are intended for use when logs less than 8 inches in diameter are scaled as their length in feet.

TABLE 29–46.—*Board feet, Doyle log scale, per 1,000 lb. of southern pine saw logs of three lengths and various diameter classes*[1] (Barton 1966)[2]

Average diameter of logs on load (inches)	Average length of load in feet		
	12	14	16
	– – – – –	*Bd. ft. log scale*/1,000 lb.	– – – – –
7.5 _____	----	44.4	51.8
8.0 _____	----	50.7	52.1
8.5 _____	----	53.6	54.5
9.0 _____	50.0	52.4	55.4
10.0 _____	53.5	57.5	60.6
11.0 _____	58.0	63.8	66.5
12.0 _____	64.0	70.0	72.1
13.0 _____	69.5	76.4	78.0
14.0 _____	75.0	82.5	83.8
15.0 _____	80.2	88.8	89.5
16.0 _____	85.6	95.0	95.3
17.0 _____	----	102.0	99.8
18.0 _____	----	107.5	107.0

[1] Data based on 600 truckloads of mixed southern pine saw logs cut in Alabama.

[2] Adapted from Martin (1965).

TABLE 29–47.—*Board feet, Doyle-Scribner log scale, in a truckload as related to number of logs and weight of load*[1] (Bair 1965)

Number of logs	Total weight of logs in thousands of pounds					
	37	38	39	40	41	42
	– – – – –		*Total bd. ft., gross Doyle-Scribner scale*		– – – – –	
35 _____	2,560	2,650	2,750	2,850	2,950	3,050
36 _____	2,530	2,620	2,720	2,820	2,920	3,020
37 _____	2,500	2,600	2,700	2,790	2,890	2,990
38 _____	2,470	2,570	2,670	2,760	2,860	2,960
39 _____	2,440	2,540	2,640	2,740	2,830	2,930
40 _____	2,410	2,510	2,610	2,710	2,810	2,900
41 _____	2,380	2,480	2,580	2,680	2,780	2,880
42 _____	2,360	2,450	2,550	2,650	2,750	2,850
43 _____	2,330	2,420	2,520	2,620	2,720	2,820
44 _____	2,300	2,400	2,490	2,590	2,690	2,790
45 _____	2,270	2,370	2,470	2,560	2,660	2,760
46 _____	2,240	2,340	2,440	2,540	2,630	2,730
47 _____	2,210	2,310	2,410	2,510	2,600	2,700
48 _____	2,180	2,280	2,380	2,480	2,580	2,670
49 _____	2,150	2,250	2,350	2,450	2,550	2,650
50 _____	2,130	2,220	2,320	2,420	2,520	2,620

[1] Data applicable to mixed southern pine species from Sabine and Angelina Counties in east Texas.

TABLE 29–48.—*Board feet, Doyle log scale, in a truckload, as related to number of logs and weight of load*[1] *(Freeman 1962)*

Number of logs	Total weight of logs in thousands of pounds										
	25	26	27	28	29	30	31	32	33	34	35
	Total bd. ft., gross Doyle scale										
30	1,590										
31	1,590	1,670									
32	1,560	1,640	1,730								
33	1,550	1,640	1,730	1,810							
34	1,540	1,600	1,690	1,780	1,860						
35	1,500	1,590	1,680	1,770	1,860						
36	1,490	1,570	1,660	1,760	1,850	1,910					
37	1,480	1,550	1,650	1,740	1,800	1,900	2,000				
38	1,470	1,530	1,630	1,720	1,790	1,890	1,980				
39		1,540	1,600	1,700	1,770	1,870	1,950	2,050	2,140		
40			1,610	1,680	1,750	1,850	1,940	2,040	2,090	2,190	
41				1,650	1,750	1,820	1,930	2,000	2,070	2,180	2,250
42				1,660	1,730	1,800	1,900	1,980	2,080	2,160	2,230
43					1,700	1,800	1,880	1,950	2,060	2,130	2,210
44						1,770	1,850	1,960	2,030	2,110	2,220
45						1,770	1,850	1,930	2,000	2,120	2,190

[1] Mixed loblolly and shortleaf pine from southeast Arkansas and northeast Louisiana.

TABLE 29–49.—*Equations for estimating board foot content, log scale, of individual logs and truckloads of logs by log weight*[1] (Row and Guttenberg 1966)

Description and equation	R^2
Single-log equations for loblolly (Louisiana logs) by two log scales	
Doyle scale	
$V=0.01525+0.1547W-0.09552\sqrt{W}$	0.957
In'lt ¼ scale	
$V=-0.01190+0.1232W$	.966
Single-log equations for Doyle scale volume by species	
Loblolly (Louisiana, Georgia, and Virginia logs combined)	
$V=0.0126+0.1492W-0.0917\sqrt{W}$	.963
Longleaf (Georgia logs)	
$V=0.0491+0.2109W-0.1932\sqrt{W}$	.917
Shortleaf (Georgia logs)	
$V=0.0248+0.1766W-0.1233\sqrt{W}$	.961
Slash (Georgia logs)	
$V=0.1089W-0.0489\sqrt{W}$	.902
Truckload equations for southern pine by two log scales	
Doyle scale	
$V^*=0.1432W^*-0.0639\sqrt{W^*N}$	.984
Int'l ¼ scale	
$V^*=0.1410W^*-0.0304\sqrt{W^*N}$	.992

[1] V = Estimated volume (log scale) of individual log, board feet.
V^* = Estimated volume (log scale) of truckload, board feet.
W = Weight of individual log, pounds.
W^* = Total weight of logs in truckload, pounds.
N = Number of logs in truckload.

TABLE 29–50.—*Weight of green southern pine saw logs, bark included, required to produce 1,000 bd. ft. of sawn lumber*[1] (Page and Bois 1961)

Scaling diameter (inches)	Loblolly and shortleaf	Longleaf	Slash
	— — — — — — *Lb./M b.f. lumber scale* — — — — — —		
5	19,400	20,000	23,600
6	14,100	16,300	19,000
7	12,900	14,500	16,800
8	11,900	13,500	15,200
9	11,300	12,800	14,200
10	10,900	12,200	13,400
11	10,500	11,800	12,800
12	10,200	11,400	12,400
13	9,900	11,200	11,900
14	9,800	11,000	11,600
15	9,600	10,900	11,300
16	9,400	10,800	11,000
Average	10,759	13,087	14,191

[1] Trees were cut in Georgia.

TABLE 29–51.—*Board foot content, Scribner log scale, of southern pine poles of form class 80* (USDA Forest Service 1959, p. 41)

Length (feet)	Pole class							
	1	2	3	4	5	6	7	9
				Bd. ft.				
25_____			70	55	45	35	25	20
30_____	125	105	85	70	55	45	35	25
35_____	155	135	115	90	75			
40_____	205	175	150	130	100			
45_____	245	210	180	145	120			
50_____	280	240	205	170				
55_____	335	295	250					
60_____	385	325	280					
65_____	420	365						
70_____	495	425						
75_____	535							
80_____	570							

TABLE 29-52.—*Weight, volume, and dimensions of southern pine poles by class and length* (American Standards Association 1963)

Class and minimum circumference and equivalent diameter of top of pole (inches)	Length	Weight[1]	Volume	Minimum circumference and equivalent diameter at 6 feet from butt	
				Circumference	Diameter
	Feet	*Lb.*	*Cu. ft.*	— — — *Inches* — — —	
Class 1 27-inch circumference 8.59-inch diameter _ _	20	710	12.91	31.0	9.78
	25	990	18.00	33.5	10.66
	30	1,279	23.25	36.5	11.62
	35	1,568	28.50	39.0	12.41
	40	1,884	34.25	41.0	13.05
	45	2,223	40.41	43.0	13.69
	50	2,585	47.00	45.0	14.32
	55	2,993	54.42	46.5	14.80
	60	3,451	62.75	48.0	15.28
	65	4,015	73.00	49.5	15.76
	70	4,620	84.00	51.0	16.23
	75	5,198	94.50	52.5	16.71
	80	5,867	106.67	54.0	17.19
	85	6,600	120.00	55.0	17.51
	90	7,462	135.67	56.0	17.82
Class 2 25-inch circumference 7.96-inch diameter _ _	20	564	10.25	29.0	9.24
	25	811	14.75	31.5	10.03
	30	1,082	19.67	34.0	10.82
	35	1,343	24.42	36.5	11.62
	40	1,623	29.50	38.5	12.25
	45	1,911	34.75	40.5	12.89
	50	2,214	40.25	42.0	13.36
	55	2,567	46.67	43.5	13.85
	60	2,943	53.50	45.0	14.32
	65	3,341	60.75	46.5	14.80
	70	3,781	68.75	48.0	15.28
	75	4,235	77.00	49.0	15.60
	80	4,739	86.17	50.5	16.07
	85	5,266	95.75	51.5	16.39
	90	5,871	106.75	53.0	16.87

TABLE 29–52.—*Weight, volume, and dimensions of southern pine poles by class and length* (American Standards Association 1963)

Class and minimum circumference and equivalent diameter of top of pole (inches)	Length	Weight[1]	Volume	Minimum circumference and equivalent diameter at 6 feet from butt	
				Circumference	Diameter
	Feet	*Lb.*	*Cu. ft.*	– – *Inches* – –	
Class 3 23-inch circumference 7.32-inch diameter _ _	20	468	8.50	27.0	8.59
	25	674	12.25	29.5	9.39
	30	921	16.75	32.0	10.18
	35	1,155	21.00	34.0	10.82
	40	1,403	25.50	36.0	11.46
	45	1,664	30.25	37.5	11.94
	50	1,925	25.00	39.0	12.41
	55	2,200	40.00	40.5	12.89
	60	2,512	45.67	42.0	13.36
	65	2,814	51.17	43.5	13.85
	70	3,144	57.17	45.0	14.32
	75	3,506	63.75	46.0	14.67
	80	3,887	70.67	47.0	14.96
	85	4,299	78.17	48.0	15.28
	90	4,730	86.00	49.0	15.60
Class 4 21-inch circumference 6.68-inch diameter _ _	20	394	7.17	25.0	7.96
	25	573	10.42	27.5	8.75
	30	784	14.25	29.5	9.39
	35	1,004	18.25	31.5	10.03
	40	1,219	22.17	33.5	10.66
	45	1,444	26.25	35.0	11.14
	50	1,687	30.67	36.5	11.62
	55	1,934	35.17	38.0	12.10
	60	2,186	39.75	39.0	12.41
	65	2,457	44.67	40.5	12.89
	70	2,732	49.67	41.5	13.21
	75	3,021	54.92	43.0	13.69
	80	3,314	60.25	44.0	14.00

TABLE 29–52.—*Weight, volume, and dimensions of southern pine poles by class and length* (American Standards Association 1963)—Continued

Class and minimum circumference and equivalent diameter of top of pole (inches)	Length	Weight[1]	Volume	Minimum circumference and equivalent diameter at 6 feet from butt	
				Circumference	Diameter
	Feet	Lb.	Cu. ft.	– – Inches – –	
Class 5 19-inch circum- ference 6.06-inch diameter _ _	20	330	6.00	23.0	7.32
	25	491	8.92	25.5	8.12
	30	660	12.00	27.5	8.75
	35	862	15.67	29.0	9.23
	40	1,059	19.25	31.0	9.87
	45	1,274	23.17	32.5	10.34
	50	1,494	27.17	34.0	10.82
	55	1,719	31.25	35.0	11.14
	60	1,953	35.50	36.0	11.46
	65	2,237	40.67	37.5	11.94
	70	2,498	45.25	38.5	12.25
Class 6 17-inch circum- ference 5.41-inch diameter _ _	20	284	5.17	21.0	6.67
	25	422	7.67	23.0	7.32
	30	550	10.00	25.0	7.96
	35	743	13.50	27.0	8.59
	40	921	16.75	28.5	9.07
	45	1,114	20.25	30.0	9.55
	50	1,329	24.17	31.5	10.03
	55	1,563	28.42	32.5	10.34
	60	1,801	32.75	33.5	10.66
Class 7 15-inch circum- ference 4.77-inch diameter _ _	20	234	4.25	19.5	6.21
	25	344	6.25	21.5	6.84
	30	454	8.25	23.5	7.48
	35	646	11.75	25.0	7.96
	40	807	14.67	26.5	8.43
	45	976	17.75	28.0	8.91
	50	1,169	21.25	29.0	9.23
Class 9 15-inch circum- ference 4.77-inch diameter _ _ _ _	20	202	3.67	17.5	5.57
	25	289	5.25	19.5	6.21
	30	371	6.25	20.5	6.52
Class 10 12-inch circum- ference 3.82-inch diameter _ _	20	161	2.92	14.0	4.46
	25	234	4.25	15.0	4.77

[1] Weight based on 55 lb./cu. ft., i.e., a specific gravity of 0.5 (ovendry weight, green volume basis) and a moisture content of about 76 percent.

TABLE 29–53.—*Theoretical lineal yield of veneer rotary-cut from bolts of various sizes according to core diameter and veneer thickness*[1]
(Borden Chemical Company 1966)

Veneer thickness and core diameter (inches)	Bolt diameter in inches								
	8	9	10	11	12	14	16	18	20
	– – – – – – – – – – *Feet* – – – – – – – – – – –								
$\frac{1}{10}$-inch thick									
5	25.2	36.3	48.7	62.4	77.3	111.2	150.1	194.5	244.0
4	31.2	42.2	54.8	68.4	83.3	117.2	156.1	200.4	249.9
3	35.8	47.6	59.2	73.0	87.9	121.8	160.7	205.1	254.4
$\frac{1}{8}$-inch thick									
5	20.4	29.3	39.2	50.1	62.4	89.8	121.2	157.0	196.9
4	25.1	34.1	44.1	55.2	67.2	94.6	126.0	161.8	201.7
3	28.8	37.4	47.8	58.9	71.0	98.3	129.8	165.5	205.4
$\frac{3}{16}$-inch thick									
5	13.5	19.4	26.1	33.4	41.4	59.6	80.5	104.2	130.4
4	16.7	22.6	29.4	36.6	44.6	62.8	83.7	107.4	133.9
3	19.2	25.5	31.8	39.1	47.1	65.3	86.6	109.9	136.4

[1] Lineal footage figures on a volumetric basis, assuming each bolt to be a perfect cylinder.

$$\text{Lineal footage} = \frac{\text{Bolt volume–core volume}}{\text{Volume of 1 lineal foot of } \frac{1}{10}\text{-}, \frac{1}{8}\text{-}, \frac{3}{16}\text{-inch veneer}}$$

TABLE 29–54.—*Tree size and percentage of weight in above-ground tree parts of 10 loblolly pine trees* (Metz and Wells 1965)

Tree age (years)	Diameter of base	Height	Portion of total ovendry weight				Total ovendry weight[2]
			Needles	Stemwood[1]	Stembark	Branches	
	Inches	*Feet*	– – – – – – – *Percent* – – – – – – –				*Lb.*
7	2.8	8.0	38.0	28.4	18.1	15.5	4.12
7	2.8	10.0	43.3	24.4	13.6	18.7	6.39
7	4.1	10.6	29.8	36.9	14.2	19.1	12.74
7	4.3	13.2	29.5	34.4	11.9	24.2	20.36
7	5.0	17.1	26.5	41.4	14.1	18.0	28.73
8	5.6	20.5	24.2	43.6	13.8	18.4	30.79
8	6.9	23.3	14.5	53.1	13.8	18.6	54.33
13	8.3	35.6	9.7	57.7	12.9	19.7	95.98
21	7.5	45.8	5.0	70.9	12.5	11.6	121.66
21	9.6	46.4	4.7	70.0	10.0	15.3	194.40

[1] All wood from the base of the tree to the terminal shoot, but excluding branches.
[2] Above-ground portions of tree.

TABLE 29–55.—*Bark volume in second-growth southern pines, as a percentage of total volume of unpeeled wood* (Demmon 1936)

D.b.h. (inches)	Species			
	Loblolly	Longleaf	Shortleaf	Slash
	– – – – – – – – *Percent* – – – – – – – –			
6	19.4	22.2	17.3	26.8
8	17.5	20.2	15.4	24.0
10	16.0	17.8	11.8	21.7
12	14.5	14.5	11.2	19.4
14	14.0	13.6	10.5	19.4

TABLE 29–56.—*Weight of bark on loblolly and shortleaf pine saw logs by scaling diameter (inside bark) and log length*[1]

Scaling diameter (inches)	Log length, feet				
	8	10	12	14	16
	– – – – – – – – – – – – *Lb.* – – – – – – – – – – – –				
8	13	16	20	23	26
10	19	24	29	34	38
12	26	33	40	46	53
14	35	43	52	61	70
16	44	55	66	77	88
18	55	69	82	96	110
20	67	83	100	116	133
22	73	99	119	139	155
24	93	117	140	163	187
26	108	136	163	190	217

[1] Computed from equation 29–26. Values above 18 inches extend beyond range of basic data. Moisture content of bark at time of weight measurement was that normal for logs in temporary storage but not under sprinklers.

TABLE 29–57.—*Weight of shortleaf and loblolly pine bark per M b.f. of saw logs, International ¼-inch scale* (Williams and Hopkins 1969, p. 84[1])

Log scaling diameter (inches)	Log length in feet				
	8	10	12	14	16
	— — — — — — — — — — *Tons* — — — — — — — — — —				
8_____	0.436	0.409	0.393	0.327	0.327
10_____	.319	.342	.320	.305	.295
12_____	.293	.300	.283	.272	.278
14_____	.270	.272	.261	.264	.257
16_____	.260	.251	.255	.250	.246
18_____	.249	.245	.242	.239	.238
20_____	.246	.238	.238	.233	.229
22_____	.234	.231	.229	.228	.224
24_____	.228	.229	.226	.221	.219
26_____	.226	.222	.220	.218	.217

[1] Computed from data of Row et al. (1965). Moisture content of bark at time of weight measurement was normal for logs in temporary storage.

TABLE 29–58.—*Green weight of logs, bark, sawdust, chippable residue, and lumber, per M b.f. of southern pine lumber sawn, by log diameter* (Applefield 1958)

Scaling diameter (inches)	Lumber	Residue chips	Sawdust and unused residues	Peeled log	Bark	Unpeeled log
	— — — — — — — — — — *Lb.* — — — — — — — — — —					
6_____	4,580	5,540	4,810	14,930	2,010	16,940
7_____	5,420	4,600	4,200	14,220	1,900	16,120
8_____	5,770	3,900	3,810	13,480	1,760	15,240
9_____	5,880	3,340	3,640	12,860	1,630	14,490
10_____	5,900	2,940	3,540	12,380	1,550	13,930
11_____	5,860	2,600	3,440	11,900	1,440	13,340
12_____	5,780	2,320	3,410	11,510	1,350	12,860
13_____	5,700	2,100	3,380	11,180	1,210	12,440
14_____	5,670	1,900	3,430	11,000	1,210	12,210
15_____	5,580	1,740	3,420	10,740	1,120	11,860

TABLE 29–59.—*Proportion of slab volume and weight in wood and bark for shortleaf pine*[1] (Todd and Anderson 1955)

Saw log scaling diameter (inches)	Volume		Weight	
	Wood	Bark	Wood	Bark
	– – – – – – – – Percent – – – – – – – –			
5	78	22	86	14
6	76	24	85	15
7	74	26	84	16
8	72	28	83	17
9	70	30	81	19
10	69	31	80	20
11	67	33	79	21
12	65	35	77	23
13	63	37	76	24
14	61	39	74	26
15	60	40	73	27
16	58	42	71	29
17	56	44	68	30
18	54	46	68	32
19	52	48	67	33
Average	65	35	77	21

[1] Average moisture content of bark was 29 percent of the green weight; that of the wood was 54 percent.

TABLE 29–60.—*Effect of log diameter and barking procedure on yield of bark-free, chippable, green residues per M b.f. of southern pine lumber cut in small sawmills* (Applefield 1960)

Source of residue and log scaling diameter (inches)	Bark-free wood	Acceptable chips
	— — — — — — Tons — — — — — —	
Slabs and edgings from debarked logs		
5	3.25	3.10
6	2.90	2.75
7	2.50	2.40
8	2.20	2.10
9	1.90	1.80
10	1.65	1.55
11	1.40	1.35
12	1.20	1.15
13	1.05	1.00
14	.95	.90
15	.85	.80
Debarked slabs and edgings		
5	2.65	2.50
6	2.30	2.20
7	2.00	1.90
8	1.80	1.70
9	1.50	1.45
10	1.30	1.25
11	1.15	1.10
12	.95	.90
13	.85	.80
14	.75	.70
15	.70	.65
Debarked slabs only		
5	2.10	2.00
6	1.90	1.80
7	1.65	1.55
8	1.40	1.35
9	1.20	1.15
10	1.05	1.00
11	.95	.90
12	.80	.75
13	.70	.65
14	.65	.60
15	.50	.50

TABLE 29–61.—*Volume of bark-free wood in a standard cord of southern pine slabs with bark attached, by log diameter and species* (Todd 1955)

Scaling diameter (inches)	Longleaf and shortleaf	Loblolly	Slash
		Cu. ft.	
6	60	58	57
8	57	54	51
10	55	50	47
12	51	46	43
14	48	43	39
16	46	39	36
18	43	36	32
20	40	32	29

TABLE 29–62.—*Weight of usable chips from residue of loblolly and shortleaf pien saw logs*[1]

Log type and scaling diameter (inches)	Log length, feet				
	8	10	12	14	16
			Lb.		
Butt logs					
8	58	72	87	101	115
10	92	115	137	160	183
12	126	157	188	220	240
14	159	199	239	279	319
16	193	242	290	338	387
18	227	284	341	398	455
20	261	327	392	457	522
22	295	369	443	516	590
24	329	411	494	576	658
26	363	454	544	635	726
Upper logs					
8	69	86	103	120	137
10	95	120	142	166	189
12	121	152	181	211	241
14	147	184	220	257	294
16	173	217	259	303	346
18	199	249	298	348	398
20	225	282	338	394	450
22	251	315	377	439	502
24	227	347	416	485	554
26	303	380	455	531	607

[1] Computed from equations 29–28 and 29–29; values above 18 inches are extensions beyond range of basic data. Weights tabulated are for green chips.

TABLE 29–63.— *Tons of usable chips, from residue of loblolly and shortleaf pine saw logs, per M b.f. International ¼-inch log scale sawn*[1]

Log type and scaling diameter (inches)	Log length, feet				
	8	10	12	14	16
	— — — — — — — — — —		Tons	— — — — — — — — — —	
Butt logs					
8	1.92	1.80	1.73	1.44	1.44
10	1.53	1.64	1.53	1.46	1.41
12	1.40	1.43	1.34	1.29	1.27
14	1.16	1.25	1.20	1.21	1.18
16	1.14	1.10	1.12	1.09	1.07
18	1.03	1.02	1.00	.99	.99
20	.97	.93	.96	.91	.90
22	.87	.86	.85	.85	.83
24	.80	.81	.80	.78	.77
26	.76	.74	.74	.73	.73
Upper logs					
8	2.29	2.16	2.06	1.71	1.71
10	1.58	1.70	1.58	1.51	1.46
12	1.34	1.38	1.29	1.24	1.27
14	1.13	1.15	1.10	1.12	1.09
16	1.02	.99	1.00	.98	.96
18	.90	.89	.88	.87	.87
20	.83	.81	.81	.79	.78
22	.74	.73	.72	.72	.71
24	.68	.68	.67	.66	.67
26	.63	.62	.62	.61	.61

[1] Computed from equations 29–28 and 29–29; values above 18 inches are extensions above range of basic data. Weights tabulated are for green chips.

TABLE 29–64.—*Weight of green sawdust from sawing a southern pine log into lumber, as affected by log length and diameter*[1]

Log scaling diameter (inches)	Log length, feet				
	8	10	12	14	16
	– – – – – – – – – – Lb. – – – – – – – – – –				
8	35	44	52	61	70
10	54	68	82	95	109
12	78	98	118	137	157
14	107	133	160	187	213
16	139	174	209	244	279
18	176	220	264	308	353
20	218	272	326	381	435
22	263	329	395	461	527
24	313	392	470	548	627
26	368	460	552	644	735

[1] Computed from equation 29–30; values above 18 inches are an extension beyond the range of the basic data.

29–4 LITERATURE CITED

American Standards Association
1963. American standard specifications and dimensions for wood poles. Amer. Standard 05.1, 15 pp. Amer Standards Assoc., N.Y.

Applefield, M.
1956. The utilization of wood residues for pulp chips. Tex. Forest Serv. Bull. 49, 121 pp.

Applefield, M.
1958. The marginal sawlog for southern yellow pine. Tex. Forest Serv. Res. Note 21, 24 pp.

Applefield, M.
1960. The production and marketing of pine wood residues by small sawmills. Tex. Forest Serv. Bull. 50, 14 pp.

Bair, W. M.
1965. Weight-scaling pine sawlogs in Texas. Tex. Forest Serv. Bull. 52, 8 p.

Barton, W. J.
1966. Weight vs. volume for use in measuring forest products. *In* Measuring the southern forest, pp. 30–42. La. State Univ. 15th Annu. Forest. Symp. Proc. 1966. La. State Univ. Press.

Bennett, F. A.
1953. Topwood volume tables for slash and longleaf pine. USDA Forest Serv. Southeast. Forest Res. Notes 42, 2 pp.

Bois, P. J.
1968. Weight of sawdust from several southern Appalachian wood species. Forest Prod. J. 18(10): 52–54.

Borden Chemical Company.
1966. Conversion tables for the southern pine industry. Borden Chemical Co. Interim Rep. 11, 8 pp. New York.

Bower, D. R.
1961. Are scales better than sticks? South. Lumberman 203(2530): 38.

Bruce, D., and Schumacher, F. X.
1935. Forest mensuration. 360 pp. N.Y.: McGraw-Hill Book Co.

Burns, P. Y.
1965. A condensation of Minor's form class volume tables for southern pine pulpwood. La. Agr. Exp. Sta., LSU Forest. Note 61, 4 pp.

Campbell, R. A.
1962. Overruns—southern pine logs. USDA Forest Serv. Southeast. Forest Exp. Sta. Res. Notes 183, 2 pp.

Carpenter, B. E., and Schroeder, J. G.
1968. Combined effects of drying, surfacing, and trimming on grade and volume of southern pine lumber. USDA Forest Serv. Res. Note SE–93, 3 pp. Southeast Forest Exp. Sta., Asheville, N.C.

Chamberlain, E. B., and Meyer, H. A.
1950. Bark volume in cordwood. TAPPI 33: 554–555.

Cole, D. E., Zobel, B. J., and Roberds, J. H.
1966. Slash, loblolly, and longleaf pine in a mixed natural stand; a comparison of their wood properties, pulp yields, and paper properties. TAPPI 49: 161–166.

Curtis, F. H.
1966. Tree weight equations—their development and use in forest management planning. Soc. Amer. Forest. Proc. 1965: 189–191.

Davis, D. S.
1963. Nomograph for weights of pulpwood logs. Pap. Ind. 45: 662.

Demmon, E. L.
1936. Influence of forest practice on the suitability of southern pine for newsprint. J. Forest. 34: 202–210.

Forbes, R. D.
1961. Forestry handbook. 1143 pp. N.Y.: Ronald Press Co.

Forest Farmers Assocation.
1966. Pulpwood. Forest Farmer 25(7): 141–143.

Freeman, E. A.
1962. Weight-scaling sawlog volume by the truckload. Forest Prod. J. 12: 473–475.

Goebel, N. B., and Warner, J. R.
1962. Volume tables for small diameter loblolly, shortleaf and Virginia pine in the Upper South Carolina Piedmont. S. C. Agr. Exp. Sta. Forest Res. Ser. 7, 7 pp.

Goggans, J. F., and Schultz, E. F., Jr.
1958. Growth of pine plantations in Alabama's coastal plain. Ala. Agr. Exp. Sta. Bull. 313, 19 pp.

Grosenbaugh, L. R.
1952. Shortcuts for cruisers and scalers. USDA Forest Serv. South. Forest Exp. Sta. Occas. Pap. 126, 24 pp.

Grosenbaugh, L. R.
1954. New tree-measurement concepts: height-accumulation, giant tree, taper and shape. USDA Forest Serv. South. Forest Exp. Sta. Occas. Pap. 134, 32 pp.

Grosenbaugh, L. R.
1967a. Rex—Fortran-4 system for combinatorial screening or conventional analysis of multivariate regressions. USDA Forest Serv. Res. Pap. PSW–44, 47 pp. Pacific Southwest Forest Exp. Sta., Berkeley, Calif.

Grosenbaugh, L. R.
1967b. STX—Fortran-4 program for estimates of tree populations from 3P sample-tree-measurements. USDA Forest Serv. Res. Pap. PSW–13 (ed 2, rev.), 76 pp. Pacific Southwest Forest and Range Exp. Sta., Berkeley, Calif.

Grosenbaugh, L. R.
1968. Sampel–tree–measurement: a new science. Forest Farmer 28(3): 10–11.

Guttenberg, S.
1967. Veneer yields from southern pine bolts. Forest Prod. J. 17(12): 30–32.

Guttenberg, S., Fassnacht, D., and Siegel, W. C.
1960. Weight-scaling southern pine saw logs. USDA Forest Serv. South. Forest Exp. Sta. Occas. Pap. 177, 6 pp.

Hawes, E. T.
1940. Volume tables, converting factors, and other information applicable to commercial timber in the South. Ed. 3, 45 pp. USDA Forest Serv., Atlanta, Ga.

Kerbes, E. L., and McIntosh, J. A.
1969. Conversion of trees to finished lumber—the volume losses. Forest. Chron. 45: 348–352.

King, W. W.
1952. Survey of sawmill residues in east Texas. Tex. Forest Serv. Tech. Rep. 3, 59 pp.

Koch, P.
1971. Process for straightening and drying southern pine 2 by 4's in 24 hours. Forest Prod. J. 21(5): 17–24.

Lane, R. D., and Schnur, G. L.
1948. Log rule comparison: International ¼-inch, Doyle, and Scribner. USDA Forest Serv. Cent. States Forest Exp. Sta., Sta. Notes 47, 6 pp.

Lehman, J. W.
1958. Utilizing pine sawmill residue for pulp chips. Tenn. Val. Authority Div. Forest Relat. Rep. 223–58, 11 pp.

Loomis, R. M., Phares, R. E., and Crosby, J. S.
1966. Estimating foliage and branchwood quantities in shortleaf pine. Forest Sci. 12: 30–39.

McGee, C. E.
1959. Weight of merchantable wood with bark from planted slash pine in the Carolina sandhills. USDA Forest Serv. Southeast. Forest Exp. Sta. Res. Note 128, 2 pp.

MacKinney, A. L., and Chaiken, L. E.
1946. Volume, yield, and growth of loblolly pine in the mid-Atlantic coastal region. USDA Forest Serv. Southeast. Forest Exp. Sta. Tech. Note 33 rev., 58 pp.

Martin, J. W.
1965. A procedure for weight scaling southern pine logs. Ala. Forest Prod. 8(10): 59–62.

Merrifield, R. G., and Foil, R. R.
1967. Volume equations for southern pine pulpwood. La. Agr. Exp. Sta. Hill Farm Facts 7, 4 pp.

Mesavage, C.
1947. Tables for estimating cubic-foot volume of timber. USDA Forest Serv. South. Forest Exp. Sta. Occas. Pap. 111, 70 pp.

Mesavage, C., and Girard, J. W.
1956. Tables for estimating board-foot volume of timber. USDA Forest Serv., 94 pp. Wash., D.C.

Metz, L. J., and Wells, C. G.
1965. Weight and nutrient content of the aboveground parts of some loblolly

pines. USDA Forest Serv. Res. Pap. SE–17, 20 pp. Southeast. Forest Exp. Sta., Asheville, N.C.

Minor, C. O.
1950. Form class volume tables for use in southern pine pulpwood timber estimating. La. Agr. Exp. Sta. Bull. 445, 39 p.

Minor, C. O.
1953a. Converting basal area to pulpwood volume. La. Agr. Exp. Sta. LSU Forest. Note 3, 1 p.

Minor, C. O.
1953b. Preliminary volume tables for use with aerial photographs. Forest Farmer 12(10): 9–10, 11.

Page, R. H., and Bois, P. J.
1961. Buying and selling southern yellow pine saw logs by weight. Ga. Forest Res. Counc. Rep. 7, 9 pp.

Page, R. H., and Saucier, J. R.
1958. Survey of wood residue in Georgia. Ga. Forest Res. Counc. Resour.-Ind. Ser. 1, 39 pp.

Perry, T. O., and Wang, C. W.
1958. Variation in the specific gravity of slash pinewood and its genetic and silvicultural implications. TAPPI 41: 178–180.

Potts, S. M.
1952. Volume tables for small-diameter loblolly and shortleaf pine trees. Tenn. Val. Authority Tech. Note 10, 23 pp.

Reynolds, R. R.
1937. Factors for converting log and tree volumes or values from one common scale to another. USDA Forest Serv. South. Forest Exp. Sta. Occas. Pap. 68, 4 pp.

Rodenbach, R. C.
1966. Southern yellow pine log overruns. USDA Forest Serv. Res. Note SE–56, 2 pp. Southeast. Forest Exp. Sta., Asheville, N.C.

Romancier, R. M.
1961. Weight and volume of plantation-grown loblolly pine. USDA Forest Serv. Southeast. Forest Exp. Sta. Res. Note 161, 2 pp.

Rothacher, R. S.
1948. Percentage distribution of tree volume by logs. J. Forest. 46: 115–118.

Row, C., and Fasick, C. F.
1966. Weight-scaling tables by electronic computer. Forest Prod. J. 16(8): 41–45.

Row, C., Fasick, C., and Guttenberg, S.
1965. Improving sawmill profits through operations research. USDA Forest Serv. Res. Pap. SO–20, 26 pp. South. Forest Exp. Sta., New Orleans, La.

Row, C., and Guttenberg, S.
1966. Determining weight-volume relationships for saw logs. Forest Prod. J. 16(5): 39–47.

Schmitt, D., and Bower, D.
1970. Volume tables for young loblolly, slash, and longleaf pines in plantations in south Mississippi. USDA Forest Serv. Res. Note SO–102, 2 pp. South. Forest Exp. Sta., New Orleans, La.

Schumacher, F. X.
1946. Volume-weight ratios of pine logs in the Virginia-North Carolina Coastal Plain. J. Forest. 44: 583–586.

Schumacher, F. X., and Jones, W. C.
1940. Empirical log rules and the allocation of sawing time to log size. J. Forest. 38: 889–896.

Siegel, W. C., and Row, C.
1960. Selling sawlogs by the ton. Forest Farmer 19(13): 8–9.

Snow, E. A.
1949. Pine bark as a source of tannin. J. Amer. Leather Chem. Assoc. 44: 504–511.

Southern Pine Inspection Bureau.
1970. Standard grading rules for southern pine lumber. 208 pp. Pensacola, Fla.: Southern Pine Inspection Bureau.

Taras, M. A.
1956. Buying pulpwood by weight as compared with volume measure. USDA Forest Serv. Southeast. Forest Exp. Sta., Sta. Pap. 74, 11 pp.

Todd, A. S., Jr.
1955. How much wood in a cord of pine slabs? USDA Forest Serv. Southeast. Forest Exp. Sta. Res. Notes 87, 1 p.

Todd, A. S., Jr. and Anderson, W. C.
1955. Size, volume, and weight of pine slabs and edgings in the South Carolina Piedmont. USDA Forest Serv. Southeast. Forest Exp. Sta., Sta. Pap. 49, 21 pp.

USDA Forest Service.
1941. National forest scaling handbook. 119 pp. Washington, D.C.: U.S. Government Printing Office.

USDA Forest Service.
1959. Volume tables, converting factors, and other information applicable to commercial timber in the South. Ed. 7, 54 pp. Div. State and Priv. Forest., Atlanta.

USDA Forest Service.
1965. Service foresters handbook. USDA Forest Serv., South. Reg., Atlanta, Ga. (Rev.) 51 pp.

USDA Forest Service.
1969. Volume tables and additional information for the Southeastern area. Ed. 8, 28 p. USDA Forest Serv. Southeast. Area State & Priv. Forest.

USDA Forest Service.
1970. Service foresters handbook. USDA Forest Serv. Southeast. Area State & Priv. Forest. 67 pp. rev.

Van Sickle, C. C.
1966. Factors for converting Midsouth pulpwood from cords to cubic feet. USDA Forest Serv. Res. Note SO–45, 2 pp. South. Forest Exp. Sta., New Orleans, La.

Wahlenberg, W. G.
1960. Loblolly Pine. 603 pp. N.C.: Duke Univ. Sch. Forest.

Williams, D. L., and Hopkins, W. C.
1969. Converting factors for southern pine products. La. Agr. Exp. Sta. Bull. 626 rev., 89 pp.

Williston, H. L.
1957. Pole grower's guide. USDA Forest Serv. South. Forest Exp. Sta. Occas. Pap. 153, 34 pp.

Yandle, D. O.
1968. Southern yellow pine tree overruns and lumber width distributions. USDA Forest Serv. Res. Pap. SE–41, 12 pp. Southeast. Forest Exp. Sta., Asheville, N.C.

INDEX

Oil from needles, 591
 chemical composition of, *592*
 distillation temperatures for, *593*
 uses for, 594
 yield and physical properties of, *592*
Oils and oil-borne preservatives, 1067
Old-house borer, 702
Oleoresin, 1476
 product yield from, 1483
Olustee process for naval stores, 1482, 1483
Open coat sanding belt, 895
Orchard heater, reference on, 1406
Organic liquids, resistance of wood to, 615
Orthogonal cutting, 759
 cutting force comparisons, by direction, 791, *796*
 definition of, 759, 760
 effects of cutting velocity on, 760
 nomenclature for, **760, 761**
 oblique and inclined cutting, 793
 parallel to grain in 90–0 direction, 761
 perpendicular to grain in 0–90 direction, 775
 perpendicular to grain in 90–90 direction, 781
 see also Orthogonal cutting, 90–0 mode
 see also Orthogonal cutting, 0–90 mode
 see also Orthogonal cutting, 90–90 mode
Orthogonal cutting, 0–90 mode, 775
 chip formation during, 775
 definition of, 760
 force during, 780, *781, 782, 783–786*
 nomenclature, **761**
Orthogonal cutting, 90–0 mode, 761
 chip formation during, 762, *766*
 definition of, 760
 forces during, **764,** *767–771,* **772,** 774
 nomenclature, **761**
Orthogonal cutting, 90–90 mode, 781
 chip formation during, 781, *789*
 definition of, 760
 forces during, **790,** *791–795*
 nomenclature, **761**
Oscillation of gangsaws, 862
Osmoplastic groundline treatment; *see* Preservatives
Osmoplastic process of treatment, 1095
Osmose (diffusion) treatment, effectiveness against termites, 680
Osmose-Osmosar; *see* Preservatives
Osmose process of treatment, 1094
Outer bark; *see* Rhytidome
Outer wood
 moisture content of, 273
 shrinking and swelling in, *292,* **299**
 see also Mature wood
Overhang of gangsaws, 862
Overlays
 bonding of, 1350
 material for, 1349
Overlays for lumber, paintable, 1349
 bond with wood, 1350

Overlays for lumber, paintable (*Continued*)
 designs for use of, 1351
 material for, 1349, 1350
 performance of, 1351
Overlays for plywood, paintable
 for concrete forms, 1355
 high-density, 1355
 medium-density, 1355
 paintable, 1355
Overlays, precast colored, 1352
Overrun, by various log scales, 1530, *1594, 1595*
 definition of, 1530
Ozone, stabilization of wood, 1133

P

Paint
 drying-oil based, 1343
 formulations of, 1348
 latex, or emulsion, 1343
 number of coats and thickness, 1347
 pigments in, 1340, 1343
 preparation for, 1345
 primers under, 1345
 repainting, 1348
 steps in applying, 1347
 technology of, 1338
 wood selection for, 1345
Paint failures
 blisters, 1346
 cracking, 1346
 moisture content related to, 1345, 1346
 peeling, 1346
 vapor barrier placement, related to, 1346
Paint systems, 1346
 drying-oil based, 1343
 for hardboard, 1356
 for plywood, 1352
 for repainting, 1348
 latex, or emulsion, 1343
 steps in painting, 1346, 1347
Paneling, finishing of, 1360
Paper
 drying of, 1017
 storage of, 752
 use of bark in, 526
 see also Pulp
Paper, kraft types characterized, 1445, 1446
Paper size, 1490
Parchmentized paper overlay, 1350
Parenchyma
 destruction by anaerobic bacteria, 650
 destruction by fungi, **650**
 horizontal, 109, **111, 112**
 longitudinal in bark, 475
 vertical, 102, **106**
Particleboard, 1191
 consumption of, **1192**
 dulling of cutting tools, 767
 equilibrium moisture content, 287, 288
 factors affecting properties of, 1199
  adhesive spread, 1200–1204
  densification ratio, 1196
  glue properties, 1204–1207

Yields and measures, residues, 1540
  bark, 1543
    pounds produced per acre per year,
      shortleaf, 586
    weight and volume in slabwood,
      1549, *1610*
    weight and volume per standard
      rough cord, 1547, *1557*
    weight and volume per tree or log,
      562, **583**, 1527, 1541, 1544,
      1607–1609
    weight per M b.f. log scale, 1547,
      1609
    weight per M b.f. lumber scale,
      1548–1550, *1609*
    density in piles, 1550
  needles, *562*, 581–586, 1541, 1542,
    1607
  pulp chips, 1551
    chip yield from chipping headrigs,
      844, 845, *846*
    chip yield from plywood mills, 1552
    chip yield from sawmills, *846*, 1542,
      1552, *1609*, *1611*, *1613*
    chip yield per cord of wood, 1552
    chip yield per M b.f. lumber sawn,
      845, *1609*, *1611*
    weight and volume of chips in piles,
      1553
  roots, *562*, 1541, 1543
  sawdust, 1553
    percentage of cubic volume con-
      verted to, *846*, 1542
    sawdust residue per log, *1614*
    sawdust residue per M b.f. (log
      scale) sawn, 1553
    sawdust residue per M b.f. (lum-
      ber scale) sawn, **1549**, 1554,
      1609

Yields and measures, residues, sawdust
  (*Continued*)
    sawdust weight per unit volume,
      1555
  shavings, 1556
  slabs and edgings, 1550
    slab yield per M b.f. log scale, 1550
    slab yield per M b.f. lumber scale,
      1550, *1611*
    solid wood content of slabs and
      edgings, 1551, *1610–1612*
  stumps and roots, *562*, **583**, 1541, 1543
  tops and branches, *562*, 1541, 1542,
    1561, *1588*, *1607*
  trim, 1542, **1549**, 1556
  see also Conversion tables
  see also Measurement units

Z

Zinc arsenate, chromated; *see* Preservatives
Zinc borate, 1127
Zinc chloride
  effectiveness against termites, 680
  effectiveness as fire retardant, 1119,
    1122, 1124
  see also Preservatives
Zinc chloride, chromated
  effectiveness as fire retardant, 1124
  see also Preservatives
Zinc chloride, copperized chromated; *see*
  Preservatives
Zinc meta arsenite
  effectiveness against termites, 680
  see also Preservatives
Zinc oxides, in paints, 1340, 1347